THE ENTIRE ORIGINAL MAUPASSANT SHORT STORIES

by *Guy de Maupassant*

Translated by
ALBERT M. C. McMASTER, B.A.
A. E. HENDERSON, B.A.
MME. QUESADA and Others

This book has been published by:

Contact: sales@nuvisionpublications.com

URL: http://www.nuvisionpublications.com

Publishing Date: 2007

ISBN# 1-59547-876-0

Please see my website for several books created for education, research and entertainment.

Specializing in rare, out-of-print books still in demand.

Contents

VOLUME I.

GUY DE MAUPASSANT… A STUDY BY POL. NEVEUX	11
BOULE DE SUIF	14
TWO FRIENDS	33
THE LANCER'S WIFE	38
THE PRISONERS	44
TWO LITTLE SOLDIERS	51
FATHER MILON	54
A COUP D'ETAT	57
LIEUTENANT LARE'S MARRIAGE	63
THE HORRIBLE	66
MADAME PARISSE	69
MADEMOISELLE FIFI	73
A DUEL	78

VOLUME II.

THE COLONEL'S IDEAS	83
MOTHER SAUVAGE	85
EPIPHANY	89
THE MUSTACHE	94
MADAME BAPTISTE	96
THE QUESTION OF LATIN	99
A MEETING	104
THE BLIND MAN	108
INDISCRETION	110
A FAMILY AFFAIR	113
BESIDE SCHOPENHAUER'S CORPSE	126

VOLUME III.

MISS HARRIET	129
LITTLE LOUISE ROQUE	139
THE DONKEY	156
MOIRON	160
THE DISPENSER OF HOLY WATER	163
A PARRICIDE	166
BERTHA	169
THE PATRON	173
THE DOOR	176

A SALE	179
THE IMPOLITE SEX	182
A WEDDING GIFT	185
THE RELIC	187

VOLUME IV.

THE MORIBUND	191
THE GAMEKEEPER	195
THE STORY OF A FARM GIRL	199
THE WRECK	207
THEODULE SABOT'S CONFESSION	213
THE WRONG HOUSE	218
THE DIAMOND NECKLACE	222
THE MARQUIS DE FUMEROL	226
THE TRIP OF LE HORLA	230
FAREWELL!	235
THE WOLF	237
THE INN	240

VOLUME V.

MONSIEUR PARENT	247
QUEEN HORTENSE	260
TIMBUCTOO	264
TOMBSTONES	268
MADEMOISELLE PEARL	271
THE THIEF	278
CLAIR DE LUNE	280
WAITER, A "BOCK"	283
AFTER	286
FORGIVENESS	289
IN THE SPRING	293
A QUEER NIGHT IN PARIS	295

VOLUME VI.

THAT COSTLY RIDE	303
USELESS BEAUTY	307
THE FATHER	315
MY UNCLE SOSTHENES	319
THE BARONESS	322
MOTHER AND SON	324
THE HAND	327

A TRESS OF HAIR	331
ON THE RIVER	334
THE CRIPPLE	337
A STROLL	339
ALEXANDRE	342
THE LOG	344
JULIE ROMAIN	347
THE RONDOLI SISTERS	351

VOLUME VII.

THE FALSE GEMS	365
FASCINATION	368
YVETTE SAMORIS	371
A VENDETTA	374
MY TWENTY-FIVE DAYS	376
"THE TERROR"	380
LEGEND OF MONT ST. MICHEL	383
A NEW YEAR'S GIFT	385
FRIEND PATIENCE	389
ABANDONED	392
THE MAISON TELLIER	397
DENIS	408
MY WIFE	412
THE UNKNOWN	415
THE APPARITION	417

VOLUME VIII.

CLOCHETTE	423
THE KISS	425
THE LEGION OF HONOR	427
THE TEST	430
FOUND ON A DROWNED MAN	434
THE ORPHAN	437
THE BEGGAR	441
THE RABBIT	443
HIS AVENGER	448
MY UNCLE JULES	451
THE MODEL	455
A VAGABOND	459
THE FISHING HOLE	463

THE SPASM	466
IN THE WOOD	469
MARTINE	472
ALL OVER	475
THE PARROT	479
THE PIECE OF STRING	482

VOLUME IX.

TOINE	487
MADAME HUSSON'S "ROSIER"	491
THE ADOPTED SON	500
COWARD	503
OLD MONGILET	507
MOONLIGHT	510
THE FIRST SNOWFALL	512
SUNDAYS OF A BOURGEOIS	517
A RECOLLECTION	532
OUR LETTERS	536
THE LOVE OF LONG AGO	540
FRIEND JOSEPH	542
THE EFFEMINATES	545
OLD AMABLE	547

VOLUME X.

THE CHRISTENING	561
THE FARMER'S WIFE	563
THE DEVIL	567
THE SNIPE	570
THE WILL	571
WALTER SCHNAFFS' ADVENTURE	574
AT SEA	578
MINUET	581
THE SON	583
THAT PIG OF A MORIN	588
SAINT ANTHONY	592
LASTING LOVE	596
PIERROT	599
A NORMANDY JOKE	602
FATHER MATTHEW	603

VOLUME XI.

THE UMBRELLA	607
BELHOMME'S BEAST	612
DISCOVERY	616
THE ACCURSED BREAD	618
THE DOWRY	620
THE DIARY OF A MADMAN	624
THE MASK	626
THE PENGUINS' ROCK	630
A FAMILY	632
SUICIDES	634
AN ARTIFICE	637
DREAMS	639
SIMON'S PAPA	641

VOLUME XII.

THE CHILD	647
A COUNTRY EXCURSION	650
ROSE	655
ROSALIE PRUDENT	658
REGRET	660
A SISTER'S CONFESSION	663
COCO	665
DEAD WOMAN'S SECRET	667
A HUMBLE DRAMA	669
MADEMOISELLE COCOTTE	672
THE CORSICAN BANDIT	674
THE GRAVE	675

VOLUME XIII.

OLD JUDAS	679
THE LITTLE CASK	681
BOITELLE	684
A WIDOW	688
THE ENGLISHMAN OF ETRETAT	690
MAGNETISM	692
A FATHER'S CONFESSION	694
A MOTHER OF MONSTERS	702
AN UNCOMFORTABLE BED	704
A PORTRAIT	705

- THE DRUNKARD 707
- THE WARDROBE 710
- THE MOUNTAIN POOL 714
- A CREMATION 716
- MISTI 719
- MADAME HERMET 722
- THE MAGIC COUCH 725

VOLUME I.

GUY DE MAUPASSANT

A STUDY BY POL. NEVEUX

"I entered literary life as a meteor, and I shall leave it like a thunderbolt." These words of Maupassant to Jose Maria de Heredia on the occasion of a memorable meeting are, in spite of their morbid solemnity, not an inexact summing up of the brief career during which, for ten years, the writer, by turns undaunted and sorrowful, with the fertility of a master hand produced poetry, novels, romances and travels, only to sink prematurely into the abyss of madness and death. . . . .

In the month of April, 1880, an article appeared in the "Le Gaulois" announcing the publication of the Soirees de Medan. It was signed by a name as yet unknown: Guy de Maupassant. After a juvenile diatribe against romanticism and a passionate attack on languorous literature, the writer extolled the study of real life, and announced the publication of the new work. It was picturesque and charming. In the quiet of evening, on an island, in the Seine, beneath poplars instead of the Neapolitan cypresses dear to the friends of Boccaccio, amid the continuous murmur of the valley, and no longer to the sound of the Pyrennean streams that murmured a faint accompaniment to the tales of Marguerite's cavaliers, the master and his disciples took turns in narrating some striking or pathetic episode of the war. And the issue, in collaboration, of these tales in one volume, in which the master jostled elbows with his pupils, took on the appearance of a manifesto, the tone of a challenge, or the utterance of a creed.

In fact, however, the beginnings had been much more simple, and they had confined themselves, beneath the trees of Medan, to deciding on a general title for the work. Zola had contributed the manuscript of the "Attaque du Moulin," and it was at Maupassant's house that the five young men gave in their contributions. Each one read his story, Maupassant being the last. When he had finished Boule de Suif, with a spontaneous impulse, with an emotion they never forgot, filled with enthusiasm at this revelation, they all rose and, without superfluous words, acclaimed him as a master.

He undertook to write the article for the Gaulois and, in cooperation with his friends, he worded it in the terms with which we are familiar, amplifying and embellishing it, yielding to an inborn taste for mystification which his youth rendered excusable. The essential point, he said, is to "unmoor" criticism.

It was unmoored. The following day Wolff wrote a polemical dissertation in the Figaro and carried away his colleagues. The volume was a brilliant success, thanks to Boule de Suif. Despite the novelty, the honesty of effort, on the part of all, no mention was made of the other stories. Relegated to the second rank, they passed without notice. From his first battle, Maupassant was master of the field in literature.

At once the entire press took him up and said what was appropriate regarding the budding celebrity. Biographers and reporters sought information concerning his life. As it was very simple and perfectly straightforward, they resorted to invention. And thus it is that at the present day Maupassant appears to us like one of those ancient heroes whose origin and death are veiled in mystery.

I will not dwell on Guy de Maupassant's younger days. His relatives, his old friends, he himself, here and there in his works, have furnished us in their letters enough valuable revelations and touching remembrances of the years preceding his literary debut. His worthy biographer, H. Edouard Maynial, after collecting intelligently all the writings, condensing and comparing them, has been able to give us some definite information regarding that early period.

I will simply recall that he was born on the 5th of August, 1850, near Dieppe, in the castle of Miromesnil which he describes in Une Vie. . . .

Maupassant, like Flaubert, was a Norman, through his mother, and through his place of birth he belonged to that strange and adventurous race, whose heroic and long voyages on tramp trading ships he liked to recall. And just as the author of "Education sentimentale" seems to have inherited in the paternal line the shrewd realism of Champagne, so de Maupassant appears to have inherited from his Lorraine ancestors their indestructible discipline and cold lucidity.

His childhood was passed at Etretat, his beautiful childhood; it was there that his instincts were awakened in the unfoldment of his prehistoric soul. Years went by in an ecstasy of physical happiness. The delight of running at full speed through fields of gorse, the charm of voyages of discovery in hollows and ravines, games beneath the dark hedges, a passion for going to sea with the fishermen and, on nights when there was no moon, for dreaming on their boats of imaginary voyages.

Mme. de Maupassant, who had guided her son's early reading, and had gazed with him at the sublime spectacle of nature, put, off as long as possible the hour of separation. One day, however, she had to take the child to the little seminary at Yvetot. Later, he became a student at the college at Rouen, and became a literary correspondent of Louis Bouilhet. It was at the latter's house on those Sundays in winter when the Norman rain drowned the sound of the bells and dashed against the window panes that the school boy learned to write poetry.

Vacation took the rhetorician back to the north of Normandy. Now it was shooting at Saint Julien l'Hospitalier, across fields, bogs, and through the woods. From that time on he sealed his pact with the earth, and those "deep and delicate roots" which attached him to his native soil began to grow. It was of Normandy, broad, fresh and virile, that he would presently demand his inspiration, fervent and eager as a boy's love; it was in her that he would take refuge when, weary of life, he would implore a truce, or when he simply wished to work and revive his energies in old-time joys. It was at this time that was born in him that voluptuous love of the sea, which in later days could alone withdraw him from the world, calm him, console him.

In 1870 he lived in the country, then he came to Paris to live; for, the family fortunes having dwindled, he had to look for a position. For several years he was a clerk in the Ministry of Marine, where he turned over musty papers, in the uninteresting company of the clerks of the admiralty.

Then he went into the department of Public Instruction, where bureaucratic servility is less intolerable. The daily duties are certainly scarcely more onerous and he had as chiefs, or colleagues, Xavier Charmes and Leon Dierx, Henry Roujon and Rene Billotte, but his office looked out on a beautiful melancholy garden with immense plane trees around which black circles of crows gathered in winter.

Maupassant made two divisions of his spare hours, one for boating, and the other for literature. Every evening in spring, every free day, he ran down to the river whose mysterious current veiled in fog or sparkling in the sun called to him and bewitched him. In the islands in the Seine between Chatou and Port-Marly, on the banks of Sartrouville and Triel he was long noted among the population of boatmen, who have now vanished, for his unwearying biceps, his cynical gaiety of good-fellowship, his unfailing practical jokes, his broad witticisms. Sometimes he would row with frantic speed, free and joyous, through the glowing sunlight on the stream; sometimes, he would wander along the coast, questioning the sailors, chatting with the ravageurs, or junk gatherers, or stretched at full length amid the irises and tansy he would lie for hours watching the frail insects that play on the surface of the stream, water spiders, or white butterflies, dragon flies, chasing each other amid the willow leaves, or frogs asleep on the lily-pads.

The rest of his life was taken up by his work. Without ever becoming despondent, silent and persistent, he accumulated manuscripts, poetry, criticisms, plays, romances and novels. Every week he docilely submitted his work to the great Flaubert, the childhood friend of his mother and his uncle Alfred Le Poittevin. The master had consented to assist the young man, to reveal to him the secrets that make chefs-d'oeuvre immortal. It was he who compelled him to make copious research and to use direct observation and who inculcated in him a horror of vulgarity and a contempt for facility.

Maupassant himself tells us of those severe initiations in the Rue Murillo, or in the tent at Croisset; he has recalled the implacable didactics of his old master, his tender brutality, the paternal advice of his generous and candid heart. For seven years Flaubert slashed, pulverized, the awkward attempts of his pupil whose success remained uncertain.

Suddenly, in a flight of spontaneous perfection, he wrote Boule de Suif. His master's joy was great and overwhelming. He died two months later.

Until the end Maupassant remained illuminated by the reflection of the good, vanished giant, by that touching reflection that comes from the dead to those souls they have so profoundly stirred. The worship of Flaubert was a religion from which nothing could distract him, neither work, nor glory, nor slow moving waves, nor balmy nights.

At the end of his short life, while his mind was still clear: he wrote to a friend: "I am always thinking of my poor Flaubert, and I say to myself that I should like to die if I were sure that anyone would think of me in the same manner."

During these long years of his novitiate Maupassant had entered the social literary circles. He would remain silent, preoccupied; and if anyone, astonished at his silence, asked him about his plans he answered simply: "I am learning my trade." However, under the pseudonym of Guy de Valmont, he had sent some articles to the newspapers, and, later, with the approval and by the advice of Flaubert, he published, in the "Republique des Lettres," poems signed by his name.

These poems, overflowing with sensuality, where the hymn to the Earth describes the transports of physical possession, where the impatience of love expresses itself in loud melancholy appeals like the calls of animals in the spring nights, are valuable chiefly inasmuch as they reveal the creature of instinct, the fawn escaped from his native forests, that Maupassant was in his early youth. But they add nothing to his glory. They are the "rhymes of a prose writer" as Jules Lemaitre said. To mould the expression of his thought according to the strictest laws, and to "narrow it down" to some extent, such was his aim. Following the example of one of his comrades of Medan, being readily carried away by precision of style and the rhythm of sentences, by the imperious rule of the ballad, of the pantoum or the chant royal, Maupassant also desired to write in metrical lines. However, he never liked this collection that he often regretted having published. His encounters with prosody had left him with that monotonous weariness that the horseman and the fencer feel after a period in the riding school, or a bout with the foils.

Such, in very broad lines, is the story of Maupassant's literary apprenticeship.

The day following the publication of "Boule de Suif," his reputation began to grow rapidly. The quality of his story was unrivalled, but at the same time it must be acknowledged that there were some who, for the sake of discussion, desired to place a young reputation in opposition to the triumphant brutality of Zola.

From this time on, Maupassant, at the solicitation of the entire press, set to work and wrote story after story. His talent, free from all influences, his individuality, are not disputed for a moment. With a quick step, steady and alert, he advanced to fame, a fame of which he himself was not aware, but which was so universal, that no contemporary author during his life ever experienced the same. The "meteor" sent out its light and its rays were prolonged without limit, in article after article, volume on volume.

He was now rich and famous . . . . He is esteemed all the more as they believe him to be rich and happy. But they do not know that this young fellow with the sunburnt face, thick neck and salient muscles whom they invariably compare to a young bull at liberty, and whose love affairs they whisper, is ill, very ill. At the very moment that success came to him, the malady that never afterwards left him came also, and, seated motionless at his side, gazed at him with its threatening countenance. He suffered from terrible headaches, followed by nights of insomnia. He had nervous attacks, which he soothed with narcotics and anesthetics, which he used freely. His sight, which had troubled him at intervals, became affected, and a celebrated oculist spoke of abnormality, asymetry of the pupils. The famous young man trembled in secret and was haunted by all kinds of terrors.

The reader is charmed at the saneness of this revived art and yet, here and there, he is surprised to discover, amid descriptions of nature that are full of humanity, disquieting flights towards the supernatural, distressing conjurations, veiled at first, of the most commonplace, the most vertiginous shuddering fits of fear, as old as the world and as eternal as the unknown. But, instead of being alarmed, he thinks that the author must be gifted with infallible intuition to follow out thus the taints in his characters, even through their most dangerous mazes. The reader does not know that these hallucinations which he describes so minutely were experienced by Maupassant himself; he does not know that the fear is in himself, the anguish of fear "which is not caused by the presence of danger, or of inevitable death, but by certain abnormal conditions, by certain mysterious influences in presence of vague dangers," the "fear of fear, the dread of that horrible sensation of incomprehensible terror."

How can one explain these physical sufferings and this morbid distress that were known for some time to his intimates alone? Alas! the explanation is only too simple. All his life, consciously or unconsciously, Maupassant fought this malady, hidden as yet, which was latent in him.

As his malady began to take a more definite form, he turned his steps towards the south, only visiting Paris to see his physicians and publishers. In the old port of Antibes beyond the causeway of Cannes, his yacht, Bel Ami, which he cherished as a brother, lay at anchor and awaited him. He took it to the white cities of the Genoese Gulf, towards the palm trees of Hyeres, or the red bay trees of Antheor.

After several tragic weeks in which, from instinct, he made a desperate fight, on the 1st of January, 1892, he felt he was hopelessly vanquished, and in a moment of supreme clearness of intellect, like Gerard de Nerval, he attempted suicide. Less fortunate than the author of Sylvia, he was unsuccessful. But his mind, henceforth "indifferent to all unhappiness," had entered into eternal darkness.

He was taken back to Paris and placed in Dr. Meuriot's sanatorium, where, after eighteen months of mechanical existence, the "meteor" quietly passed away.

BOULE DE SUIF

For several days in succession fragments of a defeated army had passed through the town. They were mere disorganized bands, not disciplined forces. The men wore long, dirty beards and tattered uniforms; they advanced in listless fashion, without a flag, without a leader. All seemed exhausted, worn out, incapable of thought or resolve, marching onward merely by force of habit, and dropping to the ground with fatigue the moment they halted. One saw, in particular, many enlisted men, peaceful citizens, men who lived quietly on their income, bending beneath the weight of their rifles; and little active volunteers, easily frightened but full of enthusiasm, as eager to attack as they were ready to take to flight; and amid these, a sprinkling of red-breeched soldiers, the pitiful remnant of a division cut down in a great battle; somber artillerymen, side by side with nondescript foot-soldiers; and, here and there, the gleaming helmet of a heavy-footed dragoon who had difficulty in keeping up with the quicker pace of the soldiers of the line. Legions of irregulars with high-sounding names "Avengers of Defeat," "Citizens of the Tomb," "Brethren in Death"—passed in their turn, looking like banditti. Their leaders, former drapers or grain merchants, or tallow or soap chandlers—warriors by force of circumstances, officers by reason of their mustachios or their money—covered with weapons, flannel and gold lace, spoke in an impressive manner, discussed plans of campaign, and behaved as though they alone bore the fortunes of dying France on their braggart shoulders; though, in truth, they frequently were afraid of their own men—scoundrels often brave beyond measure, but pillagers and debauchees.

Rumor had it that the Prussians were about to enter Rouen.

The members of the National Guard, who for the past two months had been reconnoitering with the utmost caution in the neighboring woods, occasionally shooting their own sentinels, and making ready for fight whenever a rabbit rustled in the undergrowth, had now returned to their homes. Their arms, their uniforms, all the death-dealing paraphernalia with which they had terrified all the milestones along the highroad for eight miles round, had suddenly and marvellously disappeared.

The last of the French soldiers had just crossed the Seine on their way to Pont-Audemer, through Saint-Sever and Bourg-Achard, and in their rear the vanquished general, powerless to do aught with the forlorn remnants of his army, himself dismayed at the final overthrow of a nation accustomed to victory and disastrously beaten despite its legendary bravery, walked between two orderlies.

Then a profound calm, a shuddering, silent dread, settled on the city. Many a round-paunched citizen, emasculated by years devoted to business, anxiously awaited the conquerors, trembling lest his roasting-jacks or kitchen knives should be looked upon as weapons.

Life seemed to have stopped short; the shops were shut, the streets deserted. Now and then an inhabitant, awed by the silence, glided swiftly by in the shadow of the walls. The anguish of suspense made men even desire the arrival of the enemy.

In the afternoon of the day following the departure of the French troops, a number of uhlans, coming no one knew whence, passed rapidly through the town. A little later on, a black mass descended St. Catherine's Hill, while two other invading bodies appeared respectively on the Darnetal and the Boisguillaume roads. The advance guards of the three corps arrived at precisely the same moment at the Square of the Hotel de Ville, and the German army poured through all the adjacent streets, its battalions making the pavement ring with their firm, measured tread.

Orders shouted in an unknown, guttural tongue rose to the windows of the seemingly dead, deserted houses; while behind the fast-closed shutters eager eyes peered forth at the victors-masters now of the city, its fortunes, and its lives, by "right of war." The inhabitants, in their darkened rooms, were possessed by that terror which follows in the wake of cataclysms, of deadly upheavals of the earth, against which all human skill and strength are vain. For the same thing happens whenever the established order of things is upset, when security no longer exists, when all those rights usually protected by the law of man or of Nature are at the mercy of unreasoning, savage force. The earthquake crushing a whole nation under falling roofs; the flood let loose, and engulfing in its swirling depths the corpses of drowned peasants, along with dead oxen and beams torn from shattered houses; or the army, covered with glory, murdering those who defend themselves, making prisoners of the rest, pillaging in the name of the Sword, and giving thanks to God to the thunder of cannon—all these are appalling scourges, which destroy all belief in eternal justice, all that confidence we have been taught to feel in the protection of Heaven and the reason of man.

Small detachments of soldiers knocked at each door, and then disappeared within the houses; for the vanquished saw they would have to be civil to their conquerors.

At the end of a short time, once the first terror had subsided, calm was again restored. In many houses the Prussian officer ate at the same table with the family. He was often well-bred, and, out of politeness, expressed sympathy with France and repugnance at being compelled to take part in the war. This sentiment was received with gratitude; besides, his protection might be needful some day or other. By the exercise of tact the number of men quartered in one's house might be reduced; and why should one provoke the hostility of a person on whom one's whole welfare depended? Such conduct would savor less of bravery than of fool-hardiness. And foolhardiness is no longer a failing of the citizens of Rouen as it was in the days when their city earned renown by its heroic defenses. Last of all-final argument based on the national politeness—the folk of Rouen said to one another that it was only right to be civil in one's own house, provided there was no public exhibition of familiarity with the foreigner. Out of doors, therefore, citizen and soldier did not know each other; but in the house both chatted freely, and each evening the German remained a little longer warming himself at the hospitable hearth.

Even the town itself resumed by degrees its ordinary aspect. The French seldom walked abroad, but the streets swarmed with Prussian soldiers. Moreover, the officers of the Blue Hussars, who arrogantly dragged their instruments of death along the pavements, seemed to hold the simple townsmen in but little more contempt than did the French cavalry officers who had drunk at the same cafes the year before.

But there was something in the air, a something strange and subtle, an intolerable foreign atmosphere like a penetrating odor—the odor of invasion. It permeated dwellings and places of public resort, changed the taste of food, made one imagine one's self in far-distant lands, amid dangerous, barbaric tribes.

The conquerors exacted money, much money. The inhabitants paid what was asked; they were rich. But, the wealthier a Norman tradesman becomes, the more he suffers at having to part with anything that belongs to him, at having to see any portion of his substance pass into the hands of another.

Nevertheless, within six or seven miles of the town, along the course of the river as it flows onward to Croisset, Dieppedalle and Biessart, boat-men and fishermen often hauled to the surface of the water the body of a German, bloated in his uniform, killed by a blow from knife or club, his head crushed by a stone, or perchance pushed from some bridge into the stream below. The mud of the river-bed swallowed up these obscure acts of vengeance—savage, yet legitimate; these unrecorded deeds of bravery; these silent attacks fraught with greater danger than battles fought in broad day, and surrounded, moreover, with no halo of romance. For hatred of the foreigner ever arms a few intrepid souls, ready to die for an idea.

At last, as the invaders, though subjecting the town to the strictest discipline, had not committed any of the deeds of horror with which they had been credited while on their triumphal march, the people grew bolder, and the necessities of business again animated the breasts of the local merchants. Some of these had important commercial interests at Havre —occupied at present by the French army—and wished to attempt to reach that port by overland route to Dieppe, taking the boat from there.

Through the influence of the German officers whose acquaintance they had made, they obtained a permit to leave town from the general in command.

A large four-horse coach having, therefore, been engaged for the journey, and ten passengers having given in their names to the proprietor, they decided to start on a certain Tuesday morning before daybreak, to avoid attracting a crowd.

The ground had been frozen hard for some time-past, and about three o'clock on Monday afternoon—large black clouds from the north shed their burden of snow uninterruptedly all through that evening and night.

At half-past four in the morning the travellers met in the courtyard of the Hotel de Normandie, where they were to take their seats in the coach.

They were still half asleep, and shivering with cold under their wraps. They could see one another but indistinctly in the darkness, and the mountain of heavy winter wraps in which each was swathed made them look like a gathering of obese priests in their long cassocks. But two men recognized each other, a third accosted them, and the three began to talk. "I am bringing my wife," said one. "So am I." "And I, too." The first speaker added: "We shall not return to Rouen, and if the Prussians approach Havre we will cross to England." All three, it turned out, had made the same plans, being of similar disposition and temperament.

Still the horses were not harnessed. A small lantern carried by a stable-boy emerged now and then from one dark doorway to disappear immediately in another. The stamping of horses' hoofs, deadened by the dung and straw of the stable, was heard from time to time, and from inside the building issued a man's voice, talking to the animals and swearing at them. A faint tinkle of bells showed that the harness was being got ready; this tinkle soon developed into a continuous jingling, louder or softer according to the movements of the horse, sometimes stopping altogether, then breaking out in a sudden peal accompanied by a pawing of the ground by an iron-shod hoof.

The door suddenly closed. All noise ceased.

The frozen townsmen were silent; they remained motionless, stiff with cold.

A thick curtain of glistening white flakes fell ceaselessly to the ground; it obliterated all outlines, enveloped all objects in an icy mantle of foam; nothing was to be heard throughout the length and breadth of the silent, winter-bound city save the vague, nameless rustle of falling snow—a sensation rather than a sound—the gentle mingling of light atoms which seemed to fill all space, to cover the whole world.

The man reappeared with his lantern, leading by a rope a melancholy-looking horse, evidently being led out against his inclination. The hostler placed him beside the pole, fastened the traces, and spent some time in walking round him to make sure that the harness was all right; for he could use only one hand, the other being engaged in holding the lantern. As he was about to fetch the second horse he noticed the motionless group of travellers, already white with snow, and said to them: "Why don't you get inside the coach? You'd be under shelter, at least."

This did not seem to have occurred to them, and they at once took his advice. The three men seated their wives at the far end of the coach, then got in themselves; lastly the other vague, snow-shrouded forms clambered to the remaining places without a word.

The floor was covered with straw, into which the feet sank. The ladies at the far end, having brought with them little copper foot-warmers heated by means of a kind of chemical fuel, proceeded to light these, and spent some time in expatiating in low tones on their advantages, saying over and over again things which they had all known for a long time.

At last, six horses instead of four having been harnessed to the diligence, on account of the heavy roads, a voice outside asked: "Is every one there?" To which a voice from the interior replied: "Yes," and they set out.

The vehicle moved slowly, slowly, at a snail's pace; the wheels sank into the snow; the entire body of the coach creaked and groaned; the horses slipped, puffed, steamed, and the coachman's long whip cracked incessantly, flying hither and thither, coiling up, then flinging out its length like a slender serpent, as it lashed some rounded flank, which instantly grew tense as it strained in further effort.

But the day grew apace. Those light flakes which one traveller, a native of Rouen, had compared to a rain of cotton fell no longer. A murky light filtered through dark, heavy clouds, which made the country more dazzlingly white by contrast, a whiteness broken sometimes by a row of tall trees spangled with hoarfrost, or by a cottage roof hooded in snow.

Within the coach the passengers eyed one another curiously in the dim light of dawn.

Right at the back, in the best seats of all, Monsieur and Madame Loiseau, wholesale wine merchants of the Rue Grand-Pont, slumbered opposite each other. Formerly clerk to a merchant who had failed in business, Loiseau had bought his master's interest, and made a fortune for himself. He sold very bad wine at a very low price to the retail-dealers in the country, and had the reputation, among his friends and acquaintances, of being a shrewd rascal a true Norman, full of quips and wiles. So well established was his character as a cheat that, in the mouths of the citizens of Rouen, the very name of Loiseau became a byword for sharp practice.

Above and beyond this, Loiseau was noted for his practical jokes of every description—his tricks, good or ill-natured; and no one could mention his name without adding at once: "He's an extraordinary man—Loiseau." He was undersized and potbellied, had a florid face with grayish whiskers.

His wife-tall, strong, determined, with a loud voice and decided manner —represented the spirit of order and arithmetic in the business house which Loiseau enlivened by his jovial activity.

Beside them, dignified in bearing, belonging to a superior caste, sat Monsieur Carre-Lamadon, a man of considerable importance, a king in the cotton trade, proprietor of three spinning-mills, officer of the Legion of Honor, and member of the General Council. During the whole time the Empire was in the ascendancy he remained the chief of the well-disposed Opposition, merely in order to command a higher value for his devotion when he should rally to the cause which he meanwhile opposed with "courteous weapons," to use his own expression.

Madame Carre-Lamadon, much younger than her husband, was the consolation of all the officers of good family quartered at Rouen. Pretty, slender, graceful, she sat opposite her husband, curled up in her furs, and gazing mournfully at the sorry interior of the coach.

Her neighbors, the Comte and Comtesse Hubert de Breville, bore one of the noblest and most ancient names in Normandy. The count, a nobleman advanced in years and of aristocratic bearing, strove to enhance by every artifice of the toilet, his natural resemblance to King Henry IV, who, according to a legend of which the family were inordinately proud, had been the favored lover of a De Breville lady, and father of her child —the frail one's husband having, in recognition of this fact, been made a count and governor of a province.

A colleague of Monsieur Carre-Lamadon in the General Council, Count Hubert represented the Orleanist party in his department. The story of his marriage with the daughter of a small shipowner at Nantes had always remained more or less of a mystery. But as the countess had an air of unmistakable breeding, entertained faultlessly, and was even supposed to have been loved by a son of Louis-Philippe, the nobility vied with one another in doing her honor, and her drawing-room remained the most select in the whole countryside—the only one which retained the old spirit of gallantry, and to which access was not easy.

The fortune of the Brevilles, all in real estate, amounted, it was said, to five hundred thousand francs a year.

These six people occupied the farther end of the coach, and represented Society—with an income—the strong, established society of good people with religion and principle.

It happened by chance that all the women were seated on the same side; and the countess had, moreover, as neighbors two nuns, who spent the time in fingering their long rosaries and murmuring paternosters and aves. One of them was old, and so deeply pitted with smallpox that she looked for all the world as if she had received a charge of shot full in the face. The other, of sickly appearance, had a pretty but wasted countenance, and a narrow, consumptive chest, sapped by that devouring faith which is the making of martyrs and visionaries.

A man and woman, sitting opposite the two nuns, attracted all eyes.

The man—a well-known character—was Cornudet, the democrat, the terror of all respectable people. For the past twenty years his big red beard had been on terms of intimate acquaintance with the tankards of all the republican cafes. With the help of his comrades and brethren he had dissipated a respectable fortune left him by his father, an old-established confectioner, and he now impatiently awaited the Republic, that he might at last be rewarded with the post he had earned by his revolutionary orgies. On the fourth of September—possibly as the result of a practical joke—he was led to believe that he had been appointed prefect; but when he attempted to take up the duties of the position the clerks in charge of the office refused to recognize his authority, and he was compelled in consequence to retire. A good sort of fellow in other respects, inoffensive and obliging, he had thrown himself zealously into the work of making an organized defence of the town. He had had pits dug in the level country, young forest trees felled, and traps set on all the roads; then at the approach of the enemy, thoroughly satisfied with his preparations, he had hastily returned to the town. He thought he might now do more good at Havre, where new intrenchments would soon be necessary.

The woman, who belonged to the courtesan class, was celebrated for an embonpoint unusual for her age, which had earned for her the sobriquet of "Boule de Suif" (Tallow Ball). Short and round, fat as a pig, with puffy fingers constricted at the joints, looking like rows of short sausages; with a shiny, tightly-stretched skin and an enormous bust filling out the bodice of her dress, she was yet attractive and much sought after, owing to her fresh and pleasing appearance. Her face was like a crimson apple, a peony-bud just bursting into bloom; she had two magnificent dark eyes, fringed with thick, heavy lashes, which cast a shadow into their depths; her mouth was small, ripe, kissable, and was furnished with the tiniest of white teeth.

As soon as she was recognized the respectable matrons of the party began to whisper among themselves, and the words "hussy" and "public scandal" were uttered so loudly that Boule de Suif raised her head. She forthwith cast such a challenging, bold look at her neighbors that a sudden silence fell on the company, and all lowered their eyes, with the exception of Loiseau, who watched her with evident interest.

But conversation was soon resumed among the three ladies, whom the presence of this girl had suddenly drawn together in the bonds of friendship—one might almost say in those of intimacy. They decided that they ought to combine, as it were, in their dignity as wives in face of this shameless hussy; for legitimized love always despises its easygoing brother.

The three men, also, brought together by a certain conservative instinct awakened by the presence of Cornudet, spoke of money matters in a tone expressive of contempt for the poor. Count Hubert related the losses he had sustained at the hands of the Prussians, spoke of the cattle which had been stolen from him, the crops which had been ruined, with the easy manner of a nobleman who was also a tenfold millionaire, and whom such reverses would scarcely inconvenience for a single year. Monsieur Carre-Lamadon, a man of wide experience in the cotton industry, had taken care to send six hundred thousand francs to England as provision against the rainy day he was always anticipating. As for Loiseau, he had managed to sell to the French commissariat department all the wines he had in stock, so that the state now owed him a considerable sum, which he hoped to receive at Havre.

And all three eyed one another in friendly, well-disposed fashion. Although of varying social status, they were united in the brotherhood of money—in that vast freemasonry made up of those who possess, who can jingle gold wherever they choose to put their hands into their breeches' pockets.

The coach went along so slowly that at ten o'clock in the morning it had not covered twelve miles. Three times the men of the party got out and climbed the hills on foot. The passengers were becoming uneasy, for they had counted on lunching at Totes, and it seemed now as if they would hardly arrive there before nightfall. Every one was eagerly looking out for an inn by the roadside, when, suddenly, the coach foundered in a snowdrift, and it took two hours to extricate it.

As appetites increased, their spirits fell; no inn, no wine shop could be discovered, the approach of the Prussians and the transit of the starving French troops having frightened away all business.

The men sought food in the farmhouses beside the road, but could not find so much as a crust of bread; for the suspicious peasant invariably hid his stores for fear of being pillaged by the soldiers, who, being entirely without food, would take violent possession of everything they found.

About one o'clock Loiseau announced that he positively had a big hollow in his stomach. They had all been suffering in the same way for some time, and the increasing gnawings of hunger had put an end to all conversation.

Now and then some one yawned, another followed his example, and each in turn, according to his character, breeding and social position, yawned either quietly or noisily, placing his hand before the gaping void whence issued breath condensed into vapor.

Several times Boule de Suif stooped, as if searching for something under her petticoats. She would hesitate a moment, look at her neighbors, and then quietly sit upright again. All faces were pale and drawn. Loiseau declared he would give a thousand francs for a knuckle of ham. His wife made an involuntary and quickly checked gesture of protest. It always hurt her to hear of money being squandered, and she could not even understand jokes on such a subject.

"As a matter of fact, I don't feel well," said the count. "Why did I not think of bringing provisions?" Each one reproached himself in similar fashion.

Cornudet, however, had a bottle of rum, which he offered to his neighbors. They all coldly refused except Loiseau, who took a sip, and returned the bottle with thanks, saying: "That's good stuff; it warms one up, and cheats the appetite." The alcohol put him in good humor, and he proposed they should do as the sailors did in the song: eat the fattest of the passengers. This indirect allusion to Boule de Suif shocked the respectable members of the party. No one replied; only Cornudet smiled. The two good sisters had ceased to mumble their rosary, and, with hands enfolded in their wide sleeves, sat motionless, their eyes steadfastly cast down, doubtless offering up as a sacrifice to Heaven the suffering it had sent them.

At last, at three o'clock, as they were in the midst of an apparently limitless plain, with not a single village in sight, Boule de Suif stooped quickly, and drew from underneath the seat a large basket covered with a white napkin.

From this she extracted first of all a small earthenware plate and a silver drinking cup, then an enormous dish containing two whole chickens cut into joints and imbedded in jelly. The basket was seen to contain other good things: pies, fruit, dainties of all sorts-provisions, in fine, for a three days' journey, rendering their owner independent of wayside inns. The necks of four bottles protruded from among the food. She took a chicken wing, and began to eat it daintily, together with one of those rolls called in Normandy "Regence."

All looks were directed toward her. An odor of food filled the air, causing nostrils to dilate, mouths to water, and jaws to contract painfully. The scorn of the ladies for this disreputable female grew positively ferocious; they would have liked to kill her, or throw, her and her drinking cup, her basket, and her provisions, out of the coach into the snow of the road below.

But Loiseau's gaze was fixed greedily on the dish of chicken. He said:

"Well, well, this lady had more forethought than the rest of us. Some people think of everything."

She looked up at him.

"Would you like some, sir? It is hard to go on fasting all day."

He bowed.

"Upon my soul, I can't refuse; I cannot hold out another minute. All is fair in war time, is it not, madame?" And, casting a glance on those around, he added:

"At times like this it is very pleasant to meet with obliging people."

He spread a newspaper over his knees to avoid soiling his trousers, and, with a pocketknife he always carried, helped himself to a chicken leg coated with jelly, which he thereupon proceeded to devour.

Then Boule le Suif, in low, humble tones, invited the nuns to partake of her repast. They both accepted the offer unhesitatingly, and after a few stammered words of thanks began to eat quickly, without raising their eyes. Neither did Cornudet refuse his neighbor's offer, and, in combination with the nuns, a sort of table was formed by opening out the newspaper over the four pairs of knees.

Mouths kept opening and shutting, ferociously masticating and devouring the food. Loiseau, in his corner, was hard at work, and in low tones urged his wife to follow his example. She held out for a long time, but overstrained Nature gave way at last. Her husband, assuming his politest manner, asked their "charming companion" if he might be allowed to offer Madame Loiseau a small helping.

"Why, certainly, sir," she replied, with an amiable smile, holding out the dish.

When the first bottle of claret was opened some embarrassment was caused by the fact that there was only one drinking cup, but this was passed from one to another, after being wiped. Cornudet alone, doubtless in a spirit of gallantry, raised to his own lips that part of the rim which was still moist from those of his fair neighbor.

Then, surrounded by people who were eating, and well-nigh suffocated by the odor of food, the Comte and Comtesse de Breville and Monsieur and Madame Carre-Lamadon endured that hateful form of torture which has perpetuated the name of Tantalus. All at once the manufacturer's young wife heaved a sigh which made every one turn and look at her; she was white as the snow without; her eyes closed, her head fell forward; she had fainted. Her husband, beside himself, implored the help of his neighbors. No one seemed to know what to do until the elder of the two nuns, raising the patient's head, placed Boule de Suif's drinking cup to her lips, and made her swallow a few drops of wine. The pretty invalid moved, opened her eyes, smiled, and declared in a feeble voice that she was all right again. But, to prevent a recurrence of the catastrophe, the nun made her drink a cupful of claret, adding: "It's just hunger —that's what is wrong with you."

Then Boule de Suif, blushing and embarrassed, stammered, looking at the four passengers who were still fasting:

"'Mon Dieu', if I might offer these ladies and gentlemen——"

She stopped short, fearing a snub. But Loiseau continued:

"Hang it all, in such a case as this we are all brothers and sisters and ought to assist each other. Come, come, ladies, don't stand on ceremony, for goodness' sake! Do we even know whether we shall find a house in which to pass the night? At our present rate of going we sha'n't be at Totes till midday to-morrow."

They hesitated, no one daring to be the first to accept. But the count settled the question. He turned toward the abashed girl, and in his most distinguished manner said:

"We accept gratefully, madame."

As usual, it was only the first step that cost. This Rubicon once crossed, they set to work with a will. The basket was emptied. It still contained a pate de foie gras, a lark pie, a piece of smoked tongue, Crassane pears, Pont-Leveque gingerbread, fancy cakes, and a cup full of pickled gherkins and onions—Boule de Suif, like all women, being very fond of indigestible things.

They could not eat this girl's provisions without speaking to her. So they began to talk, stiffly at first; then, as she seemed by no means forward, with greater freedom. Mesdames de Breville and Carre-Lamadon, who were accomplished women of the world, were gracious and tactful. The countess especially displayed that amiable condescension characteristic of great ladies whom no contact with baser mortals can sully, and was absolutely charming. But the sturdy Madame Loiseau, who had the soul of a gendarme, continued morose, speaking little and eating much.

Conversation naturally turned on the war. Terrible stories were told about the Prussians, deeds of bravery were recounted of the French; and all these people who were fleeing themselves were ready to pay homage to the courage of their compatriots. Personal experiences soon followed, and Bottle le Suif related with genuine emotion, and with that warmth of language not uncommon in women of her class and temperament, how it came about that she had left Rouen.

"I thought at first that I should be able to stay," she said. "My house was well stocked with provisions, and it seemed better to put up with feeding a few soldiers than to banish myself goodness knows where. But when I saw these Prussians it was too much for me! My blood boiled with rage; I wept the whole day for very shame. Oh, if only I had been a man! I looked at them from my window— the fat swine, with their pointed helmets!—and my maid held my hands to keep me from throwing my furniture down on them. Then some of them were quartered on me; I flew at the throat of the first one who entered. They are just as easy to strangle as other men! And I'd have been the death of that one if I hadn't been dragged away from him by my hair. I had to hide after that. And as soon as I could get an opportunity I left the place, and here I am."

She was warmly congratulated. She rose in the estimation of her companions, who had not been so brave; and Cornudet listened to her with the approving and benevolent smile of an apostle, the smile a priest might wear in listening to a devotee praising God; for long-bearded democrats of his type have a monopoly of patriotism, just as priests have a monopoly of religion. He held forth in turn, with dogmatic self-assurance, in the style of the proclamations daily pasted on the walls of the town, winding up with a specimen of stump oratory in which he reviled "that besotted fool of a Louis-Napoleon."

But Boule de Suif was indignant, for she was an ardent Bonapartist. She turned as red as a cherry, and stammered in her wrath: "I'd just like to have seen you in his place—you and your sort! There would have been a nice mix-up. Oh, yes! It was you who betrayed that man. It would be impossible to live in France if we were governed by such rascals as you!"

Cornudet, unmoved by this tirade, still smiled a superior, contemptuous smile; and one felt that high words were impending, when the count interposed, and, not without difficulty, succeeded in calming the exasperated woman, saying that all sincere opinions ought to be respected. But the countess and the manufacturer's wife, imbued with the unreasoning hatred of the upper classes for the Republic, and instinct, moreover, with the affection felt by all women for the pomp and circumstance of despotic government, were drawn, in spite of themselves, toward this dignified young woman, whose opinions coincided so closely with their own.

The basket was empty. The ten people had finished its contents without difficulty amid general regret that it did not hold more. Conversation went on a little longer, though it flagged somewhat after the passengers had finished eating.

Night fell, the darkness grew deeper and deeper, and the cold made Boule de Suif shiver, in spite of her plumpness. So Madame de Breville offered her her foot-warmer, the fuel of which had been several times renewed since the morning, and she accepted the offer at once, for her feet were icy cold. Mesdames Carre-Lamadon and Loiseau gave theirs to the nuns.

The driver lighted his lanterns. They cast a bright gleam on a cloud of vapor which hovered over the sweating flanks of the horses, and on the roadside snow, which seemed to unroll as they went along in the changing light of the lamps.

All was now indistinguishable in the coach; but suddenly a movement occurred in the corner occupied by Boule de Suif and Cornudet; and Loiseau, peering into the gloom, fancied he saw the big, bearded democrat move hastily to one side, as if he had received a well-directed, though noiseless, blow in the dark.

Tiny lights glimmered ahead. It was Totes. The coach had been on the road eleven hours, which, with the three hours allotted the horses in four periods for feeding and breathing, made fourteen. It entered the town, and stopped before the Hotel du Commerce.

The coach door opened; a well-known noise made all the travellers start; it was the clanging of a scabbard, on the pavement; then a voice called out something in German.

Although the coach had come to a standstill, no one got out; it looked as if they were afraid of being murdered the moment they left their seats. Thereupon the driver appeared, holding in his hand one of his lanterns, which cast a sudden glow on the interior of the coach, lighting up the double row of startled faces, mouths agape, and eyes wide open in surprise and terror.

Beside the driver stood in the full light a German officer, a tall young man, fair and slender, tightly encased in his uniform like a woman in her corset, his flat shiny cap, tilted to one side of his head, making him look like an English hotel runner. His exaggerated mustache, long and straight and tapering to a point at either end in a single blond hair that could hardly be seen, seemed to weigh down the corners of his mouth and give a droop to his lips.

In Alsatian French he requested the travellers to alight, saying stiffly:

"Kindly get down, ladies and gentlemen."

The two nuns were the first to obey, manifesting the docility of holy women accustomed to submission on every occasion. Next appeared the count and countess, followed by the manufacturer and his wife, after whom came Loiseau, pushing his larger and better half before him.

"Good-day, sir," he said to the officer as he put his foot to the ground, acting on an impulse born of prudence rather than of politeness. The other, insolent like all in authority, merely stared without replying.

Boule de Suif and Cornudet, though near the door, were the last to alight, grave and dignified before the enemy. The stout girl tried to control herself and appear calm; the democrat stroked his long russet beard with a somewhat trembling hand. Both strove to maintain their dignity, knowing well that at such a time each individual is always looked upon as more or less typical of his nation; and, also, resenting the complaisant attitude of their companions, Boule de Suif tried to wear a bolder front than her neighbors, the virtuous women, while he, feeling that it was incumbent on him to set a good example, kept up the attitude of resistance which he had first assumed when he undertook to mine the high roads round Rouen.

They entered the spacious kitchen of the inn, and the German, having demanded the passports signed by the general in command, in which were mentioned the name, description and profession of each traveller, inspected them all minutely, comparing their appearance with the written particulars.

Then he said brusquely: "All right," and turned on his heel.

They breathed freely, All were still hungry; so supper was ordered. Half an hour was required for its preparation, and while two servants were apparently engaged in getting it ready the travellers went to look at their rooms. These all opened off a long corridor, at the end of which was a glazed door with a number on it.

They were just about to take their seats at table when the innkeeper appeared in person. He was a former horse dealer—a large, asthmatic individual, always wheezing, coughing, and clearing his throat. Follenvie was his patronymic.

He called:

"Mademoiselle Elisabeth Rousset?"

Boule de Suif started, and turned round.

"That is my name."

"Mademoiselle, the Prussian officer wishes to speak to you immediately."

"To me?"

"Yes; if you are Mademoiselle Elisabeth Rousset."

She hesitated, reflected a moment, and then declared roundly:

"That may be; but I'm not going."

They moved restlessly around her; every one wondered and speculated as to the cause of this order. The count approached:

"You are wrong, madame, for your refusal may bring trouble not only on yourself but also on all your companions. It never pays to resist those in authority. Your compliance with this request cannot possibly be fraught with any danger; it has probably been made because some formality or other was forgotten."

All added their voices to that of the count; Boule de Suif was begged, urged, lectured, and at last convinced; every one was afraid of the complications which might result from headstrong action on her part. She said finally:

"I am doing it for your sakes, remember that!"

The countess took her hand.

"And we are grateful to you."

She left the room. All waited for her return before commencing the meal. Each was distressed that he or she had not been sent for rather than this impulsive, quick-tempered girl, and each mentally rehearsed platitudes in case of being summoned also.

But at the end of ten minutes she reappeared breathing hard, crimson with indignation.

"Oh! the scoundrel! the scoundrel!" she stammered.

All were anxious to know what had happened; but she declined to enlighten them, and when the count pressed the point, she silenced him with much dignity, saying:

"No; the matter has nothing to do with you, and I cannot speak of it."

Then they took their places round a high soup tureen, from which issued an odor of cabbage. In spite of this coincidence, the supper was cheerful. The cider was good; the Loiseaus and the nuns drank it from motives of economy. The others ordered wine; Cornudet demanded beer. He had his own fashion of uncorking the bottle and making the beer foam, gazing at it as he inclined his glass and then raised it to a position between the lamp and his eye that he might judge of its color. When he drank, his great beard, which matched the color of his favorite beverage, seemed to tremble with affection; his eyes positively squinted in the endeavor not to lose sight of the beloved glass, and he looked for all the world as if he were fulfilling the only function for which he was born. He seemed to have established in his mind an affinity between the two great passions of his life—pale ale and revolution—and assuredly he could not taste the one without dreaming of the other.

Monsieur and Madame Follenvie dined at the end of the table. The man, wheezing like a broken-down locomotive, was too short-winded to talk when he was eating. But the wife was not silent a moment; she told how the Prussians had impressed her on their arrival, what they did, what they said; execrating them in the first place because they cost her money, and in the second because she had two sons in the army. She addressed herself principally to the countess, flattered at the opportunity of talking to a lady of quality.

Then she lowered her voice, and began to broach delicate subjects. Her husband interrupted her from time to time, saying:

"You would do well to hold your tongue, Madame Follenvie."

But she took no notice of him, and went on:

"Yes, madame, these Germans do nothing but eat potatoes and pork, and then pork and potatoes. And don't imagine for a moment that they are clean! No, indeed! And if only you saw them drilling for hours, indeed for days, together; they all collect in a field, then they do nothing but march backward and forward, and wheel this way and that. If only they would cultivate the land, or remain at home and work on their high roads! Really, madame, these soldiers are of no earthly use! Poor people have to feed and keep them, only in order that they may learn how to kill! True, I am only an old woman with no education, but when I see them wearing themselves out marching about from morning till night, I say to myself: When there are people who make discoveries that are of use to people, why should others take so much trouble to do harm? Really, now, isn't it a terrible thing to kill people, whether they are Prussians, or English, or Poles, or French? If we revenge ourselves on any one who injures us we do wrong, and are punished for it; but when our sons are shot down like partridges, that is all right, and decorations are given to the man who kills the most. No, indeed, I shall never be able to understand it."

Cornudet raised his voice:

"War is a barbarous proceeding when we attack a peaceful neighbor, but it is a sacred duty when undertaken in defence of one's country."

The old woman looked down:

"Yes; it's another matter when one acts in self-defence; but would it not be better to kill all the kings, seeing that they make war just to amuse themselves?"

Cornudet's eyes kindled.

"Bravo, citizens!" he said.

Monsieur Carre-Lamadon was reflecting profoundly. Although an ardent admirer of great generals, the peasant woman's sturdy common sense made him reflect on the wealth which might accrue to a country by the employment of so many idle hands now maintained at a great expense, of so much unproductive force, if they were employed in those great industrial enterprises which it will take centuries to complete.

But Loiseau, leaving his seat, went over to the innkeeper and began chatting in a low voice. The big man chuckled, coughed, sputtered; his enormous carcass shook with merriment at the pleasantries of the other; and he ended by buying six casks of claret from Loiseau to be delivered in spring, after the departure of the Prussians.

The moment supper was over every one went to bed, worn out with fatigue.

But Loiseau, who had been making his observations on the sly, sent his wife to bed, and amused himself by placing first his ear, and then his eye, to the bedroom keyhole, in order to discover what he called "the mysteries of the corridor."

At the end of about an hour he heard a rustling, peeped out quickly, and caught sight of Boule de Suif, looking more rotund than ever in a dressing-gown of blue cashmere trimmed with white lace. She held a candle in her hand, and directed her steps to the numbered door at the end of the corridor. But one of the side doors was partly opened, and when, at the end of a few minutes, she returned, Cornudet, in his shirt-sleeves, followed her. They spoke in low tones, then stopped short. Boule de Suif seemed to be stoutly denying him admission to her room. Unfortunately, Loiseau could not at first hear what they said; but toward the end of the conversation they raised their voices, and he caught a few words. Cornudet was loudly insistent.

"How silly you are! What does it matter to you?" he said.

She seemed indignant, and replied:

"No, my good man, there are times when one does not do that sort of thing; besides, in this place it would be shameful."

Apparently he did not understand, and asked the reason. Then she lost her temper and her caution, and, raising her voice still higher, said:

"Why? Can't you understand why? When there are Prussians in the house! Perhaps even in the very next room!"

He was silent. The patriotic shame of this wanton, who would not suffer herself to be caressed in the neighborhood of the enemy, must have roused his dormant dignity, for after bestowing on her a simple kiss he crept softly back to his room. Loiseau, much edified, capered round the bedroom before taking his place beside his slumbering spouse.

Then silence reigned throughout the house. But soon there arose from some remote part—it might easily have been either cellar or attic—a stertorous, monotonous, regular snoring, a dull, prolonged rumbling, varied by tremors like those of a boiler under pressure of steam. Monsieur Follenvie had gone to sleep.

As they had decided on starting at eight o'clock the next morning, every one was in the kitchen at that hour; but the coach, its roof covered with snow, stood by itself in the middle of the yard, without either horses or driver. They sought the latter in the stables, coach-houses and barns —but in vain. So the men of the party resolved to scour the country for him, and sallied forth. They found themselves in the square, with the church at the farther side, and to right and left low-roofed houses where there were some Prussian soldiers. The first soldier they saw was peeling potatoes. The second, farther on, was washing out a barber's shop. Another, bearded to the eyes, was fondling a crying infant, and dandling it on his knees to quiet it; and the stout peasant women, whose men-folk were for the most part at the war, were, by means of signs, telling their obedient conquerors what work they were to do: chop wood, prepare soup, grind coffee; one of them even was doing the washing for his hostess, an infirm old grandmother.

The count, astonished at what he saw, questioned the beadle who was coming out of the presbytery. The old man answered:

"Oh, those men are not at all a bad sort; they are not Prussians, I am told; they come from somewhere farther off, I don't exactly know where. And they have all left wives and children behind them; they are not fond of war either, you may be sure! I am sure they are mourning for the men where they come from, just as we do here; and the war causes them just as much unhappiness as it does us. As a matter of fact, things are not so very bad here just now, because the soldiers do no harm, and work just as if they were in their own homes. You see, sir, poor folk always help one another; it is the great ones of this world who make war."

Cornudet indignant at the friendly understanding established between conquerors and conquered, withdrew, preferring to shut himself up in the inn.

"They are repeopling the country," jested Loiseau.

"They are undoing the harm they have done," said Monsieur Carre-Lamadon gravely.

But they could not find the coach driver. At last he was discovered in the village cafe, fraternizing cordially with the officer's orderly.

"Were you not told to harness the horses at eight o'clock?" demanded the count.

"Oh, yes; but I've had different orders since."

"What orders?"

"Not to harness at all."

"Who gave you such orders?"

"Why, the Prussian officer."

"But why?"

"I don't know. Go and ask him. I am forbidden to harness the horses, so I don't harness them—that's all."

"Did he tell you so himself?"

"No, sir; the innkeeper gave me the order from him."

"When?"

"Last evening, just as I was going to bed."

The three men returned in a very uneasy frame of mind.

They asked for Monsieur Follenvie, but the servant replied that on account of his asthma he never got up before ten o'clock. They were strictly forbidden to rouse him earlier, except in case of fire.

They wished to see the officer, but that also was impossible, although he lodged in the inn. Monsieur Follenvie alone was authorized to interview him on civil matters. So they waited. The women returned to their rooms, and occupied themselves with trivial matters.

Cornudet settled down beside the tall kitchen fireplace, before a blazing fire. He had a small table and a jug of beer placed beside him, and he smoked his pipe—a pipe which enjoyed among democrats a consideration almost equal to his own, as though it had served its country in serving Cornudet. It was a fine meerschaum, admirably colored to a black the shade of its owner's teeth, but sweet-smelling, gracefully curved, at home in its master's hand, and completing his physiognomy. And Cornudet sat motionless, his eyes fixed now on the dancing flames, now on the froth which crowned his beer; and after each draught he passed his long, thin fingers with an air of satisfaction through his long, greasy hair, as he sucked the foam from his mustache.

Loiseau, under pretence of stretching his legs, went out to see if he could sell wine to the country dealers. The count and the manufacturer began to talk politics. They forecast the future of France. One believed in the Orleans dynasty, the other in an unknown savior—a hero who should rise up in the last extremity: a Du Guesclin, perhaps a Joan of Arc? or another Napoleon the First? Ah! if only the Prince Imperial were not so young! Cornudet, listening to them, smiled like a man who holds the keys of destiny in his hands. His pipe perfumed the whole kitchen.

As the clock struck ten, Monsieur Follenvie appeared. He was immediately surrounded and questioned, but could only repeat, three or four times in succession, and without variation, the words:

"The officer said to me, just like this: 'Monsieur Follenvie, you will forbid them to harness up the coach for those travellers to-morrow. They are not to start without an order from me. You hear? That is sufficient.'"

Then they asked to see the officer. The count sent him his card, on which Monsieur Carre-Lamadon also inscribed his name and titles. The Prussian sent word that the two men would be admitted to see him after his luncheon—that is to say, about one o'clock.

The ladies reappeared, and they all ate a little, in spite of their anxiety. Boule de Suif appeared ill and very much worried.

They were finishing their coffee when the orderly came to fetch the gentlemen.

Loiseau joined the other two; but when they tried to get Cornudet to accompany them, by way of adding greater solemnity to the occasion, he declared proudly that he would never have anything to do with the Germans, and, resuming his seat in the chimney corner, he called for another jug of beer.

The three men went upstairs, and were ushered into the best room in the inn, where the officer received them lolling at his ease in an armchair, his feet on the mantelpiece, smoking a long porcelain pipe, and enveloped in a gorgeous dressing-gown, doubtless stolen from the deserted dwelling of some citizen destitute of taste in dress. He neither rose, greeted them, nor even glanced in their direction. He afforded a fine example of that insolence of bearing which seems natural to the victorious soldier.

After the lapse of a few moments he said in his halting French:

"What do you want?"

"We wish to start on our journey," said the count.

"No."

"May I ask the reason of your refusal?"

"Because I don't choose."

"I would respectfully call your attention, monsieur, to the fact that your general in command gave us a permit to proceed to Dieppe; and I do not think we have done anything to deserve this harshness at your hands."

"I don't choose—that's all. You may go."

They bowed, and retired.

The afternoon was wretched. They could not understand the caprice of this German, and the strangest ideas came into their heads. They all congregated in the kitchen, and talked the subject to death, imagining all kinds of unlikely things. Perhaps they were to be kept as hostages —but for what reason? or to be extradited as prisoners of war? or possibly they were to be held for ransom? They were panic-stricken at this last supposition. The richest among them were the most alarmed, seeing themselves forced to empty bags of gold into the insolent soldier's hands in order to buy back their lives. They racked their brains for plausible lies whereby they might conceal the fact that they were rich, and pass themselves off as poor—very poor. Loiseau took off his watch chain, and put it in his pocket. The approach of night increased their apprehension. The lamp was lighted, and as it wanted yet two hours to dinner Madame Loiseau proposed a game of trente et un. It would distract their thoughts. The rest agreed, and Cornudet himself joined the party, first putting out his pipe for politeness' sake.

The count shuffled the cards—dealt—and Boule de Suif had thirty-one to start with; soon the interest of the game assuaged the anxiety of the players. But Cornudet noticed that Loiseau and his wife were in league to cheat.

They were about to sit down to dinner when Monsieur Follenvie appeared, and in his grating voice announced:

"The Prussian officer sends to ask Mademoiselle Elisabeth Rousset if she has changed her mind yet."

Boule de Suif stood still, pale as death. Then, suddenly turning crimson with anger, she gasped out:

"Kindly tell that scoundrel, that cur, that carrion of a Prussian, that I will never consent—you understand?—never, never, never!"

The fat innkeeper left the room. Then Boule de Suif was surrounded, questioned, entreated on all sides to reveal the mystery of her visit to the officer. She refused at first; but her wrath soon got the better of her.

"What does he want? He wants to make me his mistress!" she cried.

No one was shocked at the word, so great was the general indignation. Cornudet broke his jug as he banged it down on the table. A loud outcry arose against this base soldier. All were furious. They drew together in common resistance against the foe, as if some part of the sacrifice exacted of Boule de Suif had been demanded of each. The count declared, with supreme disgust, that those people behaved like ancient barbarians. The women, above all, manifested a lively and tender sympathy for Boule de Suif. The nuns, who appeared only at meals, cast down their eyes, and said nothing.

They dined, however, as soon as the first indignant outburst had subsided; but they spoke little and thought much.

The ladies went to bed early; and the men, having lighted their pipes, proposed a game of ecarte, in which Monsieur Follenvie was invited to join, the travellers hoping to question him skillfully as to the best means of vanquishing the officer's obduracy. But he thought of nothing but his cards, would listen to nothing, reply to nothing, and repeated, time after time: "Attend to the game, gentlemen! attend to the game!" So absorbed was his attention that he even forgot to expectorate. The consequence was that his chest gave forth rumbling sounds like those of an organ. His wheezing lungs struck every note of the asthmatic scale, from deep, hollow tones to a shrill, hoarse piping resembling that of a young cock trying to crow.

He refused to go to bed when his wife, overcome with sleep, came to fetch him. So she went off alone, for she was an early bird, always up with the sun; while he was addicted to late hours, ever ready to spend the night with friends. He merely said: "Put my egg-nogg by the fire," and went on with the game. When the other men saw that nothing was to be got out of him they declared it was time to retire, and each sought his bed.

They rose fairly early the next morning, with a vague hope of being allowed to start, a greater desire than ever to do so, and a terror at having to spend another day in this wretched little inn.

Alas! the horses remained in the stable, the driver was invisible. They spent their time, for want of something better to do, in wandering round the coach.

Luncheon was a gloomy affair; and there was a general coolness toward Boule de Suif, for night, which brings counsel, had somewhat modified the judgment of her companions. In the cold light of the morning they almost bore a grudge against the girl for not having secretly sought out the Prussian, that the rest of the party might receive a joyful surprise when they awoke. What more simple?

Besides, who would have been the wiser? She might have saved appearances by telling the officer that she had taken pity on their distress. Such a step would be of so little consequence to her.

But no one as yet confessed to such thoughts.

In the afternoon, seeing that they were all bored to death, the count proposed a walk in the neighborhood of the village. Each one wrapped himself up well, and the little party set out, leaving behind only Cornudet, who preferred to sit over the fire, and the two nuns, who were in the habit of spending their day in the church or at the presbytery.

The cold, which grew more intense each day, almost froze the noses and ears of the pedestrians, their feet began to pain them so that each step was a penance, and when they reached the open country it looked so mournful and depressing in its limitless mantle of white that they all hastily retraced their steps, with bodies benumbed and hearts heavy.

The four women walked in front, and the three men followed a little in their rear.

Loiseau, who saw perfectly well how matters stood, asked suddenly "if that trollop were going to keep them waiting much longer in this Godforsaken spot." The count, always courteous, replied that they could not exact so painful a sacrifice from any woman, and that the first move must come from herself. Monsieur Carre-Lamadon remarked that if the French, as they talked of doing, made a counter attack by way of Dieppe, their encounter with the enemy must inevitably take place at Totes. This reflection made the other two anxious.

"Supposing we escape on foot?" said Loiseau.

The count shrugged his shoulders.

"How can you think of such a thing, in this snow? And with our wives? Besides, we should be pursued at once, overtaken in ten minutes, and brought back as prisoners at the mercy of the soldiery."

This was true enough; they were silent.

The ladies talked of dress, but a certain constraint seemed to prevail among them.

Suddenly, at the end of the street, the officer appeared. His tall, wasp-like, uniformed figure was outlined against the snow which bounded the horizon, and he walked, knees apart, with that motion peculiar to soldiers, who are always anxious not to soil their carefully polished boots.

He bowed as he passed the ladies, then glanced scornfully at the men, who had sufficient dignity not to raise their hats, though Loiseau made a movement to do so.

Boule de Suif flushed crimson to the ears, and the three married women felt unutterably humiliated at being met thus by the soldier in company with the girl whom he had treated with such scant ceremony.

Then they began to talk about him, his figure, and his face. Madame Carre-Lamadon, who had known many officers and judged them as a connoisseur, thought him not at all bad-looking; she even regretted that he was not a Frenchman, because in that case he would have made a very handsome hussar, with whom all the women would assuredly have fallen in love.

When they were once more within doors they did not know what to do with themselves. Sharp words even were exchanged apropos of the merest trifles. The silent dinner was quickly over, and each one went to bed early in the hope of sleeping, and thus killing time.

They came down next morning with tired faces and irritable tempers; the women scarcely spoke to Boule de Suif.

A church bell summoned the faithful to a baptism. Boule de Suif had a child being brought up by peasants at Yvetot. She did not see him once a year, and never thought of him; but the idea of the child who was about to be baptized induced a sudden wave of tenderness for her own, and she insisted on being present at the ceremony.

As soon as she had gone out, the rest of the company looked at one another and then drew their chairs together; for they realized that they must decide on some course of action. Loiseau had an inspiration: he proposed that they should ask the officer to detain Boule de Suif only, and to let the rest depart on their way.

Monsieur Follenvie was intrusted with this commission, but he returned to them almost immediately. The German, who knew human nature, had shown him the door. He intended to keep all the travellers until his condition had been complied with.

Whereupon Madame Loiseau's vulgar temperament broke bounds.

"We're not going to die of old age here!" she cried. "Since it's that vixen's trade to behave so with men I don't see that she has any right to refuse one more than another. I may as well tell you she took any lovers she could get at Rouen—even coachmen! Yes, indeed, madame—the coachman at the prefecture! I know it for a fact, for he buys his wine of us. And now that it is a question of getting us out of a difficulty she puts on virtuous airs, the drab! For my part, I think this officer has behaved very well. Why, there were three others of us, any one of whom he would undoubtedly have preferred. But no, he contents himself with the girl who is common property. He respects married women. Just think. He is master here. He had only to say: 'I wish it!' and he might have taken us by force, with the help of his soldiers."

The two other women shuddered; the eyes of pretty Madame Carre-Lamadon glistened, and she grew pale, as if the officer were indeed in the act of laying violent hands on her.

The men, who had been discussing the subject among themselves, drew near. Loiseau, in a state of furious resentment, was for delivering up "that miserable woman," bound hand and foot, into the enemy's power. But the count, descended from three generations of ambassadors, and endowed, moreover, with the lineaments of a diplomat, was in favor of more tactful measures.

"We must persuade her," he said.

Then they laid their plans.

The women drew together; they lowered their voices, and the discussion became general, each giving his or her opinion. But the conversation was not in the least coarse. The ladies, in particular, were adepts at delicate phrases and charming subtleties of expression to describe the most improper things. A stranger would have understood none of their allusions, so guarded was the language they employed. But, seeing that the thin veneer of modesty with which every woman of the world is furnished goes but a very little way below the surface, they began rather to enjoy this unedifying episode, and at bottom were hugely delighted —feeling themselves in their element, furthering the schemes of lawless love with the gusto of a gourmand cook who prepares supper for another.

Their gaiety returned of itself, so amusing at last did the whole business seem to them. The count uttered several rather risky witticisms, but so tactfully were they said that his audience could not help smiling. Loiseau in turn made some considerably broader jokes, but no one took offence; and the thought expressed with such brutal directness by his wife was uppermost in the minds of all: "Since it's the girl's trade, why should she refuse this man more than another?" Dainty Madame Carre-Lamadon seemed to think even that in Boule de Suif's place she would be less inclined to refuse him than another.

The blockade was as carefully arranged as if they were investing a fortress. Each agreed on the role which he or she was to play, the arguments to be used, the maneuvers to be executed. They decided on the plan of campaign, the stratagems they were to employ, and the surprise attacks which were to reduce this human citadel and force it to receive the enemy within its walls.

But Cornudet remained apart from the rest, taking no share in the plot.

So absorbed was the attention of all that Boule de Suif's entrance was almost unnoticed. But the count whispered a gentle "Hush!" which made the others look up. She was there. They suddenly stopped talking, and a vague embarrassment prevented them for a few moments from addressing her. But the countess, more practiced than the others in the wiles of the drawing-room, asked her:

"Was the baptism interesting?"

The girl, still under the stress of emotion, told what she had seen and heard, described the faces, the attitudes of those present, and even the appearance of the church. She concluded with the words:

"It does one good to pray sometimes."

Until lunch time the ladies contented themselves with being pleasant to her, so as to increase her confidence and make her amenable to their advice.

As soon as they took their seats at table the attack began. First they opened a vague conversation on the subject of self-sacrifice. Ancient examples were quoted: Judith and Holofernes; then, irrationally enough, Lucrece and Sextus; Cleopatra and the hostile generals whom she reduced to abject slavery by a surrender of her charms. Next was recounted an extraordinary story, born of the imagination of these ignorant millionaires, which told how the matrons of Rome seduced Hannibal, his lieutenants, and all his mercenaries at Capua. They held up to admiration all those women who from time to time have arrested the victorious progress of conquerors, made of their bodies a field of battle, a means of ruling, a weapon; who have vanquished by their heroic caresses hideous or detested beings, and sacrificed their chastity to vengeance and devotion.

All was said with due restraint and regard for propriety, the effect heightened now and then by an outburst of forced enthusiasm calculated to excite emulation.

A listener would have thought at last that the one role of woman on earth was a perpetual sacrifice of her person, a continual abandonment of herself to the caprices of a hostile soldiery.

The two nuns seemed to hear nothing, and to be lost in thought. Boule de Suif also was silent.

During the whole afternoon she was left to her reflections. But instead of calling her "madame" as they had done hitherto, her companions addressed her simply as "mademoiselle," without exactly knowing why, but as if desirous of making her descend a step in the esteem she had won, and forcing her to realize her degraded position.

Just as soup was served, Monsieur Follenvie reappeared, repeating his phrase of the evening before:

"The Prussian officer sends to ask if Mademoiselle Elisabeth Rousset has changed her mind."

Boule de Suif answered briefly:

"No, monsieur."

But at dinner the coalition weakened. Loiseau made three unfortunate remarks. Each was cudgeling his brains for further examples of self-sacrifice, and could find none, when the countess, possibly without ulterior motive, and moved simply by a vague desire to do homage to religion, began to question the elder of the two nuns on the most striking facts in the lives of the saints. Now, it fell out that many of these had committed acts which would be crimes in our eyes, but the Church readily pardons such deeds when they are accomplished for the glory of God or the good of mankind. This was a powerful argument, and the countess made the most of it. Then, whether by reason of a tacit understanding, a thinly veiled act of complaisance such as those who wear the ecclesiastical habit excel in, or whether merely as the result of sheer stupidity—a stupidity admirably adapted to further their designs—the old nun rendered formidable aid to the conspirator. They had thought her timid; she proved herself bold, talkative, bigoted. She was not troubled by the ins and outs of casuistry; her doctrines were as iron bars; her faith knew no doubt; her conscience no scruples. She looked on Abraham's sacrifice as natural enough, for she herself would not have hesitated to kill both father and mother if she had received a divine order to that effect; and nothing, in her opinion, could displease our Lord, provided the motive were praiseworthy. The countess, putting to good use the consecrated authority of her unexpected ally, led her on to make a lengthy and edifying paraphrase of that axiom enunciated by a certain school of moralists: "The end justifies the means."

"Then, sister," she asked, "you think God accepts all methods, and pardons the act when the motive is pure?"

"Undoubtedly, madame. An action reprehensible in itself often derives merit from the thought which inspires it."

And in this wise they talked on, fathoming the wishes of God, predicting His judgments, describing Him as interested in matters which assuredly concern Him but little.

All was said with the utmost care and discretion, but every word uttered by the holy woman in her nun's garb weakened the indignant resistance of the courtesan. Then the conversation drifted somewhat, and the nun began to talk of the convents of her order, of her Superior, of herself, and of her fragile little neighbor, Sister St. Nicephore. They had been sent for from Havre to nurse the hundreds of soldiers who were in hospitals, stricken with smallpox. She described these wretched invalids and their malady. And, while they themselves were detained on their way by the caprices of the Prussian officer, scores of Frenchmen might be dying, whom they would otherwise have saved! For the nursing of soldiers was the old nun's specialty; she had been in the Crimea, in Italy, in Austria; and as she told the story of her campaigns she revealed herself as one of those holy sisters of the fife and drum who seem designed by nature to follow camps, to snatch the wounded from amid the strife of battle, and to quell with a word, more effectually than any general, the rough and insubordinate troopers—a masterful woman, her seamed and pitted face itself an image of the devastations of war.

No one spoke when she had finished for fear of spoiling the excellent effect of her words.

As soon as the meal was over the travellers retired to their rooms, whence they emerged the following day at a late hour of the morning.

Luncheon passed off quietly. The seed sown the preceding evening was being given time to germinate and bring forth fruit.

In the afternoon the countess proposed a walk; then the count, as had been arranged beforehand, took Boule de Suif's arm, and walked with her at some distance behind the rest.

He began talking to her in that familiar, paternal, slightly contemptuous tone which men of his class adopt in speaking to women like her, calling her "my dear child," and talking down to her from the height of his exalted social position and stainless reputation. He came straight to the point.

"So you prefer to leave us here, exposed like yourself to all the violence which would follow on a repulse of the Prussian troops, rather than consent to surrender yourself, as you have done so many times in your life?"

The girl did not reply.

He tried kindness, argument, sentiment. He still bore himself as count, even while adopting, when desirable, an attitude of gallantry, and making pretty—nay, even tender—speeches. He exalted the service she would render them, spoke of their gratitude; then, suddenly, using the familiar "thou":

"And you know, my dear, he could boast then of having made a conquest of a pretty girl such as he won't often find in his own country."

Boule de Suif did not answer, and joined the rest of the party.

As soon as they returned she went to her room, and was seen no more. The general anxiety was at its height. What would she do? If she still resisted, how awkward for them all!

The dinner hour struck; they waited for her in vain. At last Monsieur Follenvie entered, announcing that Mademoiselle Rousset was not well, and that they might sit down to table. They all pricked up their ears. The count drew near the innkeeper, and whispered:

"Is it all right?"

"Yes."

Out of regard for propriety he said nothing to his companions, but merely nodded slightly toward them. A great sigh of relief went up from all breasts; every face was lighted up with joy.

"By Gad!" shouted Loiseau, "I'll stand champagne all round if there's any to be found in this place." And great was Madame Loiseau's dismay when the proprietor came back with four bottles in his hands. They had all suddenly become talkative and merry; a lively joy filled all hearts. The count seemed to perceive for the first time that Madame Carre-Lamadon was charming; the manufacturer paid compliments to the countess. The conversation was animated, sprightly, witty, and, although many of the jokes were in the worst possible taste, all the company were amused by them, and none offended—indignation being dependent, like other emotions, on surroundings. And the mental atmosphere had gradually become filled with gross imaginings and unclean thoughts.

At dessert even the women indulged in discreetly worded allusions. Their glances were full of meaning; they had drunk much. The count, who even in his moments of relaxation preserved a dignified demeanor, hit on a much-appreciated comparison of the condition of things with the termination of a winter spent in the icy solitude of the North Pole and the joy of shipwrecked mariners who at last perceive a southward track opening out before their eyes.

Loiseau, fairly in his element, rose to his feet, holding aloft a glass of champagne.

"I drink to our deliverance!" he shouted.

All stood up, and greeted the toast with acclamation. Even the two good sisters yielded to the solicitations of the ladies, and consented to moisten their lips with the foaming wine, which they had never before tasted. They declared it was like effervescent lemonade, but with a pleasanter flavor.

"It is a pity," said Loiseau, "that we have no piano; we might have had a quadrille."

Cornudet had not spoken a word or made a movement; he seemed plunged in serious thought, and now and then tugged furiously at his great beard, as if trying to add still further to its length. At last, toward midnight, when they were about to separate, Loiseau, whose gait was far from steady, suddenly slapped him on the back, saying thickly:

"You're not jolly to-night; why are you so silent, old man?"

Cornudet threw back his head, cast one swift and scornful glance over the assemblage, and answered:

"I tell you all, you have done an infamous thing!"

He rose, reached the door, and repeating: "Infamous!" disappeared.

A chill fell on all. Loiseau himself looked foolish and disconcerted for a moment, but soon recovered his aplomb, and, writhing with laughter, exclaimed:

"Really, you are all too green for anything!"

Pressed for an explanation, he related the "mysteries of the corridor," whereat his listeners were hugely amused. The ladies could hardly contain their delight. The count and Monsieur Carre-Lamadon laughed till they cried. They could scarcely believe their ears.

"What! you are sure? He wanted——"

"I tell you I saw it with my own eyes."

"And she refused?"

"Because the Prussian was in the next room!"

"Surely you are mistaken?"

"I swear I'm telling you the truth."

The count was choking with laughter. The manufacturer held his sides. Loiseau continued:

"So you may well imagine he doesn't think this evening's business at all amusing."

And all three began to laugh again, choking, coughing, almost ill with merriment.

Then they separated. But Madame Loiseau, who was nothing if not spiteful, remarked to her husband as they were on the way to bed that "that stuck-up little minx of a Carre-Lamadon had laughed on the wrong side of her mouth all the evening."

"You know," she said, "when women run after uniforms it's all the same to them whether the men who wear them are French or Prussian. It's perfectly sickening!"

The next morning the snow showed dazzling white tinder a clear winter sun. The coach, ready at last, waited before the door; while a flock of white pigeons, with pink eyes spotted in the centres with black, puffed out their white feathers and walked sedately between the legs of the six horses, picking at the steaming manure.

The driver, wrapped in his sheepskin coat, was smoking a pipe on the box, and all the passengers, radiant with delight at their approaching departure, were putting up provisions for the remainder of the journey.

They were waiting only for Boule de Suif. At last she appeared.

She seemed rather shamefaced and embarrassed, and advanced with timid step toward her companions, who with one accord turned aside as if they had not seen her. The count, with much dignity, took his wife by the arm, and removed her from the unclean contact.

The girl stood still, stupefied with astonishment; then, plucking up courage, accosted the manufacturer's wife with a humble "Good-morning, madame," to which the other replied merely with a slight and insolent nod, accompanied by a look of outraged virtue. Every one suddenly appeared extremely busy, and kept as far from Boule de Suif as if tier skirts had been infected with some deadly disease. Then they hurried to the coach, followed by the despised courtesan, who, arriving last of all, silently took the place she had occupied during the first part of the journey.

The rest seemed neither to see nor to know her—all save Madame Loiseau, who, glancing contemptuously in her direction, remarked, half aloud, to her husband:

"What a mercy I am not sitting beside that creature!"

The lumbering vehicle started on its way, and the journey began afresh.

At first no one spoke. Boule de Suif dared not even raise her eyes. She felt at once indignant with her neighbors, and humiliated at having yielded to the Prussian into whose arms they had so hypocritically cast her.

But the countess, turning toward Madame Carre-Lamadon, soon broke the painful silence:

"I think you know Madame d'Etrelles?"

"Yes; she is a friend of mine."

"Such a charming woman!"

"Delightful! Exceptionally talented, and an artist to the finger tips. She sings marvellously and draws to perfection."

The manufacturer was chatting with the count, and amid the clatter of the window-panes a word of their conversation was now and then distinguishable: "Shares—maturity—premium—time-limit."

Loiseau, who had abstracted from the inn the timeworn pack of cards, thick with the grease of five years' contact with half-wiped-off tables, started a game of bezique with his wife.

The good sisters, taking up simultaneously the long rosaries hanging from their waists, made the sign of the cross, and began to mutter in unison interminable prayers, their lips moving ever more and more swiftly, as if they sought which should outdistance the other in the race of orisons; from time to time they kissed a medal, and crossed themselves anew, then resumed their rapid and unintelligible murmur.

Cornudet sat still, lost in thought.

Ah the end of three hours Loiseau gathered up the cards, and remarked that he was hungry.

His wife thereupon produced a parcel tied with string, from which she extracted a piece of cold veal. This she cut into neat, thin slices, and both began to eat.

"We may as well do the same," said the countess. The rest agreed, and she unpacked the provisions which had been prepared for herself, the count, and the Carre-Lamadons. In one of those oval dishes, the lids of which are decorated with an earthenware hare, by way of showing that a game pie lies within, was a succulent delicacy consisting of the brown flesh of the game larded with streaks of bacon and flavored with other meats chopped fine. A solid wedge of Gruyere cheese, which had been wrapped in a newspaper, bore the imprint: "Items of News," on its rich, oily surface.

The two good sisters brought to light a hunk of sausage smelling strongly of garlic; and Cornudet, plunging both hands at once into the capacious pockets of his loose overcoat, produced from one four hard-boiled eggs and from the other a crust of bread. He removed the shells, threw them into the straw beneath his feet, and began to devour the eggs, letting morsels of the bright yellow yolk fall in his mighty beard, where they looked like stars.

Boule de Suif, in the haste and confusion of her departure, had not thought of anything, and, stifling with rage, she watched all these people placidly eating. At first, ill-suppressed wrath shook her whole person, and she opened her lips to shriek the truth at them, to overwhelm them with a volley of insults; but she could not utter a word, so choked was she with indignation.

No one looked at her, no one thought of her. She felt herself swallowed up in the scorn of these virtuous creatures, who had first sacrificed, then rejected her as a thing useless and unclean. Then she remembered her big basket full of the good things they had so greedily devoured: the two chickens coated in jelly, the pies, the pears, the four bottles of claret; and her fury broke forth like a cord that is overstrained, and she was on the verge of tears. She made terrible efforts at self-control, drew herself up, swallowed the sobs which choked her; but the tears rose nevertheless, shone at the brink of her eyelids, and soon two heavy drops coursed slowly down her cheeks. Others followed more quickly, like water filtering from a rock, and fell, one after another, on her rounded bosom. She sat upright, with a fixed expression, her face pale and rigid, hoping desperately that no one saw her give way.

But the countess noticed that she was weeping, and with a sign drew her husband's attention to the fact. He shrugged his shoulders, as if to say: "Well, what of it? It's not my fault." Madame Loiseau chuckled triumphantly, and murmured:

"She's weeping for shame."

The two nuns had betaken themselves once more to their prayers, first wrapping the remainder of their sausage in paper:

Then Cornudet, who was digesting his eggs, stretched his long legs under the opposite seat, threw himself back, folded his arms, smiled like a man who had just thought of a good joke, and began to whistle the Marseillaise.

The faces of his neighbors clouded; the popular air evidently did not find favor with them; they grew nervous and irritable, and seemed ready to howl as a dog does at the sound of a barrel-organ. Cornudet saw the discomfort he was creating, and whistled the louder; sometimes he even hummed the words:

> Amour sacre de la patrie,
>
> Conduis, soutiens, nos bras vengeurs,
>
> Liberte, liberte cherie,
>
> Combats avec tes defenseurs!

The coach progressed more swiftly, the snow being harder now; and all the way to Dieppe, during the long, dreary hours of the journey, first in the gathering dusk, then in the thick darkness, raising his voice above the rumbling of the vehicle, Cornudet continued with fierce obstinacy his vengeful and monotonous whistling, forcing his weary and exasperated-hearers to follow the song from end to end, to recall every word of every line, as each was repeated over and over again with untiring persistency.

And Boule de Suif still wept, and sometimes a sob she could not restrain was heard in the darkness between two verses of the song.

TWO FRIENDS

Besieged Paris was in the throes of famine. Even the sparrows on the roofs and the rats in the sewers were growing scarce. People were eating anything they could get.

As Monsieur Morissot, watchmaker by profession and idler for the nonce, was strolling along the boulevard one bright January morning, his hands in his trousers pockets and stomach empty, he suddenly came face to face with an acquaintance—Monsieur Sauvage, a fishing chum.

Before the war broke out Morissot had been in the habit, every Sunday morning, of setting forth with a bamboo rod in his hand and a tin box on his back. He took the Argenteuil train, got out at Colombes, and walked thence to the Ile Marante. The moment he arrived at this place of his dreams he began fishing, and fished till nightfall.

Every Sunday he met in this very spot Monsieur Sauvage, a stout, jolly, little man, a draper in the Rue Notre Dame de Lorette, and also an ardent fisherman. They often spent half the day side by side, rod in hand and feet dangling over the water, and a warm friendship had sprung up between the two.

Some days they did not speak; at other times they chatted; but they understood each other perfectly without the aid of words, having similar tastes and feelings.

In the spring, about ten o'clock in the morning, when the early sun caused a light mist to float on the water and gently warmed the backs of the two enthusiastic anglers, Morissot would occasionally remark to his neighbor:

"My, but it's pleasant here."

To which the other would reply:

"I can't imagine anything better!"

And these few words sufficed to make them understand and appreciate each other.

In the autumn, toward the close of day, when the setting sun shed a blood-red glow over the western sky, and the reflection of the crimson clouds tinged the whole river with red, brought a glow to the faces of the two friends, and gilded the trees, whose leaves were already turning at the first chill touch of winter, Monsieur Sauvage would sometimes smile at Morissot, and say:

"What a glorious spectacle!"

And Morissot would answer, without taking his eyes from his float:

"This is much better than the boulevard, isn't it?"

As soon as they recognized each other they shook hands cordially, affected at the thought of meeting under such changed circumstances.

Monsieur Sauvage, with a sigh, murmured:

"These are sad times!"

Morissot shook his head mournfully.

"And such weather! This is the first fine day of the year."

The sky was, in fact, of a bright, cloudless blue.

They walked along, side by side, reflective and sad.

"And to think of the fishing!" said Morissot. "What good times we used to have!"

"When shall we be able to fish again?" asked Monsieur Sauvage.

They entered a small cafe and took an absinthe together, then resumed their walk along the pavement.

Morissot stopped suddenly.

"Shall we have another absinthe?" he said.

"If you like," agreed Monsieur Sauvage.

And they entered another wine shop.

They were quite unsteady when they came out, owing to the effect of the alcohol on their empty stomachs. It was a fine, mild day, and a gentle breeze fanned their faces.

The fresh air completed the effect of the alcohol on Monsieur Sauvage. He stopped suddenly, saying:

"Suppose we go there?"

"Where?"

"Fishing."

"But where?"

"Why, to the old place. The French outposts are close to Colombes. I know Colonel Dumoulin, and we shall easily get leave to pass."

Morissot trembled with desire.

"Very well. I agree."

And they separated, to fetch their rods and lines.

An hour later they were walking side by side on the-highroad. Presently they reached the villa occupied by the colonel. He smiled at their request, and granted it. They resumed their walk, furnished with a password.

Soon they left the outposts behind them, made their way through deserted Colombes, and found themselves on the outskirts of the small vineyards which border the Seine. It was about eleven o'clock.

Before them lay the village of Argenteuil, apparently lifeless. The heights of Orgement and Sannois dominated the landscape. The great plain, extending as far as Nanterre, was empty, quite empty-a waste of dun-colored soil and bare cherry trees.

Monsieur Sauvage, pointing to the heights, murmured:

"The Prussians are up yonder!"

And the sight of the deserted country filled the two friends with vague misgivings.

The Prussians! They had never seen them as yet, but they had felt their presence in the neighborhood of Paris for months past—ruining France, pillaging, massacring, starving them. And a kind of superstitious terror mingled with the hatred they already felt toward this unknown, victorious nation.

"Suppose we were to meet any of them?" said Morissot.

"We'd offer them some fish," replied Monsieur Sauvage, with that Parisian light-heartedness which nothing can wholly quench.

Still, they hesitated to show themselves in the open country, overawed by the utter silence which reigned around them.

At last Monsieur Sauvage said boldly:

"Come, we'll make a start; only let us be careful!"

And they made their way through one of the vineyards, bent double, creeping along beneath the cover afforded by the vines, with eye and ear alert.

A strip of bare ground remained to be crossed before they could gain the river bank. They ran across this, and, as soon as they were at the water's edge, concealed themselves among the dry reeds.

Morissot placed his ear to the ground, to ascertain, if possible, whether footsteps were coming their way. He heard nothing. They seemed to be utterly alone.

Their confidence was restored, and they began to fish.

Before them the deserted Ile Marante hid them from the farther shore. The little restaurant was closed, and looked as if it had been deserted for years.

Monsieur Sauvage caught the first gudgeon, Monsieur Morissot the second, and almost every moment one or other raised his line with a little, glittering, silvery fish wriggling at the end; they were having excellent sport.

They slipped their catch gently into a close-meshed bag lying at their feet; they were filled with joy—the joy of once more indulging in a pastime of which they had long been deprived.

The sun poured its rays on their backs; they no longer heard anything or thought of anything. They ignored the rest of the world; they were fishing.

But suddenly a rumbling sound, which seemed to come from the bowels of the earth, shook the ground beneath them: the cannon were resuming their thunder.

Morissot turned his head and could see toward the left, beyond the banks of the river, the formidable outline of Mont-Valerien, from whose summit arose a white puff of smoke.

The next instant a second puff followed the first, and in a few moments a fresh detonation made the earth tremble.

Others followed, and minute by minute the mountain gave forth its deadly breath and a white puff of smoke, which rose slowly into the peaceful heaven and floated above the summit of the cliff.

Monsieur Sauvage shrugged his shoulders.

"They are at it again!" he said.

Morissot, who was anxiously watching his float bobbing up and down, was suddenly seized with the angry impatience of a peaceful man toward the madmen who were firing thus, and remarked indignantly:

"What fools they are to kill one another like that!"

"They're worse than animals," replied Monsieur Sauvage.

And Morissot, who had just caught a bleak, declared:

"And to think that it will be just the same so long as there are governments!"

"The Republic would not have declared war," interposed Monsieur Sauvage.

Morissot interrupted him:

"Under a king we have foreign wars; under a republic we have civil war."

And the two began placidly discussing political problems with the sound common sense of peaceful, matter-of-fact citizens—agreeing on one point: that they would never be free. And Mont-Valerien thundered ceaselessly, demolishing the houses of the French with its cannon balls, grinding lives of men to powder, destroying many a dream, many a cherished hope, many a prospective happiness; ruthlessly causing endless woe and suffering in the hearts of wives, of daughters, of mothers, in other lands.

"Such is life!" declared Monsieur Sauvage.

"Say, rather, such is death!" replied Morissot, laughing.

But they suddenly trembled with alarm at the sound of footsteps behind them, and, turning round, they perceived close at hand four tall, bearded men, dressed after the manner of livery servants and wearing flat caps on their heads. They were covering the two anglers with their rifles.

The rods slipped from their owners' grasp and floated away down the river.

In the space of a few seconds they were seized, bound, thrown into a boat, and taken across to the Ile Marante.

And behind the house they had thought deserted were about a score of German soldiers.

A shaggy-looking giant, who was bestriding a chair and smoking a long clay pipe, addressed them in excellent French with the words:

"Well, gentlemen, have you had good luck with your fishing?"

Then a soldier deposited at the officer's feet the bag full of fish, which he had taken care to bring away. The Prussian smiled.

"Not bad, I see. But we have something else to talk about. Listen to me, and don't be alarmed:

"You must know that, in my eyes, you are two spies sent to reconnoitre me and my movements. Naturally, I capture you and I shoot you. You pretended to be fishing, the better to disguise your real errand. You have fallen into my hands, and must take the consequences. Such is war.

"But as you came here through the outposts you must have a password for your return. Tell me that password and I will let you go."

The two friends, pale as death, stood silently side by side, a slight fluttering of the hands alone betraying their emotion.

"No one will ever know," continued the officer. "You will return peacefully to your homes, and the secret will disappear with you. If you refuse, it means death-instant death. Choose!"

They stood motionless, and did not open their lips.

The Prussian, perfectly calm, went on, with hand outstretched toward the river:

"Just think that in five minutes you will be at the bottom of that water. In five minutes! You have relations, I presume?"

Mont-Valerien still thundered.

The two fishermen remained silent. The German turned and gave an order in his own language. Then he moved his chair a little way off, that he might not be so near the prisoners, and a dozen men stepped forward, rifle in hand, and took up a position, twenty paces off.

"I give you one minute," said the officer; "not a second longer."

Then he rose quickly, went over to the two Frenchmen, took Morissot by the arm, led him a short distance off, and said in a low voice:

"Quick! the password! Your friend will know nothing. I will pretend to relent."

Morissot answered not a word.

Then the Prussian took Monsieur Sauvage aside in like manner, and made him the same proposal.

Monsieur Sauvage made no reply.

Again they stood side by side.

The officer issued his orders; the soldiers raised their rifles.

Then by chance Morissot's eyes fell on the bag full of gudgeon lying in the grass a few feet from him.

A ray of sunlight made the still quivering fish glisten like silver. And Morissot's heart sank. Despite his efforts at self-control his eyes filled with tears.

"Good-by, Monsieur Sauvage," he faltered.

"Good-by, Monsieur Morissot," replied Sauvage.

They shook hands, trembling from head to foot with a dread beyond their mastery.

The officer cried:

"Fire!"

The twelve shots were as one.

Monsieur Sauvage fell forward instantaneously. Morissot, being the taller, swayed slightly and fell across his friend with face turned skyward and blood oozing from a rent in the breast of his coat.

The German issued fresh orders.

His men dispersed, and presently returned with ropes and large stones, which they attached to the feet of the two friends; then they carried them to the river bank.

Mont-Valerien, its summit now enshrouded in smoke, still continued to thunder.

Two soldiers took Morissot by the head and the feet; two others did the same with Sauvage. The bodies, swung lustily by strong hands, were cast to a distance, and, describing a curve, fell feet foremost into the stream.

The water splashed high, foamed, eddied, then grew calm; tiny waves lapped the shore.

A few streaks of blood flecked the surface of the river.

The officer, calm throughout, remarked, with grim humor:

"It's the fishes' turn now!"

Then he retraced his way to the house.

Suddenly he caught sight of the net full of gudgeons, lying forgotten in the grass. He picked it up, examined it, smiled, and called:

"Wilhelm!"

A white-aproned soldier responded to the summons, and the Prussian, tossing him the catch of the two murdered men, said:

"Have these fish fried for me at once, while they are still alive; they'll make a tasty dish."

Then he resumed his pipe.

THE LANCER'S WIFE

I

It was after Bourbaki's defeat in the east of France. The army, broken up, decimated, and worn out, had been obliged to retreat into Switzerland after that terrible campaign, and it was only its short duration that saved a hundred and fifty thousand men from certain death. Hunger, the terrible cold, forced marches in the snow without boots, over bad mountain roads, had caused us 'francs-tireurs', especially, the greatest suffering, for we were without tents, and almost without food, always in the van when we were marching toward Belfort, and in the rear when returning by the Jura. Of our little band that had numbered twelve hundred men on the first of January, there remained only twenty-two pale, thin, ragged wretches, when we at length succeeded in reaching Swiss territory.

There we were safe, and could rest. Everybody knows what sympathy was shown to the unfortunate French army, and how well it was cared for. We all gained fresh life, and those who had been rich and happy before the war declared that they had never experienced a greater feeling of comfort than they did then. Just think. We actually had something to eat every day, and could sleep every night.

Meanwhile, the war continued in the east of France, which had been excluded from the armistice. Besancon still kept the enemy in check, and the latter had their revenge by ravaging Franche Comte. Sometimes we heard that they had approached quite close to the frontier, and we saw Swiss troops, who were to form a line of observation between us and them, set out on their march.

That pained us in the end, and, as we regained health and strength, the longing to fight took possession of us. It was disgraceful and irritating to know that within two or three leagues of us the Germans were victorious and insolent, to feel that we were protected by our captivity, and to feel that on that account we were powerless against them.

One day our captain took five or six of us aside, and spoke to us about it, long and furiously. He was a fine fellow, that captain. He had been a sublieutenant in the Zouaves, was tall and thin and as hard as steel, and during the whole campaign he had cut out their work for the Germans. He fretted in inactivity, and could not accustom himself to the idea of being a prisoner and of doing nothing.

"Confound it!" he said to us, "does it not pain you to know that there is a number of uhlans within two hours of us? Does it not almost drive you mad to know that those beggarly wretches are walking about as masters in our mountains, when six determined men might kill a whole spitful any day? I cannot endure it any longer, and I must go there."

"But how can you manage it, captain?"

"How? It is not very difficult! Just as if we had not done a thing or two within the last six months, and got out of woods that were guarded by very different men from the Swiss. The day that you wish to cross over into France, I will undertake to get you there."

"That may be; but what shall we do in France without any arms?"

"Without arms? We will get them over yonder, by Jove!"

"You are forgetting the treaty," another soldier said; "we shall run the risk of doing the Swiss an injury, if Manteuffel learns that they have allowed prisoners to return to France."

"Come," said the captain, "those are all bad reasons. I mean to go and kill some Prussians; that is all I care about. If you do not wish to do as I do, well and good; only say so at once. I can quite well go by myself; I do not require anybody's company."

Naturally we all protested, and, as it was quite impossible to make the captain alter his mind, we felt obliged to promise to go with him. We liked him too much to leave him in the lurch, as he never failed us in any extremity; and so the expedition was decided on.

II

The captain had a plan of his own, that he had been cogitating over for some time. A man in that part of the country whom he knew was going to lend him a cart and six suits of peasants' clothes. We could hide under some straw at the bottom of the wagon, which would be loaded with Gruyere cheese, which he was supposed to be going to sell in France. The captain told the sentinels that he was taking two friends with him to protect his goods, in case any one should try to rob him, which did not seem an extraordinary precaution. A Swiss officer seemed to look at the wagon in a knowing manner, but that was in order to impress his soldiers. In a word, neither officers nor men could make it out.

"Get up," the captain said to the horses, as he cracked his whip, while our three men quietly smoked their pipes. I was half suffocated in my box, which only admitted the air through those holes in front, and at the same time I was nearly frozen, for it was terribly cold.

"Get up," the captain said again, and the wagon loaded with Gruyere cheese entered France.

The Prussian lines were very badly guarded, as the enemy trusted to the watchfulness of the Swiss. The sergeant spoke North German, while our captain spoke the bad German of the Four Cantons, and so they could not understand each other. The sergeant, however, pretended to be very intelligent; and, in order to make us believe that he understood us, they allowed us to continue our journey; and, after travelling for seven hours, being continually stopped in the same manner, we arrived at a small village of the Jura in ruins, at nightfall.

What were we going to do? Our only arms were the captain's whip, our uniforms our peasants' blouses, and our food the Gruyere cheese. Our sole wealth consisted in our ammunition, packages of cartridges which we had stowed away inside some of the large cheeses. We had about a thousand of them, just two hundred each, but we needed rifles, and they must be chassepots. Luckily, however, the captain was a bold man of an inventive mind, and this was the plan that he hit upon:

While three of us remained hidden in a cellar in the abandoned village, he continued his journey as far as Besancon with the empty wagon and one man. The town was invested, but one can always make one's way into a town among the hills by crossing the tableland till within about ten miles of the walls, and then following paths and ravines on foot. They left their wagon at Omans, among the Germans, and escaped out of it at night on foot; so as to gain the heights which border the River Doubs; the next day they entered Besancon, where there were plenty of chassepots. There were nearly forty thousand of them left in the arsenal, and General Roland, a brave marine, laughed at the captain's daring project, but let him have six rifles and wished him "good luck." There he had also found his wife, who had been through all the war with us before the campaign in the East, and who had been only prevented by illness from continuing with Bourbaki's army. She had recovered, however, in spite of the cold, which was growing more and more intense, and in spite of the numberless privations that awaited her, she persisted in accompanying her husband. He was obliged to give way to her, and they all three, the captain, his wife, and our comrade, started on their expedition.

Going was nothing in comparison to returning. They were obliged to travel by night, so as to avoid meeting anybody, as the possession of six rifles would have made them liable to suspicion. But, in spite of everything, a week after leaving us, the captain and his two men were back with us again. The campaign was about to begin.

III

The first night of his arrival he began it himself, and, under pretext of examining the surrounding country, he went along the high road.

I must tell you that the little village which served as our fortress was a small collection of poor, badly built houses, which had been deserted long before. It lay on a steep slope, which terminated in a wooded plain. The country people sell the wood; they send it down the slopes, which are called coulees, locally, and which lead down to the plain, and there they stack it into piles, which they sell thrice a year to the wood merchants. The spot where this market is held in indicated by two small houses by the side of the highroad, which serve for public houses. The captain had gone down there by way of one of these coulees.

He had been gone about half an hour, and we were on the lookout at the top of the ravine, when we heard a shot. The captain had ordered us not to stir, and only to come to him when we heard him blow his trumpet. It was made of a goat's horn, and could be heard a league off; but it gave no sound, and, in spite of our cruel anxiety, we were obliged to wait in silence, with our rifles by our side.

It is nothing to go down these coulees; one just lets one's self slide down; but it is more difficult to get up again; one has to scramble up by catching hold of the hanging branches of the trees, and sometimes on all fours, by sheer strength. A whole mortal hour passed, and he did not come; nothing moved in the brushwood. The captain's wife began to grow impatient. What could he be doing? Why did he not call us? Did the shot that we had heard proceed from an enemy, and had he killed or wounded our leader, her husband? They did not know what to think, but I myself fancied either that he was dead or that his enterprise was successful; and I was merely anxious and curious to know what he had done.

Suddenly we heard the sound of his trumpet, and we were much surprised that instead of coming from below, as we had expected, it came from the village behind us. What did that mean? It was a mystery to us, but the same idea struck us all, that he had been killed, and that the Prussians were blowing the trumpet to draw us into an ambush. We therefore returned to the cottage, keeping a careful lookout with our fingers on the trigger, and hiding under the branches; but his wife, in spite of our entreaties, rushed on, leaping like a tigress. She thought that she had to avenge her husband, and had fixed the bayonet to her rifle, and we lost sight of her at the moment that we heard the trumpet again; and, a few moments later, we heard her calling out to us:

"Come on! come on! He is alive! It is he!"

We hastened on, and saw the captain smoking his pipe at the entrance of the village, but strangely enough, he was on horseback.

"Ah! ah!" he said to us, "you see that there is something to be done here. Here I am on horseback already; I knocked over an uhlan yonder, and took his horse; I suppose they were guarding the wood, but it was by drinking and swilling in clover. One of them, the sentry at the door, had not time to see me before I gave him a sugarplum in his stomach, and then, before the others could come out, I jumped on the horse and was off like a shot. Eight or ten of them followed me, I think; but I took the crossroads through the woods. I have got scratched and torn a bit, but here I am, and now, my good fellows, attention, and take care! Those brigands will not rest until they have caught us, and we must receive them with rifle bullets. Come along; let us take up our posts!"

We set out. One of us took up his position a good way from the village on the crossroads; I was posted at the entrance of the main street, where the road from the level country enters the village, while the two others, the captain and his wife, were in the middle of the village, near the church, whose tower-served for an observatory and citadel.

We had not been in our places long before we heard a shot, followed by another, and then two, then three. The first was evidently a chassepot —one recognized it by the sharp report, which sounds like the crack of a whip—while the other three came from the lancers' carbines.

The captain was furious. He had given orders to the outpost to let the enemy pass and merely to follow them at a distance if they marched toward the village, and to join me when they had gone well between the houses. Then they were to appear suddenly, take the patrol between two fires, and not allow a single man to escape; for, posted as we were, the six of us could have hemmed in ten Prussians, if needful.

"That confounded Piedelot has roused them," the captain said, "and they will not venture to come on blindfolded any longer. And then I am quite sure that he has managed to get a shot into himself somewhere or other, for we hear nothing of him. It serves him right; why did he not obey orders?" And then, after a moment, he grumbled in his beard: "After all I am sorry for the poor fellow; he is so brave, and shoots so well!"

The captain was right in his conjectures. We waited until evening, without seeing the uhlans; they had retreated after the first attack; but unfortunately we had not seen Piedelot, either. Was he dead or a prisoner? When night came, the captain proposed that we should go out and look for him, and so the three of us started. At the crossroads we found a broken rifle and some blood, while the ground was trampled down; but we did not find either a wounded man or a dead body, although we searched every thicket, and at midnight we returned without having discovered anything of our unfortunate comrade.

"It is very strange," the captain growled. "They must have killed him and thrown him into the bushes somewhere; they cannot possibly have taken him prisoner, as he would have called out for help. I cannot understand it at all." Just as he said that, bright flames shot up in the direction of the inn on the high road, which illuminated the sky.

"Scoundrels! cowards!" he shouted. "I will bet that they have set fire to the two houses on the marketplace, in order to have their revenge, and then they will scuttle off without saying a word. They will be satisfied with having killed a man and set fire to two houses. All right. It shall not pass over like that. We must go for them; they will not like to leave their illuminations in order to fight."

"It would be a great stroke of luck if we could set Piedelot free at the same time," some one said.

The five of us set off, full of rage and hope. In twenty minutes we had got to the bottom of the coulee, and had not yet seen any one when we were within a hundred yards of the inn. The fire was behind the house, and all we saw of it was the reflection above the roof. However, we were walking rather slowly, as we were afraid of an ambush, when suddenly we heard Piedelot's well-known voice. It had a strange sound, however; for it was at the same time—dull and vibrating, stifled and clear, as if he were calling out as loud as he could with a bit of rag stuffed into his mouth. He seemed to be hoarse and gasping, and the unlucky fellow kept exclaiming: "Help! Help!"

We sent all thoughts of prudence to the devil, and in two bounds we were at the back of the inn, where a terrible sight met our eyes.

IV

Piedelot was being burned alive. He was writhing in the midst of a heap of fagots, tied to a stake, and the flames were licking him with their burning tongues. When he saw us, his tongue seemed to stick in his throat; he drooped his head, and seemed as if he were going to die. It was only the affair of a moment to upset the burning pile, to scatter the embers, and to cut the ropes that fastened him.

Poor fellow! In what a terrible state we found him. The evening before he had had his left arm broken, and it seemed as if he had been badly beaten since then, for his whole body was covered with wounds, bruises and blood. The flames had also begun their work on him, and he had two large burns, one on his loins and the other on his right thigh, and his beard and hair were scorched. Poor Piedelot!

No one knows the terrible rage we felt at this sight! We would have rushed headlong at a hundred thousand Prussians; our thirst for vengeance was intense. But the cowards had run away, leaving their crime behind them. Where could we find them now? Meanwhile, however, the captain's wife was looking after Piedelot, and dressing his wounds as best she could, while the captain himself shook hands with him excitedly, and in a few minutes he came to himself.

"Good-morning, captain; good-morning, all of you," he said. "Ah! the scoundrels, the wretches! Why, twenty of them came to surprise us."

"Twenty, do you say?"

"Yes; there was a whole band of them, and that is why I disobeyed orders, captain, and fired on them, for they would have killed you all, and I preferred to stop them. That frightened them, and they did not venture to go farther than the crossroads. They were such cowards. Four of them shot at me at twenty yards, as if I had been a target, and then they slashed me with their swords. My arm was broken, so that I could only use my bayonet with one hand."

"But why did you not call for help?"

"I took good care not to do that, for you would all have come; and you would neither have been able to defend me nor yourselves, being only five against twenty."

"You know that we should not have allowed you to have been taken, poor old fellow."

"I preferred to die by myself, don't you see! I did not want to bring you here, for it would have been a mere ambush."

"Well, we will not talk about it any more. Do you feel rather easier?"

"No, I am suffocating. I know that I cannot live much longer. The brutes! They tied me to a tree, and beat me till I was half dead, and then they shook my broken arm; but I did not make a sound. I would rather have bitten my tongue out than have called out before them. Now I can tell what I am suffering and shed tears; it does one good. Thank you, my kind friends."

"Poor Piedelot! But we will avenge you, you may be sure!"

"Yes, yes; I want you to do that. There is, in particular, a woman among them who passes as the wife of the lancer whom the captain killed yesterday. She is dressed like a lancer, and she tortured me the most yesterday, and suggested burning me; and it was she who set fire to the wood. Oh! the wretch, the brute! Ah! how I am suffering! My loins, my arms!" and he fell back gasping and exhausted, writhing in his terrible agony, while the captain's wife wiped the perspiration from his forehead, and we all shed tears of grief and rage, as if we had been children. I will not describe the end to you; he died half an hour later, previously telling us in what direction the enemy had gone. When he was dead we gave ourselves time to bury him, and then we set out in pursuit of them, with our hearts full of fury and hatred.

"We will throw ourselves on the whole Prussian army, if it be necessary," the captain said; "but we will avenge Piedelot. We must catch those scoundrels. Let us swear to die, rather than not to find them; and if I am killed first, these are my orders: All the prisoners that you take are to be shot immediately, and as for the lancer's wife, she is to be tortured before she is put to death."

"She must not be shot, because she is a woman," the captain's wife said. "If you survive, I am sure that you would not shoot a woman. Torturing her will be quite sufficient; but if you are killed in this pursuit, I want one thing, and that is to fight with her; I will kill her with my own hands, and the others can do what they like with her if she kills me."

"We will outrage her! We will burn her! We will tear her to pieces! Piedelot shall be avenged!

"An eye for an eye, a tooth for a tooth!"

V

The next morning we unexpectedly fell on an outpost of uhlans four leagues away. Surprised by our sudden attack, they were not able to mount their horses, nor even to defend themselves; and in a few moments we had five prisoner, corresponding to our own number. The captain questioned them, and from their answers we felt certain that they were the same whom we had encountered the previous day. Then a very curious operation took place. One of us was told off to ascertain their sex, and nothing can describe our joy when we discovered what we were seeking among them, the female executioner who had tortured our friend.

The four others were shot on the spot, with their backs to us and close to the muzzles of our rifles; and then we turned our attention to the woman. What were we going to do with her? I must acknowledge that we were all of us in favor of shooting her. Hatred, and the wish to avenge Piedelot, had extinguished all pity in us, and we had forgotten that we were going to shoot a woman, but a woman reminded us of it, the captain's wife; at her entreaties, therefore, we determined to keep her a prisoner.

The captain's poor wife was to be severely punished for this act of clemency.

The next day we heard that the armistice had been extended to the eastern part of France, and we had to put an end to our little campaign. Two of us, who belonged to the neighborhood, returned home, so there were only four of us, all told: the captain, his wife, and two men. We belonged to Besancon, which was still being besieged in spite of the armistice.

"Let us stop here," said the captain. "I cannot believe that the war is going to end like this. The devil take it! Surely there are men still left in France; and now is the time to prove what they are made of. The spring is coming on, and the armistice is only a trap laid for the Prussians. During the time that it lasts, a new army will be raised, and some fine morning we shall fall upon them again. We shall be ready, and we have a hostage—let us remain here."

We fixed our quarters there. It was terribly cold, and we did not go out much, and somebody had always to keep the female prisoner in sight.

She was sullen, and never said anything, or else spoke of her husband, whom the captain had killed. She looked at him continually with fierce eyes, and we felt that she was tortured by a wild longing for revenge. That seemed to us to be the most suitable punishment for the terrible torments that she had made Piedelot suffer, for impotent vengeance is such intense pain!

Alas! we who knew how to avenge our comrade ought to have thought that this woman would know how to avenge her husband, and have been on our guard. It is true that one of us kept watch every night, and that at first we tied her by a long rope to the great oak bench that was fastened to the wall. But, by and by, as she had never tried to escape, in spite of her hatred for us, we relaxed our extreme prudence, and allowed her to sleep somewhere else except on the bench, and without being tied. What had we to fear? She was at the end of the room, a man was on guard at the door, and between her and the sentinel the captain's wife and two other men used to lie. She was alone and unarmed against four, so there could be no danger.

One night when we were asleep, and the captain was on guard, the lancer's wife was lying more quietly in her corner than usual, and she had even smiled for the first time since she had been our prisoner during the evening. Suddenly, however, in the middle of the night, we were all awakened by a terrible cry. We got up, groping about, and at once stumbled over a furious couple who were rolling about and fighting on the ground. It was the captain and the lancer's wife. We threw ourselves on them, and separated them in a moment. She was shouting and laughing, and he seemed to have the death rattle. All this took place in the dark. Two of us held her, and when a light was struck a terrible sight met our eyes. The captain was lying on the floor in a pool of blood, with an enormous gash in his throat, and his sword bayonet, that had been taken from his rifle, was sticking in the red, gaping wound. A few minutes afterward he died, without having been able to utter a word.

His wife did not shed a tear. Her eyes were dry, her throat was contracted, and she looked at the lancer's wife steadfastly, and with a calm ferocity that inspired fear.

"This woman belongs to me," she said to us suddenly. "You swore to me not a week ago to let me kill her as I chose, if she killed my husband; and you must keep your oath. You must fasten her securely to the fireplace, upright against the back of it, and then you can go where you like, but far from here. I will take my revenge on her myself. Leave the captain's body, and we three, he, she and I, will remain here."

We obeyed, and went away. She promised to write to us to Geneva, as we were returning thither.

VI

Two days later I received the following letter, dated the day after we had left, that had been written at an inn on the high road:

"MY FRIEND: I am writing to you, according to my promise. For the moment I am at the inn, where I have just handed my prisoner over to a Prussian officer.

"I must tell you, my friend, that this poor woman has left two children in Germany. She had followed her husband, whom she adored, as she did not wish him to be exposed to the risks of war by himself, and as her children were with their grandparents. I have learned all this since yesterday, and it has turned my ideas of vengeance into more humane feelings. At the very moment when I felt pleasure in insulting this woman, and in threatening her with the most fearful torments, in recalling Piedelot, who had been burned alive, and in threatening her with a similar death, she looked at me coldly, and said:

"'What have you got to reproach me with, Frenchwoman? You think that you will do right in avenging your husband's death, is not that so?'

"'Yes,' I replied.

"'Very well, then; in killing him, I did what you are going to do in burning me. I avenged my husband, for your husband killed him.'

"'Well,' I replied, 'as you approve of this vengeance, prepare to endure it.'

"'I do not fear it.'

"And in fact she did not seem to have lost courage. Her face was calm, and she looked at me without trembling, while I brought wood and dried leaves together, and feverishly threw on to them the powder from some cartridges, which was to make her funeral pile the more cruel.

"I hesitated in my thoughts of persecution for a moment. But the captain was there, pale and covered with blood, and he seemed to be looking at me with his large, glassy eyes, and I applied myself to my work again after kissing his pale lips. Suddenly, however, on raising my head, I saw that she was crying, and I felt rather surprised.

"'So you are frightened?' I said to her.

"'No, but when I saw you kiss your husband, I thought of mine, of all whom I love.'

"She continued to sob, but stopping suddenly, she said to me in broken words and in a low voice:

"'Have you any children?'

"A shiver rare over me, for I guessed that this poor woman had some. She asked me to look in a pocketbook which was in her bosom, and in it I saw two photographs of quite young children, a boy and a girl, with those kind, gentle, chubby faces that German children have. In it there were also two locks of light hair and a letter in a large, childish hand, and beginning with German words which meant:

"'My dear little mother.

"'I could not restrain my tears, my dear friend, and so I untied her, and without venturing to look at the face of my poor dead husband, who was not to be avenged, I went with her as far as the inn. She is free; I have just left her, and she kissed me with tears. I am going upstairs to my husband; come as soon as possible, my dear friend, to look for our two bodies.'"

I set off with all speed, and when I arrived there was a Prussian patrol at the cottage; and when I asked what it all meant, I was told that there was a captain of francs-tireurs and his wife inside, both dead. I gave their names; they saw that I knew them, and I begged to be allowed to arrange their funeral.

"Somebody has already undertaken it," was the reply. "Go in if you wish to, as you know them. You can settle about their funeral with their friend."

I went in. The captain and his wife were lying side by side on a bed, and were covered by a sheet. I raised it, and saw that the woman had inflicted a similar wound in her throat to that from which her husband had died.

At the side of the bed there sat, watching and weeping, the woman who had been mentioned to me as their best friend. It was the lancer's wife.

THE PRISONERS

There was not a sound in the forest save the indistinct, fluttering sound of the snow falling on the trees. It had been snowing since noon; a little fine snow, that covered the branches as with frozen moss, and spread a silvery covering over the dead leaves in the ditches, and covered the roads with a white, yielding carpet, and made still more intense the boundless silence of this ocean of trees.

Before the door of the forester's dwelling a young woman, her arms bare to the elbow, was chopping wood with a hatchet on a block of stone. She was tall, slender, strong-a true girl of the woods, daughter and wife of a forester.

A voice called from within the house:

"We are alone to-night, Berthine; you must come in. It is getting dark, and there may be Prussians or wolves about."

"I've just finished, mother," replied the young woman, splitting as she spoke an immense log of wood with strong, deft blows, which expanded her chest each time she raised her arms to strike. "Here I am; there's no need to be afraid; it's quite light still."

Then she gathered up her sticks and logs, piled them in the chimney corner, went back to close the great oaken shutters, and finally came in, drawing behind her the heavy bolts of the door.

Her mother, a wrinkled old woman whom age had rendered timid, was spinning by the fireside.

"I am uneasy," she said, "when your father's not here. Two women are not much good."

"Oh," said the younger woman, "I'd cheerfully kill a wolf or a Prussian if it came to that."

And she glanced at a heavy revolver hanging above the hearth.

Her husband had been called upon to serve in the army at the beginning of the Prussian invasion, and the two women had remained alone with the old father, a keeper named Nicolas Pichon, sometimes called Long-legs, who refused obstinately to leave his home and take refuge in the town.

This town was Rethel, an ancient stronghold built on a rock. Its inhabitants were patriotic, and had made up their minds to resist the invaders, to fortify their native place, and, if need be, to stand a siege as in the good old days. Twice already, under Henri IV and under Louis XIV, the people of Rethel had distinguished themselves by their heroic defence of their town. They would do as much now, by gad! or else be slaughtered within their own walls.

They had, therefore, bought cannon and rifles, organized a militia, and formed themselves into battalions and companies, and now spent their time drilling all day long in the square. All-bakers, grocers, butchers, lawyers, carpenters, booksellers, chemists-took their turn at military training at regular hours of the day, under the auspices of Monsieur Lavigne, a former noncommissioned officer in the dragoons, now a draper, having married the daughter and inherited the business of Monsieur Ravaudan, Senior.

He had taken the rank of commanding officer in Rethel, and, seeing that all the young men had gone off to the war, he had enlisted all the others who were in favor of resisting an attack. Fat men now invariably walked the streets at a rapid pace, to reduce their weight and improve their breathing, and weak men carried weights to strengthen their muscles.

And they awaited the Prussians. But the Prussians did not appear. They were not far off, however, for twice already their scouts had penetrated as far as the forest dwelling of Nicolas Pichon, called Long-legs.

The old keeper, who could run like a fox, had come and warned the town. The guns had been got ready, but the enemy had not shown themselves.

Long-legs' dwelling served as an outpost in the Aveline forest. Twice a week the old man went to the town for provisions and brought the citizens news of the outlying district.

On this particular day he had gone to announce the fact that a small detachment of German infantry had halted at his house the day before, about two o'clock in the afternoon, and had left again almost immediately. The noncommissioned officer in charge spoke French.

When the old man set out like this he took with him his dogs—two powerful animals with the jaws of lions-as a safeguard against the wolves, which were beginning to get fierce, and he left directions with the two women to barricade themselves securely within their dwelling as soon as night fell.

The younger feared nothing, but her mother was always apprehensive, and repeated continually:

"We'll come to grief one of these days. You see if we don't!"

This evening she was, if possible, more nervous than ever.

"Do you know what time your father will be back?" she asked.

"Oh, not before eleven, for certain. When he dines with the commandant he's always late."

And Berthine was hanging her pot over the fire to warm the soup when she suddenly stood still, listening attentively to a sound that had reached her through the chimney.

"There are people walking in the wood," she said; "seven or eight men at least."

The terrified old woman stopped her spinning wheel, and gasped:

"Oh, my God! And your father not here!"

She had scarcely finished speaking when a succession of violent blows shook the door.

As the woman made no reply, a loud, guttural voice shouted:

"Open the door!"

After a brief silence the same voice repeated:

"Open the door or I'll break it down!"

Berthine took the heavy revolver from its hook, slipped it into the pocket of her skirt, and, putting her ear to the door, asked:

"Who are you?" demanded the young woman. "What do you want?".

"The detachment that came here the other day," replied the voice.

"My men and I have lost our way in the forest since morning. Open the door or I'll break it down!"

The forester's daughter had no choice; she shot back the heavy bolts, threw open the ponderous shutter, and perceived in the wan light of the snow six men, six Prussian soldiers, the same who had visited the house the day before.

"What are you doing here at this time of night?" she asked dauntlessly.

"I lost my bearings," replied the officer; "lost them completely. Then I recognized this house. I've eaten nothing since morning, nor my men either."

"But I'm quite alone with my mother this evening," said Berthine.

"Never mind," replied the soldier, who seemed a decent sort of fellow. "We won't do you any harm, but you must give us something to eat. We are nearly dead with hunger and fatigue."

Then the girl moved aside.

"Come in;" she said.

Then entered, covered with snow, their helmets sprinkled with a creamy-looking froth, which gave them the appearance of meringues. They seemed utterly worn out.

The young woman pointed to the wooden benches on either side of the large table.

"Sit down," she said, "and I'll make you some soup. You certainly look tired out, and no mistake."

Then she bolted the door afresh.

She put more water in the pot, added butter and potatoes; then, taking down a piece of bacon from a hook in the chimney earner, cut it in two and slipped half of it into the pot.

The six men watched her movements with hungry eyes. They had placed their rifles and helmets in a corner and waited for supper, as well behaved as children on a school bench.

The old mother had resumed her spinning, casting from time to time a furtive and uneasy glance at the soldiers. Nothing was to be heard save the humming of the wheel, the crackling of the fire, and the singing of the water in the pot.

But suddenly a strange noise—a sound like the harsh breathing of some wild animal sniffing under the door-startled the occupants of the room.

The German officer sprang toward the rifles. Berthine stopped him with a gesture, and said, smilingly:

"It's only the wolves. They are like you—prowling hungry through the forest."

The incredulous man wanted to see with his own eyes, and as soon as the door was opened he perceived two large grayish animals disappearing with long, swinging trot into the darkness.

He returned to his seat, muttering:

"I wouldn't have believed it!"

And he waited quietly till supper was ready.

The men devoured their meal voraciously, with mouths stretched to their ears that they might swallow the more. Their round eyes opened at the same time as their jaws, and as the soup coursed down their throats it made a noise like the gurgling of water in a rainpipe.

The two women watched in silence the movements of the big red beards. The potatoes seemed to be engulfed in these moving fleeces.

But, as they were thirsty, the forester's daughter went down to the cellar to draw them some cider. She was gone some time. The cellar was small, with an arched ceiling, and had served, so people said, both as prison and as hiding-place during the Revolution. It was approached by means of a narrow, winding staircase, closed by a trap-door at the farther end of the kitchen.

When Berthine returned she was smiling mysteriously to herself. She gave the Germans her jug of cider.

Then she and her mother supped apart, at the other end of the kitchen.

The soldiers had finished eating, and were all six falling asleep as they sat round the table. Every now and then a forehead fell with a thud on the board, and the man, awakened suddenly, sat upright again.

Berthine said to the officer:

"Go and lie down, all of you, round the fire. There's lots of room for six. I'm going up to my room with my mother."

And the two women went upstairs. They could be heard locking the door and walking about overhead for a time; then they were silent.

The Prussians lay down on the floor, with their feet to the fire and their heads resting on their rolled-up cloaks. Soon all six snored loudly and uninterruptedly in six different keys.

They had been sleeping for some time when a shot rang out so loudly that it seemed directed against the very wall's of the house. The soldiers rose hastily. Two-then three-more shots were fired.

The door opened hastily, and Berthine appeared, barefooted and only half dressed, with her candle in her hand and a scared look on her face.

"There are the French," she stammered; "at least two hundred of them. If they find you here they'll burn the house down. For God's sake, hurry down into the cellar, and don't make a 'sound, whatever you do. If you make any noise we are lost."

"We'll go, we'll go," replied the terrified officer. "Which is the way?"

The young woman hurriedly raised the small, square trap-door, and the six men disappeared one after another down the narrow, winding staircase, feeling their way as they went.

But as soon as the spike of the out of the last helmet was out of sight Berthine lowered the heavy oaken lid—thick as a wall, hard as steel, furnished with the hinges and bolts of a prison cell—shot the two heavy bolts, and began to laugh long and silently, possessed with a mad longing to dance above the heads of her prisoners.

They made no sound, inclosed in the cellar as in a strong-box, obtaining air only from a small, iron-barred vent-hole.

Berthine lighted her fire again, hung the pot over it, and prepared more soup, saying to herself:

"Father will be tired to-night."

Then she sat and waited. The heavy pendulum of the clock swung to and fro with a monotonous tick.

Every now and then the young woman cast an impatient glance at the dial-a glance which seemed to say:

"I wish he'd be quick!"

But soon there was a sound of voices beneath her feet. Low, confused words reached her through the masonry which roofed the cellar. The Prussians were beginning to suspect the trick she had played them, and presently the officer came up the narrow staircase, and knocked at the trap-door.

"Open the door!" he cried.

"What do you want?" she said, rising from her seat and approaching the cellarway.

"Open the door!"

"I won't do any such thing!"

"Open it or I'll break it down!" shouted the man angrily.

She laughed.

"Hammer away, my good man! Hammer away!"

He struck with the butt-end of his gun at the closed oaken door. But it would have resisted a battering-ram.

The forester's daughter heard him go down the stairs again. Then the soldiers came one after another and tried their strength against the trapdoor. But, finding their efforts useless, they all returned to the cellar and began to talk among themselves.

The young woman heard them for a short time, then she rose, opened the door of the house; looked out into the night, and listened.

A sound of distant barking reached her ear. She whistled just as a huntsman would, and almost immediately two great dogs emerged from the darkness, and bounded to her side. She held them tight, and shouted at the top of her voice:

"Hullo, father!"

A far-off voice replied:

"Hullo, Berthine!"

She waited a few seconds, then repeated:

"Hullo, father!"

The voice, nearer now, replied:

"Hullo, Berthine!"

"Don't go in front of the vent-hole!" shouted his daughter. "There are Prussians in the cellar!"

Suddenly the man's tall figure could be seen to the left, standing between two tree trunks.

"Prussians in the cellar?" he asked anxiously. "What are they doing?"

The young woman laughed.

"They are the same as were here yesterday. They lost their way, and I've given them free lodgings in the cellar."

She told the story of how she had alarmed them by firing the revolver, and had shut them up in the cellar.

The man, still serious, asked:

"But what am I to do with them at this time of night?"

"Go and fetch Monsieur Lavigne with his men," she replied. "He'll take them prisoners. He'll be delighted."

Her father smiled.

"So he will-delighted."

"Here's some soup for you," said his daughter. "Eat it quick, and then be off."

The old keeper sat down at the table, and began to eat his soup, having first filled two plates and put them on the floor for the dogs.

The Prussians, hearing voices, were silent.

Long-legs set off a quarter of an hour later, and Berthine, with her head between her hands, waited.

The prisoners began to make themselves heard again. They shouted, called, and beat furiously with the butts of their muskets against the rigid trap-door of the cellar.

Then they fired shots through the vent-hole, hoping, no doubt, to be heard by any German detachment which chanced to be passing that way.

The forester's daughter did not stir, but the noise irritated and unnerved her. Blind anger rose in her heart against the prisoners; she would have been only too glad to kill them all, and so silence them.

Then, as her impatience grew, she watched the clock, counting the minutes as they passed.

Her father had been gone an hour and a half. He must have reached the town by now. She conjured up a vision of him telling the story to Monsieur Lavigne, who grew pale with emotion, and rang for his servant to bring him his arms and uniform. She fancied she could bear the drum as it sounded the call to arms. Frightened faces appeared at the windows. The citizen-soldiers emerged from their houses half dressed, out of breath, buckling on their belts, and hurrying to the commandant's house.

Then the troop of soldiers, with Long-legs at its head, set forth through the night and the snow toward the forest.

She looked at the clock. "They may be here in an hour."

A nervous impatience possessed her. The minutes seemed interminable. Would the time never come?

At last the clock marked the moment she had fixed on for their arrival. And she opened the door to listen for their approach. She perceived a shadowy form creeping toward the house. She was afraid, and cried out. But it was her father.

"They have sent me," he said, "to see if there is any change in the state of affairs."

"No-none."

Then he gave a shrill whistle. Soon a dark mass loomed up under the trees; the advance guard, composed of ten men.

"Don't go in front of the vent-hole!" repeated Long-legs at intervals.

And the first arrivals pointed out the much-dreaded vent-hole to those who came after.

At last the main body of the troop arrived, in all two hundred men, each carrying two hundred cartridges.

Monsieur Lavigne, in a state of intense excitement, posted them in such a fashion as to surround the whole house, save for a large space left vacant in front of the little hole on a level with the ground, through which the cellar derived its supply of air.

Monsieur Lavigne struck the trap-door a blow with his foot, and called:

"I wish to speak to the Prussian officer!"

The German did not reply.

"The Prussian officer!" again shouted the commandant.

Still no response. For the space of twenty minutes Monsieur Lavigne called on this silent officer to surrender with bag and baggage, promising him that all lives should be spared, and that he and his men should be accorded military honors. But he could extort no sign, either of consent or of defiance. The situation became a puzzling one.

The citizen-soldiers kicked their heels in the snow, slapping their arms across their chest, as cabdrivers do, to warm themselves, and gazing at the vent-hole with a growing and childish desire to pass in front of it.

At last one of them took the risk-a man named Potdevin, who was fleet of limb. He ran like a deer across the zone of danger. The experiment succeeded. The prisoners gave no sign of life.

A voice cried:

"There's no one there!"

And another soldier crossed the open space before the dangerous vent-hole. Then this hazardous sport developed into a game. Every minute a man ran swiftly from one side to the other, like a boy playing baseball, kicking up the snow behind him as he ran. They had lighted big fires of dead wood at which to warm themselves, and the, figures of the runners were illumined by the flames as they passed rapidly from the camp on the right to that on the left.

Some one shouted:

"It's your turn now, Maloison."

Maloison was a fat baker, whose corpulent person served to point many a joke among his comrades.

He hesitated. They chaffed him. Then, nerving himself to the effort, he set off at a little, waddling gait, which shook his fat paunch and made the whole detachment laugh till they cried.

"Bravo, bravo, Maloison!" they shouted for his encouragement.

He had accomplished about two-thirds of his journey when a long, crimson flame shot forth from the vent-hole. A loud report followed, and the fat baker fell face forward to the ground, uttering a frightful scream. No one went to his assistance. Then he was seen to drag himself, groaning, on all-fours through the snow until he was beyond danger, when he fainted.

He was shot in the upper part of the thigh.

After the first surprise and fright were over they laughed at him again. But Monsieur Lavigne appeared on the threshold of the forester's dwelling. He had formed his plan of attack. He called in a loud voice "I want Planchut, the plumber, and his workmen."

Three men approached.

"Take the eavestroughs from the roof."

In a quarter of an hour they brought the commandant thirty yards of pipes.

Next, with infinite precaution, he had a small round hole drilled in the trap-door; then, making a conduit with the troughs from the pump to this opening, he said, with an air of extreme satisfaction:

"Now we'll give these German gentlemen something to drink."

A shout of frenzied admiration, mingled with uproarious laughter, burst from his followers. And the commandant organized relays of men, who were to relieve one another every five minutes. Then he commanded:

"Pump!!!"

And, the pump handle having been set in motion, a stream of water trickled throughout the length of the piping, and flowed from step to step down the cellar stairs with a gentle, gurgling sound.

They waited.

An hour passed, then two, then three. The commandant, in a state of feverish agitation, walked up and down the kitchen, putting his ear to the ground every now and then to discover, if possible, what the enemy were doing and whether they would soon capitulate.

The enemy was astir now. They could be heard moving the casks about, talking, splashing through the water.

Then, about eight o'clock in the morning, a voice came from the vent-hole "I want to speak to the French officer."

Lavigne replied from the window, taking care not to put his head out too far:

"Do you surrender?"

"I surrender."

"Then put your rifles outside."

A rifle immediately protruded from the hole, and fell into the snow, then another and another, until all were disposed of. And the voice which had spoken before said:

"I have no more. Be quick! I am drowned."

"Stop pumping!" ordered the commandant.

And the pump handle hung motionless.

Then, having filled the kitchen with armed and waiting soldiers, he slowly raised the oaken trapdoor.

Four heads appeared, soaking wet, four fair heads with long, sandy hair, and one after another the six Germans emerged—scared, shivering and dripping from head to foot.

They were seized and bound. Then, as the French feared a surprise, they set off at once in two convoys, one in charge of the prisoners, and the other conducting Maloison on a mattress borne on poles.

They made a triumphal entry into Rethel.

Monsieur Lavigne was decorated as a reward for having captured a Prussian advance guard, and the fat baker received the military medal for wounds received at the hands of the enemy.

TWO LITTLE SOLDIERS

Every Sunday, as soon as they were free, the little soldiers would go for a walk. They turned to the right on leaving the barracks, crossed Courbevoie with rapid strides, as though on a forced march; then, as the houses grew scarcer, they slowed down and followed the dusty road which leads to Bezons.

They were small and thin, lost in their ill-fitting capes, too large and too long, whose sleeves covered their hands; their ample red trousers fell in folds around their ankles. Under the high, stiff shako one could just barely perceive two thin, hollow-cheeked Breton faces, with their calm, naive blue eyes. They never spoke during their journey, going straight before them, the same idea in each one's mind taking the place of conversation. For at the entrance of the little forest of Champioux they had found a spot which reminded them of home, and they did not feel happy anywhere else.

At the crossing of the Colombes and Chatou roads, when they arrived under the trees, they would take off their heavy, oppressive headgear and wipe their foreheads.

They always stopped for a while on the bridge at Bezons, and looked at the Seine. They stood there several minutes, bending over the railing, watching the white sails, which perhaps reminded them of their home, and of the fishing smacks leaving for the open.

As soon as they had crossed the Seine, they would purchase provisions at the delicatessen, the baker's, and the wine merchant's. A piece of bologna, four cents' worth of bread, and a quart of wine, made up the luncheon which they carried away, wrapped up in their handkerchiefs. But as soon as they were out of the village their gait would slacken and they would begin to talk.

Before them was a plain with a few clumps of trees, which led to the woods, a little forest which seemed to remind them of that other forest at Kermarivan. The wheat and oat fields bordered on the narrow path, and Jean Kerderen said each time to Luc Le Ganidec:

"It's just like home, just like Plounivon."

"Yes, it's just like home."

And they went on, side by side, their minds full of dim memories of home. They saw the fields, the hedges, the forests, and beaches.

Each time they stopped near a large stone on the edge of the private estate, because it reminded them of the dolmen of Locneuven.

As soon as they reached the first clump of trees, Luc Le Ganidec would cut off a small stick, and, whittling it slowly, would walk on, thinking of the folks at home.

Jean Kerderen carried the provisions.

From time to time Luc would mention a name, or allude to some boyish prank which would give them food for plenty of thought. And the home country, so dear and so distant, would little by little gain possession of their minds, sending them back through space, to the well-known forms and noises, to the familiar scenery, with the fragrance of its green fields and sea air. They no longer noticed the smells of the city. And in their dreams they saw their friends leaving, perhaps forever, for the dangerous fishing grounds.

They were walking slowly, Luc Le Ganidec and Jean Kerderen, contented and sad, haunted by a sweet sorrow, the slow and penetrating sorrow of a captive animal which remembers the days of its freedom.

And when Luc had finished whittling his stick, they came to a little nook, where every Sunday they took their meal. They found the two bricks, which they had hidden in a hedge, and they made a little fire of dry branches and roasted their sausages on the ends of their knives.

When their last crumb of bread had been eaten and the last drop of wine had been drunk, they stretched themselves out on the grass side by side, without speaking, their half-closed eyes looking away in the distance, their hands clasped as in prayer, their red-trousered legs mingling with the bright colors of the wild flowers.

Towards noon they glanced, from time to time, towards the village of Bezons, for the dairy maid would soon be coming. Every Sunday she would pass in front of them on the way to milk her cow, the only cow in the neighborhood which was sent out to pasture.

Soon they would see the girl, coming through the fields, and it pleased them to watch the sparkling sunbeams reflected from her shining pail. They never spoke of her. They were just glad to see her, without understanding why.

She was a tall, strapping girl, freckled and tanned by the open air—a girl typical of the Parisian suburbs.

Once, on noticing that they were always sitting in the same place, she said to them:

"Do you always come here?"

Luc Le Ganidec, more daring than his friend, stammered:

"Yes, we come here for our rest."

That was all. But the following Sunday, on seeing them, she smiled with the kindly smile of a woman who understood their shyness, and she asked:

"What are you doing here? Are you watching the grass grow?"

Luc, cheered up, smiled: "P'raps."

She continued: "It's not growing fast, is it?"

He answered, still laughing: "Not exactly."

She went on. But when she came back with her pail full of milk, she stopped before them and said:

"Want some? It will remind you of home."

She had, perhaps instinctively, guessed and touched the right spot.

Both were moved. Then not without difficulty, she poured some milk into the bottle in which they had brought their wine. Luc started to drink, carefully watching lest he should take more than his share. Then he passed the bottle to Jean. She stood before them, her hands on her hips, her pail at her feet, enjoying the pleasure that she was giving them. Then she went on, saying: "Well, bye-bye until next Sunday!"

For a long time they watched her tall form as it receded in the distance, blending with the background, and finally disappeared.

The following week as they left the barracks, Jean said to Luc:

"Don't you think we ought to buy her something good?"

They were sorely perplexed by the problem of choosing something to bring to the dairy maid. Luc was in favor of bringing her some chitterlings; but Jean, who had a sweet tooth, thought that candy would be the best thing. He won, and so they went to a grocery to buy two sous' worth, of red and white candies.

This time they ate more quickly than usual, excited by anticipation.

Jean was the first one to notice her. "There she is," he said; and Luc answered: "Yes, there she is."

She smiled when she saw them, and cried:

"Well, how are you to-day?"

They both answered together:

"All right! How's everything with you?"

Then she started to talk of simple things which might interest them; of the weather, of the crops, of her masters.

They didn't dare to offer their candies, which were slowly melting in Jean's pocket. Finally Luc, growing bolder, murmured:

"We have brought you something."

She asked: "Let's see it."

Then Jean, blushing to the tips of his ears, reached in his pocket, and drawing out the little paper bag, handed it to her.

She began to eat the little sweet dainties. The two soldiers sat in front of her, moved and delighted.

At last she went to do her milking, and when she came back she again gave them some milk.

They thought of her all through the week and often spoke of her: The following Sunday she sat beside them for a longer time.

The three of them sat there, side by side, their eyes looking far away in the distance, their hands clasped over their knees, and they told each other little incidents and little details of the villages where they were born, while the cow, waiting to be milked, stretched her heavy head toward the girl and mooed.

Soon the girl consented to eat with them and to take a sip of wine. Often she brought them plums pocket for plums were now ripe. Her presence enlivened the little Breton soldiers, who chattered away like two birds.

One Tuesday something unusual happened to Luc Le Ganidec; he asked for leave and did not return until ten o'clock at night.

Jean, worried and racked his brain to account for his friend's having obtained leave.

The following Friday, Luc borrowed ten sons from one of his friends, and once more asked and obtained leave for several hours.

When he started out with Jean on Sunday he seemed queer, disturbed, changed. Kerderen did not understand; he vaguely suspected something, but he could not guess what it might be.

They went straight to the usual place, and lunched slowly. Neither was hungry.

Soon the girl appeared. They watched her approach as they always did. When she was near, Luc arose and went towards her. She placed her pail on the ground and kissed him. She kissed him passionately, throwing her arms around his neck, without paying attention to Jean, without even noticing that he was there.

Poor Jean was dazed, so dazed that he could not understand. His mind was upset and his heart broken, without his even realizing why.

Then the girl sat down beside Luc, and they started to chat.

Jean was not looking at them. He understood now why his friend had gone out twice during the week. He felt the pain and the sting which treachery and deceit leave in their wake.

Luc and the girl went together to attend to the cow.

Jean followed them with his eyes. He saw them disappear side by side, the red trousers of his friend making a scarlet spot against the white road. It was Luc who sank the stake to which the cow was tethered. The girl stooped down to milk the cow, while he absent-mindedly stroked the animal's glossy neck. Then they left the pail in the grass and disappeared in the woods.

Jean could no longer see anything but the wall of leaves through which they had passed. He was unmanned so that he did not have strength to stand. He stayed there, motionless, bewildered and grieving-simple, passionate grief. He wanted to weep, to run away, to hide somewhere, never to see anyone again.

Then he saw them coming back again. They were walking slowly, hand in hand, as village lovers do. Luc was carrying the pail.

After kissing him again, the girl went on, nodding carelessly to Jean. She did not offer him any milk that day.

The two little soldiers sat side by side, motionless as always, silent and quiet, their calm faces in no way betraying the trouble in their hearts. The sun shone down on them. From time to time they could hear the plaintive lowing of the cow. At the usual time they arose to return.

Luc was whittling a stick. Jean carried the empty bottle. He left it at the wine merchant's in Bezons. Then they stopped on the bridge, as they did every Sunday, and watched the water flowing by.

Jean leaned over the railing, farther and farther, as though he had seen something in the stream which hypnotized him. Luc said to him:

"What's the matter? Do you want a drink?"

He had hardly said the last word when Jean's head carried away the rest of his body, and the little blue and red soldier fell like a shot and disappeared in the water.

Luc, paralyzed with horror, tried vainly to shout for help. In the distance he saw something move; then his friend's head bobbed up out of the water only to disappear again.

Farther down he again noticed a hand, just one hand, which appeared and again went out of sight. That was all.

The boatmen who had rushed to the scene found the body that day.

Luc ran back to the barracks, crazed, and with eyes and voice full of tears, he related the accident: "He leaned—he—he was leaning —so far over—that his head carried him away—and—he—fell —he fell——"

Emotion choked him so that he could say no more. If he had only known.

FATHER MILON

For a month the hot sun has been parching the fields. Nature is expanding beneath its rays; the fields are green as far as the eye can see. The big azure dome of the sky is unclouded. The farms of Normandy, scattered over the plains and surrounded by a belt of tall beeches, look, from a distance, like little woods. On closer view, after lowering the worm-eaten wooden bars, you imagine yourself in an immense garden, for all the ancient apple-trees, as gnarled as the peasants themselves, are in bloom. The sweet scent of their blossoms mingles with the heavy smell of the earth and the penetrating odor of the stables. It is noon. The family is eating under the shade of a pear tree planted in front of the door; father, mother, the four children, and the help—two women and three men are all there. All are silent. The soup is eaten and then a dish of potatoes fried with bacon is brought on.

From time to time one of the women gets up and takes a pitcher down to the cellar to fetch more cider.

The man, a big fellow about forty years old, is watching a grape vine, still bare, which is winding and twisting like a snake along the side of the house.

At last he says: "Father's vine is budding early this year. Perhaps we may get something from it."

The woman then turns round and looks, without saying a word.

This vine is planted on the spot where their father had been shot.

It was during the war of 1870. The Prussians were occupying the whole country. General Faidherbe, with the Northern Division of the army, was opposing them.

The Prussians had established their headquarters at this farm. The old farmer to whom it belonged, Father Pierre Milon, had received and quartered them to the best of his ability.

For a month the German vanguard had been in this village. The French remained motionless, ten leagues away; and yet, every night, some of the Uhlans disappeared.

Of all the isolated scouts, of all those who were sent to the outposts, in groups of not more than three, not one ever returned.

They were picked up the next morning in a field or in a ditch. Even their horses were found along the roads with their throats cut.

These murders seemed to be done by the same men, who could never be found.

The country was terrorized. Farmers were shot on suspicion, women were imprisoned; children were frightened in order to try and obtain information. Nothing could be ascertained.

But, one morning, Father Milon was found stretched out in the barn, with a sword gash across his face.

Two Uhlans were found dead about a mile and a half from the farm. One of them was still holding his bloody sword in his hand. He had fought, tried to defend himself. A court-martial was immediately held in the open air, in front of the farm. The old man was brought before it.

He was sixty-eight years old, small, thin, bent, with two big hands resembling the claws of a crab. His colorless hair was sparse and thin, like the down of a young duck, allowing patches of his scalp to be seen. The brown and wrinkled skin of his neck showed big veins which disappeared behind his jaws and came out again at the temples. He had the reputation of being miserly and hard to deal with.

They stood him up between four soldiers, in front of the kitchen table, which had been dragged outside. Five officers and the colonel seated themselves opposite him.

The colonel spoke in French:

"Father Milon, since we have been here we have only had praise for you. You have always been obliging and even attentive to us. But to-day a terrible accusation is hanging over you, and you must clear the matter up. How did you receive that wound on your face?"

The peasant answered nothing.

The colonel continued:

"Your silence accuses you, Father Milon. But I want you to answer me! Do you understand? Do you know who killed the two Uhlans who were found this morning near Calvaire?"

The old man answered clearly

"I did."

The colonel, surprised, was silent for a minute, looking straight at the prisoner. Father Milon stood impassive, with the stupid look of the peasant, his eyes lowered as though he were talking to the priest. Just one thing betrayed an uneasy mind; he was continually swallowing his saliva, with a visible effort, as though his throat were terribly contracted.

The man's family, his son Jean, his daughter-in-law and his two grandchildren were standing a few feet behind him, bewildered and affrighted.

The colonel went on:

"Do you also know who killed all the scouts who have been found dead, for a month, throughout the country, every morning?"

The old man answered with the same stupid look:

"I did."

"You killed them all?"

"Uh huh! I did."

"You alone? All alone?"

"Uh huh!"

"Tell me how you did it."

This time the man seemed moved; the necessity for talking any length of time annoyed him visibly. He stammered:

"I dunno! I simply did it."

The colonel continued:

"I warn you that you will have to tell me everything. You might as well make up your mind right away. How did you begin?"

The man cast a troubled look toward his family, standing close behind him. He hesitated a minute longer, and then suddenly made up his mind to obey the order.

"I was coming home one night at about ten o'clock, the night after you got here. You and your soldiers had taken more than fifty ecus worth of forage from me, as well as a cow and two sheep. I said to myself: 'As much as they take from you; just so much will you make them pay back.' And then I had other things on my mind which I will tell you. Just then I noticed one of your soldiers who was smoking his pipe by the ditch behind the barn. I went and got my scythe and crept up slowly behind him, so that he couldn't hear me. And I cut his head off with one single blow, just as I would a blade of grass, before he could say 'Booh!' If you should look at the bottom of the pond, you will find him tied up in a potato-sack, with a stone fastened to it.

"I got an idea. I took all his clothes, from his boots to his cap, and hid them away in the little wood behind the yard."

The old man stopped. The officers remained speechless, looking at each other. The questioning began again, and this is what they learned.

Once this murder committed, the man had lived with this one thought: "Kill the Prussians!" He hated them with the blind, fierce hate of the greedy yet patriotic peasant. He had his idea, as he said. He waited several days.

He was allowed to go and come as he pleased, because he had shown himself so humble, submissive and obliging to the invaders. Each night he saw the outposts leave. One night he followed them, having heard the name of the village to which the men were going, and having learned the few words of German which he needed for his plan through associating with the soldiers.

He left through the back yard, slipped into the woods, found the dead man's clothes and put them on. Then he began to crawl through the fields, following along the hedges in order to keep out of sight, listening to the slightest noises, as wary as a poacher.

As soon as he thought the time ripe, he approached the road and hid behind a bush. He waited for a while. Finally, toward midnight, he heard the sound of a galloping horse. The man put his ear to the ground in order to make sure that only one horseman was approaching, then he got ready.

An Uhlan came galloping along, carrying des patches. As he went, he was all eyes and ears. When he was only a few feet away, Father Milon dragged himself across the road, moaning: "Hilfe! Hilfe!" (Help! Help!) The horseman stopped, and recognizing a German, he thought he was wounded and dismounted, coming nearer without any suspicion, and just as he was leaning over the unknown man, he received, in the pit of his stomach, a heavy thrust from the long curved blade of the sabre. He dropped without suffering pain, quivering only in the final throes. Then the farmer, radiant with the silent joy of an old peasant, got up again, and, for his own pleasure, cut the dead man's throat. He then dragged the body to the ditch and threw it in.

The horse quietly awaited its master. Father Milon mounted him and started galloping across the plains.

About an hour later he noticed two more Uhlans who were returning home, side by side. He rode straight for them, once more crying "Hilfe! Hilfe!"

The Prussians, recognizing the uniform, let him approach without distrust. The old man passed between them like a cannon-ball, felling them both, one with his sabre and the other with a revolver.

Then he killed the horses, German horses! After that he quickly returned to the woods and hid one of the horses. He left his uniform there and again put on his old clothes; then going back into bed, he slept until morning.

For four days he did not go out, waiting for the inquest to be terminated; but on the fifth day he went out again and killed two more soldiers by the same stratagem. From that time on he did not stop. Each night he wandered about in search of adventure, killing Prussians, sometimes here and sometimes there, galloping through deserted fields, in the moonlight, a lost Uhlan, a hunter of men. Then, his task accomplished, leaving behind him the bodies lying along the roads, the old farmer would return and hide his horse and uniform.

He went, toward noon, to carry oats and water quietly to his mount, and he fed it well as he required from it a great amount of work.

But one of those whom he had attacked the night before, in defending himself slashed the old peasant across the face with his sabre.

However, he had killed them both. He had come back and hidden the horse and put on his ordinary clothes again; but as he reached home he began to feel faint, and had dragged himself as far as the stable, being unable to reach the house.

They had found him there, bleeding, on the straw.

When he had finished his tale, he suddenly lifted up his head and looked proudly at the Prussian officers.

The colonel, who was gnawing at his mustache, asked:

"You have nothing else to say?"

"Nothing more; I have finished my task; I killed sixteen, not one more or less."

"Do you know that you are going to die?"

"I haven't asked for mercy."

"Have you been a soldier?"

"Yes, I served my time. And then, you had killed my father, who was a soldier of the first Emperor. And last month you killed my youngest son, Francois, near Evreux. I owed you one for that; I paid. We are quits."

The officers were looking at each other.

The old man continued:

"Eight for my father, eight for the boy—we are quits. I did not seek any quarrel with you. I don't know you. I don't even know where you come from. And here you are, ordering me about in my home as though it were your own. I took my revenge upon the others. I'm not sorry."

And, straightening up his bent back, the old man folded his arms in the attitude of a modest hero.

The Prussians talked in a low tone for a long time. One of them, a captain, who had also lost his son the previous month, was defending the poor wretch. Then the colonel arose and, approaching Father Milon, said in a low voice:

"Listen, old man, there is perhaps a way of saving your life, it is to—"

But the man was not listening, and, his eyes fixed on the hated officer, while the wind played with the downy hair on his head, he distorted his slashed face, giving it a truly terrible expression, and, swelling out his chest, he spat, as hard as he could, right in the Prussian's face.

The colonel, furious, raised his hand, and for the second time the man spat in his face.

All the officers had jumped up and were shrieking orders at the same time.

In less than a minute the old man, still impassive, was pushed up against the wall and shot, looking smilingly the while toward Jean, his eldest son, his daughter-in-law and his two grandchildren, who witnessed this scene in dumb terror.

A COUP D'ETAT

Paris had just heard of the disaster at Sedan. A republic had been declared. All France was wavering on the brink of this madness which lasted until after the Commune. From one end of the country to the other everybody was playing soldier.

Cap-makers became colonels, fulfilling the duties of generals; revolvers and swords were displayed around big, peaceful stomachs wrapped in flaming red belts; little tradesmen became warriors commanding battalions of brawling volunteers, and swearing like pirates in order to give themselves some prestige.

The sole fact of handling firearms crazed these people, who up to that time had only handled scales, and made them, without any reason, dangerous to all. Innocent people were shot to prove that they knew how to kill; in forests which had never seen a Prussian, stray dogs, grazing cows and browsing horses were killed.

Each one thought himself called upon to play a great part in military affairs. The cafes of the smallest villages, full of uniformed tradesmen, looked like barracks or hospitals.

The town of Canneville was still in ignorance of the maddening news from the army and the capital; nevertheless, great excitement had prevailed for the last month, the opposing parties finding themselves face to face.

The mayor, Viscount de Varnetot, a thin, little old man, a conservative, who had recently, from ambition, gone over to the Empire, had seen a determined opponent arise in Dr. Massarel, a big, full-blooded man, leader of the Republican party of the neighborhood, a high official in the local masonic lodge, president of the Agricultural Society and of the firemen's banquet and the organizer of the rural militia which was to save the country.

In two weeks, he had managed to gather together sixty-three volunteers, fathers of families, prudent farmers and town merchants, and every morning he would drill them in the square in front of the town-hall.

When, perchance, the mayor would come to the municipal building, Commander Massarel, girt with pistols, would pass proudly in front of his troop, his sword in his hand, and make all of them cry: "Long live the Fatherland!" And it had been noticed that this cry excited the little viscount, who probably saw in it a menace, a threat, as well as the odious memory of the great Revolution.

On the morning of the fifth of September, the doctor, in full uniform, his revolver on the table, was giving a consultation to an old couple, a farmer who had been suffering from varicose veins for the last seven years and had waited until his wife had them also, before he would consult the doctor, when the postman brought in the paper.

M. Massarel opened it, grew pale, suddenly rose, and lifting his hands to heaven in a gesture of exaltation, began to shout at the top of his voice before the two frightened country folks:

"Long live the Republic! long live the Republic! long live the Republic!"

Then he fell back in his chair, weak from emotion.

And as the peasant resumed: "It started with the ants, which began to run up and down my legs—-" Dr. Massarel exclaimed:

"Shut up! I haven't got time to bother with your nonsense. The Republic has been proclaimed, the emperor has been taken prisoner, France is saved! Long live the Republic!"

Running to the door, he howled:

"Celeste, quick, Celeste!"

The servant, affrighted, hastened in; he was trying to talk so rapidly, that he could only stammer:

"My boots, my sword, my cartridge-box and the Spanish dagger which is on my night-table! Hasten!"

As the persistent peasant, taking advantage of a moment's silence, continued, "I seemed to get big lumps which hurt me when I walk," the physician, exasperated, roared:

"Shut up and get out! If you had washed your feet it would not have happened!"

Then, grabbing him by the collar, he yelled at him:

"Can't you understand that we are a republic, you brass-plated idiot!"

But professional sentiment soon calmed him, and he pushed the bewildered couple out, saying:

"Come back to-morrow, come back to-morrow, my friends. I haven't any time to-day."

As he equipped himself from head to foot, he gave a series of important orders to his servant:

"Run over to Lieutenant Picart and to Second Lieutenant Pommel, and tell them that I am expecting them here immediately. Also send me Torchebeuf with his drum. Quick! quick!"

When Celeste had gone out, he sat down and thought over the situation and the difficulties which he would have to surmount.

The three men arrived together in their working clothes. The commandant, who expected to see them in uniform, felt a little shocked.

"Don't you people know anything? The emperor has been taken prisoner, the Republic has been proclaimed. We must act. My position is delicate, I might even say dangerous."

He reflected for a few moments before his bewildered subordinates, then he continued:

"We must act and not hesitate; minutes count as hours in times like these. All depends on the promptness of our decision. You, Picart, go to the cure and order him to ring the alarm-bell, in order to get together the people, to whom I am going to announce the news. You, Torchebeuf beat the tattoo throughout the whole neighborhood as far as the hamlets of Gerisaie and Salmare, in order to assemble the militia in the public square. You, Pommel, get your uniform on quickly, just the coat and cap. We are going to the town-hall to demand Monsieur de Varnetot to surrender his powers to me. Do you understand?"

"Yes."

"Now carry out those orders quickly. I will go over to your house with you, Pommel, since we shall act together."

Five minutes later, the commandant and his subordinates, armed to the teeth, appeared on the square, just as the little Viscount de Varnetot, his legs encased in gaiters as for a hunting party, his gun on his shoulder, was coming down the other street at double-quick time, followed by his three green-coated guards, their swords at their sides and their guns swung over their shoulders.

While the doctor stopped, bewildered, the four men entered the town-hall and closed the door behind them.

"They have outstripped us," muttered the physician, "we must now wait for reenforcements. There is nothing to do for the present."

Lieutenant Picart now appeared on the scene.

"The priest refuses to obey," he said. "He has even locked himself in the church with the sexton and beadle."

On the other side of the square, opposite the white, tightly closed town-hall, stood the church, silent and dark, with its massive oak door studded with iron.

But just as the perplexed inhabitants were sticking their heads out of the windows or coming out on their doorsteps, the drum suddenly began to be heard, and Torchebeuf appeared, furiously beating the tattoo. He crossed the square running, and disappeared along the road leading to the fields.

The commandant drew his sword, and advanced alone to half way between the two buildings behind which the enemy had intrenched itself, and, waving his sword over his head, he roared with all his might:

"Long live the Republic! Death to traitors!"

Then he returned to his officers.

The butcher, the baker and the druggist, much disturbed, were anxiously pulling down their shades and closing their shops. The grocer alone kept open.

However, the militia were arriving by degrees, each man in a different uniform, but all wearing a black cap with gold braid, the cap being the principal part of the outfit. They were armed with old rusty guns, the old guns which had hung for thirty years on the kitchen wall; and they looked a good deal like an army of tramps.

When he had about thirty men about him, the commandant, in a few words, outlined the situation to them. Then, turning to his staff: "Let us act," he said.

The villagers were gathering together and talking the matter over.

The doctor quickly decided on a plan of campaign.

"Lieutenant Picart, you will advance under the windows of this town-hall and summon Monsieur de Varnetot, in the name of the Republic, to hand the keys over to me."

But the lieutenant, a master mason, refused:

"You're smart, you are. I don't care to get killed, thank you. Those people in there shoot straight, don't you forget it. Do your errands yourself."

The commandant grew very red.

"I command you to go in the name of discipline!"

The lieutenant rebelled:

"I'm not going to have my beauty spoiled without knowing why."

All the notables, gathered in a group near by, began to laugh. One of them cried:

"You are right, Picart, this isn't the right time."

The doctor then muttered:

"Cowards!"

And, leaving his sword and his revolver in the hands of a soldier, he advanced slowly, his eye fastened on the windows, expecting any minute to see a gun trained on him.

When he was within a few feet of the building, the doors at both ends, leading into the two schools, opened and a flood of children ran out, boys from one side, girls from the ether, and began to play around the doctor, in the big empty square, screeching and screaming, and making so much noise that he could not make himself heard.

As soon as the last child was out of the building, the two doors closed again.

Most of the youngsters finally dispersed, and the commandant called in a loud voice:

"Monsieur de Varnetot!"

A window on the first floor opened and M. de Varnetot appeared.

The commandant continued:

"Monsieur, you know that great events have just taken place which have changed the entire aspect of the government. The one which you represented no longer exists. The one which I represent is taking control. Under these painful, but decisive circumstances, I come, in the name of the new Republic, to ask you to turn over to me the office which you held under the former government."

M. de Varnetot answered:

"Doctor, I am the mayor of Canneville, duly appointed, and I shall remain mayor of Canneville until I have been dismissed by a decree from my superiors. As mayor, I am in my place in the townhall, and here I stay. Anyhow, just try to get me out."

He closed the window.

The commandant returned to his troop. But before giving any information, eyeing Lieutenant Picart from head to foot, he exclaimed:

"You're a great one, you are! You're a fine specimen of manhood! You're a disgrace to the army! I degrade you."

"I don't give a——!"

He turned away and mingled with a group of townspeople.

Then the doctor hesitated. What could he do? Attack? But would his men obey orders? And then, did he have the right to do so?

An idea struck him. He ran to the telegraph office, opposite the town-hall, and sent off three telegrams:

To the new republican government in Paris.

To the new prefect of the Seine-Inferieure, at Rouen.

To the new republican sub-prefect at Dieppe.

He explained the situation, pointed out the danger which the town would run if it should remain in the hands of the royalist mayor; offered his faithful services, asked for orders and signed, putting all his titles after his name.

Then he returned to his battalion, and, drawing ten francs from his pocket, he cried: "Here, my friends, go eat and drink; only leave me a detachment of ten men to guard against anybody's leaving the town-hall."

But ex-Lieutenant Picart, who had been talking with the watchmaker, heard him; he began to laugh, and exclaimed: "By Jove, if they come out, it'll give you a chance to get in. Otherwise I can see you standing out there for the rest of your life!"

The doctor did not reply, and he went to luncheon.

In the afternoon, he disposed his men about the town as though they were in immediate danger of an ambush.

Several times he passed in front of the town-hall and of the church without noticing anything suspicious; the two buildings looked as though empty.

The butcher, the baker and the druggist once more opened up their stores.

Everybody was talking about the affair. If the emperor were a prisoner, there must have been some kind of treason. They did not know exactly which of the republics had returned to power.

Night fell.

Toward nine o'clock, the doctor, alone, noiselessly approached the entrance of the public building, persuaded that the enemy must have gone to bed; and, as he was preparing to batter down the door with a pick-axe, the deep voice of a sentry suddenly called:

"Who goes there?"

And M. Massarel retreated as fast as his legs could carry him.

Day broke without any change in the situation.

Armed militia occupied the square. All the citizens had gathered around this troop awaiting developments. Even neighboring villagers had come to look on.

Then the doctor, seeing that his reputation was at stake, resolved to put an end to the matter in one way or another; and he was about to take some measures, undoubtedly energetic ones, when the door of the telegraph station opened and the little servant of the postmistress appeared, holding in her hands two papers.

First she went to the commandant and gave him one of the despatches; then she crossed the empty square, confused at seeing the eyes of everyone on her, and lowering her head and running along with little quick steps, she went and knocked softly at the door of the barricaded house, as though ignorant of the fact that those behind it were armed.

The door opened wide enough to let a man's hand reach out and receive the message; and the young girl returned blushing, ready to cry at being thus stared at by the whole countryside.

In a clear voice, the doctor cried:

"Silence, if you please."

When the populace had quieted down, he continued proudly:

"Here is the communication which I have received from the government."

And lifting the telegram he read:

Former mayor dismissed. Inform him immediately, More orders

following.

For the sub-prefect:

SAPIN, Councillor.

He was-triumphant; his heart was throbbing with joy and his hands were trembling; but Picart, his former subordinate, cried to him from a neighboring group:

"That's all right; but supposing the others don't come out, what good is the telegram going to do you?"

M. Massarel grew pale. He had not thought of that; if the others did not come out, he would now have to take some decisive step. It was not only his right, but his duty.

He looked anxiously at the town-hall, hoping to see the door open and his adversary give in.

The door remained closed. What could he do? The crowd was growing and closing around the militia. They were laughing.

One thought especially tortured the doctor. If he attacked, he would have to march at the head of his men; and as, with him dead, all strife would cease, it was at him and him only that M. de Varnetot and his three guards would aim. And they were good shots, very good shots, as Picart had just said. But an idea struck him and, turning to Pommel, he ordered:

"Run quickly to the druggist and ask him to lend me a towel and a stick."

The lieutenant hastened.

He would make a flag of truce, a white flag, at the sight of which the royalist heart of the mayor would perhaps rejoice.

Pommel returned with the cloth and a broom-stick. With some twine they completed the flag, and M. Massarel, grasping it in both hands and holding it in front of him, again advanced in the direction of the town-hall. When he was opposite the door, he once more called: "Monsieur de Varnetot!" The door suddenly opened and M. de Varnetot and his three guards appeared on the threshold.

Instinctively the doctor stepped back; then he bowed courteously to his enemy, and, choking with emotion, he announced: "I have come, monsieur, to make you acquainted with the orders which I have received."

The nobleman, without returning the bow, answered: "I resign, monsieur, but understand that it is neither through fear of, nor obedience to, the odious government which has usurped the power." And, emphasizing every word, he declared: "I do not wish to appear, for a single day, to serve the Republic. That's all."

Massarel, stunned, answered nothing; and M. de Varnetot, walking quickly, disappeared around the corner of the square, still followed by his escort.

The doctor, puffed up with pride, returned to the crowd. As soon as he was near enough to make himself heard, he cried: "Hurrah! hurrah! Victory crowns the Republic everywhere."

There was no outburst of joy.

The doctor continued: "We are free, you are free, independent! Be proud!"

The motionless villagers were looking at him without any signs of triumph shining in their eyes.

He looked at them, indignant at their indifference, thinking of what he could say or do in order to make an impression to electrify this calm peasantry, to fulfill his mission as a leader.

He had an inspiration and, turning to Pommel, he ordered: "Lieutenant, go get me the bust of the ex-emperor which is in the meeting room of the municipal council, and bring it here with a chair."

The man presently reappeared, carrying on his right shoulder the plaster Bonaparte, and holding in his left hand a cane-seated chair.

M. Massarel went towards him, took the chair, placed the white bust on it, then stepping back a few steps, he addressed it in a loud voice:

"Tyrant, tyrant, you have fallen down in the mud. The dying fatherland was in its death throes under your oppression. Vengeful Destiny has struck you. Defeat and shame have pursued you; you fall conquered, a prisoner of the Prussians; and from the ruins of your crumbling empire, the young and glorious Republic arises, lifting from the ground your broken sword——"

He waited for applause. Not a sound greeted his listening ear. The peasants, nonplussed, kept silent; and the white, placid, well-groomed statue seemed to look at M. Massarel with its plaster smile, ineffaceable and sarcastic.

Thus they stood, face to face, Napoleon on his chair, the physician standing three feet away. Anger seized the commandant. What could he do to move this crowd and definitely to win over public opinion?

He happened to carry his hand to his stomach, and he felt, under his red belt, the butt of his revolver.

Not another inspiration, not another word cane to his mind. Then, he drew his weapon, stepped back a few steps and shot the former monarch.

The bullet made a little black hole: like a spot, in his forehead. No sensation was created. M. Massarel shot a second time and made a second hole, then a third time, then, without stopping, he shot off the three remaining shots. Napoleon's forehead was blown away in a white powder, but his eyes, nose and pointed mustache remained intact.

Then in exasperation, the doctor kicked the chair over, and placing one foot on what remained of the bust in the position of a conqueror, he turned to the amazed public and yelled: "Thus may all traitors die!"

As no enthusiasm was, as yet, visible, the spectators appearing to be dumb with astonishment, the commandant cried to the militia: "You may go home now." And he himself walked rapidly, almost ran, towards his house.

As soon as he appeared, the servant told him that some patients had been waiting in his office for over three hours. He hastened in. They were the same two peasants as a few days before, who had returned at daybreak, obstinate and patient.

The old man immediately began his explanation:

"It began with ants, which seemed to be crawling up and down my legs——"

LIEUTENANT LARE'S MARRIAGE

Since the beginning of the campaign Lieutenant Lare had taken two cannon from the Prussians. His general had said: "Thank you, lieutenant," and had given him the cross of honor.

As he was as cautious as he was brave, wary, inventive, wily and resourceful, he was entrusted with a hundred soldiers and he organized a company of scouts who saved the army on several occasions during a retreat.

But the invading army entered by every frontier like a surging sea. Great waves of men arrived one after the other, scattering all around them a scum of freebooters. General Carrel's brigade, separated from its division, retreated continually, fighting each day, but remaining almost intact, thanks to the vigilance and agility of Lieutenant Lare, who seemed to be everywhere at the same moment, baffling all the enemy's cunning, frustrating their plans, misleading their Uhlans and killing their vanguards.

One morning the general sent for him.

"Lieutenant," said he, "here is a dispatch from General de Lacere, who will be destroyed if we do not go to his aid by sunrise to-morrow. He is at Blainville, eight leagues from here. You will start at nightfall with three hundred men, whom you will echelon along the road. I will follow you two hours later. Study the road carefully; I fear we may meet a division of the enemy."

It had been freezing hard for a week. At two o'clock it began to snow, and by night the ground was covered and heavy white swirls concealed objects hard by.

At six o'clock the detachment set out.

Two men walked alone as scouts about three yards ahead. Then came a platoon of ten men commanded by the lieutenant himself. The rest followed them in two long columns. To the right and left of the little band, at a distance of about three hundred feet on either side, some soldiers marched in pairs.

The snow, which was still falling, covered them with a white powder in the darkness, and as it did not melt on their uniforms, they were hardly distinguishable in the night amid the dead whiteness of the landscape.

From time to time they halted. One heard nothing but that indescribable, nameless flutter of falling snow—a sensation rather than a sound, a vague, ominous murmur. A command was given in a low tone and when the troop resumed its march it left in its wake a sort of white phantom standing in the snow. It gradually grew fainter and finally disappeared. It was the echelons who were to lead the army.

The scouts slackened their pace. Something was ahead of them.

"Turn to the right," said the lieutenant; "it is the Ronfi wood; the chateau is more to the left."

Presently the command "Halt" was passed along. The detachment stopped and waited for the lieutenant, who, accompanied by only ten men, had undertaken a reconnoitering expedition to the chateau.

They advanced, creeping under the trees. Suddenly they all remained motionless. Around them was a dead silence. Then, quite near them, a little clear, musical young voice was heard amid the stillness of the wood.

"Father, we shall get lost in the snow. We shall never reach Blainville."

A deeper voice replied:

"Never fear, little daughter; I know the country as well as I know my pocket."

The lieutenant said a few words and four men moved away silently, like shadows.

All at once a woman's shrill cry was heard through the darkness. Two prisoners were brought back, an old man and a young girl. The lieutenant questioned them, still in a low tone:

"Your name?"

"Pierre Bernard."

"Your profession?"

"Butler to Comte de Ronfi."

"Is this your daughter?"

'Yes!'

"What does she do?"

"She is laundress at the chateau."

"Where are you going?"

"We are making our escape."

"Why?"

"Twelve Uhlans passed by this evening. They shot three keepers and hanged the gardener. I was alarmed on account of the little one."

"Whither are you bound?"

"To Blainville."

"Why?"

"Because there is a French army there."

"Do you know the way?"

"Perfectly."

"Well then, follow us."

They rejoined the column and resumed their march across country. The old man walked in silence beside the lieutenant, his daughter walking at his side. All at once she stopped.

"Father," she said, "I am so tired I cannot go any farther."

And she sat down. She was shaking with cold and seemed about to lose consciousness. Her father wanted to carry her, but he was too old and too weak.

"Lieutenant," said he, sobbing, "we shall only impede your march. France before all. Leave us here."

The officer had given a command. Some men had started off. They came back with branches they had cut, and in a minute a litter was ready. The whole detachment had joined them by this time.

"Here is a woman dying of cold," said the lieutenant. "Who will give his cape to cover her?"

Two hundred capes were taken off. The young girl was wrapped up in these warm soldiers' capes, gently laid in the litter, and then four' hardy shoulders lifted her up, and like an Eastern queen borne by her slaves she was placed in the center of the detachment of soldiers, who resumed their march with more energy, more courage, more cheerfulness, animated by the presence of a woman, that sovereign inspiration that has stirred the old French blood to so many deeds of valor.

At the end of an hour they halted again and every one lay down in the snow. Over yonder on the level country a big, dark shadow was moving. It looked like some weird monster stretching itself out like a serpent, then suddenly coiling itself into a mass, darting forth again, then back, and then forward again without ceasing. Some whispered orders were passed around among the soldiers, and an occasional little, dry, metallic click was heard. The moving object suddenly came nearer, and twelve Uhlans were seen approaching at a gallop, one behind the other, having lost their way in the darkness. A brilliant flash suddenly revealed to them two hundred mete lying on the ground before them. A rapid fire was heard, which died away in the snowy silence, and all the twelve fell to the ground, their horses with them.

After a long rest the march was resumed. The old man whom they had captured acted as guide.

Presently a voice far off in the distance cried out: "Who goes there?"

Another voice nearer by gave the countersign.

They made another halt; some conferences took place. It had stopped snowing. A cold wind was driving the clouds, and innumerable stars were sparkling in the sky behind them, gradually paling in the rosy light of dawn.

A staff officer came forward to receive the detachment. But when he asked who was being carried in the litter, the form stirred; two little hands moved aside the big blue army capes and, rosy as the dawn, with two eyes that were brighter than the stars that had just faded from sight, and a smile as radiant as the morn, a dainty face appeared.

"It is I, monsieur."

The soldiers, wild with delight, clapped their hands and bore the young girl in triumph into the midst of the camp, that was just getting to arms. Presently General Carrel arrived on the scene. At nine o'clock the Prussians made an attack. They beat a retreat at noon.

That evening, as Lieutenant Lare, overcome by fatigue, was sleeping on a bundle of straw, he was sent for by the general. He found the commanding officer in his tent, chatting with the old man whom they had come across during the night. As soon as he entered the tent the general took his hand, and addressing the stranger, said:

"My dear comte, this is the young man of whom you were telling me just now; he is one of my best officers."

He smiled, lowered his tone, and added:

"The best."

Then, turning to the astonished lieutenant, he presented "Comte de Ronfi-Quedissac."

The old man took both his hands, saying:

"My dear lieutenant, you have saved my daughter's life. I have only one way of thanking you. You may come in a few months to tell me—if you like her."

One year later, on the very same day, Captain Lare and Miss Louise-Hortense-Genevieve de Ronfi-Quedissac were married in the church of St. Thomas Aquinas.

She brought a dowry of six thousand francs, and was said to be the prettiest bride that had been seen that year.

THE HORRIBLE

The shadows of a balmy night were slowly falling. The women remained in the drawing-room of the villa. The men, seated, or astride of garden chairs, were smoking outside the door of the house, around a table laden with cups and liqueur glasses.

Their lighted cigars shone like eyes in the darkness, which was gradually becoming more dense. They had been talking about a frightful accident which had occurred the night before—two men and three women drowned in the river before the eyes of the guests.

General de G—— remarked:

"Yes, these things are affecting, but they are not horrible.

"Horrible, that well-known word, means much more than terrible. A frightful accident like this affects, upsets, terrifies; it does not horrify. In order that we should experience horror, something more is needed than emotion, something more than the spectacle of a dreadful death; there must be a shuddering sense of mystery, or a sensation of abnormal terror, more than natural. A man who dies, even under the most tragic circumstances, does not excite horror; a field of battle is not horrible; blood is not horrible; the vilest crimes are rarely horrible.

"Here are two personal examples which have shown me what is the meaning of horror.

"It was during the war of 1870. We were retreating toward Pont-Audemer, after having passed through Rouen. The army, consisting of about twenty thousand men, twenty thousand routed men, disbanded, demoralized, exhausted, were going to disband at Havre.

"The earth was covered with snow. The night was falling. They had not eaten anything since the day before. They were fleeing rapidly, the Prussians not being far off.

"All the Norman country, sombre, dotted with the shadows of the trees surrounding the farms, stretched out beneath a black, heavy, threatening sky.

"Nothing else could be heard in the wan twilight but the confused sound, undefined though rapid, of a marching throng, an endless tramping, mingled with the vague clink of tin bowls or swords. The men, bent, round-shouldered, dirty, in many cases even in rags, dragged themselves along, hurried through the snow, with a long, broken-backed stride.

"The skin of their hands froze to the butt ends of their muskets, for it was freezing hard that night. I frequently saw a little soldier take off his shoes in order to walk barefoot, as his shoes hurt his weary feet; and at every step he left a track of blood. Then, after some time, he would sit down in a field for a few minutes' rest, and he never got up again. Every man who sat down was a dead man.

"Should we have left behind us those poor, exhausted soldiers, who fondly counted on being able to start afresh as soon as they had somewhat refreshed their stiffened legs? But scarcely had they ceased to move, and to make their almost frozen blood circulate in their veins, than an unconquerable torpor congealed them, nailed them to the ground, closed their eyes, and paralyzed in one second this overworked human mechanism. And they gradually sank down, their foreheads on their knees, without, however, falling over, for their loins and their limbs became as hard and immovable as wood, impossible to bend or to stand upright.

"And the rest of us, more robust, kept straggling on, chilled to the marrow, advancing by a kind of inertia through the night, through the snow, through that cold and deadly country, crushed by pain, by defeat, by despair, above all overcome by the abominable sensation of abandonment, of the end, of death, of nothingness.

"I saw two gendarmes holding by the arm a curious-looking little man, old, beardless, of truly surprising aspect.

"They were looking for an officer, believing that they had caught a spy. The word 'spy' at once spread through the midst of the stragglers, and they gathered in a group round the prisoner. A voice exclaimed: 'He must be shot!' And all these soldiers who were falling from utter prostration, only holding themselves on their feet by leaning on their guns, felt all of a sudden that thrill of furious and bestial anger which urges on a mob to massacre.

"I wanted to speak. I was at that time in command of a battalion; but they no longer recognized the authority of their commanding officers; they would even have shot me.

"One of the gendarmes said: 'He has been following us for the three last days. He has been asking information from every one about the artillery.'"

I took it on myself to question this person.

"What are you doing? What do you want? Why are you accompanying the army?"

"He stammered out some words in some unintelligible dialect. He was, indeed, a strange being, with narrow shoulders, a sly look, and such an agitated air in my presence that I really no longer doubted that he was a spy. He seemed very aged and feeble. He kept looking at me from under his eyes with a humble, stupid, crafty air.

"The men all round us exclaimed.

"'To the wall! To the wall!'

"I said to the gendarmes:

"'Will you be responsible for the prisoner?'

"I had not ceased speaking when a terrible shove threw me on my back, and in a second I saw the man seized by the furious soldiers, thrown down, struck, dragged along the side of the road, and flung against a tree. He fell in the snow, nearly dead already.

"And immediately they shot him. The soldiers fired at him, reloaded their guns, fired again with the desperate energy of brutes. They fought with each other to have a shot at him, filed off in front of the corpse, and kept on firing at him, as people at a funeral keep sprinkling holy water in front of a coffin.

"But suddenly a cry arose of 'The Prussians! the Prussians!'

"And all along the horizon I heard the great noise of this panic-stricken army in full flight.

"A panic, the result of these shots fired at this vagabond, had filled his very executioners with terror; and, without realizing that they were themselves the originators of the scare, they fled and disappeared in the darkness.

"I remained alone with the corpse, except for the two gendarmes whose duty compelled them to stay with me.

"They lifted up the riddled mass of bruised and bleeding flesh.

"'He must be searched,' I said. And I handed them a box of taper matches which I had in my pocket. One of the soldiers had another box. I was standing between the two.

"The gendarme who was examining the body announced:

"'Clothed in a blue blouse, a white shirt, trousers, and a pair of shoes.'

"The first match went out; we lighted a second. The man continued, as he turned out his pockets:

"'A horn-handled pocketknife, check handkerchief, a snuffbox, a bit of pack thread, a piece of bread.'

"The second match went out; we lighted a third. The gendarme, after having felt the corpse for a long time, said:

"'That is all.'

"I said:

"'Strip him. We shall perhaps find something next his skin."

"And in order that the two soldiers might help each other in this task, I stood between them to hold the lighted match. By the rapid and speedily extinguished flame of the match, I saw them take off the garments one by one, and expose to view that bleeding bundle of flesh, still warm, though lifeless.

"And suddenly one of them exclaimed:

"'Good God, general, it is a woman!'

"I cannot describe to you the strange and poignant sensation of pain that moved my heart. I could not believe it, and I knelt down in the snow before this shapeless pulp of flesh to see for myself: it was a woman.

"The two gendarmes, speechless and stunned, waited for me to give my opinion on the matter. But I did not know what to think, what theory to adopt.

"Then the brigadier slowly drawled out:

"'Perhaps she came to look for a son of hers in the artillery, whom she had not heard from.'

"And the other chimed in:

"'Perhaps, indeed, that is so.'

"And I, who had seen some very terrible things in my time, began to cry. And I felt, in the presence of this corpse, on that icy cold night, in the midst of that gloomy plain; at the sight of this mystery, at the sight of this murdered stranger, the meaning of that word 'horror.'

"I had the same sensation last year, while interrogating one of the survivors of the Flatters Mission, an Algerian sharpshooter.

"You know the details of that atrocious drama. It is possible, however, that you are unacquainted with one of them.

"The colonel travelled through the desert into the Soudan, and passed through the immense territory of the Touaregs, who, in that great ocean of sand which stretches from the Atlantic to Egypt and from the Soudan to Algeria, are a kind of pirates, resembling those who ravaged the seas in former days.

"The guides who accompanied the column belonged to the tribe of the Chambaa, of Ouargla.

"Now, one day we encamped in the middle of the desert, and the Arabs declared that, as the spring was still some distance away, they would go with all their camels to look for water.

"One man alone warned the colonel that he had been betrayed. Flatters did not believe this, and accompanied the convoy with the engineers, the doctors, and nearly all his officers.

"They were massacred round the spring, and all the camels were captured.

"The captain of the Arab Intelligence Department at Ouargla, who had remained in the camp, took command of the survivors, spahis and sharpshooters, and they began to retreat, leaving behind them the baggage and provisions, for want of camels to carry them.

"Then they started on their journey through this solitude without shade and boundless, beneath the devouring sun, which burned them from morning till night.

"One tribe came to tender its submission and brought dates as a tribute. The dates were poisoned. Nearly all the Frenchmen died, and, among them, the last officer.

"There now only remained a few spahis with their quartermaster, Pobeguin, and some native sharpshooters of the Chambaa tribe. They had still two camels left. They disappeared one night, along with two, Arabs.

"Then the survivors understood that they would be obliged to eat each other, and as soon as they discovered the flight of the two men with the two camels, those who remained separated, and proceeded to march, one by one, through the soft sand, under the glare of a scorching sun, at a distance of more than a gunshot from each other.

"So they went on all day, and when they reached a spring each of them came to drink at it in turn, as soon as each solitary marcher had moved forward the number of yards arranged upon. And thus they continued marching the whole day, raising everywhere they passed, in that level, burnt up expanse, those little columns of dust which, from a distance, indicate those who are trudging through the desert.

"But one morning one of the travellers suddenly turned round and approached the man behind him. And they all stopped to look.

"The man toward whom the famished soldier drew near did not flee, but lay flat on the ground, and took aim at the one who was coming toward him. When he believed he was within gunshot, he fired. The other was not hit, and he continued then to advance, and levelling his gun, in turn, he killed his comrade.

"Then from all directions the others rushed to seek their share. And he who had killed the fallen man, cutting the corpse into pieces, distributed it.

"And they once more placed themselves at fixed distances, these irreconcilable allies, preparing for the next murder which would bring them together.

"For two days they lived on this human flesh which they divided between them. Then, becoming famished again, he who had killed the first man began killing afresh. And again, like a butcher, he cut up the corpse and offered it to his comrades, keeping only his own portion of it.

"And so this retreat of cannibals continued.

"The last Frenchman, Pobeguin, was massacred at the side of a well, the very night before the supplies arrived.

"Do you understand now what I mean by the horrible?"

This was the story told us a few nights ago by General de G——.

MADAME PARISSE

I was sitting on the pier of the small port of Obernon, near the village of Salis, looking at Antibes, bathed in the setting sun. I had never before seen anything so wonderful and so beautiful.

The small town, enclosed by its massive ramparts, built by Monsieur de Vauban, extended into the open sea, in the middle of the immense Gulf of Nice. The great waves, coming in from the ocean, broke at its feet, surrounding it with a wreath of foam; and beyond the ramparts the houses climbed up the hill, one after the other, as far as the two towers, which rose up into the sky, like the peaks of an ancient helmet. And these two towers were outlined against the milky whiteness of the Alps, that enormous distant wall of snow which enclosed the entire horizon.

Between the white foam at the foot of the walls and the white snow on the sky-line the little city, dazzling against the bluish background of the nearest mountain ranges, presented to the rays of the setting sun a pyramid of red-roofed houses, whose facades were also white, but so different one from another that they seemed to be of all tints.

And the sky above the Alps was itself of a blue that was almost white, as if the snow had tinted it; some silvery clouds were floating just over the pale summits, and on the other side of the gulf Nice, lying close to the water, stretched like a white thread between the sea and the mountain. Two great sails, driven by a strong breeze, seemed to skim over the waves. I looked upon all this, astounded.

This view was one of those sweet, rare, delightful things that seem to permeate you and are unforgettable, like the memory of a great happiness. One sees, thinks, suffers, is moved and loves with the eyes. He who can feel with the eye experiences the same keen, exquisite and deep pleasure in looking at men and things as the man with the delicate and sensitive ear, whose soul music overwhelms.

I turned to my companion, M. Martini, a pureblooded Southerner.

"This is certainly one of the rarest sights which it has been vouchsafed to me to admire.

"I have seen Mont Saint-Michel, that monstrous granite jewel, rise out of the sand at sunrise.

"I have seen, in the Sahara, Lake Raianechergui, fifty kilometers long, shining under a moon as brilliant as our sun and breathing up toward it a white cloud, like a mist of milk.

"I have seen, in the Lipari Islands, the weird sulphur crater of the Volcanello, a giant flower which smokes and burns, an enormous yellow flower, opening out in the midst of the sea, whose stem is a volcano.

"But I have seen nothing more wonderful than Antibes, standing against the Alps in the setting sun.

"And I know not how it is that memories of antiquity haunt me; verses of Homer come into my mind; this is a city of the ancient East, a city of the odyssey; this is Troy, although Troy was very far from the sea."

M. Martini drew the Sarty guide-book out of his pocket and read: "This city was originally a colony founded by the Phocians of Marseilles, about 340 B.C. They gave it the Greek name of Antipolis, meaning counter-city, city opposite another, because it is in fact opposite to Nice, another colony from Marseilles.

"After the Gauls were conquered, the Romans turned Antibes into a municipal city, its inhabitants receiving the rights of Roman citizenship.

"We know by an epigram of Martial that at this time——"

I interrupted him:

"I don't care what she was. I tell you that I see down there a city of the Odyssey. The coast of Asia and the coast of Europe resemble each other in their shores, and there is no city on the other coast of the Mediterranean which awakens in me the memories of the heroic age as this one does."

A footstep caused me to turn my head; a woman, a large, dark woman, was walking along the road which skirts the sea in going to the cape.

"That is Madame Parisse, you know," muttered Monsieur Martini, dwelling on the final syllable.

No, I did not know, but that name, mentioned carelessly, that name of the Trojan shepherd, confirmed me in my dream.

However, I asked: "Who is this Madame Parisse?"

He seemed astonished that I did not know the story.

I assured him that I did not know it, and I looked after the woman, who passed by without seeing us, dreaming, walking with steady and slow step, as doubtless the ladies of old walked.

She was perhaps thirty-five years old and still very beautiful, though a trifle stout.

And Monsieur Martini told me the following story:

Mademoiselle Combelombe was married, one year before the war of 1870, to Monsieur Parisse, a government official. She was then a handsome young girl, as slender and lively as she has now become stout and sad.

Unwillingly she had accepted Monsieur Parisse, one of those little fat men with short legs, who trip along, with trousers that are always too large.

After the war Antibes was garrisoned by a single battalion commanded by Monsieur Jean de Carmelin, a young officer decorated during the war, and who had just received his four stripes.

As he found life exceedingly tedious in this fortress this stuffy mole-hole enclosed by its enormous double walls, he often strolled out to the cape, a kind of park or pine wood shaken by all the winds from the sea.

There he met Madame Parisse, who also came out in the summer evenings to get the fresh air under the trees. How did they come to love each other? Who knows? They met, they looked at each other, and when out of sight they doubtless thought of each other. The image of the young woman with the brown eyes, the black hair, the pale skin, this fresh, handsome Southerner, who displayed her teeth in smiling, floated before the eyes of the officer as he continued his promenade, chewing his cigar instead of smoking it; and the image of the commanding officer, in his close-fitting coat, covered with gold lace, and his red trousers, and a little blond mustache, would pass before the eyes of Madame Parisse, when her husband, half shaven and ill-clad, short-legged and big-bellied, came home to supper in the evening.

As they met so often, they perhaps smiled at the next meeting; then, seeing each other again and again, they felt as if they knew each other. He certainly bowed to her. And she, surprised, bowed in return, but very, very slightly, just enough not to appear impolite. But after two weeks she returned his salutation from a distance, even before they were side by side.

He spoke to her. Of what? Doubtless of the setting sun. They admired it together, looking for it in each other's eyes more often than on the horizon. And every evening for two weeks this was the commonplace and persistent pretext for a few minutes' chat.

Then they ventured to take a few steps together, talking of anything that came into their minds, but their eyes were already saying to each other a thousand more intimate things, those secret, charming things that are reflected in the gentle emotion of the glance, and that cause the heart to beat, for they are a better revelation of the soul than the spoken ward.

And then he would take her hand, murmuring those words which the woman divines, without seeming to hear them.

And it was agreed between them that they would love each other without evidencing it by anything sensual or brutal.

She would have remained indefinitely at this stage of intimacy, but he wanted more. And every day he urged her more hotly to give in to his ardent desire.

She resisted, would not hear of it, seemed determined not to give way.

But one evening she said to him casually: "My husband has just gone to Marseilles. He will be away four days."

Jean de Carmelin threw himself at her feet, imploring her to open her door to him that very night at eleven o'clock. But she would not listen to him, and went home, appearing to be annoyed.

The commandant was in a bad humor all the evening, and the next morning at dawn he went out on the ramparts in a rage, going from one exercise field to the other, dealing out punishment to the officers and men as one might fling stones into a crowd,

On going in to breakfast he found an envelope under his napkin with these four words: "To-night at ten." And he gave one hundred sous without any reason to the waiter.

The day seemed endless to him. He passed part of it in curling his hair and perfuming himself.

As he was sitting down to the dinner-table another envelope was handed to him, and in it he found the following telegram:

"My Love: Business completed. I return this evening on the nine o'clock train.

  PARISSE."

The commandant let loose such a vehement oath that the waiter dropped the soup-tureen on the floor.

What should he do? He certainly wanted her, that very, evening at whatever cost; and he would have her. He would resort to any means, even to arresting and imprisoning the husband. Then a mad thought struck him. Calling for paper, he wrote the following note:

MADAME: He will not come back this evening, I swear it to

you,—and I shall be, you know where, at ten o'clock. Fear nothing.

I will answer for everything, on my honor as an officer.

  JEAN DE CARMELIN.

And having sent off this letter, he quietly ate his dinner.

Toward eight o'clock he sent for Captain Gribois, the second in command, and said, rolling between his fingers the crumpled telegram of Monsieur Parisse:

"Captain, I have just received a telegram of a very singular nature, which it is impossible for me to communicate to you. You will immediately have all the gates of the city closed and guarded, so that no one, mind me, no one, will either enter or leave before six in the morning. You will also have men patrol the streets, who will compel the inhabitants to retire to their houses at nine o'clock. Any one found outside beyond that time will be conducted to his home 'manu militari'. If your men meet me this night they will at once go out of my way, appearing not to know me. You understand me?"

"Yes, commandant."

"I hold you responsible for the execution of my orders, my dear captain."

"Yes, commandant."

"Would you like to have a glass of chartreuse?"

"With great pleasure, commandant."

They clinked glasses drank down the brown liquor and Captain Gribois left the room.

The train from Marseilles arrived at the station at nine o'clock sharp, left two passengers on the platform and went on toward Nice.

One of them, tall and thin, was Monsieur Saribe, the oil merchant, and the other, short and fat, was Monsieur Parisse.

Together they set out, with their valises, to reach the city, one kilometer distant.

But on arriving at the gate of the port the guards crossed their bayonets, commanding them to retire.

Frightened, surprised, cowed with astonishment, they retired to deliberate; then, after having taken counsel one with the other, they came back cautiously to parley, giving their names.

But the soldiers evidently had strict orders, for they threatened to shoot; and the two scared travellers ran off, throwing away their valises, which impeded their flight.

Making the tour of the ramparts, they presented themselves at the gate on the route to Cannes. This likewise was closed and guarded by a menacing sentinel. Messrs. Saribe and Parisse, like the prudent men they were, desisted from their efforts and went back to the station for shelter, since it was not safe to be near the fortifications after sundown.

The station agent, surprised and sleepy, permitted them to stay till morning in the waiting-room.

And they sat there side by side, in the dark, on the green velvet sofa, too scared to think of sleeping.

It was a long and weary night for them.

At half-past six in the morning they were informed that the gates were open and that people could now enter Antibes.

They set out for the city, but failed to find their abandoned valises on the road.

When they passed through the gates of the city, still somewhat anxious, the Commandant de Carmelin, with sly glance and mustache curled up, came himself to look at them and question them.

Then he bowed to them politely, excusing himself for having caused them a bad night. But he had to carry out orders.

The people of Antibes were scared to death. Some spoke of a surprise planned by the Italians, others of the landing of the prince imperial and others again believed that there was an Orleanist conspiracy. The truth was suspected only later, when it became known that the battalion of the commandant had been sent away, to a distance and that Monsieur de Carmelin had been severely punished.

Monsieur Martini had finished his story. Madame Parisse returned, her promenade being ended. She passed gravely near me, with her eyes fixed on the Alps, whose summits now gleamed rosy in the last rays of the setting sun.

I longed to speak to her, this poor, sad woman, who would ever be thinking of that night of love, now long past, and of the bold man who for the sake of a kiss from her had dared to put a city into a state of siege and to compromise his whole future.

And to-day he had probably forgotten her, if he did not relate this audacious, comical and tender farce to his comrades over their cups.

Had she seen him again? Did she still love him? And I thought: Here is an instance of modern love, grotesque and yet heroic. The Homer who should sing of this new Helen and the adventure of her Menelaus must be gifted with the soul of a Paul de Kock. And yet the hero of this deserted woman was brave, daring, handsome, strong as Achilles and more cunning than Ulysses.

MADEMOISELLE FIFI

Major Graf Von Farlsberg, the Prussian commandant, was reading his newspaper as he lay back in a great easy-chair, with his booted feet on the beautiful marble mantelpiece where his spurs had made two holes, which had grown deeper every day during the three months that he had been in the chateau of Uville.

A cup of coffee was smoking on a small inlaid table, which was stained with liqueur, burned by cigars, notched by the penknife of the victorious officer, who occasionally would stop while sharpening a pencil, to jot down figures, or to make a drawing on it, just as it took his fancy.

When he had read his letters and the German newspapers, which his orderly had brought him, he got up, and after throwing three or four enormous pieces of green wood on the fire, for these gentlemen were gradually cutting down the park in order to keep themselves warm, he went to the window. The rain was descending in torrents, a regular Normandy rain, which looked as if it were being poured out by some furious person, a slanting rain, opaque as a curtain, which formed a kind of wall with diagonal stripes, and which deluged everything, a rain such as one frequently experiences in the neighborhood of Rouen, which is the watering-pot of France.

For a long time the officer looked at the sodden turf and at the swollen Andelle beyond it, which was overflowing its banks; he was drumming a waltz with his fingers on the window-panes, when a noise made him turn round. It was his second in command, Captain Baron van Kelweinstein.

The major was a giant, with broad shoulders and a long, fan-like beard, which hung down like a curtain to his chest. His whole solemn person suggested the idea of a military peacock, a peacock who was carrying his tail spread out on his breast. He had cold, gentle blue eyes, and a scar from a swordcut, which he had received in the war with Austria; he was said to be an honorable man, as well as a brave officer.

The captain, a short, red-faced man, was tightly belted in at the waist, his red hair was cropped quite close to his head, and in certain lights he almost looked as if he had been rubbed over with phosphorus. He had lost two front teeth one night, though he could not quite remember how, and this sometimes made him speak unintelligibly, and he had a bald patch on top of his head surrounded by a fringe of curly, bright golden hair, which made him look like a monk.

The commandant shook hands with him and drank his cup of coffee (the sixth that morning), while he listened to his subordinate's report of what had occurred; and then they both went to the window and declared that it was a very unpleasant outlook. The major, who was a quiet man, with a wife at home, could accommodate himself to everything; but the captain, who led a fast life, who was in the habit of frequenting low resorts, and enjoying women's society, was angry at having to be shut up for three months in that wretched hole.

There was a knock at the door, and when the commandant said, "Come in," one of the orderlies appeared, and by his mere presence announced that breakfast was ready. In the dining-room they met three other officers of lower rank—a lieutenant, Otto von Grossling, and two sub-lieutenants, Fritz Scheuneberg and Baron von Eyrick, a very short, fair-haired man, who was proud and brutal toward men, harsh toward prisoners and as explosive as gunpowder.

Since he had been in France his comrades had called him nothing but Mademoiselle Fifi. They had given him that nickname on account of his dandified style and small waist, which looked as if he wore corsets; of his pale face, on which his budding mustache scarcely showed, and on account of the habit he had acquired of employing the French expression, 'Fi, fi donc', which he pronounced with a slight whistle when he wished to express his sovereign contempt for persons or things.

The dining-room of the chateau was a magnificent long room, whose fine old mirrors, that were cracked by pistol bullets, and whose Flemish tapestry, which was cut to ribbons, and hanging in rags in places from sword-cuts, told too well what Mademoiselle Fifi's occupation was during his spare time.

There were three family portraits on the walls a steel-clad knight, a cardinal and a judge, who were all smoking long porcelain pipes, which had been inserted into holes in the canvas, while a lady in a long, pointed waist proudly exhibited a pair of enormous mustaches, drawn with charcoal. The officers ate their breakfast almost in silence in that mutilated room, which looked dull in the rain and melancholy in its dilapidated condition, although its old oak floor had become as solid as the stone floor of an inn.

When they had finished eating and were smoking and drinking, they began, as usual, to berate the dull life they were leading. The bottles of brandy and of liqueur passed from hand to hand, and all sat back in their chairs and took repeated sips from their glasses, scarcely removing from their mouths the long, curved stems, which terminated in china bowls, painted in a manner to delight a Hottentot.

As soon as their glasses were empty they filled them again, with a gesture of resigned weariness, but Mademoiselle Fifi emptied his every minute, and a soldier immediately gave him another. They were enveloped in a cloud of strong tobacco smoke, and seemed to be sunk in a state of drowsy, stupid intoxication, that condition of stupid intoxication of men who have nothing to do, when suddenly the baron sat up and said: "Heavens! This cannot go on; we must think of something to do." And on hearing this, Lieutenant Otto and Sub-lieutenant Fritz, who preeminently possessed the serious, heavy German countenance, said: "What, captain?"

He thought for a few moments and then replied: "What? Why, we must get up some entertainment, if the commandant will allow us." "What sort of an entertainment, captain?" the major asked, taking his pipe out of his mouth. "I will arrange all that, commandant," the baron said. "I will send Le Devoir to Rouen, and he will bring back some ladies. I know where they can be found, We will have supper here, as all the materials are at hand and; at least, we shall have a jolly evening."

Graf von Farlsberg shrugged his shoulders with a smile: "You must surely be mad, my friend."

But all the other officers had risen and surrounded their chief, saying: "Let the captain have his way, commandant; it is terribly dull here." And the major ended by yielding. "Very well," he replied, and the baron immediately sent for Le Devoir. He was an old non-commissioned officer, who had never been seen to smile, but who carried out all the orders of his superiors to the letter, no matter what they might be. He stood there, with an impassive face, while he received the baron's instructions, and then went out, and five minutes later a large military wagon, covered with tarpaulin, galloped off as fast as four horses could draw it in the pouring rain. The officers all seemed to awaken from their lethargy, their looks brightened, and they began to talk.

Although it was raining as hard as ever, the major declared that it was not so dark, and Lieutenant von Grossling said with conviction that the sky was clearing up, while Mademoiselle Fifi did not seem to be able to keep still. He got up and sat down again, and his bright eyes seemed to be looking for something to destroy. Suddenly, looking at the lady with the mustaches, the young fellow pulled out his revolver and said: "You shall not see it." And without leaving his seat he aimed, and with two successive bullets cut out both the eyes of the portrait.

"Let us make a mine!" he then exclaimed, and the conversation was suddenly interrupted, as if they had found some fresh and powerful subject of interest. The mine was his invention, his method of destruction, and his favorite amusement.

When he left the chateau, the lawful owner, Comte Fernand d'Amoys d'Uville, had not had time to carry away or to hide anything except the plate, which had been stowed away in a hole made in one of the walls. As he was very rich and had good taste, the large drawing-room, which opened into the dining-room, looked like a gallery in a museum, before his precipitate flight.

Expensive oil paintings, water colors and drawings hung against the walls, while on the tables, on the hanging shelves and in elegant glass cupboards there were a thousand ornaments: small vases, statuettes, groups of Dresden china and grotesque Chinese figures, old ivory and Venetian glass, which filled the large room with their costly and fantastic array.

Scarcely anything was left now; not that the things had been stolen, for the major would not have allowed that, but Mademoiselle Fifi would every now and then have a mine, and on those occasions all the officers thoroughly enjoyed themselves for five minutes. The little marquis went into the drawing-room to get what he wanted, and he brought back a small, delicate china teapot, which he filled with gunpowder, and carefully introduced a piece of punk through the spout. This he lighted and took his infernal machine into the next room, but he came back immediately and shut the door. The Germans all stood expectant, their faces full of childish, smiling curiosity, and as soon as the explosion had shaken the chateau, they all rushed in at once.

Mademoiselle Fifi, who got in first, clapped his hands in delight at the sight of a terra-cotta Venus, whose head had been blown off, and each picked up pieces of porcelain and wondered at the strange shape of the fragments, while the major was looking with a paternal eye at the large drawing-room, which had been wrecked after the fashion of a Nero, and was strewn with the fragments of works of art. He went out first and said with a smile: "That was a great success this time."

But there was such a cloud of smoke in the dining-room, mingled with the tobacco smoke, that they could not breathe, so the commandant opened the window, and all the officers, who had returned for a last glass of cognac, went up to it.

The moist air blew into the room, bringing with it a sort of powdery spray, which sprinkled their beards. They looked at the tall trees which were dripping with rain, at the broad valley which was covered with mist, and at the church spire in the distance, which rose up like a gray point in the beating rain.

The bells had not rung since their arrival. That was the only resistance which the invaders had met with in the neighborhood. The parish priest had not refused to take in and to feed the Prussian soldiers; he had several times even drunk a bottle of beer or claret with the hostile commandant, who often employed him as a benevolent intermediary; but it was no use to ask him for a single stroke of the bells; he would sooner have allowed himself to be shot. That was his way of protesting against the invasion, a peaceful and silent protest, the only one, he said, which was suitable to a priest, who was a man of mildness, and not of blood; and every one, for twenty-five miles round, praised Abbe Chantavoine's firmness and heroism in venturing to proclaim the public mourning by the obstinate silence of his church bells.

The whole village, enthusiastic at his resistance, was ready to back up their pastor and to risk anything, for they looked upon that silent protest as the safeguard of the national honor. It seemed to the peasants that thus they deserved better of their country than Belfort and Strassburg, that they had set an equally valuable example, and that the name of their little village would become immortalized by that; but, with that exception, they refused their Prussian conquerors nothing.

The commandant and his officers laughed among themselves at this inoffensive courage, and as the people in the whole country round showed themselves obliging and compliant toward them, they willingly tolerated their silent patriotism. Little Baron Wilhelm alone would have liked to have forced them to ring the bells. He was very angry at his superior's politic compliance with the priest's scruples, and every day begged the commandant to allow him to sound "ding-dong, ding-dong," just once, only just once, just by way of a joke. And he asked it in the coaxing, tender voice of some loved woman who is bent on obtaining her wish, but the commandant would not yield, and to console himself, Mademoiselle Fifi made a mine in the Chateau d'Uville.

The five men stood there together for five minutes, breathing in the moist air, and at last Lieutenant Fritz said with a laugh: "The ladies will certainly not have fine weather for their drive." Then they separated, each to his duty, while the captain had plenty to do in arranging for the dinner.

When they met again toward evening they began to laugh at seeing each other as spick and span and smart as on the day of a grand review. The commandant's hair did not look so gray as it was in the morning, and the captain had shaved, leaving only his mustache, which made him look as if he had a streak of fire under his nose.

In spite of the rain, they left the window open, and one of them went to listen from time to time; and at a quarter past six the baron said he heard a rumbling in the distance. They all rushed down, and presently the wagon drove up at a gallop with its four horses steaming and blowing, and splashed with mud to their girths. Five women dismounted, five handsome girls whom a comrade of the captain, to whom Le Devoir had presented his card, had selected with care.

They had not required much pressing, as they had got to know the Prussians in the three months during which they had had to do with them, and so they resigned themselves to the men as they did to the state of affairs.

They went at once into the dining-room, which looked still more dismal in its dilapidated condition when it was lighted up; while the table covered with choice dishes, the beautiful china and glass, and the plate, which had been found in the hole in the wall where its owner had hidden it, gave it the appearance of a bandits' inn, where they were supping after committing a robbery in the place. The captain was radiant, and put his arm round the women as if he were familiar with them; and when the three young men wanted to appropriate one each, he opposed them authoritatively, reserving to himself the right to apportion them justly, according to their several ranks, so as not to offend the higher powers. Therefore, to avoid all discussion, jarring, and suspicion of partiality, he placed them all in a row according to height, and addressing the tallest, he said in a voice of command:

"What is your name?" "Pamela," she replied, raising her voice. And then he said: "Number One, called Pamela, is adjudged to the commandant." Then, having kissed Blondina, the second, as a sign of proprietorship, he proffered stout Amanda to Lieutenant Otto; Eva, "the Tomato," to Sub-lieutenant

Fritz, and Rachel, the shortest of them all, a very young, dark girl, with eyes as black as ink, a Jewess, whose snub nose proved the rule which allots hooked noses to all her race, to the youngest officer, frail Count Wilhelm d'Eyrick.

They were all pretty and plump, without any distinctive features, and all had a similarity of complexion and figure.

The three young men wished to carry off their prizes immediately, under the pretext that they might wish to freshen their toilets; but the captain wisely opposed this, for he said they were quite fit to sit down to dinner, and his experience in such matters carried the day. There were only many kisses, expectant kisses.

Suddenly Rachel choked, and began to cough until the tears came into her eyes, while smoke came through her nostrils. Under pretence of kissing her, the count had blown a whiff of tobacco into her mouth. She did not fly into a rage and did not say a word, but she looked at her tormentor with latent hatred in her dark eyes.

They sat down to dinner. The commandant seemed delighted; he made Pamela sit on his right, and Blondina on his left, and said, as he unfolded his table napkin: "That was a delightful idea of yours, captain."

Lieutenants Otto and Fritz, who were as polite as if they had been with fashionable ladies, rather intimidated their guests, but Baron von Kelweinstein beamed, made obscene remarks and seemed on fire with his crown of red hair. He paid the women compliments in French of the Rhine, and sputtered out gallant remarks, only fit for a low pothouse, from between his two broken teeth.

They did not understand him, however, and their intelligence did not seem to be awakened until he uttered foul words and broad expressions, which were mangled by his accent. Then they all began to laugh at once like crazy women and fell against each other, repeating the words, which the baron then began to say all wrong, in order that he might have the pleasure of hearing them say dirty things. They gave him as much of that stuff as he wanted, for they were drunk after the first bottle of wine, and resuming their usual habits and manners, they kissed the officers to right and left of them, pinched their arms, uttered wild cries, drank out of every glass and sang French couplets and bits of German songs which they had picked up in their daily intercourse with the enemy.

Soon the men themselves became very unrestrained, shouted and broke the plates and dishes, while the soldiers behind them waited on them stolidly. The commandant was the only one who kept any restraint upon himself.

Mademoiselle Fifi had taken Rachel on his knee, and, getting excited, at one moment he kissed the little black curls on her neck and at another he pinched her furiously and made her scream, for he was seized by a species of ferocity, and tormented by his desire to hurt her. He often held her close to him and pressed a long kiss on the Jewess' rosy mouth until she lost her breath, and at last he bit her until a stream of blood ran down her chin and on to her bodice.

For the second time she looked him full in the face, and as she bathed the wound, she said: "You will have to pay for, that!" But he merely laughed a hard laugh and said: "I will pay."

At dessert champagne was served, and the commandant rose, and in the same voice in which he would have drunk to the health of the Empress Augusta, he drank: "To our ladies!" And a series of toasts began, toasts worthy of the lowest soldiers and of drunkards, mingled with obscene jokes, which were made still more brutal by their ignorance of the language. They got up, one after the other, trying to say something witty, forcing themselves to be funny, and the women, who were so drunk that they almost fell off their chairs, with vacant looks and clammy tongues applauded madly each time.

The captain, who no doubt wished to impart an appearance of gallantry to the orgy, raised his glass again and said: "To our victories over hearts." and, thereupon Lieutenant Otto, who was a species of bear from the Black Forest, jumped up, inflamed and saturated with drink, and suddenly seized by an access of alcoholic patriotism, he cried: "To our victories over France!"

Drunk as they were, the women were silent, but Rachel turned round, trembling, and said: "See here, I know some Frenchmen in whose presence you would not dare say that." But the little count, still holding her on his knee, began to laugh, for the wine had made him very merry, and said: "Ha! ha! ha! I have never met any of them myself. As soon as we show ourselves, they run away!" The girl, who was in a terrible rage, shouted into his face: "You are lying, you dirty scoundrel!"

For a moment he looked at her steadily with his bright eyes upon her, as he had looked at the portrait before he destroyed it with bullets from his revolver, and then he began to laugh: "Ah! yes, talk about them, my dear! Should we be here now if they were brave?" And, getting excited, he exclaimed: "We are the masters! France belongs to us!" She made one spring from his knee and threw herself into her chair, while he arose, held out his glass over the table and repeated: "France and the French, the woods, the fields and the houses of France belong to us!"

The others, who were quite drunk, and who were suddenly seized by military enthusiasm, the enthusiasm of brutes, seized their glasses, and shouting, "Long live Prussia!" they emptied them at a draught.

The girls did not protest, for they were reduced to silence and were afraid. Even Rachel did not say a word, as she had no reply to make. Then the little marquis put his champagne glass, which had just been refilled, on the head of the Jewess and exclaimed: "All the women in France belong to us also!"

At that she got up so quickly that the glass upset, spilling the amber-colored wine on her black hair as if to baptize her, and broke into a hundred fragments, as it fell to the floor. Her lips trembling, she defied the looks of the officer, who was still laughing, and stammered out in a voice choked with rage:

"That—that—that—is not true—for you shall not have the women of France!"

He sat down again so as to laugh at his ease; and, trying to speak with the Parisian accent, he said: "She is good, very good! Then why did you come here, my dear?" She was thunderstruck and made no reply for a moment, for in her agitation she did not understand him at first, but as soon as she grasped his meaning she said to him indignantly and vehemently: "I! I! I am not a woman, I am only a strumpet, and that is all that Prussians want."

Almost before she had finished he slapped her full in the face; but as he was raising his hand again, as if to strike her, she seized a small dessert knife with a silver blade from the table and, almost mad with rage, stabbed him right in the hollow of his neck. Something that he was going to say was cut short in his throat, and he sat there with his mouth half open and a terrible look in his eyes.

All the officers shouted in horror and leaped up tumultuously; but, throwing her chair between the legs of Lieutenant Otto, who fell down at full length, she ran to the window, opened it before they could seize her and jumped out into the night and the pouring rain.

In two minutes Mademoiselle Fifi was dead, and Fritz and Otto drew their swords and wanted to kill the women, who threw themselves at their feet and clung to their knees. With some difficulty the major stopped the slaughter and had the four terrified girls locked up in a room under the care of two soldiers, and then he organized the pursuit of the fugitive as carefully as if he were about to engage in a skirmish, feeling quite sure that she would be caught.

The table, which had been cleared immediately, now served as a bed on which to lay out the lieutenant, and the four officers stood at the windows, rigid and sobered with the stern faces of soldiers on duty, and tried to pierce through the darkness of the night amid the steady torrent of rain. Suddenly a shot was heard and then another, a long way off; and for four hours they heard from time to time near or distant reports and rallying cries, strange words of challenge, uttered in guttural voices.

In the morning they all returned. Two soldiers had been killed and three others wounded by their comrades in the ardor of that chase and in the confusion of that nocturnal pursuit, but they had not caught Rachel.

Then the inhabitants of the district were terrorized, the houses were turned topsy-turvy, the country was scoured and beaten up, over and over again, but the Jewess did not seem to have left a single trace of her passage behind her.

When the general was told of it he gave orders to hush up the affair, so as not to set a bad example to the army, but he severely censured the commandant, who in turn punished his inferiors. The general had said: "One does not go to war in order to amuse one's self and to caress prostitutes." Graf von Farlsberg, in his exasperation, made up his mind to have his revenge on the district, but as he required a pretext for showing severity, he sent for the priest and ordered him to have the bell tolled at the funeral of Baron von Eyrick.

Contrary to all expectation, the priest showed himself humble and most respectful, and when Mademoiselle Fifi's body left the Chateau d'Uville on its way to the cemetery, carried by soldiers, preceded, surrounded and followed by soldiers who marched with loaded rifles, for the first time the bell sounded its funeral knell in a lively manner, as if a friendly hand were caressing it. At night it rang again, and the next day, and every day; it rang as much as any one could desire. Sometimes even it would start at night and sound gently through the darkness, seized with a strange joy, awakened one could not tell why. All the peasants in the neighborhood declared that it was bewitched, and nobody except the priest and the sacristan would now go near the church tower. And they went because a poor girl was living there in grief and solitude and provided for secretly by those two men.

She remained there until the German troops departed, and then one evening the priest borrowed the baker's cart and himself drove his prisoner to Rouen. When they got there he embraced her, and she quickly went back on foot to the establishment from which she had come, where the proprietress, who thought that she was dead, was very glad to see her.

A short time afterward a patriot who had no prejudices, and who liked her because of her bold deed, and who afterward loved her for herself, married her and made her a lady quite as good as many others.

A DUEL

The war was over. The Germans occupied France. The whole country was pulsating like a conquered wrestler beneath the knee of his victorious opponent.

The first trains from Paris, distracted, starving, despairing Paris, were making their way to the new frontiers, slowly passing through the country districts and the villages. The passengers gazed through the windows at the ravaged fields and burned hamlets. Prussian soldiers, in their black helmets with brass spikes, were smoking their pipes astride their chairs in front of the houses which were still left standing. Others were working or talking just as if they were members of the families. As you passed through the different towns you saw entire regiments drilling in the squares, and, in spite of the rumble of the carriage-wheels, you could every moment hear the hoarse words of command.

M. Dubuis, who during the entire siege had served as one of the National Guard in Paris, was going to join his wife and daughter, whom he had prudently sent away to Switzerland before the invasion.

Famine and hardship had not diminished his big paunch so characteristic of the rich, peace-loving merchant. He had gone through the terrible events of the past year with sorrowful resignation and bitter complaints at the savagery of men. Now that he was journeying to the frontier at the close of the war, he saw the Prussians for the first time, although he had done his duty on the ramparts and mounted guard on many a cold night.

He stared with mingled fear and anger at those bearded armed men, installed all over French soil as if they were at home, and he felt in his soul a kind of fever of impotent patriotism, at the same time also the great need of that new instinct of prudence which since then has, never left us. In the same railway carriage were two Englishmen, who had come to the country as sightseers and were gazing about them with looks of quiet curiosity. They were both also stout, and kept chatting in their own language, sometimes referring to their guidebook, and reading aloud the names of the places indicated.

Suddenly the train stopped at a little village station, and a Prussian officer jumped up with a great clatter of his sabre on the double footboard of the railway carriage. He was tall, wore a tight-fitting uniform, and had whiskers up to his eyes. His red hair seemed to be on fire, and his long mustache, of a paler hue, stuck out on both sides of his face, which it seemed to cut in two.

The Englishmen at once began staring, at him with smiles of newly awakened interest, while M. Dubuis made a show of reading a newspaper. He sat concealed in his corner like a thief in presence of a gendarme.

The train started again. The Englishmen went on chatting and looking out for the exact scene of different battles; and all of a sudden, as one of them stretched out his arm toward the horizon as he pointed out a village, the Prussian officer remarked in French, extending his long legs and lolling backward:

"I killed a dozen Frenchmen in that village and took more than a hundred prisoners."

The Englishmen, quite interested, immediately asked:

"Ha! and what is the name of this village?"

The Prussian replied:

"Pharsbourg." He added: "We caught those French scoundrels by the ears."

And he glanced toward M. Dubuis, laughing conceitedly into his mustache.

The train rolled on, still passing through hamlets occupied by the victorious army. German soldiers could be seen along the roads, on the edges of fields, standing in front of gates or chatting outside cafes. They covered the soil like African locusts.

The officer said, with a wave of his hand:

"If I had been in command, I'd have taken Paris, burned everything, killed everybody. No more France!"

The Englishman, through politeness, replied simply:

"Ah! yes."

He went on:

"In twenty years all Europe, all of it, will belong to us. Prussia is more than a match for all of them."

The Englishmen, getting uneasy, no longer replied. Their faces, which had become impassive, seemed made of wax behind their long whiskers. Then the Prussian officer began to laugh. And still, lolling back, he began to sneer. He sneered at the downfall of France, insulted the prostrate enemy; he sneered at Austria, which had been recently conquered; he sneered at the valiant but fruitless defence of the departments; he sneered at the Garde Mobile and at the useless artillery. He announced that Bismarck was going to build a city of iron with the captured cannon. And suddenly he placed his boots against the thigh of M. Dubuis, who turned away his eyes, reddening to the roots of his hair.

The Englishmen seemed to have become indifferent to all that was going on, as if they were suddenly shut up in their own island, far from the din of the world.

The officer took out his pipe, and looking fixedly at the Frenchman, said:

"You haven't any tobacco—have you?"

M. Dubuis replied:

"No, monsieur."

The German resumed:

"You might go and buy some for me when the train stops."

And he began laughing afresh as he added:

"I'll give you the price of a drink."

The train whistled, and slackened its pace. They passed a station that had been burned down; and then they stopped altogether.

The German opened the carriage door, and, catching M. Dubuis by the arm, said:

"Go and do what I told you—quick, quick!"

A Prussian detachment occupied the station. Other soldiers were standing behind wooden gratings, looking on. The engine was getting up steam before starting off again. Then M. Dubuis hurriedly jumped on the platform, and, in spite of the warnings of the station master, dashed into the adjoining compartment.

He was alone! He tore open his waistcoat, his heart was beating so rapidly, and, gasping for breath, he wiped the perspiration from his forehead.

The train drew up at another station. And suddenly the officer appeared at the carriage door and jumped in, followed close behind by the two Englishmen, who were impelled by curiosity. The German sat facing the Frenchman, and, laughing still, said:

"You did not want to do what I asked you?"

M. Dubuis replied:

"No, monsieur."

The train had just left the station.

The officer said:

"I'll cut off your mustache to fill my pipe with."

And he put out his hand toward the Frenchman's face.

The Englishmen stared at them, retaining their previous impassive manner.

The German had already pulled out a few hairs, and was still tugging at the mustache, when M. Dubuis, with a back stroke of his hand, flung aside the officer's arm, and, seizing him by the collar, threw him down on the seat. Then, excited to a pitch of fury, his temples swollen and his eyes glaring, he kept throttling the officer with one hand, while with the other clenched he began to strike him violent blows in the face. The Prussian struggled, tried to draw his sword, to clinch with his adversary, who was on top of him. But M. Dubuis crushed him with his enormous weight and kept punching him without taking breath or knowing where his blows fell. Blood flowed down the face of the German, who, choking and with a rattling in his throat, spat out his broken teeth and vainly strove to shake off this infuriated man who was killing him.

The Englishmen had got on their feet and came closer in order to see better. They remained standing, full of mirth and curiosity, ready to bet for, or against, either combatant.

Suddenly M. Dubuis, exhausted by his violent efforts, rose and resumed his seat without uttering a word.

The Prussian did not attack him, for the savage assault had terrified and astonished the officer as well as causing him suffering. When he was able to breathe freely, he said:

"Unless you give me satisfaction with pistols I will kill you."

M. Dubuis replied:

"Whenever you like. I'm quite ready."

The German said:

"Here is the town of Strasbourg. I'll get two officers to be my seconds, and there will be time before the train leaves the station."

M. Dubuis, who was puffing as hard as the engine, said to the Englishmen:

"Will you be my seconds?" They both answered together:

"Oh, yes!"

And the train stopped.

In a minute the Prussian had found two comrades, who brought pistols, and they made their way toward the ramparts.

The Englishmen were continually looking at their watches, shuffling their feet and hurrying on with the preparations, uneasy lest they should be too late for the train.

M. Dubuis had never fired a pistol in his life.

They made him stand twenty paces away from his enemy. He was asked:

"Are you ready?"

While he was answering, "Yes, monsieur," he noticed that one of the Englishmen had opened his umbrella in order to keep off the rays of the sun.

A voice gave the signal:

"Fire!"

M. Dubuis fired at random without delay, and he was amazed to see the Prussian opposite him stagger, lift up his arms and fall forward, dead. He had killed the officer.

One of the Englishmen exclaimed: "Ah!" He was quivering with delight, with satisfied curiosity and joyous impatience. The other, who still kept his watch in his hand, seized M. Dubuis' arm and hurried him in double-quick time toward the station, his fellow-countryman marking time as he ran beside them, with closed fists, his elbows at his sides, "One, two; one, two!"

And all three, running abreast rapidly, made their way to the station like three grotesque figures in a comic newspaper.

The train was on the point of starting. They sprang into their carriage. Then the Englishmen, taking off their travelling caps, waved them three times over their heads, exclaiming:

"Hip! hip! hip! hurrah!"

And gravely, one after the other, they extended their right hands to M. Dubuis and then went back and sat down in their own corner.

VOLUME II.

THE COLONEL'S IDEAS

"Upon my word," said Colonel Laporte, "although I am old and gouty, my legs as stiff as two pieces of wood, yet if a pretty woman were to tell me to go through the eye of a needle, I believe I should take a jump at it, like a clown through a hoop. I shall die like that; it is in the blood. I am an old beau, one of the old school, and the sight of a woman, a pretty woman, stirs me to the tips of my toes. There!

"We are all very much alike in France in this respect; we still remain knights, knights of love and fortune, since God has been abolished whose bodyguard we really were. But nobody can ever get woman out of our hearts; there she is, and there she will remain, and we love her, and shall continue to love her, and go on committing all kinds of follies on her account as long as there is a France on the map of Europe; and even if France were to be wiped off the map, there would always be Frenchmen left.

"When I am in the presence of a woman, of a pretty woman, I feel capable of anything. By Jove! when I feel her looks penetrating me, her confounded looks which set your blood on fire, I should like to do I don't know what; to fight a duel, to have a row, to smash the furniture, in order to show that I am the strongest, the bravest, the most daring and the most devoted of men.

"But I am not the only one, certainly not; the whole French army is like me, I swear to you. From the common soldier to the general, we all start out, from the van to the rear guard, when there is a woman in the case, a pretty woman. Do you remember what Joan of Arc made us do formerly? Come. I will make a bet that if a pretty woman had taken command of the army on the eve of Sedan, when Marshal MacMahon was wounded, we should have broken through the Prussian lines, by Jove! and had a drink out of their guns.

"It was not a Trochu, but a Sainte-Genevieve, who was needed in Paris; and I remember a little anecdote of the war which proves that we are capable of everything in presence of a woman.

"I was a captain, a simple captain, at the time, and I was in command of a detachment of scouts, who were retreating through a district which swarmed with Prussians. We were surrounded, pursued, tired out and half dead with fatigue and hunger, but we were bound to reach Bar-sur-Tain before the morrow, otherwise we should be shot, cut down, massacred. I do not know how we managed to escape so far. However, we had ten leagues to go during the night, ten leagues through the night, ten leagues through the snow, and with empty stomachs, and I thought to myself:

"'It is all over; my poor devils of fellows will never be able to do it.'

"We had eaten nothing since the day before, and the whole day long we remained hidden in a barn, huddled close together, so as not to feel the cold so much, unable to speak or even move, and sleeping by fits and starts, as one does when worn out with fatigue.

"It was dark by five o'clock, that wan darkness of the snow, and I shook my men. Some of them would not get up; they were almost incapable of moving or of standing upright; their joints were stiff from cold and hunger.

"Before us there was a large expanse of flat, bare country; the snow was still falling like a curtain, in large, white flakes, which concealed everything under a thick, frozen coverlet, a coverlet of frozen wool One might have thought that it was the end of the world.

"'Come, my lads, let us start.'

"They looked at the thick white flakes that were coming down, and they seemed to think: 'We have had enough of this; we may just as well die here!' Then I took out my revolver and said:

"'I will shoot the first man who flinches.' And so they set off, but very slowly, like men whose legs were of very little use to them, and I sent four of them three hundred yards ahead to scout, and the others followed pell-mell, walking at random and without any order. I put the strongest in the rear, with orders to quicken the pace of the sluggards with the points of their bayonets in the back.

"The snow seemed as if it were going to bury us alive; it powdered our kepis and cloaks without melting, and made phantoms of us, a kind of spectres of dead, weary soldiers. I said to myself: 'We shall never get out of this except by a, miracle.'

"Sometimes we had to stop for a few minutes, on account of those who could not follow us, and then we heard nothing except the falling snow, that vague, almost undiscernible sound made by the falling flakes. Some of the men shook themselves, others did not move, and so I gave the order to set off again. They shouldered their rifles, and with weary feet we resumed our march, when suddenly the scouts fell back. Something had alarmed them; they had heard voices in front of them. I sent forward six men and a sergeant and waited.

"All at once a shrill cry, a woman's cry, pierced through the heavy silence of the snow, and in a few minutes they brought back two prisoners, an old man and a girl, whom I questioned in a low voice. They were escaping from the Prussians, who had occupied their house during the evening and had got drunk. The father was alarmed on his daughter's account, and, without even telling their servants, they had made their escape in the darkness. I saw immediately that they belonged to the better class. I invited them to accompany us, and we started off again, the old man who knew the road acting as our guide.

"It had ceased snowing, the stars appeared and the cold became intense. The girl, who was leaning on her father's arm, walked unsteadily as though in pain, and several times she murmured:

"'I have no feeling at all in my feet'; and I suffered more than she did to see that poor little woman dragging herself like that through the snow. But suddenly she stopped and said:

"'Father, I am so tired that I cannot go any further.'

"The old man wanted to carry her, but he could not even lift her up, and she sank to the ground with a deep sigh. We all gathered round her, and, as for me, I stamped my foot in perplexity, not knowing what to do, and being unwilling to abandon that man and girl like that, when suddenly one of the soldiers, a Parisian whom they had nicknamed Pratique, said:

"'Come, comrades, we must carry the young lady, otherwise we shall not show ourselves Frenchmen, confound it!'

"I really believe that I swore with pleasure. 'That is very good of you, my children,' I said; 'and I will take my share of the burden.'

"We could indistinctly see, through the darkness, the trees of a little wood on the left. Several of the men went into it, and soon came back with a bundle of branches made into a litter.

"'Who will lend his cape? It is for a pretty girl, comrades,' Pratique said, and ten cloaks were thrown to him. In a moment the girl was lying, warm and comfortable, among them, and was raised upon six shoulders. I placed myself at their head, on the right, well pleased with my position.

"We started off much more briskly, as if we had had a drink of wine, and I even heard some jokes. A woman is quite enough to electrify Frenchmen, you see. The soldiers, who had become cheerful and warm, had almost reformed their ranks, and an old 'franc-tireur' who was following the litter, waiting for his turn to replace the first of his comrades who might give out, said to one of his neighbors, loud enough for me to hear: "'I am not a young man now, but by—-, there is nothing like the women to put courage into you!'

"We went on, almost without stopping, until three o'clock in the morning, when suddenly our scouts fell back once more, and soon the whole detachment showed nothing but a vague shadow on the ground, as the men lay on the snow. I gave my orders in a low voice, and heard the harsh, metallic sound of the cocking, of rifles. For there, in the middle of the plain, some strange object was moving about. It looked like some enormous animal running about, now stretching out like a serpent, now coiling itself into a ball, darting to the right, then to the left, then stopping, and presently starting off again. But presently that wandering shape came nearer, and I saw a dozen lancers at full gallop, one behind the other. They had lost their way and were trying to find it.

"They were so near by that time that I could hear the loud breathing of their horses, the clinking of their swords and the creaking of their saddles, and cried: 'Fire!'

"Fifty rifle shots broke the stillness of the night, then there were four or five reports, and at last one single shot was heard, and when the smoke had cleared away, we saw that the twelve men and nine horses had fallen. Three of the animals were galloping away at a furious pace, and one of them was dragging the dead body of its rider, which rebounded violently from the ground; his foot had caught in the stirrup.

"One of the soldiers behind me gave a terrible laugh and said: 'There will be some widows there!'

"Perhaps he was married. A third added: 'It did not take long!'

"A head emerged from the litter.

"'What is the matter?' she asked; 'are you fighting?'

"'It is nothing, mademoiselle,' I replied; 'we have got rid of a dozen Prussians!'

"'Poor fellows!' she said. But as she was cold, she quickly disappeared beneath the cloaks again, and we started off once more. We marched on for a long time, and at last the sky began to grow lighter. The snow became quite clear, luminous and glistening, and a rosy tint appeared in the east. Suddenly a voice in the distance cried:

"'Who goes there?'

"The whole detachment halted, and I advanced to give the countersign. We had reached the French lines, and, as my men defiled before the outpost, a commandant on horseback, whom I had informed of what had taken place, asked in a sonorous voice, as he saw the litter pass him: 'What have you in there?'

"And immediately a small head covered with light hair appeared, dishevelled and smiling, and replied:

"'It is I, monsieur.'

"At this the men raised a hearty laugh, and we felt quite light-hearted, while Pratique, who was walking by the side of the litter, waved his kepi and shouted:

"'Vive la France!' And I felt really affected. I do not know why, except that I thought it a pretty and gallant thing to say.

"It seemed to me as if we had just saved the whole of France and had done something that other men could not have done, something simple and really patriotic. I shall never forget that little face, you may be sure; and if I had to give my opinion about abolishing drums, trumpets and bugles, I should propose to replace them in every regiment by a pretty girl, and that would be even better than playing the 'Marseillaise: By Jove! it would put some spirit into a trooper to have a Madonna like that, a live Madonna, by the colonel's side."

He was silent for a few moments and then continued, with an air of conviction, and nodding his head:

"All the same, we are very fond of women, we Frenchmen!"

MOTHER SAUVAGE

Fifteen years had passed since I was at Virelogne. I returned there in the autumn to shoot with my friend Serval, who had at last rebuilt his chateau, which the Prussians had destroyed.

I loved that district. It is one of those delightful spots which have a sensuous charm for the eyes. You love it with a physical love. We, whom the country enchants, keep tender memories of certain springs, certain woods, certain pools, certain hills seen very often which have stirred us like joyful events. Sometimes our thoughts turn back to a corner in a forest, or the end of a bank, or an orchard filled with flowers, seen but a single time on some bright day, yet remaining in our hearts like the image of certain women met in the street on a spring morning in their light, gauzy dresses, leaving in soul and body an unsatisfied desire which is not to be forgotten, a feeling that you have just passed by happiness.

At Virelogne I loved the whole countryside, dotted with little woods and crossed by brooks which sparkled in the sun and looked like veins carrying blood to the earth. You fished in them for crawfish, trout and eels. Divine happiness! You could bathe in places and you often found snipe among the high grass which grew along the borders of these small water courses.

I was stepping along light as a goat, watching my two dogs running ahead of me, Serval, a hundred metres to my right, was beating a field of lucerne. I turned round by the thicket which forms the boundary of the wood of Sandres and I saw a cottage in ruins.

Suddenly I remembered it as I had seen it the last time, in 1869, neat, covered with vines, with chickens before the door. What is sadder than a dead house, with its skeleton standing bare and sinister?

I also recalled that inside its doors, after a very tiring day, the good woman had given me a glass of wine to drink and that Serval had told me the history of its people. The father, an old poacher, had been killed by the gendarmes. The son, whom I had once seen, was a tall, dry fellow who also passed for a fierce slayer of game. People called them "Les Sauvage."

Was that a name or a nickname?

I called to Serval. He came up with his long strides like a crane.

I asked him:

"What's become of those people?"

This was his story:

When war was declared the son Sauvage, who was then thirty-three years old, enlisted, leaving his mother alone in the house. People did not pity the old woman very much because she had money; they knew it.

She remained entirely alone in that isolated dwelling, so far from the village, on the edge of the wood. She was not afraid, however, being of the same strain as the men folk—a hardy old woman, tall and thin, who seldom laughed and with whom one never jested. The women of the fields laugh but little in any case, that is men's business. But they themselves have sad and narrowed hearts, leading a melancholy, gloomy life. The peasants imbibe a little noisy merriment at the tavern, but their helpmates always have grave, stern countenances. The muscles of their faces have never learned the motions of laughter.

Mother Sauvage continued her ordinary existence in her cottage, which was soon covered by the snows. She came to the village once a week to get bread and a little meat. Then she returned to her house. As there was talk of wolves, she went out with a gun upon her shoulder—her son's gun, rusty and with the butt worn by the rubbing of the hand—and she was a strange sight, the tall "Sauvage," a little bent, going with slow strides over the snow, the muzzle of the piece extending beyond the black headdress, which confined her head and imprisoned her white hair, which no one had ever seen.

One day a Prussian force arrived. It was billeted upon the inhabitants, according to the property and resources of each. Four were allotted to the old woman, who was known to be rich.

They were four great fellows with fair complexion, blond beards and blue eyes, who had not grown thin in spite of the fatigue which they had endured already and who also, though in a conquered country, had remained kind and gentle. Alone with this aged woman, they showed themselves full of consideration, sparing her, as much as they could, all expense and fatigue. They could be seen, all four of them, making their toilet at the well in their shirt-sleeves in the gray dawn, splashing with great swishes of water their pink-white northern skin, while La Mere Sauvage went and came, preparing their soup. They would be seen cleaning the kitchen, rubbing the tiles, splitting wood, peeling potatoes, doing up all the housework like four good sons around their mother.

But the old woman thought always of her own son, so tall and thin, with his hooked nose and his brown eyes and his heavy mustache which made a roll of black hair upon his lip. She asked every day of each of the soldiers who were installed beside her hearth: "Do you know where the French marching regiment, No. 23, was sent? My boy is in it."

They invariably answered, "No, we don't know, don't know a thing at all." And, understanding her pain and her uneasiness—they who had mothers, too, there at home—they rendered her a thousand little services. She loved them well, moreover, her four enemies, since the peasantry have no patriotic hatred; that belongs to the upper class alone. The humble, those who pay the most because they are poor and because every new burden crushes them down; those who are killed in masses, who make the true cannon's prey because they are so many; those, in fine, who suffer most cruelly the atrocious miseries of war because they are the feeblest and offer least resistance—they hardly understand at all those bellicose ardors, that excitable sense of honor or those pretended political combinations which in six months exhaust two nations, the conqueror with the conquered.

They said in the district, in speaking of the Germans of La Mere Sauvage:

"There are four who have found a soft place."

Now, one morning, when the old woman was alone in the house, she observed, far off on the plain, a man coming toward her dwelling. Soon she recognized him; it was the postman to distribute the letters. He gave her a folded paper and she drew out of her case the spectacles which she used for sewing. Then she read:

MADAME SAUVAGE: This letter is to tell you sad news. Your boy

Victor was killed yesterday by a shell which almost cut him in two.

I was near by, as we stood next each other in the company, and he

told me about you and asked me to let you know on the same day if

anything happened to him.

I took his watch, which was in his pocket, to bring it back to you

when the war is done.

CESAIRE RIVOT,

Soldier of the 2d class, March. Reg. No. 23.

The letter was dated three weeks back.

She did not cry at all. She remained motionless, so overcome and stupefied that she did not even suffer as yet. She thought: "There's Victor killed now." Then little by little the tears came to her eyes and the sorrow filled her heart. Her thoughts came, one by one, dreadful, torturing. She would never kiss him again, her child, her big boy, never again! The gendarmes had killed the father, the Prussians had killed the son. He had been cut in two by a cannon-ball. She seemed to see the thing, the horrible thing: the head falling, the eyes open, while he chewed the corner of his big mustache as he always did in moments of anger.

What had they done with his body afterward? If they had only let her have her boy back as they had brought back her husband—with the bullet in the middle of the forehead!

But she heard a noise of voices. It was the Prussians returning from the village. She hid her letter very quickly in her pocket, and she received them quietly, with her ordinary face, having had time to wipe her eyes.

They were laughing, all four, delighted, for they brought with them a fine rabbit—stolen, doubtless—and they made signs to the old woman that there was to be something good to east.

She set herself to work at once to prepare breakfast, but when it came to killing the rabbit, her heart failed her. And yet it was not the first. One of the soldiers struck it down with a blow of his fist behind the ears.

The beast once dead, she skinned the red body, but the sight of the blood which she was touching, and which covered her hands, and which she felt cooling and coagulating, made her tremble from head to foot, and she kept seeing her big boy cut in two, bloody, like this still palpitating animal.

She sat down at table with the Prussians, but she could not eat, not even a mouthful. They devoured the rabbit without bothering themselves about her. She looked at them sideways, without speaking, her face so impassive that they perceived nothing.

All of a sudden she said: "I don't even know your names, and here's a whole month that we've been together." They understood, not without difficulty, what she wanted, and told their names.

That was not sufficient; she had them written for her on a paper, with the addresses of their families, and, resting her spectacles on her great nose, she contemplated that strange handwriting, then folded the sheet and put it in her pocket, on top of the letter which told her of the death of her son.

When the meal was ended she said to the men:

"I am going to work for you."

And she began to carry up hay into the loft where they slept.

They were astonished at her taking all this trouble; she explained to them that thus they would not be so cold; and they helped her. They heaped the stacks of hay as high as the straw roof, and in that manner they made a sort of great chamber with four walls of fodder, warm and perfumed, where they should sleep splendidly.

At dinner one of them was worried to see that La Mere Sauvage still ate nothing. She told him that she had pains in her stomach. Then she kindled a good fire to warm herself, and the four Germans ascended to their lodging-place by the ladder which served them every night for this purpose.

As soon as they closed the trapdoor the old woman removed the ladder, then opened the outside door noiselessly and went back to look for more bundles of straw, with which she filled her kitchen. She went barefoot in the snow, so softly that no sound was heard. From time to time she listened to the sonorous and unequal snoring of the four soldiers who were fast asleep.

When she judged her preparations to be sufficient, she threw one of the bundles into the fireplace, and when it was alight she scattered it over all the others. Then she went outside again and looked.

In a few seconds the whole interior of the cottage was illumined with a brilliant light and became a frightful brasier, a gigantic fiery furnace, whose glare streamed out of the narrow window and threw a glittering beam upon the snow.

Then a great cry issued from the top of the house; it was a clamor of men shouting heartrending calls of anguish and of terror. Finally the trapdoor having given way, a whirlwind of fire shot up into the loft, pierced the straw roof, rose to the sky like the immense flame of a torch, and all the cottage flared.

Nothing more was heard therein but the crackling of the fire, the cracking of the walls, the falling of the rafters. Suddenly the roof fell in and the burning carcass of the dwelling hurled a great plume of sparks into the air, amid a cloud of smoke.

The country, all white, lit up by the fire, shone like a cloth of silver tinted with red.

A bell, far off, began to toll.

The old "Sauvage" stood before her ruined dwelling, armed with her gun, her son's gun, for fear one of those men might escape.

When she saw that it was ended, she threw her weapon into the brasier. A loud report followed.

People were coming, the peasants, the Prussians.

They found the woman seated on the trunk of a tree, calm and satisfied.

A German officer, but speaking French like a son of France, demanded:

"Where are your soldiers?"

She reached her bony arm toward the red heap of fire which was almost out and answered with a strong voice:

"There!"

They crowded round her. The Prussian asked:

"How did it take fire?"

"It was I who set it on fire."

They did not believe her, they thought that the sudden disaster had made her crazy. While all pressed round and listened, she told the story from beginning to end, from the arrival of the letter to the last shriek of the men who were burned with her house, and never omitted a detail.

When she had finished, she drew two pieces of paper from her pocket, and, in order to distinguish them by the last gleams of the fire, she again adjusted her spectacles. Then she said, showing one:

"That, that is the death of Victor." Showing the other, she added, indicating the red ruins with a bend of the head: "Here are their names, so that you can write home." She quietly held a sheet of paper out to the officer, who held her by the shoulders, and she continued:

"You must write how it happened, and you must say to their mothers that it was I who did that, Victoire Simon, la Sauvage! Do not forget."

The officer shouted some orders in German. They seized her, they threw her against the walls of her house, still hot. Then twelve men drew quickly up before her, at twenty paces. She did not move. She had understood; she waited.

An order rang out, followed instantly by a long report. A belated shot went off by itself, after the others.

The old woman did not fall. She sank as though they had cut off her legs.

The Prussian officer approached. She was almost cut in two, and in her withered hand she held her letter bathed with blood.

My friend Serval added:

"It was by way of reprisal that the Germans destroyed the chateau of the district, which belonged to me."

I thought of the mothers of those four fine fellows burned in that house and of the horrible heroism of that other mother shot against the wall.

And I picked up a little stone, still blackened by the flames.

EPIPHANY

I should say I did remember that Epiphany supper during the war! exclaimed Count de Garens, an army captain.

I was quartermaster of cavalry at the time, and for a fortnight had been scouting in front of the German advance guard. The evening before we had cut down a few Uhlans and had lost three men, one of whom was that poor little Raudeville. You remember Joseph de Raudeville, of course.

Well, on that day my commanding officer ordered me to take six troopers and to go and occupy the village of Porterin, where there had been five skirmishes in three weeks, and to hold it all night. There were not twenty houses left standing, not a dozen houses in that wasps' nest. So I took ten troopers and set out about four o'clock, and at five o'clock, while it was still pitch dark, we reached the first houses of Porterin. I halted and ordered Marchas—you know Pierre de Marchas, who afterward married little Martel-Auvelin, the daughter of the Marquis de Martel-Auvelin—to go alone into the village, and to report to me what he saw.

I had selected nothing but volunteers, all men of good family. It is pleasant when on duty not to be forced to be on intimate terms with unpleasant fellows. This Marchas was as smart as possible, cunning as a fox and supple as a serpent. He could scent the Prussians as a dog can scent a hare, could discover food where we should have died of hunger without him, and obtained information from everybody, and information which was always reliable, with incredible cleverness.

In ten minutes he returned. "All right," he said; "there have been no Prussians here for three days. It is a sinister place, is this village. I have been talking to a Sister of Mercy, who is caring for four or five wounded men in an abandoned convent."

I ordered them to ride on, and we entered the principal street. On the right and left we could vaguely see roofless walls, which were hardly visible in the profound darkness. Here and there a light was burning in a room; some family had remained to keep its house standing as well as they were able; a family of brave or of poor people. The rain began to fall, a fine, icy cold rain, which froze as it fell on our cloaks. The horses stumbled against stones, against beams, against furniture. Marchas guided us, going before us on foot, and leading his horse by the bridle.

"Where are you taking us to?" I asked him. And he replied: "I have a place for us to lodge in, and a rare good one." And we presently stopped before a small house, evidently belonging to some proprietor of the middle class. It stood on the street, was quite inclosed, and had a garden in the rear.

Marchas forced open the lock by means of a big stone which he picked up near the garden gate; then he mounted the steps, smashed in the front door with his feet and shoulders, lit a bit of wax candle, which he was never without, and went before us into the comfortable apartments of some rich private individual, guiding us with admirable assurance, as if he lived in this house which he now saw for the first time.

Two troopers remained outside to take care of our horses, and Marchas said to stout Ponderel, who followed him: "The stables must be on the left; I saw that as we came in; go and put the animals up there, for we do not need them"; and then, turning to me, he said: "Give your orders, confound it all!"

This fellow always astonished me, and I replied with a laugh: "I will post my sentinels at the country approaches and will return to you here."

"How many men are you going to take?"

"Five. The others will relieve them at five o'clock in the evening."

"Very well. Leave me four to look after provisions, to do the cooking and to set the table. I will go and find out where the wine is hidden."

I went off, to reconnoitre the deserted streets until they ended in the open country, so as to post my sentries there.

Half an hour later I was back, and found Marchas lounging in a great easy-chair, the covering of which he had taken off, from love of luxury, as he said. He was warming his feet at the fire and smoking an excellent cigar, whose perfume filled the room. He was alone, his elbows resting on the arms of the chair, his head sunk between his shoulders, his cheeks flushed, his eyes bright, and looking delighted.

I heard the noise of plates and dishes in the next room, and Marchas said to me, smiling in a contented manner: "This is famous; I found the champagne under the flight of steps outside, the brandy—fifty bottles of the very finest in the kitchen garden under a pear tree, which did not seem to me to be quite straight when I looked at it by the light of my lantern. As for solids, we have two fowls, a goose, a duck, and three pigeons. They are being cooked at this moment. It is a delightful district."

I sat down opposite him, and the fire in the grate was burning my nose and cheeks. "Where did you find this wood?" I asked. "Splendid wood," he replied. "The owner's carriage. It is the paint which is causing all this flame, an essence of punch and varnish. A capital house!"

I laughed, for I saw the creature was funny, and he went on: "Fancy this being the Epiphany! I have had a bean put into the goose dressing; but there is no queen; it is really very annoying!" And I repeated like an echo: "It is annoying, but what do you want me to do in the matter?" "To find some, of course." "Some women. Women?—you must be mad?" "I managed to find the brandy under the pear tree, and the champagne under the steps; and yet there was nothing to guide me, while as for you, a petticoat is a sure bait. Go and look, old fellow."

He looked so grave, so convinced, that I could not tell whether he was joking or not, and so I replied: "Look here, Marchas, are you having a joke with me?" "I never joke on duty." "But where the devil do you expect me to find any women?" "Where you like; there must be two or three remaining in the neighborhood, so ferret them out and bring them here."

I got up, for it was too hot in front of the fire, and Marchas went off:

"Do you want an idea?" "Yes." "Go and see the priest." "The priest? What for?" "Ask him to supper, and beg him to bring a woman with him." "The priest! A woman! Ha! ha! ha!"

But Marchas continued with extraordinary gravity: "I am not laughing; go and find the priest and tell him how we are situated, and, as he must be horribly dull, he will come. But tell him that we want one woman at least, a lady, of course, since we, are all men of the world. He is sure to know his female parishioners on the tips of his fingers, and if there is one to suit us, and you manage it well, he will suggest her to you."

"Come, come, Marchas, what are you thinking of?" "My dear Garens, you can do this quite well. It will even be very funny. We are well bred, by Jove! and we will put on our most distinguished manners and our grandest style. Tell the abbe who we are, make him laugh, soften his heart, coax him and persuade him!" "No, it is impossible."

He drew his chair close to mine, and as he knew my special weakness, the scamp continued: "Just think what a swaggering thing it will be to do and how amusing to tell about; the whole army will talk about it, and it will give you a famous reputation."

I hesitated, for the adventure rather tempted me, and he persisted: "Come, my little Garens. You are the head of this detachment, and you alone can go and call on the head of the church in this neighborhood. I beg of you to go, and I promise you that after the war I will relate the whole affair in verse in the Revue de Deux Mondes. You owe this much to your men, for you have made them march enough during the last month."

I got up at last and asked: "Where is the priest's house?" "Take the second turning at the end of the street, you will see an avenue, and at the end of the avenue you will find the church. The parsonage is beside it." As I went out, he called out: "Tell him the bill of fare, to make him hungry!"

I discovered the ecclesiastic's little house without any difficulty; it was by the side of a large, ugly brick church. I knocked at the door with my fist, as there was neither bell nor knocker, and a loud voice from inside asked: "Who is there?" To which I replied: "A quartermaster of hussars."

I heard the noise of bolts and of a key being turned, and found myself face to face with a tall priest with a large stomach, the chest of a prizefighter, formidable hands projecting from turned-up sleeves, a red face, and the look of a kind man. I gave him a military salute and said: "Good-day, Monsieur le Cure."

He had feared a surprise, some marauders' ambush, and he smiled as he replied: "Good-day, my friend; come in." I followed him into a small room with a red tiled floor, in which a small fire was burning, very different to Marchas' furnace, and he gave me a chair and said: "What can I do for you?" "Monsieur, allow me first of all to introduce myself"; and I gave him my card, which he took and read half aloud: "Le Comte de Garens."

I continued: "There are eleven of us here, Monsieur l'Abbe, five on picket duty, and six installed at the house of an unknown inhabitant. The names of the six are: Garens, myself; Pierre de Marchas, Ludovic de Ponderel, Baron d'Streillis, Karl Massouligny, the painter's son, and Joseph Herbon, a young musician. I have come to ask you, in their name and my own, to do us the honor of supping with us. It is an Epiphany supper, Monsieur le Cure, and we should like to make it a little cheerful."

The priest smiled and murmured: "It seems to me to be hardly a suitable occasion for amusing one's self." And I replied: "We are fighting during the day, monsieur. Fourteen of our comrades have been killed in a month, and three fell as late as yesterday. It is war time. We stake our life at every moment; have we not, therefore, the right to amuse ourselves freely? We are Frenchmen, we like to laugh, and we can laugh everywhere. Our fathers laughed on the scaffold! This evening we should like to cheer ourselves up a little, like gentlemen, and not like soldiers; you understand me, I hope. Are we wrong?"

He replied quickly: "You are quite right, my friend, and I accept your invitation with great pleasure." Then he called out: "Hermance!"

An old bent, wrinkled, horrible peasant woman appeared and said: "What do you want?" "I shall not dine at home, my daughter." "Where are you going to dine then?" "With some gentlemen, the hussars."

I felt inclined to say: "Bring your servant with you," just to see Marchas' face, but I did not venture, and continued: "Do you know any one among your parishioners, male or female, whom I could invite as well?" He hesitated, reflected, and then said: "No, I do not know anybody!"

I persisted: "Nobody! Come, monsieur, think; it would be very nice to have some ladies, I mean to say, some married couples! I know nothing about your parishioners. The baker and his wife, the grocer, the—the—the—watchmaker—the—shoemaker—the—the druggist with Mrs. Druggist. We have a good spread and plenty of wine, and we should be enchanted to leave pleasant recollections of ourselves with the people here."

The priest thought again for a long time, and then said resolutely: "No, there is nobody." I began to laugh. "By Jove, Monsieur le Cure, it is very annoying not to have an Epiphany queen, for we have the bean. Come, think. Is there not a married mayor, or a married deputy mayor, or a married municipal councillor or a schoolmaster?" "No, all the ladies have gone away." "What, is there not in the whole place some good tradesman's wife with her good tradesman, to whom we might give this pleasure, for it would be a pleasure to them, a great pleasure under present circumstances?"

But, suddenly, the cure began to laugh, and laughed so violently that he fairly shook, and presently exclaimed: "Ha! ha! ha! I have got what you want, yes. I have got what you want! Ha! ha! ha! We will laugh and enjoy ourselves, my children; we will have some fun. How pleased the ladies will be, I say, how delighted they will be! Ha! ha! Where are you staying?"

I described the house, and he understood where it was. "Very good," he said. "It belongs to Monsieur Bertin-Lavaille. I will be there in half an hour, with four ladies! Ha! ha! ha! four ladies!"

He went out with me, still laughing, and left me, repeating: "That is capital; in half an hour at Bertin-Lavaille's house."

I returned quickly, very much astonished and very much puzzled. "Covers for how many?" Marchas asked, as soon as he saw me. "Eleven. There are six of us hussars, besides the priest and four ladies." He was thunderstruck, and I was triumphant. He repeated: "Four ladies! Did you say, four ladies?" "I said four women." "Real women?" "Real women." "Well, accept my compliments!" "I will, for I deserve them."

He got out of his armchair, opened the door, and I saw a beautiful white tablecloth on a long table, round which three hussars in blue aprons were setting out the plates and glasses. "There are some women coming!" Marchas cried. And the three men began to dance and to cheer with all their might.

Everything was ready, and we were waiting. We waited for nearly an hour, while a delicious smell of roast poultry pervaded the whole house. At last, however, a knock against the shutters made us all jump up at the same moment. Stout Ponderel ran to open the door, and in less than a minute a little Sister of Mercy appeared in the doorway. She was thin, wrinkled and timid, and successively greeted the four bewildered hussars who saw her enter. Behind her, the noise of sticks sounded on the tiled floor in the vestibule, and as soon as she had come into the drawing-room, I saw three old heads in white caps, following each other one by one, who came in, swaying with different movements, one inclining to the right, while the other inclined to the left. And three worthy women appeared, limping, dragging their legs behind them, crippled by illness and deformed through old age, three infirm old women, past service, the only three pensioners who were able to walk in the home presided over by Sister Saint-Benedict.

She had turned round to her invalids, full of anxiety for them, and then, seeing my quartermaster's stripes, she said to me: "I am much obliged to you for thinking of these poor women. They have very little pleasure in life, and you are at the same time giving them a great treat and doing them a great honor."

I saw the priest, who had remained in the dark hallway, and was laughing heartily, and I began to laugh in my turn, especially when I saw Marchas' face. Then, motioning the nun to the seats, I said:

"Sit down, sister; we are very proud and very happy that you have accepted our unpretentious invitation."

She took three chairs which stood against the wall, set them before the fire, led her three old women to them, settled them on them, took their sticks and shawls, which she put into a corner, and then, pointing to the first, a thin woman with an enormous stomach, who was evidently suffering from the dropsy, she said: "This is Mother Paumelle; whose husband was killed by falling from a roof, and whose son died in Africa; she is sixty years old." Then she pointed to another, a tall woman, whose head trembled unceasingly: "This is Mother Jean-Jean, who is sixty-seven. She is nearly blind, for her face was terribly singed in a fire, and her right leg was half burned off."

Then she pointed to the third, a sort of dwarf, with protruding, round, stupid eyes, which she rolled incessantly in all directions, "This is La Putois, an idiot. She is only forty-four."

I bowed to the three women as if I were being presented to some royal highnesses, and turning to the priest, I said: "You are an excellent man, Monsieur l'Abbe, to whom all of us here owe a debt of gratitude."

Everybody was laughing, in fact, except Marchas, who seemed furious, and just then Karl Massouligny cried: "Sister Saint-Benedict, supper is on the table!"

I made her go first with the priest, then I helped up Mother Paumelle, whose arm I took and dragged her into the next room, which was no easy task, for she seemed heavier than a lump of iron.

Stout Ponderel gave his arm to Mother Jean-Jean, who bemoaned her crutch, and little Joseph Herbon took the idiot, La Putois, to the dining-room, which was filled with the odor of the viands.

As soon as we were opposite our plates, the sister clapped her hands three times, and, with the precision of soldiers presenting arms, the women made a rapid sign of the cross, and then the priest slowly repeated the Benedictus in Latin. Then we sat down, and the two fowls appeared, brought in by Marchas, who chose to wait at table, rather than to sit down as a guest to this ridiculous repast.

But I cried: "Bring the champagne at once!" and a cork flew out with the noise of a pistol, and in spite of the resistance of the priest and of the kind sister, the three hussars, sitting by the side of the three invalids, emptied their three full glasses down their throats by force.

Massouligny, who possessed the faculty of making himself at home, and of being on good terms with every one, wherever he was, made love to Mother Paumelle in the drollest manner. The dropsical woman, who had retained her cheerfulness in spite of her misfortunes, answered him banteringly in a high falsetto voice which appeared as if it were put on, and she laughed so heartily at her neighbor's jokes that it was quite alarming. Little Herbon had seriously undertaken the task of making the idiot drunk, and Baron d'Streillis, whose wits were not always particularly sharp, was questioning old Jean-Jean about the life, the habits, and the rules of the hospital.

The nun said to Massouligny in consternation:

"Oh! oh! you will make her ill; pray do not make her laugh like that, monsieur. Oh! monsieur—" Then she got up and rushed at Herbon to take from him a full glass which he was hastily emptying down La Putois' throat, while the priest shook with laughter, and said to the sister: "Never mind; just this once, it will not hurt them. Do leave them alone."

After the two fowls they ate the duck, which was flanked by the three pigeons and the blackbird, and then the goose appeared, smoking, golden-brown, and diffusing a warm odor of hot, browned roast meat. La Paumelle, who was getting lively, clapped her hands; La Jean-Jean left off answering the baron's numerous questions, and La Putois uttered. grunts of pleasure, half cries and half sighs, as little children do when one shows them candy. "Allow me to take charge of this animal," the cure said. "I understand these sort of operations better than most people." "Certainly, Monsieur l'Abbe," and the sister said: "How would it be to open the window a little? They are too warm, and I am afraid they will be ill."

I turned to Marchas: "Open the window for a minute." He did so; the cold outer air as it came in made the candles flare, and the steam from the goose, which the cure was scientifically carving, with a table napkin round his neck, whirl about. We watched him doing it, without speaking now, for we were interested in his attractive handiwork, and seized with renewed appetite at the sight of that enormous golden-brown bird, whose limbs fell one after another into the brown gravy at the bottom of the dish. At that moment, in the midst of that greedy silence which kept us all attentive, the distant report of a shot came in at the open window.

I started to my feet so quickly that my chair fell down behind me, and I shouted: "To saddle, all of you! You, Marches, take two men and go and see what it is. I shall expect you back here in five minutes." And while the three riders went off at full gallop through the night, I got into the saddle with my three remaining hussars, in front of the steps of the villa, while the cure, the sister and the three old women showed their frightened faces at the window.

We heard nothing more, except the barking of a dog in the distance. The rain had ceased, and it was cold, very cold, and soon I heard the gallop of a horse, of a single horse, coming back. It was Marchas, and I called out to him: "Well?" "It is nothing; Francois has wounded an old peasant who refused to answer his challenge: 'Who goes there?' and who continued to advance in spite of the order to keep off; but they are bringing him here, and we shall see what is the matter."

I gave orders for the horses to be put back in the stable, and I sent my two soldiers to meet the others, and returned to the house. Then the cure, Marchas, and I took a mattress into the room to lay the wounded man on; the sister tore up a table napkin in order to make lint, while the three frightened women remained huddled up in a corner.

Soon I heard the rattle of sabres on the road, and I took a candle to show a light to the men who were returning; and they soon appeared, carrying that inert, soft, long, sinister object which a human body becomes when life no longer sustains it.

They put the wounded man on the mattress that had been prepared for him, and I saw at the first glance that he was dying. He had the death rattle and was spitting up blood, which ran out of the corners of his mouth at every gasp. The man was covered with blood! His cheeks, his beard, his hair, his neck and his clothes seemed to have been soaked, to have been dipped in a red tub; and that blood stuck to him, and had become a dull color which was horrible to look at.

The wounded man, wrapped up in a large shepherd's cloak, occasionally opened his dull, vacant eyes, which seemed stupid with astonishment, like those of animals wounded by a sportsman, which fall at his feet, more than half dead already, stupefied with terror and surprise.

The cure exclaimed: "Ah, it is old Placide, the shepherd from Les Moulins. He is deaf, poor man, and heard nothing. Ah! Oh, God! they have killed the unhappy man!" The sister had opened his blouse and shirt, and was looking at a little blue hole in his chest, which was not bleeding any more. "There is nothing to be done," she said.

The shepherd was gasping terribly and bringing up blood with every last breath, and in his throat, to the very depth of his lungs, they could hear an ominous and continued gurgling. The cure, standing in front of him, raised his right hand, made the sign of the cross, and in a slow and solemn voice pronounced the Latin words which purify men's souls, but before they were finished, the old man's body trembled violently, as if something had given way inside him, and he ceased to breathe. He was dead.

When I turned round, I saw a sight which was even more horrible than the death struggle of this unfortunate man; the three old women were standing up huddled close together, hideous, and grimacing with fear and horror. I went up to them, and they began to utter shrill screams, while La Jean-Jean, whose burned leg could no longer support her, fell to the ground at full length.

Sister Saint-Benedict left the dead man, ran up to her infirm old women, and without a word or a look for me, wrapped their shawls round them, gave them their crutches, pushed them to the door, made them go out, and disappeared with them into the dark night.

I saw that I could not even let a hussar accompany them, for the mere rattle of a sword would have sent them mad with fear.

The cure was still looking at the dead man; but at last he turned round to me and said:

"Oh! What a horrible thing!"

THE MUSTACHE

CHATEAU DE SOLLES,

July 30, 1883.

My Dear Lucy:

I have no news. We live in the drawing-room, looking out at the rain. We cannot go out in this frightful weather, so we have theatricals. How stupid they are, my dear, these drawing entertainments in the repertory of real life! All is forced, coarse, heavy. The jokes are like cannon balls, smashing everything in their passage. No wit, nothing natural, no sprightliness, no elegance. These literary men, in truth, know nothing of society. They are perfectly ignorant of how people think and talk in our set. I do not mind if they despise our customs, our conventionalities, but I do not forgive them for not knowing them. When they want to be humorous they make puns that would do for a barrack; when they try to be jolly, they give us jokes that they must have picked up on the outer boulevard in those beer houses artists are supposed to frequent, where one has heard the same students' jokes for fifty years.

So we have taken to Theatricals. As we are only two women, my husband takes the part of a soubrette, and, in order to do that, he has shaved off his mustache. You cannot imagine, my dear Lucy, how it changes him! I no longer recognize him-by day or at night. If he did not let it grow again I think I should no longer love him; he looks so horrid like this.

In fact, a man without a mustache is no longer a man. I do not care much for a beard; it almost always makes a man look untidy. But a mustache, oh, a mustache is indispensable to a manly face. No, you would never believe how these little hair bristles on the upper lip are a relief to the eye and good in other ways. I have thought over the matter a great deal but hardly dare to write my thoughts.

Words look so different on paper and the subject is so difficult, so delicate, so dangerous that it requires infinite skill to tackle it.

Well, when my husband appeared, shaven, I understood at once that I never could fall in love with a strolling actor nor a preacher, even if it were Father Didon, the most charming of all! Later when I was alone with him (my husband) it was worse still. Oh, my dear Lucy, never let yourself be kissed by a man without a mustache; their kisses have no flavor, none whatever! They no longer have the charm, the mellowness and the snap —yes, the snap—of a real kiss. The mustache is the spice.

Imagine placing to your lips a piece of dry—or moist—parchment. That is the kiss of the man without a mustache. It is not worth while.

Whence comes this charm of the mustache, will you tell me? Do I know myself? It tickles your face, you feel it approaching your mouth and it sends a little shiver through you down to the tips of your toes.

And on your neck! Have you ever felt a mustache on your neck? It intoxicates you, makes you feel creepy, goes to the tips of your fingers. You wriggle, shake your shoulders, toss back your head. You wish to get away and at the same time to remain there; it is delightful, but irritating. But how good it is!

A lip without a mustache is like a body without clothing; and one must wear clothes, very few, if you like, but still some clothing.

I recall a sentence (uttered by a politician) which has been running in my mind for three months. My husband, who keeps up with the newspapers, read me one evening a very singular speech by our Minister of Agriculture, who was called M. Meline. He may have been superseded by this time. I do not know.

I was paying no attention, but the name Meline struck me. It recalled, I do not exactly know why, the 'Scenes de la vie de boheme'. I thought it was about some grisette. That shows how scraps of the speech entered my mind. This M. Meline was making this statement to the people of Amiens, I believe, and I have ever since been trying to understand what he meant: "There is no patriotism without agriculture!" Well, I have just discovered his meaning, and I affirm in my turn that there is no love without a mustache. When you say it that way it sounds comical, does it not?

There is no love without a mustache!

"There is no patriotism without agriculture," said M. Meline, and he was right, that minister; I now understand why.

From a very different point of view the mustache is essential. It gives character to the face. It makes a man look gentle, tender, violent, a monster, a rake, enterprising! The hairy man, who does not shave off his whiskers, never has a refined look, for his features are concealed; and the shape of the jaw and the chin betrays a great deal to those who understand.

The man with a mustache retains his own peculiar expression and his refinement at the same time.

And how many different varieties of mustaches there are! Sometimes they are twisted, curled, coquettish. Those seem to be chiefly devoted to women.

Sometimes they are pointed, sharp as needles, and threatening. That kind prefers wine, horses and war.

Sometimes they are enormous, overhanging, frightful. These big ones generally conceal a fine disposition, a kindliness that borders on weakness and a gentleness that savors of timidity.

But what I adore above all in the mustache is that it is French, altogether French. It came from our ancestors, the Gauls, and has remained the insignia of our national character.

It is boastful, gallant and brave. It sips wine gracefully and knows how to laugh with refinement, while the broad-bearded jaws are clumsy in everything they do.

I recall something that made me weep all my tears and also—I see it now—made me love a mustache on a man's face.

It was during the war, when I was living with my father. I was a young girl then. One day there was a skirmish near the chateau. I had heard the firing of the cannon and of the artillery all the morning, and that evening a German colonel came and took up his abode in our house. He left the following day.

My father was informed that there were a number of dead bodies in the fields. He had them brought to our place so that they might be buried together. They were laid all along the great avenue of pines as fast as they brought them in, on both sides of the avenue, and as they began to smell unpleasant, their bodies were covered with earth until the deep trench could be dug. Thus one saw only their heads which seemed to protrude from the clayey earth and were almost as yellow, with their closed eyes.

I wanted to see them. But when I saw those two rows of frightful faces, I thought I should faint. However, I began to look at them, one by one, trying to guess what kind of men these had been.

The uniforms were concealed beneath the earth, and yet immediately, yes, immediately, my dear, I recognized the Frenchmen by their mustache!

Some of them had shaved on the very day of the battle, as though they wished to be elegant up to the last; others seemed to have a week's growth, but all wore the French mustache, very plain, the proud mustache that seems to say: "Do not take me for my bearded friend, little one; I am a brother."

And I cried, oh, I cried a great deal more than I should if I had not recognized them, the poor dead fellows.

It was wrong of me to tell you this. Now I am sad and cannot chatter any

longer. Well, good-by, dear Lucy. I send you a hearty kiss. Long live

the mustache!

JEANNE.

MADAME BAPTISTE

The first thing I did was to look at the clock as I entered the waiting-room of the station at Loubain, and I found that I had to wait two hours and ten minutes for the Paris express.

I had walked twenty miles and felt suddenly tired. Not seeing anything on the station walls to amuse me, I went outside and stood there racking my brains to think of something to do. The street was a kind of boulevard, planted with acacias, and on either side a row of houses of varying shape and different styles of architecture, houses such as one only sees in a small town, and ascended a slight hill, at the extreme end of which there were some trees, as though it ended in a park.

From time to time a cat crossed the street and jumped over the gutters carefully. A cur sniffed at every tree and hunted for scraps from the kitchens, but I did not see a single human being, and I felt listless and disheartened. What could I do with myself? I was already thinking of the inevitable and interminable visit to the small cafe at the railway station, where I should have to sit over a glass of undrinkable beer and the illegible newspaper, when I saw a funeral procession coming out of a side street into the one in which I was, and the sight of the hearse was a relief to me. It would, at any rate, give me something to do for ten minutes.

Suddenly, however, my curiosity was aroused. The hearse was followed by eight gentlemen, one of whom was weeping, while the others were chatting together, but there was no priest, and I thought to myself:

"This is a non-religious funeral," and then I reflected that a town like Loubain must contain at least a hundred freethinkers, who would have made a point of making a manifestation. What could it be, then? The rapid pace of the procession clearly proved that the body was to be buried without ceremony, and, consequently, without the intervention of the Church.

My idle curiosity framed the most complicated surmises, and as the hearse passed me, a strange idea struck me, which was to follow it, with the eight gentlemen. That would take up my time for an hour, at least, and I accordingly walked with the others, with a sad look on my face, and, on seeing this, the two last turned round in surprise, and then spoke to each other in a low voice.

No doubt they were asking each other whether I belonged to the town, and then they consulted the two in front of them, who stared at me in turn. This close scrutiny annoyed me, and to put an end to it I went up to them, and, after bowing, I said:

"I beg your pardon, gentlemen, for interrupting your conversation, but, seeing a civil funeral, I have followed it, although I did not know the deceased gentleman whom you are accompanying."

"It was a woman," one of them said.

I was much surprised at hearing this, and asked:

"But it is a civil funeral, is it not?"

The other gentleman, who evidently wished to tell me all about it, then said: "Yes and no. The clergy have refused to allow us the use of the church."

On hearing this I uttered a prolonged "A-h!" of astonishment. I could not understand it at all, but my obliging neighbor continued:

"It is rather a long story. This young woman committed suicide, and that is the reason why she cannot be buried with any religious ceremony. The gentleman who is walking first, and who is crying, is her husband."

I replied with some hesitation:

"You surprise and interest me very much, monsieur. Shall I be indiscreet if I ask you to tell me the facts of the case? If I am troubling you, forget that I have said anything about the matter."

The gentleman took my arm familiarly.

"Not at all, not at all. Let us linger a little behind the others, and I will tell it you, although it is a very sad story. We have plenty of time before getting to the cemetery, the trees of which you see up yonder, for it is a stiff pull up this hill."

And he began:

"This young woman, Madame Paul Hamot, was the daughter of a wealthy merchant in the neighborhood, Monsieur Fontanelle. When she was a mere child of eleven, she had a shocking adventure; a footman attacked her and she nearly died. A terrible criminal case was the result, and the man was sentenced to penal servitude for life.

"The little girl grew up, stigmatized by disgrace, isolated, without any companions; and grown-up people would scarcely kiss her, for they thought that they would soil their lips if they touched her forehead, and she became a sort of monster, a phenomenon to all the town. People said to each other in a whisper: 'You know, little Fontanelle,' and everybody turned away in the streets when she passed. Her parents could not even get a nurse to take her out for a walk, as the other servants held aloof from her, as if contact with her would poison everybody who came near her.

"It was pitiable to see the poor child go and play every afternoon. She remained quite by herself, standing by her maid and looking at the other children amusing themselves. Sometimes, yielding to an irresistible desire to mix with the other children, she advanced timidly, with nervous gestures, and mingled with a group, with furtive steps, as if conscious of her own disgrace. And immediately the mothers, aunts and nurses would come running from every seat and take the children entrusted to their care by the hand and drag them brutally away.

"Little Fontanelle remained isolated, wretched, without understanding what it meant, and then she began to cry, nearly heartbroken with grief, and then she used to run and hide her head in her nurse's lap, sobbing.

"As she grew up, it was worse still. They kept the girls from her, as if she were stricken with the plague. Remember that she had nothing to learn, nothing; that she no longer had the right to the symbolical wreath of orange-flowers; that almost before she could read she had penetrated that redoubtable mystery which mothers scarcely allow their daughters to guess at, trembling as they enlighten them on the night of their marriage.

"When she went through the streets, always accompanied by her governess, as if, her parents feared some fresh, terrible adventure, with her eyes cast down under the load of that mysterious disgrace which she felt was always weighing upon her, the other girls, who were not nearly so innocent as people thought, whispered and giggled as they looked at her knowingly, and immediately turned their heads absently, if she happened to look at them. People scarcely greeted her; only a few men bowed to her, and the mothers pretended not to see her, while some young blackguards called her Madame Baptiste, after the name of the footman who had attacked her.

"Nobody knew the secret torture of her mind, for she hardly ever spoke, and never laughed, and her parents themselves appeared uncomfortable in her presence, as if they bore her a constant grudge for some irreparable fault.

"An honest man would not willingly give his hand to a liberated convict, would he, even if that convict were his own son? And Monsieur and Madame Fontanelle looked on their daughter as they would have done on a son who had just been released from the hulks. She was pretty and pale, tall, slender, distinguished-looking, and she would have pleased me very much, monsieur, but for that unfortunate affair.

"Well, when a new sub-prefect was appointed here, eighteen months ago, he brought his private secretary with him. He was a queer sort of fellow, who had lived in the Latin Quarter, it appears. He saw Mademoiselle Fontanelle and fell in love with her, and when told of what occurred, he merely said:

"'Bah! That is just a guarantee for the future, and I would rather it should have happened before I married her than afterward. I shall live tranquilly with that woman.'

"He paid his addresses to her, asked for her hand and married her, and then, not being deficient in assurance, he paid wedding calls, as if nothing had happened. Some people returned them, others did not; but, at last, the affair began to be forgotten, and she took her proper place in society.

"She adored her husband as if he had been a god; for, you must remember, he had restored her to honor and to social life, had braved public opinion, faced insults, and, in a word, performed such a courageous act as few men would undertake, and she felt the most exalted and tender love for him.

"When she became enceinte, and it was known, the most particular people and the greatest sticklers opened their doors to her, as if she had been definitely purified by maternity.

"It is strange, but so it is, and thus everything was going on as well as possible until the other day, which was the feast of the patron saint of our town. The prefect, surrounded by his staff and the authorities, presided at the musical competition, and when he had finished his speech the distribution of medals began, which Paul Hamot, his private secretary, handed to those who were entitled to them.

"As you know, there are always jealousies and rivalries, which make people forget all propriety. All the ladies of the town were there on the platform, and, in his turn, the bandmaster from the village of Mourmillon came up. This band was only to receive a second-class medal, for one cannot give first-class medals to everybody, can one? But when the private secretary handed him his badge, the man threw it in his face and exclaimed:

"'You may keep your medal for Baptiste. You owe him a first-class one, also, just as you do me.'

"There were a number of people there who began to laugh. The common herd are neither charitable nor refined, and every eye was turned toward that poor lady. Have you ever seen a woman going mad, monsieur? Well, we were present at the sight! She got up and fell back on her chair three times in succession, as if she wished to make her escape, but saw that she could not make her way through the crowd, and then another voice in the crowd exclaimed:

"'Oh! Oh! Madame Baptiste!'

"And a great uproar, partly of laughter and partly of indignation, arose. The word was repeated over and over again; people stood on tiptoe to see the unhappy woman's face; husbands lifted their wives up in their arms, so that they might see her, and people asked:

"'Which is she? The one in blue?'

"The boys crowed like cocks, and laughter was heard all over the place.

"She did not move now on her state chair, but sat just as if she had been put there for the crowd to look at. She could not move, nor conceal herself, nor hide her face. Her eyelids blinked quickly, as if a vivid light were shining on them, and she breathed heavily, like a horse that is going up a steep hill, so that it almost broke one's heart to see her. Meanwhile, however, Monsieur Hamot had seized the ruffian by the throat, and they were rolling on the ground together, amid a scene of indescribable confusion, and the ceremony was interrupted.

"An hour later, as the Hamots were returning home, the young woman, who had not uttered a word since the insult, but who was trembling as if all her nerves had been set in motion by springs, suddenly sprang over the parapet of the bridge and threw herself into the river before her husband could prevent her. The water is very deep under the arches, and it was two hours before her body was recovered. Of course, she was dead."

The narrator stopped and then added:

"It was, perhaps, the best thing she could do under the circumstances. There are some things which cannot be wiped out, and now you understand why the clergy refused to have her taken into church. Ah! If it had been a religious funeral the whole town would have been present, but you can understand that her suicide added to the other affair and made families abstain from attending her funeral; and then, it is not an easy matter here to attend a funeral which is performed without religious rites."

We passed through the cemetery gates and I waited, much moved by what I had heard, until the coffin had been lowered into the grave, before I went up to the poor fellow who was sobbing violently, to press his hand warmly. He looked at me in surprise through his tears and then said:

"Thank you, monsieur." And I was not sorry that I had followed the funeral.

THE QUESTION OF LATIN

This subject of Latin that has been dinned into our ears for some time past recalls to my mind a story—a story of my youth.

I was finishing my studies with a teacher, in a big central town, at the Institution Robineau, celebrated through the entire province for the special attention paid there to the study of Latin.

For the past ten years, the Robineau Institute beat the imperial lycee of the town at every competitive examination, and all the colleges of the subprefecture, and these constant successes were due, they said, to an usher, a simple usher, M. Piquedent, or rather Pere Piquedent.

He was one of those middle-aged men quite gray, whose real age it is impossible to tell, and whose history we can guess at first glance. Having entered as an usher at twenty into the first institution that presented itself so that he could proceed to take first his degree of Master of Arts and afterward the degree of Doctor of Laws, he found himself so enmeshed in this routine that he remained an usher all his life. But his love for Latin did not leave him and harassed him like an unhealthy passion. He continued to read the poets, the prose writers, the historians, to interpret them and penetrate their meaning, to comment on them with a perseverance bordering on madness.

One day, the idea came into his head to oblige all the students in his class to answer him in Latin only; and he persisted in this resolution until at last they were capable of sustaining an entire conversation with him just as they would in their mother tongue. He listened to them, as a leader of an orchestra listens to his musicians rehearsing, and striking his desk every moment with his ruler, he exclaimed:

"Monsieur Lefrere, Monsieur Lefrere, you are committing a solecism! You forget the rule.

"Monsieur Plantel, your way of expressing yourself is altogether French and in no way Latin. You must understand the genius of a language. Look here, listen to me."

Now, it came to pass that the pupils of the Institution Robineau carried off, at the end of the year, all the prizes for composition, translation, and Latin conversation.

Next year, the principal, a little man, as cunning as an ape, whom he resembled in his grinning and grotesque appearance, had had printed on his programmes, on his advertisements, and painted on the door of his institution:

"Latin Studies a Specialty. Five first prizes carried off in the five classes of the lycee.

"Two honor prizes at the general examinations in competition with all the lycees and colleges of France."

For ten years the Institution Robineau triumphed in the same fashion. Now my father, allured by these successes, sent me as a day pupil to Robineau's—or, as we called it, Robinetto or Robinettino's—and made me take special private lessons from Pere Piquedent at the rate of five francs per hour, out of which the usher got two francs and the principal three francs. I was then eighteen, and was in the philosophy class.

These private lessons were given in a little room looking out on the street. It so happened that Pere Piquedent, instead of talking Latin to me, as he did when teaching publicly in the institution, kept telling me his troubles in French. Without relations, without friends, the poor man conceived an attachment to me, and poured out his misery to me.

He had never for the last ten or fifteen years chatted confidentially with any one.

"I am like an oak in a desert," he said—"'sicut quercus in solitudine'."

The other ushers disgusted him. He knew nobody in the town, since he had no time to devote to making acquaintances.

"Not even the nights, my friend, and that is the hardest thing on me. The dream of my life is to have a room with my own furniture, my own books, little things that belong to myself and which others may not touch. And I have nothing of my own, nothing except my trousers and my frock-coat, nothing, not even my mattress and my pillow! I have not four walls to shut myself up in, except when I come to give a lesson in this room. Do you see what this means—a man forced to spend his life without ever having the right, without ever finding the time, to shut himself up all alone, no matter where, to think, to reflect, to work, to dream? Ah! my dear boy, a key, the key of a door which one can lock—this is happiness, mark you, the only happiness!

"Here, all day long, teaching all those restless rogues, and during the night the dormitory with the same restless rogues snoring. And I have to sleep in the bed at the end of two rows of beds occupied by these youngsters whom I must look after. I can never be alone, never! If I go out I find the streets full of people, and, when I am tired of walking, I go into some cafe crowded with smokers and billiard players. I tell you what, it is the life of a galley slave."

I said:

"Why did you not take up some other line, Monsieur Piquedent?"

He exclaimed:

"What, my little friend? I am not a shoemaker, or a joiner, or a hatter, or a baker, or a hairdresser. I only know Latin, and I have no diploma which would enable me to sell my knowledge at a high price. If I were a doctor I would sell for a hundred francs what I now sell for a hundred sous; and I would supply it probably of an inferior quality, for my title would be enough to sustain my reputation."

Sometimes he would say to me:

"I have no rest in life except in the hours spent with you. Don't be afraid! you'll lose nothing by that. I'll make it up to you in the class-room by making you speak twice as much Latin as the others."

One day, I grew bolder, and offered him a cigarette. He stared at me in astonishment at first, then he gave a glance toward the door.

"If any one were to come in, my dear boy?"

"Well, let us smoke at the window," said I.

And we went and leaned our elbows on the windowsill looking on the street, holding concealed in our hands the little rolls of tobacco. Just opposite to us was a laundry. Four women in loose white waists were passing hot, heavy irons over the linen spread out before them, from which a warm steam arose.

Suddenly, another, a fifth, carrying on her arm a large basket which made her stoop, came out to take the customers their shirts, their handkerchiefs, and their sheets. She stopped on the threshold as if she were already fatigued; then, she raised her eyes, smiled as she saw us smoking, flung at us, with her left hand, which was free, the sly kiss characteristic of a free-and-easy working-woman, and went away at a slow place, dragging her feet as she went.

She was a woman of about twenty, small, rather thin, pale, rather pretty, with a roguish air and laughing eyes beneath her ill-combed fair hair.

Pere Piquedent, affected, began murmuring:

"What an occupation for a woman! Really a trade only fit for a horse."

And he spoke with emotion about the misery of the people. He had a heart which swelled with lofty democratic sentiment, and he referred to the fatiguing pursuits of the working class with phrases borrowed from Jean-Jacques Rousseau, and with sobs in his throat.

Next day, as we were leaning our elbows on the same window sill, the same woman perceived us and cried out to us:

"Good-day, scholars!" in a comical sort of tone, while she made a contemptuous gesture with her hands.

I flung her a cigarette, which she immediately began to smoke. And the four other ironers rushed out to the door with outstretched hands to get cigarettes also.

And each day a friendly intercourse was established between the working-women of the pavement and the idlers of the boarding school.

Pere Piquedent was really a comical sight. He trembled at being noticed, for he might lose his position; and he made timid and ridiculous gestures, quite a theatrical display of love signals, to which the women responded with a regular fusillade of kisses.

A perfidious idea came into my mind. One day, on entering our room, I said to the old usher in a low tone:

"You would not believe it, Monsieur Piquedent, I met the little washerwoman! You know the one I mean, the woman who had the basket, and I spoke to her!"

He asked, rather worried at my manner:

"What did she say to you?"

"She said to me—why, she said she thought you were very nice. The fact of the matter is, I believe, I believe, that she is a little in love with you." I saw that he was growing pale.

"She is laughing at me, of course. These things don't happen at my age," he replied.

I said gravely:

"How is that? You are all right."

As I felt that my trick had produced its effect on him, I did not press the matter.

But every day I pretended that I had met the little laundress and that I had spoken to her about him, so that in the end he believed me, and sent her ardent and earnest kisses.

Now it happened that one morning, on my way to the boarding school, I really came across her. I accosted her without hesitation, as if I had known her for the last ten years.

"Good-day, mademoiselle. Are you quite well?"

"Very well, monsieur, thank you."

"Will you have a cigarette?"

"Oh! not in the street."

"You can smoke it at home."

"In that case, I will."

"Let me tell you, mademoiselle, there's something you don't know."

"What is that, monsieur?"

"The old gentleman—my old professor, I mean—"

"Pere Piquedent?"

"Yes, Pere Piquedent. So you know his name?"

"Faith, I do! What of that?"

"Well, he is in love with you!"

She burst out laughing wildly, and exclaimed:

"You are only fooling."

"Oh! no, I am not fooling! He keeps talking of you all through the lesson. I bet that he'll marry you!"

She ceased laughing. The idea of marriage makes every girl serious. Then she repeated, with an incredulous air:

"This is humbug!"

"I swear to you, it's true."

She picked up her basket which she had laid down at her feet.

"Well, we'll see," she said. And she went away.

Presently when I had reached the boarding school, I took Pere Piquedent aside, and said:

"You must write to her; she is infatuated with you."

And he wrote a long letter, tenderly affectionate, full of phrases and circumlocutions, metaphors and similes, philosophy and academic gallantry; and I took on myself the responsibility of delivering it to the young woman.

She read it with gravity, with emotion; then she murmured:

"How well he writes! It is easy to see he has got education! Does he really mean to marry me?"

I replied intrepidly: "Faith, he has lost his head about you!"

"Then he must invite me to dinner on Sunday at the Ile des Fleurs."

I promised that she should be invited.

Pere Piquedent was much touched by everything I told him about her.

I added:

"She loves you, Monsieur Piquedent, and I believe her to be a decent girl. It is not right to lead her on and then abandon her."

He replied in a firm tone:

"I hope I, too, am a decent man, my friend."

I confess I had at the time no plan. I was playing a practical joke a schoolboy joke, nothing more. I had been aware of the simplicity of the old usher, his innocence and his weakness. I amused myself without asking myself how it would turn out. I was eighteen, and I had been for a long time looked upon at the lycee as a sly practical joker.

So it was agreed that Pere Piquedent and I should set out in a hack for the ferry of Queue de Vache, that we should there pick up Angele, and that I should take them into my boat, for in those days I was fond of boating. I would then bring them to the Ile des Fleurs, where the three of us would dine. I had inflicted myself on them, the better to enjoy my triumph, and the usher, consenting to my arrangement, proved clearly that he was losing his head by thus risking the loss of his position.

When we arrived at the ferry, where my boat had been moored since morning, I saw in the grass, or rather above the tall weeds of the bank, an enormous red parasol, resembling a monstrous wild poppy. Beneath the parasol was the little laundress in her Sunday clothes. I was surprised. She was really pretty, though pale; and graceful, though with a rather suburban grace.

Pere Piquedent raised his hat and bowed. She put out her hand toward him, and they stared at one another without uttering a word. Then they stepped into my boat, and I took the oars. They were seated side by side near the stern.

The usher was the first to speak.

"This is nice weather for a row in a boat."

She murmured:

"Oh! yes."

She dipped her hand into the water, skimming the surface, making a thin, transparent film like a sheet of glass, which made a soft plashing along the side of the boat.

When they were in the restaurant, she took it on herself to speak, and ordered dinner, fried fish, a chicken, and salad; then she led us on toward the isle, which she knew perfectly.

After this, she was gay, romping, and even rather tantalizing.

Until dessert, no question of love arose. I had treated them to champagne, and Pere Piquedent was tipsy. Herself slightly the worse, she called out to him:

"Monsieur Piquenez."

He said abruptly:

"Mademoiselle, Monsieur Raoul has communicated my sentiments to you."

She became as serious as a judge.

"Yes, monsieur."

"What is your reply?"

"We never reply to these questions!"

He puffed with emotion, and went on:

"Well, will the day ever come that you will like me?"

She smiled.

"You big stupid! You are very nice."

"In short, mademoiselle, do you think that, later on, we might—"

She hesitated a second; then in a trembling voice she said:

"Do you mean to marry me when you say that? For on no other condition, you know."

"Yes, mademoiselle!"

"Well, that's all right, Monsieur Piquedent!"

It was thus that these two silly creatures promised marriage to each other through the trick of a young scamp. But I did not believe that it was serious, nor, indeed, did they, perhaps.

"You know, I have nothing, not four sous," she said.

He stammered, for he was as drunk as Silenus:

"I have saved five thousand francs."

She exclaimed triumphantly:

"Then we can set up in business?"

He became restless.

"In what business?"

"What do I know? We shall see. With five thousand francs we could do many things. You don't want me to go and live in your boarding school, do you?"

He had not looked forward so far as this, and he stammered in great perplexity:

"What business could we set up in? That would not do, for all I know is Latin!"

She reflected in her turn, passing in review all her business ambitions.

"You could not be a doctor?"

"No, I have no diploma."

"Or a chemist?"

"No more than the other."

She uttered a cry of joy. She had discovered it.

"Then we'll buy a grocer's shop! Oh! what luck! we'll buy a grocer's shop. Not on a big scale, of course; with five thousand francs one does not go far."

He was shocked at the suggestion.

"No, I can't be a grocer. I am—I am—too well known: I only know Latin, that is all I know."

But she poured a glass of champagne down his throat. He drank it and was silent.

We got back into the boat. The night was dark, very dark. I saw clearly, however, that he had caught her by the waist, and that they were hugging each other again and again.

It was a frightful catastrophe. Our escapade was discovered, with the result that Pere Piquedent was dismissed. And my father, in a fit of anger, sent me to finish my course of philosophy at Ribaudet's school.

Six months later I took my degree of Bachelor of Arts. Then I went to study law in Paris, and did not return to my native town till two years later.

At the corner of the Rue de Serpent a shop caught my eye. Over the door were the words: "Colonial Products—Piquedent"; then underneath, so as to enlighten the most ignorant: "Grocery."

I exclaimed:

"'Quantum mutatus ab illo!'"

Piquedent raised his head, left his female customer, and rushed toward me with outstretched hands.

"Ah! my young friend, my young friend, here you are! What luck! what luck!"

A beautiful woman, very plump, abruptly left the cashier's desk and flung herself on my breast. I had some difficulty in recognizing her, she had grown so stout.

I asked:

"So then you're doing well?"

Piquedent had gone back to weigh the groceries.

"Oh! very well, very well, very well. I have made three thousand francs clear this year!"

"And what about Latin, Monsieur Piquedent?"

"Oh, good heavens! Latin, Latin, Latin—you see it does not keep the pot boiling!"

A MEETING

It was nothing but an accident, an accident pure and simple. On that particular evening the princess' rooms were open, and as they appeared dark after the brilliantly lighted parlors, Baron d'Etraille, who was tired of standing, inadvertently wandered into an empty bedroom.

He looked round for a chair in which to have a doze, as he was sure his wife would not leave before daylight. As soon as he became accustomed to the light of the room he distinguished the big bed with its azure-and-gold hangings, in the middle of the great room, looking like a catafalque in which love was buried, for the princess was no longer young. Behind it, a large bright surface looked like a lake seen at a distance. It was a large mirror, discreetly covered with dark drapery, that was very rarely let down, and seemed to look at the bed, which was its accomplice. One might almost fancy that it had reminiscences, and that one might see in it charming female forms and the gentle movement of loving arms.

The baron stood still for a moment, smiling, almost experiencing an emotion on the threshold of this chamber dedicated to love. But suddenly something appeared in the looking-glass, as if the phantoms which he had evoked had risen up before him. A man and a woman who had been sitting on a low couch concealed in the shadow had arisen, and the polished surface, reflecting their figures, showed that they were kissing each other before separating.

Baron d'Etraille recognized his wife and the Marquis de Cervigne. He turned and went away like a man who is fully master of himself, and waited till it was day before taking away the baroness; but he had no longer any thoughts of sleeping.

As soon as they were alone he said:

"Madame, I saw you just now in Princesse de Raynes' room; I need say no more, and I am not fond either of reproaches, acts of violence, or of ridicule. As I wish to avoid all such things, we shall separate without any scandal. Our lawyers will settle your position according to my orders. You will be free to live as you please when you are no longer under my roof; but, as you will continue to bear my name, I must warn you that should any scandal arise I shall show myself inflexible."

She tried to speak, but he stopped her, bowed, and left the room.

He was more astonished and sad than unhappy. He had loved her dearly during the first period of their married life; but his ardor had cooled, and now he often amused himself elsewhere, either in a theatre or in society, though he always preserved a certain liking for the baroness.

She was very young, hardly four-and-twenty, small, slight—too slight—and very fair. She was a true Parisian doll: clever, spoiled, elegant, coquettish, witty, with more charm than real beauty. He used to say familiarly to his brother, when speaking of her:

"My wife is charming, attractive, but—there is nothing to lay hold of. She is like a glass of champagne that is all froth; when you get to the wine it is very good, but there is too little of it, unfortunately."

He walked up and down the room in great agitation, thinking of a thousand things. At one moment he was furious, and felt inclined to give the marquis a good thrashing, or to slap his face publicly, in the club. But he decided that would not do, it would not be good form; he would be laughed at, and not his rival, and this thought wounded his vanity. So he went to bed, but could not sleep. Paris knew in a few days that the Baron and Baroness d'Etraille had agreed to an amicable separation on account of incompatibility of temper. No one suspected anything, no one laughed, and no one was astonished.

The baron, however, to avoid meeting his wife, travelled for a year, then spent the summer at the seaside, and the autumn in shooting, returning to Paris for the winter. He did not meet the baroness once.

He did not even know what people said about her. In any case, she took care to respect appearances, and that was all he asked for.

He became dreadfully bored, travelled again, restored his old castle of Villebosc, which took him two years; then for over a year he entertained friends there, till at last, tired of all these so-called pleasures, he returned to his mansion in the Rue de Lille, just six years after the separation.

He was now forty-five, with a good crop of gray hair, rather stout, and with that melancholy look characteristic of those who have been handsome, sought after, and liked, but who are deteriorating, daily.

A month after his return to Paris, he took cold on coming out of his club, and had such a bad cough that his medical man ordered him to Nice for the rest of the winter.

He reached the station only a few minutes before the departure of the train on Monday evening, and had barely time to get into a carriage, with only one other occupant, who was sitting in a corner so wrapped in furs and cloaks that he could not even make out whether it was a man or a woman, as nothing of the figure could be seen. When he perceived that he could not find out, he put on his travelling cap, rolled himself up in his rugs, and stretched out comfortably to sleep.

He did not wake until the day was breaking, and looked at once at his fellow-traveller, who had not stirred all night, and seemed still to be sound asleep.

M. d'Etraille made use of the opportunity to brush his hair and his beard, and to try to freshen himself up a little generally, for a night's travel does not improve one's appearance when one has attained a certain age.

A great poet has said:

"When we are young, our mornings are triumphant!"

Then we wake up with a cool skin, a bright eye, and glossy hair.

As one grows older one wakes up in a very different condition. Dull eyes, red, swollen cheeks, dry lips, hair and beard disarranged, impart an old, fatigued, worn-out look to the face.

The baron opened his travelling case, and improved his looks as much as possible.

The engine whistled, the train stopped, and his neighbor moved. No doubt he was awake. They started off again, and then a slanting ray of sunlight shone into the carriage and on the sleeper, who moved again, shook himself, and then his face could be seen.

It was a young, fair, pretty, plump woman, and the baron looked at her in amazement. He did not know what to think. He could really have sworn that it was his wife, but wonderfully changed for the better: stouter —why she had grown as stout as he was, only it suited her much better than it did him.

She looked at him calmly, did not seem to recognize him, and then slowly laid aside her wraps. She had that quiet assurance of a woman who is sure of herself, who feels that on awaking she is in her full beauty and freshness.

The baron was really bewildered. Was it his wife, or else as like her as any sister could be? Not having seen her for six years, he might be mistaken.

She yawned, and this gesture betrayed her. She turned and looked at him again, calmly, indifferently, as if she scarcely saw him, and then looked out of the window again.

He was upset and dreadfully perplexed, and kept looking at her sideways.

Yes; it was surely his wife. How could he possibly have doubted it? There could certainly not be two noses like that, and a thousand recollections flashed through his mind. He felt the old feeling of the intoxication of love stealing over him, and he called to mind the sweet odor of her skin, her smile when she put her arms on to his shoulders, the soft intonations of her voice, all her graceful, coaxing ways.

But how she had changed and improved! It was she and yet not she. She seemed riper, more developed, more of a woman, more seductive, more desirable, adorably desirable.

And this strange, unknown woman, whom he had accidentally met in a railway carriage, belonged to him; he had only to say to her:

"I insist upon it."

He had formerly slept in her arms, existed only in her love, and now he had found her again certainly, but so changed that he scarcely knew her. It was another, and yet it was she herself. It was some one who had been born and had formed and grown since he had left her. It was she, indeed; she whom he had loved, but who was now altered, with a more assured smile and greater self-possession. There were two women in one, mingling a great part of what was new and unknown with many sweet recollections of the past. There was something singular, disturbing, exciting about it —a kind of mystery of love in which there floated a delicious confusion. It was his wife in a new body and in new flesh which lips had never pressed.

And he thought that in a few years nearly every thing changes in us; only the outline can be recognized, and sometimes even that disappears.

The blood, the hair, the skin, all changes and is renewed, and when people have not seen each other for a long time, when they meet they find each other totally different beings, although they are the same and bear the same name.

And the heart also can change. Ideas may be modified and renewed, so that in forty years of life we may, by gradual and constant transformations, become four or five totally new and different beings.

He dwelt on this thought till it troubled him; it had first taken possession of him when he surprised her in the princess' room. He was not the least angry; it was not the same woman that he was looking at —that thin, excitable little doll of those days.

What was he to do? How should he address her? and what could he say to her? Had she recognized him?

The train stopped again. He got up, bowed, and said: "Bertha, do you want anything I could bring you?"

She looked at him from head to foot, and answered, without showing the slightest surprise, or confusion, or anger, but with the most perfect indifference:

"I do not want anything—-thank you."

He got out and walked up and down the platform a little in order to recover himself, and, as it were, to recover his senses after a fall. What should he do now? If he got into another carriage it would look as if he were running away. Should he be polite or importunate? That would look as if he were asking for forgiveness. Should he speak as if he were her master? He would look like a fool, and, besides, he really had no right to do so.

He got in again and took his place.

During his absence she had hastily arranged her dress and hair, and was now lying stretched out on the seat, radiant, and without showing any emotion.

He turned to her, and said: "My dear Bertha, since this singular chance has brought up together after a separation of six years—a quite friendly separation—are we to continue to look upon each other as irreconcilable enemies? We are shut up together, tete-a-tete, which is so much the better or so much the worse. I am not going to get into another carriage, so don't you think it is preferable to talk as friends till the end of our journey?"

She answered, quite calmly again:

"Just as you please."

Then he suddenly stopped, really not knowing what to say; but as he had plenty of assurance, he sat down on the middle seat, and said:

"Well, I see I must pay my court to you; so much the better. It is, however, really a pleasure, for you are charming. You cannot imagine how you have improved in the last six years. I do not know any woman who could give me that delightful sensation which I experienced just now when you emerged from your wraps. I really could not have thought such a change possible."

Without moving her head or looking at him, she said: "I cannot say the same with regard to you; you have certainly deteriorated a great deal."

He got red and confused, and then, with a smile of resignation, he said:

"You are rather hard."

"Why?" was her reply. "I am only stating facts. I don't suppose you intend to offer me your love? It must, therefore, be a matter of perfect indifference to you what I think about you. But I see it is a painful subject, so let us talk of something else. What have you been doing since I last saw you?"

He felt rather out of countenance, and stammered:

"I? I have travelled, done some shooting, and grown old, as you see. And you?"

She said, quite calmly: "I have taken care of appearances, as you ordered me."

He was very nearly saying something brutal, but he checked himself; and kissed his wife's hand:

"And I thank you," he said.

She was surprised. He was indeed diplomatic, and always master of himself.

He went on: "As you have acceded to my first request, shall we now talk without any bitterness?"

She made a little movement of surprise.

"Bitterness? I don't feel any; you are a complete stranger to me; I am only trying to keep up a difficult conversation."

He was still looking at her, fascinated in spite of her harshness, and he felt seized with a brutal Beside, the desire of the master.

Perceiving that she had hurt his feelings, she said:

"How old are you now? I thought you were younger than you look."

"I am forty-five"; and then he added: "I forgot to ask after Princesse de Raynes. Are you still intimate with her?"

She looked at him as if she hated him:

"Yes, I certainly am. She is very well, thank you."

They remained sitting side by side, agitated and irritated. Suddenly he said:

"My dear Bertha, I have changed my mind. You are my wife, and I expect you to come with me today. You have, I think, improved both morally and physically, and I am going to take you back again. I am your husband, and it is my right to do so."

She was stupefied, and looked at him, trying to divine his thoughts; but his face was resolute and impenetrable.

"I am very sorry," she said, "but I have made other engagements."

"So much the worse for you," was his reply. "The law gives me the power, and I mean to use it."

They were nearing Marseilles, and the train whistled and slackened speed. The baroness rose, carefully rolled up her wraps, and then, turning to her husband, said:

"My dear Raymond, do not make a bad use of this tete-a tete which I had carefully prepared. I wished to take precautions, according to your advice, so that I might have nothing to fear from you or from other people, whatever might happen. You are going to Nice, are you not?"

"I shall go wherever you go."

"Not at all; just listen to me, and I am sure that you will leave me in peace. In a few moments, when we get to the station, you will see the Princesse de Raynes and Comtesse Henriot waiting for me with their husbands. I wished them to see as, and to know that we had spent the night together in the railway carriage. Don't be alarmed; they will tell it everywhere as a most surprising fact.

"I told you just now that I had most carefully followed your advice and saved appearances. Anything else does not matter, does it? Well, in order to do so, I wished to be seen with you. You told me carefully to avoid any scandal, and I am avoiding it, for, I am afraid—I am afraid—"

She waited till the train had quite stopped, and as her friends ran up to open the carriage door, she said:

"I am afraid"—hesitating—"that there is another reason—je suis enceinte."

The princess stretched out her arms to embrace her,—and the baroness said, painting to the baron, who was dumb with astonishment, and was trying to get at the truth:

"You do not recognize Raymond? He has certainly changed a good deal, and he agreed to come with me so that I might not travel alone. We take little trips like this occasionally, like good friends who cannot live together. We are going to separate here; he has had enough of me already."

She put out her hand, which he took mechanically, and then she jumped out on to the platform among her friends, who were waiting for her.

The baron hastily shut the carriage door, for he was too much disturbed to say a word or come to any determination. He heard his wife's voice and their merry laughter as they went away.

He never saw her again, nor did he ever discover whether she had told him a lie or was speaking the truth.

THE BLIND MAN

How is it that the sunlight gives us such joy? Why does this radiance when it falls on the earth fill us with the joy of living? The whole sky is blue, the fields are green, the houses all white, and our enchanted eyes drink in those bright colors which bring delight to our souls. And then there springs up in our hearts a desire to dance, to run, to sing, a happy lightness of thought, a sort of enlarged tenderness; we feel a longing to embrace the sun.

The blind, as they sit in the doorways, impassive in their eternal darkness, remain as calm as ever in the midst of this fresh gaiety, and, not understanding what is taking place around them, they continually check their dogs as they attempt to play.

When, at the close of the day, they are returning home on the arm of a young brother or a little sister, if the child says: "It was a very fine day!" the other answers: "I could notice that it was fine. Loulou wouldn't keep quiet."

I knew one of these men whose life was one of the most cruel martyrdoms that could possibly be conceived.

He was a peasant, the son of a Norman farmer. As long as his father and mother lived, he was more or less taken care of; he suffered little save from his horrible infirmity; but as soon as the old people were gone, an atrocious life of misery commenced for him. Dependent on a sister of his, everybody in the farmhouse treated him as a beggar who is eating the bread of strangers. At every meal the very food he swallowed was made a subject of reproach against him; he was called a drone, a clown, and although his brother-in-law had taken possession of his portion of the inheritance, he was helped grudgingly to soup, getting just enough to save him from starving.

His face was very pale and his two big white eyes looked like wafers. He remained unmoved at all the insults hurled at him, so reserved that one could not tell whether he felt them.

Moreover, he had never known any tenderness, his mother having always treated him unkindly and caring very little for him; for in country places useless persons are considered a nuisance, and the peasants would be glad to kill the infirm of their species, as poultry do.

As soon as he finished his soup he went and sat outside the door in summer and in winter beside the fireside, and did not stir again all the evening. He made no gesture, no movement; only his eyelids, quivering from some nervous affection, fell down sometimes over his white, sightless orbs. Had he any intellect, any thinking faculty, any consciousness of his own existence? Nobody cared to inquire.

For some years things went on in this fashion. But his incapacity for work as well as his impassiveness eventually exasperated his relatives, and he became a laughingstock, a sort of butt for merriment, a prey to the inborn ferocity, to the savage gaiety of the brutes who surrounded him.

It is easy to imagine all the cruel practical jokes inspired by his blindness. And, in order to have some fun in return for feeding him, they now converted his meals into hours of pleasure for the neighbors and of punishment for the helpless creature himself.

The peasants from the nearest houses came to this entertainment; it was talked about from door to door, and every day the kitchen of the farmhouse was full of people. Sometimes they placed before his plate, when he was beginning to eat his soup, some cat or dog. The animal instinctively perceived the man's infirmity, and, softly approaching, commenced eating noiselessly, lapping up the soup daintily; and, when they lapped the food rather noisily, rousing the poor fellow's attention, they would prudently scamper away to avoid the blow of the spoon directed at random by the blind man!

Then the spectators ranged along the wall would burst out laughing, nudge each other and stamp their feet on the floor. And he, without ever uttering a word, would continue eating with his right hand, while stretching out his left to protect his plate.

Another time they made him chew corks, bits of wood, leaves or even filth, which he was unable to distinguish.

After this they got tired even of these practical jokes, and the brother-in-law, angry at having to support him always, struck him, cuffed him incessantly, laughing at his futile efforts to ward off or return the blows. Then came a new pleasure—the pleasure of smacking his face. And the plough-men, the servant girls and even every passing vagabond were every moment giving him cuffs, which caused his eyelashes to twitch spasmodically. He did not know where to hide himself and remained with his arms always held out to guard against people coming too close to him.

At last he was forced to beg.

He was placed somewhere on the high-road on market-days, and as soon as he heard the sound of footsteps or the rolling of a vehicle, he reached out his hat, stammering:

"Charity, if you please!"

But the peasant is not lavish, and for whole weeks he did not bring back a sou.

Then he became the victim of furious, pitiless hatred. And this is how he died.

One winter the ground was covered with snow, and it was freezing hard. His brother-in-law led him one morning a great distance along the high road in order that he might solicit alms. The blind man was left there all day; and when night came on, the brother-in-law told the people of his house that he could find no trace of the mendicant. Then he added:

"Pooh! best not bother about him! He was cold and got someone to take him away. Never fear! he's not lost. He'll turn up soon enough tomorrow to eat the soup."

Next day he did not come back.

After long hours of waiting, stiffened with the cold, feeling that he was dying, the blind man began to walk. Being unable to find his way along the road, owing to its thick coating of ice, he went on at random, falling into ditches, getting up again, without uttering a sound, his sole object being to find some house where he could take shelter.

But, by degrees, the descending snow made a numbness steal over him, and his feeble limbs being incapable of carrying him farther, he sat down in the middle of an open field. He did not get up again.

The white flakes which fell continuously buried him, so that his body, quite stiff and stark, disappeared under the incessant accumulation of their rapidly thickening mass, and nothing was left to indicate the place where he lay.

His relatives made a pretence of inquiring about him and searching for him for about a week. They even made a show of weeping.

The winter was severe, and the thaw did not set in quickly. Now, one Sunday, on their way to mass, the farmers noticed a great flight of crows, who were whirling incessantly above the open field, and then descending like a shower of black rain at the same spot, ever going and coming.

The following week these gloomy birds were still there. There was a crowd of them up in the air, as if they had gathered from all corners of the horizon, and they swooped down with a great cawing into the shining snow, which they covered like black patches, and in which they kept pecking obstinately. A young fellow went to see what they were doing and discovered the body of the blind man, already half devoured, mangled. His wan eyes had disappeared, pecked out by the long, voracious beaks.

And I can never feel the glad radiance of sunlit days without sadly remembering and pondering over the fate of the beggar who was such an outcast in life that his horrible death was a relief to all who had known him.

INDISCRETION

They had loved each other before marriage with a pure and lofty love. They had first met on the sea-shore. He had thought this young girl charming, as she passed by with her light-colored parasol and her dainty dress amid the marine landscape against the horizon. He had loved her, blond and slender, in these surroundings of blue ocean and spacious sky. He could not distinguish the tenderness which this budding woman awoke in him from the vague and powerful emotion which the fresh salt air and the grand scenery of surf and sunshine and waves aroused in his soul.

She, on the other hand, had loved him because he courted her, because he was young, rich, kind, and attentive. She had loved him because it is natural for young girls to love men who whisper sweet nothings to them.

So, for three months, they had lived side by side, and hand in hand. The greeting which they exchanged in the morning before the bath, in the freshness of the morning, or in the evening on the sand, under the stars, in the warmth of a calm night, whispered low, very low, already had the flavor of kisses, though their lips had never met.

Each dreamed of the other at night, each thought of the other on awaking, and, without yet having voiced their sentiments, each longer for the other, body and soul.

After marriage their love descended to earth. It was at first a tireless, sensuous passion, then exalted tenderness composed of tangible poetry, more refined caresses, and new and foolish inventions. Every glance and gesture was an expression of passion.

But, little by little, without even noticing it, they began to get tired of each other. Love was still strong, but they had nothing more to reveal to each other, nothing more to learn from each other, no new tale of endearment, no unexpected outburst, no new way of expressing the well-known, oft-repeated verb.

They tried, however, to rekindle the dwindling flame of the first love. Every day they tried some new trick or desperate attempt to bring back to their hearts the uncooled ardor of their first days of married life. They tried moonlight walks under the trees, in the sweet warmth of the summer evenings: the poetry of mist-covered beaches; the excitement of public festivals.

One morning Henriette said to Paul:

"Will you take me to a cafe for dinner?"

"Certainly, dearie."

"To some well-known cafe?"

"Of course!"

He looked at her with a questioning glance, seeing that she was thinking of something which she did not wish to tell.

She went on:

"You know, one of those cafes—oh, how can I explain myself?—a sporty cafe!"

He smiled: "Of course, I understand—you mean in one of the cafes which are commonly called bohemian."

"Yes, that's it. But take me to one of the big places, one where you are known, one where you have already supped—no—dined—well, you know—I—I—oh! I will never dare say it!"

"Go ahead, dearie. Little secrets should no longer exist between us."

"No, I dare not."

"Go on; don't be prudish. Tell me."

"Well, I—I—I want to be taken for your sweetheart—there! and I want the boys, who do not know that you are married, to take me for such; and you too—I want you to think that I am your sweetheart for one hour, in that place which must hold so many memories for you. There! And I will play that I am your sweetheart. It's awful, I know—I am abominably ashamed, I am as red as a peony. Don't look at me!"

He laughed, greatly amused, and answered:

"All right, we will go to-night to a very swell place where I am well known."

Toward seven o'clock they went up the stairs of one of the big cafes on the Boulevard, he, smiling, with the look of a conqueror, she, timid, veiled, delighted. They were immediately shown to one of the luxurious private dining-rooms, furnished with four large arm-chairs and a red plush couch. The head waiter entered and brought them the menu. Paul handed it to his wife.

"What do you want to eat?"

"I don't care; order whatever is good."

After handing his coat to the waiter, he ordered dinner and champagne. The waiter looked at the young woman and smiled. He took the order and murmured:

"Will Monsieur Paul have his champagne sweet or dry?"

"Dry, very dry."

Henriette was pleased to hear that this man knew her husband's name. They sat on the couch, side by side, and began to eat.

Ten candles lighted the room and were reflected in the mirrors all around them, which seemed to increase the brilliancy a thousand-fold. Henriette drank glass after glass in order to keep up her courage, although she felt dizzy after the first few glasses. Paul, excited by the memories which returned to him, kept kissing his wife's hands. His eyes were sparkling.

She was feeling strangely excited in this new place, restless, pleased, a little guilty, but full of life. Two waiters, serious, silent, accustomed to seeing and forgetting everything, to entering the room only when it was necessary and to leaving it when they felt they were intruding, were silently flitting hither and thither.

Toward the middle of the dinner, Henriette was well under the influence of champagne. She was prattling along fearlessly, her cheeks flushed, her eyes glistening.

"Come, Paul; tell me everything."

"What, sweetheart?"

"I don't dare tell you."

"Go on!"

"Have you loved many women before me?"

He hesitated, a little perplexed, not knowing whether he should hide his adventures or boast of them.

She continued:

"Oh! please tell me. How many have you loved?"

"A few."

"How many?"

"I don't know. How do you expect me to know such things?"

"Haven't you counted them?"

"Of course not."

"Then you must have loved a good many!"

"Perhaps."

"About how many? Just tell me about how many."

"But I don't know, dearest. Some years a good many, and some years only a few."

"How many a year, did you say?"

"Sometimes twenty or thirty, sometimes only four or five."

"Oh! that makes more than a hundred in all!"

"Yes, just about."

"Oh! I think that is dreadful!"

"Why dreadful?"

"Because it's dreadful when you think of it—all those women—and always—always the same thing. Oh! it's dreadful, just the same—more than a hundred women!"

He was surprised that she should think that dreadful, and answered, with the air of superiority which men take with women when they wish to make them understand that they have said something foolish:

"That's funny! If it is dreadful to have a hundred women, it's dreadful to have one."

"Oh, no, not at all!"

"Why not?"

"Because with one woman you have a real bond of love which attaches you to her, while with a hundred women it's not the same at all. There is no real love. I don't understand how a man can associate with such women."

"But they are all right."

"No, they can't be!"

"Yes, they are!"

"Oh, stop; you disgust me!"

"But then, why did you ask me how many sweethearts I had had?"

"Because——"

"That's no reason!"

"What were they-actresses, little shop-girls, or society women?"

"A few of each."

"It must have been rather monotonous toward the last."

"Oh, no; it's amusing to change."

She remained thoughtful, staring at her champagne glass. It was full —she drank it in one gulp; then putting it back on the table, she threw her arms around her husband's neck and murmured in his ear:

"Oh! how I love you, sweetheart! how I love you!"

He threw his arms around her in a passionate embrace. A waiter, who was just entering, backed out, closing the door discreetly. In about five minutes the head waiter came back, solemn and dignified, bringing the fruit for dessert. She was once more holding between her fingers a full glass, and gazing into the amber liquid as though seeking unknown things. She murmured in a dreamy voice:

"Yes, it must be fun!"

A FAMILY AFFAIR

The small engine attached to the Neuilly steam-tram whistled as it passed the Porte Maillot to warn all obstacles to get out of its way and puffed like a person out of breath as it sent out its steam, its pistons moving rapidly with a noise as of iron legs running. The train was going along the broad avenue that ends at the Seine. The sultry heat at the close of a July day lay over the whole city, and from the road, although there was not a breath of wind stirring, there arose a white, chalky, suffocating, warm dust, which adhered to the moist skin, filled the eyes and got into the lungs. People stood in the doorways of their houses to try and get a breath of air.

The windows of the steam-tram were open and the curtains fluttered in the wind. There were very few passengers inside, because on warm days people preferred the outside or the platforms. They consisted of stout women in peculiar costumes, of those shopkeepers' wives from the suburbs, who made up for the distinguished looks which they did not possess by ill-assumed dignity; of men tired from office-work, with yellow faces, stooped shoulders, and with one shoulder higher than the other, in consequence of, their long hours of writing at a desk. Their uneasy and melancholy faces also spoke of domestic troubles, of constant want of money, disappointed hopes, for they all belonged to the army of poor, threadbare devils who vegetate economically in cheap, plastered houses with a tiny piece of neglected garden on the outskirts of Paris, in the midst of those fields where night soil is deposited.

A short, corpulent man, with a puffy face, dressed all in black and wearing a decoration in his buttonhole, was talking to a tall, thin man, dressed in a dirty, white linen suit, the coat all unbuttoned, with a white Panama hat on his head. The former spoke so slowly and hesitatingly that it occasionally almost seemed as if he stammered; he was Monsieur Caravan, chief clerk in the Admiralty. The other, who had formerly been surgeon on board a merchant ship, had set up in practice in Courbevoie, where he applied the vague remnants of medical knowledge which he had retained after an adventurous life, to the wretched population of that district. His name was Chenet, and strange rumors were current as to his morality.

Monsieur Caravan had always led the normal life of a man in a Government office. For the last thirty years he had invariably gone the same way to his office every morning, and had met the same men going to business at the same time, and nearly on the same spot, and he returned home every evening by the same road, and again met the same faces which he had seen growing old. Every morning, after buying his penny paper at the corner of the Faubourg Saint Honore, he bought two rolls, and then went to his office, like a culprit who is giving himself up to justice, and got to his desk as quickly as possible, always feeling uneasy; as though he were expecting a rebuke for some neglect of duty of which he might have been guilty.

Nothing had ever occurred to change the monotonous order of his existence, for no event affected him except the work of his office, perquisites, gratuities, and promotion. He never spoke of anything but of his duties, either at the office, or at home—he had married the portionless daughter of one of his colleagues. His mind, which was in a state of atrophy from his depressing daily work, had no other thoughts, hopes or dreams than such as related to the office, and there was a constant source of bitterness that spoilt every pleasure that he might have had, and that was the employment of so many naval officials, tinsmiths, as they were called because of their silver-lace as first-class clerks; and every evening at dinner he discussed the matter hotly with his wife, who shared his angry feelings, and proved to their own satisfaction that it was in every way unjust to give places in Paris to men who ought properly to have been employed in the navy.

He was old now, and had scarcely noticed how his life was passing, for school had merely been exchanged for the office without any intermediate transition, and the ushers, at whom he had formerly trembled, were replaced by his chiefs, of whom he was terribly afraid. When he had to go into the rooms of these official despots, it made him tremble from head to foot, and that constant fear had given him a very awkward manner in their presence, a humble demeanor, and a kind of nervous stammering.

He knew nothing more about Paris than a blind man might know who was led to the same spot by his dog every day; and if he read the account of any uncommon events or scandals in his penny paper, they appeared to him like fantastic tales, which some pressman had made up out of his own head, in order to amuse the inferior employees. He did not read the political news, which his paper frequently altered as the cause which subsidized it might require, for he was not fond of innovations, and when he went through the Avenue of the Champs-Elysees every evening, he looked at the surging crowd of pedestrians, and at the stream of carriages, as a traveller might who has lost his way in a strange country.

As he had completed his thirty years of obligatory service that year, on the first of January, he had had the cross of the Legion of Honor bestowed upon him, which, in the semi-military public offices, is a recompense for the miserable slavery—the official phrase is, loyal services—of unfortunate convicts who are riveted to their desk. That unexpected dignity gave him a high and new idea of his own capacities, and altogether changed him. He immediately left off wearing light trousers and fancy waistcoats, and wore black trousers and long coats, on which his ribbon, which was very broad, showed off better. He got shaved every morning, manicured his nails more carefully, changed his linen every two days, from a legitimate sense of what was proper, and out of respect for the national Order, of which he formed a part, and from that day he was another Caravan, scrupulously clean, majestic and condescending.

At home, he said, "my cross," at every moment, and he had become so proud of it, that he could not bear to see men wearing any other ribbon in their button-holes. He became especially angry on seeing strange orders: "Which nobody ought to be allowed to wear in France," and he bore Chenet a particular grudge, as he met him on a tram-car every evening, wearing a decoration of one kind or another, white, blue, orange, or green.

The conversation of the two men, from the Arc de Triomphe to Neuilly, was always the same, and on that day they discussed, first of all, various local abuses which disgusted them both, and the Mayor of Neuilly received his full share of their censure. Then, as invariably happens in the company of medical man Caravan began to enlarge on the chapter of illness, as in that manner, he hoped to obtain a little gratuitous advice, if he was careful not to show his hand. His mother had been causing him no little anxiety for some time; she had frequent and prolonged fainting fits, and, although she was ninety, she would not take care of herself.

Caravan grew quite tender-hearted when he mentioned her great age, and more than once asked Doctor Chenet, emphasizing the word doctor—although he was not fully qualified, being only an Offcier de Sante—whether he had often met anyone as old as that. And he rubbed his hands with pleasure; not, perhaps, that he cared very much about seeing the good woman last forever here on earth, but because the long duration of his mother's life was, as it were an earnest of old age for himself, and he continued:

"In my family, we last long, and I am sure that, unless I meet with an accident, I shall not die until I am very old."

The doctor looked at him with pity, and glanced for a moment at his neighbor's red face, his short, thick neck, his "corporation," as Chenet called it to himself, his two fat, flabby legs, and the apoplectic rotundity of the old official; and raising the white Panama hat from his head, he said with a snigger:

"I am not so sure of that, old fellow; your mother is as tough as nails, and I should say that your life is not a very good one."

This rather upset Caravan, who did not speak again until the tram put them down at their destination, where the two friends got out, and Chenet asked his friend to have a glass of vermouth at the Cafe du Globe, opposite, which both of them were in the habit of frequenting. The proprietor, who was a friend of theirs, held out to them two fingers, which they shook across the bottles of the counter; and then they joined three of their friends, who were playing dominoes, and who had been there since midday. They exchanged cordial greetings, with the usual question: "Anything new?" And then the three players continued their game, and held out their hands without looking up, when the others wished them "Good-night," and then they both went home to dinner.

Caravan lived in a small two-story house in Courbevaie, near where the roads meet; the ground floor was occupied by a hair-dresser. Two bed rooms, a dining-room and a kitchen, formed the whole of their apartments, and Madame Caravan spent nearly her whole time in cleaning them up, while her daughter, Marie-Louise, who was twelve, and her son, Phillip-Auguste, were running about with all the little, dirty, mischievous brats of the neighborhood, and playing in the gutter.

Caravan had installed his mother, whose avarice was notorious in the neighborhood, and who was terribly thin, in the room above them. She was always cross, and she never passed a day without quarreling and flying into furious tempers. She would apostrophize the neighbors, who were standing at their own doors, the coster-mongers, the street-sweepers, and the street-boys, in the most violent language; and the latter, to have their revenge, used to follow her at a distance when she went out, and call out rude things after her.

A little servant from Normandy, who was incredibly giddy and thoughtless, performed the household work, and slept on the second floor in the same room as the old woman, for fear of anything happening to her in the night.

When Caravan got in, his wife, who suffered from a chronic passion for cleaning, was polishing up the mahogany chairs that were scattered about the room with a piece of flannel. She always wore cotton gloves, and adorned her head with a cap ornamented with many colored ribbons, which was always tilted over one ear; and whenever anyone caught her polishing, sweeping, or washing, she used to say:

"I am not rich; everything is very simple in my house, but cleanliness is my luxury, and that is worth quite as much as any other."

As she was gifted with sound, obstinate, practical common sense, she led her husband in everything. Every evening during dinner, and afterwards when they were in their room, they talked over the business of the office for a long time, and although she was twenty years younger than he was, he confided everything to her as if she took the lead, and followed her advice in every matter.

She had never been pretty, and now she had grown ugly; in addition to that, she was short and thin, while her careless and tasteless way of dressing herself concealed her few small feminine attractions, which might have been brought out if she had possessed any taste in dress. Her skirts were always awry, and she frequently scratched herself, no matter on what part of her person, totally indifferent as to who might see her, and so persistently, that anyone who saw her might think that she was suffering from something like the itch. The only adornments that she allowed herself were silk ribbons, which she had in great profusion, and of various colors mixed together, in the pretentious caps which she wore at home.

As soon as she saw her husband she rose and said, as she kissed his whiskers:

"Did you remember Potin, my dear?"

He fell into a chair, in consternation, for that was the fourth time on which he had forgotten a commission that he had promised to do for her.

"It is a fatality," he said; "it is no good for me to think of it all day long, for I am sure to forget it in the evening."

But as he seemed really so very sorry, she merely said, quietly:

"You will think of it to-morrow, I dare say. Anything new at the office?"

"Yes, a great piece of news; another tinsmith has been appointed second chief clerk." She became very serious, and said:

"So he succeeds Ramon; this was the very post that I wanted you to have. And what about Ramon?"

"He retires on his pension."

She became furious, her cap slid down on her shoulder, and she continued:

"There is nothing more to be done in that shop now. And what is the name of the new commissioner?"

"Bonassot."

She took up the Naval Year Book, which she always kept close at hand, and looked him up.

"'Bonassot-Toulon. Born in 1851. Student Commissioner in 1871. Sub-Commissioner in 1875.' Has he been to sea?" she continued. At that question Caravan's looks cleared up, and he laughed until his sides shook.

"As much as Balin—as much as Baffin, his chief." And he added an old office joke, and laughed more than ever:

"It would not even do to send them by water to inspect the Point-du-Jour, for they would be sick on the penny steamboats on the Seine."

But she remained as serious as if she had not heard him, and then she said in a low voice, as she scratched her chin:

"If we only had a Deputy to fall back upon. When the Chamber hears everything that is going on at the Admiralty, the Minister will be turned out——"

She was interrupted by a terrible noise on the stairs. Marie-Louise and Philippe-Auguste, who had just come in from the gutter, were slapping each other all the way upstairs. Their mother rushed at them furiously, and taking each of them by an arm she dragged them into the room, shaking them vigorously; but as soon as they saw their father, they rushed up to him, and he kissed them affectionately, and taking one of them on each knee, began to talk to them.

Philippe-Auguste was an ugly, ill-kempt little brat, dirty from head to foot, with the face of an idiot, and Marie-Louise was already like her mother—spoke like her, repeated her words, and even imitated her movements. She also asked him whether there was anything fresh at the office, and he replied merrily:

"Your friend, Ramon, who comes and dines here every Sunday, is going to leave us, little one. There is a new second head-clerk."

She looked at her father, and with a precocious child's pity, she said:

"Another man has been put over your head again."

He stopped laughing, and did not reply, and in order to create a diversion, he said, addressing his wife, who was cleaning the windows:

"How is mamma, upstairs?"

Madame Caravan left off rubbing, turned round pulled her cap up, as it had fallen quite on to her back, and said with trembling lips:

"Ah! yes; let us talk about your mother, for she has made a pretty scene. Just imagine: a short time ago Madame Lebaudin, the hairdresser's wife, came upstairs to borrow a packet of starch of me, and, as I was not at home, your mother chased her out as though she were a beggar; but I gave it to the old woman. She pretended not to hear, as she always does when one tells her unpleasant truths, but she is no more deaf than I am, as you know. It is all a sham, and the proof of it is, that she went up to her own room immediately, without saying a word."

Caravan, embarrassed, did not utter a word, and at that moment the little servant came in to announce dinner. In order to let his mother know, he took a broom-handle, which always stood in a corner, and rapped loudly on the ceiling three times, and then they went into the dining-room. Madame Caravan, junior, helped the soup, and waited for the old woman, but she did not come, and as the soup was getting cold, they began to eat slowly, and when their plates were empty, they waited again, and Madame Caravan, who was furious, attacked her husband:

"She does it on purpose, you know that as well as I do. But you always uphold her."

Not knowing which side to take, he sent Marie-Louise to fetch her grandmother, and he sat motionless, with his eyes cast down, while his wife tapped her glass angrily with her knife. In about a minute, the door flew open suddenly, and the child came in again, out of breath and very pale, and said hurriedly:

"Grandmamma has fallen on the floor."

Caravan jumped up, threw his table-napkin down, and rushed upstairs, while his wife, who thought it was some trick of her mother-in-law's, followed more slowly, shrugging her shoulders, as if to express her doubt. When they got upstairs, however, they found the old woman lying at full length in the middle of the room; and when they turned her over, they saw that she was insensible and motionless, while her skin looked more wrinkled and yellow than usual, her eyes were closed, her teeth clenched, and her thin body was stiff.

Caravan knelt down by her, and began to moan.

"My poor mother! my poor mother!" he said. But the other Madame Caravan said:

"Bah! She has only fainted again, that is all, and she has done it to prevent us from dining comfortably, you may be sure of that."

They put her on the bed, undressed her completely, and Caravan, his wife, and the servant began to rub her; but, in spite of their efforts, she did not recover consciousness, so they sent Rosalie, the servant, to fetch Doctor Chenet. He lived a long way off, on the quay, going towards Suresnes, and so it was a considerable time before he arrived. He came at last, however, and, after having looked at the old woman, felt her pulse, and listened for a heart beat, he said: "It is all over."

Caravan threw himself on the body, sobbing violently; he kissed his mother's rigid face, and wept so that great tears fell on the dead woman's face like drops of water, and, naturally, Madame Caravan, junior, showed a decorous amount of grief, and uttered feeble moans as she stood behind her husband, while she rubbed her eyes vigorously.

But, suddenly, Caravan raised himself up, with his thin hair in disorder, and, looking very ugly in his grief, said:

"But—are you sure, doctor? Are you quite sure?"

The doctor stooped over the body, and, handling it with professional dexterity, as a shopkeeper might do, when showing off his goods, he said:

"See, my dear friend, look at her eye."

He raised the eyelid, and the old woman's eye appeared altogether unaltered, unless, perhaps, the pupil was rather larger, and Caravan felt a severe shock at the sight. Then Monsieur Chenet took her thin arm, forced the fingers open, and said, angrily, as if he had been contradicted:

"Just look at her hand; I never make a mistake, you may be quite sure of that."

Caravan fell on the bed, and almost bellowed, while his wife, still whimpering, did what was necessary.

She brought the night-table, on which she spread a towel and placed four wax candles on it, which she lighted; then she took a sprig of box, which was hanging over the chimney glass, and put it between the four candles, in a plate, which she filled with clean water, as she had no holy water. But, after a moment's rapid reflection, she threw a pinch of salt into the water, no doubt thinking she was performing some sort of act of consecration by doing that, and when she had finished, she remained standing motionless, and the doctor, who had been helping her, whispered to her:

"We must take Caravan away."

She nodded assent, and, going up to her husband, who was still on his knees, sobbing, she raised him up by one arm, while Chenet took him by the other.

They put him into a chair, and his wife kissed his forehead, and then began to lecture him. Chenet enforced her words and preached firmness, courage, and resignation—the very things which are always wanting in such overwhelming misfortunes—and then both of them took him by the arms again and led him out.

He was crying like a great child, with convulsive sobs; his arms hanging down, and his legs weak, and he went downstairs without knowing what he was doing, and moving his feet mechanically. They put him into the chair which he always occupied at dinner, in front of his empty soup plate. And there he sat, without moving, his eyes fixed on his glass, and so stupefied with grief, that he could not even think.

In a corner, Madame Caravan was talking with the doctor and asking what the necessary formalities were, as she wanted to obtain practical information. At last, Monsieur Chenet, who appeared to be waiting for something, took up his hat and prepared to go, saying that he had not dined yet; whereupon she exclaimed:

"What! you have not dined? Why, stay here, doctor; don't go. You shall have whatever we have, for, of course, you understand that we do not fare sumptuously." He made excuses and refused, but she persisted, and said: "You really must stay; at times like this, people like to have friends near them, and, besides that, perhaps you will be able to persuade my husband to take some nourishment; he must keep up his strength."

The doctor bowed, and, putting down his hat, he said:

"In that case, I will accept your invitation, madame."

She gave Rosalie, who seemed to have lost her head, some orders, and then sat down, "to pretend to eat," as she said, "to keep the doctor company."

The soup was brought in again, and Monsieur Chenet took two helpings. Then there came a dish of tripe, which exhaled a smell of onions, and which Madame Caravan made up her mind to taste.

"It is excellent," the doctor said, at which she smiled, and, turning to her husband, she said:

"Do take a little, my poor Alfred, only just to put something in your stomach. Remember that you have got to pass the night watching by her!"

He held out his plate, docilely, just as he would have gone to bed, if he had been told to, obeying her in everything, without resistance and without reflection, and he ate; the doctor helped himself three times, while Madame Caravan, from time to time, fished out a large piece at the end of her fork, and swallowed it with a sort of studied indifference.

When a salad bowl full of macaroni was brought in, the doctor said:

"By Jove! That is what I am very fond of." And this time, Madame Caravan helped everybody. She even filled the saucers that were being scraped by the children, who, being left to themselves, had been drinking wine without any water, and were now kicking each other under the table.

Chenet remembered that Rossini, the composer, had been very fond of that Italian dish, and suddenly he exclaimed:

"Why! that rhymes, and one could begin some lines like this:

The Maestro Rossini

Was fond of macaroni."

Nobody listened to him, however. Madame Caravan, who had suddenly grown thoughtful, was thinking of all the probable consequences of the event, while her husband made bread pellets, which he put on the table-cloth, and looked at with a fixed, idiotic stare. As he was devoured by thirst, he was continually raising his glass full of wine to his lips, and the consequence was that his mind, which had been upset by the shock and grief, seemed to become vague, and his ideas danced about as digestion commenced.

The doctor, who, meanwhile, had been drinking away steadily, was getting visibly drunk, and Madame Caravan herself felt the reaction which follows all nervous shocks, and was agitated and excited, and, although she had drunk nothing but water, her head felt rather confused.

Presently, Chenet began to relate stories of death that appeared comical to him. For in that suburb of Paris, that is full of people from the provinces, one finds that indifference towards death which all peasants show, were it even their own father or mother; that want of respect, that unconscious brutality which is so common in the country, and so rare in Paris, and he said:

"Why, I was sent for last week to the Rue du Puteaux, and when I went, I found the patient dead and the whole family calmly sitting beside the bed finishing a bottle of aniseed cordial, which had been bought the night before to satisfy the dying man's fancy."

But Madame Caravan was not listening; she was continually thinking of the inheritance, and Caravan was incapable of understanding anything further.

Coffee was presently served, and it had been made very strong to give them courage. As every cup was well flavored with cognac, it made all their faces red, and confused their ideas still more. To make matters still worse, Chenet suddenly seized the brandy bottle and poured out "a drop for each of them just to wash their mouths out with," as he termed it, and then, without speaking any more, overcome in spite of themselves, by that feeling of animal comfort which alcohol affords after dinner, they slowly sipped the sweet cognac, which formed a yellowish syrup at the bottom of their cups.

The children had fallen asleep, and Rosalie carried them off to bed. Caravan, mechanically obeying that wish to forget oneself which possesses all unhappy persons, helped himself to brandy again several times, and his dull eyes grew bright. At last the doctor rose to go, and seizing his friend's arm, he said:

"Come with me; a little fresh air will do you good. When one is in trouble, one must not remain in one spot."

The other obeyed mechanically, put on his hat, took his stick, and went out, and both of them walked arm-in-arm towards the Seine, in the starlight night.

The air was warm and sweet, for all the gardens in the neighborhood were full of flowers at this season of the year, and their fragrance, which is scarcely perceptible during the day, seemed to awaken at the approach of night, and mingled with the light breezes which blew upon them in the darkness.

The broad avenue with its two rows of gas lamps, that extended as far as the Arc de Triomphe, was deserted and silent, but there was the distant roar of Paris, which seemed to have a reddish vapor hanging over it. It was a kind of continual rumbling, which was at times answered by the whistle of a train in the distance, travelling at full speed to the ocean, through the provinces.

The fresh air on the faces of the two men rather overcame them at first, made the doctor lose his equilibrium a little, and increased Caravan's giddiness, from which he had suffered since dinner. He walked as if he were in a dream; his thoughts were paralyzed, although he felt no great grief, for he was in a state of mental torpor that prevented him from suffering, and he even felt a sense of relief which was increased by the mildness of the night.

When they reached the bridge, they turned to the right, and got the fresh breeze from the river, which rolled along, calm and melancholy, bordered by tall poplar trees, while the stars looked as if they were floating on the water and were-moving with the current. A slight white mist that floated over the opposite banks, filled their lungs with a sensation of cold, and Caravan stopped suddenly, for he was struck by that smell from the water which brought back old memories to his mind. For, in his mind, he suddenly saw his mother again, in Picardy, as he had seen her years before, kneeling in front of their door, and washing the heaps of linen at her side in the stream that ran through their garden. He almost fancied that he could hear the sound of the wooden paddle with which she beat the linen in the calm silence of the country, and her voice, as she called out to him: "Alfred, bring me some soap." And he smelled that odor of running water, of the mist rising from the wet ground, that marshy smell, which he should never forget, and which came back to him on this very evening on which his mother had died.

He stopped, seized with a feeling of despair. A sudden flash seemed to reveal to him the extent of his calamity, and that breath from the river plunged him into an abyss of hopeless grief. His life seemed cut in half, his youth disappeared, swallowed up by that death. All the former days were over and done with, all the recollections of his youth had been swept away; for the future, there would be nobody to talk to him of what had happened in days gone by, of the people he had known of old, of his own part of the country, and of his past life; that was a part of his existence which existed no longer, and the rest might as well end now.

And then he saw "the mother" as she was when young, wearing well-worn dresses, which he remembered for such a long time that they seemed inseparable from her; he recollected her movements, the different tones of her voice, her habits, her predilections, her fits of anger, the wrinkles on her face, the movements of her thin fingers, and all her well-known attitudes, which she would never have again, and clutching hold of the doctor, he began to moan and weep. His thin legs began to tremble, his whole stout body was shaken by his sobs, all he could say was:

"My mother, my poor mother, my poor mother!"

But his companion, who was still drunk, and who intended to finish the evening in certain places of bad repute that he frequented secretly, made him sit down on the grass by the riverside, and left him almost immediately, under the pretext that he had to see a patient.

Caravan went on crying for some time, and when he had got to the end of his tears, when his grief had, so to say, run out, he again felt relief, repose and sudden tranquillity.

The moon had risen, and bathed the horizon in its soft light.

The tall poplar trees had a silvery sheen on them, and the mist on the plain looked like drifting snow; the river, in which the stars were reflected, and which had a sheen as of mother-of-pearl, was gently rippled by the wind. The air was soft and sweet, and Caravan inhaled it almost greedily, and thought that he could perceive a feeling of freshness, of calm and of superhuman consolation pervading him.

He actually resisted that feeling of comfort and relief, and kept on saying to himself: "My poor mother, my poor mother!" and tried to make himself cry, from a kind of conscientious feeling; but he could not succeed in doing so any longer, and those sad thoughts, which had made him sob so bitterly a shore time before, had almost passed away. In a few moments, he rose to go home, and returned slowly, under the influence of that serene night, and with a heart soothed in spite of himself.

When he reached the bridge, he saw that the last tramcar was ready to start, and behind it were the brightly lighted windows of the Cafe du Globe. He felt a longing to tell somebody of his loss, to excite pity, to make himself interesting. He put on a woeful face, pushed open the door, and went up to the counter, where the landlord still was. He had counted on creating a sensation, and had hoped that everybody would get up and come to him with outstretched hands, and say: "Why, what is the matter with you?" But nobody noticed his disconsolate face, so he rested his two elbows on the counter, and, burying his face in his hands, he murmured: "Mon Dieu! Mon Dieu!"

The landlord looked at him and said: "Are you ill, Monsieur Caravan?"

"No, my friend," he replied, "but my mother has just died."

"Ah!" the other exclaimed, and as a customer at the other end of the establishment asked for a glass of Bavarian beer, he went to attend to him, leaving Caravan dumfounded at his want of sympathy.

The three domino players were sitting at the same table which they had occupied before dinner, totally absorbed in their game, and Caravan went up to them, in search of pity, but as none of them appeared to notice him he made up his mind to speak.

"A great misfortune has happened to me since I was here," he said.

All three slightly raised their heads at the same instant, but keeping their eyes fixed on the pieces which they held in their hands.

"What do you say?"

"My mother has just died"; whereupon one of them said:

"Oh! the devil," with that false air of sorrow which indifferent people assume. Another, who could not find anything to say, emitted a sort of sympathetic whistle, shaking his head at the same time, and the third turned to the game again, as if he were saying to himself: "Is that all!"

Caravan had expected some of these expressions that are said to "come from the heart," and when he saw how his news was received, he left the table, indignant at their calmness at their friend's sorrow, although this sorrow had stupefied him so that he scarcely felt it any longer. When he got home his wife was waiting for him in her nightgown, and sitting in a low chair by the open window, still thinking of the inheritance.

"Undress yourself," she said; "we can go on talking."

He raised his head, and looking at the ceiling, said:

"But—there is nobody upstairs."

"I beg your pardon, Rosalie is with her, and you can go and take her place at three o'clock in the morning, when you have had some sleep."

He only partially undressed, however, so as to be ready for anything that might happen, and after tying a silk handkerchief round his head, he lay down to rest, and for some time neither of them spoke. Madame Caravan was thinking.

Her nightcap was adorned with a red bow, and was pushed rather to one side, as was the way with all the caps she wore, and presently she turned towards him and said:

"Do you know whether your mother made a will?"

He hesitated for a moment, and then replied:

"I—I do not think so. No, I am sure that she did not."

His wife looked at him, and she said, in a law, angry tone:

"I call that infamous; here we have been wearing ourselves out for ten years in looking after her, and have boarded and lodged her! Your sister would not have done so much for her, nor I either, if I had known how I was to be rewarded! Yes, it is a disgrace to her memory! I dare say that you will tell me that she paid us, but one cannot pay one's children in ready money for what they do; that obligation is recognized after death; at any rate, that is how honorable people act. So I have had all my worry and trouble for nothing! Oh, that is nice! that is very nice!"

Poor Caravan, who was almost distracted, kept on repeating:

"My dear, my dear, please, please be quiet."

She grew calmer by degrees, and, resuming her usual voice and manner, she continued:

"We must let your sister know to-morrow."

He started, and said:

"Of course we must; I had forgotten all about it; I will send her a telegram the first thing in the morning."

"No," she replied, like a woman who had foreseen everything; "no, do not send it before ten or eleven o'clock, so that we may have time to turn round before she comes. It does not take more than two hours to get here from Charenton, and we can say that you lost your head from grief. If we let her know in the course of the day, that will be soon enough, and will give us time to look round."

Caravan put his hand to his forehead, and, in the came timid voice in which he always spoke of his chief, the very thought of whom made him tremble, he said:

"I must let them know at the office."

"Why?" she replied. "On occasions like this, it is always excusable to forget. Take my advice, and don't let him know; your chief will not be able to say anything to you, and you will put him in a nice fix.

"Oh! yes, that I shall, and he will be in a terrible rage, too, when he notices my absence. Yes, you are right; it is a capital idea, and when I tell him that my mother is dead, he will be obliged to hold his tongue."

And he rubbed his hands in delight at the joke, when he thought of his chief's face; while upstairs lay the body of the dead old woman, with the servant asleep beside it.

But Madame Caravan grew thoughtful, as if she were preoccupied by something which she did not care to mention, and at last she said:

"Your mother had given you her clock, had she not—the girl playing at cup and ball?"

He thought for a moment, and then replied:

"Yes, yes; she said to me (but it was a long time ago, when she first came here): 'I shall leave the clock to you, if you look after me well.'"

Madame Caravan was reassured, and regained her serenity, and said:

"Well, then, you must go and fetch it out of her room, for if we get your sister here, she will prevent us from taking it."

He hesitated.

"Do you think so?"

That made her angry.

"I certainly think so; once it is in our possession, she will know nothing at all about where it came from; it belongs to us. It is just the same with the chest of drawers with the marble top, that is in her room; she gave it me one day when she was in a good temper. We will bring it down at the same time."

Caravan, however, seemed incredulous, and said:

"But, my dear, it is a great responsibility!"

She turned on him furiously.

"Oh! Indeed! Will you never change? You would let your children die of hunger, rather than make a move. Does not that chest of drawers belong to us, as she gave it to me? And if your sister is not satisfied, let her tell me so, me! I don't care a straw for your sister. Come, get up, and we will bring down what your mother gave us, immediately."

Trembling and vanquished, he got out of bed and began to put on his trousers, but she stopped him:

"It is not worth while to dress yourself; your underwear is quite enough. I mean to go as I am."

They both left the room in their night clothes, went upstairs quite noiselessly, opened the door and went into the room, where the four lighted tapers and the plate with the sprig of box alone seemed to be watching the old woman in her rigid repose, for Rosalie, who was lying back in the easy chair with her legs stretched out, her hands folded in her lap, and her head on one side, was also quite motionless, and was snoring with her mouth wide open.

Caravan took the clock, which was one of those grotesque objects that were produced so plentifully under the Empire. A girl in gilt bronze was holding a cup and ball, and the ball formed the pendulum.

"Give that to me," his wife said, "and take the marble slab off the chest of drawers."

He put the marble slab on his shoulder with considerable effort, and they left the room. Caravan had to stoop in the doorway, and trembled as he went downstairs, while his wife walked backwards, so as to light him, and held the candlestick in one hand, carrying the clock under the other arm.

When they were in their own room, she heaved a sigh.

"We have got over the worst part of the job," she said; "so now let us go and fetch the other things."

But the bureau drawers were full of the old woman's wearing apparel, which they must manage to hide somewhere, and Madame Caravan soon thought of a plan.

"Go and get that wooden packing case in the vestibule; it is hardly worth anything, and we may just as well put it here."

And when he had brought it upstairs they began to fill it. One by one they took out all the collars, cuffs, chemises, caps, all the well-worn things that had belonged to the poor woman lying there behind them, and arranged them methodically in the wooden box in such a manner as to deceive Madame Braux, the deceased woman's other child, who would be coming the next day.

When they had finished, they first of all carried the bureau drawers downstairs, and the remaining portion afterwards, each of them holding an end, and it was some time before they could make up their minds where it would stand best; but at last they decided upon their own room, opposite the bed, between the two windows, and as soon as it was in its place Madame Caravan filled it with her own things. The clock was placed on the chimney-piece in the dining-room, and they looked to see what the effect was, and were both delighted with it and agreed that nothing could be better. Then they retired, she blew out the candle, and soon everybody in the house was asleep.

It was broad daylight when. Caravan opened his eyes again. His mind was rather confused when he woke up, and he did not clearly remember what had happened for a few minutes; when he did, he felt a weight at his heart, and jumped out of bed, almost ready to cry again.

He hastened to the room overhead, where Rosalie was still sleeping in the same position as the night before, not having awakened once. He sent her to do her work, put fresh tapers in the place of those that had burnt out, and then he looked at his mother, revolving in his brain those apparently profound thoughts, those religious and philosophical commonplaces which trouble people of mediocre intelligence in the presence of death.

But, as his wife was calling him, he went downstairs. She had written out a list of what had to be done during the morning, and he was horrified when he saw the memorandum:

1. Report the death at the mayor's office. 2. See the doctor who had attended her. 3. Order the coffin. 4. Give notice at the church. 5. Go to the undertaker. 6. Order the notices of her death at the printer's. 7. Go to the lawyer. 8. Telegraph the news to all the family.

Besides all this, there were a number of small commissions; so he took his hat and went out. As the news had spread abroad, Madame Caravan's female friends and neighbors soon began to come in and begged to be allowed to see the body. There had been a scene between husband and wife at the hairdresser's on the ground floor about the matter, while a customer was being shaved. The wife, who was knitting steadily, said: "Well, there is one less, and as great a miser as one ever meets with. I certainly did not care for her; but, nevertheless, I must go and have a look at her."

The husband, while lathering his patient's chin, said: "That is another queer fancy! Nobody but a woman would think of such a thing. It is not enough for them to worry you during life, but they cannot even leave you at peace when you are dead:" But his wife, without being in the least disconcerted, replied: "The feeling is stronger than I am, and I must go. It has been on me since the morning. If I were not to see her, I should think about it all my life; but when I have had a good look at her, I shall be satisfied."

The knight of the razor shrugged his shoulders and remarked in a low voice to the gentleman whose cheek he was scraping: "I just ask you, what sort of ideas do you think these confounded females have? I should not amuse myself by going to see a corpse!" But his wife had heard him and replied very quietly: "But it is so, it is so." And then, putting her knitting on the counter, she went upstairs to the first floor, where she met two other neighbors, who had just come, and who were discussing the event with Madame Caravan, who was giving them the details, and they all went together to the death chamber. The four women went in softly, and, one after the other, sprinkled the bed clothes with the salt water, knelt down, made the sign of the cross while they mumbled a prayer. Then they rose from their knees and looked for some time at the corpse with round, wide-open eyes and mouths partly open, while the daughter-in-law of the dead woman, with her handkerchief to her face, pretended to be sobbing piteously.

When she turned about to walk away whom should she perceive standing close to the door but Marie-Louise and Philippe-Auguste, who were curiously taking stock of all that was going on. Then, forgetting her pretended grief, she threw herself upon them with uplifted hands, crying out in a furious voice, "Will you get out of this, you horrid brats!"

Ten minutes later, going upstairs again with another contingent of neighbors, she prayed, wept profusely, performed all her duties, and found once more her two children, who had followed her upstairs. She again boxed their ears soundly, but the next time she paid no heed to them, and at each fresh arrival of visitors the two urchins always followed in the wake, kneeling down in a corner and imitating slavishly everything they saw their mother do.

When the afternoon came the crowds of inquisitive people began to diminish, and soon there were no more visitors. Madame Caravan, returning to her own apartments, began to make the necessary preparations for the funeral ceremony, and the deceased was left alone.

The window of the room was open. A torrid heat entered, along with clouds of dust; the flames of the four candles were flickering beside the immobile corpse, and upon the cloth which covered the face, the closed eyes, the two stretched-out hands, small flies alighted, came, went and careered up and down incessantly, being the only companions of the old woman for the time being.

Marie-Louise and Philippe-Auguste, however, had now left the house and were running up and down the street. They were soon surrounded by their playmates, by little girls especially, who were older and who were much more interested in all the mysteries of life, asking questions as if they were grown people.

"Then your grandmother is dead?" "Yes, she died yesterday evening." "What does a dead person look like?"

Then Marie began to explain, telling all about the candles, the sprig of box and the face of the corpse. It was not long before great curiosity was aroused in the minds of all the children, and they asked to be allowed to go upstairs to look at the departed.

Marie-Louise at once organized a first expedition, consisting of five girls and two boys—the biggest and the most courageous. She made them take off their shoes so that they might not be discovered. The troupe filed into the house and mounted the stairs as stealthily as an army of mice.

Once in the chamber, the little girl, imitating her mother, regulated the ceremony. She solemnly walked in advance of her comrades, went down on her knees, made the sign of the cross, moved her lips as in prayer, rose, sprinkled the bed, and while the children, all crowded together, were approaching—frightened and curious and eager to look at the face and hands of the deceased—she began suddenly to simulate sobbing and to bury her eyes in her little handkerchief. Then, becoming instantly consoled, on thinking of the other children who were downstairs waiting at the door, she ran downstairs followed by the rest, returning in a minute with another group, then a third; for all the little ragamuffins of the countryside, even to the little beggars in rags, had congregated in order to participate in this new pleasure; and each time she repeated her mother's grimaces with absolute perfection.

At length, however, she became tired. Some game or other drew the children away from the house, and the old grandmother was left alone, forgotten suddenly by everybody.

The room was growing dark, and upon the dry and rigid features of the corpse the fitful flames of the candles cast patches of light.

Towards 8 o'clock Caravan ascended to the chamber of death, closed the windows and renewed the candles. He was now quite composed on entering the room, accustomed already to regard the corpse as though it had been there for months. He even went the length of declaring that, as yet, there were no signs of decomposition, making this remark just at the moment when he and his wife were about to sit down at table. "Pshaw!" she responded, "she is now stark and stiff; she will keep for a year."

The soup was eaten in silence. The children, who had been left to themselves all day, now worn out by fatigue, were sleeping soundly on their chairs, and nobody ventured to break the silence.

Suddenly the flame of the lamp went down. Madame Caravan immediately turned up the wick, a hollow sound ensued, and the light went out. They had forgotten to buy oil. To send for it now to the grocer's would keep back the dinner, and they began to look for candles, but none were to be found except the tapers which had been placed upon the table upstairs in the death chamber.

Madame Caravan, always prompt in her decisions, quickly despatched Marie-Louise to fetch two, and her return was awaited in total darkness.

The footsteps of the girl who had ascended the stairs were distinctly heard. There was silence for a few seconds and then the child descended precipitately. She threw open the door and in a choking voice murmured: "Oh! papa, grandmamma is dressing herself!"

Caravan bounded to his feet with such precipitance that his chair fell over against the wall. He stammered out: "You say? . . . . What are you saying?"

But Marie-Louise, gasping with emotion, repeated: "Grand—grand —grandmamma is putting on her clothes, she is coming downstairs."

Caravan rushed boldly up the staircase, followed by his wife, dumfounded; but he came to a standstill before the door of the second floor, overcome with terror, not daring to enter. What was he going to see? Madame Caravan, more courageous, turned the handle of the door and stepped forward into the room.

The old woman was standing up. In awakening from her lethargic sleep, before even regaining full consciousness, in turning upon her side and raising herself on her elbow, she had extinguished three of the candles which burned near the bed. Then, gaining strength, she got off the bed and began to look for her clothes. The absence of her chest of drawers had at first worried her, but, after a little, she had succeeded in finding her things at the bottom of the wooden box, and was now quietly dressing. She emptied the plateful of water, replaced the sprig of box behind the looking-glass, and arranged the chairs in their places, and was ready to go downstairs when there appeared before her her son and daughter-in-law.

Caravan rushed forward, seized her by the hands, embraced her with tears in his eyes, while his wife, who was behind him, repeated in a hypocritical tone of voice: "Oh, what a blessing! oh, what a blessing!"

But the old woman, without being at all moved, without even appearing to understand, rigid as a statue, and with glazed eyes, simply asked: "Will dinner soon be ready?"

He stammered out, not knowing what he said:

"Oh, yes, mother, we have been waiting for you."

And with an alacrity unusual in him, he took her arm, while Madame Caravan, the younger, seized the candle and lighted them downstairs, walking backwards in front of them, step by step, just as she had done the previous night for her husband, who was carrying the marble.

On reaching the first floor, she almost ran against people who were ascending the stairs. It was the Charenton family, Madame Braux, followed by her husband.

The wife, tall and stout, with a prominent stomach, opened wide her terrified eyes and was ready to make her escape. The husband, a socialist shoemaker, a little hairy man, the perfect image of a monkey, murmured quite unconcerned: "Well, what next? Is she resurrected?"

As soon as Madame Caravan recognized them, she made frantic gestures to them; then, speaking aloud, she said: "Why, here you are! What a pleasant surprise!"

But Madame Braux, dumfounded, understood nothing. She responded in a low voice: "It was your telegram that brought us; we thought that all was over."

Her husband, who was behind her, pinched her to make her keep silent. He added with a sly laugh, which his thick beard concealed: "It was very kind of you to invite us here. We set out post haste," which remark showed the hostility which had for a long time reigned between the households. Then, just as the old woman reached the last steps, he pushed forward quickly and rubbed his hairy face against her cheeks, shouting in her ear, on account of her deafness: "How well you look, mother; sturdy as usual, hey!"

Madame Braux, in her stupefaction at seeing the old woman alive, whom they all believed to be dead, dared not even embrace her; and her enormous bulk blocked up the passageway and hindered the others from advancing. The old woman, uneasy and suspicious, but without speaking, looked at everyone around her; and her little gray eyes, piercing and hard, fixed themselves now on one and now on the other, and they were so full of meaning that the children became frightened.

Caravan, to explain matters, said: "She has been somewhat ill, but she is better now; quite well, indeed, are you not, mother?"

Then the good woman, continuing to walk, replied in a husky voice, as though it came from a distance: "It was syncope. I heard you all the while."

An embarrassing silence followed. They entered the dining-room, and in a few minutes all sat down to an improvised dinner.

Only M. Braux had retained his self-possession. His gorilla features grinned wickedly, while he let fall some words of double meaning which painfully disconcerted everyone.

But the door bell kept ringing every second, and Rosalie, distracted, came to call Caravan, who rushed out, throwing down his napkin. His brother-in-law even asked him whether it was not one of his reception days, to which he stammered out in answer: "No, only a few packages; nothing more."

A parcel was brought in, which he began to open carelessly, and the mourning announcements with black borders appeared unexpectedly. Reddening up to the very eyes, he closed the package hurriedly and pushed it under his waistcoat.

His mother had not seen it! She was looking intently at her clock which stood on the mantelpiece, and the embarrassment increased in midst of a dead silence. Turning her wrinkled face towards her daughter, the old woman, in whose eyes gleamed malice, said: "On Monday you must take me away from here, so that I can see your little girl. I want so much to see her." Madame Braux, her features all beaming, exclaimed: "Yes, mother, that I will," while Madame Caravan, the younger, who had turned pale, was ready to faint with annoyance. The two men, however, gradually drifted into conversation and soon became embroiled in a political discussion. Braux maintained the most revolutionary and communistic doctrines, his eyes glowing, and gesticulating and throwing about his arms. "Property, sir," he said, "is a robbery perpetrated on the working classes; the land is the common property of every man; hereditary rights are an infamy and a disgrace." But here he suddenly stopped, looking as if he had just said something foolish, then added in softer tones: "But this is not the proper moment to discuss such things."

The door was opened and Dr. Chenet appeared. For a moment he seemed bewildered, but regaining his usual smirking expression of countenance, he jauntily approached the old woman and said: "Aha! mamma; you are better to-day. Oh! I never had any doubt but you would come round again; in fact, I said to myself as I was mounting the staircase, 'I have an idea that I shall find the old lady on her feet once more';" and as he patted her gently on the back: "Ah! she is as solid as the Pont-Neuf, she will bury us all; see if she does not."

He sat down, accepted the coffee that was offered him, and soon began to join in the conversation of the two men, backing up Braux, for he himself had been mixed up in the Commune.

The old woman, now feeling herself fatigued, wished to retire. Caravan rushed forward. She looked him steadily in the eye and said: "You, you must carry my clock and chest of drawers upstairs again without a moment's delay." "Yes, mamma," he replied, gasping; "yes, I will do so." The old woman then took the arm of her daughter and withdrew from the room. The two Caravans remained astounded, silent, plunged in the deepest despair, while Braux rubbed his hands and sipped his coffee gleefully.

Suddenly Madame Caravan, consumed with rage, rushed at him, exclaiming: "You are a thief, a footpad, a cur! I would spit in your face! I—I —would——" She could find nothing further to say, suffocating as she was with rage, while he went on sipping his coffee with a smile.

His wife returning just then, Madame Caravan attacked her sister-in-law, and the two women—the one with her enormous bulk, the other epileptic and spare, with changed voices and trembling hands flew at one another with words of abuse.

Chenet and Braux now interposed, and the latter, taking his better half by the shoulders, pushed her out of the door before him, shouting: "Go on, you slut; you talk too much"; and the two were heard in the street quarrelling until they disappeared from sight.

M. Chenet also took his departure, leaving the Caravans alone, face to face. The husband fell back on his chair, and with the cold sweat standing out in beads on his temples, murmured: "What shall I say to my chief to-morrow?"

BESIDE SCHOPENHAUER'S CORPSE

He was slowly dying, as consumptives die. I saw him each day, about two o'clock, sitting beneath the hotel windows on a bench in the promenade, looking out on the calm sea. He remained for some time without moving, in the heat of the sun, gazing mournfully at the Mediterranean. Every now and then, he cast a glance at the lofty mountains with beclouded summits that shut in Mentone; then, with a very slow movement, he would cross his long legs, so thin that they seemed like two bones, around which fluttered the cloth of his trousers, and he would open a book, always the same book. And then he did not stir any more, but read on, read on with his eye and his mind; all his wasting body seemed to read, all his soul plunged, lost, disappeared, in this book, up to the hour when the cool air made him cough a little. Then, he got up and reentered the hotel.

He was a tall German, with fair beard, who breakfasted and dined in his own room, and spoke to nobody.

A vague, curiosity attracted me to him. One day, I sat down by his side, having taken up a book, too, to keep up appearances, a volume of Musset's poems.

And I began to look through "Rolla."

Suddenly, my neighbor said to me, in good French:

"Do you know German, monsieur?"

"Not at all, monsieur."

"I am sorry for that. Since chance has thrown us side by side, I could have lent you, I could have shown you, an inestimable thing—this book which I hold in my hand."

"What is it, pray?"

"It is a copy of my master, Schopenhauer, annotated with his own hand. All the margins, as you may see, are covered with his handwriting."

I took the book from him reverently, and I gazed at these forms incomprehensible to me, but which revealed the immortal thoughts of the greatest shatterer of dreams who had ever dwelt on earth.

And Musset's verses arose in my memory:

"Hast thou found out, Voltaire, that it is bliss to die,

And does thy hideous smile over thy bleached bones fly?"

And involuntarily I compared the childish sarcasm, the religious sarcasm of Voltaire with the irresistible irony of the German philosopher whose influence is henceforth ineffaceable.

Let us protest and let us be angry, let us be indignant, or let us be enthusiastic, Schopenhauer has marked humanity with the seal of his disdain and of his disenchantment.

A disabused pleasure-seeker, he overthrew beliefs, hopes, poetic ideals and chimeras, destroyed the aspirations, ravaged the confidence of souls, killed love, dragged down the chivalrous worship of women, crushed the illusions of hearts, and accomplished the most gigantic task ever attempted by scepticism. He spared nothing with his mocking spirit, and exhausted everything. And even to-day those who execrate him seem to carry in their own souls particles of his thought.

"So, then, you were intimately acquainted with Schopenhauer?" I said to the German.

He smiled sadly.

"Up to the time of his death, monsieur."

And he spoke to me about the philosopher and told me about the almost supernatural impression which this strange being made on all who came near him.

He gave me an account of the interview of the old iconoclast with a French politician, a doctrinaire Republican, who wanted to get a glimpse of this man, and found him in a noisy tavern, seated in the midst of his disciples, dry, wrinkled, laughing with an unforgettable laugh, attacking and tearing to pieces ideas and beliefs with a single word, as a dog tears with one bite of his teeth the tissues with which he plays.

He repeated for me the comment of this Frenchman as he went away, astonished and terrified: "I thought I had spent an hour with the devil."

Then he added:

"He had, indeed, monsieur, a frightful smile, which terrified us even after his death. I can tell you an anecdote about it that is not generally known, if it would interest you."

And he began, in a languid voice, interrupted by frequent fits of coughing.

"Schopenhauer had just died, and it was arranged that we should watch, in turn, two by two, till morning.

"He was lying in a large apartment, very simple, vast and gloomy. Two wax candles were burning on the stand by the bedside.

"It was midnight when I went on watch, together with one of our comrades. The two friends whom we replaced had left the apartment, and we came and sat down at the foot of the bed.

"The face was not changed. It was laughing. That pucker which we knew so well lingered still around the corners of the lips, and it seemed to us that he was about to open his eyes, to move and to speak. His thought, or rather his thoughts, enveloped us. We felt ourselves more than ever in the atmosphere of his genius, absorbed, possessed by him. His domination seemed to be even more sovereign now that he was dead. A feeling of mystery was blended with the power of this incomparable spirit.

"The bodies of these men disappear, but they themselves remain; and in the night which follows the cessation of their heart's pulsation I assure you, monsieur, they are terrifying.

"And in hushed tones we talked about him, recalling to mind certain sayings, certain formulas of his, those startling maxims which are like jets of flame flung, in a few words, into the darkness of the Unknown Life.

"'It seems to me that he is going to speak,' said my comrade. And we stared with uneasiness bordering on fear at the motionless face, with its eternal laugh. Gradually, we began to feel ill at ease, oppressed, on the point of fainting. I faltered:

"'I don't know what is the matter with me, but, I assure you I am not well.'

"And at that moment we noticed that there was an unpleasant odor from the corpse.

"Then, my comrade suggested that we should go into the adjoining room, and leave the door open; and I assented to his proposal.

"I took one of the wax candles which burned on the stand, and I left the second behind. Then we went and sat down at the other end of the adjoining apartment, in such a position that we could see the bed and the corpse, clearly revealed by the light.

"But he still held possession of us. One would have said that his immaterial essence, liberated, free, all-powerful and dominating, was flitting around us. And sometimes, too, the dreadful odor of the decomposed body came toward us and penetrated us, sickening and indefinable.

"Suddenly a shiver passed through our bones: a sound, a slight sound, came from the death-chamber. Immediately we fixed our glances on him, and we saw, yes, monsieur, we saw distinctly, both of us, something white pass across the bed, fall on the carpet, and vanish under an armchair.

"We were on our feet before we had time to think of anything, distracted by stupefying terror, ready to run away. Then we stared at each other. We were horribly pale. Our hearts throbbed fiercely enough to have raised the clothing on our chests. I was the first to speak:

"'Did you see?'

"'Yes, I saw.'

"'Can it be that he is not dead?'

"'Why, when the body is putrefying?'

"'What are we to do?'

"My companion said in a hesitating tone:

"'We must go and look.'

"I took our wax candle and entered first, glancing into all the dark corners in the large apartment. Nothing was moving now, and I approached the bed. But I stood transfixed with stupor and fright:

"Schopenhauer was no longer laughing! He was grinning in a horrible fashion, with his lips pressed together and deep hollows in his cheeks. I stammered out:

"'He is not dead!'

"But the terrible odor ascended to my nose and stifled me. And I no longer moved, but kept staring fixedly at him, terrified as if in the presence of an apparition.

"Then my companion, having seized the other wax candle, bent forward. Next, he touched my arm without uttering a word. I followed his glance, and saw on the ground, under the armchair by the side of the bed, standing out white on the dark carpet, and open as if to bite, Schopenhauer's set of artificial teeth.

"The work of decomposition, loosening the jaws, had made it jump out of the mouth.

"I was really frightened that day, monsieur."

And as the sun was sinking toward the glittering sea, the consumptive German rose from his seat, gave me a parting bow, and retired into the hotel.

VOLUME III.

MISS HARRIET

There were seven of us on a drag, four women and three men; one of the latter sat on the box seat beside the coachman. We were ascending, at a snail's pace, the winding road up the steep cliff along the coast.

Setting out from Etretat at break of day in order to visit the ruins of Tancarville, we were still half asleep, benumbed by the fresh air of the morning. The women especially, who were little accustomed to these early excursions, half opened and closed their eyes every moment, nodding their heads or yawning, quite insensible to the beauties of the dawn.

It was autumn. On both sides of the road stretched the bare fields, yellowed by the stubble of wheat and oats which covered the soil like a beard that had been badly shaved. The moist earth seemed to steam. Larks were singing high up in the air, while other birds piped in the bushes.

The sun rose at length in front of us, bright red on the plane of the horizon, and in proportion as it ascended, growing clearer from minute to minute, the country seemed to awake, to smile, to shake itself like a young girl leaving her bed in her white robe of vapor. The Comte d'Etraille, who was seated on the box, cried:

"Look! look! a hare!" and he extended his arm toward the left, pointing to a patch of clover. The animal scurried along, almost hidden by the clover, only its large ears showing. Then it swerved across a furrow, stopped, started off again at full speed, changed its course, stopped anew, uneasy, spying out every danger, uncertain what route to take, when suddenly it began to run with great bounds, disappearing finally in a large patch of beet-root. All the men had waked up to watch the course of the animal.

Rene Lamanoir exclaimed:

"We are not at all gallant this morning," and; regarding his neighbor, the little Baroness de Serennes, who struggled against sleep, he said to her in a low tone: "You are thinking of your husband, baroness. Reassure yourself; he will not return before Saturday, so you have still four days."

She answered with a sleepy smile:

"How stupid you are!" Then, shaking off her torpor, she added: "Now, let somebody say something to make us laugh. You, Monsieur Chenal, who have the reputation of having had more love affairs than the Due de Richelieu, tell us a love story in which you have played a part; anything you like."

Leon Chenal, an old painter, who had once been very handsome, very strong, very proud of his physique and very popular with women, took his long white beard in his hand and smiled. Then, after a few moments' reflection, he suddenly became serious.

"Ladies, it will not be an amusing tale, for I am going to relate to you the saddest love affair of my life, and I sincerely hope that none of my friends may ever pass through a similar experience.

"I was twenty-five years of age and was pillaging along the coast of Normandy. I call 'pillaging' wandering about, with a knapsack on one's back, from inn to inn, under the pretext of making studies and sketching landscapes. I knew nothing more enjoyable than that happy-go-lucky wandering life, in which one is perfectly free, without shackles of any kind, without care, without preoccupation, without thinking even of the morrow. One goes in any direction one pleases, without any guide save his fancy, without any counsellor save his eyes. One stops because a running brook attracts one, because the smell of potatoes frying tickles one's olfactories on passing an inn. Sometimes it is the perfume of clematis which decides one in his choice or the roguish glance of the servant at an inn. Do not despise me for my affection for these rustics. These girls have a soul as well as senses, not to mention firm cheeks and fresh lips; while their hearty and willing kisses have the flavor of wild fruit. Love is always love, come whence it may. A heart that beats at your approach, an eye that weeps when you go away are things so rare, so sweet, so precious that they must never be despised.

"I have had rendezvous in ditches full of primroses, behind the cow stable and in barns among the straw, still warm from the heat of the day. I have recollections of coarse gray cloth covering supple peasant skin and regrets for simple, frank kisses, more delicate in their unaffected sincerity than the subtle favors of charming and distinguished women.

"But what one loves most amid all these varied adventures is the country, the woods, the rising of the sun, the twilight, the moonlight. These are, for the painter, honeymoon trips with Nature. One is alone with her in that long and quiet association. You go to sleep in the fields, amid marguerites and poppies, and when you open your eyes in the full glare of the sunlight you descry in the distance the little village with its pointed clock tower which sounds the hour of noon.

"You sit down by the side of a spring which gushes out at the foot of an oak, amid a growth of tall, slender weeds, glistening with life. You go down on your knees, bend forward and drink that cold, pellucid water which wets your mustache and nose; you drink it with a physical pleasure, as though you kissed the spring, lip to lip. Sometimes, when you find a deep hole along the course of these tiny brooks, you plunge in quite naked, and you feel on your skin, from head to foot, as it were, an icy and delicious caress, the light and gentle quivering of the stream.

"You are gay on the hills, melancholy on the edge of ponds, inspired when the sun is setting in an ocean of blood-red clouds and casts red reflections or the river. And at night, under the moon, which passes across the vault of heaven, you think of a thousand strange things which would never have occurred to your mind under the brilliant light of day.

"So, in wandering through the same country where we, are this year, I came to the little village of Benouville, on the cliff between Yport and Etretat. I came from Fecamp, following the coast, a high coast as straight as a wall, with its projecting chalk cliffs descending perpendicularly into the sea. I had walked since early morning on the short grass, smooth and yielding as a carpet, that grows on the edge of the cliff. And, singing lustily, I walked with long strides, looking sometimes at the slow circling flight of a gull with its white curved wings outlined on the blue sky, sometimes at the brown sails of a fishing bark on the green sea. In short, I had passed a happy day, a day of liberty and of freedom from care.

"A little farmhouse where travellers were lodged was pointed out to me, a kind of inn, kept by a peasant woman, which stood in the centre of a Norman courtyard surrounded by a double row of beeches.

"Leaving the coast, I reached the hamlet, which was hemmed in by great trees, and I presented myself at the house of Mother Lecacheur.

"She was an old, wrinkled and stern peasant woman, who seemed always to receive customers under protest, with a kind of defiance.

"It was the month of May. The spreading apple trees covered the court with a shower of blossoms which rained unceasingly both upon people and upon the grass.

"I said: 'Well, Madame Lecacheur, have you a room for me?'

"Astonished to find that I knew her name, she answered:

"'That depends; everything is let, but all the same I can find out."

"In five minutes we had come to an agreement, and I deposited my bag upon the earthen floor of a rustic room, furnished with a bed, two chairs, a table and a washbowl. The room looked into the large, smoky kitchen, where the lodgers took their meals with the people of the farm and the landlady, who was a widow.

"I washed my hands, after which I went out. The old woman was making a chicken fricassee for dinner in the large fireplace in which hung the iron pot, black with smoke.

"'You have travellers, then, at the present time?' said I to her.

"She answered in an offended tone of voice:

"'I have a lady, an English lady, who has reached years of maturity. She occupies the other room.'

"I obtained, by means of an extra five sous a day, the privilege of dining alone out in the yard when the weather was fine.

"My place was set outside the door, and I was beginning to gnaw the lean limbs of the Normandy chicken, to drink the clear cider and to munch the hunk of white bread, which was four days old but excellent.

"Suddenly the wooden gate which gave on the highway was opened, and a strange lady directed her steps toward the house. She was very thin, very tall, so tightly enveloped in a red Scotch plaid shawl that one might have supposed she had no arms, if one had not seen a long hand appear just above the hips, holding a white tourist umbrella. Her face was like that of a mummy, surrounded with curls of gray hair, which tossed about at every step she took and made me think, I know not why, of a pickled herring in curl papers. Lowering her eyes, she passed quickly in front of me and entered the house.

"That singular apparition cheered me. She undoubtedly was my neighbor, the English lady of mature age of whom our hostess had spoken.

"I did not see her again that day. The next day, when I had settled myself to commence painting at the end of that beautiful valley which you know and which extends as far as Etretat, I perceived, on lifting my eyes suddenly, something singular standing on the crest of the cliff, one might have said a pole decked out with flags. It was she. On seeing me, she suddenly disappeared. I reentered the house at midday for lunch and took my seat at the general table, so as to make the acquaintance of this odd character. But she did not respond to my polite advances, was insensible even to my little attentions. I poured out water for her persistently, I passed her the dishes with great eagerness. A slight, almost imperceptible, movement of the head and an English word, murmured so low that I did not understand it, were her only acknowledgments.

"I ceased occupying myself with her, although she had disturbed my thoughts.

"At the end of three days I knew as much about her as did Madame Lecacheur herself.

"She was called Miss Harriet. Seeking out a secluded village in which to pass the summer, she had been attracted to Benouville some six months before and did not seem disposed to leave it. She never spoke at table, ate rapidly, reading all the while a small book of the Protestant propaganda. She gave a copy of it to everybody. The cure himself had received no less than four copies, conveyed by an urchin to whom she had paid two sous commission. She said sometimes to our hostess abruptly, without preparing her in the least for the declaration:

"'I love the Saviour more than all. I admire him in all creation; I adore him in all nature; I carry him always in my heart.'

"And she would immediately present the old woman with one of her tracts which were destined to convert the universe.

"In, the village she was not liked. In fact, the schoolmaster having pronounced her an atheist, a kind of stigma attached to her. The cure, who had been consulted by Madame Lecacheur, responded:

"'She is a heretic, but God does not wish the death of the sinner, and I believe her to be a person of pure morals.'

"These words, 'atheist,' 'heretic,' words which no one can precisely define, threw doubts into some minds. It was asserted, however, that this English woman was rich and that she had passed her life in travelling through every country in the world because her family had cast her off. Why had her family cast her off? Because of her impiety, of course!

"She was, in fact, one of those people of exalted principles; one of those opinionated puritans, of which England produces so many; one of those good and insupportable old maids who haunt the tables d'hote of every hotel in Europe, who spoil Italy, poison Switzerland, render the charming cities of the Mediterranean uninhabitable, carry everywhere their fantastic manias their manners of petrified vestals, their indescribable toilets and a certain odor of india-rubber which makes one believe that at night they are slipped into a rubber casing.

"Whenever I caught sight of one of these individuals in a hotel I fled like the birds who see a scarecrow in a field.

"This woman, however, appeared so very singular that she did not displease me.

"Madame Lecacheur, hostile by instinct to everything that was not rustic, felt in her narrow soul a kind of hatred for the ecstatic declarations of the old maid. She had found a phrase by which to describe her, a term of contempt that rose to her lips, called forth by I know not what confused and mysterious mental ratiocination. She said: 'That woman is a demoniac.' This epithet, applied to that austere and sentimental creature, seemed to me irresistibly droll. I myself never called her anything now but 'the demoniac,' experiencing a singular pleasure in pronouncing aloud this word on perceiving her.

"One day I asked Mother Lecacheur: 'Well, what is our demoniac about to-day?'

"To which my rustic friend replied with a shocked air:

"'What do you think, sir? She picked up a toad which had had its paw crushed and carried it to her room and has put it in her washbasin and bandaged it as if it were a man. If that is not profanation I should like to know what is!'

"On another occasion, when walking along the shore she bought a large fish which had just been caught, simply to throw it back into the sea again. The sailor from whom she had bought it, although she paid him handsomely, now began to swear, more exasperated, indeed, than if she had put her hand into his pocket and taken his money. For more than a month he could not speak of the circumstance without becoming furious and denouncing it as an outrage. Oh, yes! She was indeed a demoniac, this Miss Harriet, and Mother Lecacheur must have had an inspiration in thus christening her.

"The stable boy, who was called Sapeur, because he had served in Africa in his youth, entertained other opinions. He said with a roguish air: 'She is an old hag who has seen life.'

"If the poor woman had but known!

"The little kind-hearted Celeste did not wait upon her willingly, but I was never able to understand why. Probably her only reason was that she was a stranger, of another race; of a different tongue and of another religion. She was, in fact, a demoniac!

"She passed her time wandering about the country, adoring and seeking God in nature. I found her one evening on her knees in a cluster of bushes. Having discovered something red through the leaves, I brushed aside the branches, and Miss Harriet at once rose to her feet, confused at having been found thus, fixing on me terrified eyes like those of an owl surprised in open day.

"Sometimes, when I was working among the rocks, I would suddenly descry her on the edge of the cliff like a lighthouse signal. She would be gazing in rapture at the vast sea glittering in the sunlight and the boundless sky with its golden tints. Sometimes I would distinguish her at the end of the valley, walking quickly with her elastic English step, and I would go toward her, attracted by I know not what, simply to see her illuminated visage, her dried-up, ineffable features, which seemed to glow with inward and profound happiness.

"I would often encounter her also in the corner of a field, sitting on the grass under the shadow of an apple tree, with her little religious booklet lying open on her knee while she gazed out at the distance.

"I could not tear myself away from that quiet country neighborhood, to which I was attached by a thousand links of love for its wide and peaceful landscape. I was happy in this sequestered farm, far removed from everything, but in touch with the earth, the good, beautiful, green earth. And—must I avow it?—there was, besides, a little curiosity which retained me at the residence of Mother Lecacheur. I wished to become acquainted a little with this strange Miss Harriet and to know what transpires in the solitary souls of those wandering old English women.

"We became acquainted in a rather singular manner. I had just finished a study which appeared to me to be worth something, and so it was, as it sold for ten thousand francs fifteen years later. It was as simple, however, as two and two make four and was not according to academic rules. The whole right side of my canvas represented a rock, an enormous rock, covered with sea-wrack, brown, yellow and red, across which the sun poured like a stream of oil. The light fell upon the rock as though it were aflame without the sun, which was at my back, being visible. That was all. A first bewildering study of blazing, gorgeous light.

"On the left was the sea, not the blue sea, the slate-colored sea, but a sea of jade, greenish, milky and solid beneath the deep-colored sky.

"I was so pleased with my work that I danced from sheer delight as I carried it back to the inn. I would have liked the whole world to see it at once. I can remember that I showed it to a cow that was browsing by the wayside, exclaiming as I did so: 'Look at that, my old beauty; you will not often see its like again.'

"When I had reached the house I immediately called out to Mother Lecacheur, shouting with all my might:

"'Hullo, there! Mrs. Landlady, come here and look at this.'

"The rustic approached and looked at my work with her stupid eyes which distinguished nothing and could not even tell whether the picture represented an ox or a house.

"Miss Harriet just then came home, and she passed behind me just as I was holding out my canvas at arm's length, exhibiting it to our landlady. The demoniac could not help but see it, for I took care to exhibit the thing in such a way that it could not escape her notice. She stopped abruptly and stood motionless, astonished. It was her rock which was depicted, the one which she climbed to dream away her time undisturbed.

"She uttered a British 'Aoh,' which was at once so accentuated and so flattering that I turned round to her, smiling, and said:

"'This is my latest study, mademoiselle.'

"She murmured rapturously, comically and tenderly:

"'Oh! monsieur, you understand nature as a living thing.'

"I colored and was more touched by that compliment than if it had come from a queen. I was captured, conquered, vanquished. I could have embraced her, upon my honor.

"I took my seat at table beside her as usual. For the first time she spoke, thinking aloud:

"'Oh! I do love nature.'

"I passed her some bread, some water, some wine. She now accepted these with a little smile of a mummy. I then began to talk about the scenery.

"After the meal we rose from the table together and walked leisurely across the courtyard; then, attracted doubtless by the fiery glow which the setting sun cast over the surface of the sea, I opened the gate which led to the cliff, and we walked along side by side, as contented as two persons might be who have just learned to understand and penetrate each other's motives and feelings.

"It was one of those warm, soft evenings which impart a sense of ease to flesh and spirit alike. All is enjoyment, everything charms. The balmy air, laden with the perfume of grasses and the smell of seaweed, soothes the olfactory sense with its wild fragrance, soothes the palate with its sea savor, soothes the mind with its pervading sweetness.

"We were now walking along the edge of the cliff, high above the boundless sea which rolled its little waves below us at a distance of a hundred metres. And we drank in with open mouth and expanded chest that fresh breeze, briny from kissing the waves, that came from the ocean and passed across our faces.

"Wrapped in her plaid shawl, with a look of inspiration as she faced the breeze, the English woman gazed fixedly at the great sun ball as it descended toward the horizon. Far off in the distance a three-master in full sail was outlined on the blood-red sky and a steamship, somewhat nearer, passed along, leaving behind it a trail of smoke on the horizon. The red sun globe sank slowly lower and lower and presently touched the water just behind the motionless vessel, which, in its dazzling effulgence, looked as though framed in a flame of fire. We saw it plunge, grow smaller and disappear, swallowed up by the ocean.

"Miss Harriet gazed in rapture at the last gleams of the dying day. She seemed longing to embrace the sky, the sea, the whole landscape.

"She murmured: 'Aoh! I love—I love' I saw a tear in her eye. She continued: 'I wish I were a little bird, so that I could mount up into the firmament.'

"She remained standing as I had often before seen her, perched on the cliff, her face as red as her shawl. I should have liked to have sketched her in my album. It would have been a caricature of ecstasy.

"I turned away so as not to laugh.

"I then spoke to her of painting as I would have done to a fellow artist, using the technical terms common among the devotees of the profession. She listened attentively, eagerly seeking to divine the meaning of the terms, so as to understand my thoughts. From time to time she would exclaim:

"'Oh! I understand, I understand. It is very interesting.'

"We returned home.

"The next day, on seeing me, she approached me, cordially holding out her hand; and we at once became firm friends.

"She was a good creature who had a kind of soul on springs, which became enthusiastic at a bound. She lacked equilibrium like all women who are spinsters at the age of fifty. She seemed to be preserved in a pickle of innocence, but her heart still retained something very youthful and inflammable. She loved both nature and animals with a fervor, a love like old wine fermented through age, with a sensuous love that she had never bestowed on men.

"One thing is certain, that the sight of a bitch nursing her puppies, a mare roaming in a meadow with a foal at its side, a bird's nest full of young ones, screaming, with their open mouths and their enormous heads, affected her perceptibly.

"Poor, solitary, sad, wandering beings! I love you ever since I became acquainted with Miss Harriet.

"I soon discovered that she had something she would like to tell me, but dare not, and I was amused at her timidity. When I started out in the morning with my knapsack on my back, she would accompany me in silence as far as the end of the village, evidently struggling to find words with which to begin a conversation. Then she would leave me abruptly and walk away quickly with her springy step.

"One day, however, she plucked up courage:

"I would like to see how you paint pictures. Are you willing? I have been very curious.'

"And she blushed as if she had said something very audacious.

"I conducted her to the bottom of the Petit-Val, where I had begun a large picture.

"She remained standing behind me, following all my gestures with concentrated attention. Then, suddenly, fearing perhaps that she was disturbing me, she said: 'Thank you,' and walked away.

"But she soon became more friendly, and accompanied me every day, her countenance exhibiting visible pleasure. She carried her camp stool under her arm, not permitting me to carry it. She would remain there for hours, silent and motionless, following with her eyes the point of my brush, in its every movement. When I obtained unexpectedly just the effect I wanted by a dash of color put on with the palette knife, she involuntarily uttered a little 'Ah!' of astonishment, of joy, of admiration. She had the most tender respect for my canvases, an almost religious respect for that human reproduction of a part of nature's work divine. My studies appeared to her a kind of religious pictures, and sometimes she spoke to me of God, with the idea of converting me.

"Oh, he was a queer, good-natured being, this God of hers! He was a sort of village philosopher without any great resources and without great power, for she always figured him to herself as inconsolable over injustices committed under his eyes, as though he were powerless to prevent them.

"She was, however, on excellent terms with him, affecting even to be the confidante of his secrets and of his troubles. She would say:

"'God wills' or 'God does not will,' just like a sergeant announcing to a recruit: 'The colonel has commanded.'

"At the bottom of her heart she deplored my ignorance of the intentions of the Eternal, which she endeavored to impart to me.

"Almost every day I found in my pockets, in my hat when I lifted it from the ground, in my paintbox, in my polished shoes, standing in front of my door in the morning, those little pious tracts which she no doubt, received directly from Paradise.

"I treated her as one would an old friend, with unaffected cordiality. But I soon perceived that she had changed somewhat in her manner, though, for a while, I paid little attention to it.

"When I was painting, whether in my valley or in some country lane, I would see her suddenly appear with her rapid, springy walk. She would then sit down abruptly, out of breath, as though she had been running or were overcome by some profound emotion. Her face would be red, that English red which is denied to the people of all other countries; then, without any reason, she would turn ashy pale and seem about to faint away. Gradually, however, her natural color would return and she would begin to speak.

"Then, without warning, she would break off in the middle of a sentence, spring up from her seat and walk away so rapidly and so strangely that I was at my wits' ends to discover whether I had done or said anything to displease or wound her.

"I finally came to the conclusion that those were her normal manners, somewhat modified no doubt in my honor during the first days of our acquaintance.

"When she returned to the farm, after walking for hours on the windy coast, her long curls often hung straight down, as if their springs had been broken. This had hitherto seldom given her any concern, and she would come to dinner without embarrassment all dishevelled by her sister, the breeze.

"But now she would go to her room and arrange the untidy locks, and when I would say, with familiar gallantry, which, however, always offended her:

"'You are as beautiful as a star to-day, Miss Harriet,' a blush would immediately rise to her cheeks, the blush of a young girl, of a girl of fifteen.

"Then she would suddenly become quite reserved and cease coming to watch me paint. I thought, 'This is only a fit of temper; it will blow over.' But it did not always blow over, and when I spoke to her she would answer me either with affected indifference or with sullen annoyance.

"She became by turns rude, impatient and nervous. I never saw her now except at meals, and we spoke but little. I concluded at length that I must have offended her in some way, and, accordingly, I said to her one evening:

"'Miss Harriet, why is it that you do not act toward me as formerly? What have I done to displease you? You are causing me much pain!'

"She replied in a most comical tone of anger:

"'I am just the same with you as formerly. It is not true, not true,' and she ran upstairs and shut herself up in her room.

"Occasionally she would look at me in a peculiar manner. I have often said to myself since then that those who are condemned to death must look thus when they are informed that their last day has come. In her eye there lurked a species of insanity, an insanity at once mystical and violent; and even more, a fever, an aggravated longing, impatient and impotent, for the unattained and unattainable.

"Nay, it seemed to me there was also going on within her a struggle in which her heart wrestled with an unknown force that she sought to master, and even, perhaps, something else. But what do I know? What do I know?

"It was indeed a singular revelation.

"For some time I had commenced to work, as soon as daylight appeared, on a picture the subject of which was as follows:

"A deep ravine, enclosed, surmounted by two thickets of trees and vines, extended into the distance and was lost, submerged in that milky vapor, in that cloud like cotton down that sometimes floats over valleys at daybreak. And at the extreme end of that heavy, transparent fog one saw, or, rather, surmised, that a couple of human beings were approaching, a human couple, a youth and a maiden, their arms interlaced, embracing each other, their heads inclined toward each other, their lips meeting.

"A first ray of the sun, glistening through the branches, pierced that fog of the dawn, illuminated it with a rosy reflection just behind the rustic lovers, framing their vague shadows in a silvery background. It was well done; yes, indeed, well done.

"I was working on the declivity which led to the Valley of Etretat. On this particular morning I had, by chance, the sort of floating vapor which I needed. Suddenly something rose up in front of me like a phantom; it was Miss Harriet. On seeing me she was about to flee. But I called after her, saying: 'Come here, come here, mademoiselle. I have a nice little picture for you.'

"She came forward, though with seeming reluctance. I handed her my sketch. She said nothing, but stood for a long time, motionless, looking at it, and suddenly she burst into tears. She wept spasmodically, like men who have striven hard to restrain their tears, but who can do so no longer and abandon themselves to grief, though still resisting. I sprang to my feet, moved at the sight of a sorrow I did not comprehend, and I took her by the hand with an impulse of brusque affection, a true French impulse which acts before it reflects.

"She let her hands rest in mine for a few seconds, and I felt them quiver as if all her nerves were being wrenched. Then she withdrew her hands abruptly, or, rather, snatched them away.

"I recognized that tremor, for I had felt it, and I could not be deceived. Ah! the love tremor of a woman, whether she be fifteen or fifty years of age, whether she be of the people or of society, goes so straight to my heart that I never have any hesitation in understanding it!

"Her whole frail being had trembled, vibrated, been overcome. I knew it. She walked away before I had time to say a word, leaving me as surprised as if I had witnessed a miracle and as troubled as if I had committed a crime.

"I did not go in to breakfast. I went to take a turn on the edge of the cliff, feeling that I would just as lief weep as laugh, looking on the adventure as both comic and deplorable and my position as ridiculous, believing her unhappy enough to go insane.

"I asked myself what I ought to do. It seemed best for me to leave the place, and I immediately resolved to do so.

"Somewhat sad and perplexed, I wandered about until dinner time and entered the farmhouse just when the soup had been served up.

"I sat down at the table as usual. Miss Harriet was there, eating away solemnly, without speaking to any one, without even lifting her eyes. Her manner and expression were, however, the same as usual.

"I waited patiently till the meal had been finished, when, turning toward the landlady, I said: 'Well, Madame Lecacheur, it will not be long now before I shall have to take my leave of you.'

"The good woman, at once surprised and troubled, replied in her drawling voice: 'My dear sir, what is it you say? You are going to leave us after I have become so accustomed to you?'

"I glanced at Miss Harriet out of the corner of my eye. Her countenance did not change in the least. But Celeste, the little servant, looked up at me. She was a fat girl, of about eighteen years of age, rosy, fresh, as strong as a horse, and possessing the rare attribute of cleanliness. I had kissed her at odd times in out-of-the-way corners, after the manner of travellers—nothing more.

"The dinner being at length over, I went to smoke my pipe under the apple trees, walking up and down from one end of the enclosure to the other. All the reflections which I had made during the day, the strange discovery of the morning, that passionate and grotesque attachment for me, the recollections which that revelation had suddenly called up, recollections at once charming and perplexing, perhaps also that look which the servant had cast on me at the announcement of my departure—all these things, mixed up and combined, put me now in a reckless humor, gave me a tickling sensation of kisses on the lips and in my veins a something which urged me on to commit some folly.

"Night was coming on, casting its dark shadows under the trees, when I descried Celeste, who had gone to fasten up the poultry yard at the other end of the enclosure. I darted toward her, running so noiselessly that she heard nothing, and as she got up from closing the small trapdoor by which the chickens got in and out, I clasped her in my arms and rained on her coarse, fat face a shower of kisses. She struggled, laughing all the time, as she was accustomed to do in such circumstances. Why did I suddenly loose my grip of her? Why did I at once experience a shock? What was it that I heard behind me?

"It was Miss Harriet, who had come upon us, who had seen us and who stood in front of us motionless as a spectre. Then she disappeared in the darkness.

"I was ashamed, embarrassed, more desperate at having been thus surprised by her than if she had caught me committing some criminal act.

"I slept badly that night. I was completely unnerved and haunted by sad thoughts. I seemed to hear loud weeping, but in this I was no doubt deceived. Moreover, I thought several times that I heard some one walking up and down in the house and opening the hall door.

"Toward morning I was overcome by fatigue and fell asleep. I got up late and did not go downstairs until the late breakfast, being still in a bewildered state, not knowing what kind of expression to put on.

"No one had seen Miss Harriet. We waited for her at table, but she did not appear. At length Mother Lecacheur went to her room. The English woman had gone out. She must have set out at break of day, as she was wont to do, in order to see the sun rise.

"Nobody seemed surprised at this, and we began to eat in silence.

"The weather was hot, very hot, one of those broiling, heavy days when not a leaf stirs. The table had been placed out of doors, under an apple tree, and from time to time Sapeur had gone to the cellar to draw a jug of cider, everybody was so thirsty. Celeste brought the dishes from the kitchen, a ragout of mutton with potatoes, a cold rabbit and a salad. Afterward she placed before us a dish of strawberries, the first of the season.

"As I wished to wash and freshen these, I begged the servant to go and draw me a pitcher of cold water.

"In about five minutes she returned, declaring that the well was dry. She had lowered the pitcher to the full extent of the cord and had touched the bottom, but on drawing the pitcher up again it was empty. Mother Lecacheur, anxious to examine the thing for herself, went and looked down the hole. She returned, announcing that one could see clearly something in the well, something altogether unusual. But this no doubt was bundles of straw, which a neighbor had thrown in out of spite.

"I wished to look down the well also, hoping I might be able to clear up the mystery, and I perched myself close to the brink. I perceived indistinctly a white object. What could it be? I then conceived the idea of lowering a lantern at the end of a cord. When I did so the yellow flame danced on the layers of stone and gradually became clearer. All four of us were leaning over the opening, Sapeur and Celeste having now joined us. The lantern rested on a black-and-white indistinct mass, singular, incomprehensible. Sapeur exclaimed:

"'It is a horse. I see the hoofs. It must have got out of the meadow during the night and fallen in headlong.'

"But suddenly a cold shiver froze me to the marrow. I first recognized a foot, then a leg sticking up; the whole body and the other leg were completely under water.

"I stammered out in a loud voice, trembling so violently that the lantern danced hither and thither over the slipper:

"'It is a woman! Who-who-can it be? It is Miss Harriet!'

"Sapeur alone did not manifest horror. He had witnessed many such scenes in Africa.

"Mother Lecacheur and Celeste began to utter piercing screams and ran away.

"But it was necessary to recover the corpse of the dead woman. I attached the young man securely by the waist to the end of the pulley rope and lowered him very slowly, watching him disappear in the darkness. In one hand he held the lantern and a rope in the other. Soon I recognized his voice, which seemed to come from the centre of the earth, saying:

"'Stop!'

"I then saw him fish something out of the water. It was the other leg. He then bound the two feet together and shouted anew:

"'Haul up!'

"I began to wind up, but I felt my arms crack, my muscles twitch, and I was in terror lest I should let the man fall to the bottom. When his head appeared at the brink I asked:

"'Well?' as if I expected he had a message from the drowned woman.

"We both got on the stone slab at the edge of the well and from opposite sides we began to haul up the body.

"Mother Lecacheur and Celeste watched us from a distance, concealed from view behind the wall of the house. When they saw issuing from the hole the black slippers and white stockings of the drowned person they disappeared.

"Sapeur seized the ankles, and we drew up the body of the poor woman. The head was shocking to look at, being bruised and lacerated, and the long gray hair, out of curl forevermore, hanging down tangled and disordered.

"'In the name of all that is holy! how lean she is,' exclaimed Sapeur in a contemptuous tone.

"We carried her into the room, and as the women did not put in an appearance I, with the assistance of the stable lad, dressed the corpse for burial.

"I washed her disfigured face. Under the touch of my finger an eye was slightly opened and regarded me with that pale, cold look, that terrible look of a corpse which seems to come from the beyond. I braided as well as I could her dishevelled hair and with my clumsy hands arranged on her head a novel and singular coiffure. Then I took off her dripping wet garments, baring, not without a feeling of shame, as though I had been guilty of some profanation, her shoulders and her chest and her long arms, as slim as the twigs of a tree.

"I next went to fetch some flowers, poppies, bluets, marguerites and fresh, sweet-smelling grass with which to strew her funeral couch.

"I then had to go through the usual formalities, as I was alone to attend to everything. A letter found in her pocket, written at the last moment, requested that her body be buried in the village in which she had passed the last days of her life. A sad suspicion weighed on my heart. Was it not on my account that she wished to be laid to rest in this place?

"Toward evening all the female gossips of the locality came to view the remains of the defunct, but I would not allow a single person to enter. I wanted to be alone, and I watched beside her all night.

"I looked at the corpse by the flickering light of the candles, at this unhappy woman, unknown to us all, who had died in such a lamentable manner and so far away from home. Had she left no friends, no relations behind her? What had her infancy been? What had been her life? Whence had she come thither alone, a wanderer, lost like a dog driven from home? What secrets of sufferings and of despair were sealed up in that unprepossessing body, in that poor body whose outward appearance had driven from her all affection, all love?

"How many unhappy beings there are! I felt that there weighed upon that human creature the eternal injustice of implacable nature! It was all over with her, without her ever having experienced, perhaps, that which sustains the greatest outcasts to wit, the hope of being loved once! Otherwise why should she thus have concealed herself, fled from the face of others? Why did she love everything so tenderly and so passionately, everything living that was not a man?

"I recognized the fact that she believed in a God, and that she hoped to receive compensation from the latter for all the miseries she had endured. She would now disintegrate and become, in turn, a plant. She would blossom in the sun, the cattle would browse on her leaves, the birds would bear away the seeds, and through these changes she would become again human flesh. But that which is called the soul had been extinguished at the bottom of the dark well. She suffered no longer. She had given her life for that of others yet to come.

"Hours passed away in this silent and sinister communion with the dead. A pale light at length announced the dawn of a new day; then a red ray streamed in on the bed, making a bar of light across the coverlet and across her hands. This was the hour she had so much loved. The awakened birds began to sing in the trees.

"I opened the window to its fullest extent and drew back the curtains that the whole heavens might look in upon us, and, bending over the icy corpse, I took in my hands the mutilated head and slowly, without terror or disgust, I imprinted a kiss, a long kiss, upon those lips which had never before been kissed."

Leon Chenal remained silent. The women wept. We heard on the box seat the Count d'Atraille blowing his nose from time to time. The coachman alone had gone to sleep. The horses, who no longer felt the sting of the whip, had slackened their pace and moved along slowly. The drag, hardly advancing at all, seemed suddenly torpid, as if it had been freighted with sorrow.

[Miss Harriet appeared in Le Gaulois, July 9, 1883, under the title of Miss Hastings. The story was later revised, enlarged; and partly reconstructed. This is what De Maupassant wrote to Editor Havard March 15, 1884, in an unedited letter, in regard to the title of the story that was to give its name to the volume:

"I do not believe that Hastings is a bad name, inasmuch as it is known all over the world, and recalls the greatest facts in English history. Besides, Hastings is as much a name as Duval is with us.

"The name Cherbuliez selected, Miss Revel, is no more like an English name than like a Turkish name. But here is another name as English as Hastings, and more euphonious; it is Miss Harriet. I will ask you therefore to substitute Harriet for Hastings."

It was in regard to this very tittle that De Maupassant had a disagreement with Audran and Boucheron director of the Bouffes Parisiens in October, 1890 They had given this title to an operetta about to be played at the Bouffes. It ended however, by their ceding to De Maupassant, and the title of the operetta was changed to Miss Helyett.]

LITTLE LOUISE ROQUE

The former soldier, Mederic Rompel, familiarly called Mederic by the country folks, left the post office of Roily-le-Tors at the usual hour. After passing through the village with his long stride, he cut across the meadows of Villaume and reached the bank of the Brindille, following the path along the water's edge to the village of Carvelin, where he commenced to deliver his letters. He walked quickly, following the course of the narrow river, which frothed, murmured and boiled in its grassy bed beneath an arch of willows.

Mederic went on without stopping, with only this thought in his mind: "My first letter is for the Poivron family, then I have one for Monsieur Renardet; so I must cross the wood."

His blue blouse, fastened round his waist by a black leather belt, moved in a quick, regular fashion above the green hedge of willow trees, and his stout stick of holly kept time with his steady tread.

He crossed the Brindille on a bridge consisting of a tree trunk, with a handrail of rope, fastened at either end to a stake driven into the ground.

The wood, which belonged to Monsieur Renardet, the mayor of Carvelin and the largest landowner in the district, consisted of huge old trees, straight as pillars and extending for about half a league along the left bank of the stream which served as a boundary to this immense dome of foliage. Alongside the water large shrubs had grown up in the sunlight, but under the trees one found nothing but moss, thick, soft and yielding, from which arose, in the still air, an odor of dampness and of dead wood.

Mederic slackened his pace, took off his black cap adorned with red lace and wiped his forehead, for it was by this time hot in the meadows, though it was not yet eight o'clock in the morning.

He had just recovered from the effects of the heat and resumed his quick pace when he noticed at the foot of a tree a knife, a child's small knife. When he picked it up he discovered a thimble and also a needlecase not far away.

Having taken up these objects, he thought: "I'll entrust them to the mayor," and he resumed his journey, but now he kept his eyes open, expecting to find something else.

All of a sudden he stopped short, as if he had struck against a wooden barrier. Ten paces in front of him lay stretched on her back on the moss a little girl, perfectly nude, her face covered with a handkerchief. She was about twelve years old.

Meredic advanced on tiptoe, as if he apprehended some danger, and he glanced toward the spot uneasily.

What was this? No doubt she was asleep. Then he reflected that a person does not go to sleep naked at half-past seven in the morning under the cool trees. So, then, she must be dead, and he must be face to face with a crime. At this thought a cold shiver ran through his frame, although he was an old soldier. And then a murder was such a rare thing in the country, and, above all, the murder of a child, that he could not believe his eyes. But she had no wound—nothing save a spot of blood on her leg. How, then, had she been killed?

He stopped close to her and gazed at her, while he leaned on his stick. Certainly he must know her, for he knew all the inhabitants of the district; but, not being able to get a look at her face, he could not guess her name. He stooped forward in order to take off the handkerchief which covered her face, then paused, with outstretched hand, restrained by an idea that occurred to him.

Had he the right to disarrange anything in the condition of the corpse before the official investigation? He pictured justice to himself as a kind of general whom nothing escapes and who attaches as much importance to a lost button as to the stab of a knife in the stomach. Perhaps under this handkerchief evidence could be found to sustain a charge of murder; in fact, if such proof were there it might lose its value if touched by an awkward hand.

Then he raised himself with the intention of hastening toward the mayor's residence, but again another thought held him back. If the little girl were still alive, by any chance, he could not leave her lying there in this way. He sank on his knees very gently, a little distance from her, through precaution, and extended his hand toward her foot. It was icy cold, with the terrible coldness of death which leaves us no longer in doubt. The letter carrier, as he touched her, felt his heart in his mouth, as he said himself afterward, and his mouth parched. Rising up abruptly, he rushed off under the trees toward Monsieur Renardet's house.

He walked on faster than ever, with his stick under his arm, his hands clenched and his head thrust forward, while his leathern bag, filled with letters and newspapers, kept flapping at his side.

The mayor's residence was at the end of the wood which served as a park, and one side of it was washed by the Brindille.

It was a big square house of gray stone, very old, and had stood many a siege in former days, and at the end of it was a huge tower, twenty metres high, rising out of the water.

From the top of this fortress one could formerly see all the surrounding country. It was called the Fox's tower, without any one knowing exactly why; and from this appellation, no doubt, had come the name Renardet, borne by the owners of this fief, which had remained in the same family, it was said, for more than two hundred years. For the Renardets formed part of the upper middle class, all but noble, to be met with so often in the province before the Revolution.

The postman dashed into the kitchen, where the servants were taking breakfast, and exclaimed:

"Is the mayor up? I want to speak to him at once."

Mederic was recognized as a man of standing and authority, and they understood that something serious had happened.

As soon as word was brought to Monsieur Renardet, he ordered the postman to be sent up to him. Pale and out of breath, with his cap in his hand, Mederic found the mayor seated at a long table covered with scattered papers.

He was a large, tall man, heavy and red-faced, strong as an ox, and was greatly liked in the district, although of an excessively violent disposition. Almost forty years old and a widower for the past six months, he lived on his estate like a country gentleman. His choleric temperament had often brought him into trouble from which the magistrates of Roily-le-Tors, like indulgent and prudent friends, had extricated him. Had he not one day thrown the conductor of the diligence from the top of his seat because he came near running over his retriever, Micmac? Had he not broken the ribs of a gamekeeper who abused him for having, gun in hand, passed through a neighbor's property? Had he not even caught by the collar the sub-prefect, who stopped over in the village during an administrative circuit, called by Monsieur Renardet an electioneering circuit, for he was opposed to the government, in accordance with family traditions.

The mayor asked:

"What's the matter now, Mederic?"

"I found a little girl dead in your wood."

Renardet rose to his feet, his face the color of brick.

"What do you say—a little girl?"

"Yes, m'sieu, a little girl, quite naked, on her back, with blood on her, dead—quite dead!"

The mayor gave vent to an oath:

"By God, I'd make a bet it is little Louise Roque! I have just learned that she did not go home to her mother last night. Where did you find her?"

The postman described the spot, gave full details and offered to conduct the mayor to the place.

But Renardet became brusque:

"No, I don't need you. Send the watchman, the mayor's secretary and the doctor to me at once, and resume your rounds. Quick, quick, go and tell them to meet me in the wood."

The letter carrier, a man used to discipline, obeyed and withdrew, angry and grieved at not being able to be present at the investigation.

The mayor, in his turn, prepared to go out, took his big soft hat and paused for a few seconds on the threshold of his abode. In front of him stretched a wide sward, in which were three large beds of flowers in full bloom, one facing the house and the others at either side of it. Farther on the outlying trees of the wood rose skyward, while at the left, beyond the Brindille, which at that spot widened into a pond, could be seen long meadows, an entirely green flat sweep of country, intersected by trenches and hedges of pollard willows.

To the right, behind the stables, the outhouses and all the buildings connected with the property, might be seen the village, which was wealthy, being mainly inhabited by cattle breeders.

Renardet slowly descended the steps in front of his house, and, turning to the left, gained the water's edge, which he followed at a slow pace, his hand behind his back. He walked on, with bent head, and from time to time glanced round in search of the persons he had sent for.

When he stood beneath the trees he stopped, took off his hat and wiped his forehead as Mederic had done, for the burning sun was darting its fiery rays on the earth. Then the mayor resumed his journey, stopped once more and retraced his steps. Suddenly, stooping down, he steeped his handkerchief in the stream that glided along at his feet and spread it over his head, under his hat. Drops of water flowed down his temples over his ears, which were always purple, over his strong red neck, and made their way, one after the other, under his white shirt collar.

As nobody had appeared, he began tapping with his foot, then he called out:

"Hello! Hello!"

A voice at his right answered:

"Hello! Hello!"

And the doctor appeared under the trees. He was a thin little man, an ex-military surgeon, who passed in the neighborhood for a very skillful practitioner. He limped, having been wounded while in the service, and had to use a stick to assist him in walking.

Next came the watchman and the mayor's secretary, who, having been sent for at the same time, arrived together. They looked scared, and hurried forward, out of breath, walking and running alternately to hasten their progress, and moving their arms up and down so vigorously that they seemed to do more work with them than with their legs.

Renardet said to the doctor:

"You know what the trouble is about?"

"Yes, a child found dead in the wood by Mederic."

"That's quite correct. Come on!"

They walked along, side by side, followed by the two men.

Their steps made no sound on the moss. Their eyes were gazing ahead in front of them.

Suddenly the doctor, extending his arm, said:

"See, there she is!"

Far ahead of them under the trees they saw something white on which the sun gleamed down through the branches. As they approached they gradually distinguished a human form lying there, its head toward the river, the face covered and the arms extended as though on a crucifix.

"I am fearfully warm," said the mayor, and stooping down, he again soaked his handkerchief in the water and placed it round his forehead.

The doctor hastened his steps, interested by the discovery. As soon as they were near the corpse, he bent down to examine it without touching it. He had put on his pince-nez, as one does in examining some curious object, and turned round very quietly.

He said, without rising:

"Violated and murdered, as we shall prove presently. This little girl, moreover, is almost a woman—look at her throat."

The doctor lightly drew away the handkerchief which covered her face, which looked black, frightful, the tongue protruding, the eyes bloodshot. He went on:

"By heavens! She was strangled the moment the deed was done."

He felt her neck.

"Strangled with the hands without leaving any special trace, neither the mark of the nails nor the imprint of the fingers. Quite right. It is little Louise Roque, sure enough!"

He carefully replaced the handkerchief.

"There's nothing for me to do. She's been dead for the last hour at least. We must give notice of the matter to the authorities."

Renardet, standing up, with his hands behind his back, kept staring with a stony look at the little body exposed to view on the grass. He murmured:

"What a wretch! We must find the clothes."

The doctor felt the hands, the arms, the legs. He said:

"She had been bathing no doubt. They ought to be at the water's edge."

The mayor thereupon gave directions:

"Do you, Principe" (this was his secretary), "go and find those clothes for me along the stream. You, Maxime" (this was the watchman), "hurry on toward Rouy-le-Tors and bring with you the magistrate with the gendarmes. They must be here within an hour. You understand?"

The two men started at once, and Renardet said to the doctor:

"What miscreant could have done such a deed in this part of the country?"

The doctor murmured:

"Who knows? Any one is capable of that. Every one in particular and nobody in general. No matter, it must be some prowler, some workman out of employment. Since we have become a Republic we meet only this kind of person along the roads."

Both of them were Bonapartists.

The mayor went on:

"Yes, it can only be a stranger, a passer-by, a vagabond without hearth or home."

The doctor added, with the shadow of a smile on his face:

"And without a wife. Having neither a good supper nor a good bed, he became reckless. You can't tell how many men there may be in the world capable of a crime at a given moment. Did you know that this little girl had disappeared?"

And with the end of his stick he touched one after the other the stiffened fingers of the corpse, resting on them as on the keys of a piano.

"Yes, the mother came last night to look for me about nine o'clock, the child not having come home at seven to supper. We looked for her along the roads up to midnight, but we did not think of the wood. However, we needed daylight to carry out a thorough search."

"Will you have a cigar?" said the doctor.

"Thanks, I don't care to smoke. This thing affects me so."

They remained standing beside the corpse of the young girl, so pale on the dark moss. A big blue fly was walking over the body with his lively, jerky movements. The two men kept watching this wandering speck.

The doctor said:

"How pretty it is, a fly on the skin! The ladies of the last century had good reason to paste them on their faces. Why has this fashion gone out?"

The mayor seemed not to hear, plunged as he was in deep thought.

But, all of a sudden, he turned round, surprised by a shrill noise. A woman in a cap and blue apron was running toward them under the trees. It was the mother, La Roque. As soon as she saw Renardet she began to shriek:

"My little girl! Where's my little girl!" so distractedly that she did not glance down at the ground. Suddenly she saw the corpse, stopped short, clasped her hands and raised both her arms while she uttered a sharp, heartrending cry—the cry of a wounded animal. Then she rushed toward the body, fell on her knees and snatched away the handkerchief that covered the face. When she saw that frightful countenance, black and distorted, she rose to her feet with a shudder, then sinking to the ground, face downward, she pressed her face against the ground and uttered frightful, continuous screams on the thick moss.

Her tall, thin frame, with its close-clinging dress, was palpitating, shaken with spasms. One could see her bony ankles and her dried-up calves covered with coarse blue stockings shaking horribly. She was digging the soil with her crooked fingers, as though she were trying to make a hole in which to hide herself.

The doctor, much affected, said in a low tone:

"Poor old woman!"

Renardet felt a strange sensation. Then he gave vent to a sort of loud sneeze, and, drawing his handkerchief from his pocket, he began to weep internally, coughing, sobbing and blowing his nose noisily.

He stammered:

"Damn—damn—damned pig to do this! I would like to seem him guillotined."

Principe reappeared with his hands empty. He murmured:

"I have found nothing, M'sieu le Maire, nothing at all anywhere."

The mayor, alarmed, replied in a thick voice, drowned in tears:

"What is that you could not find?"

"The little girl's clothes."

"Well—well—look again, and find them—or you'll have to answer to me."

The man, knowing that the mayor would not brook opposition, set forth again with hesitating steps, casting a timid side glance at the corpse.

Distant voices were heard under the trees, a confused sound, the noise of an approaching crowd, for Mederic had, in the course of his rounds, carried the news from door to door. The people of the neighborhood, dazed at first, had gossiped about it in the street, from one threshold to another. Then they gathered together. They talked over, discussed and commented on the event for some minutes and had now come to see for themselves.

They arrived in groups, a little faltering and uneasy through fear of the first impression of such a scene on their minds. When they saw the body they stopped, not daring to advance, and speaking low. Then they grew bolder, went on a few steps, stopped again, advanced once more, and presently formed around the dead girl, her mother, the doctor and Renardet a close circle, restless and noisy, which crowded forward at the sudden impact of newcomers. And now they touched the corpse. Some of them even bent down to feel it with their fingers. The doctor kept them back. But the mayor, waking abruptly out of his torpor, flew into a rage, and seizing Dr. Labarbe's stick, flung himself on his townspeople, stammering:

"Clear out—clear out—you pack of brutes—clear out!"

And in a second the crowd of sightseers had fallen back two hundred paces.

Mother La Roque had risen to a sitting posture and now remained weeping, with her hands clasped over her face.

The crowd was discussing the affair, and young lads' eager eyes curiously scrutinized this nude young form. Renardet perceived this, and, abruptly taking off his coat, he flung it over the little girl, who was entirely hidden from view beneath the large garment.

The secretary drew near quietly. The wood was filled with people, and a continuous hum of voices rose up under the tangled foliage of the tall trees.

The mayor, in his shirt sleeves, remained standing, with his stick in his hands, in a fighting attitude. He seemed exasperated by this curiosity on the part of the people and kept repeating:

"If one of you come nearer I'll break his head just as I would a dog's."

The peasants were greatly afraid of him. They held back. Dr. Labarbe, who was smoking, sat down beside La Roque and spoke to her in order to distract her attention. The old woman at once removed her hands from her face and replied with a flood of tearful words, emptying her grief in copious talk. She told the whole story of her life, her marriage, the death of her man, a cattle drover, who had been gored to death, the infancy of her daughter, her wretched existence as a widow without resources and with a child to support. She had only this one, her little Louise, and the child had been killed—killed in this wood. Then she felt anxious to see her again, and, dragging herself on her knees toward the corpse, she raised up one corner of the garment that covered her; then she let it fall again and began wailing once more. The crowd remained silent, eagerly watching all the mother's gestures.

But suddenly there was a great commotion at the cry of "The gendarmes! the gendarmes!"

Two gendarmes appeared in the distance, advancing at a rapid trot, escorting their captain and a little gentleman with red whiskers, who was bobbing up and down like a monkey on a big white mare.

The watchman had just found Monsieur Putoin, the magistrate, at the moment when he was mounting his horse to take his daily ride, for he posed as a good horseman, to the great amusement of the officers.

He dismounted, along with the captain, and pressed the hands of the mayor and the doctor, casting a ferret-like glance on the linen coat beneath which lay the corpse.

When he was made acquainted with all the facts, he first gave orders to disperse the crowd, whom the gendarmes drove out of the wood, but who soon reappeared in the meadow and formed a hedge, a big hedge of excited and moving heads, on the other side of the stream.

The doctor, in his turn, gave explanations, which Renardet noted down in his memorandum book. All the evidence was given, taken down and commented on without leading to any discovery. Maxime, too, came back without having found any trace of the clothes.

This disappearance surprised everybody; no one could explain it except on the theory of theft, and as her rags were not worth twenty sous, even this theory was inadmissible.

The magistrate, the mayor, the captain and the doctor set to work searching in pairs, putting aside the smallest branch along the water.

Renardet said to the judge:

"How does it happen that this wretch has concealed or carried away the clothes, and has thus left the body exposed, in sight of every one?"

The other, crafty and sagacious, answered:

"Ha! ha! Perhaps a dodge? This crime has been committed either by a brute or by a sly scoundrel. In any case, we'll easily succeed in finding him."

The noise of wheels made them turn their heads round. It was the deputy magistrate, the doctor and the registrar of the court who had arrived in their turn. They resumed their search, all chatting in an animated fashion.

Renardet said suddenly:

"Do you know that you are to take luncheon with me?"

Every one smilingly accepted the invitation, and the magistrate, thinking that the case of little Louise Roque had occupied enough attention for one day, turned toward the mayor.

"I can have the body brought to your house, can I not? You have a room in which you can keep it for me till this evening?"

The other became confused and stammered:

"Yes—no—no. To tell the truth, I prefer that it should not come into my house on account of—on account of my servants, who are already talking about ghosts in—in my tower, in the Fox's tower. You know—I could no longer keep a single one. No—I prefer not to have it in my house."

The magistrate began to smile.

"Good! I will have it taken at once to Roily for the legal examination." And, turning to his deputy, he said:

"I can make use of your trap, can I not?"

"Yes, certainly."

They all came back to the place where the corpse lay. Mother La Roque, now seated beside her daughter, was holding her hand and was staring right before her with a wandering, listless eye.

The two doctors endeavored to lead her away, so that she might not witness the dead girl's removal, but she understood at once what they wanted to do, and, flinging herself on the body, she threw both arms round it. Lying on top of the corpse, she exclaimed:

"You shall not have it—it's mine—it's mine now. They have killed her for me, and I want to keep her—you shall not have her——"

All the men, affected and not knowing how to act, remained standing around her. Renardet fell on his knees and said to her:

"Listen, La Roque, it is necessary, in order to find out who killed her. Without this, we could not find out. We must make a search for the man in order to punish him. When we have found him we'll give her up to you. I promise you this."

This explanation bewildered the woman, and a feeling of hatred manifested itself in her distracted glance.

"So then they'll arrest him?"

"Yes, I promise you that."

She rose up, deciding to let them do as they liked, but when the captain remarked:

"It is surprising that her clothes were not found," a new idea, which she had not previously thought of, abruptly entered her mind, and she asked:

"Where are her clothes? They're mine. I want them. Where have they been put?"

They explained to her that they had not been found. Then she demanded them persistently, crying and moaning.

"They're mine—I want them. Where are they? I want them!"

The more they tried to calm her the more she sobbed and persisted in her demands. She no longer wanted the body, she insisted on having the clothes, as much perhaps through the unconscious cupidity of a wretched being to whom a piece of silver represents a fortune as through maternal tenderness.

And when the little body, rolled up in blankets which had been brought out from Renardet's house, had disappeared in the vehicle, the old woman standing under the trees, sustained by the mayor and the captain, exclaimed:

"I have nothing, nothing, nothing in the world, not even her little cap —her little cap."

The cure, a young priest, had just arrived. He took it on himself to accompany the mother, and they went away together toward the village. The mother's grief was modified by the sugary words of the clergyman, who promised her a thousand compensations. But she kept repeating: "If I had only her little cap." This idea now dominated every other.

Renardet called from the distance:

"You will lunch with us, Monsieur l'Abbe—in an hour's time."

The priest turned his head round and replied:

"With pleasure, Monsieur le Maire. I'll be with you at twelve."

And they all directed their steps toward the house, whose gray front, with the large tower built on the edge of the Brindille, could be seen through the branches.

The meal lasted a long time. They talked about the crime. Everybody was of the same opinion. It had been committed by some tramp passing there by mere chance while the little girl was bathing.

Then the magistrates returned to Rouy, announcing that they would return next day at an early hour. The doctor and the cure went to their respective homes, while Renardet, after a long walk through the meadows, returned to the wood, where he remained walking till nightfall with slow steps, his hands behind his back.

He went to bed early and was still asleep next morning when the magistrate entered his room. He was rubbing his hands together with a self-satisfied air.

"Ha! ha! You are still sleeping! Well, my dear fellow, we have news this morning."

The mayor sat up in his bed.

"What, pray?"

"Oh! Something strange. You remember well how the mother clamored yesterday for some memento of her daughter, especially her little cap? Well, on opening her door this morning she found on the threshold her child's two little wooden shoes. This proves that the crime was perpetrated by some one from the district, some one who felt pity for her. Besides, the postman, Mederic, brought me the thimble, the knife and the needle case of the dead girl. So, then, the man in carrying off the clothes to hide them must have let fall the articles which were in the pocket. As for me, I attach special importance to the wooden shoes, as they indicate a certain moral culture and a faculty for tenderness on the part of the assassin. We will, therefore, if you have no objection, go over together the principal inhabitants of your district."

The mayor got up. He rang for his shaving water and said:

"With pleasure, but it will take some time, and we may begin at once."

M. Putoin sat astride a chair.

Renardet covered his chin with a white lather while he looked at himself in the glass. Then he sharpened his razor on the strop and continued:

"The principal inhabitant of Carvelin bears the name of Joseph Renardet, mayor, a rich landowner, a rough man who beats guards and coachmen—"

The examining magistrate burst out laughing.

"That's enough. Let us pass on to the next."

"The second in importance is Pelledent, his deputy, a cattle breeder, an equally rich landowner, a crafty peasant, very sly, very close-fisted on every question of money, but incapable in my opinion of having perpetrated such a crime."

"Continue," said M. Putoin.

Renardet, while proceeding with his toilet, reviewed the characters of all the inhabitants of Carvelin. After two hours' discussion their suspicions were fixed on three individuals who had hitherto borne a shady reputation—a poacher named Cavalle, a fisherman named Paquet, who caught trout and crabs, and a cattle drover named Clovis. II

The search for the perpetrator of the crime lasted all summer, but he was not discovered. Those who were suspected and arrested easily proved their innocence, and the authorities were compelled to abandon the attempt to capture the criminal.

But this murder seemed to have moved the entire country in a singular manner. There remained in every one's mind a disquietude, a vague fear, a sensation of mysterious terror, springing not merely from the impossibility of discovering any trace of the assassin, but also and above all from that strange finding of the wooden shoes in front of La Roque's door the day after the crime. The certainty that the murderer had assisted at the investigation, that he was still, doubtless, living in the village, possessed all minds and seemed to brood over the neighborhood like a constant menace.

The wood had also become a dreaded spot, a place to be avoided and supposed to be haunted.

Formerly the inhabitants went there to spend every Sunday afternoon. They used to sit down on the moss at the feet of the huge tall trees or walk along the water's edge watching the trout gliding among the weeds. The boy's used to play bowls, hide-and-seek and other games where the ground had been cleared and levelled, and the girls, in rows of four or five, would trip along, holding one another by the arms and screaming songs with their shrill voices. Now nobody ventured there for fear of finding some corpse lying on the ground.

Autumn arrived, the leaves began to fall from the tall trees, whirling round and round to the ground, and the sky could be seen through the bare branches. Sometimes, when a gust of wind swept over the tree tops, the slow, continuous rain suddenly grew heavier and became a rough storm that covered the moss with a thick yellow carpet that made a kind of creaking sound beneath one's feet.

And the sound of the falling leaves seemed like a wail and the leaves themselves like tears shed by these great, sorrowful trees, that wept in the silence of the bare and empty wood, this dreaded and deserted wood where wandered lonely the soul, the little soul of little Louise Roque.

The Brindille, swollen by the storms, rushed on more quickly, yellow and angry, between its dry banks, bordered by two thin, bare, willow hedges.

And here was Renardet suddenly resuming his walks under the trees. Every day, at sunset, he came out of his house, descended the front steps slowly and entered the wood in a dreamy fashion, with his hands in his pockets, and paced over the damp soft moss, while a legion of rooks from all the neighboring haunts came thither to rest in the tall trees and then flew off like a black cloud uttering loud, discordant cries.

Night came on, and Renardet was still strolling slowly under the trees; then, when the darkness prevented him from walking any longer, he would go back to the house and sink into his armchair in front of the glowing hearth, stretching his damp feet toward the fire.

One morning an important bit of news was circulated through the district; the mayor was having his wood cut down.

Twenty woodcutters were already at work. They had commenced at the corner nearest to the house and worked rapidly in the master's presence.

And each day the wood grew thinner, losing its trees, which fell down one by one, as an army loses its soldiers.

Renardet no longer walked up, and down. He remained from morning till night, contemplating, motionless, with his hands behind his back, the slow destruction of his wood. When a tree fell he placed his foot on it as if it were a corpse. Then he raised his eyes to the next with a kind of secret, calm impatience, as if he expected, hoped for something at the end of this slaughter.

Meanwhile they were approaching the place where little Louise Roque had been found. They came to it one evening in the twilight.

As it was dark, the sky being overcast, the woodcutters wanted to stop their work, putting off till next day the fall of an enormous beech tree, but the mayor objected to this and insisted that they should at once lop and cut down this giant, which had sheltered the crime.

When the lopper had laid it bare and the woodcutters had sapped its base, five men commenced hauling at the rope attached to the top.

The tree resisted; its powerful trunk, although notched to the centre, was as rigid as iron. The workmen, all together, with a sort of simultaneous motion,' strained at the rope, bending backward and uttering a cry which timed and regulated their efforts.

Two woodcutters standing close to the giant remained with axes in their grip, like two executioners ready to strike once more, and Renardet, motionless, with his hand on the trunk, awaited the fall with an uneasy, nervous feeling.

One of the men said to him:

"You are too near, Monsieur le Maire. When it falls it may hurt you."

He did not reply and did not move away. He seemed ready to catch the beech tree in his open arms and to cast it on the ground like a wrestler.

All at once, at the base of the tall column of wood there was a rent which seemed to run to the top, like a painful shock; it bent slightly, ready to fall, but still resisting. The men, in a state of excitement, stiffened their arms, renewed their efforts with greater vigor, and, just as the tree came crashing down, Renardet suddenly made a forward step, then stopped, his shoulders raised to receive the irresistible shock, the mortal shock which would crush him to the earth.

But the beech tree, having deviated a little, only rubbed against his loins, throwing him on his face, five metres away.

The workmen dashed forward to lift him up. He had already arisen to his knees, stupefied, with bewildered eyes and passing his hand across his forehead, as if he were awaking from an attack of madness.

When he had got to his feet once more the men, astonished, questioned him, not being able to understand what he had done. He replied in faltering tones that he had been dazed for a moment, or, rather, he had been thinking of his childhood days; that he thought he would have time to run under the tree, just as street boys rush in front of vehicles driving rapidly past; that he had played at danger; that for the past eight days he felt this desire growing stronger within him, asking himself each time a tree began to fall whether he could pass beneath it without being touched. It was a piece of stupidity, he confessed, but every one has these moments of insanity and these temptations to boyish folly.

He made this explanation in a slow tone, searching for his words, and speaking in a colorless tone.

Then he went off, saying:

"Till to-morrow, my friends-till to-morrow."

As soon as he got back to his room he sat down at his table which his lamp lighted up brightly, and, burying his head in his hands, he began to cry.

He remained thus for a long time, then wiped his eyes, raised his head and looked at the clock. It was not yet six o'clock.

He thought:

"I have time before dinner."

And he went to the door and locked it. He then came back, and, sitting down at his table, pulled out the middle drawer. Taking from it a revolver, he laid it down on his papers in full view. The barrel of the firearm glittered, giving out gleams of light.

Renardet gazed at it for some time with the uneasy glance of a drunken man. Then he rose and began to pace up and down the room.

He walked from one end of the apartment to the other, stopping from time to time, only to pace up and down again a moment afterward. Suddenly he opened the door of his dressing-room, steeped a towel in the water pitcher and moistened his forehead, as he had done on the morning of the crime.

Then he, began walking up and down again. Each time he passed the table the gleaming revolver attracted his glance, tempted his hand, but he kept watching the clock and reflected:

"I have still time."

It struck half-past six. Then he took up the revolver, opened his mouth wide with a frightful grimace and stuck the barrel into it as if he wanted to swallow it. He remained in this position for some seconds without moving, his finger on the trigger. Then, suddenly seized with a shudder of horror, he dropped the pistol on the carpet.

He fell back on his armchair, sobbing:

"I cannot. I dare not! My God! my God! How can I have the courage to kill myself?'"

There was a knock at the door. He rose up, bewildered. A servant said:

"Monsieur's dinner is ready."

He replied:

"All right. I'm coming down."

Then he picked up the revolver, locked it up again in the drawer and looked at himself in the mirror over the mantelpiece to see whether his face did not look too much troubled. It was as red as usual, a little redder perhaps. That was all. He went down and seated himself at table.

He ate slowly, like a man who wants to prolong the meal, who does not want to be alone.

Then he smoked several pipes in the hall while the table was being cleared. After that he went back to his room.

As soon as he had locked himself in he looked, under the bed, opened all the closets, explored every corner, rummaged through all the furniture. Then he lighted the candles on the mantelpiece, and, turning round several times, ran his eye all over the apartment with an anguish of terror that distorted his face, for he knew well that he would see her, as he did every night—little Louise Roque, the little girl he had attacked and afterward strangled.

Every night the odious vision came back again. First he seemed to hear a kind of roaring sound, such as is made by a threshing machine or the distant passage of a train over a bridge. Then he commenced to gasp, to suffocate, and he had to unbutton his collar and his belt. He moved about to make his blood circulate, he tried to read, he attempted to sing. It was in vain. His thoughts, in spite of himself, went back to the day of the murder and made him begin it all over again in all its most secret details, with all the violent emotions he had experienced from the first minute to the last.

He had felt on rising that morning, the morning of the horrible day, a little dizziness and headache, which he attributed to the heat, so that he remained in his room until breakfast time.

After the meal he had taken a siesta, then, toward the close of the afternoon, he had gone out to breathe the fresh, soothing breeze under the trees in the wood.

But, as soon as he was outside, the heavy, scorching air of the plain oppressed him still more. The sun, still high in the heavens, poured down on the parched soil waves of burning light. Not a breath of wind stirred the leaves. Every beast and bird, even the grasshoppers, were silent. Renardet reached the tall trees and began to walk over the moss where the Brindille produced a slight freshness of the air beneath the immense roof of branches. But he felt ill at ease. It seemed to him that an unknown, invisible hand was strangling him, and he scarcely thought of anything, having usually few ideas in his head. For the last three months only one thought haunted him, the thought of marrying again. He suffered from living alone, suffered from it morally and physically. Accustomed for ten years past to feeling a woman near him, habituated to her presence every moment, he had need, an imperious and perplexing need of such association. Since Madame Renardet's death he had suffered continually without knowing why, he had suffered at not feeling her dress brushing past him, and, above all, from no longer being able to calm and rest himself in her arms. He had been scarcely six months a widower and he was already looking about in the district for some young girl or some widow he might marry when his period of mourning was at an end.

He had a chaste soul, but it was lodged in a powerful, herculean body, and carnal imaginings began to disturb his sleep and his vigils. He drove them away; they came back again; and he murmured from time to time, smiling at himself:

"Here I am, like St. Anthony."

Having this special morning had several of these visions, the desire suddenly came into his breast to bathe in the Brindille in order to refresh himself and cool his blood.

He knew of a large deep pool, a little farther down, where the people of the neighborhood came sometimes to take a dip in summer. He went there.

Thick willow trees hid this clear body of water where the current rested and went to sleep for a while before starting on its way again. Renardet, as he appeared, thought he heard a light sound, a faint plashing which was not that of the stream on the banks. He softly put aside the leaves and looked. A little girl, quite naked in the transparent water, was beating the water with both hands, dancing about in it and dipping herself with pretty movements. She was not a child nor was she yet a woman. She was plump and developed, while preserving an air of youthful precocity, as of one who had grown rapidly. He no longer moved, overcome with surprise, with desire, holding his breath with a strange, poignant emotion. He remained there, his heart beating as if one of his sensuous dreams had just been realized, as if an impure fairy had conjured up before him this young creature, this little rustic Venus, rising from the eddies of the stream as the real Venus rose from the waves of the sea.

Suddenly the little girl came out of the water, and, without seeing him, came over to where he stood, looking for her clothes in order to dress herself. As she approached gingerly, on account of the sharp-pointed stones, he felt himself pushed toward her by an irresistible force, by a bestial transport of passion, which stirred his flesh, bewildered his mind and made him tremble from head to foot.

She remained standing some seconds behind the willow tree which concealed him from view. Then, losing his reason entirely, he pushed aside the branches, rushed on her and seized her in his arms. She fell, too terrified to offer any resistance, too terror-stricken to cry out. He seemed possessed, not understanding what he was doing.

He woke from his crime as one wakes from a nightmare. The child burst out weeping.

"Hold your tongue! Hold your tongue!" he said. "I'll give you money."

But she did not hear him and went on sobbing.

"Come now, hold your tongue! Do hold your tongue! Keep quiet!" he continued.

She kept shrieking as she tried to free herself. He suddenly realized that he was ruined, and he caught her by the neck to stop her mouth from uttering these heartrending, dreadful screams. As she continued to struggle with the desperate strength of a being who is seeking to fly from death, he pressed his enormous hands on the little throat swollen with screaming, and in a few seconds he had strangled her, so furiously did he grip her. He had not intended to kill her, but only to make her keep quiet.

Then he stood up, overwhelmed with horror.

She lay before him, her face bleeding and blackened. He was about to rush away when there sprang up in his agitated soul the mysterious and undefined instinct that guides all beings in the hour of danger.

He was going to throw the body into the water, but another impulse drove him toward the clothes, which he made into a small package. Then, as he had a piece of twine in his pocket, he tied it up and hid it in a deep portion of the stream, beneath the trunk of a tree that overhung the Brindille.

Then he went off at a rapid pace, reached the meadows, took a wide turn in order to show himself to some peasants who dwelt some distance away at the opposite side of the district, and came back to dine at the usual hour, telling his servants all that was supposed to have happened during his walk.

He slept, however, that night; he slept with a heavy, brutish sleep like the sleep of certain persons condemned to death. He did not open his eyes until the first glimmer of dawn, and he waited till his usual hour for riding, so as to excite no suspicion.

Then he had to be present at the inquiry as to the cause of death. He did so like a somnambulist, in a kind of vision which showed him men and things as in a dream, in a cloud of intoxication, with that sense of unreality which perplexes the mind at the time of the greatest catastrophes.

But the agonized cry of Mother Roque pierced his heart. At that moment he had felt inclined to cast himself at the old woman's feet and to exclaim:

"I am the guilty one!"

But he had restrained himself. He went back, however, during the night to fish up the dead girl's wooden shoes, in order to place them on her mother's threshold.

As long as the inquiry lasted, as long as it was necessary to lead justice astray he was calm, master of himself, crafty and smiling. He discussed quietly with the magistrates all the suppositions that passed through their minds, combated their opinions and demolished their arguments. He even took a keen and mournful pleasure in disturbing their investigations, in embroiling their ideas, in showing the innocence of those whom they suspected.

But as soon as the inquiry was abandoned he became gradually nervous, more excitable than he had been before, although he mastered his irritability. Sudden noises made him start with fear; he shuddered at the slightest thing and trembled sometimes from head to foot when a fly alighted on his forehead. Then he was seized with an imperious desire for motion, which impelled him to take long walks and to remain up whole nights pacing up and down his room.

It was not that he was goaded by remorse. His brutal nature did not lend itself to any shade of sentiment or of moral terror. A man of energy and even of violence, born to make war, to ravage conquered countries and to massacre the vanquished, full of the savage instincts of the hunter and the fighter, he scarcely took count of human life. Though he respected the Church outwardly, from policy, he believed neither in God nor the devil, expecting neither chastisement nor recompense for his acts in another life. His sole belief was a vague philosophy drawn from all the ideas of the encyclopedists of the last century, and he regarded religion as a moral sanction of the law, the one and the other having been invented by men to regulate social relations. To kill any one in a duel, or in war, or in a quarrel, or by accident, or for the sake of revenge, or even through bravado would have seemed to him an amusing and clever thing and would not have left more impression on his mind than a shot fired at a hare; but he had experienced a profound emotion at the murder of this child. He had, in the first place, perpetrated it in the heat of an irresistible gust of passion, in a sort of tempest of the senses that had overpowered his reason. And he had cherished in his heart, in his flesh, on his lips, even to the very tips of his murderous fingers a kind of bestial love, as well as a feeling of terrified horror, toward this little girl surprised by him and basely killed. Every moment his thoughts returned to that horrible scene, and, though he endeavored to drive this picture from his mind, though he put it aside with terror, with disgust, he felt it surging through his soul, moving about in him, waiting incessantly for the moment to reappear.

Then, as evening approached, he was afraid of the shadow falling around him. He did not yet know why the darkness seemed frightful to him, but he instinctively feared it, he felt that it was peopled with terrors. The bright daylight did not lend itself to fears. Things and beings were visible then, and only natural things and beings could exhibit themselves in the light of day. But the night, the impenetrable night, thicker than walls and empty; the infinite night, so black, so vast, in which one might brush against frightful things; the night, when one feels that a mysterious terror is wandering, prowling about, appeared to him to conceal an unknown threatening danger, close beside him.

What was it?

He knew ere long. As he sat in his armchair, rather late one evening when he could not sleep, he thought he saw the curtain of his window move. He waited, uneasily, with beating heart. The drapery did not stir; then, all of a sudden, it moved once more. He did not venture to rise; he no longer ventured to breathe, and yet he was brave. He had often fought, and he would have liked to catch thieves in his house.

Was it true that this curtain did move? he asked himself, fearing that his eyes had deceived him. It was, moreover, such a slight thing, a gentle flutter of drapery, a kind of trembling in its folds, less than an undulation caused by the wind.

Renardet sat still, with staring eyes and outstretched neck. He sprang to his feet abruptly, ashamed of his fear, took four steps, seized the drapery with both hands and pulled it wide apart. At first he saw nothing but darkened glass, resembling plates of glittering ink. The night, the vast, impenetrable night, stretched beyond as far as the invisible horizon. He remained standing in front of this illimitable shadow, and suddenly he perceived a light, a moving light, which seemed some distance away.

Then he put his face close to the window pane, thinking that a person looking for crabs might be poaching in the Brindille, for it was past midnight, and this light rose up at the edge of the stream, under the trees. As he was not yet able to see clearly, Renardet placed his hands over his eyes, and suddenly this light became an illumination, and he beheld little Louise Roque naked and bleeding on the moss. He recoiled, frozen with horror, knocked over his chair and fell over on his back. He remained there some minutes in anguish of mind; then he sat up and began to reflect. He had had a hallucination—that was all, a hallucination due to the fact that a night marauder was walking with a lantern in his hand near the water's edge. What was there astonishing, besides, in the circumstance that the recollection of his crime should sometimes bring before him the vision of the dead girl?

He rose from the ground, swallowed a glass of wine and sat down again. He was thinking:

"What am I to do if this occurs again?"

And it would occur; he felt it; he was sure of it. Already his glance was drawn toward the window; it called him; it attracted him. In order to avoid looking at it, he turned his chair round. Then he took a book and tried to read, but it seemed to him that he presently heard something stirring behind him, and he swung round his armchair on one foot.

The curtain was moving again; unquestionably, it moved this time. He could no longer have any doubt about it.

He rushed forward and grasped it so violently that he pulled it down with its pole. Then he eagerly glued his face to the glass. He saw nothing. All was black outside, and he breathed with the joy of a man whose life has just been saved.

Then he went back to his chair and sat down again, but almost immediately he felt a longing to look out once more through the window. Since the curtain had fallen down, the window made a sort of gap, fascinating and terrible, on the dark landscape. In order not to yield to this dangerous temptation, he undressed, blew out the light and closed his eyes.

Lying on his back motionless, his skin warm and moist, he awaited sleep. Suddenly a great gleam of light flashed across his eyelids. He opened them, believing that his dwelling was on fire. All was black as before, and he leaned on his elbow to try to distinguish the window which had still for him an unconquerable attraction. By dint of, straining his eyes he could perceive some stars, and he rose, groped his way across the room, discovered the panes with his outstretched hands, and placed his forehead close to them. There below, under the trees, lay the body of the little girl gleaming like phosphorus, lighting up the surrounding darkness.

Renardet uttered a cry and rushed toward his bed, where he lay till morning, his head hidden under the pillow.

From that moment his life became intolerable. He passed his days in apprehension of each succeeding night, and each night the vision came back again. As soon as he had locked himself up in his room he strove to resist it, but in vain. An irresistible force lifted him up and pushed him against the window, as if to call the phantom, and he saw it at once, lying first in the spot where the crime was committed in the position in which it had been found.

Then the dead girl rose up and came toward him with little steps just as the child had done when she came out of the river. She advanced quietly, passing straight across the grass and over the bed of withered flowers. Then she rose up in the air toward Renardet's window. She came toward him as she had come on the day of the crime. And the man recoiled before the apparition—he retreated to his bed and sank down upon it, knowing well that the little one had entered the room and that she now was standing behind the curtain, which presently moved. And until daybreak he kept staring at this curtain with a fixed glance, ever waiting to see his victim depart.

But she did not show herself any more; she remained there behind the curtain, which quivered tremulously now and then.

And Renardet, his fingers clutching the clothes, squeezed them as he had squeezed the throat of little Louise Roque.

He heard the clock striking the hours, and in the stillness the pendulum kept ticking in time with the loud beating of his heart. And he suffered, the wretched man, more than any man had ever suffered before.

Then, as soon as a white streak of light on the ceiling announced the approaching day, he felt himself free, alone at last, alone in his room; and he went to sleep. He slept several hours—a restless, feverish sleep in which he retraced in dreams the horrible vision of the past night.

When he went down to the late breakfast he felt exhausted as after unusual exertion, and he scarcely ate anything, still haunted as he was by the fear of what he had seen the night before.

He knew well, however, that it was not an apparition, that the dead do not come back, and that his sick soul, his soul possessed by one thought alone, by an indelible remembrance, was the only cause of his torture, was what brought the dead girl back to life and raised her form before his eyes, on which it was ineffaceably imprinted. But he knew, too, that there was no cure, that he would never escape from the savage persecution of his memory, and he resolved to die rather than to endure these tortures any longer.

Then he thought of how he would kill himself, It must be something simple and natural, which would preclude the idea of suicide. For he clung to his reputation, to the name bequeathed to him by his ancestors; and if his death awakened any suspicion people's thoughts might be, perhaps, directed toward the mysterious crime, toward the murderer who could not be found, and they would not hesitate to accuse him of the crime.

A strange idea came into his head, that of allowing himself to be crushed by the tree at the foot of which he had assassinated little Louise Roque. So he determined to have the wood cut down and to simulate an accident. But the beech tree refused to crush his ribs.

Returning to his house, a prey to utter despair, he had snatched up his revolver, and then did not dare to fire it.

The dinner bell summoned him. He could eat nothing, and he went upstairs again. And he did not know what to do. Now that he had escaped the first time, he felt himself a coward. Presently he would be ready, brave, decided, master of his courage and of his resolution; now he was weak and feared death as much as he did the dead girl.

He faltered:

"I dare not venture it again—I dare not venture it."

Then he glanced with terror, first at the revolver on the table and next at the curtain which hid his window. It seemed to him, moreover, that something horrible would occur as soon as his life was ended. Something? What? A meeting with her, perhaps. She was watching for him; she was waiting for him; she was calling him; and it was in order to seize him in her turn, to draw him toward the doom that would avenge her, and to lead him to die, that she appeared thus every night.

He began to cry like a child, repeating:

"I will not venture it again—I will not venture it."

Then he fell on his knees and murmured:

"My God! my God!" without believing, nevertheless, in God. And he no longer dared, in fact, to look at his window, where he knew the apparition was hiding, nor at his table, where his revolver gleamed. When he had risen up he said:

"This cannot last; there must be an end of it"

The sound of his voice in the silent room made a chill of fear pass through his limbs, but as he could not bring himself to come to a determination, as he felt certain that his finger would always refuse to pull the trigger of his revolver, he turned round to hide his head under the bedclothes and began to reflect.

He would have to find some way in which he could force himself to die, to play some trick on himself which would not permit of any hesitation on his part, any delay, any possible regrets. He envied condemned criminals who are led to the scaffold surrounded by soldiers. Oh! if he could only beg of some one to shoot him; if after confessing his crime to a true friend who would never divulge it he could procure death at his hand. But from whom could he ask this terrible service? From whom? He thought of all the people he knew. The doctor? No, he would talk about it afterward, most probably. And suddenly a fantastic idea entered his mind. He would write to the magistrate, who was on terms of close friendship with him, and would denounce himself as the perpetrator of the crime. He would in this letter confess everything, revealing how his soul had been tortured, how he had resolved to die, how he had hesitated about carrying out his resolution and what means he had employed to strengthen his failing courage. And in the name of their old friendship he would implore of the other to destroy the letter as soon as he had ascertained that the culprit had inflicted justice on himself. Renardet could rely on this magistrate; he knew him to be true, discreet, incapable of even an idle word. He was one of those men who have an inflexible conscience, governed, directed, regulated by their reason alone.

Scarcely had he formed this project when a strange feeling of joy took possession of his heart. He was calm now. He would write his letter slowly, then at daybreak he would deposit it in the box nailed to the outside wall of his office; then he would ascend his tower to watch for the postman's arrival; and when the man in the blue blouse had gone away, he would cast himself head foremost on the rocks on which the foundations rested, He would take care to be seen first by the workmen who had cut down his wood. He could climb to the projecting stone which bore the flagstaff displayed on festivals, He would smash this pole with a shake and carry it along with him as he fell.

Who would suspect that it was not an accident? And he would be killed outright, owing to his weight and the height of the tower.

Presently he got out of bed, went over to the table and began to write. He omitted nothing, not a single detail of the crime, not a single detail of the torments of his heart, and he ended by announcing that he had passed sentence on himself, that he was going to execute the criminal, and begged his friend, his old friend, to be careful that there should never be any stain on his memory.

When he had finished this letter he saw that the day had dawned.

He closed, sealed it and wrote the address. Then he descended with light steps, hurried toward the little white box fastened to the outside wall in the corner of the farmhouse, and when he had thrown into it this letter, which made his hand tremble, he came back quickly, drew the bolts of the great door and climbed up to his tower to wait for the passing of the postman, who was to bear away his death sentence.

He felt self-possessed now. Liberated! Saved!

A cold dry wind, an icy wind passed across his face. He inhaled it eagerly with open mouth, drinking in its chilling kiss. The sky was red, a wintry red, and all the plain, whitened with frost, glistened under the first rays of the sun, as if it were covered with powdered glass.

Renardet, standing up, his head bare, gazed at the vast tract of country before him, the meadows to the left and to the right the village whose chimneys were beginning to smoke in preparation for the morning meal. At his feet he saw the Brindille flowing amid the rocks, where he would soon be crushed to death. He felt new life on that beautiful frosty morning. The light bathed him, entered his being like a new-born hope. A thousand recollections assailed him, recollections of similar mornings, of rapid walks on the hard earth which rang beneath his footsteps, of happy days of shooting on the edges of pools where wild ducks sleep. All the good things that he loved, the good things of existence, rushed to his memory, penetrated him with fresh desires, awakened all the vigorous appetites of his active, powerful body.

And he was about to die! Why? He was going to kill himself stupidly because he was afraid of a shadow-afraid of nothing! He was still rich and in the prime of life. What folly! All he needed was distraction, absence, a voyage in order to forget.

This night even he had not seen the little girl because his mind was preoccupied and had wandered toward some other subject. Perhaps he would not see her any more? And even if she still haunted him in this house, certainly she would not follow him elsewhere! The earth was wide, the future was long.

Why should he die?

His glance travelled across the meadows, and he perceived a blue spot in the path which wound alongside the Brindille. It was Mederic coming to bring letters from the town and to carry away those of the village.

Renardet gave a start, a sensation of pain shot through his breast, and he rushed down the winding staircase to get back his letter, to demand it back from the postman. Little did it matter to him now whether he was seen, He hurried across the grass damp from the light frost of the previous night and arrived in front of the box in the corner of the farmhouse exactly at the same time as the letter carrier.

The latter had opened the little wooden door and drew forth the four papers deposited there by the inhabitants of the locality.

Renardet said to him:

"Good-morrow, Mederic."

"Good-morrow, Monsieur le Maire."

"I say, Mederic, I threw a letter into the box that I want back again. I came to ask you to give it back to me."

"That's all right, Monsieur le Maire—you'll get it."

And the postman raised his eyes. He stood petrified at the sight of Renardet's face. The mayor's cheeks were purple, his eyes were anxious and sunken, with black circles round them, his hair was unbrushed, his beard untrimmed, his necktie unfastened. It was evident that he had not been in bed.

The postman asked:

"Are you ill, Monsieur le Maire?"

The other, suddenly comprehending that his appearance must be unusual, lost countenance and faltered:

"Oh! no-oh! no. Only I jumped out of bed to ask you for this letter. I was asleep. You understand?"

He said in reply:

"What letter?"

"The one you are going to give back to me."

Mederic now began to hesitate. The mayor's attitude did not strike him as natural. There was perhaps a secret in that letter, a political secret. He knew Renardet was not a Republican, and he knew all the tricks and chicanery employed at elections.

He asked:

"To whom is it addressed, this letter of yours?"

"To Monsieur Putoin, the magistrate—you know, my friend, Monsieur Putoin!"

The postman searched through the papers and found the one asked for. Then he began looking at it, turning it round and round between his fingers, much perplexed, much troubled by the fear of either committing a grave offence or of making an enemy of the mayor.

Seeing his hesitation, Renardet made a movement for the purpose of seizing the letter and snatching it away from him. This abrupt action convinced Mederic that some important secret was at stake and made him resolve to do his duty, cost what it may.

So he flung the letter into his bag and fastened it up, with the reply:

"No, I can't, Monsieur le Maire. As long as it is for the magistrate, I can't."

A dreadful pang wrung Renardet's heart and he murmured:

"Why, you know me well. You are even able to recognize my handwriting. I tell you I want that paper."

"I can't."

"Look here, Mederic, you know that I'm incapable of deceiving you—I tell you I want it."

"No, I can't."

A tremor of rage passed through Renardet's soul.

"Damn it all, take care! You know that I never trifle and that I could get you out of your job, my good fellow, and without much delay, either, And then, I am the mayor of the district, after all; and I now order you to give me back that paper."

The postman answered firmly:

"No, I can't, Monsieur le Maire."

Thereupon Renardet, losing his head, caught hold of the postman's arms in order to take away his bag; but, freeing himself by a strong effort, and springing backward, the letter carrier raised his big holly stick. Without losing his temper, he said emphatically:

"Don't touch me, Monsieur le Maire, or I'll strike. Take care, I'm only doing my duty!"

Feeling that he was lost, Renardet suddenly became humble, gentle, appealing to him like a whimpering child:

"Look here, look here, my friend, give me back that letter and I'll recompense you—I'll give you money. Stop! stop! I'll give you a hundred francs, you understand—a hundred francs!"

The postman turned on his heel and started on his journey.

Renardet followed him, out of breath, stammering:

"Mederic, Mederic, listen! I'll give you a thousand francs, you understand—a thousand francs."

The postman still went on without giving any answer.

Renardet went on:

"I'll make your fortune, you understand—whatever you wish—fifty thousand francs—fifty thousand francs for that letter! What does it matter to you? You won't? Well, a hundred thousand—I say—a hundred thousand francs. Do you understand? A hundred thousand francs—a hundred thousand francs."

The postman turned back, his face hard, his eye severe:

"Enough of this, or else I'll repeat to the magistrate everything you have just said to me."

Renardet stopped abruptly. It was all over. He turned back and rushed toward his house, running like a hunted animal.

Then, in his turn, Mederic stopped and watched his flight with stupefaction. He saw the mayor reenter his house, and he waited still, as if something astonishing were about to happen.

In fact, presently the tall form of Renardet appeared on the summit of the Fox's tower. He ran round the platform like a madman. Then he seized the flagstaff and shook it furiously without succeeding in breaking it; then, all of a sudden, like a diver, with his two hands before him, he plunged into space.

Mederic rushed forward to his assistance. He saw the woodcutters going to work and called out to them, telling them an accident had occurred. At the foot of the walls they found a bleeding body, its head crushed on a rock. The Brindille surrounded this rock, and over its clear, calm waters could be seen a long red thread of mingled brains and blood.

THE DONKEY

There was not a breath of air stirring; a heavy mist was lying over the river. It was like a layer of cotton placed on the water. The banks themselves were indistinct, hidden behind strange fogs. But day was breaking and the hill was becoming visible. In the dawning light of day the plaster houses began to appear like white spots. Cocks were crowing in the barnyard.

On the other side of the river, hidden behind the fogs, just opposite Frette, a slight noise from time to time broke the dead silence of the quiet morning. At times it was an indistinct plashing, like the cautious advance of a boat, then again a sharp noise like the rattle of an oar and then the sound of something dropping in the water. Then silence.

Sometimes whispered words, coming perhaps from a distance, perhaps from quite near, pierced through these opaque mists. They passed by like wild birds which have slept in the rushes and which fly away at the first light of day, crossing the mist and uttering a low and timid sound which wakes their brothers along the shores.

Suddenly along the bank, near the village, a barely perceptible shadow appeared on the water. Then it grew, became more distinct and, coming out of the foggy curtain which hung over the river, a flatboat, manned by two men, pushed up on the grass.

The one who was rowing rose and took a pailful of fish from the bottom of the boat, then he threw the dripping net over his shoulder. His companion, who had not made a motion, exclaimed: "Say, Mailloche, get your gun and see if we can't land some rabbit along the shore."

The other one answered: "All right. I'll be with you in a minute." Then he disappeared, in order to hide their catch.

The man who had stayed in the boat slowly filled his pipe and lighted it. His name was Labouise, but he was called Chicot, and was in partnership with Maillochon, commonly called Mailloche, to practice the doubtful and undefined profession of junk-gatherers along the shore.

They were a low order of sailors and they navigated regularly only in the months of famine. The rest of the time they acted as junk-gatherers. Rowing about on the river day and night, watching for any prey, dead or alive, poachers on the water and nocturnal hunters, sometimes ambushing venison in the Saint-Germain forests, sometimes looking for drowned people and searching their clothes, picking up floating rags and empty bottles; thus did Labouise and Maillochon live easily.

At times they would set out on foot about noon and stroll along straight ahead. They would dine in some inn on the shore and leave again side by side. They would remain away for a couple of days; then one morning they would be seen rowing about in the tub which they called their boat.

At Joinville or at Nogent some boatman would be looking for his boat, which had disappeared one night, probably stolen, while twenty or thirty miles from there, on the Oise, some shopkeeper would be rubbing his hands, congratulating himself on the bargain he had made when he bought a boat the day before for fifty francs, which two men offered him as they were passing.

Maillochon reappeared with his gun wrapped up in rags. He was a man of forty or fifty, tall and thin, with the restless eye of people who are worried by legitimate troubles and of hunted animals. His open shirt showed his hairy chest, but he seemed never to have had any more hair on his face than a short brush of a mustache and a few stiff hairs under his lower lip. He was bald around the temples. When he took off the dirty cap that he wore his scalp seemed to be covered with a fluffy down, like the body of a plucked chicken.

Chicot, on the contrary, was red, fat, short and hairy. He looked like a raw beefsteak. He continually kept his left eye closed, as if he were aiming at something or at somebody, and when people jokingly cried to him, "Open your eye, Labouise!" he would answer quietly: "Never fear, sister, I open it when there's cause to."

He had a habit of calling every one "sister," even his scavenger companion.

He took up the oars again, and once more the boat disappeared in the heavy mist, which was now turned snowy white in the pink-tinted sky.

"What kind of lead did you take, Maillochon?" Labouise asked.

"Very small, number nine; that's the best for rabbits."

They were approaching the other shore so slowly, so quietly that no noise betrayed them. This bank belongs to the Saint-Germain forest and is the boundary line for rabbit hunting. It is covered with burrows hidden under the roots of trees, and the creatures at daybreak frisk about, running in and out of the holes.

Maillochon was kneeling in the bow, watching, his gun hidden on the floor. Suddenly he seized it, aimed, and the report echoed for some time throughout the quiet country.

Labouise, in a few strokes, touched the beach, and his companion, jumping to the ground, picked up a little gray rabbit, not yet dead.

Then the boat once more disappeared into the fog in order to get to the other side, where it could keep away from the game wardens.

The two men seemed to be riding easily on the water. The weapon had disappeared under the board which served as a hiding place and the rabbit was stuffed into Chicot's loose shirt.

After about a quarter of an hour Labouise asked: "Well, sister, shall we get one more?"

"It will suit me," Maillochon answered.

The boat started swiftly down the current. The mist, which was hiding both shores, was beginning to rise. The trees could be barely perceived, as through a veil, and the little clouds of fog were floating up from the water. When they drew near the island, the end of which is opposite Herblay, the two men slackened their pace and began to watch. Soon a second rabbit was killed.

Then they went down until they were half way to Conflans. Here they stopped their boat, tied it to a tree and went to sleep in the bottom of it.

From time to time Labouise would sit up and look over the horizon with his open eye. The last of the morning mist had disappeared and the large summer sun was climbing in the blue sky.

On the other side of the river the vineyard-covered hill stretched out in a semicircle. One house stood out alone at the summit. Everything was silent.

Something was moving slowly along the tow-path, advancing with difficulty. It was a woman dragging a donkey. The stubborn, stiff-jointed beast occasionally stretched out a leg in answer to its companion's efforts, and it proceeded thus, with outstretched neck and ears lying flat, so slowly that one could not tell when it would ever be out of sight.

The woman, bent double, was pulling, turning round occasionally to strike the donkey with a stick.

As soon as he saw her, Labouise exclaimed: "Say, Mailloche!"

Mailloche answered: "What's the matter?"

"Want to have some fun?"

"Of course!"

"Then hurry, sister; we're going to have a laugh."

Chicot took the oars. When he had crossed the river he stopped opposite the woman and called:

"Hey, sister!"

The woman stopped dragging her donkey and looked.

Labouise continued: "What are you doing—going to the locomotive show?"

The woman made no reply. Chicot continued:

"Say, your trotter's prime for a race. Where are you taking him at that speed?"

At last the woman answered: "I'm going to Macquart, at Champioux, to have him killed. He's worthless."

Labouise answered: "You're right. How much do you think Macquart will give you for him?"

The woman wiped her forehead on the back of her hand and hesitated, saying: "How do I know? Perhaps three francs, perhaps four."

Chicot exclaimed: "I'll give you five francs and your errand's done! How's that?"

The woman considered the matter for a second and then exclaimed: "Done!"

The two men landed. Labouise grasped the animal by the bridle. Maillochon asked in surprise:

"What do you expect to do with that carcass?"

Chicot this time opened his other eye in order to express his gaiety. His whole red face was grinning with joy. He chuckled: "Don't worry, sister. I've got my idea."

He gave five francs to the woman, who then sat down by the road to see what was going to happen. Then Labouise, in great humor, got the gun and held it out to Maillochon, saying: "Each one in turn; we're going after big game, sister. Don't get so near or you'll kill it right away! You must make the pleasure last a little."

He placed his companion about forty paces from the victim. The ass, feeling itself free, was trying to get a little of the tall grass, but it was so exhausted that it swayed on its legs as if it were about to fall.

Maillochon aimed slowly and said: "A little pepper for the ears; watch, Ghicot!" And he fired.

The tiny shot struck the donkey's long ears and he began to shake them in order to get rid of the stinging sensation. The two men were doubled up with laughter and stamped their feet with joy. The woman, indignant, rushed forward; she did not want her donkey to be tortured, and she offered to return the five francs. Labouise threatened her with a thrashing and pretended to roll up his sleeves. He had paid, hadn't he? Well, then, he would take a shot at her skirts, just to show that it didn't hurt. She went away, threatening to call the police. They could hear her protesting indignantly and cursing as she went her way.

Maillochon held out the gun to his comrade, saying: "It's your turn, Chicot."

Labouise aimed and fired. The donkey received the charge in his thighs, but the shot was so small and came from such a distance that he thought he was being stung by flies, for he began to thrash himself with his tail.

Labouise sat down to laugh more comfortably, while Maillochon reloaded the weapon, so happy that he seemed to sneeze into the barrel. He stepped forward a few paces, and, aiming at the same place that his friend had shot at, he fired again. This time the beast started, tried to kick and turned its head. At last a little blood was running. It had been wounded and felt a sharp pain, for it tried to run away with a slow, limping, jerky gallop.

Both men darted after the beast, Maillochon with a long stride, Labouise with the short, breathless trot of a little man. But the donkey, tired out, had stopped, and, with a bewildered look, was watching his two murderers approach. Suddenly he stretched his neck and began to bray.

Labouise, out of breath, had taken the gun. This time he walked right up close, as he did not wish to begin the chase over again.

When the poor beast had finished its mournful cry, like a last call for help, the man called: "Hey, Mailloche! Come here, sister; I'm going to give him some medicine." And while the other man was forcing the animal's mouth open, Chicot stuck the barrel of his gun down its throat, as if he were trying to make it drink a potion. Then he said: "Look out, sister, here she goes!"

He pressed the trigger. The donkey stumbled back a few steps, fell down, tried to get up again and finally lay on its side and closed its eyes: The whole body was trembling, its legs were kicking as if it were, trying to run. A stream of blood was oozing through its teeth. Soon it stopped moving. It was dead.

The two men went along, laughing. It was over too quickly; they had not had their money's worth. Maillochon asked: "Well, what are we going to do now?"

Labouise answered: "Don't worry, sister. Get the thing on the boat; we're going to have some fun when night comes."

They went and got the boat. The animal's body was placed on the bottom, covered with fresh grass, and the two men stretched out on it and went to sleep.

Toward noon Labouise drew a bottle of wine, some bread and butter and raw onions from a hiding place in their muddy, worm-eaten boat, and they began to eat.

When the meal was over they once more stretched out on the dead donkey and slept. At nightfall Labouise awoke and shook his comrade, who was snoring like a buzzsaw. "Come on, sister," he ordered.

Maillochon began to row. As they had plenty of time they went up the Seine slowly. They coasted along the reaches covered with water-lilies, and the heavy, mud-covered boat slipped over the lily pads and bent the flowers, which stood up again as soon as they had passed.

When they reached the wall of the Eperon, which separates the Saint-Germain forest from the Maisons-Laffitte Park, Labouise stopped his companion and explained his idea to him. Maillochon was moved by a prolonged, silent laugh.

They threw into the water the grass which had covered the body, took the animal by the feet and hid it behind some bushes. Then they got into their boat again and went to Maisons-Laffitte.

The night was perfectly black when they reached the wine shop of old man Jules. As soon as the dealer saw them he came up, shook hands with them and sat down at their table. They began to talk of one thing and another. By eleven o'clock the last customer had left and old man Jules winked at Labouise and asked: "Well, have you got any?"

Labouise made a motion with his head and answered: "Perhaps so, perhaps not!"

The dealer insisted: "Perhaps you've not nothing but gray ones?"

Chicot dug his hands into his flannel shirt, drew out the ears of a rabbit and declared: "Three francs a pair!"

Then began a long discussion about the price. Two francs sixty-five and the two rabbits were delivered. As the two men were getting up to go, old man Jules, who had been watching them, exclaimed:

"You have something else, but you won't say what."

Labouise answered: "Possibly, but it is not for you; you're too stingy."

The man, growing eager, kept asking: "What is it? Something big? Perhaps we might make a deal."

Labouise, who seemed perplexed, pretended to consult Maillochon with a glance. Then he answered in a slow voice: "This is how it is. We were in the bushes at Eperon when something passed right near us, to the left, at the end of the wall. Mailloche takes a shot and it drops. We skipped on account of the game people. I can't tell you what it is, because I don't know. But it's big enough. But what is it? If I told you I'd be lying, and you know, sister, between us everything's above-board."

Anxiously the man asked: "Think it's venison?"

Labouise answered: "Might be and then again it might not! Venison?—uh! uh!—might be a little big for that! Mind you, I don't say it's a doe, because I don't know, but it might be."

Still the dealer insisted: "Perhaps it's a buck?"

Labouise stretched out his hand, exclaiming: "No, it's not that! It's not a buck. I should have seen the horns. No, it's not a buck!"

"Why didn't you bring it with you?" asked the man.

"Because, sister, from now on I sell from where I stand. Plenty of people will buy. All you have to do is to take a walk over there, find the thing and take it. No risk for me."

The innkeeper, growing suspicious, exclaimed "Supposing he wasn't there!"

Labouise once more raised his hand and said:

"He's there, I swear!—first bush to the left. What it is, I don't know. But it's not a buck, I'm positive. It's for you to find out what it is. Twenty-five francs, cash down!"

Still the man hesitated: "Couldn't you bring it?"

Maillochon exclaimed: "No, indeed! You know our price! Take it or leave it!"

The dealer decided: "It's a bargain for twenty francs!"

And they shook hands over the deal.

Then he took out four big five-franc pieces from the cash drawer, and the two friends pocketed the money. Labouise arose, emptied his glass and left. As he was disappearing in the shadows he turned round to exclaim: "It isn't a buck. I don't know what it is!—but it's there. I'll give you back your money if you find nothing!"

And he disappeared in the darkness. Maillochon, who was following him, kept punching him in the back to express his joy.

MOIRON

As we were still talking about Pranzini, M. Maloureau, who had been attorney general under the Empire, said: "Oh! I formerly knew a very curious affair, curious for several reasons, as you will see.

"I was at that time imperial attorney in one of the provinces. I had to take up the case which has remained famous under the name of the Moiron case.

"Monsieur Moiron, who was a teacher in the north of France, enjoyed an excellent reputation throughout the whole country. He was a person of intelligence, quiet, very religious, a little taciturn; he had married in the district of Boislinot, where he exercised his profession. He had had three children, who had died of consumption, one after the other. From this time he seemed to bestow upon the youngsters confided to his care all the tenderness of his heart. With his own money he bought toys for his best scholars and for the good boys; he gave them little dinners and stuffed them with delicacies, candy and cakes: Everybody loved this good man with his big heart, when suddenly five of his pupils died, in a strange manner, one after the other. It was supposed that there was an epidemic due to the condition of the water, resulting from drought; they looked for the causes without being able to discover them, the more so that the symptoms were so peculiar. The children seemed to be attacked by a feeling of lassitude; they would not eat, they complained of pains in their stomachs, dragged along for a short time, and died in frightful suffering.

"A post-mortem examination was held over the last one, but nothing was discovered. The vitals were sent to Paris and analyzed, and they revealed the presence of no toxic substance.

"For a year nothing new developed; then two little boys, the best scholars in the class, Moiron's favorites, died within four days of each other. An examination of the bodies was again ordered, and in both of them were discovered tiny fragments of crushed glass. The conclusion arrived at was that the two youngsters must imprudently have eaten from some carelessly cleaned receptacle. A glass broken over a pail of milk could have produced this frightful accident, and the affair would have been pushed no further if Moiron's servant had not been taken sick at this time. The physician who was called in noticed the same symptoms he had seen in the children. He questioned her and obtained the admission that she had stolen and eaten some candies that had been bought by the teacher for his scholars.

"On an order from the court the schoolhouse was searched, and a closet was found which was full of toys and dainties destined for the children. Almost all these delicacies contained bits of crushed glass or pieces of broken needles!

"Moiron was immediately arrested; but he seemed so astonished and indignant at the suspicion hanging over him that he was almost released. How ever, indications of his guilt kept appearing, and baffled in my mind my first conviction, based on his excellent reputation, on his whole life, on the complete absence of any motive for such a crime.

"Why should this good, simple, religious man have killed little children, and the very children whom he seemed to love the most, whom he spoiled and stuffed with sweet things, for whom he spent half his salary in buying toys and bonbons?

"One must consider him insane to believe him guilty of this act. Now, Moiron seemed so normal, so quiet, so rational and sensible that it seemed impossible to adjudge him insane.

"However, the proofs kept growing! In none of the candies that were bought at the places where the schoolmaster secured his provisions could the slightest trace of anything suspicious be found.

"He then insisted that an unknown enemy must have opened his cupboard with a false key in order to introduce the glass and the needles into the eatables. And he made up a whole story of an inheritance dependent on the death of a child, determined on and sought by some peasant, and promoted thus by casting suspicions on the schoolmaster. This brute, he claimed, did not care about the other children who were forced to die as well.

"The story was possible. The man appeared to be so sure of himself and in such despair that we should undoubtedly have acquitted him, notwithstanding the charges against him, if two crushing discoveries had not been made, one after the other.

"The first one was a snuffbox full of crushed glass; his own snuffbox, hidden in the desk where he kept his money!

"He explained this new find in an acceptable manner, as the ruse of the real unknown criminal. But a mercer from Saint-Marlouf came to the presiding judge and said that a gentleman had several times come to his store to buy some needles; and he always asked for the thinnest needles he could find, and would break them to see whether they pleased him. The man was brought forward in the presence of a dozen or more persons, and immediately recognized Moiron. The inquest revealed that the schoolmaster had indeed gone into Saint-Marlouf on the days mentioned by the tradesman.

"I will pass over the terrible testimony of children on the choice of dainties and the care which he took to have them eat the things in his presence, and to remove the slightest traces.

"Public indignation demanded capital punishment, and it became more and more insistent, overturning all objections.

"Moiron was condemned to death, and his appeal was rejected. Nothing was left for him but the imperial pardon. I knew through my father that the emperor would not grant it.

"One morning, as I was working in my study, the visit of the prison almoner was announced. He was an old priest who knew men well and understood the habits of criminals. He seemed troubled, ill at ease, nervous. After talking for a few minutes about one thing and another, he arose and said suddenly: 'If Moiron is executed, monsieur, you will have put an innocent man to death.'

"Then he left without bowing, leaving me behind with the deep impression made by his words. He had pronounced them in such a sincere and solemn manner, opening those lips, closed and sealed by the secret of confession, in order to save a life.

"An hour later I left for Paris, and my father immediately asked that I be granted an audience with the emperor.

"The following day I was received. His majesty was working in a little reception room when we were introduced. I described the whole case, and I was just telling about the priest's visit when a door opened behind the sovereign's chair and the empress, who supposed he was alone, appeared. His majesty, Napoleon, consulted her. As soon as she had heard the matter, she exclaimed: 'This man must be pardoned. He must, since he is innocent.'

"Why did this sudden conviction of a religious woman cast a terrible doubt in my mind?

"Until then I had ardently desired a change of sentence. And now I suddenly felt myself the toy, the dupe of a cunning criminal who had employed the priest and confession as a last means of defence.

"I explained my hesitancy to their majesties. The emperor remained undecided, urged on one side by his natural kindness and held back on the other by the fear of being deceived by a criminal; but the empress, who was convinced that the priest had obeyed a divine inspiration, kept repeating: 'Never mind! It is better to spare a criminal than to kill an innocent man!' Her advice was taken. The death sentence was commuted to one of hard labor.

"A few years later I heard that Moiron had again been called to the emperor's attention on account of his exemplary conduct in the prison at Toulon and was now employed as a servant by the director of the penitentiary.

"For a long time I heard nothing more of this man. But about two years ago, while I was spending a summer near Lille with my cousin, De Larielle, I was informed one evening, just as we were sitting down to dinner, that a young priest wished to speak to me.

"I had him shown in and he begged me to come to a dying man who desired absolutely to see me. This had often happened to me in my long career as a magistrate, and, although I had been set aside by the Republic, I was still often called upon in similar circumstances. I therefore followed the priest, who led me to a miserable little room in a large tenement house.

"There I found a strange-looking man on a bed of straw, sitting with his back against the wall, in order to get his breath. He was a sort of skeleton, with dark, gleaming eyes.

"As soon as he saw me, he murmured: 'Don't you recognize me?'

"'No.'

"'I am Moiron.'

"I felt a shiver run through me, and I asked 'The schoolmaster?'

"'Yes.'

"'How do you happen to be here?'

"'The story is too long. I haven't time to tell it. I was going to die —and that priest was brought to me—and as I knew that you were here I sent for you. It is to you that I wish to confess—since you were the one who once saved my life.'

"His hands clutched the straw of his bed through the sheet and he continued in a hoarse, forcible and low tone: 'You see—I owe you the truth—I owe it to you—for it must be told to some one before I leave this earth.

"'It is I who killed the children—all of them. I did it—for revenge!

"'Listen. I was an honest, straightforward, pure man—adoring God—this good Father—this Master who teaches us to love, and not the false God, the executioner, the robber, the murderer who governs the earth. I had never done any harm; I had never committed an evil act. I was as good as it is possible to be, monsieur.

"'I married and had children, and I loved them as no father or mother ever loved their children. I lived only for them. I was wild about them. All three of them died! Why? why? What had I done? I was rebellious, furious; and suddenly my eyes were opened as if I were waking up out of a sleep. I understood that God is bad. Why had He killed my children? I opened my eyes and saw that He loves to kill. He loves only that, monsieur. He gives life but to destroy it! God, monsieur, is a murderer! He needs death every day. And He makes it of every variety, in order the better to be amused. He has invented sickness and accidents in order to give Him diversion all through the months and the years; and when He grows tired of this, He has epidemics, the plague, cholera, diphtheria, smallpox, everything possible! But this does not satisfy Him; all these things are too similar; and so from time to time He has wars, in order to see two hundred thousand soldiers killed at once, crushed in blood and in the mud, blown apart, their arms and legs torn off, their heads smashed by bullets, like eggs that fall on the ground.

"'But this is not all. He has made men who eat each other. And then, as men become better than He, He has made beasts, in order to see men hunt them, kill them and eat them. That is not all. He has made tiny little animals which live one day, flies who die by the millions in one hour, ants which we are continually crushing under our feet, and so many, many others that we cannot even imagine. And all these things are continually killing each other and dying. And the good Lord looks on and is amused, for He sees everything, the big ones as well as the little ones, those who are in the drops of water and those in the other firmaments. He watches them and is amused. Wretch!

"'Then, monsieur, I began to kill children played a trick on Him. He did not get those. It was not He, but I! And I would have killed many others, but you caught me. There!

"'I was to be executed. I! How He would have laughed! Then I asked for a priest, and I lied. I confessed to him. I lied and I lived.

"'Now, all is over. I can no longer escape from Him. I no longer fear Him, monsieur; I despise Him too much.'

"This poor wretch was frightful to see as he lay there gasping, opening an enormous mouth in order to utter words which could scarcely be heard, his breath rattling, picking at his bed and moving his thin legs under a grimy sheet as though trying to escape.

"Oh! The mere remembrance of it is frightful!

"'You have nothing more to say?' I asked.

"'No, monsieur.'

"'Then, farewell.'

"'Farewell, monsieur, till some day——'

"I turned to the ashen-faced priest, whose dark outline stood out against the wall, and asked: 'Are you going to stay here, Monsieur l'Abbe?'

"'Yes.'

"Then the dying man sneered: 'Yes, yes, He sends His vultures to the corpses.'

"I had had enough of this. I opened the door and ran away."

THE DISPENSER OF HOLY WATER

We lived formerly in a little house beside the high road outside the village. He had set up in business as a wheelwright, after marrying the daughter of a farmer of the neighborhood, and as they were both industrious, they managed to save up a nice little fortune. But they had no children, and this caused them great sorrow. Finally a son was born, whom they named Jean. They both loved and petted him, enfolding him with their affection, and were unwilling to let him be out of their sight.

When he was five years old some mountebanks passed through the country and set up their tent in the town hall square.

Jean, who had seen them pass by, made his escape from the house, and after his father had made a long search for him, he found him among the learned goats and trick dogs, uttering shouts of laughter and sitting on the knees of an old clown.

Three days later, just as they were sitting down to dinner, the wheelwright and his wife noticed that their son was not in the house. They looked for him in the garden, and as they did not find him, his father went out into the road and shouted at the top of his voice, "Jean!"

Night came on. A brown vapor arose making distant objects look still farther away and giving them a dismal, weird appearance. Three tall pines, close at hand, seemed to be weeping. Still there was no reply, but the air appeared to be full of indistinct sighing. The father listened for some time, thinking he heard a sound first in one direction, then in another, and, almost beside himself, he ran, out into the night, calling incessantly "Jean! Jean!"

He ran along thus until daybreak, filling the, darkness with his shouts, terrifying stray animals, torn by a terrible anguish and fearing that he was losing his mind. His wife, seated on the stone step of their home, sobbed until morning.

They did not find their son. They both aged rapidly in their inconsolable sorrow. Finally they sold their house and set out to search together.

They inquired of the shepherds on the hillsides, of the tradesmen passing by, of the peasants in the villages and of the authorities in the towns. But their boy had been lost a long time and no one knew anything about him. He had probably forgotten his own name by this time and also the name of his village, and his parents wept in silence, having lost hope.

Before long their money came to an end, and they worked out by the day in the farms and inns, doing the most menial work, eating what was left from the tables, sleeping on the ground and suffering from cold. Then as they became enfeebled by hard work no one would employ them any longer, and they were forced to beg along the high roads. They accosted passers-by in an entreating voice and with sad, discouraged faces; they begged a morsel of bread from the harvesters who were dining around a tree in the fields at noon, and they ate in silence seated on the edge of a ditch. An innkeeper to whom they told their story said to them one day:

"I know some one who had lost their daughter, and they found her in Paris."

They at once set out for Paris.

When they entered the great city they were bewildered by its size and by the crowds that they saw. But they knew that Jean must be in the midst of all these people, though they did not know how to set about looking for him. Then they feared that they might not recognize him, for he was only five years old when they last saw him.

They visited every place, went through all the streets, stopping whenever they saw a group of people, hoping for some providential meeting, some extraordinary luck, some compassionate fate.

They frequently walked at haphazard straight ahead, leaning one against the other, looking so sad and poverty-stricken that people would give them alms without their asking.

They spent every Sunday at the doors of the churches, watching the crowds entering and leaving, trying to distinguish among the faces one that might be familiar. Several times they thought they recognized him, but always found they had made a mistake.

In the vestibule of one of the churches which they visited the most frequently there was an old dispenser of holy Water who had become their friend. He also had a very sad history, and their sympathy for him had established a bond of close friendship between them. It ended by them all three living together in a poor lodging on the top floor of a large house situated at some distance, quite on the outskirts of the city, and the wheelwright would sometimes take his new friend's place at the church when the latter was ill.

Winter came, a very severe winter. The poor holy water sprinkler died and the parish priest appointed the wheelwright, whose misfortunes had come to his knowledge, to replace him. He went every morning and sat in the same place, on the same chair, wearing away the old stone pillar by continually leaning against it. He would gaze steadily at every man who entered the church and looked forward to Sunday with as much impatience as a schoolboy, for on that day the church was filled with people from morning till night.

He became very old, growing weaker each day from the dampness of the church, and his hope oozed away gradually.

He now knew by sight all the people who came to the services; he knew their hours, their manners, could distinguish their step on the stone pavement.

His interests had become so contracted that the entrance of a stranger in the church was for him a great event. One day two ladies came in; one was old, the other young—a mother and daughter probably. Behind them came a man who was following them. He bowed to them as they came out, and after offering them some holy water, he took the arm of the elder lady.

"That must be the fiance of the younger one," thought the wheelwright. And until evening he kept trying to recall where he had formerly seen a young man who resembled this one. But the one he was thinking of must be an old man by this time, for it seemed as if he had known him down home in his youth.

The same man frequently came again to walk home with the ladies, and this vague, distant, familiar resemblance which he could not place worried the old man so much that he made his wife come with him to see if she could help his impaired memory.

One evening as it was growing dusk the three strangers entered together. When they had passed the old man said:

"Well, do you know him?"

His wife anxiously tried to ransack her memory. Suddenly she said in a low tone:

"Yes—yes—but he is darker, taller, stouter and is dressed like a gentleman, but, father, all the same, it is your face when you were young!"

The old man started violently.

It was true. He looked like himself and also like his brother who was dead, and like his father, whom he remembered while he was yet young. The old couple were so affected that they could not speak. The three persons came out and were about to leave the church.

The man touched his finger to the holy water sprinkler. Then the old man, whose hand was trembling so that he was fairly sprinkling the ground with holy water, exclaimed:

"Jean!"

The young man stopped and looked at him.

He repeated in a lower tone:

"Jean!"

The two women looked at them without understanding.

He then said for the third time, sobbing as he did so:

"Jean!"

The man stooped down, with his face close to the old man's, and as a memory of his childhood dawned on him he replied:

"Papa Pierre, Mamma Jeanne!"

He had forgotten everything, his father's surname and the name of his native place, but he always remembered those two words that he had so often repeated: "Papa Pierre, Mamma Jeanne."

He sank to the floor, his face on the old man's knees, and he wept, kissing now his father and then his mother, while they were almost breathless from intense joy.

The two ladies also wept, understanding as they did that some great happiness had come to pass.

Then they all went to the young man's house and he told them his history. The circus people had carried him off. For three years he traveled with them in various countries. Then the troupe disbanded, and one day an old lady in a chateau had paid to have him stay with her because she liked his appearance. As he was intelligent, he was sent to school, then to college, and the old lady having no children, had left him all her money. He, for his part, had tried to find his parents, but as he could remember only the two names, "Papa Pierre, Mamma Jeanne," he had been unable to do so. Now he was about to be married, and he introduced his fiancee, who was very good and very pretty.

When the two old people had told their story in their turn he kissed them once more. They sat up very late that night, not daring to retire lest the happiness they had so long sought should escape them again while they were asleep.

But misfortune had lost its hold on them and they were happy for the rest of their lives.

A PARRICIDE

The lawyer had presented a plea of insanity. How could anyone explain this strange crime otherwise?

One morning, in the grass near Chatou, two bodies had been found, a man and a woman, well known, rich, no longer young and married since the preceding year, the woman having been a widow for three years before.

They were not known to have enemies; they had not been robbed. They seemed to have been thrown from the roadside into the river, after having been struck, one after the other, with a long iron spike.

The investigation revealed nothing. The boatmen, who had been questioned, knew nothing. The matter was about to be given up, when a young carpenter from a neighboring village, Georges Louis, nicknamed "the Bourgeois," gave himself up.

To all questions he only answered this:

"I had known the man for two years, the woman for six months. They often had me repair old furniture for them, because I am a clever workman."

And when he was asked:

"Why did you kill them?"

He would obstinately answer:

"I killed them because I wanted to kill them."

They could get nothing more out of him.

This man was undoubtedly an illegitimate child, put out to nurse and then abandoned. He had no other name than Georges Louis, but as on growing up he became particularly intelligent, with the good taste and native refinement which his acquaintances did not have, he was nicknamed "the Bourgeois," and he was never called otherwise. He had become remarkably clever in the trade of a carpenter, which he had taken up. He was also said to be a socialist fanatic, a believer in communistic and nihilistic doctrines, a great reader of bloodthirsty novels, an influential political agitator and a clever orator in the public meetings of workmen or of farmers.

His lawyer had pleaded insanity.

Indeed, how could one imagine that this workman should kill his best customers, rich and generous (as he knew), who in two years had enabled him to earn three thousand francs (his books showed it)? Only one explanation could be offered: insanity, the fixed idea of the unclassed individual who reeks vengeance on two bourgeois, on all the bourgeoisie, and the lawyer made a clever allusion to this nickname of "The Bourgeois," given throughout the neighborhood to this poor wretch. He exclaimed:

"Is this irony not enough to unbalance the mind of this poor wretch, who has neither father nor mother? He is an ardent republican. What am I saying? He even belongs to the same political party, the members of which, formerly shot or exiled by the government, it now welcomes with open arms this party to which arson is a principle and murder an ordinary occurrence.

"These gloomy doctrines, now applauded in public meetings, have ruined this man. He has heard republicans—even women, yes, women—ask for the blood of M. Gambetta, the blood of M. Grevy; his weakened mind gave way; he wanted blood, the blood of a bourgeois!

"It is not he whom you should condemn, gentlemen; it is the Commune!"

Everywhere could be heard murmurs of assent. Everyone felt that the lawyer had won his case. The prosecuting attorney did not oppose him.

Then the presiding judge asked the accused the customary question:

"Prisoner, is there anything that you wish to add to your defense?"

The man stood up.

He was a short, flaxen blond, with calm, clear, gray eyes. A strong, frank, sonorous voice came from this frail-looking boy and, at the first words, quickly changed the opinion which had been formed of him.

He spoke loud in a declamatory manner, but so distinctly that every word could be understood in the farthest corners of the big hall:

"Your honor, as I do not wish to go to an insane asylum, and as I even prefer death to that, I will tell everything.

"I killed this man and this woman because they were my parents.

"Now, listen, and judge me.

"A woman, having given birth to a boy, sent him out, somewhere, to a nurse. Did she even know where her accomplice carried this innocent little being, condemned to eternal misery, to the shame of an illegitimate birth; to more than that—to death, since he was abandoned and the nurse, no longer receiving the monthly pension, might, as they often do, let him die of hunger and neglect!

"The woman who nursed me was honest, better, more noble, more of a mother than my own mother. She brought me up. She did wrong in doing her duty. It is more humane to let them die, these little wretches who are cast away in suburban villages just as garbage is thrown away.

"I grew up with the indistinct impression that I was carrying some burden of shame. One day the other children called me a 'b——-'. They did not know the meaning of this word, which one of them had heard at home. I was also ignorant of its meaning, but I felt the sting all the same.

"I was, I may say, one of the cleverest boys in the school. I would have been a good man, your honor, perhaps a man of superior intellect, if my parents had not committed the crime of abandoning me.

"This crime was committed against me. I was the victim, they were the guilty ones. I was defenseless, they were pitiless. Their duty was to love me, they rejected me.

"I owed them life—but is life a boon? To me, at any rate, it was a misfortune. After their shameful desertion, I owed them only vengeance. They committed against me the most inhuman, the most infamous, the most monstrous crime which can be committed against a human creature.

"A man who has been insulted, strikes; a man who has been robbed, takes back his own by force. A man who has been deceived, played upon, tortured, kills; a man who has been slapped, kills; a man who has been dishonored, kills. I have been robbed, deceived, tortured, morally slapped, dishonored, all this to a greater degree than those whose anger you excuse.

"I revenged myself, I killed. It was my legitimate right. I took their happy life in exchange for the terrible one which they had forced on me.

"You will call me parricide! Were these people my parents, for whom I was an abominable burden, a terror, an infamous shame; for whom my birth was a calamity and my life a threat of disgrace? They sought a selfish pleasure; they got an unexpected child. They suppressed the child. My turn came to do the same for them.

"And yet, up to quite recently, I was ready to love them.

"As I have said, this man, my father, came to me for the first time two years ago. I suspected nothing. He ordered two pieces of furniture. I found out, later on, that, under the seal of secrecy, naturally, he had sought information from the priest.

"He returned often. He gave me a lot of work and paid me well. Sometimes he would even talk to me of one thing or another. I felt a growing affection for him.

"At the beginning of this year he brought with him his wife, my mother. When she entered she was trembling so that I thought her to be suffering from some nervous disease. Then she asked for a seat and a glass of water. She said nothing; she looked around abstractedly at my work and only answered 'yes' and 'no,' at random, to all the questions which he asked her. When she had left I thought her a little unbalanced.

"The following month they returned. She was calm, self-controlled. That day they chattered for a long time, and they left me a rather large order. I saw her three more times, without suspecting anything. But one day she began to talk to me of my life, of my childhood, of my parents. I answered: 'Madame, my parents were wretches who deserted me.' Then she clutched at her heart and fell, unconscious. I immediately thought: 'She is my mother!' but I took care not to let her notice anything. I wished to observe her.

"I, in turn, sought out information about them. I learned that they had been married since last July, my mother having been a widow for only three years. There had been rumors that they had loved each other during the lifetime of the first husband, but there was no proof of it. I was the proof—the proof which they had at first hidden and then hoped to destroy.

"I waited. She returned one evening, escorted as usual by my father. That day she seemed deeply moved, I don't know why. Then, as she was leaving, she said to me: 'I wish you success, because you seem to me to be honest and a hard worker; some day you will undoubtedly think of getting married. I have come to help you to choose freely the woman who may suit you. I was married against my inclination once and I know what suffering it causes. Now I am rich, childless, free, mistress of my fortune. Here is your dowry.'

"She held out to me a large, sealed envelope.

"I looked her straight in the eyes and then said: 'Are you my mother?'

"She drew back a few steps and hid her face in her hands so as not to see me. He, the man, my father, supported her in his arms and cried out to me: 'You must be crazy!'

"I answered: 'Not in the least. I know that you are my parents. I cannot be thus deceived. Admit it and I will keep the secret; I will bear you no ill will; I will remain what I am, a carpenter.'

"He retreated towards the door, still supporting his wife who was beginning to sob. Quickly I locked the door, put the key in my pocket and continued: 'Look at her and dare to deny that she is my mother.'

"Then he flew into a passion, very pale, terrified at the thought that the scandal, which had so far been avoided, might suddenly break out; that their position, their good name, their honor might all at once be lost. He stammered out: 'You are a rascal, you wish to get money from us! That's the thanks we get for trying to help such common people!'

"My mother, bewildered, kept repeating: 'Let's get out of here, let's get out!'

"Then, when he found the door locked, he exclaimed: 'If you do not open this door immediately, I will have you thrown into prison for blackmail and assault!'

"I had remained calm; I opened the door and saw them disappear in the darkness.

"Then I seemed to have been suddenly orphaned, deserted, pushed to the wall. I was seized with an overwhelming sadness, mingled with anger, hatred, disgust; my whole being seemed to rise up in revolt against the injustice, the meanness, the dishonor, the rejected love. I began to run, in order to overtake them along the Seine, which they had to follow in order to reach the station of Chaton.

"I soon caught up with them. It was now pitch dark. I was creeping up behind them softly, that they might not hear me. My mother was still crying. My father was saying: 'It's all your own fault. Why did you wish to see him? It was absurd in our position. We could have helped him from afar, without showing ourselves. Of what use are these dangerous visits, since we can't recognize him?'

"Then I rushed up to them, beseeching. I cried:

"'You see! You are my parents. You have already rejected me once; would you repulse me again?'

"Then, your honor, he struck me. I swear it on my honor, before the law and my country. He struck me, and as I seized him by the collar, he drew from his pocket a revolver.

"The blood rushed to my head, I no longer knew what I was doing, I had my compass in my pocket; I struck him with it as often as I could.

"Then she began to cry: 'Help! murder!' and to pull my beard. It seems that I killed her also. How do I know what I did then?

"Then, when I saw them both lying on the ground, without thinking, I threw them into the Seine.

"That's all. Now sentence me."

The prisoner sat down. After this revelation the case was carried over to the following session. It comes up very soon. If we were jurymen, what would we do with this parricide?

BERTHA

Dr. Bonnet, my old friend—one sometimes has friends older than one's self—had often invited me to spend some time with him at Riom, and, as I did not know Auvergne, I made up my mind to visit him in the summer of 1876.

I arrived by the morning train, and the first person I saw on the platform was the doctor. He was dressed in a gray suit, and wore a soft, black, wide-brimmed, high-crowned felt hat, narrow at the top like a chimney pot, a hat which hardly any one except an Auvergnat would wear, and which reminded one of a charcoal burner. Dressed like that, the doctor had the appearance of an old young man, with his spare body under his thin coat, and his large head covered with white hair.

He embraced me with that evident pleasure which country people feel when they meet long-expected friends, and, stretching out his arm, he said proudly:

"This is Auvergne!" I saw nothing before me except a range of mountains, whose summits, which resembled truncated cones, must have been extinct volcanoes.

Then, pointing to the name of the station, he said:

"Riom, the fatherland of magistrates, the pride of the magistracy, and which ought rather to be the fatherland of doctors."

"Why?" I, asked.

"Why?" he replied with a laugh. "If you transpose the letters, you have the Latin word 'mori', to die. That is the reason why I settled here, my young friend."

And, delighted at his own joke, he carried me off, rubbing his hands.

As soon as I had swallowed a cup of coffee, he made me go and see the town. I admired the druggist's house, and the other noted houses, which were all black, but as pretty as bric-a-brac, with their facades of sculptured stone. I admired the statue of the Virgin, the patroness of butchers, and he told me an amusing story about this, which I will relate some other time, and then Dr. Bonnet said to me:

"I must beg you to excuse me for a few minutes while I go and see a patient, and then I will take you to Chatel-Guyon, so as to show you the general aspect of the town, and all the mountain chain of the Puy-de-Dome before lunch. You can wait for me outside; I shall only go upstairs and come down immediately."

He left me outside one of those old, gloomy, silent, melancholy houses, which one sees in the provinces, and this one appeared to look particularly sinister, and I soon discovered the reason. All the large windows on the first floor were boarded half way up. The upper part of them alone could be opened, as if one had wished to prevent the people who were locked up in that huge stone box from looking into the street.

When the doctor came down again, I told him how it struck me, and he replied:

"You are quite right; the poor creature who is living there must never see what is going on outside. She is a madwoman, or rather an idiot, what you Normans would call a Niente. It is a miserable story, but a very singular pathological case at the same time. Shall I tell you?"

I begged him to do so, and he continued:

"Twenty years ago the owners of this house, who were my patients, had a daughter who was like all other girls, but I soon discovered that while her body became admirably developed, her intellect remained stationary.

"She began to walk very early, but she could not talk. At first I thought she was deaf, but I soon discovered that, although she heard perfectly, she did not understand anything that was said to her. Violent noises made her start and frightened her, without her understanding how they were caused.

"She grew up into a superb woman, but she was dumb, from an absolute want of intellect. I tried all means to introduce a gleam of intelligence into her brain, but nothing succeeded. I thought I noticed that she knew her nurse, though as soon as she was weaned, she failed to recognize her mother. She could never pronounce that word which is the first that children utter and the last which soldiers murmur when they are dying on the field of battle. She sometimes tried to talk, but she produced nothing but incoherent sounds.

"When the weather was fine, she laughed continually, and emitted low cries which might be compared to the twittering of birds; when it rained she cried and moaned in a mournful, terrifying manner, which sounded like the howling of a dog before a death occurs in a house.

"She was fond of rolling on the grass, as young animals do, and of running about madly, and she would clap her hands every morning, when the sun shone into her room, and would insist, by signs, on being dressed as quickly as possible, so that she might get out.

"She did not appear to distinguish between people, between her mother and her nurse, or between her father and me, or between the coachman and the cook. I particularly liked her parents, who were very unhappy on her account, and went to see them nearly every day. I dined with them quite frequently, which enabled me to remark that Bertha (they had called her Bertha) seemed to recognize the various dishes, and to prefer some to others. At that time she was twelve years old, but as fully formed in figure as a girl of eighteen, and taller than I was. Then the idea struck me of developing her greediness, and by this means of cultivating some slight power of discrimination in her mind, and to force her, by the diversity of flavors, if not to reason, at any rate to arrive at instinctive distinctions, which would of themselves constitute a kind of process that was necessary to thought. Later on, by appealing to her passions, and by carefully making use of those which could serve our purpose, we might hope to obtain a kind of reaction on her intellect, and by degrees increase the unconscious action of her brain.

"One day I put two plates before her, one of soup, and the other of very sweet vanilla cream. I made her taste each of them successively, and then I let her choose for herself, and she ate the plate of cream. In a short time I made her very greedy, so greedy that it appeared as if the only idea she had in her head was the desire for eating. She perfectly recognized the various dishes, and stretched out her hands toward those that she liked, and took hold of them eagerly, and she used to cry when they were taken from her. Then I thought I would try and teach her to come to the dining-room when the dinner bell rang. It took a long time, but I succeeded in the end. In her vacant intellect a vague correlation was established between sound and taste, a correspondence between the two senses, an appeal from one to the other, and consequently a sort of connection of ideas—if one can call that kind of instinctive hyphen between two organic functions an idea—and so I carried my experiments further, and taught her, with much difficulty, to recognize meal times by the clock.

"It was impossible for me for a long time to attract her attention to the hands, but I succeeded in making her remark the clockwork and the striking apparatus. The means I employed were very simple; I asked them not to have the bell rung for lunch, and everybody got up and went into the dining-room when the little brass hammer struck twelve o'clock, but I found great difficulty in making her learn to count the strokes. She ran to the door each time she heard the clock strike, but by degrees she learned that all the strokes had not the same value as far as regarded meals, and she frequently fixed her eyes, guided by her ears, on the dial of the clock.

"When I noticed that, I took care every day at twelve, and at six o'clock, to place my fingers on the figures twelve and six, as soon as the moment she was waiting for had arrived, and I soon noticed that she attentively followed the motion of the small brass hands, which I had often turned in her presence.

"She had understood! Perhaps I ought rather to say that she had grasped the idea. I had succeeded in getting the knowledge, or, rather, the sensation, of the time into her, just as is the case with carp, who certainly have no clocks, when they are fed every day exactly at the same time.

"When once I had obtained that result all the clocks and watches in the house occupied her attention almost exclusively. She spent her time in looking at them, listening to them, and in waiting for meal time, and once something very funny happened. The striking apparatus of a pretty little Louis XVI clock that hung at the head of her bed having got out of order, she noticed it. She sat for twenty minutes with her eyes on the hands, waiting for it to strike ten, but when the hands passed the figure she was astonished at not hearing anything; so stupefied was she, indeed, that she sat down, no doubt overwhelmed by a feeling of violent emotion such as attacks us in the face of some terrible catastrophe. And she had the wonderful patience to wait until eleven o'clock in order to see what would happen, and as she naturally heard nothing, she was suddenly either seized with a wild fit of rage at having been deceived and imposed upon by appearances, or else overcome by that fear which some frightened creature feels at some terrible mystery, and by the furious impatience of a passionate individual who meets with some obstacle; she took up the tongs from the fireplace and struck the clock so violently that she broke it to pieces in a moment.

"It was evident, therefore, that her, brain did act and calculate, obscurely it is true, and within very restricted limits, for I could never succeed in making her distinguish persons as she distinguished the time; and to stir her intellect, it was necessary to appeal to her passions, in the material sense of the word, and we soon had another, and alas! a very terrible proof of this!

"She had grown up into a splendid girl, a perfect type of a race, a sort of lovely and stupid Venus. She was sixteen, and I have rarely seen such perfection of form, such suppleness and such regular features. I said she was a Venus; yes, a fair, stout, vigorous Venus, with large, bright, vacant eyes, which were as blue as the flowers of the flax plant; she had a large mouth with full lips, the mouth of a glutton, of a sensualist, a mouth made for kisses. Well, one morning her father came into my consulting room with a strange look on his face, and, sitting down without even replying to my greeting, he said:

"'I want to speak to you about a very serious matter. Would it be possible—would it be possible for Bertha to marry?'

"'Bertha to marry! Why, it is quite impossible!'

"'Yes, I know, I know,' he replied. 'But reflect, doctor. Don't you think—perhaps—we hoped—if she had children—it would be a great shock to her, but a great happiness, and—who knows whether maternity might not rouse her intellect?'

"I was in a state of great perplexity. He was right, and it was possible that such a new situation, and that wonderful instinct of maternity, which beats in the hearts of the lower animals as it does in the heart of a woman, which makes the hen fly at a dog's jaws to defend her chickens, might bring about a revolution, an utter change in her vacant mind, and set the motionless mechanism of her thoughts in motion. And then, moreover, I immediately remembered a personal instance. Some years previously I had owned a spaniel bitch who was so stupid that I could do nothing with her, but when she had had puppies she became, if not exactly intelligent, yet almost like many other dogs who had not been thoroughly broken.

"As soon as I foresaw the possibility of this, the wish to get Bertha married grew in me, not so much out of friendship for her and her poor parents as from scientific curiosity. What would happen? It was a singular problem. I said in reply to her father:

"'Perhaps you are right. You might make the attempt, but you will never find a man to consent to marry her.'

"'I have found somebody,' he said, in a low voice.

"I was dumfounded, and said: 'Somebody really suitable? Some one of your own rank and position in society?'

"'Decidedly,' he replied.

"'Oh! And may I ask his name?'

"'I came on purpose to tell you, and to consult you. It is Monsieur Gaston du Boys de Lucelles.'

"I felt inclined to exclaim: 'The wretch!' but I held my tongue, and after a few moments' silence I said:

"'Oh! Very good. I see nothing against it.'

"The poor man shook me heartily by the hand.

"'She is to be married next month,' he said.

"Monsieur Gaston du Boys de Lucelles was a scapegrace of good family, who, after having spent all that he had inherited from his father, and having incurred debts in all kinds of doubtful ways, had been trying to discover some other means of obtaining money, and he had discovered this method. He was a good-looking young fellow, and in capital health, but fast; one of that odious race of provincial fast men, and he appeared to me to be as suitable as anyone, and could be got rid of later by making him an allowance. He came to the house to pay his addresses and to strut about before the idiot girl, who, however, seemed to please him. He brought her flowers, kissed her hands, sat at her feet, and looked at her with affectionate eyes; but she took no notice of any of his attentions, and did not make any distinction between him and the other persons who were about her.

"However, the marriage took place, and you may guess how my curiosity was aroused. I went to see Bertha the next day to try and discover from her looks whether any feelings had been awakened in her, but I found her just the same as she was every day, wholly taken up with the clock and dinner, while he, on the contrary, appeared really in love, and tried to rouse his wife's spirits and affection by little endearments and such caresses as one bestows on a kitten. He could think of nothing better.

"I called upon the married couple pretty frequently, and I soon perceived that the young woman knew her husband, and gave him those eager looks which she had hitherto only bestowed on sweet dishes.

"She followed his movements, knew his step on the stairs or in the neighboring rooms, clapped her hands when he came in, and her face was changed and brightened by the flames of profound happiness and of desire.

"She loved him with her whole body and with all her soul to the very depths of her poor, weak soul, and with all her heart, that poor heart of some grateful animal. It was really a delightful and innocent picture of simple passion, of carnal and yet modest passion, such as nature had implanted in mankind, before man had complicated and disfigured it by all the various shades of sentiment. But he soon grew tired of this ardent, beautiful, dumb creature, and did not spend more than an hour during the day with her, thinking it sufficient if he came home at night, and she began to suffer in consequence. She used to wait for him from morning till night with her eyes on the clock; she did not even look after the meals now, for he took all his away from home, Clermont, Chatel-Guyon, Royat, no matter where, as long as he was not obliged to come home.

"She began to grow thin; every other thought, every other wish, every other expectation, and every confused hope disappeared from her mind, and the hours during which she did not see him became hours of terrible suffering to her. Soon he ceased to come home regularly of nights; he spent them with women at the casino at Royat and did not come home until daybreak. But she never went to bed before he returned. She remained sitting motionless in an easy-chair, with her eyes fixed on the hands of the clock, which turned so slowly and regularly round the china face on which the hours were painted.

"She heard the trot of his horse in the distance and sat up with a start, and when he came into the room she got up with the movements of an automaton and pointed to the clock, as if to say: 'Look how late it is!'

"And he began to be afraid of this amorous and jealous, half-witted woman, and flew into a rage, as brutes do; and one night he even went so far as to strike her, so they sent for me. When I arrived she was writhing and screaming in a terrible crisis of pain, anger, passion, how do I know what? Can one tell what goes on in such undeveloped brains?

"I calmed her by subcutaneous injections of morphine, and forbade her to see that man again, for I saw clearly that marriage would infallibly kill her by degrees.

"Then she went mad! Yes, my dear friend, that idiot went mad. She is always thinking of him and waiting for him; she waits for him all day and night, awake or asleep, at this very moment, ceaselessly. When I saw her getting thinner and thinner, and as she persisted in never taking her eyes off the clocks, I had them removed from the house. I thus made it impossible for her to count the hours, and to try to remember, from her indistinct reminiscences, at what time he used to come home formerly. I hope to destroy the recollection of it in time, and to extinguish that ray of thought which I kindled with so much difficulty.

"The other day I tried an experiment. I offered her my watch; she took it and looked at it for some time; then she began to scream terribly, as if the sight of that little object had suddenly awakened her memory, which was beginning to grow indistinct. She is pitiably thin now, with hollow and glittering eyes, and she walks up and down ceaselessly, like a wild beast in its cage; I have had gratings put on the windows, boarded them up half way, and have had the seats fixed to the floor so as to prevent her from looking to see whether he is coming.

"Oh! her poor parents! What a life they must lead!"

We had got to the top of the hill, and the doctor turned round and said to me:

"Look at Riom from here."

The gloomy town looked like some ancient city. Behind it a green, wooded plain studded with towns and villages, and bathed in a soft blue haze, extended until it was lost in the distance. Far away, on my right, there was a range of lofty mountains with round summits, or else cut off flat, as if with a sword, and the doctor began to enumerate the villages, towns and hills, and to give me the history of all of them. But I did not listen to him; I was thinking of nothing but the madwoman, and I only saw her. She seemed to be hovering over that vast extent of country like a mournful ghost, and I asked him abruptly:

"What has become of the husband?"

My friend seemed rather surprised, but after a few moments' hesitation, he replied:

"He is living at Royat, on an allowance that they made him, and is quite happy; he leads a very fast life."

As we were slowly going back, both of us silent and rather low-spirited, an English dogcart, drawn by a thoroughbred horse, came up behind us and passed us rapidly. The doctor took me by the arm.

"There he is," he said.

I saw nothing except a gray felt hat, cocked over one ear above a pair of broad shoulders, driving off in a cloud of dust.

THE PATRON

We never dreamed of such good fortune! The son of a provincial bailiff, Jean Marin had come, as do so many others, to study law in the Quartier Latin. In the various beer-houses that he had frequented he had made friends with several talkative students who spouted politics as they drank their beer. He had a great admiration for them and followed them persistently from cafe to cafe, even paying for their drinks when he had the money.

He became a lawyer and pleaded causes, which he lost. However, one morning he read in the papers that one of his former comrades of the Quartier had just been appointed deputy.

He again became his faithful hound, the friend who does the drudgery, the unpleasant tasks, for whom one sends when one has need of him and with whom one does not stand on ceremony. But it chanced through some parliamentary incident that the deputy became a minister. Six months later Jean Marin was appointed a state councillor.

He was so elated with pride at first that he lost his head. He would walk through the streets just to show himself off, as though one could tell by his appearance what position he occupied. He managed to say to the shopkeepers as soon as he entered a store, bringing it in somehow in the course of the most insignificant remarks and even to the news vendors and the cabmen:

"I, who am a state councillor—"

Then, in consequence of his position as well as for professional reasons and as in duty bound through being an influential and generous man, he felt an imperious need of patronizing others. He offered his support to every one on all occasions and with unbounded generosity.

When he met any one he recognized on the boulevards he would advance to meet them with a charmed air, would take their hand, inquire after their health, and, without waiting for any questions, remark:

"You know I am state councillor, and I am entirely at your service. If I can be of any use to you, do not hesitate to call on me. In my position one has great influence."

Then he would go into some cafe with the friend he had just met and ask for a pen and ink and a sheet of paper. "Just one, waiter; it is to write a letter of recommendation."

And he wrote ten, twenty, fifty letters of recommendation a day. He wrote them to the Cafe Americain, to Bignon's, to Tortoni's, to the Maison Doree, to the Cafe Riche, to the Helder, to the Cafe Anglais, to the Napolitain, everywhere, everywhere. He wrote them to all the officials of the republican government, from the magistrates to the ministers. And he was happy, perfectly happy.

One morning as he was starting out to go to the council it began to rain. He hesitated about taking a cab, but decided not to do so and set out on foot.

The rain came down in torrents, swamping the sidewalks and inundating the streets. M. Marin was obliged to take shelter in a doorway. An old priest was standing there—an old priest with white hair. Before he became a councillor M. Marin did not like the clergy. Now he treated them with consideration, ever since a cardinal had consulted him on an important matter. The rain continued to pour down in floods and obliged the two men to take shelter in the porter's lodge so as to avoid getting wet. M. Marin, who was always itching to talk so as to let people know who he was, remarked:

"This is horrible weather, Monsieur l'Abbe."

The old priest bowed:

"Yes indeed, sir, it is very unpleasant when one comes to Paris for only a few days."

"Ah! You come from the provinces?"

"Yes, monsieur. I am only passing through on my journey."

"It certainly is very disagreeable to have rain during the few days one spends in the capital. We officials who stay here the year round, we think nothing of it."

The priest did not reply. He was looking at the street where the rain seemed to be falling less heavily. And with a sudden resolve he raised his cassock just as women raise their skirts in stepping across water.

M. Marin, seeing him start away, exclaimed:

"You will get drenched, Monsieur l'Abbe. Wait a few moments longer; the rain will be over."

The good man stopped irresistibly and then said:

"But I am in a great hurry. I have an important engagement."

M. Marin seemed quite worried.

"But you will be absolutely drenched. Might I ask in which direction you are going?"

The priest appeared to hesitate. Then he said:

"I am going in the direction of the Palais Royal."

"In that case, if you will allow me, Monsieur l'Abbe, I will offer you the shelter of my umbrella: As for me, I am going to the council. I am a councillor of state."

The old priest raised his head and looked at his neighbor and then exclaimed:

"I thank you, monsieur. I shall be glad to accept your offer."

M. Marin then took his arm and led him away. He directed him, watched over him and advised him.

"Be careful of that stream, Monsieur l'Abbe. And be very careful about the carriage wheels; they spatter you with mud sometimes from head to foot. Look out for the umbrellas of the people passing by; there is nothing more dangerous to the eyes than the tips of the ribs. Women especially are unbearable; they pay no heed to where they are going and always jab you in the face with the point of their parasols or umbrellas. And they never move aside for anybody. One would suppose the town belonged to them. They monopolize the pavement and the street. It is my opinion that their education has been greatly neglected."

And M. Marin laughed.

The priest did not reply. He walked along, slightly bent over, picking his steps carefully so as not to get mud on his boots or his cassock.

M. Marin resumed:

"I suppose you have come to Paris to divert your mind a little?"

The good man replied:

"No, I have some business to attend to."

"Ali! Is it important business? Might I venture to ask what it is? If I can be of any service to you, you may command me."

The priest seemed embarrassed. He murmured:

"Oh, it is a little personal matter; a little difficulty with—with my bishop. It would not interest you. It is a matter of internal regulation—an ecclesiastical affair."

M. Marin was eager.

"But it is precisely the state council that regulates all those things. In that case, make use of me."

"Yes, monsieur, it is to the council that I am going. You are a thousand times too kind. I have to see M. Lerepere and M. Savon and also perhaps M. Petitpas."

M. Marin stopped short.

"Why, those are my friends, Monsieur l'Abbe, my best friends, excellent colleagues, charming men. I will speak to them about you, and very highly. Count upon me."

The cure thanked him, apologizing for troubling him, and stammered out a thousand grateful promises.

M. Marin was enchanted.

"Ah, you may be proud of having made a stroke of luck, Monsieur l'Abbe. You will see—you will see that, thanks to me, your affair will go along swimmingly."

They reached the council hall. M. Marin took the priest into his office, offered him a chair in front of the fire and sat down himself at his desk and began to write.

"My dear colleague, allow me to recommend to you most highly a venerable and particularly worthy and deserving priest, M. L'Abbe——"

He stopped and asked:

"Your name, if you please?"

"L'Abbe Ceinture."

"M. l'Abbe Ceinture, who needs your good office in a little matter which he will communicate to you.

"I am pleased at this incident which gives me an opportunity, my dear colleague——"

And he finished with the usual compliments.

When he had written the three letters he handed them to his protege, who took his departure with many protestations of gratitude.

M. Marin attended to some business and then went home, passed the day quietly, slept well, woke in a good humor and sent for his newspapers.

The first he opened was a radical sheet. He read:

"OUR CLERGY AND OUR GOVERNMENT OFFICIALS

"We shall never make an end of enumerating the misdeeds of the clergy. A certain priest, named Ceinture, convicted of conspiracy against the present government, accused of base actions to which we will not even allude, suspected besides of being a former Jesuit, metamorphosed into a simple priest, suspended by a bishop for causes that are said to be unmentionable and summoned to Paris to give an explanation of his conduct, has found an ardent defender in the man named Marin, a councillor of state, who was not afraid to give this frocked malefactor the warmest letters of recommendation to all the republican officials, his colleagues.

"We call the, attention of the ministry to the unheard of attitude of this councillor of state——"

M. Marin bounded out of bed, dressed himself and hastened to his colleague, Petitpas, who said to him:

"How now? You were crazy to recommend to me that old conspirator!"

M. Marin, bewildered, stammered out:

"Why no—you see—I was deceived. He looked such an honest man. He played me a trick—a disgraceful trick! I beg that you will sentence him severely, very severely. I am going to write. Tell me to whom I should write about having him punished. I will go and see the attorney-general and the archbishop of Paris—yes, the archbishop."

And seating himself abruptly at M. Petitpas' desk, he wrote:

"Monseigneur, I have the honor to bring to your grace's notice the fact that I have recently been made a victim of the intrigues and lies of a certain Abbe Ceinture, who imposed on my kind-heartedness.

"Deceived by the representations of this ecclesiastic, I was led——"

Then, having signed and sealed his letter, he turned to his colleague and exclaimed:

"See here; my dear friend, let this be a warning to you never to recommend any one again."

THE DOOR

"Bah!" exclaimed Karl Massouligny, "the question of complaisant husbands is a difficult one. I have seen many kinds, and yet I am unable to give an opinion about any of them. I have often tried to determine whether they are blind, weak or clairvoyant. I believe that there are some which belong to each of these categories.

"Let us quickly pass over the blind ones. They cannot rightly be called complaisant, since they do not know, but they are good creatures who cannot see farther than their nose. It is a curious and interesting thing to notice the ease with which men and women can, be deceived. We are taken in by the slightest trick of those who surround us, by our children, our friends, our servants, our tradespeople. Humanity is credulous, and in order to discover deceit in others, we do not display one-tenth the shrewdness which we use when we, in turn, wish to deceive some one else.

"Clairvoyant husbands may be divided into three classes: Those who have some interest, pecuniary, ambitious or otherwise, in their wife's having love affairs. These ask only to safeguard appearances as much as possible, and they are satisfied.

"Next come those who get angry. What a beautiful novel one could write about them!

"Finally the weak ones! Those who are afraid of scandal.

"There are also those who are powerless, or, rather, tired, who flee from the duties of matrimony through fear of ataxia or apoplexy, who are satisfied to see a friend run these risks.

"But I once met a husband of a rare species, who guarded against the common accident in a strange and witty manner.

"In Paris I had made the acquaintance of an elegant, fashionable couple. The woman, nervous, tall, slender, courted, was supposed to have had many love adventures. She pleased me with her wit, and I believe that I pleased her also. I courted her, a trial courting to which she answered with evident provocations. Soon we got to tender glances, hand pressures, all the little gallantries which precede the final attack.

"Nevertheless, I hesitated. I consider that, as a rule, the majority of society intrigues, however short they may be, are not worth the trouble which they give us and the difficulties which may arise. I therefore mentally compared the advantages and disadvantages which I might expect, and I thought I noticed that the husband suspected me.

"One evening, at a ball, as I was saying tender things to the young woman in a little parlor leading from the big hall where the dancing was going on, I noticed in a mirror the reflection of some one who was watching me. It was he. Our looks met and then I saw him turn his head and walk away.

"I murmured: 'Your husband is spying on us.'

"She seemed dumbfounded and asked: 'My husband?'

"'Yes, he has been watching us for some time:

"'Nonsense! Are you sure?'

"'Very sure.'

"'How strange! He is usually extraordinarily pleasant to all my. friends.'

"'Perhaps he guessed that I love you!'

"'Nonsense! You are not the first one to pay attention to me. Every woman who is a little in view drags behind her a herd of admirers.'

"'Yes. But I love you deeply.'

"'Admitting that that is true, does a husband ever guess those things?'

"'Then he is not jealous?'

"'No-no!'

"She thought for an instant and then continued: 'No. I do not think that I ever noticed any jealousy on his part.'

"'Has he never-watched you?'

"'No. As I said, he is always agreeable to my friends.'

"From that day my courting became much more assiduous. The woman did not please me any more than before, but the probable jealousy of her husband tempted me greatly.

"As for her, I judged her coolly and clearly. She had a certain worldly charm, due to a quick, gay, amiable and superficial mind, but no real, deep attraction. She was, as I have already said, an excitable little being, all on the surface, with rather a showy elegance. How can I explain myself? She was an ornament, not a home.

"One day, after taking dinner with her, her husband said to me, just as I was leaving: 'My dear friend' (he now called me 'friend'), 'we soon leave for the country. It is a great pleasure to my wife and myself to entertain people whom we like. We would be very pleased to have you spend a month with us. It would be very nice of you to do so.'

"I was dumbfounded, but I accepted.

"A month later I arrived at their estate of Vertcresson, in Touraine. They were waiting for me at the station, five miles from the chateau. There were three of them, she, the husband and a gentleman unknown to me, the Comte de Morterade, to whom I was introduced. He appeared to be delighted to make my acquaintance, and the strangest ideas passed through my mind while we trotted along the beautiful road between two hedges. I was saying to myself: 'Let's see, what can this mean? Here is a husband who cannot doubt that his wife and I are on more than friendly terms, and yet he invites me to his house, receives me like an old friend and seems to say: "Go ahead, my friend, the road is clear!"'

"Then I am introduced to a very pleasant gentleman, who seems already to have settled down in the house, and—and who is perhaps trying to get out of it, and who seems as pleased at my arrival as the husband himself.

"Is it some former admirer who wishes to retire? One might think so. But, then, would these two men tacitly have come to one of these infamous little agreements so common in society? And it is proposed to me that I should quietly enter into the pact and carry it out. All hands and arms are held out to me. All doors and hearts are open to me.

"And what about her? An enigma. She cannot be ignorant of everything. However—however—Well, I cannot understand it.

"The dinner was very gay and cordial. On leaving the table the husband and his friend began to play cards, while I went out on the porch to look at the moonlight with madame. She seemed to be greatly affected by nature, and I judged that the moment for my happiness was near. That evening she was really delightful. The country had seemed to make her more tender. Her long, slender waist looked pretty on this stone porch beside a great vase in which grew some flowers. I felt like dragging her out under the trees, throwing myself at her feet and speaking to her words of love.

"Her husband's voice called 'Louise!'

"'Yes, dear.'

"'You are forgetting the tea.'

"'I'll go and see about it, my friend.'

"We returned to the house, and she gave us some tea. When the two men had finished playing cards, they were visibly tired. I had to go to my room. I did not get to sleep till late, and then I slept badly.

"An excursion was decided upon for the following afternoon, and we went in an open carriage to visit some ruins. She and I were in the back of the vehicle and they were opposite us, riding backward. The conversation was sympathetic and agreeable. I am an orphan, and it seemed to me as though I had just found my family, I felt so at home with them.

"Suddenly, as she had stretched out her foot between her husband's legs, he murmured reproachfully: 'Louise, please don't wear out your old shoes yourself. There is no reason for being neater in Paris than in the country.'

"I lowered my eyes. She was indeed wearing worn-out shoes, and I noticed that her stockings were not pulled up tight.

"She had blushed and hidden her foot under her dress. The friend was looking out in the distance with an indifferent and unconcerned look.

"The husband offered me a cigar, which I accepted. For a few days it was impossible for me to be alone with her for two minutes; he was with us everywhere. He was delightful to me, however.

"One morning he came to get me to take a walk before breakfast, and the conversation happened to turn on marriage. I spoke a little about solitude and about how charming life can be made by the affection of a woman. Suddenly he interrupted me, saying: 'My friend, don't talk about things you know nothing about. A woman who has no other reason for loving you will not love you long. All the little coquetries which make them so exquisite when they do not definitely belong to us cease as soon as they become ours. And then—the respectable women—that is to say our wives—are—are not—in fact do not understand their profession of wife. Do you understand?'

"He said no more, and I could not guess his thoughts.

"Two days after this conversation he called me to his room quite early, in order to show me a collection of engravings. I sat in an easy chair opposite the big door which separated his apartment from his wife's, and behind this door I heard some one walking and moving, and I was thinking very little of the engravings, although I kept exclaiming: 'Oh, charming! delightful! exquisite!'

"He suddenly said: 'Oh, I have a beautiful specimen in the next room. I'll go and get it.'

"He ran to the door quickly, and both sides opened as though for a theatrical effect.

"In a large room, all in disorder, in the midst of skirts, collars, waists lying around on the floor, stood a tall, dried-up creature. The lower part of her body was covered with an old, worn-out silk petticoat, which was hanging limply on her shapeless form, and she was standing in front of a mirror brushing some short, sparse blond hairs. Her arms formed two acute angles, and as she turned around in astonishment I saw under a common cotton chemise a regular cemetery of ribs, which were hidden from the public gaze by well-arranged pads.

"The husband uttered a natural exclamation and came back, closing the doors, and said: 'Gracious! how stupid I am! Oh, how thoughtless! My wife will never forgive me for that!'

"I already felt like thanking him. I left three days later, after cordially shaking hands with the two men and kissing the lady's fingers. She bade me a cold good-by."

Karl Massouligny was silent. Some one asked: "But what was the friend?"

"I don't know—however—however he looked greatly distressed to see me leaving so soon."

A SALE

The defendants, Cesaire-Isidore Brument and Prosper-Napoleon Cornu, appeared before the Court of Assizes of the Seine-Inferieure, on a charge of attempted murder, by drowning, of Mme. Brument, lawful wife of the first of the aforenamed.

The two prisoners sat side by side on the traditional bench. They were two peasants; the first was small and stout, with short arms, short legs, and a round head with a red pimply face, planted directly on his trunk, which was also round and short, and with apparently no neck. He was a raiser of pigs and lived at Cacheville-la-Goupil, in the district of Criquetot.

Cornu (Prosper-Napoleon) was thin, of medium height, with enormously long arms. His head was on crooked, his jaw awry, and he squinted. A blue blouse, as long as a shirt, hung down to his knees, and his yellow hair, which was scanty and plastered down on his head, gave his face a worn-out, dirty look, a dilapidated look that was frightful. He had been nicknamed "the cure" because he could imitate to perfection the chanting in church, and even the sound of the serpent. This talent attracted to his cafe—for he was a saloon keeper at Criquetot—a great many customers who preferred the "mass at Cornu" to the mass in church.

Mme. Brument, seated on the witness bench, was a thin peasant woman who seemed to be always asleep. She sat there motionless, her hands crossed on her knees, gazing fixedly before her with a stupid expression.

The judge continued his interrogation.

"Well, then, Mme. Brument, they came into your house and threw you into a barrel full of water. Tell us the details. Stand up."

She rose. She looked as tall as a flag pole with her cap which looked like a white skull cap. She said in a drawling tone:

"I was shelling beans. Just then they came in. I said to myself, 'What is the matter with them? They do not seem natural, they seem up to some mischief.' They watched me sideways, like this, especially Cornu, because he squints. I do not like to see them together, for they are two good-for-nothings when they are in company. I said: 'What do you want with me?' They did not answer. I had a sort of mistrust——"

The defendant Brument interrupted the witness hastily, saying:

"I was full."

Then Cornu, turning towards his accomplice said in the deep tones of an organ:

"Say that we were both full, and you will be telling no lie."

The judge, severely:

"You mean by that that you were both drunk?"

Brument: "There can be no question about it."

Cornu: "That might happen to anyone."

The judge to the victim: "Continue your testimony, woman Brument."

"Well, Brument said to me, 'Do you wish to earn a hundred sous?' 'Yes,' I replied, seeing that a hundred sous are not picked up in a horse's tracks. Then he said: 'Open your eyes and do as I do,' and he went to fetch the large empty barrel which is under the rain pipe in the corner, and he turned it over and brought it into my kitchen, and stuck it down in the middle of the floor, and then he said to me: 'Go and fetch water until it is full.'

"So I went to the pond with two pails and carried water, and still more water for an hour, seeing that the barrel was as large as a vat, saving your presence, m'sieu le president.

"All this time Brument and Cornu were drinking a glass, and then another glass, and then another. They were finishing their drinks when I said to them: 'You are full, fuller than this barrel.' And Brument answered me. 'Do not worry, go on with your work, your turn will come, each one has his share.' I paid no attention to what he said as he was full.

"When the barrel was full to the brim, I said: 'There, that's done.'

"And then Cornu gave me a hundred sous, not Brument, Cornu; it was Cornu gave them to me. And Brument said: 'Do you wish to earn a hundred sous more?' 'Yes,' I said, for I am not accustomed to presents like that. Then he said: 'Take off your clothes!

"'Take off my clothes?'

"'Yes,' he said.

"'How many shall I take off?'

"'If it worries you at all, keep on your chemise, that won't bother us.'

"A hundred sous is a hundred sous, and I have to undress myself; but I did not fancy undressing before those two good-for-nothings. I took off my cap, and then my jacket, and then my skirt, and then my sabots. Brument said, 'Keep on your stockings, also; we are good fellows.'

"And Cornu said, too, 'We are good fellows.'

"So there I was, almost like mother Eve. And they got up from their chairs, but could not stand straight, they were so full, saving your presence, M'sieu le president.

"I said to myself: 'What are they up to?'

"And Brument said: 'Are you ready?'

"And Cornu said: 'I'm ready!'

"And then they took me, Brument by the head, and Cornu by the feet, as one might take, for instance, a sheet that has been washed. Then I began to bawl.

"And Brument said: 'Keep still, wretched creature!'

"And they lifted me up in the air and put me into the barrel, which was full of water, so that I had a check of the circulation, a chill to my very insides.

"And Brument said: 'Is that all?'

"Cornu said: 'That is all.'

"Brument said: 'The head is not in, that will make a difference in the measure.'

"Cornu said: 'Put in her head.'

"And then Brument pushed down my head as if to drown me, so that the water ran into my nose, so that I could already see Paradise. And he pushed it down, and I disappeared.

"And then he must have been frightened. He pulled me out and said: 'Go and get dry, carcass.'

"As for me, I took to my heels and ran as far as M. le cure's. He lent me a skirt belonging to his servant, for I was almost in a state of nature, and he went to fetch Maitre Chicot, the country watchman who went to Criquetot to fetch the police who came to my house with me.

"Then we found Brument and Cornu fighting each other like two rams.

"Brument was bawling: 'It isn't true, I tell you that there is at least a cubic metre in it. It is the method that was no good.'

"Cornu bawled: 'Four pails, that is almost half a cubic metre. You need not reply, that's what it is.'

"The police captain put them both under arrest. I have no more to tell."

She sat down. The audience in the court room laughed. The jurors looked at one another in astonishment. The judge said:

"Defendant Cornu, you seem to have been the instigator of this infamous plot. What have you to say?"

And Cornu rose in his turn.

"Judge," he replied, "I was full."

The Judge answered gravely:

"I know it. Proceed."

"I will. Well, Brument came to my place about nine o'clock, and ordered two drinks, and said: 'There's one for you, Cornu.' I sat down opposite him and drank, and out of politeness, I offered him a glass. Then he returned the compliment and so did I, and so it went on from glass to glass until noon, when we were full.

"Then Brument began to cry. That touched me. I asked him what was the matter. He said: 'I must have a thousand francs by Thursday.' That cooled me off a little, you understand. Then he said to me all at once: 'I will sell you my wife.'

"I was full, and I was a widower. You understand, that stirred me up. I did not know his wife, but she was a woman, wasn't she? I asked him: 'How much would you sell her for?'

"He reflected, or pretended to reflect. When one is full one is not very clear-headed, and he replied: 'I will sell her by the cubic metre.'

"That did not surprise me, for I was as drunk as he was, and I knew what a cubic metre is in my business. It is a thousand litres, that suited me.

"But the price remained to be settled. All depends on the quality. I said: 'How much do you want a cubic metre?'

"He answered: 'Two thousand francs.'

"I gave a bound like a rabbit, and then I reflected that a woman ought not to measure more than three hundred litres. So I said: 'That's too dear.'

"He answered: 'I cannot do it for less. I should lose by it.'

"You understand, one is not a dealer in hogs for nothing. One understands one's business. But, if he is smart, the seller of bacon, I am smarter, seeing that I sell them also. Ha, Ha, Ha! So I said to him: 'If she were new, I would not say anything, but she has been married to you for some time, so she is not as fresh as she was. I will give you fifteen hundred francs a cubic metre, not a sou more. Will that suit you?'

"He answered: 'That will do. That's a bargain!'

"I agreed, and we started out, arm in arm. We must help each other in this world.

"But a fear came to me: 'How can you measure her unless you put her into the liquid?'

"Then he explained his idea, not without difficulty for he was full. He said to me: 'I take a barrel, and fill it with water to the brim. I put her in it. All the water that comes out we will measure, that is the way to fix it.'

"I said: 'I see, I understand. But this water that overflows will run away; how are you going to gather it up?'

"Then he began stuffing me and explained to me that all we should have to do would be to refill the barrel with the water his wife had displaced as soon as she should have left. All the water we should pour in would be the measure. I supposed about ten pails; that would be a cubic metre. He isn't a fool, all the same, when he is drunk, that old horse.

"To be brief, we reached his house and I took a look at its mistress. A beautiful woman she certainly was not. Anyone can see her, for there she is. I said to myself: 'I am disappointed, but never mind, she will be of value; handsome or ugly, it is all the same, is it not, monsieur le president?' And then I saw that she was as thin as a rail. I said to myself: 'She will not measure four hundred litres.' I understand the matter, it being in liquids.

"She told you about the proceeding. I even let her keep on her chemise and stockings, to my own disadvantage.

"When that was done she ran away. I said: 'Look out, Brument! she is escaping.'

"He replied: 'Do not be afraid. I will catch her all right. She will have to come back to sleep, I will measure the deficit.'

"We measured. Not four pailfuls. Ha, Ha, Ha!"

The witness began to laugh so persistently that a gendarme was obliged to punch him in the back. Having quieted down, he resumed:

"In short, Brument exclaimed: 'Nothing doing, that is not enough.' I bawled and bawled, and bawled again, he punched me, I hit back. That would have kept on till the Day of judgment, seeing we were both drunk.

"Then came the gendarmes! They swore at us, they took us off to prison. I want damages."

He sat down.

Brument confirmed in every particular the statements of his accomplice. The jury, in consternation, retired to deliberate.

At the end of an hour they returned a verdict of acquittal for the defendants, with some severe strictures on the dignity of marriage, and establishing the precise limitations of business transactions.

Brument went home to the domestic roof accompanied by his wife.

Cornu went back to his business.

THE IMPOLITE SEX

Madame de X. to Madame de L.

ETRETAT, Friday.

My Dear Aunt:

I am coming to see you without anyone knowing it. I shall be at Les Fresnes on the 2d of September, the day before the hunting season opens, as I do not want to miss it, so that I may tease these gentlemen. You are too good, aunt, and you will allow them, as you usually do when there are no strange guests, to come to table, under pretext of fatigue, without dressing or shaving for the occasion.

They are delighted, of course, when I am not present. But I shall be there and will hold a review, like a general, at dinner time; and, if I find a single one of them at all careless in dress, no matter how little, I mean to send them down to the kitchen with the servants.

The men of to-day have so little consideration for others and so little good manners that one must be always severe with them. We live indeed in an age of vulgarity. When they quarrel, they insult each other in terms worthy of longshoremen, and, in our presence, they do not conduct themselves even as well as our servants. It is at the seaside that you see this most clearly. They are to be found there in battalions, and you can judge them in the lump. Oh! what coarse beings they are!

Just imagine, in a train, a gentleman who looked well, as I thought at first sight, thanks to his tailor, carefully took off his boots in order to put on a pair of old shoes! Another, an old man who was probably some wealthy upstart (these are the most ill-bred), while sitting opposite to me, had the delicacy to place his two feet on the seat quite close to me. This is a positive fact.

At the watering-places the vulgarity is unrestrained. I must here make one admission—that my indignation is perhaps due to the fact that I am not accustomed to associate, as a rule, with the sort of people one comes across here, for I should be less shocked by their manners if I had the opportunity of observing them oftener. In the office of the hotel I was nearly thrown down by a young man who snatched the key over my head. Another knocked against me so violently without begging my pardon or lifting his hat, coming away from a ball at the Casino, that it gave me a pain in the chest. It is the same way with all of them. Watch them addressing ladies on the terrace; they scarcely ever bow. They merely raise their hands to their headgear. But, indeed, as they are all more or less bald, it is the best plan.

But what exasperates and disgusts me particularly is the liberty they take of talking in public, without any kind of precaution, about the most revolting adventures. When two men are together, they relate to each other, in the broadest language and with the most abominable comments really horrible stories, without caring in the slightest degree whether a woman's ear is within reach of their voices. Yesterday, on the beach, I was forced to leave the place where I was sitting in order not to be any longer the involuntary confidante of an obscene anecdote, told in such immodest language that I felt just as humiliated as indignant at having heard it. Would not the most elementary good-breeding teach them to speak in a lower tone about such matters when we are near at hand. Etretat is, moreover, the country of gossip and scandal. From five to seven o'clock you can see people wandering about in quest of scandal, which they retail from group to group. As you remarked to me, my dear aunt, tittle-tattle is the mark of petty individuals and petty minds. It is also the consolation of women who are no longer loved or sought after. It is enough for me to observe the women who are fondest of gossiping to be persuaded that you are quite right.

The other day I was present at a musical evening at the Casino, given by a remarkable artist, Madame Masson, who sings in a truly delightful manner. I took the opportunity of applauding the admirable Coquelin, as well as two charming vaudeville performers, M——and Meillet. I met, on this occasion, all the bathers who were at the beach. It is no great distinction this year.

Next day I went to lunch at Yport. I noticed a tall man with a beard, coming out of a large house like a castle. It was the painter, Jean Paul Laurens. He is not satisfied apparently with imprisoning the subjects of his pictures, he insists on imprisoning himself.

Then I found myself seated on the shingle close to a man still young, of gentle and refined appearance, who was reading poetry. But he read it with such concentration, with such passion, I may say, that he did not even raise his eyes towards me. I was somewhat astonished and asked the proprietor of the baths, without appearing to be much concerned, the name of this gentleman. I laughed to myself a little at this reader of rhymes; he seemed behind the age, for a man. This person, I thought, must be a simpleton. Well, aunt, I am now infatuated about this stranger. Just fancy, his name is Sully Prudhomme! I went back and sat down beside him again so as to get a good look at him. His face has an expression of calmness and of penetration. Somebody came to look for him, and I heard his voice, which is sweet and almost timid. He would certainly not tell obscene stories aloud in public or knock up against ladies without apologizing. He is assuredly a man of refinement, but his refinement is of an almost morbid, sensitive character, I will try this winter to get an introduction to him.

I have no more news, my dear aunt, and I must finish this letter in

haste, as the mail will soon close. I kiss your hands and your cheeks.

Your devoted niece,

BERTHE DE X.

P. S.—I should add, however, by way of justification of French politeness, that our fellow-countrymen are, when travelling, models of good manners in comparison with the abominable English, who seem to have been brought up in a stable, so careful are they not to discommode themselves in any way, while they always discommode their neighbors.

Madame de L. to Madame de X.

LES FRESNES, Saturday.

My Dear Child:

Many of the things you have said to me are very sensible, but that does not prevent you from being wrong. Like you, I used formerly to feel very indignant at the impoliteness of men, who, as I supposed, constantly treated me with neglect; but, as I grew older and reflected on everything, putting aside coquetry, and observing things without taking any part in them myself, I perceived this much—that if men are not always polite, women are always indescribably rude.

We imagine that we should be permitted to do anything, my darling, and at the same time we consider that we have a right to the utmost respect, and in the most flagrant manner we commit actions devoid of that elementary good-breeding of which you speak so feelingly.

I find, on the contrary, that men consider us much more than we consider them. Besides, darling, men must needs be, and are, what we make them. In a state of society, where women are all true gentlewomen, all men would become gentlemen.

Come now; just observe and reflect.

Look at two women meeting in the street. What an attitude each assumes towards the other! What disparaging looks! What contempt they throw into each glance! How they toss their heads while they inspect each other to find something to condemn! And, if the footpath is narrow, do you think one woman would make room for another, or would beg pardon as she sweeps by? Never! When two men jostle each other by accident in some narrow lane, each of them bows and at the same time gets out of the other's way, while we women press against each other stomach to stomach, face to face, insolently staring each other out of countenance.

Look at two women who are acquaintances meeting on a staircase outside the door of a friend's drawing-room, one of them just leaving, the other about to go in. They begin to talk to each other and block up all the landing. If anyone happens to be coming up behind them, man or woman, do you imagine that they will put themselves half an inch out of their way? Never! never!

I was waiting myself, with my watch in my hands, one day last winter at a certain drawing-room door. And, behind me, two gentlemen were also waiting without showing any readiness, as I did, to lose their temper. The reason was that they had long grown accustomed to our unconscionable insolence.

The other day, before leaving Paris, I went to dine with no less a person than your husband, in the Champs Elysees, in order to enjoy the fresh air. Every table was occupied. The waiter asked us to wait and there would soon be a vacant table.

At that moment I noticed an elderly lady of noble figure, who, having paid for her dinner, seemed on the point of going away. She saw me, scanned me from head to foot, and did not budge. For more than a quarter of an hour she sat there, immovable, putting on her gloves, and calmly staring at those who were waiting like myself. Now, two young men who were just finishing their dinner, having seen me in their turn, hastily summoned the waiter, paid what they owed, and at once offered me their seats, even insisting on standing while waiting for their change. And, bear in mind, my fair niece, that I am no longer pretty, like you, but old and white-haired.

It is we, you see, who should be taught politeness, and the task would be such a difficult one that Hercules himself would not be equal to it. You speak to me about Etretat and about the people who indulged in "tittle-tattle" along the beach of that delightful watering-place. It is a spot now lost to me, a thing of the past, but I found much amusement therein days gone by.

There were only a few of us, people in good society, really good society, and a few artists, and we all fraternized. We paid little attention to gossip in those days.

As we had no monotonous Casino, where people only gather for show, where they whisper, where they dance stupidly, where they succeed in thoroughly boring one another, we sought some other way of passing our evenings pleasantly. Now, just guess what came into the head of one of our husbands? Nothing less than to go and dance each night in one of the farm-houses in the neighborhood.

We started out in a group with a street-organ, generally played by Le Poittevin, the painter, with a cotton nightcap on his head. Two men carried lanterns. We followed in procession, laughing and chattering like a pack of fools.

We woke up the farmer and his servant-maids and farm hands. We got them to make onion soup (horror!), and we danced under the apple trees, to the sound of the barrel-organ. The cocks waking up began to crow in the darkness of the out-houses; the horses began prancing on the straw of their stables. The cool air of the country caressed our cheeks with the smell of grass and of new-mown hay.

How long ago it is! How long ago it is! It is thirty years since then!

I do not want you, my darling, to come for the opening of the hunting

season. Why spoil the pleasure of our friends by inflicting on them

fashionable toilettes on this day of vigorous exercise in the country?

This is the way, child, that men are spoiled. I embrace you. Your old

aunt,

GENEVIEVE DE L.

A WEDDING GIFT

For a long time Jacques Bourdillere had sworn that he would never marry, but he suddenly changed his mind. It happened suddenly, one summer, at the seashore.

One morning as he lay stretched out on the sand, watching the women coming out of the water, a little foot had struck him by its neatness and daintiness. He raised his eyes and was delighted with the whole person, although in fact he could see nothing but the ankles and the head emerging from a flannel bathrobe carefully held closed. He was supposed to be sensual and a fast liver. It was therefore by the mere grace of the form that he was at first captured. Then he was held by the charm of the young girl's sweet mind, so simple and good, as fresh as her cheeks and lips.

He was presented to the family and pleased them. He immediately fell madly in love. When he saw Berthe Lannis in the distance, on the long yellow stretch of sand, he would tingle to the roots of his hair. When he was near her he would become silent, unable to speak or even to think, with a kind of throbbing at his heart, and a buzzing in his ears, and a bewilderment in his mind. Was that love?

He did not know or understand, but he had fully decided to have this child for his wife.

Her parents hesitated for a long time, restrained by the young man's bad reputation. It was said that he had an old sweetheart, one of these binding attachments which one always believes to be broken off and yet which always hold.

Besides, for a shorter or longer period, he loved every woman who came within reach of his lips.

Then he settled down and refused, even once, to see the one with whom he had lived for so long. A friend took care of this woman's pension and assured her an income. Jacques paid, but he did not even wish to hear of her, pretending even to ignore her name. She wrote him letters which he never opened. Every week he would recognize the clumsy writing of the abandoned woman, and every week a greater anger surged within him against her, and he would quickly tear the envelope and the paper, without opening it, without reading one single line, knowing in advance the reproaches and complaints which it contained.

As no one had much faith in his constancy, the test was prolonged through the winter, and Berthe's hand was not granted him until the spring. The wedding took place in Paris at the beginning of May.

The young couple had decided not to take the conventional wedding trip, but after a little dance for the younger cousins, which would not be prolonged after eleven o'clock, in order that this day of lengthy ceremonies might not be too tiresome, the young pair were to spend the first night in the parental home and then, on the following morning, to leave for the beach so dear to their hearts, where they had first known and loved each other.

Night had come, and the dance was going on in the large parlor. 'The two had retired into a little Japanese boudoir hung with bright silks and dimly lighted by the soft rays of a large colored lantern hanging from the ceiling like a gigantic egg. Through the open window the fresh air from outside passed over their faces like a caress, for the night was warm and calm, full of the odor of spring.

They were silent, holding each other's hands and from time to time squeezing them with all their might. She sat there with a dreamy look, feeling a little lost at this great change in her life, but smiling, moved, ready to cry, often also almost ready to faint from joy, believing the whole world to be changed by what had just happened to her, uneasy, she knew not why, and feeling her whole body and soul filled with an indefinable and delicious lassitude.

He was looking at her persistently with a fixed smile. He wished to speak, but found nothing to say, and so sat there, expressing all his ardor by pressures of the hand. From time to time he would murmur: "Berthe!" And each time she would raise her eyes to him with a look of tenderness; they would look at each other for a second and then her look, pierced and fascinated by his, would fall.

They found no thoughts to exchange. They had been left alone, but occasionally some of the dancers would cast a rapid glance at them, as though they were the discreet and trusty witnesses of a mystery.

A door opened and a servant entered, holding on a tray a letter which a messenger had just brought. Jacques, trembling, took this paper, overwhelmed by a vague and sudden fear, the mysterious terror of swift misfortune.

He looked for a longtime at the envelope, the writing on which he did not know, not daring to open it, not wishing to read it, with a wild desire to put it in his pocket and say to himself: "I'll leave that till to-morrow, when I'm far away!" But on one corner two big words, underlined, "Very urgent," filled him with terror. Saying, "Please excuse me, my dear," he tore open the envelope. He read the paper, grew frightfully pale, looked over it again, and, slowly, he seemed to spell it out word for word.

When he raised his head his whole expression showed how upset he was. He stammered: "My dear, it's—it's from my best friend, who has had a very great misfortune. He has need of me immediately—for a matter of life or death. Will you excuse me if I leave you for half an hour? I'll be right back."

Trembling and dazed, she stammered: "Go, my dear!" not having been his wife long enough to dare to question him, to demand to know. He disappeared. She remained alone, listening to the dancing in the neighboring parlor.

He had seized the first hat and coat he came to and rushed downstairs three steps at a time. As he was emerging into the street he stopped under the gas-jet of the vestibule and reread the letter. This is what it said:

SIR: A girl by the name of Ravet, an old sweetheart of yours, it

seems, has just given birth to a child that she says is yours. The

mother is about to die and is begging for you. I take the liberty to

write and ask you if you can grant this last request to a woman who

seems to be very unhappy and worthy of pity.

Yours truly,   DR. BONNARD.

When he reached the sick-room the woman was already on the point of death. He did not recognize her at first. The doctor and two nurses were taking care of her. And everywhere on the floor were pails full of ice and rags covered with blood. Water flooded the carpet; two candles were burning on a bureau; behind the bed, in a little wicker crib, the child was crying, and each time it would moan the mother, in torture, would try to move, shivering under her ice bandages.

She was mortally wounded, killed by this birth. Her life was flowing from her, and, notwithstanding the ice and the care, the merciless hemorrhage continued, hastening her last hour.

She recognized Jacques and wished to raise her arms. They were so weak that she could not do so, but tears coursed down her pallid cheeks. He dropped to his knees beside the bed, seized one of her hands and kissed it frantically. Then, little by little, he drew close to the thin face, which started at the contact. One of the nurses was lighting them with a candle, and the doctor was watching them from the back of the room.

Then she said in a voice which sounded as though it came from a distance: "I am going to die, dear. Promise to stay to the end. Oh! don't leave me now. Don't leave me in my last moments!"

He kissed her face and her hair, and, weeping, he murmured: "Do not be uneasy; I will stay."

It was several minutes before she could speak again, she was so weak. She continued: "The little one is yours. I swear it before God and on my soul. I swear it as I am dying! I have never loved another man but you —promise to take care of the child."

He was trying to take this poor pain-racked body in his arms. Maddened by remorse and sorrow, he stammered: "I swear to you that I will bring him up and love him. He shall never leave me."

Then she tried to kiss Jacques. Powerless to lift her head, she held out her white lips in an appeal for a kiss. He approached his lips to respond to this piteous entreaty.

As soon as she felt a little calmer, she murmured: "Bring him here and let me see if you love him."

He went and got the child. He placed him gently on the bed between them, and the little one stopped crying. She murmured: "Don't move any more!" And he was quiet. And he stayed there, holding in his burning hand this other hand shaking in the chill of death, just as, a while ago, he had been holding a hand trembling with love. From time to time he would cast a quick glance at the clock, which marked midnight, then one o'clock, then two.

The physician had returned. The two nurses, after noiselessly moving about the room for a while, were now sleeping on chairs. The child was asleep, and the mother, with eyes shut, appeared also to be resting.

Suddenly, just as pale daylight was creeping in behind the curtains, she stretched out her arms with such a quick and violent motion that she almost threw her baby on the floor. A kind of rattle was heard in her throat, then she lay on her back motionless, dead.

The nurses sprang forward and declared: "All is over!"

He looked once more at this woman whom he had so loved, then at the clock, which pointed to four, and he ran away, forgetting his overcoat, in the evening dress, with the child in his arms.

After he had left her alone the young wife had waited, calmly enough at first, in the little Japanese boudoir. Then, as she did not see him return, she went back to the parlor with an indifferent and calm appearance, but terribly anxious. When her mother saw her alone she asked: "Where is your husband?" She answered: "In his room; he is coming right back."

After an hour, when everybody had questioned her, she told about the letter, Jacques' upset appearance and her fears of an accident.

Still they waited. The guests left; only the nearest relatives remained. At midnight the bride was put to bed, sobbing bitterly. Her mother and two aunts, sitting around the bed, listened to her crying, silent and in despair. The father had gone to the commissary of police to see if he could obtain some news.

At five o'clock a slight noise was heard in the hall. A door was softly opened and closed. Then suddenly a little cry like the mewing of a cat was heard throughout the silent house.

All the women started forward and Berthe sprang ahead of them all, pushing her way past her aunts, wrapped in a bathrobe.

Jacques stood in the middle of the room, pale and out of breath, holding an infant in his arms. The four women looked at him, astonished; but Berthe, who had suddenly become courageous, rushed forward with anguish in her heart, exclaiming: "What is it? What's the matter?"

He looked about him wildly and answered shortly:

"I—I have a child and the mother has just died."

And with his clumsy hands he held out the screaming infant.

Without saying a word, Berthe seized the child, kissed it and hugged it to her. Then she raised her tear-filled eyes to him, asking: "Did you say that the mother was dead?" He answered: "Yes—just now—in my arms. I had broken with her since summer. I knew nothing. The physician sent for me."

Then Berthe murmured: "Well, we will bring up the little one."

THE RELIC

"To the Abbe Louis d'Ennemare, at Soissons.

"My Dear Abbe.

"My marriage with your cousin is broken off in the most stupid way, all on account of an idiotic trick which I almost involuntarily played my intended. In my perplexity I turn to you, my old school chum, for you may be able to help me out of the difficulty. If you can, I shall be grateful to you until I die.

"You know Gilberte, or, rather, you think you know her, but do we ever understand women? All their opinions, their ideas, their creeds, are a surprise to us. They are all full of twists and turns, cf the unforeseen, of unintelligible arguments, of defective logic and of obstinate ideas, which seem final, but which they alter because a little bird came and perched on the window ledge.

"I need not tell you that your cousin is very religious, as she was brought up by the White (or was it the Black?) Ladies at Nancy. You know that better than I do, but what you perhaps do not know is, that she is just as excitable about other matters as she is about religion. Her head flies away, just as a leaf is whirled away by the wind; and she is a true woman, or, rather, girl, for she is moved or made angry in a moment, starting off at a gallop in affection, just as she does in hatred, and returning in the same manner; and she is pretty—as you know, and more charming than I can say—as you will never know.

"Well, we became engaged, and I adored her, as I adore her still, and she appeared to love me.

"One evening, I received a telegram summoning me to Cologne for a consultation, which might be followed by a serious and difficult operation, and as I had to start the next morning, I went to wish Gilberte good-by, and tell her why I could not dine with them on Wednesday, but would do so on Friday, the day of my return. Ah! Beware of Fridays, for I assure you they are unlucky!

"When I told her that I had to go to Germany, I saw that her eyes filled with tears, but when I said I should be back very soon, she clapped her hands, and said:

"'I am very glad you are going, then! You must bring me back something; a mere trifle, just a souvenir, but a souvenir that you have chosen for me. You must guess what I should like best, do you hear? And then I shall see whether you have any imagination.'

"She thought for a few moments, and then added:

"'I forbid you to spend more than twenty francs on it. I want it for the intention, and for a remembrance of your penetration, and not for its intrinsic value.'

"And then, after another moment's silence, she said, in a low voice, and with downcast eyes:

"'If it costs you nothing in money, but is something very ingenious and pretty, I will—I will kiss you.'

"The next day I was in Cologne. It was a case of a terrible accident, which had plunged a whole family into despair, and a difficult amputation was necessary. They lodged me in the house; I might say, they almost locked me up, and I saw nobody but people in tears, who almost deafened me with their lamentations; I operated on a man who appeared to be in a moribund state, and who nearly died under my hands, and with whom I remained two nights; and then, when I saw that there was a chance of his recovery, I drove to the station. I had, however, made a mistake in the trains, and I had an hour to wait, and so I wandered about the streets, still thinking of my poor patient, when a man accosted me. I do not know German, and he was totally ignorant of French, but at last I made out that he was offering me some relics. I thought of Gilberte, for I knew her fanatical devotion, and here was my present ready to hand, so I followed the man into a shop where religious objects were for sale, and I bought a small piece of a bone of one of the Eleven Thousand Virgins.

"The pretended relic was inclosed in a charming old silver box, and that determined my choice, and, putting my purchase into my pocket, I went to the railway station, and so on to Paris.

"As soon as I got home, I wished to examine my purchase again, and on taking hold of it, I found that the box was open, and the relic missing! I searched in vain in my pocket, and turned it inside out; the small bit of bone, which was no bigger than half a pin, had disappeared.

"You know, my dear little Abbe, that my faith is not very fervent, but, as my friend, you are magnanimous enough to put up with my lukewarmness, and to leave me alone, and to wait for the future, so you say. But I absolutely disbelieve in the relics of secondhand dealers in piety, and you share my doubts in that respect. Therefore, the loss of that bit of sheep's carcass did not grieve me, and I easily procured a similar fragment, which I carefully fastened inside my jewel-box, and then I went to see my intended.

"As soon as she saw me, she ran up to me, smiling and eager, and, said to me:

"'What have you brought me?'

"I pretended to have forgotten, but she did not believe me, and I made her beg, and even beseech me. But when I saw that she was devoured by curiosity, I gave her the sacred silver box. She appeared overjoyed.

"'A relic! Oh! A relic!'

"And she kissed the box passionately, so that I was ashamed of my deception. She was not quite satisfied, however, and her uneasiness soon turned to terrible fear, and looking straight into my eyes, she said:

"'Are you sure-that it is genuine?'

"'Absolutely certain.'

"'How can you be so certain?'

"I was trapped; for to say that I had bought it of a man in the streets would be my destruction. What was I to say? A wild idea struck me, and I said, in a low, mysterious voice:

"'I stole it for you.'

"She looked at me with astonishment and delight in her large eyes.

"'Oh! You stole it? Where?'

"'In the cathedral; in the very shrine of the Eleven Thousand Virgins.'

"Her heart beat with pleasure, and she murmured:

"'Oh! Did you really do that-for me? Tell me-all about it!'

"That was the climax; I could not retract what I had said. I made up a fanciful story; with precise details: I had given the custodian of the building a hundred francs to be allowed to go about the building by myself; the shrine was being repaired, but I happened to be there at the breakfast hour of the workmen and clergy; by removing a small panel, I had been enabled to seize a small piece of bone (oh! so small), among a quantity of others (I said a quantity, as I thought of the amount that the remains of the skeletons of eleven thousand virgins must produce). Then I went to a goldsmith's and bought a casket worthy of the relic; and I was not sorry to let her know that the silver box cost me five hundred francs.

"But she did not think of that; she listened to me, trembling, in an ecstasy, and whispering: 'How I love you!' she threw herself into my arms.

"Just note this: I had committed sacrilege for her sake. I had committed a theft; I had violated a church; I had violated a shrine; violated and stolen holy relics, and for that she adored me, thought me perfect, tender, divine. Such is woman, my dear Abbe, every woman.

"For two months I was the most admirable of lovers. In her room, she had made a kind of magnificent chapel in which to keep this bit of mutton chop, which, as she thought, had made me commit that divine love-crime, and she worked up her religious enthusiasm in front of it every morning and evening. I had asked her to keep the matter secret, for fear, as I said, that I might be arrested, condemned, and given over to Germany, and she kept her promise.

"Well, at the beginning of the summer, she was seized with an irresistible desire to see the scene of my exploit, and she teased her father so persistently (without telling him her secret reason), that he took her to Cologne, but without telling me of their trip, according to his daughter's wish.

"I need not tell you that I had not seen the interior of the cathedral. I do not know where the tomb (if there be a tomb) of the Eleven Thousand Virgins is; and then, it appears, it is unapproachable, alas!

"A week afterward, I received ten lines, breaking off our engagement, and then an explanatory letter from her father, whom she had, somewhat late, taken into her confidence.

"At the sight of the shrine, she had suddenly seen through my trickery and my lie, and at the same time discovered my real innocence of any crime. Having asked the keeper of the relics whether any robbery had been committed, the man began to laugh, and pointed out to them how impossible such a crime was. But, from the moment that I had not plunged my profane hand into venerable relics, I was no longer worthy of my fair-haired, sensitive betrothed.

"I was forbidden the house; I begged and prayed in vain; nothing could move the fair devotee, and I became ill from grief. Well, last week, her cousin, Madame d'Arville, who is your cousin also, sent me word that she should like to see me, and when I called, she told me on what conditions I might obtain my pardon, and here they are. I must bring her a relic, a real, authentic relic of some virgin and martyr, certified to be such by our Holy Father, the Pope, and I am going mad from embarrassment and anxiety.

"I will go to Rome, if needful, but I cannot call on the Pope unexpectedly, to tell him my stupid misadventure; and, besides, I doubt whether they allow private individuals to have relics. Could not you give me an introduction to some cardinal, or even to some French prelate who possesses some remains of a female saint? Or, perhaps, you may have the precious object she wants in your collection?

"Help me out of my difficulty, my dear Abbe, and I promise you that I will be converted ten years sooner than I otherwise should be!

"Madame d'Arville, who takes the matter seriously, said to me the other day:

"'Poor Gilberte will never marry.'

"My dear old schoolmate, will you allow your cousin to die the victim of a stupid piece of subterfuge on my part? Pray prevent her from being virgin eleven thousand and one.

"Pardon me, I am unworthy, but I embrace you, and love you with all my heart.

"Your old friend,

"HENRI FONTAL."

VOLUME IV.

THE MORIBUND

The warm autumn sun was beating down on the farmyard. Under the grass, which had been cropped close by the cows, the earth soaked by recent rains, was soft and sank in under the feet with a soggy noise, and the apple trees, loaded with apples, were dropping their pale green fruit in the dark green grass.

Four young heifers, tied in a line, were grazing and at times looking toward the house and lowing. The fowls made a colored patch on the dung-heap before the stable, scratching, moving about and cackling, while two roosters crowed continually, digging worms for their hens, whom they were calling with a loud clucking.

The wooden gate opened and a man entered. He might have been forty years old, but he looked at least sixty, wrinkled, bent, walking slowly, impeded by the weight of heavy wooden shoes full of straw. His long arms hung down on both sides of his body. When he got near the farm a yellow cur, tied at the foot of an enormous pear tree, beside a barrel which served as his kennel, began at first to wag his tail and then to bark for joy. The man cried:

"Down, Finot!"

The dog was quiet.

A peasant woman came out of the house. Her large, flat, bony body was outlined under a long woollen jacket drawn in at the waist. A gray skirt, too short, fell to the middle of her legs, which were encased in blue stockings. She, too, wore wooden shoes, filled with straw. The white cap, turned yellow, covered a few hairs which were plastered to the scalp, and her brown, thin, ugly, toothless face had that wild, animal expression which is often to be found on the faces of the peasants.

The man asked:

"How is he gettin' along?"

The woman answered:

"The priest said it's the end—that he will never live through the night."

Both of them went into the house.

After passing through the kitchen, they entered a low, dark room, barely lighted by one window, in front of which a piece of calico was hanging. The big beams, turned brown with age and smoke, crossed the room from one side to the other, supporting the thin floor of the garret, where an army of rats ran about day and night.

The moist, lumpy earthen floor looked greasy, and, at the back of the room, the bed made an indistinct white spot. A harsh, regular noise, a difficult, hoarse, wheezing breathing, like the gurgling of water from a broken pump, came from the darkened couch where an old man, the father of the peasant woman, was dying.

The man and the woman approached the dying man and looked at him with calm, resigned eyes.

The son-in-law said:

"I guess it's all up with him this time; he will not last the night."

The woman answered:

"He's been gurglin' like that ever since midday." They were silent. The father's eyes were closed, his face was the color of the earth and so dry that it looked like wood. Through his open mouth came his harsh, rattling breath, and the gray linen sheet rose and fell with each respiration.

The son-in-law, after a long silence, said:

"There's nothing more to do; I can't help him. It's a nuisance, just the same, because the weather is good and we've got a lot of work to do."

His wife seemed annoyed at this idea. She reflected a few moments and then said:

"He won't be buried till Saturday, and that will give you all day tomorrow."

The peasant thought the matter over and answered:

"Yes, but to-morrow I'll have to invite the people to the funeral. That means five or six hours to go round to Tourville and Manetot, and to see everybody."

The woman, after meditating two or three minutes, declared:

"It isn't three o'clock yet. You could begin this evening and go all round the country to Tourville. You can just as well say that he's dead, seem' as he's as good as that now."

The man stood perplexed for a while, weighing the pros and cons of the idea. At last he declared:

"Well, I'll go!"

He was leaving the room, but came back after a minute's hesitation:

"As you haven't got anythin' to do you might shake down some apples to bake and make four dozen dumplings for those who come to the funeral, for one must have something to cheer them. You can light the fire with the wood that's under the shed. It's dry."

He left the room, went back into the kitchen, opened the cupboard, took out a six-pound loaf of bread, cut off a slice, and carefully gathered the crumbs in the palm of his hand and threw them into his mouth, so as not to lose anything. Then, with the end of his knife, he scraped out a little salt butter from the bottom of an earthen jar, spread it on his bread and began to eat slowly, as he did everything.

He recrossed the farmyard, quieted the dog, which had started barking again, went out on the road bordering on his ditch, and disappeared in the direction of Tourville.

As soon as she was alone, the woman began to work. She uncovered the meal-bin and made the dough for the dumplings. She kneaded it a long time, turning it over and over again, punching, pressing, crushing it. Finally she made a big, round, yellow-white ball, which she placed on the corner of the table.

Then she went to get her apples, and, in order not to injure the tree with a pole, she climbed up into it by a ladder. She chose the fruit with care, only taking the ripe ones, and gathering them in her apron.

A voice called from the road:

"Hey, Madame Chicot!"

She turned round. It was a neighbor, Osime Favet, the mayor, on his way to fertilize his fields, seated on the manure-wagon, with his feet hanging over the side. She turned round and answered:

"What can I do for you, Maitre Osime?"

"And how is the father?"

She cried:

"He is as good as dead. The funeral is Saturday at seven, because there's lots of work to be done."

The neighbor answered:

"So! Good luck to you! Take care of yourself."

To his kind remarks she answered:"

"Thanks; the same to you."

And she continued picking apples.

When she went back to the house, she went over to look at her father, expecting to find him dead. But as soon as she reached the door she heard his monotonous, noisy rattle, and, thinking it a waste of time to go over to him, she began to prepare her dumplings. She wrapped up the fruit, one by one, in a thin layer of paste, then she lined them up on the edge of the table. When she had made forty-eight dumplings, arranged in dozens, one in front of the other, she began to think of preparing supper, and she hung her kettle over the fire to cook potatoes, for she judged it useless to heat the oven that day, as she had all the next day in which to finish the preparations.

Her husband returned at about five. As soon as he had crossed the threshold he asked:

"Is it over?"

She answered:

"Not yet; he's still gurglin'."

They went to look at him. The old man was in exactly the same condition. His hoarse rattle, as regular as the ticking of a clock, was neither quicker nor slower. It returned every second, the tone varying a little, according as the air entered or left his chest.

His son-in-law looked at him and then said:

"He'll pass away without our noticin' it, just like a candle."

They returned to the kitchen and started to eat without saying a word. When they had swallowed their soup, they ate another piece of bread and butter. Then, as soon as the dishes were washed, they returned to the dying man.

The woman, carrying a little lamp with a smoky wick, held it in front of her father's face. If he had not been breathing, one would certainly have thought him dead.

The couple's bed was hidden in a little recess at the other end of the room. Silently they retired, put out the light, closed their eyes, and soon two unequal snores, one deep and the other shriller, accompanied the uninterrupted rattle of the dying man.

The rats ran about in the garret.

The husband awoke at the first streaks of dawn. His father-in-law was still alive. He shook his wife, worried by the tenacity of the old man.

"Say, Phemie, he don't want to quit. What would you do?"

He knew that she gave good advice.

She answered:

"You needn't be afraid; he can't live through the day. And the mayor won't stop our burying him tomorrow, because he allowed it for Maitre Renard's father, who died just during the planting season."

He was convinced by this argument, and left for the fields.

His wife baked the dumplings and then attended to her housework.

At noon the old man was not dead. The people hired for the day's work came by groups to look at him. Each one had his say. Then they left again for the fields.

At six o'clock, when the work was over, the father was still breathing. At last his son-in-law was frightened.

"What would you do now, Phemie?"

She no longer knew how to solve the problem. They went to the mayor. He promised that he would close his eyes and authorize the funeral for the following day. They also went to the health officer, who likewise promised, in order to oblige Maitre Chicot, to antedate the death certificate. The man and the woman returned, feeling more at ease.

They went to bed and to sleep, just as they did the preceding day, their sonorous breathing blending with the feeble breathing of the old man.

When they awoke, he was not yet dead.

Then they began to be frightened. They stood by their father, watching him with distrust, as though he had wished to play them a mean trick, to deceive them, to annoy them on purpose, and they were vexed at him for the time which he was making them lose.

The son-in-law asked:

"What am I goin' to do?"

She did not know. She answered:

"It certainly is annoying!"

The guests who were expected could not be notified. They decided to wait and explain the case to them.

Toward a quarter to seven the first ones arrived. The women in black, their heads covered with large veils, looking very sad. Then men, ill at ease in their homespun coats, were coming forward more slowly, in couples, talking business.

Maitre Chicot and his wife, bewildered, received them sorrowfully, and suddenly both of them together began to cry as they approached the first group. They explained the matter, related their difficulty, offered chairs, bustled about, tried to make excuses, attempting to prove that everybody would have done as they did, talking continually and giving nobody a chance to answer.

They were going from one person to another:

"I never would have thought it; it's incredible how he can last this long!"

The guests, taken aback, a little disappointed, as though they had missed an expected entertainment, did not know what to do, some remaining seated others standing. Several wished to leave. Maitre Chicot held them back:

"You must take something, anyhow! We made some dumplings; might as well make use of 'em."

The faces brightened at this idea. The yard was filling little by little; the early arrivals were telling the news to those who had arrived later. Everybody was whispering. The idea of the dumplings seemed to cheer everyone up.

The women went in to take a look at the dying man. They crossed themselves beside the bed, muttered a prayer and went out again. The men, less anxious for this spectacle, cast a look through the window, which had been opened.

Madame Chicot explained her distress:

"That's how he's been for two days, neither better nor worse. Doesn't he sound like a pump that has gone dry?"

When everybody had had a look at the dying man, they thought of the refreshments; but as there were too many people for the kitchen to hold, the table was moved out in front of the door. The four dozen golden dumplings, tempting and appetizing, arranged in two big dishes, attracted the eyes of all. Each one reached out to take his, fearing that there would not be enough. But four remained over.

Maitre Chicot, his mouth full, said:

"Father would feel sad if he were to see this. He loved them so much when he was alive."

A big, jovial peasant declared:

"He won't eat any more now. Each one in his turn."

This remark, instead of making the guests sad, seemed to cheer them up. It was their turn now to eat dumplings.

Madame Chicot, distressed at the expense, kept running down to the cellar continually for cider. The pitchers were emptied in quick succession. The company was laughing and talking loud now. They were beginning to shout as they do at feasts.

Suddenly an old peasant woman who had stayed beside the dying man, held there by a morbid fear of what would soon happen to herself, appeared at the window and cried in a shrill voice:

"He's dead! he's dead!"

Everybody was silent. The women arose quickly to go and see. He was indeed dead. The rattle had ceased. The men looked at each other, looking down, ill at ease. They hadn't finished eating the dumplings. Certainly the rascal had not chosen a propitious moment. The Chicots were no longer weeping. It was over; they were relieved.

They kept repeating:

"I knew it couldn't 'last. If he could only have done it last night, it would have saved us all this trouble."

Well, anyhow, it was over. They would bury him on Monday, that was all, and they would eat some more dumplings for the occasion.

The guests went away, talking the matter over, pleased at having had the chance to see him and of getting something to eat.

And when the husband and wife were alone, face to face, she said, her face distorted with grief:

"We'll have to bake four dozen more dumplings! Why couldn't he have made up his mind last night?"

The husband, more resigned, answered:

"Well, we'll not have to do this every day."

THE GAMEKEEPER

It was after dinner, and we were talking about adventures and accidents which happened while out shooting.

An old friend, known to all of us, M. Boniface, a great sportsman and a connoisseur of wine, a man of wonderful physique, witty and gay, and endowed with an ironical and resigned philosophy, which manifested itself in caustic humor, and never in melancholy, suddenly exclaimed:

"I know a story, or rather a tragedy, which is somewhat peculiar. It is not at all like those which one hears of usually, and I have never told it, thinking that it would interest no one.

"It is not at all sympathetic. I mean by that, that it does not arouse the kind of interest which pleases or which moves one agreeably.

"Here is the story:

"I was then about thirty-five years of age, and a most enthusiastic sportsman.

"In those days I owned a lonely bit of property in the neighborhood of Jumieges, surrounded by forests and abounding in hares and rabbits. I was accustomed to spending four or five days alone there each year, there not being room enough to allow of my bringing a friend with me.

"I had placed there as gamekeeper, an old retired gendarme, a good man, hot-tempered, a severe disciplinarian, a terror to poachers and fearing nothing. He lived all alone, far from the village, in a little house, or rather hut, consisting of two rooms downstairs, with kitchen and store-room, and two upstairs. One of them, a kind of box just large enough to accommodate a bed, a cupboard and a chair, was reserved for my use.

"Old man Cavalier lived in the other one. When I said that he was alone in this place, I was wrong. He had taken his nephew with him, a young scamp about fourteen years old, who used to go to the village and run errands for the old man.

"This young scapegrace was long and lanky, with yellow hair, so light that it resembled the fluff of a plucked chicken, so thin that he seemed bald. Besides this, he had enormous feet and the hands of a giant.

"He was cross-eyed, and never looked at anyone. He struck me as being in the same relation to the human race as ill-smelling beasts are to the animal race. He reminded me of a polecat.

"He slept in a kind of hole at the top of the stairs which led to the two rooms.

"But during my short sojourns at the Pavilion—so I called the hut —Marius would give up his nook to an old woman from Ecorcheville, called Celeste, who used to come and cook for me, as old man Cavalier's stews were not sufficient for my healthy appetite.

"You now know the characters and the locality. Here is the story:

"It was on the fifteenth of October, 1854—I shall remember that date as long as I live.

"I left Rouen on horseback, followed by my dog Bock, a big Dalmatian hound from Poitou, full-chested and with a heavy jaw, which could retrieve among the bushes like a Pont-Andemer spaniel.

"I was carrying my satchel slung across my back and my gun diagonally across my chest. It was a cold, windy, gloomy day, with clouds scurrying across the sky.

"As I went up the hill at Canteleu, I looked over the broad valley of the Seine, the river winding in and out along its course as far as the eye could see. To the right the towers of Rouen stood out against the sky, and to the left the landscape was bounded by the distant slopes covered with trees. Then I crossed the forest of Roumare and, toward five o'clock, reached the Pavilion, where Cavalier and Celeste were expecting me.

"For ten years I had appeared there at the same time, in the same manner; and for ten years the same faces had greeted me with the same words:

"'Welcome, master! We hope your health is good.'

"Cavalier had hardly changed. He withstood time like an old tree; but Celeste, especially in the past four years, had become unrecognizable.

"She was bent almost double, and, although still active, when she walked her body was almost at right angles to her legs.

"The old woman, who was very devoted to me, always seemed affected at seeing me again, and each time, as I left, she would say:

"'This may be the last time, master.'

"The sad, timid farewell of this old servant, this hopeless resignation to the inevitable fate which was not far off for her, moved me strangely each year.

"I dismounted, and while Cavalier, whom I had greeted, was leading my horse to the little shed which served as a stable, I entered the kitchen, which also served as dining-room, followed by Celeste.

"Here the gamekeeper joined us. I saw at first glance that something was the matter. He seemed preoccupied, ill at ease, worried.

"I said to him:

"'Well, Cavalier, is everything all right?'

"He muttered:

"'Yes and no. There are things I don't like.'

"I asked:

"'What? Tell me about it.'

"But he shook his head.

"'No, not yet, monsieur. I do not wish to bother you with my little troubles so soon after your arrival.'

"I insisted, but he absolutely refused to give me any information before dinner. From his expression, I could tell that it was something very serious.

"Not knowing what to say to him, I asked:

"'How about game? Much of it this year?'

"'Oh, yes! You'll find all you want. Thank heaven, I looked out for that.'

"He said this with so much seriousness, with such sad solemnity, that it was really almost funny. His big gray mustache seemed almost ready to drop from his lips.

"Suddenly I remembered that I had not yet seen his nephew.

"'Where is Marius? Why does he not show himself?'

"The gamekeeper started, looking me suddenly in the face:

"Well, monsieur, I had rather tell you the whole business right away; it's on account of him that I am worrying.'

"'Ah! Well, where is he?'

"'Over in the stable, monsieur. I was waiting for the right time to bring him out.'

"'What has he done?'

"'Well, monsieur——'

"The gamekeeper, however, hesitated, his voice altered and shaky, his face suddenly furrowed by the deep lines of an old man.

"He continued slowly:

"'Well, I found out, last winter, that someone was poaching in the woods of Roseraies, but I couldn't seem to catch the man. I spent night after night on the lookout for him. In vain. During that time they began poaching over by Ecorcheville. I was growing thin from vexation. But as for catching the trespasser, impossible! One might have thought that the rascal was forewarned of my plans.

"'But one day, while I was brushing Marius' Sunday trousers, I found forty cents in his pocket. Where did he get it?

"'I thought the matter over for about a week, and I noticed that he used to go out; he would leave the house just as I was coming home to go to bed—yes, monsieur.

"'Then I started to watch him, without the slightest suspicion of the real facts. One morning, just after I had gone to bed before him, I got right up again, and followed him. For shadowing a man, there is nobody like me, monsieur.

"'And I caught him, Marius, poaching on your land, monsieur; he my nephew, I your keeper!

"'The blood rushed to my head, and I almost killed him on the spot, I hit him so hard. Oh! yes, I thrashed him all right. And I promised him that he would get another beating from my hand, in your presence, as an example.

"'There! I have grown thin from sorrow. You know how it is when one is worried like that. But tell me, what would you have done? The boy has no father or mother, and I am the last one of his blood; I kept him, I couldn't drive him out, could I?

"'I told him that if it happened again I would have no more pity for him, all would be over. There! Did I do right, monsieur?'

"I answered, holding out my hand:

"'You did well, Cavalier; you are an honest man.'

"He rose.

"'Thank you, monsieur. Now I am going to fetch him. I must give him his thrashing, as an example.'

"I knew that it was hopeless to try and turn the old man from his idea. I therefore let him have his own way.

"He got the rascal and brought him back by the ear.

"I was seated on a cane chair, with the solemn expression of a judge.

"Marius seemed to have grown; he was homelier even than the year before, with his evil, sneaking expression.

"His big hands seemed gigantic.

"His uncle pushed him up to me, and, in his soldierly voice, said:

"'Beg the gentleman's pardon.'

"The boy didn't say a word.

"Then putting one arm round him, the former gendarme lifted him right off the ground, and began to whack him with such force that I rose to stop the blows.

"The boy was now howling: 'Mercy! mercy! mercy! I promise——'

"Cavalier put him back on the ground and forced him to his knees:

"'Beg for pardon,' he said.

"With eyes lowered, the scamp murmured:

"'I ask for pardon!'

"Then his uncle lifted him to his feet, and dismissed him with a cuff which almost knocked him down again.

"He made his escape, and I did not see him again that evening.

"Cavalier appeared overwhelmed.'

"'He is a bad egg,' he said.

"And throughout the whole dinner, he kept repeating:

"'Oh! that worries me, monsieur, that worries me.'

"I tried to comfort him, but in vain.

"I went to bed early, so that I might start out at daybreak.

"My dog was already asleep on the floor, at the foot of my bed, when I put out the light.

"I was awakened toward midnight by the furious barking of my dog Bock. I immediately noticed that my room was full of smoke. I jumped out of bed, struck a light, ran to the door and opened it. A cloud of flames burst in. The house was on fire.

"I quickly closed the heavy oak door and, drawing on my trousers, I first lowered the dog through the window, by means of a rope made of my sheets; then, having thrown out the rest of my clothes, my game-bag and my gun, I in turn escaped the same way.

"I began to shout with all my might: 'Cavalier! Cavalier! Cavalier!'

"But the gamekeeper did not wake up. He slept soundly like an old gendarme.

"However, I could see through the lower windows that the whole ground-floor was nothing but a roaring furnace; I also noticed that it had been filled with straw to make it burn readily.

"Somebody must purposely have set fire to the place!

"I continued shrieking wildly: 'Cavalier!'

"Then the thought struck me that the smoke might be suffocating him. An idea came to me. I slipped two cartridges into my gun, and shot straight at his window.

"The six panes of glass shattered into the room in a cloud of glass. This time the old man had heard me, and he appeared, dazed, in his nightshirt, bewildered by the glare which illumined the whole front of his 'house.

"I cried to him:

"'Your house is on fire! Escape through the window! Quick! Quick!'

"The flames were coming out through all the cracks downstairs, were licking along the wall, were creeping toward him and going to surround him. He jumped and landed on his feet, like a cat.

"It was none too soon. The thatched roof cracked in the middle, right over the staircase, which formed a kind of flue for the fire downstairs; and an immense red jet jumped up into the air, spreading like a stream of water and sprinkling a shower of sparks around the hut. In a few seconds it was nothing but a pool of flames.

"Cavalier, thunderstruck, asked:

"'How did the fire start?'

"I answered:

"'Somebody lit it in the kitchen.'

"He muttered:

"'Who could have started the fire?'

"And I, suddenly guessing, answered:

"'Marius!'

"The old man understood. He stammered:

"'Good God! That is why he didn't return.'

"A terrible thought flashed through my mind. I cried:

"'And Celeste! Celeste!'

"He did not answer. The house caved in before us, forming only an enormous, bright, blinding brazier, an awe-inspiring funeral-pile, where the poor woman could no longer be anything but a glowing ember, a glowing ember of human flesh.

"We had not heard a single cry.

"As the fire crept toward the shed, I suddenly bethought me of my horse, and Cavalier ran to free it.

"Hardly had he opened the door of the stable, when a supple, nimble body darted between his legs, and threw him on his face. It was Marius, running for all he was worth.

"The man was up in a second. He tried to run after the wretch, but, seeing that he could not catch him, and maddened by an irresistible anger, yielding to one of those thoughtless impulses which we cannot foresee or prevent, he picked up my gun, which was lying on the ground. near him, put it to his shoulder, and, before I could make a motion, he pulled the trigger without even noticing whether or not the weapon was loaded.

"One of the cartridges which I had put in to announce the fire was still intact, and the charge caught the fugitive right in the back,—throwing him forward on the ground, bleeding profusely. He immediately began to claw the earth with his hands and with his knees, as though trying to run on all fours like a rabbit who has been mortally wounded, and sees the hunter approaching.

"I rushed forward to the boy, but I could already hear the death-rattle. He passed away before the fire was extinguished, without having said a word.

"Cavalier, still in his shirt, his legs bare, was standing near us, motionless, dazed.

"When the people from the village arrived, my gamekeeper was taken away, like an insane man.

"I appeared at the trial as witness, and related the facts in detail, without changing a thing. Cavalier was acquitted. He disappeared that very day, leaving the country.

"I have never seen him since.

"There, gentlemen, that is my story."

THE STORY OF A FARM GIRL

PART I

As the weather was very fine, the people on the farm had hurried through their dinner and had returned to the fields.

The servant, Rose, remained alone in the large kitchen, where the fire was dying out on the hearth beneath the large boiler of hot water. From time to time she dipped out some water and slowly washed her dishes, stopping occasionally to look at the two streaks of light which the sun threw across the long table through the window, and which showed the defects in the glass.

Three venturesome hens were picking up the crumbs under the chairs, while the smell of the poultry yard and the warmth from the cow stall came in through the half-open door, and a cock was heard crowing in the distance.

When she had finished her work, wiped down the table, dusted the mantelpiece and put the plates on the high dresser close to the wooden clock with its loud tick-tock, she drew a long breath, as she felt rather oppressed, without exactly knowing why. She looked at the black clay walls, the rafters that were blackened with smoke and from which hung spiders' webs, smoked herrings and strings of onions, and then she sat down, rather overcome by the stale odor from the earthen floor, on which so many things had been continually spilled and which the heat brought out. With this there was mingled the sour smell of the pans of milk which were set out to raise the cream in the adjoining dairy.

She wanted to sew, as usual, but she did not feel strong enough, and so she went to the door to get a mouthful of fresh air, which seemed to do her good.

The fowls were lying on the steaming dunghill; some of them were scratching with one claw in search of worms, whlle the cock stood up proudly in their midst. When he crowed, the cocks in all the neighboring farmyards replied to him, as if they were uttering challenges from farm to farm.

The girl looked at them without thinking, and then she raised her eyes and was almost dazzled at the sight of the apple trees in blossom. Just then a colt, full of life and friskiness, jumped over the ditches and then stopped suddenly, as if surprised at being alone.

She also felt inclined to run; she felt inclined to move and to stretch her limbs and to repose in the warm, breathless air. She took a few undecided steps and closed her eyes, for she was seized with a feeling of animal comfort, and then she went to look for eggs in the hen loft. There were thirteen of them, which she took in and put into the storeroom; but the smell from the kitchen annoyed her again, and she went out to sit on the grass for a time.

The farmyard, which was surrounded by trees, seemed to be asleep. The tall grass, amid which the tall yellow dandelions rose up like streaks of yellow light, was of a vivid, fresh spring green. The apple trees cast their shade all round them, and the thatched roofs, on which grew blue and yellow irises, with their sword-like leaves, steamed as if the moisture of the stables and barns were coming through the straw. The girl went to the shed, where the carts and buggies were kept. Close to it, in a ditch, there was a large patch of violets, whose fragrance was spread abroad, while beyond the slope the open country could be seen, where grain was growing, with clumps of trees in places, and groups of laborers here and there, who looked as small as dolls, and white horses like toys, who were drawing a child's cart, driven by a man as tall as one's finger.

She took up a bundle of straw, threw it into the ditch and sat down upon it. Then, not feeling comfortable, she undid it, spread it out and lay down upon it at full length on her back, with both arms under her head and her legs stretched out.

Gradually her eyes closed, and she was falling into a state of delightful languor. She was, in fact, almost asleep when she felt two hands on her bosom, and she sprang up at a bound. It was Jacques, one of the farm laborers, a tall fellow from Picardy, who had been making love to her for a long time. He had been herding the sheep, and, seeing her lying down in the shade, had come up stealthily and holding his breath, with glistening eyes and bits of straw in his hair.

He tried to kiss her, but she gave him a smack in the face, for she was as strong as he, and he was shrewd enough to beg her pardon; so they sat down side by side and talked amicably. They spoke about the favorable weather, of their master, who was a good fellow, then of their neighbors, of all the people in the country round, of themselves, of their village, of their youthful days, of their recollections, of their relations, who had left them for a long time, and it might be forever. She grew sad as she thought of it, while he, with one fixed idea in his head, drew closer to her.

"I have not seen my mother for a long time," she said. "It is very hard to be separated like that," and she directed her looks into the distance, toward the village in the north which she had left.

Suddenly, however, he seized her by the neck and kissed her again, but she struck him so violently in the face with her clenched fist that his nose began to bleed, and he got up and laid his head against the stem of a tree. When she saw that, she was sorry, and going up to him, she said: "Have I hurt you?" He, however, only laughed. "No, it was a mere nothing; only she had hit him right on the middle of the nose. What a devil!" he said, and he looked at her with admiration, for she had inspired him with a feeling of respect and of a very different kind of admiration which was the beginning of a real love for that tall, strong wench. When the bleeding had stopped, he proposed a walk, as he was afraid of his neighbor's heavy hand, if they remained side by side like that much longer; but she took his arm of her own accord, in the avenue, as if they had been out for an evening's walk, and said: "It is not nice of you to despise me like that, Jacques." He protested, however. No, he did not despise her. He was in love with her, that was all.

"So you really want to marry me?" she asked.

He hesitated and then looked at her sideways, while she looked straight ahead of her. She had fat, red cheeks, a full bust beneath her cotton jacket; thick, red lips; and her neck, which was almost bare, was covered with small beads of perspiration. He felt a fresh access of desire, and, putting his lips to her ear, he murmured: "Yes, of course I do."

Then she threw her arms round his neck and kissed him till they were both out of breath. From that moment the eternal story of love began between them. They plagued one another in corners; they met in the moonlight beside the haystack and gave each other bruises on the legs, under the table, with their heavy nailed boots. By degrees, however, Jacques seemed to grow tired of her; he avoided her, scarcely spoke to her, and did not try any longer to meet her alone, which made her sad and anxious; and soon she found that she was enceinte.

At first she was in a state of consternation, but then she got angry, and her rage increased every day because she could not meet him, as he avoided her most carefully. At last, one night, when every one in the farmhouse was asleep, she went out noiselessly in her petticoat, with bare feet, crossed the yard and opened the door of the stable where Jacques was lying in a large box of straw above his horses. He pretended to snore when he heard her coming, but she knelt down by his side and shook him until he sat up.

"What do you want?" he then asked her. And with clenched teeth, and trembling with anger, she replied: "I want—I want you to marry me, as you promised." But he only laughed and replied: "Oh! if a man were to marry all the girls with whom he has made a slip, he would have more than enough to do."

Then she seized him by the throat, threw him or his back, so that he could not get away from her, and, half strangling him, she shouted into his face:

"I am enceinte, do you hear? I am enceinte!"

He gasped for breath, as he was almost choked, and so they remained, both of them, motionless and without speaking, in the dark silence, which was only broken by the noise made by a horse as he, pulled the hay out of the manger and then slowly munched it.

When Jacques found that she was the stronger, he stammered out: "Very well, I will marry you, as that is the case." But she did not believe his promises. "It must be at once," she said. "You must have the banns put up." "At once," he replied. "Swear solemnly that you will." He hesitated for a few moments and then said: "I swear it, by Heaven!"

Then she released her grasp and went away without another word.

She had no chance of speaking to him for several days; and, as the stable was now always locked at night, she was afraid to make any noise, for fear of creating a scandal. One morning, however, she saw another man come in at dinner time, and she said: "Has Jacques left?" "Yes;" the man replied; "I have got his place."

This made her tremble so violently that she could not take the saucepan off the fire; and later, when they were all at work, she went up into her room and cried, burying her head in the bolster, so that she might not be heard. During the day, however, she tried to obtain some information without exciting any suspicion, but she was so overwhelmed by the thoughts of her misfortune that she fancied that all the people whom she asked laughed maliciously. All she learned, however, was that he had left the neighborhood altogether.

PART II

Then a cloud of constant misery began for her. She worked mechanically, without thinking of what she was doing, with one fixed idea in her head:

"Suppose people were to know."

This continual feeling made her so incapable of reasoning that she did not even try to think of any means of avoiding the disgrace that she knew must ensue, which was irreparable and drawing nearer every day, and which was as sure as death itself. She got up every morning long before the others and persistently tried to look at her figure in a piece of broken looking-glass, before which she did her hair, as she was very anxious to know whether anybody would notice a change in her, and, during the day, she stopped working every few minutes to look at herself from top to toe, to see whether her apron did not look too short.

The months went on, and she scarcely spoke now, and when she was asked a question, did not appear to understand; but she had a frightened look, haggard eyes and trembling hands, which made her master say to her occasionally: "My poor girl, how stupid you have grown lately."

In church she hid behind a pillar, and no longer ventured to go to confession, as she feared to face the priest, to whom she attributed superhuman powers, which enabled him to read people's consciences; and at meal times the looks of her fellow servants almost made her faint with mental agony; and she was always fancying that she had been found out by the cowherd, a precocious and cunning little lad, whose bright eyes seemed always to be watching her.

One morning the postman brought her a letter, and as she had never received one in her life before she was so upset by it that she was obliged to sit down. Perhaps it was from him? But, as she could not read, she sat anxious and trembling with that piece of paper, covered with ink, in her hand. After a time, however, she put it into her pocket, as she did not venture to confide her secret to any one. She often stopped in her work to look at those lines written at regular intervals, and which terminated in a signature, imagining vaguely that she would suddenly discover their meaning, until at last, as she felt half mad with impatience and anxiety, she went to the schoolmaster, who told her to sit down and read to her as follows:

"MY DEAR DAUGHTER: I write to tell you that I am very ill. Our neighbor, Monsieur Dentu, begs you to come, if you can.

"From your affectionate mother,

"CESAIRE DENTU, Deputy Mayor."

She did not say a word and went away, but as soon as she was alone her legs gave way under her, and she fell down by the roadside and remained there till night.

When she got back, she told the farmer her bad news, and he allowed her to go home for as long as she liked, and promised to have her work done by a charwoman and to take her back when she returned.

Her mother died soon after she got there, and the next day Rose gave birth to a seven-months child, a miserable little skeleton, thin enough to make anybody shudder, and which seemed to be suffering continually, to judge from the painful manner in which it moved its poor little hands, which were as thin as a crab's legs; but it lived for all that. She said she was married, but could not be burdened with the child, so she left it with some neighbors, who promised to take great care of it, and she went back to the farm.

But now in her heart, which had been wounded so long, there arose something like brightness, an unknown love for that frail little creature which she had left behind her, though there was fresh suffering in that very love, suffering which she felt every hour and every minute, because she was parted from her child. What pained her most, however, was the mad longing to kiss it, to press it in her arms, to feel the warmth of its little body against her breast. She could not sleep at night; she thought of it the whole day long, and in the evening, when her work was done, she would sit in front of the fire and gaze at it intently, as people do whose thoughts are far away.

They began to talk about her and to tease-her about her lover. They asked her whether he was tall, handsome and rich. When was the wedding to be and the christening? And often she ran away to cry by herself, for these questions seemed to hurt her like the prick of a pin; and, in order to forget their jokes, she began to work still more energetically, and, still thinking of her child, she sought some way of saving up money for it, and determined to work so that her master would be obliged to raise her wages.

By degrees she almost monopolized the work and persuaded him to get rid of one servant girl, who had become useless since she had taken to working like two; she economized in the bread, oil and candles; in the corn, which they gave to the chickens too extravagantly, and in the fodder for the horses and cattle, which was rather wasted. She was as miserly about her master's money as if it had been her own; and, by dint of making good bargains, of getting high prices for all their produce, and by baffling the peasants' tricks when they offered anything for sale, he, at last, entrusted her with buying and selling everything, with the direction of all the laborers, and with the purchase of provisions necessary for the household; so that, in a short time, she became. indispensable to him. She kept such a strict eye on everything about her that, under her direction, the farm prospered wonderfully, and for five miles around people talked of "Master Vallin's servant," and the farmer himself said everywhere: "That girl is worth more than her weight in gold."

But time passed by, and her wages remained the same. Her hard work was accepted as something that was due from every good servant, and as a mere token of good will; and she began to think rather bitterly that if the farmer could put fifty or a hundred crowns extra into the bank every month, thanks to her, she was still only earning her two hundred francs a year, neither more nor less; and so she made up her mind to ask for an increase of wages. She went to see the schoolmaster three times about it, but when she got there, she spoke about something else. She felt a kind of modesty in asking for money, as if it were something disgraceful; but, at last, one day, when the farmer was having breakfast by himself in the kitchen, she said to him, with some embarrassment, that she wished to speak to him particularly. He raised his head in surprise, with both his hands on the table, holding his knife, with its point in the air, in one, and a piece of bread in the other, and he looked fixedly at, the girl, who felt uncomfortable under his gaze, but asked for a week's holiday, so that she might get away, as she was not very well. He acceded to her request immediately, and then added, in some embarrassment himself:

"When you come back, I shall have something to say to you myself."

PART III

The child was nearly eight months old, and she did not recognize it. It had grown rosy and chubby all over, like a little roll of fat. She threw herself on it, as if it had been some prey, and kissed it so violently that it began to scream with terror; and then she began to cry herself, because it did not know her, and stretched out its arms to its nurse as soon as it saw her. But the next day it began to know her, and laughed when it saw her, and she took it into the fields, and ran about excitedly with it, and sat down under the shade of the trees; and then, for the first time in her life, she opened her heart to somebody, although he could not understand her, and told him her troubles; how hard her work was, her anxieties and her hopes, and she quite tired the child with the violence of her caresses.

She took the greatest pleasure in handling it, in washing and dressing it, for it seemed to her that all this was the confirmation of her maternity; and she would look at it, almost feeling surprised 'that it was hers, and would say to herself in a low voice as she danced it in her arms: "It is my baby, it's my baby."

She cried all the way home as she returned to the farm and had scarcely got in before her master called her into his room; and she went, feeling astonished and nervous, without knowing why.

"Sit down there," he said. She sat down, and for some moments they remained side by side, in some embarrassment, with their arms hanging at their sides, as if they did not know what to do with them, and looking each other in the face, after the manner of peasants.

The farmer, a stout, jovial, obstinate man of forty-five, who had lost two wives, evidently felt embarrassed, which was very unusual with him; but, at last, he made up his mind, and began to speak vaguely, hesitating a little, and looking out of the window as he talked. "How is it, Rose," he said, "that you have never thought of settling in life?" She grew as pale as death, and, seeing that she gave him no answer, he went on: "You are a good, steady, active and economical girl; and a wife like you would make a man's fortune."

She did not move, but looked frightened; she did not even try to comprehend his meaning, for her thoughts were in a whirl, as if at the approach of some great danger; so, after waiting for a few seconds, he went on: "You see, a farm without a mistress can never succeed, even with a servant like you." Then he stopped, for he did not know what else to say, and Rose looked at him with the air of a person who thinks that he is face to face with a murderer and ready to flee at the slightest movement he may make; but, after waiting for about five minutes, he asked her: "Well, will it suit you?" "Will what suit me, master?" And he said quickly: "Why, to marry me, by Heaven!"

She jumped up, but fell back on her chair, as if she had been struck, and there she remained motionless, like a person who is overwhelmed by some great misfortune. At last the farmer grew impatient and said: "Come, what more do you want?" She looked at him, almost in terror, then suddenly the tears came into her eyes and she said twice in a choking voice: "I cannot, I cannot!" "Why not?" he asked. "Come, don't be silly; I will give you until tomorrow to think it over."

And he hurried out of the room, very glad to have got through with the matter, which had troubled him a good deal, for he had no doubt that she would the next morning accept a proposal which she could never have expected and which would be a capital bargain for him, as he thus bound a woman to his interests who would certainly bring him more than if she had the best dowry in the district.

Neither could there be any scruples about an unequal match between them, for in the country every one is very nearly equal; the farmer works with his laborers, who frequently become masters in their turn, and the female servants constantly become the mistresses of the establishments without its making any change in their life or habits.

Rose did not go to bed that night. She threw herself, dressed as she was, on her bed, and she had not even the strength to cry left in her, she was so thoroughly dumfounded. She remained quite inert, scarcely knowing that she had a body, and without being at all able to collect her thoughts, though, at moments, she remembered something of what had happened, and then she was frightened at the idea of what might happen. Her terror increased, and every time the great kitchen clock struck the hour she broke out in a perspiration from grief. She became bewildered, and had the nightmare; her candle went out, and then she began to imagine that some one had cast a spell over her, as country people so often imagine, and she felt a mad inclination to run away, to escape and to flee before her misfortune, like a ship scudding before the wind. An owl hooted; she shivered, sat up, passed her hands over her face, her hair, and all over her body, and then she went downstairs, as if she were walking in her sleep. When she got into the yard she stooped down, so as not to be seen by any prowling scamp, for the moon, which was setting, shed a bright light over the fields. Instead of opening the gate she scrambled over the fence, and as soon as she was outside she started off. She went on straight before her, with a quick, springy trot, and from time to time she unconsciously uttered a piercing cry. Her long shadow accompanied her, and now and then some night bird flew over her head, while the dogs in the farmyards barked as they heard her pass; one even jumped over the ditch, and followed her and tried to bite her, but she turned round and gave such a terrible yell that the frightened animal ran back and cowered in silence in its kennel.

The stars grew dim, and the birds began to twitter; day was breaking. The girl was worn out and panting; and when the sun rose in the purple sky, she stopped, for her swollen feet refused to go any farther; but she saw a pond in the distance, a large pond whose stagnant water looked like blood under the reflection of this new day, and she limped on slowly with her hand on her heart, in order to dip both her feet in it. She sat down on a tuft of grass, took off her heavy shoes, which were full of dust, pulled off her stockings and plunged her legs into the still water, from which bubbles were rising here and there.

A feeling of delicious coolness pervaded her from head to foot, and suddenly, while she was looking fixedly at the deep pool, she was seized with dizziness, and with a mad longing to throw herself into it. All her sufferings would be over in there, over forever. She no longer thought of her child; she only wanted peace, complete rest, and to sleep forever, and she got up with raised arms and took two steps forward. She was in the water up to her thighs, and she was just about to throw her self in when sharp, pricking pains in her ankles made her jump back, and she uttered a cry of despair, for, from her knees to the tips of her feet, long black leeches were sucking her lifeblood, and were swelling as they adhered to her flesh. She did not dare to touch them, and screamed with horror, so that her cries of despair attracted a peasant, who was driving along at some distance, to the spot. He pulled off the leeches one by one, applied herbs to the wounds, and drove the girl to her master's farm in his gig.

She was in bed for a fortnight, and as she was sitting outside the door on the first morning that she got up, the farmer suddenly came and planted himself before her. "Well," he said, "I suppose the affair is settled isn't it?" She did not reply at first, and then, as he remained standing and looking at her intently with his piercing eyes, she said with difficulty: "No, master, I cannot." He immediately flew into a rage.

"You cannot, girl; you cannot? I should just like to know the reason why?" She began to cry, and repeated: "I cannot." He looked at her, and then exclaimed angrily: "Then I suppose you have a lover?" "Perhaps that is it," she replied, trembling with shame.

The man got as red as a poppy, and stammered out in a rage: "Ah! So you confess it, you slut! And pray who is the fellow? Some penniless, half-starved ragamuffin, without a roof to his head, I suppose? Who is it, I say?" And as she gave him no answer, he continued: "Ah! So you will not tell me. Then I will tell you; it is Jean Baudu?"—"No, not he," she exclaimed. "Then it is Pierre Martin?"—"Oh! no, master."

And he angrily mentioned all the young fellows in the neighborhood, while she denied that he had hit upon the right one, and every moment wiped her eyes with the corner of her blue apron. But he still tried to find it out, with his brutish obstinacy, and, as it were, scratching at her heart to discover her secret, just as a terrier scratches at a hole to try and get at the animal which he scents inside it. Suddenly, however, the man shouted: "By George! It is Jacques, the man who was here last year. They used to say that you were always talking together, and that you thought about getting married."

Rose was choking, and she grew scarlet, while her tears suddenly stopped and dried up on her cheeks, like drops of water on hot iron, and she exclaimed: "No, it is not he, it is not he!" "Is that really a fact?" asked the cunning peasant, who partly guessed the truth; and she replied, hastily: "I will swear it; I will swear it to you—" She tried to think of something by which to swear, as she did not venture to invoke sacred things, but he interrupted her: "At any rate, he used to follow you into every corner and devoured you with his eyes at meal times. Did you ever give him your promise, eh?"

This time she looked her master straight in the face. "No, never, never; I will solemnly swear to you that if he were to come to-day and ask me to marry him I would have nothing to do with him." She spoke with such an air of sincerity that the farmer hesitated, and then he continued, as if speaking to himself: "What, then? You have not had a misfortune, as they call it, or it would have been known, and as it has no consequences, no girl would refuse her master on that account. There must be something at the bottom of it, however."

She could say nothing; she had not the strength to speak, and he asked her again: "You will not?" "I cannot, master," she said, with a sigh, and he turned on his heel.

She thought she had got rid of him altogether and spent the rest of the day almost tranquilly, but was as exhausted as if she had been turning the thrashing machine all day in the place of the old white horse, and she went to bed as soon as she could and fell asleep immediately. In the middle of the night, however, two hands touching the bed woke her. She trembled with fear, but immediately recognized the farmer's voice, when he said to her: "Don't be frightened, Rose; I have come to speak to you." She was surprised at first, but when he tried to take liberties with her she understood and began to tremble violently, as she felt quite alone in the darkness, still heavy from sleep, and quite unprotected, with that man standing near her. She certainly did not consent, but she resisted carelessly struggling against that instinct which is always strong in simple natures and very imperfectly protected by the undecided will of inert and gentle races. She turned her head now to the wall, and now toward the room, in order to avoid the attentions which the farmer tried to press on her, but she was weakened by fatigue, while he became brutal, intoxicated by desire.

They lived together as man and wife, and one morning he said to her: "I have put up our banns, and we will get married next month."

She did not reply, for what could she say? She did not resist, for what could she do?

PART IV

She married him. She felt as if she were in a pit with inaccessible sides from which she could never get out, and all kinds of misfortunes were hanging over her head, like huge rocks, which would fall on the first occasion. Her husband gave her the impression of a man whom she had robbed, and who would find it out some day or other. And then she thought of her child, who was the cause of her misfortunes, but who was also the cause of all her happiness on earth, and whom she went to see twice a year, though she came back more unhappy each time.

But she gradually grew accustomed to her life, her fears were allayed, her heart was at rest, and she lived with an easier mind, though still with some vague fear floating in it. And so years went on, until the child was six. She was almost happy now, when suddenly the farmer's temper grew very bad.

For two or three years he seemed to have been nursing some secret anxiety, to be troubled by some care, some mental disturbance, which was gradually increasing. He remained sitting at table after dinner, with his head in his hands, sad and devoured by sorrow. He always spoke hastily, sometimes even brutally, and it even seemed as if he had a grudge against his wife, for at times he answered her roughly, almost angrily.

One day, when a neighbor's boy came for some eggs, and she spoke rather crossly to him, as she was very busy, her husband suddenly came in and said to her in his unpleasant voice: "If that were your own child you would not treat him so." She was hurt and did not reply, and then she went back into the house, with all her grief awakened afresh; and at dinner the farmer neither spoke to her nor looked at her, and he seemed to hate her, to despise her, to know something about the affair at last. In consequence she lost her composure, and did not venture to remain alone with him after the meal was over, but left the room and hastened to the church.

It was getting dusk; the narrow nave was in total darkness, but she heard footsteps in the choir, for the sacristan was preparing the tabernacle lamp for the night. That spot of trembling light, which was lost in the darkness of the arches, looked to Rose like her last hope, and with her eyes fixed on it, she fell on her knees. The chain rattled as the little lamp swung up into the air, and almost immediately the small bell rang out the Angelus through the increasing mist. She went up to him, as he was going out.

"Is Monsieur le Cure at home?" she asked. "Of course he is; this is his dinnertime." She trembled as she rang the bell of the parsonage. The priest was just sitting down to dinner, and he made her sit down also. "Yes, yes, I know all about it; your husband has mentioned the matter to me that brings you here." The poor woman nearly fainted, and the priest continued: "What do you want, my child?" And he hastily swallowed several spoonfuls of soup, some of which dropped on to his greasy cassock. But Rose did not venture to say anything more, and she got up to go, but the priest said: "Courage."

And she went out and returned to the farm without knowing what she was doing. The farmer was waiting for her, as the laborers had gone away during her absence, and she fell heavily at his feet, and, shedding a flood of tears, she said to him: "What have you got against me?"

He began to shout and to swear: "What have I got against you? That I have no children, by—-. When a man takes a wife it is not that they may live alone together to the end of their days. That is what I have against you. When a cow has no calves she is not worth anything, and when a woman has no children she is also not worth anything."

She began to cry, and said: "It is not my fault! It is not my fault!" He grew rather more gentle when he heard that, and added: "I do not say that it is, but it is very provoking, all the same."

PART V

From that day forward she had only one thought: to have a child another child; she confided her wish to everybody, and, in consequence of this, a neighbor told her of an infallible method. This was, to make her husband drink a glass of water with a pinch of ashes in it every evening. The farmer consented to try it, but without success; so they said to each other: "Perhaps there are some secret ways?" And they tried to find out. They were told of a shepherd who lived ten leagues off, and so Vallin one day drove off to consult him. The shepherd gave him a loaf on which he had made some marks; it was kneaded up with herbs, and each of them was to eat a piece of it, but they ate the whole loaf without obtaining any results from it.

Next, a schoolmaster unveiled mysteries and processes of love which were unknown in the country, but infallible, so he declared; but none of them had the desired effect. Then the priest advised them to make a pilgrimage to the shrine at Fecamp. Rose went with the crowd and prostrated herself in the abbey, and, mingling her prayers with the coarse desires of the peasants around her, she prayed that she might be fruitful a second time; but it was in vain, and then she thought that she was being punished for her first fault, and she was seized by terrible grief. She was wasting away with sorrow; her husband was also aging prematurely, and was wearing himself out in useless hopes.

Then war broke out between them; he called her names and beat her. They quarrelled all day long, and when they were in their room together at night he flung insults and obscenities at her, choking with rage, until one night, not being able to think of any means of making her suffer more he ordered her to get up and go and stand out of doors in the rain until daylight. As she did not obey him, he seized her by the neck and began to strike her in the face with his fists, but she said nothing and did not move. In his exasperation he knelt on her stomach, and with clenched teeth, and mad with rage, he began to beat her. Then in her despair she rebelled, and flinging him against the wall with a furious gesture, she sat up, and in an altered voice she hissed: "I have had a child, I have had one! I had it by Jacques; you know Jacques. He promised to marry me, but he left this neighborhood without keeping his word."

The man was thunderstruck and could hardly speak, but at last he stammered out: "What are you saying? What are you saying?" Then she began to sob, and amid her tears she continued: "That was the reason why I did not want to marry you. I could not tell you, for you would have left me without any bread for my child. You have never had any children, so you cannot understand, you cannot understand!"

He said again, mechanically, with increasing surprise: "You have a child? You have a child?"

"You took me by force, as I suppose you know? I did not want to marry you," she said, still sobbing.

Then he got up, lit the candle, and began to walk up and down, with his arms behind him. She was cowering on the bed and crying, and suddenly he stopped in front of her, and said: "Then it is my fault that you have no children?" She gave him no answer, and he began to walk up and down again, and then, stopping again, he continued: "How old is your child?" "Just six," she whispered. "Why did you not tell me about it?" he asked. "How could I?" she replied, with a sigh.

He remained standing, motionless. "Come, get up," he said. She got up with some difficulty, and then, when she was standing on the floor, he suddenly began to laugh with the hearty laugh of his good days, and, seeing how surprised she was, he added: "Very well, we will go and fetch the child, as you and I can have none together."

She was so scared that if she had had the strength she would assuredly have run away, but the farmer rubbed his hands and said: "I wanted to adopt one, and now we have found one. I asked the cure about an orphan some time ago."

Then, still laughing, he kissed his weeping and agitated wife on both cheeks, and shouted out, as though she could not hear him: "Come along, mother, we will go and see whether there is any soup left; I should not mind a plateful."

She put on her petticoat and they went downstairs; and While she was kneeling in front of the fireplace and lighting the fire under the saucepan, he continued to walk up and down the kitchen with long strides, repeating:

"Well, I am really glad of this; I am not saying it for form's sake, but I am glad, I am really very glad."

THE WRECK

It was yesterday, the 31st of December.

I had just finished breakfast with my old friend Georges Garin when the servant handed him a letter covered with seals and foreign stamps.

Georges said:

"Will you excuse me?"

"Certainly."

And so he began to read the letter, which was written in a large English handwriting, crossed and recrossed in every direction. He read them slowly, with serious attention and the interest which we only pay to things which touch our hearts.

Then he put the letter on the mantelpiece and said:

"That was a curious story! I've never told you about it, I think. Yet it was a sentimental adventure, and it really happened to me. That was a strange New Year's Day, indeed! It must have been twenty years ago, for I was then thirty and am now fifty years old.

"I was then an inspector in the Maritime Insurance Company, of which I am now director. I had arranged to pass New Year's Day in Paris—since it is customary to make that day a fete—when I received a letter from the manager, asking me to proceed at once to the island of Re, where a three-masted vessel from Saint-Nazaire, insured by us, had just been driven ashore. It was then eight o'clock in the morning. I arrived at the office at ten to get my advices, and that evening I took the express, which put me down in La Rochelle the next day, the 31st of December.

"I had two hours to wait before going aboard the boat for Re. So I made a tour of the town. It is certainly a queer city, La Rochelle, with strong characteristics of its own streets tangled like a labyrinth, sidewalks running under endless arcaded galleries like those of the Rue de Rivoli, but low, mysterious, built as if to form a suitable setting for conspirators and making a striking background for those old-time wars, the savage heroic wars of religion. It is indeed the typical old Huguenot city, conservative, discreet, with no fine art to show, with no wonderful monuments, such as make Rouen; but it is remarkable for its severe, somewhat sullen look; it is a city of obstinate fighters, a city where fanaticism might well blossom, where the faith of the Calvinists became enthusiastic and which gave birth to the plot of the 'Four Sergeants.'

"After I had wandered for some time about these curious streets, I went aboard the black, rotund little steamboat which was to take me to the island of Re. It was called the Jean Guiton. It started with angry puffings, passed between the two old towers which guard the harbor, crossed the roadstead and issued from the mole built by Richelieu, the great stones of which can be seen at the water's edge, enclosing the town like a great necklace. Then the steamboat turned to the right.

"It was one of those sad days which give one the blues, tighten the heart and take away all strength and energy and force-a gray, cold day, with a heavy mist which was as wet as rain, as cold as frost, as bad to breathe as the steam of a wash-tub.

"Under this low sky of dismal fog the shallow, yellow, sandy sea of all practically level beaches lay without a wrinkle, without a movement, without life, a sea of turbid water, of greasy water, of stagnant water. The Jean Guiton passed over it, rolling a little from habit, dividing the smooth, dark blue water and leaving behind a few waves, a little splashing, a slight swell, which soon calmed down.

"I began to talk to the captain, a little man with small feet, as round as his boat and rolling in the same manner. I wanted some details of the disaster on which I was to draw up a report. A great square-rigged three-master, the Marie Joseph, of Saint-Nazaire, had gone ashore one night in a hurricane on the sands of the island of Re.

"The owner wrote us that the storm had thrown the ship so far ashore that it was impossible to float her and that they had to remove everything which could be detached with the utmost possible haste. Nevertheless I must examine the situation of the wreck, estimate what must have been her condition before the disaster and decide whether all efforts had been used to get her afloat. I came as an agent of the company in order to give contradictory testimony, if necessary, at the trial.

"On receipt of my report, the manager would take what measures he might think necessary to protect our interests.

"The captain of the Jean Guiton knew all about the affair, having been summoned with his boat to assist in the attempts at salvage.

"He told me the story of the disaster. The Marie Joseph, driven by a furious gale lost her bearings completely in the night, and steering by chance over a heavy foaming sea—'a milk-soup sea,' said the captain—had gone ashore on those immense sand banks which make the coasts of this country look like limitless Saharas when the tide is low.

"While talking I looked around and ahead. Between the ocean and the lowering sky lay an open space where the eye could see into the distance. We were following a coast. I asked:

"'Is that the island of Re?'

"'Yes, sir.'

"And suddenly the captain stretched his right hand out before us, pointed to something almost imperceptible in the open sea, and said:

"'There's your ship!'

"'The Marie Joseph!'

"'Yes.'

"I was amazed. This black, almost imperceptible speck, which looked to me like a rock, seemed at least three miles from land.

"I continued:

"'But, captain, there must be a hundred fathoms of water in that place.'

"He began to laugh.

"'A hundred fathoms, my child! Well, I should say about two!'

"He was from Bordeaux. He continued:

"'It's now nine-forty, just high tide. Go down along the beach with your hands in your pockets after you've had lunch at the Hotel du Dauphin, and I'll wager that at ten minutes to three, or three o'clock, you'll reach the wreck without wetting your feet, and have from an hour and three-quarters to two hours aboard of her; but not more, or you'll be caught. The faster the sea goes out the faster it comes back. This coast is as flat as a turtle! But start away at ten minutes to five, as I tell you, and at half-past seven you will be again aboard of the Jean Guiton, which will put you down this same evening on the quay at La Rochelle.'

"I thanked the captain and I went and sat down in the bow of the steamer to get a good look at the little city of Saint-Martin, which we were now rapidly approaching.

"It was just like all small seaports which serve as capitals of the barren islands scattered along the coast—a large fishing village, one foot on sea and one on shore, subsisting on fish and wild fowl, vegetables and shell-fish, radishes and mussels. The island is very low and little cultivated, yet it seems to be thickly populated. However, I did not penetrate into the interior.

"After breakfast I climbed across a little promontory, and then, as the tide was rapidly falling, I started out across the sands toward a kind of black rock which I could just perceive above the surface of the water, out a considerable distance.

"I walked quickly over the yellow plain. It was elastic, like flesh and seemed to sweat beneath my tread. The sea had been there very lately. Now I perceived it at a distance, escaping out of sight, and I no longer could distinguish the line which separated the sands from ocean. I felt as though I were looking at a gigantic supernatural work of enchantment. The Atlantic had just now been before me, then it had disappeared into the sands, just as scenery disappears through a trap; and I was now walking in the midst of a desert. Only the feeling, the breath of the salt-water, remained in me. I perceived the smell of the wrack, the smell of the sea, the good strong smell of sea coasts. I walked fast; I was no longer cold. I looked at the stranded wreck, which grew in size as I approached, and came now to resemble an enormous shipwrecked whale.

"It seemed fairly to rise out of the ground, and on that great, flat, yellow stretch of sand assumed wonderful proportions. After an hour's walk I at last reached it. It lay upon its side, ruined and shattered, its broken bones showing as though it were an animal, its bones of tarred wood pierced with great bolts. The sand had already invaded it, entering it by all the crannies, and held it and refused to let it go. It seemed to have taken root in it. The bow had entered deep into this soft, treacherous beach, while the stern, high in air, seemed to cast at heaven, like a cry of despairing appeal, the two white words on the black planking, Marie Joseph.

"I climbed upon this carcass of a ship by the lowest side; then, having reached the deck, I went below. The daylight, which entered by the stove-in hatches and the cracks in the sides, showed me dimly long dark cavities full of demolished woodwork. They contained nothing but sand, which served as foot-soil in this cavern of planks.

"I began to take some notes about the condition of the ship. I was seated on a broken empty cask, writing by the light of a great crack, through which I could perceive the boundless stretch of the strand. A strange shivering of cold and loneliness ran over my skin from time to time, and I would often stop writing for a moment to listen to the mysterious noises in the derelict: the noise of crabs scratching the planking with their crooked claws; the noise of a thousand little creatures of the sea already crawling over this dead body or else boring into the wood.

"Suddenly, very near me, I heard human voices. I started as though I had seen a ghost. For a second I really thought I was about to see drowned men rise from the sinister depths of the hold, who would tell me about their death. At any rate, it did not take me long to swing myself on deck. There, standing by the bows, was a tall Englishman with three young misses. Certainly they were a good deal more frightened at seeing this sudden apparition on the abandoned three-master than I was at seeing them. The youngest girl turned and ran, the two others threw their arms round their father. As for him, he opened his mouth—that was the only sign of emotion which he showed.

"Then, after several seconds, he spoke:

"'Mosieu, are you the owner of this ship?'

"'I am.'

"'May I go over it?'

"'You may.'

"Then he uttered a long sentence in English, in which I only distinguished the word 'gracious,' repeated several times.

"As he was looking for a place to climb up I showed him the easiest way, and gave him a hand. He climbed up. Then we helped up the three girls, who had now quite recovered their composure. They were charming, especially the oldest, a blonde of eighteen, fresh as a flower, and very dainty and pretty! Ah, yes! the pretty Englishwomen have indeed the look of tender sea fruit. One would have said of this one that she had just risen out of the sands and that her hair had kept their tint. They all, with their exquisite freshness, make you think of the delicate colors of pink sea-shells and of shining pearls hidden in the unknown depths of the ocean.

"She spoke French a little better than her father and acted as interpreter. I had to tell all about the shipwreck, and I romanced as though I had been present at the catastrophe. Then the whole family descended into the interior of the wreck. As soon as they had penetrated into this sombre, dimly lit cavity they uttered cries of astonishment and admiration. Suddenly the father and his three daughters were holding sketch-books in their hands, which they had doubtless carried hidden somewhere in their heavy weather-proof clothes, and were all beginning at once to make pencil sketches of this melancholy and weird place.

"They had seated themselves side by side on a projecting beam, and the four sketch-books on the eight knees were being rapidly covered with little black lines which were intended to represent the half-opened hulk of the Marie Joseph.

"I continued to inspect the skeleton of the ship, and the oldest girl talked to me while she worked.

"They had none of the usual English arrogance; they were simple honest hearts of that class of continuous travellers with which England covers the globe. The father was long and thin, with a red face framed in white whiskers, and looking like a living sandwich, a piece of ham carved like a face between two wads of hair. The daughters, who had long legs like young storks, were also thin-except the oldest. All three were pretty, especially the tallest.

"She had such a droll way of speaking, of laughing, of understanding and of not understanding, of raising her eyes to ask a question (eyes blue as the deep ocean), of stopping her drawing a moment to make a guess at what you meant, of returning once more to work, of saying 'yes' or 'no'—that I could have listened and looked indefinitely.

"Suddenly she murmured:

"'I hear a little sound on this boat.'

"I listened and I immediately distinguished a low, steady, curious sound. I rose and looked out of the crack and gave a scream. The sea had come up to us; it would soon surround us!

"We were on deck in an instant. It was too late. The water circled us about and was running toward the coast at tremendous speed. No, it did not run, it glided, crept, spread like an immense, limitless blot. The water was barely a few centimeters deep, but the rising flood had gone so far that we no longer saw the vanishing line of the imperceptible tide.

"The Englishman wanted to jump. I held him back. Flight was impossible because of the deep places which we had been obliged to go round on our way out and into which we should fall on our return.

"There was a minute of horrible anguish in our hearts. Then the little English girl began to smile and murmured:

"'It is we who are shipwrecked.'

"I tried to laugh, but fear held me, a fear which was cowardly and horrid and base and treacherous like the tide. All the danger which we ran appeared to me at once. I wanted to shriek: 'Help!' But to whom?

"The two younger girls were clinging to their father, who looked in consternation at the measureless sea which hedged us round about.

"The night fell as swiftly as the ocean rose—a lowering, wet, icy night.

"I said:

"'There's nothing to do but to stay on the ship:

"The Englishman answered:

"'Oh, yes!'

"And we waited there a quarter of an hour, half an hour, indeed I don't know how long, watching that creeping water growing deeper as it swirled around us, as though it were playing on the beach, which it had regained.

"One of the young girls was cold, and we went below to shelter ourselves from the light but freezing wind that made our skins tingle.

"I leaned over the hatchway. The ship was full of water. So we had to cower against the stern planking, which shielded us a little.

"Darkness was now coming on, and we remained huddled together. I felt the shoulder of the little English girl trembling against mine, her teeth chattering from time to time. But I also felt the gentle warmth of her body through her ulster, and that warmth was as delicious to me as a kiss. We no longer spoke; we sat motionless, mute, cowering down like animals in a ditch when a hurricane is raging. And, nevertheless, despite the night, despite the terrible and increasing danger, I began to feel happy that I was there, glad of the cold and the peril, glad of the long hours of darkness and anguish that I must pass on this plank so near this dainty, pretty little girl.

"I asked myself, 'Why this strange sensation of well-being and of joy?'

"Why! Does one know? Because she was there? Who? She, a little unknown English girl? I did not love her, I did not even know her. And for all that, I was touched and conquered. I wanted to save her, to sacrifice myself for her, to commit a thousand follies! Strange thing! How does it happen that the presence of a woman overwhelms us so? Is it the power of her grace which enfolds us? Is it the seduction of her beauty and youth, which intoxicates one like wine?

"Is it not rather the touch of Love, of Love the Mysterious, who seeks constantly to unite two beings, who tries his strength the instant he has put a man and a woman face to face?

"The silence of the darkness became terrible, the stillness of the sky dreadful, because we could hear vaguely about us a slight, continuous sound, the sound of the rising tide and the monotonous plashing of the water against the ship.

"Suddenly I heard the sound of sobs. The youngest of the girls was crying. Her father tried to console her, and they began to talk in their own tongue, which I did not understand. I guessed that he was reassuring her and that she was still afraid.

"I asked my neighbor:

"'You are not too cold, are you, mademoiselle?'

"'Oh, yes. I am very cold.'

"I offered to give her my cloak; she refused it.

"But I had taken it off and I covered her with it against her will. In the short struggle her hand touched mine. It made a delicious thrill run through my body.

"For some minutes the air had been growing brisker, the dashing of the water stronger against the flanks of the ship. I raised myself; a great gust of wind blew in my face. The wind was rising!

"The Englishman perceived this at the same time that I did and said simply:

"'This is bad for us, this——'

"Of course it was bad, it was certain death if any breakers, however feeble, should attack and shake the wreck, which was already so shattered and disconnected that the first big sea would carry it off.

"So our anguish increased momentarily as the squalls grew stronger and stronger. Now the sea broke a little, and I saw in the darkness white lines appearing and disappearing, lines of foam, while each wave struck the Marie Joseph and shook her with a short quiver which went to our hearts.

"The English girl was trembling. I felt her shiver against me. And I had a wild desire to take her in my arms.

"Down there, before and behind us, to the left and right, lighthouses were shining along the shore—lighthouses white, yellow and red, revolving like the enormous eyes of giants who were watching us, waiting eagerly for us to disappear. One of them in especial irritated me. It went out every thirty seconds and it lit up again immediately. It was indeed an eye, that one, with its lid incessantly lowered over its fiery glance.

"From time to time the Englishman struck a match to see the hour; then he put his watch back in his pocket. Suddenly he said to me, over the heads of his daughters, with tremendous gravity:

"'I wish you a happy New Year, Mosieu.'

"It was midnight. I held out my hand, which he pressed. Then he said something in English, and suddenly he and his daughters began to sing 'God Save the Queen,' which rose through the black and silent air and vanished into space.

"At first I felt a desire to laugh; then I was seized by a powerful, strange emotion.

"It was something sinister and superb, this chant of the shipwrecked, the condemned, something like a prayer and also like something grander, something comparable to the ancient 'Ave Caesar morituri te salutant.'

"When they had finished I asked my neighbor to sing a ballad alone, anything she liked, to make us forget our terrors. She consented, and immediately her clear young voice rang out into the night. She sang something which was doubtless sad, because the notes were long drawn out and hovered, like wounded birds, above the waves.

"The sea was rising now and beating upon our wreck. As for me, I thought only of that voice. And I thought also of the sirens. If a ship had passed near by us what would the sailors have said? My troubled spirit lost itself in the dream! A siren! Was she not really a siren, this daughter of the sea, who had kept me on this worm-eaten ship and who was soon about to go down with me deep into the waters?

"But suddenly we were all five rolling on the deck, because the Marie Joseph had sunk on her right side. The English girl had fallen upon me, and before I knew what I was doing, thinking that my last moment was come, I had caught her in my arms and kissed her cheek, her temple and her hair.

"The ship did not move again, and we, we also, remained motionless.

"The father said, 'Kate!' The one whom I was holding answered 'Yes' and made a movement to free herself. And at that moment I should have wished the ship to split in two and let me fall with her into the sea.

"The Englishman continued:

"'A little rocking; it's nothing. I have my three daughters safe.'

"Not having seen the oldest, he had thought she was lost overboard!

"I rose slowly, and suddenly I made out a light on the sea quite close to us. I shouted; they answered. It was a boat sent out in search of us by the hotelkeeper, who had guessed at our imprudence.

"We were saved. I was in despair. They picked us up off our raft and they brought us back to Saint-Martin.

"The Englishman began to rub his hand and murmur:

"'A good supper! A good supper!'

"We did sup. I was not gay. I regretted the Marie Joseph.

"We had to separate the next day after much handshaking and many promises to write. They departed for Biarritz. I wanted to follow them.

"I was hard hit. I wanted to ask this little girl to marry me. If we had passed eight days together, I should have done so! How weak and incomprehensible a man sometimes is!

"Two years passed without my hearing a word from them. Then I received a letter from New York. She was married and wrote to tell me. And since then we write to each other every year, on New Year's Day. She tells me about her life, talks of her children, her sisters, never of her husband! Why? Ah! why? And as for me, I only talk of the Marie Joseph. That was perhaps the only woman I have ever loved—no—that I ever should have loved. Ah, well! who can tell? Circumstances rule one. And then—and then—all passes. She must be old now; I should not know her. Ah! she of the bygone time, she of the wreck! What a creature! Divine! She writes me her hair is white. That caused me terrible pain. Ah! her yellow hair. No, my English girl exists no longer. How sad it all is!"

THEODULE SABOT'S CONFESSION

When Sabot entered the inn at Martinville it was a signal for laughter. What a rogue he was, this Sabot! There was a man who did not like priests, for instance! Oh, no, oh, no! He did not spare them, the scamp.

Sabot (Theodule), a master carpenter, represented liberal thought in Martinville. He was a tall, thin, than, with gray, cunning eyes, and thin lips, and wore his hair plastered down on his temples. When he said: "Our holy father, the pope" in a certain manner, everyone laughed. He made a point of working on Sunday during the hour of mass. He killed his pig each year on Monday in Holy Week in order to have enough black pudding to last till Easter, and when the priest passed by, he always said by way of a joke: "There goes one who has just swallowed his God off a salver."

The priest, a stout man and also very tall, dreaded him on account of his boastful talk which attracted followers. The Abbe Maritime was a politic man, and believed in being diplomatic. There had been a rivalry between them for ten years, a secret, intense, incessant rivalry. Sabot was municipal councillor, and they thought he would become mayor, which would inevitably mean the final overthrow of the church.

The elections were about to take place. The church party was shaking in its shoes in Martinville.

One morning the cure set out for Rouen, telling his servant that he was going to see the archbishop. He returned in two days with a joyous, triumphant air. And everyone knew the following day that the chancel of the church was going to be renovated. A sum of six hundred francs had been contributed by the archbishop out of his private fund. All the old pine pews were to be removed, and replaced by new pews made of oak. It would be a big carpentering job, and they talked about it that very evening in all the houses in the village.

Theodule Sabot was not laughing.

When he went through the village the following morning, the neighbors, friends and enemies, all asked him, jokingly:

"Are you going to do the work on the chancel of the church?"

He could find nothing to say, but he was furious, he was good and angry.

Ill-natured people added:

"It is a good piece of work; and will bring in not less than two or three per cent. profit."

Two days later, they heard that the work of renovation had been entrusted to Celestin Chambrelan, the carpenter from Percheville. Then this was denied, and it was said that all the pews in the church were going to be changed. That would be well worth the two thousand francs that had been demanded of the church administration.

Theodule Sabot could not sleep for thinking about it. Never, in all the memory of man, had a country carpenter undertaken a similar piece of work. Then a rumor spread abroad that the cure felt very grieved that he had to give this work to a carpenter who was a stranger in the community, but that Sabot's opinions were a barrier to his being entrusted with the job.

Sabot knew it well. He called at the parsonage just as it was growing dark. The servant told him that the cure was at church. He went to the church.

Two attendants on the altar of the Virgin, two soar old maids, were decorating the altar for the month of Mary, under the direction of the priest, who stood in the middle of the chancel with his portly paunch, directing the two women who, mounted on chairs, were placing flowers around the tabernacle.

Sabot felt ill at ease in there, as though he were in the house of his greatest enemy, but the greed of gain was gnawing at his heart. He drew nearer, holding his cap in his hand, and not paying any attention to the "demoiselles de la Vierge," who remained standing startled, astonished, motionless on their chairs.

He faltered:

"Good morning, monsieur le cure."

The priest replied without looking at him, all occupied as he was with the altar:

"Good morning, Mr. Carpenter."

Sabot, nonplussed, knew not what to say next. But after a pause he remarked:

"You are making preparations?"

Abbe Maritime replied:

"Yes, we are near the month of Mary."

"Why, why," remarked Sabot and then was silent. He would have liked to retire now without saying anything, but a glance at the chancel held him back. He saw sixteen seats that had to be remade, six to the right and eight to the left, the door of the sacristy occupying the place of two. Sixteen oak seats, that would be worth at most three hundred francs, and by figuring carefully one might certainly make two hundred francs on the work if one were not clumsy.

Then he stammered out:

"I have come about the work."

The cure appeared surprised. He asked:

"What work?"

"The work to be done," murmured Sabot, in dismay.

Then the priest turned round and looking him straight in the eyes, said:

"Do you mean the repairs in the chancel of my church?"

At the tone of the abbe, Theodule Sabot felt a chill run down his back and he once more had a longing to take to his heels. However, he replied humbly:

"Why, yes, monsieur le cure."

Then the abbe folded his arms across his large stomach and, as if filled with amazement, said:

"Is it you—you—you, Sabot—who have come to ask me for this . . . You—the only irreligious man in my parish! Why, it would be a scandal, a public scandal! The archbishop would give me a reprimand, perhaps transfer me."

He stopped a few seconds, for breath, and then resumed in a calmer tone: "I can understand that it pains you to see a work of such importance entrusted to a carpenter from a neighboring parish. But I cannot do otherwise, unless—but no—it is impossible—you would not consent, and unless you did, never."

Sabot now looked at the row of benches in line as far as the entrance door. Christopher, if they were going to change all those!

And he asked:

"What would you require of me? Tell me."

The priest, in a firm tone replied:

"I must have an extraordinary token of your good intentions."

"I do not say—I do not say; perhaps we might come to an understanding," faltered Sabot.

"You will have to take communion publicly at high mass next Sunday," declared the cure.

The carpenter felt he was growing pale, and without replying, he asked:

"And the benches, are they going to be renovated?"

The abbe replied with confidence:

"Yes, but later on."

Sabot resumed:

"I do not say, I do not say. I am not calling it off, I am consenting to religion, for sure. But what rubs me the wrong way is, putting it in practice; but in this case I will not be refractory."

The attendants of the Virgin, having got off their chairs had concealed themselves behind the altar; and they listened pale with emotion.

The cure, seeing he had gained the victory, became all at once very friendly, quite familiar.

"That is good, that is good. That was wisely said, and not stupid, you understand. You will see, you will see."

Sabot smiled and asked with an awkward air:

"Would it not be possible to put off this communion just a trifle?"

But the priest replied, resuming his severe expression:

"From the moment that the work is put into your hands, I want to be assured of your conversion."

Then he continued more gently:

"You will come to confession to-morrow; for I must examine you at least twice."

"Twice?" repeated Sabot.

"Yes."

The priest smiled.

"You understand perfectly that you must have a general cleaning up, a thorough cleansing. So I will expect you to-morrow."

The carpenter, much agitated, asked:

"Where do you do that?"

"Why—in the confessional."

"In—that box, over there in the corner? The fact is—is—that it does not suit me, your box."

"How is that?"

"Seeing that—seeing that I am not accustomed to that, and also I am rather hard of hearing."

The cure was very affable and said:

"Well, then! you shall come to my house and into my parlor. We will have it just the two of us, tete-a-tete. Does that suit you?"

"Yes, that is all right, that will suit me, but your box, no."

"Well, then, to-morrow after the days work, at six o'clock."

"That is understood, that is all right, that is agreed on. To-morrow, monsieur le cure. Whoever draws back is a skunk!"

And he held out his great rough hand which the priest grasped heartily with a clap that resounded through the church.

Theodule Sabot was not easy in his mind all the following day. He had a feeling analogous to the apprehension one experiences when a tooth has to be drawn. The thought recurred to him at every moment: "I must go to confession this evening." And his troubled mind, the mind of an atheist only half convinced, was bewildered with a confused and overwhelming dread of the divine mystery.

As soon as he had finished his work, he betook himself to the parsonage. The cure was waiting for him in the garden, reading his breviary as he walked along a little path. He appeared radiant and greeted him with a good-natured laugh.

"Well, here we are! Come in, come in, Monsieur Sabot, no one will eat you."

And Sabot preceded him into the house. He faltered:

"If you do not mind I should like to get through with this little matter at once."

The cure replied:

"I am at your service. I have my surplice here. One minute and I will listen to you."

The carpenter, so disturbed that he had not two ideas in his head, watched him as he put on the white vestment with its pleated folds. The priest beckoned to him and said:

"Kneel down on this cushion."

Sabot remained standing, ashamed of having to kneel. He stuttered:

"Is it necessary?"

But the abbe had become dignified.

"You cannot approach the penitent bench except on your knees."

And Sabot knelt down.

"Repeat the confiteor," said the priest.

"What is that?" asked Sabot.

"The confiteor. If you do not remember it, repeat after me, one by one, the words I am going to say." And the cure repeated the sacred prayer, in a slow tone, emphasizing the words which the carpenter repeated after him. Then he said:

"Now make your confession."

But Sabot was silent, not knowing where to begin. The abbe then came to his aid.

"My child, I will ask you questions, since you don't seem familiar with these things. We will take, one by one, the commandments of God. Listen to me and do not be disturbed. Speak very frankly and never fear that you may say too much.

"'One God alone, thou shalt adore,

And love him perfectly.'

"Have you ever loved anything, or anybody, as well as you loved God? Have you loved him with all your soul, all your heart, all the strength of your love?"

Sabot was perspiring with the effort of thinking. He replied:

"No. Oh, no, m'sieu le cure. I love God as much as I can. That is —yes—I love him very much. To say that I do not love my children, no—I cannot say that. To say that if I had to choose between them and God, I could not be sure. To say that if I had to lose a hundred francs for the love of God, I could not say about that. But I love him well, for sure, I love him all the same." The priest said gravely "You must love Him more than all besides." And Sabot, meaning well, declared "I will do what I possibly can, m'sieu le cure." The abbe resumed:

"'God's name in vain thou shalt not take

Nor swear by any other thing.'

"Did you ever swear?"

"No-oh, that, no! I never swear, never. Sometimes, in a moment of anger, I may say sacre nom de Dieu! But then, I never swear."

"That is swearing," cried the priest, and added seriously:

"Do not do it again.

"'Thy Sundays thou shalt keep

 In serving God devoutly.'

"What do you do on Sunday?"

This time Sabot scratched his ear.

"Why, I serve God as best I can, m'sieu le cure. I serve him—at home. I work on Sunday."

The cure interrupted him, saying magnanimously:

"I know, you will do better in future. I will pass over the following commandments, certain that you have not transgressed the two first. We will take from the sixth to the ninth. I will resume:

 "'Others' goods thou shalt not take

 Nor keep what is not thine.'

"Have you ever taken in any way what belonged to another?"

But Theodule Sabot became indignant.

"Of course not, of course not! I am an honest man, m'sieu le cure, I swear it, for sure. To say that I have not sometimes charged for a few more hours of work to customers who had means, I could not say that. To say that I never add a few centimes to bills, only a few, I would not say that. But to steal, no! Oh, not that, no!"

The priest resumed severely:

"To take one single centime constitutes a theft. Do not do it again.

 'False witness thou shalt not bear,

 Nor lie in any way.'

"Have you ever told a lie?"

"No, as to that, no. I am not a liar. That is my quality. To say that I have never told a big story, I would not like to say that. To say that I have never made people believe things that were not true when it was to my own interest, I would not like to say that. But as for lying, I am not a liar."

The priest simply said:

"Watch yourself more closely." Then he continued:

 "'The works of the flesh thou shalt not desire

 Except in marriage only.'

"Did you ever desire, or live with, any other woman than your wife?"

Sabot exclaimed with sincerity:

"As to that, no; oh, as to that, no, m'sieu le Cure. My poor wife, deceive her! No, no! Not so much as the tip of a finger, either in thought or in act. That is the truth."

They were silent a few seconds, then, in a lower tone, as though a doubt had arisen in his mind, he resumed:

"When I go to town, to say that I never go into a house, you know, one of the licensed houses, just to laugh and talk and see something different, I could not say that. But I always pay, monsieur le cure, I always pay. From the moment you pay, without anyone seeing or knowing you, no one can get you into trouble."

The cure did not insist, and gave him absolution.

Theodule Sabot did the work on the chancel, and goes to communion every month.

THE WRONG HOUSE

Quartermaster Varajou had obtained a week's leave to go and visit his sister, Madame Padoie. Varajou, who was in garrison at Rennes and was leading a pretty gay life, finding himself high and dry, wrote to his sister saying that he would devote a week to her. It was not that he cared particularly for Mme. Padoie, a little moralist, a devotee, and always cross; but he needed money, needed it very badly, and he remembered that, of all his relations, the Padoies were the only ones whom he had never approached on the subject.

Pere Varajou, formerly a horticulturist at Angers, but now retired from business, had closed his purse strings to his scapegrace son and had hardly seen him for two years. His daughter had married Padoie, a former treasury clerk, who had just been appointed tax collector at Vannes.

Varajou, on leaving the train, had some one direct him to the house of his brother-in-law, whom he found in his office arguing with the Breton peasants of the neighborhood. Padoie rose from his seat, held out his hand across the table littered with papers, murmured, "Take a chair. I will be at liberty in a moment," sat down again and resumed his discussion.

The peasants did not understand his explanations, the collector did not understand their line of argument. He spoke French, they spoke Breton, and the clerk who acted as interpreter appeared not to understand either.

It lasted a long time, a very long time. Varajou looked at his brother-in-law and thought: "What a fool!" Padoie must have been almost fifty. He was tall, thin, bony, slow, hairy, with heavy arched eyebrows. He wore a velvet skull cap with a gold cord vandyke design round it. His look was gentle, like his actions. His speech, his gestures, his thoughts, all were soft. Varajou said to himself, "What a fool!"

He, himself, was one of those noisy roysterers for whom the greatest pleasures in life are the cafe and abandoned women. He understood nothing outside of these conditions of existence.

A boisterous braggart, filled with contempt for the rest of the world, he despised the entire universe from the height of his ignorance. When he said: "Nom d'un chien, what a spree!" he expressed the highest degree of admiration of which his mind was capable.

Having finally got rid of his peasants, Padoie inquired:

"How are you?"

"Pretty well, as you see. And how are you?"

"Quite well, thank you. It is very kind of you to have thought of coming to see us."

"Oh, I have been thinking of it for some time; but, you know, in the military profession one has not much freedom."

"Oh, I know, I know. All the same, it is very kind of you."

"And Josephine, is she well?"

"Yes, yes, thank you; you will see her presently." "Where is she?"

"She is making some calls. We have a great many friends here; it is a very nice town."

"I thought so."

The door opened and Mme. Padoie appeared. She went over to her brother without any eagerness, held her cheek for him to kiss, and asked:

"Have you been here long?"

"No, hardly half an hour."

"Oh, I thought the train would be late. Will you come into the parlor?"

They went into the adjoining room, leaving Padoie to his accounts and his taxpayers. As soon as they were alone, she said:

"I have heard nice things about you!"

"What have you heard?"

"It seems that you are behaving like a blackguard, getting drunk and contracting debts."

He appeared very much astonished.

"I! never in the world!"

"Oh, do not deny it, I know it."

He attempted to defend himself, but she gave him such a lecture that he could say nothing more.

She then resumed:

"We dine at six o'clock, and you can amuse yourself until then. I cannot entertain you, as I have so many things to do."

When he was alone he hesitated as to whether he should sleep or take a walk. He looked first at the door leading to his room and then at the hall door, and decided to go out. He sauntered slowly through the quiet Breton town, so sleepy, so calm, so dead, on the shores of its inland bay that is called "le Morbihan." He looked at the little gray houses, the occasional pedestrians, the empty stores, and he murmured:

"Vannes is certainly not gay, not lively. It was a sad idea, my coming here."

He reached the harbor, the desolate harbor, walked back along a lonely, deserted boulevard, and got home before five o'clock. Then he threw himself on his bed to sleep till dinner time. The maid woke him, knocking at the door.

"Dinner is ready, sir:"

He went downstairs. In the damp dining-room with the paper peeling from the walls near the floor, he saw a soup tureen on a round table without any table cloth, on which were also three melancholy soup-plates.

M. and Mme. Padoie entered the room at the same time as Varajou. They all sat down to table, and the husband and wife crossed themselves over the pit of their stomachs, after which Padoie helped the soup, a meat soup. It was the day for pot-roast.

After the soup, they had the beef, which was done to rags, melted, greasy, like pap. The officer ate slowly, with disgust, weariness and rage.

Mme. Padoie said to her husband:

"Are you going to the judge's house this evening?"

"Yes, dear."

"Do not stay late. You always get so tired when you go out. You are not made for society, with your poor health."

She then talked about society in Vannes, of the excellent social circle in which the Padoies moved, thanks to their religious sentiments.

A puree of potatoes and a dish of pork were next served, in honor of the guest. Then some cheese, and that was all. No coffee.

When Varajou saw that he would have to spend the evening tete-a-tete with his sister, endure her reproaches, listen to her sermons, without even a glass of liqueur to help him to swallow these remonstrances, he felt that he could not stand the torture, and declared that he was obliged to go to the police station to have something attended to regarding his leave of absence. And he made his escape at seven o'clock.

He had scarcely reached the street before he gave himself a shake like a dog coming out of the water. He muttered:

"Heavens, heavens, heavens, what a galley slave's life!"

And he set out to look for a cafe, the best in the town. He found it on a public square, behind two gas lamps. Inside the cafe, five or six men, semi-gentlemen, and not noisy, were drinking and chatting quietly, leaning their elbows on the small tables, while two billiard players walked round the green baize, where the balls were hitting each other as they rolled.

One heard them counting:

"Eighteen-nineteen. No luck. Oh, that's a good stroke! Well played! Eleven. You should have played on the red. Twenty. Froze! Froze! Twelve. Ha! Wasn't I right?"

Varajou ordered:

"A demi-tasse and a small decanter of brandy, the best." Then he sat down and waited for it.

He was accustomed to spending his evenings off duty with his companions, amid noise and the smoke of pipes. This silence, this quiet, exasperated him. He began to drink; first the coffee, then the brandy, and asked for another decanter. He now wanted to laugh, to shout, to sing, to fight some one. He said to himself:

"Gee, I am half full. I must go and have a good time."

And he thought he would go and look for some girls to amuse him. He called the waiter:

"Hey, waiter."

"Yes, sir."

"Tell me, where does one amuse oneself here?"

The man looked stupid, and replied:

"I do not know, sir. Here, I suppose!"

"How do you mean here? What do you call amusing oneself, yourself?"

"I do not know, sir, drinking good beer or good wine."

"Ah, go away, dummy, how about the girls?"

"The girls, ah! ah!"

"Yes, the girls, where can one find any here?"

"Girls?"

"Why, yes, girls!"

The boy approached and lowering his voice, said: "You want to know where they live?"

"Why, yes, the devil!"

"You take the second street to the left and then the first to the right. It is number fifteen."

"Thank you, old man. There is something for you."

"Thank you, sir."

And Varajou went out of the cafe, repeating, "Second to the left, first to the right, number 15." But at the end of a few seconds he thought, "second to the left yes. But on leaving the cafe must I walk to the right or the left? Bah, it cannot be helped, we shall see."

And he walked on, turned down the second street to the left, then the first to the right and looked for number 15. It was a nice looking house, and one could see behind the closed blinds that the windows were lighted up on the first floor. The hall door was left partly open, and a lamp was burning in the vestibule. The non-commissioned officer thought to himself:

"This looks all right."

He went in and, as no one appeared, he called out:

"Hallo there, hallo!"

A little maid appeared and looked astonished at seeing a soldier. He said:

"Good-morning, my child. Are the ladies upstairs?"

"Yes, sir."

"In the parlor?"

"Yes, sir."

"May I go up?"

"Yes, sir."

"The door opposite the stairs?"

"Yes, sir."

He ascended the stairs, opened a door and saw sitting in a room well lighted up by two lamps, a chandelier, and two candelabras with candles in them, four ladies in evening dress, apparently expecting some one.

Three of them, the younger ones, remained seated, with rather a formal air, on some crimson velvet chairs; while the fourth, who was about forty-five, was arranging some flowers in a vase. She was very stout, and wore a green silk dress with low neck and short sleeves, allowing her red neck, covered with powder, to escape as a huge flower might from its corolla.

The officer saluted them, saying:

"Good-day, ladies."

The older woman turned round, appeared surprised, but bowed.

"Good-morning, sir."

He sat down. But seeing that they did not welcome him eagerly, he thought that possibly only commissioned officers were admitted to the house, and this made him uneasy. But he said:

"Bah, if one comes in, we can soon tell."

He then remarked:

"Are you all well?"

The large lady, no doubt the mistress of the house, replied:

"Very well, thank you!"

He could think of nothing else to say, and they were all silent. But at last, being ashamed of his bashfulness, and with an awkward laugh, he said:

"Do not people have any amusement in this country? I will pay for a bottle of wine."

He had not finished his sentence when the door opened, and in walked Padoie dressed in a black suit.

Varajou gave a shout of joy, and rising from his seat, he rushed at his brother-in-law, put his arms round him and waltzed him round the room, shouting:

"Here is Padoie! Here is Padoie! Here is Padoie!"

Then letting go of the tax collector he exclaimed as he looked him in the face:

"Oh, oh, oh, you scamp, you scamp! You are out for a good time, too. Oh, you scamp! And my sister! Are you tired of her, say?"

As he thought of all that he might gain through this unexpected situation, the forced loan, the inevitable blackmail, he flung himself on the lounge and laughed so heartily that the piece of furniture creaked all over.

The three young ladies, rising simultaneously, made their escape, while the older woman retreated to the door looking as though she were about to faint.

And then two gentlemen appeared in evening dress, and wearing the ribbon of an order. Padoie rushed up to them.

"Oh, judge—he is crazy, he is crazy. He was sent to us as a convalescent. You can see that he is crazy."

Varajou was sitting up now, and not being able to understand it all, he guessed that he had committed some monstrous folly. Then he rose, and turning to his brother-in-law, said:

"What house is this?"

But Padoie, becoming suddenly furious, stammered out:

"What house—what—what house is this? Wretch—scoundrel—villain—what house, indeed? The house of the judge—of the judge of the Supreme Court—of the Supreme Court—of the Supreme Court—Oh, oh—rascal! —rascal!—rascal!"

THE DIAMOND NECKLACE

The girl was one of those pretty and charming young creatures who sometimes are born, as if by a slip of fate, into a family of clerks. She had no dowry, no expectations, no way of being known, understood, loved, married by any rich and distinguished man; so she let herself be married to a little clerk of the Ministry of Public Instruction.

She dressed plainly because she could not dress well, but she was unhappy as if she had really fallen from a higher station; since with women there is neither caste nor rank, for beauty, grace and charm take the place of family and birth. Natural ingenuity, instinct for what is elegant, a supple mind are their sole hierarchy, and often make of women of the people the equals of the very greatest ladies.

Mathilde suffered ceaselessly, feeling herself born to enjoy all delicacies and all luxuries. She was distressed at the poverty of her dwelling, at the bareness of the walls, at the shabby chairs, the ugliness of the curtains. All those things, of which another woman of her rank would never even have been conscious, tortured her and made her angry. The sight of the little Breton peasant who did her humble housework aroused in her despairing regrets and bewildering dreams. She thought of silent antechambers hung with Oriental tapestry, illumined by tall bronze candelabra, and of two great footmen in knee breeches who sleep in the big armchairs, made drowsy by the oppressive heat of the stove. She thought of long reception halls hung with ancient silk, of the dainty cabinets containing priceless curiosities and of the little coquettish perfumed reception rooms made for chatting at five o'clock with intimate friends, with men famous and sought after, whom all women envy and whose attention they all desire.

When she sat down to dinner, before the round table covered with a tablecloth in use three days, opposite her husband, who uncovered the soup tureen and declared with a delighted air, "Ah, the good soup! I don't know anything better than that," she thought of dainty dinners, of shining silverware, of tapestry that peopled the walls with ancient personages and with strange birds flying in the midst of a fairy forest; and she thought of delicious dishes served on marvellous plates and of the whispered gallantries to which you listen with a sphinxlike smile while you are eating the pink meat of a trout or the wings of a quail.

She had no gowns, no jewels, nothing. And she loved nothing but that. She felt made for that. She would have liked so much to please, to be envied, to be charming, to be sought after.

She had a friend, a former schoolmate at the convent, who was rich, and whom she did not like to go to see any more because she felt so sad when she came home.

But one evening her husband reached home with a triumphant air and holding a large envelope in his hand.

"There," said he, "there is something for you."

She tore the paper quickly and drew out a printed card which bore these words:

The Minister of Public Instruction and Madame Georges Ramponneau

request the honor of M. and Madame Loisel's company at the palace of

the Ministry on Monday evening, January 18th.

Instead of being delighted, as her husband had hoped, she threw the invitation on the table crossly, muttering:

"What do you wish me to do with that?"

"Why, my dear, I thought you would be glad. You never go out, and this is such a fine opportunity. I had great trouble to get it. Every one wants to go; it is very select, and they are not giving many invitations to clerks. The whole official world will be there."

She looked at him with an irritated glance and said impatiently:

"And what do you wish me to put on my back?"

He had not thought of that. He stammered:

"Why, the gown you go to the theatre in. It looks very well to me."

He stopped, distracted, seeing that his wife was weeping. Two great tears ran slowly from the corners of her eyes toward the corners of her mouth.

"What's the matter? What's the matter?" he answered.

By a violent effort she conquered her grief and replied in a calm voice, while she wiped her wet cheeks:

"Nothing. Only I have no gown, and, therefore, I can't go to this ball. Give your card to some colleague whose wife is better equipped than I am."

He was in despair. He resumed:

"Come, let us see, Mathilde. How much would it cost, a suitable gown, which you could use on other occasions—something very simple?"

She reflected several seconds, making her calculations and wondering also what sum she could ask without drawing on herself an immediate refusal and a frightened exclamation from the economical clerk.

Finally she replied hesitating:

"I don't know exactly, but I think I could manage it with four hundred francs."

He grew a little pale, because he was laying aside just that amount to buy a gun and treat himself to a little shooting next summer on the plain of Nanterre, with several friends who went to shoot larks there of a Sunday.

But he said:

"Very well. I will give you four hundred francs. And try to have a pretty gown."

The day of the ball drew near and Madame Loisel seemed sad, uneasy, anxious. Her frock was ready, however. Her husband said to her one evening:

"What is the matter? Come, you have seemed very queer these last three days."

And she answered:

"It annoys me not to have a single piece of jewelry, not a single ornament, nothing to put on. I shall look poverty-stricken. I would almost rather not go at all."

"You might wear natural flowers," said her husband. "They're very stylish at this time of year. For ten francs you can get two or three magnificent roses."

She was not convinced.

"No; there's nothing more humiliating than to look poor among other women who are rich."

"How stupid you are!" her husband cried. "Go look up your friend, Madame Forestier, and ask her to lend you some jewels. You're intimate enough with her to do that."

She uttered a cry of joy:

"True! I never thought of it."

The next day she went to her friend and told her of her distress.

Madame Forestier went to a wardrobe with a mirror, took out a large jewel box, brought it back, opened it and said to Madame Loisel:

"Choose, my dear."

She saw first some bracelets, then a pearl necklace, then a Venetian gold cross set with precious stones, of admirable workmanship. She tried on the ornaments before the mirror, hesitated and could not make up her mind to part with them, to give them back. She kept asking:

"Haven't you any more?"

"Why, yes. Look further; I don't know what you like."

Suddenly she discovered, in a black satin box, a superb diamond necklace, and her heart throbbed with an immoderate desire. Her hands trembled as she took it. She fastened it round her throat, outside her high-necked waist, and was lost in ecstasy at her reflection in the mirror.

Then she asked, hesitating, filled with anxious doubt:

"Will you lend me this, only this?"

"Why, yes, certainly."

She threw her arms round her friend's neck, kissed her passionately, then fled with her treasure.

The night of the ball arrived. Madame Loisel was a great success. She was prettier than any other woman present, elegant, graceful, smiling and wild with joy. All the men looked at her, asked her name, sought to be introduced. All the attaches of the Cabinet wished to waltz with her. She was remarked by the minister himself.

She danced with rapture, with passion, intoxicated by pleasure, forgetting all in the triumph of her beauty, in the glory of her success, in a sort of cloud of happiness comprised of all this homage, admiration, these awakened desires and of that sense of triumph which is so sweet to woman's heart.

She left the ball about four o'clock in the morning. Her husband had been sleeping since midnight in a little deserted anteroom with three other gentlemen whose wives were enjoying the ball.

He threw over her shoulders the wraps he had brought, the modest wraps of common life, the poverty of which contrasted with the elegance of the ball dress. She felt this and wished to escape so as not to be remarked by the other women, who were enveloping themselves in costly furs.

Loisel held her back, saying: "Wait a bit. You will catch cold outside. I will call a cab."

But she did not listen to him and rapidly descended the stairs. When they reached the street they could not find a carriage and began to look for one, shouting after the cabmen passing at a distance.

They went toward the Seine in despair, shivering with cold. At last they found on the quay one of those ancient night cabs which, as though they were ashamed to show their shabbiness during the day, are never seen round Paris until after dark.

It took them to their dwelling in the Rue des Martyrs, and sadly they mounted the stairs to their flat. All was ended for her. As to him, he reflected that he must be at the ministry at ten o'clock that morning.

She removed her wraps before the glass so as to see herself once more in all her glory. But suddenly she uttered a cry. She no longer had the necklace around her neck!

"What is the matter with you?" demanded her husband, already half undressed.

She turned distractedly toward him.

"I have—I have—I've lost Madame Forestier's necklace," she cried.

He stood up, bewildered.

"What!—how? Impossible!"

They looked among the folds of her skirt, of her cloak, in her pockets, everywhere, but did not find it.

"You're sure you had it on when you left the ball?" he asked.

"Yes, I felt it in the vestibule of the minister's house."

"But if you had lost it in the street we should have heard it fall. It must be in the cab."

"Yes, probably. Did you take his number?"

"No. And you—didn't you notice it?"

"No."

They looked, thunderstruck, at each other. At last Loisel put on his clothes.

"I shall go back on foot," said he, "over the whole route, to see whether I can find it."

He went out. She sat waiting on a chair in her ball dress, without strength to go to bed, overwhelmed, without any fire, without a thought.

Her husband returned about seven o'clock. He had found nothing.

He went to police headquarters, to the newspaper offices to offer a reward; he went to the cab companies—everywhere, in fact, whither he was urged by the least spark of hope.

She waited all day, in the same condition of mad fear before this terrible calamity.

Loisel returned at night with a hollow, pale face. He had discovered nothing.

"You must write to your friend," said he, "that you have broken the clasp of her necklace and that you are having it mended. That will give us time to turn round."

She wrote at his dictation.

At the end of a week they had lost all hope. Loisel, who had aged five years, declared:

"We must consider how to replace that ornament."

The next day they took the box that had contained it and went to the jeweler whose name was found within. He consulted his books.

"It was not I, madame, who sold that necklace; I must simply have furnished the case."

Then they went from jeweler to jeweler, searching for a necklace like the other, trying to recall it, both sick with chagrin and grief.

They found, in a shop at the Palais Royal, a string of diamonds that seemed to them exactly like the one they had lost. It was worth forty thousand francs. They could have it for thirty-six.

So they begged the jeweler not to sell it for three days yet. And they made a bargain that he should buy it back for thirty-four thousand francs, in case they should find the lost necklace before the end of February.

Loisel possessed eighteen thousand francs which his father had left him. He would borrow the rest.

He did borrow, asking a thousand francs of one, five hundred of another, five louis here, three louis there. He gave notes, took up ruinous obligations, dealt with usurers and all the race of lenders. He compromised all the rest of his life, risked signing a note without even knowing whether he could meet it; and, frightened by the trouble yet to come, by the black misery that was about to fall upon him, by the prospect of all the physical privations and moral tortures that he was to suffer, he went to get the new necklace, laying upon the jeweler's counter thirty-six thousand francs.

When Madame Loisel took back the necklace Madame Forestier said to her with a chilly manner:

"You should have returned it sooner; I might have needed it."

She did not open the case, as her friend had so much feared. If she had detected the substitution, what would she have thought, what would she have said? Would she not have taken Madame Loisel for a thief?

Thereafter Madame Loisel knew the horrible existence of the needy. She bore her part, however, with sudden heroism. That dreadful debt must be paid. She would pay it. They dismissed their servant; they changed their lodgings; they rented a garret under the roof.

She came to know what heavy housework meant and the odious cares of the kitchen. She washed the dishes, using her dainty fingers and rosy nails on greasy pots and pans. She washed the soiled linen, the shirts and the dishcloths, which she dried upon a line; she carried the slops down to the street every morning and carried up the water, stopping for breath at every landing. And dressed like a woman of the people, she went to the fruiterer, the grocer, the butcher, a basket on her arm, bargaining, meeting with impertinence, defending her miserable money, sou by sou.

Every month they had to meet some notes, renew others, obtain more time.

Her husband worked evenings, making up a tradesman's accounts, and late at night he often copied manuscript for five sous a page.

This life lasted ten years.

At the end of ten years they had paid everything, everything, with the rates of usury and the accumulations of the compound interest.

Madame Loisel looked old now. She had become the woman of impoverished households—strong and hard and rough. With frowsy hair, skirts askew and red hands, she talked loud while washing the floor with great swishes of water. But sometimes, when her husband was at the office, she sat down near the window and she thought of that gay evening of long ago, of that ball where she had been so beautiful and so admired.

What would have happened if she had not lost that necklace? Who knows? who knows? How strange and changeful is life! How small a thing is needed to make or ruin us!

But one Sunday, having gone to take a walk in the Champs Elysees to refresh herself after the labors of the week, she suddenly perceived a woman who was leading a child. It was Madame Forestier, still young, still beautiful, still charming.

Madame Loisel felt moved. Should she speak to her? Yes, certainly. And now that she had paid, she would tell her all about it. Why not?

She went up.

"Good-day, Jeanne."

The other, astonished to be familiarly addressed by this plain good-wife, did not recognize her at all and stammered:

"But—madame!—I do not know—You must have mistaken."

"No. I am Mathilde Loisel."

Her friend uttered a cry.

"Oh, my poor Mathilde! How you are changed!"

"Yes, I have had a pretty hard life, since I last saw you, and great poverty—and that because of you!"

"Of me! How so?"

"Do you remember that diamond necklace you lent me to wear at the ministerial ball?"

"Yes. Well?"

"Well, I lost it."

"What do you mean? You brought it back."

"I brought you back another exactly like it. And it has taken us ten years to pay for it. You can understand that it was not easy for us, for us who had nothing. At last it is ended, and I am very glad."

Madame Forestier had stopped.

"You say that you bought a necklace of diamonds to replace mine?"

"Yes. You never noticed it, then! They were very similar."

And she smiled with a joy that was at once proud and ingenuous.

Madame Forestier, deeply moved, took her hands.

"Oh, my poor Mathilde! Why, my necklace was paste! It was worth at most only five hundred francs!"

THE MARQUIS DE FUMEROL

Roger de Tourneville was whiffing a cigar and blowing out small clouds of smoke every now and then, as he sat astride a chair amid a party of friends. He was talking.

"We were at dinner when a letter was brought in which my father opened. You know my father, who thinks that he is king of France ad interim. I call him Don Quixote, because for twelve years he has been running a tilt against the windmill of the Republic, without quite knowing whether it was in the cause of the Bourbons or the Orleanists. At present he is bearing the lance in the cause of the Orleanists alone, because there is no one else left. In any case, he thinks himself the first gentleman of France, the best known, the most influential, the head of the party; and as he is an irremovable senator, he thinks that the thrones of the neighboring kings are very insecure.

"As for my mother, she is my father's soul, she is the soul of the kingdom and of religion, and the scourge of all evil-thinkers.

"Well, a letter was brought in while we were at dinner, and my father opened and read it, and then he said to mother: 'Your brother is dying.' She grew very pale. My uncle was scarcely ever mentioned in the house, and I did not know him at all; all I knew from public talk was, that he had led, and was still leading, a gay life. After having spent his fortune in fast living, he was now in small apartments in the Rue des Martyrs.

"An ancient peer of France and former colonel of cavalry, it was said that he believed in neither God nor devil. Not believing, therefore, in a future life he had abused the present life in every way, and had become a live wound in my mother's heart.

"'Give me that letter, Paul,' she said, and when she read it, I asked for it in my turn. Here it is:

'Monsieur le Comte, I think I ought to let you know that your

brother-in-law, the Comte Fumerol, is going to die. Perhaps you

would like to make some arrangements, and do not forget I told you.

Your servant,

'MELANIE.'

"'We must take counsel,' papa murmured. 'In my position, I ought to watch over your brother's last moments.'

"Mamma continued: 'I will send for Abbe Poivron and ask his advice, and then I will go to my brother with the abbe and Roger. Remain here, Paul, for you must not compromise yourself; but a woman can, and ought to do these things. For a politician in your position, it is another matter. It would be a fine thing for one of your opponents to be able to bring one of your most laudable actions up against you.' 'You are right,' my father said. 'Do as you think best, my dear wife.'

"A quarter of an hour, later, the Abbe Poivron came into the drawing-room, and the situation was explained to him, analyzed and discussed in all its bearings. If the Marquis de Fumerol, one of the greatest names in France, were to die without the ministrations of religion, it would assuredly be a terrible blow to the nobility in general, and to the Count de Tourneville in particular, and the freethinkers would be triumphant. The liberal newspapers would sing songs of victory for six months; my mother's name would be dragged through the mire and brought into the prose of Socialistic journals, and my father's name would be smirched. It was impossible that such a thing should be.

"A crusade was therefore immediately decided upon, which was to be led by the Abbe Poivron, a little, fat, clean, priest with a faint perfume about him, a true vicar of a large church in a noble and rich quarter.

"The landau was ordered and we all three set out, my mother, the cure and I, to administer the last sacraments to my uncle.

"It had been decided first of all we should see Madame Melanie who had written the letter, and who was most likely the porter's wife, or my uncle's servant, and I dismounted, as an advance guard, in front of a seven-story house and went into a dark passage, where I had great difficulty in finding the porter's den. He looked at me distrustfully, and I said:

"'Madame Melanie, if you please.' 'Don't know her!' 'But I have received a letter from her.' 'That may be, but I don't know her. Are you asking for a lodger?' 'No, a servant probably. She wrote me about a place.' 'A servant?—a servant? Perhaps it is the marquis'. Go and see, the fifth story on the left.'

"As soon as he found I was not asking for a doubtful character he became more friendly and came as far as the corridor with me. He was a tall, thin man with white whiskers, the manners of a beadle and majestic gestures.

"I climbed up a long spiral staircase, the railing of which I did not venture to touch, and I gave three discreet knocks at the left-hand door on the fifth story. It opened immediately, and an enormous dirty woman appeared before me. She barred the entrance with her extended arms which she placed against the two doorposts, and growled:

"'What do you want?' 'Are you Madame Melanie?' 'Yes.' 'I am the Visconte de Tourneville.' 'Ah! All right! Come in.' 'Well, the fact is, my mother is downstairs with a priest.' 'Oh! All right; go and bring them up; but be careful of the porter.'

"I went downstairs and came up again with my mother, who was followed by the abbe, and I fancied that I heard other footsteps behind us. As soon as we were in the kitchen, Melanie offered us chairs, and we all four sat down to deliberate.

"'Is he very ill?' my mother asked. 'Oh! yes, madame; he will not be here long.' 'Does he seem disposed to receive a visit from a priest?' 'Oh! I do not think so.' 'Can I see him?' 'Well—yes madame—only —only—those young ladies are with him.' 'What young ladies?' 'Why—why—his lady friends, of course.' 'Oh!' Mamma had grown scarlet, and the Abbe Poivron had lowered his eyes.

"The affair began to amuse me, and I said: 'Suppose I go in first? I shall see how he receives me, and perhaps I shall be able to prepare him to receive you.'

"My mother, who did not suspect any trick, replied: 'Yes, go, my dear.' But a woman's voice cried out: 'Melanie!'

"The servant ran out and said: 'What do you want, Mademoiselle Claire?' 'The omelette; quickly.' 'In a minute, mademoiselle.' And coming back to us, she explained this summons.

"They had ordered a cheese omelette at two o'clock as a slight collation. And she at once began to break the eggs into a salad bowl, and to whip them vigorously, while I went out on the landing and pulled the bell, so as to formally announce my arrival. Melanie opened the door to me, and made me sit down in an ante-room, while she went to tell my uncle that I had come; then she came back and asked me to go in, while the abbe hid behind the door, so that he might appear at the first signal.

"I was certainly very much surprised at the sight of my uncle, for he was very handsome, very solemn and very elegant, the old rake.

"Sitting, almost lying, in a large armchair, his legs wrapped in blankets, his hands, his long, white hands, over the arms of the chair, he was waiting for death with the dignity of a patriarch. His white beard fell on his chest, and his hair, which was also white, mingled with it on his cheeks.

"Standing behind his armchair, as if to defend him against me, were two young women, who looked at me with bold eyes. In their petticoats and morning wrappers, with bare arms, with coal black hair twisted in a knot on the nape of their neck, with embroidered, Oriental slippers, which showed their ankles and silk stockings, they looked like the figures in some symbolical painting, by the side of the dying man. Between the easy-chair and the bed, there was a table covered with a white cloth, on which two plates, two glasses, two forks and two knives, were waiting for the cheese omelette which had been ordered some time before of Melanie.

"My uncle said in a weak, almost breathless, but clear voice:

"'Good-morning, my child; it is rather late in the day to come and see me; our acquaintanceship will not last long.' I stammered out, 'It was not my fault, uncle:' 'No; I know that,' he replied. 'It is your father and mother's fault more than yours. How are they?' 'Pretty well, thank you. When they heard that you were ill, they sent me to ask after you.' 'Ah! Why did they not come themselves?'

"I looked up at the two girls and said gently: 'It is not their fault if they could not come, uncle. But it would be difficult for my father, and impossible for my mother to come in here.' The old man did not reply, but raised his hand toward mine, and I took the pale, cold hand and held it in my own.

"The door opened, Melanie came in with the omelette and put it on the table, and the two girls immediately sat down at the table, and began to eat without taking their eyes off me. Then I said: 'Uncle, it would give great pleasure to my mother to embrace you.' 'I also,' he murmured, 'should like——' He said no more, and I could think of nothing to propose to him, and there was silence except for the noise of the plates and that vague sound of eating.

"Now, the abbe, who was listening behind the door, seeing our embarrassment, and thinking we had won the game, thought the time had come to interpose, and showed himself. My uncle was so stupefied at sight of him that at first he remained motionless; and then he opened his mouth as if he meant to swallow up the priest, and shouted to him in a strong, deep, furious voice: 'What are you doing here?'

"The abbe, who was used to difficult situations, came forward into the room, murmuring: 'I have come in your sister's name, Monsieur le Marquis; she has sent me. She would be happy, monsieur—'

"But the marquis was not listening. Raising one hand, he pointed to the door with a proud, tragic gesture, and said angrily and breathing hard: 'Leave this room—go out—robber of souls. Go out from here, you violator of consciences. Go out from here, you pick-lock of dying men's doors!'

"The abbe retreated, and I also went to the door, beating a retreat with the priest; the two young women, who had the best of it, got up, leaving their omelette only half eaten, and went and stood on either side of my uncle's easy-chair, putting their hands on his arms to calm him, and to protect him against the criminal enterprises of the Family, and of Religion.

"The abbe and I rejoined my mother in the kitchen, and Melanie again offered us chairs. 'I knew quite well that this method would not work; we must try some other means, otherwise he will escape us.' And they began deliberating afresh, my mother being of one opinion and the abbe of another, while I held a third.

"We had been discussing the matter in a low voice for half an hour, perhaps, when a great noise of furniture being moved and of cries uttered by my uncle, more vehement and terrible even than the former had been, made us all four jump up.

"Through the doors and walls we could hear him shouting: 'Go out—out —rascals—humbugs, get out, scoundrels—get out—get out!'

"Melanie rushed in, but came back immediately to call me to help her, and I hastened in. Opposite to my uncle, who was terribly excited by anger, almost standing up and vociferating, stood two men, one behind the other, who seemed to be waiting till he should be dead with rage.

"By his ridiculous long coat, his long English shoes, his manners of a tutor out of a position, his high collar, white necktie and straight hair, his humble face of a false priest of a bastard religion, I immediately recognized the first as a Protestant minister.

"The second was the porter of the house, who belonged to the reformed religion and had followed us, and having seen our defeat, had gone to fetch his own pastor, in hopes that he might meet a better reception. My uncle seemed mad with rage! If the sight of the Catholic priest, of the priest of his ancestors, had irritated the Marquis de Fumerol, who had become a freethinker, the sight of his porter's minister made him altogether beside himself. I therefore took the two men by the arm and threw them out of the room so roughly that they bumped against each other twice, between the two doors which led to the staircase; and then I disappeared in my turn and returned to the kitchen, which was our headquarters in order to take counsel with my mother and the abbe.

"But Melanie came back in terror, sobbing out:

"'He is dying—he is dying—come immediately—he is dying.'

"My mother rushed out. My uncle had fallen to the ground, and lay full length along the floor, without moving. I fancy he was already dead. My mother was superb at that moment! She went straight up to the two girls who were kneeling by the body and trying to raise it up, and pointing to the door with irresistible authority, dignity and majesty, she said: 'Now it is time for you to leave the room.'

"And they went out without a word of protest. I must add, that I was getting ready to turn them out as unceremoniously as I had done the parson and the porter.

"Then the Abbe Poivron administered the last sacraments to my uncle with all the customary prayers, and remitted all his sins, while my mother sobbed as she knelt near her brother. Suddenly, however, she exclaimed: 'He recognized me; he pressed my hand; I am sure he recognized me!!!— and that he thanked me! Oh, God, what happiness!'

"Poor mamma! If she had known or guessed for whom those thanks were intended!

"They laid my uncle on his bed; he was certainly dead this time.

"'Madame,' Melanie said, 'we have no sheets to bury him in; all the linen belongs to these two young ladies,' and when I looked at the omelette which they had not finished, I felt inclined to laugh and to cry at the same time. There are some humorous moments and some humorous situations in life, occasionally!

"We gave my uncle a magnificent fungal, with five speeches at the grave. Baron de Croiselles, the senator, showed in admirable terms that God always returns victorious into well-born souls which have temporarily been led into error. All the members of the Royalist and Catholic party followed the funeral procession with the enthusiasm of victors, as they spoke of that beautiful death after a somewhat troublous life."

Viscount Roger ceased speaking; his audience was laughing. Then somebody said: "Bah! That is the story of all conversions in extremis."

THE TRIP OF LE HORLA

On the morning of July 8th I received the following telegram: "Fine day. Always my predictions. Belgian frontier. Baggage and servants left at noon at the social session. Beginning of manoeuvres at three. So I will wait for you at the works from five o'clock on. Jovis."

At five o'clock sharp I entered the gas works of La Villette. It might have been mistaken for the colossal ruins of an old town inhabited by Cyclops. There were immense dark avenues separating heavy gasometers standing one behind another, like monstrous columns, unequally high and, undoubtedly, in the past the supports of some tremendous, some fearful iron edifice.

The balloon was lying in the courtyard and had the appearance of a cake made of yellow cloth, flattened on the ground under a rope. That is called placing a balloon in a sweep-net, and, in fact, it appeared like an enormous fish.

Two or three hundred people were looking at it, sitting or standing, and some were examining the basket, a nice little square basket for a human cargo, bearing on its side in gold letters on a mahogany plate the words: Le Horla.

Suddenly the people began to stand back, for the gas was beginning to enter into the balloon through a long tube of yellow cloth, which lay on the soil, swelling and undulating like an enormous worm. But another thought, another picture occurs to every mind. It is thus that nature itself nourishes beings until their birth. The creature that will rise soon begins to move, and the attendants of Captain Jovis, as Le Horla grew larger, spread and put in place the net which covers it, so that the pressure will be regular and equally distributed at every point.

The operation is very delicate and very important, for the resistance of the cotton cloth of which the balloon is made is figured not in proportion to the contact surface of this cloth with the net, but in proportion to the links of the basket.

Le Horla, moreover, has been designed by M. Mallet, constructed under his own eyes and made by himself. Everything had been made in the shops of M. Jovis by his own working staff and nothing was made outside.

We must add that everything was new in this balloon, from the varnish to the valve, those two essential parts of a balloon. Both must render the cloth gas-proof, as the sides of a ship are waterproof. The old varnishes, made with a base of linseed oil, sometimes fermented and thus burned the cloth, which in a short time would tear like a piece of paper.

The valves were apt to close imperfectly after being opened and when the covering called "cataplasme" was injured. The fall of M. L'Hoste in the open sea during the night proved the imperfection of the old system.

The two discoveries of Captain Jovis, the varnish principally, are of inestimable value in the art of ballooning.

The crowd has begun to talk, and some men, who appear to be specialists, affirm with authority that we shall come down before reaching the fortifications. Several other things have been criticized in this novel type of balloon with which we are about to experiment with so much pleasure and success.

It is growing slowly but surely. Some small holes and scratches made in transit have been discovered, and we cover them and plug them with a little piece of paper applied on the cloth while wet. This method of repairing alarms and mystifies the public.

While Captain Jovis and his assistants are busy with the last details, the travellers go to dine in the canteen of the gas-works, according to the established custom.

When we come out again the balloon is swaying, enormous and transparent, a prodigious golden fruit, a fantastic pear which is still ripening, covered by the last rays of the setting sun. Now the basket is attached, the barometers are brought, the siren, which we will blow to our hearts' content, is also brought, also the two trumpets, the eatables, the overcoats and raincoats, all the small articles that can go with the men in that flying basket.

As the wind pushes the balloon against the gasometers, it is necessary to steady it now and then, to avoid an accident at the start.

Captain Jovis is now ready and calls all the passengers.

Lieutenant Mallet jumps aboard, climbing first on the aerial net between the basket and the balloon, from which he will watch during the night the movements of Le Horla across the skies, as the officer on watch, standing on starboard, watches the course of a ship.

M. Etierine Beer gets in after him, then comes M. Paul Bessand, then M. Patrice Eyries and I get in last.

But the basket is too heavy for the balloon, considering the long trip to be taken, and M. Eyries has to get out, not without great regret.

M. Joliet, standing erect on the edge of the basket, begs the ladies, in very gallant terms, to stand aside a little, for he is afraid he might throw sand on their hats in rising. Then he commands:

"Let it loose," and, cutting with one stroke of his knife the ropes that hold the balloon to the ground, he gives Le Horla its liberty.

In one second we fly skyward. Nothing can be heard; we float, we rise, we fly, we glide. Our friends shout with glee and applaud, but we hardly hear them, we hardly see them. We are already so far, so high! What? Are we really leaving these people down there? Is it possible? Paris spreads out beneath us, a dark bluish patch, cut by its streets, from which rise, here and there, domes, towers, steeples, then around it the plain, the country, traversed by long roads, thin and white, amidst green fields of a tender or dark green, and woods almost black.

The Seine appears like a coiled snake, asleep, of which we see neither head nor tail; it crosses Paris, and the entire field resembles an immense basin of prairies and forests dotted here and there by mountains, hardly visible in the horizon.

The sun, which we could no longer see down below, now reappears as though it were about to rise again, and our balloon seems to be lighted; it must appear like a star to the people who are looking up. M. Mallet every few seconds throws a cigarette paper into-space and says quietly: "We are rising, always rising," while Captain Jovis, radiant with joy, rubs his hands together and repeats: "Eh? this varnish? Isn't it good?"

In fact, we can see whether we are rising or sinking only by throwing a cigarette paper out of the basket now and then. If this paper appears to fall down like a stone, it means that the balloon is rising; if it appears to shoot skyward the balloon is descending.

The two barometers mark about five hundred meters, and we gaze with enthusiastic admiration at the earth we are leaving and to which we are not attached in any way; it looks like a colored map, an immense plan of the country. All its noises, however, rise to our ears very distinctly, easily recognizable. We hear the sound of the wheels rolling in the streets, the snap of a whip, the cries of drivers, the rolling and whistling of trains and the laughter of small boys running after one another. Every time we pass over a village the noise of children's voices is heard above the rest and with the greatest distinctness. Some men are calling us; the locomotives whistle; we answer with the siren, which emits plaintive, fearfully shrill wails like the voice of a weird being wandering through the world.

We perceive lights here and there, some isolated fire in the farms, and lines of gas in the towns. We are going toward the northwest, after roaming for some time over the little lake of Enghien. Now we see a river; it is the Oise, and we begin to argue about the exact spot we are passing. Is that town Creil or Pontoise—the one with so many lights? But if we were over Pontoise we could see the junction of the Seine and the Oise; and that enormous fire to the left, isn't it the blast furnaces of Montataire? So then we are above Creil. The view is superb; it is dark on the earth, but we are still in the light, and it is now past ten o'clock. Now we begin to hear slight country noises, the double cry of the quail in particular, then the mewing of cats and the barking of dogs. Surely the dogs have scented the balloon; they have seen it and have given the alarm. We can hear them barking all over the plain and making the identical noise they make when baying at the moon. The cows also seem to wake up in the barns, for we can hear them lowing; all the beasts are scared and moved before the aerial monster that is passing.

The delicious odors of the soil rise toward us, the smell of hay, of flowers, of the moist, verdant earth, perfuming the air-a light air, in fact, so light, so sweet, so delightful that I realize I never was so fortunate as to breathe before. A profound sense of well-being, unknown to me heretofore, pervades me, a well-being of body and spirit, composed of supineness, of infinite rest, of forgetfulness, of indifference to everything and of this novel sensation of traversing space without any of the sensations that make motion unbearable, without noise, without shocks and without fear.

At times we rise and then descend. Every few minutes Lieutenant Mallet, suspended in his cobweb of netting, says to Captain Jovis: "We are descending; throw down half a handful." And the captain, who is talking and laughing with us, with a bag of ballast between his legs, takes a handful of sand out of the bag and throws it overboard.

Nothing is more amusing, more delicate, more interesting than the manoeuvring of a balloon. It is an enormous toy, free and docile, which obeys with surprising sensitiveness, but it is also, and before all, the slave of the wind, which we cannot control. A pinch of sand, half a sheet of paper, one or two drops of water, the bones of a chicken which we had just eaten, thrown overboard, makes it go up quickly.

A breath of cool, damp air rising from the river or the wood we are traversing makes the balloon descend two hundred metres. It does not vary when passing over fields of ripe grain, and it rises when it passes over towns.

The earth sleeps now, or, rather, men sleep on the earth, for the beasts awakened by the sight of our balloon announce our approach everywhere. Now and then the rolling of a train or the whistling of a locomotive is plainly distinguishable. We sound our siren as we pass over inhabited places; and the peasants, terrified in their beds, must surely tremble and ask themselves if the Angel Gabriel is not passing by.

A strong and continuous odor of gas can be plainly observed. We must have encountered a current of warm air, and the balloon expands, losing its invisible blood by the escape-valve, which is called the appendix, and which closes of itself as soon as the expansion ceases.

We are rising. The earth no longer gives back the echo of our trumpets; we have risen almost two thousand feet. It is not light enough for us to consult the instruments; we only know that the rice paper falls from us like dead butterflies, that we are rising, always rising. We can no longer see the earth; a light mist separates us from it; and above our head twinkles a world of stars.

A silvery light appears before us and makes the sky turn pale, and suddenly, as if it were rising from unknown depths behind the horizon below us rises the moon on the edge of a cloud. It seems to be coming from below, while we are looking down upon it from a great height, leaning on the edge of our basket like an audience on a balcony. Clear and round, it emerges from the clouds and slowly rises in the sky.

The earth no longer seems to exist, it is buried in milky vapors that resemble a sea. We are now alone in space with the moon, which looks like another balloon travelling opposite us; and our balloon, which shines in the air, appears like another, larger moon, a world wandering in the sky amid the stars, through infinity. We no longer speak, think nor live; we float along through space in delicious inertia. The air which is bearing us up has made of us all beings which resemble itself, silent, joyous, irresponsible beings, intoxicated by this stupendous flight, peculiarly alert, although motionless. One is no longer conscious of one's flesh or one's bones; one's heart seems to have ceased beating; we have become something indescribable, birds who do not even have to flap their wings.

All memory has disappeared from our minds, all trouble from our thoughts; we have no more regrets, plans nor hopes. We look, we feel, we wildly enjoy this fantastic journey; nothing in the sky but the moon and ourselves! We are a wandering, travelling world, like our sisters, the planets; and this little world carries five men who have left the earth and who have almost forgotten it. We can now see as plainly as in daylight; we look at each other, surprised at this brightness, for we have nothing to look at but ourselves and a few silvery clouds floating below us. The barometers mark twelve hundred metres, then thirteen, fourteen, fifteen hundred; and the little rice papers still fall about us.

Captain Jovis claims that the moon has often made balloons act thus, and that the upward journey will continue.

We are now at two thousand metres; we go up to two thousand three hundred and fifty; then the balloon stops: We blow the siren and are surprised that no one answers us from the stars.

We are now going down rapidly. M. Mallet keeps crying: "Throw out more ballast! throw out more ballast!" And the sand and stones that we throw over come back into our faces, as if they were going up, thrown from below toward the stars, so rapid is our descent.

Here is the earth! Where are we? It is now past midnight, and we are crossing a broad, dry, well-cultivated country, with many roads and well populated.

To the right is a large city and farther away to the left is another. But suddenly from the earth appears a bright fairy light; it disappears, reappears and once more disappears. Jovis, intoxicated by space, exclaims: "Look, look at this phenomenon of the moon in the water. One can see nothing more beautiful at night!"

Nothing indeed can give one an idea of the wonderful brightness of these spots of light which are not fire, which do not look like reflections, which appear quickly here or there and immediately go out again. These shining lights appear on the winding rivers at every turn, but one hardly has time to see them as the balloon passes as quickly as the wind.

We are now quite near the earth, and Beer exclaims:—"Look at that! What is that running over there in the fields? Isn't it a dog?" Indeed, something is running along the ground with great speed, and this something seems to jump over ditches, roads, trees with such ease that we could not understand what it might be. The captain laughed: "It is the shadow of our balloon. It will grow as we descend."

I distinctly hear a great noise of foundries in the distance. And, according to the polar star, which we have been observing all night, 'and which I have so often watched and consulted from the bridge of my little yacht on the Mediterranean, we are heading straight for Belgium.

Our siren and our two horns are continually calling. A few cries from some truck driver or belated reveler answer us. We bellow: "Where are we?" But the balloon is going so rapidly that the bewildered man has not even time to answer us. The growing shadow of Le Horla, as large as a child's ball, is fleeing before us over the fields, roads and woods. It goes along steadily, preceding us by about a quarter of a mile; and now I am leaning out of the basket, listening to the roaring of the wind in the trees and across the harvest fields. I say to Captain Jovis: "How the wind blows!"

He answers: "No, those are probably waterfalls." I insist, sure of my ear that knows the sound of the wind, from hearing it so often whistle through the rigging. Then Jovis nudges me; he fears to frighten his happy, quiet passengers, for he knows full well that a storm is pursuing us.

At last a man manages to understand us; he answers: "Nord!" We get the same reply from another.

Suddenly the lights of a town, which seems to be of considerable size, appear before us. Perhaps it is Lille. As we approach it, such a wonderful flow of fire appears below us that I think myself transported into some fairyland where precious stones are manufactured for giants.

It seems that it is a brick factory. Here are others, two, three. The fusing material bubbles, sparkles, throws out blue, red, yellow, green sparks, reflections from giant diamonds, rubies, emeralds, turquoises, sapphires, topazes. And near by are great foundries roaring like apocalyptic lions; high chimneys belch forth their clouds of smoke and flame, and we can hear the noise of metal striking against metal.

"Where are we?"

The voice of some joker or of a crazy person answers: "In a balloon!"

"Where are we?"

"At Lille!"

We were not mistaken. We are already out of sight of the town, and we see Roubaix to the right, then some well-cultivated, rectangular fields, of different colors according to the crops, some yellow, some gray or brown. But the clouds are gathering behind us, hiding the moon, whereas toward the east the sky is growing lighter, becoming a clear blue tinged with red. It is dawn. It grows rapidly, now showing us all the little details of the earth, the trains, the brooks, the cows, the goats. And all this passes beneath us with surprising speed. One hardly has time to notice that other fields, other meadows, other houses have already disappeared. Cocks are crowing, but the voice of ducks drowns everything. One might think the world to be peopled, covered with them, they make so much noise.

The early rising peasants are waving their arms and crying to us: "Let yourselves drop!" But we go along steadily, neither rising nor falling, leaning over the edge of the basket and watching the world fleeing under our feet.

Jovis sights another city far off in the distance. It approaches; everywhere are old church spires. They are delightful, seen thus from above. Where are we? Is this Courtrai? Is it Ghent?

We are already very near it, and we see that it is surrounded by water and crossed in every direction by canals. One might think it a Venice of the north. Just as we are passing so near to a church tower that our long guy-rope almost touches it, the chimes begin to ring three o'clock. The sweet, clear sounds rise to us from this frail roof which we have almost touched in our wandering course. It is a charming greeting, a friendly welcome from Holland. We answer with our siren, whose raucous voice echoes throughout the streets.

It was Bruges. But we have hardly lost sight of it when my neighbor, Paul Bessand, asks me: "Don't you see something over there, to the right, in front of us? It looks like a river."

And, indeed, far ahead of us stretches a bright highway, in the light of the dawning day. Yes, it looks like a river, an immense river full of islands.

"Get ready for the descent," cried the captain. He makes M. Mallet leave his net and return to the basket; then we pack the barometers and everything that could be injured by possible shocks. M. Bessand exclaims: "Look at the masts over there to the left! We are at the sea!"

Fogs had hidden it from us until then. The sea was everywhere, to the left and opposite us, while to our right the Scheldt, which had joined the Moselle, extended as far as the sea, its mouths vaster than a lake.

It was necessary to descend within a minute or two. The rope to the escape-valve, which had been religiously enclosed in a little white bag and placed in sight of all so that no one would touch it, is unrolled, and M. Mallet holds it in his hand while Captain Jovis looks for a favorable landing.

Behind us the thunder was rumbling and not a single bird followed our mad flight.

"Pull!" cried Jovis.

We were passing over a canal. The basket trembled and tipped over slightly. The guy-rope touched the tall trees on both banks. But our speed is so great that the long rope now trailing does not seem to slow down, and we pass with frightful rapidity over a large farm, from which the bewildered chickens, pigeons and ducks fly away, while the cows, cats and dogs run, terrified, toward the house.

Just one-half bag of ballast is left. Jovis throws it overboard, and Le Horla flies lightly across the roof.

The captain once more cries: "The escape-valve!"

M. Mallet reaches for the rope and hangs to it, and we drop like an arrow. With a slash of a knife the cord which retains the anchor is cut, and we drag this grapple behind us, through a field of beets. Here are the trees.

"Take care! Hold fast! Look out for your heads!"

We pass over them. Then a strong shock shakes us. The anchor has taken hold.

"Look out! Take a good hold! Raise yourselves by your wrists. We are going to touch ground."

The basket does indeed strike the earth. Then it flies up again. Once more it falls and bounds upward again, and at last it settles on the ground, while the balloon struggles madly, like a wounded beast.

Peasants run toward us, but they do not dare approach. They were a long time before they decided to come and deliver us, for one cannot set foot on the ground until the bag is almost completely deflated.

Then, almost at the same time as the bewildered men, some of whom showed their astonishment by jumping, with the wild gestures of savages, all the cows that were grazing along the coast came toward us, surrounding our balloon with a strange and comical circle of horns, big eyes and blowing nostrils.

With the help of the accommodating and hospitable Belgian peasants, we were able in a short time to pack up all our material and carry it to the station at Heyst, where at twenty minutes past eight we took the train for Paris.

The descent occurred at three-fifteen in the morning, preceding by only a few seconds the torrent of rain and the blinding lightning of the storm which had been chasing us before it.

Thanks to Captain Jovis, of whom I had heard much from my colleague, Paul Ginisty—for both of them had fallen together and voluntarily into the sea opposite Mentone—thanks to this brave man, we were able to see, in a single night, from far up in the sky, the setting of the sun, the rising of the moon and the dawn of day and to go from Paris to the mouth of the Scheldt through the skies.

[This story appeared in "Figaro" on July 16, 1887, under the title:

"From Paris to Heyst."]

FAREWELL!

The two friends were getting near the end of their dinner. Through the cafe windows they could see the Boulevard, crowded with people. They could feel the gentle breezes which are wafted over Paris on warm summer evenings and make you feel like going out somewhere, you care not where, under the trees, and make you dream of moonlit rivers, of fireflies and of larks.

One of the two, Henri Simon, heaved a deep sigh and said:

"Ah! I am growing old. It's sad. Formerly, on evenings like this, I felt full of life. Now, I only feel regrets. Life is short!"

He was perhaps forty-five years old, very bald and already growing stout.

The other, Pierre Carnier, a trifle older, but thin and lively, answered:

"Well, my boy, I have grown old without noticing it in the least. I have always been merry, healthy, vigorous and all the rest. As one sees oneself in the mirror every day, one does not realize the work of age, for it is slow, regular, and it modifies the countenance so gently that the changes are unnoticeable. It is for this reason alone that we do not die of sorrow after two or three years of excitement. For we cannot understand the alterations which time produces. In order to appreciate them one would have to remain six months without seeing one's own face —then, oh, what a shock!

"And the women, my friend, how I pity the poor beings! All their joy, all their power, all their life, lies in their beauty, which lasts ten years.

"As I said, I aged without noticing it; I thought myself practically a youth, when I was almost fifty years old. Not feeling the slightest infirmity, I went about, happy and peaceful.

"The revelation of my decline came to me in a simple and terrible manner, which overwhelmed me for almost six months—then I became resigned.

"Like all men, I have often been in love, but most especially once.

"I met her at the seashore, at Etretat, about twelve years ago, shortly after the war. There is nothing prettier than this beach during the morning bathing hour. It is small, shaped like a horseshoe, framed by high while cliffs, which are pierced by strange holes called the 'Portes,' one stretching out into the ocean like the leg of a giant, the other short and dumpy. The women gather on the narrow strip of sand in this frame of high rocks, which they make into a gorgeous garden of beautiful gowns. The sun beats down on the shores, on the multicolored parasols, on the blue-green sea; and all is gay, delightful, smiling. You sit down at the edge of the water and you watch the bathers. The women come down, wrapped in long bath robes, which they throw off daintily when they reach the foamy edge of the rippling waves; and they run into the water with a rapid little step, stopping from time to time for a delightful little thrill from the cold water, a short gasp.

"Very few stand the test of the bath. It is there that they can be judged, from the ankle to the throat. Especially on leaving the water are the defects revealed, although water is a powerful aid to flabby skin.

"The first time that I saw this young woman in the water, I was delighted, entranced. She stood the test well. There are faces whose charms appeal to you at first glance and delight you instantly. You seem to have found the woman whom you were born to love. I had that feeling and that shock.

"I was introduced, and was soon smitten worse than I had ever been before. My heart longed for her. It is a terrible yet delightful thing thus to be dominated by a young woman. It is almost torture, and yet infinite delight. Her look, her smile, her hair fluttering in the wind, the little lines of her face, the slightest movement of her features, delighted me, upset me, entranced me. She had captured me, body and soul, by her gestures, her manners, even by her clothes, which seemed to take on a peculiar charm as soon as she wore them. I grew tender at the sight of her veil on some piece of furniture, her gloves thrown on a chair. Her gowns seemed to me inimitable. Nobody had hats like hers.

"She was married, but her husband came only on Saturday, and left on Monday. I didn't concern myself about him, anyhow. I wasn't jealous of him, I don't know why; never did a creature seem to me to be of less importance in life, to attract my attention less than this man.

"But she! how I loved her! How beautiful, graceful and young she was! She was youth, elegance, freshness itself! Never before had I felt so strongly what a pretty, distinguished, delicate, charming, graceful being woman is. Never before had I appreciated the seductive beauty to be found in the curve of a cheek, the movement of a lip, the pinkness of an ear, the shape of that foolish organ called the nose.

"This lasted three months; then I left for America, overwhelmed with sadness. But her memory remained in me, persistent, triumphant. From far away I was as much hers as I had been when she was near me. Years passed by, and I did not forget her. The charming image of her person was ever before my eyes and in my heart. And my love remained true to her, a quiet tenderness now, something like the beloved memory of the most beautiful and the most enchanting thing I had ever met in my life.

"Twelve years are not much in a lifetime! One does not feel them slip by. The years follow each other gently and quickly, slowly yet rapidly, each one is long and yet so soon over! They add up so rapidly, they leave so few traces behind them, they disappear so completely, that, when one turns round to look back over bygone years, one sees nothing and yet one does not understand how one happens to be so old. It seemed to me, really, that hardly a few months separated me from that charming season on the sands of Etretat.

"Last spring I went to dine with some friends at Maisons-Laffitte.

"Just as the train was leaving, a big, fat lady, escorted by four little girls, got into my car. I hardly looked at this mother hen, very big, very round, with a face as full as the moon framed in an enormous, beribboned hat.

"She was puffing, out of breath from having been forced to walk quickly. The children began to chatter. I unfolded my paper and began to read.

"We had just passed Asnieres, when my neighbor suddenly turned to me and said:

"'Excuse me, sir, but are you not Monsieur Garnier?'

"'Yes, madame.'

"Then she began to laugh, the pleased laugh of a good woman; and yet it was sad.

"'You do not seem to recognize me.'

"I hesitated. It seemed to me that I had seen that face somewhere; but where? when? I answered:

"'Yes—and no. I certainly know you, and yet I cannot recall your name.'

"She blushed a little:

"'Madame Julie Lefevre.'

"Never had I received such a shock. In a second it seemed to me as though it were all over with me! I felt that a veil had been torn from my eyes and that I was going to make a horrible and heartrending discovery.

"So that was she! That big, fat, common woman, she! She had become the mother of these four girls since I had last her. And these little beings surprised me as much as their mother. They were part of her; they were big girls, and already had a place in life. Whereas she no longer counted, she, that marvel of dainty and charming gracefulness. It seemed to me that I had seen her but yesterday, and this is how I found her again! Was it possible? A poignant grief seized my heart; and also a revolt against nature herself, an unreasoning indignation against this brutal, infarious act of destruction.

"I looked at her, bewildered. Then I took her hand in mine, and tears came to my eyes. I wept for her lost youth. For I did not know this fat lady.

"She was also excited, and stammered:

"'I am greatly changed, am I not? What can you expect—everything has its time! You see, I have become a mother, nothing but a good mother. Farewell to the rest, that is over. Oh! I never expected you to recognize me if we met. You, too, have changed. It took me quite a while to be sure that I was not mistaken. Your hair is all white. Just think! Twelve years ago! Twelve years! My oldest girl is already ten.'

"I looked at the child. And I recognized in her something of her mother's old charm, but something as yet unformed, something which promised for the future. And life seemed to me as swift as a passing train.

"We had reached. Maisons-Laffitte. I kissed my old friend's hand. I had found nothing utter but the most commonplace remarks. I was too much upset to talk.

"At night, alone, at home, I stood in front of the mirror for a long time, a very long time. And I finally remembered what I had been, finally saw in my mind's eye my brown mustache, my black hair and the youthful expression of my face. Now I was old. Farewell!"

THE WOLF

This is what the old Marquis d'Arville told us after St. Hubert's dinner at the house of the Baron des Ravels.

We had killed a stag that day. The marquis was the only one of the guests who had not taken part in this chase. He never hunted.

During that long repast we had talked about hardly anything but the slaughter of animals. The ladies themselves were interested in bloody and exaggerated tales, and the orators imitated the attacks and the combats of men against beasts, raised their arms, romanced in a thundering voice.

M. d Arville talked well, in a certain flowery, high-sounding, but effective style. He must have told this story frequently, for he told it fluently, never hesitating for words, choosing them with skill to make his description vivid.

Gentlemen, I have never hunted, neither did my father, nor my grandfather, nor my great-grandfather. This last was the son of a man who hunted more than all of you put together. He died in 1764. I will tell you the story of his death.

His name was Jean. He was married, father of that child who became my great-grandfather, and he lived with his younger brother, Francois d'Arville, in our castle in Lorraine, in the midst of the forest.

Francois d'Arville had remained a bachelor for love of the chase.

They both hunted from one end of the year to the other, without stopping and seemingly without fatigue. They loved only hunting, understood nothing else, talked only of that, lived only for that.

They had at heart that one passion, which was terrible and inexorable. It consumed them, had completely absorbed them, leaving room for no other thought.

They had given orders that they should not be interrupted in the chase for any reason whatever. My great-grandfather was born while his father was following a fox, and Jean d'Arville did not stop the chase, but exclaimed: "The deuce! The rascal might have waited till after the view —halloo!"

His brother Franqois was still more infatuated. On rising he went to see the dogs, then the horses, then he shot little birds about the castle until the time came to hunt some large game.

In the countryside they were called M. le Marquis and M. le Cadet, the nobles then not being at all like the chance nobility of our time, which wishes to establish an hereditary hierarchy in titles; for the son of a marquis is no more a count, nor the son of a viscount a baron, than a son of a general is a colonel by birth. But the contemptible vanity of today finds profit in that arrangement.

My ancestors were unusually tall, bony, hairy, violent and vigorous. The younger, still taller than the older, had a voice so strong that, according to a legend of which he was proud, all the leaves of the forest shook when he shouted.

When they were both mounted to set out hunting, it must have been a superb sight to see those two giants straddling their huge horses.

Now, toward the midwinter of that year, 1764, the frosts were excessive, and the wolves became ferocious.

They even attacked belated peasants, roamed at night outside the houses, howled from sunset to sunrise, and robbed the stables.

And soon a rumor began to circulate. People talked of a colossal wolf with gray fur, almost white, who had eaten two children, gnawed off a woman's arm, strangled all the watch dogs in the district, and even come without fear into the farmyards. The people in the houses affirmed that they had felt his breath, and that it made the flame of the lights flicker. And soon a panic ran through all the province. No one dared go out any more after nightfall. The darkness seemed haunted by the image of the beast.

The brothers d'Arville determined to find and kill him, and several times they brought together all the gentlemen of the country to a great hunt.

They beat the forests and searched the coverts in vain; they never met him. They killed wolves, but not that one. And every night after a battue the beast, as if to avenge himself, attacked some traveller or killed some one's cattle, always far from the place where they had looked for him.

Finally, one night he stole into the pigpen of the Chateau d'Arville and ate the two fattest pigs.

The brothers were roused to anger, considering this attack as a direct insult and a defiance. They took their strong bloodhounds, used to pursue dangerous animals, and they set off to hunt, their hearts filled with rage.

From dawn until the hour when the empurpled sun descended behind the great naked trees, they beat the woods without finding anything.

At last, furious and disgusted, both were returning, walking their horses along a lane bordered with hedges, and they marvelled that their skill as huntsmen should be baffled by this wolf, and they were suddenly seized with a mysterious fear.

The elder said:

"That beast is not an ordinary one. You would say it had a mind like a man."

The younger answered:

"Perhaps we should have a bullet blessed by our cousin, the bishop, or pray some priest to pronounce the words which are needed."

Then they were silent.

Jean continued:

"Look how red the sun is. The great wolf will do some harm to-night."

He had hardly finished speaking when his horse reared; that of Franqois began to kick. A large thicket covered with dead leaves opened before them, and a mammoth beast, entirely gray, jumped up and ran off through the wood.

Both uttered a kind of grunt of joy, and bending over the necks of their heavy horses, they threw them forward with an impulse from all their body, hurling them on at such a pace, urging them, hurrying them away, exciting them so with voice and with gesture and with spur that the experienced riders seemed to be carrying the heavy beasts between 4 their thighs and to bear them off as if they were flying.

Thus they went, plunging through the thickets, dashing across the beds of streams, climbing the hillsides, descending the gorges, and blowing the horn as loud as they could to attract their people and the dogs.

And now, suddenly, in that mad race, my ancestor struck his forehead against an enormous branch which split his skull; and he fell dead on the ground, while his frightened horse took himself off, disappearing in the gloom which enveloped the woods.

The younger d'Arville stopped quick, leaped to the earth, seized his brother in his arms, and saw that the brains were escaping from the wound with the blood.

Then he sat down beside the body, rested the head, disfigured and red, on his knees, and waited, regarding the immobile face of his elder brother. Little by little a fear possessed him, a strange fear which he had never felt before, the fear of the dark, the fear of loneliness, the fear of the deserted wood, and the fear also of the weird wolf who had just killed his brother to avenge himself upon them both.

The gloom thickened; the acute cold made the trees crack. Francois got up, shivering, unable to remain there longer, feeling himself growing faint. Nothing was to be heard, neither the voice of the dogs nor the sound of the horns-all was silent along the invisible horizon; and this mournful silence of the frozen night had something about it terrific and strange.

He seized in his immense hands the great body of Jean, straightened it, and laid it across the saddle to carry it back to the chateau; then he went on his way softly, his mind troubled as if he were in a stupor, pursued by horrible and fear-giving images.

And all at once, in the growing darkness a great shape crossed his path. It was the beast. A shock of terror shook the hunter; something cold, like a drop of water, seemed to glide down his back, and, like a monk haunted of the devil, he made a great sign of the cross, dismayed at this abrupt return of the horrible prowler. But his eyes fell again on the inert body before him, and passing abruptly from fear to anger, he shook with an indescribable rage.

Then he spurred his horse and rushed after the wolf.

He followed it through the copses, the ravines, and the tall trees, traversing woods which he no longer recognized, his eyes fixed on the white speck which fled before him through the night.

His horse also seemed animated by a force and strength hitherto unknown. It galloped straight ahead with outstretched neck, striking against trees, and rocks, the head and the feet of the dead man thrown across the saddle. The limbs tore out his hair; the brow, beating the huge trunks, spattered them with blood; the spurs tore their ragged coats of bark. Suddenly the beast and the horseman issued from the forest and rushed into a valley, just as the moon appeared above the mountains. The valley here was stony, inclosed by enormous rocks.

Francois then uttered a yell of joy which the echoes repeated like a peal of thunder, and he leaped from his horse, his cutlass in his hand.

The beast, with bristling hair, the back arched, awaited him, its eyes gleaming like two stars. But, before beginning battle, the strong hunter, seizing his brother, seated him on a rock, and, placing stones under his head, which was no more than a mass of blood, he shouted in the ears as if he was talking to a deaf man: "Look, Jean; look at this!"

Then he attacked the monster. He felt himself strong enough to overturn a mountain, to bruise stones in his hands. The beast tried to bite him, aiming for his stomach; but he had seized the fierce animal by the neck, without even using his weapon, and he strangled it gently, listening to the cessation of breathing in its throat and the beatings of its heart. He laughed, wild with joy, pressing closer and closer his formidable embrace, crying in a delirium of joy, "Look, Jean, look!" All resistance ceased; the body of the wolf became limp. He was dead.

Franqois took him up in his arms and carried him to the feet of the elder brother, where he laid him, repeating, in a tender voice: "There, there, there, my little Jean, see him!"

Then he replaced on the saddle the two bodies, one upon the other, and rode away.

He returned to the chateau, laughing and crying, like Gargantua at the birth of Pantagruel, uttering shouts of triumph, and boisterous with joy as he related the death of the beast, and grieving and tearing his beard in telling of that of his brother.

And often, later, when he talked again of that day, he would say, with tears in his eyes: "If only poor Jean could have seen me strangle the beast, he would have died content, that I am sure!"

The widow of my ancestor inspired her orphan son with that horror of the chase which has transmitted itself from father to son as far down as myself.

The Marquis d'Arville was silent. Some one asked:

"That story is a legend, isn't it?"

And the story teller answered:

"I swear to you that it is true from beginning to end."

Then a lady declared, in a little, soft voice

"All the same, it is fine to have passions like that."

THE INN

Resembling in appearance all the wooden hostelries of the High Alps situated at the foot of glaciers in the barren rocky gorges that intersect the summits of the mountains, the Inn of Schwarenbach serves as a resting place for travellers crossing the Gemini Pass.

It remains open for six months in the year and is inhabited by the family of Jean Hauser; then, as soon as the snow begins to fall and to fill the valley so as to make the road down to Loeche impassable, the father and his three sons go away and leave the house in charge of the old guide, Gaspard Hari, with the young guide, Ulrich Kunsi, and Sam, the great mountain dog.

The two men and the dog remain till the spring in their snowy prison, with nothing before their eyes except the immense white slopes of the Balmhorn, surrounded by light, glistening summits, and are shut in, blocked up and buried by the snow which rises around them and which envelops, binds and crushes the little house, which lies piled on the roof, covering the windows and blocking up the door.

It was the day on which the Hauser family were going to return to Loeche, as winter was approaching, and the descent was becoming dangerous. Three mules started first, laden with baggage and led by the three sons. Then the mother, Jeanne Hauser, and her daughter Louise mounted a fourth mule and set off in their turn and the father followed them, accompanied by the two men in charge, who were to escort the family as far as the brow of the descent. First of all they passed round the small lake, which was now frozen over, at the bottom of the mass of rocks which stretched in front of the inn, and then they followed the valley, which was dominated on all sides by the snow-covered summits.

A ray of sunlight fell into that little white, glistening, frozen desert and illuminated it with a cold and dazzling flame. No living thing appeared among this ocean of mountains. There was no motion in this immeasurable solitude and no noise disturbed the profound silence.

By degrees the young guide, Ulrich Kunsi, a tall, long-legged Swiss, left old man Hauser and old Gaspard behind, in order to catch up the mule which bore the two women. The younger one looked at him as he approached and appeared to be calling him with her sad eyes. She was a young, fairhaired little peasant girl, whose milk-white cheeks and pale hair looked as if they had lost their color by their long abode amid the ice. When he had got up to the animal she was riding he put his hand on the crupper and relaxed his speed. Mother Hauser began to talk to him, enumerating with the minutest details all that he would have to attend to during the winter. It was the first time that he was going to stay up there, while old Hari had already spent fourteen winters amid the snow, at the inn of Schwarenbach.

Ulrich Kunsi listened, without appearing to understand and looked incessantly at the girl. From time to time he replied: "Yes, Madame Hauser," but his thoughts seemed far away and his calm features remained unmoved.

They reached Lake Daube, whose broad, frozen surface extended to the end of the valley. On the right one saw the black, pointed, rocky summits of the Daubenhorn beside the enormous moraines of the Lommern glacier, above which rose the Wildstrubel. As they approached the Gemmi pass, where the descent of Loeche begins, they suddenly beheld the immense horizon of the Alps of the Valais, from which the broad, deep valley of the Rhone separated them.

In the distance there was a group of white, unequal, flat, or pointed mountain summits, which glistened in the sun; the Mischabel with its two peaks, the huge group of the Weisshorn, the heavy Brunegghorn, the lofty and formidable pyramid of Mount Cervin, that slayer of men, and the Dent-Blanche, that monstrous coquette.

Then beneath them, in a tremendous hole, at the bottom of a terrific abyss, they perceived Loeche, where houses looked as grains of sand which had been thrown into that enormous crevice that is ended and closed by the Gemmi and which opens, down below, on the Rhone.

The mule stopped at the edge of the path, which winds and turns continually, doubling backward, then, fantastically and strangely, along the side of the mountain as far as the almost invisible little village at its feet. The women jumped into the snow and the two old men joined them. "Well," father Hauser said, "good-by, and keep up your spirits till next year, my friends," and old Hari replied: "Till next year."

They embraced each other and then Madame Hauser in her turn offered her cheek, and the girl did the same.

When Ulrich Kunsi's turn came, he whispered in Louise's ear, "Do not forget those up yonder," and she replied, "No," in such a low voice that he guessed what she had said without hearing it. "Well, adieu," Jean Hauser repeated, "and don't fall ill." And going before the two women, he commenced the descent, and soon all three disappeared at the first turn in the road, while the two men returned to the inn at Schwarenbach.

They walked slowly, side by side, without speaking. It was over, and they would be alone together for four or five months. Then Gaspard Hari began to relate his life last winter. He had remained with Michael Canol, who was too old now to stand it, for an accident might happen during that long solitude. They had not been dull, however; the only thing was to make up one's mind to it from the first, and in the end one would find plenty of distraction, games and other means of whiling away the time.

Ulrich Kunsi listened to him with his eyes on the ground, for in his thoughts he was following those who were descending to the village. They soon came in sight of the inn, which was, however, scarcely visible, so small did it look, a black speck at the foot of that enormous billow of snow, and when they opened the door Sam, the great curly dog, began to romp round them.

"Come, my boy," old Gaspard said, "we have no women now, so we must get our own dinner ready. Go and peel the potatoes." And they both sat down on wooden stools and began to prepare the soup.

The next morning seemed very long to Kunsi. Old Hari smoked and spat on the hearth, while the young man looked out of the window at the snow-covered mountain opposite the house.

In the afternoon he went out, and going over yesterday's ground again, he looked for the traces of the mule that had carried the two women. Then when he had reached the Gemmi Pass, he laid himself down on his stomach and looked at Loeche.

The village, in its rocky pit, was not yet buried under the snow, from which it was sheltered by the pine woods which protected it on all sides. Its low houses looked like paving stones in a large meadow from above. Hauser's little daughter was there now in one of those gray-colored houses. In which? Ulrich Kunsi was too far away to be able to make them out separately. How he would have liked to go down while he was yet able!

But the sun had disappeared behind the lofty crest of the Wildstrubel and the young man returned to the chalet. Daddy Hari was smoking, and when he saw his mate come in he proposed a game of cards to him, and they sat down opposite each other, on either side of the table. They played for a long time a simple game called brisque and then they had supper and went to bed.

The following days were like the first, bright and cold, without any fresh snow. Old Gaspard spent his afternoons in watching the eagles and other rare birds which ventured on those frozen heights, while Ulrich returned regularly to the Gemmi Pass to look at the village. Then they played cards, dice or dominoes and lost and won a trifle, just to create an interest in the game.

One morning Hari, who was up first, called his companion. A moving, deep and light cloud of white spray was falling on them noiselessly and was by degrees burying them under a thick, heavy coverlet of foam. That lasted four days and four nights. It was necessary to free the door and the windows, to dig out a passage and to cut steps to get over this frozen powder, which a twelve hours' frost had made as hard as the granite of the moraines.

They lived like prisoners and did not venture outside their abode. They had divided their duties, which they performed regularly. Ulrich Kunsi undertook the scouring, washing and everything that belonged to cleanliness. He also chopped up the wood while Gaspard Hari did the cooking and attended to the fire. Their regular and monotonous work was interrupted by long games at cards or dice, and they never quarrelled, but were always calm and placid. They were never seen impatient or ill-humored, nor did they ever use hard words, for they had laid in a stock of patience for their wintering on the top of the mountain.

Sometimes old Gaspard took his rifle and went after chamois, and occasionally he killed one. Then there was a feast in the inn at Schwarenbach and they revelled in fresh meat. One morning he went out as usual. The thermometer outside marked eighteen degrees of frost, and as the sun had not yet risen, the hunter hoped to surprise the animals at the approaches to the Wildstrubel, and Ulrich, being alone, remained in bed until ten o'clock. He was of a sleepy nature, but he would not have dared to give way like that to his inclination in the presence of the old guide, who was ever an early riser. He breakfasted leisurely with Sam, who also spent his days and nights in sleeping in front of the fire; then he felt low-spirited and even frightened at the solitude, and was-seized by a longing for his daily game of cards, as one is by the craving of a confirmed habit, and so he went out to meet his companion, who was to return at four o'clock.

The snow had levelled the whole deep valley, filled up the crevasses, obliterated all signs of the two lakes and covered the rocks, so that between the high summits there was nothing but an immense, white, regular, dazzling and frozen surface. For three weeks Ulrich had not been to the edge of the precipice from which he had looked down on the village, and he wanted to go there before climbing the slopes which led to Wildstrubel. Loeche was now also covered by the snow and the houses could scarcely be distinguished, covered as they were by that white cloak.

Then, turning to the right, he reached the Loemmern glacier. He went along with a mountaineer's long strides, striking the snow, which was as hard as a rock, with his iron-pointed stick, and with his piercing eyes he looked for the little black, moving speck in the distance, on that enormous, white expanse.

When he reached the end of the glacier he stopped and asked himself whether the old man had taken that road, and then he began to walk along the moraines with rapid and uneasy steps. The day was declining, the snow was assuming a rosy tint, and a dry, frozen wind blew in rough gusts over its crystal surface. Ulrich uttered a long, shrill, vibrating call. His voice sped through the deathlike silence in which the mountains were sleeping; it reached the distance, across profound and motionless waves of glacial foam, like the cry of a bird across the waves of the sea. Then it died away and nothing answered him.

He began to walk again. The sun had sunk yonder behind the mountain tops, which were still purple with the reflection from the sky, but the depths of the valley were becoming gray, and suddenly the young man felt frightened. It seemed to him as if the silence, the cold, the solitude, the winter death of these mountains were taking possession of him, were going to stop and to freeze his blood, to make his limbs grow stiff and to turn him into a motionless and frozen object, and he set off running, fleeing toward his dwelling. The old man, he thought, would have returned during his absence. He had taken another road; he would, no doubt, be sitting before the fire, with a dead chamois at his feet. He soon came in sight of the inn, but no smoke rose from it. Ulrich walked faster and opened the door. Sam ran up to him to greet him, but Gaspard Hari had not returned. Kunsi, in his alarm, turned round suddenly, as if he had expected to find his comrade hidden in a corner. Then he relighted the fire and made the soup, hoping every moment to see the old man come in. From time to time he went out to see if he were not coming. It was quite night now, that wan, livid night of the mountains, lighted by a thin, yellow crescent moon, just disappearing behind the mountain tops.

Then the young man went in and sat down to warm his hands and feet, while he pictured to himself every possible accident. Gaspard might have broken a leg, have fallen into a crevasse, taken a false step and dislocated his ankle. And, perhaps, he was lying on the snow, overcome and stiff with the cold, in agony of mind, lost and, perhaps, shouting for help, calling with all his might in the silence of the night.. But where? The mountain was so vast, so rugged, so dangerous in places, especially at that time of the year, that it would have required ten or twenty guides to walk for a week in all directions to find a man in that immense space. Ulrich Kunsi, however, made up his mind to set out with Sam if Gaspard did not return by one in the morning, and he made his preparations.

He put provisions for two days into a bag, took his steel climbing iron, tied a long, thin, strong rope round his waist, and looked to see that his iron-shod stick and his axe, which served to cut steps in the ice, were in order. Then he waited. The fire was burning on the hearth, the great dog was snoring in front of it, and the clock was ticking, as regularly as a heart beating, in its resounding wooden case. He waited, with his ears on the alert for distant sounds, and he shivered when the wind blew against the roof and the walls. It struck twelve and he trembled: Then, frightened and shivering, he put some water on the fire, so that he might have some hot coffee before starting, and when the clock struck one he got up, woke Sam, opened the door and went off in the direction of the Wildstrubel. For five hours he mounted, scaling the rocks by means of his climbing irons, cutting into the ice, advancing continually, and occasionally hauling up the dog, who remained below at the foot of some slope that was too steep for him, by means of the rope. It was about six o'clock when he reached one of the summits to which old Gaspard often came after chamois, and he waited till it should be daylight.

The sky was growing pale overhead, and a strange light, springing nobody could tell whence, suddenly illuminated the immense ocean of pale mountain summits, which extended for a hundred leagues around him. One might have said that this vague brightness arose from the snow itself and spread abroad in space. By degrees the highest distant summits assumed a delicate, pink flesh color, and the red sun appeared behind the ponderous giants of the Bernese Alps.

Ulrich Kunsi set off again, walking like a hunter, bent over, looking for tracks, and saying to his dog: "Seek, old fellow, seek!"

He was descending the mountain now, scanning the depths closely, and from time to time shouting, uttering aloud, prolonged cry, which soon died away in that silent vastness. Then he put his ear to the ground to listen. He thought he could distinguish a voice, and he began to run and shouted again, but he heard nothing more and sat down, exhausted and in despair. Toward midday he breakfasted and gave Sam, who was as tired as himself, something to eat also, and then he recommenced his search.

When evening came he was still walking, and he had walked more than thirty miles over the mountains. As he was too far away to return home and too tired to drag himself along any further, he dug a hole in the snow and crouched in it with his dog under a blanket which he had brought with him. And the man and the dog lay side by side, trying to keep warm, but frozen to the marrow nevertheless. Ulrich scarcely slept, his mind haunted by visions and his limbs shaking with cold.

Day was breaking when he got up. His legs were as stiff as iron bars and his spirits so low that he was ready to cry with anguish, while his heart was beating so that he almost fell over with agitation, when he thought he heard a noise.

Suddenly he imagined that he also was going to die of cold in the midst of this vast solitude, and the terror of such a death roused his energies and gave him renewed vigor. He was descending toward the inn, falling down and getting up again, and followed at a distance by Sam, who was limping on three legs, and they did not reach Schwarenbach until four o'clock in the afternoon. The house was empty and the young man made a fire, had something to eat and went to sleep, so worn out that he did not think of anything more.

He slept for a long time, for a very long time, an irresistible sleep. But suddenly a voice, a cry, a name, "Ulrich!" aroused him from his profound torpor and made him sit up in bed. Had he been dreaming? Was it one of those strange appeals which cross the dreams of disquieted minds? No, he heard it still, that reverberating cry-which had entered his ears and remained in his flesh-to the tips of his sinewy fingers. Certainly somebody had cried out and called "Ulrich!" There was somebody there near the house, there could be no doubt of that, and he opened the door and shouted, "Is it you, Gaspard?" with all the strength of his lungs. But there was no reply, no murmur, no groan, nothing. It was quite dark and the snow looked wan.

The wind had risen, that icy wind that cracks the rocks and leaves nothing alive on those deserted heights, and it came in sudden gusts, which were more parching and more deadly than the burning wind of the desert, and again Ulrich shouted: "Gaspard! Gaspard! Gaspard." And then he waited again. Everything was silent on the mountain.

Then he shook with terror and with a bound he was inside the inn, when he shut and bolted the door, and then he fell into a chair trembling all over, for he felt certain that his comrade had called him at the moment he was expiring.

He was sure of that, as sure as one is of being alive or of eating a piece of bread. Old Gaspard Hari had been dying for two days and three nights somewhere, in some hole, in one of those deep, untrodden ravines whose whiteness is more sinister than subterranean darkness. He had been dying for two days and three nights and he had just then died, thinking of his comrade. His soul, almost before it was released, had taken its flight to the inn where Ulrich was sleeping, and it had called him by that terrible and mysterious power which the spirits of the dead have to haunt the living. That voiceless soul had cried to the worn-out soul of the sleeper; it had uttered its last farewell, or its reproach, or its curse on the man who had not searched carefully enough.

And Ulrich felt that it was there, quite close to him, behind the wall, behind the door which he had just fastened. It was wandering about, like a night bird which lightly touches a lighted window with his wings, and the terrified young man was ready to scream with horror. He wanted to run away, but did not dare to go out; he did not dare, and he should never dare to do it in the future, for that phantom would remain there day and night, round the inn, as long as the old man's body was not recovered and had not been deposited in the consecrated earth of a churchyard.

When it was daylight Kunsi recovered some of his courage at the return of the bright sun. He prepared his meal, gave his dog some food and then remained motionless on a chair, tortured at heart as he thought of the old man lying on the snow, and then, as soon as night once more covered the mountains, new terrors assailed him. He now walked up and down the dark kitchen, which was scarcely lighted by the flame of one candle, and he walked from one end of it to the other with great strides, listening, listening whether the terrible cry of the other night would again break the dreary silence outside. He felt himself alone, unhappy man, as no man had ever been alone before! He was alone in this immense desert of Snow, alone five thousand feet above the inhabited earth, above human habitation, above that stirring, noisy, palpitating life, alone under an icy sky! A mad longing impelled him to run away, no matter where, to get down to Loeche by flinging himself over the precipice; but he did not even dare to open the door, as he felt sure that the other, the dead man, would bar his road, so that he might not be obliged to remain up there alone:

Toward midnight, tired with walking, worn out by grief and fear, he at last fell into a doze in his chair, for he was afraid of his bed as one is of a haunted spot. But suddenly the strident cry of the other evening pierced his ears, and it was so shrill that Ulrich stretched out his arms to repulse the ghost, and he fell backward with his chair.

Sam, who was awakened by the noise, began to howl as frightened dogs do howl, and he walked all about the house trying to find out where the danger came from. When he got to the door, he sniffed beneath it, smelling vigorously, with his coat bristling and his tail stiff, while he growled angrily. Kunsi, who was terrified, jumped up, and, holding his chair by one leg, he cried: "Don't come in, don't come in, or I shall kill you." And the dog, excited by this threat, barked angrily at that invisible enemy who defied his master's voice. By degrees, however, he quieted down and came back and stretched himself in front of the fire, but he was uneasy and kept his head up and growled between his teeth.

Ulrich, in turn, recovered his senses, but as he felt faint with terror, he went and got a bottle of brandy out of the sideboard, and he drank off several glasses, one after anther, at a gulp. His ideas became vague, his courage revived and a feverish glow ran through his veins.

He ate scarcely anything the next day and limited himself to alcohol, and so he lived for several days, like a drunken brute. As soon as he thought of Gaspard Hari, he began to drink again, and went on drinking until he fell to the ground, overcome by intoxication. And there he remained lying on his face, dead drunk, his limbs benumbed, and snoring loudly. But scarcely had he digested the maddening and burning liquor than the same cry, "Ulrich!" woke him like a bullet piercing his brain, and he got up, still staggering, stretching out his hands to save himself from falling, and calling to Sam to help him. And the dog, who appeared to be going mad like his master, rushed to the door, scratched it with his claws and gnawed it with his long white teeth, while the young man, with his head thrown back drank the brandy in draughts, as if it had been cold water, so that it might by and by send his thoughts, his frantic terror, and his memory to sleep again.

In three weeks he had consumed all his stock of ardent spirits. But his continual drunkenness only lulled his terror, which awoke more furiously than ever as soon as it was impossible for him to calm it. His fixed idea then, which had been intensified by a month of drunkenness, and which was continually increasing in his absolute solitude, penetrated him like a gimlet. He now walked about the house like a wild beast in its cage, putting his ear to the door to listen if the other were there and defying him through the wall. Then, as soon as he dozed, overcome by fatigue, he heard the voice which made him leap to his feet.

At last one night, as cowards do when driven to extremities, he sprang to the door and opened it, to see who was calling him and to force him to keep quiet, but such a gust of cold wind blew into his face that it chilled him to the bone, and he closed and bolted the door again immediately, without noticing that Sam had rushed out. Then, as he was shivering with cold, he threw some wood on the fire and sat down in front of it to warm himself, but suddenly he started, for somebody was scratching at the wall and crying. In desperation he called out: "Go away!" but was answered by another long, sorrowful wail.

Then all his remaining senses forsook him from sheer fright. He repeated: "Go away!" and turned round to try to find some corner in which to hide, while the other person went round the house still crying and rubbing against the wall. Ulrich went to the oak sideboard, which was full of plates and dishes and of provisions, and lifting it up with superhuman strength, he dragged it to the door, so as to form a barricade. Then piling up all the rest of the furniture, the mattresses, palliasses and chairs, he stopped up the windows as one does when assailed by an enemy.

But the person outside now uttered long, plaintive, mournful groans, to which the young man replied by similar groans, and thus days and nights passed without their ceasing to howl at each other. The one was continually walking round the house and scraped the walls with his nails so vigorously that it seemed as if he wished to destroy them, while the other, inside, followed all his movements, stooping down and holding his ear to the walls and replying to all his appeals with terrible cries. One evening, however, Ulrich heard nothing more, and he sat down, so overcome by fatigue, that he went to sleep immediately and awoke in the morning without a thought, without any recollection of what had happened, just as if his head had been emptied during his heavy sleep, but he felt hungry, and he ate.

The winter was over and the Gemmi Pass was practicable again, so the Hauser family started off to return to their inn. As soon as they had reached the top of the ascent the women mounted their mule and spoke about the two men whom they would meet again shortly. They were, indeed, rather surprised that neither of them had come down a few days before, as soon as the road was open, in order to tell them all about their long winter sojourn. At last, however, they saw the inn, still covered with snow, like a quilt. The door and the window were closed, but a little smoke was coming out of the chimney, which reassured old Hauser. On going up to the door, however, he saw the skeleton of an animal which had been torn to pieces by the eagles, a large skeleton lying on its side.

They all looked close at it and the mother said:

"That must be Sam," and then she shouted: "Hi, Gaspard!" A cry from the interior of the house answered her and a sharp cry that one might have thought some animal had uttered it. Old Hauser repeated, "Hi, Gaspard!" and they heard another cry similar to the first.

Then the three men, the father and the two sons, tried to open the door, but it resisted their efforts. From the empty cow-stall they took a beam to serve as a battering-ram and hurled it against the door with all their might. The wood gave way and the boards flew into splinters. Then the house was shaken by a loud voice, and inside, behind the side board which was overturned, they saw a man standing upright, with his hair falling on his shoulders and a beard descending to his breast, with shining eyes, and nothing but rags to cover him. They did not recognize him, but Louise Hauser exclaimed:

"It is Ulrich, mother." And her mother declared that it was Ulrich, although his hair was white.

He allowed them to go up to him and to touch him, but he did not reply to any of their questions, and they were obliged to take him to Loeche, where the doctors found that he was mad, and nobody ever found out what had become of his companion.

Little Louise Hauser nearly died that summer of decline, which the physicians attributed to the cold air of the mountains.

VOLUME V.

MONSIEUR PARENT

George's father was sitting in an iron chair, watching his little son with concentrated affection and attention, as little George piled up the sand into heaps during one of their walks. He would take up the sand with both hands, make a mound of it, and put a chestnut leaf on top. His father saw no one but him in that public park full of people.

The sun was just disappearing behind the roofs of the Rue Saint-Lazare, but still shed its rays obliquely on that little, overdressed crowd. The chestnut trees were lighted up by its yellow rays, and the three fountains before the lofty porch of the church had the appearance of liquid silver.

Monsieur Parent, accidentally looking up at the church clock, saw that he was five minutes late. He got up, took the child by the arm, shook his dress, which was covered with sand, wiped his hands, and led him in the direction of the Rue Blanche. He walked quickly, so as not to get in after his wife, and the child could not keep up with him. He took him up and carried him, though it made him pant when he had to walk up the steep street. He was a man of forty, already turning gray, and rather stout. At last he reached his house. An old servant who had brought him up, one of those trusted servants who are the tyrants of families, opened the door to him.

"Has madame come in yet?" he asked anxiously.

The servant shrugged her shoulders:

"When have you ever known madame to come home at half-past six, monsieur?"

"Very well; all the better; it will give me time to change my things, for I am very warm."

The servant looked at him with angry and contemptuous pity. "Oh, I can see that well enough," she grumbled. "You are covered with perspiration, monsieur. I suppose you walked quickly and carried the child, and only to have to wait until half-past seven, perhaps, for madame. I have made up my mind not to have dinner ready on time. I shall get it for eight o'clock, and if, you have to wait, I cannot help it; roast meat ought not to be burnt!"

Monsieur Parent pretended not to hear, but went into his own room, and as soon as he got in, locked the door, so as to be alone, quite alone. He was so used now to being abused and badly treated that he never thought himself safe except when he was locked in.

What could he do? To get rid of Julie seemed to him such a formidable thing to do that he hardly ventured to think of it, but it was just as impossible to uphold her against his wife, and before another month the situation would become unbearable between the two. He remained sitting there, with his arms hanging down, vaguely trying to discover some means to set matters straight, but without success. He said to himself: "It is lucky that I have George; without him I should-be very miserable."

Just then the clock struck seven, and he started up. Seven o'clock, and he had not even changed his clothes. Nervous and breathless, he undressed, put on a clean shirt, hastily finished his toilet, as if he had been expected in the next room for some event of extreme importance, and went into the drawing-room, happy at having nothing to fear. He glanced at the newspaper, went and looked out of the window, and then sat down again, when the door opened, and the boy came in, washed, brushed, and smiling. Parent took him up in his arms and kissed him passionately; then he tossed him into the air, and held him up to the ceiling, but soon sat down again, as he was tired with all his exertion. Then, taking George on his knee, he made him ride a-cock-horse. The child laughed and clapped his hands and shouted with pleasure, as did his father, who laughed until his big stomach shook, for it amused him almost more than it did the child.

Parent loved him with all the heart of a weak, resigned, ill-used man. He loved him with mad bursts of affection, with caresses and with all the bashful tenderness which was hidden in him, and which had never found an outlet, even at the early period of his married life, for his wife had always shown herself cold and reserved.

Just then Julie came to the door, with a pale face and glistening eyes, and said in a voice which trembled with exasperation: "It is half-past seven, monsieur."

Parent gave an uneasy and resigned look at the clock and replied: "Yes, it certainly is half-past seven."

"Well, my dinner is quite ready now."

Seeing the storm which was coming, he tried to turn it aside. "But did you not tell me when I came in that it would not be ready before eight?"

"Eight! what are you thinking about? You surely do not mean to let the child dine at eight o'clock? It would ruin his stomach. Just suppose that he only had his mother to look after him! She cares a great deal about her child. Oh, yes, we will speak about her; she is a mother! What a pity it is that there should be any mothers like her!"

Parent thought it was time to cut short a threatened scene. "Julie," he said, "I will not allow you to speak like that of your mistress. You understand me, do you not? Do not forget it in the future."

The old servant, who was nearly choked with surprise, turned and went out, slamming the door so violently after her that the lustres on the chandelier rattled, and for some seconds it sounded as if a number of little invisible bells were ringing in the drawing-room.

Eight o'clock struck, the door opened, and Julie came in again. She had lost her look of exasperation, but now she put on an air of cold and determined resolution, which was still more formidable.

"Monsieur," she said, "I served your mother until the day of her death, and I have attended to you from your birth until now, and I think it may be said that I am devoted to the family." She waited for a reply, and Parent stammered:

"Why, yes, certainly, my good Julie."

"You know quite well," she continued, "that I have never done anything for the sake of money, but always for your sake; that I have never deceived you nor lied to you, that you have never had to find fault with me—"

"Certainly, my good Julie."

"Very well, then, monsieur; it cannot go on any longer like this. I have said nothing, and left you in your ignorance, out of respect and liking for you, but it is too much, and every one in the neighborhood is laughing at you. Everybody knows about it, and so I must tell you also, although I do not like to repeat it. The reason why madame comes in at any time she chooses is that she is doing abominable things."

He seemed stupefied and not to understand, and could only stammer out:

"Hold your tongue; you know I have forbidden you——"

But she interrupted him with irresistible resolution. "No, monsieur, I must tell you everything now. For a long time madame has been carrying on with Monsieur Limousin. I have seen them kiss scores of times behind the door. Ah! you may be sure that if Monsieur Limousin had been rich, madame would never have married Monsieur Parent. If you remember how the marriage was brought about, you would understand the matter from beginning to end."

Parent had risen, and stammered out, his face livid: "Hold your tongue —hold your tongue, or——"

She went on, however: "No, I mean to tell you everything. She married you from interest, and she deceived you from the very first day. It was all settled between them beforehand. You need only reflect for a few moments to understand it, and then, as she was not satisfied with having married you, as she did not love you, she has made your life miserable, so miserable that it has almost broken my heart when I have seen it."

He walked up and down the room with hands clenched, repeating: "Hold your tongue—hold your tongue——" For he could find nothing else to say. The old servant, however, would not yield; she seemed resolved on everything.

George, who had been at first astonished and then frightened at those angry voices, began to utter shrill screams, and remained behind his father, with his face puckered up and his mouth open, roaring.

His son's screams exasperated Parent, and filled him with rage and courage. He rushed at Julie with both arms raised, ready to strike her, exclaiming: "Ah! you wretch. You will drive the child out of his senses." He already had his hand on her, when she screamed in his face:

"Monsieur, you may beat me if you like, me who reared you, but that will not prevent your wife from deceiving you, or alter the fact that your child is not yours——"

He stopped suddenly, let his arms fall, and remained standing opposite to her, so overwhelmed that he could understand nothing more.

"You need only to look at the child," she added, "to know who is its father! He is the very image of Monsieur Limousin. You need only look at his eyes and forehead. Why, a blind man could not be mistaken in him."

He had taken her by the shoulders, and was now shaking her with all his might. "Viper, viper!" he said. "Go out the room, viper! Go out, or I shall kill you! Go out! Go out!"

And with a desperate effort he threw her into the next room. She fell across the table, which was laid for dinner, breaking the glasses. Then, rising to her feet, she put the table between her master and herself. While he was pursuing her, in order to take hold of her again, she flung terrible words at him.

"You need only go out this evening after dinner, and come in again immediately, and you will see! You will see whether I have been lying! Just try it, and you will see." She had reached the kitchen door and escaped, but he ran after her, up the back stairs to her bedroom, into which she had locked herself, and knocking at the door, he said:

"You will leave my house this very instant!"

"You may be certain of that, monsieur," was her reply. "In an hour's time I shall not be here any longer."

He then went slowly downstairs again, holding on to the banister so as not to fall, and went back to the drawing-room, where little George was sitting on the floor, crying. He fell into a chair, and looked at the child with dull eyes. He understood nothing, knew nothing more; he felt dazed, stupefied, mad, as if he had just fallen on his head, and he scarcely even remembered the dreadful things the servant had told him. Then, by degrees, his mind, like muddy water, became calmer and clearer, and the abominable revelations began to work in his heart.

He was no longer thinking of George. The child was quiet now and sitting on the carpet; but, seeing that no notice was being taken of him, he began to cry. His father ran to him, took him in his arms, and covered him with kisses. His child remained to him, at any rate! What did the rest matter? He held him in his arms and pressed his lips to his light hair, and, relieved and composed, he whispered:

"George—my little George—my dear little George——" But he suddenly remembered what Julie had said! Yes, she had said that he was Limousin's child. Oh! it could not be possible, surely. He could not believe it, could not doubt, even for a moment, that he was his own child. It was one of those low scandals which spring from servants' brains! And he repeated: "George—my dear little George." The youngster was quiet again, now that his father was fondling him.

Parent felt the warmth of the little chest penetrate through his clothes, and it filled him with love, courage, and happiness; that gentle warmth soothed him, fortified him and saved him. Then he put the small, curly head away from him a little, and looked at it affectionately, still repeating: "George! Oh, my little George!" But suddenly he thought:

"Suppose he were to resemble Limousin, after all!" He looked at him with haggard, troubled eyes, and tried to discover whether there was any likeness in his forehead, in his nose, mouth, or cheeks. His thoughts wandered as they do when a person is going mad, and his child's face changed in his eyes, and assumed a strange look and improbable resemblances.

The hall bell rang. Parent gave a bound as if a bullet had gone through him. "There she is," he said. "What shall I do?" And he ran and locked himself up in his room, to have time to bathe his eyes. But in a few moments another ring at the bell made him jump again, and then he remembered that Julie had left, without the housemaid knowing it, and so nobody would go to open the door. What was he to do? He went himself, and suddenly he felt brave, resolute, ready for dissimulation and the struggle. The terrible blow had matured him in a few moments. He wished to know the truth, he desired it with the rage of a timid man, and with the tenacity of an easy-going man who has been exasperated.

Nevertheless, he trembled. Does one know how much excited cowardice there often is in boldness? He went to the door with furtive steps, and stopped to listen; his heart beat furiously. Suddenly, however, the noise of the bell over his head startled him like an explosion. He seized the lock, turned the key, and opening the door, saw his wife and Limousin standing before him on the stairs.

With an air of astonishment, which also betrayed a little irritation, she said:

"So you open the door now? Where is Julie?"

His throat felt tight and his breathing was labored as he tried to. reply, without being able to utter a word.

"Are you dumb?" she continued. "I asked you where Julie is?"

"She—she—has—gone——" he managed to stammer.

His wife began to get angry. "What do you mean by gone? Where has she gone? Why?"

By degrees he regained his coolness. He felt an intense hatred rise up in him for that insolent woman who was standing before him.

"Yes, she has gone altogether. I sent her away."

"You have sent away Julie? Why, you must be mad."

"Yes, I sent her away because she was insolent, and because—because she was ill-using the child."

"Julie?"

"Yes—Julie."

"What was she insolent about?"

"About you."

"About me?"

"Yes, because the dinner was burnt, and you did not come in."

"And she said——"

"She said—offensive things about you—which I ought not—which I could not listen to——"

"What did she, say?"

"It is no good repeating them."

"I want to hear them."

"She said it was unfortunate for a man like me to be married to a woman like you, unpunctual, careless, disorderly, a bad mother, and a bad wife."

The young woman had gone into the anteroom, followed by Limousin, who did not say a word at this unexpected condition of things. She shut the door quickly, threw her cloak on a chair, and going straight up to her husband, she stammered out:

"You say? You say? That I am——"

Very pale and calm, he replied: "I say nothing, my dear. I am simply repeating what Julie said to me, as you wanted to know what it was, and I wish you to remark that I turned her off just on account of what she said."

She trembled with a violent longing to tear out his beard and scratch his face. In his voice and manner she felt that he was asserting his position as master. Although she had nothing to say by way of reply, she tried to assume the offensive by saying something unpleasant. "I suppose you have had dinner?" she asked.

"No, I waited for you."

She shrugged her shoulders impatiently. "It is very stupid of you to wait after half-past seven," she said. "You might have guessed that I was detained, that I had a good many things to do, visits and shopping,"

And then, suddenly, she felt that she wanted to explain how she had spent her time, and told him in abrupt, haughty words that, having to buy some furniture in a shop a long distance off, very far off, in the Rue de Rennes, she had met Limousin at past seven o'clock on the Boulevard Saint-Germain, and that then she had gone with him to have something to eat in a restaurant, as she did not like to go to one by herself, although she was faint with hunger. That was how she had dined with Limousin, if it could be called dining, for they had only some soup and half a chicken, as they were in a great hurry to get back.

Parent replied simply: "Well, you were quite right. I am not finding fault with you."

Then Limousin, who, had not spoken till then, and who had been half hidden behind Henriette, came forward and put out his hand, saying: "Are you very well?"

Parent took his hand, and shaking it gently, replied: "Yes, I am very well."

But the young woman had felt a reproach in her husband's last words. "Finding fault! Why do you speak of finding fault? One might think that you meant to imply something."

"Not at all," he replied, by way of excuse. "I simply meant that I was not at all anxious although you were late, and that I did not find fault with you for it."

She, however, took the high hand, and tried to find a pretext for a quarrel. "Although I was late? One might really think that it was one o'clock in the morning, and that I spent my nights away from home."

"Certainly not, my dear. I said late because I could find no other word. You said you should be back at half-past six, and you returned at half-past eight. That was surely being late. I understand it perfectly well. I am not at all surprised, even. But—but—I can hardly use any other word."

"But you pronounce them as if I had been out all night."

"Oh, no-oh, no!"

She saw that he would yield on every point, and she was going into her own room, when at last she noticed that George was screaming, and then she asked, with some feeling: "What is the matter with the child?"

"I told you that Julie had been rather unkind to him."

"What has the wretch been doing to him?"

"Oh nothing much. She gave him a push, and he fell down."

She wanted to see her child, and ran into the dining room, but stopped short at the sight of the table covered with spilt wine, with broken decanters and glasses and overturned saltcellars. "Who did all that mischief?" she asked.

"It was Julie, who——" But she interrupted him furiously:

"That is too much, really! Julie speaks of me as if I were a shameless woman, beats my child, breaks my plates and dishes, turns my house upside down, and it appears that you think it all quite natural."

"Certainly not, as I have got rid of her."

"Really! You have got rid of her! But you ought to have given her in charge. In such cases, one ought to call in the Commissary of Police!"

"But—my dear—I really could not. There was no reason. It would have been very difficult——"

She shrugged her shoulders disdainfully. "There! you will never be anything but a poor, wretched fellow, a man without a will, without any firmness or energy. Ah! she must have said some nice things to you, your Julie, to make you turn her off like that. I should like to have been here for a minute, only for a minute." Then she opened the drawing-room door and ran to George, took him into her arms and kissed him, and said: "Georgie, what is it, my darling, my pretty one, my treasure?"

Then, suddenly turning to another idea, she said: "But the child has had no dinner? You have had nothing to eat, my pet?"

"No, mamma."

Then she again turned furiously upon her husband. "Why, you must be mad, utterly mad! It is half-past eight, and George has had no dinner!"

He excused himself as best he could, for he had nearly lost his wits through the overwhelming scene and the explanation, and felt crushed by this ruin of his life. "But, my dear, we were waiting for you, as I did not wish to dine without you. As you come home late every day, I expected you every moment."

She threw her bonnet, which she had kept on till then, into an easy-chair, and in an angry voice she said: "It is really intolerable to have to do with people who can understand nothing, who can divine nothing and do nothing by themselves. So, I suppose, if I were to come in at twelve o'clock at night, the child would have had nothing to eat? Just as if you could not have understood that, as it was after half-past seven, I was prevented from coming home, that I had met with some hindrance!"

Parent trembled, for he felt that his anger was getting the upper hand, but Limousin interposed, and turning toward the young woman, said:

"My dear friend, you, are altogether unjust. Parent could not guess that you would come here so late, as you never do so, and then, how could you expect him to get over the difficulty all by himself, after having sent away Julie?"

But Henriette was very angry, and replied:

"Well, at any rate, he must get over the difficulty himself, for I will not help him," she replied. "Let him settle it!" And she went into her own room, quite forgetting that her child had not had anything to eat.

Limousin immediately set to work to help his friend. He picked up the broken glasses which strewed the table and took them out, replaced the plates and knives and forks, and put the child into his high chair, while Parent went to look for the chambermaid to wait at table. The girl came in, in great astonishment, as she had heard nothing in George's room, where she had been working. She soon, however, brought in the soup, a burnt leg of mutton, and mashed potatoes.

Parent sat by the side of the child, very much upset and distressed at all that had happened. He gave the boy his dinner, and endeavored to eat something himself, but he could only swallow with an effort, as his throat felt paralyzed. By degrees he was seized with an insane desire to look at Limousin, who was sitting opposite to him, making bread pellets, to see whether George was like him, but he did not venture to raise his eyes for some time. At last, however, he made up his mind to do so, and gave a quick, sharp look at the face which he knew so well, although he almost fancied that he had never examined it carefully. It looked so different to what he had imagined. From time to time he looked at Limousin, trying to recognize a likeness in the smallest lines of his face, in the slightest features, and then he looked at his son, under the pretext of feeding him.

Two words were sounding in his ears: "His father! his father! his father!" They buzzed in his temples at every beat of his heart. Yes, that man, that tranquil man who was sitting on the other side of the table, was, perhaps, the father of his son, of George, of his little George. Parent left off eating; he could not swallow any more. A terrible pain, one of those attacks of pain which make men scream, roll on the ground, and bite the furniture, was tearing at his entrails, and he felt inclined to take a knife and plunge it into his stomach. He started when he heard the door open. His wife came in. "I am hungry," she said; "are not you, Limousin?"

He hesitated a little, and then said: "Yes, I am, upon my word." She had the leg of mutton brought in again. Parent asked himself "Have they had dinner? Or are they late because they have had a lovers' meeting?"

They both ate with a very good appetite. Henriette was very calm, but laughed and joked. Her husband watched her furtively. She had on a pink teagown trimmed with white lace, and her fair head, her white neck and her plump hands stood out from that coquettish and perfumed dress as though it were a sea shell edged with foam.

What fun they must be making of him, if he had been their dupe since the first day! Was it possible to make a fool of a man, of a worthy man, because his father had left him a little money? Why could one not see into people's souls? How was it that nothing revealed to upright hearts the deceits of infamous hearts? How was it that voices had the same sound for adoring as for lying? Why was a false, deceptive look the same as a sincere one? And he watched them, waiting to catch a gesture, a word, an intonation. Then suddenly he thought: "I will surprise them this evening," and he said:

"My dear, as I have dismissed Julie, I will see about getting another girl this very day. I will go at once to procure one by to-morrow morning, so I may not be in until late."

"Very well," she replied; "go. I shall not stir from here. Limousin will keep me company. We will wait for you." Then, turning to the maid, she said: "You had better put George to bed, and then you can clear away and go up to your room."

Parent had got up; he was unsteady on his legs, dazed and bewildered, and saying, "I shall see you again later on," he went out, holding on to the wall, for the floor seemed to roll like a ship. George had been carried out by his nurse, while Henriette and Limousin went into the drawing-room.

As soon as the door was shut, he said: "You must be mad, surely, to torment your husband as you do?"

She immediately turned on him: "Ah! Do you know that I think the habit you have got into lately, of looking upon Parent as a martyr, is very unpleasant?"

Limousin threw himself into an easy-chair and crossed his legs. "I am not setting him up as a martyr in the least, but I think that, situated as we are, it is ridiculous to defy this man as you do, from morning till night."

She took a cigarette from the mantelpiece, lighted it, and replied: "But I do not defy him; quite the contrary. Only he irritates me by his stupidity, and I treat him as he deserves."

Limousin continued impatiently: "What you are doing is very foolish! I am only asking you to treat your husband gently, because we both of us require him to trust us. I think that you ought to see that."

They were close together: he, tall, dark, with long whiskers and the rather vulgar manners of a good-looking man who is very well satisfied with himself; she, small, fair, and pink, a little Parisian, born in the back room of a shop, half cocotte and half bourgeoise, brought up to entice customers to the store by her glances, and married, in consequence, to a simple, unsophisticated man, who saw her outside the door every morning when he went out and every evening when he came home.

"But do you not understand; you great booby," she said, "that I hate him just because he married me, because he bought me, in fact; because everything that he says and does, everything that he thinks, acts on my nerves? He exasperates me every moment by his stupidity, which you call his kindness; by his dullness, which you call his confidence, and then, above all, because he is my husband, instead of you. I feel him between us, although he does not interfere with us much. And then—-and then! No, it is, after all, too idiotic of him not to guess anything! I wish he would, at any rate, be a little jealous. There are moments when I feel inclined to say to him: 'Do you not see, you stupid creature, that Paul is my lover?'"

"It is quite incomprehensible that you cannot understand how hateful he is to me, how he irritates me. You always seem to like him, and you shake hands with him cordially. Men are very extraordinary at times."

"One must know how to dissimulate, my dear."

"It is no question of dissimulation, but of feeling. One might think that, when you men deceive one another, you like each other better on that account, while we women hate a man from the moment that we have betrayed him."

"I do not see why one should hate an excellent fellow because one is friendly with his wife."

"You do not see it? You do not see it? You all of you are wanting in refinement of feeling. However, that is one of those things which one feels and cannot express. And then, moreover, one ought not. No, you would not understand; it is quite useless! You men have no delicacy of feeling."

And smiling, with the gentle contempt of an impure woman, she put both her hands on his shoulders and held up her lips to him. He stooped down and clasped her closely in his arms, and their lips met. And as they stood in front of the mantel mirror, another couple exactly like them embraced behind the clock.

They had heard nothing, neither the noise of the key nor the creaking of the door, but suddenly Henriette, with a loud cry, pushed Limousin away with both her arms, and they saw Parent looking at them, livid with rage, without his shoes on and his hat over his forehead. He looked at each, one after the other, with a quick glance of his eyes and without moving his head. He appeared beside himself. Then, without saying a word, he threw himself on Limousin, seized him as if he were going to strangle him, and flung him into the opposite corner of the room so violently that the other lost his balance, and, beating the air with his hand, struck his head violently against the wall.

When Henriette saw that her husband was going to murder her lover, she threw herself on Parent, seized him by the neck, and digging her ten delicate, rosy fingers into his neck, she squeezed him so tightly, with all the vigor of a desperate woman, that the blood spurted out under her nails, and she bit his shoulder, as if she wished to tear it with her teeth. Parent, half-strangled and choking, loosened his hold on Limousin, in order to shake off his wife, who was hanging to his neck. Putting his arms round her waist, he flung her also to the other end of the drawing-room.

Then, as his passion was short-lived, like that of most good-tempered men, and his strength was soon exhausted, he remained standing between the two, panting, worn out, not knowing what to do next. His brutal fury had expended itself in that effort, like the froth of a bottle of champagne, and his unwonted energy ended in a gasping for breath. As soon as he could speak, however, he said:

"Go away—both of you—immediately! Go away!"

Limousin remained motionless in his corner, against the wall, too startled to understand anything as yet, too frightened to move a finger; while Henriette, with her hands resting on a small, round table, her head bent forward, her hair hanging down, the bodice of her dress unfastened, waited like a wild animal which is about to spring. Parent continued in a stronger voice: "Go away immediately. Get out of the house!"

His wife, however, seeing that he had got over his first exasperation grew bolder, drew herself up, took two steps toward him, and, grown almost insolent, she said: "Have you lost your head? What is the matter with you? What is the meaning of this unjustifiable violence?"

But he turned toward her, and raising his fist to strike her, he stammered out: "Oh—oh—this is too much, too much! I heard everything! Everything—do you understand? Everything! You wretch—you wretch! You are two wretches! Get out of the house, both of you! Immediately, or I shall kill you! Leave the house!"

She saw that it was all over, and that he knew everything; that she could not prove her innocence, and that she must comply. But all her impudence had returned to her, and her hatred for the man, which was aggravated now, drove her to audacity, made her feel the need of bravado, and of defying him, and she said in a clear voice: "Come, Limousin; as he is going to turn me out of doors, I will go to your lodgings with you."

But Limousin did not move, and Parent, in a fresh access of rage, cried out: "Go, will you? Go, you wretches! Or else—or else——" He seized a chair and whirled it over his head.

Henriette walked quickly across the room, took her lover by the arm, dragged him from the wall, to which he appeared fixed, and led him toward the door, saying: "Do come, my friend—you see that the man is mad. Do come!"

As she went out she turned round to her husband, trying to think of something that she could do, something that she could invent to wound him to the heart as she left the house, and an idea struck her, one of those venomous, deadly ideas in which all a woman's perfidy shows itself, and she said resolutely: "I am going to take my child with me."

Parent was stupefied, and stammered: "Your—your—child? You dare to talk of your child? You venture—you venture to ask for your child—after-after—Oh, oh, that is too much! Go, you vile creature! Go!"

She went up to him again, almost smiling, almost avenged already, and defying him, standing close to him, and face to face, she said: "I want my child, and you have no right to keep him, because he is not yours—do you understand? He is not yours! He is Limousin's!"

And Parent cried out in bewilderment: "You lie—you lie—worthless woman!"

But she continued: "You fool! Everybody knows it except you. I tell you, this is his father. You need only look at him to see it."

Parent staggered backward, and then he suddenly turned round, took a candle, and rushed into the next room; returning almost immediately, carrying little George wrapped up in his bedclothes. The child, who had been suddenly awakened, was crying from fright. Parent threw him into his wife's arms, and then, without speaking, he pushed her roughly out toward the stairs, where Limousin was waiting, from motives of prudence.

Then he shut the door again, double-locked and bolted it, but had scarcely got back into the drawing-room when he fell to the floor at full length.

Parent lived alone, quite alone. During the five weeks that followed their separation, the feeling of surprise at his new life prevented him from thinking much. He had resumed his bachelor life, his habits of lounging, about, and took his meals at a restaurant, as he had done formerly. As he wished to avoid any scandal, he made his wife an allowance, which was arranged by their lawyers. By degrees, however, the thought of the child began to haunt him. Often, when he was at home alone at night, he suddenly thought he heard George calling out "Papa," and his heart would begin to beat, and he would get up quickly and open the door, to see whether, by chance, the child might have returned, as dogs or pigeons do. Why should a child have less instinct than an animal? On finding that he was mistaken, he would sit down in his armchair again and think of the boy. He would think of him for hours and whole days. It was not only a moral, but still more a physical obsession, a nervous longing to kiss him, to hold and fondle him, to take him on his knees and dance him. He felt the child's little arms around his neck, his little mouth pressing a kiss on his beard, his soft hair tickling his cheeks, and the remembrance of all those childish ways made him suffer as a man might for some beloved woman who has left him. Twenty or a hundred times a day he asked himself the question whether he was or was not George's father, and almost before he was in bed every night he recommenced the same series of despairing questionings.

He especially dreaded the darkness of the evening, the melancholy feeling of the twilight. Then a flood of sorrow invaded his heart, a torrent of despair which seemed to overwhelm him and drive him mad. He was as afraid of his own thoughts as men are of criminals, and he fled before them as one does from wild beasts. Above all things, he feared his empty, dark, horrible dwelling and the deserted streets, in which, here and there, a gas lamp flickered, where the isolated foot passenger whom one hears in the distance seems to be a night prowler, and makes one walk faster or slower, according to whether he is coming toward you or following you.

And in spite of himself, and by instinct, Parent went in the direction of the broad, well-lighted, populous streets. The light and the crowd attracted him, occupied his mind and distracted his thoughts, and when he was tired of walking aimlessly about among the moving crowd, when he saw the foot passengers becoming more scarce and the pavements less crowded, the fear of solitude and silence drove him into some large cafe full of drinkers and of light. He went there as flies go to a candle, and he would sit down at one of the little round tables and ask for a "bock," which he would drink slowly, feeling uneasy every time a customer got up to go. He would have liked to take him by the arm, hold him back, and beg him to stay a little longer, so much did he dread the time when the waiter should come up to him and say sharply: "Come, monsieur, it is closing time!"

He thus got into the habit of going to the beer houses, where the continual elbowing of the drinkers brings you in contact with a familiar and silent public, where the heavy clouds of tobacco smoke lull disquietude, while the heavy beer dulls the mind and calms the heart. He almost lived there. He was scarcely up before he went there to find people to distract his glances and his thoughts, and soon, as he felt too lazy to move, he took his meals there.

After every meal, during more than an hour, he sipped three or four small glasses of brandy, which stupefied him by degrees, and then his head drooped on his chest, he shut his eyes, and went to sleep. Then, awaking, he raised himself on the red velvet seat, straightened his waistcoat, pulled down his cuffs, and took up the newspapers again, though he had already seen them in the morning, and read them all through again, from beginning to end. Between four and five o'clock he went for a walk on the boulevards, to get a little fresh air, as he used to say, and then came back to the seat which had been reserved for him, and asked for his absinthe. He would talk to the regular customers whose acquaintance he had made. They discussed the news of the day and political events, and that carried him on till dinner time; and he spent the evening as he had the afternoon, until it was time to close. That was a terrible moment for him when he was obliged to go out into the dark, into his empty room full of dreadful recollections, of horrible thoughts, and of mental agony. He no longer saw any of his old friends, none of his relatives, nobody who might remind him of his past life. But as his apartments were a hell to him, he took a room in a large hotel, a good room on the ground floor, so as to see the passers-by. He was no longer alone in that great building. He felt people swarming round him, he heard voices in the adjoining rooms, and when his former sufferings tormented him too much at the sight of his bed, which was turned down, and of his solitary fireplace, he went out into the wide passages and walked up and down them like a sentinel, before all the closed doors, and looked sadly at the shoes standing in couples outside them, women's little boots by the side of men's thick ones, and he thought that, no doubt, all these people were happy, and were sleeping in their warm beds. Five years passed thus; five miserable years. But one day, when he was taking his usual walk between the Madeleine and the Rue Drouot, he suddenly saw a lady whose bearing struck him. A tall gentleman and a child were with her, and all three were walking in front of him. He asked himself where he had seen them before, when suddenly he recognized a movement of her hand; it was his wife, his wife with Limousin and his child, his little George.

His heart beat as if it would suffocate him, but he did not stop, for he wished to see them, and he followed them. They looked like a family of the better middle class. Henriette was leaning on Paul's arm, and speaking to him in a low voice, and looking at him sideways occasionally. Parent got a side view of her and recognized her pretty features, the movements of her lips, her smile, and her coaxing glances. But the child chiefly took up his attention. How tall and strong he was! Parent could not see his face, but only his long, fair curls. That tall boy with bare legs, who was walking by his mother's side like a little man, was George. He saw them suddenly, all three, as they stopped in front of a shop. Limousin had grown very gray, had aged and was thinner; his wife, on the contrary, was as young looking as ever, and had grown stouter. George he would not have recognized, he was so different from what he had been formerly.

They went on again and Parent followed them. He walked on quickly, passed them, and then turned round, so as to meet them face to face. As he passed the child he felt a mad longing to take him into his arms and run off with him, and he knocked against him as if by accident. The boy turned round and looked at the clumsy man angrily, and Parent hurried away, shocked, hurt, and pursued by that look. He went off like a thief, seized with a horrible fear lest he should have been seen and recognized by his wife and her lover. He went to his cafe without stopping, and fell breathless into his chair. That evening he drank three absinthes. For four months he felt the pain of that meeting in his heart. Every night he saw the three again, happy and tranquil, father, mother, and child walking on the boulevard before going in to dinner, and that new vision effaced the old one. It was another matter, another hallucination now, and also a fresh pain. Little George, his little George, the child he had so much loved and so often kissed, disappeared in the far distance, and he saw a new one, like a brother of the first, a little boy with bare legs, who did not know him! He suffered terribly at that thought. The child's love was dead; there was no bond between them; the child would not have held out his arms when he saw him. He had even looked at him angrily.

Then, by degrees he grew calmer, his mental torture diminished, the image that had appeared to his eyes and which haunted his nights became more indistinct and less frequent. He began once more to live nearly like everybody else, like all those idle people who drink beer off marble-topped tables and wear out their clothes on the threadbare velvet of the couches.

He grew old amid the smoke from pipes, lost his hair under the gas lights, looked upon his weekly bath, on his fortnightly visit to the barber's to have his hair cut, and on the purchase of a new coat or hat as an event. When he got to his cafe in a new hat he would look at himself in the glass for a long time before sitting down, and take it off and put it on again several times, and at last ask his friend, the lady at the bar, who was watching him with interest, whether she thought it suited him.

Two or three times a year he went to the theatre, and in the summer he sometimes spent his evenings at one of the open-air concerts in the Champs Elysees. And so the years followed each other slow, monotonous, and short, because they were quite uneventful.

He very rarely now thought of the dreadful drama which had wrecked his life; for twenty years had passed since that terrible evening. But the life he had led since then had worn him out. The landlord of his cafe would often say to him: "You ought to pull yourself together a little, Monsieur Parent; you should get some fresh air and go into the country. I assure you that you have changed very much within the last few months." And when his customer had gone out be used to say to the barmaid: "That poor Monsieur Parent is booked for another world; it is bad never to get out of Paris. Advise him to go out of town for a day occasionally; he has confidence in you. Summer will soon be here; that will put him straight."

And she, full of pity and kindness for such a regular customer, said to Parent every day: "Come, monsieur, make up your mind to get a little fresh air. It is so charming in the country when the weather is fine. Oh, if I could, I would spend my life there!"

By degrees he was seized with a vague desire to go just once and see whether it was really as pleasant there as she said, outside the walls of the great city. One morning he said to her:

"Do you know where one can get a good luncheon in the neighborhood of Paris?"

"Go to the Terrace at Saint-Germain; it is delightful there!"

He had been there formerly, just when he became engaged. He made up his mind to go there again, and he chose a Sunday, for no special reason, but merely because people generally do go out on Sundays, even when they have nothing to do all the week; and so one Sunday morning he went to Saint-Germain. He felt low-spirited and vexed at having yielded to that new longing, and at having broken through his usual habits. He was thirsty; he would have liked to get out at every station and sit down in the cafe which he saw outside and drink a "bock" or two, and then take the first train back to Paris. The journey seemed very long to him. He could remain sitting for whole days, as long as he had the same motionless objects before his eyes, but he found it very trying and fatiguing to remain sitting while he was being whirled along, and to see the whole country fly by, while he himself was motionless.

However, he found the Seine interesting every time he crossed it. Under the bridge at Chatou he saw some small boats going at great speed under the vigorous strokes of the bare-armed oarsmen, and he thought: "There are some fellows who are certainly enjoying themselves!" The train entered the tunnel just before you get to the station at Saint-Germain, and presently stopped at the platform. Parent got out, and walked slowly, for he already felt tired, toward the Terrace, with his hands behind his back, and when he got to the iron balustrade, stopped to look at the distant horizon. The immense plain spread out before him vast as the sea, green and studded with large villages, almost as populous as towns. The sun bathed the whole landscape in its full, warm light. The Seine wound like an endless serpent through the plain, flowed round the villages and along the slopes. Parent inhaled the warm breeze, which seemed to make his heart young again, to enliven his spirits, and to vivify his blood, and said to himself:

"Why, it is delightful here."

Then he went on a few steps, and stopped again to look about him. The utter misery of his existence seemed to be brought into full relief by the intense light which inundated the landscape. He saw his twenty years of cafe life—dull, monotonous, heartbreaking. He might have traveled as others did, have gone among foreigners, to unknown countries beyond the sea, have interested himself somewhat in everything which other men are passionately devoted to, in arts and science; he might have enjoyed life in a thousand forms, that mysterious life which is either charming or painful, constantly changing, always inexplicable and strange. Now, however, it was too late. He would go on drinking "bock" after "bock" until he died, without any family, without friends, without hope, without any curiosity about anything, and he was seized with a feeling of misery and a wish to run away, to hide himself in Paris, in his cafe and his lethargy! All the thoughts, all the dreams, all the desires which are dormant in the slough of stagnating hearts had reawakened, brought to life by those rays of sunlight on the plain.

Parent felt that if he were to remain there any longer he should lose his reason, and he made haste to get to the Pavilion Henri IV for lunch, to try and forget his troubles under—the influence of wine and alcohol, and at any rate to have some one to speak to.

He took a small table in one of the arbors, from which one can see all the surrounding country, ordered his lunch, and asked to be served at once. Then some more people arrived and sat down at tables near him. He felt more comfortable; he was no longer alone. Three persons were eating luncheon near him. He looked at them two or three times without seeing them clearly, as one looks at total strangers. Suddenly a woman's voice sent a shiver through him which seemed to penetrate to his very marrow. "George," it said, "will you carve the chicken?"

And another voice replied: "Yes, mamma."

Parent looked up, and he understood; he guessed immediately who those people were! He should certainly not have known them again. His wife had grown quite white and very stout, an elderly, serious, respectable lady, and she held her head forward as she ate for fear of spotting her dress, although she had a table napkin tucked under her chin. George had become a man. He had a slight beard, that uneven and almost colorless beard which adorns the cheeks of youths. He wore a high hat, a white waistcoat, and a monocle, because it looked swell, no doubt. Parent looked at him in astonishment. Was that George, his son? No, he did not know that young man; there could be nothing in common between them. Limousin had his back to him, and was eating; with his shoulders rather bent.

All three of them seemed happy and satisfied; they came and took luncheon in the country at well-known restaurants. They had had a calm and pleasant existence, a family existence in a warm and comfortable house, filled with all those trifles which make life agreeable, with affection, with all those tender words which people exchange continually when they love each other. They had lived thus, thanks to him, Parent, on his money, after having deceived him, robbed him, ruined him! They had condemned him, the innocent, simple-minded, jovial man, to all the miseries of solitude, to that abominable life which he had led, between the pavement and a bar-room, to every mental torture and every physical misery! They had made him a useless, aimless being, a waif in the world, a poor old man without any pleasures, any prospects, expecting nothing from anybody or anything. For him, the world was empty, because he loved nothing in the world. He might go among other nations, or go about the streets, go into all the houses in Paris, open every room, but he would not find inside any door the beloved face, the face of wife or child which smiles when it sees you. This idea worked upon him more than any other, the idea of a door which one opens, to see and to embrace somebody behind it.

And that was the fault of those three wretches! The fault of that worthless woman, of that infamous friend, and of that tall, light-haired lad who put on insolent airs. Now he felt as angry with the child as he did with the other two. Was he not Limousin's son? Would Limousin have kept him and loved him otherwise? Would not Limousin very quickly have got rid of the mother and of the child if he had not felt sure that it was his, positively his? Does anybody bring up other people's children? And now they were there, quite close to him, those three who had made him suffer so much.

Parent looked at them, irritated and excited at the recollection of all his sufferings and of his despair, and was especially exasperated at their placid and satisfied looks. He felt inclined to kill them, to throw his siphon of Seltzer water at them, to split open Limousin's head as he every moment bent it over his plate, raising it again immediately.

He would have his revenge now, on the spot, as he had them under his hand. But how? He tried to think of some means, he pictured such dreadful things as one reads of in the newspapers occasionally, but could not hit on anything practical. And he went on drinking to excite himself, to give himself courage not to allow such an opportunity to escape him, as he might never have another.

Suddenly an idea struck him, a terrible idea; and he left off drinking to mature it. He smiled as he murmured: "I have them, I have them! We will see; we will see!"

They finished their luncheon slowly, conversing with perfect unconcern. Parent could not hear what they were saying, but he saw their quiet gestures. His wife's face especially exasperated him. She had assumed a haughty air, the air of a comfortable, devout woman, of an unapproachable, devout woman, sheathed in principles, iron-clad in virtue. They paid their bill and got up from table. Parent then noticed Limousin. He might have been taken for a retired diplomat, for he looked a man of great importance, with his soft white whiskers, the tips of which touched his coat collar.

They walked away. Parent rose and followed them. First they went up and down the terrace, and calmly admired the landscape, and then they went. into the forest. Parent followed them at a distance, hiding himself so as not to excite their suspicion too soon.

Parent came up to them by degrees, breathing hard with emotion and fatigue, for he was unused to walking now. He soon came up to them, but was seized with fear, an inexplicable fear, and he passed them, so as to turn round and meet them face to face. He walked on, his heart beating, feeling that they were just behind him now, and he said to himself: "Come, now is the time. Courage! courage! Now is the moment!"

He turned round. They were all three sitting on the grass, at the foot of a huge tree, and were still chatting. He made up his mind, and walked back rapidly; stopping in front of them in the middle of the road, he said abruptly, in a voice broken by emotion:

"It is I! Here I am! I suppose you did not expect me?"

They all three stared at this man, who seemed to be insane. He continued:

"One would suppose that you did not know me again. Just look at me! I am Parent, Henri Parent. You thought it was all over, and that you would never see me again. Ah! but here I am once more, you see, and now we will have an explanation."

Henriette, terrified, hid her face in her hands, murmuring: "Oh! Good heavens!"

Seeing this stranger, who seemed to be threatening his mother, George sprang up, ready to seize him by the collar. Limousin, thunderstruck, looked in horror at this apparition, who, after gasping for breath, continued:

"So now we will have an explanation; the proper moment has come! Ah! you deceived me, you condemned me to the life of a convict, and you thought that I should never catch you!"

The young man took him by the shoulders and pushed him back.

"Are you mad?" he asked. "What do you want? Go on your way immediately, or I shall give you a thrashing!"

"What do I want?" replied Parent. "I want to tell you who these people are."

George, however, was in a rage, and shook him; and was even going to strike him.

"Let me go," said Parent. "I am your father. There, see whether they recognize me now, the wretches!"

The young man, thunderstruck, unclenched his fists and turned toward his mother. Parent, as soon as he was released, approached her.

"Well," he said, "tell him yourself who I am! Tell him that my name is Henri Parent, that I am his father because his name is George Parent, because you are my wife, because you are all three living on my money, on the allowance of ten thousand francs which I have made you since I drove you out of my house. Will you tell him also why I drove you out? Because I surprised you with this beggar, this wretch, your lover! Tell him what I was, an honorable man, whom you married for money, and whom you deceived from the very first day. Tell him who you are, and who I am——"

He stammered and gasped for breath in his rage. The woman exclaimed in a heartrending voice:

"Paul, Paul, stop him; make him be quiet! Do not let him say this before my son!"

Limousin had also risen to his feet. He said in a very low voice: "Hold your tongue! Hold your tongue! Do you understand what you are doing?"

"I quite know what I am doing," resumed Parent, "and that is not all. There is one thing that I will know, something that has tormented me for twenty years." Then, turning to George, who was leaning against a tree in consternation, he said:

"Listen to me. When she left my house she thought it was not enough to have deceived me, but she also wanted to drive me to despair. You were my only consolation, and she took you with her, swearing that I was not your father, but, that he was your father. Was she lying? I do not know. I have been asking myself the question for the last twenty years." He went close up to her, tragic and terrible, and, pulling away her hands, with which she had covered her face, he continued:

"Well, now! I call upon you to tell me which of us two is the father of this young man; he or I, your husband or your lover. Come! Come! tell us."

Limousin rushed at him. Parent pushed him back, and, sneering in his fury, he said: "Ah! you are brave now! You are braver than you were that day when you ran downstairs because you thought I was going to murder you. Very well! If she will not reply, tell me yourself. You ought to know as well as she. Tell me, are you this young fellow's father? Come! Come! Tell me!"

He turned to his wife again. "If you will not tell me, at any rate tell your son. He is a man, now, and he has the right to know who his father is. I do not know, and I never did know, never, never! I cannot tell you, my boy."

He seemed to be losing his senses; his voice grew shrill and he worked his arms about as if he had an epileptic 'fit.

"Come! . . . Give me an answer. She does not know . . . I will make a bet that she does not know . . . No . . . she does not know, by Jove! Ha! ha! ha! Nobody knows . . . nobody . . . How can one know such things?

"You will not know either, my boy, you will not know any more than I do . . . never. . . . Look here . . . Ask her you will find that she does not know . . . I do not know either . . . nor does he, nor do you, nobody knows. You can choose . . . You can choose . . . yes, you can choose him or me. . . Choose.

"Good evening . . . It is all over. If she makes up her mind to tell you, you will come and let me know, will you not? I am living at the Hotel des Continents . . . I should be glad to know . . . Good evening . . . I hope you will enjoy yourselves very much . . ."

And he went away gesticulating, talking to himself under the tall trees, in the quiet, the cool air, which was full of the fragrance of growing plants. He did not turn round to look at them, but went straight on, walking under the stimulus of his rage, under a storm of passion, with that one fixed idea in his mind. All at once he found himself outside the station. A train was about to start and he got in.

During the journey his anger calmed down, he regained his senses and returned to Paris, astonished at his own boldness, full of aches and pains as if he had broken some bones. Nevertheless, he went to have a "bock" at his brewery.

When she saw him come in, Mademoiselle Zoe asked in surprise: "What! back already? are you tired?"

"Yes—yes, I am tired . . . very tired . . . You know, when one is not used to going out. . . I've had enough of it. I shall not go into the country again. It would have been better to have stayed here. For the future, I shall not stir out."

She could not persuade him to tell her about his little excursion, much as she wished to.

For the first time in his life he got thoroughly drunk that night, and had to be carried home.

QUEEN HORTENSE

In Argenteuil she was called Queen Hortense. No one knew why. Perhaps it was because she had a commanding tone of voice; perhaps because she was tall, bony, imperious; perhaps because she governed a kingdom of servants, chickens, dogs, cats, canaries, parrots, all so dear to an old maid's heart. But she did not spoil these familiar friends; she had for them none of those endearing names, none of the foolish tenderness which women seem to lavish on the soft fur of a purring cat. She governed these beasts with authority; she reigned.

She was indeed an old maid—one of those old maids with a harsh voice and angular motions, whose very soul seems to be hard. She never would stand contradiction, argument, hesitation, indifference, laziness nor fatigue. She had never been heard to complain, to regret anything, to envy anyone. She would say: "Everyone has his share," with the conviction of a fatalist. She did not go to church, she had no use for priests, she hardly believed in God, calling all religious things "weeper's wares."

For thirty years she had lived in her little house, with its tiny garden running along the street; she had never changed her habits, only changing her servants pitilessly, as soon as they reached twenty-one years of age.

When her dogs, cats and birds would die of old age, or from an accident, she would replace them without tears and without regret; with a little spade she would bury the dead animal in a strip of ground, throwing a few shovelfuls of earth over it and stamping it down with her feet in an indifferent manner.

She had a few friends in town, families of clerks who went to Paris every day. Once in a while she would be invited out, in the evening, to tea. She would inevitably fall asleep, and she would have to be awakened, when it was time for her to go home. She never allowed anyone to accompany her, fearing neither light nor darkness. She did not appear to like children.

She kept herself busy doing countless masculine tasks—carpentering, gardening, sawing or chopping wood, even laying bricks when it was necessary.

She had relatives who came to see her twice a year, the Cimmes and the Colombels, her two sisters having married, one of them a florist and the other a retired merchant. The Cimmes had no children; the Colombels had three: Henri, Pauline and Joseph. Henri was twenty, Pauline seventeen and Joseph only three.

There was no love lost between the old maid and her relatives.

In the spring of the year 1882 Queen Hortense suddenly fell sick. The neighbors called in a physician, whom she immediately drove out. A priest then having presented himself, she jumped out of bed, in order to throw him out of the house.

The young servant, in despair, was brewing her some tea.

After lying in bed for three days the situation appeared so serious that the barrel-maker, who lived next door, to the right, acting on advice from the doctor, who had forcibly returned to the house, took it upon himself to call together the two families.

They arrived by the same train, towards ten in the morning, the Colombels bringing little Joseph with them.

When they got to the garden gate, they saw the servant seated in the chair against the wall, crying.

The dog was sleeping on the door mat in the broiling sun; two cats, which looked as though they might be dead, were stretched out in front of the two windows, their eyes closed, their paws and tails stretched out at full length.

A big clucking hen was parading through the garden with a whole regiment of yellow, downy chicks, and a big cage hanging from the wall and covered with pimpernel, contained a population of birds which were chirping away in the warmth of this beautiful spring morning.

In another cage, shaped like a chalet, two lovebirds sat motionless side by side on their perch.

M. Cimme, a fat, puffing person, who always entered first everywhere, pushing aside everyone else, whether man or woman, when it was necessary, asked:

"Well, Celeste, aren't things going well?"

The little servant moaned through her tears:

"She doesn't even recognize me any more. The doctor says it's the end."

Everybody looked around.

Mme. Cimme and Mme. Colombel immediately embraced each other, without saying a word. They locked very much alike, having always worn their hair in Madonna bands, and loud red French cashmere shawls.

Cimme turned to his brother-in-law, a pale, sal, low-complexioned, thin man, wasted by stomach complaints, who limped badly, and said in a serious tone of voice:

"Gad! It was high time."

But no one dared to enter the dying woman's room on the ground floor. Even Cimme made way for the others. Colombel was the first to make up his mind, and, swaying from side to side like the mast of a ship, the iron ferule of his cane clattering on the paved hall, he entered.

The two women were the next to venture, and M. Cimmes closed the procession.

Little Joseph had remained outside, pleased at the sight of the dog.

A ray of sunlight seemed to cut the bed in two, shining just on the hands, which were moving nervously, continually opening and closing. The fingers were twitching as though moved by some thought, as though trying to point out a meaning or idea, as though obeying the dictates of a will. The rest of the body lay motionless under the sheets. The angular frame showed not a single movement. The eyes remained closed.

The family spread out in a semi-circle and, without a word, they began to watch the contracted chest and the short, gasping breathing. The little servant had followed them and was still crying.

At last Cimme asked:

"Exactly what did the doctor say?"

The girl stammered:

"He said to leave her alone, that nothing more could be done for her."

But suddenly the old woman's lips began to move. She seemed to be uttering silent words, words hidden in the brain of this dying being, and her hands quickened their peculiar movements.

Then she began to speak in a thin, high voice, which no one had ever heard, a voice which seemed to come from the distance, perhaps from the depths of this heart which had always been closed.

Cimme, finding this scene painful, walked away on tiptoe. Colombel, whose crippled leg was growing tired, sat down.

The two women remained standing.

Queen Hortense was now babbling away, and no one could understand a word. She was pronouncing names, many names, tenderly calling imaginary people.

"Come here, Philippe, kiss your mother. Tell me, child, do you love your mamma? You, Rose, take care of your little sister while I am away. And don't leave her alone. Don't play with matches!"

She stopped for a while, then, in a louder voice, as though she were calling someone: "Henriette!" then waited a moment and continued:

"Tell your father that I wish to speak to him before he goes to business." And suddenly: "I am not feeling very well to-day, darling; promise not to come home late. Tell your employer that I am sick. You know, it isn't safe to leave the children alone when I am in bed. For dinner I will fix you up a nice dish of rice. The little ones like that very much. Won't Claire be happy?"

And she broke into a happy, joyous laugh, such as they had never heard: "Look at Jean, how funny he looks! He has smeared jam all over his face, the little pig! Look, sweetheart, look; isn't he funny?"

Colombel, who was continually lifting his tired leg from place to place, muttered:

"She is dreaming that she has children and a husband; it is the beginning of the death agony."

The two sisters had not yet moved, surprised, astounded.

The little maid exclaimed:

"You must take off your shawls and your hits! Would you like to go into the parlor?"

They went out without having said a word. And Colombel followed them, limping, once more leaving the dying woman alone.

When they were relieved of their travelling garments, the women finally sat down. Then one of the cats left its window, stretched, jumped into the room and on to Mme. Cimme's knees. She began to pet it.

In the next room could be heard the voice of the dying woman, living, in this last hour, the life for which she had doubtless hoped, living her dreams themselves just when all was over for her.

Cimme, in the garden, was playing with little Joseph and the dog, enjoying himself in the whole hearted manner of a countryman, having completely forgotten the dying woman.

But suddenly he entered the house and said to the girl:

"I say, my girl, are we not going to have luncheon? What do you ladies wish to eat?"

They finally agreed on an omelet, a piece of steak with new potatoes, cheese and coffee.

As Mme. Colombel was fumbling in her pocket for her purse, Cimme stopped her, and, turning to the maid: "Have you got any money?"

She answered:

"Yes, monsieur."

"How much?"

"Fifteen francs."

"That's enough. Hustle, my girl, because I am beginning to get very hungry:"

Mme. Cimme, looking out over the climbing vines bathed in sunlight, and at the two turtle-doves on the roof opposite, said in an annoyed tone of voice:

"What a pity to have had to come for such a sad occasion. It is so nice in the country to-day."

Her sister sighed without answering, and Colombel mumbled, thinking perhaps of the walk ahead of him:

"My leg certainly is bothering me to-day:"

Little Joseph and the dog were making a terrible noise; one was shrieking with pleasure, the other was barking wildly. They were playing hide-and-seek around the three flower beds, running after each other like mad.

The dying woman continued to call her children, talking with each one, imagining that she was dressing them, fondling them, teaching them how to read: "Come on! Simon repeat: A, B, C, D. You are not paying attention, listen—D, D, D; do you hear me? Now repeat—"

Cimme exclaimed: "Funny what people say when in that condition."

Mme. Colombel then asked:

"Wouldn't it be better if we were to return to her?"

But Cimme dissuaded her from the idea:

"What's the use? You can't change anything. We are just as comfortable here."

Nobody insisted. Mme. Cimme observed the two green birds called love-birds. In a few words she praised this singular faithfulness and blamed the men for not imitating these animals. Cimme began to laugh, looked at his wife and hummed in a teasing way: "Tra-la-la, tra-la-la" as though to cast a good deal of doubt on his own, Cimme's, faithfulness:

Colombel was suffering from cramps and was rapping the floor with his cane.

The other cat, its tail pointing upright to the sky, now came in.

They sat down to luncheon at one o'clock.

As soon as he had tasted the wine, Colombel, for whom only the best of Bordeaux had been prescribed, called the servant back:

"I say, my girl, is this the best stuff that you have in the cellar?"

"No, monsieur; there is some better wine, which was only brought out when you came."

"Well, bring us three bottles of it."

They tasted the wine and found it excellent, not because it was of a remarkable vintage, but because it had been in the cellar fifteen years. Cimme declared:

"That is regular invalid's wine."

Colombel, filled with an ardent desire to gain possession of this Bordeaux, once more questioned the girl:

"How much of it is left?"

"Oh! Almost all, monsieur; mamz'elle never touched it. It's in the bottom stack."

Then he turned to his brother-in-law:

"If you wish, Cimme, I would be willing to exchange something else for this wine; it suits my stomach marvellously."

The chicken had now appeared with its regiment of young ones. The two women were enjoying themselves throwing crumbs to them.

Joseph and the dog, who had eaten enough, were sent back to the garden.

Queen Hortense was still talking, but in a low, hushed voice, so that the words could no longer be distinguished.

When they had finished their coffee all went in to observe the condition of the sick woman. She seemed calm.

They went outside again and seated themselves in a circle in the garden, in order to complete their digestion.

Suddenly the dog, who was carrying something in his mouth, began to run around the chairs at full speed. The child was chasing him wildly. Both disappeared into the house.

Cimme fell asleep, his well-rounded paunch bathed in the glow of the shining sun.

The dying woman once more began to talk in a loud voice. Then suddenly she shrieked.

The two women and Colombel rushed in to see what was the matter. Cimme, waking up, did not budge, because, he did not wish to witness such a scene.

She was sitting up, with haggard eyes. Her dog, in order to escape being pursued by little Joseph, had jumped up on the bed, run over the sick woman, and entrenched behind the pillow, was looking down at his playmate with snapping eyes, ready to jump down and begin the game again. He was holding in his mouth one of his mistress' slippers, which he had torn to pieces and with which he had been playing for the last hour.

The child, frightened by this woman who had suddenly risen in front of him, stood motionless before the bed.

The hen had also come in, and frightened by the noise, had jumped up on a chair and was wildly calling her chicks, who were chirping distractedly around the four legs of the chair.

Queen Hortense was shrieking:

"No, no, I don't want to die, I don't want to! I don't want to! Who will bring up my children? Who will take care of them? Who will love them? No, I don't want to!—I don't——"

She fell back. All was over.

The dog, wild with excitement, jumped about the room, barking.

Colombel ran to the window, calling his brother-in-law:

"Hurry up, hurry up! I think that she has just gone."

Then Cimme, resigned, arose and entered the room, mumbling

"It didn't take as long as I thought it would!"

TIMBUCTOO

The boulevard, that river of humanity, was alive with people in the golden light of the setting sun. The whole sky was red, blinding, and behind the Madeleine an immense bank of flaming clouds cast a shower of light the whole length of the boulevard, vibrant as the heat from a brazier.

The gay, animated crowd went by in this golden mist and seemed to be glorified. Their faces were gilded, their black hats and clothes took on purple tints, the patent leather of their shoes cast bright reflections on the asphalt of the sidewalk.

Before the cafes a mass of men were drinking opalescent liquids that looked like precious stones dissolved in the glasses.

In the midst of the drinkers two officers in full uniform dazzled all eyes with their glittering gold lace. They chatted, happy without asking why, in this glory of life, in this radiant light of sunset, and they looked at the crowd, the leisurely men and the hurrying women who left a bewildering odor of perfume as they passed by.

All at once an enormous negro, dressed in black, with a paunch beneath his jean waistcoat, which was covered with charms, his face shining as if it had been polished, passed before them with a triumphant air. He laughed at the passers-by, at the news venders, at the dazzling sky, at the whole of Paris. He was so tall that he overtopped everyone else, and when he passed all the loungers turned round to look at his back.

But he suddenly perceived the officers and darted towards them, jostling the drinkers in his path. As soon as he reached their table he fixed his gleaming and delighted eyes upon them and the corners of his mouth expanded to his ears, showing his dazzling white teeth like a crescent moon in a black sky. The two men looked in astonishment at this ebony giant, unable to understand his delight.

With a voice that made all the guests laugh, he said:

"Good-day, my lieutenant."

One of the officers was commander of a battalion, the other was a colonel. The former said:

"I do not know you, sir. I am at a loss to know what you want of me."

"Me like you much, Lieutenant Vedie, siege of Bezi, much grapes, find me."

The officer, utterly bewildered, looked at the man intently, trying to refresh his memory. Then he cried abruptly:

"Timbuctoo?"

The negro, radiant, slapped his thigh as he uttered a tremendous laugh and roared:

"Yes, yes, my lieutenant; you remember Timbuctoo, ya. How do you do?"

The commandant held out his hand, laughing heartily as he did so. Then Timbuctoo became serious. He seized the officer's hand and, before the other could prevent it, he kissed it, according to negro and Arab custom. The officer embarrassed, said in a severe tone:

"Come now, Timbuctoo, we are not in Africa. Sit down there and tell me how it is I find you here."

Timbuctoo swelled himself out and, his words falling over one another, replied hurriedly:

"Make much money, much, big restaurant, good food; Prussians, me, much steal, much, French cooking; Timbuctoo cook to the emperor; two thousand francs mine. Ha, ha, ha, ha!"

And he laughed, doubling himself up, roaring, with wild delight in his glances.

When the officer, who understood his strange manner of expressing himself, had questioned him he said:

"Well, au revoir, Timbuctoo. I will see you again."

The negro rose, this time shaking the hand that was extended to him and, smiling still, cried:

"Good-day, good-day, my lieutenant!"

He went off so happy that he gesticulated as he walked, and people thought he was crazy.

"Who is that brute?" asked the colonel.

"A fine fellow and a brave soldier. I will tell you what I know about him. It is funny enough.

"You know that at the commencement of the war of 1870 I was shut up in Bezieres, that this negro calls Bezi. We were not besieged, but blockaded. The Prussian lines surrounded us on all sides, outside the reach of cannon, not firing on us, but slowly starving us out.

"I was then lieutenant. Our garrison consisted of soldier of all descriptions, fragments of slaughtered regiments, some that had run away, freebooters separated from the main army, etc. We had all kinds, in fact even eleven Turcos [Algerian soldiers in the service of France], who arrived one evening no one knew whence or how. They appeared at the gates of the city, exhausted, in rags, starving and dirty. They were handed over to me.

"I saw very soon that they were absolutely undisciplined, always in the street and always drunk. I tried putting them in the police station, even in prison, but nothing was of any use. They would disappear, sometimes for days at a time, as if they had been swallowed up by the earth, and then come back staggering drunk. They had no money. Where did they buy drink and how and with what?

"This began to worry me greatly, all the more as these savages interested me with their everlasting laugh and their characteristics of overgrown frolicsome children.

"I then noticed that they blindly obeyed the largest among them, the one you have just seen. He made them do as he pleased, planned their mysterious expeditions with the all-powerful and undisputed authority of a leader. I sent for him and questioned him. Our conversation lasted fully three hours, for it was hard for me to understand his remarkable gibberish. As for him, poor devil, he made unheard-of efforts to make himself intelligible, invented words, gesticulated, perspired in his anxiety, mopping his forehead, puffing, stopping and abruptly beginning again when he thought he had found a new method of explaining what he wanted to say.

"I gathered finally that he was the son of a big chief, a sort of negro king of the region around Timbuctoo. I asked him his name. He repeated something like 'Chavaharibouhalikranafotapolara.' It seemed simpler to me to give him the name of his native place, 'Timbuctoo.' And a week later he was known by no other name in the garrison.

"But we were all wildly anxious to find out where this African ex-prince procured his drinks. I discovered it in a singular manner.

"I was on the ramparts one morning, watching the horizon, when I perceived something moving about in a vineyard. It was near the time of vintage, the grapes were ripe, but I was not thinking of that. I thought that a spy was approaching the town, and I organized a complete expedition to catch the prowler. I took command myself, after obtaining permission from the general.

"I sent out by three different gates three little companies, which were to meet at the suspected vineyard and form a cordon round it. In order to cut off the spy's retreat, one of these detachments had to make at least an hour's march. A watch on the walls signalled to me that the person I had seen had not left the place. We went along in profound silence, creeping, almost crawling, along the ditches. At last we reached the spot assigned.

"I abruptly disbanded my soldiers, who darted into the vineyard and found Timbuctoo on hands and knees travelling around among the vines and eating grapes, or rather devouring them as a dog eats his sop, snatching them in mouthfuls from the vine with his teeth.

"I wanted him to get up, but he could not think of it. I then understood why he was crawling on his hands and knees. As soon as we stood him on his feet he began to wabble, then stretched out his arms and fell down on his nose. He was more drunk than I have ever seen anyone.

"They brought him home on two poles. He never stopped laughing all the way back, gesticulating with his arms and legs.

"This explained the mystery. My men also drank the juice of the grapes, and when they were so intoxicated they could not stir they went to sleep in the vineyard. As for Timbuctoo, his love of the vineyard was beyond all belief and all bounds. He lived in it as did the thrushes, whom he hated with the jealous hate of a rival. He repeated incessantly: 'The thrushes eat all the grapes, captain!'

"One evening I was sent for. Something had been seen on the plain coming in our direction. I had not brought my field-glass and I could not distinguish things clearly. It looked like a great serpent uncoiling itself—a convoy. How could I tell?

"I sent some men to meet this strange caravan, which presently made its triumphal entry. Timbuctoo and nine of his comrades were carrying on a sort of altar made of camp stools eight severed, grinning and bleeding heads. The African was dragging along a horse to whose tail another head was fastened, and six other animals followed, adorned in the same manner.

"This is what I learned: Having started out to the vineyard, my Africans had suddenly perceived a detachment of Prussians approaching a village. Instead of taking to their heels, they hid themselves, and as soon as the Prussian officers dismounted at an inn to refresh themselves, the eleven rascals rushed on them, put to flight the lancers, who thought they were being attacked by the main army, killed the two sentries, then the colonel and the five officers of his escort.

"That day I kissed Timbuctoo. I saw, however, that he walked with difficulty and thought he was wounded. He laughed and said:

"'Me provisions for my country.'

"Timbuctoo was not fighting for glory, but for gain. Everything he found that seemed to him to be of the slightest value, especially anything that glistened, he put in his pocket. What a pocket! An abyss that began at his hips and reached to his ankles. He had retained an old term used by the troopers and called it his 'profonde,' and it was his 'profonde' in fact.

"He had taken the gold lace off the Prussian uniforms, the brass off their helmets, detached their buttons, etc., and had thrown them all into his 'profonde,' which was full to overflowing.

"Each day he pocketed every glistening object that came beneath his observation, pieces of tin or pieces of silver, and sometimes his contour was very comical.

"He intended to carry all that back to the land of ostriches, whose brother he might have been, this son of a king, tormented with the longing to gobble up all objects that glistened. If he had not had his 'profonde' what would he have done? He doubtless would have swallowed them.

"Each morning his pocket was empty. He had, then, some general store where his riches were piled up. But where? I could not discover it.

"The general, on being informed of Timbuctoo's mighty act of valor, had the headless bodies that had been left in the neighboring village interred at once, that it might not be discovered that they were decapitated. The Prussians returned thither the following day. The mayor and seven prominent inhabitants were shot on the spot, by way of reprisal, as having denounced the Prussians.

"Winter was here. We were exhausted and desperate. There were skirmishes now every day. The famished men could no longer march. The eight 'Turcos' alone (three had been killed) remained fat and shiny, vigorous and always ready to fight. Timbuctoo was even getting fatter. He said to me one day:

"'You much hungry; me good meat.'

"And he brought me an excellent filet. But of what? We had no more cattle, nor sheep, nor goats, nor donkeys, nor pigs. It was impossible to get a horse. I thought of all this after I had devoured my meat. Then a horrible idea came to me. These negroes were born close to a country where they eat human beings! And each day such a number of soldiers were killed around the town! I questioned Timbuctoo. He would not answer. I did not insist, but from that time on I declined his presents.

"He worshipped me. One night snow took us by surprise at the outposts. We were seated, on the ground. I looked with pity at those poor negroes shivering beneath this white frozen shower. I was very cold and began to cough. At once I felt something fall on me like a large warm quilt. It was Timbuctoo's cape that he had thrown on my shoulders.

"I rose and returned his garment, saying:

"'Keep it, my boy; you need it more than I do.'

"'Non, my lieutenant, for you; me no need. Me hot, hot!'

"And he looked at me entreatingly.

"'Come, obey orders. Keep your cape; I insist,' I replied.

"He then stood up, drew his sword, which he had sharpened to an edge like a scythe, and holding in his other hand the large cape which I had refused, said:

"'If you not keep cape, me cut. No one cape.'

"And he would have done it. So I yielded.

"Eight days later we capitulated. Some of us had been able to escape, the rest were to march out of the town and give themselves up to the conquerors.

"I went towards the exercising ground, where we were all to meet, when I was dumfounded at the sight of a gigantic negro dressed in white duck and wearing a straw hat. It was Timbuctoo. He was beaming and was walking with his hands in his pockets in front of a little shop where two plates and two glasses were displayed.

"'What are you doing?' I said.

"'Me not go. Me good cook; me make food for Colonel Algeria. Me eat Prussians; much steal, much.'

"There were ten degrees of frost. I shivered at sight of this negro in white duck. He took me by the arm and made me go inside. I noticed an immense flag that he was going to place outside his door as soon as we had left, for he had some shame."

I read this sign, traced by the hand of some accomplice

"'ARMY KITCHEN OF M. TIMBUCTOO,

"'Formerly Cook to H. M. the Emperor.

"'A Parisian Artist. Moderate Prices.'

"In spite of the despair that was gnawing at my heart, I could not help laughing, and I left my negro to his new enterprise.

"Was not that better than taking him prisoner?

"You have just seen that he made a success of it, the rascal.

"Bezieres to-day belongs to the Germans. The 'Restaurant Timbuctoo' is the beginning of a retaliation."

TOMBSTONES

The five friends had finished dinner, five men of the world, mature, rich, three married, the two others bachelors. They met like this every month in memory of their youth, and after dinner they chatted until two o'clock in the morning. Having remained intimate friends, and enjoying each other's society, they probably considered these the pleasantest evenings of their lives. They talked on every subject, especially of what interested and amused Parisians. Their conversation was, as in the majority of salons elsewhere, a verbal rehash of what they had read in the morning papers.

One of the most lively of them was Joseph de Bardon, a celibate living the Parisian life in its fullest and most whimsical manner. He was not a debauche nor depraved, but a singular, happy fellow, still young, for he was scarcely forty. A man of the world in its widest and best sense, gifted with a brilliant, but not profound, mind, with much varied knowledge, but no true erudition, ready comprehension without true understanding, he drew from his observations, his adventures, from everything he saw, met with and found, anecdotes at once comical and philosophical, and made humorous remarks that gave him a great reputation for cleverness in society.

He was the after dinner speaker and had his own story each time, upon which they counted, and he talked without having to be coaxed.

As he sat smoking, his elbows on the table, a petit verre half full beside his plate, half torpid in an atmosphere of tobacco blended with steaming coffee, he seemed to be perfectly at home. He said between two whiffs:

"A curious thing happened to me some time ago."

"Tell it to us," they all exclaimed at once.

"With pleasure. You know that I wander about Paris a great deal, like book collectors who ransack book stalls. I just look at the sights, at the people, at all that is passing by and all that is going on.

"Toward the middle of September—it was beautiful weather—I went out one afternoon, not knowing where I was going. One always has a vague wish to call on some pretty woman or other. One chooses among them in one's mental picture gallery, compares them in one's mind, weighs the interest with which they inspire you, their comparative charms and finally decides according to the influence of the day. But when the sun is very bright and the air warm, it takes away from you all desire to make calls.

"The sun was bright, the air warm. I lighted a cigar and sauntered aimlessly along the outer boulevard. Then, as I strolled on, it occurred to me to walk as far as Montmartre and go into the cemetery.

"I am very fond of cemeteries. They rest me and give me a feeling of sadness; I need it. And, besides, I have good friends in there, those that one no longer goes to call on, and I go there from time to time.

"It is in this cemetery of Montmartre that is buried a romance of my life, a sweetheart who made a great impression on me, a very emotional, charming little woman whose memory, although it causes me great sorrow, also fills me with regrets—regrets of all kinds. And I go to dream beside her grave. She has finished with life.

"And then I like cemeteries because they are immense cities filled to overflowing with inhabitants. Think how many dead people there are in this small space, think of all the generations of Parisians who are housed there forever, veritable troglodytes enclosed in their little vaults, in their little graves covered with a stone or marked by a cross, while living beings take up so much room and make so much noise —imbeciles that they are!

"Then, again, in cemeteries there are monuments almost as interesting as in museums. The tomb of Cavaignac reminded me, I must confess without making any comparison, of the chef d'oeuvre of Jean Goujon: the recumbent statue of Louis de Breze in the subterranean chapel of the Cathedral of Rouen. All modern and realistic art has originated there, messieurs. This dead man, Louis de Breze, is more real, more terrible, more like inanimate flesh still convulsed with the death agony than all the tortured corpses that are distorted to-day in funeral monuments.

"But in Montmartre one can yet admire Baudin's monument, which has a degree of grandeur; that of Gautier, of Murger, on which I saw the other day a simple, paltry wreath of immortelles, yellow immortelles, brought thither by whom? Possibly by the last grisette, very old and now janitress in the neighborhood. It is a pretty little statue by Millet, but ruined by dirt and neglect. Sing of youth, O Murger!

"Well, there I was in Montmartre Cemetery, and was all at once filled with sadness, a sadness that is not all pain, a kind of sadness that makes you think when you are in good health, 'This place is not amusing, but my time has not come yet.'

"The feeling of autumn, of the warm moisture which is redolent of the death of the leaves, and the weakened, weary, anaemic sun increased, while rendering it poetical, the sensation of solitude and of finality that hovered over this spot which savors of human mortality.

"I walked along slowly amid these streets of tombs, where the neighbors do not visit each other, do not sleep together and do not read the newspapers. And I began to read the epitaphs. That is the most amusing thing in the world. Never did Labiche or Meilhac make me laugh as I have laughed at the comical inscriptions on tombstones. Oh, how much superior to the books of Paul de Kock for getting rid of the spleen are these marble slabs and these crosses where the relatives of the deceased have unburdened their sorrow, their desires for the happiness of the vanished ones and their hope of rejoining them—humbugs!

"But I love above all in this cemetery the deserted portion, solitary, full of great yews and cypresses, the older portion, belonging to those dead long since, and which will soon be taken into use again; the growing trees nourished by the human corpses cut down in order to bury in rows beneath little slabs of marble those who have died more recently.

"When I had sauntered about long enough to refresh my mind I felt that I would soon have had enough of it and that I must place the faithful homage of my remembrance on my little friend's last resting place. I felt a tightening of the heart as I reached her grave. Poor dear, she was so dainty, so loving and so white and fresh—and now—if one should open the grave—

"Leaning over the iron grating, I told her of my sorrow in a low tone, which she doubtless did not hear, and was moving away when I saw a woman in black, in deep mourning, kneeling on the next grave. Her crape veil was turned back, uncovering a pretty fair head, the hair in Madonna bands looking like rays of dawn beneath her sombre headdress. I stayed.

"Surely she must be in profound grief. She had covered her face with her hands and, standing there in meditation, rigid as a statue, given up to her grief, telling the sad rosary of her remembrances within the shadow of her concealed and closed eyes, she herself seemed like a dead person mourning another who was dead. All at once a little motion of her back, like a flutter of wind through a willow, led me to suppose that she was going to cry. She wept softly at first, then louder, with quick motions of her neck and shoulders. Suddenly she uncovered her eyes. They were full of tears and charming, the eyes of a bewildered woman, with which she glanced about her as if awaking from a nightmare. She looked at me, seemed abashed and hid her face completely in her hands. Then she sobbed convulsively, and her head slowly bent down toward the marble. She leaned her forehead on it, and her veil spreading around her, covered the white corners of the beloved tomb, like a fresh token of mourning. I heard her sigh, then she sank down with her cheek on the marble slab and remained motionless, unconscious.

"I darted toward her, slapped her hands, blew on her eyelids, while I read this simple epitaph: 'Here lies Louis-Theodore Carrel, Captain of Marine Infantry, killed by the enemy at Tonquin. Pray for him.'

"He had died some months before. I was affected to tears and redoubled my attentions. They were successful. She regained consciousness. I appeared very much moved. I am not bad looking, I am not forty. I saw by her first glance that she would be polite and grateful. She was, and amid more tears she told me her history in detached fragments as well as her gasping breath would allow, how the officer was killed at Tonquin when they had been married a year, how she had married him for love, and being an orphan, she had only the usual dowry.

"I consoled her, I comforted her, raised her and lifted her on her feet. Then I said:

"'Do not stay here. Come.'

"'I am unable to walk,' she murmured.

"'I will support you.'

"'Thank you, sir; you are good. Did you also come to mourn for some one?'

"'Yes, madame.'

"'A dead friend?'

"'Yes, madame.'

"'Your wife?'

"'A friend.'

"'One may love a friend as much as they love their wife. Love has no law.'

"'Yes, madame.'

"And we set off together, she leaning on my arm, while I almost carried her along the paths of the cemetery. When we got outside she faltered:

"'I feel as if I were going to be ill.'

"'Would you like to go in anywhere, to take something?'

"'Yes, monsieur.'

"I perceived a restaurant, one of those places where the mourners of the dead go to celebrate the funeral. We went in. I made her drink a cup of hot tea, which seemed to revive her. A faint smile came to her lips. She began to talk about herself. It was sad, so sad to be always alone in life, alone in one's home, night and day, to have no one on whom one can bestow affection, confidence, intimacy.

"That sounded sincere. It sounded pretty from her mouth. I was touched. She was very young, perhaps twenty. I paid her compliments, which she took in good part. Then, as time was passing, I suggested taking her home in a carriage. She accepted, and in the cab we sat so close that our shoulders touched.

"When the cab stopped at her house she murmured: 'I do not feel equal to going upstairs alone, for I live on the fourth floor. You have been so good. Will you let me take your arm as far as my own door?'

"I agreed with eagerness. She ascended the stairs slowly, breathing hard. Then, as we stood at her door, she said:

"'Come in a few moments so that I may thank you.'

"And, by Jove, I went in. Everything was modest, even rather poor, but simple and in good taste.

"We sat down side by side on a little sofa and she began to talk again about her loneliness. She rang for her maid, in order to offer me some wine. The maid did not come. I was delighted, thinking that this maid probably came in the morning only, what one calls a charwoman.

"She had taken off her hat. She was really pretty, and she gazed at me with her clear eyes, gazed so hard and her eyes were so clear that I was terribly tempted. I caught her in my arms and rained kisses on her eyelids, which she closed suddenly.

"She freed herself and pushed me away, saying:

"'Have done, have done.'

"But I next kissed her on the mouth and she did not resist, and as our glances met after thus outraging the memory of the captain killed in Tonquin, I saw that she had a languid, resigned expression that set my mind at rest.

"I became very attentive and, after chatting for some time, I said:

"'Where do you dine?'

"'In a little restaurant in the neighborhood.'

"'All alone?'

"'Why, yes.'

"'Will you dine with me?'

"'Where?'

"'In a good restaurant on the Boulevard.'

"She demurred a little. I insisted. She yielded, saying by way of apology to herself: 'I am so lonely—so lonely.' Then she added:

"'I must put on something less sombre,' and went into her bedroom. When she reappeared she was dressed in half-mourning, charming, dainty and slender in a very simple gray dress. She evidently had a costume for the cemetery and one for the town.

"The dinner was very enjoyable. She drank some champagne, brightened up, grew lively and I went home with her.

"This friendship, begun amid the tombs, lasted about three weeks. But one gets tired of everything, especially of women. I left her under pretext of an imperative journey. She made me promise that I would come and see her on my return. She seemed to be really rather attached to me.

"Other things occupied my attention, and it was about a month before I thought much about this little cemetery friend. However, I did not forget her. The recollection of her haunted me like a mystery, like a psychological problem, one of those inexplicable questions whose solution baffles us.

"I do not know why, but one day I thought I might possibly meet her in the Montmartre Cemetery, and I went there.

"I walked about a long time without meeting any but the ordinary visitors to this spot, those who have not yet broken off all relations with their dead. The grave of the captain killed at Tonquin had no mourner on its marble slab, no flowers, no wreath.

"But as I wandered in another direction of this great city of the dead I perceived suddenly, at the end of a narrow avenue of crosses, a couple in deep mourning walking toward me, a man and a woman. Oh, horrors! As they approached I recognized her. It was she!

"She saw me, blushed, and as I brushed past her she gave me a little signal, a tiny little signal with her eye, which meant: 'Do not recognize me!' and also seemed to say, 'Come back to see me again, my dear!'

"The man was a gentleman, distingue, chic, an officer of the Legion of Honor, about fifty years old. He was supporting her as I had supported her myself when we were leaving the cemetery.

"I went my way, filled with amazement, asking myself what this all meant, to what race of beings belonged this huntress of the tombs? Was she just a common girl, one who went to seek among the tombs for men who were in sorrow, haunted by the recollection of some woman, a wife or a sweetheart, and still troubled by the memory of vanished caresses? Was she unique? Are there many such? Is it a profession? Do they parade the cemetery as they parade the street? Or else was she only impressed with the admirable, profoundly philosophical idea of exploiting love recollections, which are revived in these funereal places?

"And I would have liked to know whose widow she was on that special day."

MADEMOISELLE PEARL

I

What a strange idea it was for me to choose Mademoiselle Pearl for queen that evening!

Every year I celebrate Twelfth Night with my old friend Chantal. My father, who was his most intimate friend, used to take me round there when I was a child. I continued the custom, and I doubtless shall continue it as long as I live and as long as there is a Chantal in this world.

The Chantals lead a peculiar existence; they live in Paris as though they were in Grasse, Evetot, or Pont-a-Mousson.

They have a house with a little garden near the observatory. They live there as though they were in the country. Of Paris, the real Paris, they know nothing at all, they suspect nothing; they are so far, so far away! However, from time to time, they take a trip into it. Mademoiselle Chantal goes to lay in her provisions, as it is called in the family. This is how they go to purchase their provisions:

Mademoiselle Pearl, who has the keys to the kitchen closet (for the linen closets are administered by the mistress herself), Mademoiselle Pearl gives warning that the supply of sugar is low, that the preserves are giving out, that there is not much left in the bottom of the coffee bag. Thus warned against famine, Mademoiselle Chantal passes everything in review, taking notes on a pad. Then she puts down a lot of figures and goes through lengthy calculations and long discussions with Mademoiselle Pearl. At last they manage to agree, and they decide upon the quantity of each thing of which they will lay in a three months' provision; sugar, rice, prunes, coffee, preserves, cans of peas, beans, lobster, salt or smoked fish, etc., etc. After which the day for the purchasing is determined on and they go in a cab with a railing round the top and drive to a large grocery store on the other side of the river in the new sections of the town.

Madame Chantal and Mademoiselle Pearl make this trip together, mysteriously, and only return at dinner time, tired out, although still excited, and shaken up by the cab, the roof of which is covered with bundles and bags, like an express wagon.

For the Chantals all that part of Paris situated on the other side of the Seine constitutes the new quarter, a section inhabited by a strange, noisy population, which cares little for honor, spends its days in dissipation, its nights in revelry, and which throws money out of the windows. From time to time, however, the young girls are taken to the Opera-Comique or the Theatre Francais, when the play is recommended by the paper which is read by M. Chantal.

At present the young ladies are respectively nineteen and seventeen. They are two pretty girls, tall and fresh, very well brought up, in fact, too well brought up, so much so that they pass by unperceived like two pretty dolls. Never would the idea come to me to pay the slightest attention or to pay court to one of the young Chantal ladies; they are so immaculate that one hardly dares speak to them; one almost feels indecent when bowing to them.

As for the father, he is a charming man, well educated, frank, cordial, but he likes calm and quiet above all else, and has thus contributed greatly to the mummifying of his family in order to live as he pleased in stagnant quiescence. He reads a lot, loves to talk and is readily affected. Lack of contact and of elbowing with the world has made his moral skin very tender and sensitive. The slightest thing moves him, excites him, and makes him suffer.

The Chantals have limited connections carefully chosen in the neighborhood. They also exchange two or three yearly visits with relatives who live in the distance.

As for me, I take dinner with them on the fifteenth of August and on Twelfth Night. That is as much one of my duties as Easter communion is for a Catholic.

On the fifteenth of August a few friends are invited, but on Twelfth Night I am the only stranger.

Well, this year, as every former year, I went to the Chantals' for my Epiphany dinner.

According to my usual custom, I kissed M. Chantal, Madame Chantal and Mademoiselle Pearl, and I made a deep bow to the Misses Louise and Pauline. I was questioned about a thousand and one things, about what had happened on the boulevards, about politics, about how matters stood in Tong-King, and about our representatives in Parliament. Madame Chantal, a fat lady, whose ideas always gave me the impression of being carved out square like building stones, was accustomed to exclaiming at the end of every political discussion: "All that is seed which does not promise much for the future!" Why have I always imagined that Madame Chantal's ideas are square? I don't know; but everything that she says takes that shape in my head: a big square, with four symmetrical angles. There are other people whose ideas always strike me as being round and rolling like a hoop. As soon as they begin a sentence on any subject it rolls on and on, coming out in ten, twenty, fifty round ideas, large and small, which I see rolling along, one behind the other, to the end of the horizon. Other people have pointed ideas—but enough of this.

We sat down as usual and finished our dinner without anything out of the ordinary being said. At dessert the Twelfth Night cake was brought on. Now, M. Chantal had been king every year. I don't know whether this was the result of continued chance or a family convention, but he unfailingly found the bean in his piece of cake, and he would proclaim Madame Chantal to be queen. Therefore, I was greatly surprised to find something very hard, which almost made me break a tooth, in a mouthful of cake. Gently I took this thing from my mouth and I saw that it was a little porcelain doll, no bigger than a bean. Surprise caused me to exclaim:

"Ah!" All looked at me, and Chantal clapped his hands and cried: "It's Gaston! It's Gaston! Long live the king! Long live the king!"

All took up the chorus: "Long live the king!" And I blushed to the tip of my ears, as one often does, without any reason at all, in situations which are a little foolish. I sat there looking at my plate, with this absurd little bit of pottery in my fingers, forcing myself to laugh and not knowing what to do or say, when Chantal once more cried out: "Now, you must choose a queen!"

Then I was thunderstruck. In a second a thousand thoughts and suppositions flashed through my mind. Did they expect me to pick out one of the young Chantal ladies? Was that a trick to make me say which one I prefer? Was it a gentle, light, direct hint of the parents toward a possible marriage? The idea of marriage roams continually in houses with grown-up girls, and takes every shape and disguise, and employs every subterfuge. A dread of compromising myself took hold of me as well as an extreme timidity before the obstinately correct and reserved attitude of the Misses Louise and Pauline. To choose one of them in preference to the other seemed to me as difficult as choosing between two drops of water; and then the fear of launching myself into an affair which might, in spite of me, lead me gently into matrimonial ties, by means as wary and imperceptible and as calm as this insignificant royalty—the fear of all this haunted me.

Suddenly I had an inspiration, and I held out to Mademoiselle Pearl the symbolical emblem. At first every one was surprised, then they doubtless appreciated my delicacy and discretion, for they applauded furiously. Everybody was crying: "Long live the queen! Long live the queen!"

As for herself, poor old maid, she was so amazed that she completely lost control of herself; she was trembling and stammering: "No—no—oh! no—not me—please—not me—I beg of you——"

Then for the first time in my life I looked at Mademoiselle Pearl and wondered what she was.

I was accustomed to seeing her in this house, just as one sees old upholstered armchairs on which one has been sitting since childhood without ever noticing them. One day, with no reason at all, because a ray of sunshine happens to strike the seat, you suddenly think: "Why, that chair is very curious"; and then you discover that the wood has been worked by a real artist and that the material is remarkable. I had never taken any notice of Mademoiselle Pearl.

She was a part of the Chantal family, that was all. But how? By what right? She was a tall, thin person who tried to remain in the background, but who was by no means insignificant. She was treated in a friendly manner, better than a housekeeper, not so well as a relative. I suddenly observed several shades of distinction which I had never noticed before. Madame Chantal said: "Pearl." The young ladies: "Mademoiselle Pearl," and Chantal only addressed her as "Mademoiselle," with an air of greater respect, perhaps.

I began to observe her. How old could she be? Forty? Yes, forty. She was not old, she made herself old. I was suddenly struck by this fact. She fixed her hair and dressed in a ridiculous manner, and, notwithstanding all that, she was not in the least ridiculous, she had such simple, natural gracefulness, veiled and hidden. Truly, what a strange creature! How was it I had never observed her before? She dressed her hair in a grotesque manner with little old maid curls, most absurd; but beneath this one could see a large, calm brow, cut by two deep lines, two wrinkles of long sadness, then two blue eyes, large and tender, so timid, so bashful, so humble, two beautiful eyes which had kept the expression of naive wonder of a young girl, of youthful sensations, and also of sorrow, which had softened without spoiling them.

Her whole face was refined and discreet, a face the expression of which seemed to have gone out without being used up or faded by the fatigues and great emotions of life.

What a dainty mouth! and such pretty teeth! But one would have thought that she did not dare smile.

Suddenly I compared her to Madame Chantal! Undoubtedly Mademoiselle Pearl was the better of the two, a hundred times better, daintier, prouder, more noble. I was surprised at my observation. They were pouring out champagne. I held my glass up to the queen and, with a well-turned compliment, I drank to her health. I could see that she felt inclined to hide her head in her napkin. Then, as she was dipping her lips in the clear wine, everybody cried: "The queen drinks! the queen drinks!" She almost turned purple and choked. Everybody was laughing; but I could see that all loved her.

As soon as dinner was over Chantal took me by the arm. It was time for his cigar, a sacred hour. When alone he would smoke it out in the street; when guests came to dinner he would take them to the billiard room and smoke while playing. That evening they had built a fire to celebrate Twelfth Night; my old friend took his cue, a very fine one, and chalked it with great care; then he said:

"You break, my boy!"

He called me "my boy," although I was twenty-five, but he had known me as a young child.

I started the game and made a few carroms. I missed some others, but as the thought of Mademoiselle Pearl kept returning to my mind, I suddenly asked:

"By the way, Monsieur Chantal, is Mademoiselle Pearl a relative of yours?"

Greatly surprised, he stopped playing and looked at me:

"What! Don't you know? Haven't you heard about Mademoiselle Pearl?"

"No."

"Didn't your father ever tell you?"

"No."

"Well, well, that's funny! That certainly is funny! Why, it's a regular romance!"

He paused, and then continued:

"And if you only knew how peculiar it is that you should ask me that to-day, on Twelfth Night!"

"Why?"

"Why? Well, listen. Forty-one years ago to day, the day of the Epiphany, the following events occurred: We were then living at Roily-le-Tors, on the ramparts; but in order that you may understand, I must first explain the house. Roily is built on a hill, or, rather, on a mound which overlooks a great stretch of prairie. We had a house there with a beautiful hanging garden supported by the old battlemented wall; so that the house was in the town on the streets, while the garden overlooked the plain. There was a door leading from the garden to the open country, at the bottom of a secret stairway in the thick wall—the kind you read about in novels. A road passed in front of this door, which was provided with a big bell; for the peasants, in order to avoid the roundabout way, would bring their provisions up this way.

"You now understand the place, don't you? Well, this year, at Epiphany, it had been snowing for a week. One might have thought that the world was coming to an end. When we went to the ramparts to look over the plain, this immense white, frozen country, which shone like varnish, would chill our very souls. One might have thought that the Lord had packed the world in cotton to put it away in the storeroom for old worlds. I can assure you that it was dreary looking.

"We were a very numerous family at that time my father, my mother, my uncle and aunt, my two brothers and four cousins; they were pretty little girls; I married the youngest. Of all that crowd, there are only three of us left: my wife, I, and my sister-in-law, who lives in Marseilles. Zounds! how quickly a family like that dwindles away! I tremble when I think of it! I was fifteen years old then, since I am fifty-six now.

"We were going to celebrate the Epiphany, and we were all happy, very happy! Everybody was in the parlor, awaiting dinner, and my oldest brother, Jacques, said: 'There has been a dog howling out in the plain for about ten minutes; the poor beast must be lost.'

"He had hardly stopped talking when the garden bell began to ring. It had the deep sound of a church bell, which made one think of death. A shiver ran through everybody. My father called the servant and told him to go outside and look. We waited in complete silence; we were thinking of the snow which covered the ground. When the man returned he declared that he had seen nothing. The dog kept up its ceaseless howling, and always from the same spot.

"We sat down to dinner; but we were all uneasy, especially the young people. Everything went well up to the roast, then the bell began to ring again, three times in succession, three heavy, long strokes which vibrated to the tips of our fingers and which stopped our conversation short. We sat there looking at each other, fork in the air, still listening, and shaken by a kind of supernatural fear.

"At last my mother spoke: 'It's surprising that they should have waited so long to come back. Do not go alone, Baptiste; one of these gentlemen will accompany you.'

"My Uncle Francois arose. He was a kind of Hercules, very proud of his strength, and feared nothing in the world. My father said to him: 'Take a gun. There is no telling what it might be.'

"But my uncle only took a cane and went out with the servant.

"We others remained there trembling with fear and apprehension, without eating or speaking. My father tried to reassure us: 'Just wait and see,' he said; 'it will be some beggar or some traveller lost in the snow. After ringing once, seeing that the door was not immediately opened, he attempted again to find his way, and being unable to, he has returned to our door.'

"Our uncle seemed to stay away an hour. At last he came back, furious, swearing: 'Nothing at all; it's some practical joker! There is nothing but that damned dog howling away at about a hundred yards from the walls. If I had taken a gun I would have killed him to make him keep quiet.'

"We sat down to dinner again, but every one was excited; we felt that all was not over, that something was going to happen, that the bell would soon ring again.

"It rang just as the Twelfth Night cake was being cut. All the men jumped up together. My Uncle, Francois, who had been drinking champagne, swore so furiously that he would murder it, whatever it might be, that my mother and my aunt threw themselves on him to prevent his going. My father, although very calm and a little helpless (he limped ever since he had broken his leg when thrown by a horse), declared, in turn, that he wished to find out what was the matter and that he was going. My brothers, aged eighteen and twenty, ran to get their guns; and as no one was paying any attention to me I snatched up a little rifle that was used in the garden and got ready to accompany the expedition.

"It started out immediately. My father and uncle were walking ahead with Baptiste, who was carrying a lantern. My brothers, Jacques and Paul, followed, and I trailed on behind in spite of the prayers of my mother, who stood in front of the house with her sister and my cousins.

"It had been snowing again for the last hour, and the trees were weighted down. The pines were bending under this heavy, white garment, and looked like white pyramids or enormous sugar cones, and through the gray curtains of small hurrying flakes could be seen the lighter bushes which stood out pale in the shadow. The snow was falling so thick that we could hardly see ten feet ahead of us. But the lantern threw a bright light around us. When we began to go down the winding stairway in the wall I really grew frightened. I felt as though some one were walking behind me, were going to grab me by the shoulders and carry me away, and I felt a strong desire to return; but, as I would have had to cross the garden all alone, I did not dare. I heard some one opening the door leading to the plain; my uncle began to swear again, exclaiming: 'By—-! He has gone again! If I can catch sight of even his shadow, I'll take care not to miss him, the swine!'

"It was a discouraging thing to see this great expanse of plain, or, rather, to feel it before us, for we could not see it; we could only see a thick, endless veil of snow, above, below, opposite us, to the right, to the left, everywhere. My uncle continued:

"'Listen! There is the dog howling again; I will teach him how I shoot. That will be something gained, anyhow.'

"But my father, who was kind-hearted, went on:

"'It will be much better to go on and get the poor animal, who is crying for hunger. The poor fellow is barking for help; he is calling like a man in distress. Let us go to him.'

"So we started out through this mist, through this thick continuous fall of snow, which filled the air, which moved, floated, fell, and chilled the skin with a burning sensation like a sharp, rapid pain as each flake melted. We were sinking in up to our knees in this soft, cold mass, and we had to lift our feet very high in order to walk. As we advanced the dog's voice became clearer and stronger. My uncle cried: 'Here he is!' We stopped to observe him as one does when he meets an enemy at night.

"I could see nothing, so I ran up to the others, and I caught sight of him; he was frightful and weird-looking; he was a big black shepherd's dog with long hair and a wolf's head, standing just within the gleam of light cast by our lantern on the snow. He did not move; he was silently watching us.

"My uncle said: 'That's peculiar, he is neither advancing nor retreating. I feel like taking a shot at him.'

"My father answered in a firm voice: 'No, we must capture him.'

"Then my brother Jacques added: 'But he is not alone. There is something behind him."

"There was indeed something behind him, something gray, impossible to distinguish. We started out again cautiously. When he saw us approaching the dog sat down. He did not look wicked. Instead, he seemed pleased at having been able to attract the attention of some one.

"My father went straight to him and petted him. The dog licked his hands. We saw that he was tied to the wheel of a little carriage, a sort of toy carriage entirely wrapped up in three or four woolen blankets. We carefully took off these coverings, and as Baptiste approached his lantern to the front of this little vehicle, which looked like a rolling kennel, we saw in it a little baby sleeping peacefully.

"We were so astonished that we couldn't speak.

"My father was the first to collect his wits, and as he had a warm heart and a broad mind, he stretched his hand over the roof of the carriage and said: 'Poor little waif, you shall be one of us!' And he ordered my brother Jacques to roll the foundling ahead of us. Thinking out loud, my father continued:

"'Some child of love whose poor mother rang at my door on this night of Epiphany in memory of the Child of God.'

"He once more stopped and called at the top of his lungs through the night to the four corners of the heavens: 'We have found it!' Then, putting his hand on his brother's shoulder, he murmured: 'What if you had shot the dog, Francois?'

"My uncle did not answer, but in the darkness he crossed himself, for, notwithstanding his blustering manner, he was very religious.

"The dog, which had been untied, was following us.

"Ah! But you should have seen us when we got to the house! At first we had a lot of trouble in getting the carriage up through the winding stairway; but we succeeded and even rolled it into the vestibule.

"How funny mamma was! How happy and astonished! And my four little cousins (the youngest was only six), they looked like four chickens around a nest. At last we took the child from the carriage. It was still sleeping. It was a girl about six weeks old. In its clothes we found ten thousand francs in gold, yes, my boy, ten thousand francs!—which papa saved for her dowry. Therefore, it was not a child of poor people, but, perhaps, the child of some nobleman and a little bourgeoise of the town—or again—we made a thousand suppositions, but we never found out anything-never the slightest clue. The dog himself was recognized by no one. He was a stranger in the country. At any rate, the person who rang three times at our door must have known my parents well, to have chosen them thus.

"That is how, at the age of six weeks, Mademoiselle Pearl entered the Chantal household.

"It was not until later that she was called Mademoiselle Pearl. She was at first baptized 'Marie Simonne Claire,' Claire being intended, for her family name.

"I can assure you that our return to the diningroom was amusing, with this baby now awake and looking round her at these people and these lights with her vague blue questioning eyes.

"We sat down to dinner again and the cake was cut. I was king, and for queen I took Mademoiselle Pearl, just as you did to-day. On that day she did not appreciate the honor that was being shown her.

"Well, the child was adopted and brought up in the family. She grew, and the years flew by. She was so gentle and loving and minded so well that every one would have spoiled her abominably had not my mother prevented it.

"My mother was an orderly woman with a great respect for class distinctions. She consented to treat little Claire as she did her own sons, but, nevertheless, she wished the distance which separated us to be well marked, and our positions well established. Therefore, as soon as the child could understand, she acquainted her with her story and gently, even tenderly, impressed on the little one's mind that, for the Chantals, she was an adopted daughter, taken in, but, nevertheless, a stranger. Claire understood the situation with peculiar intelligence and with surprising instinct; she knew how to take the place which was allotted her, and to keep it with so much tact, gracefulness and gentleness that she often brought tears to my father's eyes. My mother herself was often moved by the passionate gratitude and timid devotion of this dainty and loving little creature that she began calling her: 'My daughter.' At times, when the little one had done something kind and good, my mother would raise her spectacles on her forehead, a thing which always indicated emotion with her, and she would repeat: 'This child is a pearl, a perfect pearl!' This name stuck to the little Claire, who became and remained for us Mademoiselle Pearl."

II

M. Chantal stopped. He was sitting on the edge of the billiard table, his feet hanging, and was playing with a ball with his left hand, while with his right he crumpled a rag which served to rub the chalk marks from the slate. A little red in the face, his voice thick, he was talking away to himself now, lost in his memories, gently drifting through the old scenes and events which awoke in his mind, just as we walk through old family gardens where we were brought up and where each tree, each walk, each hedge reminds us of some occurrence.

I stood opposite him leaning against the wall, my hands resting on my idle cue.

After a slight pause he continued:

"By Jove! She was pretty at eighteen—and graceful—and perfect. Ah! She was so sweet—and good and true—and charming! She had such eyes—blue-transparent—clear—such eyes as I have never seen since!"

He was once more silent. I asked: "Why did she never marry?"

He answered, not to me, but to the word "marry" which had caught his ear: "Why? why? She never would—she never would! She had a dowry of thirty thousand francs, and she received several offers—but she never would! She seemed sad at that time. That was when I married my cousin, little Charlotte, my wife, to whom I had been engaged for six years."

I looked at M. Chantal, and it seemed to me that I was looking into his very soul, and I was suddenly witnessing one of those humble and cruel tragedies of honest, straightforward, blameless hearts, one of those secret tragedies known to no one, not even the silent and resigned victims. A rash curiosity suddenly impelled me to exclaim:

"You should have married her, Monsieur Chantal!"

He started, looked at me, and said:

"I? Marry whom?"

"Mademoiselle Pearl."

"Why?"

"Because you loved her more than your cousin."

He stared at me with strange, round, bewildered eyes and stammered:

"I loved her—I? How? Who told you that?"

"Why, anyone can see that—and it's even on account of her that you delayed for so long your marriage to your cousin who had been waiting for you for six years."

He dropped the ball which he was holding in his left hand, and, seizing the chalk rag in both hands, he buried his face in it and began to sob. He was weeping with his eyes, nose and mouth in a heartbreaking yet ridiculous manner, like a sponge which one squeezes. He was coughing, spitting and blowing his nose in the chalk rag, wiping his eyes and sneezing; then the tears would again begin to flow down the wrinkles on his face and he would make a strange gurgling noise in his throat. I felt bewildered, ashamed; I wanted to run away, and I no longer knew what to say, do, or attempt.

Suddenly Madame Chantal's voice sounded on the stairs. "Haven't you men almost finished smoking your cigars?"

I opened the door and cried: "Yes, madame, we are coming right down."

Then I rushed to her husband, and, seizing him by the shoulders, I cried: "Monsieur Chantal, my friend Chantal, listen to me; your wife is calling; pull yourself together, we must go downstairs."

He stammered: "Yes—yes—I am coming—poor girl! I am coming—tell her that I am coming."

He began conscientiously to wipe his face on the cloth which, for the last two or three years, had been used for marking off the chalk from the slate; then he appeared, half white and half red, his forehead, nose, cheeks and chin covered with chalk, and his eyes swollen, still full of tears.

I caught him by the hands and dragged him into his bedroom, muttering: "I beg your pardon, I beg your pardon, Monsieur Chantal, for having caused you such sorrow—but—I did not know—you—you understand."

He squeezed my hand, saying: "Yes—yes—there are difficult moments."

Then he plunged his face into a bowl of water. When he emerged from it he did not yet seem to me to be presentable; but I thought of a little stratagem. As he was growing worried, looking at himself in the mirror, I said to him: "All you have to do is to say that a little dust flew into your eye and you can cry before everybody to your heart's content."

He went downstairs rubbing his eyes with his handkerchief. All were worried; each one wished to look for the speck, which could not be found; and stories were told of similar cases where it had been necessary to call in a physician.

I went over to Mademoiselle Pearl and watched her, tormented by an ardent curiosity, which was turning to positive suffering. She must indeed have been pretty, with her gentle, calm eyes, so large that it looked as though she never closed them like other mortals. Her gown was a little ridiculous, a real old maid's gown, which was unbecoming without appearing clumsy.

It seemed to me as though I were looking into her soul, just as I had into Monsieur Chantal's; that I was looking right from one end to the other of this humble life, so simple and devoted. I felt an irresistible longing to question her, to find out whether she, too, had loved him; whether she also had suffered, as he had, from this long, secret, poignant grief, which one cannot see, know, or guess, but which breaks forth at night in the loneliness of the dark room. I was watching her, and I could observe her heart beating under her waist, and I wondered whether this sweet, candid face had wept on the soft pillow and she had sobbed, her whole body shaken by the violence of her anguish.

I said to her in a low voice, like a child who is breaking a toy to see what is inside: "If you could have seen Monsieur Chantal crying a while ago it would have moved you."

She started, asking: "What? He was weeping?"

"Ah, yes, he was indeed weeping!"

"Why?"

She seemed deeply moved. I answered:

"On your account."

"On my account?"

"Yes. He was telling me how much he had loved you in the days gone by; and what a pang it had given him to marry his cousin instead of you."

Her pale face seemed to grow a little longer; her calm eyes, which always remained open, suddenly closed so quickly that they seemed shut forever. She slipped from her chair to the floor, and slowly, gently sank down as would a fallen garment.

I cried: "Help! help! Mademoiselle Pearl is ill."

Madame Chantal and her daughters rushed forward, and while they were looking for towels, water and vinegar, I grabbed my hat and ran away.

I walked away with rapid strides, my heart heavy, my mind full of remorse and regret. And yet sometimes I felt pleased; I felt as though I had done a praiseworthy and necessary act. I was asking myself: "Did I do wrong or right?" They had that shut up in their hearts, just as some people carry a bullet in a closed wound. Will they not be happier now? It was too late for their torture to begin over again and early enough for them to remember it with tenderness.

And perhaps some evening next spring, moved by a beam of moonlight falling through the branches on the grass at their feet, they will join and press their hands in memory of all this cruel and suppressed suffering; and, perhaps, also this short embrace may infuse in their veins a little of this thrill which they would not have known without it, and will give to those two dead souls, brought to life in a second, the rapid and divine sensation of this intoxication, of this madness which gives to lovers more happiness in an instant than other men can gather during a whole lifetime!

THE THIEF

While apparently thinking of something else, Dr. Sorbier had been listening quietly to those amazing accounts of burglaries and daring deeds that might have been taken from the trial of Cartouche. "Assuredly," he exclaimed, "assuredly, I know of no viler fault nor any meaner action than to attack a girl's innocence, to corrupt her, to profit by a moment of unconscious weakness and of madness, when her heart is beating like that of a frightened fawn, and her pure lips seek those of her tempter; when she abandons herself without thinking of the irremediable stain, nor of her fall, nor of the morrow.

"The man who has brought this about slowly, viciously, who can tell with what science of evil, and who, in such a case, has not steadiness and self-restraint enough to quench that flame by some icy words, who has not sense enough for two, who cannot recover his self-possession and master the runaway brute within him, and who loses his head on the edge of the precipice over which she is going to fall, is as contemptible as any man who breaks open a lock, or as any rascal on the lookout for a house left defenceless and unprotected or for some easy and dishonest stroke of business, or as that thief whose various exploits you have just related to us.

"I, for my part, utterly refuse to absolve him, even when extenuating circumstances plead in his favor, even when he is carrying on a dangerous flirtation, in which a man tries in vain to keep his balance, not to exceed the limits of the game, any more than at lawn tennis; even when the parts are inverted and a man's adversary is some precocious, curious, seductive girl, who shows you immediately that she has nothing to learn and nothing to experience, except the last chapter of love, one of those girls from whom may fate always preserve our sons, and whom a psychological novel writer has christened 'The Semi-Virgins.'

"It is, of course, difficult and painful for that coarse and unfathomable vanity which is characteristic of every man, and which might be called 'malism', not to stir such a charming fire, difficult to act the Joseph and the fool, to turn away his eyes, and, as it were, to put wax into his ears, like the companions of Ulysses when they were attracted by the divine, seductive songs of the Sirens, difficult only to touch that pretty table covered with a perfectly new cloth, at which you are invited to take a seat before any one else, in such a suggestive voice, and are requested to quench your thirst and to taste that new wine, whose fresh and strange flavor you will never forget. But who would hesitate to exercise such self-restraint if, when he rapidly examines his conscience, in one of those instinctive returns to his sober self in which a man thinks clearly and recovers his head, he were to measure the gravity of his fault, consider it, think of its consequences, of the reprisals, of the uneasiness which he would always feel in the future, and which would destroy the repose and happiness of his life?

"You may guess that behind all these moral reflections, such as a graybeard like myself may indulge in, there is a story hidden, and, sad as it is, I am sure it will interest you on account of the strange heroism it shows."

He was silent for a few moments, as if to classify his recollections, and, with his elbows resting on the arms of his easy-chair and his eyes looking into space, he continued in the slow voice of a hospital professor who is explaining a case to his class of medical students, at a bedside:

"He was one of those men who, as our grandfathers used to say, never met with a cruel woman, the type of the adventurous knight who was always foraging, who had something of the scamp about him, but who despised danger and was bold even to rashness. He was ardent in the pursuit of pleasure, and had an irresistible charm about him, one of those men in whom we excuse the greatest excesses as the most natural things in the world. He had run through all his money at gambling and with pretty girls, and so became, as it were, a soldier of fortune. He amused himself whenever and however he could, and was at that time quartered at Versailles.

"I knew him to the very depths of his childlike heart, which was only too easily seen through and sounded, and I loved him as some old bachelor uncle loves a nephew who plays him tricks, but who knows how to coax him. He had made me his confidant rather than his adviser, kept me informed of his slightest pranks, though he always pretended to be speaking about one of his friends, and not about himself; and I must confess that his youthful impetuosity, his careless gaiety, and his amorous ardor sometimes distracted my thoughts and made me envy the handsome, vigorous young fellow who was so happy at being alive, that I had not the courage to check him, to show him the right road, and to call out to him: 'Take care!' as children do at blind man's buff.

"And one day, after one of those interminable cotillons, where the couples do not leave each other for hours, and can disappear together without anybody thinking of noticing them, the poor fellow at last discovered what love was, that real love which takes up its abode in the very centre of the heart and in the brain, and is proud of being there, and which rules like a sovereign and a tyrannous master, and he became desperately enamored of a pretty but badly brought up girl, who was as disquieting and wayward as she was pretty.

"She loved him, however, or rather she idolized him despotically, madly, with all her enraptured soul and all her being. Left to do as she pleased by imprudent and frivolous parents, suffering from neurosis, in consequence of the unwholesome friendships which she contracted at the convent school, instructed by what she saw and heard and knew was going on around her, in spite of her deceitful and artificial conduct, knowing that neither her father nor her mother, who were very proud of their race as well as avaricious, would ever agree to let her marry the man whom she had taken a liking to, that handsome fellow who had little besides vision, ideas and debts, and who belonged to the middle-class, she laid aside all scruples, thought of nothing but of becoming his, no matter what might be the cost.

"By degrees, the unfortunate man's strength gave way, his heart softened, and he allowed himself to be carried away by that current which buffeted him, surrounded him, and left him on the shore like a waif and a stray.

"They wrote letters full of madness to each other, and not a day passed without their meeting, either accidentally, as it seemed, or at parties and balls. She had yielded her lips to him in long, ardent caresses, which had sealed their compact of mutual passion."

The doctor stopped, and his eyes suddenly filled with tears, as these former troubles came back to his mind; and then, in a hoarse voice, he went on, full of the horror of what he was going to relate:

"For months he scaled the garden wall, and, holding his breath and listening for the slightest noise, like a burglar who is going to break into a house, he went in by the servants' entrance, which she had left open, slunk barefoot down a long passage and up the broad staircase, which creaked occasionally, to the second story, where his sweetheart's room was, and stayed there for hours.

"One night, when it was darker than usual, and he was hurrying lest he should be later than the time agreed on, he knocked up against a piece of furniture in the anteroom and upset it. It so happened that the girl's mother had not gone to sleep, either because she had a sick headache, or else be cause she had sat up late over some novel, and, frightened at that unusual noise which disturbed the silence of the house, she jumped out of bed, opened the door, saw some one indistinctly running away and keeping close to the wall, and, immediately thinking that there were burglars in the house, she aroused her husband and the servants by her frantic screams. The unfortunate man understood the situation; and, seeing what a terrible fix he was in, and preferring to be taken for a common thief to dishonoring his adored one's name, he ran into the drawing-room, felt on the tables and what-nots, filled his pockets at random with valuable bric-a-brac, and then cowered down behind the grand piano, which barred the corner of a large room.

"The servants, who had run in with lighted candles, found him, and, overwhelming him with abuse, seized him by the collar and dragged him, panting and apparently half dead with shame and terror, to the nearest police station. He defended himself with intentional awkwardness when he was brought up for trial, kept up his part with the most perfect self-possession and without any signs of the despair and anguish that he felt in his heart, and, condemned and degraded and made to suffer martyrdom in his honor as a man and a soldier—he was an officer—he did not protest, but went to prison as one of those criminals whom society gets rid of like noxious vermin.

"He died there of misery and of bitterness of spirit, with the name of the fair-haired idol, for whom he had sacrificed himself, on his lips, as if it had been an ecstatic prayer, and he intrusted his will 'to the priest who administered extreme unction to him, and requested him to give it to me. In it, without mentioning anybody, and without in the least lifting the veil, he at last explained the enigma, and cleared himself of those accusations the terrible burden of which he had borne until his last breath.

"I have always thought myself, though I do not know why, that the girl married and had several charming children, whom she brought up with the austere strictness and in the serious piety of former days!"

CLAIR DE LUNE

Abbe Marignan's martial name suited him well. He was a tall, thin priest, fanatic, excitable, yet upright. All his beliefs were fixed, never varying. He believed sincerely that he knew his God, understood His plans, desires and intentions.

When he walked with long strides along the garden walk of his little country parsonage, he would sometimes ask himself the question: "Why has God done this?" And he would dwell on this continually, putting himself in the place of God, and he almost invariably found an answer. He would never have cried out in an outburst of pious humility: "Thy ways, O Lord, are past finding out."

He said to himself: "I am the servant of God; it is right for me to know the reason of His deeds, or to guess it if I do not know it."

Everything in nature seemed to him to have been created in accordance with an admirable and absolute logic. The "whys" and "becauses" always balanced. Dawn was given to make our awakening pleasant, the days to ripen the harvest, the rains to moisten it, the evenings for preparation for slumber, and the dark nights for sleep.

The four seasons corresponded perfectly to the needs of agriculture, and no suspicion had ever come to the priest of the fact that nature has no intentions; that, on the contrary, everything which exists must conform to the hard demands of seasons, climates and matter.

But he hated woman—hated her unconsciously, and despised her by instinct. He often repeated the words of Christ: "Woman, what have I to do with thee?" and he would add: "It seems as though God, Himself, were dissatisfied with this work of His." She was the tempter who led the first man astray, and who since then had ever been busy with her work of damnation, the feeble creature, dangerous and mysteriously affecting one. And even more than their sinful bodies, he hated their loving hearts.

He had often felt their tenderness directed toward himself, and though he knew that he was invulnerable, he grew angry at this need of love that is always vibrating in them.

According to his belief, God had created woman for the sole purpose of tempting and testing man. One must not approach her without defensive precautions and fear of possible snares. She was, indeed, just like a snare, with her lips open and her arms stretched out to man.

He had no indulgence except for nuns, whom their vows had rendered inoffensive; but he was stern with them, nevertheless, because he felt that at the bottom of their fettered and humble hearts the everlasting tenderness was burning brightly—that tenderness which was shown even to him, a priest.

He felt this cursed tenderness, even in their docility, in the low tones of their voices when speaking to him, in their lowered eyes, and in their resigned tears when he reproved them roughly. And he would shake his cassock on leaving the convent doors, and walk off, lengthening his stride as though flying from danger.

He had a niece who lived with her mother in a little house near him. He was bent upon making a sister of charity of her.

She was a pretty, brainless madcap. When the abbe preached she laughed, and when he was angry with her she would give him a hug, drawing him to her heart, while he sought unconsciously to release himself from this embrace which nevertheless filled him with a sweet pleasure, awakening in his depths the sensation of paternity which slumbers in every man.

Often, when walking by her side, along the country road, he would speak to her of God, of his God. She never listened to him, but looked about her at the sky, the grass and flowers, and one could see the joy of life sparkling in her eyes. Sometimes she would dart forward to catch some flying creature, crying out as she brought it back: "Look, uncle, how pretty it is! I want to hug it!" And this desire to "hug" flies or lilac blossoms disquieted, angered, and roused the priest, who saw, even in this, the ineradicable tenderness that is always budding in women's hearts.

Then there came a day when the sexton's wife, who kept house for Abbe Marignan, told him, with caution, that his niece had a lover.

Almost suffocated by the fearful emotion this news roused in him, he stood there, his face covered with soap, for he was in the act of shaving.

When he had sufficiently recovered to think and speak he cried: "It is not true; you lie, Melanie!"

But the peasant woman put her hand on her heart, saying: "May our Lord judge me if I lie, Monsieur le Cure! I tell you, she goes there every night when your sister has gone to bed. They meet by the river side; you have only to go there and see, between ten o'clock and midnight."

He ceased scraping his chin, and began to walk up and down impetuously, as he always did when he was in deep thought. When he began shaving again he cut himself three times from his nose to his ear.

All day long he was silent, full of anger and indignation. To his priestly hatred of this invincible love was added the exasperation of her spiritual father, of her guardian and pastor, deceived and tricked by a child, and the selfish emotion shown by parents when their daughter announces that she has chosen a husband without them, and in spite of them.

After dinner he tried to read a little, but could not, growing more and, more angry. When ten o'clock struck he seized his cane, a formidable oak stick, which he was accustomed to carry in his nocturnal walks when visiting the sick. And he smiled at the enormous club which he twirled in a threatening manner in his strong, country fist. Then he raised it suddenly and, gritting his teeth, brought it down on a chair, the broken back of which fell over on the floor.

He opened the door to go out, but stopped on the sill, surprised by the splendid moonlight, of such brilliance as is seldom seen.

And, as he was gifted with an emotional nature, one such as had all those poetic dreamers, the Fathers of the Church, he felt suddenly distracted and moved by all the grand and serene beauty of this pale night.

In his little garden, all bathed in soft light, his fruit trees in a row cast on the ground the shadow of their slender branches, scarcely in full leaf, while the giant honeysuckle, clinging to the wall of his house, exhaled a delicious sweetness, filling the warm moonlit atmosphere with a kind of perfumed soul.

He began to take long breaths, drinking in the air as drunkards drink wine, and he walked along slowly, delighted, marveling, almost forgetting his niece.

As soon as he was outside of the garden, he stopped to gaze upon the plain all flooded with the caressing light, bathed in that tender, languishing charm of serene nights. At each moment was heard the short, metallic note of the cricket, and distant nightingales shook out their scattered notes—their light, vibrant music that sets one dreaming, without thinking, a music made for kisses, for the seduction of moonlight.

The abbe walked on again, his heart failing, though he knew not why. He seemed weakened, suddenly exhausted; he wanted to sit down, to rest there, to think, to admire God in His works.

Down yonder, following the undulations of the little river, a great line of poplars wound in and out. A fine mist, a white haze through which the moonbeams passed, silvering it and making it gleam, hung around and above the mountains, covering all the tortuous course of the water with a kind of light and transparent cotton.

The priest stopped once again, his soul filled with a growing and irresistible tenderness.

And a doubt, a vague feeling of disquiet came over him; he was asking one of those questions that he sometimes put to himself.

"Why did God make this? Since the night is destined for sleep, unconsciousness, repose, forgetfulness of everything, why make it more charming than day, softer than dawn or evening? And does why this seductive planet, more poetic than the sun, that seems destined, so discreet is it, to illuminate things too delicate and mysterious for the light of day, make the darkness so transparent?

"Why does not the greatest of feathered songsters sleep like the others? Why does it pour forth its voice in the mysterious night?

"Why this half-veil cast over the world? Why these tremblings of the heart, this emotion of the spirit, this enervation of the body? Why this display of enchantments that human beings do not see, since they are lying in their beds? For whom is destined this sublime spectacle, this abundance of poetry cast from heaven to earth?"

And the abbe could not understand.

But see, out there, on the edge of the meadow, under the arch of trees bathed in a shining mist, two figures are walking side by side.

The man was the taller, and held his arm about his sweetheart's neck and kissed her brow every little while. They imparted life, all at once, to the placid landscape in which they were framed as by a heavenly hand. The two seemed but a single being, the being for whom was destined this calm and silent night, and they came toward the priest as a living answer, the response his Master sent to his questionings.

He stood still, his heart beating, all upset; and it seemed to him that he saw before him some biblical scene, like the loves of Ruth and Boaz, the accomplishment of the will of the Lord, in some of those glorious stories of which the sacred books tell. The verses of the Song of Songs began to ring in his ears, the appeal of passion, all the poetry of this poem replete with tenderness.

And he said unto himself: "Perhaps God has made such nights as these to idealize the love of men."

He shrank back from this couple that still advanced with arms intertwined. Yet it was his niece. But he asked himself now if he would not be disobeying God. And does not God permit love, since He surrounds it with such visible splendor?

And he went back musing, almost ashamed, as if he had intruded into a temple where he had, no right to enter.

WAITER, A "BOCK"

Why did I go into that beer hall on that particular evening? I do not know. It was cold; a fine rain, a flying mist, veiled the gas lamps with a transparent fog, made the side walks reflect the light that streamed from the shop windows—lighting up the soft slush and the muddy feet of the passers-by.

I was going nowhere in particular; was simply having a short walk after dinner. I had passed the Credit Lyonnais, the Rue Vivienne, and several other streets. I suddenly descried a large beer hall which was more than half full. I walked inside, with no object in view. I was not the least thirsty.

I glanced round to find a place that was not too crowded, and went and sat down by the side of a man who seemed to me to be old, and who was smoking a two-sous clay pipe, which was as black as coal. From six to eight glasses piled up on the table in front of him indicated the number of "bocks" he had already absorbed. At a glance I recognized a "regular," one of those frequenters of beer houses who come in the morning when the place opens, and do not leave till evening when it is about to close. He was dirty, bald on top of his head, with a fringe of iron-gray hair falling on the collar of his frock coat. His clothes, much too large for him, appeared to have been made for him at a time when he was corpulent. One could guess that he did not wear suspenders, for he could not take ten steps without having to stop to pull up his trousers. Did he wear a vest? The mere thought of his boots and of that which they covered filled me with horror. The frayed cuffs were perfectly black at the edges, as were his nails.

As soon as I had seated myself beside him, this individual said to me in a quiet tone of voice:

"How goes it?"

I turned sharply round and closely scanned his features, whereupon he continued:

"I see you do not recognize me."

"No, I do not."

"Des Barrets."

I was stupefied. It was Count Jean des Barrets, my old college chum.

I seized him by the hand, and was so dumbfounded that I could find nothing to say. At length I managed to stammer out:

"And you, how goes it with you?"

He responded placidly:

"I get along as I can."

"What are you doing now?" I asked.

"You see what I am doing," he answered quit resignedly.

I felt my face getting red. I insisted:

"But every day?"

"Every day it is the same thing," was his reply, accompanied with a thick puff of tobacco smoke.

He then tapped with a sou on the top of the marble table, to attract the attention of the waiter, and called out:

"Waiter, two 'bocks.'"

A voice in the distance repeated:

"Two bocks for the fourth table."

Another voice, more distant still, shouted out:

"Here they are!"

Immediately a man with a white apron appeared, carrying two "bocks," which he set down, foaming, on the table, spilling some of the yellow liquid on the sandy floor in his haste.

Des Barrets emptied his glass at a single draught and replaced it on the table, while he sucked in the foam that had been left on his mustache. He next asked:

"What is there new?"

I really had nothing new to tell him. I stammered:

"Nothing, old man. I am a business man."

In his monotonous tone of voice he said:

"Indeed, does it amuse you?"

"No, but what can I do? One must do something!"

"Why should one?"

"So as to have occupation."

"What's the use of an occupation? For my part, I do nothing at all, as you see, never anything. When one has not a sou I can understand why one should work. But when one has enough to live on, what's the use? What is the good of working? Do you work for yourself, or for others? If you work for yourself, you do it for your own amusement, which is all right; if you work for others, you are a fool."

Then, laying his pipe on the marble table, he called out anew:

"Waiter, a 'bock.'" And continued: "It makes me thirsty to keep calling so. I am not accustomed to that sort of thing. Yes, yes, I do nothing. I let things slide, and I am growing old. In dying I shall have nothing to regret. My only remembrance will be this beer hall. No wife, no children, no cares, no sorrows, nothing. That is best."

He then emptied the glass which had been brought him, passed his tongue over his lips, and resumed his pipe.

I looked at him in astonishment, and said:

"But you have not always been like that?"

"Pardon me; ever since I left college."

"That is not a proper life to lead, my dear fellow; it is simply horrible. Come, you must have something to do, you must love something, you must have friends."

"No, I get up at noon, I come here, I have my breakfast, I drink my beer, I remain until the evening, I have my dinner, I drink beer. Then about half-past one in the morning, I go home to bed, because the place closes up; that annoys me more than anything. In the last ten years I have passed fully six years on this bench, in my corner; and the other four in my bed, nowhere else. I sometimes chat with the regular customers."

"But when you came to Paris what did you do at first?"

"I paid my devoirs to the Cafe de Medicis."

"What next?"

"Next I crossed the water and came here."

"Why did you take that trouble?"

"What do you mean? One cannot remain all one's life in the Latin Quarter. The students make too much noise. Now I shall not move again. Waiter, a 'bock.'"

I began to think that he was making fun of me, and I continued:

"Come now, be frank. You have been the victim of some great sorrow; some disappointment in love, no doubt! It is easy to see that you are a man who has had some trouble. What age are you?"

"I am thirty, but I look forty-five, at least."

I looked him straight in the face. His wrinkled, ill-shaven face gave one the impression that he was an old man. On the top of his head a few long hairs waved over a skin of doubtful cleanliness. He had enormous eyelashes, a heavy mustache, and a thick beard. Suddenly I had a kind of vision, I know not why, of a basin filled with dirty water in which all that hair had been washed. I said to him:

"You certainly look older than your age. You surely must have experienced some great sorrow."

He replied:

"I tell you that I have not. I am old because I never go out into the air. Nothing makes a man deteriorate more than the life of a cafe."

I still could not believe him.

"You must surely also have been married? One could not get as bald-headed as you are without having been in love."

He shook his head, shaking dandruff down on his coat as he did so.

"No, I have always been virtuous."

And, raising his eyes toward the chandelier which heated our heads, he said:

"If I am bald, it is the fault of the gas. It destroys the hair. Waiter, a 'bock.' Are you not thirsty?"

"No, thank you. But you really interest me. Since when have you been so morbid? Your life is not normal, it is not natural. There is something beneath it all."

"Yes, and it dates from my infancy. I received a great shock when I was very young, and that turned my life into darkness which will last to the end."

"What was it?"

"You wish to know about it? Well, then, listen. You recall, of course, the castle in which I was brought up, for you used to spend five or six months there during vacation. You remember that large gray building, in the middle of a great park, and the long avenues of oaks which opened to the four points of the compass. You remember my father and mother, both of whom were ceremonious, solemn, and severe.

"I worshipped my mother; I was afraid of my father; but I respected both, accustomed always as I was to see every one bow before them. They were Monsieur le Comte and Madame la Comtesse to all the country round, and our neighbors, the Tannemares, the Ravelets, the Brennevilles, showed them the utmost consideration.

"I was then thirteen years old. I was happy, pleased with everything, as one is at that age, full of the joy of life.

"Well, toward the end of September, a few days before returning to college, as I was playing about in the shrubbery of the park, among the branches and leaves, as I was crossing a path, I saw my father and mother, who were walking along.

"I recall it as though it were yesterday. It was a very windy day. The whole line of trees swayed beneath the gusts of wind, groaning, and seeming to utter cries-those dull, deep cries that forests give out during a tempest.

"The falling leaves, turning yellow, flew away like birds, circling and falling, and then running along the path like swift animals.

"Evening came on. It was dark in the thickets. The motion of the wind and of the branches excited me, made me tear about as if I were crazy, and howl in imitation of the wolves.

"As soon as I perceived my parents, I crept furtively toward them, under the branches, in order to surprise them, as though I had been a veritable prowler. But I stopped in fear a few paces from them. My father, who was in a terrible passion, cried:

"'Your mother is a fool; moreover, it is not a question of your mother. It is you. I tell you that I need this money, and I want you to sign this.'

"My mother replied in a firm voice:

"'I will not sign it. It is Jean's fortune. I shall guard it for him and I will not allow you to squander it with strange women, as you have your own heritage.'

"Then my father, trembling with rage, wheeled round and, seizing his wife by the throat, began to slap her with all his might full in the face with his disengaged hand.

"My mother's hat fell off, her hair became loosened and fell over her shoulders; she tried to parry the blows, but she could not do so. And my father, like a madman, kept on striking her. My mother rolled over on the ground, covering her face with her hands. Then he turned her over on her back in order to slap her still more, pulling away her hands, which were covering her face.

"As for me, my friend, it seemed as though the world was coming to an end, that the eternal laws had changed. I experienced the overwhelming dread that one has in presence of things supernatural, in presence of irreparable disasters. My childish mind was bewildered, distracted. I began to cry with all my might, without knowing why; a prey to a fearful dread, sorrow, and astonishment. My father heard me, turned round, and, on seeing me, started toward me. I believe that he wanted to kill me, and I fled like a hunted animal, running straight ahead into the thicket.

"I ran perhaps for an hour, perhaps for two. I know not. Darkness set in. I sank on the grass, exhausted, and lay there dismayed, frantic with fear, and devoured by a sorrow capable of breaking forever the heart of a poor child. I was cold, hungry, perhaps. At length day broke. I was afraid to get up, to walk, to return home, to run farther, fearing to encounter my father, whom I did not wish to see again.

"I should probably have died of misery and of hunger at the foot of a tree if the park guard had not discovered me and led me home by force.

"I found my parents looking as usual. My mother alone spoke to me "'How you frightened me, you naughty boy. I lay awake the whole night.'

"I did not answer, but began to weep. My father did not utter a single word.

"Eight days later I returned to school.

"Well, my friend, it was all over with me. I had witnessed the other side of things, the bad side. I have not been able to perceive the good side since that day. What has taken place in my mind, what strange phenomenon has warped my ideas, I do not know. But I no longer had a taste for anything, a wish for anything, a love for anybody, a desire for anything whatever, any ambition, or any hope. And I always see my poor mother on the ground, in the park, my father beating her. My mother died some years later; my, father still lives. I have not seen him since. Waiter, a 'bock.'"

A waiter brought him his "bock," which he swallowed at a gulp. But, in taking up his pipe again, trembling as he was, he broke it. "Confound it!" he said, with a gesture of annoyance. "That is a real sorrow. It will take me a month to color another!"

And he called out across the vast hall, now reeking with smoke and full of men drinking, his everlasting: "Garcon, un 'bock'—and a new pipe."

AFTER

"My darlings," said the comtesse, "you might go to bed."

The three children, two girls and a boy, rose and kissed their grandmother. Then they said goodnight to M. le Cure, who had dined at the chateau, as was his custom every Thursday.

The Abbe Mauduit lifted two of the children on his knees, passing his long arms clad in black round their necks, and kissing them tenderly on the forehead as he drew their heads toward him as a father might.

Then he set them down on the ground, and the little beings went off, the boy ahead, and the girls following.

"You are fond of children, M. le Cure," said the comtesse.

"Very fond, madame."

The old woman raised her bright eyes toward the priest.

"And—has your solitude never weighed too heavily on you?"

"Yes, sometimes."

He became silent, hesitated, and then added: "But I was never made for ordinary life."

"What do you know about it?"

"Oh! I know very well. I was made to be a priest; I followed my vocation."

The comtesse kept staring at him:

"Come now, M. le Cure, tell me this—tell me how it was you resolved to renounce forever all that makes the rest of us love life—all that consoles and sustains us? What is it that drove you, impelled you, to separate yourself from the great natural path of marriage and the family? You are neither an enthusiast nor a fanatic, neither a gloomy person nor a sad person. Was it some incident, some sorrow, that led you to take life vows?"

The Abbe Mauduit rose and approached the fire, then, holding toward the flame his big shoes, such as country priests generally wear, he seemed still hesitating as to what reply he should make.

He was a tall old man with white hair, and for the last twenty years had been pastor of the parish of Saint-Antoine-du-Rocher. The peasants said of him: "There's a good man for you!" And indeed he was a good man, benevolent, friendly to all, gentle, and, to crown all, generous. Like Saint Martin, he would have cut his cloak in two. He laughed readily, and wept also, on slight provocation, just like a woman—which prejudiced him more or less in the hard minds of the country folk.

The old Comtesse de Saville, living in retirement in her chateau of Rocher, in order to bring up her grandchildren, after the successive deaths of her son and her daughter-in-law, was very much attached to her cure, and used to say of him: "What a heart he has!"

He came every Thursday to spend the evening with the comtesse, and they were close friends, with the frank and honest friendship of old people.

She persisted:

"Look here, M. le Cure! it is your turn now to make a confession!"

He repeated: "I was not made for ordinary life. I saw it fortunately in time, and I have had many proofs since that I made no mistake on the point:

"My parents, who were mercers in Verdiers, and were quite well to do, had great ambitions for me. They sent me to a boarding school while I was very young. No one knows what a boy may suffer at school through the mere fact of separation, of isolation. This monotonous life without affection is good for some, and detestable for others. Young people are often more sensitive than one supposes, and by shutting them up thus too soon, far from those they love, we may develop to an exaggerated extent a sensitiveness which is overwrought and may become sickly and dangerous.

"I scarcely ever played; I had no companions; I passed my hours in homesickness; I spent the whole night weeping in my bed. I sought to bring before my mind recollections of home, trifling memories of little things, little events. I thought incessantly of all I had left behind there. I became almost imperceptibly an over-sensitive youth to whom the slightest annoyances were terrible griefs.

"In this way I remained taciturn, self-absorbed, without expansion, without confidants. This mental excitement was going on secretly and surely. The nerves of children are quickly affected, and one should see to it that they live a tranquil life until they are almost fully developed. But who ever reflects that, for certain boys, an unjust imposition may be as great a pang as the death of a friend in later years? Who can explain why certain young temperaments are liable to terrible emotions for the slightest cause, and may eventually become morbid and incurable?

"This was my case. This faculty of regret developed in me to such an extent that my existence became a martyrdom.

"I did not speak about it; I said nothing about it; but gradually I became so sensitive that my soul resembled an open wound. Everything that affected me gave me painful twitchings, frightful shocks, and consequently impaired my health. Happy are the men whom nature has buttressed with indifference and armed with stoicism.

"I reached my sixteenth year. An excessive timidity had arisen from this abnormal sensitiveness. Feeling myself unprotected from all the attacks of chance or fate, I feared every contact, every approach, every current. I lived as though I were threatened by an unknown and always expected misfortune. I did not venture either to speak or do anything in public. I had, indeed, the feeling that life, is a battle, a dreadful conflict in which one receives terrible blows, grievous, mortal wounds. In place of cherishing, like all men, a cheerful anticipation of the morrow, I had only a confused fear of it, and felt in my own mind a desire to conceal myself to avoid that combat in which I would be vanquished and slain.

"As soon as my studies were finished, they gave me six months' time to choose a career. A very simple occurrence showed me clearly, all of a sudden, the diseased condition of my mind, made me understand the danger, and determined me to flee from it.

"Verdiers is a little town surrounded with plains and woods. In the central street stands my parents' house. I now passed my days far from this dwelling which I had so much regretted, so much desired. Dreams had reawakened in me, and I walked alone in the fields in order to let them escape and fly away. My father and mother, quite occupied with business, and anxious about my future, talked to me only about their profits or about my possible plans. They were fond of me after the manner of hardheaded, practical people; they had more reason than heart in their affection for me. I lived imprisoned in my thoughts, and vibrating with my eternal sensitiveness.

"Now, one evening, after a long walk, as I was making my way home with great strides so as not to be late, I saw a dog trotting toward me. He was a species of red spaniel, very lean, with long curly ears.

"When he was ten paces away from me he stopped. I did the same. Then he began wagging his tail, and came over to me with short steps and nervous movements of his whole body, bending down on his paws as if appealing to me, and softly shaking his head. I spoke to him. He then began to crawl along in such a sad, humble, suppliant manner that I felt the tears coming into my eyes. I approached him; he ran away, then he came back again; and I bent down on one knee trying to coax him to approach me, with soft words. At last, he was within reach of my hands, and I gently and very carefully stroked him.

"He gained courage, gradually rose and, placing his paws on my shoulders, began to lick my face. He followed me to the house.

"This was really the first being I had passionately loved, because he returned my affection. My attachment to this animal was certainly exaggerated and ridiculous. It seemed to me in a confused sort of way that we were two brothers, lost on this earth, and therefore isolated and without defense, one as well as the other. He never again quitted my side. He slept at the foot of my bed, ate at the table in spite of the objections of my parents, and followed me in my solitary walks.

"I often stopped at the side of a ditch, and sat down in the grass. Sam immediately rushed up, lay down at my feet, and lifted up my hand with his muzzle that I might caress him.

"One day toward the end of June, as we were on the road from Saint-Pierre de Chavrol, I saw the diligence from Pavereau coming along. Its four horses were going at a gallop, with its yellow body, and its imperial with the black leather hood. The coachman cracked his whip; a cloud of dust rose up under the wheels of the heavy vehicle, then floated behind, just as a cloud would do.

"Suddenly, as the vehicle came close to me, Sam, perhaps frightened by the noise and wishing to join me, jumped in front of it. A horse's hoof knocked him down. I saw him roll over, turn round, fall back again beneath the horses' feet, then the coach gave two jolts, and behind it I saw something quivering in the dust on the road. He was nearly cut in two; all his intestines were hanging out and blood was spurting from the wound. He tried to get up, to walk, but he could only move his two front paws, and scratch the ground with them, as if to make a hole. The two others were already dead. And he howled dreadfully, mad with pain.

"He died in a few minutes. I cannot describe how much I felt and suffered. I was confined to my room for a month.

"One night, my father, enraged at seeing me so affected by such a trifling occurrence, exclaimed:

"'How will it be when you have real griefs—if you lose your wife or children?'

"His words haunted me and I began to see my condition clearly. I understood why all the small miseries of each day assumed in my eyes the importance of a catastrophe; I saw that I was organized in such a way that I suffered dreadfully from everything, that every painful impression was multiplied by my diseased sensibility, and an atrocious fear of life took possession of me. I was without passions, without ambitions; I resolved to sacrifice possible joys in order to avoid sure sorrows. Existence is short, but I made up my mind to spend it in the service of others, in relieving their troubles and enjoying their happiness. Having no direct experience of either one or the other, I should only experience a milder form of emotion.

"And if you only knew how, in spite of this, misery tortures me, ravages me! But what would formerly have been an intolerable affliction has become commiseration, pity.

"These sorrows which cross my path at every moment, I could not endure if they affected me directly. I could not have seen one of my children die without dying myself. And I have, in spite of everything, preserved such a mysterious, overwhelming fear of events that the sight of the postman entering my house makes a shiver pass every day through my veins, and yet I have nothing to be afraid of now."

The Abbe Mauduit ceased speaking. He stared into the fire in the huge grate, as if he saw there mysterious things, all the unknown of the existence he might have passed had he been more fearless in the face of suffering.

He added, then, in a subdued tone:

"I was right. I was not made for this world."

The comtesse said nothing at first; but at length, after a long silence, she remarked:

"For my part, if I had not my grandchildren, I believe I would not have the courage to live."

And the cure rose up without saying another word.

As the servants were asleep in the kitchen, she accompanied him herself to the door, which looked out on the garden, and she saw his tall shadow, lit up by the reflection of the lamp, disappearing through the gloom of night.

Then she came back and sat down before the fire, and pondered over many things we never think of when we are young.

FORGIVENESS

She had been brought up in one of those families who live entirely to themselves, apart from all the rest of the world. Such families know nothing of political events, although they are discussed at table; for changes in the Government take place at such a distance from them that they are spoken of as one speaks of a historical event, such as the death of Louis XVI or the landing of Napoleon.

Customs are modified in course of time, fashions succeed one another, but such variations are taken no account of in the placid family circle where traditional usages prevail year after year. And if some scandalous episode or other occurs in the neighborhood, the disreputable story dies a natural death when it reaches the threshold of the house. The father and mother may, perhaps, exchange a few words on the subject when alone together some evening, but they speak in hushed tones—for even walls have ears. The father says, with bated breath:

"You've heard of that terrible affair in the Rivoil family?"

And the mother answers:

"Who would have dreamed of such a thing? It's dreadful."

The children suspected nothing, and arrive in their turn at years of discretion with eyes and mind blindfolded, ignorant of the real side of life, not knowing that people do not think as they speak, and do not speak as they act; or aware that they should live at war, or at all events, in a state of armed peace, with the rest of mankind; not suspecting the fact that the simple are always deceived, the sincere made sport of, the good maltreated.

Some go on till the day of their death in this blind probity and loyalty and honor, so pure-minded that nothing can open their eyes.

Others, undeceived, but without fully understanding, make mistakes, are dismayed, and become desperate, believing themselves the playthings of a cruel fate, the wretched victims of adverse circumstances, and exceptionally wicked men.

The Savignols married their daughter Bertha at the age of eighteen. She wedded a young Parisian, George Baron by name, who had dealings on the Stock Exchange. He was handsome, well-mannered, and apparently all that could be desired. But in the depths of his heart he somewhat despised his old-fashioned parents-in-law, whom he spoke of among his intimates as "my dear old fossils."

He belonged to a good family, and the girl was rich. They settled down in Paris.

She became one of those provincial Parisians whose name is legion. She remained in complete ignorance of the great city, of its social side, its pleasures and its customs—just as she remained ignorant also of life, its perfidy and its mysteries.

Devoted to her house, she knew scarcely anything beyond her own street; and when she ventured into another part of Paris it seemed to her that she had accomplished a long and arduous journey into some unknown, unexplored city. She would then say to her husband in the evening:

"I have been through the boulevards to-day."

Two or three times a year her husband took her to the theatre. These were events the remembrance of which never grew dim; they provided subjects of conversation for long afterward.

Sometimes three months afterward she would suddenly burst into laughter, and exclaim:

"Do you remember that actor dressed up as a general, who crowed like a cock?"

Her friends were limited to two families related to her own. She spoke of them as "the Martinets" and "the Michelins."

Her husband lived as he pleased, coming home when it suited him —sometimes not until dawn— alleging business, but not putting himself out overmuch to account for his movements, well aware that no suspicion would ever enter his wife's guileless soul.

But one morning she received an anonymous letter.

She was thunderstruck—too simple-minded to understand the infamy of unsigned information and to despise the letter, the writer of which declared himself inspired by interest in her happiness, hatred of evil, and love of truth.

This missive told her that her husband had had for two years past, a sweetheart, a young widow named Madame Rosset, with whom he spent all his evenings.

Bertha knew neither how to dissemble her grief nor how to spy on her husband. When he came in for lunch she threw the letter down before him, burst into tears, and fled to her room.

He had time to take in the situation and to prepare his reply. He knocked at his wife's door. She opened it at once, but dared not look at him. He smiled, sat down, drew her to his knee, and in a tone of light raillery began:

"My dear child, as a matter of fact, I have a friend named Madame Rosset, whom I have known for the last ten years, and of whom I have a very high opinion. I may add that I know scores of other people whose names I have never mentioned to you, seeing that you do not care for society, or fresh acquaintances, or functions of any sort. But, to make short work of such vile accusations as this, I want you to put on your things after lunch, and we'll go together and call on this lady, who will very soon become a friend of yours, too, I am quite sure."

She embraced her husband warmly, and, moved by that feminine spirit of curiosity which will not be lulled once it is aroused, consented to go and see this unknown widow, of whom she was, in spite of everything, just the least bit jealous. She felt instinctively that to know a danger is to be already armed against it.

She entered a small, tastefully furnished flat on the fourth floor of an attractive house. After waiting five minutes in a drawing-room rendered somewhat dark by its many curtains and hangings, a door opened, and a very dark, short, rather plump young woman appeared, surprised and smiling.

George introduced them:

"My wife—Madame Julie Rosset."

The young widow uttered a half-suppressed cry of astonishment and joy, and ran forward with hands outstretched. She had not hoped, she said, to have this pleasure, knowing that Madame Baron never saw any one, but she was delighted to make her acquaintance. She was so fond of George (she said "George" in a familiar, sisterly sort of way) that, she had been most anxious to know his young wife and to make friends with her, too.

By the end of a month the two new friends were inseparable. They saw each other every day, sometimes twice a day, and dined together every evening, sometimes at one house, sometimes at the other. George no longer deserted his home, no longer talked of pressing business. He adored his own fireside, he said.

When, after a time, a flat in the house where Madame Rosset lived became vacant Madame Baron hastened to take it, in order to be near her friend and spend even more time with her than hitherto.

And for two whole years their friendship was without a cloud, a friendship of heart and mind—absolute, tender, devoted. Bertha could hardly speak without bringing in Julie's name. To her Madame Rosset represented perfection.

She was utterly happy, calm and contented.

But Madame Rosset fell ill. Bertha hardly left her side. She spent her nights with her, distracted with grief; even her husband seemed inconsolable.

One morning the doctor, after leaving the invalid's bedside, took George and his wife aside, and told them that he considered Julie's condition very grave.

As soon as he had gone the grief-stricken husband and wife sat down opposite each other and gave way to tears. That night they both sat up with the patient. Bertha tenderly kissed her friend from time to time, while George stood at the foot of the bed, his eyes gazing steadfastly on the invalid's face.

The next day she was worse.

But toward evening she declared she felt better, and insisted that her friends should go back to their own apartment to dinner.

They were sitting sadly in the dining-room, scarcely even attempting to eat, when the maid gave George a note. He opened it, turned pale as death, and, rising from the table, said to his wife in a constrained voice:

"Wait for me. I must leave you a moment. I shall be back in ten minutes. Don't go away on any account."

And he hurried to his room to get his hat.

Bertha waited for him, a prey to fresh anxiety. But, docile in everything, she would not go back to her friend till he returned.

At length, as he did not reappear, it occurred to her to visit his room and see if he had taken his gloves. This would show whether or not he had had a call to make.

She saw them at the first glance. Beside them lay a crumpled paper, evidently thrown down in haste.

She recognized it at once as the note George had received.

And a burning temptation, the first that had ever assailed her urged her to read it and discover the cause of her husband's abrupt departure. Her rebellious conscience protester' but a devouring and fearful curiosity prevailed. She seized the paper, smoothed it out, recognized the tremulous, penciled writing as Julie's, and read:

"Come alone and kiss me, my poor dear. I am dying."

At first she did not understand, the idea of Julie's death being her uppermost thought. But all at once the true meaning of what she read burst in a flash upon her; this penciled note threw a lurid light upon her whole existence, revealed the whole infamous truth, all the treachery and perfidy of which she had been the victim. She understood the long years of deceit, the way in which she had been made their puppet. She saw them again, sitting side by side in the evening, reading by lamplight out of the same book, glancing at each other at the end of each page.

And her poor, indignant, suffering, bleeding heart was cast into the depths of a despair which knew no bounds.

Footsteps drew near; she fled, and shut herself in her own room.

Presently her husband called her:

"Come quickly! Madame Rosset is dying."

Bertha appeared at her door, and with trembling lips replied:

"Go back to her alone; she does not need me."

He looked at her stupidly, dazed with grief, and repeated:

"Come at once! She's dying, I tell you!"

Bertha answered:

"You would rather it were I."

Then at last he understood, and returned alone to the dying woman's bedside.

He mourned her openly, shamelessly, indifferent to the sorrow of the wife who no longer spoke to him, no longer looked at him; who passed her life in solitude, hedged round with disgust, with indignant anger, and praying night and day to God.

They still lived in the same house, however, and sat opposite each other at table, in silence and despair.

Gradually his sorrow grew less acute; but she did not forgive him.

And so their life went on, hard and bitter for them both.

For a whole year they remained as complete strangers to each other as if they had never met. Bertha nearly lost her reason.

At last one morning she went out very early, and returned about eight o'clock bearing in her hands an enormous bouquet of white roses. And she sent word to her husband that she wanted to speak to him. He came-anxious and uneasy.

"We are going out together," she said. "Please carry these flowers; they are too heavy for me."

A carriage took them to the gate of the cemetery, where they alighted. Then, her eyes filling with tears, she said to George:

"Take me to her grave."

He trembled, and could not understand her motive; but he led the way, still carrying the flowers. At last he stopped before a white marble slab, to which he pointed without a word.

She took the bouquet from him, and, kneeling down, placed it on the grave. Then she offered up a silent, heartfelt prayer.

Behind her stood her husband, overcome by recollections of the past.

She rose, and held out her hands to him.

"If you wish it, we will be friends," she said.

IN THE SPRING

With the first day of spring, when the awakening earth puts on its garment of green, and the warm, fragrant air fans our faces and fills our lungs and appears even to penetrate to our hearts, we experience a vague, undefined longing for freedom, for happiness, a desire to run, to wander aimlessly, to breathe in the spring. The previous winter having been unusually severe, this spring feeling was like a form of intoxication in May, as if there were an overabundant supply of sap.

One morning on waking I saw from my window the blue sky glowing in the sun above the neighboring houses. The canaries hanging in the windows were singing loudly, and so were the servants on every floor; a cheerful noise rose up from the streets, and I went out, my spirits as bright as the day, to go—I did not exactly know where. Everybody I met seemed to be smiling; an air of happiness appeared to pervade everything in the warm light of returning spring. One might almost have said that a breeze of love was blowing through the city, and the sight of the young women whom I saw in the streets in their morning toilets, in the depths of whose eyes there lurked a hidden tenderness, and who walked with languid grace, filled my heart with agitation.

Without knowing how or why, I found myself on the banks of the Seine. Steamboats were starting for Suresnes, and suddenly I was seized by an unconquerable desire to take a walk through the woods. The deck of the Mouche was covered with passengers, for the sun in early spring draws one out of the house, in spite of themselves, and everybody moves about, goes and comes and talks to his neighbor.

I had a girl neighbor; a little work-girl, no doubt, who possessed the true Parisian charm: a little head, with light curly hair, which looked like a shimmer of light as it danced in the wind, came down to her ears, and descended to the nape of her neck, where it became such fine, light-colored clown that one could scarcely see it, but felt an irresistible desire to shower kisses on it.

Under my persistent gaze, she turned her head toward me, and then immediately looked down, while a slight crease at the side of her mouth, that was ready to break out into a smile, also showed a fine, silky, pale down which the sun was gilding a little.

The calm river grew wider; the atmosphere was warm and perfectly still, but a murmur of life seemed to fill all space.

My neighbor raised her eyes again, and this time, as I was still looking at her, she smiled decidedly. She was charming, and in her passing glance I saw a thousand things, which I had hitherto been ignorant of, for I perceived unknown depths, all the charm of tenderness, all the poetry which we dream of, all the happiness which we are continually in search of. I felt an insane longing to open my arms and to carry her off somewhere, so as to whisper the sweet music of words of love into her ears.

I was just about to address her when somebody touched me on the shoulder, and as I turned round in some surprise, I saw an ordinary-looking man, who was neither young nor old, and who gazed at me sadly.

"I should like to speak to you," he said.

I made a grimace, which he no doubt saw, for he added:

"It is a matter of importance."

I got up, therefore, and followed him to the other end of the boat and then he said:

"Monsieur, when winter comes, with its cold, wet and snowy weather, your doctor says to you constantly: 'Keep your feet warm, guard against chills, colds, bronchitis, rheumatism and pleurisy.'

"Then you are very careful, you wear flannel, a heavy greatcoat and thick shoes, but all this does not prevent you from passing two months in bed. But when spring returns, with its leaves and flowers, its warm, soft breezes and its smell of the fields, all of which causes you vague disquiet and causeless emotion, nobody says to you:

"'Monsieur, beware of love! It is lying in ambush everywhere; it is watching for you at every corner; all its snares are laid, all its weapons are sharpened, all its guiles are prepared! Beware of love! Beware of love! It is more dangerous than brandy, bronchitis or pleurisy! It never forgives and makes everybody commit irreparable follies.'

"Yes, monsieur, I say that the French Government ought to put large public notices on the walls, with these words: 'Return of spring. French citizens, beware of love!' just as they put: 'Beware of paint:

"However, as the government will not do this, I must supply its place, and I say to you: 'Beware of love!' for it is just going to seize you, and it is my duty to inform you of it, just as in Russia they inform any one that his nose is frozen."

I was much astonished at this individual, and assuming a dignified manner, I said:

"Really, monsieur, you appear to me to be interfering in a matter which is no concern of yours."

He made an abrupt movement and replied:

"Ah! monsieur, monsieur! If I see that a man is in danger of being drowned at a dangerous spot, ought I to let him perish? So just listen to my story and you will see why I ventured to speak to you like this.

"It was about this time last year that it occurred. But, first of all, I must tell you that I am a clerk in the Admiralty, where our chiefs, the commissioners, take their gold lace as quill-driving officials seriously, and treat us like forecastle men on board a ship. Well, from my office I could see a small bit of blue sky and the swallows, and I felt inclined to dance among my portfolios.

"My yearning for freedom grew so intense that, in spite of my repugnance, I went to see my chief, a short, bad-tempered man, who was always in a rage. When I told him that I was not well, he looked at me and said: 'I do not believe it, monsieur, but be off with you! Do you think that any office can go on with clerks like you?' I started at once and went down the Seine. It was a day like this, and I took the Mouche, to go as far as Saint Cloud. Ah! what a good thing it would have been if my chief had refused me permission to leave the office that day!

"I seemed to myself to expand in the sun. I loved everything—the steamer, the river, the trees, the houses and my fellow-passengers. I felt inclined to kiss something, no matter what; it was love, laying its snare. Presently, at the Trocadero, a girl, with a small parcel in her hand, came on board and sat down opposite me. She was decidedly pretty, but it is surprising, monsieur, how much prettier women seem to us when the day is fine at the beginning of the spring. Then they have an intoxicating charm, something quite peculiar about them. It is just like drinking wine after cheese.

"I looked at her and she also looked at me, but only occasionally, as that girl did at you, just now; but at last, by dint of looking at each other constantly, it seemed to me that we knew each other well enough to enter into conversation, and I spoke to her and she replied. She was decidedly pretty and nice and she intoxicated me, monsieur!

"She got out at Saint-Cloud, and I followed her. She went and delivered her parcel, and when she returned the boat had just started. I walked by her side, and the warmth of the 'air made us both sigh. 'It would be very nice in the woods,' I said. 'Indeed, it would!' she replied. 'Shall we go there for a walk, mademoiselie?'

"She gave me a quick upward look, as if to see exactly what I was like, and then, after a little hesitation, she accepted my proposal, and soon we were there, walking side by side. Under the foliage, which was still rather scanty, the tall, thick, bright green grass was inundated by the sun, and the air was full of insects that were also making love to one another, and birds were singing in all directions. My companion began to jump and to run, intoxicated by the air and the smell of the country, and I ran and jumped, following her example. How silly we are at times, monsieur!

"Then she sang unrestrainedly a thousand things, opera airs and the song of Musette! The song of Musette! How poetical it seemed to me, then! I almost cried over it. Ah! Those silly songs make us lose our heads; and, believe me, never marry a woman who sings in the country, especially if she sings the song of Musette!

"She soon grew tired, and sat down on a grassy slope, and I sat at her feet and took her hands, her little hands, that were so marked with the needle, and that filled me with emotion. I said to myself:

"'These are the sacred marks of toil.' Oh! monsieur, do you know what those sacred marks of toil mean? They mean all the gossip of the workroom, the whispered scandal, the mind soiled by all the filth that is talked; they mean lost chastity, foolish chatter, all the wretchedness of their everyday life, all the narrowness of ideas which belongs to women of the lower orders, combined to their fullest extent in the girl whose fingers bear the sacred marks of toil.

"Then we looked into each other's eyes for a long while. Oh! what power a woman's eye has! How it agitates us, how it invades our very being, takes possession of us, and dominates us! How profound it seems, how full of infinite promises! People call that looking into each other's souls! Oh! monsieur, what humbug! If we could see into each other's souls, we should be more careful of what we did. However, I was captivated and was crazy about her and tried to take her into my arms, but she said: 'Paws off!'. Then I knelt down and opened my heart to her and poured out all the affection that was suffocating me. She seemed surprised at my change of manner and gave me a sidelong glance, as if to say, 'Ah! so that is the way women make a fool of you, old fellow! Very well, we will see.'

"In love, monsieur, we are always novices, and women artful dealers.

"No doubt I could have had her, and I saw my own stupidity later, but what I wanted was not a woman's person, it was love, it was the ideal. I was sentimental, when I ought to have been using my time to a better purpose.

"As soon as she had had enough of my declarations of affection, she got up, and we returned to Saint-Cloud, and I did not leave her until we got to Paris; but she had looked so sad as we were returning, that at last I asked her what was the matter. 'I am thinking,' she replied, 'that this has been one of those days of which we have but few in life.' My heart beat so that it felt as if it would break my ribs.

"I saw her on the following Sunday, and the next Sunday, and every Sunday. I took her to Bougival, Saint-Germain, Maisons-Lafitte, Poissy; to every suburban resort of lovers.

"The little jade, in turn, pretended to love me, until, at last, I altogether lost my head, and three months later I married her.

"What can you expect, monsieur, when a man is a clerk, living alone, without any relations, or any one to advise him? One says to one's self: 'How sweet life would be with a wife!'

"And so one gets married and she calls you names from morning till night, understands nothing, knows nothing, chatters continually, sings the song of Musette at the, top of her voice (oh! that song of Musette, how tired one gets of it!); quarrels with the charcoal dealer, tells the janitor all her domestic details, confides all the secrets of her bedroom to the neighbor's servant, discusses her husband with the tradespeople and has her head so stuffed with stupid stories, with idiotic superstitions, with extraordinary ideas and monstrous prejudices, that I—for what I have said applies more particularly to myself—shed tears of discouragement every time I talk to her."

He stopped, as he was rather out of breath and very much moved, and I looked at him, for I felt pity for this poor, artless devil, and I was just going to give him some sort of answer, when the boat stopped. We were at Saint-Cloud.

The little woman who had so taken my fancy rose from her seat in order to land. She passed close to me, and gave me a sidelong glance and a furtive smile, one of those smiles that drive you wild. Then she jumped on the landing-stage. I sprang forward to follow her, but my neighbor laid hold of my arm. I shook myself loose, however, whereupon he seized the skirt of my coat and pulled me back, exclaiming: "You shall not go! you shall not go!" in such a loud voice that everybody turned round and laughed, and I remained standing motionless and furious, but without venturing to face scandal and ridicule, and the steamboat started.

The little woman on the landing-stage looked at me as I went off with an air of disappointment, while my persecutor rubbed his hands and whispered to me:

"You must acknowledge that I have done you a great service."

A QUEER NIGHT IN PARIS

Mattre Saval, notary at Vernon, was passionately fond of music. Although still young he was already bald; he was always carefully shaven, was somewhat corpulent as was suitable, and wore a gold pince-nez instead of spectacles. He was active, gallant and cheerful and was considered quite an artist in Vernon. He played the piano and the violin, and gave musicals where the new operas were interpreted.

He had even what is called a bit of a voice; nothing but a bit, very little bit of a voice; but he managed it with so much taste that cries of "Bravo!" "Exquisite!" "Surprising!" "Adorable!" issued from every throat as soon as he had murmured the last note.

He subscribed to a music publishing house in Paris, and they sent him the latest music, and from time to time he sent invitations after this fashion to the elite of the town:

"You are invited to be present on Monday evening at the house of M. Saval, notary, Vernon, at the first rendering of 'Sais.'"

A few officers, gifted with good voices, formed the chorus. Two or three lady amateurs also sang. The notary filled the part of leader of the orchestra with so much correctness that the bandmaster of the 190th regiment of the line said of him, one day, at the Cafe de l'Europe.

"Oh! M. Saval is a master. It is a great pity that he did not adopt the career of an artist."

When his name was mentioned in a drawing-room, there was always somebody found to declare: "He is not an amateur; he is an artist, a genuine artist."

And two or three persons repeated, in a tone of profound conviction:

"Oh! yes, a genuine artist," laying particular stress on the word "genuine."

Every time that a new work was interpreted at a big Parisian theatre M. Saval paid a visit to the capital.

Now, last year, according to his custom, he went to hear Henri VIII. He then took the express which arrives in Paris at 4:30 P.M., intending to return by the 12:35 A.M. train, so as not to have to sleep at a hotel. He had put on evening dress, a black coat and white tie, which he concealed under his overcoat with the collar turned up.

As soon as he set foot on the Rue d'Amsterdam, he felt himself in quite jovial mood. He said to himself:

"Decidedly, the air of Paris does not resemble any other air. It has in it something indescribably stimulating, exciting, intoxicating, which fills you with a strange longing to dance about and to do many other things. As soon as I arrive here, it seems to me, all of a sudden, that I have taken a bottle of champagne. What a life one can lead in this city in the midst of artists! Happy are the elect, the great men who make themselves a reputation in such a city! What an existence is theirs!"

And he made plans; he would have liked to know some of these celebrated men, to talk about them in Vernon, and to spend an evening with them from time to time in Paris.

But suddenly an idea struck him. He had heard allusions to little cafes in the outer boulevards at which well-known painters, men of letters, and even musicians gathered, and he proceeded to go up to Montmartre at a slow pace.

He had two hours before him. He wanted to look about him. He passed in front of taverns frequented by belated bohemians, gazing at the different faces, seeking to discover the artists. Finally, he came to the sign of "The Dead Rat," and, allured by the name, he entered.

Five or six women, with their elbows resting on the marble tables, were talking in low tones about their love affairs, the quarrels of Lucie and Hortense, and the scoundrelism of Octave. They were no longer young, were too fat or too thin, tired out, used up. You could see that they were almost bald; and they drank beer like men.

M. Saval sat down at some distance from them and waited, for the hour for taking absinthe was at hand.

A tall young man soon came in and took a seat beside him. The landlady called him M. "Romantin." The notary quivered. Was this the Romantin who had taken a medal at the last Salon?

The young man made a sign to the waiter.

"You will bring up my dinner at once, and then carry to my new studio, 15 Boulevard de Clichy, thirty bottles of beer, and the ham I ordered this morning. We are going to have a housewarming."

M. Saval immediately ordered dinner. Then, he took off his overcoat, so that his dress suit and his white tie could be seen. His neighbor did not seem to notice him. He had taken up a newspaper, and was reading it. M. Saval glanced sideways at him, burning with the desire to speak to him.

Two young men entered, in red vests and with peaked beards, in the fashion of Henry III. They sat down opposite Romantin.

The first of the pair said:

"Is it for this evening?"

Romantin pressed his hand.

"I believe you, old chap, and everyone will be there. I have Bonnat, Guillemet, Gervex, Beraud, Hebert, Duez, Clairin, and Jean-Paul Laurens. It will be a stunning affair! And women, too! Wait till you see! Every actress without exception—of course I mean, you know, all those who have nothing to do this evening."

The landlord of the establishment came across.

"Do you often have this housewarming?"

The painter replied:

"I believe you, every three months, each quarter."

M. Saval could not restrain himself any longer, and in a hesitating voice said:

"I beg your pardon for intruding on you, monsieur, but I heard your name mentioned, and I would be very glad to know if you really are M. Romantin, whose work in the last Salon I have so much admired?"

The painter answered:

"I am the very person, monsieur."

The notary then paid the artist a very well-turned compliment, showing that he was a man of culture.

The painter, gratified, thanked him politely in reply.

Then they chattered. Romantin returned to the subject of his house-warming, going into details as to the magnificence of the forthcoming entertainment.

M. Saval questioned him as to all the men he was going to receive, adding:

"It would be an extraordinary piece of good fortune for a stranger to meet at one time so many celebrities assembled in the studio of an artist of your rank."

Romantin, vanquished, replied:

"If it would be agreeable to you, come."

M. Saval accepted the invitation with enthusiasm, reflecting:

"I shall have time enough to see Henri VIII."

Both of them had finished their meal. The notary insisted on paying the two bills, wishing to repay his neighbor's civilities. He also paid for the drinks of the young fellows in red velvet; then he left the establishment with the painter.

They stopped in front of a very long, low house, the first story having the appearance of an interminable conservatory. Six studios stood in a row with their fronts facing the boulevards.

Romantin was the first to enter, and, ascending the stairs, he opened a door, and lighted a match and then a candle.

They found themselves in an immense apartment, the furniture of which consisted of three chairs, two easels, and a few sketches standing on the ground along the walls. M. Saval remained standing at the door somewhat astonished.

The painter remarked:

"Here you are! we've got to the spot; but everything has yet to be done."

Then, examining the high, bare apartment, its ceiling disappearing in the darkness, he said:

"We might make a great deal out of this studio."

He walked round it, surveying it with the utmost attention, then went on:

"I know someone who might easily give a helping hand. Women are incomparable for hanging drapery. But I sent her to the country for to-day in order to get her off my hands this evening. It is not that she bores me, but she is too much lacking in the ways of good society. It would be embarrassing to my guests."

He reflected for a few seconds, and then added:

"She is a good girl, but not easy to deal with. If she knew that I was holding a reception, she would tear out my eyes."

M. Saval had not even moved; he did not understand.

The artist came over to him.

"Since I have invited you, you will assist ma about something."

The notary said emphatically:

"Make any use of me you please. I am at your disposal."

Romantin took off his jacket.

"Well, citizen, to work!' We are first going to clean up."

He went to the back of the easel, on which there was a canvas representing a cat, and seized a very worn-out broom.

"I say! Just brush up while I look after the lighting."

M. Saval took the broom, inspected it, and then began to sweep the floor very awkwardly, raising a whirlwind of dust.

Romantin, disgusted, stopped him: "Deuce take it! you don't know how to sweep the floor! Look at me!"

And he began to roll before him a heap of grayish sweepings, as if he had done nothing else all his life. Then, he gave bark the broom to the notary, who imitated him.

In five minutes, such a cloud of dust filled the studio that Rormantin asked:

"Where are you? I can't see you any longer."

M. Saval, who was coughing, came near to him. The painter said:

"How would you set about making a chandelier?"

The other, surprised, asked:

"What chandelier?"

"Why, a chandelier to light the room—a chandelier with wax-candles."

The notary did not understand.

He answered: "I don't know."

The painter began to jump about, cracking his fingers.

"Well, monseigneur, I have found out a way."

Then he went on more calmly:

"Have you got five francs about you?"

M. Saval replied:

"Why, yes."

The artist said: "Well! you'll go out and buy for me five francs' worth of wax-candles while I go and see the cooper."

And he pushed the notary in his evening coat into the street. At the end of five minutes, they had returned, one of them with the wax-candles and the other with the hoop of a cask. Then Romantin plunged his hand into a cupboard, and drew forth twenty empty bottles, which he fixed in the form of a crown around the hoop.

He then went downstairs to borrow a ladder from the janitress, after having explained that he had made interest with the old woman by painting the portrait of her cat, exhibited on the easel.

When he returned with the ladder, he said to M. Saval:

"Are you active?"

The other, without understanding, answered:

"Why, yes."

"Well, you just climb up there, and fasten this chandelier for me to the ring of the ceiling. Then, you put a wax-candle in each bottle, and light it. I tell you I have a genius for lighting up. But off with your coat, damn it! You are just like a Jeames."

The door was opened brusquely. A woman appeared, her eyes flashing, and remained standing on the threshold.

Romantin gazed at her with a look of terror.

She waited some seconds, crossing her arms over her breast, and then in a shrill, vibrating, exasperated voice said:

"Ha! you dirty scoundrel, is this the way you leave me?"

Romantin made no reply. She went on:

"Ha! you scoundrel! You did a nice thing in parking me off to the country. You'll soon see the way I'll settle your jollification. Yes, I'm going to receive your friends."

She grew warmer.

"I'm going to slap their faces with the bottles and the wax-candles——"

Romantin said in a soft tone:

"Mathilde——"

But she did not pay any attention to him; she went on:

"Wait a little, my fine fellow! wait a little!"

Romantin went over to her, and tried to take her by the hands.

"Mathilde——"

But she was now fairly under way; and on she went, emptying the vials of her wrath with strong words and reproaches. They flowed out of her mouth like, a stream sweeping a heap of filth along with it. The words pouring forth seemed struggling for exit. She stuttered, stammered, yelled, suddenly recovering her voice to cast forth an insult or a curse.

He seized her hands without her having noticed it. She did not seem to see anything, so taken up was she in scolding and relieving her feelings. And suddenly she began to weep. The tears flowed from her eyes, but this did not stop her complaints. But her words were uttered in a screaming falsetto voice with tears in it and interrupted by sobs. She commenced afresh twice or three times, till she stopped as if something were choking her, and at last she ceased with a regular flood of tears.

Then he clasped her in his arms and kissed her hair, affected himself.

"Mathilde, my little Mathilde, listen. You must be reasonable. You know, if I give a supper-party to my friends, it is to thank these gentlemen for the medal I got at the Salon. I cannot receive women. You ought to understand that. It is not the same with artists as with other people."

She stammered, in the midst of her tears:

"Why didn't you tell me this?"

He replied:

"It was in order not to annoy you, not to give you pain. Listen, I'm going to see you home. You will be very sensible, very nice; you will remain quietly waiting for me in bed, and I'll come back as soon as it's over."

She murmured:

"Yes, but you will not begin over again?"

"No, I swear to you!"

He turned towards M. Saval, who had at last hooked on the chandelier:

"My dear friend, I am coming back in five minutes. If anyone arrives in my absence, do the honors for me, will you not?"

And he carried off Mathilde, who kept drying her eyes with her handkerchief as she went along.

Left to himself, M. Saval succeeded in putting everything around him in order. Then he lighted the wax-candles, and waited.

He waited for a quarter of an hour, half an hour, an hour. Romantin did not return. Then, suddenly there was a dreadful noise on the stairs, a song shouted out in chorus by twenty mouths and a regular march like that of a Prussian regiment. The whole house was shaken by the steady tramp of feet. The door flew open, and a motley throng appeared—men and women in file, two and two holding each other by the arm and stamping their heels on the ground to mark time, advanced into the studio like a snake uncoiling itself. They howled:

"Come, and let us all be merry,

Pretty maids and soldiers gay!"

M. Saval, thunderstruck, remained standing in evening dress under the chandelier. The procession of revellers caught sight of him, and uttered a shout:

"A Jeames! A Jeames!"

And they began whirling round him, surrounding him with a circle of vociferations. Then they took each other by the hand and went dancing about madly.

He attempted to explain:

"Messieurs—messieurs—mesdames——"

But they did not listen to him. They whirled about, they jumped, they brawled.

At last, the dancing ceased. M. Saval said:

"Gentlemen——"

A tall young fellow, fair-haired and bearded to the nose, interrupted him:

"What's your name, my friend?"

The notary, quite scared, said:

"I am M. Saval."

A voice exclaimed:

"You mean Baptiste."

A woman said:

"Let the poor waiter alone! You'll end by making him get angry. He's paid to wait on us, and not to be laughed at by us."

Then, M. Saval noticed that each guest had brought his own provisions. One held a bottle of wine, and the other a pie. This one had a loaf of bread, and one a ham.

The tall, fair young fellow placed in his hands an enormous sausage, and gave orders:

"Here, go and arrange the sideboard in the corner over there. Put the bottles at the left and the provisions at the right."

Saval, getting quite distracted, exclaimed: "But, messieurs, I am a notary!"

There was a moment's silence and then a wild outburst of laughter. One suspicious gentleman asked:

"How came you to be here?"

He explained, telling about his project of going to the opera, his departure from Vernon, his arrival in Paris, and the way in which he had spent the evening.

They sat around him to listen to him; they greeted him with words of applause, and called him Scheherazade.

Romantin did not return. Other guests arrived. M. Saval was presented to them so that he might begin his story over again. He declined; they forced him to relate it. They seated and tied him on one of three chairs between two women who kept constantly filling his glass. He drank; he laughed; he talked; he sang, too. He tried to waltz with his chair, and fell on the ground.

From that moment, he forgot everything. It seemed to him, however, that they undressed him, put him to bed, and that he was nauseated.

When he awoke, it was broad daylight, and he lay stretched with his feet against a cupboard, in a strange bed.

An old woman with a broom in her hand was glaring angrily at him. At last, she said:

"Clear out, you blackguard! Clear out! What right has anyone to get drunk like this?"

He sat up in bed, feeling very ill at ease. He asked:

"Where am I?"

"Where are you, you dirty scamp? You are drunk. Take your rotten carcass out of here as quick as you can—and lose no time about it!"

He wanted to get up. He found that he was in no condition to do so. His clothes had disappeared. He blurted out:

"Madame, I——Then he remembered. What was he to do? He asked:

"Did Monsieur Romantin come back?"

The doorkeeper shouted:

"Will you take your dirty carcass out of this, so that he at any rate may not catch you here?"

M. Saval said, in a state of confusion:

"I haven't got my clothes; they have been taken away from me."

He had to wait, to explain his situation, give notice to his friends, and borrow some money to buy clothes. He did not leave Paris till evening. And when people talk about music to him in his beautiful drawing-room in Vernon, he declares with an air of authority that painting is a very inferior art.

VOLUME VI.

THAT COSTLY RIDE

The household lived frugally on the meager income derived from the husband's insignificant appointments. Two children had been born of the marriage, and the earlier condition of the strictest economy had become one of quiet, concealed, shamefaced misery, the poverty of a noble family—which in spite of misfortune never forgets its rank.

Hector de Gribelin had been educated in the provinces, under the paternal roof, by an aged priest. His people were not rich, but they managed to live and to keep up appearances.

At twenty years of age they tried to find him a position, and he entered the Ministry of Marine as a clerk at sixty pounds a year. He foundered on the rock of life like all those who have not been early prepared for its rude struggles, who look at life through a mist, who do not know how to protect themselves, whose special aptitudes and faculties have not been developed from childhood, whose early training has not developed the rough energy needed for the battle of life or furnished them with tool or weapon.

His first three years of office work were a martyrdom.

He had, however, renewed the acquaintance of a few friends of his family —elderly people, far behind the times, and poor like himself, who lived in aristocratic streets, the gloomy thoroughfares of the Faubourg Saint-Germain; and he had created a social circle for himself.

Strangers to modern life, humble yet proud, these needy aristocrats lived in the upper stories of sleepy, old-world houses. From top to bottom of their dwellings the tenants were titled, but money seemed just as scarce on the ground floor as in the attics.

Their eternal prejudices, absorption in their rank, anxiety lest they should lose caste, filled the minds and thoughts of these families once so brilliant, now ruined by the idleness of the men of the family. Hector de Gribelin met in this circle a young girl as well born and as poor as himself and married her.

They had two children in four years.

For four years more the husband and wife, harassed by poverty, knew no other distraction than the Sunday walk in the Champs-Elysees and a few evenings at the theatre (amounting in all to one or two in the course of the winter) which they owed to free passes presented by some comrade or other.

But in the spring of the following year some overtime work was entrusted to Hector de Gribelin by his chief, for which he received the large sum of three hundred francs.

The day he brought the money home he said to his wife:

"My dear Henrietta, we must indulge in some sort of festivity—say an outing for the children."

And after a long discussion it was decided that they should go and lunch one day in the country.

"Well," cried Hector, "once will not break us, so we'll hire a wagonette for you, the children and the maid. And I'll have a saddle horse; the exercise will do me good."

The whole week long they talked of nothing but the projected excursion.

Every evening, on his return from the office, Hector caught up his elder son, put him astride his leg, and, making him bounce up and down as hard as he could, said:

"That's how daddy will gallop next Sunday."

And the youngster amused himself all day long by bestriding chairs, dragging them round the room and shouting:

"This is daddy on horseback!"

The servant herself gazed at her master with awestruck eyes as she thought of him riding alongside the carriage, and at meal-times she listened with all her ears while he spoke of riding and recounted the exploits of his youth, when he lived at home with his father. Oh, he had learned in a good school, and once he felt his steed between his legs he feared nothing—nothing whatever!

Rubbing his hands, he repeated gaily to his wife:

"If only they would give me a restive animal I should be all the better pleased. You'll see how well I can ride; and if you like we'll come back by the Champs-Elysees just as all the people are returning from the Bois. As we shall make a good appearance, I shouldn't at all object to meeting some one from the ministry. That is all that is necessary to insure the respect of one's chiefs."

On the day appointed the carriage and the riding horse arrived at the same moment before the door. Hector went down immediately to examine his mount. He had had straps sewn to his trousers and flourished in his hand a whip he had bought the evening before.

He raised the horse's legs and felt them one after another, passed his hand over the animal's neck, flank and hocks, opened his mouth, examined his teeth, declared his age; and then, the whole household having collected round him, he delivered a discourse on the horse in general and the specimen before him in particular, pronouncing the latter excellent in every respect.

When the rest of the party had taken their seats in the carriage he examined the saddle-girth; then, putting his foot in the stirrup, he sprang to the saddle. The animal began to curvet and nearly threw his rider.

Hector, not altogether at his ease, tried to soothe him:

"Come, come, good horse, gently now!"

Then, when the horse had recovered his equanimity and the rider his nerve, the latter asked:

"Are you ready?"

The occupants of the carriage replied with one voice:

"Yes."

"Forward!" he commanded.

And the cavalcade set out.

All looks were centered on him. He trotted in the English style, rising unnecessarily high in the saddle; looking at times as if he were mounting into space. Sometimes he seemed on the point of falling forward on the horse's mane; his eyes were fixed, his face drawn, his cheeks pale.

His wife, holding one of the children on her knees, and the servant, who was carrying the other, continually cried out:

"Look at papa! look at papa!"

And the two boys, intoxicated by the motion of the carriage, by their delight and by the keen air, uttered shrill cries. The horse, frightened by the noise they made, started off at a gallop, and while Hector was trying to control his steed his hat fell off, and the driver had to get down and pick it up. When the equestrian had recovered it he called to his wife from a distance:

"Don't let the children shout like that! They'll make the horse bolt!"

They lunched on the grass in the Vesinet woods, having brought provisions with them in the carriage.

Although the driver was looking after the three horses, Hector rose every minute to see if his own lacked anything; he patted him on the neck and fed him with bread, cakes and sugar.

"He's an unequal trotter," he declared. "He certainly shook me up a little at first, but, as you saw, I soon got used to it. He knows his master now and won't give any more trouble."

As had been decided, they returned by the Champs-Elysees.

That spacious thoroughfare literally swarmed with vehicles of every kind, and on the sidewalks the pedestrians were so numerous that they looked like two indeterminate black ribbons unfurling their length from the Arc de Triomphe to the Place de la Concorde. A flood of sunlight played on this gay scene, making the varnish of the carriages, the steel of the harness and the handles of the carriage doors shine with dazzling brilliancy.

An intoxication of life and motion seemed to have invaded this assemblage of human beings, carriages and horses. In the distance the outlines of the Obelisk could be discerned in a cloud of golden vapor.

As soon as Hector's horse had passed the Arc de Triomphe he became suddenly imbued with fresh energy, and, realizing that his stable was not far off, began to trot rapidly through the maze of wheels, despite all his rider's efforts to restrain him.

The carriage was now far behind. When the horse arrived opposite the Palais de l'Industrie he saw a clear field before him, and, turning to the right, set off at a gallop.

An old woman wearing an apron was crossing the road in leisurely fashion. She happened to be just in Hector's way as he arrived on the scene riding at full speed. Powerless to control his mount, he shouted at the top of his voice:

"Hi! Look out there! Hi!"

She must have been deaf, for she continued peacefully on her way until the awful moment when, struck by the horse's chest as by a locomotive under full steam, she rolled ten paces off, turning three somersaults on the way.

Voices yelled:

"Stop him!"

Hector, frantic with terror, clung to the horse's mane and shouted:

"Help! help!"

A terrible jolt hurled him, as if shot from a gun, over his horse's ears and cast him into the arms of a policeman who was running up to stop him.

In the space of a second a furious, gesticulating, vociferating group had gathered round him. An old gentleman with a white mustache, wearing a large round decoration, seemed particularly exasperated. He repeated:

"Confound it! When a man is as awkward as all that he should remain at home and not come killing people in the streets, if he doesn't know how to handle a horse."

Four men arrived on the scene, carrying the old woman. She appeared to be dead. Her skin was like parchment, her cap on one side and she was covered with dust.

"Take her to a druggist's," ordered the old gentleman, "and let us go to the commissary of police."

Hector started on his way with a policeman on either side of him, a third was leading his horse. A crowd followed them—and suddenly the wagonette appeared in sight. His wife alighted in consternation, the servant lost her head, the children whimpered. He explained that he would soon be at home, that he had knocked a woman down and that there was not much the matter. And his family, distracted with anxiety, went on their way.

When they arrived before the commissary the explanation took place in few words. He gave his name—Hector de Gribelin, employed at the Ministry of Marine; and then they awaited news of the injured woman. A policeman who had been sent to obtain information returned, saying that she had recovered consciousness, but was complaining of frightful internal pain. She was a charwoman, sixty-five years of age, named Madame Simon.

When he heard that she was not dead Hector regained hope and promised to defray her doctor's bill. Then he hastened to the druggist's. The door way was thronged; the injured woman, huddled in an armchair, was groaning. Her arms hung at her sides, her face was drawn. Two doctors were still engaged in examining her. No bones were broken, but they feared some internal lesion.

Hector addressed her:

"Do you suffer much?"

"Oh, yes!"

"Where is the pain?"

"I feel as if my stomach were on fire."

A doctor approached.

"Are you the gentleman who caused the accident?"

"I am."

"This woman ought to be sent to a home. I know one where they would take her at six francs a day. Would you like me to send her there?"

Hector was delighted at the idea, thanked him and returned home much relieved.

His wife, dissolved in tears, was awaiting him. He reassured her.

"It's all right. This Madame Simon is better already and will be quite well in two or three days. I have sent her to a home. It's all right."

When he left his office the next day he went to inquire for Madame Simon. He found her eating rich soup with an air of great satisfaction.

"Well?" said he.

"Oh, sir," she replied, "I'm just the same. I feel sort of crushed—not a bit better."

The doctor declared they must wait and see; some complication or other might arise.

Hector waited three days, then he returned. The old woman, fresh-faced and clear-eyed, began to whine when she saw him:

"I can't move, sir; I can't move a bit. I shall be like this for the rest of my days."

A shudder passed through Hector's frame. He asked for the doctor, who merely shrugged his shoulders and said:

"What can I do? I can't tell what's wrong with her. She shrieks when they try to raise her. They can't even move her chair from one place to another without her uttering the most distressing cries. I am bound to believe what she tells me; I can't look into her inside. So long as I have no chance of seeing her walk I am not justified in supposing her to be telling lies about herself."

The old woman listened, motionless, a malicious gleam in her eyes.

A week passed, then a fortnight, then a month. Madame Simon did not leave her armchair. She ate from morning to night, grew fat, chatted gaily with the other patients and seemed to enjoy her immobility as if it were the rest to which she was entitled after fifty years of going up and down stairs, of turning mattresses, of carrying coal from one story to another, of sweeping and dusting.

Hector, at his wits' end, came to see her every day. Every day he found her calm and serene, declaring:

"I can't move, sir; I shall never be able to move again."

Every evening Madame de Gribelin, devoured with anxiety, said:

"How is Madame Simon?"

And every time he replied with a resignation born of despair:

"Just the same; no change whatever."

They dismissed the servant, whose wages they could no longer afford. They economized more rigidly than ever. The whole of the extra pay had been swallowed up.

Then Hector summoned four noted doctors, who met in consultation over the old woman. She let them examine her, feel her, sound her, watching them the while with a cunning eye.

"We must make her walk," said one.

"But, sirs, I can't!" she cried. "I can't move!"

Then they took hold of her, raised her and dragged her a short distance, but she slipped from their grasp and fell to the floor, groaning and giving vent to such heartrending cries that they carried her back to her seat with infinite care and precaution.

They pronounced a guarded opinion—agreeing, however, that work was an impossibility to her.

And when Hector brought this news to his wife she sank on a chair, murmuring:

"It would be better to bring her here; it would cost us less."

He started in amazement.

"Here? In our own house? How can you think of such a thing?"

But she, resigned now to anything, replied with tears in her eyes:

"But what can we do, my love? It's not my fault!"

USELESS BEAUTY

I

About half-past five one afternoon at the end of June when the sun was shining warm and bright into the large courtyard, a very elegant victoria with two beautiful black horses drew up in front of the mansion.

The Comtesse de Mascaret came down the steps just as her husband, who was coming home, appeared in the carriage entrance. He stopped for a few moments to look at his wife and turned rather pale. The countess was very beautiful, graceful and distinguished looking, with her long oval face, her complexion like yellow ivory, her large gray eyes and her black hair; and she got into her carriage without looking at him, without even seeming to have noticed him, with such a particularly high-bred air, that the furious jealousy by which he had been devoured for so long again gnawed at his heart. He went up to her and said: "You are going for a drive?"

She merely replied disdainfully: "You see I am!"

"In the Bois de Boulogne?"

"Most probably."

"May I come with you?"

"The carriage belongs to you."

Without being surprised at the tone in which she answered him, he got in and sat down by his wife's side and said: "Bois de Boulogne." The footman jumped up beside the coachman, and the horses as usual pranced and tossed their heads until they were in the street. Husband and wife sat side by side without speaking. He was thinking how to begin a conversation, but she maintained such an obstinately hard look that he did not venture to make the attempt. At last, however, he cunningly, accidentally as it were, touched the countess' gloved hand with his own, but she drew her arm away with a movement which was so expressive of disgust that he remained thoughtful, in spite of his usual authoritative and despotic character, and he said: "Gabrielle!"

"What do you want?"

"I think you are looking adorable."

She did not reply, but remained lying back in the carriage, looking like an irritated queen. By that time they were driving up the Champs Elysees, toward the Arc de Triomphe. That immense monument, at the end of the long avenue, raised its colossal arch against the red sky and the sun seemed to be descending on it, showering fiery dust on it from the sky.

The stream of carriages, with dashes of sunlight reflected in the silver trappings of the harness and the glass of the lamps, flowed on in a double current toward the town and toward the Bois, and the Comte de Mascaret continued: "My dear Gabrielle!"

Unable to control herself any longer, she replied in an exasperated voice: "Oh! do leave me in peace, pray! I am not even allowed to have my carriage to myself now." He pretended not to hear her and continued: "You never have looked so pretty as you do to-day."

Her patience had come to an end, and she replied with irrepressible anger: "You are wrong to notice it, for I swear to you that I will never have anything to do with you in that way again."

The count was decidedly stupefied and upset, and, his violent nature gaining the upper hand, he exclaimed: "What do you mean by that?" in a tone that betrayed rather the brutal master than the lover. She replied in a low voice, so that the servants might not hear amid the deafening noise of the wheels: "Ah! What do I mean by that? What do I mean by that? Now I recognize you again! Do you want me to tell everything?"

"Yes."

"Everything that has weighed on my heart since I have been the victim of your terrible selfishness?"

He had grown red with surprise and anger and he growled between his closed teeth: "Yes, tell me everything."

He was a tall, broad-shouldered man, with a big red beard, a handsome man, a nobleman, a man of the world, who passed as a perfect husband and an excellent father, and now, for the first time since they had started, she turned toward him and looked him full in the face: "Ah! You will hear some disagreeable things, but you must know that I am prepared for everything, that I fear nothing, and you less than any one to-day."

He also was looking into her eyes and was already shaking with rage as he said in a low voice: "You are mad."

"No, but I will no longer be the victim of the hateful penalty of maternity, which you have inflicted on me for eleven years! I wish to take my place in society as I have the right to do, as all women have the right to do."

He suddenly grew pale again and stammered: "I do not understand you."

"Oh! yes; you understand me well enough. It is now three months since I had my last child, and as I am still very beautiful, and as, in spite of all your efforts you cannot spoil my figure, as you just now perceived, when you saw me on the doorstep, you think it is time that I should think of having another child."

"But you are talking nonsense!"

"No, I am not, I am thirty, and I have had seven children, and we have been married eleven years, and you hope that this will go on for ten years longer, after which you will leave off being jealous."

He seized her arm and squeezed it, saying: "I will not allow you to talk to me like that much longer."

"And I shall talk to you till the end, until I have finished all I have to say to you, and if you try to prevent me, I shall raise my voice so that the two servants, who are on the box, may hear. I only allowed you to come with me for that object, for I have these witnesses who will oblige you to listen to me and to contain yourself, so now pay attention to what I say. I have always felt an antipathy to you, and I have always let you see it, for I have never lied, monsieur. You married me in spite of myself; you forced my parents, who were in embarrassed circumstances, to give me to you, because you were rich, and they obliged me to marry you in spite of my tears.

"So you bought me, and as soon as I was in your power, as soon as I had become your companion, ready to attach myself to you, to forget your coercive and threatening proceedings, in order that I might only remember that I ought to be a devoted wife and to love you as much as it might be possible for me to love you, you became jealous, you, as no man has ever been before, with the base, ignoble jealousy of a spy, which was as degrading to you as it was to me. I had not been married eight months when you suspected me of every perfidiousness, and you even told me so. What a disgrace! And as you could not prevent me from being beautiful and from pleasing people, from being called in drawing-rooms and also in the newspapers one of the most beautiful women in Paris, you tried everything you could think of to keep admirers from me, and you hit upon the abominable idea of making me spend my life in a constant state of motherhood, until the time should come when I should disgust every man. Oh, do not deny it. I did not understand it for some time, but then I guessed it. You even boasted about it to your sister, who told me of it, for she is fond of me and was disgusted at your boorish coarseness.

"Ah! Remember how you have behaved in the past! How for eleven years you have compelled me to give up all society and simply be a mother to your children. And then you would grow disgusted with me and I was sent into the country, the family chateau, among fields and meadows. And when I reappeared, fresh, pretty and unspoiled, still seductive and constantly surrounded by admirers, hoping that at last I should live a little more like a rich young society woman, you were seized with jealousy again, and you began once more to persecute me with that infamous and hateful desire from which you are suffering at this moment by my side. And it is not the desire of possessing me—for I should never have refused myself to you, but it is the wish to make me unsightly.

"And then that abominable and mysterious thing occurred which I was a long time in understanding (but I grew sharp by dint of watching your thoughts and actions): You attached yourself to your children with all the security which they gave you while I bore them. You felt affection for them, with all your aversion to me, and in spite of your ignoble fears, which were momentarily allayed by your pleasure in seeing me lose my symmetry.

"Oh! how often have I noticed that joy in you! I have seen it in your eyes and guessed it. You loved your children as victories, and not because they were of your own blood. They were victories over me, over my youth, over my beauty, over my charms, over the compliments which were paid me and over those that were whispered around me without being paid to me personally. And you are proud of them, you make a parade of them, you take them out for drives in your break in the Bois de Boulogne and you give them donkey rides at Montmorency. You take them to theatrical matinees so that you may be seen in the midst of them, so that the people may say: 'What a kind father' and that it may be repeated——"

He had seized her wrist with savage brutality, and he squeezed it so violently that she was quiet and nearly cried out with the pain and he said to her in a whisper:

"I love my children, do you hear? What you have just told me is disgraceful in a mother. But you belong to me; I am master—your master—I can exact from you what I like and when I like—and I have the law-on my side."

He was trying to crush her fingers in the strong grip of his large, muscular hand, and she, livid with pain, tried in vain to free them from that vise which was crushing them. The agony made her breathe hard and the tears came into her eyes. "You see that I am the master and the stronger," he said. When he somewhat loosened his grip, she asked him: "Do you think that I am a religious woman?"

He was surprised and stammered "Yes."

"Do you think that I could lie if I swore to the truth of anything to you before an altar on which Christ's body is?"

"No."

"Will you go with me to some church?"

"What for?"

"You shall see. Will you?"

"If you absolutely wish it, yes."

She raised her voice and said: "Philippe!" And the coachman, bending down a little, without taking his eyes from his horses, seemed to turn his ear alone toward his mistress, who continued: "Drive to St. Philippe-du-Roule." And the-victoria, which had reached the entrance of the Bois de Boulogne returned to Paris.

Husband and wife did not exchange a word further during the drive, and when the carriage stopped before the church Madame de Mascaret jumped out and entered it, followed by the count, a few yards distant. She went, without stopping, as far as the choir-screen, and falling on her knees at a chair, she buried her face in her hands. She prayed for a long time, and he, standing behind her could see that she was crying. She wept noiselessly, as women weep when they are in great, poignant grief. There was a kind of undulation in her body, which ended in a little sob, which was hidden and stifled by her fingers.

But the Comte de Mascaret thought that the situation was lasting too long, and he touched her on the shoulder. That contact recalled her to herself, as if she had been burned, and getting up, she looked straight into his eyes. "This is what I have to say to you. I am afraid of nothing, whatever you may do to me. You may kill me if you like. One of your children is not yours, and one only; that I swear to you before God, who hears me here. That was the only revenge that was possible for me in return for all your abominable masculine tyrannies, in return for the penal servitude of childbearing to which you have condemned me. Who was my lover? That you never will know! You may suspect every one, but you never will find out. I gave myself to him, without love and without pleasure, only for the sake of betraying you, and he also made me a mother. Which is the child? That also you never will know. I have seven; try to find out! I intended to tell you this later, for one has not avenged oneself on a man by deceiving him, unless he knows it. You have driven me to confess it today. I have now finished."

She hurried through the church toward the open door, expecting to hear behind her the quick step: of her husband whom she had defied and to be knocked to the ground by a blow of his fist, but she heard nothing and reached her carriage. She jumped into it at a bound, overwhelmed with anguish and breathless with fear. So she called out to the coachman: "Home!" and the horses set off at a quick trot.

II

The Comtesse de Mascaret was waiting in her room for dinner time as a criminal sentenced to death awaits the hour of his execution. What was her husband going to do? Had he come home? Despotic, passionate, ready for any violence as he was, what was he meditating, what had he made up his mind to do? There was no sound in the house, and every moment she looked at the clock. Her lady's maid had come and dressed her for the evening and had then left the room again. Eight o'clock struck and almost at the same moment there were two knocks at the door, and the butler came in and announced dinner.

"Has the count come in?"

"Yes, Madame la Comtesse. He is in the diningroom."

For a little moment she felt inclined to arm herself with a small revolver which she had bought some time before, foreseeing the tragedy which was being rehearsed in her heart. But she remembered that all the children would be there, and she took nothing except a bottle of smelling salts. He rose somewhat ceremoniously from his chair. They exchanged a slight bow and sat down. The three boys with their tutor, Abbe Martin, were on her right and the three girls, with Miss Smith, their English governess, were on her left. The youngest child, who was only three months old, remained upstairs with his nurse.

The abbe said grace as usual when there was no company, for the children did not come down to dinner when guests were present. Then they began dinner. The countess, suffering from emotion, which she had not calculated upon, remained with her eyes cast down, while the count scrutinized now the three boys and now the three girls with an uncertain, unhappy expression, which travelled from one to the other. Suddenly pushing his wineglass from him, it broke, and the wine was spilt on the tablecloth, and at the slight noise caused by this little accident the countess started up from her chair; and for the first time they looked at each other. Then, in spite of themselves, in spite of the irritation of their nerves caused by every glance, they continued to exchange looks, rapid as pistol shots.

The abbe, who felt that there was some cause for embarrassment which he could not divine, attempted to begin a conversation and tried various subjects, but his useless efforts gave rise to no ideas and did not bring out a word. The countess, with feminine tact and obeying her instincts of a woman of the world, attempted to answer him two or three times, but in vain. She could not find words, in the perplexity of her mind, and her own voice almost frightened her in the silence of the large room, where nothing was heard except the slight sound of plates and knives and forks.

Suddenly her husband said to her, bending forward: "Here, amid your children, will you swear to me that what you told me just now is true?"

The hatred which was fermenting in her veins suddenly roused her, and replying to that question with the same firmness with which she had replied to his looks, she raised both her hands, the right pointing toward the boys and the left toward the girls, and said in a firm, resolute voice and without any hesitation: "On the head of my children, I swear that I have told you the truth."

He got up and throwing his table napkin on the table with a movement of exasperation, he turned round and flung his chair against the wall, and then went out without another word, while she, uttering a deep sigh, as if after a first victory, went on in a calm voice: "You must not pay any attention to what your father has just said, my darlings; he was very much upset a short time ago, but he will be all right again in a few days."

Then she talked with the abbe and Miss Smith and had tender, pretty words for all her children, those sweet, tender mother's ways which unfold little hearts.

When dinner was over she went into the drawing-room, all her children following her. She made the elder ones chatter, and when their bedtime came she kissed them for a long time and then went alone into her room.

She waited, for she had no doubt that the count would come, and she made up her mind then, as her children were not with her, to protect herself as a woman of the world as she would protect her life, and in the pocket of her dress she put the little loaded revolver which she had bought a few days previously. The hours went by, the hours struck, and every sound was hushed in the house. Only the cabs, continued to rumble through the streets, but their noise was only heard vaguely through the shuttered and curtained windows.

She waited, full of nervous energy, without any fear of him now, ready for anything, and almost triumphant, for she had found means of torturing him continually during every moment of his life.

But the first gleam of dawn came in through the fringe at the bottom of her curtain without his having come into her room, and then she awoke to the fact, with much amazement, that he was not coming. Having locked and bolted her door, for greater security, she went to bed at last and remained there, with her eyes open, thinking and barely understanding it all, without being able to guess what he was going to do.

When her maid brought her tea she at the same time handed her a letter from her husband. He told her that he was going to undertake a longish journey and in a postscript added that his lawyer would provide her with any sums of money she might require for all her expenses.

III

It was at the opera, between two acts of "Robert the Devil." In the stalls the men were standing up, with their hats on, their waistcoats cut very low so as to show a large amount of white shirt front, in which gold and jewelled studs glistened, and were looking at the boxes full of ladies in low dresses covered with diamonds and pearls, who were expanding like flowers in that illuminated hothouse, where the beauty of their faces and the whiteness of their shoulders seemed to bloom in order to be gazed at, amid the sound of the music and of human voices.

Two friends, with their backs to the orchestra, were scanning those rows of elegance, that exhibition of real or false charms, of jewels, of luxury and of pretension which displayed itself in all parts of the Grand Theatre, and one of them, Roger de Salnis, said to his companion, Bernard Grandin:

"Just look how beautiful the Comtesse de Mascaret still is."

The older man in turn looked through his opera glasses at a tall lady in a box opposite. She appeared to be still very young, and her striking beauty seemed to attract all eyes in every corner of the house. Her pale complexion, of an ivory tint, gave her the appearance of a statue, while a small diamond coronet glistened on her black hair like a streak of light.

When he had looked at her for some time, Bernard Grandin replied with a jocular accent of sincere conviction: "You may well call her beautiful!"

"How old do you think she is?"

"Wait a moment. I can tell you exactly, for I have known her since she was a child and I saw her make her debut into society when she was quite a girl. She is—she is—thirty—thirty-six."

"Impossible!"

"I am sure of it."

"She looks twenty-five."

"She has had seven children."

"It is incredible."

"And what is more, they are all seven alive, as she is a very good mother. I occasionally go to the house, which is a very quiet and pleasant one, where one may see the phenomenon of the family in the midst of society."

"How very strange! And have there never been any reports about her?"

"Never."

"But what about her husband? He is peculiar, is he not?"

"Yes and no. Very likely there has been a little drama between them, one of those little domestic dramas which one suspects, never finds out exactly, but guesses at pretty closely."

"What is it?"

"I do not know anything about it. Mascaret leads a very fast life now, after being a model husband. As long as he remained a good spouse he had a shocking temper, was crabbed and easily took offence, but since he has been leading his present wild life he has become quite different, But one might surmise that he has some trouble, a worm gnawing somewhere, for he has aged very much."

Thereupon the two friends talked philosophically for some minutes about the secret, unknowable troubles which differences of character or perhaps physical antipathies, which were not perceived at first, give rise to in families, and then Roger de Salnis, who was still looking at Madame de Mascaret through his opera glasses, said: "It is almost incredible that that woman can have had seven children!"

"Yes, in eleven years; after which, when she was thirty, she refused to have any more, in order to take her place in society, which she seems likely to do for many years."

"Poor women!"

"Why do you pity them?"

"Why? Ah! my dear fellow, just consider! Eleven years in a condition of motherhood for such a woman! What a hell! All her youth, all her beauty, every hope of success, every poetical ideal of a brilliant life sacrificed to that abominable law of reproduction which turns the normal woman into a mere machine for bringing children into the world."

"What would you have? It is only Nature!"

"Yes, but I say that Nature is our enemy, that we must always fight against Nature, for she is continually bringing us back to an animal state. You may be sure that God has not put anything on this earth that is clean, pretty, elegant or accessory to our ideal; the human brain has done it. It is man who has introduced a little grace, beauty, unknown charm and mystery into creation by singing about it, interpreting it, by admiring it as a poet, idealizing it as an artist and by explaining it through science, doubtless making mistakes, but finding ingenious reasons, hidden grace and beauty, unknown charm and mystery in the various phenomena of Nature. God created only coarse beings, full of the germs of disease, who, after a few years of bestial enjoyment, grow old and infirm, with all the ugliness and all the want of power of human decrepitude. He seems to have made them only in order that they may reproduce their species in an ignoble manner and then die like ephemeral insects. I said reproduce their species in an ignoble manner and I adhere to that expression. What is there as a matter of fact more ignoble and more repugnant than that act of reproduction of living beings, against which all delicate minds always have revolted and always will revolt? Since all the organs which have been invented by this economical and malicious Creator serve two purposes, why did He not choose another method of performing that sacred mission, which is the noblest and the most exalted of all human functions? The mouth, which nourishes the body by means of material food, also diffuses abroad speech and thought. Our flesh renews itself of its own accord, while we are thinking about it. The olfactory organs, through which the vital air reaches the lungs, communicate all the perfumes of the world to the brain: the smell of flowers, of woods, of trees, of the sea. The ear, which enables us to communicate with our fellow men, has also allowed us to invent music, to create dreams, happiness, infinite and even physical pleasure by means of sound! But one might say that the cynical and cunning Creator wished to prohibit man from ever ennobling and idealizing his intercourse with women. Nevertheless man has found love, which is not a bad reply to that sly Deity, and he has adorned it with so much poetry that woman often forgets the sensual part of it. Those among us who are unable to deceive themselves have invented vice and refined debauchery, which is another way of laughing at God and paying homage, immodest homage, to beauty.

"But the normal man begets children just like an animal coupled with another by law.

"Look at that woman! Is it not abominable to think that such a jewel, such a pearl, born to be beautiful, admired, feted and adored, has spent eleven years of her life in providing heirs for the Comte de Mascaret?"

Bernard Grandin replied with a laugh: "There is a great deal of truth in all that, but very few people would understand you."

Salnis became more and more animated. "Do you know how I picture God myself?" he said. "As an enormous, creative organ beyond our ken, who scatters millions of worlds into space, just as one single fish would deposit its spawn in the sea. He creates because it is His function as God to do so, but He does not know what He is doing and is stupidly prolific in His work and is ignorant of the combinations of all kinds which are produced by His scattered germs. The human mind is a lucky little local, passing accident which was totally unforeseen, and condemned to disappear with this earth and to recommence perhaps here or elsewhere the same or different with fresh combinations of eternally new beginnings. We owe it to this little lapse of intelligence on His part that we are very uncomfortable in this world which was not made for us, which had not been prepared to receive us, to lodge and feed us or to satisfy reflecting beings, and we owe it to Him also that we have to struggle without ceasing against what are still called the designs of Providence, when we are really refined and civilized beings."

Grandin, who was listening to him attentively as he had long known the surprising outbursts of his imagination, asked him: "Then you believe that human thought is the spontaneous product of blind divine generation?"

"Naturally! A fortuitous function of the nerve centres of our brain, like the unforeseen chemical action due to new mixtures and similar also to a charge of electricity, caused by friction or the unexpected proximity of some substance, similar to all phenomena caused by the infinite and fruitful fermentation of living matter.

"But, my dear fellow, the truth of this must be evident to any one who looks about him. If the human mind, ordained by an omniscient Creator, had been intended to be what it has become, exacting, inquiring, agitated, tormented—so different from mere animal thought and resignation—would the world which was created to receive the beings which we now are have been this unpleasant little park for small game, this salad patch, this wooded, rocky and spherical kitchen garden where your improvident Providence had destined us to live naked, in caves or under trees, nourished on the flesh of slaughtered animals, our brethren, or on raw vegetables nourished by the sun and the rain?

"But it is sufficient to reflect for a moment, in order to understand that this world was not made for such creatures as we are. Thought, which is developed by a miracle in the nerves of the cells in our brain, powerless, ignorant and confused as it is, and as it will always remain, makes all of us who are intellectual beings eternal and wretched exiles on earth.

"Look at this earth, as God has given it to those who inhabit it. Is it not visibly and solely made, planted and covered with forests for the sake of animals? What is there for us? Nothing. And for them, everything, and they have nothing to do but to eat or go hunting and eat each other, according to their instincts, for God never foresaw gentleness and peaceable manners; He only foresaw the death of creatures which were bent on destroying and devouring each other. Are not the quail, the pigeon and the partridge the natural prey of the hawk? the sheep, the stag and the ox that of the great flesh-eating animals, rather than meat to be fattened and served up to us with truffles, which have been unearthed by pigs for our special benefit?

"As to ourselves, the more civilized, intellectual and refined we are, the more we ought to conquer and subdue that animal instinct, which represents the will of God in us. And so, in order to mitigate our lot as brutes, we have discovered and made everything, beginning with houses, then exquisite food, sauces, sweetmeats, pastry, drink, stuffs, clothes, ornaments, beds, mattresses, carriages, railways and innumerable machines, besides arts and sciences, writing and poetry. Every ideal comes from us as do all the amenities of life, in order to make our existence as simple reproducers, for which divine Providence solely intended us, less monotonous and less hard.

"Look at this theatre. Is there not here a human world created by us, unforeseen and unknown to eternal fate, intelligible to our minds alone, a sensual and intellectual distraction, which has been invented solely by and for that discontented and restless little animal, man?

"Look at that woman, Madame de Mascaret. God intended her to live in a cave, naked or wrapped up in the skins of wild animals. But is she not better as she is? But, speaking of her, does any one know why and how her brute of a husband, having such a companion by his side, and especially after having been boorish enough to make her a mother seven times, has suddenly left her, to run after bad women?"

Grandin replied: "Oh! my dear fellow, this is probably the only reason. He found that raising a family was becoming too expensive, and from reasons of domestic economy he has arrived at the same principles which you lay down as a philosopher."

Just then the curtain rose for the third act, and they turned round, took off their hats and sat down.

IV

The Comte and Comtesse Mascaret were sitting side by side in the carriage which was taking them home from the Opera, without speaking but suddenly the husband said to his wife: "Gabrielle!"

"What do you want?"

"Don't you think that this has lasted long enough?"

"What?"

"The horrible punishment to which you have condemned me for the last six years?"

"What do you want? I cannot help it."

"Then tell me which of them it is."

"Never."

"Think that I can no longer see my children or feel them round me, without having my heart burdened with this doubt. Tell me which of them it is, and I swear that I will forgive you and treat it like the others."

"I have not the right to do so."

"Do you not see that I can no longer endure this life, this thought which is wearing me out, or this question which I am constantly asking myself, this question which tortures me each time I look at them? It is driving me mad."

"Then you have suffered a great deal?" she said.

"Terribly. Should I, without that, have accepted the horror of living by your side, and the still greater horror of feeling and knowing that there is one among them whom I cannot recognize and who prevents me from loving the others?"

"Then you have really suffered very much?" she repeated.

And he replied in a constrained and sorrowful voice:

"Yes, for do I not tell you every day that it is intolerable torture to me? Should I have remained in that house, near you and them, if I did not love them? Oh! You have behaved abominably toward me. All the affection of my heart I have bestowed upon my children, and that you know. I am for them a father of the olden time, as I was for you a husband of one of the families of old, for by instinct I have remained a natural man, a man of former days. Yes, I will confess it, you have made me terribly jealous, because you are a woman of another race, of another soul, with other requirements. Oh! I shall never forget the things you said to me, but from that day I troubled myself no more about you. I did not kill you, because then I should have had no means on earth of ever discovering which of our— of your children is not mine. I have waited, but I have suffered more than you would believe, for I can no longer venture to love them, except, perhaps, the two eldest; I no longer venture to look at them, to call them to me, to kiss them; I cannot take them on my knee without asking myself, 'Can it be this one?' I have been correct in my behavior toward you for six years, and even kind and complaisant. Tell me the truth, and I swear that I will do nothing unkind."

He thought, in spite of the darkness of the carriage, that he could perceive that she was moved, and feeling certain that she was going to speak at last, he said: "I beg you, I beseech you to tell me" he said.

"I have been more guilty than you think perhaps," she replied, "but I could no longer endure that life of continual motherhood, and I had only one means of driving you from me. I lied before God and I lied, with my hand raised to my children's head, for I never have wronged you."

He seized her arm in the darkness, and squeezing it as he had done on that terrible day of their drive in the Bois de Boulogne, he stammered:

"Is that true?"

"It is true."

But, wild with grief, he said with a groan: "I shall have fresh doubts that will never end! When did you lie, the last time or now? How am I to believe you at present? How can one believe a woman after that? I shall never again know what I am to think. I would rather you had said to me, 'It is Jacques or it is Jeanne.'"

The carriage drove into the courtyard of the house and when it had drawn up in front of the steps the count alighted first, as usual, and offered his wife his arm to mount the stairs. As soon as they reached the first floor he said: "May I speak to you for a few moments longer?" And she replied, "I am quite willing."

They went into a small drawing-room and a footman, in some surprise, lighted the wax candles. As soon as he had left the room and they were alone the count continued: "How am I to know the truth? I have begged you a thousand times to speak, but you have remained dumb, impenetrable, inflexible, inexorable, and now to-day you tell me that you have been lying. For six years you have actually allowed me to believe such a thing! No, you are lying now, I do not know why, but out of pity for me, perhaps?"

She replied in a sincere and convincing manner: "If I had not done so, I should have had four more children in the last six years!"

"Can a mother speak like that?"

"Oh!" she replied, "I do not feel that I am the mother of children who never have been born; it is enough for me to be the mother of those that I have and to love them with all my heart. I am a woman of the civilized world, monsieur—we all are—and we are no longer, and we refuse to be, mere females to restock the earth."

She got up, but he seized her hands. "Only one word, Gabrielle. Tell me the truth!"

"I have just told you. I never have dishonored you."

He looked her full in the face, and how beautiful she was, with her gray eyes, like the cold sky. In her dark hair sparkled the diamond coronet, like a radiance. He suddenly felt, felt by a kind of intuition, that this grand creature was not merely a being destined to perpetuate the race, but the strange and mysterious product of all our complicated desires which have been accumulating in us for centuries but which have been turned aside from their primitive and divine object and have wandered after a mystic, imperfectly perceived and intangible beauty. There are some women like that, who blossom only for our dreams, adorned with every poetical attribute of civilization, with that ideal luxury, coquetry and esthetic charm which surround woman, a living statue that brightens our life.

Her husband remained standing before her, stupefied at his tardy and obscure discovery, confusedly hitting on the cause of his former jealousy and understanding it all very imperfectly, and at last lie said: "I believe you, for I feel at this moment that you are not lying, and before I really thought that you were."

She put out her hand to him: "We are friends then?"

He took her hand and kissed it and replied: "We are friends. Thank you, Gabrielle."

Then he went out, still looking at her, and surprised that she was still so beautiful and feeling a strange emotion arising in him.

THE FATHER

I

He was a clerk in the Bureau of Public Education and lived at Batignolles. He took the omnibus to Paris every morning and always sat opposite a girl, with whom he fell in love.

She was employed in a shop and went in at the same time every day. She was a little brunette, one of those girls whose eyes are so dark that they look like black spots, on a complexion like ivory. He always saw her coming at the corner of the same street, and she generally had to run to catch the heavy vehicle, and sprang upon the steps before the horses had quite stopped. Then she got inside, out of breath, and, sitting down, looked round her.

The first time that he saw her, Francois Tessier liked the face. One sometimes meets a woman whom one longs to clasp in one's arms without even knowing her. That girl seemed to respond to some chord in his being, to that sort of ideal of love which one cherishes in the depths of the heart, without knowing it.

He looked at her intently, not meaning to be rude, and she became embarrassed and blushed. He noticed it, and tried to turn away his eyes; but he involuntarily fixed them upon her again every moment, although he tried to look in another direction; and, in a few days, they seemed to know each other without having spoken. He gave up his place to her when the omnibus was full, and got outside, though he was very sorry to do it. By this time she had got so far as to greet him with a little smile; and, although she always dropped her eyes under his looks, which she felt were too ardent, yet she did not appear offended at being looked at in such a manner.

They ended by speaking. A kind of rapid friendship had become established between them, a daily freemasonry of half an hour, and that was certainly one of the most charming half hours in his life to him. He thought of her all the rest of the day, saw her image continually during the long office hours. He was haunted and bewitched by that floating and yet tenacious recollection which the form of a beloved woman leaves in us, and it seemed to him that if he could win that little person it would be maddening happiness to him, almost above human realization.

Every morning she now shook hands with him, and he preserved the sense of that touch and the recollection of the gentle pressure of her little fingers until the next day, and he almost fancied that he preserved the imprint on his palm. He anxiously waited for this short omnibus ride, while Sundays seemed to him heartbreaking days. However, there was no doubt that she loved him, for one Saturday, in spring, she promised to go and lunch with him at Maisons-Laffitte the next day.

II

She was at the railway station first, which surprised him, but she said: "Before going, I want to speak to you. We have twenty minutes, and that is more than I shall take for what I have to say."

She trembled as she hung on his arm, and looked down, her cheeks pale, as she continued: "I do not want you to be deceived in me, and I shall not go there with you, unless you promise, unless you swear—not to do—not to do anything—that is at all improper."

She had suddenly become as red as a poppy, and said no more. He did not know what to reply, for he was happy and disappointed at the same time. He should love her less, certainly, if he knew that her conduct was light, but then it would be so charming, so delicious to have a little flirtation.

As he did not say anything, she began to speak again in an agitated voice and with tears in her eyes. "If you do not promise to respect me altogether, I shall return home." And so he squeezed her arm tenderly and replied: "I promise, you shall only do what you like." She appeared relieved in mind, and asked, with a smile: "Do you really mean it?" And he looked into her eyes and replied: "I swear it" "Now you may take the tickets," she said.

During the journey they could hardly speak, as the carriage was full, and when they reached Maisons-Laffite they went toward the Seine. The sun, which shone full on the river, on the leaves and the grass, seemed to be reflected in their hearts, and they went, hand in hand, along the bank, looking at the shoals of little fish swimming near the bank, and they walked on, brimming over with happiness, as if they were walking on air.

At last she said: "How foolish you must think me!"

"Why?" he asked. "To come out like this, all alone with you."

"Certainly not; it is quite natural." "No, no; it is not natural for me —because I do not wish to commit a fault, and yet this is how girls fall. But if you only knew how wretched it is, every day the same thing, every day in the month and every month in the year. I live quite alone with mamma, and as she has had a great deal of trouble, she is not very cheerful. I do the best I can, and try to laugh in spite of everything, but I do not always succeed. But, all the same, it was wrong in me to come, though you, at any rate, will not be sorry."

By way of an answer, he kissed her ardently on the ear that was nearest him, but she moved from him with an abrupt movement, and, getting suddenly angry, exclaimed: "Oh! Monsieur Francois, after what you swore to me!" And they went back to Maisons-Laffitte.

They had lunch at the Petit-Havre, a low house, buried under four enormous poplar trees, by the side of the river. The air, the heat, the weak white wine and the sensation of being so close together made them silent; their faces were flushed and they had a feeling of oppression; but, after the coffee, they regained their high spirits, and, having crossed the Seine, started off along the bank, toward the village of La Frette. Suddenly he asked: "What-is your name?"

"Louise."

"Louise," he repeated and said nothing more.

The girl picked daisies and made them into a great bunch, while he sang vigorously, as unrestrained as a colt that has been turned into a meadow. On their left a vine-covered slope followed the river. Francois stopped motionless with astonishment: "Oh, look there!" he said.

The vines had come to an end, and the whole slope was covered with lilac bushes in flower. It was a purple wood! A kind of great carpet of flowers stretched over the earth, reaching as far as the village, more than two miles off. She also stood, surprised and delighted, and murmured: "Oh! how pretty!" And, crossing a meadow, they ran toward that curious low hill, which, every year, furnishes all the lilac that is drawn through Paris on the carts of the flower venders.

There was a narrow path beneath the trees, so they took it, and when they came to a small clearing, sat down.

Swarms of flies were buzzing around them and making a continuous, gentle sound, and the sun, the bright sun of a perfectly still day, shone over the bright slopes and from that forest of blossoms a powerful fragrance was borne toward them, a breath of perfume, the breath of the flowers.

A church clock struck in the distance, and they embraced gently, then, without the knowledge of anything but that kiss, lay down on the grass. But she soon came to herself with the feeling of a great misfortune, and began to cry and sob with grief, with her face buried in her hands.

He tried to console her, but she wanted to start to return and to go home immediately; and she kept saying, as she walked along quickly: "Good heavens! good heavens!"

He said to her: "Louise! Louise! Please let us stop here." But now her cheeks were red and her eyes hollow, and, as soon as they got to the railway station in Paris, she left him without even saying good-by.

III

When he met her in the omnibus, next day, she appeared to him to be changed and thinner, and she said to him: "I want to speak to you; we will get down at the Boulevard."

As soon as they were on the pavement, she said:

"We must bid each other good-by; I cannot meet you again." "But why?" he asked. "Because I cannot; I have been culpable, and I will not be so again."

Then he implored her, tortured by his love, but she replied firmly: "No, I cannot, I cannot." He, however, only grew all the more excited and promised to marry her, but she said again: "No," and left him.

For a week he did not see her. He could not manage to meet her, and, as he did not know her address, he thought that he had lost her altogether. On the ninth day, however, there was a ring at his bell, and when he opened the door, she was there. She threw herself into his arms and did not resist any longer, and for three months they were close friends. He was beginning to grow tired of her, when she whispered something to him, and then he had one idea and wish: to break with her at any price. As, however, he could not do that, not knowing how to begin, or what to say, full of anxiety through fear of the consequences of his rash indiscretion, he took a decisive step: one night he changed his lodgings and disappeared.

The blow was so heavy that she did not look, for the man who had abandoned her, but threw herself at her mother's knees and confessed her misfortune, and, some months after, gave birth to a boy. IV

Years passed, and Francois Tessier grew old, without there having been any alteration in his life. He led the dull, monotonous life of an office clerk, without hope and without expectation. Every day he got up at the same time, went through the same streets, went through the same door, past the same porter, went into the same office, sat in the same chair, and did the same work. He was alone in the world, alone during the day in the midst of his different colleagues, and alone at night in his bachelor's lodgings, and he laid by a hundred francs a month against old age.

Every Sunday he went to the Champs-Elysees, to watch the elegant people, the carriages and the pretty women, and the next day he used to say to one of his colleagues: "The return of the carriages from the Bois du Boulogne was very brilliant yesterday." One fine Sunday morning, however, he went into the Parc Monceau, where the mothers and nurses, sitting on the sides of the walks, watched the children playing, and suddenly Francois Tessier started. A woman passed by, holding two children by the hand, a little boy of about ten and a little girl of four. It was she!

He walked another hundred yards anti then fell into a chair, choking with emotion. She had not recognized him, and so he came back, wishing to see her again. She was sitting down now, and the boy was standing by her side very quietly, while the little girl was making sand castles. It was she, it was certainly she, but she had the reserved appearance of a lady, was dressed simply, and looked self-possessed and dignified. He looked at her from a distance, for he did not venture to go near; but the little boy raised his head, and Francois Tessier felt himself tremble. It was his own son, there could be no doubt of that. And, as he looked at him, he thought he could recognize himself as he appeared in an old photograph taken years ago. He remained hidden behind a tree, waiting for her to go that he might follow her.

He did not sleep that night. The idea of the child especially tormented him. His son! Oh, if he could only have known, have been sure! But what could he have done? However, he went to the house where she lived and asked about her. He was told that a neighbor, an honorable man of strict morals, had been touched by her distress and had married her; he knew the fault she had committed and had married her, and had even recognized the child, his, Francois Tessier's child, as his own.

He returned to the Parc Monceau every Sunday, for then he always saw her, and each time he was seized with a mad, an irresistible longing to take his son into his arms, to cover him with kisses and to steal him, to carry him off.

He suffered horribly in his wretched isolation as an old bachelor, with nobody to care for him, and he also suffered atrocious mental torture, torn by paternal tenderness springing from remorse, longing and jealousy and from that need of loving one's own children which nature has implanted in all. At last he determined to make a despairing attempt, and, going up to her, as she entered the park, he said, standing in the middle of the path, pale and with trembling lips: "You do not recognize me." She raised her eyes, looked at him, uttered an exclamation of horror, of terror, and, taking the two children by the hand, she rushed away, dragging them after her, while he went home and wept inconsolably.

Months passed without his seeing her again, but he suffered, day and night, for he was a prey to his paternal love. He would gladly have died, if he could only have kissed his son; he would have committed murder, performed any task, braved any danger, ventured anything. He wrote to her, but she did not reply, and, after writing her some twenty letters, he saw that there was no hope of altering her determination, and then he formed the desperate resolution of writing to her husband, being quite prepared to receive a bullet from a revolver, if need be. His letter only consisted of a few lines, as follows:

"Monsieur: You must have a perfect horror of my name, but I am so wretched, so overcome by misery that my only hope is in you, and, therefore, I venture to request you to grant me an interview of only five minutes.

"I have the honor, etc."

The next day he received the reply:

"Monsieur: I shall expect you to-morrow, Tuesday, at five o'clock."

As he went up the staircase, Francois Tessier's heart beat so violently that he had to stop several times. There was a dull and violent thumping noise in his breast, as of some animal galloping; and he could breathe only with difficulty, and had to hold on to the banisters, in order not to fall.

He rang the bell on the third floor, and when a maid servant had opened the door, he asked: "Does Monsieur Flamel live here?" "Yes, monsieur. Kindly come in."

He was shown into the drawing-room; he was alone, and waited, feeling bewildered, as in the midst of a catastrophe, until a door opened, and a man came in. He was tall, serious and rather stout, and wore a black frock coat, and pointed to a chair with his hand. Francois Tessier sat down, and then said, with choking breath: "Monsieur—monsieur—I do not know whether you know my name—whether you know——"

Monsieur Flamel interrupted him. "You need not tell it me, monsieur, I know it. My wife has spoken to me about you." He spoke in the dignified tone of voice of a good man who wishes to be severe, and with the commonplace stateliness of an honorable man, and Francois Tessier continued:

"Well, monsieur, I want to say this: I am dying of grief, of remorse, of shame, and I would like once, only once to kiss the child."

Monsieur Flamel got up and rang the bell, and when the servant came in, he said: "Will you bring Louis here?" When she had gone out, they remained face to face, without speaking, as they had nothing more to say to one another, and waited. Then, suddenly, a little boy of ten rushed into the room and ran up to the man whom he believed to be his father, but he stopped when he saw the stranger, and Monsieur Flamel kissed him and said: "Now, go and kiss that gentleman, my dear." And the child went up to the stranger and looked at him.

Francois Tessier had risen. He let his hat fall, and was ready to fall himself as he looked at his son, while Monsieur Flamel had turned away, from a feeling of delicacy, and was looking out of the window.

The child waited in surprise; but he picked up the hat and gave it to the stranger. Then Francois, taking the child up in his arms, began to kiss him wildly all over his face; on his eyes, his cheeks, his mouth, his hair; and the youngster, frightened at the shower of kisses, tried to avoid them, turned away his head, and pushed away the man's face with his little hands. But suddenly Francois Tessier put him down and cried: "Good-by! good-by!" And he rushed out of the room as if he had been a thief.

MY UNCLE SOSTHENES

Some people are Freethinkers from sheer stupidity. My Uncle Sosthenes was one of these. Some people are often religious for the same reason. The very sight of a priest threw my uncle into a violent rage. He would shake his fist and make grimaces at him, and would then touch a piece of iron when the priest's back was turned, forgetting that the latter action showed a belief after all, the belief in the evil eye. Now, when beliefs are unreasonable, one should have all or none at all. I myself am a Freethinker; I revolt at all dogmas, but feel no anger toward places of worship, be they Catholic, Apostolic, Roman, Protestant, Greek, Russian, Buddhist, Jewish, or Mohammedan.

My uncle was a Freemason, and I used to declare that they are stupider than old women devotees. That is my opinion, and I maintain it; if we must have any religion at all, the old one is good enough for me.

What is their object? Mutual help to be obtained by tickling the palms of each other's hands. I see no harm in it, for they put into practice the Christian precept: "Do unto others as ye would they should do unto you." The only difference consists in the tickling, but it does not seem worth while to make such a fuss about lending a poor devil half a crown.

To all my arguments my uncle's reply used to be:

"We are raising up a religion against a religion; Free Thought will kill clericalism. Freemasonry is the stronghold, of those who are demolishing all deities."

"Very well, my dear uncle," I would reply—in my heart I felt inclined to say, "You old idiot! it is just that which I am blaming you for. Instead of destroying, you are organizing competition; it is only a case of lowering prices. And then, if you admitted only Freethinkers among you, I could understand it, but you admit anybody. You have a number of Catholics among you, even the leaders of the party. Pius IX is said to have been one of you before he became pope. If you call a society with such an organization a bulwark against clericalism, I think it is an extremely weak one."

"My dear boy," my uncle would reply, with a wink, "we are most to be dreaded in politics; slowly and surely we are everywhere undermining the monarchical spirit."

Then I broke out: "Yes, you are very clever! If you tell me that Freemasonry is an election machine, I will grant it. I will never deny that it is used as a machine to control candidates of all shades; if you say that it is only used to hoodwink people, to drill them to go to the polls as soldiers are sent under fire, I agree with you; if you declare that it is indispensable to all political ambitions because it changes all its members into electoral agents, I should say to you: 'That is as clear as the sun.' But when you tell me that it serves to undermine the monarchical spirit, I can only laugh in your face.

"Just consider that gigantic and secret democratic association which had Prince Napoleon for its grand master under the Empire; which has the Crown Prince for its grand master in Germany, the Czar's brother in Russia, and to which the Prince of Wales and King Humbert, and nearly all the crowned heads of the globe belong."

"You are quite right," my uncle said; "but all these persons are serving our projects without guessing it."

I felt inclined to tell him he was talking a pack of nonsense.

It was, however, indeed a sight to see my uncle when he had a Freemason to dinner.

On meeting they shook hands in a manner that was irresistibly funny; one could see that they were going through a series of secret, mysterious signs.

Then my uncle would take his friend into a corner to tell him something important, and at dinner they had a peculiar way of looking at each other, and of drinking to each other, in a manner as if to say: "We know all about it, don't we?"

And to think that there are millions on the face of the globe who are amused at such monkey tricks! I would sooner be a Jesuit.

Now, in our town there really was an old Jesuit who was my uncle's detestation. Every time he met him, or if he only saw him at a distance, he used to say: "Get away, you toad." And then, taking my arm, he would whisper to me:

"See here, that fellow will play me a trick some day or other, I feel sure of it."

My uncle spoke quite truly, and this was how it happened, and through my fault.

It was close on Holy Week, and my uncle made up his mind to give a dinner on Good Friday, a real dinner, with his favorite chitterlings and black puddings. I resisted as much as I could, and said:

"I shall eat meat on that day, but at home, quite by myself. Your manifestation, as you call it, is an idiotic idea. Why should you manifest? What does it matter to you if people do not eat any meat?"

But my uncle would not be persuaded. He asked three of his friends to dine with him at one of the best restaurants in the town, and as he was going to pay the bill I had certainly, after all, no scruples about manifesting.

At four o'clock we took a conspicuous place in the most frequented restaurant in the town, and my uncle ordered dinner in a loud voice for six o'clock.

We sat down punctually, and at ten o'clock we had not yet finished. Five of us had drunk eighteen bottles of choice, still wine and four of champagne. Then my uncle proposed what he was in the habit of calling "the archbishop's circuit." Each man put six small glasses in front of him, each of them filled with a different liqueur, and they had all to be emptied at one gulp, one after another, while one of the waiters counted twenty. It was very stupid, but my uncle thought it was very suitable to the occasion.

At eleven o'clock he was as drunk as a fly. So we had to take him home in a cab and put him to bed, and one could easily foresee that his anti-clerical demonstration would end in a terrible fit of indigestion.

As I was going back to my lodgings, being rather drunk myself, with a cheerful drunkenness, a Machiavellian idea struck me which satisfied all my sceptical instincts.

I arranged my necktie, put on a look of great distress, and went and, rang loudly at the old Jesuit's door. As he was deaf he made me wait a longish while, but at length appeared at his window in a cotton nightcap and asked what I wanted.

I shouted out at the top of my voice:

"Make haste, reverend sir, and open the door; a poor, despairing, sick man is in need of your spiritual ministrations."

The good, kind man put on his trousers as quickly as he could, and came down without his cassock. I told him in a breathless voice that my uncle, the Freethinker, had been taken suddenly ill, and fearing it was going to be something serious, he had been seized with a sudden dread of death, and wished to see the priest and talk to him; to have his advice and comfort, to make his peace with the Church, and to confess, so as to be able to cross the dreaded threshold at peace with himself; and I added in a mocking tone:

"At any rate, he wishes it, and if it does him no good it can do him no harm."

The old Jesuit, who was startled, delighted, and almost trembling, said to me:

"Wait a moment, my son; I will come with you." But I replied: "Pardon me, reverend father, if I do not go with you; but my convictions will not allow me to do so. I even refused to come and fetch you, so I beg you not to say that you have seen me, but to declare that you had a presentiment—a sort of revelation of his illness."

The priest consented and went off quickly; knocked at my uncle's door, and was soon let in; and I saw the black cassock disappear within that stronghold of Free Thought.

I hid under a neighboring gateway to wait results. Had he been well, my uncle would have half-murdered the Jesuit, but I knew that he would scarcely be able to move an arm, and I asked myself gleefully what sort of a scene would take place between these antagonists, what disputes, what arguments, what a hubbub, and what would be the issue of the situation, which my uncle's indignation would render still more tragic?

I laughed till my sides ached, and said half aloud: "Oh, what a joke, what a joke!"

Meanwhile it was getting very cold, and I noticed that the Jesuit stayed a long time, and I thought: "They are having an argument, I suppose."

One, two, three hours passed, and still the reverend father did not come out. What had happened? Had my uncle died in a fit when he saw him, or had he killed the cassocked gentleman? Perhaps they had mutually devoured each other? This last supposition appeared very unlikely, for I fancied that my uncle was quite incapable of swallowing a grain more nourishment at that moment.

At last the day broke.

I was very uneasy, and, not venturing to go into the house myself, went to one of my friends who lived opposite. I woke him up, explained matters to him, much to his amusement and astonishment, and took possession of his window.

At nine o'clock he relieved me, and I got a little sleep. At two o'clock I, in my turn, replaced him. We were utterly astonished.

At six o'clock the Jesuit left, with a very happy and satisfied look on his face, and we saw him go away with a quiet step.

Then, timid and ashamed, I went and knocked at the door of my uncle's house; and when the servant opened it I did not dare to ask her any questions, but went upstairs without saying a word.

My uncle was lying, pale and exhausted, with weary, sorrowful eyes and heavy arms, on his bed. A little religious picture was fastened to one of the bed curtains with a pin.

"Why, uncle," I said, "in bed still? Are you not well?"

He replied in a feeble voice:

"Oh, my dear boy, I have been very ill, nearly dead."

"How was that, uncle?"

"I don't know; it was most surprising. But what is stranger still is that the Jesuit priest who has just left—you know, that excellent man whom I have made such fun of—had a divine revelation of my state, and came to see me."

I was seized with an almost uncontrollable desire to laugh, and with difficulty said: "Oh, really!"

"Yes, he came. He heard a voice telling him to get up and come to me, because I was going to die. I was a revelation."

I pretended to sneeze, so as not to burst out laughing; I felt inclined to roll on the ground with amusement.

In about a minute I managed to say indignantly:

"And you received him, uncle? You, a Freethinker, a Freemason? You did not have him thrown out of doors?"

He seemed confused, and stammered:

"Listen a moment, it is so astonishing—so astonishing and providential! He also spoke to me about my father; it seems he knew him formerly."

"Your father, uncle? But that is no reason for receiving a Jesuit."

"I know that, but I was very ill, and he looked after me most devotedly all night long. He was perfect; no doubt he saved my life; those men all know a little of medicine."

"Oh! he looked after you all night? But you said just now that he had only been gone a very short time."

"That is quite true; I kept him to breakfast after all his kindness. He had it at a table by my bedside while I drank a cup of tea."

"And he ate meat?"

My uncle looked vexed, as if I had said something very uncalled for, and then added:

"Don't joke, Gaston; such things are out of place at times. He has shown me more devotion than many a relation would have done, and I expect to have his convictions respected."

This rather upset me, but I answered, nevertheless: "Very well, uncle; and what did you do after breakfast?"

"We played a game of bezique, and then he repeated his breviary while I read a little book which he happened to have in his pocket, and which was not by any means badly written."

"A religious book, uncle?"

"Yes, and no, or, rather—no. It is the history of their missions in Central Africa, and is rather a book of travels and adventures. What these men have done is very grand."

I began to feel that matters were going badly, so I got up. "Well, good-by, uncle," I said, "I see you are going to give up Freemasonry for religion; you are a renegade."

He was still rather confused, and stammered:

"Well, but religion is a sort of Freemasonry."

"When is your Jesuit coming back?" I asked.

"I don't—I don't know exactly; to-morrow, perhaps; but it is not certain."

I went out, altogether overwhelmed.

My joke turned out very badly for me! My uncle became thoroughly converted, and if that had been all I should not have cared so much. Clerical or Freemason, to me it is all the same; six of one and half a dozen of the other; but the worst of it is that he has just made his will—yes, made his will—and he has disinherited me in favor of that rascally Jesuit!

THE BARONESS

"Come with me," said my friend Boisrene, "you will see some very interesting bric-a-brac and works of art there."

He conducted me to the first floor of an elegant house in one of the big streets of Paris. We were welcomed by a very pleasing man, with excellent manners, who led us from room to room, showing us rare things, the price of which he mentioned carelessly. Large sums, ten, twenty, thirty, fifty thousand francs, dropped from his lips with such grace and ease that one could not doubt that this gentleman-merchant had millions shut up in his safe.

I had known him by reputation for a long time Very bright, clever, intelligent, he acted as intermediary in all sorts of transactions. He kept in touch with all the richest art amateurs in Paris, and even of Europe and America, knowing their tastes and preferences; he apprised them by letter, or by wire if they lived in a distant city, as soon as he knew of some work of art which might suit them.

Men of the best society had had recourse to him in times of difficulty, either to find money for gambling, or to pay off a debt, or to sell a picture, a family jewel, or a tapestry.

It was said that he never refused his services when he saw a chance of gain.

Boisrene seemed very intimate with this strange merchant. They must have worked together in many a deal. I observed the man with great interest.

He was tall, thin, bald, and very elegant. His soft, insinuating voice had a peculiar, tempting charm which seemed to give the objects a special value. When he held anything in his hands, he turned it round and round, looking at it with such skill, refinement, and sympathy that the object seemed immediately to be beautiful and transformed by his look and touch. And its value increased in one's estimation, after the object had passed from the showcase into his hands.

"And your Crucifix," said Boisrene, "that beautiful Renaissance Crucifix which you showed me last year?"

The man smiled and answered:

"It has been sold, and in a very peculiar manner. There is a real Parisian story for you! Would you like to hear it?"

"With pleasure."

"Do you know the Baroness Samoris?"

"Yes and no. I have seen her once, but I know what she is!"

"You know—everything?"

"Yes."

"Would you mind telling me, so that I can see whether you are not mistaken?"

"Certainly. Mme. Samoris is a woman of the world who has a daughter, without anyone having known her husband. At any rate, she is received in a certain tolerant, or blind society. She goes to church and devoutly partakes of Communion, so that everyone may know it, and she never compromises herself. She expects her daughter to marry well. Is that correct?"

"Yes, but I will complete your information. She is a woman who makes herself respected by her admirers in spite of everything. That is a rare quality, for in this manner she can get what she wishes from a man. The man whom she has chosen without his suspecting it courts her for a long time, longs for her timidly, wins her with astonishment and possesses her with consideration. He does not notice that he is paying, she is so tactful; and she maintains her relations on such a footing of reserve and dignity that he would slap the first man who dared doubt her in the least. And all this in the best of faith.

"Several times I have been able to render little services to this woman. She has no secrets from me.

"Toward the beginning of January she came to me in order to borrow thirty thousand francs. Naturally, I did not lend them to her; but, as I wished to oblige her, I told her to explain her situation to me completely, so that I might see whether there was not something I could do for her.

"She told me her troubles in such cautious language that she could not have spoken more delicately of her child's first communion. I finally managed to understand that times were hard, and that she was penniless.

"The commercial crisis, political unrest, rumors of war, had made money scarce even in the hands of her clients. And then, of course, she was very particular.

"She would associate only with a man in the best of society, who could strengthen her reputation as well as help her financially. A reveller, no matter how rich, would have compromised her forever, and would have made the marriage of her daughter quite doubtful.

"She had to maintain her household expenses and continue to entertain, in order not to lose the opportunity of finding, among her numerous visitors, the discreet and distinguished friend for whom she was waiting, and whom she would choose.

"I showed her that my thirty thousand francs would have but little likelihood of returning to me; for, after spending them all, she would have to find at least sixty thousand more, in a lump, to pay me back.

"She seemed very disheartened when she heard this. I did not know just what to do, when an idea, a really fine idea, struck me.

"I had just bought this Renaissance Crucifix which I showed you, an admirable piece of workmanship, one of the finest of its land that I have ever seen.

"'My dear friend,' I said to her, 'I am going to send you that piece of ivory. You will invent some ingenious, touching, poetic story, anything that you wish, to explain your desire for parting with it. It is, of course, a family heirloom left you by your father.

"'I myself will send you amateurs, or will bring them to you. The rest concerns you. Before they come I will drop you a line about their position, both social and financial. This Crucifix is worth fifty thousand francs; but I will let it go for thirty thousand. The difference will belong to you.'

"She considered the matter seriously for several minutes, and then answered: 'Yes, it is, perhaps, a good idea. I thank you very-much.'

"The next day I sent her my Crucifix, and the same evening the Baron de Saint-Hospital.

"For three months I sent her my best clients, from a business point of view. But I heard nothing more from her.

"One day I received a visit from a foreigner who spoke very little French. I decided to introduce him personally to the baroness, in order to see how she was getting along.

"A footman in black livery received us and ushered us into a quiet little parlor, furnished with taste, where we waited for several minutes. She appeared, charming as usual, extended her hand to me and invited us to be seated; and when I had explained the reason of my visit, she rang.

"The footman appeared.

"'See if Mlle. Isabelle can let us go into her oratory.' The young girl herself brought the answer. She was about fifteen years of age, modest and good to look upon in the sweet freshness of her youth. She wished to conduct us herself to her chapel.

"It was a kind of religious boudoir where a silver lamp was burning before the Crucifix, my Crucifix, on a background of black velvet. The setting was charming and very clever. The child crossed herself and then said:

"'Look, gentlemen. Isn't it beautiful?'

"I took the object, examined it and declared it to be remarkable. The foreigner also examined it, but he seemed much more interested in the two women than in the crucifix.

"A delicate odor of incense, flowers and perfume pervaded the whole house. One felt at home there. This really was a comfortable home, where one would have liked to linger.

"When we had returned to the parlor I delicately broached the subject of the price. Mme. Samoris, lowering her eyes, asked fifty thousand francs.

"Then she added: 'If you wish to see it again, monsieur, I very seldom go out before three o'clock; and I can be found at home every day.'

"In the street the stranger asked me for some details about the baroness, whom he had found charming. But I did not hear anything more from either of them.

"Three months passed by.

"One morning, hardly two weeks ago, she came here at about lunch time, and, placing a roll of bills in my hand, said: 'My dear, you are an angel! Here are fifty thousand francs; I am buying your crucifix, and I am paying twenty thousand francs more for it than the price agreed upon, on condition that you always—always send your clients to me—for it is sill for sale.'"

MOTHER AND SON

A party of men were chatting in the smoking room after dinner. We were talking of unexpected legacies, strange inheritances. Then M. le Brument, who was sometimes called "the illustrious judge" and at other times "the illustrious lawyer," went and stood with his back to the fire.

"I have," said he, "to search for an heir who disappeared under peculiarly distressing circumstances. It is one of those simple and terrible dramas of ordinary life, a thing which possibly happens every day, and which is nevertheless one of the most dreadful things I know. Here are the facts:

"Nearly six months ago I was called to the bedside of a dying woman. She said to me:

"'Monsieur, I want to intrust to you the most delicate, the most difficult, and the most wearisome mission that can be conceived. Be good enough to notice my will, which is there on the table. A sum of five thousand francs is left to you as a fee if you do not succeed, and of a hundred thousand francs if you do succeed. I want you to find my son after my death.'

"She asked me to assist her to sit up in bed, in order that she might talk with greater ease, for her voice, broken and gasping, was whistling in her throat.

"It was a very wealthy establishment. The luxurious apartment, of an elegant simplicity, was upholstered with materials as thick as walls, with a soft inviting surface.

"The dying woman continued:

"'You are the first to hear my horrible story. I will try to have strength enough to finish it. You must know all, in order that you, whom I know to be a kind-hearted man as well as a man of the world, may have a sincere desire to aid me with all your power.

"'Listen to me:

"'Before my marriage, I loved a young man, whose suit was rejected by my family because he was not rich enough. Not long afterward, I married a man of great wealth. I married him through ignorance, through obedience, through indifference, as young girls do marry.

"'I had a child, a boy. My husband died in the course of a few years.

"'He whom I had loved had married, in his turn. When he saw that I was a widow, he was crushed by grief at knowing he was not free. He came to see me; he wept and sobbed so bitterly, that it was enough to break my heart. He came to see me at first as a friend. Perhaps I ought not to have received him. What could I do? I was alone, so sad, so solitary, so hopeless! And I loved him still. What sufferings we women have sometimes to endure!

"'I had only him in the world, my parents being dead. He came frequently; he spent whole evenings with me. I should not have let him come so often, seeing that he was married. But I had not enough will-power to prevent him from coming.

"'How can I tell it?—he became my lover. How did this come about? Can I explain it? Can any one explain such things? Do you think it could be otherwise when two human beings are drawn to each other by the irresistible force of mutual affection? Do you believe, monsieur, that it is always in our power to resist, that we can keep up the struggle forever, and refuse to yield to the prayers, the supplications, the tears, the frenzied words, the appeals on bended knees, the transports of passion, with which we are pursued by the man we adore, whom we want to gratify even in his slightest wishes, whom we desire to crown with every possible happiness, and whom, if we are to be guided by a worldly code of honor, we must drive to despair? What strength would it not require? What a renunciation of happiness? what self-denial? and even what virtuous selfishness?

"'In short, monsieur, I was his mistress; and I was happy. I became—and this was my greatest weakness and my greatest piece of cowardice-I became his wife's friend.

"'We brought up my son together; we made a man of him, a thorough man, intelligent, full of sense and resolution, of large and generous ideas. The boy reached the age of seventeen.

"'He, the young man, was fond of my—my lover, almost as fond of him as I was myself, for he had been equally cherished and cared for by both of us. He used to call him his 'dear friend,' and respected him immensely, having never received from him anything but wise counsels and an example of integrity, honor, and probity. He looked upon him as an old loyal and devoted comrade of his mother, as a sort of moral father, guardian, protector—how am I to describe it?

"'Perhaps the reason why he never asked any questions was that he had been accustomed from his earliest years to see this man in my house, at my side, and at his side, always concerned about us both.

"'One evening the three of us were to dine together—this was my chief amusement—and I waited for the two men, asking myself which of them would be the first to arrive. The door opened; it was my old friend. I went toward him, with outstretched arms; and he pressed my lips in a long, delicious kiss.

"'All of a sudden, a slight sound, a faint rustling, that mysterious sensation which indicates the presence of another person, made us start and turn round abruptly. Jean, my son, stood there, livid, staring at us.

"'There was a moment of atrocious confusion. I drew back, holding out my hand toward my son as if in supplication; but I could not see him. He had gone.

"'We remained facing each other—my lover and I—crushed, unable to utter a word. I sank into an armchair, and I felt a desire, a vague, powerful desire, to flee, to go out into the night, and to disappear forever. Then convulsive sobs rose in my throat, and I wept, shaken with spasms, my heart breaking, all my nerves writhing with the horrible sensation of an irreparable, misfortune, and with that dreadful sense of shame which, in such moments as this, fills a mother's heart.

"'He looked at me in a terrified manner, not venturing to approach, to speak to me, or to touch me, for fear of the boy's return. At last he said:

"'I am going to follow him-to talk to him—to explain matters to him. In short, I must see him and let him know——"

"'And he hurried away.

"'I waited—waited in a distracted frame of mind, trembling at the least sound, starting with fear and with some unutterably strange and intolerable emotion at every slight crackling of the fire in the grate.

"'I waited an hour, two hours, feeling my heart swell with a dread I had never before experienced, such anguish that I would not wish the greatest criminal to endure ten minutes of such misery. Where was my son? What was he doing?

"'About midnight, a messenger brought me a note from my lover. I still know its contents by heart:

"'Has your son returned? I did not find him. I am down here. I do not want to go up at this hour."

"'I wrote in pencil on the same slip of paper:

"'Jean has not returned. You must find him."

"'And I 'remained all night in the armchair, waiting for him.

"'I felt as if I were going mad. I longed to run wildly about, to roll on the ground. And yet I did not even stir, but kept waiting hour after hour. What was going to happen? I tried to imagine, to guess. But I could form no conception, in spite of my efforts, in spite of the tortures of my soul!

"'And now I feared that they might meet. What would they do in that case? What would my son do? My mind was torn with fearful doubts, with terrible suppositions.

"'You can understand my feelings, can you not, monsieur? "'My chambermaid, who knew nothing, who understood nothing, came into the room every moment, believing, naturally, that I had lost my reason. I sent her away with a word or a movement of the hand. She went for the doctor, who found me in the throes of a nervous attack.

"'I was put to bed. I had brain fever.

"'When I regained consciousness, after a long illness, I saw beside my bed my—lover—alone.

"'I exclaimed:

"'My son? Where is my son?

"'He made no reply. I stammered:

"'Dead-dead. Has he committed suicide?

"'No, no, I swear it. But we have not found him in spite of all my efforts.

"'Then, becoming suddenly exasperated and even indignant—for women are subject to such outbursts of unaccountable and unreasoning anger—I said:

"'I forbid you to come near me or to see me again unless you find him. Go away!

"He did go away.

"'I have never seen one or the other of them since, monsieur, and thus I have lived for the last twenty years.

"'Can you imagine what all this meant to me? Can you understand this monstrous punishment, this slow, perpetual laceration of a mother's heart, this abominable, endless waiting? Endless, did I say? No; it is about to end, for I am dying. I am dying without ever again seeing either of them—either one or the other!

"'He—the man I loved—has written to me every day for the last twenty years; and I—I have never consented to see him, even for one second; for I had a strange feeling that, if he were to come back here, my son would make his appearance at the same moment. Oh! my son! my son! Is he dead? Is he living? Where is he hiding? Over there, perhaps, beyond the great ocean, in some country so far away that even its very name is unknown to me! Does he ever think of me? Ah! if he only knew! How cruel one's children are! Did he understand to what frightful suffering he condemned me, into what depths of despair, into what tortures, he cast me while I was still in the prime of life, leaving me to suffer until this moment, when I am about to die—me, his mother, who loved him with all the intensity of a mother's love? Oh! isn't it cruel, cruel?

"'You will tell him all this, monsieur—will you not? You will repeat to him my last words:

"'My child, my dear, dear child, be less harsh toward poor women! Life is already brutal and savage enough in its dealings with them. My dear son, think of what the existence of your poor mother has been ever since the day you left her. My dear child, forgive her, and love her, now that she is dead, for she has had to endure the most frightful penance ever inflicted on a woman."

"She gasped for breath, trembling, as if she had addressed the last words to her son and as if he stood by her bedside.

"Then she added:

"'You will tell him also, monsieur, that I never again saw-the other.'

"Once more she ceased speaking, then, in a broken voice, she said:

"'Leave me now, I beg of you. I want to die all alone, since they are not with me.'"

Maitre Le Brument added:

"And I left the house, monsieurs, crying like a fool, so bitterly, indeed, that my coachman turned round to stare at me.

"And to think that, every day, dramas like this are being enacted all around us!

"I have not found the son—that son—well, say what you like about him, but I call him that criminal son!"

THE HAND

All were crowding around M. Bermutier, the judge, who was giving his opinion about the Saint-Cloud mystery. For a month this in explicable crime had been the talk of Paris. Nobody could make head or tail of it.

M. Bermutier, standing with his back to the fireplace, was talking, citing the evidence, discussing the various theories, but arriving at no conclusion.

Some women had risen, in order to get nearer to him, and were standing with their eyes fastened on the clean-shaven face of the judge, who was saying such weighty things. They, were shaking and trembling, moved by fear and curiosity, and by the eager and insatiable desire for the horrible, which haunts the soul of every woman. One of them, paler than the others, said during a pause:

"It's terrible. It verges on the supernatural. The truth will never be known."

The judge turned to her:

"True, madame, it is likely that the actual facts will never be discovered. As for the word 'supernatural' which you have just used, it has nothing to do with the matter. We are in the presence of a very cleverly conceived and executed crime, so well enshrouded in mystery that we cannot disentangle it from the involved circumstances which surround it. But once I had to take charge of an affair in which the uncanny seemed to play a part. In fact, the case became so confused that it had to be given up."

Several women exclaimed at once:

"Oh! Tell us about it!"

M. Bermutier smiled in a dignified manner, as a judge should, and went on:

"Do not think, however, that I, for one minute, ascribed anything in the case to supernatural influences. I believe only in normal causes. But if, instead of using the word 'supernatural' to express what we do not understand, we were simply to make use of the word 'inexplicable,' it would be much better. At any rate, in the affair of which I am about to tell you, it is especially the surrounding, preliminary circumstances which impressed me. Here are the facts:

"I was, at that time, a judge at Ajaccio, a little white city on the edge of a bay which is surrounded by high mountains.

"The majority of the cases which came up before me concerned vendettas. There are some that are superb, dramatic, ferocious, heroic. We find there the most beautiful causes for revenge of which one could dream, enmities hundreds of years old, quieted for a time but never extinguished; abominable stratagems, murders becoming massacres and almost deeds of glory. For two years I heard of nothing but the price of blood, of this terrible Corsican prejudice which compels revenge for insults meted out to the offending person and all his descendants and relatives. I had seen old men, children, cousins murdered; my head was full of these stories.

"One day I learned that an Englishman had just hired a little villa at the end of the bay for several years. He had brought with him a French servant, whom he had engaged on the way at Marseilles.

"Soon this peculiar person, living alone, only going out to hunt and fish, aroused a widespread interest. He never spoke to any one, never went to the town, and every morning he would practice for an hour or so with his revolver and rifle.

"Legends were built up around him. It was said that he was some high personage, fleeing from his fatherland for political reasons; then it was affirmed that he was in hiding after having committed some abominable crime. Some particularly horrible circumstances were even mentioned.

"In my judicial position I thought it necessary to get some information about this man, but it was impossible to learn anything. He called himself Sir John Rowell.

"I therefore had to be satisfied with watching him as closely as I could, but I could see nothing suspicious about his actions.

"However, as rumors about him were growing and becoming more widespread, I decided to try to see this stranger myself, and I began to hunt regularly in the neighborhood of his grounds.

"For a long time I watched without finding an opportunity. At last it came to me in the shape of a partridge which I shot and killed right in front of the Englishman. My dog fetched it for me, but, taking the bird, I went at once to Sir John Rowell and, begging his pardon, asked him to accept it.

"He was a big man, with red hair and beard, very tall, very broad, a kind of calm and polite Hercules. He had nothing of the so-called British stiffness, and in a broad English accent he thanked me warmly for my attention. At the end of a month we had had five or six conversations.

"One night, at last, as I was passing before his door, I saw him in the garden, seated astride a chair, smoking his pipe. I bowed and he invited me to come in and have a glass of beer. I needed no urging.

"He received me with the most punctilious English courtesy, sang the praises of France and of Corsica, and declared that he was quite in love with this country.

"Then, with great caution and under the guise of a vivid interest, I asked him a few questions about his life and his plans. He answered without embarrassment, telling me that he had travelled a great deal in Africa, in the Indies, in America. He added, laughing:

"'I have had many adventures.'

"Then I turned the conversation on hunting, and he gave me the most curious details on hunting the hippopotamus, the tiger, the elephant and even the gorilla.

"I said:

"'Are all these animals dangerous?'

"He smiled:

"'Oh, no! Man is the worst.'

"And he laughed a good broad laugh, the wholesome laugh of a contented Englishman.

"'I have also frequently been man-hunting.'

"Then he began to talk about weapons, and he invited me to come in and see different makes of guns.

"His parlor was draped in black, black silk embroidered in gold. Big yellow flowers, as brilliant as fire, were worked on the dark material.

"He said:

"'It is a Japanese material.'

"But in the middle of the widest panel a strange thing attracted my attention. A black object stood out against a square of red velvet. I went up to it; it was a hand, a human hand. Not the clean white hand of a skeleton, but a dried black hand, with yellow nails, the muscles exposed and traces of old blood on the bones, which were cut off as clean as though it had been chopped off with an axe, near the middle of the forearm.

"Around the wrist, an enormous iron chain, riveted and soldered to this unclean member, fastened it to the wall by a ring, strong enough to hold an elephant in leash.

"I asked:

"'What is that?'

"The Englishman answered quietly:

"'That is my best enemy. It comes from America, too. The bones were severed by a sword and the skin cut off with a sharp stone and dried in the sun for a week.'

"I touched these human remains, which must have belonged to a giant. The uncommonly long fingers were attached by enormous tendons which still had pieces of skin hanging to them in places. This hand was terrible to see; it made one think of some savage vengeance.

"I said:

"'This man must have been very strong.'

"The Englishman answered quietly:

"'Yes, but I was stronger than he. I put on this chain to hold him.'

"I thought that he was joking. I said:

"'This chain is useless now, the hand won't run away.'

"Sir John Rowell answered seriously:

"'It always wants to go away. This chain is needed.'

"I glanced at him quickly, questioning his face, and I asked myself:

"'Is he an insane man or a practical joker?'

"But his face remained inscrutable, calm and friendly. I turned to other subjects, and admired his rifles.

"However, I noticed that he kept three loaded revolvers in the room, as though constantly in fear of some attack.

"I paid him several calls. Then I did not go any more. People had become used to his presence; everybody had lost interest in him.

"A whole year rolled by. One morning, toward the end of November, my servant awoke me and announced that Sir John Rowell had been murdered during the night.

"Half an hour later I entered the Englishman's house, together with the police commissioner and the captain of the gendarmes. The servant, bewildered and in despair, was crying before the door. At first I suspected this man, but he was innocent.

"The guilty party could never be found.

"On entering Sir John's parlor, I noticed the body, stretched out on its back, in the middle of the room.

"His vest was torn, the sleeve of his jacket had been pulled off, everything pointed to, a violent struggle.

"The Englishman had been strangled! His face was black, swollen and frightful, and seemed to express a terrible fear. He held something between his teeth, and his neck, pierced by five or six holes which looked as though they had been made by some iron instrument, was covered with blood.

"A physician joined us. He examined the finger marks on the neck for a long time and then made this strange announcement:

"'It looks as though he had been strangled by a skeleton.'

"A cold chill seemed to run down my back, and I looked over to where I had formerly seen the terrible hand. It was no longer there. The chain was hanging down, broken.

"I bent over the dead man and, in his contracted mouth, I found one of the fingers of this vanished hand, cut—or rather sawed off by the teeth down to the second knuckle.

"Then the investigation began. Nothing could be discovered. No door, window or piece of furniture had been forced. The two watch dogs had not been aroused from their sleep.

"Here, in a few words, is the testimony of the servant:

"For a month his master had seemed excited. He had received many letters, which he would immediately burn.

"Often, in a fit of passion which approached madness, he had taken a switch and struck wildly at this dried hand riveted to the wall, and which had disappeared, no one knows how, at the very hour of the crime.

"He would go to bed very late and carefully lock himself in. He always kept weapons within reach. Often at night he would talk loudly, as though he were quarrelling with some one.

"That night, somehow, he had made no noise, and it was only on going to open the windows that the servant had found Sir John murdered. He suspected no one.

"I communicated what I knew of the dead man to the judges and public officials. Throughout the whole island a minute investigation was carried on. Nothing could be found out.

"One night, about three months after the crime, I had a terrible nightmare. I seemed to see the horrible hand running over my curtains and walls like an immense scorpion or spider. Three times I awoke, three times I went to sleep again; three times I saw the hideous object galloping round my room and moving its fingers like legs.

"The following day the hand was brought me, found in the cemetery, on the grave of Sir John Rowell, who had been buried there because we had been unable to find his family. The first finger was missing.

"Ladies, there is my story. I know nothing more."

The women, deeply stirred, were pale and trembling. One of them exclaimed:

"But that is neither a climax nor an explanation! We will be unable to sleep unless you give us your opinion of what had occurred."

The judge smiled severely:

"Oh! Ladies, I shall certainly spoil your terrible dreams. I simply believe that the legitimate owner of the hand was not dead, that he came to get it with his remaining one. But I don't know how. It was a kind of vendetta."

One of the women murmured:

"No, it can't be that."

And the judge, still smiling, said:

"Didn't I tell you that my explanation would not satisfy you?"

A TRESS OF HAIR

The walls of the cell were bare and white washed. A narrow grated window, placed so high that one could not reach it, lighted this sinister little room. The mad inmate, seated on a straw chair, looked at us with a fixed, vacant and haunted expression. He was very thin, with hollow cheeks and hair almost white, which one guessed might have turned gray in a few months. His clothes appeared to be too large for his shrunken limbs, his sunken chest and empty paunch. One felt that this man's mind was destroyed, eaten by his thoughts, by one thought, just as a fruit is eaten by a worm. His craze, his idea was there in his brain, insistent, harassing, destructive. It wasted his frame little by little. It—the invisible, impalpable, intangible, immaterial idea—was mining his health, drinking his blood, snuffing out his life.

What a mystery was this man, being killed by an ideal! He aroused sorrow, fear and pity, this madman. What strange, tremendous and deadly thoughts dwelt within this forehead which they creased with deep wrinkles which were never still?

"He has terrible attacks of rage," said the doctor to me. "His is one of the most peculiar cases I have ever seen. He has seizures of erotic and macaberesque madness. He is a sort of necrophile. He has kept a journal in which he sets forth his disease with the utmost clearness. In it you can, as it were, put your finger on it. If it would interest you, you may go over this document."

I followed the doctor into his office, where he handed me this wretched man's diary, saying: "Read it and tell me what you think of it." I read as follows:

"Until the age of thirty-two I lived peacefully, without knowing love. Life appeared very simple, very pleasant and very easy. I was rich. I enjoyed so many things that I had no passion for anything in particular. It was good to be alive! I awoke happy every morning and did those things that pleased me during the day and went to bed at night contented, in the expectation of a peaceful tomorrow and a future without anxiety.

"I had had a few flirtations without my heart being touched by any true passion or wounded by any of the sensations of true love. It is good to live like that. It is better to love, but it is terrible. And yet those who love in the ordinary way must experience ardent happiness, though less than mine possibly, for love came to me in a remarkable manner.

"As I was wealthy, I bought all kinds of old furniture and old curiosities, and I often thought of the unknown hands that had touched these objects, of the eyes that had admired them, of the hearts that had loved them; for one does love things! I sometimes remained hours and hours looking at a little watch of the last century. It was so tiny, so pretty with its enamel and gold chasing. And it kept time as on the day when a woman first bought it, enraptured at owning this dainty trinket. It had not ceased to vibrate, to live its mechanical life, and it had kept up its regular tick-tock since the last century. Who had first worn it on her bosom amid the warmth of her clothing, the heart of the watch beating beside the heart of the woman? What hand had held it in its warm fingers, had turned it over and then wiped the enamelled shepherds on the case to remove the slight moisture from her fingers? What eyes had watched the hands on its ornamental face for the expected, the beloved, the sacred hour?

"How I wished I had known her, seen her, the woman who had selected this exquisite and rare object! She is dead! I am possessed with a longing for women of former days. I love, from afar, all those who have loved. The story of those dead and gone loves fills my heart with regrets. Oh, the beauty, the smiles, the youthful caresses, the hopes! Should not all that be eternal?

"How I have wept whole nights-thinking of those poor women of former days, so beautiful, so loving, so sweet, whose arms were extended in an embrace, and who now are dead! A kiss is immortal! It goes from lips to lips, from century to century, from age to age. Men receive them, give them and die.

"The past attracts me, the present terrifies me because the future means death. I regret all that has gone by. I mourn all who have lived; I should like to check time, to stop the clock. But time goes, it goes, it passes, it takes from me each second a little of myself for the annihilation of to-morrow. And I shall never live again.

"Farewell, ye women of yesterday. I love you!

"But I am not to be pitied. I found her, the one I was waiting for, and through her I enjoyed inestimable pleasure.

"I was sauntering in Paris on a bright, sunny morning, with a happy heart and a high step, looking in at the shop windows with the vague interest of an idler. All at once I noticed in the shop of a dealer in antiques a piece of Italian furniture of the seventeenth century. It was very handsome, very rare. I set it down as being the work of a Venetian artist named Vitelli, who was celebrated in his day.

"I went on my way.

"Why did the remembrance of that piece of furniture haunt me with such insistence that I retraced my steps? I again stopped before the shop, in order to take another look at it, and I felt that it tempted me.

"What a singular thing temptation is! One gazes at an object, and, little by little, it charms you, it disturbs you, it fills your thoughts as a woman's face might do. The enchantment of it penetrates your being, a strange enchantment of form, color and appearance of an inanimate object. And one loves it, one desires it, one wishes to have it. A longing to own it takes possession of you, gently at first, as though it were timid, but growing, becoming intense, irresistible.

"And the dealers seem to guess, from your ardent gaze, your secret and increasing longing.

"I bought this piece of furniture and had it sent home at once. I placed it in my room.

"Oh, I am sorry for those who do not know the honeymoon of the collector with the antique he has just purchased. One looks at it tenderly and passes one's hand over it as if it were human flesh; one comes back to it every moment, one is always thinking of it, wherever ore goes, whatever one does. The dear recollection of it pursues you in the street, in society, everywhere; and when you return home at night, before taking off your gloves or your hat; you go and look at it with the tenderness of a lover.

"Truly, for eight days I worshipped this piece of furniture. I opened its doors and pulled out the drawers every few moments. I handled it with rapture, with all the intense joy of possession.

"But one evening I surmised, while I was feeling the thickness of one of the panels, that there must be a secret drawer in it: My heart began to beat, and I spent the night trying to discover this secret cavity.

"I succeeded on the following day by driving a knife into a slit in the wood. A panel slid back and I saw, spread out on a piece of black velvet, a magnificent tress of hair.

"Yes, a woman's hair, an immense coil of fair hair, almost red, which must have been cut off close to the head, tied with a golden cord.

"I stood amazed, trembling, confused. An almost imperceptible perfume, so ancient that it seemed to be the spirit of a perfume, issued from this mysterious drawer and this remarkable relic.

"I lifted it gently, almost reverently, and took it out of its hiding place. It at once unwound in a golden shower that reached to the floor, dense but light; soft and gleaming like the tail of a comet.

"A strange emotion filled me. What was this? When, how, why had this hair been shut up in this drawer? What adventure, what tragedy did this souvenir conceal? Who had cut it off? A lover on a day of farewell, a husband on a day of revenge, or the one whose head it had graced on the day of despair?

"Was it as she was about to take the veil that they had cast thither that love dowry as a pledge to the world of the living? Was it when they were going to nail down the coffin of the beautiful young corpse that the one who had adored her had cut off her tresses, the only thing that he could retain of her, the only living part of her body that would not suffer decay, the only thing he could still love, and caress, and kiss in his paroxysms of grief?

"Was it not strange that this tress should have remained as it was in life, when not an atom of the body on which it grew was in existence?

"It fell over my fingers, tickled the skin with a singular caress, the caress of a dead woman. It affected me so that I felt as though I should weep.

"I held it in my hands for a long time, then it seemed as if it disturbed me, as though something of the soul had remained in it. And I put it back on the velvet, rusty from age, and pushed in the drawer, closed the doors of the antique cabinet and went out for a walk to meditate.

"I walked along, filled with sadness and also with unrest, that unrest that one feels when in love. I felt as though I must have lived before, as though I must have known this woman.

"And Villon's lines came to my mind like a sob:

Tell me where, and in what place

Is Flora, the beautiful Roman,

Hipparchia and Thais

Who was her cousin-german?

Echo answers in the breeze

O'er river and lake that blows,

Their beauty was above all praise,

But where are last year's snows?

The queen, white as lilies,

Who sang as sing the birds,

Bertha Broadfoot, Beatrice, Alice,

Ermengarde, princess of Maine,

And Joan, the good Lorraine,

Burned by the English at Rouen,

Where are they, Virgin Queen?

And where are last year's snows?

"When I got home again I felt an irresistible longing to see my singular treasure, and I took it out and, as I touched it, I felt a shiver go all through me.

"For some days, however, I was in my ordinary condition, although the thought of that tress of hair was always present to my mind.

"Whenever I came into the house I had to see it and take it in my, hands. I turned the key of the cabinet with the same hesitation that one opens the door leading to one's beloved, for in my hands and my heart I felt a confused, singular, constant sensual longing to plunge my hands in the enchanting golden flood of those dead tresses.

"Then, after I had finished caressing it and had locked the cabinet I felt as if it were a living thing, shut up in there, imprisoned; and I longed to see it again. I felt again the imperious desire to take it in my hands, to touch it, to even feel uncomfortable at the cold, slippery, irritating, bewildering contact.

"I lived thus for a month or two, I forget how long. It obsessed me, haunted me. I was happy and tormented by turns, as when one falls in love, and after the first vows have been exchanged.

"I shut myself in the room with it to feel it on my skin, to bury my lips in it, to kiss it. I wound it round my face, covered my eyes with the golden flood so as to see the day gleam through its gold.

"I loved it! Yes, I loved it. I could not be without it nor pass an hour without looking at it.

"And I waited—I waited—for what? I do not know—For her!

"One night I woke up suddenly, feeling as though I were not alone in my room.

"I was alone, nevertheless, but I could not go to sleep again, and, as I was tossing about feverishly, I got up to look at the golden tress. It seemed softer than usual, more life-like. Do the dead come back? I almost lost consciousness as I kissed it. I took it back with me to bed and pressed it to my lips as if it were my sweetheart.

"Do the dead come back? She came back. Yes, I saw her; I held her in my arms, just as she was in life, tall, fair and round. She came back every evening—the dead woman, the beautiful, adorable, mysterious unknown.

"My happiness was so great that I could not conceal it. No lover ever tasted such intense, terrible enjoyment. I loved her so well that I could not be separated from her. I took her with me always and everywhere. I walked about the town with her as if she were my wife, and took her to the theatre, always to a private box. But they saw her—they guessed—they arrested me. They put me in prison like a criminal. They took her. Oh, misery!"

Here the manuscript stopped. And as I suddenly raised my astonished eyes to the doctor a terrific cry, a howl of impotent rage and of exasperated longing resounded through the asylum.

"Listen," said the doctor. "We have to douse the obscene madman with water five times a day. Sergeant Bertrand was the only one who was in love with the dead."

Filled with astonishment, horror and pity, I stammered out:

"But—that tress—did it really exist?"

The doctor rose, opened a cabinet full of phials and instruments and tossed over a long tress of fair hair which flew toward me like a golden bird.

I shivered at feeling its soft, light touch on my hands. And I sat there, my heart beating with disgust and desire, disgust as at the contact of anything accessory to a crime and desire as at the temptation of some infamous and mysterious thing.

The doctor said as he shrugged his shoulders:

"The mind of man is capable of anything."

ON THE RIVER

I rented a little country house last summer on the banks of the Seine, several leagues from Paris, and went out there to sleep every evening. After a few days I made the acquaintance of one of my neighbors, a man between thirty and forty, who certainly was the most curious specimen I ever met. He was an old boating man, and crazy about boating. He was always beside the water, on the water, or in the water. He must have been born in a boat, and he will certainly die in a boat at the last.

One evening as we were walking along the banks of the Seine I asked him to tell me some stories about his life on the water. The good man at once became animated, his whole expression changed, he became eloquent, almost poetical. There was in his heart one great passion, an absorbing, irresistible passion-the river.

Ah, he said to me, how many memories I have, connected with that river that you see flowing beside us! You people who live in streets know nothing about the river. But listen to a fisherman as he mentions the word. To him it is a mysterious thing, profound, unknown, a land of mirages and phantasmagoria, where one sees by night things that do not exist, hears sounds that one does not recognize, trembles without knowing why, as in passing through a cemetery—and it is, in fact, the most sinister of cemeteries, one in which one has no tomb.

The land seems limited to the river boatman, and on dark nights, when there is no moon, the river seems limitless. A sailor has not the same feeling for the sea. It is often remorseless and cruel, it is true; but it shrieks, it roars, it is honest, the great sea; while the river is silent and perfidious. It does not speak, it flows along without a sound; and this eternal motion of flowing water is more terrible to me than the high waves of the ocean.

Dreamers maintain that the sea hides in its bosom vast tracts of blue where those who are drowned roam among the big fishes, amid strange forests and crystal grottoes. The river has only black depths where one rots in the slime. It is beautiful, however, when it sparkles in the light of the rising sun and gently laps its banks covered with whispering reeds.

The poet says, speaking of the ocean,

"O waves, what mournful tragedies ye know

—Deep waves, the dread of kneeling mothers' hearts!

Ye tell them to each other as ye roll

On flowing tide, and this it is that gives

The sad despairing tones unto your voice

As on ye roll at eve by mounting tide."

Well, I think that the stories whispered by the slender reeds, with their little soft voices, must be more sinister than the lugubrious tragedies told by the roaring of the waves.

But as you have asked for some of my recollections, I will tell you of a singular adventure that happened to me ten years ago.

I was living, as I am now, in Mother Lafon's house, and one of my closest friends, Louis Bernet who has now given up boating, his low shoes and his bare neck, to go into the Supreme Court, was living in the village of C., two leagues further down the river. We dined together every day, sometimes at his house, sometimes at mine.

One evening as I was coming home along and was pretty tired, rowing with difficulty my big boat, a twelve-footer, which I always took out at night, I stopped a few moments to draw breath near the reed-covered point yonder, about two hundred metres from the railway bridge.

It was a magnificent night, the moon shone brightly, the river gleamed, the air was calm and soft. This peacefulness tempted me. I thought to myself that it would be pleasant to smoke a pipe in this spot. I took up my anchor and cast it into the river.

The boat floated downstream with the current, to the end of the chain, and then stopped, and I seated myself in the stern on my sheepskin and made myself as comfortable as possible. There was not a sound to be heard, except that I occasionally thought I could perceive an almost imperceptible lapping of the water against the bank, and I noticed taller groups of reeds which assumed strange shapes and seemed, at times, to move.

The river was perfectly calm, but I felt myself affected by the unusual silence that surrounded me. All the creatures, frogs and toads, those nocturnal singers of the marsh, were silent.

Suddenly a frog croaked to my right, and close beside me. I shuddered. It ceased, and I heard nothing more, and resolved to smoke, to soothe my mind. But, although I was a noted colorer of pipes, I could not smoke; at the second draw I was nauseated, and gave up trying. I began to sing. The sound of my voice was distressing to me. So I lay still, but presently the slight motion of the boat disturbed me. It seemed to me as if she were making huge lurches, from bank to bank of the river, touching each bank alternately. Then I felt as though an invisible force, or being, were drawing her to the surface of the water and lifting her out, to let her fall again. I was tossed about as in a tempest. I heard noises around me. I sprang to my feet with a single bound. The water was glistening, all was calm.

I saw that my nerves were somewhat shaky, and I resolved to leave the spot. I pulled the anchor chain, the boat began to move; then I felt a resistance. I pulled harder, the anchor did not come up; it had caught on something at the bottom of the river and I could not raise it. I began pulling again, but all in vain. Then, with my oars, I turned the boat with its head up stream to change the position of the anchor. It was no use, it was still caught. I flew into a rage and shook the chain furiously. Nothing budged. I sat down, disheartened, and began to reflect on my situation. I could not dream of breaking this chain, or detaching it from the boat, for it was massive and was riveted at the bows to a piece of wood as thick as my arm. However, as the weather was so fine I thought that it probably would not be long before some fisherman came to my aid. My ill-luck had quieted me. I sat down and was able, at length, to smoke my pipe. I had a bottle of rum; I drank two or three glasses, and was able to laugh at the situation. It was very warm; so that, if need be, I could sleep out under the stars without any great harm.

All at once there was a little knock at the side of the boat. I gave a start, and a cold sweat broke out all over me. The noise was, doubtless, caused by some piece of wood borne along by the current, but that was enough, and I again became a prey to a strange nervous agitation. I seized the chain and tensed my muscles in a desperate effort. The anchor held firm. I sat down again, exhausted.

The river had slowly become enveloped in a thick white fog which lay close to the water, so that when I stood up I could see neither the river, nor my feet, nor my boat; but could perceive only the tops of the reeds, and farther off in the distance the plain, lying white in the moonlight, with big black patches rising up from it towards the sky, which were formed by groups of Italian poplars. I was as if buried to the waist in a cloud of cotton of singular whiteness, and all sorts of strange fancies came into my mind. I thought that someone was trying to climb into my boat which I could no longer distinguish, and that the river, hidden by the thick fog, was full of strange creatures which were swimming all around me. I felt horribly uncomfortable, my forehead felt as if it had a tight band round it, my heart beat so that it almost suffocated me, and, almost beside myself, I thought of swimming away from the place. But then, again, the very idea made me tremble with fear. I saw myself, lost, going by guesswork in this heavy fog, struggling about amid the grasses and reeds which I could not escape, my breath rattling with fear, neither seeing the bank, nor finding my boat; and it seemed as if I would feel myself dragged down by the feet to the bottom of these black waters.

In fact, as I should have had to ascend the stream at least five hundred metres before finding a spot free from grasses and rushes where I could land, there were nine chances to one that I could not find my way in the fog and that I should drown, no matter how well I could swim.

I tried to reason with myself. My will made me resolve not to be afraid, but there was something in me besides my will, and that other thing was afraid. I asked myself what there was to be afraid of. My brave "ego" ridiculed my coward "ego," and never did I realize, as on that day, the existence in us of two rival personalities, one desiring a thing, the other resisting, and each winning the day in turn.

This stupid, inexplicable fear increased, and became terror. I remained motionless, my eyes staring, my ears on the stretch with expectation. Of what? I did not know, but it must be something terrible. I believe if it had occurred to a fish to jump out of the water, as often happens, nothing more would have been required to make me fall over, stiff and unconscious.

However, by a violent effort I succeeded in becoming almost rational again. I took up my bottle of rum and took several pulls. Then an idea came to me, and I began to shout with all my might towards all the points of the compass in succession. When my throat was absolutely paralyzed I listened. A dog was howling, at a great distance.

I drank some more rum and stretched myself out at the bottom of the boat. I remained there about an hour, perhaps two, not sleeping, my eyes wide open, with nightmares all about me. I did not dare to rise, and yet I intensely longed to do so. I delayed it from moment to moment. I said to myself: "Come, get up!" and I was afraid to move. At last I raised myself with infinite caution as though my life depended on the slightest sound that I might make; and looked over the edge of the boat. I was dazzled by the most marvellous, the most astonishing sight that it is possible to see. It was one of those phantasmagoria of fairyland, one of those sights described by travellers on their return from distant lands, whom we listen to without believing.

The fog which, two hours before, had floated on the water, had gradually cleared off and massed on the banks, leaving the river absolutely clear; while it formed on either bank an uninterrupted wall six or seven metres high, which shone in the moonlight with the dazzling brilliance of snow. One saw nothing but the river gleaming with light between these two white mountains; and high above my head sailed the great full moon, in the midst of a bluish, milky sky.

All the creatures in the water were awake. The frogs croaked furiously, while every few moments I heard, first to the right and then to the left, the abrupt, monotonous and mournful metallic note of the bullfrogs. Strange to say, I was no longer afraid. I was in the midst of such an unusual landscape that the most remarkable things would not have astonished me.

How long this lasted I do not know, for I ended by falling asleep. When I opened my eyes the moon had gone down and the sky was full of clouds. The water lapped mournfully, the wind was blowing, it was pitch dark. I drank the rest of the rum, then listened, while I trembled, to the rustling of the reeds and the foreboding sound of the river. I tried to see, but could not distinguish my boat, nor even my hands, which I held up close to my eyes.

Little by little, however, the blackness became less intense. All at once I thought I noticed a shadow gliding past, quite near me. I shouted, a voice replied; it was a fisherman. I called him; he came near and I told him of my ill-luck. He rowed his boat alongside of mine and, together, we pulled at the anchor chain. The anchor did not move. Day came, gloomy gray, rainy and cold, one of those days that bring one sorrows and misfortunes. I saw another boat. We hailed it. The man on board of her joined his efforts to ours, and gradually the anchor yielded. It rose, but slowly, slowly, loaded down by a considerable weight. At length we perceived a black mass and we drew it on board. It was the corpse of an old women with a big stone round her neck.

THE CRIPPLE

The following adventure happened to me about 1882. I had just taken the train and settled down in a corner, hoping that I should be left alone, when the door suddenly opened again and I heard a voice say: "Take care, monsieur, we are just at a crossing; the step is very high."

Another voice answered: "That's all right, Laurent, I have a firm hold on the handle."

Then a head appeared, and two hands seized the leather straps hanging on either side of the door and slowly pulled up an enormous body, whose feet striking on the step, sounded like two canes. When the man had hoisted his torso into the compartment I noticed, at the loose edge of his trousers, the end of a wooden leg, which was soon followed by its mate. A head appeared behind this traveller and asked; "Are you all right, monsieur?"

"Yes, my boy."

"Then here are your packages and crutches."

And a servant, who looked like an old soldier, climbed in, carrying in his arms a stack of bundles wrapped in black and yellow papers and carefully tied; he placed one after the other in the net over his master's head. Then he said: "There, monsieur, that is all. There are five of them—the candy, the doll the drum, the gun, and the pate de foies gras."

"Very well, my boy."

"Thank you, Laurent; good health!"

The man closed the door and walked away, and I looked at my neighbor. He was about thirty-five, although his hair was almost white; he wore the ribbon of the Legion of Honor; he had a heavy mustache and was quite stout, with the stoutness of a strong and active man who is kept motionless on account of some infirmity. He wiped his brow, sighed, and, looking me full in the face, he asked: "Does smoking annoy you, monsieur?"

"No, monsieur."

Surely I knew that eye, that voice, that face. But when and where had I seen them? I had certainly met that man, spoken to him, shaken his hand. That was a long, long time ago. It was lost in the haze wherein the mind seems to feel around blindly for memories and pursues them like fleeing phantoms without being able to seize them. He, too, was observing me, staring me out of countenance, with the persistence of a man who remembers slightly but not completely. Our eyes, embarrassed by this persistent contact, turned away; then, after a few minutes, drawn together again by the obscure and tenacious will of working memory, they met once more, and I said: "Monsieur, instead of staring at each other for an hour or so, would it not be better to try to discover where we have known each other?"

My neighbor answered graciously: "You are quite right, monsieur."

I named myself: "I am Henri Bonclair, a magistrate."

He hesitated for a few minutes; then, with the vague look and voice which accompany great mental tension, he said: "Oh, I remember perfectly. I met you twelve years ago, before the war, at the Poincels!"

"Yes, monsieur. Ah! Ah! You are Lieutenant Revaliere?"

"Yes. I was Captain Revaliere even up to the time when I lost my feet —both of them together from one cannon ball."

Now that we knew each other's identity we looked at each other again. I remembered perfectly the handsome, slender youth who led the cotillons with such frenzied agility and gracefulness that he had been nicknamed "the fury." Going back into the dim, distant past, I recalled a story which I had heard and forgotten, one of those stories to which one listens but forgets, and which leave but a faint impression upon the memory.

There was something about love in it. Little by little the shadows cleared up, and the face of a young girl appeared before my eyes. Then her name struck me with the force of an explosion: Mademoiselle de Mandel. I remembered everything now. It was indeed a love story, but quite commonplace. The young girl loved this young man, and when I had met them there was already talk of the approaching wedding. The youth seemed to be very much in love, very happy.

I raised my eye to the net, where all the packages which had been brought in by the servant were trembling from the motion of the train, and the voice of the servant came back to me, as if he had just finished speaking. He had said: "There, monsieur, that is all. There are five of them: the candy, the doll, the drum, the gun, and the pate de foies gras."

Then, in a second, a whole romance unfolded itself in my head. It was like all those which I had already read, where the young lady married notwithstanding the catastrophe, whether physical or financial; therefore, this officer who had been maimed in the war had returned, after the campaign, to the young girl who had given him her promise, and she had kept her word.

I considered that very beautiful, but simple, just as one, considers simple all devotions and climaxes in books or in plays. It always seems, when one reads or listens to these stories of magnanimity, that one could sacrifice one's self with enthusiastic pleasure and overwhelming joy. But the following day, when an unfortunate friend comes to borrow some money, there is a strange revulsion of feeling.

But, suddenly, another supposition, less poetic and more realistic, replaced the first one. Perhaps he had married before the war, before this frightful accident, and she, in despair and resignation, had been forced to receive, care for, cheer, and support this husband, who had departed, a handsome man, and had returned without his feet, a frightful wreck, forced into immobility, powerless anger, and fatal obesity.

Was he happy or in torture? I was seized with an irresistible desire to know his story, or, at least, the principal points, which would permit me to guess that which he could not or would not tell me. Still thinking the matter over, I began talking to him. We had exchanged a few commonplace words; and I raised my eyes to the net, and thought: "He must have three children: the bonbons are for his wife, the doll for his little girl, the drum and the gun for his sons, and this pate de foies gras for himself."

Suddenly I asked him: "Are you a father, monsieur?"

He answered: "No, monsieur."

I suddenly felt confused, as if I had been guilty of some breach of etiquette, and I continued: "I beg your pardon. I had thought that you were when I heard your servant speaking about the toys. One listens and draws conclusions unconsciously."

He smiled and then murmured: "No, I am not even married. I am still at the preliminary stage."

I pretended suddenly to remember, and said:

"Oh! that's true! When I knew you, you were engaged to Mademoiselle de Mandel, I believe."

"Yes, monsieur, your memory is excellent."

I grew very bold and added: "I also seem to remember hearing that Mademoiselle de Mandel married Monsieur—Monsieur—"

He calmly mentioned the name: "Monsieur de Fleurel."

"Yes, that's it! I remember it was on that occasion that I heard of your wound."

I looked him full in the face, and he blushed. His full face, which was already red from the oversupply of blood, turned crimson. He answered quickly, with a sudden ardor of a man who is pleading a cause which is lost in his mind and in his heart, but which he does not wish to admit.

"It is wrong, monsieur, to couple my name with that of Madame de Fleurel. When I returned from the war-without my feet, alas! I never would have permitted her to become my wife. Was it possible? When one marries, monsieur, it is not in order to parade one's generosity; it is in order to live every day, every hour, every minute, every second beside a man; and if this man is disfigured, as I am, it is a death sentence to marry him! Oh, I understand, I admire all sacrifices and devotions when they have a limit, but I do not admit that a woman should give up her whole life, all joy, all her dreams, in order to satisfy the admiration of the gallery. When I hear, on the floor of my room, the tapping of my wooden legs and of my crutches, I grow angry enough to strangle my servant. Do you think that I would permit a woman to do what I myself am unable to tolerate? And, then, do you think that my stumps are pretty?"

He was silent. What could I say? He certainly was right. Could I blame her, hold her in contempt, even say that she was wrong? No. However, the end which conformed to the rule, to the truth, did not satisfy my poetic appetite. These heroic deeds demand a beautiful sacrifice, which seemed to be lacking, and I felt a certain disappointment. I suddenly asked: "Has Madame de Fleurel any children?"

"Yes, one girl and two boys. It is for them that I am bringing these toys. She and her husband are very kind to me."

The train was going up the incline to Saint-Germain. It passed through the tunnels, entered the station, and stopped. I was about to offer my arm to the wounded officer, in order to help him descend, when two hands were stretched up to him through the open door.

"Hello! my dear Revaliere!"

"Ah! Hello, Fleurel!"

Standing behind the man, the woman, still beautiful, was smiling and waving her hands to him. A little girl, standing beside her, was jumping for joy, and two young boys were eagerly watching the drum and the gun, which were passing from the car into their father's hands.

When the cripple was on the ground, all the children kissed him. Then they set off, the little girl holding in her hand the small varnished rung of a crutch, just as she might walk beside her big friend and hold his thumb.

A STROLL

When Old Man Leras, bookkeeper for Messieurs Labuze and Company, left the store, he stood for a minute bewildered at the glory of the setting sun. He had worked all day in the yellow light of a small jet of gas, far in the back of the store, on a narrow court, as deep as a well. The little room where he had been spending his days for forty years was so dark that even in the middle of summer one could hardly see without gaslight from eleven until three.

It was always damp and cold, and from this hole on which his window opened came the musty odor of a sewer.

For forty years Monsieur Leras had been arriving every morning in this prison at eight o'clock, and he would remain there until seven at night, bending over his books, writing with the industry of a good clerk.

He was now making three thousand francs a year, having started at fifteen hundred. He had remained a bachelor, as his means did not allow him the luxury of a wife, and as he had never enjoyed anything, he desired nothing. From time to time, however, tired of this continuous and monotonous work, he formed a platonic wish: "Gad! If I only had an income of fifteen thousand francs, I would take life easy."

He had never taken life easy, as he had never had anything but his monthly salary. His life had been uneventful, without emotions, without hopes. The faculty of dreaming with which every one is blessed had never developed in the mediocrity of his ambitions.

When he was twenty-one he entered the employ of Messieurs Labuze and Company. And he had never left them.

In 1856 he had lost his father and then his mother in 1859. Since then the only incident in his life was when he moved, in 1868, because his landlord had tried to raise his rent.

Every day his alarm clock, with a frightful noise of rattling chains, made him spring out of bed at 6 o'clock precisely.

Twice, however, this piece of mechanism had been out of order—once in 1866 and again in 1874; he had never been able to find out the reason why. He would dress, make his bed, sweep his room, dust his chair and the top of his bureau. All this took him an hour and a half.

Then he would go out, buy a roll at the Lahure Bakery, in which he had seen eleven different owners without the name ever changing, and he would eat this roll on the way to the office.

His entire existence had been spent in the narrow, dark office, which was still decorated with the same wall paper. He had entered there as a young man, as assistant to Monsieur Brument, and with the desire to replace him.

He had taken his place and wished for nothing more.

The whole harvest of memories which other men reap in their span of years, the unexpected events, sweet or tragic loves, adventurous journeys, all the occurrences of a free existence, all these things had remained unknown to him.

Days, weeks, months, seasons, years, all were alike to him. He got up every day at the same hour, started out, arrived at the office, ate luncheon, went away, had dinner and went to bed without ever interrupting the regular monotony of similar actions, deeds and thoughts.

Formerly he used to look at his blond mustache and wavy hair in the little round mirror left by his predecessor. Now, every evening before leaving, he would look at his white mustache and bald head in the same mirror. Forty years had rolled by, long and rapid, dreary as a day of sadness and as similar as the hours of a sleepless night. Forty years of which nothing remained, not even a memory, not even a misfortune, since the death of his parents. Nothing.

That day Monsieur Leras stood by the door, dazzled at the brilliancy of the setting sun; and instead of returning home he decided to take a little stroll before dinner, a thing which happened to him four or five times a year.

He reached the boulevards, where people were streaming along under the green trees. It was a spring evening, one of those first warm and pleasant evenings which fill the heart with the joy of life.

Monsieur Leras went along with his mincing old man's step; he was going along with joy in his heart, at peace with the world. He reached the Champs-Elysees, and he continued to walk, enlivened by the sight of the young people trotting along.

The whole sky was aflame; the Arc de Triomphe stood out against the brilliant background of the horizon, like a giant surrounded by fire. As he approached the immense monument, the old bookkeeper noticed that he was hungry, and he went into a wine dealer's for dinner.

The meal was served in front of the store, on the sidewalk. It consisted of some mutton, salad and asparagus. It was the best dinner that Monsieur Leras had had in a long time. He washed down his cheese with a small bottle of burgundy, had his after-dinner cup of coffee, a thing which he rarely took, and finally a little pony of brandy.

When he had paid he felt quite youthful, even a little moved. And he said to himself: "What a fine evening! I will continue my stroll as far as the entrance to the Bois de Boulogne. It will do me good." He set out. An old tune which one of his neighbors used to sing kept returning to his mind. He kept on humming it over and over again. A hot, still night had fallen over Paris. Monsieur Leras walked along the Avenue du Bois de Boulogne and watched the cabs drive by. They kept coming with their shining lights, one behind the other, giving horn a glimpse of the couples inside, the women in their light dresses and the men dressed in black.

It was one long procession of lovers, riding under the warm, starlit sky. They kept on coming in rapid succession. They passed by in the carriages, silent, side by side, lost in their dreams, in the emotion of desire, in the anticipation of the approaching embrace. The warm shadows seemed to be full of floating kisses. A sensation of tenderness filled the air. All these carriages full of tender couples, all these people intoxicated with the same idea, with the same thought, seemed to give out a disturbing, subtle emanation.

At last Monsieur Leras grew a little tired of walking, and he sat down on a bench to watch these carriages pass by with their burdens of love. Almost immediately a woman walked up to him and sat down beside him. "Good-evening, papa," she said.

He answered: "Madame, you are mistaken."

She slipped her arm through his, saying: "Come along, now; don't be foolish. Listen——"

He arose and walked away, with sadness in his heart. A few yards away another woman walked up to him and asked: "Won't you sit down beside me?" He said: "What makes you take up this life?"

She stood before him and in an altered, hoarse, angry voice exclaimed:

"Well, it isn't for the fun of it, anyhow!"

He insisted in a gentle voice: "Then what makes you?"

She grumbled: "I've got to live! Foolish question!" And she walked away, humming.

Monsieur Leras stood there bewildered. Other women were passing near him, speaking to him and calling to him. He felt as though he were enveloped in darkness by something disagreeable.

He sat down again on a bench. The carriages were still rolling by. He thought: "I should have done better not to come here; I feel all upset." He began to think of all this venal or passionate love, of all these kisses, sold or given, which were passing by it front of him. Love! He scarcely knew it. In his lifetime he had only known two or three women, his means forcing him to live a quiet life, and he looked back at the life which he had led, so different from everybody else, so dreary, so mournful, so empty.

Some people are really unfortunate. And suddenly, as though a veil had been torn from his eyes, he perceived the infinite misery, the monotony of his existence: the past, present and future misery; his last day similar to his first one, with nothing before him, behind him or about him, nothing in his heart or any place.

The stream of carriages was still going by. In the rapid passage of the open carriage he still saw the two silent, loving creatures. It seemed to him that the whole of humanity was flowing on before him, intoxicated with joy, pleasure and happiness. He alone was looking on. To-morrow he would again be alone, always alone, more so than any one else. He stood up, took a few steps, and suddenly he felt as tired as though he had taken a long journey on foot, and he sat down on the next bench.

What was he waiting for? What was he hoping for? Nothing. He was thinking of how pleasant it must be in old age to return home and find the little children. It is pleasant to grow old when one is surrounded by those beings who owe their life to you, who love you, who caress you, who tell you charming and foolish little things which warm your heart and console you for everything.

And, thinking of his empty room, clean and sad, where no one but himself ever entered, a feeling of distress filled his soul; and the place seemed to him more mournful even than his little office. Nobody ever came there; no one ever spoke in it. It was dead, silent, without the echo of a human voice. It seems as though walls retain something of the people who live within them, something of their manner, face and voice. The very houses inhabited by happy families are gayer than the dwellings of the unhappy. His room was as barren of memories as his life. And the thought of returning to this place, all alone, of getting into his bed, of again repeating all the duties and actions of every evening, this thought terrified him. As though to escape farther from this sinister home, and from the time when he would have to return to it, he arose and walked along a path to a wooded corner, where he sat down on the grass.

About him, above him, everywhere, he heard a continuous, tremendous, confused rumble, composed of countless and different noises, a vague and throbbing pulsation of life: the life breath of Paris, breathing like a giant.

The sun was already high and shed a flood of light on the Bois de Boulogne. A few carriages were beginning to drive about and people were appearing on horseback.

A couple was walking through a deserted alley.

Suddenly the young woman raised her eyes and saw something brown in the branches. Surprised and anxious, she raised her hand, exclaiming: "Look! what is that?"

Then she shrieked and fell into the arms of her companion, who was forced to lay her on the ground.

The policeman who had been called cut down an old man who had hung himself with his suspenders.

Examination showed that he had died the evening before. Papers found on him showed that he was a bookkeeper for Messieurs Labuze and Company and that his name was Leras.

His death was attributed to suicide, the cause of which could not be suspected. Perhaps a sudden access of madness!

ALEXANDRE

At four o'clock that day, as on every other day, Alexandre rolled the three-wheeled chair for cripples up to the door of the little house; then, in obedience to the doctor's orders, he would push his old and infirm mistress about until six o'clock.

When he had placed the light vehicle against the step, just at the place where the old lady could most easily enter it, he went into the house; and soon a furious, hoarse old soldier's voice was heard cursing inside the house: it issued from the master, the retired ex-captain of infantry, Joseph Maramballe.

Then could be heard the noise of doors being slammed, chairs being pushed about, and hasty footsteps; then nothing more. After a few seconds, Alexandre reappeared on the threshold, supporting with all his strength Madame Maramballe, who was exhausted from the exertion of descending the stairs. When she was at last settled in the rolling chair, Alexandre passed behind it, grasped the handle, and set out toward the river.

Thus they crossed the little town every day amid the respectful greeting, of all. These bows were perhaps meant as much for the servant as for the mistress, for if she was loved and esteemed by all, this old trooper, with his long, white, patriarchal beard, was considered a model domestic.

The July sun was beating down unmercifully on the street, bathing the low houses in its crude and burning light. Dogs were sleeping on the sidewalk in the shade of the houses, and Alexandre, a little out of breath, hastened his footsteps in order sooner to arrive at the avenue which leads to the water.

Madame Maramballe was already slumbering under her white parasol, the point of which sometimes grazed along the man's impassive face. As soon as they had reached the Allee des Tilleuls, she awoke in the shade of the trees, and she said in a kindly voice: "Go more slowly, my poor boy; you will kill yourself in this heat."

Along this path, completely covered by arched linden trees, the Mavettek flowed in its winding bed bordered by willows.

The gurgling of the eddies and the splashing of the little waves against the rocks lent to the walk the charming music of babbling water and the freshness of damp air. Madame Maramballe inhaled with deep delight the humid charm of this spot and then murmured: "Ah! I feel better now! But he wasn't in a good humor to-day."

Alexandre answered: "No, madame."

For thirty-five years he had been in the service of this couple, first as officer's orderly, then as simple valet who did not wish to leave his masters; and for the last six years, every afternoon, he had been wheeling his mistress about through the narrow streets of the town. From this long and devoted service, and then from this daily tete-a-tete, a kind of familiarity arose between the old lady and the devoted servant, affectionate on her part, deferential on his.

They talked over the affairs of the house exactly as if they were equals. Their principal subject of conversation and of worry was the bad disposition of the captain, soured by a long career which had begun with promise, run along without promotion, end ended without glory.

Madame Maramballe continued: "He certainly was not in a good humor today. This happens too often since he has left the service."

And Alexandre, with a sigh, completed his mistress's thoughts, "Oh, madame might say that it happens every day and that it also happened before leaving the army."

"That is true. But the poor man has been so unfortunate. He began with a brave deed, which obtained for him the Legion of Honor at the age of twenty; and then from twenty to fifty he was not able to rise higher than captain, whereas at the beginning he expected to retire with at least the rank of colonel."

"Madame might also admit that it was his fault. If he had not always been as cutting as a whip, his superiors would have loved and protected him better. Harshness is of no use; one should try to please if one wishes to advance. As far as his treatment of us is concerned, it is also our fault, since we are willing to remain with him, but with others it's different."

Madame Maramballe was thinking. Oh, for how many years had she thus been thinking of the brutality of her husband, whom she had married long ago because he was a handsome officer, decorated quite young, and full of promise, so they said! What mistakes one makes in life!

She murmured: "Let us stop a while, my poor Alexandre, and you rest on that bench:"

It was a little worm-eaten bench, placed at a turn in the alley. Every time they came in this direction Alexandre was accustomed to making a short pause on this seat.

He sat down and with a proud and familiar gesture he took his beautiful white beard in his hand, and, closing his, fingers over it, ran them down to the point, which he held for a minute at the pit of his stomach, as if once more to verify the length of this growth.

Madame Maramballe continued: "I married him; it is only just and natural that I should bear his injustice; but what I do not understand is why you also should have supported it, my good Alexandre!"

He merely shrugged his shoulders and answered: "Oh! I—madame."

She added: "Really. I have often wondered. When I married him you were his orderly and you could hardly do otherwise than endure him. But why did you remain with us, who pay you so little and who treat you so badly, when you could have done as every one else does, settle down, marry, have a family?"

He answered: "Oh, madame! with me it's different."

Then he was silent; but he kept pulling his beard as if he were ringing a bell within him, as if he were trying to pull it out, and he rolled his eyes like a man who is greatly embarrassed.

Madame Maramballe was following her own train of thought: "You are not a peasant. You have an education—"

He interrupted her proudly: "I studied surveying, madame."

"Then why did you stay with us, and blast your prospects?"

He stammered: "That's it! that's it! it's the fault of my dispositton."

"How so, of your disposition?"

"Yes, when I become attached to a person I become attached to him, that's all."

She began to laugh: "You are not going to try to tell me that Maramballe's sweet disposition caused you to become attached to him for life."

He was fidgeting about on his bench visibly embarrassed, and he muttered behind his long beard:

"It was not he, it was you!"

The old lady, who had a sweet face, with a snowy line of curly white hair between her forehead and her bonnet, turned around in her chair and observed her servant with a surprised look, exclaiming: "I, my poor Alexandre! How so?"

He began to look up in the air, then to one side, then toward the distance, turning his head as do timid people when forced to admit shameful secrets. At last he exclaimed, with the courage of a trooper who is ordered to the line of fire: "You see, it's this way—the first time I brought a letter to mademoiselle from the lieutenant, mademoiselle gave me a franc and a smile, and that settled it."

Not understanding well, she questioned him "Explain yourself."

Then he cried out, like a malefactor who is admitting a fatal crime: "I had a sentiment for madame! There!"

She answered nothing, stopped looking at him, hung her head, and thought. She was good, full of justice, gentleness, reason, and tenderness. In a second she saw the immense devotion of this poor creature, who had given up everything in order to live beside her, without saying anything. And she felt as if she could cry. Then, with a sad but not angry expression, she said: "Let us return home."

He rose and began to push the wheeled chair.

As they approached the village they saw Captain Maramballe coming toward them. As soon as he joined them he asked his wife, with a visible desire of getting angry: "What have we for dinner?"

"Some chicken with flageolets."

He lost his temper: "Chicken! chicken! always chicken! By all that's holy, I've had enough chicken! Have you no ideas in your head, that you make me eat chicken every day?"

She answered, in a resigned tone: "But, my dear, you know that the doctor has ordered it for you. It's the best thing for your stomach. If your stomach were well, I could give you many things which I do not dare set before you now."

Then, exasperated, he planted himself in front of Alexandre, exclaiming: "Well, if my stomach is out of order it's the fault of that brute. For thirty-five years he has been poisoning me with his abominable cooking."

Madame Maramballe suddenly turned about completely, in order to see the old domestic. Their eyes met, and in this single glance they both said "Thank you!" to each other.

THE LOG

The drawing-room was small, full of heavy draperies and discreetly fragrant. A large fire burned in the grate and a solitary lamp at one end of the mantelpiece threw a soft light on the two persons who were talking.

She, the mistress of the house, was an old lady with white hair, but one of those old ladies whose unwrinkled skin is as smooth as the finest paper, and scented, impregnated with perfume, with the delicate essences which she had used in her bath for so many years.

He was a very old friend, who had never married, a constant friend, a companion in the journey of life, but nothing more.

They had not spoken for about a minute, and were both looking at the fire, dreaming of no matter what, in one of those moments of friendly silence between people who have no need to be constantly talking in order to be happy together, when suddenly a large log, a stump covered with burning roots, fell out. It fell over the firedogs into the drawing-room and rolled on to the carpet, scattering great sparks around it. The old lady, with a little scream, sprang to her feet to run away, while he kicked the log back on to the hearth and stamped out all the burning sparks with his boots.

When the disaster was remedied, there was a strong smell of burning, and, sitting down opposite to his friend, the man looked at her with a smile and said, as he pointed to the log:

"That is the reason why I never married."

She looked at him in astonishment, with the inquisitive gaze of women who wish to know everything, that eye which women have who are no longer very young,—in which a complex, and often roguish, curiosity is reflected, and she asked:

"How so?"

"Oh, it is a long story," he replied; "a rather sad and unpleasant story.

"My old friends were often surprised at the coldness which suddenly sprang up between one of my best friends whose Christian name was Julien, and myself. They could not understand how two such intimate and inseparable friends, as we had been, could suddenly become almost strangers to one another, and I will tell you the reason of it.

"He and I used to live together at one time. We were never apart, and the friendship that united us seemed so strong that nothing could break it.

"One evening when he came home, he told me that he was going to get married, and it gave me a shock as if he had robbed me or betrayed me. When a man's friend marries, it is all over between them. The jealous affection of a woman, that suspicious, uneasy and carnal affection, will not tolerate the sturdy and frank attachment, that attachment of the mind, of the heart, and that mutual confidence which exists between two men.

"You see, however great the love may be that unites them a man and a woman are always strangers in mind and intellect; they remain belligerents, they belong to different races. There must always be a conqueror and a conquered, a master and a slave; now the one, now the other—they are never two equals. They press each other's hands, those hands trembling with amorous passion; but they never press them with a long, strong, loyal pressure, with that pressure which seems to open hearts and to lay them bare in a burst of sincere, strong, manly affection. Philosophers of old, instead of marrying, and procreating as a consolation for their old age children, who would abandon them, sought for a good, reliable friend, and grew old with him in that communion of thought which can only exist between men.

"Well, my friend Julien married. His wife was pretty, charming, a little, curly-haired blonde, plump and lively, who seemed to worship him. At first I went but rarely to their house, feeling myself de trop. But, somehow, they attracted me to their home; they were constantly inviting me, and seemed very fond of me. Consequently, by degrees, I allowed myself to be allured by the charm of their life. I often dined with them, and frequently, when I returned home at night, thought that I would do as he had done, and get married, as my empty house now seemed very dull.

"They appeared to be very much in love, and were never apart.

"Well, one evening Julien wrote and asked me to go to dinner, and I naturally went.

"'My dear fellow,' he said, 'I must go out directly afterward on business, and I shall not be back until eleven o'clock; but I shall be back at eleven precisely, and I reckon on you to keep Bertha company.'

"The young woman smiled.

"'It was my idea,' she said, 'to send for you.'

"I held out my hand to her.

"'You are as nice as ever, I said, and I felt a long, friendly pressure of my fingers, but I paid no attention to it; so we sat down to dinner, and at eight o'clock Julien went out.

"As soon as he had gone, a kind of strange embarrassment immediately seemed to arise between his wife and me. We had never been alone together yet, and in spite of our daily increasing intimacy, this tete-a-tete placed us in a new position. At first I spoke vaguely of those indifferent matters with which one fills up an embarrassing silence, but she did not reply, and remained opposite to me with her head down in an undecided manner, as if she were thinking over some difficult subject, and as I was at a loss for small talk, I held my tongue. It is surprising how hard it is at times to find anything to say.

"And then also I felt something in the air, something I could not express, one of those mysterious premonitions that warn one of another person's secret intentions in regard to yourself, whether they be good or evil.

"That painful silence lasted some time, and then Bertha said to me:

"'Will you kindly put a log on the fire for it is going out.'

"So I opened the box where the wood was kept, which was placed just where yours is, took out the largest log and put it on top of the others, which were three parts burned, and then silence again reigned in the room.

"In a few minutes the log was burning so brightly that it scorched our faces, and the young woman raised her eyes to mine—eyes that had a strange look to me.

"'It is too hot now,' she said; 'let us go and sit on the sofa over there.'

"So we went and sat on the sofa, and then she said suddenly, looking me full in the face:

"'What would you do if a woman were to tell you that she was in love with you?'

"'Upon my word,' I replied, very much at a loss for an answer, 'I cannot foresee such a case; but it would depend very much upon the woman.'

"She gave a hard, nervous, vibrating laugh; one of those false laughs which seem as if they must break thin glass, and then she added: 'Men are never either venturesome or spiteful.' And, after a moment's silence, she continued: 'Have you ever been in love, Monsieur Paul?' I was obliged to acknowledge that I certainly had, and she asked me to tell her all about it. Whereupon I made up some story or other. She listened to me attentively, with frequent signs of disapproval and contempt, and then suddenly she said:

"'No, you understand nothing about the subject. It seems to me that real love must unsettle the mind, upset the nerves and distract the head; that it must—how shall I express it?—be dangerous, even terrible, almost criminal and sacrilegious; that it must be a kind of treason; I mean to say that it is bound to break laws, fraternal bonds, sacred obligations; when love is tranquil, easy, lawful and without dangers, is it really love?'

"I did not know what answer to give her, and I made this philosophical reflection to myself: 'Oh! female brain, here; indeed, you show yourself!'

"While speaking, she had assumed a demure saintly air; and, resting on the cushions, she stretched herself out at full length, with her head on my shoulder, and her dress pulled up a little so as to show her red stockings, which the firelight made look still brighter. In a minute or two she continued:

"'I suppose I have frightened you?' I protested against such a notion, and she leaned against my breast altogether, and without looking at me, she said: 'If I were to tell you that I love you, what would you do?'

"And before I could think of an answer, she had thrown her arms around my neck, had quickly drawn my head down, and put her lips to mine.

"Oh! My dear friend, I can tell you that I did not feel at all happy! What! deceive Julien? become the lover of this little, silly, wrong-headed, deceitful woman, who was, no doubt, terribly sensual, and whom her husband no longer satisfied.

"To betray him continually, to deceive him, to play at being in love merely because I was attracted by forbidden fruit, by the danger incurred and the friendship betrayed! No, that did not suit me, but what was I to do? To imitate Joseph would be acting a very stupid and, moreover, difficult part, for this woman was enchanting in her perfidy, inflamed by audacity, palpitating and excited. Let the man who has never felt on his lips the warm kiss of a woman who is ready to give herself to him throw the first stone at me.

"Well, a minute more—you understand what I mean? A minute more, and—I should have been—no, she would have been!—I beg your pardon, he would have been—when a loud noise made us both jump up. The log had fallen into the room, knocking over the fire irons and the fender, and on to the carpet, which it had scorched, and had rolled under an armchair, which it would certainly set alight.

"I jumped up like a madman, and, as I was replacing on the fire that log which had saved me, the door opened hastily, and Julien came in.

"'I am free,' he said, with evident pleasure. 'The business was over two hours sooner than I expected!'

"Yes, my dear friend, without that log, I should have been caught in the very act, and you know what the consequences would have been!

"You may be sure that I took good care never to be found in a similar situation again, never, never. Soon afterward I saw that Julien was giving me the 'cold shoulder,' as they say. His wife was evidently undermining our friendship. By degrees he got rid of me, and we have altogether ceased to meet.

"I never married, which ought not to surprise you, I think."

JULIE ROMAIN

Two years ago this spring I was making a walking tour along the shore of the Mediterranean. Is there anything more pleasant than to meditate while walking at a good pace along a highway? One walks in the sunlight, through the caressing breeze, at the foot of the mountains, along the coast of the sea. And one dreams! What a flood of illusions, loves, adventures pass through a pedestrian's mind during a two hours' march! What a crowd of confused and joyous hopes enter into you with the mild, light air! You drink them in with the breeze, and they awaken in your heart a longing for happiness which increases with the hun ger induced by walking. The fleeting, charming ideas fly and sing like birds.

I was following that long road which goes from Saint Raphael to Italy, or, rather, that long, splendid panoramic highway which seems made for the representation of all the love-poems of earth. And I thought that from Cannes, where one poses, to Monaco, where one gambles, people come to this spot of the earth for hardly any other purpose than to get embroiled or to throw away money on chance games, displaying under this delicious sky and in this garden of roses and oranges all base vanities and foolish pretensions and vile lusts, showing up the human mind such as it is, servile, ignorant, arrogant and full of cupidity.

Suddenly I saw some villas in one of those ravishing bays that one meets at every turn of the mountain; there were only four or five fronting the sea at the foot of the mountains, and behind them a wild fir wood slopes into two great valleys, that were untraversed by roads. I stopped short before one of these chalets, it was so pretty: a small white house with brown trimmings, overrun with rambler roses up to the top.

The garden was a mass of flowers, of all colors and all kinds, mixed in a coquettish, well-planned disorder. The lawn was full of them, big pots flanked each side of every step of the porch, pink or yellow clusters framed each window, and the terrace with the stone balustrade, which enclosed this pretty little dwelling, had a garland of enormous red bells, like drops of blood. Behind the house I saw a long avenue of orange trees in blossom, which went up to the foot of the mountain.

Over the door appeared the name, "Villa d'Antan," in small gold letters.

I asked myself what poet or what fairy was living there, what inspired, solitary being had discovered this spot and created this dream house, which seemed to nestle in a nosegay.

A workman was breaking stones up the street, and I went to him to ask the name of the proprietor of this jewel.

"It is Madame Julie Romain," he replied.

Julie Romain! In my childhood, long ago, I had heard them speak of this great actress, the rival of Rachel.

No woman ever was more applauded and more loved—especially more loved! What duets and suicides on her account and what sensational adventures! How old was this seductive woman now? Sixty, seventy, seventy-five! Julie Romain here, in this house! The woman who had been adored by the greatest musician and the most exquisite poet of our land! I still remember the sensation (I was then twelve years of age) which her flight to Sicily with the latter, after her rupture with the former, caused throughout France.

She had left one evening, after a premiere, where the audience had applauded her for a whole half hour, and had recalled her eleven times in succession. She had gone away with the poet, in a post-chaise, as was the fashion then; they had crossed the sea, to love each other in that antique island, the daughter of Greece, in that immense orange wood which surrounds Palermo, and which is called the "Shell of Gold."

People told of their ascension of Mount Etna and how they had leaned over the immense crater, arm in arm, cheek to cheek, as if to throw themselves into the very abyss.

Now he was dead, that maker of verses so touching and so profound that they turned, the heads of a whole generation, so subtle and so mysterious that they opened a new world to the younger poets.

The other one also was dead—the deserted one, who had attained through her musical periods that are alive in the memories of all, periods of triumph and of despair, intoxicating triumph and heartrending despair.

And she was there, in that house veiled by flowers.

I did not hesitate, but rang the bell.

A small servant answered, a boy of eighteen with awkward mien and clumsy hands. I wrote in pencil on my card a gallant compliment to the actress, begging her to receive me. Perhaps, if she knew my name, she would open her door to me.

The little valet took it in, and then came back, asking me to follow him. He led me to a neat and decorous salon, furnished in the Louis-Philippe style, with stiff and heavy furniture, from which a little maid of sixteen, slender but not pretty, took off the covers in my honor.

Then I was left alone.

On the walls hung three portraits, that of the actress in one of her roles, that of the poet in his close-fitting greatcoat and the ruffled shirt then in style, and that of the musician seated at a piano.

She, blond, charming, but affected, according to the fashion of her day, was smiling, with her pretty mouth and blue eyes; the painting was careful, fine, elegant, but lifeless.

Those faces seemed to be already looking upon posterity.

The whole place had the air of a bygone time, of days that were done and men who had vanished.

A door opened and a little woman entered, old, very old, very small, with white hair and white eyebrows, a veritable white mouse, and as quick and furtive of movement.

She held out her hand to me, saying in a voice still fresh, sonorous and vibrant:

"Thank you, monsieur. How kind it is of the men of to-day to remember the women of yesterday! Sit down."

I told her that her house had attracted me, that I had inquired for the proprietor's name, and that, on learning it, I could not resist the desire to ring her bell.

"This gives me all the more pleasure, monsieur," she replied, "as it is the first time that such a thing has happened. When I received your card, with the gracious note, I trembled as if an old friend who had disappeared for twenty years had been announced to me. I am like a dead body, whom no one remembers, of whom no one will think until the day when I shall actually die; then the newspapers will mention Julie Romain for three days, relating anecdotes and details of my life, reviving memories, and praising me greatly. Then all will be over with me."

After a few moments of silence, she continued:

"And this will not be so very long now. In a few months, in a few days, nothing will remain but a little skeleton of this little woman who is now alive."

She raised her eyes toward her portrait, which smiled down upon this caricature of herself; then she looked at those of the two men, the disdainful poet and the inspired musician, who seemed to say: "What does this ruin want of us?"

An indefinable, poignant, irresistible sadness overwhelmed my heart, the sadness of existences that have had their day, but who are still debating with their memories, like a person drowning in deep water.

From my seat I could see on the highroad the handsome carriages that were whirling from Nice to Monaco; inside them I saw young, pretty, rich and happy women and smiling, satisfied men. Following my eye, she understood my thought and murmured with a smile of resignation:

"One cannot both be and have been."

"How beautiful life must have been for you!" I said.

She heaved a great sigh.

"Beautiful and sweet! And for that reason I regret it so much."

I saw that she was disposed to talk of herself, so I began to question her, gently and discreetly, as one might touch bruised flesh.

She spoke of her successes, her intoxications and her friends, of her whole triumphant existence.

"Was it on the stage that you found your most intense joys, your true happiness?" I asked.

"Oh, no!" she replied quickly.

I smiled; then, raising her eyes to the two portraits, she said, with a sad glance:

"It was with them."

"Which one?" I could not help asking.

"Both. I even confuse them up a little now in my old woman's memory, and then I feel remorse."

"Then, madame, your acknowledgment is not to them, but to Love itself. They were merely its interpreters."

"That is possible. But what interpreters!"

"Are you sure that you have not been, or that you might not have been, loved as well or better by a simple man, but not a great man, who would have offered to you his whole life and heart, all his thoughts, all his days, his whole being, while these gave you two redoubtable rivals, Music and Poetry?"

"No, monsieur, no!" she exclaimed emphatically, with that still youthful voice, which caused the soul to vibrate. "Another one might perhaps have loved me more, but he would not have loved me as these did. Ah! those two sang to me of the music of love as no one else in the world could have sung of it. How they intoxicated me! Could any other man express what they knew so well how to express in tones and in words? Is it enough merely to love if one cannot put all the poetry and all the music of heaven and earth into love? And they knew how to make a woman delirious with songs and with words. Yes, perhaps there was more of illusion than of reality in our passion; but these illusions lift you into the clouds, while realities always leave you trailing in the dust. If others have loved me more, through these two I have understood, felt and worshipped love."

Suddenly she began to weep.

She wept silently, shedding tears of despair.

I pretended not to see, looking off into the distance. She resumed, after a few minutes:

"You see, monsieur, with nearly every one the heart ages with the body. But this has not happened with me. My body is sixty-nine years old, while my poor heart is only twenty. And that is the reason why I live all alone, with my flowers and my dreams."

There was a long silence between us. She grew calmer and continued, smiling:

"How you would laugh at me, if you knew, if you knew how I pass my evenings, when the weather is fine. I am ashamed and I pity myself at the same time."

Beg as I might, she would not tell me what she did. Then I rose to leave.

"Already!" she exclaimed.

And as I said that I wished to dine at Monte Carlo, she asked timidly:

"Will you not dine with me? It would give me a great deal of pleasure."

I accepted at once. She rang, delighted, and after giving some orders to the little maid she took me over her house.

A kind of glass-enclosed veranda, filled with shrubs, opened into the dining-room, revealing at the farther end the long avenue of orange trees extending to the foot of the mountain. A low seat, hidden by plants, indicated that the old actress often came there to sit down.

Then we went into the garden, to look at the flowers. Evening fell softly, one of those calm, moist evenings when the earth breathes forth all her perfumes. Daylight was almost gone when we sat down at table. The dinner was good and it lasted a long time, and we became intimate friends, she and I, when she understood what a profound sympathy she had aroused in my heart. She had taken two thimblefuls of wine, as the phrase goes, and had grown more confiding and expansive.

"Come, let us look at the moon," she said. "I adore the good moon. She has been the witness of my most intense joys. It seems to me that all my memories are there, and that I need only look at her to bring them all back to me. And even—some times—in the evening—I offer to myself a pretty play—yes, pretty—if you only knew! But no, you would laugh at me. I cannot—I dare not—no, no—really—no."

I implored her to tell me what it was.

"Come, now! come, tell me; I promise you that I will not laugh. I swear it to you—come, now!"

She hesitated. I took her hands—those poor little hands, so thin and so cold!—and I kissed them one after the other, several times, as her lovers had once kissed them. She was moved and hesitated.

"You promise me not to laugh?"

"Yes, I swear it to you."

"Well, then, come."

She rose, and as the little domestic, awkward in his green livery, removed the chair behind her, she whispered quickly a few words into his ear.

"Yes, madame, at once," he replied.

She took my arm and led me to the veranda.

The avenue of oranges was really splendid to see. The full moon made a narrow path of silver, a long bright line, which fell on the yellow sand, between the round, opaque crowns of the dark trees.

As these trees were in bloom, their strong, sweet perfume filled the night, and swarming among their dark foliage I saw thousands of fireflies, which looked like seeds fallen from the stars.

"Oh, what a setting for a love scene!" I exclaimed.

She smiled.

"Is it not true? Is it not true? You will see!"

And she made me sit down beside her.

"This is what makes one long for more life. But you hardly think of these things, you men of to-day. You are speculators, merchants and men of affairs.

"You no longer even know how to talk to us. When I say 'you,' I mean young men in general. Love has been turned into a liaison which very often begins with an unpaid dressmaker's bill. If you think the bill is dearer than the woman, you disappear; but if you hold the woman more highly, you pay it. Nice morals—and a nice kind of love!"

She took my hand.

"Look!"

I looked, astonished and delighted. Down there at the end of the avenue, in the moonlight, were two young people, with their arms around each other's waist. They were walking along, interlaced, charming, with short, little steps, crossing the flakes of light; which illuminated them momentarily, and then sinking back into the shadow. The youth was dressed in a suit of white satin, such as men wore in the eighteenth century, and had on a hat with an ostrich plume. The girl was arrayed in a gown with panniers, and the high, powdered coiffure of the handsome dames of the time of the Regency.

They stopped a hundred paces from us, and standing in the middle of the avenue, they kissed each other with graceful gestures.

Suddenly I recognized the two little servants. Then one of those dreadful fits of laughter that convulse you made me writhe in my chair. But I did not laugh aloud. I resisted, convulsed and feeling almost ill, as a man whose leg is cut off resists the impulse to cry out.

As the young pair turned toward the farther end of the avenue they again became delightful. They went farther and farther away, finally disappearing as a dream disappears. I no longer saw them. The avenue seemed a sad place.

I took my leave at once, so as not to see them again, for I guessed that this little play would last a long time, awakening, as it did, a whole past of love and of stage scenery; the artificial past, deceitful and seductive, false but charming, which still stirred the heart of this amorous old comedienne.

THE RONDOLI SISTERS

I

I set out to see Italy thoroughly on two occasions, and each time I was stopped at the frontier and could not get any further. So I do not know Italy, said my friend, Charles Jouvent. And yet my two attempts gave me a charming idea of the manners of that beautiful country. Some time, however, I must visit its cities, as well as the museums and works of art with which it abounds. I will make another attempt to penetrate into the interior, which I have not yet succeeded in doing.

You don't understand me, so I will explain: In the spring of 1874 I was seized with an irresistible desire to see Venice, Florence, Rome and Naples. I am, as you know, not a great traveller; it appears to me a useless and fatiguing business. Nights spent in a train, the disturbed slumbers of the railway carriage, with the attendant headache, and stiffness in every limb, the sudden waking in that rolling box, the unwashed feeling, with your eyes and hair full of dust, the smell of the coal on which one's lungs feed, those bad dinners in the draughty refreshment rooms are, according to my ideas, a horrible way of beginning a pleasure trip.

After this introduction, we have the miseries of the hotel; of some great hotel full of people, and yet so empty; the strange room and the doubtful bed!

I am most particular about my bed; it is the sanctuary of life. We entrust our almost naked and fatigued bodies to it so that they may be reanimated by reposing between soft sheets and feathers.

There we find the most delightful hours of our existence, the hours of love and of sleep. The bed is sacred, and should be respected, venerated and loved by us as the best and most delightful of our earthly possessions.

I cannot lift up the sheets of a hotel bed without a shudder of disgust. Who has occupied it the night before? Perhaps dirty, revolting people have slept in it. I begin, then, to think of all the horrible people with whom one rubs shoulders every day, people with suspicious-looking skin which makes one think of the feet and all the rest! I call to mind those who carry about with them the sickening smell of garlic or of humanity. I think of those who are deformed and unhealthy, of the perspiration emanating from the sick, of everything that is ugly and filthy in man.

And all this, perhaps, in the bed in which I am about to sleep! The mere idea of it makes me feel ill as I get into it.

And then the hotel dinners—those dreary table d'hote dinners in the midst of all sorts of extraordinary people, or else those terrible solitary dinners at a small table in a restaurant, feebly lighted by a wretched composite candle under a shade.

Again, those terribly dull evenings in some unknown town! Do you know anything more wretched than the approach of dusk on such an occasion? One goes about as if almost in a dream, looking at faces that one never has seen before and never will see again; listening to people talking about matters which are quite indifferent to you in a language that perhaps you do not understand. You have a terrible feeling, almost as if you were lost, and you continue to walk on so as not to be obliged to return to the hotel, where you would feel more lost still because you are at home, in a home which belongs to anyone who can pay for it; and at last you sink into a chair of some well-lighted cafe, whose gilding and lights oppress you a thousand times more than the shadows in the streets. Then you feel so abominably lonely sitting in front of the glass of flat bock beer that a kind of madness seizes you, the longing to go somewhere or other, no matter where, as long as you need not remain in front of that marble table amid those dazzling lights.

And then, suddenly, you are aware that you are really alone in the world, always and everywhere, and that in places which we know, the familiar jostlings give us the illusion only of human fraternity. At such moments of self-abandonment and sombre isolation in distant cities one thinks broadly, clearly and profoundly. Then one suddenly sees the whole of life outside the vision of eternal hope, apart from the deceptions of our innate habits, and of our expectations of happiness, which we indulge in dreams never to be realized.

It is only by going a long distance from home that we can fully understand how short-lived and empty everything near at hand is; by searching for the unknown, we perceive how commonplace and evanescent everything is; only by wandering over the face of the earth can we understand how small the world is, and how very much alike it is everywhere.

How well I know, and how I hate and almost fear, those haphazard walks through unknown streets; and this was the reason why, as nothing would induce me to undertake a tour in Italy by myself, I made up my mind to accompany my friend Paul Pavilly.

You know Paul, and how he idealizes women. To him the earth is habitable only because they are there; the sun gives light and is warm because it shines upon them; the air is soft and balmy because it blows upon their skin and ruffles the soft hair on their temples; and the moon is charming because it makes them dream and imparts a languorous charm to love. Every act and action of Paul's has woman for its motive; all his thoughts, all his efforts and hopes are centered in them.

When I mentioned Italy to Paul he at first absolutely refused to leave Paris. I, however, began to tell him of the adventures I had on my travels. I assured him that all Italian women are charming, and I made him hope for the most refined pleasures at Naples, thanks to certain letters of introduction which I had; and so at last he allowed himself to be persuaded.

II

We took the express one Thursday evening, Paul and I. Hardly anyone goes south at that time of the year, so that we had the carriages to ourselves, and both of us were in a bad temper on leaving Paris, sorry for having yielded to the temptation of this journey, and regretting Marly, the Seine, and our lazy boating excursions, and all those pleasures in and near Paris which are so dear to every true Parisian.

As soon as the train started Paul stuck himself in his corner, and said, "It is most idiotic to go all that distance," and as it was too late for him to change his mind then, I said, "Well, you should not have come."

He made no answer, and I felt very much inclined to laugh when I saw how furious he looked. He is certainly always rather like a squirrel, but then every one of us has retained the type of some animal or other as the mark of his primitive origin. How many people have jaws like a bulldog, or heads like goats, rabbits, foxes, horses, or oxen. Paul is a squirrel turned into a man. He has its bright, quick eyes, its hair, its pointed nose, its small, fine, supple, active body, and a certain mysterious resemblance in its general bearing; in fact, a similarity of movement, of gesture, and of bearing which might almost be taken for a recollection.

At last we both went to sleep with that uncomfortable slumber of the railway carriage, which is interrupted by horrible cramps in the arms and neck, and by the sudden stoppages of the train.

We woke up as we were passing along the Rhone. Soon the continued noise of crickets came in through the windows, that cry which seems to be the voice of the warm earth, the song of Provence; and seemed to instill into our looks, our breasts, and our souls the light and happy feeling of the south, that odor of the parched earth, of the stony and light soil of the olive with its gray-green foliage.

When the train stopped again a railway guard ran along the train calling out "Valence" in a sonorous voice, with an accent that again gave us a taste of that Provence which the shrill note of the crickets had already imparted to us.

Nothing fresh happened till we got to Marseilles, where we alighted for breakfast, but when we returned to our carriage we found a woman installed there.

Paul, with a delighted glance at me, gave his short mustache a mechanical twirl, and passed his fingers through his, hair, which had become slightly out of order with the night's journey. Then he sat down opposite the newcomer.

Whenever I happen to see a striking new face, either in travelling or in society, I always have the strongest inclination to find out what character, mind, and intellectual capacities are hidden beneath those features.

She was a young and pretty woman, certainly a native of the south of France, with splendid eyes, beautiful wavy black hair, which was so thick and long that it seemed almost too heavy for her head. She was dressed with a certain southern bad taste which made her look a little vulgar. Her regular features had none of the grace and finish of the refined races, of that slight delicacy which members of the aristocracy inherit from their birth, and which is the hereditary mark of thinner blood.

Her bracelets were too big to be of gold; she wore earrings with large white stones that were certainly not diamonds, and she belonged unmistakably to the People. One surmised that she would talk too loud, and shout on every occasion with exaggerated gestures.

When the train started she remained motionless in her place, in the attitude of a woman who was indignant, without even looking at us.

Paul began to talk to me, evidently with an eye to effect, trying to attract her attention, as shopkeepers expose their choice wares to catch the notice of passersby.

She, however, did not appear to be paying the least attention.

"Toulon! Ten minutes to wait! Refreshment room!" the porters shouted.

Paul motioned to me to get out, and as soon as we had done so, he said:

"I wonder who on earth she can be?"

I began to laugh. "I am sure I don't know, and I don't in the least care."

He was quite excited.

"She is an uncommonly fresh and pretty girl. What eyes she has, and how cross she looks. She must have been dreadfully worried, for she takes no notice of anything."

"You will have all your trouble for nothing," I growled.

He began to lose his temper.

"I am not taking any trouble, my dear fellow. I think her an extremely pretty woman, that is all. If one could only speak to her! But I don't know how to begin. Cannot you give me an idea? Can't you guess who she is?"

"Upon my word, I cannot. However, I should rather think she is some strolling actress who is going to rejoin her company after a love adventure."

He seemed quite upset, as if I had said something insulting.

"What makes you think that? On the contrary, I think she looks most respectable."

"Just look at her bracelets," I said, "her earrings and her whole dress. I should not be the least surprised if she were a dancer or a circus rider, but most likely a dancer. Her whole style smacks very much of the theatre."

He evidently did not like the idea.

"She is much too young, I am sure; why, she is hardly twenty."

"Well," I replied, "there are many things which one can do before one is twenty; dancing and elocution are among them."

"Take your seats for Nice, Vintimiglia," the guards and porters called.

We got in; our fellow passenger was eating an orange, and certainly she did not do it elegantly. She had spread her pocket-handkerchief on her knees, and the way in which she tore off the peel and opened her mouth to put in the pieces, and then spat the pips out of the window, showed that her training had been decidedly vulgar.

She seemed, also, more put out than ever, and swallowed the fruit with an exceedingly comic air of rage.

Paul devoured her with his eyes, and tried to attract her attention and excite her curiosity; but in spite of his talk, and of the manner in which he brought in well-known names, she did not pay the least attention to him.

After passing Frejus and St. Raphael, the train passed through a veritable garden, a paradise of roses, and groves of oranges and lemons covered with fruits and flowers at the same time. That delightful coast from Marseilles to Genoa is a kingdom of perfumes in a home of flowers.

June is the time to see it in all its beauty, when in every narrow valley and on every slope, the most exquisite flowers are growing luxuriantly. And the roses! fields, hedges, groves of roses. They climb up the walls, blossom on the roofs, hang from the trees, peep out from among the bushes; they are white, red, yellow, large and small, single, with a simple self-colored dress, or full and heavy in brilliant toilettes.

Their breath makes the air heavy and relaxing, and the still more penetrating odor of the orange blossoms sweetens the atmosphere till it might almost be called the refinement of odor.

The shore, with its brown rocks, was bathed by the motionless Mediterranean. The hot summer sun stretched like a fiery cloth over the mountains, over the long expanses of sand, and over the motionless, apparently solid blue sea. The train went on through the tunnels, along the slopes, above the water, on straight, wall-like viaducts, and a soft, vague, saltish smell, a smell of drying seaweed, mingled at times with the strong, heavy perfume of the flowers.

But Paul neither saw, looked at, nor smelled anything, for our fellow traveller engrossed all his attention.

When we reached Cannes, as he wished to speak to me he signed to me to get out, and as soon as I did so, he took me by the arm.

"Do you know, she is really charming. Just look at her eyes; and I never saw anything like her hair."

"Don't excite yourself," I replied, "or else address her, if you have any intentions that way. She does not look unapproachable; I fancy, although she appear to be a little bit grumpy."

"Why don't you speak to her?" he said.

"I don't know what to say, for I am always terribly stupid at first; I can never make advances to a woman in the street. I follow them, go round and round them, and quite close to them, but never know what to say at first. I only once tried to enter into conversation with a woman in that way. As I clearly saw that she was waiting for me to make overtures, and as I felt bound to say something, I stammered out, 'I hope you are quite well, madame?' She laughed in my face, and I made my escape."

I promised Paul to do all I could to bring about a conversation, and when we had taken our places again, I politely asked our neighbor:

"Have you any objection to the smell of tobacco, madame?"

She merely replied, "Non capisco."

So she was an Italian! I felt an absurd inclination to laugh. As Paul did not understand a word of that language, I was obliged to act as his interpreter, so I said in Italian:

"I asked you, madame, whether you had any objection to tobacco smoke?"

With an angry look she replied, "Che mi fa!"

She had neither turned her head nor looked at me, and I really did not know whether to take this "What do I care" for an authorization, a refusal, a real sign of indifference, or for a mere "Let me alone."

"Madame," I replied, "if you mind the smell of tobacco in the least—"

She again said, "Mica," in a tone which seemed to mean, "I wish to goodness you would leave me alone!" It was, however, a kind of permission, so I said to Paul:

"You may smoke."

He looked at me in that curious sort of way that people have when they try to understand others who are talking in a strange language before them, and asked me:

"What did you say to her?"

"I asked whether we might smoke, and she said we might do whatever we liked."

Whereupon I lighted my cigar.

"Did she say anything more?"

"If you had counted her words you would have noticed that she used exactly six, two of which gave me to understand that she knew no French, so four remained, and much can be said in four words."

Paul seemed quite unhappy, disappointed, and at sea, so to speak.

But suddenly the Italian asked me, in that tone of discontent which seemed habitual to her, "Do you know at what time we shall get to Genoa?"

"At eleven o'clock," I replied. Then after a moment I went on:

"My friend and I are also going to Genoa, and if we can be of any service to you, we shall be very happy, as you are quite alone." But she interrupted with such a "Mica!" that I did not venture on another word.

"What did she say?" Paul asked.

"She said she thought you were charming."

But he was in no humor for joking, and begged me dryly not to make fun of him; so I translated her question and my polite offer, which had been so rudely rejected.

Then he really became as restless as a caged squirrel.

"If we only knew," he said, "what hotel she was going to, we would go to the same. Try to find out so as to have another opportunity to make her talk."

It was not particularly easy, and I did not know what pretext to invent, desirous as I was to make the acquaintance of this unapproachable person.

We passed Nice, Monaco, Mentone, and the train stopped at the frontier for the examination of luggage.

Although I hate those ill-bred people who breakfast and dine in railway-carriages, I went and bought a quantity of good things to make one last attack on her by their means. I felt sure that this girl must, ordinarily, be by no means inaccessible. Something had put her out and made her irritable, but very little would suffice, a mere word or some agreeable offer, to decide her and vanquish her.

We started again, and we three were still alone. I spread my eatables on the seat. I cut up the fowl, put the slices of ham neatly on a piece of paper, and then carefully laid out our dessert, strawberries, plums, cherries and cakes, close to the girl.

When she saw that we were about to eat she took a piece of chocolate and two little crisp cakes out of her pocket and began to munch them.

"Ask her to have some of ours," Paul said in a whisper.

"That is exactly what I wish to do, but it is rather a difficult matter."

As she, however, glanced from time to time at our provisions, I felt sure that she would still be hungry when she had finished what she had with her; so, as soon as her frugal meal was over, I said to her:

"It would be very kind of you if you would take some of this fruit."

Again she said "Mica!" but less crossly than before.

"Well, then," I said, "may I offer you a little wine? I see you have not drunk anything. It is Italian wine, and as we are now in your own country, we should be very pleased to see such a pretty Italian mouth accept the offer of its French neighbors."

She shook her head slightly, evidently wishing to refuse, but very desirous of accepting, and her mica this time was almost polite. I took the flask, which was covered with straw in the Italian fashion, and filling the glass, I offered it to her.

"Please drink it," I said, "to bid us welcome to your country."

She took the glass with her usual look, and emptied it at a draught, like a woman consumed with thirst, and then gave it back to me without even saying "Thank you."

I then offered her the cherries. "Please take some," I said; "we shall be so glad if you will."

Out of her corner she looked at all the fruit spread out beside her, and said so rapidly that I could scarcely follow her: "A me non piacciono ne le ciriegie ne le susine; amo soltano le fragole."

"What does she say?" Paul asked.

"That she does riot care for cherries or plums, but only for strawberries."

I put a newspaper full of wild strawberries on her lap, and she ate them quickly, tossing them into her mouth from some distance in a coquettish and charming manner.

When she had finished the little red heap, which soon disappeared under the rapid action of her hands, I asked her:

"What may I offer you now?"

"I will take a little chicken," she replied.

She certainly devoured half of it, tearing it to pieces with the rapid movements of her jaws like some carnivorous animal. Then she made up her mind to have some cherries, which she "did not like," and then some plums, then some little cakes. Then she said, "I have had enough," and sat back in her corner.

I was much amused, and tried to make her eat more, insisting, in fact, till she suddenly flew into a rage, and flung such a furious mica at me, that I would no longer run the risk of spoiling her digestion.

I turned to my friend. "My poor Paul," I said, "I am afraid we have had our trouble for nothing."

The night came on, one of those hot summer nights which extend their warm shade over the burning and exhausted earth. Here and there, in the distance, by the sea, on capes and promontories, bright stars, which I was, at times, almost inclined to confound with lighthouses, began to shine on the dark horizon:

The scent of the orange trees became more penetrating, and we breathed with delight, distending our lungs to inhale it more deeply. The balmy air was soft, delicious, almost divine.

Suddenly I noticed something like a shower of stars under the dense shade of the trees along the line, where it was quite dark. It might have been taken for drops of light, leaping, flying, playing and running among the leaves, or for small stars fallen from the skies in order to have an excursion on the earth; but they were only fireflies dancing a strange fiery ballet in the perfumed air.

One of them happened to come into our carriage, and shed its intermittent light, which seemed to be extinguished one moment and to be burning the next. I covered the carriage-lamp with its blue shade and watched the strange fly careering about in its fiery flight. Suddenly it settled on the dark hair of our neighbor, who was half dozing after dinner. Paul seemed delighted, with his eyes fixed on the bright, sparkling spot, which looked like a living jewel on the forehead of the sleeping woman.

The Italian woke up about eleven o'clock, with the bright insect still in her hair. When I saw her move, I said: "We are just getting to Genoa, madame," and she murmured, without answering me, as if possessed by some obstinate and embarrassing thought:

"What am I going to do, I wonder?"

And then she suddenly asked:

"Would you like me to come with you?"

I was so taken aback that I really did not understand her.

"With us? How do you mean?"

She repeated, looking more and more furious:

"Would you like me to be your guide now, as soon as we get out of the train?"

"I am quite willing; but where do you want to go."

She shrugged her shoulders with an air of supreme indifference.

"Wherever you like; what does it matter to me?" She repeated her "Che mi fa" twice.

"But we are going to the hotel."

"Very well, let us all go to the hotel," she said, in a contemptuous voice.

I turned to Paul, and said:

"She wishes to know whether we should like her to come with us."

My friend's utter surprise restored my self-possession. He stammered:

"With us? Where to? What for? How?"

"I don't know, but she made this strange proposal to me in a most irritated voice. I told her that we were going to the hotel, and she said: 'Very well, let us all go there!' I suppose she is without a penny. She certainly has a very strange way of making acquaintances."

Paul, who 'was very much excited, exclaimed:

"I am quite agreeable. Tell her that we will go wherever she likes." Then, after a moment's hesitation, he said uneasily:

"We must know, however, with whom she wishes to go—with you or with me?"

I turned to the Italian, who did not even seem to be listening to us, and said:

"We shall be very happy to have you with us, but my friend wishes to know whether you will take my arm or his?"

She opened her black eyes wide with vague surprise, and said, "Che ni fa?"

I was obliged to explain myself. "In Italy, I believe, when a man looks after a woman, fulfils all her wishes, and satisfies all her caprices, he is called a patito. Which of us two will you take for your patito?"

Without the slightest hesitation she replied:

"You!"

I turned to Paul. "You see, my friend, she chooses me; you have no chance."

"All the better for you," he replied in a rage. Then, after thinking for a few moments, he went on:

"Do you really care about taking this creature with you? She will spoil our journey. What are we to do with this woman, who looks like I don't know what? They will not take us in at any decent hotel."

I, however, just began to find the Italian much nicer than I had thought her at first, and I was now very desirous to take her with us. The idea delighted me.

I replied, "My dear fellow, we have accepted, and it is too late to recede. You were the first to advise me to say 'Yes.'"

"It is very stupid," he growled, "but do as you please."

The train whistled, slackened speed, and we ran into the station.

I got out of the carriage, and offered my new companion my hand. She jumped out lightly, and I gave her my arm, which she took with an air of seeming repugnance. As soon as we had claimed our luggage we set off into the town, Paul walking in utter silence.

"To what hotel shall we go?" I asked him. "It may be difficult to get into the City of Paris with a woman, especially with this Italian."

Paul interrupted me. "Yes, with an Italian who looks more like a dancer than a duchess. However, that is no business of mine. Do just as you please."

I was in a state of perplexity. I had written to the City of Paris to retain our rooms, and now I did not know what to do.

Two commissionaires followed us with our luggage. I continued: "You might as well go on first, and say that we are coming; and give the landlord to understand that I have a—a friend with me and that we should like rooms quite by themselves for us three, so as not to be brought in contact with other travellers. He will understand, and we will decide according to his answer."

But Paul growled, "Thank you, such commissions and such parts do not suit me, by any means. I did not come here to select your apartments or to minister to your pleasures."

But I was urgent: "Look here, don't be angry. It is surely far better to go to a good hotel than to a bad one, and it is not difficult to ask the landlord for three separate bedrooms and a dining-room."

I put a stress on three, and that decided him.

He went on first, and I saw him go into a large hotel while I remained on the other side of the street, with my fair Italian, who did not say a word, and followed the porters with the luggage.

Paul came back at last, looking as dissatisfied as my companion.

"That is settled," he said, "and they will take us in; but here are only two bedrooms. You must settle it as you can."

I followed him, rather ashamed of going in with such a strange companion.

There were two bedrooms separated by a small sitting-room. I ordered a cold supper, and then I turned to the Italian with a perplexed look.

"We have only been able to get two rooms, so you must choose which you like."

She replied with her eternal "Che mi fa!" I thereupon took up her little black wooden trunk, such as servants use, and took it into the room on the right, which I had chosen for her. A bit of paper was fastened to the box, on which was written, Mademoiselle Francesca Rondoli, Genoa.

"Your name is Francesca?" I asked, and she nodded her head, without replying.

"We shall have supper directly," I continued. "Meanwhile, I dare say you would like to arrange your toilette a little?"

She answered with a 'mica', a word which she employed just as frequently as 'Che me fa', but I went on: "It is always pleasant after a journey."

Then I suddenly remembered that she had not, perhaps, the necessary requisites, for she appeared to me in a very singular position, as if she had just escaped from some disagreeable adventure, and I brought her my dressing-case.

I put out all the little instruments for cleanliness and comfort which it contained: a nail-brush, a new toothbrush—I always carry a selection of them about with me—my nail-scissors, a nail-file, and sponges. I uncorked a bottle of eau de cologne, one of lavender-water, and a little bottle of new-mown hay, so that she might have a choice. Then I opened my powder-box, and put out the powder-puff, placed my fine towels over the water-jug, and a piece of new soap near the basin.

She watched my movements with a look of annoyance in her wide-open eyes, without appearing either astonished or pleased at my forethought.

"Here is all that you require," I then said; "I will tell you when supper is ready."

When I returned to the sitting-room I found that Paul had shut himself in the other room, so I sat down to wait.

A waiter went to and fro, bringing plates and glasses. He laid the table slowly, then put a cold chicken on it, and told me that all was ready.

I knocked gently at Mademoiselle Rondoli's door. "Come in," she said, and when I did so I was struck by a strong, heavy smell of perfumes, as if I were in a hairdresser's shop.

The Italian was sitting on her trunk in an attitude either of thoughtful discontent or absent-mindedness. The towel was still folded over the waterjug that was full of water, and the soap, untouched and dry, was lying beside the empty basin; but one would have thought that the young woman had used half the contents of the bottles of perfume. The eau de cologne, however, had been spared, as only about a third of it had gone; but to make up for that she had used a surprising amount of lavender-water and new-mown hay. A cloud of violet powder, a vague white mist, seemed still to be floating in the air, from the effects of her over-powdering her face and neck. It seemed to cover her eyelashes, eyebrows, and the hair on her temples like snow, while her cheeks were plastered with it, and layers of it covered her nostrils, the corners of her eyes, and her chin.

When she got up she exhaled such a strong odor of perfume that it almost made me feel faint.

When we sat down to supper, I found that Paul was in a most execrable temper, and I could get nothing out of him but blame, irritable words, and disagreeable remarks.

Mademoiselle Francesca ate like an ogre, and as soon as she had finished her meal she threw herself upon the sofa in the sitting-room. Sitting down beside her, I said gallantly, kissing her hand:

"Shall I have the bed prepared, or will you sleep on the couch?"

"It is all the same to me. 'Che mi fa'!"

Her indifference vexed me.

"Should you like to retire at once?"

"Yes; I am very sleepy."

She got up, yawned, gave her hand to Paul, who took it with a furious look, and I lighted her into the bedroom. A disquieting feeling haunted me. "Here is all you want," I said again.

The next morning she got up early, like a woman who is accustomed to work. She woke me by doing so, and I watched her through my half-closed eyelids.

She came and went without hurrying herself, as if she were astonished at having nothing to do. At length she went to the dressing-table, and in a moment emptied all my bottles of perfume. She certainly also used some water, but very little.

When she was quite dressed, she sat down on her trunk again, and clasping one knee between her hands, she seemed to be thinking.

At that moment I pretended to first notice her, and said:

"Good-morning, Francesca."

Without seeming in at all a better temper than the previous night, she murmured, "Good-morning!"

When I asked her whether she had slept well, she nodded her head, and jumping out of bed, I went and kissed her.

She turned her face toward me like a child who is being kissed against its will; but I took her tenderly in my arms, and gently pressed my lips on her eyelids, which she closed with evident distaste under my kisses on her fresh cheek and full lips, which she turned away.

"You don't seem to like being kissed," I said to her.

"Mica!" was her only answer.

I sat down on the trunk by her side, and passing my arm through hers, I said: "Mica! mica! mica! in reply to everything. I shall call you Mademoiselle Mica, I think."

For the first time I fancied that I saw the shadow of a smile on her lips, but it passed by so quickly that I may have been mistaken.

"But if you never say anything but Mica, I shall not know what to do to please you. Let me see; what shall we do to-day?"

She hesitated a moment, as if some fancy had flitted through her head, and then she said carelessly: "It is all the same to me; whatever you like."

"Very well, Mademoiselle Mica, we will have a carriage and go for a drive."

"As you please," she said.

Paul was waiting for us in the dining-room, looking as bored as third parties usually do in love affairs. I assumed a delighted air, and shook hands with him with triumphant energy.

"What are you thinking of doing?" he asked.

"First of all, we will go and see a little of the town, and then we might get a carriage and take a drive in the neighborhood."

We breakfasted almost in silence, and then set out. I dragged Francesca from palace to palace, and she either looked at nothing or merely glanced carelessly at the various masterpieces. Paul followed us, growling all sorts of disagreeable things. Then we all three took a drive in silence into the country and returned to dinner.

The next day it was the same thing and the next day again; and on the third Paul said to me: "Look here, I am going to leave you; I am not going to stop here for three weeks watching you make love to this creature."

I was perplexed and annoyed, for to my great surprise I had become singularly attached to Francesca. A man is but weak and foolish, carried away by the merest trifle, and a coward every time that his senses are excited or mastered. I clung to this unknown girl, silent and dissatisfied as she always was. I liked her somewhat ill-tempered face, the dissatisfied droop of her mouth, the weariness of her look; I liked her fatigued movements, the contemptuous way in which she let me kiss her, the very indifference of her caresses. A secret bond, that mysterious bond of physical love, which does not satisfy, bound me to her. I told Paul so, quite frankly. He treated me as if I were a fool, and then said:

"Very well, take her with you."

But she obstinately refused to leave Genoa, without giving any reason. I besought, I reasoned, I promised, but all was of no avail, and so I stayed on.

Paul declared that he would go by himself, and went so far as to pack up his portmanteau; but he remained all the same.

Thus a fortnight passed. Francesca was always silent and irritable, lived beside me rather than with me, responded to all my requirements and all my propositions with her perpetual Che mi fa, or with her no less perpetual Mica.

My friend became more and more furious, but my only answer was, "You can go if you are tired of staying. I am not detaining you."

Then he called me names, overwhelmed me with reproaches, and exclaimed: "Where do you think I can go now? We had three weeks at our disposal, and here is a fortnight gone! I cannot continue my journey now; and, in any case, I am not going to Venice, Florence and Rome all by myself. But you will pay for it, and more dearly than you think, most likely. You are not going to bring a man all the way from Paris in order to shut him up at a hotel in Genoa with an Italian adventuress."

When I told him, very calmly, to return to Paris, he exclaimed that he intended to do so the very next day; but the next day he was still there, still in a rage and swearing.

By this time we began to be known in the streets through which we wandered from morning till night. Sometimes French people would turn round astonished at meeting their fellow-countrymen in the company of this girl with her striking costume, who looked singularly out of place, not to say compromising, beside us.

She used to walk along, leaning on my arm, without looking at anything. Why did she remain with me, with us, who seemed to do so little to amuse her? Who was she? Where did she come from? What was she doing? Had she any plan or idea? Where did she live? As an adventuress, or by chance meetings? I tried in vain to find out and to explain it. The better I knew her the more enigmatical she became. She seemed to be a girl of poor family who had been taken away, and then cast aside and lost. What did she think would become of her, or whom was she waiting for? She certainly did not appear to be trying to make a conquest of me, or to make any real profit out of me.

I tried to question her, to speak to her of her childhood and family; but she never gave me an answer. I stayed with her, my heart unfettered and my senses enchained, never wearied of holding her in my arms, that proud and quarrelsome woman, captivated by my senses, or rather carried away, overcome by a youthful, healthy, powerful charm, which emanated from her fragrant person and from the well-molded lines of her body.

Another week passed, and the term of my journey was drawing on, for I had to be back in Paris by the eleventh of July. By this time Paul had come to take his part in the adventure, though still grumbling at me, while I invented pleasures, distractions and excursions to amuse Francesca and my friend; and in order to do this I gave myself a great amount of trouble.

One day I proposed an excursion to Sta Margarita, that charming little town in the midst of gardens, hidden at the foot of a slope which stretches far into the sea up to the village of Portofino. We three walked along the excellent road which goes along the foot of the mountain. Suddenly Francesca said to me: "I shall not be able to go with you to-morrow; I must go and see some of my relatives."

That was all; I did not ask her any questions, as I was quite sure she would not answer me.

The next morning she got up very early. When she spoke to me it was in a constrained and hesitating voice:

"If I do not come back again, shall you come and fetch me?"

"Most certainly I shall," was my reply. "Where shall I go to find you?"

Then she explained: "You must go into the Street Victor-Emmanuel, down the Falcone road and the side street San-Rafael and into the furniture shop in the building at the right at the end of a court, and there you must ask for Madame Rondoli. That is the place."

And so she went away, leaving me rather astonished.

When Paul saw that I was alone, he stammered out: "Where; is Francesca?" And when I told him what had happened, he exclaimed:

"My dear fellow, let us make use of our opportunity, and bolt; as it is, our time is up. Two days, more or less, make no difference. Let us go at once; go and pack up your things. Off we go!"

But I refused. I could not, as I told him, leave the girl in that manner after such companionship for nearly three weeks. At any rate, I ought to say good-by to her, and make her accept a present; I certainly had no intention of behaving badly to her.

But he would not listen; he pressed and worried me, but I would not give way.

I remained indoors for several hours, expecting Francesca's return, but she did not come, and at last, at dinner, Paul said with a triumphant air:

"She has flown, my dear fellow; it is certainly very strange."

I must acknowledge that I was surprised and rather vexed. He laughed in my face, and made fun of me.

"It is not exactly a bad way of getting rid of you, though rather primitive. 'Just wait for me, I shall be back in a moment,' they often say. How long are you going to wait? I should not wonder if you were foolish enough to go and look for her at the address she gave you. 'Does Madame Rondoli live here, please?' 'No, monsieur.' I'll bet that you are longing to go there."

"Not in the least," I protested, "and I assure you that if she does not come back to-morrow morning I shall leave by the express at eight o'clock. I shall have waited twenty-four hours, and that is enough; my conscience will be quite clear."

I spent an uneasy and unpleasant evening, for I really had at heart a very tender feeling for her. I went to bed at twelve o'clock, and hardly slept at all. I got up at six, called Paul, packed up my things, and two hours later we set out for France together.

III

The next year, at just about the same period, I was seized as one is with a periodical fever, with a new desire to go to Italy, and I immediately made up my mind to carry it into effect. There is no doubt that every really well-educated man ought to see Florence, Venice and Rome. This travel has, also, the additional advantage of providing many subjects of conversation in society, and of giving one an opportunity for bringing forward artistic generalities which appear profound.

This time I went alone, and I arrived at Genoa at the same time as the year before, but without any adventure on the road. I went to the same hotel, and actually happened to have the same room.

I was hardly in bed when the recollection of Francesca which, since the evening before, had been floating vaguely through my mind, haunted me with strange persistency. I thought of her nearly the whole night, and by degrees the wish to see her again seized me, a confused desire at first, which gradually grew stronger and more intense. At last I made up my mind to spend the next day in Genoa to try to find her, and if I should not succeed, to take the evening train.

Early in the morning I set out on my search. I remembered the directions she had given me when she left me, perfectly—Victor-Emmanuel Street, house of the furniture-dealer, at the bottom of the yard on the right.

I found it without the least difficulty, and I knocked at the door of a somewhat dilapidated-looking dwelling. It was opened by a stout woman, who must have been very handsome, but who actually was only very dirty. Although she had too much embonpoint, she still bore the lines of majestic beauty; her untidy hair fell over her forehead and shoulders, and one fancied one could see her floating about in an enormous dressing-gown covered with spots of dirt and grease. Round her neck she wore a great gilt necklace, and on her wrists were splendid bracelets of Genoa filigree work.

In rather a hostile manner she asked me what I wanted, and I replied by requesting her to tell me whether Francesca Rondoli lived there.

"What do you want with her?" she asked.

"I had the pleasure of meeting her last year, and I should like to see her again."

The old woman looked at me suspiciously.

"Where did you meet her?" she asked.

"Why, here in Genoa itself."

"What is your name?"

I hesitated a moment, and then I told her. I had hardly done so when the Italian put out her arms as if to embrace me. "Oh! you are the Frenchman how glad I am to see you! But what grief you caused the poor child! She waited for you a month; yes, a whole month. At first she thought you would come to fetch her. She wanted to see whether you loved her. If you only knew how she cried when she saw that you were not coming! She cried till she seemed to have no tears left. Then she went to the hotel, but you had gone. She thought that most likely you were travelling in Italy, and that you would return by Genoa to fetch her, as she would not go with you. And she waited more than a month, monsieur; and she was so unhappy; so unhappy. I am her mother."

I really felt a little disconcerted, but I regained my self-possession, and asked:

"Where is she now?"

"She has gone to Paris with a painter, a delightful man, who loves her very much, and who gives her everything that she wants. Just look at what she sent me; they are very pretty, are they not?"

And she showed me, with quite southern animation, her heavy bracelets and necklace. "I have also," she continued, "earrings with stones in them, a silk dress, and some rings; but I only wear them on grand occasions. Oh! she is very happy, monsieur, very happy. She will be so pleased when I tell her you have been here. But pray come in and sit down. You will take something or other, surely?"

But I refused, as I now wished to get away by the first train; but she took me by the arm and pulled me in, saying:

"Please, come in; I must tell her that you have been in here."

I found myself in a small, rather dark room, furnished with only a table and a few chairs.

She continued: "Oh, she is very happy now, very happy. When you met her in the train she was very miserable; she had had an unfortunate love affair in Marseilles, and she was coming home, poor child. But she liked you at once, though she was still rather sad, you understand. Now she has all she wants, and she writes and tells me everything that she does. His name is Bellemin, and they say he is a great painter in your country. He fell in love with her at first sight. But you will take a glass of sirup?—it is very good. Are you quite alone, this year?"

"Yes," I said, "quite alone."

I felt an increasing inclination to laugh, as my first disappointment was dispelled by what Mother Rondoli said. I was obliged; however, to drink a glass of her sirup.

"So you are quite alone?" she continued. "How sorry I am that Francesca is not here now; she would have been company for you all the time you stayed. It is not very amusing to go about all by oneself, and she will be very sorry also."

Then, as I was getting up to go, she exclaimed:

"But would you not like Carlotta to go with you? She knows all the walks very well. She is my second daughter, monsieur."

No doubt she took my look of surprise for consent, for she opened the inner door and called out up the dark stairs which I could not see:

"Carlotta! Carlotta! make haste down, my dear child."

I tried to protest, but she would not listen.

"No; she will be very glad to go with you; she is very nice, and much more cheerful than her sister, and she is a good girl, a very good girl, whom I love very much."

In a few moments a tall, slender, dark girl appeared, her hair hanging down, and her youthful figure showing unmistakably beneath an old dress of her mother's.

The latter at once told her how matters stood.

"This is Francesca's Frenchman, you know, the one whom she knew last year. He is quite alone, and has come to look for her, poor fellow; so I told him that you would go with him to keep him company."

The girl looked at me with her handsome dark eyes, and said, smiling:

"I have no objection, if he wishes it"

I could not possibly refuse, and merely said:

"Of course, I shall be very glad of your company."

Her mother pushed her out. "Go and get dressed directly; put on your blue dress and your hat with the flowers, and make haste."

As soon as she had left the room the old woman explained herself: "I have two others, but they are much younger. It costs a lot of money to bring up four children. Luckily the eldest is off my hands at present."

Then she told all about herself, about her husband, who had been an employee on the railway, but who was dead, and she expatiated on the good qualities of Carlotta, her second girl, who soon returned, dressed, as her sister had been, in a striking, peculiar manner.

Her mother examined her from head to foot, and, after finding everything right, she said:

"Now, my children, you can go." Then turning to the girl, she said: "Be sure you are back by ten o'clock to-night; you know the door is locked then." The answer was:

"All right, mamma; don't alarm yourself."

She took my arm and we went wandering about the streets, just as I had wandered the previous year with her sister.

We returned to the hotel for lunch, and then I took my new friend to Santa Margarita, just as I had taken her sister the year previously.

During the whole fortnight which I had at my disposal, I took Carlotta to all the places of interest in and about Genoa. She gave me no cause to regret her sister.

She cried when I left her, and the morning of my departure I gave her four bracelets for her mother, besides a substantial token of my affection for herself.

One of these days I intend to return to Italy, and I cannot help remembering with a certain amount of uneasiness, mingled with hope, that Madame Rondoli has two more daughters.

VOLUME VII.

THE FALSE GEMS

Monsieur Lantin had met the young girl at a reception at the house of the second head of his department, and had fallen head over heels in love with her.

She was the daughter of a provincial tax collector, who had been dead several years. She and her mother came to live in Paris, where the latter, who made the acquaintance of some of the families in her neighborhood, hoped to find a husband for her daughter.

They had very moderate means, and were honorable, gentle, and quiet.

The young girl was a perfect type of the virtuous woman in whose hands every sensible young man dreams of one day intrusting his happiness. Her simple beauty had the charm of angelic modesty, and the imperceptible smile which constantly hovered about the lips seemed to be the reflection of a pure and lovely soul. Her praises resounded on every side. People never tired of repeating: "Happy the man who wins her love! He could not find a better wife."

Monsieur Lantin, then chief clerk in the Department of the Interior, enjoyed a snug little salary of three thousand five hundred francs, and he proposed to this model young girl, and was accepted.

He was unspeakably happy with her. She governed his household with such clever economy that they seemed to live in luxury. She lavished the most delicate attentions on her husband, coaxed and fondled him; and so great was her charm that six years after their marriage, Monsieur Lantin discovered that he loved his wife even more than during the first days of their honeymoon.

He found fault with only two of her tastes: Her love for the theatre, and her taste for imitation jewelry. Her friends (the wives of some petty officials) frequently procured for her a box at the theatre, often for the first representations of the new plays; and her husband was obliged to accompany her, whether he wished it or not, to these entertainments which bored him excessively after his day's work at the office.

After a time, Monsieur Lantin begged his wife to request some lady of her acquaintance to accompany her, and to bring her home after the theatre. She opposed this arrangement, at first; but, after much persuasion, finally consented, to the infinite delight of her husband.

Now, with her love for the theatre, came also the desire for ornaments. Her costumes remained as before, simple, in good taste, and always modest; but she soon began to adorn her ears with huge rhinestones, which glittered and sparkled like real diamonds. Around her neck she wore strings of false pearls, on her arms bracelets of imitation gold, and combs set with glass jewels.

Her husband frequently remonstrated with her, saying:

"My dear, as you cannot afford to buy real jewelry, you ought to appear adorned with your beauty and modesty alone, which are the rarest ornaments of your sex."

But she would smile sweetly, and say:

"What can I do? I am so fond of jewelry. It is my only weakness. We cannot change our nature."

Then she would wind the pearl necklace round her fingers, make the facets of the crystal gems sparkle, and say:

"Look! are they not lovely? One would swear they were real."

Monsieur Lantin would then answer, smilingly:

"You have bohemian tastes, my dear."

Sometimes, of an evening, when they were enjoying a tete-a-tote by the fireside, she would place on the tea table the morocco leather box containing the "trash," as Monsieur Lantin called it. She would examine the false gems with a passionate attention, as though they imparted some deep and secret joy; and she often persisted in passing a necklace around her husband's neck, and, laughing heartily, would exclaim: "How droll you look!" Then she would throw herself into his arms, and kiss him affectionately.

One evening, in winter, she had been to the opera, and returned home chilled through and through. The next morning she coughed, and eight days later she died of inflammation of the lungs.

Monsieur Lantin's despair was so great that his hair became white in one month. He wept unceasingly; his heart was broken as he remembered her smile, her voice, every charm of his dead wife.

Time did not assuage his grief. Often, during office hours, while his colleagues were discussing the topics of the day, his eyes would suddenly fill with tears, and he would give vent to his grief in heartrending sobs. Everything in his wife's room remained as it was during her lifetime; all her furniture, even her clothing, being left as it was on the day of her death. Here he was wont to seclude himself daily and think of her who had been his treasure-the joy of his existence.

But life soon became a struggle. His income, which, in the hands of his wife, covered all household expenses, was now no longer sufficient for his own immediate wants; and he wondered how she could have managed to buy such excellent wine and the rare delicacies which he could no longer procure with his modest resources.

He incurred some debts, and was soon reduced to absolute poverty. One morning, finding himself without a cent in his pocket, he resolved to sell something, and immediately the thought occurred to him of disposing of his wife's paste jewels, for he cherished in his heart a sort of rancor against these "deceptions," which had always irritated him in the past. The very sight of them spoiled, somewhat, the memory of his lost darling.

To the last days of her life she had continued to make purchases, bringing home new gems almost every evening, and he turned them over some time before finally deciding to sell the heavy necklace, which she seemed to prefer, and which, he thought, ought to be worth about six or seven francs; for it was of very fine workmanship, though only imitation.

He put it in his pocket, and started out in search of what seemed a reliable jeweler's shop. At length he found one, and went in, feeling a little ashamed to expose his misery, and also to offer such a worthless article for sale.

"Sir," said he to the merchant, "I would like to know what this is worth."

The man took the necklace, examined it, called his clerk, and made some remarks in an undertone; he then put the ornament back on the counter, and looked at it from a distance to judge of the effect.

Monsieur Lantin, annoyed at all these ceremonies, was on the point of saying: "Oh! I know well 'enough it is not worth anything," when the jeweler said: "Sir, that necklace is worth from twelve to fifteen thousand francs; but I could not buy it, unless you can tell me exactly where it came from."

The widower opened his eyes wide and remained gaping, not comprehending the merchant's meaning. Finally he stammered: "You say—are you sure?" The other replied, drily: "You can try elsewhere and see if any one will offer you more. I consider it worth fifteen thousand at the most. Come back; here, if you cannot do better."

Monsieur Lantin, beside himself with astonishment, took up the necklace and left the store. He wished time for reflection.

Once outside, he felt inclined to laugh, and said to himself: "The fool! Oh, the fool! Had I only taken him at his word! That jeweler cannot distinguish real diamonds from the imitation article."

A few minutes after, he entered another store, in the Rue de la Paix. As soon as the proprietor glanced at the necklace, he cried out:

"Ah, parbleu! I know it well; it was bought here."

Monsieur Lantin, greatly disturbed, asked:

"How much is it worth?"

"Well, I sold it for twenty thousand francs. I am willing to take it back for eighteen thousand, when you inform me, according to our legal formality, how it came to be in your possession."

This time, Monsieur Lantin was dumfounded. He replied:

"But—but—examine it well. Until this moment I was under the impression that it was imitation."

The jeweler asked:

"What is your name, sir?"

"Lantin—I am in the employ of the Minister of the Interior. I live at number sixteen Rue des Martyrs."

The merchant looked through his books, found the entry, and said: "That necklace was sent to Madame Lantin's address, sixteen Rue des Martyrs, July 20, 1876."

The two men looked into each other's eyes—the widower speechless with astonishment; the jeweler scenting a thief. The latter broke the silence.

"Will you leave this necklace here for twenty-four hours?" said he; "I will give you a receipt."

Monsieur Lantin answered hastily: "Yes, certainly." Then, putting the ticket in his pocket, he left the store.

He wandered aimlessly through the streets, his mind in a state of dreadful confusion. He tried to reason, to understand. His wife could not afford to purchase such a costly ornament. Certainly not.

But, then, it must have been a present!—a present!—a present, from whom? Why was it given her?

He stopped, and remained standing in the middle of the street. A horrible doubt entered his mind— She? Then, all the other jewels must have been presents, too! The earth seemed to tremble beneath him—the tree before him to be falling; he threw up his arms, and fell to the ground, unconscious. He recovered his senses in a pharmacy, into which the passers-by had borne him. He asked to be taken home, and, when he reached the house, he shut himself up in his room, and wept until nightfall. Finally, overcome with fatigue, he went to bed and fell into a heavy sleep.

The sun awoke him next morning, and he began to dress slowly to go to the office. It was hard to work after such shocks. He sent a letter to his employer, requesting to be excused. Then he remembered that he had to return to the jeweler's. He did not like the idea; but he could not leave the necklace with that man. He dressed and went out.

It was a lovely day; a clear, blue sky smiled on the busy city below. Men of leisure were strolling about with their hands in their pockets.

Monsieur Lantin, observing them, said to himself: "The rich, indeed, are happy. With money it is possible to forget even the deepest sorrow. One can go where one pleases, and in travel find that distraction which is the surest cure for grief. Oh if I were only rich!"

He perceived that he was hungry, but his pocket was empty. He again remembered the necklace. Eighteen thousand francs! Eighteen thousand francs! What a sum!

He soon arrived in the Rue de la Paix, opposite the jeweler's. Eighteen thousand francs! Twenty times he resolved to go in, but shame kept him back. He was hungry, however—very hungry—and not a cent in his pocket. He decided quickly, ran across the street, in order not to have time for reflection, and rushed into the store.

The proprietor immediately came forward, and politely offered him a chair; the clerks glanced at him knowingly.

"I have made inquiries, Monsieur Lantin," said the jeweler, "and if you are still resolved to dispose of the gems, I am ready to pay you the price I offered."

"Certainly, sir," stammered Monsieur Lantin.

Whereupon the proprietor took from a drawer eighteen large bills, counted, and handed them to Monsieur Lantin, who signed a receipt; and, with trembling hand, put the money into his pocket.

As he was about to leave the store, he turned toward the merchant, who still wore the same knowing smile, and lowering his eyes, said:

"I have—I have other gems, which came from the same source. Will you buy them, also?"

The merchant bowed: "Certainly, sir."

Monsieur Lantin said gravely: "I will bring them to you." An hour later, he returned with the gems.

The large diamond earrings were worth twenty thousand francs; the bracelets, thirty-five thousand; the rings, sixteen thousand; a set of emeralds and sapphires, fourteen thousand; a gold chain with solitaire pendant, forty thousand—making the sum of one hundred and forty-three thousand francs.

The jeweler remarked, jokingly:

"There was a person who invested all her savings in precious stones."

Monsieur Lantin replied, seriously:

"It is only another way of investing one's money."

That day he lunched at Voisin's, and drank wine worth twenty francs a bottle. Then he hired a carriage and made a tour of the Bois. He gazed at the various turnouts with a kind of disdain, and could hardly refrain from crying out to the occupants:

"I, too, am rich!—I am worth two hundred thousand francs."

Suddenly he thought of his employer. He drove up to the bureau, and entered gaily, saying:

"Sir, I have come to resign my position. I have just inherited three hundred thousand francs."

He shook hands with his former colleagues, and confided to them some of his projects for the future; he then went off to dine at the Cafe Anglais.

He seated himself beside a gentleman of aristocratic bearing; and, during the meal, informed the latter confidentially that he had just inherited a fortune of four hundred thousand francs.

For the first time in his life, he was not bored at the theatre, and spent the remainder of the night in a gay frolic.

Six months afterward, he married again. His second wife was a very virtuous woman; but had a violent temper. She caused him much sorrow.

FASCINATION

I can tell you neither the name of the country, nor the name of the man. It was a long, long way from here on a fertile and burning shore. We had been walking since the morning along the coast, with the blue sea bathed in sunlight on one side of us, and the shore covered with crops on the other. Flowers were growing quite close to the waves, those light, gentle, lulling waves. It was very warm, a soft warmth permeated with the odor of the rich, damp, fertile soil. One fancied one was inhaling germs.

I had been told, that evening, that I should meet with hospitality at the house of a Frenchman who lived in an orange grove at the end of a promontory. Who was he? I did not know. He had come there one morning ten years before, and had bought land which he planted with vines and sowed with grain. He had worked, this man, with passionate energy, with fury. Then as he went on from month to month, year to year, enlarging his boundaries, cultivating incessantly the strong virgin soil, he accumulated a fortune by his indefatigable labor.

But he kept on working, they said. Rising at daybreak, he would remain in the fields till evening, superintending everything without ceasing, tormented by one fixed idea, the insatiable desire for money, which nothing can quiet, nothing satisfy. He now appeared to be very rich. The sun was setting as I reached his house. It was situated as described, at the end of a promontory in the midst of a grove of orange trees. It was a large square house, quite plain, and overlooked the sea. As I approached, a man wearing a long beard appeared in the doorway. Having greeted him, I asked if he would give me shelter for the night. He held out his hand and said, smiling:

"Come in, monsieur, consider yourself at home."

He led me into a room, and put a man servant at my disposal with the perfect ease and familiar graciousness of a man-of-the-world. Then he left me saying:

"We will dine as soon as you are ready to come downstairs."

We took dinner, sitting opposite each other, on a terrace facing the sea. I began to talk about this rich, distant, unknown land. He smiled, as he replied carelessly:

"Yes, this country is beautiful. But no country satisfies one when they are far from the one they love."

"You regret France?"

"I regret Paris."

"Why do you not go back?"

"Oh, I will return there."

And gradually we began to talk of French society, of the boulevards, and things Parisian. He asked me questions that showed he knew all about these things, mentioned names, all the familiar names in vaudeville known on the sidewalks.

"Whom does one see at Tortoni's now?

"Always the same crowd, except those who died." I looked at him attentively, haunted by a vague recollection. I certainly had seen that head somewhere. But where? And when? He seemed tired, although he was vigorous; and sad, although he was determined. His long, fair beard fell on his chest. He was somewhat bald and had heavy eyebrows and a thick mustache.

The sun was sinking into the sea, turning the vapor from the earth into a fiery mist. The orange blossoms exhaled their powerful, delicious fragrance. He seemed to see nothing besides me, and gazing steadfastly he appeared to discover in the depths of my mind the far-away, beloved and well-known image of the wide, shady pavement leading from the Madeleine to the Rue Drouot.

"Do you know Boutrelle?"

"Yes, indeed."

"Has he changed much?"

"Yes, his hair is quite white."

"And La Ridamie?"

"The same as ever."

"And the women? Tell me about the women. Let's see. Do you know Suzanne Verner?"

"Yes, very much. But that is over."

"Ah! And Sophie Astier?"

"Dead."

"Poor girl. Did you—did you know—"

But he ceased abruptly: And then, in a changed voice, his face suddenly turning pale, he continued:

"No, it is best that I should not speak of that any more, it breaks my heart."

Then, as if to change the current of his thoughts he rose.

"Would you like to go in?" he said.

"Yes, I think so."

And he preceded me into the house. The downstairs rooms were enormous, bare and mournful, and had a deserted look. Plates and glasses were scattered on the tables, left there by the dark-skinned servants who wandered incessantly about this spacious dwelling.

Two rifles were banging from two nails, on the wall; and in the corners of the rooms were spades, fishing poles, dried palm leaves, every imaginable thing set down at random when people came home in the evening and ready to hand when they went out at any time, or went to work.

My host smiled as he said:

"This is the dwelling, or rather the kennel, of an exile, but my own room is cleaner. Let us go there."

As I entered I thought I was in a second-hand store, it was so full of things of all descriptions, strange things of various kinds that one felt must be souvenirs. On the walls were two pretty paintings by well-known artists, draperies, weapons, swords and pistols, and exactly in the middle, on the principal panel, a square of white satin in a gold frame.

Somewhat surprised, I approached to look at it, and perceived a hairpin fastened in the centre of the glossy satin. My host placed his hand on my shoulder.

"That," said he, "is the only thing that I look at here, and the only thing that I have seen for ten years. M. Prudhomme said: 'This sword is the most memorable day of my life.' I can say: 'This hairpin is all my life.'"

I sought for some commonplace remark, and ended by saying:

"You have suffered on account of some woman?"

He replied abruptly:

"Say, rather, that I am suffering like a wretch."

"But come out on my balcony. A name rose to my lips just now which I dared not utter; for if you had said 'Dead' as you did of Sophie Astier, I should have fired a bullet into my brain, this very day."

We had gone out on the wide balcony from whence we could see two gulfs, one to the right and the other to the left, enclosed by high gray mountains. It was just twilight and the reflection of the sunset still lingered in the sky.

He continued:

"Is Jeanne de Limours still alive?"

His eyes were fastened on mine and were full of a trembling anxiety. I smiled.

"Parbleu—she is prettier than ever."

"Do you know her?"

"Yes."

He hesitated and then said:

"Very well?"

"No."

He took my hand.

"Tell me about her," he said.

"Why, I have nothing to tell. She is one of the most charming women, or, rather, girls, and the most admired in Paris. She leads a delightful existence and lives like a princess, that is all."

"I love her," he murmured in a tone in which he might have said "I am going to die." Then suddenly he continued:

"Ah! For three years we lived in a state of terror and delight. I almost killed her five or six times. She tried to pierce my eyes with that hairpin that you saw just now. Look, do you see that little white spot beneath my left eye? We loved each other. How can I explain that infatuation? You would not understand it."

"There must be a simple form of love, the result of the mutual impulse of two hearts and two souls. But there is also assuredly an atrocious form, that tortures one cruelly, the result of the occult blending of two unlike personalities who detest each other at the same time that they adore one another."

"In three years this woman had ruined me. I had four million francs which she squandered in her calm manner, quietly, eat them up with a gentle smile that seemed to fall from her eyes on to her lips."

"You know her? There is something irresistible about her. What is it? I do not know. Is it those gray eyes whose glance penetrates you like a gimlet and remains there like the point of an arrow? It is more likely the gentle, indifferent and fascinating smile that she wears like a mask. Her slow grace pervades you little by little; exhales from her like a perfume, from her slim figure that scarcely sways as she passes you, for she seems to glide rather than walk; from her pretty voice with its slight drawl that would seem to be the music of her smile; from her gestures, also, which are never exaggerated, but always appropriate, and intoxicate your vision with their harmony. For three years she was the only being that existed for me on the earth! How I suffered; for she deceived me as she deceived everyone! Why? For no reason; just for the pleasure of deceiving. And when I found it out, when I treated her as a common girl and a beggar, she said quietly: 'Are we married?'

"Since I have been here I have thought so much about her that at last I understand her. She is Manon Lescaut come back to life. It is Manon, who could not love without deceiving; Marion for whom love, amusement, money, are all one."

He was silent. After a few minutes he resumed:

"When I had spent my last sou on her she said simply:

"'You understand, my dear boy, that I cannot live on air and weather. I love you very much, better than anyone, but I must live. Poverty and I could not keep house together."

"And if I should tell you what a horrible life I led with her! When I looked at her I would just as soon have killed her as kissed her. When I looked at her . . . I felt a furious desire to open my arms to embrace and strangle her. She had, back of her eyes, something false and intangible that made me execrate her; and that was, perhaps, the reason I loved her so well. The eternal feminine, the odious and seductive feminine, was stronger in her than in any other woman. She was full of it, overcharged, as with a venomous and intoxicating fluid. She was a woman to a greater extent than any one has ever been."

"And when I went out with her she would look at all men in such a manner that she seemed to offer herself to each in a single glance. This exasperated me, and still it attached me to her all the more. This creature in just walking along the street belonged to everyone, in spite of me, in spite of herself, by the very fact of her nature, although she had a modest, gentle carriage. Do you understand?

"And what torture! At the theatre, at the restaurant she seemed to belong to others under my very eyes. And as soon as I left her she did belong to others.

"It is now ten years since I saw her and I love her better than ever."

Night spread over the earth. A strong perfume of orange blossoms pervaded the air. I said:

"Will you see her again?"

"Parbleu! I now have here, in land and money, seven to eight thousand francs. When I reach a million I shall sell out and go away. I shall have enough to live on with her for a year—one whole year. And then, good-bye, my life will be finished."

"But after that?" I asked.

"After that, I do not know. That will be all, I may possibly ask her to take me as a valet de chambre."

YVETTE SAMORIS

"The Comtesse Samoris."

"That lady in black over there?"

"The very one. She's wearing mourning for her daughter, whom she killed."

"You don't mean that seriously? How did she die?"

"Oh! it is a very simple story, without any crime in it, any violence."

"Then what really happened?"

"Almost nothing. Many courtesans are born to be virtuous women, they say; and many women called virtuous are born to be courtesans—is that not so? Now, Madame Samoris, who was born a courtesan, had a daughter born a virtuous woman, that's all."

"I don't quite understand you."

"I'll—explain what I mean. The comtesse is nothing but a common, ordinary parvenue originating no one knows where. A Hungarian or Wallachian countess or I know not what. She appeared one winter in apartments she had taken in the Champs Elysees, that quarter for adventurers and adventuresses, and opened her drawing-room to the first comer or to any one that turned up.

"I went there. Why? you will say. I really can't tell you. I went there, as every one goes to such places because the women are facile and the men are dishonest. You know that set composed of filibusters with varied decorations, all noble, all titled, all unknown at the embassies, with the exception of those who are spies. All talk of their honor without the slightest occasion for doing so, boast of their ancestors, tell you about their lives, braggarts, liars, sharpers, as dangerous as the false cards they have up their sleeves, as delusive as their names—in short, the aristocracy of the bagnio.

"I adore these people. They are interesting to study, interesting to know, amusing to understand, often clever, never commonplace like public functionaries. Their wives are always pretty, with a slight flavor of foreign roguery, with the mystery of their existence, half of it perhaps spent in a house of correction. They have, as a rule, magnificent eyes and incredible hair. I adore them also.

"Madame Samoris is the type of these adventuresses, elegant, mature and still beautiful. Charming feline creatures, you feel that they are vicious to the marrow of their bones. You find them very amusing when you visit them; they give card parties; they have dances and suppers; in short, they offer you all the pleasures of social life.

"And she had a daughter—a tall, fine-looking girl, always ready for amusement, always full of laughter and reckless gaiety—a true adventuress' daughter—but, at the same time, an innocent, unsophisticated, artless girl, who saw nothing, knew nothing, understood nothing of all the things that happened in her father's house.

"The girl was simply a puzzle to me. She was a mystery. She lived amid those infamous surroundings with a quiet, tranquil ease that was either terribly criminal or else the result of innocence. She sprang from the filth of that class like a beautiful flower fed on corruption."

"How do you know about them?"

"How do I know? That's the funniest part of the business! One morning there was a ring at my door, and my valet came up to tell me that M. Joseph Bonenthal wanted to speak to me. I said directly:

"'And who is this gentleman?' My valet replied: 'I don't know, monsieur; perhaps 'tis some one that wants employment.' And so it was. The man wanted me to take him as a servant. I asked him where he had been last. He answered: 'With the Comtesse Samoris.' 'Ah!' said I, 'but my house is not a bit like hers.' 'I know that well, monsieur,' he said, 'and that's the very reason I want to take service with monsieur. I've had enough of these people: a man may stay a little while with them, but he won't remain long with them.' I required an additional man servant at the time and so I took him.

"A month later Mademoiselle Yvette Samoris died mysteriously, and here are all the details of her death I could gather from Joseph, who got them from his sweetheart, the comtesse's chambermaid.

"It was a ball night, and two newly arrived guests were chatting behind a door. Mademoiselle Yvette, who had just been dancing, leaned against this door to get a little air.

"They did not see her approaching, but she heard what they were saying. And this was what they said:

"'But who is the father of the girl?'

"'A Russian, it appears; Count Rouvaloff. He never comes near the mother now.'

"'And who is the reigning prince to-day?'

"'That English prince standing near the window; Madame Samoris adores him. But her adoration of any one never lasts longer than a month or six weeks. Nevertheless, as you see, she has a large circle of admirers. All are called—and nearly all are chosen. That kind of thing costs a good deal, but—hang it, what can you expect?'

"'And where did she get this name of Samoris?'

"'From the only man perhaps that she ever loved—a Jewish banker from Berlin who goes by the name of Samuel Morris.'

"'Good. Thanks. Now that I know what kind of woman she is and have seen her, I'm off!'

"What a shock this was to the mind of a young girl endowed with all the instincts of a virtuous woman! What despair overwhelmed that simple soul! What mental tortures quenched her unbounded gaiety, her delightful laughter, her exultant satisfaction with life! What a conflict took place in that youthful heart up to the moment when the last guest had left! Those were things that Joseph could not tell me. But, the same night, Yvette abruptly entered her mother's room just as the comtesse was getting into bed, sent out the lady's maid, who was close to the door, and, standing erect and pale and with great staring eyes, she said:

"'Mamma, listen to what I heard a little while ago during the ball.'

"And she repeated word for word the conversation just as I told it to you.

"The comtesse was so stunned that she did not know what to say in reply at first. When she recovered her self-possession she denied everything and called God to witness that there was no truth in the story.

"The young girl went away, distracted but not convinced. And she began to watch her mother.

"I remember distinctly the strange alteration that then took place in her. She became grave and melancholy. She would fix on us her great earnest eyes as if she wanted to read what was at the bottom of our hearts. We did not know what to think of her and used to imagine that she was looking out for a husband.

"One evening she overheard her mother talking to her admirer and later saw them together, and her doubts were confirmed. She was heartbroken, and after telling her mother what she had seen, she said coldly, like a man of business laying down the terms of an agreement:

"'Here is what I have determined to do, mamma: We will both go away to some little town, or rather into the country. We will live there quietly as well as we can. Your jewelry alone may be called a fortune. If you wish to marry some honest man, so much the better; still better will it be if I can find one. If you don't consent to do this, I will kill myself.'

"This time the comtesse ordered her daughter to go to bed and never to speak again in this manner, so unbecoming in the mouth of a child toward her mother.

"Yvette's answer to this was: 'I give you a month to reflect. If, at the end of that month, we have not changed our way of living, I will kill myself, since there is no other honorable issue left to my life.'

"And she left the room.

"At the end of a month the Comtesse Samoris had resumed her usual entertainments, as though nothing had occurred. One day, under the pretext that she had a bad toothache, Yvette purchased a few drops of chloroform from a neighboring chemist. The next day she purchased more, and every time she went out she managed to procure small doses of the narcotic. She filled a bottle with it.

"One morning she was found in bed, lifeless and already quite cold, with a cotton mask soaked in chloroform over her face.

"Her coffin was covered with flowers, the church was hung in white. There was a large crowd at the funeral ceremony.

"Ah! well, if I had known—but you never can know—I would have married that girl, for she was infernally pretty."

"And what became of the mother?"

"Oh! she shed a lot of tears over it. She has only begun to receive visits again for the past week."

"And what explanation is given of the girl's death?"

"Oh! they pretended that it was an accident caused by a new stove, the mechanism of which got out of order. As a good many such accidents have occurred, the thing seemed probable enough."

A VENDETTA

The widow of Paolo Saverini lived alone with her son in a poor little house on the outskirts of Bonifacio. The town, built on an outjutting part of the mountain, in places even overhanging the sea, looks across the straits, full of sandbanks, towards the southernmost coast of Sardinia. Beneath it, on the other side and almost surrounding it, is a cleft in the cliff like an immense corridor which serves as a harbor, and along it the little Italian and Sardinian fishing boats come by a circuitous route between precipitous cliffs as far as the first houses, and every two weeks the old, wheezy steamer which makes the trip to Ajaccio.

On the white mountain the houses, massed together, makes an even whiter spot. They look like the nests of wild birds, clinging to this peak, overlooking this terrible passage, where vessels rarely venture. The wind, which blows uninterruptedly, has swept bare the forbidding coast; it drives through the narrow straits and lays waste both sides. The pale streaks of foam, clinging to the black rocks, whose countless peaks rise up out of the water, look like bits of rag floating and drifting on the surface of the sea.

The house of widow Saverini, clinging to the very edge of the precipice, looks out, through its three windows, over this wild and desolate picture.

She lived there alone, with her son Antonia and their dog "Semillante," a big, thin beast, with a long rough coat, of the sheep-dog breed. The young man took her with him when out hunting.

One night, after some kind of a quarrel, Antoine Saverini was treacherously stabbed by Nicolas Ravolati, who escaped the same evening to Sardinia.

When the old mother received the body of her child, which the neighbors had brought back to her, she did not cry, but she stayed there for a long time motionless, watching him. Then, stretching her wrinkled hand over the body, she promised him a vendetta. She did not wish anybody near her, and she shut herself up beside the body with the dog, which howled continuously, standing at the foot of the bed, her head stretched towards her master and her tail between her legs. She did not move any more than did the mother, who, now leaning over the body with a blank stare, was weeping silently and watching it.

The young man, lying on his back, dressed in his jacket of coarse cloth, torn at the chest, seemed to be asleep. But he had blood all over him; on his shirt, which had been torn off in order to administer the first aid; on his vest, on his trousers, on his face, on his hands. Clots of blood had hardened in his beard and in his hair.

His old mother began to talk to him. At the sound of this voice the dog quieted down.

"Never fear, my boy, my little baby, you shall be avenged. Sleep, sleep; you shall be avenged. Do you hear? It's your mother's promise! And she always keeps her word, your mother does, you know she does."

Slowly she leaned over him, pressing her cold lips to his dead ones.

Then Semillante began to howl again with a long, monotonous, penetrating, horrible howl.

The two of them, the woman and the dog, remained there until morning.

Antoine Saverini was buried the next day and soon his name ceased to be mentioned in Bonifacio.

He had neither brothers nor cousins. No man was there to carry on the vendetta. His mother, the old woman, alone pondered over it.

On the other side of the straits she saw, from morning until night, a little white speck on the coast. It was the little Sardinian village Longosardo, where Corsican criminals take refuge when they are too closely pursued. They compose almost the entire population of this hamlet, opposite their native island, awaiting the time to return, to go back to the "maquis." She knew that Nicolas Ravolati had sought refuge in this village.

All alone, all day long, seated at her window, she was looking over there and thinking of revenge. How could she do anything without help—she, an invalid and so near death? But she had promised, she had sworn on the body. She could not forget, she could not wait. What could she do? She no longer slept at night; she had neither rest nor peace of mind; she thought persistently. The dog, dozing at her feet, would sometimes lift her head and howl. Since her master's death she often howled thus, as though she were calling him, as though her beast's soul, inconsolable too, had also retained a recollection that nothing could wipe out.

One night, as Semillante began to howl, the mother suddenly got hold of an idea, a savage, vindictive, fierce idea. She thought it over until morning. Then, having arisen at daybreak she went to church. She prayed, prostrate on the floor, begging the Lord to help her, to support her, to give to her poor, broken-down body the strength which she needed in order to avenge her son.

She returned home. In her yard she had an old barrel, which acted as a cistern. She turned it over, emptied it, made it fast to the ground with sticks and stones. Then she chained Semillante to this improvised kennel and went into the house.

She walked ceaselessly now, her eyes always fixed on the distant coast of Sardinia. He was over there, the murderer.

All day and all night the dog howled. In the morning the old woman brought her some water in a bowl, but nothing more; no soup, no bread.

Another day went by. Semillante, exhausted, was sleeping. The following day her eyes were shining, her hair on end and she was pulling wildly at her chain.

All this day the old woman gave her nothing to eat. The beast, furious, was barking hoarsely. Another night went by.

Then, at daybreak, Mother Saverini asked a neighbor for some straw. She took the old rags which had formerly been worn by her husband and stuffed them so as to make them look like a human body.

Having planted a stick in the ground, in front of Semillante's kennel, she tied to it this dummy, which seemed to be standing up. Then she made a head out of some old rags.

The dog, surprised, was watching this straw man, and was quiet, although famished. Then the old woman went to the store and bought a piece of black sausage. When she got home she started a fire in the yard, near the kennel, and cooked the sausage. Semillante, frantic, was jumping about, frothing at the mouth, her eyes fixed on the food, the odor of which went right to her stomach.

Then the mother made of the smoking sausage a necktie for the dummy. She tied it very tight around the neck with string, and when she had finished she untied the dog.

With one leap the beast jumped at the dummy's throat, and with her paws on its shoulders she began to tear at it. She would fall back with a piece of food in her mouth, then would jump again, sinking her fangs into the string, and snatching few pieces of meat she would fall back again and once more spring forward. She was tearing up the face with her teeth and the whole neck was in tatters.

The old woman, motionless and silent, was watching eagerly. Then she chained the beast up again, made her fast for two more days and began this strange performance again.

For three months she accustomed her to this battle, to this meal conquered by a fight. She no longer chained her up, but just pointed to the dummy.

She had taught her to tear him up and to devour him without even leaving any traces in her throat.

Then, as a reward, she would give her a piece of sausage.

As soon as she saw the man, Semillante would begin to tremble. Then she would look up to her mistress, who, lifting her finger, would cry, "Go!" in a shrill tone.

When she thought that the proper time had come, the widow went to confession and, one Sunday morning she partook of communion with an ecstatic fervor. Then, putting on men's clothes and looking like an old tramp, she struck a bargain with a Sardinian fisherman who carried her and her dog to the other side of the straits.

In a bag she had a large piece of sausage. Semillante had had nothing to eat for two days. The old woman kept letting her smell the food and whetting her appetite.

They got to Longosardo. The Corsican woman walked with a limp. She went to a baker's shop and asked for Nicolas Ravolati. He had taken up his old trade, that of carpenter. He was working alone at the back of his store.

The old woman opened the door and called:

"Hallo, Nicolas!"

He turned around. Then releasing her dog, she cried:

"Go, go! Eat him up! eat him up!"

The maddened animal sprang for his throat. The man stretched out his arms, clasped the dog and rolled to the ground. For a few seconds he squirmed, beating the ground with his feet. Then he stopped moving, while Semillante dug her fangs into his throat and tore it to ribbons. Two neighbors, seated before their door, remembered perfectly having seen an old beggar come out with a thin, black dog which was eating something that its master was giving him.

At nightfall the old woman was at home again. She slept well that night.

MY TWENTY-FIVE DAYS

I had just taken possession of my room in the hotel, a narrow den between two papered partitions, through which I could hear every sound made by my neighbors; and I was beginning to arrange my clothes and linen in the wardrobe with a long mirror, when I opened the drawer which is in this piece of furniture. I immediately noticed a roll of paper. Having opened it, I spread it out before me, and read this title:

My Twenty-five Days.

It was the diary of a guest at the watering place, of the last occupant of my room, and had been forgotten at the moment of departure.

These notes may be of some interest to sensible and healthy persons who never leave their own homes. It is for their benefit that I transcribe them without altering a letter.

"CHATEL-GUYON, July 15th.

"At the first glance it is not lively, this country. However, I am going to spend twenty-five days here, to have my liver and stomach treated, and to get thin. The twenty-five days of any one taking the baths are very like the twenty-eight days of the reserves; they are all devoted to fatigue duty, severe fatigue duty. To-day I have done nothing as yet; I have been getting settled. I have made the acquaintance of the locality and of the doctor. Chatel-Guyon consists of a stream in which flows yellow water, in the midst of several hillocks on which are a casino, some houses, and some stone crosses. On the bank of the stream, at the end of the valley, may be seen a square building surrounded by a little garden; this is the bathing establishment. Sad people wander around this building—the invalids. A great silence reigns in the walks shaded by trees, for this is not a pleasure resort, but a true health resort; one takes care of one's health as a business, and one gets well, so it seems.

"Those who know affirm, even, that the mineral springs perform true miracles here. However, no votive offering is hung around the cashier's office.

"From time to time a gentleman or a lady comes over to a kiosk with a slate roof, which shelters a woman of smiling and gentle aspect, and a spring boiling in a basin of cement: Not a word is exchanged between the invalid and the female custodian of the healing water. She hands the newcomer a little glass in which air bubbles sparkle in the transparent liquid. The guest drinks and goes off with a grave step to resume his interrupted walk beneath the trees.

"No noise in the little park, no breath of air in the leaves; no voice passes through this silence. One ought to write at the entrance to this district: 'No one laughs here; they take care of their health.'

"The people who chat resemble mutes who merely open their mouths to simulate sounds, so afraid are they that their voices might escape.

"In the hotel, the same silence. It is a big hotel, where you dine solemnly with people of good position, who have nothing to say to each other. Their manners bespeak good breeding, and their faces reflect the conviction of a superiority of which it might be difficult for some to give actual proofs.

"At two o'clock I made my way up to the Casino, a little wooden but perched on a hillock, which one reaches by a goat path. But the view from that height is admirable. Chatel-Guyon is situated in a very narrow valley, exactly between the, plain and the mountain. I perceive, at the left, the first great billows of the mountains of Auvergne, covered with woods, and here and there big gray patches, hard masses of lava, for we are at the foot of the extinct volcanoes. At the right, through the narrow cut of the valley, I discover a plain, infinite as the sea, steeped in a bluish fog which lets one only dimly discern the villages, the towns, the yellow fields of ripe grain, and the green squares of meadowland shaded with apple trees. It is the Limagne, an immense level, always enveloped in a light veil of vapor.

"The night has come. And now, after having dined alone, I write these lines beside my open window. I hear, over there, in front of me, the little orchestra of the Casino, which plays airs just as a foolish bird might sing all alone in the desert.

"A dog barks at intervals. This great calm does one good. Goodnight.

"July 16th.—Nothing new. I have taken a bath and then a shower bath. I have swallowed three glasses of water, and I have walked along the paths in the park, a quarter of an hour between each glass, then half an hour after the last. I have begun my twenty-five days.

"July 17th.—Remarked two mysterious, pretty women who are taking their baths and their meals after every one else has finished.

"July 18th.—Nothing new.

"July 19th.—Saw the two pretty women again. They have style and a little indescribable air which I like very much.

"July 20th.—Long walk in a charming wooded valley, as far as the Hermitage of Sans-Souci. This country is delightful, although sad; but so calm; so sweet, so green. One meets along the mountain roads long wagons loaded with hay, drawn by two cows at a slow pace or held back by them in going down the slopes with a great effort of their heads, which are yoked together. A man with a big black hat on his head is driving them with a slender stick, tipping them on the side or on the forehead; and often with a simple gesture, an energetic and serious gesture, he suddenly halts them when the excessive load precipitates their journey down the too rugged descents.

"The air is good to inhale in these valleys. And, if it is very warm, the dust bears with it a light odor of vanilla and of the stable, for so many cows pass over these routes that they leave reminders everywhere. And this odor is a perfume, when it would be a stench if it came from other animals.

"July 21st.—Excursion to the valley of the Enval. It is a narrow gorge inclosed by superb rocks at the very foot of the mountain. A stream flows amid the heaped-up boulders.

"As I reached the bottom of this ravine I heard women's voices, and I soon perceived the two mysterious ladies of my hotel, who were chatting, seated on a stone.

"The occasion appeared to me a good one, and I introduced myself without hesitation. My overtures were received without embarrassment. We walked back together to the hotel. And we talked about Paris. They knew, it seemed, many people whom I knew, too. Who can they be?

"I shall see them to-morrow. There is nothing more amusing than such meetings as this.

"July 22d.—Day passed almost entirely with the two unknown ladies. They are very pretty, by Jove!—one a brunette and the other a blonde. They say they are widows. H'm?

"I offered to accompany them to Royat tomorrow, and they accepted my offer.

"Chatel-Guyon is less sad than I thought on my arrival.

"July 23d.—Day spent at Royat. Royat is a little patch of hotels at the bottom of a valley, at the gate of Clermont-Ferrand. A great many people there. A large park full of life. Superb view of the Puyde-Dome, seen at the end of a perspective of valleys.

"My fair companions are very popular, which is flattering to me. The man who escorts a pretty woman always believes himself crowned with an aureole; with much more reason, the man who is accompanied by one on each side of him. Nothing is so pleasant as to dine in a fashionable restaurant with a female companion at whom everybody stares, and there is nothing better calculated to exalt a man in the estimation of his neighbors.

"To go to the Bois, in a trap drawn by a sorry nag, or to go out into the boulevard escorted by a plain woman, are the two most humiliating things that could happen to a sensitive heart that values the opinion of others. Of all luxuries, woman is the rarest and the most distinguished; she is the one that costs most and which we desire most; she is, therefore the one that we should seek by preference to exhibit to the jealous eyes of the world.

"To exhibit to the world a pretty woman leaning on your arm is to excite, all at once, every kind of jealousy. It is as much as to say: 'Look here! I am rich, since I possess this rare and costly object; I have taste, since I have known how to discover this pearl; perhaps, even, I am loved by her, unless I am deceived by her, which would still prove that others also consider her charming.

"But, what a disgrace it is to walk about town with an ugly woman!

"And how many humiliating things this gives people to understand!

"In the first place, they assume she must be your wife, for how could it be supposed that you would have an unattractive sweetheart? A true woman may be ungraceful; but then, her ugliness implies a thousand disagreeable things for you. One supposes you must be a notary or a magistrate, as these two professions have a monopoly of grotesque and well-dowered spouses. Now, is this not distressing to a man? And then, it seems to proclaim to the public that you have the odious courage, and are even under a legal obligation, to caress that ridiculous face and that ill-shaped body, and that you will, without doubt, be shameless enough to make a mother of this by no means desirable being—which is the very height of the ridiculous.

"July 24th.—I never leave the side of the two unknown widows, whom I am beginning to know quite well. This country is delightful and our hotel is excellent. Good season. The treatment is doing me an immense amount of good.

"July 25th.—Drive in a landau to the lake of Tazenat. An exquisite and unexpected jaunt decided on at luncheon. We started immediately on rising from table. After a long journey through the mountains we suddenly perceived an admirable little lake, quite round, very blue, clear as glass, and situated at the bottom of an extinct crater. One side of this immense basin is barren, the other is wooded. In the midst of the trees is a small house where sleeps a good-natured, intellectual man, a sage who passes his days in this Virgilian region. He opens his dwelling for us. An idea comes into my head. I exclaim:

"'Supposing we bathe?'

"'Yes,' they said, 'but costumes.'

"'Bah! we are in the wilderness.'

"And we did bathe!

"If I were a poet, how I would describe this unforgettable vision of those lissome young forms in the transparency of the water! The high, sloping sides shut in the lake, motionless, gleaming and round, as a silver coin; the sun pours into it a flood of warm light; and along the rocks the fair forms move in the almost invisible water in which the swimmers seemed suspended. On the sand at the bottom of the lake one could see their shadows as they moved along.

"July 26th.—Some persons seem to look with shocked and disapproving eyes at my rapid intimacy with the two fair widows. There are some people, then, who imagine that life consists in being bored. Everything that appears to be amusing becomes immediately a breach of good breeding or morality. For them duty has inflexible and mortally tedious rules.

"I would draw their attention, with all respect, to the fact that duty is not the same for Mormons, Arabs Zulus, Turks, Englishmen, and Frenchmen, and that there are very virtuous people among all these nations.

"I will cite a single example. As regards women, duty begins in England at nine years of age; in France at fifteen. As for me, I take a little of each people's notion of duty, and of the whole I make a result comparable to the morality of good King Solomon.

"July 27th.—Good news. I have lost 620 grams in weight. Excellent, this water of Chatel-Guyon! I am taking the widows to dine at Riom. A sad town whose anagram constitutes it an objectionable neighbor to healing springs: Riom, Mori.

"July 28th.—Hello, how's this! My two widows have been visited by two gentlemen who came to look for them. Two widowers, without doubt. They are leaving this evening. They have written to me on fancy notepaper.

"July 29th.—Alone! Long excursion on foot to the extinct crater of Nachere. Splendid view.

"July 30th.—Nothing. I am taking the treatment.

"July 31st.—Ditto. Ditto. This pretty country is full of polluted streams. I am drawing the notice of the municipality to the abominable sewer which poisons the road in front of the hotel. All the kitchen refuse of the establishment is thrown into it. This is a good way to breed cholera.

"August 1st.—Nothing. The treatment.

"August 2d.—Admirable walk to Chateauneuf, a place of sojourn for rheumatic patients, where everybody is lame. Nothing can be queerer than this population of cripples!

"August 3d.—Nothing. The treatment.

"August 4th.—Ditto. Ditto.

"August 5th.—Ditto. Ditto.

"August 6th.—Despair! I have just weighed myself. I have gained 310 grams. But then?

"August 7th.—Drove sixty-six kilometres in a carriage on the mountain. I will not mention the name of the country through respect for its women.

"This excursion had been pointed out to me as a beautiful one, and one that was rarely made. After four hours on the road, I arrived at a rather pretty village on the banks of a river in the midst of an admirable wood of walnut trees. I had not yet seen a forest of walnut trees of such dimensions in Auvergne. It constitutes, moreover, all the wealth of the district, for it is planted on the village common. This common was formerly only a hillside covered with brushwood. The authorities had tried in vain to get it cultivated. There was scarcely enough pasture on it to feed a few sheep.

"To-day it is a superb wood, thanks to the women, and it has a curious name: it is called the Sins of the Cure.

"Now I must say that the women of the mountain districts have the reputation of being light, lighter than in the plain. A bachelor who meets them owes them at least a kiss; and if he does not take more he is only a blockhead. If we consider this fairly, this way of looking at the matter is the only one that is logical and reasonable. As woman, whether she be of the town or the country, has her natural mission to please man, man should always show her that she pleases him. If he abstains from every sort of demonstration, this means that he considers her ugly; it is almost an insult to her. If I were a woman, I would not receive, a second time, a man who failed to show me respect at our first meeting, for I would consider that he had failed in appreciation of my beauty, my charm, and my feminine qualities.

"So the bachelors of the village X often proved to the women of the district that they found them to their taste, and, as the cure was unable to prevent these demonstrations, as gallant as they were natural, he resolved to utilize them for the benefit of the general prosperity. So he imposed as a penance on every woman who had gone wrong that she should plant a walnut tree on the common. And every night lanterns were seen moving about like will-o'-the-wisps on the hillock, for the erring ones scarcely like to perform their penance in broad daylight.

"In two years there was no longer any room on the lands belonging to the village, and to-day they calculate that there are more than three thousand trees around the belfry which rings out the services amid their foliage. These are the Sins of the Cure.

"Since we have been seeking for so many ways of rewooding France, the Administration of Forests might surely enter into some arrangement with the clergy to employ a method so simple as that employed by this humble cure.

"August 7th.—Treatment.

"August 8th.—I am packing up my trunks and saying good-by to the charming little district so calm and silent, to the green mountain, to the quiet valleys, to the deserted Casino, from which you can see, almost veiled by its light, bluish mist, the immense plain of the Limagne.

"I shall leave to-morrow."

Here the manuscript stopped. I will add nothing to it, my impressions of the country not having been exactly the same as those of my predecessor. For I did not find the two widows!

"THE TERROR"

You say you cannot possibly understand it, and I believe you. You think I am losing my mind? Perhaps I am, but for other reasons than those you imagine, my dear friend.

Yes, I am going to be married, and will tell you what has led me to take that step.

I may add that I know very little of the girl who is going to become my wife to-morrow; I have only seen her four or five times. I know that there is nothing unpleasing about her, and that is enough for my purpose. She is small, fair, and stout; so, of course, the day after to-morrow I shall ardently wish for a tall, dark, thin woman.

She is not rich, and belongs to the middle classes. She is a girl such as you may find by the gross, well adapted for matrimony, without any apparent faults, and with no particularly striking qualities. People say of her:

"Mlle. Lajolle is a very nice girl," and tomorrow they will say: "What a very nice woman Madame Raymon is." She belongs, in a word, to that immense number of girls whom one is glad to have for one's wife, till the moment comes when one discovers that one happens to prefer all other women to that particular woman whom one has married.

"Well," you will say to me, "what on earth did you get married for?"

I hardly like to tell you the strange and seemingly improbable reason that urged me on to this senseless act; the fact, however, is that I am afraid of being alone.

I don't know how to tell you or to make you understand me, but my state of mind is so wretched that you will pity me and despise me.

I do not want to be alone any longer at night. I want to feel that there is some one close to me, touching me, a being who can speak and say something, no matter what it be.

I wish to be able to awaken somebody by my side, so that I may be able to ask some sudden question, a stupid question even, if I feel inclined, so that I may hear a human voice, and feel that there is some waking soul close to me, some one whose reason is at work; so that when I hastily light the candle I may see some human face by my side—because—because —I am ashamed to confess it— because I am afraid of being alone.

Oh, you don't understand me yet.

I am not afraid of any danger; if a man were to come into the room, I should kill him without trembling. I am not afraid of ghosts, nor do I believe in the supernatural. I am not afraid of dead people, for I believe in the total annihilation of every being that disappears from the face of this earth.

Well—yes, well, it must be told: I am afraid of myself, afraid of that horrible sensation of incomprehensible fear.

You may laugh, if you like. It is terrible, and I cannot get over it. I am afraid of the walls, of the furniture, of the familiar objects; which are animated, as far as I am concerned, by a kind of animal life. Above all, I am afraid of my own dreadful thoughts, of my reason, which seems as if it were about to leave me, driven away by a mysterious and invisible agony.

At first I feel a vague uneasiness in my mind, which causes a cold shiver to run all over me. I look round, and of course nothing is to be seen, and I wish that there were something there, no matter what, as long as it were something tangible. I am frightened merely because I cannot understand my own terror.

If I speak, I am afraid of my own voice. If I walk, I am afraid of I know not what, behind the door, behind the curtains, in the cupboard, or under my bed, and yet all the time I know there is nothing anywhere, and I turn round suddenly because I am afraid of what is behind me, although there is nothing there, and I know it.

I become agitated. I feel that my fear increases, and so I shut myself up in my own room, get into bed, and hide under the clothes; and there, cowering down, rolled into a ball, I close my eyes in despair, and remain thus for an indefinite time, remembering that my candle is alight on the table by my bedside, and that I ought to put it out, and yet—I dare not do it.

It is very terrible, is it not, to be like that?

Formerly I felt nothing of all that. I came home quite calm, and went up and down my apartment without anything disturbing my peace of mind. Had any one told me that I should be attacked by a malady—for I can call it nothing else—of most improbable fear, such a stupid and terrible malady as it is, I should have laughed outright. I was certainly never afraid of opening the door in the dark. I went to bed slowly, without locking it, and never got up in the middle of the night to make sure that everything was firmly closed.

It began last year in a very strange manner on a damp autumn evening. When my servant had left the room, after I had dined, I asked myself what I was going to do. I walked up and down my room for some time, feeling tired without any reason for it, unable to work, and even without energy to read. A fine rain was falling, and I felt unhappy, a prey to one of those fits of despondency, without any apparent cause, which make us feel inclined to cry, or to talk, no matter to whom, so as to shake off our depressing thoughts.

I felt that I was alone, and my rooms seemed to me to be more empty than they had ever been before. I was in the midst of infinite and overwhelming solitude. What was I to do? I sat down, but a kind of nervous impatience seemed to affect my legs, so I got up and began to walk about again. I was, perhaps, rather feverish, for my hands, which I had clasped behind me, as one often does when walking slowly, almost seemed to burn one another. Then suddenly a cold shiver ran down my back, and I thought the damp air might have penetrated into my rooms, so I lit the fire for the first time that year, and sat down again and looked at the flames. But soon I felt that I could not possibly remain quiet, and so I got up again and determined to go out, to pull myself together, and to find a friend to bear me company.

I could not find anyone, so I walked to the boulevard to try and meet some acquaintance or other there.

It was wretched everywhere, and the wet pavement glistened in the gaslight, while the oppressive warmth of the almost impalpable rain lay heavily over the streets and seemed to obscure the light of the lamps.

I went on slowly, saying to myself: "I shall not find a soul to talk to."

I glanced into several cafes, from the Madeleine as far as the Faubourg Poissoniere, and saw many unhappy-looking individuals sitting at the tables who did not seem even to have enough energy left to finish the refreshments they had ordered.

For a long time I wandered aimlessly up and down, and about midnight I started for home. I was very calm and very tired. My janitor opened the door at once, which was quite unusual for him, and I thought that another lodger had probably just come in.

When I go out I always double-lock the door of my room, and I found it merely closed, which surprised me; but I supposed that some letters had been brought up for me in the course of the evening.

I went in, and found my fire still burning so that it lighted up the room a little, and, while in the act of taking up a candle, I noticed somebody sitting in my armchair by the fire, warming his feet, with his back toward me.

I was not in the slightest degree frightened. I thought, very naturally, that some friend or other had come to see me. No doubt the porter, to whom I had said I was going out, had lent him his own key. In a moment I remembered all the circumstances of my return, how the street door had been opened immediately, and that my own door was only latched and not locked.

I could see nothing of my friend but his head, and he had evidently gone to sleep while waiting for me, so I went up to him to rouse him. I saw him quite distinctly; his right arm was hanging down and his legs were crossed; the position of his head, which was somewhat inclined to the left of the armchair, seemed to indicate that he was asleep. "Who can it be?" I asked myself. I could not see clearly, as the room was rather dark, so I put out my hand to touch him on the shoulder, and it came in contact with the back of the chair. There was nobody there; the seat was empty.

I fairly jumped with fright. For a moment I drew back as if confronted by some terrible danger; then I turned round again, impelled by an imperious standing upright, panting with fear, so upset that I could not collect my thoughts, and ready to faint.

But I am a cool man, and soon recovered myself. I thought: "It is a mere hallucination, that is all," and I immediately began to reflect on this phenomenon. Thoughts fly quickly at such moments.

I had been suffering from an hallucination, that was an incontestable fact. My mind had been perfectly lucid and had acted regularly and logically, so there was nothing the matter with the brain. It was only my eyes that had been deceived; they had had a vision, one of those visions which lead simple folk to believe in miracles. It was a nervous seizure of the optical apparatus, nothing more; the eyes were rather congested, perhaps.

I lit my candle, and when I stooped down to the fire in doing so I noticed that I was trembling, and I raised myself up with a jump, as if somebody had touched me from behind.

I was certainly not by any means calm.

I walked up and down a little, and hummed a tune or two. Then I double-locked the door and felt rather reassured; now, at any rate, nobody could come in.

I sat down again and thought over my adventure for a long time; then I went to bed and blew out my light.

For some minutes all went well; I lay quietly on my back, but presently an irresistible desire seized me to look round the room, and I turned over on my side.

My fire was nearly out, and the few glowing embers threw a faint light on the floor by the chair, where I fancied I saw the man sitting again.

I quickly struck a match, but I had been mistaken; there was nothing there. I got up, however, and hid the chair behind my bed, and tried to get to sleep, as the room was now dark; but I had not forgotten myself for more than five minutes, when in my dream I saw all the scene which I had previously witnessed as clearly as if it were reality. I woke up with a start, and having lit the candle, sat up in bed, without venturing even to try to go to sleep again.

Twice, however, sleep overcame me for a few moments in spite of myself, and twice I saw the same thing again, till I fancied I was going mad. When day broke, however, I thought that I was cured, and slept peacefully till noon.

It was all past and over. I had been feverish, had had the nightmare. I know not what. I had been ill, in fact, but yet thought I was a great fool.

I enjoyed myself thoroughly that evening. I dined at a restaurant and afterward went to the theatre, and then started for home. But as I got near the house I was once more seized by a strange feeling of uneasiness. I was afraid of seeing him again. I was not afraid of him, not afraid of his presence, in which I did not believe; but I was afraid of being deceived again. I was afraid of some fresh hallucination, afraid lest fear should take possession of me.

For more than an hour I wandered up and down the pavement; then, feeling that I was really too foolish, I returned home. I breathed so hard that I could hardly get upstairs, and remained standing outside my door for more than ten minutes; then suddenly I had a courageous impulse and my will asserted itself. I inserted my key into the lock, and went into the apartment with a candle in my hand. I kicked open my bedroom door, which was partly open, and cast a frightened glance toward the fireplace. There was nothing there. A-h! What a relief and what a delight! What a deliverance! I walked up and down briskly and boldly, but I was not altogether reassured, and kept turning round with a jump; the very shadows in the corners disquieted me.

I slept badly, and was constantly disturbed by imaginary noises, but did not see him; no, that was all over.

Since that time I have been afraid of being alone at night. I feel that the spectre is there, close to me, around me; but it has not appeared to me again.

And supposing it did, what would it matter, since I do not believe in it, and know that it is nothing?

However, it still worries me, because I am constantly thinking of it. His right arm hanging down and his head inclined to the left like a man who was asleep—I don't want to think about it!

Why, however, am I so persistently possessed with this idea? His feet were close to the fire!

He haunts me; it is very stupid, but who and what is he? I know that he does not exist except in my cowardly imagination, in my fears, and in my agony. There—enough of that!

Yes, it is all very well for me to reason with myself, to stiffen my backbone, so to say; but I cannot remain at home because I know he is there. I know I shall not see him again; he will not show himself again; that is all over. But he is there, all the same, in my thoughts. He remains invisible, but that does not prevent his being there. He is behind the doors, in the closed cupboard, in the wardrobe, under the bed, in every dark corner. If I open the door or the cupboard, if I take the candle to look under the bed and throw a light on the dark places he is there no longer, but I feel that he is behind me. I turn round, certain that I shall not see him, that I shall never see him again; but for all that, he is behind me.

It is very stupid, it is dreadful; but what am I to do? I cannot help it.

But if there were two of us in the place I feel certain that he would not be there any longer, for he is there just because I am alone, simply and solely because I am alone!

LEGEND OF MONT ST. MICHEL

I had first seen it from Cancale, this fairy castle in the sea. I got an indistinct impression of it as of a gray shadow outlined against the misty sky. I saw it again from Avranches at sunset. The immense stretch of sand was red, the horizon was red, the whole boundless bay was red. The rocky castle rising out there in the distance like a weird, seignorial residence, like a dream palace, strange and beautiful-this alone remained black in the crimson light of the dying day.

The following morning at dawn I went toward it across the sands, my eyes fastened on this, gigantic jewel, as big as a mountain, cut like a cameo, and as dainty as lace. The nearer I approached the greater my admiration grew, for nothing in the world could be more wonderful or more perfect.

As surprised as if I had discovered the habitation of a god, I wandered through those halls supported by frail or massive columns, raising my eyes in wonder to those spires which looked like rockets starting for the sky, and to that marvellous assemblage of towers, of gargoyles, of slender and charming ornaments, a regular fireworks of stone, granite lace, a masterpiece of colossal and delicate architecture.

As I was looking up in ecstasy a Lower Normandy peasant came up to me and told me the story of the great quarrel between Saint Michael and the devil.

A sceptical genius has said: "God made man in his image and man has returned the compliment."

This saying is an eternal truth, and it would be very curious to write the history of the local divinity of every continent as well as the history of the patron saints in each one of our provinces. The negro has his ferocious man-eating idols; the polygamous Mahometan fills his paradise with women; the Greeks, like a practical people, deified all the passions.

Every village in France is under the influence of some protecting saint, modelled according to the characteristics of the inhabitants.

Saint Michael watches over Lower Normandy, Saint Michael, the radiant and victorious angel, the sword-carrier, the hero of Heaven, the victorious, the conqueror of Satan.

But this is how the Lower Normandy peasant, cunning, deceitful and tricky, understands and tells of the struggle between the great saint and the devil.

To escape from the malice of his neighbor, the devil, Saint Michael built himself, in the open ocean, this habitation worthy of an archangel; and only such a saint could build a residence of such magnificence.

But as he still feared the approaches of the wicked one, he surrounded his domains by quicksands, more treacherous even than the sea.

The devil lived in a humble cottage on the hill, but he owned all the salt marshes, the rich lands where grow the finest crops, the wooded valleys and all the fertile hills of the country, while the saint a ruled only over the sands. Therefore Satan was rich, whereas Saint Michael was as poor as a church mouse.

After a few years of fasting the saint grew tired of this state of affairs and began to think of some compromise with the devil, but the matter was by no means easy, as Satan kept a good hold on his crops.

He thought the thing over for about six months; then one morning he walked across to the shore. The demon was eating his soup in front of his door when he saw the saint. He immediately rushed toward him, kissed the hem of his sleeve, invited him in and offered him refreshments.

Saint Michael drank a bowl of milk and then began: "I have come here to propose to you a good bargain."

The devil, candid and trustful, answered: "That will suit me."

"Here it is. Give me all your lands."

Satan, growing alarmed, wished to speak "But—"

She saint continued: "Listen first. Give me all your lands. I will take care of all the work, the ploughing, the sowing, the fertilizing, everything, and we will share the crops equally. How does that suit you?"

The devil, who was naturally lazy, accepted. He only demanded in addition a few of those delicious gray mullet which are caught around the solitary mount. Saint Michael promised the fish.

They grasped hands and spat on the ground to show that it was a bargain, and the saint continued: "See here, so that you will have nothing to complain of, choose that part of the crops which you prefer: the part that grows above ground or the part that stays in the ground." Satan cried out: "I will take all that will be above ground."

"It's a bargain!" said the saint. And he went away.

Six months later, all over the immense domain of the devil, one could see nothing but carrots, turnips, onions, salsify, all the plants whose juicy roots are good and savory and whose useless leaves are good for nothing but for feeding animals.

Satan wished to break the contract, calling Saint Michael a swindler.

But the saint, who had developed quite a taste for agriculture, went back to see the devil and said:

"Really, I hadn't thought of that at all; it was just an accident, no fault of mine. And to make things fair with you, this year I'll let you take everything that is under the ground."

"Very well," answered Satan.

The following spring all the evil spirit's lands were covered with golden wheat, oats as big as beans, flax, magnificent colza, red clover, peas, cabbage, artichokes, everything that develops into grains or fruit in the sunlight.

Once more Satan received nothing, and this time he completely lost his temper. He took back his fields and remained deaf to all the fresh propositions of his neighbor.

A whole year rolled by. From the top of his lonely manor Saint Michael looked at the distant and fertile lands and watched the devil direct the work, take in his crops and thresh the wheat. And he grew angry, exasperated at his powerlessness.

As he was no longer able to deceive Satan, he decided to wreak vengeance on him, and he went out to invite him to dinner for the following Monday.

"You have been very unfortunate in your dealings with me," he said; "I know it, but I don't want any ill feeling between us, and I expect you to dine with me. I'll give you some good things to eat."

Satan, who was as greedy as he was lazy, accepted eagerly. On the day appointed he donned his finest clothes and set out for the castle.

Saint Michael sat him down to a magnificent meal. First there was a 'vol-au-vent', full of cocks' crests and kidneys, with meat-balls, then two big gray mullet with cream sauce, a turkey stuffed with chestnuts soaked in wine, some salt-marsh lamb as tender as cake, vegetables which melted in the mouth and nice hot pancake which was brought on smoking and spreading a delicious odor of butter.

They drank new, sweet, sparkling cider and heady red wine, and after each course they whetted their appetites with some old apple brandy.

The devil drank and ate to his heart's content; in fact he took so much that he was very uncomfortable, and began to retch.

Then Saint Michael arose in anger and cried in a voice like thunder: "What! before me, rascal! You dare—before me—"

Satan, terrified, ran away, and the saint, seizing a stick, pursued him. They ran through the halls, turning round the pillars, running up the staircases, galloping along the cornices, jumping from gargoyle to gargoyle. The poor devil, who was woefully ill, was running about madly and trying hard to escape. At last he found himself at the top of the last terrace, right at the top, from which could be seen the immense bay, with its distant towns, sands and pastures. He could no longer escape, and the saint came up behind him and gave him a furious kick, which shot him through space like a cannonball.

He shot through the air like a javelin and fell heavily before the town of Mortain. His horns and claws stuck deep into the rock, which keeps through eternity the traces of this fall of Satan.

He stood up again, limping, crippled until the end of time, and as he looked at this fatal castle in the distance, standing out against the setting sun, he understood well that he would always be vanquished in this unequal struggle, and he went away limping, heading for distant countries, leaving to his enemy his fields, his hills, his valleys and his marshes.

And this is how Saint Michael, the patron saint of Normandy, vanquished the devil.

Another people would have dreamed of this battle in an entirely different manner.

A NEW YEAR'S GIFT

Jacques de Randal, having dined at home alone, told his valet he might go out, and he sat down at his table to write some letters.

He ended every year in this manner, writing and dreaming. He reviewed the events of his life since last New Year's Day, things that were now all over and dead; and, in proportion as the faces of his friends rose up before his eyes, he wrote them a few lines, a cordial New Year's greeting on the first of January.

So he sat down, opened a drawer, took out of it a woman's photograph, gazed at it a few moments, and kissed it. Then, having laid it beside a sheet of notepaper, he began:

"MY DEAR IRENE: You must by this time have received the little

souvenir I sent, you addressed to the maid. I have shut myself up

this evening in order to tell you——"

The pen here ceased to move. Jacques rose up and began walking up and down the room.

For the last ten months he had had a sweetheart, not like the others, a woman with whom one engages in a passing intrigue, of the theatrical world or the demi-monde, but a woman whom he loved and won. He was no longer a young man, although he was still comparatively young for a man, and he looked on life seriously in a positive and practical spirit.

Accordingly, he drew up the balance sheet of his passion, as he drew up every year the balance sheet of friendships that were ended or freshly contracted, of circumstances and persons that had entered into his life.

His first ardor of love having grown calmer, he asked himself with the precision of a merchant making a calculation what was the state of his heart with regard to her, and he tried to form an idea of what it would be in the future.

He found there a great and deep affection; made up of tenderness, gratitude and the thousand subtleties which give birth to long and powerful attachments.

A ring at the bell made him start. He hesitated. Should he open the door? But he said to himself that one must always open the door on New Year's night, to admit the unknown who is passing by and knocks, no matter who it may be.

So he took a wax candle, passed through the antechamber, drew back the bolts, turned the key, pulled the door back, and saw his sweetheart standing pale as a corpse, leaning against the wall.

He stammered:

"What is the matter with you?"

She replied:

"Are you alone?"

"Yes."

"Without servants?"

"Yes."

"You are not going out?"

"No."

She entered with the air of a woman who knew the house. As soon as she was in the drawing-room, she sank down on the sofa, and, covering her face with her hands, began to weep bitterly.

He knelt down at her feet, and tried to remove her hands from her eyes, so that he might look at them, and exclaimed:

"Irene, Irene, what is the matter with you? I implore you to tell me what is the matter with you?"

Then, amid her sobs, she murmured:

"I can no longer live like this."

"Live like this? What do you mean?"

"Yes. I can no longer live like this. I have endured so much. He struck me this afternoon."

"Who? Your husband?"

"Yes, my husband."

"Ah!"

He was astonished, having never suspected that her husband could be brutal. He was a man of the world, of the better class, a clubman, a lover of horses, a theatergoer and an expert swordsman; he was known, talked about, appreciated everywhere, having very courteous manners, a very mediocre intellect, an absence of education and of the real culture needed in order to think like all well-bred people, and finally a respect for conventionalities.

He appeared to devote himself to his wife, as a man ought to do in the case of wealthy and well-bred people. He displayed enough of anxiety about her wishes, her health, her dresses, and, beyond that, left her perfectly free.

Randal, having become Irene's friend, had a right to the affectionate hand-clasp which every husband endowed with good manners owes to his wife's intimate acquaintance. Then, when Jacques, after having been for some time the friend, became the lover, his relations with the husband were more cordial, as is fitting.

Jacques had never dreamed that there were storms in this household, and he was bewildered at this unexpected revelation.

He asked:

"How did it happen? Tell me."

Thereupon she related a long story, the entire history of her life since the day of her marriage, the first disagreement arising out of a mere nothing, then becoming accentuated at every new difference of opinion between two dissimilar dispositions.

Then came quarrels, a complete separation, not apparent, but real; next, her husband showed himself aggressive, suspicious, violent. Now, he was jealous, jealous of Jacques, and that very day, after a scene, he had struck her.

She added with decision: "I will not go back to him. Do with me what you like."

Jacques sat down opposite to her, their knees touching. He took her hands:

"My dear love, you are going to commit a gross, an irreparable folly. If you want to leave your husband, put him in the wrong, so that your position as a woman of the world may be saved."

She asked, as she looked at him uneasily:

"Then, what do you advise me?"

"To go back home and to put up with your life there till the day when you can obtain either a separation or a divorce, with the honors of war."

"Is not this thing which you advise me to do a little cowardly?"

"No; it is wise and sensible. You have a high position, a reputation to protect, friends to preserve and relations to deal with. You must not lose all these through a mere caprice."

She rose up, and said with violence:

"Well, no! I cannot stand it any longer! It is at an end! it is at an end!"

Then, placing her two hands on her lover's shoulders, and looking him straight in the face, she asked:

"Do you love me?"

"Yes."

"Really and truly?"

"Yes."

"Then take care of me."

He exclaimed:

"Take care of you? In my own house? Here? Why, you are mad. It would mean losing you forever; losing you beyond hope of recall! You are mad!"

She replied, slowly and seriously, like a woman who feels the weight of her words:

"Listen, Jacques. He has forbidden me to see you again, and I will not play this comedy of coming secretly to your house. You must either lose me or take me."

"My dear Irene, in that case, obtain your divorce, and I will marry you."

"Yes, you will marry me in—two years at the soonest. Yours is a patient love."

"Look here! Reflect! If you remain here he'll come to-morrow to take you away, seeing that he is your husband, seeing that he has right and law on his side."

"I did not ask you to keep me in your own house, Jacques, but to take me anywhere you like. I thought you loved me enough to do that. I have made a mistake. Good-by!"

She turned round and went toward the door so quickly that he was only able to catch hold of her when she was outside the room:

"Listen, Irene."

She struggled, and would not listen to him. Her eyes were full of tears, and she stammered:

"Let me alone! let me alone! let me alone!"

He made her sit down by force, and once more falling on his knees at her feet, he now brought forward a number of arguments and counsels to make her understand the folly and terrible risk of her project. He omitted nothing which he deemed necessary to convince her, finding even in his very affection for her incentives to persuasion.

As she remained silent and cold as ice, he begged of her, implored of her to listen to him, to trust him, to follow his advice.

When he had finished speaking, she only replied:

"Are you disposed to let me go away now? Take away your hands, so that I may rise to my feet."

"Look here, Irene."

"Will you let me go?"

"Irene—is your resolution irrevocable?"

"Will you let me go."

"Tell me only whether this resolution, this mad resolution of yours, which you will bitterly regret, is irrevocable?"

"Yes—let me go!"

"Then stay. You know well that you are at home here. We shall go away to-morrow morning."

She rose to her feet in spite of him, and said in a hard tone:

"No. It is too late. I do not want sacrifice; I do not want devotion."

"Stay! I have done what I ought to do; I have said what I ought to say. I have no further responsibility on your behalf. My conscience is at peace. Tell me what you want me to do, and I will obey."'

She resumed her seat, looked at him for a long time, and then asked, in a very calm voice:

"Well, then, explain."

"Explain what? What do you wish me to explain?"

"Everything—everything that you thought about before changing your mind. Then I will see what I ought to do."

"But I thought about nothing at all. I had to warn you that you were going to commit an act of folly. You persist; then I ask to share in this act of folly, and I even insist on it."

"It is not natural to change one's mind so quickly."

"Listen, my dear love. It is not a question here of sacrifice or devotion. On the day when I realized that I loved you, I said to myself what every lover ought to say to himself in the same case: 'The man who loves a woman, who makes an effort to win her, who gets her, and who takes her, enters into a sacred contract with himself and with her. That is, of course, in dealing with a woman like you, not a woman with a fickle heart and easily impressed.'

"Marriage which has a great social value, a great legal value, possesses in my eyes only a very slight moral value, taking into account the conditions under which it generally takes place.

"Therefore, when a woman, united by this lawful bond, but having no attachment to her husband, whom she cannot love, a woman whose heart is free, meets a man whom she cares for, and gives herself to him, when a man who has no other tie, takes a woman in this way, I say that they pledge themselves toward each other by this mutual and free agreement much more than by the 'Yes' uttered in the presence of the mayor.

"I say that, if they are both honorable persons, their union must be more intimate, more real, more wholesome, than if all the sacraments had consecrated it.

"This woman risks everything. And it is exactly because she knows it, because she gives everything, her heart, her body, her soul, her honor, her life, because she has foreseen all miseries, all dangers all catastrophes, because she dares to do a bold act, an intrepid act, because she is prepared, determined to brave everything—her husband, who might kill her, and society, which may cast her out. This is why she is worthy of respect in the midst of her conjugal infidelity; this is why her lover, in taking her, should also foresee everything, and prefer her to every one else whatever may happen. I have nothing more to say. I spoke in the beginning like a sensible man whose duty it was to warn you; and now I am only a man—a man who loves you—Command, and I obey."

Radiant, she closed his mouth with a kiss, and said in a low tone:

"It is not true, darling! There is nothing the matter! My husband does not suspect anything. But I wanted to see, I wanted to know, what you would do I wished for a New Year's gift—the gift of your heart—another gift besides the necklace you sent me. You have given it to me. Thanks! thanks! God be thanked for the happiness you have given me!"

FRIEND PATIENCE

"What became of Leremy?"

"He is captain in the Sixth Dragoons."

"And Pinson?"

"He's a subprefect."

"And Racollet?"

"Dead."

We were searching for other names which would remind us of the youthful faces of our younger days. Once in a while we had met some of these old comrades, bearded, bald, married, fathers of several children, and the realization of these changes had given us an unpleasant shudder, reminding us how short life is, how everything passes away, how everything changes. My friend asked me:

"And Patience, fat Patience?"

I almost, howled:

"Oh! as for him, just listen to this. Four or five years ago I was in Limoges, on a tour of inspection, and I was waiting for dinner time. I was seated before the big cafe in the Place du Theatre, just bored to death. The tradespeople were coming by twos, threes or fours, to take their absinthe or vermouth, talking all the time of their own or other people's business, laughing loudly, or lowering their voices in order to impart some important or delicate piece of news.

"I was saying to myself: 'What shall I do after dinner?' And I thought of the long evening in this provincial town, of the slow, dreary walk through unknown streets, of the impression of deadly gloom which these provincial people produce on the lonely traveller, and of the whole oppressive atmosphere of the place.

"I was thinking of all these things as I watched the little jets of gas flare up, feeling my loneliness increase with the falling shadows.

"A big, fat man sat down at the next table and called in a stentorian voice:

"'Waiter, my bitters!'

"The 'my' came out like the report of a cannon. I immediately understood that everything was his in life, and not another's; that he had his nature, by Jove, his appetite, his trousers, his everything, his, more absolutely and more completely than anyone else's. Then he looked round him with a satisfied air. His bitters were brought, and he ordered:

"'My newspaper!'

"I wondered: 'Which newspaper can his be?' The title would certainly reveal to me his opinions, his theories, his principles, his hobbies, his weaknesses.

"The waiter brought the Temps. I was surprised. Why the Temps, a serious, sombre, doctrinaire, impartial sheet? I thought:

"'He must be a serious man with settled and regular habits; in short, a good bourgeois.'

"He put on his gold-rimmed spectacles, leaned back before beginning to read, and once more glanced about him. He noticed me, and immediately began to stare at me in an annoying manner. I was even going to ask the reason for this attention, when he exclaimed from his seat:

"'Well, by all that's holy, if this isn't Gontran Lardois.'

"I answered:

"'Yes, monsieur, you are not mistaken.'

"Then he quickly rose and came toward me with hands outstretched:

"'Well, old man, how are you?'

"As I did not recognize him at all I was greatly embarrassed. I stammered:

"'Why-very well-and-you?'

"He began to laugh "'I bet you don't recognize me.'

"'No, not exactly. It seems—however—'

"He slapped me on the back:

"'Come on, no joking! I am Patience, Robert Patience, your friend, your chum.'

"I recognized him. Yes, Robert Patience, my old college chum. It was he. I took his outstretched hand:

"'And how are you?'

"'Fine!'

"His smile was like a paean of victory.

"He asked:

"'What are you doing here?'

"I explained that I was government inspector of taxes.

"He continued, pointing to my red ribbon:

"'Then you have-been a success?'

"I answered:

"'Fairly so. And you?'

"'I am doing well!'

"'What are you doing?'

"'I'm in business.'

"'Making money?'

"'Heaps. I'm very rich. But come around to lunch, to-morrow noon, 17 Rue du Coq-qui-Chante; you will see my place.'

"He seemed to hesitate a second, then continued:

"'Are you still the good sport that you used to be?'

"'I—I hope so.'

"'Not married?'

"'No.'

"'Good. And do you still love a good time and potatoes?'

"I was beginning to find him hopelessly vulgar. Nevertheless, I answered "'Yes.'

"'And pretty girls?'

"'Most assuredly.'

"He began to laugh good-humoredly.

"'Good, good! Do you remember our first escapade, in Bordeaux, after that dinner at Routie's? What a spree!'

"I did, indeed, remember that spree; and the recollection of it cheered me up. This called to mind other pranks. He would say:

"'Say, do you remember the time when we locked the proctor up in old man Latoque's cellar?'

"And he laughed and banged the table with his fist, and then he continued:

"'Yes-yes-yes-and do you remember the face of the geography teacher, M. Marin, the day we set off a firecracker in the globe, just as he was haranguing about the principal volcanoes of the earth?'

"Then suddenly I asked him:

"'And you, are you married?'

"He exclaimed:

"'Ten years, my boy, and I have four children, remarkable youngsters; but you'll see them and their mother.'

"We were talking rather loud; the people around us looked at us in surprise.

"Suddenly my friend looked at his watch, a chronometer the size of a pumpkin, and he cried:

"'Thunder! I'm sorry, but I'll have to leave you; I am never free at night.'

"He rose, took both my hands, shook them as though he were trying to wrench my arms from their sockets, and exclaimed:

"'So long, then; till to-morrow noon!'

"'So long!'

"I spent the morning working in the office of the collector-general of the Department. The chief wished me to stay to luncheon, but I told him that I had an engagement with a friend. As he had to go out, he accompanied me.

"I asked him:

"'Can you tell me how I can find the Rue du Coq-qui-Chante?'

"He answered:

"'Yes, it's only five minutes' walk from here. As I have nothing special to do, I will take you there.'

"We started out and soon found ourselves there. It was a wide, fine-looking street, on the outskirts of the town. I looked at the houses and I noticed No. 17. It was a large house with a garden behind it. The facade, decorated with frescoes, in the Italian style, appeared to me as being in bad taste. There were goddesses holding vases, others swathed in clouds. Two stone cupids supported the number of the house.

"I said to the treasurer:

"'Here is where I am going.'

"I held my hand out to him. He made a quick, strange gesture, said nothing and shook my hand.

"I rang. A maid appeared. I asked:

"'Monsieur Patience, if you please?'

"She answered:

"'Right here, sir. Is it to monsieur that you wish to speak?'

"'Yes.'

"The hall was decorated with paintings from the brush of some local artist. Pauls and Virginias were kissing each other under palm trees bathed in a pink light. A hideous Oriental lantern was ranging from the ceiling. Several doors were concealed by bright hangings.

"But what struck me especially was the odor. It was a sickening and perfumed odor, reminding one of rice powder and the mouldy smell of a cellar. An indefinable odor in a heavy atmosphere as oppressive as that of public baths. I followed the maid up a marble stairway, covered with a green, Oriental carpet, and was ushered into a sumptubus parlor.

"Left alone, I looked about me.

"The room was richly furnished, but in the pretentious taste of a parvenu. Rather fine engravings of the last century represented women with powdered hair dressed high surprised by gentlemen in interesting positions. Another lady, lying in a large bed, was teasing with her foot a little dog, lost in the sheets. One drawing showed four feet, bodies concealed behind a curtain. The large room, surrounded by soft couches, was entirely impregnated with that enervating and insipid odor which I had already noticed. There seemed to be something suspicious about the walls, the hangings, the exaggerated luxury, everything.

"I approached the window to look into the garden. It was very big, shady, beautiful. A wide path wound round a grass plot in the midst of which was a fountain, entered a shrubbery and came out farther away. And, suddenly, yonder, in the distance, between two clumps of bushes, three women appeared. They were walking slowly, arm in arm, clad in long, white tea-gowns covered with lace. Two were blondes and the other was dark-haired. Almost immediately they disappeared again behind the trees. I stood there entranced, delighted with this short and charming apparition, which brought to my mind a whole world of poetry. They had scarcely allowed themselves to be seen, in just the proper light, in that frame of foliage, in the midst of that mysterious, delightful park. It seemed to me that I had suddenly seen before me the great ladies of the last century, who were depicted in the engravings on the wall. And I began to think of the happy, joyous, witty and amorous times when manners were so graceful and lips so approachable.

"A deep voice male me jump. Patience had come in, beaming, and held out his hands to me.

"He looked into my eyes with the sly look which one takes when divulging secrets of love, and, with a Napoleonic gesture, he showed me his sumptuous parlor, his park, the three women, who had reappeared in the back of it, then, in a triumphant voice, where the note of pride was prominent, he said:

"'And to think that I began with nothing—my wife and my sister-in-law!'"

ABANDONED

"I really think you must be mad, my dear, to go for a country walk in such weather as this. You have had some very strange notions for the last two months. You drag me to the seaside in spite of myself, when you have never once had such a whim during all the forty-four years that we have been married. You chose Fecamp, which is a very dull town, without consulting me in the matter, and now you are seized with such a rage for walking, you who hardly ever stir out on foot, that you want to take a country walk on the hottest day of the year. Ask d'Apreval to go with you, as he is ready to gratify all your whims. As for me, I am going back to have a nap."

Madame de Cadour turned to her old friend and said:

"Will you come with me, Monsieur d'Apreval?"

He bowed with a smile, and with all the gallantry of former years:

"I will go wherever you go," he replied.

"Very well, then, go and get a sunstroke," Monsieur de Cadour said; and he went back to the Hotel des Bains to lie down for an hour or two.

As soon as they were alone, the old lady and her old companion set off, and she said to him in a low voice, squeezing his hand:

"At last! at last!"

"You are mad," he said in a whisper. "I assure you that you are mad. Think of the risk you are running. If that man—"

She started.

"Oh! Henri, do not say that man, when you are speaking of him."

"Very well," he said abruptly, "if our son guesses anything, if he has any suspicions, he will have you, he will have us both in his power. You have got on without seeing him for the last forty years. What is the matter with you to-day?"

They had been going up the long street that leads from the sea to the town, and now they turned to the right, to go to Etretat. The white road stretched in front of him, then under a blaze of brilliant sunshine, so they went on slowly in the burning heat. She had taken her old friend's arm, and was looking straight in front of her, with a fixed and haunted gaze, and at last she said:

"And so you have not seen him again, either?"

"No, never."

"Is it possible?"

"My dear friend, do not let us begin that discussion again. I have a wife and children and you have a husband, so we both of us have much to fear from other people's opinion."

She did not reply; she was thinking of her long past youth and of many sad things that had occurred. How well she recalled all the details of their early friendship, his smiles, the way he used to linger, in order to watch her until she was indoors. What happy days they were, the only really delicious days she had ever enjoyed, and how quickly they were over!

And then—her discovery—of the penalty she paid! What anguish!

Of that journey to the South, that long journey, her sufferings, her constant terror, that secluded life in the small, solitary house on the shores of the Mediterranean, at the bottom of a garden, which she did not venture to leave. How well she remembered those long days which she spent lying under an orange tree, looking up at the round, red fruit, amid the green leaves. How she used to long to go out, as far as the sea, whose fresh breezes came to her over the wall, and whose small waves she could hear lapping on the beach. She dreamed of its immense blue expanse sparkling under the sun, with the white sails of the small vessels, and a mountain on the horizon. But she did not dare to go outside the gate. Suppose anybody had recognized her!

And those days of waiting, those last days of misery and expectation! The impending suffering, and then that terrible night! What misery she had endured, and what a night it was! How she had groaned and screamed! She could still see the pale face of her lover, who kissed her hand every moment, and the clean-shaven face of the doctor and the nurse's white cap.

And what she felt when she heard the child's feeble cries, that wail, that first effort of a human's voice!

And the next day! the next day! the only day of her life on which she had seen and kissed her son; for, from that time, she had never even caught a glimpse of him.

And what a long, void existence hers had been since then, with the thought of that child always, always floating before her. She had never seen her son, that little creature that had been part of herself, even once since then; they had taken him from her, carried him away, and had hidden him. All she knew was that he had been brought up by some peasants in Normandy, that he had become a peasant himself, had married well, and that his father, whose name he did not know, had settled a handsome sum of money on him.

How often during the last forty years had she wished to go and see him and to embrace him! She could not imagine to herself that he had grown! She always thought of that small human atom which she had held in her arms and pressed to her bosom for a day.

How often she had said to M. d'Apreval: "I cannot bear it any longer; I must go and see him."

But he had always stopped her and kept her from going. She would be unable to restrain and to master herself; their son would guess it and take advantage of her, blackmail her; she would be lost.

"What is he like?" she said.

"I do not know. I have not seen him again, either."

"Is it possible? To have a son and not to know him; to be afraid of him and to reject him as if he were a disgrace! It is horrible."

They went along the dusty road, overcome by the scorching sun, and continually ascending that interminable hill.

"One might take it for a punishment," she continued; "I have never had another child, and I could no longer resist the longing to see him, which has possessed me for forty years. You men cannot understand that. You must remember that I shall not live much longer, and suppose I should never see him, never have seen him! . . . Is it possible? How could I wait so long? I have thought about him every day since, and what a terrible existence mine has been! I have never awakened, never, do you understand, without my first thoughts being of him, of my child. How is he? Oh, how guilty I feel toward him! Ought one to fear what the world may say in a case like this? I ought to have left everything to go after him, to bring him up and to show my love for him. I should certainly have been much happier, but I did not dare, I was a coward. How I have suffered! Oh, how those poor, abandoned children must hate their mothers!"

She stopped suddenly, for she was choked by her sobs. The whole valley was deserted and silent in the dazzling light and the overwhelming heat, and only the grasshoppers uttered their shrill, continuous chirp among the sparse yellow grass on both sides of the road.

"Sit down a little," he said.

She allowed herself to be led to the side of the ditch and sank down with her face in her hands. Her white hair, which hung in curls on both sides of her face, had become tangled. She wept, overcome by profound grief, while he stood facing her, uneasy and not knowing what to say, and he merely murmured: "Come, take courage."

She got up.

"I will," she said, and wiping her eyes, she began to walk again with the uncertain step of an elderly woman.

A little farther on the road passed beneath a clump of trees, which hid a few houses, and they could distinguish the vibrating and regular blows of a blacksmith's hammer on the anvil; and presently they saw a wagon standing on the right side of the road in front of a low cottage, and two men shoeing a horse under a shed.

Monsieur d'Apreval went up to them.

"Where is Pierre Benedict's farm?" he asked.

"Take the road to the left, close to the inn, and then go straight on; it is the third house past Poret's. There is a small spruce fir close to the gate; you cannot make a mistake."

They turned to the left. She was walking very slowly now, her legs threatened to give way, and her heart was beating so violently that she felt as if she should suffocate, while at every step she murmured, as if in prayer:

"Oh! Heaven! Heaven!"

Monsieur d'Apreval, who was also nervous and rather pale, said to her somewhat gruffly:

"If you cannot manage to control your feelings, you will betray yourself at once. Do try and restrain yourself."

"How can I?" she replied. "My child! When I think that I am going to see my child."

They were going along one of those narrow country lanes between farmyards, that are concealed beneath a double row of beech trees at either side of the ditches, and suddenly they found themselves in front of a gate, beside which there was a young spruce fir.

"This is it," he said.

She stopped suddenly and looked about her. The courtyard, which was planted with apple trees, was large and extended as far as the small thatched dwelling house. On the opposite side were the stable, the barn, the cow house and the poultry house, while the gig, the wagon and the manure cart were under a slated outhouse. Four calves were grazing under the shade of the trees and black hens were wandering all about the enclosure.

All was perfectly still; the house door was open, but nobody was to be seen, and so they went in, when immediately a large black dog came out of a barrel that was standing under a pear tree, and began to bark furiously.

There were four bee-hives on boards against the wall of the house.

Monsieur d'Apreval stood outside and called out:

"Is anybody at home?"

Then a child appeared, a little girl of about ten, dressed in a chemise and a linen, petticoat, with dirty, bare legs and a timid and cunning look. She remained standing in the doorway, as if to prevent any one going in.

"What do you want?" she asked.

"Is your father in?"

"No."

"Where is he?"

"I don't know."

"And your mother?"

"Gone after the cows."

"Will she be back soon?"

"I don't know."

Then suddenly the lady, as if she feared that her companion might force her to return, said quickly:

"I shall not go without having seen him."

"We will wait for him, my dear friend."

As they turned away, they saw a peasant woman coming toward the house, carrying two tin pails, which appeared to be heavy and which glistened brightly in the sunlight.

She limped with her right leg, and in her brown knitted jacket, that was faded by the sun and washed out by the rain, she looked like a poor, wretched, dirty servant.

"Here is mamma," the child said.

When she got close to the house, she looked at the strangers angrily and suspiciously, and then she went in, as if she had not seen them. She looked old and had a hard, yellow, wrinkled face, one of those wooden faces that country people so often have.

Monsieur d'Apreval called her back.

"I beg your pardon, madame, but we came in to know whether you could sell us two glasses of milk."

She was grumbling when she reappeared in the door, after putting down her pails.

"I don't sell milk," she replied.

"We are very thirsty," he said, "and madame is very tired. Can we not get something to drink?"

The peasant woman gave them an uneasy and cunning glance and then she made up her mind.

"As you are here, I will give you some," she said, going into the house, and almost immediately the child came out and brought two chairs, which she placed under an apple tree, and then the mother, in turn, brought out two bowls of foaming milk, which she gave to the visitors. She did not return to the house, however, but remained standing near them, as if to watch them and to find out for what purpose they had come there.

"You have come from Fecamp?" she said.

"Yes," Monsieur d'Apreval replied, "we are staying at Fecamp for the summer."

And then, after a short silence, he continued:

"Have you any fowls you could sell us every week?"

The woman hesitated for a moment and then replied:

"Yes, I think I have. I suppose you want young ones?"

"Yes, of course."

"'What do you pay for them in the market?"

D'Apreval, who had not the least idea, turned to his companion:

"What are you paying for poultry in Fecamp, my dear lady?"

"Four francs and four francs fifty centimes," she said, her eyes full of tears, while the farmer's wife, who was looking at her askance, asked in much surprise:

"Is the lady ill, as she is crying?"

He did not know what to say, and replied with some hesitation:

"No—no—but she lost her watch as we came along, a very handsome watch, and that troubles her. If anybody should find it, please let us know."

Mother Benedict did not reply, as she thought it a very equivocal sort of answer, but suddenly she exclaimed:

"Oh, here is my husband!"

She was the only one who had seen him, as she was facing the gate. D'Apreval started and Madame de Cadour nearly fell as she turned round suddenly on her chair.

A man bent nearly double, and out of breath, stood there, ten-yards from them, dragging a cow at the end of a rope. Without taking any notice of the visitors, he said:

"Confound it! What a brute!"

And he went past them and disappeared in the cow house.

Her tears had dried quickly as she sat there startled, without a word and with the one thought in her mind, that this was her son, and D'Apreval, whom the same thought had struck very unpleasantly, said in an agitated voice:

"Is this Monsieur Benedict?"

"Who told you his name?" the wife asked, still rather suspiciously.

"The blacksmith at the corner of the highroad," he replied, and then they were all silent, with their eyes fixed on the door of the cow house, which formed a sort of black hole in the wall of the building. Nothing could be seen inside, but they heard a vague noise, movements and footsteps and the sound of hoofs, which were deadened by the straw on the floor, and soon the man reappeared in the door, wiping his forehead, and came toward the house with long, slow strides. He passed the strangers without seeming to notice them and said to his wife:

"Go and draw me a jug of cider; I am very thirsty."

Then he went back into the house, while his wife went into the cellar and left the two Parisians alone.

"Let us go, let us go, Henri," Madame de Cadour said, nearly distracted with grief, and so d'Apreval took her by the arm, helped her to rise, and sustaining her with all his strength, for he felt that she was nearly fainting, he led her out, after throwing five francs on one of the chairs.

As soon as they were outside the gate, she began to sob and said, shaking with grief:

"Oh! oh! is that what you have made of him?"

He was very pale and replied coldly:

"I did what I could. His farm is worth eighty thousand francs, and that is more than most of the sons of the middle classes have."

They returned slowly, without speaking a word. She was still crying; the tears ran down her cheeks continually for a time, but by degrees they stopped, and they went back to Fecamp, where they found Monsieur de Cadour waiting dinner for them. As soon as he saw them, he began to laugh and exclaimed:

"So my wife has had a sunstroke, and I am very glad of it. I really think she has lost her head for some time past!"

Neither of them replied, and when the husband asked them, rubbing his hands:

"Well, I hope that, at least, you have had a pleasant walk?"

Monsieur d'Apreval replied:

"A delightful walk, I assure you; perfectly delightful."

THE MAISON TELLIER

They went there every evening about eleven o'clock, just as they would go to the club. Six or eight of them; always the same set, not fast men, but respectable tradesmen, and young men in government or some other employ, and they would drink their Chartreuse, and laugh with the girls, or else talk seriously with Madame Tellier, whom everybody respected, and then they would go home at twelve o'clock! The younger men would sometimes stay later.

It was a small, comfortable house painted yellow, at the corner of a street behind Saint Etienne's Church, and from the windows one could see the docks full of ships being unloaded, the big salt marsh, and, rising beyond it, the Virgin's Hill with its old gray chapel.

Madame Tellier, who came of a respectable family of peasant proprietors in the Department of the Eure, had taken up her profession, just as she would have become a milliner or dressmaker. The prejudice which is so violent and deeply rooted in large towns, does not exist in the country places in Normandy. The peasant says:

"It is a paying-business," and he sends his daughter to keep an establishment of this character just as he would send her to keep a girls' school.

She had inherited the house from an old uncle, to whom it had belonged. Monsieur and Madame Tellier, who had formerly been innkeepers near Yvetot, had immediately sold their house, as they thought that the business at Fecamp was more profitable, and they arrived one fine morning to assume the direction of the enterprise, which was declining on account of the absence of the proprietors. They were good people enough in their way, and soon made themselves liked by their staff and their neighbors.

Monsieur died of apoplexy two years later, for as the new place kept him in idleness and without any exercise, he had grown excessively stout, and his health had suffered. Since she had been a widow, all the frequenters of the establishment made much of her; but people said that, personally, she was quite virtuous, and even the girls in the house could not discover anything against her. She was tall, stout and affable, and her complexion, which had become pale in the dimness of her house, the shutters of which were scarcely ever opened, shone as if it had been varnished. She had a fringe of curly false hair, which gave her a juvenile look, that contrasted strongly with the ripeness of her figure. She was always smiling and cheerful, and was fond of a joke, but there was a shade of reserve about her, which her occupation had not quite made her lose. Coarse words always shocked her, and when any young fellow who had been badly brought up called her establishment a hard name, she was angry and disgusted.

In a word, she had a refined mind, and although she treated her women as friends, yet she very frequently used to say that "she and they were not made of the same stuff."

Sometimes during the week she would hire a carriage and take some of her girls into the country, where they used to enjoy themselves on the grass by the side of the little river. They were like a lot of girls let out from school, and would run races and play childish games. They had a cold dinner on the grass, and drank cider, and went home at night with a delicious feeling of fatigue, and in the carriage they kissed Madame' Tellier as their kind mother, who was full of goodness and complaisance.

The house had two entrances. At the corner there was a sort of tap-room, which sailors and the lower orders frequented at night, and she had two girls whose special duty it was to wait on them with the assistance of Frederic, a short, light-haired, beardless fellow, as strong as a horse. They set the half bottles of wine and the jugs of beer on the shaky marble tables before the customers, and then urged the men to drink.

The three other girls—there were only five of them—formed a kind of aristocracy, and they remained with the company on the first floor, unless they were wanted downstairs and there was nobody on the first floor. The salon de Jupiter, where the tradesmen used to meet, was papered in blue, and embellished with a large drawing representing Leda and the swan. The room was reached by a winding staircase, through a narrow door opening on the street, and above this door a lantern inclosed in wire, such as one still sees in some towns, at the foot of the shrine of some saint, burned all night long.

The house, which was old and damp, smelled slightly of mildew. At times there was an odor of eau de Cologne in the passages, or sometimes from a half-open door downstairs the noisy mirth of the common men sitting and drinking rose to the first floor, much to the disgust of the gentlemen who were there. Madame Tellier, who was on friendly terms with her customers, did not leave the room, and took much interest in what was going on in the town, and they regularly told her all the news. Her serious conversation was a change from the ceaseless chatter of the three women; it was a rest from the obscene jokes of those stout individuals who every evening indulged in the commonplace debauchery of drinking a glass of liqueur in company with common women.

The names of the girls on the first floor were Fernande, Raphaele, and Rosa, the Jade. As the staff was limited, madame had endeavored that each member of it should be a pattern, an epitome of the feminine type, so that every customer might find as nearly as possible the realization of his ideal. Fernande represented the handsome blonde; she was very tall, rather fat, and lazy; a country girl, who could not get rid of her freckles, and whose short, light, almost colorless, tow-like hair, like combed-out hemp, barely covered her head.

Raphaele, who came from Marseilles, played the indispensable part of the handsome Jewess, and was thin, with high cheekbones, which were covered with rouge, and black hair covered with pomatum, which curled on her forehead. Her eyes would have been handsome, if the right one had not had a speck in it. Her Roman nose came down over a square jaw, where two false upper teeth contrasted strangely with the bad color of the rest.

Rosa was a little roll of fat, nearly all body, with very short legs, and from morning till night she sang songs, which were alternately risque or sentimental, in a harsh voice; told silly, interminable tales, and only stopped talking in order to eat, and left off eating in order to talk; she was never still, and was active as a squirrel, in spite of her embonpoint and her short legs; her laugh, which was a torrent of shrill cries, resounded here and there, ceaselessly, in a bedroom, in the loft, in the cafe, everywhere, and all about nothing.

The two women on the ground floor, Lodise, who was nicknamed La Cocotte, and Flora, whom they called Balancoise, because she limped a little, the former always dressed as the Goddess of Liberty, with a tri-colored sash, and the other as a Spanish woman, with a string of copper coins in her carroty hair, which jingled at every uneven step, looked like cooks dressed up for the carnival. They were like all other women of the lower orders, neither uglier nor better looking than they usually are.

They looked just like servants at an inn, and were generally called "the two pumps."

A jealous peace, which was, however, very rarely disturbed, reigned among these five women, thanks to Madame Tellier's conciliatory wisdom, and to her constant good humor, and the establishment, which was the only one of the kind in the little town, was very much frequented. Madame Tellier had succeeded in giving it such a respectable appearance, she was so amiable and obliging to everybody, her good heart was so well known, that she was treated with a certain amount of consideration. The regular customers spent money on her, and were delighted when she was especially friendly toward them, and when they met during the day, they would say: "Until this evening, you know where," just as men say: "At the club, after dinner." In a word, Madame Tellier's house was somewhere to go to, and they very rarely missed their daily meetings there.

One evening toward the end of May, the first arrival, Monsieur Poulin, who was a timber merchant, and had been mayor, found the door shut. The lantern behind the grating was not alight; there was not a sound in the house; everything seemed dead. He knocked, gently at first, but then more loudly, but nobody answered the door. Then he went slowly up the street, and when he got to the market place he met Monsieur Duvert, the gunmaker, who was going to the same place, so they went back together, but did not meet with any better success. But suddenly they heard a loud noise, close to them, and on going round the house, they saw a number of English and French sailors, who were hammering at the closed shutters of the taproom with their fists.

The two tradesmen immediately made their escape, but a low "Pst!" stopped them; it was Monsieur Tournevau, the fish curer, who had recognized them, and was trying to attract their attention. They told him what had happened, and he was all the more annoyed, as he was a married man and father of a family, and only went on Saturdays. That was his regular evening, and now he should be deprived of this dissipation for the whole week.

The three men went as far as the quay together, and on the way they met young Monsieur Philippe, the banker's son, who frequented the place regularly, and Monsieur Pinipesse, the collector, and they all returned to the Rue aux Juifs together, to make a last attempt. But the exasperated sailors were besieging the house, throwing stones at the shutters, and shouting, and the five first-floor customers went away as quickly as possible, and walked aimlessly about the streets.

Presently they met Monsieur Dupuis, the insurance agent, and then Monsieur Vasse, the Judge of the Tribunal of Commerce, and they took a long walk, going to the pier first of all, where they sat down in a row on the granite parapet and watched the rising tide, and when the promenaders had sat there for some time, Monsieur Tournevau said:

"This is not very amusing!"

"Decidedly not," Monsieur Pinipesse replied, and they started off to walk again.

After going through the street alongside the hill, they returned over the wooden bridge which crosses the Retenue, passed close to the railway, and came out again on the market place, when, suddenly, a quarrel arose between Monsieur Pinipesse, the collector, and Monsieur Tournevau about an edible mushroom which one of them declared he had found in the neighborhood.

As they were out of temper already from having nothing to do, they would very probably have come to blows, if the others had not interfered. Monsieur Pinipesse went off furious, and soon another altercation arose between the ex-mayor, Monsieur Poulin, and Monsieur Dupuis, the insurance agent, on the subject of the tax collector's salary and the profits which he might make. Insulting remarks were freely passing between them, when a torrent of formidable cries was heard, and the body of sailors, who were tired of waiting so long outside a closed house, came into the square. They were walking arm in arm, two and two, and formed a long procession, and were shouting furiously. The townsmen hid themselves in a doorway, and the yelling crew disappeared in the direction of the abbey. For a long time they still heard the noise, which diminished like a storm in the distance, and then silence was restored. Monsieur Poulin and Monsieur Dupuis, who were angry with each other, went in different directions, without wishing each other good-by.

The other four set off again, and instinctively went in the direction of Madame Tellier's establishment, which was still closed, silent, impenetrable. A quiet, but obstinate drunken man was knocking at the door of the lower room, antd then stopped and called Frederic, in a low voice, but finding that he got no answer, he sat down on the doorstep, and waited the course of events.

The others were just going to retire, when the noisy band of sailors reappeared at the end of the street. The French sailors were shouting the "Marseillaise," and the Englishmen "Rule Britannia." There was a general lurching against the wall, and then the drunken fellows went on their way toward the quay, where a fight broke out between the two nations, in the course of which an Englishman had his arm broken and a Frenchman his nose split.

The drunken man who had waited outside the door, was crying by that time, as drunken men and children cry when they are vexed, and the others went away. By degrees, calm was restored in the noisy town; here and there, at moments, the distant sound of voices could be heard, and then died away in the distance.

One man only was still wandering about, Monsieur Tournevau, the fish curer, who was annoyed at having to wait until the following Saturday, and he hoped something would turn up, he did not know what; but he was exasperated at the police for thus allowing an establishment of such public utility, which they had under their control, to be closed.

He went back to it and examined the walls, trying to find out some reason, and on the shutter he saw a notice stuck up. He struck a wax match and read the following, in a large, uneven hand: "Closed on account of the Confirmation."

Then he went away, as he saw it was useless to remain, and left the drunken man lying on the pavement fast asleep, outside that inhospitable door.

The next day, all the regular customers, one after the other, found some reason for going through the street, with a bundle of papers under their arm to keep them in countenance, and with a furtive glance they all read that mysterious notice:

"Closed on account of the Confirmation."

PART II

Madame Tellier had a brother, who was a carpenter in their native place, Virville, in the Department of Eure. When she still kept the inn at Yvetot, she had stood godmother to that brother's daughter, who had received the name of Constance—Constance Rivet; she herself being a Rivet on her father's side. The carpenter, who knew that his sister was in a good position, did not lose sight of her, although they did not meet often, for they were both kept at home by their occupations, and lived a long way from each other. But as the girl was twelve years old, and going to be confirmed, he seized that opportunity to write to his sister, asking her to come and be present at the ceremony. Their old parents were dead, and as she could not well refuse her goddaughter, she accepted the invitation. Her brother, whose name was Joseph, hoped that by dint of showing his sister attention, she might be induced to make her will in the girl's favor, as she had no children of her own.

His sister's occupation did not trouble his scruples in the least, and, besides, nobody knew anything about it at Virville. When they spoke of her, they only said: "Madame Tellier is living at Fecamp," which might mean that she was living on her own private income. It was quite twenty leagues from Fecamp to Virville, and for a peasant, twenty leagues on land is as long a journey as crossing the ocean would be to city people. The people at Virville had never been further than Rouen, and nothing attracted the people from Fecamp to a village of five hundred houses in the middle of a plain, and situated in another department; at any rate, nothing was known about her business.

But the Confirmation was coming on, and Madame Tellier was in great embarrassment. She had no substitute, and did not at all care to leave her house, even for a day; for all the rivalries between the girls upstairs and those downstairs would infallibly break out. No doubt Frederic would get drunk, and when he was in that state, he would knock anybody down for a mere word. At last, however, she made up her mind to take them all with her, with the exception of the man, to whom she gave a holiday until the next day but one.

When she asked her brother, he made no objection, but undertook to put them all up for a night, and so on Saturday morning the eight-o'clock express carried off Madame Tellier and her companions in a second-class carriage. As far as Beuzeville they were alone, and chattered like magpies, but at that station a couple got in. The man, an old peasant, dressed in a blue blouse with a turned-down collar, wide sleeves tight at the wrist, ornamented with white embroidery, wearing an old high hat with long nap, held an enormous green umbrella in one hand, and a large basket in the other, from which the heads of three frightened ducks protruded. The woman, who sat up stiffly in her rustic finery, had a face like a fowl, with a nose that was as pointed as a bill. She sat down opposite her husband and did not stir, as she was startled at finding herself in such smart company.

There was certainly an array of striking colors in the carriage. Madame Tellier was dressed in blue silk from head to foot, and had on a dazzling red imitation French cashmere shawl. Fernande was puffing in a Scotch plaid dress, of which her companions had laced the bodice as tight as they could, forcing up her full bust, that was continually heaving up and down. Raphaele, with a bonnet covered with feathers, so that it looked like a bird's nest, had on a lilac dress with gold spots on it, and there was something Oriental about it that suited her Jewish face. Rosa had on a pink skirt with large flounces, and looked like a very fat child, an obese dwarf; while the two Pumps looked as if they had cut their dresses out of old flowered curtains dating from the Restoration.

As soon as they were no longer alone in the compartment, the ladies put on staid looks, and began to talk of subjects which might give others a high opinion of them. But at Bolbeck a gentleman with light whiskers, a gold chain, and wearing two or three rings, got in, and put several parcels wrapped in oilcloth on the rack over his head. He looked inclined for a joke, and seemed a good-hearted fellow.

"Are you ladies changing your quarters?" he said, and that question embarrassed them all considerably. Madame Tellier, however, quickly regained her composure, and said sharply, to avenge the honor of her corps:

"I think you might try and be polite!"

He excused himself, and said: "I beg your pardon, I ought to have said your nunnery."

She could not think of a retort, so, perhaps thinking she had said enough, madame gave him a dignified bow and compressed her lips.

Then the gentleman, who was sitting between Rosa and the old peasant, began to wink knowingly at the ducks whose heads were sticking out of the basket, and when he felt that he had fixed the attention of his public, he began to tickle them under the bills and spoke funnily to them to make the company smile.

"We have left our little pond, quack! quack! to make the acquaintance of the little spit, qu-ack! qu-ack!"

The unfortunate creatures turned their necks away, to avoid his caresses, and made desperate efforts to get out of their wicker prison, and then, suddenly, all at once, uttered the most lamentable quacks of distress. The women exploded with laughter. They leaned forward and pushed each other, so as to see better; they were very much interested in the ducks, and the gentleman redoubled his airs, his wit and his teasing.

Rosa joined in, and leaning over her neighbor's legs, she kissed the three animals on the head, and immediately all the girls wanted to kiss them, in turn, and as they did so the gentleman took them on his knee, jumped them up and down and pinched their arms. The two peasants, who were even in greater consternation than their poultry, rolled their eyes as if they were possessed, without venturing to move, and their old wrinkled faces had not a smile, not a twitch.

Then the gentleman, who was a commercial traveller, offered the ladies suspenders by way of a joke, and taking up one of his packages, he opened it. It was a joke, for the parcel contained garters. There were blue silk, pink silk, red silk, violet silk, mauve silk garters, and the buckles were made of two gilt metal cupids embracing each other. The girls uttered exclamations of delight and looked at them with that gravity natural to all women when they are considering an article of dress. They consulted one another by their looks or in a whisper, and replied in the same manner, and Madame Tellier was longingly handling a pair of orange garters that were broader and more imposing looking than the rest; really fit for the mistress of such an establishment.

The gentleman waited, for he had an idea.

"Come, my kittens," he said, "you must try them on."

There was a torrent of exclamations, and they squeezed their petticoats between their legs, but he quietly waited his time and said: "Well, if you will not try them on I shall pack them up again."

And he added cunningly: "I offer any pair they like to those who will try them on."

But they would not, and sat up very straight and looked dignified.

But the two Pumps looked so distressed that he renewed his offer to them, and Flora, especially, visibly hesitated, and he insisted: "Come, my dear, a little courage! Just look at that lilac pair; it will suit your dress admirably."

That decided her, and pulling up her dress she showed a thick leg fit for a milkmaid, in a badly fitting, coarse stocking. The commercial traveller stooped down and fastened the garter. When he had done this, he gave her the lilac pair and asked: "Who next?"

"I! I!" they all shouted at once, and he began on Rosa, who uncovered a shapeless, round thing without any ankle, a regular "sausage of a leg," as Raphaele used to say.

Lastly, Madame Tellier herself put out her leg, a handsome, muscular Norman leg, and in his surprise and pleasure, the commercial traveller gallantly took off his hat to salute that master calf, like a true French cavalier.

The two peasants, who were speechless from surprise, glanced sideways out of the corner of one eye, and they looked so exactly like fowls that the man with the light whiskers, when he sat up, said: "Co—co—ri—co" under their very noses, and that gave rise to another storm of amusement.

The old people got out at Motteville with their basket, their ducks and their umbrella, and they heard the woman say to her husband as they went away:

"They are no good and are off to that cursed place, Paris."

The funny commercial traveller himself got out at Rouen, after behaving so coarsely that Madame Tellier was obliged sharply to put him in his right place, and she added, as a moral: "This will teach us not to talk to the first comer."

At Oissel they changed trains, and at a little station further on Monsieur Joseph Rivet was waiting for them with a large cart with a number of chairs in it, drawn by a white horse.

The carpenter politely kissed all the ladies and then helped them into his conveyance.

Three of them sat on three chairs at the back, Raphaele, Madame Tellier and her brother on the three chairs in front, while Rosa, who had no seat, settled herself as comfortably as she could on tall Fernande's knees, and then they set off.

But the horse's jerky trot shook the cart so terribly that the chairs began to dance and threw the travellers about, to the right and to the left, as if they were dancing puppets, which made them scream and make horrible grimaces.

They clung on to the sides of the vehicle, their bonnets fell on their backs, over their faces and on their shoulders, and the white horse went on stretching out his head and holding out his little hairless tail like a rat's, with which he whisked his buttocks from time to time.

Joseph Rivet, with one leg on the shafts and the other doubled under him, held the reins with his elbows very high, and kept uttering a kind of clucking sound, which made the horse prick up its ears and go faster.

The green country extended on either side of the road, and here and there the colza in flower presented a waving expanse of yellow, from which arose a strong, wholesome, sweet and penetrating odor, which the wind carried to some distance.

The cornflowers showed their little blue heads amid the rye, and the women wanted to pick them, but Monsieur Rivet refused to stop.

Then, sometimes, a whole field appeared to be covered with blood, so thick were the poppies, and the cart, which looked as if it were filled with flowers of more brilliant hue, jogged on through fields bright with wild flowers, and disappeared behind the trees of a farm, only to reappear and to go on again through the yellow or green standing crops, which were studded with red or blue.

One o'clock struck as they drove up to the carpenter's door. They were tired out and pale with hunger, as they had eaten nothing since they left home. Madame Rivet ran out and made them alight, one after another, and kissed them as soon as they were on the ground, and she seemed as if she would never tire of kissing her sister-in-law, whom she apparently wanted to monopolize. They had lunch in the workshop, which had been cleared out for the next day's dinner.

The capital omelet, followed by boiled chitterlings and washed down with good hard cider, made them all feel comfortable.

Rivet had taken a glass so that he might drink with them, and his wife cooked, waited on them, brought in the dishes, took them out and asked each of them in a whisper whether they had everything they wanted. A number of boards standing against the walls and heaps of shavings that had been swept into the corners gave out a smell of planed wood, a smell of a carpenter's shop, that resinous odor which penetrates to the lungs.

They wanted to see the little girl, but she had gone to church and would not be back again until evening, so they all went out for a stroll in the country.

It was a small village, through which the highroad passed. Ten or a dozen houses on either side of the single street were inhabited by the butcher, the grocer, the carpenter, the innkeeper, the shoemaker and the baker.

The church was at the end of the street and was surrounded by a small churchyard, and four immense lime-trees, which stood just outside the porch, shaded it completely. It was built of flint, in no particular style, and had a slate-roofed steeple. When you got past it, you were again in the open country, which was varied here and there by clumps of trees which hid the homesteads.

Rivet had given his arm to his sister, out of politeness, although he was in his working clothes, and was walking with her in a dignified manner. His wife, who was overwhelmed by Raphaele's gold-striped dress, walked between her and Fernande, and roly-poly Rosa was trotting behind with Louise and Flora, the Seesaw, who was limping along, quite tired out.

The inhabitants came to their doors, the children left off playing, and a window curtain would be raised, so as to show a muslin cap, while an old woman with a crutch, who was almost blind, crossed herself as if it were a religious procession, and they all gazed for a long time at those handsome ladies from town, who had come so far to be present at the confirmation of Joseph Rivet's little girl, and the carpenter rose very much in the public estimation.

As they passed the church they heard some children singing. Little shrill voices were singing a hymn, but Madame Tellier would not let them go in, for fear of disturbing the little cherubs.

After the walk, during which Joseph Rivet enumerated the principal landed proprietors, spoke about the yield of the land and the productiveness of the cows and sheep, he took his tribe of women home and installed them in his house, and as it was very small, they had to put them into the rooms, two and two.

Just for once Rivet would sleep in the workshop on the shavings; his wife was to share her bed with her sister-in-law, and Fernande and Raphaele were to sleep together in the next room. Louise and Flora were put into the kitchen, where they had a mattress on the floor, and Rosa had a little dark cupboard to herself at the top of the stairs, close to the loft, where the candidate for confirmation was to sleep.

When the little girl came in she was overwhelmed with kisses; all the women wished to caress her with that need of tender expansion, that habit of professional affection which had made them kiss the ducks in the railway carriage.

They each of them took her on their knees, stroked her soft, light hair and pressed her in their arms with vehement and spontaneous outbursts of affection, and the child, who was very good and religious, bore it all patiently.

As the day had been a fatiguing one for everybody, they all went to bed soon after dinner. The whole village was wrapped in that perfect stillness of the country, which is almost like a religious silence, and the girls, who were accustomed to the noisy evenings of their establishment, felt rather impressed by the perfect repose of the sleeping village, and they shivered, not with cold, but with those little shivers of loneliness which come over uneasy and troubled hearts.

As soon as they were in bed, two and two together, they clasped each other in their arms, as if to protect themselves against this feeling of the calm and profound slumber of the earth. But Rosa, who was alone in her little dark cupboard, felt a vague and painful emotion come over her.

She was tossing about in bed, unable to get to sleep, when she heard the faint sobs of a crying child close to her head, through the partition. She was frightened, and called out, and was answered by a weak voice, broken by sobs. It was the little girl, who was always used to sleeping in her mother's room, and who was afraid in her small attic.

Rosa was delighted, got up softly so as not to awaken any one, and went and fetched the child. She took her into her warm bed, kissed her and pressed her to her bosom, lavished exaggerated manifestations of tenderness on her, and at last grew calmer herself and went to sleep. And till morning the candidate for confirmation slept with her head on Rosa's bosom.

At five o'clock the little church bell, ringing the Angelus, woke the women, who usually slept the whole morning long.

The villagers were up already, and the women went busily from house to house, carefully bringing short, starched muslin dresses or very long wax tapers tied in the middle with a bow of silk fringed with gold, and with dents in the wax for the fingers.

The sun was already high in the blue sky, which still had a rosy tint toward the horizon, like a faint remaining trace of dawn. Families of fowls were walking about outside the houses, and here and there a black cock, with a glistening breast, raised his head, which was crowned by his red comb, flapped his wings and uttered his shrill crow, which the other cocks repeated.

Vehicles of all sorts came from neighboring parishes, stopping at the different houses, and tall Norman women dismounted, wearing dark dresses, with kerchiefs crossed over the bosom, fastened with silver brooches a hundred years old.

The men had put on their blue smocks over their new frock-coats or over their old dress-coats of green-cloth, the two tails of which hung down below their blouses. When the horses were in the stable there was a double line of rustic conveyances along the road: carts, cabriolets, tilburies, wagonettes, traps of every shape and age, tipping forward on their shafts or else tipping backward with the shafts up in the air.

The carpenter's house was as busy as a bee-hive. The women, in dressing-jackets and petticoats, with their thin, short hair, which looked faded and worn, hanging down their backs, were busy dressing the child, who was standing quietly on a table, while Madame Tellier was directing the movements of her battalion. They washed her, did her hair, dressed her, and with the help of a number of pins, they arranged the folds of her dress and took in the waist, which was too large.

Then, when she was ready, she was told to sit down and not to move, and the women hurried off to get ready themselves.

The church bell began to ring again, and its tinkle was lost in the air, like a feeble voice which is soon drowned in space. The candidates came out of the houses and went toward the parochial building, which contained the two schools and the mansion house, and which stood quite at one end of the village, while the church was situated at the other.

The parents, in their very best clothes, followed their children, with embarrassed looks, and those clumsy movements of a body bent by toil.

The little girls disappeared in a cloud of muslin, which looked like whipped cream, while the lads, who looked like embryo waiters in a cafe and whose heads shone with pomatum, walked with their legs apart, so as not to get any dust or dirt on their black trousers.

It was something for a family, to be proud of, when a large number of relatives, who had come from a distance, surrounded the child, and the carpenter's triumph was complete.

Madame Tellier's regiment, with its leader at its head, followed Constance; her father gave his arm to his sister, her mother walked by the side of Raphaele, Fernande with Rosa and Louise and Flora together, and thus they proceeded majestically through the village, like a general's staff in full uniform, while the effect on the village was startling.

At the school the girls ranged themselves under the Sister of Mercy and the boys under the schoolmaster, and they started off, singing a hymn as they went. The boys led the way, in two files, between the two rows of vehicles, from which the horses had been taken out, and the girls followed in the same order; and as all the people in the village had given the town ladies the precedence out of politeness, they came immediately behind the girls, and lengthened the double line of the procession still more, three on the right and three on the left, while their dresses were as striking as a display of fireworks.

When they went into the church the congregation grew quite excited. They pressed against each other, turned round and jostled one another in order to see, and some of the devout ones spoke almost aloud, for they were so astonished at the sight of those ladies whose dresses were more elaborate than the priest's vestments.

The mayor offered them his pew, the first one on the right, close to the choir, and Madame Tellier sat there with her sister-in-law, Fernande and Raphaele. Rosa, Louise and Flora occupied the second seat, in company with the carpenter.

The choir was full of kneeling children, the girls on one side and the boys on the other, and the long wax tapers which they held looked like lances pointing in all directions, and three men were standing in front of the lectern, singing as loud as they could.

They prolonged the syllables of the sonorous Latin indefinitely, holding on to "Amens" with interminable "a-a's," which the reed stop of the organ sustained in a monotonous, long-drawn-out tone.

A child's shrill voice took up the reply, and from time to time a priest sitting in a stall and wearing a biretta got up, muttered something and sat down again, while the three singers continued, their eyes fixed on the big book of plain chant lying open before them on the outstretched wings of a wooden eagle.

Then silence ensued and the service went on. Toward the close Rosa, with her head in both hands, suddenly thought of her mother, her village church and her first communion. She almost fancied that that day had returned, when she was so small anti was almost hidden in her white dress, and she began to cry.

First of all she wept silently, and the tears dropped slowly from her eyes, but her emotion in creased with her recollections, and she began to sob. She took out her pocket handkerchief, wiped her eyes and held it to her mouth, so as not to scream, but it was in vain. A sort of rattle escaped her throat, and she was answered by two other profound, heartbreaking sobs, for her two neighbors, Louise and Flora, who were kneeling near her, overcome by similar recollections, were sobbing by her side, amid a flood of tears; and as tears are contagious, Madame Tellier soon in turn found that her eyes were wet, and on turning to her sister-in-law, she saw that all the occupants of her seat were also crying.

Soon, throughout the church, here and there, a wife, a mother, a sister, seized by the strange sympathy of poignant emotion, and affected at the sight of those handsome ladies on their knees, shaken with sobs was moistening her cambric pocket handkerchief and pressing her beating heart with her left hand.

Just as the sparks from an engine will set fire to dry grass, so the tears of Rosa and of her companions infected the whole congregation in a moment. Men, women, old men and lads in new smocks were soon all sobbing, and something superhuman seemed to be hovering over their heads—a spirit, the powerful breath of an invisible and all powerful Being.

Suddenly a species of madness seemed to pervade the church, the noise of a crowd in a state of frenzy, a tempest of sobs and stifled cries. It came like gusts of wind which blow the trees in a forest, and the priest, paralyzed by emotion, stammered out incoherent prayers, without finding words, ardent prayers of the soul soaring to heaven.

The people behind him gradually grew calmer. The cantors, in all the dignity of their white surplices, went on in somewhat uncertain voices, and the reed stop itself seemed hoarse, as if the instrument had been weeping; the priest, however, raised his hand to command silence and went and stood on the chancel steps, when everybody was silent at once.

After a few remarks on what had just taken place, and which he attributed to a miracle, he continued, turning to the seats where the carpenter's guests were sitting; "I especially thank you, my dear sisters, who have come from such a distance, and whose presence among us, whose evident faith and ardent piety have set such a salutary example to all. You have edified my parish; your emotion has warmed all hearts; without you, this great day would not, perhaps, have had this really divine character. It is sufficient, at times, that there should be one chosen lamb, for the Lord to descend on His flock."

His voice failed him again, from emotion, and he said no more, but concluded the service.

They now left the church as quickly as possible; the children themselves were restless and tired with such a prolonged tension of the mind. The parents left the church by degrees to see about dinner.

There was a crowd outside, a noisy crowd, a babel of loud voices, where the shrill Norman accent was discernible. The villagers formed two ranks, and when the children appeared, each family took possession of their own.

The whole houseful of women caught hold of Constance, surrounded her and kissed her, and Rosa was especially demonstrative. At last she took hold of one hand, while Madame Tellier took the other, and Raphaele and Fernande held up her long muslin skirt, so that it might not drag in the dust; Louise and Flora brought up the rear with Madame Rivet; and the child, who was very silent and thoughtful, set off for home in the midst of this guard of honor.

Dinner was served in the workshop on long boards supported by trestles, and through the open door they could see all the enjoyment that was going on in the village. Everywhere they were feasting, and through every window were to be seen tables surrounded by people in their Sunday best, and a cheerful noise was heard in every house, while the men sat in their shirt-sleeves, drinking glass after glass of cider.

In the carpenter's house the gaiety maintained somewhat of an air of reserve, the consequence of the emotion of the girls in the morning, and Rivet was the only one who was in a jolly mood, and he was drinking to excess. Madame Tellier looked at the clock every moment, for, in order not to lose two days running, they must take the 3:55 train, which would bring them to Fecamp by dark.

The carpenter tried very hard to distract her attention, so as to keep his guests until the next day, but he did not succeed, for she never joked when there was business on hand, and as soon as they had had their coffee she ordered her girls to make haste and get ready, and then, turning to her brother, she said:

"You must put in the horse immediately," and she herself went to finish her last preparations.

When she came down again, her sister-in-law was waiting to speak to her about the child, and a long conversation took place, in which, however, nothing was settled. The carpenter's wife was artful and pretended to be very much affected, and Madame Tellier, who was holding the girl on her knee, would not pledge herself to anything definite, but merely gave vague promises—she would not forget her, there was plenty of time, and besides, they would meet again.

But the conveyance did not come to the door and the women did not come downstairs. Upstairs they even heard loud laughter, romping, little screams, and much clapping of hands, and so, while the carpenter's wife went to the stable to see whether the cart was ready, madame went upstairs.

Rivet, who was very drunk, was plaguing Rosa, who was half choking with laughter. Louise and Flora were holding him by the arms and trying to calm him, as they were shocked at his levity after that morning's ceremony; but Raphaele and Fernande were urging him on, writhing and holding their sides with laughter, and they uttered shrill cries at every rebuff the drunken fellow received.

The man was furious, his face was red, and he was trying to shake off the two women who were clinging to him, while he was pulling Rosa's skirt with all his might and stammering incoherently.

But Madame Tellier, who was very indignant, went up to her brother, seized him by the shoulders, and threw him out of the room with such violence that he fell against the wall in the passage, and a minute afterward they heard him pumping water on his head in the yard, and when he reappeared with the cart he was quite calm.

They started off in the same way as they had come the day before, and the little white horse started off with his quick, dancing trot. Under the hot sun, their fun, which had been checked during dinner, broke out again. The girls now were amused at the jolting of the cart, pushed their neighbors' chairs, and burst out laughing every moment.

There was a glare of light over the country, which dazzled their eyes, and the wheels raised two trails of dust along the highroad. Presently, Fernande, who was fond of music, asked Rosa to sing something, and she boldly struck up the "Gros Cure de Meudon," but Madame Tellier made her stop immediately, as she thought it a very unsuitable song for such a day, and she added:

"Sing us something of Beranger's." And so, after a moment's hesitation, Rosa began Beranger's song "The Grandmother" in her worn-out voice, and all the girls, and even Madame Tellier herself, joined in the chorus:

> "How I regret
>
> My dimpled arms,
>
> My nimble legs,
>
> And vanished charms."

"That is first rate," Rivet declared, carried away by the rhythm, and they shouted the refrain to every verse, while Rivet beat time on the shaft with his foot, and with the reins on the back of the horse, who, as if he himself were carried away by the rhythm, broke into a wild gallop, and threw all the women in a heap, one on top of the other, on the bottom of the conveyance.

They got up, laughing as if they were mad, and the Gong went on, shouted at the top of their voices, beneath the burning sky, among the ripening grain, to the rapid gallop of the little horse, who set off every time the refrain was sung, and galloped a hundred yards, to their great delight, while occasionally a stone-breaker by the roadside sat up and looked at the load of shouting females through his wire spectacles.

When they got out at the station, the carpenter said:

"I am sorry you are going; we might have had some good times together." But Madame Tellier replied very sensibly: "Everything has its right time, and we cannot always be enjoying ourselves." And then he had a sudden inspiration:

"Look here, I will come and see you at Fecamp next month." And he gave Rosa a roguish and knowing look.

"Come," his sister replied, "you must be sensible; you may come if you like, but you are not to be up to any of your tricks."

He did not reply, and as they heard the whistle of the train, he immediately began to kiss them all. When it came to Rosa's turn, he tried to get to her mouth, which she, however, smiling with her lips closed, turned away from him each time by a rapid movement of her head to one side. He held her in his arms, but he could not attain his object, as his large whip, which he was holding in his hand and waving behind the girl's back in desperation, interfered with his movements.

"Passengers for Rouen, take your seats!" a guard cried, and they got in. There was a slight whistle, followed by a loud whistle from the engine, which noisily puffed cut its first jet of steam, while the wheels began to turn a little with a visible effort, and Rivet left the station and ran along by the track to get another look at Rosa, and as the carriage passed him, he began to crack his whip and to jump, while he sang at the top of his voice:

"How I regret

My dimpled arms,

My nimble legs,

And vanished charms."

And then he watched a white pocket-handkerchief, which somebody was waving, as it disappeared in the distance.

PART III

They slept the peaceful sleep of a quiet conscience, until they got to Rouen, and when they returned to the house, refreshed and rested, Madame Tellier could not help saying:

"It was all very well, but I was longing to get home."

They hurried over their supper, and then, when they had put on their usual evening costume, waited for their regular customers, and the little colored lamp outside the door told the passers-by that Madame Tellier had returned, and in a moment the news spread, nobody knew how or through whom.

Monsieur Philippe, the banker's son, even carried his friendliness so far as to send a special messenger to Monsieur Tournevau, who was in the bosom of his family.

The fish curer had several cousins to dinner every Sunday, and they were having coffee, when a man came in with a letter in his hand. Monsieur Tournevau was much excited; he opened the envelope and grew pale; it contained only these words in pencil:

"The cargo of cod has been found; the ship has come into port; good business for you. Come immediately."

He felt in his pockets, gave the messenger two sons, and suddenly blushing to his ears, he said: "I must go out." He handed his wife the laconic and mysterious note, rang the bell, and when the servant came in, he asked her to bring him has hat and overcoat immediately. As soon as he was in the street, he began to hurry, and the way seemed to him to be twice as long as usual, in consequence of his impatience.

Madame Tellier's establishment had put on quite a holiday look. On the ground floor, a number of sailors were making a deafening noise, and Louise and Flora drank with one and the other, and were being called for in every direction at once.

The upstairs room was full by nine o'clock. Monsieur Vasse, the Judge of the Tribunal of Commerce, Madame Tellier's regular but Platonic wooer, was talking to her in a corner in a low voice, and they were both smiling, as if they were about to come to an understanding.

Monsieur Poulin, the ex-mayor, was talking to Rosa, and she was running her hands through the old gentleman's white whiskers.

Tall Fernande was on the sofa, her feet on the coat of Monsieur Pinipesse, the tax collector, and leaning back against young Monsieur Philippe, her right arm around his neck, while she held a cigarette in her left hand.

Raphaele appeared to be talking seriously with Monsieur Dupuis, the insurance agent, and she finished by saying: "Yes, I will, yes."

Just then, the door opened suddenly, and Monsieur Tournevau came in, and was greeted with enthusiastic cries of "Long live Tournevau!" And Raphaele, who was dancing alone up and down the room, went and threw herself into his arms. He seized her in a vigorous embrace and, without saying a word, lifted her up as if she had been a feather.

Rosa was chatting to the ex-mayor, kissing him and puffing; both his whiskers at the same time, in order to keep his head straight.

Fernanae and Madame Tellier remained with the four men, and Monsieur Philippe exclaimed: "I will pay for some champagne; get three bottles, Madame Tellier." And Fernande gave him a hug, and whispered to him: "Play us a waltz, will you?" So he rose and sat down at the old piano in the corner, and managed to get a hoarse waltz out of the depths of the instrument.

The tall girl put her arms round the tax collector, Madame Tellier let Monsieur Vasse take her round the waist, and the two couples turned round, kissing as they danced. Monsieur Vasse, who had formerly danced in good society, waltzed with such elegance that Madame Tellier was quite captivated.

Frederic brought the champagne; the first cork popped, and Monsieur Philippe played the introduction to a quadrille, through which the four dancers walked in society fashion, decorously, with propriety, deportment, bows and curtsies, and then they began to drink.

Monsieur Philippe next struck up a lively polka, and Monsieur Tournevau started off with the handsome Jewess, whom he held without letting her feet touch the ground. Monsieur Pinipesse and Monsieur Vasse had started off with renewed vigor, and from time to time one or other couple would stop to toss off a long draught of sparkling wine, and that dance was threatening to become never-ending, when Rosa opened the door.

"I want to dance," she exclaimed. And she caught hold of Monsieur Dupuis, who was sitting idle on the couch, and the dance began again.

But the bottles were empty. "I will pay for one," Monsieur Tournevau said. "So will I," Monsieur Vasse declared. "And. I will do the same," Monsieur Dupuis remarked.

They all began to clap their hands, and it soon became a regular ball, and from time to time Louise and Flora ran upstairs quickly and had a few turns, while their customers downstairs grew impatient, and then they returned regretfully to the tap-room. At midnight they were still dancing.

Madame Tellier let them amuse themselves while she had long private talks in corners with Monsieur Vasse, as if to settle the last details of something that had already been settled.

At last, at one o'clock, the two married men, Monsieur Tournevau and Monsieur Pinipesse, declared that they were going home, and wanted to pay. Nothing was charged for except the champagne, and that cost only six francs a bottle, instead of ten, which was the usual price, and when they expressed their surprise at such generosity, Madame Tellier, who was beaming, said to them:

"We don't have a holiday every day."

DENIS

To Leon Chapron.

Marambot opened the letter which his servant Denis gave him and smiled.

For twenty years Denis has been a servant in this house. He was a short, stout, jovial man, who was known throughout the countryside as a model servant. He asked:

"Is monsieur pleased? Has monsieur received good news?"

M. Marambot was not rich. He was an old village druggist, a bachelor, who lived on an income acquired with difficulty by selling drugs to the farmers. He answered:

"Yes, my boy. Old man Malois is afraid of the law-suit with which I am threatening him. I shall get my money to-morrow. Five thousand francs are not liable to harm the account of an old bachelor."

M. Marambot rubbed his hands with satisfaction. He was a man of quiet temperament, more sad than gay, incapable of any prolonged effort, careless in business.

He could undoubtedly have amassed a greater income had he taken advantage of the deaths of colleagues established in more important centers, by taking their places and carrying on their business. But the trouble of moving and the thought of all the preparations had always stopped him. After thinking the matter over for a few days, he would be satisfied to say:

"Bah! I'll wait until the next time. I'll not lose anything by the delay. I may even find something better."

Denis, on the contrary, was always urging his master to new enterprises. Of an energetic temperament, he would continually repeat:

"Oh! If I had only had the capital to start out with, I could have made a fortune! One thousand francs would do me."

M. Marambot would smile without answering and would go out in his little garden, where, his hands behind his back, he would walk about dreaming.

All day long, Denis sang the joyful refrains of the folk-songs of the district. He even showed an unusual activity, for he cleaned all the windows of the house, energetically rubbing the glass, and singing at the top of his voice.

M. Marambot, surprised at his zeal, said to him several times, smiling:

"My boy, if you work like that there will be nothing left for you to do to-morrow."

The following day, at about nine o'clock in the morning, the postman gave Denis four letters for his master, one of them very heavy. M. Marambot immediately shut himself up in his room until late in the afternoon. He then handed his servant four letters for the mail. One of them was addressed to M. Malois; it was undoubtedly a receipt for the money.

Denis asked his master no questions; he appeared to be as sad and gloomy that day as he had seemed joyful the day before.

Night came. M. Marambot went to bed as usual and slept.

He was awakened by a strange noise. He sat up in his bed and listened. Suddenly the door opened, and Denis appeared, holding in one hand a candle and in the other a carving knife, his eyes staring, his face contracted as though moved by some deep emotion; he was as pale as a ghost.

M. Marambot, astonished, thought that he was sleep-walking, and he was going to get out of bed and assist him when the servant blew out the light and rushed for the bed. His master stretched out his hands to receive the shock which knocked him over on his back; he was trying to seize the hands of his servant, whom he now thought to be crazy, in order to avoid the blows which the latter was aiming at him.

He was struck by the knife; once in the shoulder, once in the forehead and the third time in the chest. He fought wildly, waving his arms around in the darkness, kicking and crying:

"Denis! Denis! Are you mad? Listen, Denis!"

But the latter, gasping for breath, kept up his furious attack always striking, always repulsed, sometimes with a kick, sometimes with a punch, and rushing forward again furiously.

M. Marambot was wounded twice more, once in the leg and once in the stomach. But, suddenly, a thought flashed across his mind, and he began to shriek:

"Stop, stop, Denis, I have not yet received my money!"

The man immediately ceased, and his master could hear his labored breathing in the darkness.

M. Marambot then went on:

"I have received nothing. M. Malois takes back what he said, the law-suit will take place; that is why you carried the letters to the mail. Just read those on my desk."

With a final effort, he reached for his matches and lit the candle.

He was covered with blood. His sheets, his curtains, and even the walls, were spattered with red. Denis, standing in the middle of the room, was also bloody from head to foot.

When he saw the blood, M. Marambot thought himself dead, and fell unconscious.

At break of day he revived. It was some time, however, before he regained his senses, and was able to understand or remember. But, suddenly, the memory of the attack and of his wounds returned to him, and he was filled with such terror that he closed his eyes in order not to see anything. After a few minutes he grew calmer and began to think. He had not died' immediately, therefore he might still recover. He felt weak, very weak; but he had no real pain, although he noticed an uncomfortable smarting sensation in several parts of his body. He also felt icy cold, and all wet, and as though wrapped up in bandages. He thought that this dampness came from the blood which he had lost; and he shivered at the dreadful thought of this red liquid which had come from his veins and covered his bed. The idea of seeing this terrible spectacle again so upset him that he kept his eyes closed with all his strength, as though they might open in spite of himself.

What had become of Denis? He had probably escaped.

But what could he, Marambot, do now? Get up? Call for help? But if he should make the slightest motions, his wounds would undoubtedly open up again and he would die from loss of blood.

Suddenly he heard the door of his room open. His heart almost stopped. It was certainly Denis who was coming to finish him up. He held his breath in order to make the murderer think that he had been successful.

He felt his sheet being lifted up, and then someone feeling his stomach. A sharp pain near his hip made him start. He was being very gently washed with cold water. Therefore, someone must have discovered the misdeed and he was being cared for. A wild joy seized him; but prudently, he did not wish to show that he was conscious. He opened one eye, just one, with the greatest precaution.

He recognized Denis standing beside him, Denis himself! Mercy! He hastily closed his eye again.

Denis! What could he be doing? What did he want? What awful scheme could he now be carrying out?

What was he doing? Well, he was washing him in order to hide the traces of his crime! And he would now bury him in the garden, under ten feet of earth, so that no one could discover him! Or perhaps under the wine cellar! And M. Marambot began to tremble like a leaf. He kept saying to himself: "I am lost, lost!" He closed his eyes so as not to see the knife as it descended for the final stroke. It did not come. Denis was now lifting him up and bandaging him. Then he began carefully to dress the wound on his leg, as his master had taught him to do.

There was no longer any doubt. His servant, after wishing to kill him, was trying to save him.

Then M. Marambot, in a dying voice, gave him the practical piece of advice:

"Wash the wounds in a dilute solution of carbolic acid!"

Denis answered:

"This is what I am doing, monsieur."

M. Marambot opened both his eyes. There was no sign of blood either on the bed, on the walls, or on the murderer. The wounded man was stretched out on clean white sheets.

The two men looked at each other.

Finally M. Marambot said calmly:

"You have been guilty of a great crime."

Denis answered:

"I am trying to make up for it, monsieur. If you will not tell on me, I will serve you as faithfully as in the past."

This was no time to anger his servant. M. Marambot murmured as he closed his eyes:

"I swear not to tell on you."

Denis saved his master. He spent days and nights without sleep, never leaving the sick room, preparing drugs, broths, potions, feeling his pulse, anxiously counting the beats, attending him with the skill of a trained nurse and the devotion of a son.

He continually asked:

"Well, monsieur, how do you feel?"

M. Marambot would answer in a weak voice:

"A little better, my boy, thank you."

And when the sick man would wake up at night, he would often see his servant seated in an armchair, weeping silently.

Never had the old druggist been so cared for, so fondled, so spoiled. At first he had said to himself:

"As soon as I am well I shall get rid of this rascal."

He was now convalescing, and from day to day he would put off dismissing his murderer. He thought that no one would ever show him such care and attention, for he held this man through fear; and he warned him that he had left a document with a lawyer denouncing him to the law if any new accident should occur.

This precaution seemed to guarantee him against any future attack; and he then asked himself if it would not be wiser to keep this man near him, in order to watch him closely.

Just as formerly, when he would hesitate about taking some larger place of business, he could not make up his mind to any decision.

"There is always time," he would say to himself.

Denis continued to show himself an admirable servant. M. Marambot was well. He kept him.

One morning, just as he was finishing breakfast, he suddenly heard a great noise in the kitchen. He hastened in there. Denis was struggling with two gendarmes. An officer was taking notes on his pad.

As soon as he saw his master, the servant began to sob, exclaiming:

"You told on me, monsieur, that's not right, after what you had promised me. You have broken your word of honor, Monsieur Marambot; that is not right, that's not right!"

M. Marambot, bewildered and distressed at being suspected, lifted his hand:

"I swear to you before the Lord, my boy that I did not tell on you. I haven't the slightest idea how the police could have found out about your attack on me."

The officer started:

"You say that he attacked you, M. Marambot?"

The bewildered druggist answered:

"Yes—but I did not tell on him—I haven't said a word—I swear it—he has served me excellently from that time on—"

The officer pronounced severely:

"I will take down your testimony. The law will take notice of this new action, of which it was ignorant, Monsieur Marambot. I was commissioned to arrest your servant for the theft of two ducks surreptitiously taken by him from M. Duhamel of which act there are witnesses. I shall make a note of your information."

Then, turning toward his men, he ordered:

"Come on, bring him along!"

The two gendarmes dragged Denis out.

The lawyer used a plea of insanity, contrasting the two misdeeds in order to strengthen his argument. He had clearly proved that the theft of the two ducks came from the same mental condition as the eight knife-wounds in the body of Maramlot. He had cunningly analyzed all the phases of this transitory condition of mental aberration, which could, doubtless, be cured by a few months' treatment in a reputable sanatorium. He had spoken in enthusiastic terms of the continued devotion of this faithful servant, of the care with which he had surrounded his master, wounded by him in a moment of alienation.

Touched by this memory, M. Marambot felt the tears rising to his eyes.

The lawyer noticed it, opened his arms with a broad gesture, spreading out the long black sleeves of his robe like the wings of a bat, and exclaimed:

"Look, look, gentleman of the jury, look at those tears. What more can I say for my client? What speech, what argument, what reasoning would be worth these tears of his master? They, speak louder than I do, louder than the law; they cry: 'Mercy, for the poor wandering mind of a while ago! They implore, they pardon, they bless!"

He was silent and sat down.

Then the judge, turning to Marambot, whose testimony had been excellent for his servant, asked him:

"But, monsieur, even admitting that you consider this man insane, that does not explain why you should have kept him. He was none the less dangerous."

Marambot, wiping his eyes, answered:

"Well, your honor, what can you expect? Nowadays it's so hard to find good servants—I could never have found a better one."

Denis was acquitted and put in a sanatorium at his master's expense.

MY WIFE

It had been a stag dinner. These men still came together once in a while without their wives as they had done when they were bachelors. They would eat for a long time, drink for a long time; they would talk of everything, stir up those old and joyful memories which bring a smile to the lip and a tremor to the heart. One of them was saying: "Georges, do you remember our excursion to Saint-Germain with those two little girls from Montmartre?"

"I should say I do!"

And a little detail here or there would be remembered, and all these things brought joy to the hearts.

The conversation turned on marriage, and each one said with a sincere air: "Oh, if it were to do over again!" Georges Duportin added: "It's strange how easily one falls into it. You have fully decided never to marry; and then, in the springtime, you go to the country; the weather is warm; the summer is beautiful; the fields are full of flowers; you meet a young girl at some friend's house—crash! all is over. You return married!"

Pierre Letoile exclaimed: "Correct! that is exactly my case, only there were some peculiar incidents—"

His friend interrupted him: "As for you, you have no cause to complain. You have the most charming wife in the world, pretty, amiable, perfect! You are undoubtedly the happiest one of us all."

The other one continued: "It's not my fault."

"How so?"

"It is true that I have a perfect wife, but I certainly married her much against my will."

"Nonsense!"

"Yes—this is the adventure. I was thirty-five, and I had no more idea of marrying than I had of hanging myself. Young girls seemed to me to be inane, and I loved pleasure.

"During the month of May I was invited to the wedding of my cousin, Simon d'Erabel, in Normandy. It was a regular Normandy wedding. We sat down at the table at five o'clock in the evening and at eleven o'clock we were still eating. I had been paired off, for the occasion, with a Mademoiselle Dumoulin, daughter of a retired colonel, a young, blond, soldierly person, well formed, frank and talkative. She took complete possession of me for the whole day, dragged me into the park, made me dance willy-nilly, bored me to death. I said to myself: 'That's all very well for to-day, but tomorrow I'll get out. That's all there is to it!'

"Toward eleven o'clock at night the women retired to their rooms; the men stayed, smoking while they drank or drinking while they smoked, whichever you will.

"Through the open window we could see the country folks dancing. Farmers and peasant girls were jumping about in a circle yelling at the top of their lungs a dance air which was feebly accompanied by two violins and a clarinet. The wild song of the peasants often completely drowned the sound of the instruments, and the weak music, interrupted by the unrestrained voices, seemed to come to us in little fragments of scattered notes. Two enormous casks, surrounded by flaming torches, contained drinks for the crowd. Two men were kept busy rinsing the glasses or bowls in a bucket and immediately holding them under the spigots, from which flowed the red stream of wine or the golden stream of pure cider; and the parched dancers, the old ones quietly, the girls panting, came up, stretched out their arms and grasped some receptacle, threw back their heads and poured down their throats the drink which they preferred. On a table were bread, butter, cheese and sausages. Each one would step up from time to time and swallow a mouthful, and under the starlit sky this healthy and violent exercise was a pleasing sight, and made one also feel like drinking from these enormous casks and eating the crisp bread and butter with a raw onion.

"A mad desire seized me to take part in this merrymaking, and I left my companions. I must admit that I was probably a little tipsy, but I was soon entirely so.

"I grabbed the hand of a big, panting peasant woman and I jumped her about until I was out of breath.

"Then I drank some wine and reached for another girl. In order to refresh myself afterward, I swallowed a bowlful of cider, and I began to bounce around as if possessed.

"I was very light on my feet. The boys, delighted, were watching me and trying to imitate me; the girls all wished to dance with me, and jumped about heavily with the grace of cows.

"After each dance I drank a glass of wine or a glass of cider, and toward two o'clock in the morning I was so drunk that I could hardly stand up.

"I realized my condition and tried to reach my room. Everybody was asleep and the house was silent and dark.

"I had no matches and everybody was in bed. As soon as I reached the vestibule I began to, feel dizzy. I had a lot of trouble to find the banister. At last, by accident, my hand came in contact with it, and I sat down on the first step of the stairs in order to try to gather my scattered wits.

"My room was on the second floor; it was the third door to the left. Fortunately I had not forgotten that. Armed with this knowledge, I arose, not without difficulty, and I began to ascend, step by step. In my hands I firmly gripped the iron railing in order not to fall, and took great pains to make no noise.

"Only three or four times did my foot miss the steps, and I went down on my knees; but thanks to the energy of my arms and the strength of my will, I avoided falling completely.

"At last I reached the second floor and I set out in my journey along the hall, feeling my way by the walls. I felt one door; I counted: 'One'; but a sudden dizziness made me lose my hold on the wall, make a strange turn and fall up against the other wall. I wished to turn in a straight line: The crossing was long and full of hardships. At last I reached the shore, and, prudently, I began to travel along again until I met another door. In order to be sure to make no mistake, I again counted out loud: 'Two.' I started out on my walk again. At last I found the third door. I said: 'Three, that's my room,' and I turned the knob. The door opened. Notwithstanding my befuddled state, I thought: 'Since the door opens, this must be home.' After softly closing the door, I stepped out in the darkness. I bumped against something soft: my easy-chair. I immediately stretched myself out on it.

"In my condition it would not have been wise to look for my bureau, my candles, my matches. It would have taken me at least two hours. It would probably have taken me that long also to undress; and even then I might not have succeeded. I gave it up.

"I only took my shoes off; I unbuttoned my waistcoat, which was choking me, I loosened my trousers and went to sleep.

"This undoubtedly lasted for a long time. I was suddenly awakened by a deep voice which was saying: 'What, you lazy girl, still in bed? It's ten o'clock!'

"A woman's voice answered: 'Already! I was so tired yesterday.'

"In bewilderment I wondered what this dialogue meant. Where was I? What had I done? My mind was wandering, still surrounded by a heavy fog. The first voice continued: 'I'm going to raise your curtains.'

"I heard steps approaching me. Completely at a loss what to do, I sat up. Then a hand was placed on my head. I started. The voice asked: 'Who is there?' I took good care not to answer. A furious grasp seized me. I in turn seized him, and a terrific struggle ensued. We were rolling around, knocking over the furniture and crashing against the walls. A woman's voice was shrieking: 'Help! help!'

"Servants, neighbors, frightened women crowded around us. The blinds were open and the shades drawn. I was struggling with Colonel Dumoulin.

"I had slept beside his daughter's bed!

"When we were separated, I escaped to my room, dumbfounded. I locked myself in and sat down with my feet on a chair, for my shoes had been left in the young girl's room.

"I heard a great noise through the whole house, doors being opened and closed, whisperings and rapid steps.

"After half an hour some one knocked on my door. I cried: 'Who is there?' It was my uncle, the bridegroom's father. I opened the door:

"He was pale and furious, and he treated me harshly: 'You have behaved like a scoundrel in my house, do you hear?' Then he added more gently 'But, you young fool, why the devil did you let yourself get caught at ten o'clock in the morning? You go to sleep like a log in that room, instead of leaving immediately—immediately after.'

"I exclaimed: 'But, uncle, I assure you that nothing occurred. I was drunk and got into the wrong room.'

"He shrugged his shoulders! 'Don't talk nonsense.' I raised my hand, exclaiming: 'I swear to you on my honor.' My uncle continued: 'Yes, that's all right. It's your duty to say that.'

"I in turn grew angry and told him the whole unfortunate occurrence. He looked at me with a bewildered expression, not knowing what to believe. Then he went out to confer with the colonel.

"I heard that a kind of jury of the mothers had been formed, to which were submitted the different phases of the situation.

"He came back an hour later, sat down with the dignity of a judge and began: 'No matter what may be the situation, I can see only one way out of it for you; it is to marry Mademoiselle Dumoulin.'

"I bounded out of the chair, crying: 'Never! never!'

"Gravely he asked: 'Well, what do you expect to do?'

"I answered simply: 'Why—leave as soon as my shoes are returned to me.'

"My uncle continued: 'Please do not jest. The colonel has decided to blow your brains out as soon as he sees you. And you may be sure that he does not threaten idly. I spoke of a duel and he answered: "No, I tell you that I will blow his brains out."'

"'Let us now examine the question from another point of view. Either you have misbehaved yourself—and then so much the worse for you, my boy; one should not go near a young girl—or else, being drunk, as you say, you made a mistake in the room. In this case, it's even worse for you. You shouldn't get yourself into such foolish situations. Whatever you may say, the poor girl's reputation is lost, for a drunkard's excuses are never believed. The only real victim in the matter is the girl. Think it over.'

"He went away, while I cried after him: 'Say what you will, I'll not marry her!'

"I stayed alone for another hour. Then my aunt came. She was crying. She used every argument. No one believed my story. They could not imagine that this young girl could have forgotten to lock her door in a house full of company. The colonel had struck her. She had been crying the whole morning. It was a terrible and unforgettable scandal. And my good aunt added: 'Ask for her hand, anyhow. We may, perhaps, find some way out of it when we are drawing up the papers.'

"This prospect relieved me. And I agreed to write my proposal. An hour later I left for Paris. The following day I was informed that I had been accepted.

"Then, in three weeks, before I had been able to find any excuse, the banns were published, the announcement sent out, the contract signed, and one Monday morning I found myself in a church, beside a weeping young girl, after telling the magistrate that I consented to take her as my companion—for better, for worse.

"I had not seen her since my adventure, and I glanced at her out of the corner of my eye with a certain malevolent surprise. However, she was not ugly—far from it. I said to myself: 'There is some one who won't laugh every day.'

"She did not look at me once until, the evening, and she did not say a single word.

"Toward the middle of the night I entered the bridal chamber with the full intention of letting her know my resolutions, for I was now master. I found her sitting in an armchair, fully dressed, pale and with red eyes. As soon as I entered she rose and came slowly toward me saying: 'Monsieur, I am ready to do whatever you may command. I will kill myself if you so desire'

"The colonel's daughter was as pretty as she could be in this heroic role. I kissed her; it was my privilege.

"I soon saw that I had not got a bad bargain. I have now been married five years. I do not regret it in the least."

Pierre Letoile was silent. His companions were laughing. One of them said: "Marriage is indeed a lottery; you must never choose your numbers. The haphazard ones are the best."

Another added by way of conclusion: "Yes, but do not forget that the god of drunkards chose for Pierre."

THE UNKNOWN

We were speaking of adventures, and each one of us was relating his story of delightful experiences, surprising meetings, on the train, in a hotel, at the seashore. According to Roger des Annettes, the seashore was particularly favorable to the little blind god.

Gontran, who was keeping mum, was asked what he thought of it.

"I guess Paris is about the best place for that," he said. "Woman is like a precious trinket, we appreciate her all the more when we meet her in the most unexpected places; but the rarest ones are only to be found in Paris."

He was silent for a moment, and then continued:

"By Jove, it's great! Walk along the streets on some spring morning. The little women, daintily tripping along, seem to blossom out like flowers. What a delightful, charming sight! The dainty perfume of violet is everywhere. The city is gay, and everybody notices the women. By Jove, how tempting they are in their light, thin dresses, which occasionally give one a glimpse of the delicate pink flesh beneath!

"One saunters along, head up, mind alert, and eyes open. I tell you it's great! You see her in the distance, while still a block away; you already know that she is going to please you at closer quarters. You can recognize her by the flower on her hat, the toss of her head, or her gait. She approaches, and you say to yourself: 'Look out, here she is!' You come closer to her and you devour her with your eyes.

"Is it a young girl running errands for some store, a young woman returning from church, or hastening to see her lover? What do you care? Her well-rounded bosom shows through the thin waist. Oh, if you could only take her in your arms and fondle and kiss her! Her glance may be timid or bold, her hair light or dark. What difference does it make? She brushes against you, and a cold shiver runs down your spine. Ah, how you wish for her all day! How many of these dear creatures have I met this way, and how wildly in love I would have been had I known them more intimately.

"Have you ever noticed that the ones we would love the most distractedly are those whom we never meet to know? Curious, isn't it? From time to time we barely catch a glimpse of some woman, the mere sight of whom thrills our senses. But it goes no further. When I think of all the adorable creatures that I have elbowed in the streets of Paris, I fairly rave. Who are they! Where are they? Where can I find them again? There is a proverb which says that happiness often passes our way; I am sure that I have often passed alongside the one who could have caught me like a linnet in the snare of her fresh beauty."

Roger des Annettes had listened smilingly. He answered: "I know that as well as you do. This is what happened to me: About five years ago, for the first time I met, on the Pont de la Concorde, a young woman who made a wonderful impression on me. She was dark, rather stout, with glossy hair, and eyebrows which nearly met above two dark eyes. On her lip was a scarcely perceptible down, which made one dream-dream as one dreams of beloved woods, on seeing a bunch of wild violets.

She had a small waist and a well-developed bust, which seemed to present a challenge, offer a temptation. Her eyes were like two black spots on white enamel. Her glance was strange, vacant, unthinking, and yet wonderfully beautiful.

"I imagined that she might be a Jewess. I followed her, and then turned round to look at her, as did many others. She walked with a swinging gait that was not graceful, but somehow attracted one. At the Place de la Concorde she took a carriage, and I stood there like a fool, moved by the strongest desire that had ever assailed me.

"For about three weeks I thought only of her; and then her memory passed out of my mind.

"Six months later I descried her in the Rue de la Paix again. On seeing her I felt the same shock that one experiences on seeing a once dearly loved woman. I stopped that I might better observe her. When she passed close enough to touch me I felt as though I were standing before a red hot furnace. Then, when she had passed by, I noticed a delicious sensation, as of a cooling breeze blowing over my face. I did not follow her. I was afraid of doing something foolish. I was afraid of myself.

"She haunted all my dreams.

"It was a year before I saw her again. But just as the sun was going down on one beautiful evening in May I recognized her walking along the Avenue des Champs-Elysees. The Arc de Triomphe stood out in bold relief against the fiery glow of the sky. A golden haze filled the air; it was one of those delightful spring evenings which are the glory of Paris.

"I followed her, tormented by a desire to address her, to kneel before her, to pour forth the emotion which was choking me. Twice I passed by her only to fall back, and each time as I passed by I felt this sensation, as of scorching heat, which I had noticed in the Rue de la Paix.

"She glanced at me, and then I saw her enter a house on the Rue de Presbourg. I waited for her two hours and she did not come out. Then I decided to question the janitor. He seemed not to understand me. 'She must be visiting some one,' he said.

"The next time I was eight months without seeing her. But one freezing morning in January, I was walking along the Boulevard Malesherbes at a dog trot, so as to keep warm, when at the corner I bumped into a woman and knocked a small package out of her hand. I tried to apologize. It was she!

"At first I stood stock still from the shock; then having returned to her the package which she had dropped, I said abruptly:

"'I am both grieved and delighted, madame, to have jostled you. For more than two years I have known you, admired you, and had the most ardent wish to be presented to you; nevertheless I have been unable to find out who you are, or where you live. Please excuse these foolish words. Attribute them to a passionate desire to be numbered among your acquaintances. Such sentiments can surely offend you in no way! You do not know me. My name is Baron Roger des Annettes. Make inquiries about me, and you will find that I am a gentleman. Now, if you refuse my request, you will throw me into abject misery. Please be good to me and tell me how I can see you.'

"She looked at me with her strange vacant stare, and answered smilingly:

"'Give me your address. I will come and see you.'

"I was so dumfounded that I must have shown my surprise. But I quickly gathered my wits together and gave her a visiting card, which she slipped into her pocket with a quick, deft movement.

"Becoming bolder, I stammered:

"'When shall I see you again?'

"She hesitated, as though mentally running over her list of engagements, and then murmured:

"'Will Sunday morning suit you?'

"'I should say it would!'

"She went on, after having stared at me, judged, weighed and analyzed me with this heavy and vacant gaze which seemed to leave a quieting and deadening impression on the person towards whom it was directed.

"Until Sunday my mind was occupied day and night trying to guess who she might be and planning my course of conduct towards her. I finally decided to buy her a jewel, a beautiful little jewel, which I placed in its box on the mantelpiece, and left it there awaiting her arrival.

"I spent a restless night waiting for her.

"At ten o'clock she came, calm and quiet, and with her hand outstretched, as though she had known me for years. Drawing up a chair, I took her hat and coat and furs, and laid them aside. And then, timidly, I took her hand in mine; after that all went on without a hitch.

"Ah, my friends! what a bliss it is, to stand at a discreet distance and watch the hidden pink and blue ribbons, partly concealed, to observe the hazy lines of the beloved one's form, as they become visible through the last of the filmy garments! What a delight it is to watch the ostrich-like modesty of those who are in reality none too modest. And what is so pretty as their motions!

"Her back was turned towards me, and suddenly, my eyes were irresistibly drawn to a large black spot right between her shoulders. What could it be? Were my eyes deceiving me? But no, there it was, staring me in the face! Then my mind reverted to the faint down on her lip, the heavy eyebrows almost meeting over her coal-black eyes, her glossy black hair —I should have been prepared for some surprise.

"Nevertheless I was dumfounded, and my mind was haunted by dim visions of strange adventures. I seemed to see before me one of the evil genii of the Thousand and One Nights, one of these dangerous and crafty creatures whose mission it is to drag men down to unknown depths. I thought of Solomon, who made the Queen of Sheba walk on a mirror that he might be sure that her feet were not cloven.

"And when the time came for me to sing of love to her, my voice forsook me. At first she showed surprise, which soon turned to anger; and she said, quickly putting on her wraps:

"'It was hardly worth while for me to go out of my way to come here.'

"I wanted her to accept the ring which I had bought for her, but she replied haughtily: 'For whom do you take me, sir?' I blushed to the roots of my hair. She left without saying another word.

"There is my whole adventure. But the worst part of it is that I am now madly in love with her. I can't see a woman without thinking of her. All the others disgust me, unless they remind me of her. I cannot kiss a woman without seeing her face before me, and without suffering the torture of unsatisfied desire. She is always with me, always there, dressed or nude, my true love. She is there, beside the other one, visible but intangible. I am almost willing to believe that she was bewitched, and carried a talisman between her shoulders.

"Who is she? I don't know yet. I have met her once or twice since. I bowed, but she pretended not to recognize me. Who is she? An Oriental? Yes, doubtless an oriental Jewess! I believe that she must be a Jewess! But why? Why? I don't know!"

THE APPARITION

The subject of sequestration of the person came up in speaking of a recent lawsuit, and each of us had a story to tell—a true story, he said. We had been spending the evening together at an old family mansion in the Rue de Grenelle, just a party of intimate friends. The old Marquis de la Tour-Samuel, who was eighty-two, rose, and, leaning his elbow on the mantelpiece, said in his somewhat shaky voice:

"I also know of something strange, so strange that it has haunted me all my life. It is now fifty-six years since the incident occurred, and yet not a month passes that I do not see it again in a dream, so great is the impression of fear it has left on my mind. For ten minutes I experienced such horrible fright that ever since then a sort of constant terror has remained with me. Sudden noises startle me violently, and objects imperfectly distinguished at night inspire me with a mad desire to flee from them. In short, I am afraid of the dark!

"But I would not have acknowledged that before I reached my present age. Now I can say anything. I have never receded before real danger, ladies. It is, therefore, permissible, at eighty-two years of age, not to be brave in presence of imaginary danger.

"That affair so completely upset me, caused me such deep and mysterious and terrible distress, that I never spoke of it to any one. I will now tell it to you exactly as it happened, without any attempt at explanation.

"In July, 1827, I was stationed at Rouen. One day as I was walking along the quay I met a man whom I thought I recognized without being able to recall exactly who he was. Instinctively I made a movement to stop. The stranger perceived it and at once extended his hand.

"He was a friend to whom I had been deeply attached as a youth. For five years I had not seen him; he seemed to have aged half a century. His hair was quite white and he walked bent over as though completely exhausted. He apparently understood my surprise, and he told me of the misfortune which had shattered his life.

"Having fallen madly in love with a young girl, he had married her, but after a year of more than earthly happiness she died suddenly of an affection of the heart. He left his country home on the very day of her burial and came to his town house in Rouen, where he lived, alone and unhappy, so sad and wretched that he thought constantly of suicide.

"'Since I have found you again in this manner,' he said, 'I will ask you to render me an important service. It is to go and get me out of the desk in my bedroom—our bedroom—some papers of which I have urgent need. I cannot send a servant or a business clerk, as discretion and absolute silence are necessary. As for myself, nothing on earth would induce me to reenter that house. I will give you the key of the room, which I myself locked on leaving, and the key of my desk, also a few words for my gardener, telling him to open the chateau for you. But come and breakfast with me tomorrow and we will arrange all that.'

"I promised to do him the slight favor he asked. It was, for that matter, only a ride which I could make in an hour on horseback, his property being but a few miles distant from Rouen.

"At ten o'clock the following day I breakfasted, tete-a-tete, with my friend, but he scarcely spoke.

"He begged me to pardon him; the thought of the visit I was about to make to that room, the scene of his dead happiness, overcame him, he said. He, indeed, seemed singularly agitated and preoccupied, as though undergoing some mysterious mental struggle.

"At length he explained to me exactly what I had to do. It was very simple. I must take two packages of letters and a roll of papers from the first right-hand drawer of the desk, of which I had the key. He added:

"'I need not beg you to refrain from glancing at them.'

"I was wounded at that remark and told him so somewhat sharply. He stammered:

"'Forgive me, I suffer so,' and tears came to his eyes.

"At about one o'clock I took leave of him to accomplish my mission.

"'The weather was glorious, and I trotted across the fields, listening to the song of the larks and the rhythmical clang of my sword against my boot. Then I entered the forest and walked my horse. Branches of trees caressed my face as I passed, and now and then I caught a leaf with my teeth and chewed it, from sheer gladness of heart at being alive and vigorous on such a radiant day.

"As I approached the chateau I took from my pocket the letter I had for the gardener, and was astonished at finding it sealed. I was so irritated that I was about to turn back without having fulfilled my promise, but reflected that I should thereby display undue susceptibility. My friend in his troubled condition might easily have fastened the envelope without noticing that he did so.

"The manor looked as if it had been abandoned for twenty years. The open gate was falling from its hinges, the walks were overgrown with grass and the flower beds were no longer distinguishable.

"The noise I made by kicking at a shutter brought out an old man from a side door. He seemed stunned with astonishment at seeing me. On receiving my letter, he read it, reread it, turned it over and over, looked me up and down, put the paper in his pocket and finally said:

"'Well, what is it you wish?'

"I replied shortly:

"'You ought to know, since you have just read your master's orders. I wish to enter the chateau.'

"He seemed overcome.

"'Then you are going in—into her room?'

"I began to lose patience.

"'Damn it! Are you presuming to question me?'

"He stammered in confusion:

"'No—sir—but—but it has not been opened since—since the-death. If you will be kind enough to wait five minutes I will go and—and see if—'

"I interrupted him angrily:

"'See here, what do you mean by your tricks?

"'You know very well you cannot enter the room, since here is the key!'

"He no longer objected.

"'Then, sir, I will show you the way.'

"'Show me the staircase and leave me. I'll find my way without you.'

"'But—sir—indeed—'

"This time I lost patience, and pushing him aside, went into the house.

"I first went through the kitchen, then two rooms occupied by this man and his wife. I then crossed a large hall, mounted a staircase and recognized the door described by my friend.

"I easily opened it, and entered the apartment. It was so dark that at first I could distinguish nothing. I stopped short, disagreeably affected by that disagreeable, musty odor of closed, unoccupied rooms. As my eyes slowly became accustomed to the darkness I saw plainly enough a large and disordered bedroom, the bed without sheets but still retaining its mattresses and pillows, on one of which was a deep impression, as though an elbow or a head had recently rested there.

"The chairs all seemed out of place. I noticed that a door, doubtless that of a closet, had remained half open.

"I first went to the window, which I opened to let in the light, but the fastenings of the shutters had grown so rusty that I could not move them. I even tried to break them with my sword, but without success. As I was growing irritated over my useless efforts and could now see fairly well in the semi-darkness, I gave up the hope of getting more light, and went over to the writing desk.

"I seated myself in an armchair and, letting down the lid of the desk, I opened the drawer designated. It was full to the top. I needed but three packages, which I knew how to recognize, and began searching for them.

"I was straining my eyes in the effort to read the superscriptions when I seemed to hear, or, rather, feel, something rustle back of me. I paid no attention, believing that a draught from the window was moving some drapery. But in a minute or so another movement, almost imperceptible, sent a strangely disagreeable little shiver over my skin. It was so stupid to be affected, even slightly, that self-respect prevented my turning around. I had just found the second package I needed and was about to lay my hand on the third when a long and painful sigh, uttered just at my shoulder, made me bound like a madman from my seat and land several feet off. As I jumped I had turned round my hand on the hilt of my sword, and, truly, if I had not felt it at my side I should have taken to my heels like a coward.

"A tall woman dressed in white, stood gazing at me from the back of the chair where I had been sitting an instant before.

"Such a shudder ran through all my limbs that I nearly fell backward. No one who has not experienced it can understand that frightful, unreasoning terror! The mind becomes vague, the heart ceases to beat, the entire body grows as limp as a sponge.

"I do not believe in ghosts, nevertheless I collapsed from a hideous dread of the dead, and I suffered, oh! I suffered in a few moments more than in all the rest of my life from the irresistible terror of the supernatural. If she had not spoken I should have died perhaps. But she spoke, she spoke in a sweet, sad voice that set my nerves vibrating. I dare not say that I became master of myself and recovered my reason. No! I was terrified and scarcely knew what I was doing. But a certain innate pride, a remnant of soldierly instinct, made me, almost in spite of myself, maintain a bold front. She said:

"'Oh, sir, you can render me a great service.'

"I wanted to reply, but it was impossible for me to pronounce a word. Only a vague sound came from my throat. She continued:

"'Will you? You can save me, cure me. I suffer frightfully. I suffer, oh! how I suffer!' and she slowly seated herself in my armchair, still looking at me.

"'Will you?' she said.

"I nodded in assent, my voice still being paralyzed.

"Then she held out to me a tortoise-shell comb and murmured:

"'Comb my hair, oh! comb my hair; that will cure me; it must be combed. Look at my head—how I suffer; and my hair pulls so!'

"Her hair, unbound, very long and very black, it seemed to me, hung over the back of the armchair and touched the floor.

"Why did I promise? Why did I take that comb with a shudder, and why did I hold in my hands her long black hair that gave my skin a frightful cold sensation, as though I were handling snakes? I cannot tell.

"That sensation has remained in my fingers, and I still tremble in recalling it.

"I combed her hair. I handled, I know not how, those icy locks. I twisted, knotted, and unknotted, and braided them. She sighed, bowed her head, seemed happy. Suddenly she said, 'Thank you!' snatched the comb from my hands and fled by the door that I had noticed ajar.

"Left alone, I experienced for several seconds the horrible agitation of one who awakens from a nightmare. At length I regained my senses. I ran to the window and with a mighty effort burst open the shutters, letting a flood of light into the room. Immediately I sprang to the door by which that being had departed. I found it closed and immovable!

"Then the mad desire to flee overcame me like a panic the panic which soldiers know in battle. I seized the three packets of letters on the open desk, ran from the room, dashed down the stairs four steps at a time, found myself outside, I know not how, and, perceiving my horse a few steps off, leaped into the saddle and galloped away.

"I stopped only when I reached Rouen and alighted at my lodgings. Throwing the reins to my orderly, I fled to my room and shut myself in to reflect. For an hour I anxiously asked myself if I were not the victim of a hallucination. Undoubtedly I had had one of those incomprehensible nervous attacks those exaltations of mind that give rise to visions and are the stronghold of the supernatural. And I was about to believe I had seen a vision, had a hallucination, when, as I approached the window, my eyes fell, by chance, upon my breast. My military cape was covered with long black hairs! One by one, with trembling fingers, I plucked them off and threw them away.

"I then called my orderly. I was too disturbed, too upset to go and see my friend that day, and I also wished to reflect more fully upon what I ought to tell him. I sent him his letters, for which he gave the soldier a receipt. He asked after me most particularly, and, on being told I was ill—had had a sunstroke—appeared exceedingly anxious. Next morning I went to him, determined to tell him the truth. He had gone out the evening before and had not yet returned. I called again during the day; my friend was still absent. After waiting a week longer without news of him, I notified the authorities and a judicial search was instituted. Not the slightest trace of his whereabouts or manner of disappearance was discovered.

"A minute inspection of the abandoned chateau revealed nothing of a suspicious character. There was no indication that a woman had been concealed there.

"After fruitless researches all further efforts were abandoned, and for fifty-six years I have heard nothing; I know no more than before."

VOLUME VIII.

CLOCHETTE

How strange those old recollections are which haunt us, without our being able to get rid of them.

This one is so very old that I cannot understand how it has clung so vividly and tenaciously to my memory. Since then I have seen so many sinister things, which were either affecting or terrible, that I am astonished at not being able to pass a single day without the face of Mother Bellflower recurring to my mind's eye, just as I knew her formerly, now so long ago, when I was ten or twelve years old.

She was an old seamstress who came to my parents' house once a week, every Thursday, to mend the linen. My parents lived in one of those country houses called chateaux, which are merely old houses with gable roofs, to which are attached three or four farms lying around them.

The village, a large village, almost a market town, was a few hundred yards away, closely circling the church, a red brick church, black with age.

Well, every Thursday Mother Clochette came between half-past six and seven in the morning, and went immediately into the linen-room and began to work. She was a tall, thin, bearded or rather hairy woman, for she had a beard all over her face, a surprising, an unexpected beard, growing in improbable tufts, in curly bunches which looked as if they had been sown by a madman over that great face of a gendarme in petticoats. She had them on her nose, under her nose, round her nose, on her chin, on her cheeks; and her eyebrows, which were extraordinarily thick and long, and quite gray, bushy and bristling, looked exactly like a pair of mustaches stuck on there by mistake.

She limped, not as lame people generally do, but like a ship at anchor. When she planted her great, bony, swerving body on her sound leg, she seemed to be preparing to mount some enormous wave, and then suddenly she dipped as if to disappear in an abyss, and buried herself in the ground. Her walk reminded one of a storm, as she swayed about, and her head, which was always covered with an enormous white cap, whose ribbons fluttered down her back, seemed to traverse the horizon from north to south and from south to north, at each step.

I adored Mother Clochette. As soon as I was up I went into the linen-room where I found her installed at work, with a foot-warmer under her feet. As soon as I arrived, she made me take the foot-warmer and sit upon it, so that I might not catch cold in that large, chilly room under the roof.

"That draws the blood from your throat," she said to me.

She told me stories, whilst mending the linen with her long crooked nimble fingers; her eyes behind her magnifying spectacles, for age had impaired her sight, appeared enormous to me, strangely profound, double.

She had, as far as I can remember the things which she told me and by which my childish heart was moved, the large heart of a poor woman. She told me what had happened in the village, how a cow had escaped from the cow-house and had been found the next morning in front of Prosper Malet's windmill, looking at the sails turning, or about a hen's egg which had been found in the church belfry without any one being able to understand what creature had been there to lay it, or the story of Jean-Jean Pila's dog, who had been ten leagues to bring back his master's breeches which a tramp had stolen whilst they were hanging up to dry out of doors, after he had been in the rain. She told me these simple adventures in such a manner, that in my mind they assumed the proportions of never-to-be-forgotten dramas, of grand and mysterious poems; and the ingenious stories invented by the poets which my mother told me in the evening, had none of the flavor, none of the breadth or vigor of the peasant woman's narratives.

Well, one Tuesday, when I had spent all the morning in listening to Mother Clochette, I wanted to go upstairs to her again during the day after picking hazelnuts with the manservant in the wood behind the farm. I remember it all as clearly as what happened only yesterday.

On opening the door of the linen-room, I saw the old seamstress lying on the ground by the side of her chair, with her face to the ground and her arms stretched out, but still holding her needle in one hand and one of my shirts in the other. One of her legs in a blue stocking, the longer one, no doubt, was extended under her chair, and her spectacles glistened against the wall, as they had rolled away from her.

I ran away uttering shrill cries. They all came running, and in a few minutes I was told that Mother Clochette was dead.

I cannot describe the profound, poignant, terrible emotion which stirred my childish heart. I went slowly down into the drawing-room and hid myself in a dark corner, in the depths of an immense old armchair, where I knelt down and wept. I remained there a long time, no doubt, for night came on. Suddenly somebody came in with a lamp, without seeing me, however, and I heard my father and mother talking with the medical man, whose voice I recognized.

He had been sent for immediately, and he was explaining the causes of the accident, of which I understood nothing, however. Then he sat down and had a glass of liqueur and a biscuit.

He went on talking, and what he then said will remain engraved on my mind until I die! I think that I can give the exact words which he used.

"Ah!" said he, "the poor woman! She broke her leg the day of my arrival here, and I had not even had time to wash my hands after getting off the diligence before I was sent for in all haste, for it was a bad case, very bad.

"She was seventeen, and a pretty girl, very pretty! Would any one believe it? I have never told her story before, and nobody except myself and one other person who is no longer living in this part of the country ever knew it. Now that she is dead, I may be less discreet.

"Just then a young assistant-teacher came to live in the village; he was a handsome, well-made fellow, and looked like a non-commissioned officer. All the girls ran after him, but he paid no attention to them, partly because he was very much afraid of his superior, the schoolmaster, old Grabu, who occasionally got out of bed the wrong foot first.

"Old Grabu already employed pretty Hortense who has just died here, and who was afterwards nicknamed Clochette. The assistant master singled out the pretty young girl, who was, no doubt, flattered at being chosen by this impregnable conqueror; at any rate, she fell in love with him, and he succeeded in persuading her to give him a first meeting in the hay-loft behind the school, at night, after she had done her day's sewing.

"She pretended to go home, but instead of going downstairs when she left the Grabus' she went upstairs and hid among the hay, to wait for her lover. He soon joined her, and was beginning to say pretty things to her, when the door of the hay-loft opened and the schoolmaster appeared, and asked: 'What are you doing up there, Sigisbert?' Feeling sure that he would be caught, the young schoolmaster lost his presence of mind and replied stupidly: 'I came up here to rest a little amongst the bundles of hay, Monsieur Grabu.'

"The loft was very large and absolutely dark, and Sigisbert pushed the frightened girl to the further end and said: 'Go over there and hide yourself. I shall lose my position, so get away and hide yourself.'

"When the schoolmaster heard the whispering, he continued: 'Why, you are not by yourself?' 'Yes, I am, Monsieur Grabu!' 'But you are not, for you are talking.' 'I swear I am, Monsieur Grabu.' 'I will soon find out,' the old man replied, and double locking the door, he went down to get a light.

"Then the young man, who was a coward such as one frequently meets, lost his head, and becoming furious all of a sudden, he repeated: 'Hide yourself, so that he may not find you. You will keep me from making a living for the rest of my life; you will ruin my whole career. Do hide yourself!' They could hear the key turning in the lock again, and Hortense ran to the window which looked out on the street, opened it quickly, and then said in a low and determined voice: 'You will come and pick me up when he is gone,' and she jumped out.

"Old Grabu found nobody, and went down again in great surprise, and a quarter of an hour later, Monsieur Sigisbert came to me and related his adventure. The girl had remained at the foot of the wall unable to get up, as she had fallen from the second story, and I went with him to fetch her. It was raining in torrents, and I brought the unfortunate girl home with me, for the right leg was broken in three places, and the bones had come trough the flesh. She did not complain, and merely said, with admirable resignation: 'I am punished, well punished!'

"I sent for assistance and for the work-girl's relatives and told them a, made-up story of a runaway carriage which had knocked her down and lamed her outside my door. They believed me, and the gendarmes for a whole month tried in vain to find the author of this accident.

"That is all! And I say that this woman was a heroine and belonged to the race of those who accomplish the grandest deeds of history.

"That was her only love affair, and she died a virgin. She was a martyr, a noble soul, a sublimely devoted woman! And if I did not absolutely admire her, I should not have told you this story, which I would never tell any one during her life; you understand why."

The doctor ceased. Mamma cried and papa said some words which I did not catch; then they left the room and I remained on my knees in the armchair and sobbed, whilst I heard a strange noise of heavy footsteps and something knocking against the side of the staircase.

They were carrying away Clochette's body.

THE KISS

My Little Darling: So you are crying from morning until night and from night until morning, because your husband leaves you; you do not know what to do and so you ask your old aunt for advice; you must consider her quite an expert. I don't know as much as you think I do, and yet I am not entirely ignorant of the art of loving, or, rather, of making one's self loved, in which you are a little lacking. I can admit that at my age.

You say that you are all attention, love, kisses and caresses for him. Perhaps that is the very trouble; I think you kiss him too much.

My dear, we have in our hands the most terrible power in the world: LOVE.

Man is gifted with physical strength, and he exercises force. Woman is gifted with charm, and she rules with caresses. It is our weapon, formidable and invincible, but we should know how to use it.

Know well that we are the mistresses of the world! To tell the history of Love from the beginning of the world would be to tell the history of man himself: Everything springs from it, the arts, great events, customs, wars, the overthrow of empires.

In the Bible you find Delila, Judith; in fables we find Omphale, Helen; in history the Sabines, Cleopatra and many others.

Therefore we reign supreme, all-powerful. But, like kings, we must make use of delicate diplomacy.

Love, my dear, is made up of imperceptible sensations. We know that it is as strong as death, but also as frail as glass. The slightest shock breaks it, and our power crumbles, and we are never able to raise it again.

We have the power of making ourselves adored, but we lack one tiny thing, the understanding of the various kinds of caresses. In embraces we lose the sentiment of delicacy, while the man over whom we rule remains master of himself, capable of judging the foolishness of certain words. Take care, my dear; that is the defect in our armor. It is our Achilles' heel.

Do you know whence comes our real power? From the kiss, the kiss alone! When we know how to hold out and give up our lips we can become queens.

The kiss is only a preface, however, but a charming preface. More charming than the realization itself. A preface which can always be read over again, whereas one cannot always read over the book.

Yes, the meeting of lips is the most perfect, the most divine sensation given to human beings, the supreme limit of happiness: It is in the kiss alone that one sometimes seems to feel this union of souls after which we strive, the intermingling of hearts, as it were.

Do you remember the verses of Sully-Prudhomme:

> Caresses are nothing but anxious bliss,
>
> Vain attempts of love to unite souls through a kiss.

One caress alone gives this deep sensation of two beings welded into one —it is the kiss. No violent delirium of complete possession is worth this trembling approach of the lips, this first moist and fresh contact, and then the long, lingering, motionless rapture.

Therefore, my dear, the kiss is our strongest weapon, but we must take care not to dull it. Do not forget that its value is only relative, purely conventional. It continually changes according to circumstances, the state of expectancy and the ecstasy of the mind. I will call attention to one example.

Another poet, Francois Coppee, has written a line which we all remember, a line which we find delightful, which moves our very hearts.

After describing the expectancy of a lover, waiting in a room one winter's evening, his anxiety, his nervous impatience, the terrible fear of not seeing her, he describes the arrival of the beloved woman, who at last enters hurriedly, out of breath, bringing with her part of the winter breeze, and he exclaims:

> Oh! the taste of the kisses first snatched through the veil.

Is that not a line of exquisite sentiment, a delicate and charming observation, a perfect truth? All those who have hastened to a clandestine meeting, whom passion has thrown into the arms of a man, well do they know these first delicious kisses through the veil; and they tremble at the memory of them. And yet their sole charm lies in the circumstances, from being late, from the anxious expectancy, but from the purely—or, rather, impurely, if you prefer—sensual point of view, they are detestable.

Think! Outside it is cold. The young woman has walked quickly; the veil is moist from her cold breath. Little drops of water shine in the lace. The lover seizes her and presses his burning lips to her liquid breath. The moist veil, which discolors and carries the dreadful odor of chemical dye, penetrates into the young man's mouth, moistens his mustache. He does not taste the lips of his beloved, he tastes the dye of this lace moistened with cold breath. And yet, like the poet, we would all exclaim:

> Oh! the taste of the kisses first snatched through the veil.

Therefore, the value of this caress being entirely a matter of convention, we must be careful not to abuse it.

Well, my dear, I have several times noticed that you are very clumsy. However, you were not alone in that fault; the majority of women lose their authority by abusing the kiss with untimely kisses. When they feel that their husband or their lover is a little tired, at those times when the heart as well as the body needs rest, instead of understanding what is going on within him, they persist in giving inopportune caresses, tire him by the obstinacy of begging lips and give caresses lavished with neither rhyme nor reason.

Trust in the advice of my experience. First, never kiss your husband in public, in the train, at the restaurant. It is bad taste; do not give in to your desires. He would feel ridiculous and would never forgive you.

Beware of useless kisses lavished in intimacy. I am sure that you abuse them. For instance, I remember one day that you did something quite shocking. Probably you do not remember it.

All three of us were together in the drawing-room, and, as you did not stand on ceremony before me, your husband was holding you on his knees and kissing you at great length on the neck, the lips and throat. Suddenly you exclaimed: "Oh! the fire!" You had been paying no attention to it, and it was almost out. A few lingering embers were glowing on the hearth. Then he rose, ran to the woodbox, from which he dragged two enormous logs with great difficulty, when you came to him with begging lips, murmuring:

"Kiss me!" He turned his head with difficulty and tried to hold up the logs at the same time. Then you gently and slowly placed your mouth on that of the poor fellow, who remained with his neck out of joint, his sides twisted, his arms almost dropping off, trembling with fatigue and tired from his desperate effort. And you kept drawing out this torturing kiss, without seeing or understanding. Then when you freed him, you began to grumble: "How badly you kiss!" No wonder!

Oh, take care of that! We all have this foolish habit, this unconscious need of choosing the most inconvenient moments. When he is carrying a glass of water, when he is putting on his shoes, when he is tying his scarf—in short, when he finds himself in any uncomfortable position —then is the time which we choose for a caress which makes him stop for a whole minute in the middle of a gesture with the sole desire of getting rid of us!

Do not think that this criticism is insignificant. Love, my dear, is a delicate thing. The least little thing offends it; know that everything depends on the tact of our caresses. An ill-placed kiss may do any amount of harm.

Try following my advice.

>Your old aunt,

>COLLETTE.

This story appeared in the Gaulois in November, 1882, under the pseudonym of "Maufrigneuse."

THE LEGION OF HONOR

HOW HE GOT THE LEGION OF HONOR

From the time some people begin to talk they seem to have an overmastering desire or vocation.

Ever since he was a child, M. Caillard had only had one idea in his head —to wear the ribbon of an order. When he was still quite a small boy he used to wear a zinc cross of the Legion of Honor pinned on his tunic, just as other children wear a soldier's cap, and he took his mother's hand in the street with a proud air, sticking out his little chest with its red ribbon and metal star so that it might show to advantage.

His studies were not a success, and he failed in his examination for Bachelor of Arts; so, not knowing what to do, he married a pretty girl, as he had plenty of money of his own.

They lived in Paris, as many rich middle-class people do, mixing with their own particular set, and proud of knowing a deputy, who might perhaps be a minister some day, and counting two heads of departments among their friends.

But M. Caillard could not get rid of his one absorbing idea, and he felt constantly unhappy because he had not the right to wear a little bit of colored ribbon in his buttonhole.

When he met any men who were decorated on the boulevards, he looked at them askance, with intense jealousy. Sometimes, when he had nothing to do in the afternoon, he would count them, and say to himself: "Just let me see how many I shall meet between the Madeleine and the Rue Drouot."

Then he would walk slowly, looking at every coat with a practiced eye for the little bit of red ribbon, and when he had got to the end of his walk he always repeated the numbers aloud.

"Eight officers and seventeen knights. As many as that! It is stupid to sow the cross broadcast in that fashion. I wonder how many I shall meet going back?"

And he returned slowly, unhappy when the crowd of passers-by interfered with his vision.

He knew the places where most were to be found. They swarmed in the Palais Royal. Fewer were seen in the Avenue de l'Opera than in the Rue de la Paix, while the right side of the boulevard was more frequented by them than the left.

They also seemed to prefer certain cafes and theatres. Whenever he saw a group of white-haired old gentlemen standing together in the middle of the pavement, interfering with the traffic, he used to say to himself:

"They are officers of the Legion of Honor," and he felt inclined to take off his hat to them.

He had often remarked that the officers had a different bearing to the mere knights. They carried their head differently, and one felt that they enjoyed a higher official consideration and a more widely extended importance.

Sometimes, however, the worthy man would be seized with a furious hatred for every one who was decorated; he felt like a Socialist toward them.

Then, when he got home, excited at meeting so many crosses—just as a poor, hungry wretch might be on passing some dainty provision shop—he used to ask in a loud voice:

"When shall we get rid of this wretched government?"

And his wife would be surprised, and ask:

"What is the matter with you to-day?"

"I am indignant," he replied, "at the injustice I see going on around us. Oh, the Communards were certainly right!"

After dinner he would go out again and look at the shops where the decorations were sold, and he examined all the emblems of various shapes and colors. He would have liked to possess them all, and to have walked gravely at the head of a procession, with his crush hat under his arm and his breast covered with decorations, radiant as a star, amid a buzz of admiring whispers and a hum of respect.

But, alas! he had no right to wear any decoration whatever.

He used to say to himself: "It is really too difficult for any man to obtain the Legion of Honor unless he is some public functionary. Suppose I try to be appointed an officer of the Academy!"

But he did not know how to set about it, and spoke on the subject to his wife, who was stupefied.

"Officer of the Academy! What have you done to deserve it?"

He got angry. "I know what I am talking about. I only want to know how to set about it. You are quite stupid at times."

She smiled. "You are quite right. I don't understand anything about it."

An idea struck him: "Suppose you were to speak to M. Rosselin, the deputy; he might be able to advise me. You understand I cannot broach the subject to him directly. It is rather difficult and delicate, but coming from you it might seem quite natural."

Mme. Caillard did what he asked her, and M. Rosselin promised to speak to the minister about it; and then Caillard began to worry him, till the deputy told him he must make a formal application and put forward his claims.

"What were his charms?" he said. "He was not even a Bachelor of Arts." However, he set to work and produced a pamphlet, with the title, "The People's Right to Instruction," but he could not finish it for want of ideas.

He sought for easier subjects, and began several in succession. The first was, "The Instruction of Children by Means of the Eye." He wanted gratuitous theatres to be established in every poor quarter of Paris for little children. Their parents were to take them there when they were quite young, and, by means of a magic lantern, all the notions of human knowledge were to be imparted to them. There were to be regular courses. The sight would educate the mind, while the pictures would remain impressed on the brain, and thus science would, so to say, be made visible. What could be more simple than to teach universal history, natural history, geography, botany, zoology, anatomy, etc., etc., in this manner?

He had his ideas printed in pamphlets, and sent a copy to each deputy, ten to each minister, fifty to the President of the Republic, ten to each Parisian, and five to each provincial newspaper.

Then he wrote on "Street Lending-Libraries." His idea was to have little pushcarts full of books drawn about the streets. Everyone would have a right to ten volumes a month in his home on payment of one sou.

"The people," M. Caillard said, "will only disturb itself for the sake of its pleasures, and since it will not go to instruction, instruction must come to it," etc., etc.

His essays attracted no attention, but he sent in his application, and he got the usual formal official reply. He thought himself sure of success, but nothing came of it.

Then he made up his mind to apply personally. He begged for an interview with the Minister of Public Instruction, and he was received by a young subordinate, who was very grave and important, and kept touching the knobs of electric bells to summon ushers, and footmen, and officials inferior to himself. He declared to M. Caillard that his matter was going on quite favorably, and advised him to continue his remarkable labors, and M. Caillard set at it again.

M. Rosselin, the deputy, seemed now to take a great interest in his success, and gave him a lot of excellent, practical advice. He, himself, was decorated, although nobody knew exactly what he had done to deserve such a distinction.

He told Caillard what new studies he ought to undertake; he introduced him to learned societies which took up particularly obscure points of science, in the hope of gaining credit and honors thereby; and he even took him under his wing at the ministry.

One day, when he came to lunch with his friend—for several months past he had constantly taken his meals there—he said to him in a whisper as he shook hands: "I have just obtained a great favor for you. The Committee of Historical Works is going to intrust you with a commission. There are some researches to be made in various libraries in France."

Caillard was so delighted that he could scarcely eat or drink, and a week later he set out. He went from town to town, studying catalogues, rummaging in lofts full of dusty volumes, and was hated by all the librarians.

One day, happening to be at Rouen, he thought he should like to go and visit his wife, whom he had not seen for more than a week, so he took the nine o'clock train, which would land him at home by twelve at night.

He had his latchkey, so he went in without making any noise, delighted at the idea of the surprise he was going to give her. She had locked herself in. How tiresome! However, he cried out through the door:

"Jeanne, it is I!"

She must have been very frightened, for he heard her jump out of her bed and speak to herself, as if she were in a dream. Then she went to her dressing room, opened and closed the door, and went quickly up and down her room barefoot two or three times, shaking the furniture till the vases and glasses sounded. Then at last she asked:

"Is it you, Alexander?"

"Yes, yes," he replied; "make haste and open the door."

As soon as she had done so, she threw herself into his arms, exclaiming:

"Oh, what a fright! What a surprise! What a pleasure!"

He began to undress himself methodically, as he did everything, and took from a chair his overcoat, which he was in the habit of hanging up in the hall. But suddenly he remained motionless, struck dumb with astonishment—there was a red ribbon in the buttonhole:

"Why," he stammered, "this—this—this overcoat has got the ribbon in it!"

In a second, his wife threw herself on him, and, taking it from his hands, she said:

"No! you have made a mistake—give it to me."

But he still held it by one of the sleeves, without letting it go, repeating in a half-dazed manner:

"Oh! Why? Just explain—Whose overcoat is it? It is not mine, as it has the Legion of Honor on it."

She tried to take it from him, terrified and hardly able to say:

"Listen—listen! Give it to me! I must not tell you! It is a secret. Listen to me!"

But he grew angry and turned pale.

"I want to know how this overcoat comes to be here? It does not belong to me."

Then she almost screamed at him:

"Yes, it does; listen! Swear to me—well—you are decorated!"

She did not intend to joke at his expense.

He was so overcome that he let the overcoat fall and dropped into an armchair.

"I am—you say I am—decorated?"

"Yes, but it is a secret, a great secret."

She had put the glorious garment into a cupboard, and came to her husband pale and trembling.

"Yes," she continued, "it is a new overcoat that I have had made for you. But I swore that I would not tell you anything about it, as it will not be officially announced for a month or six weeks, and you were not to have known till your return from your business journey. M. Rosselin managed it for you."

"Rosselin!" he contrived to utter in his joy. "He has obtained the decoration for me? He—Oh!"

And he was obliged to drink a glass of water.

A little piece of white paper fell to the floor out of the pocket of the overcoat. Caillard picked it up; it was a visiting card, and he read out:

"Rosselin-Deputy."

"You see how it is," said his wife.

He almost cried with joy, and, a week later, it was announced in the Journal Officiel that M. Caillard had been awarded the Legion of Honor on account of his exceptional services.

THE TEST

The Bondels were a happy family, and although they frequently quarrelled about trifles, they soon became friends again.

Bondel was a merchant who had retired from active business after saving enough to allow him to live quietly; he had rented a little house at Saint-Germain and lived there with his wife. He was a quiet man with very decided opinions; he had a certain degree of education and read serious newspapers; nevertheless, he appreciated the gaulois wit. Endowed with a logical mind, and that practical common sense which is the master quality of the industrial French bourgeois, he thought little, but clearly, and reached a decision only after careful consideration of the matter in hand. He was of medium size, with a distinguished look, and was beginning to turn gray.

His wife, who was full of serious qualities, had also several faults. She had a quick temper and a frankness that bordered upon violence. She bore a grudge a long time. She had once been pretty, but had now become too stout and too red; but in her neighborhood at Saint-Germain she still passed for a very beautiful woman, who exemplified health and an uncertain temper.

Their dissensions almost always began at breakfast, over some trivial matter, and they often continued all day and even until the following day. Their simple, common, limited life imparted seriousness to the most unimportant matters, and every topic of conversation became a subject of dispute. This had not been so in the days when business occupied their minds, drew their hearts together, and gave them common interests and occupation.

But at Saint-Germain they saw fewer people. It had been necessary to make new acquaintances, to create for themselves a new world among strangers, a new existence devoid of occupations. Then the monotony of loneliness had soured each of them a little; and the quiet happiness which they had hoped and waited for with the coming of riches did not appear.

One June morning, just as they were sitting down to breakfast, Bondel asked:

"Do you know the people who live in the little red cottage at the end of the Rue du Berceau?"

Madame Bondel was out of sorts. She answered:

"Yes and no; I am acquainted with them, but I do not care to know them."

"Why not? They seem to be very nice."

"Because—"

"This morning I met the husband on the terrace and we took a little walk together."

Seeing that there was danger in the air, Bendel added: "It was he who spoke to me first."

His wife looked at him in a displeased manner. She continued: "You would have done just as well to avoid him."

"Why?"

"Because there are rumors about them."

"What kind?"

"Oh! rumors such as one often hears!"

M. Bondel was, unfortunately, a little hasty. He exclaimed:

"My dear, you know that I abhor gossip. As for those people, I find them very pleasant."

She asked testily: "The wife also?"

"Why, yes; although I have barely seen her."

The discussion gradually grew more heated, always on the same subject for lack of others. Madame Bondel obstinately refused to say what she had heard about these neighbors, allowing things to be understood without saying exactly what they were. Bendel would shrug his shoulders, grin, and exasperate his wife. She finally cried out: "Well! that gentleman is deceived by his wife, there!"

The husband answered quietly: "I can't see how that affects the honor of a man."

She seemed dumfounded: "What! you don't see?—you don't see?—well, that's too much! You don't see!—why, it's a public scandal! he is disgraced!"

He answered: "Ah! by no means! Should a man be considered disgraced because he is deceived, because he is betrayed, robbed? No, indeed! I'll grant you that that may be the case for the wife, but as for him—"

She became furious, exclaiming: "For him as well as for her. They are both in disgrace; it's a public shame."

Bondel, very calm, asked: "First of all, is it true? Who can assert such a thing as long as no one has been caught in the act?"

Madame Bondel was growing uneasy; she snapped: "What? Who can assert it? Why, everybody! everybody! it's as clear as the nose on your face. Everybody knows it and is talking about it. There is not the slightest doubt."

He was grinning: "For a long time people thought that the sun revolved around the earth. This man loves his wife and speaks of her tenderly and reverently. This whole business is nothing but lies!"

Stamping her foot, she stammered: "Do you think that that fool, that idiot, knows anything about it?"

Bondel did not grow angry; he was reasoning clearly: "Excuse me. This gentleman is no fool. He seemed to me, on the contrary, to be very intelligent and shrewd; and you can't make me believe that a man with brains doesn't notice such a thing in his own house, when the neighbors, who are not there, are ignorant of no detail of this liaison—for I'll warrant that they know everything."

Madame Bondel had a fit of angry mirth, which irritated her husband's nerves. She laughed: "Ha! ha! ha! they're all the same! There's not a man alive who could discover a thing like that unless his nose was stuck into it!"

The discussion was wandering to other topics now. She was exclaiming over the blindness of deceived husbands, a thing which he doubted and which she affirmed with such airs of personal contempt that he finally grew angry. Then the discussion became an angry quarrel, where she took the side of the women and he defended the men. He had the conceit to declare: "Well, I swear that if I had ever been deceived, I should have noticed it, and immediately, too. And I should have taken away your desire for such things in such a manner that it would have taken more than one doctor to set you on foot again!"

Boiling with anger, she cried out to him: "You! you! why, you're as big a fool as the others, do you hear!"

He still maintained: "I can swear to you that I am not!"

She laughed so impertinently that he felt his heart beat and a chill run down his back. For the third time he said:

"I should have seen it!"

She rose, still laughing in the same manner. She slammed the door and left the room, saying: "Well! if that isn't too much!"

Bondel remained alone, ill at ease. That insolent, provoking laugh had touched him to the quick. He went outside, walked, dreamed. The realization of the loneliness of his new life made him sad and morbid. The neighbor, whom he had met that morning, came to him with outstretched hands. They continued their walk together. After touching on various subjects they came to talk of their wives. Both seemed to have something to confide, something inexpressible, vague, about these beings associated with their lives; their wives. The neighbor was saying:

"Really, at times, one might think that they bear some particular ill-will toward their husband, just because he is a husband. I love my wife—I love her very much; I appreciate and respect her; well! there are times when she seems to have more confidence and faith in our friends than in me."

Bondel immediately thought: "There is no doubt; my wife was right!"

When he left this man he began to think things over again. He felt in his soul a strange confusion of contradictory ideas, a sort of interior burning; that mocking, impertinent laugh kept ringing in his ears and seemed to say: "Why; you are just the same as the others, you fool!" That was indeed bravado, one of those pieces of impudence of which a woman makes use when she dares everything, risks everything, to wound and humiliate the man who has aroused her ire. This poor man must also be one of those deceived husbands, like so many others. He had said sadly: "There are times when she seems to have more confidence and faith in our friends than in me." That is how a husband formulated his observations on the particular attentions of his wife for another man. That was all. He had seen nothing more. He was like the rest—all the rest!

And how strangely Bondel's own wife had laughed as she said: "You, too —you, too." How wild and imprudent these creatures are who can arouse such suspicions in the heart for the sole purpose of revenge!

He ran over their whole life since their marriage, reviewed his mental list of their acquaintances, to see whether she had ever appeared to show more confidence in any one else than in himself. He never had suspected any one, he was so calm, so sure of her, so confident.

But, now he thought of it, she had had a friend, an intimate friend, who for almost a year had dined with them three times a week. Tancret, good old Tancret, whom he, Bendel, loved as a brother and whom he continued to see on the sly, since his wife, he did not know why, had grown angry at the charming fellow.

He stopped to think, looking over the past with anxious eyes. Then he grew angry at himself for harboring this shameful insinuation of the defiant, jealous, bad ego which lives in all of us. He blamed and accused himself when he remembered the visits and the demeanor of this friend whom his wife had dismissed for no apparent reason. But, suddenly, other memories returned to him, similar ruptures due to the vindictive character of Madame Bondel, who never pardoned a slight. Then he laughed frankly at himself for the doubts which he had nursed; and he remembered the angry looks of his wife as he would tell her, when he returned at night: "I saw good old Tancret, and he wished to be remembered to you," and he reassured himself.

She would invariably answer: "When you see that gentleman you can tell him that I can very well dispense with his remembrances." With what an irritated, angry look she would say these words! How well one could feel that she did not and would not forgive—and he had suspected her even for a second? Such foolishness!

But why did she grow so angry? She never had given the exact reason for this quarrel. She still bore him that grudge! Was it?—But no—no—and Bondel declared that he was lowering himself by even thinking of such things.

Yes, he was undoubtedly lowering himself, but he could not help thinking of it, and he asked himself with terror if this thought which had entered into his mind had not come to stop, if he did not carry in his heart the seed of fearful torment. He knew himself; he was a man to think over his doubts, as formerly he would ruminate over his commercial operations, for days and nights, endlessly weighing the pros and the cons.

He was already becoming excited; he was walking fast and losing his calmness. A thought cannot be downed. It is intangible, cannot be caught, cannot be killed.

Suddenly a plan occurred to him; it was bold, so bold that at first he doubted whether he would carry it out.

Each time that he met Tancret, his friend would ask for news of Madame Bondel, and Bondel would answer: "She is still a little angry." Nothing more. Good Lord! What a fool he had been! Perhaps!

Well, he would take the train to Paris, go to Tancret, and bring him back with him that very evening, assuring him that his wife's mysterious anger had disappeared. But how would Madame Bondel act? What a scene there would be! What anger! what scandal! What of it?—that would be revenge! When she should come face to face with him, unexpectedly, he certainly ought to be able to read the truth in their expressions.

He immediately went to the station, bought his ticket, got into the car, and as soon as he felt himself being carried away by the train, he felt a fear, a kind of dizziness, at what he was going to do. In order not to weaken, back down, and return alone, he tried not to think of the matter any longer, to bring his mind to bear on other affairs, to do what he had decided to do with a blind resolution; and he began to hum tunes from operettas and music halls until he reached Paris.

As soon as he found himself walking along the streets that led to Tancret's, he felt like stopping, He paused in front of several shops, noticed the prices of certain objects, was interested in new things, felt like taking a glass of beer, which was not his usual custom; and as he approached his friend's dwelling he ardently hoped not meet him. But Tancret was at home, alone, reading. He jumped up in surprise, crying: "Ah! Bondel! what luck!"

Bondel, embarrassed, answered: "Yes, my dear fellow, I happened to be in Paris, and I thought I'd drop in and shake hands with you."

"That's very nice, very nice! The more so that for some time you have not favored me with your presence very often."

"Well, you see—even against one's will, one is often influenced by surrounding conditions, and as my wife seemed to bear you some ill-will"

"Jove! 'seemed'—she did better than that, since she showed me the door."

"What was the reason? I never heard it."

"Oh! nothing at all—a bit of foolishness—a discussion in which we did not both agree."

"But what was the subject of this discussion?"

"A lady of my acquaintance, whom you may perhaps know by name, Madame Boutin."

"Ah! really. Well, I think that my wife has forgotten her grudge, for this very morning she spoke to me of you in very pleasant terms."

Tancret started and seemed so dumfounded that for a few minutes he could find nothing to say. Then he asked: "She spoke of me—in pleasant terms?"

"Yes."

"You are sure?"

"Of course I am. I am not dreaming."

"And then?"

"And then—as I was coming to Paris I thought that I would please you by coming to tell you the good news."

"Why, yes—why, yes—"

Bondel appeared to hesitate; then, after a short pause, he added: "I even had an idea."

"What is it?"

"To take you back home with me to dinner."

Tancret, who was naturally prudent, seemed a little worried by this proposition, and he asked: "Oh! really—is it possible? Are we not exposing ourselves to—to—a scene?"

"No, no, indeed!"

"Because, you know, Madame Bendel bears malice for a long time."

"Yes, but I can assure you that she no longer bears you any ill—will. I am even convinced that it will be a great pleasure for her to see you thus, unexpectedly."

"Really?"

"Yes, really!"

"Well, then! let us go along. I am delighted. You see, this misunderstanding was very unpleasant for me."

They set out together toward the Saint-Lazare station, arm in arm. They made the trip in silence. Both seemed absorbed in deep meditation. Seated in the car, one opposite the other, they looked at each other without speaking, each observing that the other was pale.

Then they left the train and once more linked arms as if to unite against some common danger. After a walk of a few minutes they stopped, a little out of breath, before Bondel's house. Bondel ushered his friend into the parlor, called the servant, and asked: "Is madame at home?"

"Yes, monsieur."

"Please ask her to come down at once."

They dropped into two armchairs and waited. Both were filled with the same longing to escape before the appearance of the much-feared person.

A well-known, heavy tread could be heard descending the stairs. A hand moved the knob, and both men watched the brass handle turn. Then the door opened wide, and Madame Bondel stopped and looked to see who was there before she entered. She looked, blushed, trembled, retreated a step, then stood motionless, her cheeks aflame and her hands resting against the sides of the door frame.

Tancret, as pale as if about to faint, had arisen, letting fall his hat, which rolled along the floor. He stammered out: "Mon Dieu—madame—it is I—I thought—I ventured—I was so sorry—"

As she did not answer, he continued: "Will you forgive me?"

Then, quickly, carried away by some impulse, she walked toward him with her hands outstretched; and when he had taken, pressed, and held these two hands, she said, in a trembling, weak little voice, which was new to her husband:

"Ah! my dear friend—how happy I am!"

And Bondel, who was watching them, felt an icy chill run over him, as if he had been dipped in a cold bath.

FOUND ON A DROWNED MAN

Madame, you ask me whether I am laughing at you? You cannot believe that a man has never been in love. Well, then, no, no, I have never loved, never!

Why is this? I really cannot tell. I have never experienced that intoxication of the heart which we call love! Never have I lived in that dream, in that exaltation, in that state of madness into which the image of a woman casts us. I have never been pursued, haunted, roused to fever heat, lifted up to Paradise by the thought of meeting, or by the possession of, a being who had suddenly become for me more desirable than any good fortune, more beautiful than any other creature, of more consequence than the whole world! I have never wept, I have never suffered on account of any of you. I have not passed my nights sleepless, while thinking of her. I have no experience of waking thoughts bright with thought and memories of her. I have never known the wild rapture of hope before her arrival, or the divine sadness of regret when she went from me, leaving behind her a delicate odor of violet powder.

I have never been in love.

I have also often asked myself why this is. And truly I can scarcely tell. Nevertheless I have found some reasons for it; but they are of a metaphysical character, and perhaps you will not be able to appreciate them.

I suppose I am too critical of women to submit to their fascination. I ask you to forgive me for this remark. I will explain what I mean. In every creature there is a moral being and a physical being. In order to love, it would be necessary for me to find a harmony between these two beings which I have never found. One always predominates; sometimes the moral, sometimes the physical.

The intellect which we have a right to require in a woman, in order to love her, is not the same as the virile intellect. It is more, and it is less. A woman must be frank, delicate, sensitive, refined, impressionable. She has no need of either power or initiative in thought, but she must have kindness, elegance, tenderness, coquetry and that faculty of assimilation which, in a little while, raises her to an equality with him who shares her life. Her greatest quality must be tact, that subtle sense which is to the mind what touch is to the body. It reveals to her a thousand little things, contours, angles and forms on the plane of the intellectual.

Very frequently pretty women have not intellect to correspond with their personal charms. Now, the slightest lack of harmony strikes me and pains me at the first glance. In friendship this is not of importance. Friendship is a compact in which one fairly shares defects and merits. We may judge of friends, whether man or woman, giving them credit for what is good, and overlooking what is bad in them, appreciating them at their just value, while giving ourselves up to an intimate, intense and charming sympathy.

In order to love, one must be blind, surrender one's self absolutely, see nothing, question nothing, understand nothing. One must adore the weakness as well as the beauty of the beloved object, renounce all judgment, all reflection, all perspicacity.

I am incapable of such blindness and rebel at unreasoning subjugation. This is not all. I have such a high and subtle idea of harmony that nothing can ever fulfill my ideal. But you will call me a madman. Listen to me. A woman, in my opinion, may have an exquisite soul and charming body without that body and that soul being in perfect harmony with one another. I mean that persons who have noses made in a certain shape should not be expected to think in a certain fashion. The fat have no right to make use of the same words and phrases as the thin. You, who have blue eyes, madame, cannot look at life and judge of things and events as if you had black eyes. The shade of your eyes should correspond, by a sort of fatality, with the shade of your thought. In perceiving these things, I have the scent of a bloodhound. Laugh if you like, but it is so.

And yet, once I imagined that I was in love for an hour, for a day. I had foolishly yielded to the influence of surrounding circumstances. I allowed myself to be beguiled by a mirage of Dawn. Would you like me to tell you this short story?

I met, one evening, a pretty, enthusiastic little woman who took a poetic fancy to spend a night with me in a boat on a river. I would have preferred a room and a bed; however, I consented to the river and the boat.

It was in the month of June. My fair companion chose a moonlight night in order the better to stimulate her imagination.

We had dined at a riverside inn and set out in the boat about ten o'clock. I thought it a rather foolish kind of adventure, but as my companion pleased me I did not worry about it. I sat down on the seat facing her; I seized the oars, and off we starred.

I could not deny that the scene was picturesque. We glided past a wooded isle full of nightingales, and the current carried us rapidly over the river covered with silvery ripples. The tree toads uttered their shrill, monotonous cry; the frogs croaked in the grass by the river's bank, and the lapping of the water as it flowed on made around us a kind of confused murmur almost imperceptible, disquieting, and gave us a vague sensation of mysterious fear.

The sweet charm of warm nights and of streams glittering in the moonlight penetrated us. It was delightful to be alive and to float along thus, and to dream and to feel at one's side a sympathetic and beautiful young woman.

I was somewhat affected, somewhat agitated, somewhat intoxicated by the pale brightness of the night and the consciousness of my proximity to a lovely woman.

"Come and sit beside me," she said.

I obeyed.

She went on:

"Recite some poetry for me."

This appeared to be rather too much. I declined; she persisted. She certainly wanted to play the game, to have a whole orchestra of sentiment, from the moon to the rhymes of poets. In the end I had to yield, and, as if in mockery, I repeated to her a charming little poem by Louis Bouilhet, of which the following are the last verses:

"I hate the poet who with tearful eye

Murmurs some name while gazing tow'rds a star,

Who sees no magic in the earth or sky,

Unless Lizette or Ninon be not far.

"The bard who in all Nature nothing sees

Divine, unless a petticoat he ties

Amorously to the branches of the trees

Or nightcap to the grass, is scarcely wise.

"He has not heard the Eternal's thunder tone,

The voice of Nature in her various moods,

Who cannot tread the dim ravines alone,

And of no woman dream mid whispering woods."

I expected some reproaches. Nothing of the sort. She murmured:

"How true it is!"

I was astonished. Had she understood?

Our boat had gradually approached the bank and become entangled in the branches of a willow which impeded its progress. I placed my arm round my companion's waist, and very gently approached my lips towards her neck. But she repulsed me with an abrupt, angry movement.

"Have done, pray! How rude you are!"

I tried to draw her toward me. She resisted, caught hold of the tree, and was near flinging us both into the water. I deemed it prudent to cease my importunities.

She said:

"I would rather capsize you. I feel so happy. I want to dream. This is so delightful." Then, in a slightly malicious tone, she added:

"Have you already forgotten the verses you repeated to me just now?"

She was right. I became silent.

She went on:

"Come, now!"

And I plied the oars once more.

I began to think the night long and my position ridiculous.

My companion said to me:

"Will you make me a promise?"

"Yes. What is it?"

"To remain quiet, well-behaved and discreet, if I permit you—"

"What? Say what you mean!"

"Here is what I mean: I want to lie down on my back at the bottom of the boat with you by my side. But I forbid you to touch me, to embrace me —in short—to caress me."

I promised. She said warningly:

"If you move, 'I'll capsize the boat."

And then we lay down side by side, our eyes turned toward the sky, while the boat glided slowly through the water. We were rocked by its gentle motion. The slight sounds of the night came to us more distinctly in the bottom of the boat, sometimes causing us to start. And I felt springing up within me a strange, poignant emotion, an infinite tenderness, something like an irresistible impulse to open my arms in order to embrace, to open my heart in order to love, to give myself, to give my thoughts, my body, my life, my entire being to some one.

My companion murmured, like one in a dream:

"Where are we; Where are we going? It seems to me that I am leaving the earth. How sweet it is! Ah, if you loved me—a little!!!"

My heart began to throb. I had no answer to give. It seemed to me that I loved her. I had no longer any violent desire. I felt happy there by her side, and that was enough for me.

And thus we remained for a long, long time without stirring. We had clasped each other's hands; some delightful force rendered us motionless, an unknown force stronger than ourselves, an alliance, chaste, intimate, absolute, of our beings lying there side by side, belonging to each other without contact. What was this? How do I know? Love, perhaps?

Little by little the dawn appeared. It was three o'clock in the morning. Slowly a great brightness spread over the sky. The boat knocked up against something. I rose up. We had come close to a tiny islet.

But I remained enchanted, in an ecstasy. Before us stretched the firmament, red, pink, violet, spotted with fiery clouds resembling golden vapor. The river was glowing with purple and three houses on one side of it seemed to be burning.

I bent toward my companion. I was going to say, "Oh! look!" But I held my tongue, quite dazed, and I could no longer see anything except her. She, too, was rosy, with rosy flesh tints with a deeper tinge that was partly a reflection of the hue of the sky. Her tresses were rosy; her eyes were rosy; her teeth were rosy; her dress, her laces, her smile, all were rosy. And in truth I believed, so overpowering was the illusion, that the dawn was there in the flesh before me.

She rose softly to her feet, holding out her lips to me; and I moved toward her, trembling, delirious feeling indeed that I was going to kiss Heaven, to kiss happiness, to kiss a dream that had become a woman, to kiss the ideal which had descended into human flesh.

She said to me: "You have a caterpillar in your hair." And, suddenly, I felt as sad as if I had lost all hope in life.

That is all, madame. It is puerile, silly, stupid. But I am sure that since that day it would be impossible for me to love. And yet—who can tell?

[The young man upon whom this letter was found was yesterday taken out of the Seine between Bougival and Marly. An obliging bargeman, who had searched the pockets in order to ascertain the name of the deceased, brought this paper to the author.]

THE ORPHAN

Mademoiselle Source had adopted this boy under very sad circumstances. She was at the time thirty-six years old. Being disfigured through having as a child slipped off her nurse's lap into the fireplace and burned her face shockingly, she had determined not to marry, for she did not want any man to marry her for her money.

A neighbor of hers, left a widow just before her child was born, died in giving birth, without leaving a sou. Mademoiselle Source took the new-born child, put him out to nurse, reared him, sent him to a boarding-school, then brought him home in his fourteenth year, in order to have in her empty house somebody who would love her, who would look after her, and make her old age pleasant.

She had a little country place four leagues from Rennes, and she now dispensed with a servant; her expenses having increased to more than double since this orphan's arrival, her income of three thousand francs was no longer sufficient to support three persons.

She attended to the housekeeping and cooking herself, and sent out the boy on errands, letting him also occupy himself in cultivating the garden. He was gentle, timid, silent, and affectionate. And she experienced a deep happiness, a fresh happiness when he kissed her without surprise or horror at her disfigurement. He called her "Aunt," and treated her as a mother.

In the evening they both sat down at the fireside, and she made nice little dainties for him. She heated some wine and toasted a slice of bread, and it made a charming little meal before going to bed. She often took him on her knees and covered him with kisses, murmuring tender words in his ear. She called him: "My little flower, my cherub, my adored angel, my divine jewel." He softly accepted her caresses, hiding his head on the old maid's shoulder. Although he was now nearly fifteen, he had remained small and weak, and had a rather sickly appearance.

Sometimes Mademoiselle Source took him to the city, to see two married female relatives of hers, distant cousins, who were living in the suburbs, and who were the only members of her family in existence. The two women had always found fault with her, for having adopted this boy, on account of the inheritance; but for all that, they gave her a cordial welcome, having still hopes of getting a share for themselves, a third, no doubt, if what she possessed were only equally divided.

She was happy, very happy, always occupied with her adopted child. She bought books for him to improve his mind, and he became passionately fond of reading.

He no longer climbed on her knee to pet her as he had formerly done; but, instead, would go and sit down in his little chair in the chimney-corner and open a volume. The lamp placed at the edge of the Tittle table above his head shone on his curly hair, and on a portion of his forehead; he did not move, he did not raise his eyes or make any gesture. He read on, interested, entirely absorbed in the story he was reading.

Seated opposite to him, she would gaze at him earnestly, astonished at his studiousness, often on the point of bursting into tears.

She said to him occasionally: "You will fatigue yourself, my treasure!" hoping that he would raise his head, and come across to embrace her; but he did not even answer her; he had not heard or understood what she was saying; he paid no attention to anything save what he read in those pages.

For two years he devoured an incalculable number of volumes. His character changed.

After this, he asked Mademoiselle Source several times for money, which she gave him. As he always wanted more, she ended by refusing, for she was both methodical and decided, and knew how to act rationally when it was necessary to do so. By dint of entreaties he obtained a large sum from her one night; but when he begged her for more a few days later, she showed herself inflexible, and did not give way to him further, in fact.

He appeared to be satisfied with her decision.

He again became quiet, as he had formerly been, remaining seated for entire hours, without moving, plunged in deep reverie. He now did not even talk to Madame Source, merely answering her remarks with short, formal words. Nevertheless, he was agreeable and attentive in his manner toward her; but he never embraced her now.

She had by this time grown slightly afraid of him when they sat facing one another at night on opposite sides of the fireplace. She wanted to wake him up, to make him say something, no matter what, that would break this dreadful silence, which was like the darkness of a wood. But he did not appear to listen to her, and she shuddered with the terror of a poor feeble woman when she had spoken to him five or six times successively without being able to get a word out of him.

What was the matter with him? What was going on in that closed-up head? When she had remained thus two or three hours opposite him, she felt as if she were going insane, and longed to rush away and to escape into the open country in order to avoid that mute, eternal companionship and also some vague danger, which she could not define, but of which she had a presentiment.

She frequently wept when she was alone. What was the matter with him? When she expressed a wish, he unmurmuringly carried it into execution. When she wanted anything brought from the city, he immediately went there to procure it. She had no complaint to make of him; no, indeed! And yet—

Another year flitted by, and it seemed to her that a fresh change had taken place in the mind of the young man. She perceived it; she felt it; she divined it. How? No matter! She was sure she was not mistaken; but she could not have explained in what manner the unknown thoughts of this strange youth had changed.

It seemed to her that, until now, he had been like a person in a hesitating frame of mind, who had suddenly arrived at a determination. This idea came to her one evening as she met his glance, a fixed, singular glance which she had not seen in his face before.

Then he commenced to watch her incessantly, and she wished she could hide herself in order to avoid that cold eye riveted on her.

He kept staring at her, evening after evening, for hours together, only averting his eyes when she said, utterly unnerved:

"Do not look at me like that, my child!"

Then he would lower his head.

But the moment her back was turned she once more felt that his eyes were upon her. Wherever she went, he pursued her with his persistent gaze.

Sometimes, when she was walking in her little garden, she suddenly noticed him hidden behind a bush, as if he were lying in wait for her; and, again, when she sat in front of the house mending stockings while he was digging some vegetable bed, he kept continually watching her in a surreptitious manner, as he worked.

It was in vain that she asked him:

"What's the matter with you, my boy? For the last three years, you have become very different. I don't recognize you. Do tell me what ails you, and what you are thinking of."

He invariably replied, in a quiet, weary tone:

"Why, nothing ails me, aunt!"

And when she persisted:

"Ah! my child, answer me, answer me when I speak to you. If you knew what grief you caused me, you would always answer, and you would not look at me that way. Have you any trouble? Tell me! I'll comfort you!"

He went away, with a tired air, murmuring:

"But there is nothing the matter with me, I assure you."

He had not grown much, having always a childish look, although his features were those of a man. They were, however, hard and badly cut. He seemed incomplete, abortive, only half finished, and disquieting as a mystery. He was a self-contained, unapproachable being, in whom there seemed always to be some active, dangerous mental labor going on. Mademoiselle Source was quite conscious of all this, and she could not sleep at night, so great was her anxiety. Frightful terrors, dreadful nightmares assailed her. She shut herself up in her own room, and barricaded the door, tortured by fear.

What was she afraid of? She could not tell.

She feared everything, the night, the walls, the shadows thrown by the moon on the white curtains of the windows, and, above all, she feared him.

Why?

What had she to fear? Did she know what it was?

She could live this way no longer! She felt certain that a misfortune threatened her, a frightful misfortune.

She set forth secretly one morning, and went into the city to see her relatives. She told them about the matter in a gasping voice. The two women thought she was going mad and tried to reassure her.

She said:

"If you knew the way he looks at me from morning till night. He never takes his eyes off me! At times, I feel a longing to cry for help, to call in the neighbors, so much am I afraid. But what could I say to them? He does nothing but look at me."

The two female cousins asked:

"Is he ever brutal to you? Does he give you sharp answers?"

She replied:

"No, never; he does everything I wish; he works hard: he is steady; but I am so frightened that I care nothing for that. He is planning something, I am certain of that—quite certain. I don't care to remain all alone like that with him in the country."

The relatives, astonished at her words, declared that people would be amazed, would not understand; and they advised her to keep silent about her fears and her plans, without, however, dissuading her from coming to reside in the city, hoping in that way that the entire inheritance would eventually fall into their hands.

They even promised to assist her in selling her house, and in finding another, near them.

Mademoiselle Source returned home. But her mind was so much upset that she trembled at the slightest noise, and her hands shook whenever any trifling disturbance agitated her.

Twice she went again to consult her relatives, quite determined now not to remain any longer in this way in her lonely dwelling. At last, she found a little cottage in the suburbs, which suited her, and she privately bought it.

The signature of the contract took place on a Tuesday morning, and Mademoiselle Source devoted the rest of the day to the preparations for her change of residence.

At eight o'clock in the evening she got into the diligence which passed within a few hundred yards of her house, and she told the conductor to put her down in the place where she usually alighted. The man called out to her as he whipped his horses:

"Good evening, Mademoiselle Source—good night!"

She replied as she walked on:

"Good evening, Pere Joseph." Next morning, at half-past seven, the postman who conveyed letters to the village noticed at the cross-road, not far from the high road, a large splash of blood not yet dry. He said to himself: "Hallo! some boozer must have had a nose bleed."

But he perceived ten paces farther on a pocket handkerchief also stained with blood. He picked it up. The linen was fine, and the postman, in alarm, made his way over to the ditch, where he fancied he saw a strange object.

Mademoiselle Source was lying at the bottom on the grass, her throat cut with a knife.

An hour later, the gendarmes, the examining magistrate, and other authorities made an inquiry as to the cause of death.

The two female relatives, called as witnesses, told all about the old maid's fears and her last plans.

The orphan was arrested. After the death of the woman who had adopted him, he wept from morning till night, plunged, at least to all appearance, in the most violent grief.

He proved that he had spent the evening up to eleven o'clock in a cafe. Ten persons had seen him, having remained there till his departure.

The driver of the diligence stated that he had set down the murdered woman on the road between half-past nine and ten o'clock.

The accused was acquitted. A will, drawn up a long time before, which had been left in the hands of a notary in Rennes, made him sole heir. So he inherited everything.

For a long time, the people of the country boycotted him, as they still suspected him. His house, that of the dead woman, was looked upon as accursed. People avoided him in the street.

But he showed himself so good-natured, so open, so familiar, that gradually these horrible doubts were forgotten. He was generous, obliging, ready to talk to the humblest about anything, as long as they cared to talk to him.

The notary, Maitre Rameau, was one of the first to take his part, attracted by his smiling loquacity. He said at a dinner, at the tax collector's house:

"A man who speaks with such facility and who is always in good humor could not have such a crime on his conscience."

Touched by his argument, the others who were present reflected, and they recalled to mind the long conversations with this man who would almost compel them to stop at the road corners to listen to his ideas, who insisted on their going into his house when they were passing by his garden, who could crack a joke better than the lieutenant of the gendarmes himself, and who possessed such contagious gaiety that, in spite of the repugnance with which he inspired them, they could not keep from always laughing in his company.

All doors were opened to him after a time.

He is to-day the mayor of his township.

THE BEGGAR

He had seen better days, despite his present misery and infirmities.

At the age of fifteen both his legs had been crushed by a carriage on the Varville highway. From that time forth he begged, dragging himself along the roads and through the farmyards, supported by crutches which forced his shoulders up to his ears. His head looked as if it were squeezed in between two mountains.

A foundling, picked up out of a ditch by the priest of Les Billettes on the eve of All Saints' Day and baptized, for that reason, Nicholas Toussaint, reared by charity, utterly without education, crippled in consequence of having drunk several glasses of brandy given him by the baker (such a funny story!) and a vagabond all his life afterward—the only thing he knew how to do was to hold out his hand for alms.

At one time the Baroness d'Avary allowed him to sleep in a kind of recess spread with straw, close to the poultry yard in the farm adjoining the chateau, and if he was in great need he was sure of getting a glass of cider and a crust of bread in the kitchen. Moreover, the old lady often threw him a few pennies from her window. But she was dead now.

In the villages people gave him scarcely anything—he was too well known. Everybody had grown tired of seeing him, day after day for forty years, dragging his deformed and tattered person from door to door on his wooden crutches. But he could not make up his mind to go elsewhere, because he knew no place on earth but this particular corner of the country, these three or four villages where he had spent the whole of his miserable existence. He had limited his begging operations and would not for worlds have passed his accustomed bounds.

He did not even know whether the world extended for any distance beyond the trees which had always bounded his vision. He did not ask himself the question. And when the peasants, tired of constantly meeting him in their fields or along their lanes, exclaimed: "Why don't you go to other villages instead of always limping about here?" he did not answer, but slunk away, possessed with a vague dread of the unknown—the dread of a poor wretch who fears confusedly a thousand things— new faces, taunts, insults, the suspicious glances of people who do not know him and the policemen walking in couples on the roads. These last he always instinctively avoided, taking refuge in the bushes or behind heaps of stones when he saw them coming.

When he perceived them in the distance, 'With uniforms gleaming in the sun, he was suddenly possessed with unwonted agility—the agility of a wild animal seeking its lair. He threw aside his crutches, fell to the ground like a limp rag, made himself as small as possible and crouched like a bare under cover, his tattered vestments blending in hue with the earth on which he cowered.

He had never had any trouble with the police, but the instinct to avoid them was in his blood. He seemed to have inherited it from the parents he had never known.

He had no refuge, no roof for his head, no shelter of any kind. In summer he slept out of doors and in winter he showed remarkable skill in slipping unperceived into barns and stables. He always decamped before his presence could be discovered. He knew all the holes through which one could creep into farm buildings, and the handling of his crutches having made his arms surprisingly muscular he often hauled himself up through sheer strength of wrist into hay-lofts, where he sometimes remained for four or five days at a time, provided he had collected a sufficient store of food beforehand.

He lived like the beasts of the field. He was in the midst of men, yet knew no one, loved no one, exciting in the breasts of the peasants only a sort of careless contempt and smoldering hostility. They nicknamed him "Bell," because he hung between his two crutches like a church bell between its supports.

For two days he had eaten nothing. No one gave him anything now. Every one's patience was exhausted. Women shouted to him from their doorsteps when they saw him coming:

"Be off with you, you good-for-nothing vagabond! Why, I gave you a piece of bread only three days ago!"

And he turned on his crutches to the next house, where he was received in the same fashion.

The women declared to one another as they stood at their doors:

"We can't feed that lazy brute all the year round!"

And yet the "lazy brute" needed food every day.

He had exhausted Saint-Hilaire, Varville and Les Billettes without getting a single copper or so much as a dry crust. His only hope was in Tournolles, but to reach this place he would have to walk five miles along the highroad, and he felt so weary that he could hardly drag himself another yard. His stomach and his pocket were equally empty, but he started on his way.

It was December and a cold wind blew over the fields and whistled through the bare branches of the trees; the clouds careered madly across the black, threatening sky. The cripple dragged himself slowly along, raising one crutch after the other with a painful effort, propping himself on the one distorted leg which remained to him.

Now and then he sat down beside a ditch for a few moments' rest. Hunger was gnawing his vitals, and in his confused, slow-working mind he had only one idea-to eat-but how this was to be accomplished he did not know. For three hours he continued his painful journey. Then at last the sight of the trees of the village inspired him with new energy.

The first peasant he met, and of whom he asked alms, replied:

"So it's you again, is it, you old scamp? Shall I never be rid of you?"

And "Bell" went on his way. At every door he got nothing but hard words. He made the round of the whole village, but received not a halfpenny for his pains.

Then he visited the neighboring farms, toiling through the muddy land, so exhausted that he could hardly raise his crutches from the ground. He met with the same reception everywhere. It was one of those cold, bleak days, when the heart is frozen and the temper irritable, and hands do not open either to give money or food.

When he had visited all the houses he knew, "Bell" sank down in the corner of a ditch running across Chiquet's farmyard. Letting his crutches slip to the ground, he remained motionless, tortured by hunger, but hardly intelligent enough to realize to the full his unutterable misery.

He awaited he knew not what, possessed with that vague hope which persists in the human heart in spite of everything. He awaited in the corner of the farmyard in the biting December wind, some mysterious aid from Heaven or from men, without the least idea whence it was to arrive. A number of black hens ran hither and thither, seeking their food in the earth which supports all living things. Ever now and then they snapped up in their beaks a grain of corn or a tiny insect; then they continued their slow, sure search for nutriment.

"Bell" watched them at first without thinking of anything. Then a thought occurred rather to his stomach than to his mind—the thought that one of those fowls would be good to eat if it were cooked over a fire of dead wood.

He did not reflect that he was going to commit a theft. He took up a stone which lay within reach, and, being of skillful aim, killed at the first shot the fowl nearest to him. The bird fell on its side, flapping its wings. The others fled wildly hither and thither, and "Bell," picking up his crutches, limped across to where his victim lay.

Just as he reached the little black body with its crimsoned head he received a violent blow in his back which made him let go his hold of his crutches and sent him flying ten paces distant. And Farmer Chiquet, beside himself with rage, cuffed and kicked the marauder with all the fury of a plundered peasant as "Bell" lay defenceless before him.

The farm hands came up also and joined their master in cuffing the lame beggar. Then when they were tired of beating him they carried him off and shut him up in the woodshed, while they went to fetch the police.

"Bell," half dead, bleeding and perishing with hunger, lay on the floor. Evening came—then night—then dawn. And still he had not eaten.

About midday the police arrived. They opened the door of the woodshed with the utmost precaution, fearing resistance on the beggar's part, for Farmer Chiquet asserted that he had been attacked by him and had had great, difficulty in defending himself.

The sergeant cried:

"Come, get up!"

But "Bell" could not move. He did his best to raise himself on his crutches, but without success. The police, thinking his weakness feigned, pulled him up by main force and set him between the crutches.

Fear seized him—his native fear of a uniform, the fear of the game in presence of the sportsman, the fear of a mouse for a cat-and by the exercise of almost superhuman effort he succeeded in remaining upright.

"Forward!" said the sergeant. He walked. All the inmates of the farm watched his departure. The women shook their fists at him the men scoffed at and insulted him. He was taken at last! Good riddance! He went off between his two guards. He mustered sufficient energy—the energy of despair—to drag himself along until the evening, too dazed to know what was happening to him, too frightened to understand.

People whom he met on the road stopped to watch him go by and peasants muttered:

"It's some thief or other."

Toward evening he reached the country town. He had never been so far before. He did not realize in the least what he was there for or what was to become of him. All the terrible and unexpected events of the last two days, all these unfamiliar faces and houses struck dismay into his heart.

He said not a word, having nothing to say because he understood nothing. Besides, he had spoken to no one for so many years past that he had almost lost the use of his tongue, and his thoughts were too indeterminate to be put into words.

He was shut up in the town jail. It did not occur to the police that he might need food, and he was left alone until the following day. But when in the early morning they came to examine him he was found dead on the floor. Such an astonishing thing!

THE RABBIT

Old Lecacheur appeared at the door of his house between five and a quarter past five in the morning, his usual hour, to watch his men going to work.

He was only half awake, his face was red, and with his right eye open and the left nearly closed, he was buttoning his braces over his fat stomach with some difficulty, at the same time looking into every corner of the farmyard with a searching glance. The sun darted its oblique rays through the beech trees by the side of the ditch and athwart the apple trees outside, and was making the cocks crow on the dunghill, and the pigeons coo on the roof. The smell of the cow stable came through the open door, and blended in the fresh morning air with the pungent odor of the stable, where the horses were neighing, with their heads turned toward the light.

As soon as his trousers were properly fastened, Lecacheur came out, and went, first of all, toward the hen house to count the morning's eggs, for he had been afraid of thefts for some time; but the servant girl ran up to him with lifted arms and cried:

"Master! master! they have stolen a rabbit during the night."

"A rabbit?"

"Yes, master, the big gray rabbit, from the hutch on the left"; whereupon the farmer completely opened his left eye, and said, simply:

"I must see about that."

And off he went to inspect it. The hutch had been broken open and the rabbit was gone. Then he became thoughtful, closed his right eye again, and scratched his nose, and after a little consideration, he said to the frightened girl, who was standing stupidly before her master:

"Go and fetch the gendarmes; say I expect them as soon as possible."

Lecacheur was mayor of the village, Pavigny-le-Gras, and ruled it like a master, on account of his money and position, and as soon as the servant had disappeared in the direction of the village, which was only about five hundred yards off, he went into the house to have his morning coffee and to discuss the matter with his wife, whom he found on her knees in front of the fire, trying to make it burn quickly, and as soon as he got to the door, he said:

"Somebody has stolen the gray rabbit."

She turned round so suddenly that she found herself sitting on the floor, and looking at her husband with distressed eyes, she said:

"What is it, Cacheux? Somebody has stolen a rabbit?"

"The big gray one."

She sighed.

"What a shame! Who can have done it?"

She was a little, thin, active, neat woman, who knew all about farming. Lecacheur had his own ideas about the matter.

"It must be that fellow, Polyte."

His wife got up suddenly and said in a furious voice:

"He did it! he did it! You need not look for any one else. He did it! You have said it, Cacheux!"

All her peasant's fury, all her avarice, all her rage of a saving woman against the man of whom she had always been suspicious, and against the girl whom she had always suspected, showed themselves in the contraction of her mouth, and the wrinkles in the cheeks and forehead of her thin, exasperated face.

"And what have you done?" she asked.

"I have sent for the gendarmes."

This Polyte was a laborer, who had been employed on the farm for a few days, and who had been dismissed by Lecacheur for an insolent answer. He was an old soldier, and was supposed to have retained his habits of marauding and debauchery front his campaigns in Africa. He did anything for a livelihood, but whether he were a mason, a navvy, a reaper, whether he broke stones or lopped trees, he was always lazy, and so he remained nowhere for long, and had, at times, to change his neighborhood to obtain work.

From the first day that he came to the farm, Lecacheur's wife had detested him, and now she was sure that he had committed the theft.

In about half an hour the two gendarmes arrived. Brigadier Senateur was very tall and thin, and Gendarme Lenient short and fat. Lecacheur made them sit down, and told them the affair, and then they went and saw the scene of the theft, in order to verify the fact that the hutch had been broken open, and to collect all the proofs they could. When they got back to the kitchen, the mistress brought in some wine, filled their glasses, and asked with a distrustful look:

"Shall you catch him?"

The brigadier, who had his sword between his legs, appeared thoughtful. Certainly, he was sure of taking him, if he was pointed out to him, but if not, he could not answer for being able to discover him, himself, and after reflecting for a long time, he put this simple question:

"Do you know the thief?"

And Lecacheur replied, with a look of Normandy slyness in his eyes:

"As for knowing him, I do not, as I did not see him commit the theft. If I had seen him, I should have made him eat it raw, skin and flesh, without a drop of cider to wash it down. But as for saying who it is, I cannot, although I believe it is that good-for-nothing Polyte."

Then he related at length his troubles with Polyte, his leaving his service, his bad reputation, things which had been told him, accumulating insignificant and minute proofs, and then, the brigadier, who had been listening very attentively while he emptied his glass and filled it again with an indifferent air, turned to his gendarme and said:

"We must go and look in the cottage of Severin's wife." At which the gendarme smiled and nodded three times.

Then Madame Lecacheur came to them, and very quietly, with all a peasant's cunning, questioned the brigadier in her turn. That shepherd Severin, a simpleton, a sort of brute who had been brought up and had grown up among his bleating flocks, and who knew scarcely anything besides them in the world, had nevertheless preserved the peasant's instinct for saving, at the bottom of his heart. For years and years he must have hidden in hollow trees and crevices in the rocks all that he earned, either as a shepherd or by curing animals' sprains—for the bonesetter's secret had been handed down to him by the old shepherd whose place he took-by touch or word, and one day he bought a small property, consisting of a cottage and a field, for three thousand francs.

A few months later it became known that he was going to marry a servant, notorious for her bad morals, the innkeeper's servant. The young fellows said that the girl, knowing that he was pretty well off, had been to his cottage every night, and had taken him, captured him, led him on to matrimony, little by little night by night.

And then, having been to the mayor's office and to church, she now lived in the house which her man had bought, while he continued to tend his flocks, day and night, on the plains.

And the brigadier added:

"Polyte has been sleeping there for three weeks, for the thief has no place of his own to go to!"

The gendarme made a little joke:

"He takes the shepherd's blankets."

Madame Lecacheur, who was seized by a fresh access of rage, of rage increased by a married woman's anger against debauchery, exclaimed:

"It is she, I am sure. Go there. Ah, the blackguard thieves!"

But the brigadier was quite unmoved.

"One minute," he said. "Let us wait until twelve o'clock, as he goes and dines there every day. I shall catch them with it under their noses."

The gendarme smiled, pleased at his chief's idea, and Lecacheur also smiled now, for the affair of the shepherd struck him as very funny; deceived husbands are always a joke.

Twelve o'clock had just struck when the brigadier, followed by his man, knocked gently three times at the door of a little lonely house, situated at the corner of a wood, five hundred yards from the village.

They had been standing close against the wall, so as not to be seen from within, and they waited. As nobody answered, the brigadier knocked again in a minute or two. It was so quiet that the house seemed uninhabited; but Lenient, the gendarme, who had very quick ears, said that he heard somebody moving about inside, and then Senateur got angry. He would not allow any one to resist the authority of the law for a moment, and, knocking at the door with the hilt of his sword, he cried out:

"Open the door, in the name of the law."

As this order had no effect, he roared out:

"If you do not obey, I shall smash the lock. I am the brigadier of the gendarmerie, by G—! Here, Lenient."

He had not finished speaking when the door opened and Senateur saw before him a fat girl, with a very red, blowzy face, with drooping breasts, a big stomach and broad hips, a sort of animal, the wife of the shepherd Severin, and he went into the cottage.

"I have come to pay you a visit, as I want to make a little search," he said, and he looked about him. On the table there was a plate, a jug of cider and a glass half full, which proved that a meal was in progress. Two knives were lying side by side, and the shrewd gendarme winked at his superior officer.

"It smells good," the latter said.

"One might swear that it was stewed rabbit," Lenient added, much amused.

"Will you have a glass of brandy?" the peasant woman asked.

"No, thank you; I only want the skin of the rabbit that you are eating."

She pretended not to understand, but she was trembling.

"What rabbit?"

The brigadier had taken a seat, and was calmly wiping his forehead.

"Come, come, you are not going to try and make us believe that you live on couch grass. What were you eating there all by yourself for your dinner?"

"I? Nothing whatever, I swear to you. A mite of butter on my bread."

"You are a novice, my good woman. A mite of butter on your bread. You are mistaken; you ought to have said: a mite of butter on the rabbit. By G—, your butter smells good! It is special butter, extra good butter, butter fit for a wedding; certainly, not household butter!"

The gendarme was shaking with laughter, and repeated:

"Not household butter certainly."

As Brigadier Senateur was a joker, all the gendarmes had grown facetious, and the officer continued:

"Where is your butter?"

"My butter?"

"Yes, your butter."

"In the jar."

"Then where is the butter jar?"

"Here it is."

She brought out an old cup, at the bottom of which there was a layer of rancid salt butter, and the brigadier smelled of it, and said, with a shake of his head:

"It is not the same. I want the butter that smells of the rabbit. Come, Lenient, open your eyes; look under the sideboard, my good fellow, and I will look under the bed."

Having shut the door, he went up to the bed and tried to move it; but it was fixed to the wall, and had not been moved for more than half a century, apparently. Then the brigadier stooped, and made his uniform crack. A button had flown off.

"Lenient," he said.

"Yes, brigadier?"

"Come here, my lad, and look under the bed; I am too tall. I will look after the sideboard."

He got up and waited while his man executed his orders.

Lenient, who was short and stout, took off his kepi, laid himself on his stomach, and, putting his face on the floor, looked at the black cavity under the bed, and then, suddenly, he exclaimed:

"All right, here we are!"

"What have you got? The rabbit?"

"No, the thief."

"The thief! Pull him out, pull him out!"

The gendarme had put his arms under the bed and laid hold of something, and he was pulling with all his might, and at last a foot, shod in a thick boot, appeared, which he was holding in his right hand. The brigadier took it, crying:

"Pull! Pull!"

And Lenient, who was on his knees by that time, was pulling at the other leg. But it was a hard job, for the prisoner kicked out hard, and arched up his back under the bed.

"Courage! courage! pull! pull!" Senateur cried, and they pulled him with all their strength, so that the wooden slat gave way, and he came out as far as his head; but at last they got that out also, and they saw the terrified and furious face of Polyte, whose arms remained stretched out under the bed.

"Pull away!" the brigadier kept on exclaiming. Then they heard a strange noise, and as the arms followed the shoulders, and the hands the arms, they saw in the hands the handle of a saucepan, and at the end of the handle the saucepan itself, which contained stewed rabbit.

"Good Lord! good Lord!" the brigadier shouted in his delight, while Lenient took charge of the man; the rabbit's skin, an overwhelming proof, was discovered under the mattress, and then the gendarmes returned in triumph to the village with their prisoner and their booty.

A week later, as the affair had made much stir, Lecacheur, on going into the mairie to consult the schoolmaster, was told that the shepherd Severin had been waiting for him for more than an hour, and he found him sitting on a chair in a corner, with his stick between his legs. When he saw the mayor, he got up, took off his cap, and said:

"Good-morning, Maitre Cacheux"; and then he remained standing, timid and embarrassed.

"What do you want?" the former said.

"This is it, monsieur. Is it true that somebody stole one of your rabbits last week?"

"Yes, it is quite true, Severin."

"Who stole the rabbit?"

"Polyte Ancas, the laborer."

"Right! right! And is it also true that it was found under my bed?"

"What do you mean, the rabbit?"

"The rabbit and then Polyte."

"Yes, my poor Severin, quite true, but who told you?"

"Pretty well everybody. I understand! And I suppose you know all about marriages, as you marry people?"

"What about marriage?"

"With regard to one's rights."

"What rights?"

"The husband's rights and then the wife's rights."

"Of course I do."

"Oh! Then just tell me, M'sieu Cacheux, has my wife the right to go to bed with Polyte?"

"What, to go to bed with Polyte?"

"Yes, has she any right before the law, and, seeing that she is my wife, to go to bed with Polyte?"

"Why, of course not, of course not."

"If I catch him there again, shall I have the right to thrash him and her also?"

"Why—why—why, yes."

"Very well, then; I will tell you why I want to know. One night last week, as I had my suspicions, I came in suddenly, and they were not behaving properly. I chucked Polyte out, to go and sleep somewhere else; but that was all, as I did not know what my rights were. This time I did not see them; I only heard of it from others. That is over, and we will not say any more about it; but if I catch them again—by G—, if I catch them again, I will make them lose all taste for such nonsense, Maitre Cacheux, as sure as my name is Severin."

HIS AVENGER

When M. Antoine Leuillet married the widow, Madame Mathilde Souris, he had already been in love with her for ten years.

M. Souris has been his friend, his old college chum. Leuillet was very much attached to him, but thought he was somewhat of a simpleton. He would often remark: "That poor Souris who will never set the world on fire."

When Souris married Miss Mathilde Duval, Leuillet was astonished and somewhat annoyed, as he was slightly devoted to her, himself. She was the daughter of a neighbor, a former proprietor of a draper's establishment who had retired with quite a small fortune. She married Souris for his money.

Then Leuillet thought he would start a flirtation with his friend's wife. He was a good-looking man, intelligent and also rich. He thought it would be all plain sailing, but he was mistaken. Then he really began to admire her with an admiration that his friendship for the husband obliged him to keep within the bounds of discretion, making him timid and embarrassed. Madame Souris believing that his presumptions had received a wholesome check now treated him as a good friend. This went on for nine years.

One morning a messenger brought Leuillet a distracted note from the poor woman. Souris had just died suddenly from the rupture of an aneurism. He was dreadfully shocked, for they were just the same age. But almost immediately a feeling of profound joy, of intense relief, of emancipation filled his being. Madame Souris was free.

He managed, however, to assume the sad, sympathetic expression that was appropriate, waited the required time, observed all social appearances. At the end of fifteen months he married the widow.

This was considered to be a very natural, and even a generous action. It was the act of a good friend of an upright man.

He was happy at last, perfectly happy.

They lived in the most cordial intimacy, having understood and appreciated each other from the first. They had no secrets from one another and even confided to each other their most secret thoughts. Leuillet loved his wife now with a quiet and trustful affection; he loved her as a tender, devoted companion who is an equal and a confidante. But there lingered in his mind a strange and inexplicable bitterness towards the defunct Souris, who had first been the husband of this woman, who had had the flower of her youth and of her soul, and had even robbed her of some of her poetry. The memory of the dead husband marred the happiness of the living husband, and this posthumous jealousy tormented his heart by day and by night.

The consequence was he talked incessantly of Souris, asked about a thousand personal and secret minutia, wanted to know all about his habits and his person. And he sneered at him even in his grave, recalling with self-satisfaction his whims, ridiculing his absurdities, dwelling on his faults.

He would call to his wife all over the house:

"Hallo, Mathilde!"

"Here I am, dear."

"Come here a moment."

She would come, always smiling, knowing well that he would say something about Souris and ready to flatter her new husband's inoffensive mania.

"Tell me, do you remember one day how Souris insisted on explaining to me that little men always commanded more affection than big men?"

And he made some remarks that were disparaging to the deceased, who was a small man, and decidedly flattering to himself, Leuillet, who was a tall man.

Mme. Leuillet allowed him to think he was right, quite right, and she laughed heartily, gently ridiculing her former husband for the sake of pleasing the present one, who always ended by saying:

"All the same, what a ninny that Souris was!"

They were happy, quite happy, and Leuillet never ceased to show his devotion to his wife.

One night, however, as they lay awake, Leuillet said as he kissed his wife:

"See here, dearie."

"Well?"

"Was Souris—I don't exactly know how to say it—was Souris very loving?"

She gave him a kiss for reply and murmured "Not as loving as you are, mon chat."

He was flattered in his self-love and continued:

"He must have been—a ninny—was he not?"

She did not reply. She only smiled slyly and hid her face in her husband's neck.

"He must have been a ninny and not—not—not smart?"

She shook her head slightly to imply, "No—not at all smart."

He continued:

"He must have been an awful nuisance, eh?"

This time she was frank and replied:

"Oh yes!"

He kissed her again for this avowal and said:

"What a brute he was! You were not happy with him?"

"No," she replied. "It was not always pleasant."

Leuillet was delighted, forming in his mind a comparison, much in his own favor, between his wife's former and present position. He was silent for a time, and then with a burst of laughter he asked:

"Tell me?"

"What?"

"Will you be frank, very frank with me?"

"Why yes, my dear."

"Well then, tell me truly did you never feel tempted to—to—to deceive that imbecile Souris?"

Mme. Leuillet said: "Oh!" pretending to be shocked and hid her face again on her husband's shoulder. But he saw that she was laughing.

"Come now, own up," he persisted. "He looked like a ninny, that creature! It would be funny, so funny! Good old Souris! Come, come, dearie, you do not mind telling me, me, of all people."

He insisted on the "me" thinking that if she had wished to deceive Souris she would have chosen him, and he was trembling in anticipation of her avowal, sure that if she had not been a virtuous woman she would have encouraged his own attentions.

But she did not answer, laughing still, as at the recollection of something exceedingly comical.

Leuillet, in his turn began to laugh, thinking he might have been the lucky man, and he muttered amid his mirth: "That poor Souris, that poor Souris, oh, yes, he looked like a fool!"

Mme. Leuillet was almost in spasms of laughter.

"Come, confess, be frank. You know I will not mind."

Then she stammered out, almost choking with laughter: "Yes, yes."

"Yes, what?" insisted her husband. "Come, tell all."

She was quieter now and putting her mouth to her husband's ear, she whispered: "Yes, I did deceive him."

He felt a chill run down his back and to his very bones, and he stammered out, dumfounded: "You—you—deceived him—criminally?"

She still thought he was amused and replied: "Yes—yes, absolutely."

He was obliged to sit up to recover his breath, he was so shocked and upset at what he had heard.

She had become serious, understanding too late what she had done.

"With whom?" said Leuillet at length.

She was silent seeking some excuse.

"A young man," she replied at length.

He turned suddenly toward her and said drily:

"I did not suppose it was the cook. I want to know what young man, do you hear?"

She did not answer.

He snatched the covers from her face, repeating:

"I want to know what young man, do you hear?"

Then she said sorrowfully: "I was only in fun." But he was trembling with rage. "What? How? You were only in fun? You were making fun of me, then? But I am not satisfied, do you hear? I want the name of the young man!"

She did not reply, but lay there motionless.

He took her by the arm and squeezed it, saying: "Do you understand me, finally? I wish you to reply when I speak to you."

"I think you are going crazy," she said nervously, "let me alone!"

He was wild with rage, not knowing what to say, exasperated, and he shook her with all his might, repeating:

"Do you hear me, do you hear me?"

She made an abrupt effort to disengage herself and the tips of her fingers touched her husband's nose. He was furious, thinking she had tried to hit him, and he sprang upon her holding her down; and boxing her ears with all his might, he cried: "Take that, and that, there, there, wretch!"

When he was out of breath and exhausted, he rose and went toward the dressing table to prepare a glass of eau sucree with orange flower, for he felt as if he should faint.

She was weeping in bed, sobbing bitterly, for she felt as if her happiness was over, through her own fault.

Then, amidst her tears, she stammered out:

"Listen, Antoine, come here, I told you a lie, you will understand, listen."

And prepared to defend herself now, armed with excuses and artifice, she raised her disheveled head with its nightcap all awry.

Turning toward her, he approached, ashamed of having struck her, but feeling in the bottom of his heart as a husband, a relentless hatred toward this woman who had deceived the former husband, Souris.

MY UNCLE JULES

A white-haired old man begged us for alms. My companion, Joseph Davranche, gave him five francs. Noticing my surprised look, he said:

"That poor unfortunate reminds me of a story which I shall tell you, the memory of which continually pursues me. Here it is:

"My family, which came originally from Havre, was not rich. We just managed to make both ends meet. My father worked hard, came home late from the office, and earned very little. I had two sisters.

"My mother suffered a good deal from our reduced circumstances, and she often had harsh words for her husband, veiled and sly reproaches. The poor man then made a gesture which used to distress me. He would pass his open hand over his forehead, as if to wipe away perspiration which did not exist, and he would answer nothing. I felt his helpless suffering. We economized on everything, and never would accept an invitation to dinner, so as not to have to return the courtesy. All our provisions were bought at bargain sales. My sisters made their own gowns, and long discussions would arise on the price of a piece of braid worth fifteen centimes a yard. Our meals usually consisted of soup and beef, prepared with every kind of sauce.

"They say it is wholesome and nourishing, but I should have preferred a change.

"I used to go through terrible scenes on account of lost buttons and torn trousers.

"Every Sunday, dressed in our best, we would take our walk along the breakwater. My father, in a frock coat, high hat and kid gloves, would offer his arm to my mother, decked out and beribboned like a ship on a holiday. My sisters, who were always ready first, would await the signal for leaving; but at the last minute some one always found a spot on my father's frock coat, and it had to be wiped away quickly with a rag moistened with benzine.

"My father, in his shirt sleeves, his silk hat on his head, would await the completion of the operation, while my mother, putting on her spectacles, and taking off her gloves in order not to spoil them, would make haste.

"Then we set out ceremoniously. My sisters marched on ahead, arm in arm. They were of marriageable age and had to be displayed. I walked on the left of my mother and my father on her right. I remember the pompous air of my poor parents in these Sunday walks, their stern expression, their stiff walk. They moved slowly, with a serious expression, their bodies straight, their legs stiff, as if something of extreme importance depended upon their appearance.

"Every Sunday, when the big steamers were returning from unknown and distant countries, my father would invariably utter the same words:

"'What a surprise it would be if Jules were on that one! Eh?'

"My Uncle Jules, my father's brother, was the only hope of the family, after being its only fear. I had heard about him since childhood, and it seemed to me that I should recognize him immediately, knowing as much about him as I did. I knew every detail of his life up to the day of his departure for America, although this period of his life was spoken of only in hushed tones.

"It seems that he had led a bad life, that is to say, he had squandered a little money, which action, in a poor family, is one of the greatest crimes. With rich people a man who amuses himself only sows his wild oats. He is what is generally called a sport. But among needy families a boy who forces his parents to break into the capital becomes a good-for-nothing, a rascal, a scamp. And this distinction is just, although the action be the same, for consequences alone determine the seriousness of the act.

"Well, Uncle Jules had visibly diminished the inheritance on which my father had counted, after he had swallowed his own to the last penny. Then, according to the custom of the times, he had been shipped off to America on a freighter going from Havre to New York.

"Once there, my uncle began to sell something or other, and he soon wrote that he was making a little money and that he soon hoped to be able to indemnify my father for the harm he had done him. This letter caused a profound emotion in the family. Jules, who up to that time had not been worth his salt, suddenly became a good man, a kind-hearted fellow, true and honest like all the Davranches.

"One of the captains told us that he had rented a large shop and was doing an important business.

"Two years later a second letter came, saying: 'My dear Philippe, I am writing to tell you not to worry about my health, which is excellent. Business is good. I leave to-morrow for a long trip to South America. I may be away for several years without sending you any news. If I shouldn't write, don't worry. When my fortune is made I shall return to Havre. I hope that it will not be too long and that we shall all live happily together . . . .'

"This letter became the gospel of the family. It was read on the slightest provocation, and it was shown to everybody.

"For ten years nothing was heard from Uncle Jules; but as time went on my father's hope grew, and my mother, also, often said:

"'When that good Jules is here, our position will be different. There is one who knew how to get along!'

"And every Sunday, while watching the big steamers approaching from the horizon, pouring out a stream of smoke, my father would repeat his eternal question:

"'What a surprise it would be if Jules were on that one! Eh?'

"We almost expected to see him waving his handkerchief and crying:

"'Hey! Philippe!'

"Thousands of schemes had been planned on the strength of this expected return; we were even to buy a little house with my uncle's money—a little place in the country near Ingouville. In fact, I wouldn't swear that my father had not already begun negotiations.

"The elder of my sisters was then twenty-eight, the other twenty-six. They were not yet married, and that was a great grief to every one.

"At last a suitor presented himself for the younger one. He was a clerk, not rich, but honorable. I have always been morally certain that Uncle Jules' letter, which was shown him one evening, had swept away the young man's hesitation and definitely decided him.

"He was accepted eagerly, and it was decided that after the wedding the whole family should take a trip to Jersey.

"Jersey is the ideal trip for poor people. It is not far; one crosses a strip of sea in a steamer and lands on foreign soil, as this little island belongs to England. Thus, a Frenchman, with a two hours' sail, can observe a neighboring people at home and study their customs.

"This trip to Jersey completely absorbed our ideas, was our sole anticipation, the constant thought of our minds.

"At last we left. I see it as plainly as if it had happened yesterday. The boat was getting up steam against the quay at Granville; my father, bewildered, was superintending the loading of our three pieces of baggage; my mother, nervous, had taken the arm of my unmarried sister, who seemed lost since the departure of the other one, like the last chicken of a brood; behind us came the bride and groom, who always stayed behind, a thing that often made me turn round.

"The whistle sounded. We got on board, and the vessel, leaving the breakwater, forged ahead through a sea as flat as a marble table. We watched the coast disappear in the distance, happy and proud, like all who do not travel much.

"My father was swelling out his chest in the breeze, beneath his frock coat, which had that morning been very carefully cleaned; and he spread around him that odor of benzine which always made me recognize Sunday. Suddenly he noticed two elegantly dressed ladies to whom two gentlemen were offering oysters. An old, ragged sailor was opening them with his knife and passing them to the gentlemen, who would then offer them to the ladies. They ate them in a dainty manner, holding the shell on a fine handkerchief and advancing their mouths a little in order not to spot their dresses. Then they would drink the liquid with a rapid little motion and throw the shell overboard.

"My father was probably pleased with this delicate manner of eating oysters on a moving ship. He considered it good form, refined, and, going up to my mother and sisters, he asked:

"'Would you like me to offer you some oysters?'

"My mother hesitated on account of the expense, but my two sisters immediately accepted. My mother said in a provoked manner:

"'I am afraid that they will hurt my stomach. Offer the children some, but not too much, it would make them sick.' Then, turning toward me, she added:

"'As for Joseph, he doesn't need any. Boys shouldn't be spoiled.'

"However, I remained beside my mother, finding this discrimination unjust. I watched my father as he pompously conducted my two sisters and his son-in-law toward the ragged old sailor.

"The two ladies had just left, and my father showed my sisters how to eat them without spilling the liquor. He even tried to give them an example, and seized an oyster. He attempted to imitate the ladies, and immediately spilled all the liquid over his coat. I heard my mother mutter:

"'He would do far better to keep quiet.'

"But, suddenly, my father appeared to be worried; he retreated a few steps, stared at his family gathered around the old shell opener, and quickly came toward us. He seemed very pale, with a peculiar look. In a low voice he said to my mother:

"'It's extraordinary how that man opening the oysters looks like Jules.'

"Astonished, my mother asked:

"'What Jules?'

"My father continued:

"'Why, my brother. If I did not know that he was well off in America, I should think it was he.'

"Bewildered, my mother stammered:

"'You are crazy! As long as you know that it is not he, why do you say such foolish things?'

"But my father insisted:

"'Go on over and see, Clarisse! I would rather have you see with your own eyes.'

"She arose and walked to her daughters. I, too, was watching the man. He was old, dirty, wrinkled, and did not lift his eyes from his work.

"My mother returned. I noticed that she was trembling. She exclaimed quickly:

"'I believe that it is he. Why don't you ask the captain? But be very careful that we don't have this rogue on our hands again!'

"My father walked away, but I followed him. I felt strangely moved.

"The captain, a tall, thin man, with blond whiskers, was walking along the bridge with an important air as if he were commanding the Indian mail steamer.

"My father addressed him ceremoniously, and questioned him about his profession, adding many compliments:

"'What might be the importance of Jersey? What did it produce? What was the population? The customs? The nature of the soil?' etc., etc.

"'You have there an old shell opener who seems quite interesting. Do you know anything about him?'

"The captain, whom this conversation began to weary, answered dryly:

"'He is some old French tramp whom I found last year in America, and I brought him back. It seems that he has some relatives in Havre, but that he doesn't wish to return to them because he owes them money. His name is Jules—Jules Darmanche or Darvanche or something like that. It seems that he was once rich over there, but you can see what's left of him now.'

"My father turned ashy pale and muttered, his throat contracted, his eyes haggard.

"'Ah! ah! very well, very well. I'm not in the least surprised. Thank you very much, captain.'

"He went away, and the astonished sailor watched him disappear. He returned to my mother so upset that she said to him:

"'Sit down; some one will notice that something is the matter.'

"He sank down on a bench and stammered:

"'It's he! It's he!'

"Then he asked:

"'What are we going to do?'

"She answered quickly:

"'We must get the children out of the way. Since Joseph knows everything, he can go and get them. We must take good care that our son-in-law doesn't find out.'

"My father seemed absolutely bewildered. He murmured:

"'What a catastrophe!'

"Suddenly growing furious, my mother exclaimed:

"'I always thought that that thief never would do anything, and that he would drop down on us again! As if one could expect anything from a Davranche!'

"My father passed his hand over his forehead, as he always did when his wife reproached him. She added:

"'Give Joseph some money so that he can pay for the oysters. All that it needed to cap the climax would be to be recognized by that beggar. That would be very pleasant! Let's get down to the other end of the boat, and take care that that man doesn't come near us!'

"They gave me five francs and walked away.

"Astonished, my sisters were awaiting their father. I said that mamma had felt a sudden attack of sea-sickness, and I asked the shell opener:

"'How much do we owe you, monsieur?'

"I felt like laughing: he was my uncle! He answered:

"'Two francs fifty.'

"I held out my five francs and he returned the change. I looked at his hand; it was a poor, wrinkled, sailor's hand, and I looked at his face, an unhappy old face. I said to myself:

"'That is my uncle, the brother of my father, my uncle!'

"I gave him a ten-cent tip. He thanked me:

"'God bless you, my young sir!'

"He spoke like a poor man receiving alms. I couldn't help thinking that he must have begged over there! My sisters looked at me, surprised at my generosity. When I returned the two francs to my father, my mother asked me in surprise:

"'Was there three francs' worth? That is impossible.'

"I answered in a firm voice

"'I gave ten cents as a tip.'

"My mother started, and, staring at me, she exclaimed:

"'You must be crazy! Give ten cents to that man, to that vagabond—'

"She stopped at a look from my father, who was pointing at his son-in-law. Then everybody was silent.

"Before us, on the distant horizon, a purple shadow seemed to rise out of the sea. It was Jersey.

"As we approached the breakwater a violent desire seized me once more to see my Uncle Jules, to be near him, to say to him something consoling, something tender. But as no one was eating any more oysters, he had disappeared, having probably gone below to the dirty hold which was the home of the poor wretch."

THE MODEL

Curving like a crescent moon, the little town of Etretat, with its white cliffs, its white, shingly beach and its blue sea, lay in the sunlight at high noon one July day. At either extremity of this crescent its two "gates," the smaller to the right, the larger one at the left, stretched forth—one a dwarf and the other a colossal limb—into the water, and the bell tower, almost as tall as the cliff, wide below, narrowing at the top, raised its pointed summit to the sky.

On the sands beside the water a crowd was seated watching the bathers. On the terrace of, the Casino another crowd, seated or walking, displayed beneath the brilliant sky a perfect flower patch of bright costumes, with red and blue parasols embroidered with large flowers in silk.

On the walk at the end of the terrace, other persons, the restful, quiet ones, were walking slowly, far from the dressy throng.

A young man, well known and celebrated as a painter, Jean Sumner, was walking with a dejected air beside a wheeled chair in which sat a young woman, his wife. A manservant was gently pushing the chair, and the crippled woman was gazing sadly at the brightness of the sky, the gladness of the day, and the happiness of others.

They did not speak. They did not look at each other.

"Let us stop a while," said the young woman.

They stopped, and the painter sat down on a camp stool that the servant handed him.

Those who were passing behind the silent and motionless couple looked at them compassionately. A whole legend of devotion was attached to them. He had married her in spite of her infirmity, touched by her affection for him, it was said.

Not far from there, two young men were chatting, seated on a bench and looking out into the horizon.

"No, it is not true; I tell you that I am well acquainted with Jean Sumner."

"But then, why did he marry her? For she was a cripple when she married, was she not?"

"Just so. He married her—he married her—just as every one marries, parbleu! because he was an idiot!"

"But why?"

"But why—but why, my friend? There is no why. People do stupid things just because they do stupid things. And, besides, you know very well that painters make a specialty of foolish marriages. They almost always marry models, former sweethearts, in fact, women of doubtful reputation, frequently. Why do they do this? Who can say? One would suppose that constant association with the general run of models would disgust them forever with that class of women. Not at all. After having posed them they marry them. Read that little book, so true, so cruel and so beautiful, by Alphonse Daudet: 'Artists' Wives.'

"In the case of the couple you see over there the accident occurred in a special and terrible manner. The little woman played a frightful comedy, or, rather, tragedy. She risked all to win all. Was she sincere? Did she love Jean? Shall we ever know? Who is able to determine precisely how much is put on and how much is real in the actions of a woman? They are always sincere in an eternal mobility of impressions. They are furious, criminal, devoted, admirable and base in obedience to intangible emotions. They tell lies incessantly without intention, without knowing or understanding why, and in spite of it all are absolutely frank in their feelings and sentiments, which they display by violent, unexpected, incomprehensible, foolish resolutions which overthrow our arguments, our customary poise and all our selfish plans. The unforeseenness and suddenness of their determinations will always render them undecipherable enigmas as far as we are concerned. We continually ask ourselves:

"'Are they sincere? Are they pretending?'

"But, my friend, they are sincere and insincere at one and the same time, because it is their nature to be extremists in both and to be neither one nor the other.

"See the methods that even the best of them employ to get what they desire. They are complex and simple, these methods. So complex that we can never guess at them beforehand, and so simple that after having been victimized we cannot help being astonished and exclaiming: 'What! Did she make a fool of me so easily as that?'

"And they always succeed, old man, especially when it is a question of getting married.

"But this is Sumner's story:

"The little woman was a model, of course. She posed for him. She was pretty, very stylish-looking, and had a divine figure, it seems. He fancied that he loved her with his whole soul. That is another strange thing. As soon as one likes a woman one sincerely believes that they could not get along without her for the rest of their life. One knows that one has felt the same way before and that disgust invariably succeeded gratification; that in order to pass one's existence side by side with another there must be not a brutal, physical passion which soon dies out, but a sympathy of soul, temperament and temper. One should know how to determine in the enchantment to which one is subjected whether it proceeds from the physical, from a certain sensuous intoxication, or from a deep spiritual charm.

"Well, he believed himself in love; he made her no end of promises of fidelity, and was devoted to her.

"She was really attractive, gifted with that fashionable flippancy that little Parisians so readily affect. She chattered, babbled, made foolish remarks that sounded witty from the manner in which they were uttered. She used graceful gesture's which were calculated to attract a painter's eye. When she raised her arms, when she bent over, when she got into a carriage, when she held out her hand to you, her gestures were perfect and appropriate.

"For three months Jean never noticed that, in reality, she was like all other models.

"He rented a little house for her for the summer at Andresy.

"I was there one evening when for the first time doubts came into my friend's mind.

"As it was a beautiful evening we thought we would take a stroll along the bank of the river. The moon poured a flood of light on the trembling water, scattering yellow gleams along its ripples in the currents and all along the course of the wide, slow river.

"We strolled along the bank, a little enthused by that vague exaltation that these dreamy evenings produce in us. We would have liked to undertake some wonderful task, to love some unknown, deliciously poetic being. We felt ourselves vibrating with raptures, longings, strange aspirations. And we were silent, our beings pervaded by the serene and living coolness of the beautiful night, the coolness of the moonlight, which seemed to penetrate one's body, permeate it, soothe one's spirit, fill it with fragrance and steep it in happiness.

"Suddenly Josephine (that is her name) uttered an exclamation:

"'Oh, did you see the big fish that jumped, over there?'

"He replied without looking, without thinking:

"'Yes, dear.'

"She was angry.

"'No, you did not see it, for your back was turned.'

"He smiled.

"'Yes, that's true. It is so delightful that I am not thinking of anything.'

"She was silent, but at the end of a minute she felt as if she must say something and asked:

"'Are you going to Paris to-morrow?'

"'I do not know,' he replied.

"She was annoyed again.

"'Do you think it is very amusing to walk along without speaking? People talk when they are not stupid.'

"He did not reply. Then, feeling with her woman's instinct that she was going to make him angry, she began to sing a popular air that had harassed our ears and our minds for two years:

"'Je regardais en fair.'

"He murmured:

"'Please keep quiet.'

"She replied angrily:

"'Why do you wish me to keep quiet?'

"'You spoil the landscape for us!' he said.

"Then followed a scene, a hateful, idiotic scene, with unexpected reproaches, unsuitable recriminations, then tears. Nothing was left unsaid. They went back to the house. He had allowed her to talk without replying, enervated by the beauty of the scene and dumfounded by this storm of abuse.

"Three months later he strove wildly to free himself from those invincible and invisible bonds with which such a friendship chains our lives. She kept him under her influence, tyrannizing over him, making his life a burden to him. They quarreled continually, vituperating and finally fighting each other.

"He wanted to break with her at any cost. He sold all his canvases, borrowed money from his friends, realizing twenty thousand francs (he was not well known then), and left them for her one morning with a note of farewell.

"He came and took refuge with me.

"About three o'clock that afternoon there was a ring at the bell. I went to the door. A woman sprang toward me, pushed me aside, came in and went into my atelier. It was she!

"He had risen when he saw her coming.'

"She threw the envelope containing the banknotes at his feet with a truly noble gesture and said in a quick tone:

"'There's your money. I don't want it!'

"She was very pale, trembling and ready undoubtedly to commit any folly. As for him, I saw him grow pale also, pale with rage and exasperation, ready also perhaps to commit any violence.

"He asked:

"'What do you want?'

"She replied:

"'I do not choose to be treated like a common woman. You implored me to accept you. I asked you for nothing. Keep me with you!'

"He stamped his foot.

"'No, that's a little too much! If you think you are going—'

"I had seized his arm.

"'Keep still, Jean. . . Let me settle it.'

"I went toward her and quietly, little by little, I began to reason with her, exhausting all the arguments that are used under similar circumstances. She listened to me, motionless, with a fixed gaze, obstinate and silent.

"Finally, not knowing what more to say, and seeing that there would be a scene, I thought of a last resort and said:

"'He loves you still, my dear, but his family want him to marry some one, and you understand—'

"She gave a start and exclaimed:

"'Ah! Ah! Now I understand:

"And turning toward him, she said:

"'You are—you are going to get married?'

"He replied decidedly" 'Yes.'

"She took a step forward.

"'If you marry, I will kill myself! Do you hear?'

"He shrugged his shoulders and replied:

"'Well, then kill yourself!'

"She stammered out, almost choking with her violent emotion:

"'What do you say? What do you say? What do you say? Say it again!'

"He repeated:

"'Well, then kill yourself if you like!'

"With her face almost livid, she replied:

"'Do not dare me! I will throw myself from the window!'

"He began to laugh, walked toward the window, opened it, and bowing with the gesture of one who desires to let some one else precede him, he said:

"'This is the way. After you!'

"She looked at him for a second with terrible, wild, staring eyes. Then, taking a run as if she were going to jump a hedge in the country, she rushed past me and past him, jumped over the sill and disappeared.

"I shall never forget the impression made on me by that open window after I had seen that body pass through it to fall to the ground. It appeared to me in a second to be as large as the heavens and as hollow as space. And I drew back instinctively, not daring to look at it, as though I feared I might fall out myself.

"Jean, dumfounded, stood motionless.

"They brought the poor girl in with both legs broken. She will never walk again.

"Jean, wild with remorse and also possibly touched with gratitude, made up his mind to marry her.

"There you have it, old man."

It was growing dusk. The young woman felt chilly and wanted to go home, and the servant wheeled the invalid chair in the direction of the village. The painter walked beside his wife, neither of them having exchanged a word for an hour.

This story appeared in Le Gaulois, December 17, 1883.

A VAGABOND

He was a journeyman carpenter, a good workman and a steady fellow, twenty-seven years old, but, although the eldest son, Jacques Randel had been forced to live on his family for two months, owing to the general lack of work. He had walked about seeking work for over a month and had left his native town, Ville-Avary, in La Manche, because he could find nothing to do and would no longer deprive his family of the bread they needed themselves, when he was the strongest of them all. His two sisters earned but little as charwomen. He went and inquired at the town hall, and the mayor's secretary told him that he would find work at the Labor Agency, and so he started, well provided with papers and certificates, and carrying another pair of shoes, a pair of trousers and a shirt in a blue handkerchief at the end of his stick.

And he had walked almost without stopping, day and night, along interminable roads, in sun and rain, without ever reaching that mysterious country where workmen find work. At first he had the fixed idea that he must only work as a carpenter, but at every carpenter's shop where he applied he was told that they had just dismissed men on account of work being so slack, and, finding himself at the end of his resources, he made up his mind to undertake any job that he might come across on the road. And so by turns he was a navvy, stableman, stonecutter; he split wood, lopped the branches of trees, dug wells, mixed mortar, tied up fagots, tended goats on a mountain, and all for a few pence, for he only obtained two or three days' work occasionally by offering himself at a shamefully low price, in order to tempt the avarice of employers and peasants.

And now for a week he had found nothing, and had no money left, and nothing to eat but a piece of bread, thanks to the charity of some women from whom he had begged at house doors on the road. It was getting dark, and Jacques Randel, jaded, his legs failing him, his stomach empty, and with despair in his heart, was walking barefoot on the grass by the side of the road, for he was taking care of his last pair of shoes, as the other pair had already ceased to exist for a long time. It was a Saturday, toward the end of autumn. The heavy gray clouds were being driven rapidly through the sky by the gusts of wind which whistled among the trees, and one felt that it would rain soon. The country was deserted at that hour on the eve of Sunday. Here and there in the fields there rose up stacks of wheat straw, like huge yellow mushrooms, and the fields looked bare, as they had already been sown for the next year.

Randel was hungry, with the hunger of some wild animal, such a hunger as drives wolves to attack men. Worn out and weakened with fatigue, he took longer strides, so as not to take so many steps, and with heavy head, the blood throbbing in his temples, with red eyes and dry mouth, he grasped his stick tightly in his hand, with a longing to strike the first passerby who might be going home to supper.

He looked at the sides of the road, imagining he saw potatoes dug up and lying on the ground before his eyes; if he had found any he would have gathered some dead wood, made a fire in the ditch and have had a capital supper off the warm, round vegetables with which he would first of all have warmed his cold hands. But it was too late in the year, and he would have to gnaw a raw beetroot which he might pick up in a field as he had done the day before.

For the last two days he had talked to himself as he quickened his steps under the influence of his thoughts. He had never thought much hitherto, as he had given all his mind, all his simple faculties to his mechanical work. But now fatigue and this desperate search for work which he could not get, refusals and rebuffs, nights spent in the open air lying on the grass, long fasting, the contempt which he knew people with a settled abode felt for a vagabond, and that question which he was continually asked, "Why do you not remain at home?" distress at not being able to use his strong arms which he felt so full of vigor, the recollection of the relations he had left at home and who also had not a penny, filled him by degrees with rage, which had been accumulating every day, every hour, every minute, and which now escaped his lips in spite of himself in short, growling sentences.

As he stumbled over the stones which tripped his bare feet, he grumbled: "How wretched! how miserable! A set of hogs—to let a man die of hunger—a carpenter—a set of hogs—not two sous—not two sous—and now it is raining—a set of hogs!"

He was indignant at the injustice of fate, and cast the blame on men, on all men, because nature, that great, blind mother, is unjust, cruel and perfidious, and he repeated through his clenched teeth:

"A set of hogs" as he looked at the thin gray smoke which rose from the roofs, for it was the dinner hour. And, without considering that there is another injustice which is human, and which is called robbery and violence, he felt inclined to go into one of those houses to murder the inhabitants and to sit down to table in their stead.

He said to himself: "I have no right to live now, as they are letting me die of hunger, and yet I only ask for work—a set of hogs!" And the pain in his limbs, the gnawing in his heart rose to his head like terrible intoxication, and gave rise to this simple thought in his brain: "I have the right to live because I breathe and because the air is the common property of everybody. So nobody has the right to leave me without bread!"

A fine, thick, icy cold rain was coming down, and he stopped and murmured: "Oh, misery! Another month of walking before I get home." He was indeed returning home then, for he saw that he should more easily find work in his native town, where he was known—and he did not mind what he did—than on the highroads, where everybody suspected him. As the carpentering business was not prosperous, he would turn day laborer, be a mason's hodman, a ditcher, break stones on the road. If he only earned a franc a day, that would at any rate buy him something to eat.

He tied the remains of his last pocket handkerchief round his neck to prevent the cold rain from running down his back and chest, but he soon found that it was penetrating the thin material of which his clothes were made, and he glanced about him with the agonized look of a man who does not know where to hide his body and to rest his head, and has no place of shelter in the whole world.

Night came on and wrapped the country in obscurity, and in the distance, in a meadow, he saw a dark spot on the grass; it was a cow, and so he got over the ditch by the roadside and went up to her without exactly knowing what he was doing. When he got close to her she raised her great head to him, and he thought: "If I only had a jug I could get a little milk." He looked at the cow and the cow looked at him and then, suddenly giving her a kick in the side, he said: "Get up!"

The animal got up slowly, letting her heavy udders bang down. Then the man lay down on his back between the animal's legs and drank for a long time, squeezing her warm, swollen teats, which tasted of the cowstall, with both hands, and he drank as long as she gave any milk. But the icy rain began to fall more heavily, and he saw no place of shelter on the whole of that bare plain. He was cold, and he looked at a light which was shining among the trees in the window of a house.

The cow had lain down again heavily, and he sat down by her side and stroked her head, grateful for the nourishment she had given him. The animal's strong, thick breath, which came out of her nostrils like two jets of steam in the evening air, blew on the workman's face, and he said: "You are not cold inside there!" He put his hands on her chest and under her stomach to find some warmth there, and then the idea struck him that he might pass the night beside that large, warm animal. So he found a comfortable place and laid his head on her side, and then, as he was worn out with fatigue, fell asleep immediately.

He woke up, however, several times, with his back or his stomach half frozen, according as he put one or the other against the animal's flank. Then he turned over to warm and dry that part of his body which had remained exposed to the night air, and soon went soundly to sleep again. The crowing of a cock woke him; the day was breaking, it was no longer raining, and the sky was bright. The cow was resting with her muzzle on the ground, and he stooped down, resting on his hands, to kiss those wide, moist nostrils, and said: "Good-by, my beauty, until next time. You are a nice animal. Good-by." Then he put on his shoes and went off, and for two hours walked straight before him, always following the same road, and then he felt so tired that he sat down on the grass. It was broad daylight by that time, and the church bells were ringing; men in blue blouses, women in white caps, some on foot, some in carts, began to pass along the road, going to the neighboring villages to spend Sunday with friends or relations.

A stout peasant came in sight, driving before him a score of frightened, bleating sheep, with the help of an active dog. Randel got up, and raising his cap, said: "You do not happen to have any work for a man who is dying of hunger?" But the other, giving an angry look at the vagabond, replied: "I have no work for fellows whom I meet on the road."

And the carpenter went back and sat down by the side of the ditch again. He waited there for a long time, watching the country people pass and looking for a kind, compassionate face before he renewed his request, and finally selected a man in an overcoat, whose stomach was adorned with a gold chain. "I have been looking for work," he said, "for the last two months and cannot find any, and I have not a sou in my pocket." But the would-be gentleman replied: "You should have read the notice which is stuck up at the entrance to the village: 'Begging is prohibited within the boundaries of this parish.' Let me tell you that I am the mayor, and if you do not get out of here pretty quickly I shall have you arrested."

Randel, who was getting angry, replied: "Have me arrested if you like; I should prefer it, for, at any rate, I should not die of hunger." And he went back and sat down by the side of his ditch again, and in about a quarter of an hour two gendarmes appeared on the road. They were walking slowly side by side, glittering in the sun with their shining hats, their yellow accoutrements and their metal buttons, as if to frighten evildoers, and to put them to flight at a distance. He knew that they were coming after him, but he did not move, for he was seized with a sudden desire to defy them, to be arrested by them, and to have his revenge later.

They came on without appearing to have seen him, walking heavily, with military step, and balancing themselves as if they were doing the goose step; and then, suddenly, as they passed him, appearing to have noticed him, they stopped and looked at him angrily and threateningly, and the brigadier came up to him and asked: "What are you doing here?" "I am resting," the man replied calmly. "Where do you come from?" "If I had to tell you all the places I have been to it would take me more than an hour." "Where are you going to?" "To Ville-Avary." "Where is that?" "In La Manche." "Is that where you belong?" "It is." "Why did you leave it?" "To look for work."

The brigadier turned to his gendarme and said in the angry voice of a man who is exasperated at last by an oft-repeated trick: "They all say that, these scamps. I know all about it." And then he continued: "Have you any papers?" "Yes, I have some." "Give them to me."

Randel took his papers out of his pocket, his certificates, those poor, worn-out, dirty papers which were falling to pieces, and gave them to the soldier, who spelled them through, hemming and hawing, and then, having seen that they were all in order, he gave them back to Randel with the dissatisfied look of a man whom some one cleverer than himself has tricked.

After a few moments' further reflection, he asked him: "Have you any money on you?" "No." "None whatever?" "None." "Not even a sou?" "Not even a son!" "How do you live then?" "On what people give me." "Then you beg?" And Randel answered resolutely: "Yes, when I can."

Then the gendarme said: "I have caught you on the highroad in the act of vagabondage and begging, without any resources or trade, and so I command you to come with me." The carpenter got up and said: "Wherever you please." And, placing himself between the two soldiers, even before he had received the order to do so, he added: "Well, lock me up; that will at any rate put a roof over my head when it rains."

And they set off toward the village, the red tiles of which could be seen through the leafless trees, a quarter of a league off. Service was about to begin when they went through the village. The square was full of people, who immediately formed two lines to see the criminal pass. He was being followed by a crowd of excited children. Male and female peasants looked at the prisoner between the two gendarmes, with hatred in their eyes and a longing to throw stones at him, to tear his skin with their nails, to trample him under their feet. They asked each other whether he had committed murder or robbery. The butcher, who was an ex-'spahi', declared that he was a deserter. The tobacconist thought that he recognized him as the man who had that very morning passed a bad half-franc piece off on him, and the ironmonger declared that he was the murderer of Widow Malet, whom the police had been looking for for six months.

In the municipal court, into which his custodians took him, Randel saw the mayor again, sitting on the magisterial bench, with the schoolmaster by his side. "Aha! aha!" the magistrate exclaimed, "so here you are again, my fine fellow. I told you I should have you locked up. Well, brigadier, what is he charged with?"

"He is a vagabond without house or home, Monsieur le Maire, without any resources or money, so he says, who was arrested in the act of begging, but he is provided with good testimonials, and his papers are all in order."

"Show me his papers," the mayor said. He took them, read them, reread, returned them and then said: "Search him." So they searched him, but found nothing, and the mayor seemed perplexed, and asked the workman:

"What were you doing on the road this morning?" "I was looking for work." "Work? On the highroad?" "How do you expect me to find any if I hide in the woods?"

They looked at each other with the hatred of two wild beasts which belong to different hostile species, and the magistrate continued: "I am going to have you set at liberty, but do not be brought up before me again." To which the carpenter replied: "I would rather you locked me up; I have had enough running about the country." But the magistrate replied severely: "be silent." And then he said to the two gendarmes: "You will conduct this man two hundred yards from the village and let him continue his journey."

"At any rate, give me something to eat," the workman said, but the other grew indignant: "Have we nothing to do but to feed you? Ah! ah! ah! that is rather too much!" But Randel went on firmly: "If you let me nearly die of hunger again, you will force me to commit a crime, and then, so much the worse for you other fat fellows."

The mayor had risen and he repeated: "Take him away immediately or I shall end by getting angry."

The two gendarmes thereupon seized the carpenter by the arms and dragged him out. He allowed them to do it without resistance, passed through the village again and found himself on the highroad once more; and when the men had accompanied him two hundred yards beyond the village, the brigadier said: "Now off with you and do not let me catch you about here again, for if I do, you will know it."

Randel went off without replying or knowing where he was going. He walked on for a quarter of an hour or twenty minutes, so stupefied that he no longer thought of anything. But suddenly, as he was passing a small house, where the window was half open, the smell of the soup and boiled meat stopped him suddenly, and hunger, fierce, devouring, maddening hunger, seized him and almost drove him against the walls of the house like a wild beast.

He said aloud in a grumbling voice: "In Heaven's name! they must give me some this time!" And he began to knock at the door vigorously with his stick, and as no one came he knocked louder and called out: "Hey! hey! you people in there, open the door!" And then, as nothing stirred, he went up to the window and pushed it wider open with his hand, and the close warm air of the kitchen, full of the smell of hot soup, meat and cabbage, escaped into the cold outer air, and with a bound the carpenter was in the house. Two places were set at the table, and no doubt the proprietors of the house, on going to church, had left their dinner on the fire, their nice Sunday boiled beef and vegetable soup, while there was a loaf of new bread on the chimney-piece, between two bottles which seemed full.

Randel seized the bread first of all and broke it with as much violence as if he were strangling a man, and then he began to eat voraciously, swallowing great mouthfuls quickly. But almost immediately the smell of the meat attracted him to the fireplace, and, having taken off the lid of the saucepan, he plunged a fork into it and brought out a large piece of beef tied with a string. Then he took more cabbage, carrots and onions until his plate was full, and, having put it on the table, he sat down before it, cut the meat into four pieces, and dined as if he had been at home. When he had eaten nearly all the meat, besides a quantity of vegetables, he felt thirsty and took one of the bottles off the mantelpiece.

Scarcely had he poured the liquor into his glass when he saw it was brandy. So much the better; it was warming and would instill some fire into his veins, and that would be all right, after being so cold; and he drank some. He certainly enjoyed it, for he had grown unaccustomed to it, and he poured himself out another glassful, which he drank at two gulps. And then almost immediately he felt quite merry and light-hearted from the effects of the alcohol, just as if some great happiness filled his heart.

He continued to eat, but more slowly, and dipping his bread into the soup. His skin had become burning, and especially his forehead, where the veins were throbbing. But suddenly the church bells began to ring. Mass was over, and instinct rather than fear, the instinct of prudence, which guides all beings and makes them clear-sighted in danger, made the carpenter get up. He put the remains of the loaf into one pocket and the brandy bottle into the other, and he furtively went to the window and looked out into the road. It was still deserted, so he jumped out and set off walking again, but instead of following the highroad he ran across the fields toward a wood he saw a little way off.

He felt alert, strong, light-hearted, glad of what he had done, and so nimble that he sprang over the enclosure of the fields at a single bound, and as soon as he was under the trees he took the bottle out of his pocket again and began to drink once more, swallowing it down as he walked, and then his ideas began to get confused, his eyes grew dim, and his legs as elastic as springs, and he started singing the old popular song:

> "Oh! what joy, what joy it is,
>
> To pick the sweet, wild strawberries."

He was now walking on thick, damp, cool moss, and that soft carpet under his feet made him feel absurdly inclined to turn head over heels as he used to do when a child, so he took a run, turned a somersault, got up and began over again. And between each time he began to sing again:

"Oh! what joy, what joy it is,

To pick the sweet, wild strawberries."

Suddenly he found himself above a deep road, and in the road he saw a tall girl, a servant, who was returning to the village with two pails of milk. He watched, stooping down, and with his eyes as bright as those of a dog who scents a quail, but she saw him raised her head and said: "Was that you singing like that?" He did not reply, however, but jumped down into the road, although it was a fall of at least six feet and when she saw him suddenly standing in front of her, she exclaimed: "Oh! dear, how you frightened me!"

But he did not hear her, for he was drunk, he was mad, excited by another requirement which was more imperative than hunger, more feverish than alcohol; by the irresistible fury of the man who has been deprived of everything for two months, and who is drunk; who is young, ardent and inflamed by all the appetites which nature has implanted in the vigorous flesh of men.

The girl started back from him, frightened at his face, his eyes, his half-open mouth, his outstretched hands, but he seized her by the shoulders, and without a word, threw her down in the road.

She let her two pails fall, and they rolled over noisily, and all the milk was spilt, and then she screamed lustily, but it was of no avail in that lonely spot.

When she got up the thought of her overturned pails suddenly filled her with fury, and, taking off one of her wooden sabots, she threw it at the man to break his head if he did not pay her for her milk.

But he, mistaking the reason of this sudden violent attack, somewhat sobered, and frightened at what he had done, ran off as fast as he could, while she threw stones at him, some of which hit him in the back.

He ran for a long time, very long, until he felt more tired than he had ever been before. His legs were so weak that they could scarcely carry him; all his ideas were confused, he lost recollection of everything and could no longer think about anything, and so he sat down at the foot of a tree, and in five minutes was fast asleep. He was soon awakened, however, by a rough shake, and, on opening his eyes, he saw two cocked hats of shiny leather bending over him, and the two gendarmes of the morning, who were holding him and binding his arms.

"I knew I should catch you again," said the brigadier jeeringly. But Randel got up without replying. The two men shook him, quite ready to ill treat him if he made a movement, for he was their prey now. He had become a jailbird, caught by those hunters of criminals who would not let him go again.

"Now, start!" the brigadier said, and they set off. It was late afternoon, and the autumn twilight was setting in over the land, and in half an hour they reached the village, where every door was open, for the people had heard what had happened. Peasants and peasant women and girls, excited with anger, as if every man had been robbed and every woman attacked, wished to see the wretch brought back, so that they might overwhelm him with abuse. They hooted him from the first house in the village until they reached the Hotel de Ville, where the mayor was waiting for him to be himself avenged on this vagabond, and as soon as he saw him approaching he cried:

"Ah! my fine fellow! here we are!" And he rubbed his hands, more pleased than he usually was, and continued: "I said so. I said so, the moment I saw him in the road."

And then with increased satisfaction:

"Oh, you blackguard! Oh, you dirty blackguard! You will get your twenty years, my fine fellow!"

THE FISHING HOLE

"Cuts and wounds which caused death." Such was the charge upon which Leopold Renard, upholsterer, was summoned before the Court of Assizes.

Round him were the principal witnesses, Madame Flameche, widow of the victim, and Louis Ladureau, cabinetmaker, and Jean Durdent, plumber.

Near the criminal was his wife, dressed in black, an ugly little woman, who looked like a monkey dressed as a lady.

This is how Renard (Leopold) recounted the drama.

"Good heavens, it is a misfortune of which I was the prime victim all the time, and with which my will has nothing to do. The facts are their own commentary, Monsieur le President. I am an honest man, a hard-working man, an upholsterer, living in the same street for the last sixteen years, known, liked, respected and esteemed by all, as my neighbors can testify, even the porter's wife, who is not amiable every day. I am fond of work, I am fond of saving, I like honest men and respectable amusements. That is what has ruined me, so much the worse for me; but as my will had nothing to do with it, I continue to respect myself.

"Every Sunday for the last five years my wife and I have spent the day at Passy. We get fresh air, and, besides, we are fond of fishing. Oh! we are as fond of it as we are of little onions. Melie inspired me with that enthusiasm, the jade, and she is more enthusiastic than I am, the scold, seeing that all the mischief in this business is her fault, as you will see immediately.

"I am strong and mild tempered, without a pennyworth of malice in me. But she! oh! la! la! she looks like nothing; she is short and thin. Very well, she does more mischief than a weasel. I do not deny that she has some good qualities; she has some, and very important ones for a man in business. But her character! Just ask about it in the neighborhood, and even the porter's wife, who has just sent me about my business—she will tell you something about it.

"Every day she used to find fault with my mild temper: 'I would not put up with this! I would not put up with that.' If I had listened to her, Monsieur le President, I should have had at least three hand-to-hand fights a month . . . ."

Madame Renard interrupted him: "And for good reasons, too; they laugh best who laugh last."

He turned toward her frankly: "Well, I can't blame you, since you were not the cause of it."

Then, facing the President again, he said:

"I will continue. We used to go to Passy every Saturday evening, so as to begin fishing at daybreak the next morning. It is a habit which has become second nature with us, as the saying is. Three years ago this summer I discovered a place, oh! such a spot. Oh, dear, dear! In the shade, eight feet of water at least and perhaps ten, a hole with cavities under the bank, a regular nest for fish and a paradise for the fisherman. I might look upon that fishing hole as my property, Monsieur le President, as I was its Christopher Columbus. Everybody in the neighborhood knew it, without making any opposition. They would say: 'That is Renard's place'; and nobody would have gone there, not even Monsieur Plumeau, who is well known, be it said without any offense, for poaching on other people's preserves.

"Well, I returned to this place of which I felt certain, just as if I had owned it. I had scarcely got there on Saturday, when I got into Delila, with my wife. Delila is my Norwegian boat, which I had built by Fournaire, and which is light and safe. Well, as I said, we got into the boat and we were going to set bait, and for setting bait there is none to be compared with me, and they all know it. You want to know with what I bait? I cannot answer that question; it has nothing to do with the accident. I cannot answer; that is my secret. There are more than three hundred people who have asked me; I have been offered glasses of brandy and liqueur, fried fish, matelotes, to make me tell. But just go and try whether the chub will come. Ah! they have tempted my stomach to get at my secret, my recipe. Only my wife knows, and she will not tell it any more than I will. Is not that so, Melie?"

The president of the court interrupted him.

"Just get to the facts as soon as you can," and the accused continued: "I am getting to them, I am getting to them. Well, on Saturday, July 8, we left by the twenty-five past five train and before dinner we went to set bait as usual. The weather promised to keep fine and I said to Melie: 'All right for tomorrow.' And she replied: 'If looks like it,' We never talk more than that together.

"And then we returned to dinner. I was happy and thirsty, and that was the cause of everything. I said to Melie: 'Look here, Melie, it is fine weather, suppose I drink a bottle of 'Casque a meche'.' That is a weak white wine which we have christened so, because if you drink too much of it it prevents you from sleeping and takes the place of a nightcap. Do you understand me?

"She replied: 'You can do as you please, but you will be ill again and will not be able to get up tomorrow.' That was true, sensible and prudent, clear-sighted, I must confess. Nevertheless I could not resist, and I drank my bottle. It all came from that.

"Well, I could not sleep. By Jove! it kept me awake till two o'clock in the morning, and then I went to sleep so soundly that I should not have heard the angel sounding his trump at the last judgment.

"In short, my wife woke me at six o'clock and I jumped out of bed, hastily put on my trousers and jersey, washed my face and jumped on board Delila. But it was too late, for when I arrived at my hole it was already occupied! Such a thing had never happened to me in three years, and it made me feel as if I were being robbed under my own eyes. I said to myself: 'Confound it all! confound it!' And then my wife began to nag at me. 'Eh! what about your 'Casque a meche'? Get along, you drunkard! Are you satisfied, you great fool?' I could say nothing, because it was all true, but I landed all the same near the spot and tried to profit by what was left. Perhaps after all the fellow might catch nothing and go away.

"He was a little thin man in white linen coat and waistcoat and a large straw hat, and his wife, a fat woman, doing embroidery, sat behind him.

"When she saw us take up our position close to them she murmured: 'Are there no other places on the river?' My wife, who was furious, replied: 'People who have any manners make inquiries about the habits of the neighborhood before occupying reserved spots.'

"As I did not want a fuss, I said to her: 'Hold your tongue, Melie. Let them alone, let them alone; we shall see.'

"Well, we fastened Delila under the willows and had landed and were fishing side by side, Melie and I, close to the two others. But here, monsieur, I must enter into details.

"We had only been there about five minutes when our neighbor's line began to jerk twice, thrice; and then he pulled out a chub as thick as my thigh; rather less, perhaps, but nearly as big! My heart beat, the perspiration stood on my forehead and Melie said to me: 'Well, you sot, did you see that?'

"Just then Monsieur Bru, the grocer of Poissy, who is fond of gudgeon fishing, passed in a boat and called out to me: 'So somebody has taken your usual place, Monsieur Renard?' And I replied: 'Yes, Monsieur Bru, there are some people in this world who do not know the rules of common politeness.'

"The little man in linen pretended not to hear, nor his fat lump of a wife, either."

Here the president interrupted him a second time: "Take care, you are insulting the widow, Madame Flameche, who is present."

Renard made his excuses: "I beg your pardon, I beg your pardon; my anger carried me away. Well, not a quarter of an hour had passed when the little man caught another chub, and another almost immediately, and another five minutes later.

"Tears were in my eyes, and I knew that Madame Renard was boiling with rage, for she kept on nagging at me: 'Oh, how horrid! Don't you see that he is robbing you of your fish? Do you think that you will catch anything? Not even a frog, nothing whatever. Why, my hands are tingling, just to think of it.'

"But I said to myself: 'Let us wait until twelve o'clock. Then this poacher will go to lunch and I shall get my place again. As for me, Monsieur le President, I lunch on that spot every Sunday. We bring our provisions in Delila. But there! At noon the wretch produced a chicken in a newspaper, and while he was eating, he actually caught another chub!

"Melie and I had a morsel also, just a bite, a mere nothing, for our heart was not in it.

"Then I took up my newspaper to aid my digestion. Every Sunday I read the Gil Blas in the shade by the side of the water. It is Columbine's day, you know; Columbine, who writes the articles in the Gil Blas. I generally put Madame Renard into a rage by pretending to know this Columbine. It is not true, for I do not know her and have never seen her, but that does not matter. She writes very well, and then she says things that are pretty plain for a woman. She suits me and there are not many of her sort.

"Well, I began to tease my wife, but she got angry immediately, and very angry, so I held my tongue. At that moment our two witnesses who are present here, Monsieur Ladureau and Monsieur Durdent, appeared on the other side of the river. We knew each other by sight. The little man began to fish again and he caught so many that I trembled with vexation and his wife said: 'It is an uncommonly good spot, and we will come here always, Desire.' As for me, a cold shiver ran down my back, and Madame Renard kept repeating: 'You are not a man; you have the blood of a chicken in your veins'; and suddenly I said to her: 'Look here, I would rather go away or I shall be doing something foolish.'

"And she whispered to me, as if she had put a red-hot iron under my nose: 'You are not a man. Now you are going to run away and surrender your place! Go, then, Bazaine!'

"I felt hurt, but yet I did not move, while the other fellow pulled out a bream: Oh, I never saw such a large one before, never! And then my wife began to talk aloud, as if she were thinking, and you can see her tricks. She said: 'That is what one might call stolen fish, seeing that we set the bait ourselves. At any rate, they ought to give us back the money we have spent on bait.'

"Then the fat woman in the cotton dress said in her turn: 'Do you mean to call us thieves, madame?' Explanations followed and compliments began to fly. Oh, Lord! those creatures know some good ones. They shouted so loud that our two witnesses, who were on the other bank, began to call out by way of a joke: 'Less noise over there; you will interfere with your husbands' fishing.'

"The fact is that neither the little man nor I moved any more than if we had been two tree stumps. We remained there, with our eyes fixed on the water, as if we had heard nothing; but, by Jove! we heard all the same. 'You are a thief! You are nothing better than a tramp! You are a regular jade!' and so on and so on. A sailor could not have said more.

"Suddenly I heard a noise behind me and turned round. It was the other one, the fat woman, who had attacked my wife with her parasol. Whack, whack! Melie got two of them. But she was furious, and she hits hard when she is in a rage. She caught the fat woman by the hair and then thump! thump! slaps in the face rained down like ripe plums. I should have let them fight it out: women together, men together. It does not do to mix the blows. But the little man in the linen jacket jumped up like a devil and was going to rush at my wife. Ah! no, no, not that, my friend! I caught the gentleman with the end of my fist, and crash! crash! One on the nose, the other in the stomach. He threw up his arms and legs and fell on his back into the river, just into the hole.

"I should have fished him out most certainly, Monsieur le President, if I had had time. But, to make matters worse, the fat woman had the upper hand and was pounding Melie for all she was worth. I know I ought not to have interfered while the man was in the water, but I never thought that he would drown and said to myself: 'Bah, it will cool him.'

"I therefore ran up to the women to separate them and all I received was scratches and bites. Good Lord, what creatures! Well, it took me five minutes, and perhaps ten, to separate those two viragos. When I turned round there was nothing to be seen.

"The water was as smooth as a lake and the others yonder kept shouting: 'Fish him out! fish him out!' It was all very well to say that, but I cannot swim and still less dive.

"At last the man from the dam came and two gentlemen with boathooks, but over a quarter of an hour had passed. He was found at the bottom of the hole, in eight feet of water, as I have said. There he was, the poor little man, in his linen suit! Those are the facts such as I have sworn to. I am innocent, on my honor."

The witnesses having given testimony to the same effect, the accused was acquitted.

THE SPASM

The hotel guests slowly entered the dining-room and took their places. The waiters did not hurry themselves, in order to give the late comers a chance and thus avoid the trouble of bringing in the dishes a second time. The old bathers, the habitues, whose season was almost over, glanced, gazed toward the door whenever it opened, to see what new faces might appear.

This is the principal distraction of watering places. People look forward to the dinner hour in order to inspect each day's new arrivals, to find out who they are, what they do, and what they think. We always have a vague desire to meet pleasant people, to make agreeable acquaintances, perhaps to meet with a love adventure. In this life of elbowings, unknown strangers assume an extreme importance. Curiosity is aroused, sympathy is ready to exhibit itself, and sociability is the order of the day.

We cherish antipathies for a week and friendships for a month; we see people with different eyes, when we view them through the medium of acquaintanceship at watering places. We discover in men suddenly, after an hour's chat, in the evening after dinner, under the trees in the park where the healing spring bubbles up, a high intelligence and astonishing merits, and a month afterward we have completely forgotten these new friends, who were so fascinating when we first met them.

Permanent and serious ties are also formed here sooner than anywhere else. People see each other every day; they become acquainted very quickly, and their affection is tinged with the sweetness and unrestraint of long-standing intimacies. We cherish in after years the dear and tender memories of those first hours of friendship, the memory of those first conversations in which a soul was unveiled, of those first glances which interrogate and respond to questions and secret thoughts which the mouth has not as yet uttered, the memory of that first cordial confidence, the memory of that delightful sensation of opening our hearts to those who seem to open theirs to us in return.

And the melancholy of watering places, the monotony of days that are all alike, proves hourly an incentive to this heart expansion.

Well, this evening, as on every other evening, we awaited the appearance of strange faces.

Only two appeared, but they were very remarkable, a man and a woman —father and daughter. They immediately reminded me of some of Edgar Poe's characters; and yet there was about them a charm, the charm associated with misfortune. I looked upon them as the victims of fate. The man was very tall and thin, rather stooped, with perfectly white hair, too white for his comparatively youthful physiognomy; and there was in his bearing and in his person that austerity peculiar to Protestants. The daughter, who was probably twenty-four or twenty-five, was small in stature, and was also very thin, very pale, and she had the air of one who was worn out with utter lassitude. We meet people like this from time to time, who seem too weak for the tasks and the needs of daily life, too weak to move about, to walk, to do all that we do every day. She was rather pretty; with a transparent, spiritual beauty. And she ate with extreme slowness, as if she were almost incapable of moving her arms.

It must have been she, assuredly, who had come to take the waters.

They sat facing me, on the opposite side of the table; and I at once noticed that the father had a very singular, nervous twitching.

Every time he wanted to reach an object, his hand described a sort of zigzag before it succeeded in reaching what it was in search of, and after a little while this movement annoyed me so that I turned aside my head in order not to see it.

I noticed, too, that the young girl, during meals, wore a glove on her left hand.

After dinner I went for a stroll in the park of the bathing establishment. This led toward the little Auvergnese station of Chatel-Guyon, hidden in a gorge at the foot of the high mountain, from which flowed so many boiling springs, arising from the deep bed of extinct volcanoes. Over yonder, above our heads, the domes of extinct craters lifted their ragged peaks above the rest in the long mountain chain. For Chatel-Guyon is situated at the entrance to the land of mountain domes.

Beyond it stretches out the region of peaks, and, farther on again the region of precipitous summits.

The "Puy de Dome" is the highest of the domes, the Peak of Sancy is the loftiest of the peaks, and Cantal is the most precipitous of these mountain heights.

It was a very warm evening, and I was walking up and down a shady path, listening to the opening, strains of the Casino band, which was playing on an elevation overlooking the park.

And I saw the father and the daughter advancing slowly in my direction. I bowed as one bows to one's hotel companions at a watering place; and the man, coming to a sudden halt, said to me:

"Could you not, monsieur, tell us of a nice walk to take, short, pretty, and not steep; and pardon my troubling you?"

I offered to show them the way toward the valley through which the little river flowed, a deep valley forming a gorge between two tall, craggy, wooded slopes.

They gladly accepted my offer.

And we talked, naturally, about the virtue of the waters.

"Oh," he said, "my daughter has a strange malady, the seat of which is unknown. She suffers from incomprehensible nervous attacks. At one time the doctors think she has an attack of heart disease, at another time they imagine it is some affection of the liver, and at another they declare it to be a disease of the spine. To-day this protean malady, that assumes a thousand forms and a thousand modes of attack, is attributed to the stomach, which is the great caldron and regulator of the body. This is why we have come here. For my part, I am rather inclined to think it is the nerves. In any case it is very sad."

Immediately the remembrance of the violent spasmodic movement of his hand came back to my mind, and I asked him:

"But is this not the result of heredity? Are not your own nerves somewhat affected?"

He replied calmly:

"Mine? Oh, no-my nerves have always been very steady."

Then, suddenly, after a pause, he went on:

"Ah! You were alluding to the jerking movement of my hand every time I try to reach for anything? This arises from a terrible experience which I had. Just imagine, this daughter of mine was actually buried alive!"

I could only utter, "Ah!" so great were my astonishment and emotion.

He continued:

"Here is the story. It is simple. Juliette had been subject for some time to serious attacks of the heart. We believed that she had disease of that organ, and were prepared for the worst.

"One day she was carried into the house cold, lifeless, dead. She had fallen down unconscious in the garden. The doctor certified that life was extinct. I watched by her side for a day and two nights. I laid her with my own hands in the coffin, which I accompanied to the cemetery, where she was deposited in the family vault. It is situated in the very heart of Lorraine.

"I wished to have her interred with her jewels, bracelets, necklaces, rings, all presents which she had received from me, and wearing her first ball dress.

"You may easily imagine my state of mind when I re-entered our home. She was the only one I had, for my wife had been dead for many years. I found my way to my own apartment in a half-distracted condition, utterly exhausted, and sank into my easy-chair, without the capacity to think or the strength to move. I was nothing better now than a suffering, vibrating machine, a human being who had, as it were, been flayed alive; my soul was like an open wound.

"My old valet, Prosper, who had assisted me in placing Juliette in her coffin, and aided me in preparing her for her last sleep, entered the room noiselessly, and asked:

"'Does monsieur want anything?'

"I merely shook my head in reply.

"'Monsieur is wrong,' he urged. 'He will injure his health. Would monsieur like me to put him to bed?'

"I answered: 'No, let me alone!'

"And he left the room.

"I know not how many hours slipped away. Oh, what a night, what a night! It was cold. My fire had died out in the huge grate; and the wind, the winter wind, an icy wind, a winter hurricane, blew with a regular, sinister noise against the windows.

"How many hours slipped away? There I was without sleeping, powerless, crushed, my eyes wide open, my legs stretched out, my body limp, inanimate, and my mind torpid with despair. Suddenly the great doorbell, the great bell of the vestibule, rang out.

"I started so that my chair cracked under me. The solemn, ponderous sound vibrated through the empty country house as through a vault. I turned round to see what the hour was by the clock. It was just two in the morning. Who could be coming at such an hour?

"And, abruptly, the bell again rang twice. The servants, without doubt, were afraid to get up. I took a wax candle and descended the stairs. I was on the point of asking: 'Who is there?'

"Then I felt ashamed of my weakness, and I slowly drew back the heavy bolts. My heart was throbbing wildly. I was frightened. I opened the door brusquely, and in the darkness I distinguished a white figure, standing erect, something that resembled an apparition.

"I recoiled petrified with horror, faltering:

"'Who-who-who are you?'

"A voice replied:

"'It is I, father.'

"It was my daughter.

"I really thought I must be mad, and I retreated backward before this advancing spectre. I kept moving away, making a sign with my hand,' as if to drive the phantom away, that gesture which you have noticed—that gesture which has remained with me ever since.

"'Do not be afraid, papa,' said the apparition. 'I was not dead. Somebody tried to steal my rings and cut one of my fingers; the blood began to flow, and that restored me to life.'

"And, in fact, I could see that her hand was covered with blood.

"I fell on my knees, choking with sobs and with a rattling in my throat.

"Then, when I had somewhat collected my thoughts, though I was still so bewildered that I scarcely realized the awesome happiness that had befallen me, I made her go up to my room and sit dawn in my easy-chair; then I rang excitedly for Prosper to get him to rekindle the fire and to bring some wine, and to summon assistance.

"The man entered, stared at my daughter, opened his mouth with a gasp of alarm and stupefaction, and then fell back dead.

"It was he who had opened the vault, who had mutilated and then abandoned my daughter; for he could not efface the traces of the theft. He had not even taken the trouble to put back the coffin into its place, feeling sure, besides, that he would not be suspected by me, as I trusted him absolutely.

"You see, monsieur, that we are very unfortunate people."

He was silent.

The night had fallen, casting its shadows over the desolate, mournful vale, and a sort of mysterious fear possessed me at finding myself by the side of those strange beings, of this young girl who had come back from the tomb, and this father with his uncanny spasm.

I found it impossible to make any comment on this dreadful story. I only murmured:

"What a horrible thing!"

Then, after a minute's silence, I added:

"Let us go indoors. I think it is growing cool."

And we made our way back to the hotel.

IN THE WOOD

As the mayor was about to sit down to breakfast, word was brought to him that the rural policeman, with two prisoners, was awaiting him at the Hotel de Ville. He went there at once and found old Hochedur standing guard before a middle-class couple whom he was regarding with a severe expression on his face.

The man, a fat old fellow with a red nose and white hair, seemed utterly dejected; while the woman, a little roundabout individual with shining cheeks, looked at the official who had arrested them, with defiant eyes.

"What is it? What is it, Hochedur?"

The rural policeman made his deposition: He had gone out that morning at his usual time, in order to patrol his beat from the forest of Champioux as far as the boundaries of Argenteuil. He had not noticed anything unusual in the country except that it was a fine day, and that the wheat was doing well, when the son of old Bredel, who was going over his vines, called out to him: "Here, Daddy Hochedur, go and have a look at the outskirts of the wood. In the first thicket you will find a pair of pigeons who must be a hundred and thirty years old between them!"

He went in the direction indicated, entered the thicket, and there he heard words which made him suspect a flagrant breach of morality. Advancing, therefore, on his hands and knees as if to surprise a poacher, he had arrested the couple whom he found there.

The mayor looked at the culprits in astonishment, for the man was certainly sixty, and the woman fifty-five at least, and he began to question them, beginning with the man, who replied in such a weak voice that he could scarcely be heard.

"What is your name?"

"Nicholas Beaurain."

"Your occupation?"

"Haberdasher, in the Rue des Martyrs, in Paris."

"What were you doing in the wood?"

The haberdasher remained silent, with his eyes on his fat paunch, and his hands hanging at his sides, and the mayor continued:

"Do you deny what the officer of the municipal authorities states?"

"No, monsieur."

"So you confess it?"

"Yes, monsieur."

"What have you to say in your defence?"

"Nothing, monsieur."

"Where did you meet the partner in your misdemeanor?"

"She is my wife, monsieur."

"Your wife?"

"Yes, monsieur."

"Then—then—you do not live together-in Paris?"

"I beg your pardon, monsieur, but we are living together!"

"But in that case—you must be mad, altogether mad, my dear sir, to get caught playing lovers in the country at ten o'clock in the morning."

The haberdasher seemed ready to cry with shame, and he muttered: "It was she who enticed me! I told her it was very stupid, but when a woman once gets a thing into her head—you know—you cannot get it out."

The mayor, who liked a joke, smiled and replied: "In your case, the contrary ought to have happened. You would not be here, if she had had the idea only in her head."

Then Monsieur Beauain was seized with rage and turning to his wife, he said: "Do you see to what you have brought us with your poetry? And now we shall have to go before the courts at our age, for a breach of morals! And we shall have to shut up the shop, sell our good will, and go to some other neighborhood! That's what it has come to."

Madame Beaurain got up, and without looking at her husband, she explained herself without embarrassment, without useless modesty, and almost without hesitation.

"Of course, monsieur, I know that we have made ourselves ridiculous. Will you allow me to plead my cause like an advocate, or rather like a poor woman? And I hope that you will be kind enough to send us home, and to spare us the disgrace of a prosecution.

"Years ago, when I was young, I made Monsieur Beaurain's acquaintance one Sunday in this neighborhood. He was employed in a draper's shop, and I was a saleswoman in a ready-made clothing establishment. I remember it as if it were yesterday. I used to come and spend Sundays here occasionally with a friend of mine, Rose Leveque, with whom I lived in the Rue Pigalle, and Rose had a sweetheart, while I had none. He used to bring us here, and one Saturday he told me laughing that he should bring a friend with him the next day. I quite understood what he meant, but I replied that it would be no good; for I was virtuous, monsieur.

"The next day we met Monsieur Beaurain at the railway station, and in those days he was good-looking, but I had made up my mind not to encourage him, and I did not. Well, we arrived at Bezons. It was a lovely day, the sort of day that touches your heart. When it is fine even now, just as it used to be formerly, I grow quite foolish, and when I am in the country I utterly lose my head. The green grass, the swallows flying so swiftly, the smell of the grass, the scarlet poppies, the daisies, all that makes me crazy. It is like champagne when one is not accustomed to it!

"Well, it was lovely weather, warm and bright, and it seemed to penetrate your body through your eyes when you looked and through your mouth when you breathed. Rose and Simon hugged and kissed each other every minute, and that gave me a queer feeling! Monsieur Beaurain and I walked behind them, without speaking much, for when people do not know each other, they do not find anything to talk about. He looked timid, and I liked to see his embarrassment. At last we got to the little wood; it was as cool as in a bath there, and we four sat down. Rose and her lover teased me because I looked rather stern, but you will understand that I could not be otherwise. And then they began to kiss and hug again, without putting any more restraint upon themselves than if we had not been there; and then they whispered together, and got up and went off among the trees, without saying a word. You may fancy what I looked like, alone with this young fellow whom I saw for the first time. I felt so confused at seeing them go that it gave me courage, and I began to talk. I asked him what his business was, and he said he was a linen draper's assistant, as I told you just now. We talked for a few minutes, and that made him bold, and he wanted to take liberties with me, but I told him sharply to keep his place. Is not that true, Monsieur Beaurain?"

Monsieur Beaurain, who was looking at his feet in confusion, did not reply, and she continued: "Then he saw that I was virtuous, and he began to make love to me nicely, like an honorable man, and from that time he came every Sunday, for he was very much in love with me. I was very fond of him also, very fond of him! He was a good-looking fellow, formerly, and in short he married me the next September, and we started in business in the Rue des Martyrs.

"It was a hard struggle for some years, monsieur. Business did not prosper, and we could not afford many country excursions, and, besides, we had got out of the way of them. One has other things in one's head, and thinks more of the cash box than of pretty speeches, when one is in business. We were growing old by degrees without perceiving it, like quiet people who do not think much about love. One does not regret anything as long as one does not notice what one has lost.

"And then, monsieur, business became better, and we were tranquil as to the future! Then, you see, I do not exactly know what went on in my mind, no, I really do not know, but I began to dream like a little boarding-school girl. The sight of the little carts full of flowers which are drawn about the streets made me cry; the smell of violets sought me out in my easy-chair, behind my cash box, and made my heart beat! Then I would get up and go out on the doorstep to look at the blue sky between the roofs. When one looks up at the sky from the street, it looks like a river which is descending on Paris, winding as it flows, and the swallows pass to and fro in it like fish. These ideas are very stupid at my age! But how can one help it, monsieur, when one has worked all one's life? A moment comes in which one perceives that one could have done something else, and that one regrets, oh! yes, one feels intense regret! Just think, for twenty years I might have gone and had kisses in the woods, like other women. I used to think how delightful it would be to lie under the trees and be in love with some one! And I thought of it every day and every night! I dreamed of the moonlight on the water, until I felt inclined to drown myself.

"I did not venture to speak to Monsieur Beaurain about this at first. I knew that he would make fun of me, and send me back to sell my needles and cotton! And then, to speak the truth, Monsieur Beaurain never said much to me, but when I looked in the glass, I also understood quite well that I no longer appealed to any one!

"Well, I made up my mind, and I proposed to him an excursion into the country, to the place where we had first become acquainted. He agreed without mistrusting anything, and we arrived here this morning, about nine o'clock.

"I felt quite young again when I got among the wheat, for a woman's heart never grows old! And really, I no longer saw my husband as he is at present, but just as he was formerly! That I will swear to you, monsieur. As true as I am standing here I was crazy. I began to kiss him, and he was more surprised than if I had tried to murder him. He kept saying to me: 'Why, you must be mad! You are mad this morning! What is the matter with you?' I did not listen to him, I only listened to my own heart, and I made him come into the wood with me. That is all. I have spoken the truth, Monsieur le Maire, the whole truth."

The mayor was a sensible man. He rose from his chair, smiled, and said: "Go in peace, madame, and when you again visit our forests, be more discreet."

MARTINE

It came to him one Sunday after mass. He was walking home from church along the by-road that led to his house when he saw ahead of him Martine, who was also going home.

Her father walked beside his daughter with the important gait of a rich farmer. Discarding the smock, he wore a short coat of gray cloth and on his head a round-topped hat with wide brim.

She, laced up in a corset which she wore only once a week, walked along erect, with her squeezed-in waist, her broad shoulders and prominent hips, swinging herself a little. She wore a hat trimmed with flowers, made by a milliner at Yvetot, and displayed the back of her full, round, supple neck, reddened by the sun and air, on which fluttered little stray locks of hair.

Benoist saw only her back; but he knew well the face he loved, without, however, having ever noticed it more closely than he did now.

Suddenly he said: "Nom d'un nom, she is a fine girl, all the same, that Martine." He watched her as she walked, admiring her hastily, feeling a desire taking possession of him. He did not long to see her face again, no. He kept gazing at her figure, repeating to himself: "Nom d'un nom, she is a fine girl."

Martine turned to the right to enter "La Martiniere," the farm of her father, Jean Martin, and she cast a glance behind her as she turned round. She saw Benoist, who looked to her very comical. She called out: "Good-morning, Benoist." He replied: "Good-morning, Martine; good-morning, mait Martin," and went on his way.

When he reached home the soup was on the table. He sat down opposite his mother beside the farm hand and the hired man, while the maid servant went to draw some cider.

He ate a few spoonfuls, then pushed away his plate. His mother said:

"Don't you feel well?"

"No. I feel as if I had some pap in my stomach and that takes away my appetite."

He watched the others eating, as he cut himself a piece of bread from time to time and carried it lazily to his mouth, masticating it slowly. He thought of Martine. "She is a fine girl, all the same." And to think that he had not noticed it before, and that it came to him, just like that, all at once, and with such force that he could not eat.

He did not touch the stew. His mother said:

"Come, Benoist, try and eat a little; it is loin of mutton, it will do you good. When one has no appetite, they should force themselves to eat."

He swallowed a few morsels, then, pushing away his plate, said:

"No. I can't go that, positively."

When they rose from table he walked round the farm, telling the farm hand he might go home and that he would drive up the animals as he passed by them.

The country was deserted, as it was the day of rest. Here and there in a field of clover cows were moving along heavily, with full bellies, chewing their cud under a blazing sun. Unharnessed plows were standing at the end of a furrow; and the upturned earth ready for the seed showed broad brown patches of stubble of wheat and oats that had lately been harvested.

A rather dry autumn wind blew across the plain, promising a cool evening after the sun had set. Benoist sat down on a ditch, placed his hat on his knees as if he needed to cool off his head, and said aloud in the stillness of the country: "If you want a fine girl, she is a fine girl."

He thought of it again at night, in his bed, and in the morning when he awoke.

He was not sad, he was not discontented, he could not have told what ailed him. It was something that had hold of him, something fastened in his mind, an idea that would not leave him and that produced a sort of tickling sensation in his heart.

Sometimes a big fly is shut up in a room. You hear it flying about, buzzing, and the noise haunts you, irritates you. Suddenly it stops; you forget it; but all at once it begins again, obliging you to look up. You cannot catch it, nor drive it away, nor kill it, nor make it keep still. As soon as it settles for a second, it starts off buzzing again.

The recollection of Martine disturbed Benoist's mind like an imprisoned fly.

Then he longed to see her again and walked past the Martiniere several times. He saw her, at last, hanging out some clothes on a line stretched between two apple trees.

It was a warm day. She had on only a short skirt and her chemise, showing the curves of her figure as she hung up the towels. He remained there, concealed by the hedge, for more than an hour, even after she had left. He returned home more obsessed with her image than ever.

For a month his mind was full of her, he trembled when her name was mentioned in his presence. He could not eat, he had night sweats that kept him from sleeping.

On Sunday, at mass, he never took his eyes off her. She noticed it and smiled at him, flattered at his appreciation.

One evening, he suddenly met her in the road. She stopped short when she saw him coming. Then he walked right up to her, choking with fear and emotion, but determined to speak to her. He began falteringly:

"See here, Martine, this cannot go on like this any longer."

She replied as if she wanted to tease him:

"What cannot go on any longer, Benoist?"

"My thinking of you as many hours as there are in the day," he answered.

She put her hands on her hips.

"I do not oblige you to do so."

"Yes, it is you," he stammered; "I cannot sleep, nor rest, nor eat, nor anything."

"What do you need to cure you of all that?" she asked.

He stood there in dismay, his arms swinging, his eyes staring, his mouth agape.

She hit him a punch in the stomach and ran off.

From that day they met each other along the roadside, in by-roads or else at twilight on the edge of a field, when he was going home with his horses and she was driving her cows home to the stable.

He felt himself carried, cast toward her by a strong impulse of his heart and body. He would have liked to squeeze her, strangle her, eat her, make her part of himself. And he trembled with impotence, impatience, rage, to think she did not belong to him entirely, as if they were one being.

People gossiped about it in the countryside. They said they were engaged. He had, besides, asked her if she would be his wife, and she had answered "Yes."

They, were waiting for an opportunity to talk to their parents about it.

But, all at once, she stopped coming to meet him at the usual hour. He did not even see her as he wandered round the farm. He could only catch a glimpse of her at mass on Sunday. And one Sunday, after the sermon, the priest actually published the banns of marriage between Victoire-Adelaide Martin and Josephin-Isidore Vallin.

Benoist felt a sensation in his hands as if the blood had been drained off. He had a buzzing in the ears; and could hear nothing; and presently he perceived that his tears were falling on his prayer book.

For a month he stayed in his room. Then he went back to his work.

But he was not cured, and it was always in his mind. He avoided the roads that led past her home, so that he might not even see the trees in the yard, and this obliged him to make a great circuit morning and evening.

She was now married to Vallin, the richest farmer in the district. Benoist and he did not speak now, though they had been comrades from childhood.

One evening, as Benoist was passing the town hall, he heard that she was enceinte. Instead of experiencing a feeling of sorrow, he experienced, on the contrary, a feeling of relief. It was over, now, all over. They were more separated by that than by her marriage. He really preferred that it should be so.

Months passed, and more months. He caught sight of her, occasionally, going to the village with a heavier step than usual. She blushed as she saw him, lowered her head and quickened her pace. And he turned out of his way so as not to pass her and meet her glance.

He dreaded the thought that he might one morning meet her face to face, and be obliged to speak to her. What could he say to her now, after all he had said formerly, when he held her hands as he kissed her hair beside her cheeks? He often thought of those meetings along the roadside. She had acted horridly after all her promises.

By degrees his grief diminished, leaving only sadness behind. And one day he took the old road that led past the farm where she now lived. He looked at the roof from a distance. It was there, in there, that she lived with another! The apple trees were in bloom, the cocks crowed on the dung hill. The whole dwelling seemed empty, the farm hands had gone to the fields to their spring toil. He stopped near the gate and looked into the yard. The dog was asleep outside his kennel, three calves were walking slowly, one behind the other, towards the pond. A big turkey was strutting before the door, parading before the turkey hens like a singer at the opera.

Benoist leaned against the gate post and was suddenly seized with a desire to weep. But suddenly, he heard a cry, a loud cry for help coming from the house. He was struck with dismay, his hands grasping the wooden bars of the gate, and listened attentively. Another cry, a prolonged, heartrending cry, reached his ears, his soul, his flesh. It was she who was crying like that! He darted inside, crossed the grass patch, pushed open the door, and saw her lying on the floor, her body drawn up, her face livid, her eyes haggard, in the throes of childbirth.

He stood there, trembling and paler than she was, and stammered:

"Here I am, here I am, Martine!"

She replied in gasps:

"Oh, do not leave me, do not leave me, Benoist!"

He looked at her, not knowing what to say, what to do. She began to cry out again:

"Oh, oh, it is killing me. Oh, Benoist!"

She writhed frightfully.

Benoist was suddenly seized with a frantic longing to help her, to quiet her, to remove her pain. He leaned over, lifted her up and laid her on her bed; and while she kept on moaning he began to take off her clothes, her jacket, her skirt and her petticoat. She bit her fists to keep from crying out. Then he did as he was accustomed to doing for cows, ewes, and mares: he assisted in delivering her and found in his hands a large infant who was moaning.

He wiped it off and wrapped it up in a towel that was drying in front of the fire, and laid it on a bundle of clothes ready for ironing that was on the table. Then he went back to the mother.

He took her up and placed her on the floor again, then he changed the bedclothes and put her back into bed. She faltered:

"Thank you, Benoist, you have a noble heart." And then she wept a little as if she felt regretful.

He did not love her any longer, not the least bit. It was all over. Why? How? He could not have said. What had happened had cured him better than ten years of absence.

She asked, exhausted and trembling:

"What is it?"

He replied calmly:

"It is a very fine girl."

Then they were silent again. At the end of a few moments, the mother, in a weak voice, said:

"Show her to me, Benoist."

He took up the little one and was showing it to her as if he were holding the consecrated wafer, when the door opened, and Isidore Vallin appeared.

He did not understand at first, then all at once he guessed.

Benoist, in consternation, stammered out:

"I was passing, I was just passing by when f heard her crying out, and I came—there is your child, Vallin!"

Then the husband, his eyes full of tears, stepped forward, took the little mite of humanity that he held out to him, kissed it, unable to speak from emotion for a few seconds; then placing the child on the bed, he held out both hands to Benoist, saying:

"Your hand upon it, Benoist. From now on we understand each other. If you are willing, we will be a pair of friends, a pair of friends!" And Benoist replied: "Indeed I will, certainly, indeed I will."

ALL OVER

Compte de Lormerin had just finished dressing. He cast a parting glance at the large mirror which occupied an entire panel in his dressing-room and smiled.

He was really a fine-looking man still, although quite gray. Tall, slight, elegant, with no sign of a paunch, with a small mustache of doubtful shade, which might be called fair, he had a walk, a nobility, a "chic," in short, that indescribable something which establishes a greater difference between two men than would millions of money. He murmured:

"Lormerin is still alive!"

And he went into the drawing-room where his correspondence awaited him.

On his table, where everything had its place, the work table of the gentleman who never works, there were a dozen letters lying beside three newspapers of different opinions. With a single touch he spread out all these letters, like a gambler giving the choice of a card; and he scanned the handwriting, a thing he did each morning before opening the envelopes.

It was for him a moment of delightful expectancy, of inquiry and vague anxiety. What did these sealed mysterious letters bring him? What did they contain of pleasure, of happiness, or of grief? He surveyed them with a rapid sweep of the eye, recognizing the writing, selecting them, making two or three lots, according to what he expected from them. Here, friends; there, persons to whom he was indifferent; further on, strangers. The last kind always gave him a little uneasiness. What did they want from him? What hand had traced those curious characters full of thoughts, promises, or threats?

This day one letter in particular caught his eye. It was simple, nevertheless, without seeming to reveal anything; but he looked at it uneasily, with a sort of chill at his heart. He thought: "From whom can it be? I certainly know this writing, and yet I can't identify it."

He raised it to a level with his face, holding it delicately between two fingers, striving to read through the envelope, without making up his mind to open it.

Then he smelled it, and snatched up from the table a little magnifying glass which he used in studying all the niceties of handwriting. He suddenly felt unnerved. "Whom is it from? This hand is familiar to me, very familiar. I must have often read its tracings, yes, very often. But this must have been a long, long time ago. Whom the deuce can it be from? Pooh! it's only somebody asking for money."

And he tore open the letter. Then he read:

> MY DEAR FRIEND: You have, without doubt, forgotten me, for it is now twenty-five years since we saw each other. I was young; I am old. When I bade you farewell, I left Paris in order to follow into the provinces my husband, my old husband, whom you used to call "my hospital." Do you remember him? He died five years ago, and now I am returning to Paris to get my daughter married, for I have a daughter, a beautiful girl of eighteen, whom you have never seen. I informed you of her birth, but you certainly did not pay much attention to so trifling an event.
>
> You are still the handsome Lormerin; so I have been told. Well, if you still recollect little Lise, whom you used to call Lison, come and dine with her this evening, with the elderly Baronne de Vance your ever faithful friend, who, with some emotion, although happy, reaches out to you a devoted hand, which you must clasp, but no longer kiss, my poor Jaquelet.
>
> LISE DE VANCE.

Lormerin's heart began to throb. He remained sunk in his armchair with the letter on his knees, staring straight before him, overcome by a poignant emotion that made the tears mount up to his eyes!

If he had ever loved a woman in his life it was this one, little Lise, Lise de Vance, whom he called "Ashflower," on account of the strange color of her hair and the pale gray of her eyes. Oh! what a dainty, pretty, charming creature she was, this frail baronne, the wife of that gouty, pimply baron, who had abruptly carried her off to the provinces, shut her up, kept her in seclusion through jealousy, jealousy of the handsome Lormerin.

Yes, he had loved her, and he believed that he too, had been truly loved. She familiarly gave him, the name of Jaquelet, and would pronounce that word in a delicious fashion.

A thousand forgotten memories came back to him, far, off and sweet and melancholy now. One evening she had called on him on her way home from a ball, and they went for a stroll in the Bois de Boulogne, she in evening dress, he in his dressing-jacket. It was springtime; the weather was beautiful. The fragrance from her bodice embalmed the warm air-the odor of her bodice, and perhaps, too, the fragrance of her skin. What a divine night! When they reached the lake, as the moon's rays fell across the branches into the water, she began to weep. A little surprised, he asked her why.

"I don't know. The moon and the water have affected me. Every time I see poetic things I have a tightening at the heart, and I have to cry."

He smiled, affected himself, considering her feminine emotion charming —the unaffected emotion of a poor little woman, whom every sensation overwhelms. And he embraced her passionately, stammering:

"My little Lise, you are exquisite."

What a charming love affair, short-lived and dainty, it had been and over all too quickly, cut short in the midst of its ardor by this old brute of a baron, who had carried off his wife, and never let any one see her afterward.

Lormerin had forgotten, in fact, at the end of two or three months. One woman drives out another so quickly in Paris, when one is a bachelor! No matter; he had kept a little altar for her in his heart, for he had loved her alone! He assured himself now that this was so.

He rose, and said aloud: "Certainly, I will go and dine with her this evening!"

And instinctively he turned toward the mirror to inspect himself from head to foot. He reflected: "She must look very old, older than I look." And he felt gratified at the thought of showing himself to her still handsome, still fresh, of astonishing her, perhaps of filling her with emotion, and making her regret those bygone days so far, far distant!

He turned his attention to the other letters. They were of no importance.

The whole day he kept thinking of this ghost of other days. What was she like now? How strange it was to meet in this way after twenty-five years! But would he recognize her?

He made his toilet with feminine coquetry, put on a white waistcoat, which suited him better with the coat than a black one, sent for the hairdresser to give him a finishing touch With the curling iron, for he had preserved his hair, and started very early in order to show his eagerness to see her.

The first thing he saw on entering a pretty drawing-room newly furnished was his own portrait, an old faded photograph, dating from the days when he was a beau, hanging on the wall in an antique silk frame.

He sat down and waited. A door opened behind him. He rose up abruptly, and, turning round, beheld an old woman with white hair who extended both hands toward him.

He seized them, kissed them one after the other several times; then, lifting up his head, he gazed at the woman he had loved.

Yes, it was an old lady, an old lady whom he did not recognize, and who, while she smiled, seemed ready to weep.

He could not abstain from murmuring:

"Is it you, Lise?"

She replied:

"Yes, it is I; it is I, indeed. You would not have known me, would you? I have had so much sorrow—so much sorrow. Sorrow has consumed my life. Look at me now—or, rather, don't look at me! But how handsome you have kept—and young! If I had by chance met you in the street I would have exclaimed: 'Jaquelet!'. Now, sit down and let us, first of all, have a chat. And then I will call my daughter, my grown-up daughter. You'll see how she resembles me—or, rather, how I resembled her—no, it is not quite that; she is just like the 'me' of former days—you shall see! But I wanted to be alone with you first. I feared that there would be some emotion on my side, at the first moment. Now it is all over; it is past. Pray be seated, my friend."

He sat down beside her, holding her hand; but he did not know what to say; he did not know this woman—it seemed to him that he had never seen her before. Why had he come to this house? What could he talk about? Of the long ago? What was there in common between him and her? He could no longer recall anything in presence of this grandmotherly face. He could no longer recall all the nice, tender things, so sweet, so bitter, that had come to his mind that morning when he thought of the other, of little Lise, of the dainty Ashflower. What, then, had become of her, the former one, the one he had loved? That woman of far-off dreams, the blonde with gray eyes, the young girl who used to call him "Jaquelet" so prettily?

They remained side by side, motionless, both constrained, troubled, profoundly ill at ease.

As they talked only commonplaces, awkwardly and spasmodically and slowly, she rose and pressed the button of the bell.

"I am going to call Renee," she said.

There was a tap at the door, then the rustle of a dress; then a young voice exclaimed:

"Here I am, mamma!"

Lormerin remained bewildered as at the sight of an apparition.

He stammered:

"Good-day, mademoiselle"

Then, turning toward the mother:

"Oh! it is you!"

In fact, it was she, she whom he had known in bygone days, the Lise who had vanished and come back! In her he found the woman he had won twenty-five years before. This one was even younger, fresher, more childlike.

He felt a wild desire to open his arms, to clasp her to his heart again, murmuring in her ear:

"Good-morning, Lison!"

A man-servant announced:

"Dinner is ready, madame."

And they proceeded toward the dining-room.

What passed at this dinner? What did they say to him, and what could he say in reply? He found himself plunged in one of those strange dreams which border on insanity. He gazed at the two women with a fixed idea in his mind, a morbid, self-contradictory idea:

"Which is the real one?"

The mother smiled again repeating over and over:

"Do you remember?" And it was in the bright eyes of the young girl that he found again his memories of the past. Twenty times he opened his mouth to say to her: "Do you remember, Lison?" forgetting this white-haired lady who was looking at him tenderly.

And yet, there were moments when, he no longer felt sure, when he lost his head. He could see that the woman of to-day was not exactly the woman of long ago. The other one, the former one, had in her voice, in her glances, in her entire being, something which he did not find again. And he made prodigious efforts of mind to recall his lady love, to seize again what had escaped from her, what this resuscitated one did not possess.

The baronne said:

"You have lost your old vivacity, my poor friend."

He murmured:

"There are many other things that I have lost!"

But in his heart, touched with emotion, he felt his old love springing to life once more, like an awakened wild beast ready to bite him.

The young girl went on chattering, and every now and then some familiar intonation, some expression of her mother's, a certain style of speaking and thinking, that resemblance of mind and manner which people acquire by living together, shook Lormerin from head to foot. All these things penetrated him, making the reopened wound of his passion bleed anew.

He got away early, and took a turn along the boulevard. But the image of this young girl pursued him, haunted him, quickened his heart, inflamed his blood. Apart from the two women, he now saw only one, a young one, the old one come back out of the past, and he loved her as he had loved her in bygone years. He loved her with greater ardor, after an interval of twenty-five years.

He went home to reflect on this strange and terrible thing, and to think what he should do.

But, as he was passing, with a wax candle in his hand, before the glass, the large glass in which he had contemplated himself and admired himself before he started, he saw reflected there an elderly, gray-haired man; and suddenly he recollected what he had been in olden days, in the days of little Lise. He saw himself charming and handsome, as he had been when he was loved! Then, drawing the light nearer, he looked at himself more closely, as one inspects a strange thing with a magnifying glass, tracing the wrinkles, discovering those frightful ravages, which he had not perceived till now.

And he sat down, crushed at the sight of himself, at the sight of his lamentable image, murmuring:

"All over, Lormerin!"

THE PARROT

I

Everybody in Fecamp knew Mother Patin's story. She had certainly been unfortunate with her husband, for in his lifetime he used to beat her, just as wheat is threshed in the barn.

He was master of a fishing bark and had married her, formerly, because she was pretty, although poor.

Patin was a good sailor, but brutal. He used to frequent Father Auban's inn, where he would usually drink four or five glasses of brandy, on lucky days eight or ten glasses and even more, according to his mood. The brandy was served to the customers by Father Auban's daughter, a pleasing brunette, who attracted people to the house only by her pretty face, for nothing had ever been gossiped about her.

Patin, when he entered the inn, would be satisfied to look at her and to compliment her politely and respectfully. After he had had his first glass of brandy he would already find her much nicer; at the second he would wink; at the third he would say. "If you were only willing, Mam'zelle Desiree——" without ever finishing his sentence; at the fourth he would try to hold her back by her skirt in order to kiss her; and when he went as high as ten it was Father Auban who brought him the remaining drinks.

The old innkeeper, who knew all the tricks of the trade, made Desiree walk about between the tables in order to increase the consumption of drinks; and Desiree, who was a worthy daughter of Father Auban, flitted around among the benches and joked with them, her lips smiling and her eyes sparkling.

Patin got so well accustomed to Desiree's face that he thought of it even while at sea, when throwing out his nets, in storms or in calms, on moonlit or dark evenings. He thought of her while holding the tiller in the stern of his boat, while his four companions were slumbering with their heads on their arms. He always saw her, smiling, pouring out the yellow brandy with a peculiar shoulder movement and then exclaiming as she turned away: "There, now; are you satisfied?"

He saw her so much in his mind's eye that he was overcome by an irresistible desire to marry her, and, not being able to hold out any longer, he asked for her hand.

He was rich, owned his own vessel, his nets and a little house at the foot of the hill on the Retenue, whereas Father Auban had nothing. The marriage was therefore eagerly agreed upon and the wedding took place as soon as possible, as both parties were desirous for the affair to be concluded as early as convenient.

Three days after the wedding Patin could no longer understand how he had ever imagined Desiree to be different from other women. What a fool he had been to encumber himself with a penniless creature, who had undoubtedly inveigled him with some drug which she had put in his brandy!

He would curse all day lung, break his pipe with his teeth and maul his crew. After he had sworn by every known term at everything that came his way he would rid himself of his remaining anger on the fish and lobsters, which he pulled from the nets and threw into the baskets amid oaths and foul language. When he returned home he would find his wife, Father Auban's daughter, within reach of his mouth and hand, and it was not long before he treated her like the lowest creature in the world. As she listened calmly, accustomed to paternal violence, he grew exasperated at her quiet, and one evening he beat her. Then life at his home became unbearable.

For ten years the principal topic of conversation on the Retenue was about the beatings that Patin gave his wife and his manner of cursing at her for the least thing. He could, indeed, curse with a richness of vocabulary in a roundness of tone unequalled by any other man in Fecamp. As soon as his ship was sighted at the entrance of the harbor, returning from the fishing expedition, every one awaited the first volley he would hurl from the bridge as soon as he perceived his wife's white cap.

Standing at the stern he would steer, his eye fixed on the bows and on the sail, and, notwithstanding the difficulty of the narrow passage and the height of the turbulent waves, he would search among the watching women and try to recognize his wife, Father Auban's daughter, the wretch!

Then, as soon as he saw her, notwithstanding the noise of the wind and waves, he would let loose upon her with such power and volubility that every one would laugh, although they pitied her greatly. When he arrived at the dock he would relieve his mind, while unloading the fish, in such an expressive manner that he attracted around him all the loafers of the neighborhood. The words left his mouth sometimes like shots from a cannon, short and terrible, sometimes like peals of thunder, which roll and rumble for five minutes, such a hurricane of oaths that he seemed to have in his lungs one of the storms of the Eternal Father.

When he left his ship and found himself face to face with her, surrounded by all the gossips of the neighborhood, he would bring up a new cargo of insults and bring her back to their dwelling, she in front, he behind, she weeping, he yelling at her.

At last, when alone with her behind closed doors, he would thrash her on the slightest pretext. The least thing was sufficient to make him raise his hand, and when he had once begun he did not stop, but he would throw into her face the true motive for his anger. At each blow he would roar: "There, you beggar! There, you wretch! There, you pauper! What a bright thing I did when I rinsed my mouth with your rascal of a father's apology for brandy."

The poor woman lived in continual fear, in a ceaseless trembling of body and soul, in everlasting expectation of outrageous thrashings.

This lasted ten years. She was so timorous that she would grow pale whenever she spoke to any one, and she thought of nothing but the blows with which she was threatened; and she became thinner, more yellow and drier than a smoked fish.

II

One night, when her husband was at sea, she was suddenly awakened by the wild roaring of the wind!

She sat up in her bed, trembling, but, as she hear nothing more, she lay down again; almost immediately there was a roar in the chimney which shook the entire house; it seemed to cross the heavens like a pack of furious animals snorting and roaring.

Then she arose and rushed to the harbor. Other women were arriving from all sides, carrying lanterns. The men also were gathering, and all were watching the foaming crests of the breaking wave.

The storm lasted fifteen hours. Eleven sailors never returned; Patin was among them.

In the neighborhood of Dieppe the wreck of his bark, the Jeune-Amelie, was found. The bodies of his sailors were found near Saint-Valery, but his body was never recovered. As his vessel seemed to have been cut in two, his wife expected and feared his return for a long time, for if there had been a collision he alone might have been picked up and carried afar off.

Little by little she grew accustomed to the thought that she was rid of him, although she would start every time that a neighbor, a beggar or a peddler would enter suddenly.

One afternoon, about four years after the disappearance of her husband, while she was walking along the Rue aux Juifs, she stopped before the house of an old sea captain who had recently died and whose furniture was for sale. Just at that moment a parrot was at auction. He had green feathers and a blue head and was watching everybody with a displeased look. "Three francs!" cried the auctioneer. "A bird that can talk like a lawyer, three francs!"

A friend of the Patin woman nudged her and said:

"You ought to buy that, you who are rich. It would be good company for you. That bird is worth more than thirty francs. Anyhow, you can always sell it for twenty or twenty-five!"

Patin's widow added fifty centimes, and the bird was given her in a little cage, which she carried away. She took it home, and, as she was opening the wire door in order to give it something to drink, he bit her finger and drew blood.

"Oh, how naughty he is!" she said.

Nevertheless she gave it some hemp-seed and corn and watched it pruning its feathers as it glanced warily at its new home and its new mistress. On the following morning, just as day was breaking, the Patin woman distinctly heard a loud, deep, roaring voice calling: "Are you going to get up, carrion?"

Her fear was so great that she hid her head under the sheets, for when Patin was with her as soon as he would open his eyes he would shout those well-known words into her ears.

Trembling, rolled into a ball, her back prepared for the thrashing which she already expected, her face buried in the pillows, she murmured: "Good Lord! he is here! Good Lord! he is here! Good Lord! he has come back!"

Minutes passed; no noise disturbed the quiet room. Then, trembling, she stuck her head out of the bed, sure that he was there, watching, ready to beat her. Except for a ray of sun shining through the window, she saw nothing, and she said to her self: "He must be hidden."

She waited a long time and then, gaining courage, she said to herself: "I must have dreamed it, seeing there is nobody here."

A little reassured, she closed her eyes, when from quite near a furious voice, the thunderous voice of the drowned man, could be heard crying: "Say! when in the name of all that's holy are you going to get up, you b——?"

She jumped out of bed, moved by obedience, by the passive obedience of a woman accustomed to blows and who still remembers and always will remember that voice! She said: "Here I am, Patin; what do you want?"

Put Patin did not answer. Then, at a complete loss, she looked around her, then in the chimney and under the bed and finally sank into a chair, wild with anxiety, convinced that Patin's soul alone was there, near her, and that he had returned in order to torture her.

Suddenly she remembered the loft, in order to reach which one had to take a ladder. Surely he must have hidden there in order to surprise her. He must have been held by savages on some distant shore, unable to escape until now, and he had returned, worse that ever. There was no doubting the quality of that voice. She raised her head and asked: "Are you up there, Patin?"

Patin did not answer. Then, with a terrible fear which made her heart tremble, she climbed the ladder, opened the skylight, looked, saw nothing, entered, looked about and found nothing. Sitting on some straw, she began to cry, but while she was weeping, overcome by a poignant and supernatural terror, she heard Patin talking in the room below.

He seemed less angry and he was saying: "Nasty weather! Fierce wind! Nasty weather! I haven't eaten, damn it!"

She cried through the ceiling: "Here I am, Patin; I am getting your meal ready. Don't get angry."

She ran down again. There was no one in the room. She felt herself growing weak, as if death were touching her, and she tried to run and get help from the neighbors, when a voice near her cried out: "I haven't had my breakfast, by G—!"

And the parrot in his cage watched her with his round, knowing, wicked eye. She, too, looked at him wildly, murmuring: "Ah! so it's you!"

He shook his head and continued: "Just you wait! I'll teach you how to loaf."

What happened within her? She felt, she understood that it was he, the dead man, who had come back, who had disguised himself in the feathers of this bird in order to continue to torment her; that he would curse, as formerly, all day long, and bite her, and swear at her, in order to attract the neighbors and make them laugh. Then she rushed for the cage and seized the bird, which scratched and tore her flesh with its claws and beak. But she held it with all her strength between her hands. She threw it on the ground and rolled over it with the frenzy of one possessed. She crushed it and finally made of it nothing but a little green, flabby lump which no longer moved or spoke. Then she wrapped it in a cloth, as in a shroud, and she went out in her nightgown, barefoot; she crossed the dock, against which the choppy waves of the sea were beating, and she shook the cloth and let drop this little, dead thing, which looked like so much grass. Then she returned, threw herself on her knees before the empty cage, and, overcome by what she had done, kneeled and prayed for forgiveness, as if she had committed some heinous crime.

THE PIECE OF STRING

It was market-day, and from all the country round Goderville the peasants and their wives were coming toward the town. The men walked slowly, throwing the whole body forward at every step of their long, crooked legs. They were deformed from pushing the plough which makes the left-shoulder higher, and bends their figures side-ways; from reaping the grain, when they have to spread their legs so as to keep on their feet. Their starched blue blouses, glossy as though varnished, ornamented at collar and cuffs with a little embroidered design and blown out around their bony bodies, looked very much like balloons about to soar, whence issued two arms and two feet.

Some of these fellows dragged a cow or a calf at the end of a rope. And just behind the animal followed their wives beating it over the back with a leaf-covered branch to hasten its pace, and carrying large baskets out of which protruded the heads of chickens or ducks. These women walked more quickly and energetically than the men, with their erect, dried-up figures, adorned with scanty little shawls pinned over their flat bosoms, and their heads wrapped round with a white cloth, enclosing the hair and surmounted by a cap.

Now a char-a-banc passed by, jogging along behind a nag and shaking up strangely the two men on the seat, and the woman at the bottom of the cart who held fast to its sides to lessen the hard jolting.

In the market-place at Goderville was a great crowd, a mingled multitude of men and beasts. The horns of cattle, the high, long-napped hats of wealthy peasants, the head-dresses of the women came to the surface of that sea. And the sharp, shrill, barking voices made a continuous, wild din, while above it occasionally rose a huge burst of laughter from the sturdy lungs of a merry peasant or a prolonged bellow from a cow tied fast to the wall of a house.

It all smelled of the stable, of milk, of hay and of perspiration, giving off that half-human, half-animal odor which is peculiar to country folks.

Maitre Hauchecorne, of Breaute, had just arrived at Goderville and was making his way toward the square when he perceived on the ground a little piece of string. Maitre Hauchecorne, economical as are all true Normans, reflected that everything was worth picking up which could be of any use, and he stooped down, but painfully, because he suffered from rheumatism. He took the bit of thin string from the ground and was carefully preparing to roll it up when he saw Maitre Malandain, the harness maker, on his doorstep staring at him. They had once had a quarrel about a halter, and they had borne each other malice ever since. Maitre Hauchecorne was overcome with a sort of shame at being seen by his enemy picking up a bit of string in the road. He quickly hid it beneath his blouse and then slipped it into his breeches, pocket, then pretended to be still looking for something on the ground which he did not discover and finally went off toward the market-place, his head bent forward and his body almost doubled in two by rheumatic pains.

He was at once lost in the crowd, which kept moving about slowly and noisily as it chaffered and bargained. The peasants examined the cows, went off, came back, always in doubt for fear of being cheated, never quite daring to decide, looking the seller square in the eye in the effort to discover the tricks of the man and the defect in the beast.

The women, having placed their great baskets at their feet, had taken out the poultry, which lay upon the ground, their legs tied together, with terrified eyes and scarlet combs.

They listened to propositions, maintaining their prices in a decided manner with an impassive face or perhaps deciding to accept the smaller price offered, suddenly calling out to the customer who was starting to go away:

"All right, I'll let you have them, Mait' Anthime."

Then, little by little, the square became empty, and when the Angelus struck midday those who lived at a distance poured into the inns.

At Jourdain's the great room was filled with eaters, just as the vast court was filled with vehicles of every sort—wagons, gigs, chars-a-bancs, tilburies, innumerable vehicles which have no name, yellow with mud, misshapen, pieced together, raising their shafts to heaven like two arms, or it may be with their nose on the ground and their rear in the air.

Just opposite to where the diners were at table the huge fireplace, with its bright flame, gave out a burning heat on the backs of those who sat at the right. Three spits were turning, loaded with chickens, with pigeons and with joints of mutton, and a delectable odor of roast meat and of gravy flowing over crisp brown skin arose from the hearth, kindled merriment, caused mouths to water.

All the aristocracy of the plough were eating there at Mait' Jourdain's, the innkeeper's, a dealer in horses also and a sharp fellow who had made a great deal of money in his day.

The dishes were passed round, were emptied, as were the jugs of yellow cider. Every one told of his affairs, of his purchases and his sales. They exchanged news about the crops. The weather was good for greens, but too wet for grain.

Suddenly the drum began to beat in the courtyard before the house. Every one, except some of the most indifferent, was on their feet at once and ran to the door, to the windows, their mouths full and napkins in their hand.

When the public crier had finished his tattoo he called forth in a jerky voice, pausing in the wrong places:

"Be it known to the inhabitants of Goderville and in general to all persons present at the market that there has been lost this morning on the Beuzeville road, between nine and ten o'clock, a black leather pocketbook containing five hundred francs and business papers. You are requested to return it to the mayor's office at once or to Maitre Fortune Houlbreque, of Manneville. There will be twenty francs reward."

Then the man went away. They heard once more at a distance the dull beating of the drum and the faint voice of the crier. Then they all began to talk of this incident, reckoning up the chances which Maitre Houlbreque had of finding or of not finding his pocketbook again.

The meal went on. They were finishing their coffee when the corporal of gendarmes appeared on the threshold.

He asked:

"Is Maitre Hauchecorne, of Breaute, here?"

Maitre Hauchecorne, seated at the other end of the table answered:

"Here I am, here I am."

And he followed the corporal.

The mayor was waiting for him, seated in an armchair. He was the notary of the place, a tall, grave man of pompous speech.

"Maitre Hauchecorne," said he, "this morning on the Beuzeville road, you were seen to pick up the pocketbook lost by Maitre Houlbreque, of Manneville."

The countryman looked at the mayor in amazement frightened already at this suspicion which rested on him, he knew not why.

"I—I picked up that pocketbook?"

"Yes, YOU."

"I swear I don't even know anything about it."

"You were seen."

"I was seen—I? Who saw me?"

"M. Malandain, the harness-maker."

Then the old man remembered, understood, and, reddening with anger, said:

"Ah! he saw me, did he, the rascal? He saw me picking up this string here, M'sieu le Maire."

And fumbling at the bottom of his pocket, he pulled out of it the little end of string.

But the mayor incredulously shook his head:

"You will not make me believe, Maitre Hauchecorne, that M. Malandain, who is a man whose word can be relied on, has mistaken this string for a pocketbook."

The peasant, furious, raised his hand and spat on the ground beside him as if to attest his good faith, repeating:

"For all that, it is God's truth, M'sieu le Maire. There! On my soul's salvation, I repeat it."

The mayor continued:

"After you picked up the object in question, you even looked about for some time in the mud to see if a piece of money had not dropped out of it."

The good man was choking with indignation and fear.

"How can they tell—how can they tell such lies as that to slander an honest man! How can they?"

His protestations were in vain; he was not believed.

He was confronted with M. Malandain, who repeated and sustained his testimony. They railed at one another for an hour. At his own request Maitre Hauchecorne was searched. Nothing was found on him.

At last the mayor, much perplexed, sent him away, warning him that he would inform the public prosecutor and ask for orders.

The news had spread. When he left the mayor's office the old man was surrounded, interrogated with a curiosity which was serious or mocking, as the case might be, but into which no indignation entered. And he began to tell the story of the string. They did not believe him. They laughed.

He passed on, buttonholed by every one, himself buttonholing his acquaintances, beginning over and over again his tale and his protestations, showing his pockets turned inside out to prove that he had nothing in them.

They said to him:

"You old rogue!"

He grew more and more angry, feverish, in despair at not being believed, and kept on telling his story.

The night came. It was time to go home. He left with three of his neighbors, to whom he pointed out the place where he had picked up the string, and all the way he talked of his adventure.

That evening he made the round of the village of Breaute for the purpose of telling every one. He met only unbelievers.

He brooded over it all night long.

The next day, about one in the afternoon, Marius Paumelle, a farm hand of Maitre Breton, the market gardener at Ymauville, returned the pocketbook and its contents to Maitre Holbreque, of Manneville.

This man said, indeed, that he had found it on the road, but not knowing how to read, he had carried it home and given it to his master.

The news spread to the environs. Maitre Hauchecorne was informed. He started off at once and began to relate his story with the denoument. He was triumphant.

"What grieved me," said he, "was not the thing itself, do you understand, but it was being accused of lying. Nothing does you so much harm as being in disgrace for lying."

All day he talked of his adventure. He told it on the roads to the people who passed, at the cabaret to the people who drank and next Sunday when they came out of church. He even stopped strangers to tell them about it. He was easy now, and yet something worried him without his knowing exactly what it was. People had a joking manner while they listened. They did not seem convinced. He seemed to feel their remarks behind his back.

On Tuesday of the following week he went to market at Godeville, prompted solely by the need of telling his story.

Malandain, standing on his doorstep, began to laugh as he saw him pass. Why?

He accosted a farmer of Criquetot, who did not let hire finish, and giving him a punch in the pit of the stomach cried in his face: "Oh, you great rogue!" Then he turned his heel upon him.

Maitre Hauchecorne remained speechless and grew more and more uneasy. Why had they called him "great rogue"?

When seated at table in Jourdain's tavern he began again to explain the whole affair.

A horse dealer of Montivilliers shouted at him:

"Get out, get out, you old scamp! I know all about your old string."

Hauchecorne stammered:

"But since they found it again, the pocketbook!"

But the other continued:

"Hold your tongue, daddy; there's one who finds it and there's another who returns it. And no one the wiser."

The farmer was speechless. He understood at last. They accused him of having had the pocketbook brought back by an accomplice, by a confederate.

He tried to protest. The whole table began to laugh.

He could not finish his dinner, and went away amid a chorus of jeers.

He went home indignant, choking with rage, with confusion, the more cast down since with his Norman craftiness he was, perhaps, capable of having done what they accused him of and even of boasting of it as a good trick. He was dimly conscious that it was impossible to prove his innocence, his craftiness being so well known. He felt himself struck to the heart by the injustice of the suspicion.

He began anew to tell his tale, lengthening his recital every day, each day adding new proofs, more energetic declarations and more sacred oaths, which he thought of, which he prepared in his hours of solitude, for his mind was entirely occupied with the story of the string. The more he denied it, the more artful his arguments, the less he was believed.

"Those are liars proofs," they said behind his back.

He felt this. It preyed upon him and he exhausted himself in useless efforts.

He was visibly wasting away.

Jokers would make him tell the story of "the piece of string" to amuse them, just as you make a soldier who has been on a campaign tell his story of the battle. His mind kept growing weaker and about the end of December he took to his bed.

He passed away early in January, and, in the ravings of death agony, he protested his innocence, repeating:

"A little bit of string—a little bit of string. See, here it is, M'sieu le Maire."

VOLUME IX.

TOINE

He was known for thirty miles round was father Toine—fat Toine, Toine-my-extra, Antoine Macheble, nicknamed Burnt-Brandy—the innkeeper of Tournevent.

It was he who had made famous this hamlet buried in a niche in the valley that led down to the sea, a poor little peasants' hamlet consisting of ten Norman cottages surrounded by ditches and trees.

The houses were hidden behind a curve which had given the place the name of Tournevent. It seemed to have sought shelter in this ravine overgrown with grass and rushes, from the keen, salt sea wind—the ocean wind that devours and burns like fire, that drys up and withers like the sharpest frost of winter, just as birds seek shelter in the furrows of the fields in time of storm.

But the whole hamlet seemed to be the property of Antoine Macheble, nicknamed Burnt-Brandy, who was called also Toine, or Toine-My-Extra-Special, the latter in consequence of a phrase current in his mouth:

"My Extra-Special is the best in France:"

His "Extra-Special" was, of course, his cognac.

For the last twenty years he had served the whole countryside with his Extra-Special and his "Burnt-Brandy," for whenever he was asked: "What shall I drink, Toine?" he invariably answered: "A burnt-brandy, my son-in-law; that warms the inside and clears the head—there's nothing better for your body."

He called everyone his son-in-law, though he had no daughter, either married or to be married.

Well known indeed was Toine Burnt-Brandy, the stoutest man in all Normandy. His little house seemed ridiculously small, far too small and too low to hold him; and when people saw him standing at his door, as he did all day long, they asked one another how he could possibly get through the door. But he went in whenever a customer appeared, for it was only right that Toine should be invited to take his thimbleful of whatever was drunk in his wine shop.

His inn bore the sign: "The Friends' Meeting-Place"—and old Toine was, indeed, the friend of all. His customers came from Fecamp and Montvilliers, just for the fun of seeing him and hearing him talk; for fat Toine would have made a tombstone laugh. He had a way of chaffing people without offending them, or of winking to express what he didn't say, of slapping his thighs when he was merry in such a way as to make you hold your sides, laughing. And then, merely to see him drink was a curiosity. He drank everything that was offered him, his roguish eyes twinkling, both with the enjoyment of drinking and at the thought of the money he was taking in. His was a double pleasure: first, that of drinking; and second, that of piling up the cash.

You should have heard him quarrelling with his wife! It was worth paying for to see them together. They had wrangled all the thirty years they had been married; but Toine was good-humored, while his better-half grew angry. She was a tall peasant woman, who walked with long steps like a stork, and had a head resembling that of an angry screech-owl. She spent her time rearing chickens in a little poultry-yard behind the inn, and she was noted for her success in fattening them for the table.

Whenever the gentry of Fecamp gave a dinner they always had at least one of Madame Toine's chickens to be in the fashion.

But she was born ill-tempered, and she went through life in a mood of perpetual discontent. Annoyed at everyone, she seemed to be particularly annoyed at her husband. She disliked his gaiety, his reputation, his rude health, his embonpoint. She treated him as a good-for-nothing creature because he earned his money without working, and as a glutton because he ate and drank as much as ten ordinary men; and not a day went by without her declaring spitefully:

"You'd be better in the stye along with the pigs! You're so fat it makes me sick to look at you!"

And she would shout in his face:

"Wait! Wait a bit! We'll see! You'll burst one of these fine days like a sack of corn-you old bloat, you!"

Toine would laugh heartily, patting his corpulent person, and replying:

"Well, well, old hen, why don't you fatten up your chickens like that? just try!"

And, rolling his sleeves back from his enormous arm, he said:

"That would make a fine wing now, wouldn't it?"

And the customers, doubled up with laughter, would thump the table with their fists and stamp their feet on the floor.

The old woman, mad with rage, would repeat:

"Wait a bit! Wait a bit! You'll see what'll happen. He'll burst like a sack of grain!"

And off she would go, amid the jeers and laughter of the drinkers.

Toine was, in fact, an astonishing sight, he was so fat, so heavy, so red. He was one of those enormous beings with whom Death seems to be amusing himself—playing perfidious tricks and pranks, investing with an irresistibly comic air his slow work of destruction. Instead of manifesting his approach, as with others, in white hairs, in emaciation, in wrinkles, in the gradual collapse which makes the onlookers say: "Gad! how he has changed!" he took a malicious pleasure in fattening Toine, in making him monstrous and absurd, in tingeing his face with a deep crimson, in giving him the appearance of superhuman health, and the changes he inflicts on all were in the case of Toine laughable, comic, amusing, instead of being painful and distressing to witness.

"Wait a bit! Wait a bit!" said his wife. "You'll see."

At last Toine had an apoplectic fit, and was paralyzed in consequence. The giant was put to bed in the little room behind the partition of the drinking-room that he might hear what was said and talk to his friends, for his head was quite clear although his enormous body was helplessly inert. It was hoped at first that his immense legs would regain some degree of power; but this hope soon disappeared, and Toine spent his days and nights in the bed, which was only made up once a week, with the help of four neighbors who lifted the innkeeper, each holding a limb, while his mattress was turned.

He kept his spirits, nevertheless; but his gaiety was of a different kind—more timid, more humble; and he lived in a constant, childlike fear of his wife, who grumbled from morning till night:

"Look at him there—the great glutton! the good-for-nothing creature, the old boozer! Serve him right, serve him right!"

He no longer answered her. He contented himself with winking behind the old woman's back, and turning over on his other side—the only movement of which he was now capable. He called this exercise a "tack to the north" or a "tack to the south."

His great distraction nowadays was to listen to the conversations in the bar, and to shout through the wall when he recognized a friend's voice:

"Hallo, my son-in-law! Is that you, Celestin?"

And Celestin Maloisel answered:

"Yes, it's me, Toine. Are you getting about again yet, old fellow?"

"Not exactly getting about," answered Toine. "But I haven't grown thin; my carcass is still good."

Soon he got into the way of asking his intimates into his room to keep him company, although it grieved him to see that they had to drink without him. It pained him to the quick that his customers should be drinking without him.

"That's what hurts worst of all," he would say: "that I cannot drink my Extra-Special any more. I can put up with everything else, but going without drink is the very deuce."

Then his wife's screech-owl face would appear at the window, and she would break in with the words:

"Look at him! Look at him now, the good-for-nothing wretch! I've got to feed him and wash him just as if he were a pig!"

And when the old woman had gone, a cock with red feathers would sometimes fly up to the window sill and looking into the room with his round inquisitive eye, would begin to crow loudly. Occasionally, too, a few hens would flutter as far as the foot of the bed, seeking crumbs on the floor. Toine's friends soon deserted the drinking room to come and chat every afternoon beside the invalid's bed. Helpless though he was, the jovial Toine still provided them with amusement. He would have made the devil himself laugh. Three men were regular in their attendance at the bedside: Celestin Maloisel, a tall, thin fellow, somewhat gnarled, like the trunk of an apple-tree; Prosper Horslaville, a withered little man with a ferret nose, cunning as a fox; and Cesaire Paumelle, who never spoke, but who enjoyed Toine's society all the same.

They brought a plank from the yard, propped it upon the edge of the bed, and played dominoes from two till six.

But Toine's wife soon became insufferable. She could not endure that her fat, lazy husband should amuse himself at games while lying in his bed; and whenever she caught him beginning a game she pounced furiously on the dominoes, overturned the plank, and carried all away into the bar, declaring that it was quite enough to have to feed that fat, lazy pig without seeing him amusing himself, as if to annoy poor people who had to work hard all day long.

Celestin Maloisel and Cesaire Paumelle bent their heads to the storm, but Prosper Horslaville egged on the old woman, and was only amused at her wrath.

One day, when she was more angry than usual, he said:

"Do you know what I'd do if I were you?"

She fixed her owl's eyes on him, and waited for his next words.

Prosper went on:

"Your man is as hot as an oven, and he never leaves his bed—well, I'd make him hatch some eggs."

She was struck dumb at the suggestion, thinking that Prosper could not possibly be in earnest. But he continued:

"I'd put five under one arm, and five under the other, the same day that I set a hen. They'd all come out at the same time; then I'd take your husband's chickens to the hen to bring up with her own. You'd rear a fine lot that way."

"Could it be done?" asked the astonished old woman.

"Could it be done?" echoed the man. "Why not? Since eggs can be hatched in a warm box why shouldn't they be hatched in a warm bed?"

She was struck by this reasoning, and went away soothed and reflective.

A week later she entered Toine's room with her apron full of eggs, and said:

"I've just put the yellow hen on ten eggs. Here are ten for you; try not to break them."

"What do you want?" asked the amazed Toine.

"I want you to hatch them, you lazy creature!" she answered.

He laughed at first; then, finding she was serious, he got angry, and refused absolutely to have the eggs put under his great arms, that the warmth of his body might hatch them.

But the old woman declared wrathfully:

"You'll get no dinner as long as you won't have them. You'll see what'll happen."

Tome was uneasy, but answered nothing.

When twelve o'clock struck, he called out:

"Hullo, mother, is the soup ready?"

"There's no soup for you, lazy-bones," cried the old woman from her kitchen.

He thought she must be joking, and waited a while. Then he begged, implored, swore, "tacked to the north" and "tacked to the south," and beat on the wall with his fists, but had to consent at last to five eggs being placed against his left side; after which he had his soup.

When his friends arrived that afternoon they thought he must be ill, he seemed so constrained and queer.

They started the daily game of dominoes. But Tome appeared to take no pleasure in it, and reached forth his hand very slowly, and with great precaution.

"What's wrong with your arm?" asked Horslaville.

"I have a sort of stiffness in the shoulder," answered Toine.

Suddenly they heard people come into the inn. The players were silent.

It was the mayor with the deputy. They ordered two glasses of Extra-Special, and began to discuss local affairs. As they were talking in somewhat low tones Toine wanted to put his ear to the wall, and, forgetting all about his eggs, he made a sudden "tack to the north," which had the effect of plunging him into the midst of an omelette.

At the loud oath he swore his wife came hurrying into the room, and, guessing what had happened, stripped the bedclothes from him with lightning rapidity. She stood at first without moving or uttering a syllable, speechless with indignation at sight of the yellow poultice sticking to her husband's side.

Then, trembling with fury, she threw herself on the paralytic, showering on him blows such as those with which she cleaned her linen on the seashore. Tome's three friends were choking with laughter, coughing, spluttering and shouting, and the fat innkeeper himself warded his wife's attacks with all the prudence of which he was capable, that he might not also break the five eggs at his other side.

Tome was conquered. He had to hatch eggs, he had to give up his games of dominoes and renounce movement of any sort, for the old woman angrily deprived him of food whenever he broke an egg.

He lay on his back, with eyes fixed on the ceiling, motionless, his arms raised like wings, warming against his body the rudimentary chickens enclosed in their white shells.

He spoke now only in hushed tones; as if he feared a noise as much as motion, and he took a feverish interest in the yellow hen who was accomplishing in the poultry-yard the same task as he.

"Has the yellow hen eaten her food all right?" he would ask his wife.

And the old woman went from her fowls to her husband and from her husband to her fowls, devoured by anxiety as to the welfare of the little chickens who were maturing in the bed and in the nest.

The country people who knew the story came, agog with curiosity, to ask news of Toine. They entered his room on tiptoe, as one enters a sick-chamber, and asked:

"Well! how goes it?"

"All right," said Toine; "only it keeps me fearfully hot."

One morning his wife entered in a state of great excitement, and declared:

"The yellow hen has seven chickens! Three of the eggs were addled."

Toine's heart beat painfully. How many would he have?

"Will it soon be over?" he asked, with the anguish of a woman who is about to become a mother.

"It's to be hoped so!" answered the old woman crossly, haunted by fear of failure.

They waited. Friends of Toine who had got wind that his time was drawing near arrived, and filled the little room.

Nothing else was talked about in the neighboring cottages. Inquirers asked one another for news as they stood at their doors.

About three o'clock Toine fell asleep. He slumbered half his time nowadays. He was suddenly awakened by an unaccustomed tickling under his right arm. He put his left hand on the spot, and seized a little creature covered with yellow down, which fluttered in his hand.

His emotion was so great that he cried out, and let go his hold of the chicken, which ran over his chest. The bar was full of people at the time. The customers rushed to Toine's room, and made a circle round him as they would round a travelling showman; while Madame Toine picked up the chicken, which had taken refuge under her husband's beard.

No one spoke, so great was the tension. It was a warm April day. Outside the window the yellow hen could be heard calling to her newly-fledged brood.

Toine, who was perspiring with emotion and anxiety, murmured:

"I have another now—under the left arm."

His' wife plunged her great bony hand into the bed, and pulled out a second chicken with all the care of a midwife.

The neighbors wanted to see it. It was passed from one to another, and examined as if it were a phenomenon.

For twenty minutes no more hatched out, then four emerged at the same moment from their shells.

There was a great commotion among the lookers-on. And Toine smiled with satisfaction, beginning to take pride in this unusual sort of paternity. There were not many like him! Truly, he was a remarkable specimen of humanity!

"That makes six!" he declared. "Great heavens, what a christening we'll have!"

And a loud laugh rose from all present. Newcomers filled the bar. They asked one another:

"How many are there?"

"Six."

Toine's wife took this new family to the hen, who clucked loudly, bristled her feathers, and spread her wings wide to shelter her growing brood of little ones.

"There's one more!" cried Toine.

He was mistaken. There were three! It was an unalloyed triumph! The last chicken broke through its shell at seven o'clock in the evening. All the eggs were good! And Toine, beside himself with joy, his brood hatched out, exultant, kissed the tiny creature on the back, almost suffocating it. He wanted to keep it in his bed until morning, moved by a mother's tenderness toward the tiny being which he had brought to life, but the old woman carried it away like the others, turning a deaf ear to her husband's entreaties.

The delighted spectators went off to spread the news of the event, and Horslaville, who was the last to go, asked:

"You'll invite me when the first is cooked, won't you, Toine?"

At this idea a smile overspread the fat man's face, and he answered:

"Certainly I'll invite you, my son-in-law."

MADAME HUSSON'S "ROSIER"

We had just left Gisors, where I was awakened to hearing the name of the town called out by the guards, and I was dozing off again when a terrific shock threw me forward on top of a large lady who sat opposite me.

One of the wheels of the engine had broken, and the engine itself lay across the track. The tender and the baggage car were also derailed, and lay beside this mutilated engine, which rattled, groaned, hissed, puffed, sputtered, and resembled those horses that fall in the street with their flanks heaving, their breast palpitating, their nostrils steaming and their whole body trembling, but incapable of the slightest effort to rise and start off again.

There were no dead or wounded; only a few with bruises, for the train was not going at full speed. And we looked with sorrow at the great crippled iron creature that could not draw us along any more, and that blocked the track, perhaps for some time, for no doubt they would have to send to Paris for a special train to come to our aid.

It was then ten o'clock in the morning, and I at once decided to go back to Gisors for breakfast.

As I was walking along I said to myself:

"Gisors, Gisors—why, I know someone there!

"Who is it? Gisors? Let me see, I have a friend in this town." A name suddenly came to my mind, "Albert Marambot." He was an old school friend whom I had not seen for at least twelve years, and who was practicing medicine in Gisors. He had often written, inviting me to come and see him, and I had always promised to do so, without keeping my word. But at last I would take advantage of this opportunity.

I asked the first passer-by:

"Do you know where Dr. Marambot lives?"

He replied, without hesitation, and with the drawling accent of the Normans:

"Rue Dauphine."

I presently saw, on the door of the house he pointed out, a large brass plate on which was engraved the name of my old chum. I rang the bell, but the servant, a yellow-haired girl who moved slowly, said with a Stupid air:

"He isn't here, he isn't here."

I heard a sound of forks and of glasses and I cried:

"Hallo, Marambot!"

A door opened and a large man, with whiskers and a cross look on his face, appeared, carrying a dinner napkin in his hand.

I certainly should not have recognized him. One would have said he was forty-five at least, and, in a second, all the provincial life which makes one grow heavy, dull and old came before me. In a single flash of thought, quicker than the act of extending my hand to him, I could see his life, his manner of existence, his line of thought and his theories of things in general. I guessed at the prolonged meals that had rounded out his stomach, his after-dinner naps from the torpor of a slow indigestion aided by cognac, and his vague glances cast on the patient while he thought of the chicken that was roasting before the fire. His conversations about cooking, about cider, brandy and wine, the way of preparing certain dishes and of blending certain sauces were revealed to me at sight of his puffy red cheeks, his heavy lips and his lustreless eyes.

"You do not recognize me. I am Raoul Aubertin," I said.

He opened his arms and gave me such a hug that I thought he would choke me.

"You have not breakfasted, have you?"

"No."

"How fortunate! I was just sitting down to table and I have an excellent trout."

Five minutes later I was sitting opposite him at breakfast. I said:

"Are you a bachelor?"

"Yes, indeed."

"And do you like it here?"

"Time does not hang heavy; I am busy. I have patients and friends. I eat well, have good health, enjoy laughing and shooting. I get along."

"Is not life very monotonous in this little town?"

"No, my dear boy, not when one knows how to fill in the time. A little town, in fact, is like a large one. The incidents and amusements are less varied, but one makes more of them; one has fewer acquaintances, but one meets them more frequently. When you know all the windows in a street, each one of them interests you and puzzles you more than a whole street in Paris.

"A little town is very amusing, you know, very amusing, very amusing. Why, take Gisors. I know it at the tips of my fingers, from its beginning up to the present time. You have no idea what queer history it has."

"Do you belong to Gisors?"

"I? No. I come from Gournay, its neighbor and rival. Gournay is to Gisors what Lucullus was to Cicero. Here, everything is for glory; they say 'the proud people of Gisors.' At Gournay, everything is for the stomach; they say 'the chewers of Gournay.' Gisors despises Gournay, but Gournay laughs at Gisors. It is a very comical country, this."

I perceived that I was eating something very delicious, hard-boiled eggs wrapped in a covering of meat jelly flavored with herbs and put on ice for a few moments. I said as I smacked my lips to compliment Marambot:

"That is good."

He smiled.

"Two things are necessary, good jelly, which is hard to get, and good eggs. Oh, how rare good eggs are, with the yolks slightly reddish, and with a good flavor! I have two poultry yards, one for eggs and the other for chickens. I feed my laying hens in a special manner. I have my own ideas on the subject. In an egg, as in the meat of a chicken, in beef, or in mutton, in milk, in everything, one perceives, and ought to taste, the juice, the quintessence of all the food on which the animal has fed. How much better food we could have if more attention were paid to this!"

I laughed as I said:

"You are a gourmand?"

"Parbleu. It is only imbeciles who are not. One is a gourmand as one is an artist, as one is learned, as one is a poet. The sense of taste, my friend, is very delicate, capable of perfection, and quite as worthy of respect as the eye and the ear. A person who lacks this sense is deprived of an exquisite faculty, the faculty of discerning the quality of food, just as one may lack the faculty of discerning the beauties of a book or of a work of art; it means to be deprived of an essential organ, of something that belongs to higher humanity; it means to belong to one of those innumerable classes of the infirm, the unfortunate, and the fools of which our race is composed; it means to have the mouth of an animal, in a word, just like the mind of an animal. A man who cannot distinguish one kind of lobster from another; a herring—that admirable fish that has all the flavors, all the odors of the sea—from a mackerel or a whiting; and a Cresane from a Duchess pear, may be compared to a man who should mistake Balzac for Eugene Sue; a symphony of Beethoven for a military march composed by the bandmaster of a regiment; and the Apollo Belvidere for the statue of General de Blaumont.

"Who is General de Blaumont?"

"Oh, that's true, you do not know. It is easy to tell that you do not belong to Gisors. I told you just now, my dear boy, that they called the inhabitants of this town 'the proud people of Gisors,' and never was an epithet better deserved. But let us finish breakfast first, and then I will tell you about our town and take you to see it."

He stopped talking every now and then while he slowly drank a glass of wine which he gazed at affectionately as he replaced the glass on the table.

It was amusing to see him, with a napkin tied around his neck, his cheeks flushed, his eyes eager, and his whiskers spreading round his mouth as it kept working.

He made me eat until I was almost choking. Then, as I was about to return to the railway station, he seized me by the arm and took me through the streets. The town, of a pretty, provincial type, commanded by its citadel, the most curious monument of military architecture of the seventh century to be found in France, overlooks, in its turn, a long, green valley, where the large Norman cows graze and ruminate in the pastures.

The doctor quoted:

"'Gisors, a town of 4,000 inhabitants in the department of Eure, mentioned in Caesar's Commentaries: Caesaris ostium, then Caesartium, Caesortium, Gisortium, Gisors.' I shall not take you to visit the old Roman encampment, the remains of which are still in existence."

I laughed and replied:

"My dear friend, it seems to me that you are affected with a special malady that, as a doctor, you ought to study; it is called the spirit of provincialism."

He stopped abruptly.

"The spirit of provincialism, my friend, is nothing but natural patriotism," he said. "I love my house, my town and my province because I discover in them the customs of my own village; but if I love my country, if I become angry when a neighbor sets foot in it, it is because I feel that my home is in danger, because the frontier that I do not know is the high road to my province. For instance, I am a Norman, a true Norman; well, in spite of my hatred of the German and my desire for revenge, I do not detest them, I do not hate them by instinct as I hate the English, the real, hereditary natural enemy of the Normans; for the English traversed this soil inhabited by my ancestors, plundered and ravaged it twenty times, and my aversion to this perfidious people was transmitted to me at birth by my father. See, here is the statue of the general."

"What general?"

"General Blaumont! We had to have a statue. We are not 'the proud people of Gisors' for nothing! So we discovered General de Blaumont. Look in this bookseller's window."

He drew me towards the bookstore, where about fifteen red, yellow and blue volumes attracted the eye. As I read the titles, I began to laugh idiotically. They read:

Gisors, its origin, its future, by M. X. . . ., member of several learned societies; History of Gisors, by the Abbe A . . .; Gasors from the time of Caesar to the present day, by M. B. . . ., Landowner; Gisors and its environs, by Doctor C. D. . . .; The Glories of Gisors, by a Discoverer.

"My friend," resumed Marambot, "not a year, not a single year, you understand, passes without a fresh history of Gisors being published here; we now have twenty-three."

"And the glories of Gisors?" I asked.

"Oh, I will not mention them all, only the principal ones. We had first General de Blaumont, then Baron Davillier, the celebrated ceramist who explored Spain and the Balearic Isles, and brought to the notice of collectors the wonderful Hispano-Arabic china. In literature we have a very clever journalist, now dead, Charles Brainne, and among those who are living, the very eminent editor of the Nouvelliste de Rouen, Charles Lapierre . . . and many others, many others."

We were traversing along street with a gentle incline, with a June sun beating down on it and driving the residents into their houses.

Suddenly there appeared at the farther end of the street a drunken man who was staggering along, with his head forward his arms and legs limp. He would walk forward rapidly three, six, or ten steps and then stop. When these energetic movements landed him in the middle of the road he stopped short and swayed on his feet, hesitating between falling and a fresh start. Then he would dart off in any direction, sometimes falling against the wall of a house, against which he seemed to be fastened, as though he were trying to get in through the wall. Then he would suddenly turn round and look ahead of him, his mouth open and his eyes blinking in the sunlight, and getting away from the wall by a movement of the hips, he started off once more.

A little yellow dog, a half-starved cur, followed him, barking; stopping when he stopped, and starting off when he started.

"Hallo," said Marambot, "there is Madame Husson's 'Rosier'.

"Madame Husson's 'Rosier'," I exclaimed in astonishment. "What do you mean?"

The doctor began to laugh.

"Oh, that is what we call drunkards round here. The name comes from an old story which has now become a legend, although it is true in all respects."

"Is it an amusing story?"

"Very amusing."

"Well, then, tell it to me."

"I will."

There lived formerly in this town a very upright old lady who was a great guardian of morals and was called Mme. Husson. You know, I am telling you the real names and not imaginary ones. Mme. Husson took a special interest in good works, in helping the poor and encouraging the deserving. She was a little woman with a quick walk and wore a black wig. She was ceremonious, polite, on very good terms with the Almighty in the person of Abby Malon, and had a profound horror, an inborn horror of vice, and, in particular, of the vice the Church calls lasciviousness. Any irregularity before marriage made her furious, exasperated her till she was beside herself.

Now, this was the period when they presented a prize as a reward of virtue to any girl in the environs of Paris who was found to be chaste. She was called a Rosiere, and Mme. Husson got the idea that she would institute a similar ceremony at Gisors. She spoke about it to Abbe Malon, who at once made out a list of candidates.

However, Mme. Husson had a servant, an old woman called Francoise, as upright as her mistress. As soon as the priest had left, madame called the servant and said:

"Here, Francoise, here are the girls whose names M. le cure has submitted to me for the prize of virtue; try and find out what reputation they bear in the district."

And Francoise set out. She collected all the scandal, all the stories, all the tattle, all the suspicions. That she might omit nothing, she wrote it all down together with her memoranda in her housekeeping book, and handed it each morning to Mme. Husson, who, after adjusting her spectacles on her thin nose, read as follows:

      Bread..........................four sous

      Milk............................two sous

      Butter ....eight sous

Malvina Levesque got into trouble last year with Mathurin Poilu.

      Leg of mutton...................twenty-five sous

      Salt............................one sou

Rosalie Vatinel was seen in the Riboudet woods with Cesaire Pienoir, by

Mme. Onesime, the ironer, on July the 20th about dusk.

      Radishes........................one sou

      Vinegar.........................two sous

      Oxalic acid.....................two sous

Josephine Durdent, who is not believed to have committed a fault, although she corresponds with young Oportun, who is in service in Rouen, and who sent her a present of a cap by diligence.

Not one came out unscathed in this rigorous inquisition. Francoise inquired of everyone, neighbors, drapers, the principal, the teaching sisters at school, and gathered the slightest details.

As there is not a girl in the world about whom gossips have not found something to say, there was not found in all the countryside one young girl whose name was free from some scandal.

But Mme. Husson desired that the "Rosiere" of Gisors, like Caesar's wife, should be above suspicion, and she was horrified, saddened and in despair at the record in her servant's housekeeping account-book.

They then extended their circle of inquiries to the neighboring villages; but with no satisfaction.

They consulted the mayor. His candidates failed. Those of Dr. Barbesol were equally unlucky, in spite of the exactness of his scientific vouchers.

But one morning Francoise, on returning from one of her expeditions, said to her mistress:

"You see, madame, that if you wish to give a prize to anyone, there is only Isidore in all the country round."

Mme. Husson remained thoughtful. She knew him well, this Isidore, the son of Virginie the greengrocer. His proverbial virtue had been the delight of Gisors for several years, and served as an entertaining theme of conversation in the town, and of amusement to the young girls who loved to tease him. He was past twenty-one, was tall, awkward, slow and timid; helped his mother in the business, and spent his days picking over fruit and vegetables, seated on a chair outside the door.

He had an abnormal dread of a petticoat and cast down his eyes whenever a female customer looked at him smilingly, and this well-known timidity made him the butt of all the wags in the country.

Bold words, coarse expressions, indecent allusions, brought the color to his cheeks so quickly that Dr. Barbesol had nicknamed him "the thermometer of modesty." Was he as innocent as he looked? ill-natured people asked themselves. Was it the mere presentiment of unknown and shameful mysteries or else indignation at the relations ordained as the concomitant of love that so strongly affected the son of Virginie the greengrocer? The urchins of the neighborhood as they ran past the shop would fling disgusting remarks at him just to see him cast down his eyes. The girls amused themselves by walking up and down before him, cracking jokes that made him go into the store. The boldest among them teased him to his face just to have a laugh, to amuse themselves, made appointments with him and proposed all sorts of things.

So Madame Husson had become thoughtful.

Certainly, Isidore was an exceptional case of notorious, unassailable virtue. No one, among the most sceptical, most incredulous, would have been able, would have dared, to suspect Isidore of the slightest infraction of any law of morality. He had never been seen in a cafe, never been seen at night on the street. He went to bed at eight o'clock and rose at four. He was a perfection, a pearl.

But Mme. Husson still hesitated. The idea of substituting a boy for a girl, a "rosier" for a "rosiere," troubled her, worried her a little, and she resolved to consult Abbe Malon.

The abbe responded:

"What do you desire to reward, madame? It is virtue, is it not, and nothing but virtue? What does it matter to you, therefore, if it is masculine or feminine? Virtue is eternal; it has neither sex nor country; it is 'Virtue.'"

Thus encouraged, Mme. Husson went to see the mayor.

He approved heartily.

"We will have a fine ceremony," he said. "And another year if we can find a girl as worthy as Isidore we will give the reward to her. It will even be a good example that we shall set to Nanterre. Let us not be exclusive; let us welcome all merit."

Isidore, who had been told about this, blushed deeply and seemed happy.

The ceremony was fixed for the 15th of August, the festival of the Virgin Mary and of the Emperor Napoleon. The municipality had decided to make an imposing ceremony and had built the platform on the couronneaux, a delightful extension of the ramparts of the old citadel where I will take you presently.

With the natural revulsion of public feeling, the virtue of Isidore, ridiculed hitherto, had suddenly become respected and envied, as it would bring him in five hundred francs besides a savings bank book, a mountain of consideration, and glory enough and to spare. The girls now regretted their frivolity, their ridicule, their bold manners; and Isidore, although still modest and timid, had now a little contented air that bespoke his internal satisfaction.

The evening before the 15th of August the entire Rue Dauphine was decorated with flags. Oh, I forgot to tell you why this street had been called Rue Dauphine.

It seems that the wife or mother of the dauphin, I do not remember which one, while visiting Gisors had been feted so much by the authorities that during a triumphal procession through the town she stopped before one of the houses in this street, halting the procession, and exclaimed:

"Oh, the pretty house! How I should like to go through it! To whom does it belong?"

They told her the name of the owner, who was sent for and brought, proud and embarrassed, before the princess. She alighted from her carriage, went into the house, wishing to go over it from top to bottom, and even shut herself in one of the rooms alone for a few seconds.

When she came out, the people, flattered at this honor paid to a citizen of Gisors, shouted "Long live the dauphine!" But a rhymester wrote some words to a refrain, and the street retained the title of her royal highness, for

> "The princess, in a hurry,
>
> Without bell, priest, or beadle,
>
> But with some water only,
>
> Had baptized it."

But to come back to Isidore.

They had scattered flowers all along the road as they do for processions at the Fete-Dieu, and the National Guard was present, acting on the orders of their chief, Commandant Desbarres, an old soldier of the Grand Army, who pointed with pride to the beard of a Cossack cut with a single sword stroke from the chin of its owner by the commandant during the retreat in Russia, and which hung beside the frame containing the cross of the Legion of Honor presented to him by the emperor himself.

The regiment that he commanded was, besides, a picked regiment celebrated all through the province, and the company of grenadiers of Gisors was called on to attend all important ceremonies for a distance of fifteen to twenty leagues. The story goes that Louis Philippe, while reviewing the militia of Eure, stopped in astonishment before the company from Gisors, exclaiming:

"Oh, who are those splendid grenadiers?"

"The grenadiers of Gisors," replied the general.

"I might have known it," murmured the king.

So Commandant Desbarres came at the head of his men, preceded by the band, to get Isidore in his mother's store.

After a little air had been played by the band beneath the windows, the "Rosier" himself appeared—on the threshold. He was dressed in white duck from head to foot and wore a straw hat with a little bunch of orange blossoms as a cockade.

The question of his clothes had bothered Mme. Husson a good deal, and she hesitated some time between the black coat of those who make their first communion and an entire white suit. But Francoise, her counsellor, induced her to decide on the white suit, pointing out that the Rosier would look like a swan.

Behind him came his guardian, his godmother, Mme. Husson, in triumph. She took his arm to go out of the store, and the mayor placed himself on the other side of the Rosier. The drums beat. Commandant Desbarres gave the order "Present arms!" The procession resumed its march towards the church amid an immense crowd of people who has gathered from the neighboring districts.

After a short mass and an affecting discourse by Abbe Malon, they continued on their way to the couronneaux, where the banquet was served in a tent.

Before taking their seats at table, the mayor gave an address. This is it, word for word. I learned it by heart:

"Young man, a woman of means, beloved by the poor and respected by the rich, Mme. Husson, whom the whole country is thanking here, through me, had the idea, the happy and benevolent idea, of founding in this town a prize for, virtue, which should serve as a valuable encouragement to the inhabitants of this beautiful country.

"You, young man, are the first to be rewarded in this dynasty of goodness and chastity. Your name will remain at the head of this list of the most deserving, and your life, understand me, your whole life, must correspond to this happy commencement. To-day, in presence of this noble woman, of these soldier-citizens who have taken up their arms in your honor, in presence of this populace, affected, assembled to applaud you, or, rather, to applaud virtue, in your person, you make a solemn contract with the town, with all of us, to continue until your death the excellent example of your youth.

"Do not forget, young man, that you are the first seed cast into this field of hope; give us the fruits that we expect of you."

The mayor advanced three steps, opened his arms and pressed Isidore to his heart.

The "Rosier" was sobbing without knowing why, from a confused emotion, from pride and a vague and happy feeling of tenderness.

Then the mayor placed in one hand a silk purse in which gold tingled —five hundred francs in gold!— and in his other hand a savings bank book. And he said in a solemn tone:

"Homage, glory and riches to virtue."

Commandant Desbarres shouted "Bravo!" the grenadiers vociferated, and the crowd applauded.

Mme. Husson wiped her eyes, in her turn. Then they all sat down at the table where the banquet was served.

The repast was magnificent and seemed interminable. One course followed another; yellow cider and red wine in fraternal contact blended in the stomach of the guests. The rattle of plates, the sound of voices, and of music softly played, made an incessant deep hum, and was dispersed abroad in the clear sky where the swallows were flying. Mme. Husson occasionally readjusted her black wig, which would slip over on one side, and chatted with Abbe Malon. The mayor, who was excited, talked politics with Commandant Desbarres, and Isidore ate, drank, as if he had never eaten or drunk before. He helped himself repeatedly to all the dishes, becoming aware for the first time of the pleasure of having one's belly full of good things which tickle the palate in the first place. He had let out a reef in his belt and, without speaking, and although he was a little uneasy at a wine stain on his white waistcoat, he ceased eating in order to take up his glass and hold it to his mouth as long as possible, to enjoy the taste slowly.

It was time for the toasts. They were many and loudly applauded. Evening was approaching and they had been at the table since noon. Fine, milky vapors were already floating in the air in the valley, the light night-robe of streams and meadows; the sun neared the horizon; the cows were lowing in the distance amid the mists of the pasture. The feast was over. They returned to Gisors. The procession, now disbanded, walked in detachments. Mme. Husson had taken Isidore's arm and was giving him a quantity of urgent, excellent advice.

They stopped at the door of the fruit store, and the "Rosier" was left at his mother's house. She had not come home yet. Having been invited by her family to celebrate her son's triumph, she had taken luncheon with her sister after having followed the procession as far as the banqueting tent.

So Isidore remained alone in the store, which was growing dark. He sat down on a chair, excited by the wine and by pride, and looked about him. Carrots, cabbages, and onions gave out their strong odor of vegetables in the closed room, that coarse smell of the garden blended with the sweet, penetrating odor of strawberries and the delicate, slight, evanescent fragrance of a basket of peaches.

The "Rosier" took one of these and ate it, although he was as full as an egg. Then, all at once, wild with joy, he began to dance about the store, and something rattled in his waistcoat.

He was surprised, and put his hand in his pocket and brought out the purse containing the five hundred francs, which he had forgotten in his agitation. Five hundred francs! What a fortune! He poured the gold pieces out on the counter and spread them out with his big hand with a slow, caressing touch so as to see them all at the same time. There were twenty-five, twenty-five round gold pieces, all gold! They glistened on the wood in the dim light and he counted them over and over, one by one. Then he put them back in the purse, which he replaced in his pocket.

Who will ever know or who can tell what a terrible conflict took place in the soul of the "Rosier" between good and evil, the tumultuous attack of Satan, his artifices, the temptations which he offered to this timid virgin heart? What suggestions, what imaginations, what desires were not invented by the evil one to excite and destroy this chosen one? He seized his hat, Mme. Husson's saint, his hat, which still bore the little bunch of orange blossoms, and going out through the alley at the back of the house, he disappeared in the darkness.

Virginie, the fruiterer, on learning that her son had returned, went home at once, and found the house empty. She waited, without thinking anything about it at first; but at the end of a quarter of an hour she made inquiries. The neighbors had seen Isidore come home and had not seen him go out again. They began to look for him, but could not find him. His mother, in alarm, went to the mayor. The mayor knew nothing, except that he had left him at the door of his home. Mme. Husson had just retired when they informed her that her protege had disappeared. She immediately put on her wig, dressed herself and went to Virginie's house. Virginie, whose plebeian soul was readily moved, was weeping copiously amid her cabbages, carrots and onions.

They feared some accident had befallen him. What could it be? Commandant Desbarres notified the police, who made a circuit of the town, and on the high road to Pontoise they found the little bunch of orange blossoms. It was placed on a table around which the authorities were deliberating. The "Rosier" must have been the victim of some stratagem, some trick, some jealousy; but in what way? What means had been employed to kidnap this innocent creature, and with what object?

Weary of looking for him without any result, Virginie, alone, remained watching and weeping.

The following evening, when the coach passed by on its return from Paris, Gisors learned with astonishment that its "Rosier" had stopped the vehicle at a distance of about two hundred metres from the town, had climbed up on it and paid his fare, handing over a gold piece and receiving the change, and that he had quietly alighted in the centre of the great city.

There was great excitement all through the countryside. Letters passed between the mayor and the chief of police in Paris, but brought no result.

The days followed one another, a week passed.

Now, one morning, Dr. Barbesol, who had gone out early, perceived, sitting on a doorstep, a man dressed in a grimy linen suit, who was sleeping with his head leaning against the wall. He approached him and recognized Isidore. He tried to rouse him, but did not succeed in doing so. The ex-"Rosier" was in that profound, invincible sleep that is alarming, and the doctor, in surprise, went to seek assistance to help him in carrying the young man to Boncheval's drugstore. When they lifted him up they found an empty bottle under him, and when the doctor sniffed at it, he declared that it had contained brandy. That gave a suggestion as to what treatment he would require. They succeeded in rousing him.

Isidore was drunk, drunk and degraded by a week of guzzling, drunk and so disgusting that a ragman would not have touched him. His beautiful white duck suit was a gray rag, greasy, muddy, torn, and destroyed, and he smelt of the gutter and of vice.

He was washed, sermonized, shut up, and did not leave the house for four days. He seemed ashamed and repentant. They could not find on him either his purse, containing the five hundred francs, or the bankbook, or even his silver watch, a sacred heirloom left by his father, the fruiterer.

On the fifth day he ventured into the Rue Dauphine, Curious glances followed him and he walked along with a furtive expression in his eyes and his head bent down. As he got outside the town towards the valley they lost sight of him; but two hours later he returned laughing and rolling against the walls. He was drunk, absolutely drunk.

Nothing could cure him.

Driven from home by his mother, he became a wagon driver, and drove the charcoal wagons for the Pougrisel firm, which is still in existence.

His reputation as a drunkard became so well known and spread so far that even at Evreux they talked of Mme. Husson's "Rosier," and the sots of the countryside have been given that nickname.

A good deed is never lost.

Dr. Marambot rubbed his hands as he finished his story. I asked:

"Did you know the 'Rosier'?"

"Yes. I had the honor of closing his eyes."

"What did he die of?"

"An attack of delirium tremens, of course."

We had arrived at the old citadel, a pile of ruined walls dominated by the enormous tower of St. Thomas of Canterbury and the one called the Prisoner's Tower.

Marambot told me the story of this prisoner, who, with the aid of a nail, covered the walls of his dungeon with sculptures, tracing the reflections of the sun as it glanced through the narrow slit of a loophole.

I also learned that Clothaire II had given the patrimony of Gisors to his cousin, Saint Romain, bishop of Rouen; that Gisors ceased to be the capital of the whole of Vexin after the treaty of Saint-Clair-sur-Epte; that the town is the chief strategic centre of all that portion of France, and that in consequence of this advantage she was taken and retaken over and over again. At the command of William the Red, the eminent engineer, Robert de Bellesme, constructed there a powerful fortress that was attacked later by Louis le Gros, then by the Norman barons, was defended by Robert de Candos, was finally ceded to Louis le Gros by Geoffry Plantagenet, was retaken by the English in consequence of the treachery of the Knights-Templars, was contested by Philippe-Augustus and Richard the Lionhearted, was set on fire by Edward III of England, who could not take the castle, was again taken by the English in 1419, restored later to Charles VIII by Richard de Marbury, was taken by the Duke of Calabria occupied by the League, inhabited by Henry IV, etc., etc.

And Marambot, eager and almost eloquent, continued:

"What beggars, those English! And what sots, my boy; they are all 'Rosiers,' those hypocrites!"

Then, after a silence, stretching out his arm towards the tiny river that glistened in the meadows, he said:

"Did you know that Henry Monnier was one of the most untiring fishermen on the banks of the Epte?"

"No, I did not know it."

"And Bouffe, my boy, Bouffe was a painter on glass."

"You are joking!"

"No, indeed. How is it you do not know these things?"

THE ADOPTED SON

The two cottages stood beside each other at the foot of a hill near a little seashore resort. The two peasants labored hard on the unproductive soil to rear their little ones, and each family had four.

Before the adjoining doors a whole troop of urchins played and tumbled about from morning till night. The two eldest were six years old, and the youngest were about fifteen months; the marriages, and afterward the births, having taken place nearly simultaneously in both families.

The two mothers could hardly distinguish their own offspring among the lot, and as for the fathers, they were altogether at sea. The eight names danced in their heads; they were always getting them mixed up; and when they wished to call one child, the men often called three names before getting the right one.

The first of the two cottages, as you came up from the bathing beach, Rolleport, was occupied by the Tuvaches, who had three girls and one boy; the other house sheltered the Vallins, who had one girl and three boys.

They all subsisted frugally on soup, potatoes and fresh air. At seven o'clock in the morning, then at noon, then at six o'clock in the evening, the housewives got their broods together to give them their food, as the gooseherds collect their charges. The children were seated, according to age, before the wooden table, varnished by fifty years of use; the mouths of the youngest hardly reaching the level of the table. Before them was placed a bowl filled with bread, soaked in the water in which the potatoes had been boiled, half a cabbage and three onions; and the whole line ate until their hunger was appeased. The mother herself fed the smallest.

A small pot roast on Sunday was a feast for all; and the father on this day sat longer over the meal, repeating: "I wish we could have this every day."

One afternoon, in the month of August, a phaeton stopped suddenly in front of the cottages, and a young woman, who was driving the horses, said to the gentleman sitting at her side:

"Oh, look at all those children, Henri! How pretty they are, tumbling about in the dust, like that!"

The man did not answer, accustomed to these outbursts of admiration, which were a pain and almost a reproach to him. The young woman continued:

"I must hug them! Oh, how I should like to have one of them—that one there—the little tiny one!"

Springing down from the carriage, she ran toward the children, took one of the two youngest—a Tuvache child—and lifting it up in her arms, she kissed him passionately on his dirty cheeks, on his tousled hair daubed with earth, and on his little hands, with which he fought vigorously, to get away from the caresses which displeased him.

Then she got into the carriage again, and drove off at a lively trot. But she returned the following week, and seating herself on the ground, took the youngster in her arms, stuffed him with cakes; gave candies to all the others, and played with them like a young girl, while the husband waited patiently in the carriage.

She returned again; made the acquaintance of the parents, and reappeared every day with her pockets full of dainties and pennies.

Her name was Madame Henri d'Hubieres.

One morning, on arriving, her husband alighted with her, and without stopping to talk to the children, who now knew her well, she entered the farmer's cottage.

They were busy chopping wood for the fire. They rose to their feet in surprise, brought forward chairs, and waited expectantly.

Then the woman, in a broken, trembling voice, began:

"My good people, I have come to see you, because I should like—I should like to take—your little boy with me—"

The country people, too bewildered to think, did not answer.

She recovered her breath, and continued: "We are alone, my husband and I. We would keep it. Are you willing?"

The peasant woman began to understand. She asked:

"You want to take Charlot from us? Oh, no, indeed!"

Then M. d'Hubieres intervened:

"My wife has not made her meaning clear. We wish to adopt him, but he will come back to see you. If he turns out well, as there is every reason to expect, he will be our heir. If we, perchance, should have children, he will share equally with them; but if he should not reward our care, we should give him, when he comes of age, a sum of twenty thousand francs, which shall be deposited immediately in his name, with a lawyer. As we have thought also of you, we should pay you, until your death, a pension of one hundred francs a month. Do you understand me?"

The woman had arisen, furious.

"You want me to sell you Charlot? Oh, no, that's not the sort of thing to ask of a mother! Oh, no! That would be an abomination!"

The man, grave and deliberate, said nothing; but approved of what his wife said by a continued nodding of his head.

Madame d'Hubieres, in dismay, began to weep; turning to her husband, with a voice full of tears, the voice of a child used to having all its wishes gratified, she stammered:

"They will not do it, Henri, they will not do it."

Then he made a last attempt: "But, my friends, think of the child's future, of his happiness, of—"

The peasant woman, however, exasperated, cut him short:

"It's all considered! It's all understood! Get out of here, and don't let me see you again—the idea of wanting to take away a child like that!"

Madame d'Hubieres remembered that there were two children, quite little, and she asked, through her tears, with the tenacity of a wilful and spoiled woman:

"But is the other little one not yours?"

Father Tuvache answered: "No, it is our neighbors'. You can go to them if you wish." And he went back into his house, whence resounded the indignant voice of his wife.

The Vallins were at table, slowly eating slices of bread which they parsimoniously spread with a little rancid butter on a plate between the two.

M. d'Hubieres recommenced his proposals, but with more insinuations, more oratorical precautions, more shrewdness.

The two country people shook their heads, in sign of refusal, but when they learned that they were to have a hundred francs a month, they considered the matter, consulting one another by glances, much disturbed. They kept silent for a long time, tortured, hesitating. At last the woman asked: "What do you say to it, man?" In a weighty tone he said: "I say that it's not to be despised."

Madame d'Hubieres, trembling with anguish, spoke of the future of their child, of his happiness, and of the money which he could give them later.

The peasant asked: "This pension of twelve hundred francs, will it be promised before a lawyer?"

M. d'Hubieres responded: "Why, certainly, beginning with to-morrow."

The woman, who was thinking it over, continued:

"A hundred francs a month is not enough to pay for depriving us of the child. That child would be working in a few years; we must have a hundred and twenty francs."

Tapping her foot with impatience, Madame d'Hubieres granted it at once, and, as she wished to carry off the child with her, she gave a hundred francs extra, as a present, while her husband drew up a paper. And the young woman, radiant, carried off the howling brat, as one carries away a wished-for knick-knack from a shop.

The Tuvaches, from their door, watched her departure, silent, serious, perhaps regretting their refusal.

Nothing more was heard of little Jean Vallin. The parents went to the lawyer every month to collect their hundred and twenty francs. They had quarrelled with their neighbors, because Mother Tuvache grossly insulted them, continually, repeating from door to door that one must be unnatural to sell one's child; that it was horrible, disgusting, bribery. Sometimes she would take her Charlot in her arms, ostentatiously exclaiming, as if he understood:

"I didn't sell you, I didn't! I didn't sell you, my little one! I'm not rich, but I don't sell my children!"

The Vallins lived comfortably, thanks to the pension. That was the cause of the unappeasable fury of the Tuvaches, who had remained miserably poor. Their eldest went away to serve his time in the army; Charlot alone remained to labor with his old father, to support the mother and two younger sisters.

He had reached twenty-one years when, one morning, a brilliant carriage stopped before the two cottages. A young gentleman, with a gold watch-chain, got out, giving his hand to an aged, white-haired lady. The old lady said to him: "It is there, my child, at the second house." And he entered the house of the Vallins as though at home.

The old mother was washing her aprons; the infirm father slumbered at the chimney-corner. Both raised their heads, and the young man said:

"Good-morning, papa; good-morning, mamma!"

They both stood up, frightened! In a flutter, the peasant woman dropped her soap into the water, and stammered:

"Is it you, my child? Is it you, my child?"

He took her in his arms and hugged her, repeating: "Good-morning, mamma," while the old man, all a-tremble, said, in his calm tone which he never lost: "Here you are, back again, Jean," as if he had just seen him a month ago.

When they had got to know one another again, the parents wished to take their boy out in the neighborhood, and show him. They took him to the mayor, to the deputy, to the cure, and to the schoolmaster.

Charlot, standing on the threshold of his cottage, watched him pass. In the evening, at supper, he said to the old people: "You must have been stupid to let the Vallins' boy be taken."

The mother answered, obstinately: "I wouldn't sell my child."

The father remained silent. The son continued:

"It is unfortunate to be sacrificed like that."

Then Father Tuvache, in an angry tone, said:

"Are you going to reproach us for having kept you?" And the young man said, brutally:

"Yes, I reproach you for having been such fools. Parents like you make the misfortune of their children. You deserve that I should leave you." The old woman wept over her plate. She moaned, as she swallowed the spoonfuls of soup, half of which she spilled: "One may kill one's self to bring up children!"

Then the boy said, roughly: "I'd rather not have been born than be what I am. When I saw the other, my heart stood still. I said to myself: 'See what I should have been now!'" He got up: "See here, I feel that I would do better not to stay here, because I would throw it up to you from morning till night, and I would make your life miserable. I'll never forgive you for that!"

The two old people were silent, downcast, in tears.

He continued: "No, the thought of that would be too much. I'd rather look for a living somewhere else."

He opened the door. A sound of voices came in at the door. The Vallins were celebrating the return of their child.

COWARD

In society he was called "Handsome Signoles." His name was Vicomte Gontran-Joseph de Signoles.

An orphan, and possessed of an ample fortune, he cut quite a dash, as it is called. He had an attractive appearance and manner, could talk well, had a certain inborn elegance, an air of pride and nobility, a good mustache, and a tender eye, that always finds favor with women.

He was in great request at receptions, waltzed to perfection, and was regarded by his own sex with that smiling hostility accorded to the popular society man. He had been suspected of more than one love affair, calculated to enhance the reputation of a bachelor. He lived a happy, peaceful life—a life of physical and mental well-being. He had won considerable fame as a swordsman, and still more as a marksman.

"When the time comes for me to fight a duel," he said, "I shall choose pistols. With such a weapon I am sure to kill my man."

One evening, having accompanied two women friends of his with their husbands to the theatre, he invited them to take some ice cream at Tortoni's after the performance. They had been seated a few minutes in the restaurant when Signoles noticed that a man was staring persistently at one of the ladies. She seemed annoyed, and lowered her eyes. At last she said to her husband:

"There's a man over there looking at me. I don't know him; do you?"

The husband, who had noticed nothing, glanced across at the offender, and said:

"No; not in the least."

His wife continued, half smiling, half angry:

"It's very tiresome! He quite spoils my ice cream."

The husband shrugged his shoulders.

"Nonsense! Don't take any notice of him. If we were to bother our heads about all the ill-mannered people we should have no time for anything else."

But the vicomte abruptly left his seat. He could not allow this insolent fellow to spoil an ice for a guest of his. It was for him to take cognizance of the offence, since it was through him that his friends had come to the restaurant. He went across to the man and said:

"Sir, you are staring at those ladies in a manner I cannot permit. I must ask you to desist from your rudeness."

The other replied:

"Let me alone, will you!"

"Take care, sir," said the vicomte between his teeth, "or you will force me to extreme measures."

The man replied with a single word—a foul word, which could be heard from one end of the restaurant to the other, and which startled every one there. All those whose backs were toward the two disputants turned round; all the others raised their heads; three waiters spun round on their heels like tops; the two lady cashiers jumped, as if shot, then turned their bodies simultaneously, like two automata worked by the same spring.

There was dead silence. Then suddenly a sharp, crisp sound. The vicomte had slapped his adversary's face. Every one rose to interfere. Cards were exchanged.

When the vicomte reached home he walked rapidly up and down his room for some minutes. He was in a state of too great agitation to think connectedly. One idea alone possessed him: a duel. But this idea aroused in him as yet no emotion of any kind. He had done what he was bound to do; he had proved himself to be what he ought to be. He would be talked about, approved, congratulated. He repeated aloud, speaking as one does when under the stress of great mental disturbance:

"What a brute of a man!" Then he sat down, and began to reflect. He would have to find seconds as soon as morning came. Whom should he choose? He bethought himself of the most influential and best-known men of his acquaintance. His choice fell at last on the Marquis de la Tour-Noire and Colonel Bourdin-a nobleman and a soldier. That would be just the thing. Their names would carry weight in the newspapers. He was thirsty, and drank three glasses of water, one after another; then he walked up and down again. If he showed himself brave, determined, prepared to face a duel in deadly earnest, his adversary would probably draw back and proffer excuses. He picked up the card he had taken from his pocket and thrown on a table. He read it again, as he had already read it, first at a glance in the restaurant, and afterward on the way home in the light of each gas lamp: "Georges Lamil, 51 Rue Moncey." That was all.

He examined closely this collection of letters, which seemed to him mysterious, fraught with many meanings. Georges Lamil! Who was the man? What was his profession? Why had he stared so at the woman? Was it not monstrous that a stranger, an unknown, should thus all at once upset one's whole life, simply because it had pleased him to stare rudely at a woman? And the vicomte once more repeated aloud:

"What a brute!"

Then he stood motionless, thinking, his eyes still fixed on the card. Anger rose in his heart against this scrap of paper—a resentful anger, mingled with a strange sense of uneasiness. It was a stupid business altogether! He took up a penknife which lay open within reach, and deliberately stuck it into the middle of the printed name, as if he were stabbing some one.

So he would have to fight! Should he choose swords or pistols?—for he considered himself as the insulted party. With the sword he would risk less, but with the pistol there was some chance of his adversary backing out. A duel with swords is rarely fatal, since mutual prudence prevents the combatants from fighting close enough to each other for a point to enter very deep. With pistols he would seriously risk his life; but, on the other hand, he might come out of the affair with flying colors, and without a duel, after all.

"I must be firm," he said. "The fellow will be afraid."

The sound of his own voice startled him, and he looked nervously round the room. He felt unstrung. He drank another glass of water, and then began undressing, preparatory to going to bed.

As soon as he was in bed he blew out the light and shut his eyes.

"I have all day to-morrow," he reflected, "for setting my affairs in order. I must sleep now, in order to be calm when the time comes."

He was very warm in bed, but he could not succeed in losing consciousness. He tossed and turned, remained for five minutes lying on his back, then changed to his left side, then rolled over to his right. He was thirsty again, and rose to drink. Then a qualm seized him:

"Can it be possible that I am afraid?"

Why did his heart beat so uncontrollably at every well-known sound in his room? When the clock was about to strike, the prefatory grating of its spring made him start, and for several seconds he panted for breath, so unnerved was he.

He began to reason with himself on the possibility of such a thing: "Could I by any chance be afraid?"

No, indeed; he could not be afraid, since he was resolved to proceed to the last extremity, since he was irrevocably determined to fight without flinching. And yet he was so perturbed in mind and body that he asked himself:

"Is it possible to be afraid in spite of one's self?"

And this doubt, this fearful question, took possession of him. If an irresistible power, stronger than his own will, were to quell his courage, what would happen? He would certainly go to the place appointed; his will would force him that far. But supposing, when there, he were to tremble or faint? And he thought of his social standing, his reputation, his name.

And he suddenly determined to get up and look at himself in the glass. He lighted his candle. When he saw his face reflected in the mirror he scarcely recognized it. He seemed to see before him a man whom he did not know. His eyes looked disproportionately large, and he was very pale.

He remained standing before the mirror. He put out his tongue, as if to examine the state of his health, and all at once the thought flashed into his mind:

"At this time the day after to-morrow I may be dead."

And his heart throbbed painfully.

"At this time the day after to-morrow I may be dead. This person in front of me, this 'I' whom I see in the glass, will perhaps be no more. What! Here I am, I look at myself, I feel myself to be alive—and yet in twenty-four hours I may be lying on that bed, with closed eyes, dead, cold, inanimate."

He turned round, and could see himself distinctly lying on his back on the couch he had just quitted. He had the hollow face and the limp hands of death.

Then he became afraid of his bed, and to avoid seeing it went to his smoking-room. He mechanically took a cigar, lighted it, and began walking back and forth. He was cold; he took a step toward the bell, to wake his valet, but stopped with hand raised toward the bell rope.

"He would see that I am afraid!"

And, instead of ringing, he made a fire himself. His hands quivered nervously as they touched various objects. His head grew dizzy, his thoughts confused, disjointed, painful; a numbness seized his spirit, as if he had been drinking.

And all the time he kept on saying:

"What shall I do? What will become of me?"

His whole body trembled spasmodically; he rose, and, going to the window, drew back the curtains.

The day—a summer day-was breaking. The pink sky cast a glow on the city, its roofs, and its walls. A flush of light enveloped the awakened world, like a caress from the rising sun, and the glimmer of dawn kindled new hope in the breast of the vicomte. What a fool he was to let himself succumb to fear before anything was decided—before his seconds had interviewed those of Georges Lamil, before he even knew whether he would have to fight or not!

He bathed, dressed, and left the house with a firm step.

He repeated as he went:

"I must be firm—very firm. I must show that I am not afraid."

His seconds, the marquis and the colonel, placed themselves at his disposal, and, having shaken him warmly by the hand, began to discuss details.

"You want a serious duel?" asked the colonel.

"Yes—quite serious," replied the vicomte.

"You insist on pistols?" put in the marquis.

"Yes."

"Do you leave all the other arrangements in our hands?"

With a dry, jerky voice the vicomte answered:

"Twenty paces—at a given signal—the arm to be raised, not lowered—shots to be exchanged until one or other is seriously wounded."

"Excellent conditions," declared the colonel in a satisfied tone. "You are a good shot; all the chances are in your favor."

And they parted. The vicomte returned home to, wait for them. His agitation, only temporarily allayed, now increased momentarily. He felt, in arms, legs and chest, a sort of trembling—a continuous vibration; he could not stay still, either sitting or standing. His mouth was parched, and he made every now and then a clicking movement of the tongue, as if to detach it from his palate.

He attempted, to take luncheon, but could not eat. Then it occurred to him to seek courage in drink, and he sent for a decanter of rum, of which he swallowed, one after another, six small glasses.

A burning warmth, followed by a deadening of the mental faculties, ensued. He said to himself:

"I know how to manage. Now it will be all right!"

But at the end of an hour he had emptied the decanter, and his agitation was worse than ever. A mad longing possessed him to throw himself on the ground, to bite, to scream. Night fell.

A ring at the bell so unnerved him that he had not the strength to rise to receive his seconds.

He dared not even to speak to them, wish them good-day, utter a single word, lest his changed voice should betray him.

"All is arranged as you wished," said the colonel. "Your adversary claimed at first the privilege of the offended part; but he yielded almost at once, and accepted your conditions. His seconds are two military men."

"Thank you," said the vicomte.

The marquis added:

"Please excuse us if we do not stay now, for we have a good deal to see to yet. We shall want a reliable doctor, since the duel is not to end until a serious wound has been inflicted; and you know that bullets are not to be trifled with. We must select a spot near some house to which the wounded party can be carried if necessary. In fact, the arrangements will take us another two or three hours at least."

The vicomte articulated for the second time:

"Thank you."

"You're all right?" asked the colonel. "Quite calm?"

"Perfectly calm, thank you."

The two men withdrew.

When he was once more alone he felt as though he should go mad. His servant having lighted the lamps, he sat down at his table to write some letters. When he had traced at the top of a sheet of paper the words: "This is my last will and testament," he started from his seat, feeling himself incapable of connected thought, of decision in regard to anything.

So he was going to fight! He could no longer avoid it. What, then, possessed him? He wished to fight, he was fully determined to fight, and yet, in spite of all his mental effort, in spite of the exertion of all his will power, he felt that he could not even preserve the strength necessary to carry him through the ordeal. He tried to conjure up a picture of the duel, his own attitude, and that of his enemy.

Every now and then his teeth chattered audibly. He thought he would read, and took down Chateauvillard's Rules of Dueling. Then he said:

"Is the other man practiced in the use of the pistol? Is he well known? How can I find out?"

He remembered Baron de Vaux's book on marksmen, and searched it from end to end. Georges Lamil was not mentioned. And yet, if he were not an adept, would he have accepted without demur such a dangerous weapon and such deadly conditions?

He opened a case of Gastinne Renettes which stood on a small table, and took from it a pistol. Next he stood in the correct attitude for firing, and raised his arm. But he was trembling from head to foot, and the weapon shook in his grasp.

Then he said to himself:

"It is impossible. I cannot fight like this."

He looked at the little black, death-spitting hole at the end of the pistol; he thought of dishonor, of the whispers at the clubs, the smiles in his friends' drawing-rooms, the contempt of women, the veiled sneers of the newspapers, the insults that would be hurled at him by cowards.

He still looked at the weapon, and raising the hammer, saw the glitter of the priming below it. The pistol had been left loaded by some chance, some oversight. And the discovery rejoiced him, he knew not why.

If he did not maintain, in presence of his opponent, the steadfast bearing which was so necessary to his honor, he would be ruined forever. He would be branded, stigmatized as a coward, hounded out of society! And he felt, he knew, that he could not maintain that calm, unmoved demeanor. And yet he was brave, since the thought that followed was not even rounded to a finish in his mind; but, opening his mouth wide, he suddenly plunged the barrel of the pistol as far back as his throat, and pressed the trigger.

When the valet, alarmed at the report, rushed into the room he found his master lying dead upon his back. A spurt of blood had splashed the white paper on the table, and had made a great crimson stain beneath the words:

"This is my last will and testament."

OLD MONGILET

In the office old Mongilet was considered a type. He was a good old employee, who had never been outside Paris but once in his life.

It was the end of July, and each of us, every Sunday, went to roll in the grass, or soak in the water in the country near by. Asnieres, Argenteuil, Chatou, Borgival, Maisons, Poissy, had their habitues and their ardent admirers. We argued about the merits and advantages of all these places, celebrated and delightful to all Parsian employees.

Daddy Mongilet declared:

"You are like a lot of sheep! It must be pretty, this country you talk of!"

"Well, how about you, Mongilet? Don't you ever go on an excursion?"

"Yes, indeed. I go in an omnibus. When I have had a good luncheon, without any hurry, at the wine shop down there, I look up my route with a plan of Paris, and the time table of the lines and connections. And then I climb up on the box, open my umbrella and off we go. Oh, I see lots of things, more than you, I bet! I change my surroundings. It is as though I were taking a journey across the world, the people are so different in one street and another. I know my Paris better than anyone. And then, there is nothing more amusing than the entresols. You would not believe what one sees in there at a glance. One guesses at domestic scenes simply at sight of the face of a man who is roaring; one is amused on passing by a barber's shop, to see the barber leave his customer whose face is covered with lather to look out in the street. One exchanges heartfelt glances with the milliners just for fun, as one has no time to alight. Ah, how many things one sees!

"It is the drama, the real, the true, the drama of nature, seen as the horses trot by. Heavens! I would not give my excursions in the omnibus for all your stupid excursions in the woods."

"Come and try it, Mongilet, come to the country once just to see."

"I was there once," he replied, "twenty years ago, and you will never catch me there again."

"Tell us about it, Mongilet."

"If you wish to hear it. This is how it was:

"You knew Boivin, the old editorial clerk, whom we called Boileau?"

"Yes, perfectly."

"He was my office chum. The rascal had a house at Colombes and always invited me to spend Sunday with him. He would say:

"'Come along, Maculotte [he called me Maculotte for fun]. You will see what a nice excursion we will take.'

"I let myself be entrapped like an animal, and set out, one morning by the 8 o'clock train. I arrived at a kind of town, a country town where there is nothing to see, and I at length found my way to an old wooden door with an iron bell, at the end of an alley between two walls.

"I rang, and waited a long time, and at last the door was opened. What was it that opened it? I could not tell at the first glance. A woman or an ape? The creature was old, ugly, covered with old clothes that looked dirty and wicked. It had chicken's feathers in its hair and looked as though it would devour me.

"'What do you want?' she said.

"'Mr. Boivin.'

"'What do you want of him, of Mr. Boivin?'

"I felt ill at ease on being questioned by this fury. I stammered: 'Why-he expects me.'

"'Ah, it is you who have come to luncheon?'

"'Yes,' I stammered, trembling.

"Then, turning toward the house, she cried in an angry tone:

"'Boivin, here is your man!'

"It was my friend's wife. Little Boivin appeared immediately on the threshold of a sort of barrack of plaster covered with zinc, that looked like a foot stove. He wore white duck trousers covered with stains and a dirty Panama hat.

"After shaking my hands warmly, he took me into what he called his garden. It was at the end of another alleyway enclosed by high walls and was a little square the size of a pocket handkerchief, surrounded by houses that were so high that the sun, could reach it only two or three hours in the day. Pansies, pinks, wallflowers and a few rose bushes were languishing in this well without air, and hot as an oven from the refraction of heat from the roofs.

"'I have no trees,' said Boivin, 'but the neighbors' walls take their place. I have as much shade as in a wood.'

"Then he took hold of a button of my coat and said in a low tone:

"'You can do me a service. You saw the wife. She is not agreeable, eh? To-day, as I had invited you, she gave me clean clothes; but if I spot them all is lost. I counted on you to water my plants.'

"I agreed. I took off my coat, rolled up my sleeves, and began to work the handle of a kind of pump that wheezed, puffed and rattled like a consumptive as it emitted a thread of water like a Wallace drinking fountain. It took me ten minutes to water it and I was in a bath of perspiration. Boivin directed me:

"'Here—this plant—a little more; enough—now this one.'

"The watering pot leaked and my feet got more water than the flowers. The bottoms of my trousers were soaking and covered with mud. And twenty times running I kept it up, soaking my feet afresh each time, and perspiring anew as I worked the handle of the pump. And when I was tired out and wanted to stop, Boivin, in a tone of entreaty, said as he put his hand on my arm:

"Just one more watering pot full—just one, and that will be all.'

"To thank me he gave me a rose, a big rose, but hardly had it touched my button-hole than it fell to pieces, leaving only a hard little green knot as a decoration. I was surprised, but said nothing.

"Mme. Boivin's voice was heard in the distance:

"'Are you ever coming? When you know that luncheon is ready!'

"We went toward the foot stove. If the garden was in the shade, the house, on the other hand, was in the blazing sun, and the sweating room in the Turkish bath is not as hot as was my friend's dining room.

"Three plates at the side of which were some half-washed forks, were placed on a table of yellow wood in the middle of which stood an earthenware dish containing boiled beef and potatoes. We began to eat.

"A large water bottle full of water lightly colored with wine attracted my attention. Boivin, embarrassed, said to his wife:

"'See here, my dear, just on a special occasion, are you not going to give us some plain wine?'

"She looked at him furiously.

"'So that you may both get tipsy, is that it, and stay here gabbing all day? A fig for your special occasion!'

"He said no more. After the stew she brought in another dish of potatoes cooked with bacon. When this dish was finished, still in silence, she announced:

"'That is all! Now get out!'

"Boivin looked at her in astonishment.

"'But the pigeon—the pigeon you plucked this morning?'

"She put her hands on her hips:

"'Perhaps you have not had enough? Because you bring people here is no reason why we should devour all that there is in the house. What is there for me to eat this evening?'

"We rose. Solvin whispered

"'Wait for me a second, and we will skip.'

"He went into the kitchen where his wife had gone, and I overheard him say:

"'Give me twenty sous, my dear.'

"'What do you want with twenty sons?'

"'Why, one does not know what may happen. It is always better to have some money.'

"She yelled so that I should hear:

"'No, I will not give it to you! As the man has had luncheon here, the least he can do is to pay your expenses for the day.'

"Boivin came back to fetch me. As I wished to be polite I bowed to the mistress of the house, stammering:

"'Madame—many thanks—kind welcome.'

"'That's all right,' she replied. 'But do not bring him back drunk, for you will have to answer to me, you know!'

"We set out. We had to cross a perfectly bare plain under the burning sun. I attempted to gather a flower along the road and gave a cry of pain. It had hurt my hand frightfully. They call these plants nettles. And, everywhere, there was a smell of manure, enough to turn your stomach.

"Boivin said, 'Have a little patience and we will reach the river bank.'

"We reached the river. Here there was an odor of mud and dirty water, and the sun blazed down on the water so that it burned my eyes. I begged Boivin to go under cover somewhere. He took me into a kind of shanty filled with men, a river boatmen's tavern.

"He said:

"'This does not look very grand, but it is very comfortable.'

"I was hungry. I ordered an omelet. But to and behold, at the second glass of wine, that beggar, Boivin, lost his head, and I understand why his wife gave him water diluted.

"He got up, declaimed, wanted to show his strength, interfered in a quarrel between two drunken men who were fighting, and, but for the landlord, who came to the rescue, we should both have been killed.

"I dragged him away, holding him up until we reached the first bush where I deposited him. I lay down beside him and, it seems, I fell asleep. We must certainly have slept a long time, for it was dark when I awoke. Boivin was snoring at my side. I shook him; he rose but he was still drunk, though a little less so.

"We set out through the darkness across the plain. Boivin said he knew the way. He made me turn to the left, then to the right, then to the left. We could see neither sky nor earth, and found ourselves lost in the midst of a kind of forest of wooden stakes, that came as high as our noses. It was a vineyard and these were the supports. There was not a single light on the horizon. We wandered about in this vineyard for about an hour or two, hesitating, reaching out our arms without finding any limit, for we kept retracing our steps.

"At length Boivin fell against a stake that tore his cheek and he remained in a sitting posture on the ground, uttering with all his might long and resounding hallos, while I screamed 'Help! Help!' as loud as I could, lighting candle-matches to show the way to our rescuers, and also to keep up my courage.

"At last a belated peasant heard us and put us on our right road. I took Boivin to his home, but as I was leaving him on the threshold of his garden, the door opened suddenly and his wife appeared, a candle in her hand. She frightened me horribly.

"As soon as she saw her husband, whom she must have been waiting for since dark, she screamed, as she darted toward me:

"'Ah, scoundrel, I knew you would bring him back drunk!'

"My, how I made my escape, running all the way to the station, and as I thought the fury was pursuing me I shut myself in an inner room as the train was not due for half an hour.

"That is why I never married, and why I never go out of Paris."

MOONLIGHT

Madame Julie Roubere was expecting her elder sister, Madame Henriette Letore, who had just returned from a trip to Switzerland.

The Letore household had left nearly five weeks before. Madame Henriette had allowed her husband to return alone to their estate in Calvados, where some business required his attention, and had come to spend a few days in Paris with her sister. Night came on. In the quiet parlor Madame Roubere was reading in the twilight in an absent-minded way, raising her, eyes whenever she heard a sound.

At last, she heard a ring at the door, and her sister appeared, wrapped in a travelling cloak. And without any formal greeting, they clasped each other in an affectionate embrace, only desisting for a moment to give each other another hug. Then they talked about their health, about their respective families, and a thousand other things, gossiping, jerking out hurried, broken sentences as they followed each other about, while Madame Henriette was removing her hat and veil.

It was now quite dark. Madame Roubere rang for a lamp, and as soon as it was brought in, she scanned her sister's face, and was on the point of embracing her once more. But she held back, scared and astonished at the other's appearance.

On her temples Madame Letore had two large locks of white hair. All the rest of her hair was of a glossy, raven-black hue; but there alone, at each side of her head, ran, as it were, two silvery streams which were immediately lost in the black mass surrounding them. She was, nevertheless, only twenty-four years old, and this change had come on suddenly since her departure for Switzerland.

Without moving, Madame Roubere gazed at her in amazement, tears rising to her eyes, as she thought that some mysterious and terrible calamity must have befallen her sister. She asked:

"What is the matter with you, Henriette?"

Smiling with a sad face, the smile of one who is heartsick, the other replied:

"Why, nothing, I assure you. Were you noticing my white hair?"

But Madame Roubere impetuously seized her by the shoulders, and with a searching glance at her, repeated:

"What is the matter with you? Tell me what is the matter with you. And if you tell me a falsehood, I'll soon find it out."

They remained face to face, and Madame Henriette, who looked as if she were about to faint, had two pearly tears in the corners of her drooping eyes.

Her sister continued:

"What has happened to you? What is the matter with you? Answer me!"

Then, in a subdued voice, the other murmured:

"I have—I have a lover."

And, hiding her forehead on the shoulder of her younger sister, she sobbed.

Then, when she had grown a little calmer, when the heaving of her breast had subsided, she commenced to unbosom herself, as if to cast forth this secret from herself, to empty this sorrow of hers into a sympathetic heart.

Thereupon, holding each other's hands tightly clasped, the two women went over to a sofa in a dark corner of the room, into which they sank, and the younger sister, passing her arm over the elder one's neck, and drawing her close to her heart, listened.

"Oh! I know that there was no excuse for me; I do not understand myself, and since that day I feel as if I were mad. Be careful, my child, about yourself—be careful! If you only knew how weak we are, how quickly we yield, and fall. It takes so little, so little, so little, a moment of tenderness, one of those sudden fits of melancholy which come over you, one of those longings to open, your arms, to love, to cherish something, which we all have at certain moments.

"You know my husband, and you know how fond I am of him; but he is mature and sensible, and cannot even comprehend the tender vibrations of a woman's heart. He is always the same, always good, always smiling, always kind, always perfect. Oh! how I sometimes have wished that he would clasp me roughly in his arms, that he would embrace me with those slow, sweet kisses which make two beings intermingle, which are like mute confidences! How I have wished that he were foolish, even weak, so that he should have need of me, of my caresses, of my tears!

"This all seems very silly; but we women are made like that. How can we help it?

"And yet the thought of deceiving him never entered my mind. Now it has happened, without love, without reason, without anything, simply because the moon shone one night on the Lake of Lucerne.

"During the month when we were travelling together, my husband, with his calm indifference, paralyzed my enthusiasm, extinguished my poetic ardor. When we were descending the mountain paths at sunrise, when as the four horses galloped along with the diligence, we saw, in the transparent morning haze, valleys, woods, streams, and villages, I clasped my hands with delight, and said to him: 'How beautiful it is, dear! Give me a kiss! Kiss me now!' He only answered, with a smile of chilling kindliness: 'There is no reason why we should kiss each other because you like the landscape.'

"And his words froze me to the heart. It seems to me that when people love each other, they ought to feel more moved by love than ever, in the presence of beautiful scenes.

"In fact, I was brimming over with poetry which he kept me from expressing. I was almost like a boiler filled with steam and hermetically sealed.

"One evening (we had for four days been staying in a hotel at Fluelen) Robert, having one of his sick headaches, went to bed immediately after dinner, and I went to take a walk all alone along the edge of the lake.

"It was a night such as one reads of in fairy tales. The full moon showed itself in the middle of the sky; the tall mountains, with their snowy crests, seemed to wear silver crowns; the waters of the lake glittered with tiny shining ripples. The air was mild, with that kind of penetrating warmth which enervates us till we are ready to faint, to be deeply affected without any apparent cause. But how sensitive, how vibrating the heart is at such moments! how quickly it beats, and how intense is its emotion!

"I sat down on the grass, and gazed at that vast, melancholy, and fascinating lake, and a strange feeling arose in me; I was seized with an insatiable need of love, a revolt against the gloomy dullness of my life. What! would it never be my fate to wander, arm in arm, with a man I loved, along a moon-kissed bank like this? Was I never to feel on my lips those kisses so deep, delicious, and intoxicating which lovers exchange on nights that seem to have been made by God for tenderness? Was I never to know ardent, feverish love in the moonlit shadows of a summer's night?

"And I burst out weeping like a crazy woman. I heard something stirring behind me. A man stood there, gazing at me. When I turned my head round, he recognized me, and, advancing, said:

"'You are weeping, madame?'

"It was a young barrister who was travelling with his mother, and whom we had often met. His eyes had frequently followed me.

"I was so confused that I did not know what answer to give or what to think of the situation. I told him I felt ill.

"He walked on by my side in a natural and respectful manner, and began talking to me about what we had seen during our trip. All that I had felt he translated into words; everything that made me thrill he understood perfectly, better than I did myself. And all of a sudden he repeated some verses of Alfred de Musset. I felt myself choking, seized with indescribable emotion. It seemed to me that the mountains themselves, the lake, the moonlight, were singing to me about things ineffably sweet.

"And it happened, I don't know how, I don't know why, in a sort of hallucination.

"As for him, I did not see him again till the morning of his departure.

"He gave me his card!"

And, sinking into her sister's arms, Madame Letore broke into groans —almost into shrieks.

Then, Madame Roubere, with a self-contained and serious air, said very gently:

"You see, sister, very often it is not a man that we love, but love itself. And your real lover that night was the moonlight."

THE FIRST SNOWFALL

The long promenade of La Croisette winds in a curve along the edge of the blue water. Yonder, to the right, Esterel juts out into the sea in the distance, obstructing the view and shutting out the horizon with its pretty southern outline of pointed summits, numerous and fantastic.

To the left, the isles of Sainte Marguerite and Saint Honorat, almost level with the water, display their surface, covered with pine trees.

And all along the great gulf, all along the tall mountains that encircle Cannes, the white villa residences seem to be sleeping in the sunlight. You can see them from a distance, the white houses, scattered from the top to the bottom of the mountains, dotting the dark greenery with specks like snow.

Those near the water have gates opening on the wide promenade which is washed by the quiet waves. The air is soft and balmy. It is one of those warm winter days when there is scarcely a breath of cool air. Above the walls of the gardens may be seen orange trees and lemon trees full of golden fruit. Ladies are walking slowly across the sand of the avenue, followed by children rolling hoops, or chatting with gentlemen.

A young woman has just passed out through the door of her coquettish little house facing La Croisette. She stops for a moment to gaze at the promenaders, smiles, and with an exhausted air makes her way toward an empty bench facing the sea. Fatigued after having gone twenty paces, she sits down out of breath. Her pale face seems that of a dead woman. She coughs, and raises to her lips her transparent fingers as if to stop those paroxysms that exhaust her.

She gazes at the sky full of sunshine and swallows, at the zigzag summits of the Esterel over yonder, and at the sea, the blue, calm, beautiful sea, close beside her.

She smiles again, and murmurs:

"Oh! how happy I am!"

She knows, however, that she is going to die, that she will never see the springtime, that in a year, along the same promenade, these same people who pass before her now will come again to breathe the warm air of this charming spot, with their children a little bigger, with their hearts all filled with hopes, with tenderness, with happiness, while at the bottom of an oak coffin, the poor flesh which is still left to her to-day will have decomposed, leaving only her bones lying in the silk robe which she has selected for a shroud.

She will be no more. Everything in life will go on as before for others. For her, life will be over, over forever. She will be no more. She smiles, and inhales as well as she can, with her diseased lungs, the perfumed air of the gardens.

And she sinks into a reverie.

She recalls the past. She had been married, four years ago, to a Norman gentleman. He was a strong young man, bearded, healthy-looking, with wide shoulders, narrow mind, and joyous disposition.

They had been united through financial motives which she knew nothing about. She would willingly have said No. She said Yes, with a movement of the head, in order not to thwart her father and mother. She was a Parisian, gay, and full of the joy of living.

Her husband brought her home to his Norman chateau. It was a huge stone building surrounded by tall trees of great age. A high clump of pine trees shut out the view in front. On the right, an opening in the trees presented a view of the plain, which stretched out in an unbroken level as far as the distant, farmsteads. A cross-road passed before the gate and led to the high road three kilometres away.

Oh! she recalls everything, her arrival, her first day in her new abode, and her isolated life afterward.

When she stepped out of the carriage, she glanced at the old building, and laughingly exclaimed:

"It does not look cheerful!"

Her husband began to laugh in his turn, and replied:

"Pooh! we get used to it! You'll see. I never feel bored in it, for my part."

That day they passed their time in embracing each other, and she did not find it too long. This lasted fully a month. The days passed one after the other in insignificant yet absorbing occupations. She learned the value and the importance of the little things of life. She knew that people can interest themselves in the price of eggs, which cost a few centimes more or less according to the seasons.

It was summer. She went to the fields to see the men harvesting. The brightness of the sunshine found an echo in her heart.

The autumn came. Her husband went out shooting. He started in the morning with his two dogs Medor and Mirza. She remained alone, without grieving, moreover, at Henry's absence. She was very fond of him, but she did not miss him. When he returned home, her affection was especially bestowed on the dogs. She took care of them every evening with a mother's tenderness, caressed them incessantly, gave them a thousand charming little names which she had no idea of applying to her husband.

He invariably told her all about his sport. He described the places where he found partridges, expressed his astonishment at not having caught any hares in Joseph Ledentu's clever, or else appeared indignant at the conduct of M. Lechapelier, of Havre, who always went along the edge of his property to shoot the game that he, Henry de Parville, had started.

She replied: "Yes, indeed! it is not right," thinking of something else all the while.

The winter came, the Norman winter, cold and rainy. The endless floods of rain came down tin the slates of the great gabled roof, rising like a knife blade toward the sky. The roads seemed like rivers of mud, the country a plain of mud, and no sound could be heard save that of water falling; no movement could be seen save the whirling flight of crows that settled down like a cloud on a field and then hurried off again.

About four o'clock, the army of dark, flying creatures came and perched in the tall beeches at the left of the chateau, emitting deafening cries. During nearly an hour, they flew from tree top to tree top, seemed to be fighting, croaked, and made a black disturbance in the gray branches. She gazed at them each evening with a weight at her heart, so deeply was she impressed by the lugubrious melancholy of the darkness falling on the deserted country.

Then she rang for the lamp, and drew near the fire. She burned heaps of wood without succeeding in warming the spacious apartments reeking with humidity. She was cold all day long, everywhere, in the drawing-room, at meals, in her own apartment. It seemed to her she was cold to the marrow of her bones. Her husband only came in to dinner; he was always out shooting, or else he was superintending sowing the seed, tilling the soil, and all the work of the country.

He would come back jovial, and covered with mud, rubbing his hands as he exclaimed:

"What wretched weather!"

Or else:

"A fire looks comfortable!"

Or sometimes:

"Well, how are you to-day? Are you in good spirits?"

He was happy, in good health, without desires, thinking of nothing save this simple, healthy, and quiet life.

About December, when the snow had come, she suffered so much from the icy-cold air of the chateau which seemed to have become chilled in passing through the centuries just as human beings become chilled with years, that she asked her husband one evening:

"Look here, Henry! You ought to have a furnace put into the house; it would dry the walls. I assure you that I cannot keep warm from morning till night."

At first he was stunned at this extravagant idea of introducing a furnace into his manor-house. It would have seemed more natural to him to have his dogs fed out of silver dishes. He gave a tremendous laugh from the bottom of his chest as he exclaimed:

"A furnace here! A furnace here! Ha! ha! ha! what a good joke!"

She persisted:

"I assure you, dear, I feel frozen; you don't feel it because you are always moving about; but all the same, I feel frozen."

He replied, still laughing:

"Pooh! you'll get used to it, and besides it is excellent for the health. You will only be all the better for it. We are not Parisians, damn it! to live in hot-houses. And, besides, the spring is quite near."

About the beginning of January, a great misfortune befell her. Her father and mother died in a carriage accident. She came to Paris for the funeral. And her sorrow took entire possession of her mind for about six months.

The mildness of the beautiful summer days finally roused her, and she lived along in a state of sad languor until autumn.

When the cold weather returned, she was brought face to face, for the first time, with the gloomy future. What was she to do? Nothing. What was going to happen to her henceforth? Nothing. What expectation, what hope, could revive her heart? None. A doctor who was consulted declared that she would never have children.

Sharper, more penetrating still than the year before, the cold made her suffer continually.

She stretched out her shivering hands to the big flames. The glaring fire burned her face; but icy whiffs seemed to glide down her back and to penetrate between her skin and her underclothing. And she shivered from head to foot. Innumerable draughts of air appeared to have taken up their abode in the apartment, living, crafty currents of air as cruel as enemies. She encountered them at every moment; they blew on her incessantly their perfidious and frozen hatred, now on her face, now on her hands, and now on her back.

Once more she spoke of a furnace; but her husband listened to her request as if she were asking for the moon. The introduction of such an apparatus at Parville appeared to him as impossible as the discovery of the Philosopher's Stone.

Having been at Rouen on business one day, he brought back to his wife a dainty foot warmer made of copper, which he laughingly called a "portable furnace"; and he considered that this would prevent her henceforth from ever being cold.

Toward the end of December she understood that she could not always live like this, and she said timidly one evening at dinner:

"Listen, dear! Are we, not going to spend a week or two in Paris before spring:"

He was stupefied.

"In Paris? In Paris? But what are we to do there? Ah! no by Jove! We are better off here. What odd ideas come into your head sometimes."

She faltered:

"It might distract us a little."

He did not understand.

"What is it you want to distract you? Theatres, evening parties, dinners in town? You knew, however, when you came here, that you ought not to expect any distractions of this kind!"

She saw a reproach in these words, and in the tone in which they were uttered. She relapsed into silence. She was timid and gentle, without resisting power and without strength of will.

In January the cold weather returned with violence. Then the snow covered the earth.

One evening, as she watched the great black cloud of crows dispersing among the trees, she began to weep, in spite of herself.

Her husband came in. He asked in great surprise:

"What is the matter with you?"

He was happy, quite happy, never having dreamed of another life or other pleasures. He had been born and had grown up in this melancholy district. He felt contented in his own house, at ease in body and mind.

He did not understand that one might desire incidents, have a longing for changing pleasures; he did not understand that it does not seem natural to certain beings to remain in the same place during the four seasons; he seemed not to know that spring, summer, autumn, and winter have, for multitudes of persons, fresh amusements in new places.

She could say nothing in reply, and she quickly dried her eyes. At last she murmured in a despairing tone:

"I am—I—I am a little sad—I am a little bored."

But she was terrified at having even said so much, and added very quickly:

"And, besides—I am—I am a little cold."

This last plea made him angry.

"Ah! yes, still your idea of the furnace. But look here, deuce take it! you have not had one cold since you came here."

Night came on. She went up to her room, for she had insisted on having a separate apartment. She went to bed. Even in bed she felt cold. She thought:

"It will be always like this, always, until I die."

And she thought of her husband. How could he have said:

"You—have not had one cold since you came here"?

She would have to be ill, to cough before he could understand what she suffered!

And she was filled with indignation, the angry indignation of a weak, timid being.

She must cough. Then, perhaps, he would take pity on her. Well, she would cough; he should hear her coughing; the doctor should be called in; he should see, her husband, he should see.

She got out of bed, her legs and her feet bare, and a childish idea made her smile:

"I want a furnace, and I must have it. I shall cough so much that he'll have to put one in the house."

And she sat down in a chair in her nightdress. She waited an hour, two hours. She shivered, but she did not catch cold. Then she resolved on a bold expedient.

She noiselessly left her room, descended the stairs, and opened the gate into the garden.

The earth, covered with snows seemed dead. She abruptly thrust forward her bare foot, and plunged it into the icy, fleecy snow. A sensation of cold, painful as a wound, mounted to her heart. However, she stretched out the other leg, and began to descend the steps slowly.

Then she advanced through the grass saying to herself:

"I'll go as far as the pine trees."

She walked with quick steps, out of breath, gasping every time she plunged her foot into the snow.

She touched the first pine tree with her hand, as if to assure herself that she had carried out her plan to the end; then she went back into the house. She thought two or three times that she was going to fall, so numbed and weak did she feel. Before going in, however, she sat down in that icy fleece, and even took up several handfuls to rub on her chest.

Then she went in and got into bed. It seemed to her at the end of an hour that she had a swarm of ants in her throat, and that other ants were running all over her limbs. She slept, however.

Next day she was coughing and could not get up.

She had inflammation of the lungs. She became delirious, and in her delirium she asked for a furnace. The doctor insisted on having one put in. Henry yielded, but with visible annoyance.

She was incurable. Her lungs were seriously affected, and those about her feared for her life.

"If she remains here, she will not last until the winter," said the doctor.

She was sent south. She came to Cannes, made the acquaintance of the sun, loved the sea, and breathed the perfume of orange blossoms.

Then, in the spring, she returned north.

But she now lived with the fear of being cured, with the fear of the long winters of Normandy; and as soon as she was better she opened her window by night and recalled the sweet shores of the Mediterranean.

And now she is going to die. She knows it and she is happy.

She unfolds a newspaper which she has not already opened, and reads this heading:

"The first snow in Paris."

She shivers and then smiles. She looks across at the Esterel, which is becoming rosy in the rays of the setting sun. She looks at the vast blue sky, so blue, so very blue, and the vast blue sea, so very blue also, and she rises from her seat.

And then she returned to the house with slow steps, only stopping to cough, for she had remained out too long and she was cold, a little cold.

She finds a letter from her husband. She opens it, still smiling, and she reads:

> "MY DEAR LOVE: I hope you are well, and that you do not regret too much our beautiful country. For some days last we have had a good frost, which presages snow. For my part, I adore this weather, and you my believe that I do not light your damned furnace."

She ceases reading, quite happy at the thought that she had her furnace put in. Her right hand, which holds the letter, falls slowly on her lap, while she raises her left hand to her mouth, as if to calm the obstinate cough which is racking her chest.

SUNDAYS OF A BOURGEOIS

PREPARATIONS FOR THE EXCURSION

M. Patissot, born in Paris, after having failed in his examinations at the College Henri IV., like many others, had entered the government service through the influence of one of his aunts, who kept a tobacco store where the head of one of the departments bought his provisions.

He advanced very slowly, and would, perhaps, have died a fourth-class clerk without the aid of a kindly Providence, which sometimes watches over our destiny. He is today fifty-two years old, and it is only at this age that he is beginning to explore, as a tourist, all that part of France which lies between the fortifications and the provinces.

The story of his advance might be useful to many employees, just as the tale of his excursions may be of value to many Parisians who will take them as a model for their own outings, and will thus, through his example, avoid certain mishaps which occurred to him.

In 1854 he only enjoyed a salary of 1,800 francs. Through a peculiar trait of his character he was unpopular with all his superiors, who let him languish in the eternal and hopeless expectation of the clerk's ideal, an increase of salary. Nevertheless he worked; but he did not know how to make himself appreciated. He had too much self-respect, he claimed. His self-respect consisted in never bowing to his superiors in a low and servile manner, as did, according to him, certain of his colleagues, whom he would not mention. He added that his frankness embarrassed many people, for, like all the rest, he protested against injustice and the favoritism shown to persons entirely foreign to the bureaucracy. But his indignant voice never passed beyond the little cage where he worked.

First as a government clerk, then as a Frenchman and finally as a man who believed in order he would adhere to whatever government was established, having an unbounded reverence for authority, except for that of his chiefs.

Each time that he got the chance he would place himself where he could see the emperor pass, in order to have the honor of taking his hat off to him; and he would go away puffed up with pride at having bowed to the head of the state.

From his habit of observing the sovereign he did as many others do; he imitated the way he trimmed his beard or arranged his hair, the cut of his clothes, his walk, his mannerisms. Indeed, how many men in each country seemed to be the living images of the head of the government! Perhaps he vaguely resembled Napoleon III., but his hair was black; therefore he dyed it, and then the likeness was complete; and when he met another gentleman in the street also imitating the imperial countenance he was jealous and looked at him disdainfully. This need of imitation soon became his hobby, and, having heard an usher at the Tuilleries imitate the voice of the emperor, he also acquired the same intonations and studied slowness.

He thus became so much like his model that they might easily have been mistaken for each other, and certain high dignitaries were heard to remark that they found it unseemly and even vulgar; the matter was mentioned to the prime minister, who ordered that the employee should appear before him. But at the sight of him he began to laugh and repeated two or three times: "That's funny, really funny!" This was repeated, and the following day Patissot's immediate superior recommended that his subordinate receive an increase of salary of three hundred francs. He received it immediately.

From that time on his promotions came regularly, thanks to his ape-like faculty of imitation. The presentiment that some high honor might come to him some day caused his chiefs to speak to him with deference.

When the Republic was proclaimed it was a disaster for him. He felt lost, done for, and, losing his head, he stopped dyeing his hair, shaved his face clean and had his hair cut short, thus acquiring a paternal and benevolent expression which could not compromise him in any way.

Then his chiefs took revenge for the long time during which he had imposed upon them, and, having all turned Republican through an instinct of self preservation, they cut down his salary and delayed his promotion. He, too, changed his opinions. But the Republic not being a palpable and living person whom one can resemble, and the presidents succeeding each other with rapidity, he found himself plunged in the greatest embarrassment, in terrible distress, and, after an unsuccessful imitation of his last ideal, M. Thiers, he felt a check put on all his attempts at imitation. He needed a new manifestation of his personality. He searched for a long time; then, one morning, he arrived at the office wearing a new hat which had on the side a small red, white and blue rosette. His colleagues were astounded; they laughed all that day, the next day, all the week, all the month. But the seriousness of his demeanor at last disconcerted them, and once more his superiors became anxious. What mystery could be hidden under this sign? Was it a simple manifestation of patriotism, or an affirmation of his allegiance to the Republic, or perhaps the badge of some powerful association? But to wear it so persistently he must surely have some powerful and hidden protection. It would be well to be on one's guard, especially as he received all pleasantries with unruffled calmness. After that he was treated with respect, and his sham courage saved him; he was appointed head clerk on the first of January, 1880. His whole life had been spent indoors. He hated noise and bustle, and because of this love of rest and quiet he had remained a bachelor. He spent his Sundays reading tales of adventure and ruling guide lines which he afterward offered to his colleagues. In his whole existence he had only taken three vacations of a week each, when he was changing his quarters. But sometimes, on a holiday, he would leave by an excursion train for Dieppe or Havre in order to elevate his mind by the inspiring sight of the sea.

He was full of that common sense which borders on stupidity. For a long time he had been living quietly, with economy, temperate through prudence, chaste by temperament, when suddenly he was assailed by a terrible apprehension. One evening in the street he suddenly felt an attack of dizziness which made him fear a stroke of apoplexy. He hastened to a physician and for five francs obtained the following prescription:

> M. X-, fifty-five years old, bachelor, clerk. Full-blooded, danger of apoplexy. Cold-water applications, moderate nourishment, plenty of exercise. MONTELLIER, M.D.

Patissot was greatly distressed, and for a whole month, in his office, he kept a wet towel wrapped around his head like a turban while the water continually dripped on his work, which he would have to do over again. Every once in a while he would read the prescription over, probably in the hope of finding some hidden meaning, of penetrating into the secret thought of the physician, and also of discovering some forms of exercise which, might perhaps make him immune from apoplexy.

Then he consulted his friends, showing them the fateful paper. One advised boxing. He immediately hunted up an instructor, and, on the first day, he received a punch in the nose which immediately took away all his ambition in this direction. Single-stick made him gasp for breath, and he grew so stiff from fencing that for two days and two nights he could not get sleep. Then a bright idea struck him. It was to walk, every Sunday, to some suburb of Paris and even to certain places in the capital which he did not know.

For a whole week his mind was occupied with thoughts of the equipment which you need for these excursions; and on Sunday, the 30th of May, he began his preparations. After reading all the extraordinary advertisements which poor, blind and halt beggars distribute on the street corners, he began to visit the stores with the intention of looking about him only and of buying later on. First of all, he visited a so-called American shoe store, where heavy travelling shoes were shown him. The clerk brought out a kind of ironclad contrivance, studded with spikes like a harrow, which he claimed to be made from Rocky Mountain bison skin. He was so carried away with them that he would willingly have bought two pair, but one was sufficient. He carried them away under his arm, which soon became numb from the weight. He next invested in a pair of corduroy trousers, such as carpenters wear, and a pair of oiled canvas leggings. Then he needed a knapsack for his provisions, a telescope so as to recognize villages perched on the slope of distant hills, and finally, a government survey map to enable him to find his way about without asking the peasants toiling in the fields. Lastly, in order more comfortably to stand the heat, he decided to purchase a light alpaca jacket offered by the famous firm of Raminau, according to their advertisement, for the modest sum of six francs and fifty centimes. He went to this store and was welcomed by a distinguished-looking young man with a marvellous head of hair, nails as pink as those of a lady and a pleasant smile. He showed him the garment. It did not correspond with the glowing style of the advertisement. Then Patissot hesitatingly asked, "Well, monsieur, will it wear well?" The young man turned his eyes away in well-feigned embarrassment, like an honest man who does not wish to deceive a customer, and, lowering his eyes, he said in a hesitating manner: "Dear me, monsieur, you understand that for six francs fifty we cannot turn out an article like this for instance." And he showed him a much finer jacket than the first one. Patissot examined it and asked the price. "Twelve francs fifty." It was very tempting, but before deciding, he once more questioned the big young man, who was observing him attentively. "And—is that good? Do you guarantee it?" "Oh! certainly, monsieur, it is quite goad! But, of course, you must not get it wet! Yes, it's really quite good, but you understand that there are goods and goods. It's excellent for the price. Twelve francs fifty, just think. Why, that's nothing at all. Naturally a twenty-five-franc coat is much better. For twenty-five francs you get a superior quality, as strong as linen, and which wears even better. If it gets wet a little ironing will fix it right up. The color never fades, and it does not turn red in the sunlight. It is the warmest and lightest material out." He unfolded his wares, holding them up, shaking them, crumpling and stretching them in order to show the excellent quality of the cloth. He talked on convincingly, dispelling all hesitation by words and gesture. Patissot was convinced; he bought the coat. The pleasant salesman, still talking, tied up the bundle and continued praising the value of the purchase. When it was paid for he was suddenly silent. He bowed with a superior air, and, holding the door open, he watched his customer disappear, both arms filled with bundles and vainly trying to reach his hat to bow.

M. Patissot returned home and carefully studied the map. He wished to try on his shoes, which were more like skates than shoes, owing to the spikes. He slipped and fell, promising himself to be more careful in the future. Then he spread out all his purchases on a chair and looked at them for a long time. He went to sleep with this thought: "Isn't it strange that I didn't think before of taking an excursion to the country?"

During the whole week Patissot worked without ambition. He was dreaming of the outing which he had planned for the following Sunday, and he was seized by a sudden longing for the country, a desire of growing tender over nature, this thirst for rustic scenes which overwhelms the Parisians in spring time.

Only one person gave him any attention; it was a silent old copying clerk named Boivin, nicknamed Boileau. He himself lived in the country and had a little garden which he cultivated carefully; his needs were small, and he was perfectly happy, so they said. Patissot was now able to understand his tastes and the similarity of their ideals made them immediately fast friends. Old man Boivin said to him:

"Do I like fishing, monsieur? Why, it's the delight of my life!"

Then Patissot questioned him with deep interest. Boivin named all the fish who frolicked under this dirty water—and Patissot thought he could see them. Boivin told about the different hooks, baits, spots and times suitable for each kind. And Patissot felt himself more like a fisherman than Boivin himself. They decided that the following Sunday they would meet for the opening of the season for the edification of Patissot, who was delighted to have found such an experienced instructor.

FISHING EXCURSION

The day before the one when he was, for the first time in his life, to throw a hook into a river, Monsieur Patissot bought, for eighty centimes, "How to Become a Perfect Fisherman." In this work he learned many useful things, but he was especially impressed by the style, and he retained the following passage:

"In a word, if you wish, without books, without rules, to fish successfully, to the left or to the right, up or down stream, in the masterly manner that halts at no difficulty, then fish before, during and after a storm, when the clouds break and the sky is streaked with lightning, when the earth shakes with the grumbling thunder; it is then that, either through hunger or terror, all the fish forget their habits in a turbulent flight.

"In this confusion follow or neglect all favorable signs, and just go on fishing; you will march to victory!"

In order to catch fish of all sizes, he bought three well-perfected poles, made to be used as a cane in the city, which, on the river, could be transformed into a fishing rod by a simple jerk. He bought some number fifteen hooks for gudgeon, number twelve for bream, and with his number seven he expected to fill his basket with carp. He bought no earth worms because he was sure of finding them everywhere; but he laid in a provision of sand worms. He had a jar full of them, and in the evening he watched them with interest. The hideous creatures swarmed in their bath of bran as they do in putrid meat. Patissot wished to practice baiting his hook. He took up one with disgust, but he had hardly placed the curved steel point against it when it split open. Twenty times he repeated this without success, and he might have continued all night had he not feared to exhaust his supply of vermin.

He left by the first train. The station was full of people equipped with fishing lines. Some, like Patissot's, looked like simple bamboo canes; others, in one piece, pointed their slender ends to the skies. They looked like a forest of slender sticks, which mingled and clashed like swords or swayed like masts over an ocean of broad-brimmed straw hats.

When the train started fishing rods could be seen sticking out of all the windows and doors, giving to the train the appearance of a huge, bristly caterpillar winding through the fields.

Everybody got off at Courbevoie and rushed for the stage for Bezons. A crowd of fishermen crowded on top of the coach, holding their rods in their hands, giving the vehicle the appearance of a porcupine.

All along the road men were travelling in the same direction as though on a pilgrimage to an unknown Jerusalem. They were carrying those long, slender sticks resembling those carried by the faithful returning from Palestine. A tin box on a strap was fastened to their backs. They were in a hurry.

At Bezons the river appeared. People were lined along bath banks, men in frock coats, others in duck suits, others in blouses, women, children and even young girls of marriageable age; all were fishing.

Patissot started for the dam where his friend Boivin was waiting for him. The latter greeted him rather coolly. He had just made the acquaintance of a big, fat man of about fifty, who seemed very strong and whose skin was tanned. All three hired a big boat and lay off almost under the fall of the dam, where the fish are most plentiful.

Boivin was immediately ready. He baited his line and threw it out, and then sat motionless, watching the little float with extraordinary concentration. From time to time he would jerk his line out of the water and cast it farther out. The fat gentleman threw out his well-baited hooks, put his line down beside him, filled his pipe, lit it, crossed his arms, and, without another glance at the cork, he watched the water flow by. Patissot once more began trying to stick sand worms on his hooks. After about five minutes of this occupation he called to Boivin; "Monsieur Boivin, would you be so kind as to help me put these creatures on my hook? Try as I will, I can't seem to succeed." Boivin raised his head: "Please don't disturb me, Monsieur Patissot; we are not here for pleasure!" However, he baited the line, which Patissot then threw out, carefully imitating all the motions of his friend.

The boat was tossing wildly, shaken by the waves, and spun round like a top by the current, although anchored at both ends. Patissot, absorbed in the sport, felt a vague kind of uneasiness; he was uncomfortably heavy and somewhat dizzy.

They caught nothing. Little Boivin, very nervous, was gesticulating and shaking his head in despair. Patissot was as sad as though some disaster had overtaken him. The fat gentleman alone, still motionless, was quietly smoking without paying any attention to his line. At last Patissot, disgusted, turned toward him and said in a mournful voice:

"They are not biting, are they?"

He quietly replied:

"Of course not!"

Patissot surprised, looked at him.

"Do you ever catch many?"

"Never!"

"What! Never?"

The fat man, still smoking like a factory chimney, let out the following words, which completely upset his neighbor:

"It would bother me a lot if they did bite. I don't come here to fish; I come because I'm very comfortable here; I get shaken up as though I were at sea. If I take a line along, it's only to do as others do."

Monsieur Patissot, on the other hand, did not feel at all well. His discomfort, at first vague, kept increasing, and finally took on a definite form. He felt, indeed, as though he were being tossed by the sea, and he was suffering from seasickness. After the first attack had calmed down, he proposed leaving, but Boivin grew so furious that they almost came to blows. The fat man, moved by pity, rowed the boat back, and, as soon as Patissot had recovered from his seasickness, they bethought themselves of luncheon.

Two restaurants presented themselves. One of them, very small, looked like a beer garden, and was patronized by the poorer fishermen. The other one, which bore the imposing name of "Linden Cottage," looked like a middle-class residence and was frequented by the aristocracy of the rod. The two owners, born enemies, watched each other with hatred across a large field, which separated them, and where the white house of the dam keeper and of the inspector of the life-saving department stood out against the green grass. Moreover, these two officials disagreed, one of them upholding the beer garden and the other one defending the Elms, and the internal feuds which arose in these three houses reproduced the whole history of mankind.

Boivin, who knew the beer garden, wished to go there, exclaiming: "The food is very good, and it isn't expensive; you'll see. Anyhow, Monsieur Patissot, you needn't expect to get me tipsy the way you did last Sunday. My wife was furious, you know; and she has sworn never to forgive you!"

The fat gentleman declared that he would only eat at the Elms, because it was an excellent place and the cooking was as good as in the best restaurants in Paris.

"Do as you wish," declared Boivin; "I am going where I am accustomed to go." He left. Patissot, displeased at his friend's actions, followed the fat gentleman.

They ate together, exchanged ideas, discussed opinions and found that they were made for each other.

After the meal everyone started to fish again, but the two new friends left together. Following along the banks, they stopped near the railroad bridge and, still talking, they threw their lines in the water. The fish still refused to bite, but Patissot was now making the best of it.

A family was approaching. The father, whose whiskers stamped him as a judge, was holding an extraordinarily long rod; three boys of different sizes were carrying poles of different lengths, according to age; and the mother, who was very stout, gracefully manoeuvred a charming rod with a ribbon tied to the handle. The father bowed and asked:

"Is this spot good, gentlemen?" Patissot was going to speak, when his friend answered: "Fine!" The whole family smiled and settled down beside the fishermen. The Patissot was seized with a wild desire to catch a fish, just one, any kind, any size, in order to win the consideration of these people; so he began to handle his rod as he had seen Boivin do in the morning. He would let the cork follow the current to the end of the line, jerk the hooks out of the water, make them describe a large circle in the air and throw them out again a little higher up. He had even, as he thought, caught the knack of doing this movement gracefully. He had just jerked his line out rapidly when he felt it caught in something behind him. He tugged, and a scream burst from behind him. He perceived, caught on one of his hooks, and describing in the air a curve like a meteor, a magnificent hat which he placed right in the middle of the river.

He turned around, bewildered, dropping his pole, which followed the hat down the stream, while the fat gentleman, his new friend, lay on his back and roared with laughter. The lady, hatless and astounded, choked with anger; her husband was outraged and demanded the price of the hat, and Patissot paid about three times its value.

Then the family departed in a very dignified manner.

Patissot took another rod, and, until nightfall, he gave baths to sand worms. His neighbor was sleeping peacefully on the grass. Toward seven in the evening he awoke.

"Let's go away from here!" he said.

Then Patissot withdrew his line, gave a cry and sat down hard from astonishment. At the end of the string was a tiny little fish. When they looked at him more closely they found that he had been hooked through the stomach; the hook had caught him as it was being drawn out of the water.

Patissot was filled with a boundless, triumphant joy; he wished to have the fish fried for himself alone.

During the dinner the friends grew still more intimate. He learned that the fat gentleman lived at Argenteuil and had been sailing boats for thirty years without losing interest in the sport. He accepted to take luncheon with him the following Sunday and to take a sail in his friend's clipper, Plongeon. He became so interested in the conversation that he forgot all about his catch. He did not remember it until after the coffee, and he demanded that it be brought him. It was alone in the middle of a platter, and looked like a yellow, twisted match, But he ate it with pride and relish, and at night, on the omnibus, he told his neighbors that he had caught fourteen pounds of fish during the day.

TWO CELEBRITIES

Monsieur Patissot had promised his friend, the boating man, that he would spend the following Sunday with him. An unforeseen occurrence changed his plan. One evening, on the boulevard, he met one of his cousins whom he saw but very seldom. He was a pleasant journalist, well received in all classes of society, who offered to show Patissot many interesting things.

"What are you going to do next Sunday?"

"I'm going boating at Argenteuil."

"Come on! Boating is an awful bore; there is no variety to it. Listen —I'll take you along with me. I'll introduce you to two celebrities. We will visit the homes of two artists."

"But I have been ordered to go to the country!"

"That's just where we'll go. On the way we'll call on Meissonier, at his place in Poissy; then we'll walk over to Medan, where Zola lives. I have been commissioned to obtain his next novel for our newspaper."

Patissot, wild with joy, accepted the invitation. He even bought a new frock coat, as his own was too much worn to make a good appearance. He was terribly afraid of saying something foolish either to the artist or to the man of letters, as do people who speak of an art which they have never professed.

He mentioned his fears to his cousin, who laughed and answered: "Pshaw! Just pay them compliments, nothing but compliments, always compliments; in that way, if you say anything foolish it will be overlooked. Do you know Meissonier's paintings?"

"I should say I do."

"Have you read the Rougon-Macquart series?"

"From first to last."

"That's enough. Mention a painting from time to time, speak of a novel here and there and add:

"'Superb! Extraordinary! Delightful technique! Wonderfully powerful!' In that way you can always get along. I know that those two are very blase about everything, but admiration always pleases an artist."

Sunday morning they left for Poissy.

Just a few steps from the station, at the end of the church square, they found Meissonier's property. After passing through a low door, painted red, which led into a beautiful alley of vines, the journalist stopped and, turning toward his companion, asked:

"What is your idea of Meissonier?"

Patissot hesitated. At last he decided: "A little man, well groomed, clean shaven, a soldierly appearance." The other smiled: "All right, come along." A quaint building in the form of a chalet appeared to the left; and to the right side, almost opposite, was the main house. It was a strange-looking building, where there was a mixture of everything, a mingling of Gothic fortress, manor, villa, hut, residence, cathedral, mosque, pyramid, a, weird combination of Eastern and Western architecture. The style was complicated enough to set a classical architect crazy, and yet there was something whimsical and pretty about it. It had been invented and built under the direction of the artist.

They went in; a collection of trunks encumbered a little parlor. A little man appeared, dressed in a jumper. The striking thing about him was his beard. He bowed to the journalist, and said: "My dear sir, I hope that you will excuse me; I only returned yesterday, and everything is all upset here. Please be seated." The other refused, excusing himself: "My dear master, I only dropped in to pay my respects while passing by." Patissot, very much embarrassed, was bowing at every word of his friend's, as though moving automatically, and he murmured, stammering: "What a su—su—superb property!" The artist, flattered, smiled, and suggested visiting it.

He led them first to a little pavilion of feudal aspect, where his former studio was. Then they crossed a parlor, a dining-room, a vestibule full of beautiful works of art, of beautiful Beauvais, Gobelin and Flanders tapestries. But the strange external luxury of ornamentation became, inside, a revel of immense stairways. A magnificent grand stairway, a secret stairway in one tower, a servants' stairway in another, stairways everywhere! Patissot, by chance, opened a door and stepped back astonished. It was a veritable temple, this place of which respectable people only mention the name in English, an original and charming sanctuary in exquisite taste, fitted up like a pagoda, and the decoration of which must certainly have caused a great effort.

They next visited the park, which was complex, varied, with winding paths and full of old trees. But the journalist insisted on leaving; and, with many thanks, he took leave of the master: As they left they met a gardener; Patissot asked him: "Has Monsieur Meissonier owned this place for a long time?" The man answered: "Oh, monsieur! that needs explaining. I guess he bought the grounds in 1846. But, as for the house! he has already torn down and rebuilt that five or six times. It must have cost him at least two millions!" As Patissot left he was seized with an immense respect for this man, not on account of his success, glory or talent, but for putting so much money into a whim, because the bourgeois deprive themselves of all pleasure in order to hoard money.

After crossing Poissy, they struck out on foot along the road to Medan. The road first followed the Seine, which is dotted with charming islands at this place. Then they went up a hill and crossed the pretty village of Villaines, went down a little; and finally reached the neighborhood inhabited by the author of the Rougon-Macquart series.

A pretty old church with two towers appeared on the left. They walked along a short distance, and a passing farmer directed them to the writer's dwelling.

Before entering, they examined the house. A large building, square and new, very high, seemed, as in the fable of the mountain and the mouse, to have given birth to a tiny little white house, which nestled near it. This little house was the original dwelling, and had been built by the former owner. The tower had been erected by Zola.

They rang the bell. An enormous dog, a cross between a Saint Bernard and a Newfoundland, began to howl so terribly that Patissot felt a vague desire to retrace his steps. But a servant ran forward, calmed "Bertrand," opened the door, and took the journalist's card in order to carry it to his master.

"I hope that he will receive us!" murmured Patissot. "It would be too bad if we had come all this distance not to see him."

His companion smiled and answered: "Never fear, I have a plan for getting in."

But the servant, who had returned, simply asked them to follow him.

They entered the new building, and Patissot, who was quite enthusiastic, was panting as he climbed a stairway of ancient style which led to the second story.

At the same time he was trying to picture to himself this man whose glorious name echoes at present in all corners of the earth, amid the exasperated hatred of some, the real or feigned indignation of society, the envious scorn of several of his colleagues, the respect of a mass of readers, and the frenzied admiration of a great number. He expected to see a kind of bearded giant, of awe-inspiring aspect, with a thundering voice and an appearance little prepossessing at first.

The door opened on a room of uncommonly large dimensions, broad and high, lighted by an enormous window looking out over the valley. Old tapestries covered the walls; on the left, a monumental fireplace, flanked by two stone men, could have burned a century-old oak in one day. An immense table littered with books, papers and magazines stood in the middle of this apartment so vast and grand that it first engrossed the eye, and the attention was only afterward drawn to the man, stretched out when they entered on an Oriental divan where twenty persons could have slept. He took a few steps toward them, bowed, motioned to two seats, and turned back to his divan, where he sat with one leg drawn under him. A book lay open beside him, and in his right hand he held an ivory paper-cutter, the end of which he observed from time to time with one eye, closing the other with the persistency of a near-sighted person.

While the journalist explained the purpose of the visit, and the writer listened to him without yet answering, at times staring at him fixedly, Patissot, more and more embarrassed, was observing this celebrity.

Hardly forty, he was of medium height, fairly stout, and with a good-natured look. His head (very similar to those found in many Italian paintings of the sixteenth century), without being beautiful in the plastic sense of the word, gave an impression of great strength of character, power and intelligence. Short hair stood up straight on the high, well-developed forehead. A straight nose stopped short, as if cut off suddenly above the upper lip which was covered with a black mustache; over the whole chin was a closely-cropped beard. The dark, often ironical look was piercing, one felt that behind it there was a mind always actively at work observing people, interpreting words, analyzing gestures, uncovering the heart. This strong, round head was appropriate to his name, quick and short, with the bounding resonance of the two vowels.

When the journalist had fully explained his proposition, the writer answered him that he did not wish to make any definite arrangement, that he would, however, think the matter over, that his plans were not yet sufficiently defined. Then he stopped. It was a dismissal, and the two men, a little confused, arose. A desire seized Patissot; he wished this well-known person to say something to him, anything, some word which he could repeat to his colleagues; and, growing bold, he stammered: "Oh, monsieur! If you knew how I appreciate your works!" The other bowed, but answered nothing. Patissot became very bold and continued: "It is a great honor for me to speak to you to-day." The writer once more bowed, but with a stiff and impatient look. Patissot noticed it, and, completely losing his head, he added as he retreated: "What a su—su —superb property!"

Then, in the heart of the man of letters, the landowner awoke, and, smiling, he opened the window to show them the immense stretch of view. An endless horizon broadened out on all sides, giving a view of Triel, Pisse-Fontaine, Chanteloup, all the heights of Hautrie, and the Seine as far as the eye could see. The two visitors, delighted, congratulated him, and the house was opened to them. They saw everything, down to the dainty kitchen, whose walls and even ceilings were covered with porcelain tiles ornamented with blue designs, which excited the wonder of the farmers.

"How did you happen to buy this place?" asked the journalist.

The novelist explained that, while looking for a cottage to hire for the summer, he had found the little house, which was for sale for several thousand francs, a song, almost nothing. He immediately bought it.

"But everything that you have added must have cost you a good deal!"

The writer smiled, and answered: "Yes, quite a little."

The two men left. The journalist, taking Patissot by the arm, was philosophizing in a low voice:

"Every general has his Waterloo," he said; "every Balzac has his Jardies, and every artist living in the country feels like a landed proprietor."

They took the train at the station of Villaines, and, on the way home, Patissot loudly mentioned the names of the famous painter and of the great novelist as though they were his friends. He even allowed people to think that he had taken luncheon with one and dinner with the other.

BEFORE THE CELEBRATION

The celebration is approaching and preliminary quivers are already running through the streets, just as the ripples disturb the water preparatory to a storm. The shops, draped with flags, display a variety of gay-colored bunting materials, and the dry-goods people deceive one about the three colors as grocers do about the weight of candles. Little by little, hearts warm up to the matter; people speak about it in the street after dinner; ideas are exchanged:

"What a celebration it will be, my friend; what a celebration!"

"Have you heard the news? All the rulers are coming incognito, as bourgeois, in order to see it."

"I hear that the Emperor of Russia has arrived; he expects to go about everywhere with the Prince of Wales."

"It certainly will be a fine celebration!"

It is going to a celebration; what Monsieur Patissot, Parisian bourgeois, calls a celebration; one of these nameless tumults which, for fifteen hours, roll from one end of the city to the other, every ugly specimen togged out in its finest, a mob of perspiring bodies, where side by side are tossed about the stout gossip bedecked in red, white and blue ribbons, grown fat behind her counter and panting from lack of breath, the rickety clerk with his wife and brat in tow, the laborer carrying his youngster astride his neck, the bewildered provincial with his foolish, dazed expression, the groom, barely shaved and still spreading the perfume of the stable. And the foreigners dressed like monkeys, English women like giraffes, the water-carrier, cleaned up for the occasion, and the innumerable phalanx of little bourgeois, inoffensive little people, amused at everything. All this crowding and pressing, the sweat and dust, and the turmoil, all these eddies of human flesh, trampling of corns beneath the feet of your neighbors, this city all topsy-turvy, these vile odors, these frantic efforts toward nothing, the breath of millions of people, all redolent of garlic, give to Monsieur Patissot all the joy which it is possible for his heart to hold.

After reading the proclamation of the mayor on the walls of his district he had made his preparations.

This bit of prose said:

> I wish to call your attention particularly to the part of
>
> individuals in this celebration. Decorate your homes, illuminate
>
> your windows. Get together, open up a subscription in order to give
>
> to your houses and to your street a more brilliant and more artistic
>
> appearance than the neighboring houses and streets.

Then Monsieur Patissot tried to imagine how he could give to his home an artistic appearance.

One serious obstacle stood in the way. His only window looked out on a courtyard, a narrow, dark shaft, where only the rats could have seen his three Japanese lanterns.

He needed a public opening. He found it. On the first floor of his house lived a rich man, a nobleman and a royalist, whose coachman, also a reactionary, occupied a garret-room on the sixth floor, facing the street. Monsieur Patissot supposed that by paying (every conscience can be bought) he could obtain the use of the room for the day. He proposed five francs to this citizen of the whip for the use of his room from noon till midnight. The offer was immediately accepted.

Then he began to busy himself with the decorations. Three flags, four lanterns, was that enough to give to this box an artistic appearance—to express all the noble feelings of his soul? No; assuredly not! But, notwithstanding diligent search and nightly meditation, Monsieur Patissot could think of nothing else. He consulted his neighbors, who were surprised at the question; he questioned his colleagues—every one had bought lanterns and flags, some adding, for the occasion, red, white and blue bunting.

Then he began to rack his brains for some original idea. He frequented the cafes, questioning the patrons; they lacked imagination. Then one morning he went out on top of an omnibus. A respectable-looking gentleman was smoking a cigar beside him, a little farther away a laborer was smoking his pipe upside down, near the driver two rough fellows were joking, and clerks of every description were going to business for three cents.

Before the stores stacks of flags were resplendent under the rising sun. Patissot turned to his neighbor.

"It is going to be a fine celebration," he said. The gentleman looked at him sideways and answered in a haughty manner:

"That makes no difference to me!"

"You are not going to take part in it?" asked the surprised clerk. The other shook his head disdainfully and declared:

"They make me tired with their celebrations! Whose celebration is it? The government's? I do not recognize this government, monsieur!"

But Patissot, as government employee, took on his superior manner, and answered in a stern voice:

"Monsieur, the Republic is the government."

His neighbor was not in the least disturbed, and, pushing his hands down in his pockets, he exclaimed:

"Well, and what then? It makes no difference to me. Whether it's for the Republic or something else, I don't care! What I want, monsieur, is to know my government. I saw Charles X. and adhered to him, monsieur; I saw Louis-Philippe and adhered to him, monsieur; I saw Napoleon and adhered to him; but I have never seen the Republic."

Patissot, still serious, answered:

"The Republic, monsieur, is represented by its president!"

The other grumbled:

"Well, them, show him to me!"

Patissot shrugged his shoulders.

"Every one can see him; he's not shut up in a closet!"

Suddenly the fat man grew angry.

"Excuse me, monsieur, he cannot be seen. I have personally tried more than a hundred times, monsieur. I have posted myself near the Elysee; he did not come out. A passer-by informed me that he was playing billiards in the cafe opposite; I went to the cafe opposite; he was not there. I had been promised that he would go to Melun for the convention; I went to Melun, I did not see him. At last I became weary. I did not even see Monsieur Gambetta, and I do not know a single deputy."

He was, growing excited:

"A government, monsieur, is made to be seen; that's what it's there for, and for nothing else. One must be able to know that on such and such a day at such an hour the government will pass through such and such a street. Then one goes there and is satisfied."

Patissot, now calm, was enjoying his arguments.

"It is true," he said, "that it is agreeable to know the people by whom one is governed."

The gentleman continued more gently:

"Do you know how I would manage the celebration? Well, monsieur, I would have a procession of gilded cars, like the chariots used at the crowning of kings; in them I would parade all the members of the government, from the president to the deputies, throughout Paris all day long. In that manner, at least, every one would know by sight the personnel of the state."

But one of the toughs near the coachman turned around, exclaiming:

"And the fatted ox, where would you put him?"

A laugh ran round the two benches. Patissot understood the objection, and murmured:

"It might not perhaps be very dignified."

The gentleman thought the matter over and admitted it.

"Then," he said, "I would place them in view some place, so that every one could see them without going out of his way; on the Triumphal Arch at the Place de l'Etoile, for instance; and I would have the whole population pass before them. That would be very imposing."

Once more the tough turned round and said:

"You'd have to take telescopes to see their faces."

The gentleman did not answer; he continued:

"It's just like the presentation of the flags! There ought, to be some pretext, a mimic war ought to be organized, and the banners would be awarded to the troops as a reward. I had an idea about which I wrote to the minister; but he has not deigned to answer me. As the taking of the Bastille has been chosen for the date of the national celebration, a reproduction of this event might be made; there would be a pasteboard Bastille, fixed up by a scene-painter and concealing within its walls the whole Column of July. Then, monsieur, the troop would attack. That would be a magnificent spectacle as well as a lesson, to see the army itself overthrow the ramparts of tyranny. Then this Bastille would be set fire to and from the midst of the flames would appear the Column with the genius of Liberty, symbol of a new order and of the freedom of the people."

This time every one was listening to him and finding his idea excellent. An old gentleman exclaimed:

"That is a great idea, monsieur, which does you honor. It is to be regretted that the government did not adopt it."

A young man declared that actors ought to recite the "Iambes" of Barbier through the streets in order to teach the people art and liberty simultaneously.

These propositions excited general enthusiasm. Each one wished to have his word; all were wrought up. From a passing hand-organ a few strains of the Marseillaise were heard; the laborer started the song, and everybody joined in, roaring the chorus. The exalted nature of the song and its wild rhythm fired the driver, who lashed his horses to a gallop. Monsieur Patissot was bawling at the top of his lungs, and the passengers inside, frightened, were wondering what hurricane had struck them.

At last they stopped, and Monsieur Patissot, judging his neighbor to be a man of initiative, consulted him about the preparations which he expected to make:

"Lanterns and flags are all right,"' said Patissot; "but I prefer something better."

The other thought for a long time, but found nothing. Then, in despair, the clerk bought three flags and four lanterns.

AN EXPERIMENT IN LOVE

Many poets think that nature is incomplete without women, and hence, doubtless, come all the flowery comparisons which, in their songs, make our natural companion in turn a rose, a violet, a tulip, or something of that order. The need of tenderness which seizes us at dusk, when the evening mist begins to roll in from the hills, and when all the perfumes of the earth intoxicate us, is but imperfectly satisfied by lyric invocations. Monsieur Patissot, like all others, was seized with a wild desire for tenderness, for sweet kisses exchanged along a path where sunshine steals in at times, for the pressure of a pair of small hands, for a supple waist bending under his embrace.

He began to look at love as an unbounded pleasure, and, in his hours of reverie, he thanked the Great Unknown for having put so much charm into the caresses of human beings. But he needed a companion, and he did not know where to find one. On the advice of a friend, he went to the Folies-Bergere. There he saw a complete assortment. He was greatly perplexed to choose between them, for the desires of his heart were chiefly composed of poetic impulses, and poetry did not seem to be the strong point of these young ladies with penciled eyebrows who smiled at him in such a disturbing manner, showing the enamel of their false teeth. At last his choice fell on a young beginner who seemed poor and timid and whose sad look seemed to announce a nature easily influenced-by poetry.

He made an appointment with her for the following day at nine o'clock at the Saint-Lazare station. She did not come, but she was kind enough to send a friend in her stead.

She was a tall, red-haired girl, patriotically dressed in three colors, and covered by an immense tunnel hat, of which her head occupied the centre. Monsieur Patissot, a little disappointed, nevertheless accepted this substitute. They left for Maisons-Laffite, where regattas and a grand Venetian festival had been announced.

As soon as they were in the car, which was already occupied by two gentlemen who wore the red ribbon and three ladies who must at least have been duchesses, they were so dignified, the big red-haired girl, who answered the name of Octavie, announced to Patissot, in a screeching voice, that she was a fine girl fond of a good time and loving the country because there she could pick flowers and eat fried fish. She laughed with a shrillness which almost shattered the windows, familiarly calling her companion "My big darling."

Shame overwhelmed Patissot, who as a government employee, had to observe a certain amount of decorum. But Octavie stopped talking, glancing at her neighbors, seized with the overpowering desire which haunts all women of a certain class to make the acquaintance of respectable women. After about five minutes she thought she had found an opening, and, drawing from her pocket a Gil-Blas, she politely offered it to one of the amazed ladies, who declined, shaking her head. Then the big, red-haired girl began saying things with a double meaning, speaking of women who are stuck up without being any better than the others; sometimes she would let out a vulgar word which acted like a bomb exploding amid the icy dignity of the passengers.

At last they arrived. Patissot immediately wished to gain the shady nooks of the park, hoping that the melancholy of the forest would quiet the ruffled temper of his companion. But an entirely different effect resulted. As soon as she was amid the leaves and grass she began to sing at the top of her lungs snatches from operas which had stuck in her frivolous mind, warbling and trilling, passing from "Robert le Diable" to the "Muette," lingering especially on a sentimental love-song, whose last verses she sang in a voice as piercing as a gimlet.

Then suddenly she grew hungry. Patissot, who was still awaiting the hoped-for tenderness, tried in vain to retain her. Then she grew angry, exclaiming:

"I am not here for a dull time, am I?"

He had to take her to the Petit-Havre restaurant, which was near the place where the regatta was to be held.

She ordered an endless luncheon, a succession of dishes substantial enough to feed a regiment. Then, unable to wait, she called for relishes. A box of sardines was brought; she started in on it as though she intended to swallow the box itself. But when she had eaten two or three of the little oily fish she declared that she was no longer hungry and that she wished to see the preparations for the race.

Patissot, in despair and in his turn seized with hunger, absolutely refused to move. She started off alone, promising to return in time for the dessert. He began to eat in lonely silence, not knowing how to lead this rebellious nature to the realization of his dreams.

As she did not return he set out in search of her. She had found some friends, a troop of boatmen, in scanty garb, sunburned to the tips of their ears, and gesticulating, who were loudly arranging the details of the race in front of the house of Fourmaise, the builder.

Two respectable-looking gentlemen, probably the judges, were listening attentively. As soon as she saw Patissot, Octavie, who was leaning on the tanned arm of a strapping fellow who probably had more muscle than brains, whispered a few words in his ears. He answered:

"That's an agreement."

She returned to the clerk full of joy, her eyes sparkling, almost caressing.

"Let's go for a row," said she.

Pleased to see her so charming, he gave in to this new whim and procured a boat. But she obstinately refused to go to the races, notwithstanding Patissot's wishes.

"I had rather be alone with you, darling."

His heart thrilled. At last!

He took off his coat and began to row madly.

An old dilapidated mill, whose worm-eaten wheels hung over the water, stood with its two arches across a little arm of the river. Slowly they passed beneath it, and, when they were on the other side, they noticed before them a delightful little stretch of river, shaded by great trees which formed an arch over their heads. The little stream flowed along, winding first to the right and then to the left, continually revealing new scenes, broad fields on one side and on the other side a hill covered with cottages. They passed before a bathing establishment almost entirely hidden by the foliage, a charming country spot where gentlemen in clean gloves and beribboned ladies displayed all the ridiculous awkwardness of elegant people in the country. She cried joyously:

"Later on we will take a dip there."

Farther on, in a kind of bay, she wished to stop, coaxing:

"Come here, honey, right close to me."

She put her arm around his neck and, leaning her head on his shoulder, she murmured:

"How nice it is! How delightful it is on the water!"

Patissot was reveling in happiness. He was thinking of those foolish boatmen who, without ever feeling the penetrating charm of the river banks and the delicate grace of the reeds, row along out of breath, perspiring and tired out, from the tavern where they take luncheon to the tavern where they take dinner.

He was so comfortable that he fell asleep. When he awoke, he was alone. He called, but no one answered. Anxious, he climbed up on the side of the river, fearing that some accident might have happened.

Then, in the distance, coming in his direction, he saw a long, slender gig which four oarsmen as black as negroes were driving through the water like an arrow. It came nearer, skimming over the water; a woman was holding the tiller. Heavens! It looked—it was she! In order to regulate the rhythm of the stroke, she was singing in her shrill voice a boating song, which she interrupted for a minute as she got in front of Patissot. Then, throwing him a kiss, she cried:

"You big goose!"

A DINNER AND SOME OPINIONS

On the occasion of the national celebration Monsieur Antoine Perdrix, chief of Monsieur Patissot's department, was made a knight of the Legion of Honor. He had been in service for thirty years under preceding governments, and for ten years under the present one. His employees, although grumbling a little at being thus rewarded in the person of their chief, thought it wise, nevertheless, to offer him a cross studded with paste diamonds. The new knight, in turn, not wishing to be outdone, invited them all to dinner for the following Sunday, at his place at Asnieres.

The house, decorated with Moorish ornaments, looked like a cafe concert, but its location gave it value, as the railroad cut through the whole garden, passing within a hundred and fifty feet of the porch. On the regulation plot of grass stood a basin of Roman cement, containing goldfish and a stream of water the size of that which comes from a syringe, which occasionally made microscopic rainbows at which the guests marvelled.

The feeding of this irrigator was the constant preoccupation of Monsieur Perdrix, who would sometimes get up at five o'clock in the morning in order to fill the tank. Then, in his shirt sleeves, his big stomach almost bursting from his trousers, he would pump wildly, so that on returning from the office he could have the satisfaction of letting the fountain play and of imagining that it was cooling off the garden.

On the night of the official dinner all the guests, one after the other, went into ecstasies over the surroundings, and each time they heard a train in the distance, Monsieur Perdrix would announce to them its destination: Saint-Germain, Le Havre, Cherbourg, or Dieppe, and they would playfully wave to the passengers leaning from the windows.

The whole office force was there. First came Monsieur Capitaine, the assistant chief; Monsieur Patissot, chief clerk; then Messieurs de Sombreterre and Vallin, elegant young employees who only came to the office when they had to; lastly Monsieur Rade, known throughout the ministry for the absurd doctrines which he upheld, and the copying clerk, Monsieur Boivin.

Monsieur Rade passed for a character. Some called him a dreamer or an idealist, others a revolutionary; every one agreed that he was very clumsy. Old, thin and small, with bright eyes and long, white hair, he had all his life professed a profound contempt for administrative work. A book rummager and a great reader, with a nature continually in revolt against everything, a seeker of truth and a despiser of popular prejudices, he had a clear and paradoxical manner of expressing his opinions which closed the mouths of self-satisfied fools and of those that were discontented without knowing why. People said: "That old fool of a Rade," or else: "That harebrained Rade"; and the slowness, of his promotion seemed to indicate the reason, according to commonplace minds. His freedom of speech often made—his colleagues tremble; they asked themselves with terror how he had been able to keep his place as long as he had. As soon as they had seated themselves, Monsieur Perdrix thanked his "collaborators" in a neat little speech, promising them his protection, the more valuable as his power grew, and he ended with a stirring peroration in which he thanked and glorified a government so liberal and just that it knows how to seek out the worthy from among the humble.

Monsieur Capitaine, the assistant chief, answered in the name of the office, congratulated, greeted, exalted, sang the praises of all; frantic applause greeted these two bits of eloquence. After that they settled down seriously to the business of eating.

Everything went well up to the dessert; lack of conversation went unnoticed. But after the coffee a discussion arose, and Monsieur Rade let himself loose and soon began to overstep the bounds of discretion.

They naturally discussed love, and a breath of chivalry intoxicated this room full of bureaucrats; they praised and exalted the superior beauty of woman, the delicacy of hex soul, her aptitude for exquisite things, the correctness of her judgment, and the refinement of her sentiments. Monsieur Rade began to protest, energetically refusing to credit the so-called "fair" sex with all the qualities they ascribed to it; then, amidst the general indignation, he quoted some authors:

"Schopenhauer, gentlemen, Schopenhauer, the great philosopher, revered by all Germany, says: 'Man's intelligence must have been terribly deadened by love in order to call this sex with the small waist, narrow shoulders, large hips and crooked legs, the fair sex. All its beauty lies in the instinct of love. Instead of calling it the fair, it would have been better to call it the unaesthetic sex. Women have neither the appreciation nor the knowledge of music, any more than they have of poetry or of the plastic arts; with them it is merely an apelike imitation, pure pretence, affectation cultivated from their desire to please.'"

"The man who said that is an idiot," exclaimed Monsieur de Sombreterre.

Monsieur Rade smilingly continued:

"And how about Rousseau, gentlemen? Here is his opinion: 'Women, as a rule, love no art, are skilled in none, and have no talent.'"

Monsieur de Sombreterre disdainfully shrugged his shoulders:

"Then Rousseau is as much of a fool as the other, that's all."

Monsieur Rade, still smiling, went on:

"And this is what Lord Byron said, who, nevertheless, loved women: 'They should be well fed and well dressed, but not allowed to mingle with society. They should also be taught religion, but they should ignore poetry and politics, only being allowed to read religious works or cook-books.'"

Monsieur Rade continued:

"You see, gentlemen, all of them study painting and music. But not a single one of them has ever painted a remarkable picture or composed a great opera! Why, gentlemen? Because they are the 'sexes sequior', the secondary sex in every sense of the word, made to be kept apart, in the background."

Monsieur Patissot was growing angry, and exclaimed:

"And how about Madame Sand, monsieur?"

"She is the one exception, monsieur, the one exception. I will quote to you another passage from another great philosopher, this one an Englishman, Herbert Spencer. Here is what he says: 'Each sex is capable, under the influence of abnormal stimulation, of manifesting faculties ordinarily reserved for the other one. Thus, for instance, in extreme cases a special excitement may cause the breasts of men to give milk; children deprived of their mothers have often thus been saved in time of famine. Nevertheless, we do not place this faculty of giving milk among the male attributes. It is the same with female intelligence, which, in certain cases, will give superior products, but which is not to be considered in an estimate of the feminine nature as a social factor.'"

All Monsieur Patissot's chivalric instincts were wounded and he declared:

"You are not a Frenchman, monsieur. French gallantry is a form of patriotism."

Monsieur Rade retorted:

"I have very little patriotism, monsieur, as little as I can get along with."

A coolness settled over the company, but he continued quietly:

"Do you admit with me that war is a barbarous thing; that this custom of killing off people constitutes a condition of savagery; that it is odious, when life is the only real good, to see governments, whose duty is to protect the lives of their subjects, persistently looking for means of destruction? Am I not right? Well, if war is a terrible thing, what about patriotism, which is the idea at the base of it? When a murderer kills he has a fixed idea; it is to steal. When a good man sticks his bayonet through another good man, father of a family, or, perhaps, a great artist, what idea is he following out?"

Everybody was shocked.

"When one has such thoughts, one should not express them in public."

M. Patissot continued:

"There are, however, monsieur, principles which all good people recognize."

M. Rade asked: "Which ones?"

Then very solemnly, M. Patissot pronounced: "Morality, monsieur."

M. Rade was beaming; he exclaimed:

"Just let me give you one example, gentlemen, one little example. What is your opinion of the gentlemen with the silk caps who thrive along the boulevard's on the delightful traffic which you know, and who make a living out of it?"

A look of disgust ran round the table:

"Well, gentlemen! only a century ago, when an elegant gentleman, very ticklish about his honor, had for—friend—a beautiful and rich lady, it was considered perfectly proper to live at her expense and even to squander her whole fortune. This game was considered delightful. This only goes to show that the principles of morality are by no means settled—and that—"

M. Perdrix, visibly embarrassed, stopped him:

"M. Rade, you are sapping the very foundations of society. One must always have principles. Thus, in politics, here is M. de Sombreterre, who is a Legitimist; M. Vallin, an Orleanist; M. Patissot and myself, Republicans; we all have very different principles, and yet we agree very well because we have them."

But M. Rade exclaimed:

"I also have principles, gentlemen, very distinct ones."

M. Patissot raised his head and coldly asked:

"It would please me greatly to know them, monsieur."

M. Rade did not need to be coaxed.

"Here they are, monsieur:

"First principle—Government by one person is a monstrosity.

"Second principle—Restricted suffrage is an injustice.

"Third principle—Universal suffrage is idiotic.

"To deliver up millions of men, superior minds, scientists, even geniuses, to the caprice and will of a being who, in an instant of gaiety, madness, intoxication or love, would not hesitate to sacrifice everything for his exalted fancy, would spend the wealth of the country amassed by others with difficulty, would have thousands of men slaughtered on the battle-fields, all this appears to me—a simple logician—a monstrous aberration.

"But, admitting that a country must govern itself, to exclude, on some always debatable pretext, a part of the citizens from the administration of affairs is such an injustice that it seems to me unworthy of a further discussion.

"There remains universal suffrage. I suppose that you will agree with me that geniuses are a rarity. Let us be liberal and say that there are at present five in France. Now, let us add, perhaps, two hundred men with a decided talent, one thousand others possessing various talents, and ten thousand superior intellects. This is a staff of eleven thousand two hundred and five minds. After that you have the army of mediocrities followed by the multitude of fools. As the mediocrities and the fools always form the immense majority, it is impossible for them to elect an intelligent government.

"In order to be fair I admit that logically universal suffrage seems to me the only admissible principle, but it is impracticable. Here are the reasons why:

"To make all the living forces of the country cooperate in the government, to represent all the interests, to take into account all the rights, is an ideal dream, but hardly practicable, because the only force which can be measured is that very one which should be neglected, the stupid strength of numbers, According to your method, unintelligent numbers equal genius, knowledge, learning, wealth and industry. When you are able to give to a member of the Institute ten thousand votes to a ragman's one, one hundred votes for a great land-owner as against his farmer's ten, then you will have approached an equilibrium of forces and obtained a national representation which will really represent the strength of the nation. But I challenge you to do it.

"Here are my conclusions:

"Formerly, when a man was a failure at every other profession he turned photographer; now he has himself elected a deputy. A government thus composed will always be sadly lacking, incapable of evil as well as of good. On the other hand, a despot, if he be stupid, can do a lot of harm, and, if he be intelligent (a thing which is very scarce), he may do good.

"I cannot decide between these two forms of government; I declare myself to be an anarchist, that is to say, a partisan of that power which is the most unassuming, the least felt, the most liberal, in the broadest sense of the word, and revolutionary at the same time; by that I mean the everlasting enemy of this same power, which can in no way be anything but defective. That's all!"

Cries of indignation rose about the table, and all, whether Legitimist, Orleanist or Republican through force of circumstances, grew red with anger. M. Patissot especially was choking with rage, and, turning toward M. Rade, he cried:

"Then, monsieur, you believe in nothing?"

The other answered quietly:

"You're absolutely correct, monsieur."

The anger felt by all the guests prevented M. Rade from continuing, and M. Perdrix, as chief, closed the discussion.

"Enough, gentlemen! We each have our opinion, and we have no intention of changing it."

All agreed with the wise words. But M. Rade, never satisfied, wished to have the last word.

"I have, however, one moral," said he. "It is simple and always applicable. One sentence embraces the whole thought; here it is: 'Never do unto another that which you would not have him do unto you.' I defy you to pick any flaw in it, while I will undertake to demolish your most sacred principles with three arguments."

This time there was no answer. But as they were going home at night, by couples, each one was saying to his companion: "Really, M. Rade goes much too far. His mind must surely be unbalanced. He ought to be appointed assistant chief at the Charenton Asylum."

A RECOLLECTION

How many recollections of youth come to me in the soft sunlight of early spring! It was an age when all was pleasant, cheerful, charming, intoxicating. How exquisite are the remembrances of those old springtimes!

Do you recall, old friends and brothers, those happy years when life was nothing but a triumph and an occasion for mirth? Do you recall the days of wanderings around Paris, our jolly poverty, our walks in the fresh, green woods, our drinks in the wine-shops on the banks of the Seine and our commonplace and delightful little flirtations?

I will tell you about one of these. It was twelve years ago and already appears to me so old, so old that it seems now as if it belonged to the other end of life, before middle age, this dreadful middle age from which I suddenly perceived the end of the journey.

I was then twenty-five. I had just come to Paris. I was in a government office, and Sundays were to me like unusual festivals, full of exuberant happiness, although nothing remarkable occurred.

Now it is Sunday every day, but I regret the time when I had only one Sunday in the week. How enjoyable it was! I had six francs to spend!

On this particular morning I awoke with that sense of freedom that all clerks know so well—the sense of emancipation, of rest, of quiet and of independence.

I opened my window. The weather was charming. A blue sky full of sunlight and swallows spread above the town.

I dressed quickly and set out, intending to spend the day in the woods breathing the air of the green trees, for I am originally a rustic, having been brought up amid the grass and the trees.

Paris was astir and happy in the warmth and the light. The front of the houses was bathed in sunlight, the janitress' canaries were singing in their cages and there was an air of gaiety in the streets, in the faces of the inhabitants, lighting them up with a smile as if all beings and all things experienced a secret satisfaction at the rising of the brilliant sun.

I walked towards the Seine to take the Swallow, which would land me at Saint-Cloud.

How I loved waiting for the boat on the wharf:

It seemed to me that I was about to set out for the ends of the world, for new and wonderful lands. I saw the boat approaching yonder, yonder under the second bridge, looking quite small with its plume of smoke, then growing larger and ever larger, as it drew near, until it looked to me like a mail steamer.

It came up to the wharf and I went on board. People were there already in their Sunday clothes, startling toilettes, gaudy ribbons and bright scarlet designs. I took up a position in the bows, standing up and looking at the quays, the trees, the houses and the bridges disappearing behind us. And suddenly I perceived the great viaduct of Point du Jour which blocked the river. It was the end of Paris, the beginning of the country, and behind the double row of arches the Seine, suddenly spreading out as though it had regained space and liberty, became all at once the peaceful river which flows through the plains, alongside the wooded hills, amid the meadows, along the edge of the forests.

After passing between two islands the Swallow went round a curved verdant slope dotted with white houses. A voice called out: "Bas Meudon" and a little further on, "Sevres," and still further, "Saint-Cloud."

I went on shore and walked hurriedly through the little town to the road leading to the wood.

I had brought with me a map of the environs of Paris, so that I might not lose my way amid the paths which cross in every direction these little forests where Parisians take their outings.

As soon as I was unperceived I began to study my guide, which seemed to be perfectly clear. I was to turn to the right, then to the left, then again to the left and I should reach Versailles by evening in time for dinner.

I walked slowly beneath the young leaves, drinking in the air, fragrant with the odor of young buds and sap. I sauntered along, forgetful of musty papers, of the offices, of my chief, my colleagues, my documents, and thinking of the good things that were sure to come to me, of all the veiled unknown contained in the future. A thousand recollections of childhood came over me, awakened by these country odors, and I walked along, permeated with the fragrant, living enchantment, the emotional enchantment of the woods warmed by the sun of June.

At times I sat down to look at all sorts of little flowers growing on a bank, with the names of which I was familiar. I recognized them all just as if they were the ones I had seen long ago in the country. They were yellow, red, violet, delicate, dainty, perched on long stems or close to the ground. Insects of all colors and shapes, short, long, of peculiar form, frightful, and microscopic monsters, climbed quietly up the stalks of grass which bent beneath their weight.

Then I went to sleep for some hours in a hollow and started off again, refreshed by my doze.

In front of me lay an enchanting pathway and through its somewhat scanty foliage the sun poured down drops of light on the marguerites which grew there. It stretched out interminably, quiet and deserted, save for an occasional big wasp, who would stop buzzing now and then to sip from a flower, and then continue his way.

All at once I perceived at the end of the path two persons, a man and a woman, coming towards me. Annoyed at being disturbed in my quiet walk, I was about to dive into the thicket, when I thought I heard someone calling me. The woman was, in fact, shaking her parasol, and the man, in his shirt sleeves, his coat over one arm, was waving the other as a signal of distress.

I went towards them. They were walking hurriedly, their faces very red, she with short, quick steps and he with long strides. They both looked annoyed and fatigued.

The woman asked:

"Can you tell me, monsieur, where we are? My fool of a husband made us lose our way, although he pretended he knew the country perfectly."

I replied confidently:

"Madame, you are going towards Saint-Cloud and turning your back on Versailles."

With a look of annoyed pity for her husband, she exclaimed:

"What, we are turning our back on Versailles? Why, that is just where we want to dine!"

"I am going there also, madame."

"Mon Dieu, mon Dieu, mon Dieu!" she repeated, shrugging her shoulders, and in that tone of sovereign contempt assumed by women to express their exasperation.

She was quite young, pretty, a brunette with a slight shadow on her upper lip.

As for him, he was perspiring and wiping his forehead. It was assuredly a little Parisian bourgeois couple. The man seemed cast down, exhausted and distressed.

"But, my dear friend, it was you—" he murmured.

She did not allow him to finish his sentence.

"It was I! Ah, it is my fault now! Was it I who wanted to go out without getting any information, pretending that I knew how to find my way? Was it I who wanted to take the road to the right on top of the hill, insisting that I recognized the road? Was it I who undertook to take charge of Cachou—"

She had not finished speaking when her husband, as if he had suddenly gone crazy, gave a piercing scream, a long, wild cry that could not be described in any language, but which sounded like 'tuituit'.

The young woman did not appear to be surprised or moved and resumed:

"No, really, some people are so stupid and they pretend they know everything. Was it I who took the train to Dieppe last year instead of the train to Havre—tell me, was it I? Was it I who bet that M. Letourneur lived in Rue des Martyres? Was it I who would not believe that Celeste was a thief?"

She went on, furious, with a surprising flow of language, accumulating the most varied, the most unexpected and the most overwhelming accusations drawn from the intimate relations of their daily life, reproaching her husband for all his actions, all his ideas, all his habits, all his enterprises, all his efforts, for his life from the time of their marriage up to the present time.

He strove to check her, to calm her and stammered:

"But, my dear, it is useless—before monsieur. We are making ourselves ridiculous. This does not interest monsieur."

And he cast mournful glances into the thicket as though he sought to sound its peaceful and mysterious depths, in order to flee thither, to escape and hide from all eyes, and from time to time he uttered a fresh scream, a prolonged and shrill "tuituit." I took this to be a nervous affection.

The young woman, suddenly turning towards me: and changing her tone with singular rapidity, said:

"If monsieur will kindly allow us, we will accompany him on the road, so as not to lose our way again, and be obliged, possibly, to sleep in the wood."

I bowed. She took my arm and began to talk about a thousand things —about herself, her life, her family, her business. They were glovers in the Rue, Saint-Lazare.

Her husband walked beside her, casting wild glances into the thick wood and screaming "tuituit" every few moments.

At last I inquired:

"Why do you scream like that?"

"I have lost my poor dog," he replied in a tone of discouragement and despair.

"How is that—you have lost your dog?"

"Yes. He was just a year old. He had never been outside the shop. I wanted to take him to have a run in the woods. He had never seen the grass nor the leaves and he was almost wild. He began to run about and bark and he disappeared in the wood. I must also add that he was greatly afraid of the train. That may have driven him mad. I kept on calling him, but he has not come back. He will die of hunger in there."

Without turning towards her husband, the young woman said:

"If you had left his chain on, it would not have happened. When people are as stupid as you are they do not keep a dog."

"But, my dear, it was you—" he murmured timidly.

She stopped short, and looking into his eyes as if she were going to tear them out, she began again to cast in his face innumerable reproaches.

It was growing dark. The cloud of vapor that covers the country at dusk was slowly rising and there was a poetry in the air, induced by the peculiar and enchanting freshness of the atmosphere that one feels in the woods at nightfall.

Suddenly the young man stopped, and feeling his body feverishly, exclaimed:

"Oh, I think that I—"

She looked at him.

"Well, what?"

"I did not notice that I had my coat on my arm."

"Well—?"

"I have lost my pocketbook—my money was in it."

She shook with anger and choked with indignation.

"That was all that was lacking. How stupid you are! how stupid you are! Is it possible that I could have married such an idiot! Well, go and look for it, and see that you find it. I am going on to Versailles with monsieur. I do not want to sleep in the wood."

"Yes, my dear," he replied gently. "Where shall I find you?"

A restaurant had been recommended to me. I gave him the address.

He turned back and, stooping down as he searched the ground with anxious eyes, he moved away, screaming "tuituit" every few moments.

We could see him for some time until the growing darkness concealed all but his outline, but we heard his mournful "tuituit," shriller and shriller as the night grew darker.

As for me, I stepped along quickly and happily in the soft twilight, with this little unknown woman leaning on my arm. I tried to say pretty things to her, but could think of nothing. I remained silent, disturbed, enchanted.

Our path was suddenly crossed by a high road. To the right I perceived a town lying in a valley.

What was this place? A man was passing. I asked him. He replied:

"Bougival."

I was dumfounded.

"What, Bougival? Are you sure?"

"Parbleu, I belong there!"

The little woman burst into an idiotic laugh.

I proposed that we should take a carriage and drive to Versailles. She replied:

"No, indeed. This is very funny and I am very hungry. I am really quite calm. My husband will find his way all right. It is a treat to me to be rid of him for a few hours."

We went into a restaurant beside the water and I ventured to ask for a private compartment. We had some supper. She sang, drank champagne, committed all sorts of follies.

That was my first serious flirtation.

OUR LETTERS

Eight hours of railway travel induce sleep for some persons and insomnia for others with me, any journey prevents my sleeping on the following night.

At about five o'clock I arrived at the estate of Abelle, which belongs to my friends, the Murets d'Artus, to spend three weeks there. It is a pretty house, built by one of their grandfathers in the style of the latter half of the last century. Therefore it has that intimate character of dwellings that have always been inhabited, furnished and enlivened by the same people. Nothing changes; nothing alters the soul of the dwelling, from which the furniture has never been taken out, the tapestries never unnailed, thus becoming worn out, faded, discolored, on the same walls. None of the old furniture leaves the place; only from time to time it is moved a little to make room for a new piece, which enters there like a new-born infant in the midst of brothers and sisters.

The house is on a hill in the center of a park which slopes down to the river, where there is a little stone bridge. Beyond the water the fields stretch out in the distance, and here one can see the cows wandering around, pasturing on the moist grass; their eyes seem full of the dew, mist and freshness of the pasture. I love this dwelling, just as one loves a thing which one ardently desires to possess. I return here every autumn with infinite delight; I leave with regret.

After I had dined with this friendly family, by whom I was received like a relative, I asked my friend, Paul Muret: "Which room did you give me this year?"

"Aunt Rose's room."

An hour later, followed by her three children, two little girls and a boy, Madame Muret d'Artus installed me in Aunt Rose's room, where I had not yet slept.

When I was alone I examined the walls, the furniture, the general aspect of the room, in order to attune my mind to it. I knew it but little, as I had entered it only once or twice, and I looked indifferently at a pastel portrait of Aunt Rose, who gave her name to the room.

This old Aunt Rose, with her curls, looking at me from behind the glass, made very little impression on my mind. She looked to me like a woman of former days, with principles and precepts as strong on the maxims of morality as on cooking recipes, one of these old aunts who are the bugbear of gaiety and the stern and wrinkled angel of provincial families.

I never had heard her spoken of; I knew nothing of her life or of her death. Did she belong to this century or to the preceding one? Had she left this earth after a calm or a stormy existence? Had she given up to heaven the pure soul of an old maid, the calm soul of a spouse, the tender one of a mother, or one moved by love? What difference did it make? The name alone, "Aunt Rose," seemed ridiculous, common, ugly.

I picked up a candle and looked at her severe face, hanging far up in an old gilt frame. Then, as I found it insignificant, disagreeable, even unsympathetic, I began to examine the furniture. It dated from the period of Louis XVI, the Revolution and the Directorate. Not a chair, not a curtain had entered this room since then, and it gave out the subtle odor of memories, which is the combined odor of wood, cloth, chairs, hangings, peculiar to places wherein have lived hearts that have loved and suffered.

I retired but did not sleep. After I had tossed about for an hour or two, I decided to get up and write some letters.

I opened a little mahogany desk with brass trimmings, which was placed between the two windows, in hope of finding some ink and paper; but all I found was a quill-pen, very much worn, and chewed at the end. I was about to close this piece of furniture, when a shining spot attracted my attention it looked like the yellow head of a nail. I scratched it with my finger, and it seemed to move. I seized it between two finger-nails, and pulled as hard as I could. It came toward me gently. It was a long gold pin which had been slipped into a hole in the wood and remained hidden there.

Why? I immediately thought that it must have served to work some spring which hid a secret, and I looked. It took a long time. After about two hours of investigation, I discovered another hole opposite the first one, but at the bottom of a groove. Into this I stuck my pin: a little shelf sprang toward my face, and I saw two packages of yellow letters, tied with a blue ribbon.

I read them. Here are two of them:

> So you wish me to return to you your letters, my dearest friend.
> Here they are, but it pains me to obey. Of what are you afraid?
> That I might lose them? But they are under lock and key. Do you
> fear that they might be stolen? I guard against that, for they are
> my dearest treasure.
>
> Yes, it pains me deeply. I wondered whether, perhaps you might not
> be feeling some regret! Not regret at having loved me, for I know
> that you still do, but the regret of having expressed on white paper
> this living love in hours when your heart did not confide in me, but
> in the pen that you held in your hand. When we love, we have need
> of confession, need of talking or writing, and we either talk or
> write. Words fly away, those sweet words made of music, air and
> tenderness, warm and light, which escape as soon as they are
> uttered, which remain in the memory alone, but which one can neither
> see, touch nor kiss, as one can with the words written by your hand.
>
> Your letters? Yes, I am returning them to you! But with what
> sorrow!
>
> Undoubtedly, you must have had an after thought of delicate shame at
> expressions that are ineffaceable. In your sensitive and timid soul
> you must have regretted having written to a man that you loved him.
> You remembered sentences that called up recollections, and you said
> to yourself: "I will make ashes of those words."
>
> Be satisfied, be calm. Here are your letters. I love you.

MY FRIEND:

No, you have not understood me, you have not guessed. I do not regret, and I never shall, that I told you of my affection.

I will always write to you, but you must return my letters to me as soon as you have read them.

I shall shock you, my friend, when I tell you the reason for this demand. It is not poetic, as you imagined, but practical. I am afraid, not of you, but of some mischance. I am guilty. I do not wish my fault to affect others than myself.

Understand me well. You and I may both die. You might fall off your horse, since you ride every day; you might die from a sudden attack, from a duel, from heart disease, from a carriage accident, in a thousand ways. For, if there is only one death, there are more ways of its reaching us than there are days or us to live.

Then your sisters, your brother, or your sister-in-law might find my letters! Do you think that they love me? I doubt it. And then, even if they adored me, is it possible for two women and one man to know a secret—such a secret!—and not to tell of it?

I seem to be saying very disagreeable things, speaking first of your death, and then suspecting the discreetness of your relatives.

But don't all of us die sooner or later? And it is almost certain that one of us will precede the other under the ground. We must therefore foresee all dangers, even that one.

As for me, I will keep your letters beside mine, in the secret of my little desk. I will show them to you there, sleeping side by side in their silken hiding place, full of our love, like lovers in a tomb.

You will say to me: "But if you should die first, my dear, your husband will find these letters."

Oh! I fear nothing. First of all, he does not know the secret of my desk, and then he will not look for it. And even if he finds it after my death, I fear nothing.

Did you ever stop to think of all the love letters that have been found after death? I have been thinking of this for a long time, and that is the reason I decided to ask you for my letters.

Think that never, do you understand, never, does a woman burn, tear or destroy the letters in which it is told her that she is loved. That is our whole life, our whole hope, expectation and dream. These little papers which bear our name in caressing terms are relics which we adore; they are chapels in which we are the saints. Our love letters are our titles to beauty, grace, seduction, the intimate vanity of our womanhood; they are the treasures of our heart. No, a woman does not destroy these secret and delicious archives of her life.

But, like everybody else, we die, and then—then these letters are found! Who finds them? The husband. Then what does he do? Nothing. He burns them.

Oh, I have thought a great deal about that! Just think that every day women are dying who have been loved; every day the traces and proofs of their fault fall into the hands of their husbands, and that there is never a scandal, never a duel.

Think, my dear, of what a man's heart is. He avenges himself on a living woman; he fights with the man who has dishonored her, kills him while she lives, because, well, why? I do not know exactly why. But, if, after her death, he finds similar proofs, he burns them and no one is the wiser, and he continues to shake hands with the friend of the dead woman, and feels quite at ease that these letters should not have fallen into strange hands, and that they are destroyed.

Oh, how many men I know among my friends who must have burned such proofs, and who pretend to know nothing, and yet who would have fought madly had they found them when she was still alive! But she is dead. Honor has changed. The tomb is the boundary of conjugal sinning.

Therefore, I can safely keep our letters, which, in your hands, would be a menace to both of us. Do you dare to say that I am not right?

I love you and kiss you.

I raised my eyes to the portrait of Aunt Rose, and as I looked at her severe, wrinkled face, I thought of all those women's souls which we do not know, and which we suppose to be so different from what they really are, whose inborn and ingenuous craftiness we never can penetrate, their quiet duplicity; and a verse of De Vigny returned to my memory:

"Always this comrade whose heart is uncertain."

THE LOVE OF LONG AGO

The old-fashioned chateau was built on a wooded knoll in the midst of tall trees with dark-green foliage; the park extended to a great distance, in one direction to the edge of the forest, in another to the distant country. A few yards from the front of the house was a huge stone basin with marble ladies taking a bath; other, basins were seen at intervals down to the foot of the slope, and a stream of water fell in cascades from one basin to another.

From the manor house, which preserved the grace of a superannuated coquette, down to the grottos incrusted with shell-work, where slumbered the loves of a bygone age, everything in this antique demesne had retained the physiognomy of former days. Everything seemed to speak still of ancient customs, of the manners of long ago, of former gallantries, and of the elegant trivialities so dear to our grandmothers.

In a parlor in the style of Louis XV, whose walls were covered with shepherds paying court to shepherdesses, beautiful ladies in hoop-skirts, and gallant gentlemen in wigs, a very old woman, who seemed dead as soon as she ceased to move, was almost lying down in a large easy-chair, at each side of which hung a thin, mummy-like hand.

Her dim eyes were gazing dreamily toward the distant horizon as if they sought to follow through the park the visions of her youth. Through the open window every now and then came a breath of air laden with the odor of grass and the perfume of flowers. It made her white locks flutter around her wrinkled forehead and old memories float through her brain.

Beside her, on a tapestried stool, a young girl, with long fair hair hanging in braids down her back, was embroidering an altar-cloth. There was a pensive expression in her eyes, and it was easy to see that she was dreaming, while her agile fingers flew over her work.

But the old lady turned round her head, and said:

"Berthe, read me something out of the newspapers, that I may still know sometimes what is going on in the world."

The young girl took up a newspaper, and cast a rapid glance over it.

"There is a great deal about politics, grandmamma; shall I pass that over?"

"Yes, yes, darling. Are there no love stories? Is gallantry, then, dead in France, that they no longer talk about abductions or adventures as they did formerly?"

The girl made a long search through the columns of the newspaper.

"Here is one," she said. "It is entitled 'A Love Drama!'"

The old woman smiled through her wrinkles. "Read that for me," she said.

And Berthe commenced. It was a case of vitriol throwing. A wife, in order to avenge herself on her husband's mistress, had burned her face and eyes. She had left the Court of Assizes acquitted, declared to be innocent, amid the applause of the crowd.

The grandmother moved about excitedly in her chair, and exclaimed:

"This is horrible—why, it is perfectly horrible!

"See whether you can find anything else to read to me, darling."

Berthe again made a search; and farther down among the reports of criminal cases, she read:

"'Gloomy Drama. A shop girl, no longer young, allowed herself to be led astray by a young man. Then, to avenge herself on her lover, whose heart proved fickle, she shot him with a revolver. The unhappy man is maimed for life. The jury, all men of moral character, condoning the illicit love of the murderess, honorably acquitted her.'"

This time the old grandmother appeared quite shocked, and, in a trembling voice, she said:

"Why, you people are mad nowadays. You are mad! The good God has given you love, the only enchantment in life. Man has added to this gallantry the only distraction of our dull hours, and here you are mixing up with it vitriol and revolvers, as if one were to put mud into a flagon of Spanish wine."

Berthe did not seem to understand her grandmother's indignation.

"But, grandmamma, this woman avenged herself. Remember she was married, and her husband deceived her."

The grandmother gave a start.

"What ideas have they been filling your head with, you young girls of today?"

Berthe replied:

"But marriage is sacred, grandmamma."

The grandmother's heart, which had its birth in the great age of gallantry, gave a sudden leap.

"It is love that is sacred," she said. "Listen, child, to an old woman who has seen three generations, and who has had a long, long experience of men and women. Marriage and love have nothing in common. We marry to found a family, and we form families in order to constitute society. Society cannot dispense with marriage. If society is a chain, each family is a link in that chain. In order to weld those links, we always seek metals of the same order. When we marry, we must bring together suitable conditions; we must combine fortunes, unite similar races and aim at the common interest, which is riches and children. We marry only once my child, because the world requires us to do so, but we may love twenty times in one lifetime because nature has made us like this. Marriage, you see, is law, and love is an instinct which impels us, sometimes along a straight, and sometimes along a devious path. The world has made laws to combat our instincts—it was necessary to make them; but our instincts are always stronger, and we ought not to resist them too much, because they come from God; while the laws only come from men. If we did not perfume life with love, as much love as possible, darling, as we put sugar into drugs for children, nobody would care to take it just as it is."

Berthe opened her eyes wide in astonishment. She murmured:

"Oh! grandmamma, we can only love once."

The grandmother raised her trembling hands toward Heaven, as if again to invoke the defunct god of gallantries. She exclaimed indignantly:

"You have become a race of serfs, a race of common people. Since the Revolution, it is impossible any longer to recognize society. You have attached big words to every action, and wearisome duties to every corner of existence; you believe in equality and eternal passion. People have written poetry telling you that people have died of love. In my time poetry was written to teach men to love every woman. And we! when we liked a gentleman, my child, we sent him a page. And when a fresh caprice came into our hearts, we were not slow in getting rid of the last Lover—unless we kept both of them."

The old woman smiled a keen smile, and a gleam of roguery twinkled in her gray eye, the intellectual, skeptical roguery of those people who did not believe that they were made of the same clay as the rest, and who lived as masters for whom common beliefs were not intended.

The young girl, turning very pale, faltered out:

"So, then, women have no honor?"

The grandmother ceased to smile. If she had kept in her soul some of Voltaire's irony, she had also a little of Jean Jacques's glowing philosophy: "No honor! because we loved, and dared to say so, and even boasted of it? But, my child, if one of us, among the greatest ladies in France, had lived without a lover, she would have had the entire court laughing at her. Those who wished to live differently had only to enter a convent. And you imagine, perhaps, that your husbands will love but you alone, all their lives. As if, indeed, this could be the case. I tell you that marriage is a thing necessary in order that society should exist, but it is not in the nature of our race, do you understand? There is only one good thing in life, and that is love. And how you misunderstand it! how you spoil it! You treat it as something solemn like a sacrament, or something to be bought, like a dress."

The young girl caught the old woman's trembling hands in her own.

"Hold your tongue, I beg of you, grandmamma!"

And, on her knees, with tears in her eyes, she prayed to Heaven to bestow on her a great passion, one sole, eternal passion in accordance with the dream of modern poets, while the grandmother, kissing her on the forehead, quite imbued still with that charming, healthy reason with which gallant philosophers tinctured the thought of the eighteenth century, murmured:

"Take care, my poor darling! If you believe in such folly as that, you will be very unhappy."

FRIEND JOSEPH

They had been great friends all winter in Paris. As is always the case, they had lost sight of each other after leaving school, and had met again when they were old and gray-haired. One of them had married, but the other had remained in single blessedness.

M. de Meroul lived for six months in Paris and for six months in his little chateau at Tourbeville. Having married the daughter of a neighboring, squire, he had lived a good and peaceful life in the indolence of a man who has nothing to do. Of a calm and quiet disposition, and not over-intelligent he used to spend his time quietly regretting the past, grieving over the customs and institutions of the day and continually repeating to his wife, who would lift her eyes, and sometimes her hands, to heaven, as a sign of energetic assent: "Good gracious! What a government!"

Madame de Meroul resembled her husband intellectually as though she had been his sister. She knew, by tradition, that one should above all respect the Pope and the King!

And she loved and respected them from the bottom of her heart, without knowing them, with a poetic fervor, with an hereditary devotion, with the tenderness of a wellborn woman. She was good to, the marrow of her bones. She had had no children, and never ceased mourning the fact.

On meeting his old friend, Joseph Mouradour, at a ball, M. de Meroul was filled with a deep and simple joy, for in their youth they had been intimate friends.

After the first exclamations of surprise at the changes which time had wrought in their bodies and countenances, they told each other about their lives since they had last met.

Joseph Mouradour, who was from the south of France, had become a government official. His manner was frank; he spoke rapidly and without restraint, giving his opinions without any tact. He was a Republican, one of those good fellows who do not believe in standing on ceremony, and who exercise an almost brutal freedom of speech.

He came to his friend's house and was immediately liked for his easy cordiality, in spite of his radical ideas. Madame de Meroul would exclaim:

"What a shame! Such a charming man!"

Monsieur de Meroul would say to his friend in a serious and confidential tone of voice; "You have no idea the harm that you are doing your country." He loved him all the same, for nothing is stronger than the ties of childhood taken up again at a riper age. Joseph Mouradour bantered the wife and the husband, calling them "my amiable snails," and sometimes he would solemnly declaim against people who were behind the times, against old prejudices and traditions.

When he was once started on his democratic eloquence, the couple, somewhat ill at ease, would keep silent from politeness and good-breeding; then the husband would try to turn the conversation into some other channel in order to avoid a clash. Joseph Mouradour was only seen in the intimacy of the family.

Summer came. The Merouls had no greater pleasure than to receive their friends at their country home at Tourbeville. It was a good, healthy pleasure, the enjoyments of good people and of country proprietors. They would meet their friends at the neighboring railroad station and would bring them back in their carriage, always on the lookout for compliments on the country, on its natural features, on the condition of the roads, on the cleanliness of the farm-houses, on the size of the cattle grazing in the fields, on everything within sight.

They would call attention to the remarkable speed with which their horse trotted, surprising for an animal that did heavy work part of the year behind a plow; and they would anxiously await the opinion of the newcomer on their family domain, sensitive to the least word, and thankful for the slightest good intention.

Joseph Mouradour was invited, and he accepted the invitation.

Husband and wife had come to the train, delighted to welcome him to their home. As soon as he saw them, Joseph Mouradour jumped from the train with a briskness which increased their satisfaction. He shook their hands, congratulated them, overwhelmed them with compliments.

All the way home he was charming, remarking on the height of the trees, the goodness of the crops and the speed of the horse.

When he stepped on the porch of the house, Monsieur de Meroul said, with a certain friendly solemnity:

"Consider yourself at home now."

Joseph Mouradour answered:

"Thanks, my friend; I expected as much. Anyhow, I never stand on ceremony with my friends. That's how I understand hospitality."

Then he went upstairs to dress as a farmer, he said, and he came back all togged out in blue linen, with a little straw hat and yellow shoes, a regular Parisian dressed for an outing. He also seemed to become more vulgar, more jovial, more familiar; having put on with his country clothes a free and easy manner which he judged suitable to the surroundings. His new manners shocked Monsieur and Madame de Meroul a little, for they always remained serious and dignified, even in the country, as though compelled by the two letters preceding their name to keep up a certain formality even in the closest intimacy.

After lunch they all went out to visit the farms, and the Parisian astounded the respectful peasants by his tone of comradeship.

In the evening the priest came to dinner, an old, fat priest, accustomed to dining there on Sundays, but who had been especially invited this day in honor of the new guest.

Joseph, on seeing him, made a wry face. Then he observed him with surprise, as though he were a creature of some peculiar race, which he had never been able to observe at close quarters. During the meal he told some rather free stories, allowable in the intimacy of the family, but which seemed to the Merouls a little out of place in the presence of a minister of the Church. He did not say, "Monsieur l'abbe," but simply, "Monsieur." He embarrassed the priest greatly by philosophical discussions about diverse superstitions current all over the world. He said: "Your God, monsieur, is of those who should be respected, but also one of those who should be discussed. Mine is called Reason; he has always been the enemy of yours."

The Merouls, distressed, tried to turn the trend of the conversation. The priest left very early.

Then the husband said, very quietly:

"Perhaps you went a little bit too far with the priest."

But Joseph immediately exclaimed:

"Well, that's pretty good! As if I would be on my guard with a shaveling! And say, do me the pleasure of not imposing him on me any more at meals. You can both make use of him as much as you wish, but don't serve him up to your friends, hang it!"

"But, my friends, think of his holy—"

Joseph Mouradour interrupted him:

"Yes, I know; they have to be treated like 'rosieres.' But let them respect my convictions, and I will respect theirs!"

That was all for that day.

As soon as Madame de Meroul entered the parlor, the next morning, she noticed in the middle of the table three newspapers which made her start the Voltaire, the Republique-Francaise and the Justice. Immediately Joseph Mouradour, still in blue, appeared on the threshold, attentively reading the Intransigeant. He cried:

"There's a great article in this by Rochefort. That fellow is a wonder!"

He read it aloud, emphasizing the parts which especially pleased him, so carried away by enthusiasm that he did not notice his friend's entrance. Monsieur de Meroul was holding in his hand the Gaulois for himself, the Clarion for his wife.

The fiery prose of the master writer who overthrew the empire, spouted with violence, sung in the southern accent, rang throughout the peaceful parsons seemed to spatter the walls and century-old furniture with a hail of bold, ironical and destructive words.

The man and the woman, one standing, the other sitting, were listening with astonishment, so shocked that they could not move.

In a burst of eloquence Mouradour finished the last paragraph, then exclaimed triumphantly:

"Well! that's pretty strong!"

Then, suddenly, he noticed the two sheets which his friend was carrying, and he, in turn, stood speechless from surprise. Quickly walking toward him he demanded angrily:

"What are you doing with those papers?"

Monsieur de Meroul answered hesitatingly:

"Why—those—those are my papers!"

"Your papers! What are you doing—making fun of me? You will do me the pleasure of reading mine; they will limber up your ideas, and as for yours—there! that's what I do with them."

And before his astonished host could stop him, he had seized the two newspapers and thrown them out of the window. Then he solemnly handed the Justice to Madame de Meroul, the Voltaire to her husband, while he sank down into an arm-chair to finish reading the Intransigeant.

The couple, through delicacy, made a pretense of reading a little, they then handed him back the Republican sheets, which they handled gingerly, as though they might be poisoned.

He laughed and declared:

"One week of this regime and I will have you converted to my ideas."

In truth, at the end of a week he ruled the house. He had closed the door against the priest, whom Madame de Meroul had to visit secretly; he had forbidden the Gaulois and the Clarion to be brought into the house, so that a servant had to go mysteriously to the post-office to get them, and as soon as he entered they would be hidden under sofa cushions; he arranged everything to suit himself—always charming, always good-natured, a jovial and all-powerful tyrant.

Other friends were expected, pious and conservative friends. The unhappy couple saw the impossibility of having them there then, and, not knowing what to do, one evening they announced to Joseph Mouradour that they would be obliged to absent themselves for a few days, on business, and they begged him to stay on alone. He did not appear disturbed, and answered:

"Very well, I don't mind! I will wait here as long as you wish. I have already said that there should be no formality between friends. You are perfectly right-go ahead and attend to your business. It will not offend me in the least; quite the contrary, it will make me feel much more completely one of the family. Go ahead, my friends, I will wait for you!"

Monsieur and Madame de Meroul left the following day.

He is still waiting for them.

THE EFFEMINATES

How often we hear people say, "He is charming, that man, but he is a girl, a regular girl." They are alluding to the effeminates, the bane of our land.

For we are all girl-like men in France—that is, fickle, fanciful, innocently treacherous, without consistency in our convictions or our will, violent and weak as women are.

But the most irritating of girl—men is assuredly the Parisian and the boulevardier, in whom the appearance of intelligence is more marked and who combines in himself all the attractions and all the faults of those charming creatures in an exaggerated degree in virtue of his masculine temperament.

Our Chamber of Deputies is full of girl-men. They form the greater number of the amiable opportunists whom one might call "The Charmers." These are they who control by soft words and deceitful promises, who know how to shake hands in such a manner as to win hearts, how to say "My dear friend" in a certain tactful way to people he knows the least, to change his mind without suspecting it, to be carried away by each new idea, to be sincere in their weathercock convictions, to let themselves be deceived as they deceive others, to forget the next morning what he affirmed the day before.

The newspapers are full of these effeminate men. That is probably where one finds the most, but it is also where they are most needed. The Journal des Debats and the Gazette de France are exceptions.

Assuredly, every good journalist must be somewhat effeminate—that is, at the command of the public, supple in following unconsciously the shades of public opinion, wavering and varying, sceptical and credulous, wicked and devout, a braggart and a true man, enthusiastic and ironical, and always convinced while believing in nothing.

Foreigners, our anti-types, as Mme. Abel called them, the stubborn English and the heavy Germans, regard us with a certain amazement mingled with contempt, and will continue to so regard us till the end of time. They consider us frivolous. It is not that, it is that we are girls. And that is why people love us in spite of our faults, why they come back to us despite the evil spoken of us; these are lovers' quarrels! The effeminate man, as one meets him in this world, is so charming that he captivates you after five minutes' chat. His smile seems made for you; one cannot believe that his voice does not assume specially tender intonations on their account. When he leaves you it seems as if one had known him for twenty years. One is quite ready to lend him money if he asks for it. He has enchanted you, like a woman.

If he commits any breach of manners towards you, you cannot bear any malice, he is so pleasant when you next meet him. If he asks your pardon you long to ask pardon of him. Does he tell lies? You cannot believe it. Does he put you off indefinitely with promises that he does not keep? One lays as much store by his promises as though he had moved heaven and earth to render them a service.

When he admires anything he goes into such raptures that he convinces you. He once adored Victor Hugo, whom he now treats as a back number. He would have fought for Zola, whom he has abandoned for Barbey and d'Aurevilly. And when he admires, he permits no limitation, he would slap your face for a word. But when he becomes scornful, his contempt is unbounded and allows of no protest.

In fact, he understands nothing.

Listen to two girls talking.

"Then you are angry with Julia?" "I slapped her face." "What had she done?" "She told Pauline that I had no money thirteen months out of twelve, and Pauline told Gontran—you understand." "You were living together in the Rue Clanzel?" "We lived together four years in the Rue Breda; we quarrelled about a pair of stockings that she said I had worn —it wasn't true—silk stockings that she had bought at Mother Martin's. Then I gave her a pounding and she left me at once. I met her six months ago and she asked me to come and live with her, as she has rented a flat that is twice too large."

One goes on one's way and hears no more. But on the following Sunday as one is on the way to Saint Germain two young women get into the same railway carriage. One recognizes one of them at once; it is Julia's enemy. The other is Julia!

And there are endearments, caresses, plans. "Say, Julia—listen, Julia," etc.

The girl-man has his friendships of this kind. For three months he cannot bear to leave his old Jack, his dear Jack. There is no one but Jack in the world. He is the only one who has any intelligence, any sense, any talent. He alone amounts to anything in Paris. One meets them everywhere together, they dine together, walk about in company, and every evening walk home with each other back and forth without being able to part with one another.

Three months later, if Jack is mentioned:

"There is a drinker, a sorry fellow, a scoundrel for you. I know him well, you may be sure. And he is not even honest, and ill-bred," etc., etc.

Three months later, and they are living together.

But one morning one hears that they have fought a duel, then embraced each other, amid tears, on the duelling ground.

Just now they are the dearest friends in the world, furious with each other half the year, abusing and loving each other by turns, squeezing each other's hands till they almost crush the bones, and ready to run each other through the body for a misunderstanding.

For the relations of these effeminate men are uncertain. Their temper is by fits and starts, their delight unexpected, their affection turn-about-face, their enthusiasm subject to eclipse. One day they love you, the next day they will hardly look at you, for they have in fact a girl's nature, a girl's charm, a girl's temperament, and all their sentiments are like the affections of girls.

They treat their friends as women treat their pet dogs.

It is the dear little Toutou whom they hug, feed with sugar, allow to sleep on the pillow, but whom they would be just as likely to throw out of a window in a moment of impatience, whom they turn round like a sling, holding it by the tail, squeeze in their arms till they almost strangle it, and plunge, without any reason, in a pail of cold water.

Then, what a strange thing it is when one of these beings falls in love with a real girl! He beats her, she scratches him, they execrate each other, cannot bear the sight of each other and yet cannot part, linked together by no one knows what mysterious psychic bonds. She deceives him, he knows it, sobs and forgives her. He despises and adores her without seeing that she would be justified in despising him. They are both atrociously unhappy and yet cannot separate. They cast invectives, reproaches and abominable accusations at each other from morning till night, and when they have reached the climax and are vibrating with rage and hatred, they fall into each other's arms and kiss each other ardently.

The girl-man is brave and a coward at the same time. He has, more than another, the exalted sentiment of honor, but is lacking in the sense of simple honesty, and, circumstances favoring him, would defalcate and commit infamies which do not trouble his conscience, for he obeys without questioning the oscillations of his ideas, which are always impulsive.

To him it seems permissible and almost right to cheat a haberdasher. He considers it honorable not to pay his debts, unless they are gambling debts—that is, somewhat shady. He dupes people whenever the laws of society admit of his doing so. When he is short of money he borrows in all ways, not always being scrupulous as to tricking the lenders, but he would, with sincere indignation, run his sword through anyone who should suspect him of only lacking in politeness.

OLD AMABLE

PART I

The humid gray sky seemed to weigh down on the vast brown plain. The odor of autumn, the sad odor of bare, moist lands, of fallen leaves, of dead grass made the stagnant evening air more thick and heavy. The peasants were still at work, scattered through the fields, waiting for the stroke of the Angelus to call them back to the farmhouses, whose thatched roofs were visible here and there through the branches of the leafless trees which protected the apple-gardens against the wind.

At the side of the road, on a heap of clothes, a very small boy seated with his legs apart was playing with a potato, which he now and then let fall on his dress, whilst five women were bending down planting slips of colza in the adjoining plain. With a slow, continuous movement, all along the mounds of earth which the plough had just turned up, they drove in sharp wooden stakes and in the hole thus formed placed the plant, already a little withered, which sank on one side; then they patted down the earth and went on with their work.

A man who was passing, with a whip in his hand, and wearing wooden shoes, stopped near the child, took it up and kissed it. Then one of the women rose up and came across to him. She was a big, red haired girl, with large hips, waist and shoulders, a tall Norman woman, with yellow hair in which there was a blood-red tint.

She said in a resolute voice:

"Why, here you are, Cesaire—well?"

The man, a thin young fellow with a melancholy air, murmured:

"Well, nothing at all—always the same thing."

"He won't have it?"

"He won't have it."

"What are you going to do?"

"What do you say I ought to do?"

"Go see the cure."

"I will."

"Go at once!"

"I will."

And they stared at each other. He held the child in his arms all the time. He kissed it once more and then put it down again on the woman's clothes.

In the distance, between two farm-houses, could be seen a plough drawn by a horse and driven by a man. They moved on very gently, the horse, the plough and the laborer, in the dim evening twilight.

The woman went on:

"What did your father say?"

"He said he would not have it."

"Why wouldn't he have it?"

The young man pointed toward the child whom he had just put back on the ground, then with a glance he drew her attention to the man drawing the plough yonder there.

And he said emphatically:

"Because 'tis his—this child of yours."

The girl shrugged her shoulders and in an angry tone said:

"Faith, every one knows it well—that it is Victor's. And what about it after all? I made a slip. Am I the only woman that did? My mother also made a slip before me, and then yours did the same before she married your dad! Who is it that hasn't made a slip in the country? I made a slip with Victor because he took advantage of me while I was asleep in the barn, it's true, and afterward it happened between us when I wasn't asleep. I certainly would have married him if he weren't a servant man. Am I a worse woman for that?"

The man said simply:

"As for me, I like you just as you are, with or without the child. It's only my father that opposes me. All the same, I'll see about settling the business."

She answered:

"Go to the cure at once."

"I'm going to him."

And he set forth with his heavy peasant's tread, while the girl, with her hands on her hips, turned round to plant her colza.

In fact, the man who thus went off, Cesaire Houlbreque, the son of deaf old Amable Houlbreque, wanted to marry, in spite of his father, Celeste Levesque, who had a child by Victor Lecoq, a mere laborer on her parents' farm, who had been turned out of doors for this act.

The hierarchy of caste, however, does not exist in the country, and if the laborer is thrifty, he becomes, by taking a farm in his turn, the equal of his former master.

So Cesaire Houlbieque went off, his whip under his arm, brooding over his own thoughts and lifting up one after the other his heavy wooden shoes daubed with clay. Certainly he desired to marry Celeste Levesque. He wanted her with her child because she was the wife he wanted. He could not say why, but he knew it, he was sure of it. He had only to look at her to be convinced of it, to feel quite queer, quite stirred up, simply stupid with happiness. He even found a pleasure in kissing the little boy, Victor's little boy, because he belonged to her.

And he gazed, without hate, at the distant outline of the man who was driving his plough along the horizon.

But old Amable did not want this marriage. He opposed it with the obstinacy of a deaf man, with a violent obstinacy.

Cesaire in vain shouted in his ear, in that ear which still heard a few sounds:

"I'll take good care of you, daddy. I tell you she's a good girl and strong, too, and also thrifty."

The old man repeated:

"As long as I live I won't see her your wife."

And nothing could get the better of him, nothing could make him waver. One hope only was left to Cesaire. Old Amable was afraid of the cure through the apprehension of death which he felt drawing nigh; he had not much fear of God, nor of the Devil, nor of Hell, nor of Purgatory, of which he had no conception, but he dreaded the priest, who represented to him burial, as one might fear the doctors through horror of diseases. For the last tight days Celeste, who knew this weakness of the old man, had been urging Cesaire to go and find the cure, but Cesaire always hesitated, because he had not much liking for the black robe, which represented to him hands always stretched out for collections or for blessed bread.

However, he had made up his mind, and he proceeded toward the presbytery, thinking in what manner he would speak about his case.

The Abbe Raffin, a lively little priest, thin and never shaved, was awaiting his dinner-hour while warming his feet at his kitchen fire.

As soon as he saw the peasant entering he asked, merely turning his head:

"Well, Cesaire, what do you want?"

"I'd like to have a talk with you, M. le Cure."

The man remained standing, intimidated, holding his cap in one hand and his whip in the other.

"Well, talk."

Cesaire looked at the housekeeper, an old woman who dragged her feet while putting on the cover for her master's dinner at the corner of the table in front of the window.

He stammered:

"'Tis—'tis a sort of confession."

Thereupon the Abbe Raffin carefully surveyed his peasant. He saw his confused countenance, his air of constraint, his wandering eyes, and he gave orders to the housekeeper in these words:

"Marie, go away for five minutes to your room, while I talk to Cesaire."

The servant cast on the man an angry glance and went away grumbling.

The clergyman went on:

"Come, now, tell your story."

The young fellow still hesitated, looked down at his wooden shoes, moved about his cap, then, all of a sudden, he made up his mind:

"Here it is: I want to marry Celeste Levesque."

"Well, my boy, what's there to prevent you?"

"The father won't have it."

"Your father?"

"Yes, my father."

"What does your father say?"

"He says she has a child."

"She's not the first to whom that happened, since our Mother Eve."

"A child by Victor Lecoq, Anthime Loisel's servant man."

"Ha! ha! So he won't have it?"

"He won't have it."

"What! not at all?"

"No, no more than an ass that won't budge an inch, saving your presence."

"What do you say to him yourself in order to make him decide?"

"I say to him that she's a good girl, and strong, too, and thrifty also."

"And this does not make him agree to it. So you want me to speak to him?"

"Exactly. You speak to him."

"And what am I to tell your father?"

"Why, what you tell people in your sermons to make them give you sous."

In the peasant's mind every effort of religion consisted in loosening the purse strings, in emptying the pockets of men in order to fill the heavenly coffer. It was a kind of huge commercial establishment, of which the cures were the clerks; sly, crafty clerks, sharp as any one must be who does business for the good God at the expense of the country people.

He knew full well that the priests rendered services, great services to the poorest, to the sick and dying, that they assisted, consoled, counselled, sustained, but all this by means of money, in exchange for white pieces, for beautiful glittering coins, with which they paid for sacraments and masses, advice and protection, pardon of sins and indulgences, purgatory and paradise according to the yearly income and the generosity of the sinner.

The Abbe Raffin, who knew his man and who never lost his temper, burst out laughing.

"Well, yes, I'll tell your father my little story; but you, my lad, you'll come to church."

Houlbreque extended his hand in order to give a solemn assurance:

"On the word of a poor man, if you do this for me, I promise that I will."

"Come, that's all right. When do you wish me to go and find your father?"

"Why, the sooner the better-to-night, if you can."

"In half an hour, then, after supper."

"In half an hour."

"That's understood. So long, my lad."

"Good-by till we meet again, Monsieur le Cure; many thanks."

"Not at all, my lad."

And Cesaire Houlbreque returned home, his heart relieved of a great weight.

He held on lease a little farm, quite small, for they were not rich, his father and he. Alone with a female servant, a little girl of fifteen, who made the soup, looked after the fowls, milked the cows and churned the butter, they lived frugally, though Cesaire was a good cultivator. But they did not possess either sufficient lands or sufficient cattle to earn more than the indispensable.

The old man no longer worked. Sad, like all deaf people, crippled with pains, bent double, twisted, he went through the fields leaning on his stick, watching the animals and the men with a hard, distrustful eye. Sometimes he sat down on the side of the road and remained there without moving for hours, vaguely pondering over the things that had engrossed his whole life, the price of eggs, and corn, the sun and the rain which spoil the crops or make them grow. And, worn out with rheumatism, his old limbs still drank in the humidity of the soul, as they had drunk in for the past sixty years, the moisture of the walls of his low house thatched with damp straw.

He came back at the close of the day, took his place at the end of the table in the kitchen and when the earthen bowl containing the soup had been placed before him he placed round it his crooked fingers, which seemed to have kept the round form of the bowl and, winter and summer, he warmed his hands, before commencing to eat, so as to lose nothing, not even a particle of the heat that came from the fire, which costs a great deal, neither one drop of soup into which fat and salt have to be put, nor one morsel of bread, which comes from the wheat.

Then he climbed up a ladder into a loft, where he had his straw-bed, while his son slept below stairs at the end of a kind of niche near the chimneypiece and the servant shut herself up in a kind of cellar, a black hole which was formerly used to store the potatoes.

Cesaire and his father scarcely ever talked to each other. From time to time only, when there was a question of selling a crop or buying a calf, the young man would ask his father's advice, and, making a speaking-trumpet of his two hands, he would bawl out his views into his ear, and old Amable either approved of them or opposed them in a slow, hollow voice that came from the depths of his stomach.

So one evening Cesaire, approaching him as if about to discuss the purchase of a horse or a heifer, communicated to him at the top of his voice his intention to marry Celeste Levesque.

Then the father got angry. Why? On the score of morality? No, certainly. The virtue of a girl is of slight importance in the country. But his avarice, his deep, fierce instinct for saving, revolted at the idea that his son should bring up a child which he had not begotten himself. He had thought suddenly, in one second, of the soup the little fellow would swallow before becoming useful on the farm. He had calculated all the pounds of bread, all the pints of cider that this brat would consume up to his fourteenth year, and a mad anger broke loose from him against Cesaire, who had not bestowed a thought on all this.

He replied in an unusually strong voice:

"Have you lost your senses?"

Thereupon Cesaire began to enumerate his reasons, to speak about Celeste's good qualities, to prove that she would be worth a thousand times what the child would cost. But the old man doubted these advantages, while he could have no doubts as to the child's existence; and he replied with emphatic repetition, without giving any further explanation:

"I will not have it! I will not have it! As long as I live, this won't be done!" And at this point they had remained for the last three months without one or the other giving in, resuming at least once a week the same discussion, with the same arguments, the same words, the same gestures and the same fruitlessness.

It was then that Celeste had advised Cesaire to go and ask for the cure's assistance.

On arriving home the peasant found his father already seated at table, for he came late through his visit to the presbytery.

They dined in silence, face to face, ate a little bread and butter after the soup and drank a glass of cider. Then they remained motionless in their chairs, with scarcely a glimmer of light, the little servant girl having carried off the candle in order to wash the spoons, wipe the glasses and cut the crusts of bread to be ready for next morning's breakfast.

There was a knock, at the door, which was immediately opened, and the priest appeared. The old man raised toward him an anxious eye full of suspicion, and, foreseeing danger, he was getting ready to climb up his ladder when the Abbe Raffin laid his hand on his shoulder and shouted close to his temple:

"I want to have a talk with you, Father Amable."

Cesaire had disappeared, taking advantage of the door being open. He did not want to listen, for he was afraid and did not want his hopes to crumble slowly with each obstinate refusal of his father. He preferred to learn the truth at once, good or bad, later on; and he went out into the night. It was a moonless, starless night, one of those misty nights when the air seems thick with humidity. A vague odor of apples floated through the farmyard, for it was the season when the earliest apples were gathered, the "early ripe," as they are called in the cider country. As Cesaire passed along by the cattlesheds the warm smell of living beasts asleep on manure was exhaled through the narrow windows, and he heard the stamping of the horses, who were standing at the end of the stable, and the sound of their jaws tearing and munching the hay on the racks.

He went straight ahead, thinking about Celeste. In this simple nature, whose ideas were scarcely more than images generated directly by objects, thoughts of love only formulated themselves by calling up before the mind the picture of a big red-haired girl standing in a hollow road and laughing, with her hands on her hips.

It was thus he saw her on the day when he first took a fancy for her. He had, however, known her from infancy, but never had he been so struck by her as on that morning. They had stopped to talk for a few minutes and then he went away, and as he walked along he kept repeating:

"Faith, she's a fine girl, all the same. 'Tis a pity she made a slip with Victor."

Till evening he kept thinking of her and also on the following morning.

When he saw her again he felt something tickling the end of his throat, as if a cock's feather had been driven through his mouth into his chest, and since then, every time he found himself near her, he was astonished at this nervous tickling which always commenced again.

In three months he made up his mind to marry her, so much did she please him. He could not have said whence came this power over him, but he explained it in these words:

"I am possessed by her," as if the desire for this girl within him were as dominating as one of the powers of hell. He scarcely bothered himself about her transgression. It was a pity, but, after all, it did her no harm, and he bore no grudge against Victor Lecoq.

But if the cure should not succeed, what was he to do? He did not dare to think of it, the anxiety was such a torture to him.

He reached the presbytery and seated himself near the little gateway to wait for the priest's return.

He was there perhaps half an hour when he heard steps on the road, and although the night was very dark, he presently distinguished the still darker shadow of the cassock.

He rose up, his legs giving way under him, not even venturing to speak, not daring to ask a question.

The clergyman perceived him and said gaily:

"Well, my lad, it's all right."

Cesaire stammered:

"All right, 'tisn't possible."

"Yes, my lad, but not without trouble. What an old ass your father is!"

The peasant repeated:

"'Tisn't possible!"

"Why, yes. Come and look me up to-morrow at midday in order to settle about the publication of the banns."

The young man seized the cure's hand. He pressed it, shook it, bruised it as he stammered:

"True-true-true, Monsieur le Cure, on the word of an honest man, you'll see me to-morrow-at your sermon."

PART II

The wedding took place in the middle of December. It was simple, the bridal pair not being rich. Cesaire, attired in new clothes, was ready since eight o'clock in the morning to go and fetch his betrothed and bring her to the mayor's office, but it was too early. He seated himself before the kitchen table and waited for the members of the family and the friends who were to accompany him.

For the last eight days it had been snowing, and the brown earth, the earth already fertilized by the autumn sowing, had become a dead white, sleeping under a great sheet of ice.

It was cold in the thatched houses adorned with white caps, and the round apples in the trees of the enclosures seemed to be flowering, covered with white as they had been in the pleasant month of their blossoming.

This day the big clouds to the north, the big great snow clouds, had disappeared and the blue sky showed itself above the white earth on which the rising sun cast silvery reflections.

Cesaire looked straight before him through the window, thinking of nothing, quite happy.

The door opened, two women entered, peasant women in their Sunday clothes, the aunt and the cousin of the bridegroom; then three men, his cousins; then a woman who was a neighbor. They sat down on chairs and remained, motionless and silent, the women on one side of the kitchen, the men on the other, suddenly seized with timidity, with that embarrassed sadness which takes possession of people assembled for a ceremony. One of the cousins soon asked:

"Is it not the hour?"

Cesaire replied:

"I am much afraid it is."

"Come on! Let us start," said another.

Those rose up. Then Cesaire, whom a feeling of uneasiness had taken possession of, climbed up the ladder of the loft to see whether his father was ready. The old man, always as a rule an early riser, had not yet made his appearance. His son found him on his bed of straw, wrapped up in his blanket, with his eyes open and a malicious gleam in them.

He bawled into his ear: "Come, daddy, get up. It's time for the wedding."

The deaf man murmured-in a doleful tone:

"I can't get up. I have a sort of chill over me that freezes my back. I can't stir."

The young man, dumbfounded, stared at him, guessing that this was a dodge.

"Come, daddy; you must make an effort."

"I can't do it."

"Look here! I'll help you."

And he stooped toward the old man, pulled off his blanket, caught him by the arm and lifted him up. But old Amable began to whine, "Ooh! ooh! ooh! What suffering! Ooh! I can't. My back is stiffened up. The cold wind must have rushed in through this cursed roof."

"Well, you'll get no dinner, as I'm having a spread at Polyte's inn. This will teach you what comes of acting mulishly."

And he hurried down the ladder and started out, accompanied by his relatives and guests.

The men had turned up the bottoms of their trousers so as not to get them wet in the snow. The women held up their petticoats and showed their lean ankles with gray woollen stockings and their bony shanks resembling broomsticks. And they all moved forward with a swinging gait, one behind the other, without uttering a word, moving cautiously, for fear of losing the road which was-hidden beneath the flat, uniform, uninterrupted stretch of snow.

As they approached the farmhouses they saw one or two persons waiting to join them, and the procession went on without stopping and wound its way forward, following the invisible outlines of the road, so that it resembled a living chaplet of black beads undulating through the white countryside.

In front of the bride's door a large group was stamping up and down the open space awaiting the bridegroom. When he appeared they gave him a loud greeting, and presently Celeste came forth from her room, clad in a blue dress, her shoulders covered with a small red shawl and her head adorned with orange flowers.

But every one asked Cesaire:

"Where's your father?"

He replied with embarrassment:

"He couldn't move on account of the pains."

And the farmers tossed their heads with a sly, incredulous air.

They directed their steps toward the mayor's office. Behind the pair about to be wedded a peasant woman carried Victor's child, as if it were going to be baptized; and the risen, in pairs now, with arms linked, walked through the snow with the movements of a sloop at sea.

After having been united by the mayor in the little municipal house the pair were made one by the cure, in his turn, in the modest house of God. He blessed their union by promising them fruitfulness, then he preached to them on the matrimonial virtues, the simple and healthful virtues of the country, work, concord and fidelity, while the child, who was cold, began to fret behind the bride.

As soon as the couple reappeared on the threshold of the church shots were discharged from the ditch of the cemetery. Only the barrels of the guns could be seen whence came forth rapid jets of smoke; then a head could be seen gazing at the procession. It was Victor Lecoq celebrating the marriage of his old sweetheart, wishing her happiness and sending her his good wishes with explosions of powder. He had employed some friends of his, five or six laboring men, for these salvos of musketry. It was considered a nice attention.

The repast was given in Polyte Cacheprune's inn. Twenty covers were laid in the great hall where people dined on market days, and the big leg of mutton turning before the spit, the fowls browned under their own gravy, the chitterlings sputtering over the bright, clear fire filled the house with a thick odor of live coal sprinkled with fat—the powerful, heavy odor of rustic fare.

They sat down to table at midday and the soup was poured at once into the plates. All faces had already brightened up; mouths opened to utter loud jokes and eyes were laughing with knowing winks. They were going to amuse themselves and no mistake.

The door opened, and old Amable appeared. He seemed in a bad humor and his face wore a scowl as he dragged himself forward on his sticks, whining at every step to indicate his suffering. As soon as they saw him they stopped talking, but suddenly his neighbor, Daddy Malivoire, a big joker, who knew all the little tricks and ways of people, began to yell, just as Cesaire used to do, by making a speaking-trumpet of his hands.

"Hallo, my cute old boy, you have a good nose on you to be able to smell Polyte's cookery from your own house!"

A roar of laughter burst forth from the throats of those present. Malivoire, excited by his success, went on:

"There's nothing for the rheumatics like a chitterling poultice! It keeps your belly warm, along with a glass of three-six!"

The men uttered shouts, banged the table with their fists, laughed, bending on one side and raising up their bodies again as if they were working a pump. The women clucked like hens, while the servants wriggled, standing against the walls. Old Amable was the only one that did not laugh, and, without making any reply, waited till they made room for him.

They found a place for him in the middle of the table, facing his daughter-in-law, and, as soon as he was seated, he began to eat. It was his son who was paying, after all; it was right he should take his share. With each ladleful of soup that went into his stomach, with each mouthful of bread or meat crushed between his gums, with each glass of cider or wine that flowed through his gullet he thought he was regaining something of his own property, getting back a little of his money which all those gluttons were devouring, saving in fact a portion of his own means. And he ate in silence with the obstinacy of a miser who hides his coppers, with the same gloomy persistence with which he formerly performed his daily labors.

But all of a sudden he noticed at the end of the table Celeste's child on a woman's lap, and his eye remained fixed on the little boy. He went on eating, with his glance riveted on the youngster, into whose mouth the woman who minded him every now and then put a little morsel which he nibbled at. And the old man suffered more from the few mouthfuls sucked by this little chap than from all that the others swallowed.

The meal lasted till evening. Then every one went back home.

Cesaire raised up old Amable.

"Come, daddy, we must go home," said he.

And he put the old man's two sticks in his hands.

Celeste took her child in her arms, and they went on slowly through the pale night whitened by the snow. The deaf old man, three-fourths tipsy, and even more malicious under the influence of drink, refused to go forward. Several times he even sat down with the object of making his daughter-in-law catch cold, and he kept whining, without uttering a word, giving vent to a sort of continuous groaning as if he were in pain.

When they reached home he at once climbed up to his loft, while Cesaire made a bed for the child near the deep niche where he was going to lie down with his wife. But as the newly wedded pair could not sleep immediately, they heard the old man for a long time moving about on his bed of straw, and he even talked aloud several times, whether it was that he was dreaming or that he let his thoughts escape through his mouth, in spite of himself, not being able to keep them back, under the obsession of a fixed idea.

When he came down his ladder next morning he saw his daughter-in-law looking after the housekeeping.

She cried out to him:

"Come, daddy, hurry on! Here's some good soup."

And she placed at the end of the table the round black earthen bowl filled with steaming liquid. He sat down without giving any answer, seized the hot bowl, warmed his hands with it in his customary fashion, and, as it was very cold, even pressed it against his breast to try to make a little of the living heat of the boiling liquid enter into him, into his old body stiffened by so many winters.

Then he took his sticks and went out into the fields, covered with ice, till it was time for dinner, for he had seen Celeste's youngster still asleep in a big soap-box.

He did not take his place in the household. He lived in the thatched house, as in bygone days, but he seemed not to belong to it any longer, to be no longer interested in anything, to look upon those people, his son, the wife and the child as strangers whom he did not know, to whom he never spoke.

The winter glided by. It was long and severe.

Then the early spring made the seeds sprout forth again, and the peasants once more, like laborious ants, passed their days in the fields, toiling from morning till night, under the wind and under the rain, along the furrows of brown earth which brought forth the bread of men.

The year promised well for the newly married pair. The crops grew thick and strong. There were no late frosts, and the apples bursting into bloom scattered on the grass their rosy white snow which promised a hail of fruit for the autumn.

Cesaire toiled hard, rose early and left off work late, in order to save the expense of a hired man.

His wife said to him sometimes:

"You'll make yourself ill in the long run."

He replied:

"Certainly not. I'm a good judge."

Nevertheless one evening he came home so fatigued that he had to get to bed without supper. He rose up next morning at the usual hour, but he could not eat, in spite of his fast on the previous night, and he had to come back to the house in the middle of the afternoon in order to go to bed again. In the course of the night he began to cough; he turned round on his straw couch, feverish, with his forehead burning, his tongue dry and his throat parched by a burning thirst.

However, at daybreak he went toward his grounds, but next morning the doctor had to be sent for and pronounced him very ill with inflammation of the lungs.

And he no longer left the dark recess in which he slept. He could be heard coughing, gasping and tossing about in this hole. In order to see him, to give his medicine and to apply cupping-glasses they had to bring a candle to the entrance. Then one could see his narrow head with his long matted beard underneath a thick lacework of spiders' webs, which hung and floated when stirred by the air. And the hands of the sick man seemed dead under the dingy sheets.

Celeste watched him with restless activity, made him take physic, applied blisters to him, went back and forth in the house, while old Amable remained at the edge of his loft, watching at a distance the gloomy cavern where his son lay dying. He did not come near him, through hatred of the wife, sulking like an ill-tempered dog.

Six more days passed, then one morning, as Celeste, who now slept on the ground on two loose bundles of straw, was going to see whether her man was better, she no longer heard his rapid breathing from the interior of his recess. Terror stricken, she asked:

"Well Cesaire, what sort of a night had you?"

He did not answer. She put out her hand to touch him, and the flesh on his face felt cold as ice. She uttered a great cry, the long cry of a woman overpowered with fright. He was dead.

At this cry the deaf old man appeared at the top of his ladder, and when he saw Celeste rushing to call for help, he quickly descended, placed his hand on his son's face, and suddenly realizing what had happened, went to shut the door from the inside, to prevent the wife from re-entering and resuming possession of the dwelling, since his son was no longer living.

Then he sat down on a chair by the dead man's side.

Some of the neighbors arrived, called out and knocked. He did not hear them. One of them broke the glass of the window and jumped into the room. Others followed. The door was opened again and Celeste reappeared, all in tears, with swollen face and bloodshot eyes. Then old Amable, vanquished, without uttering a word, climbed back to his loft.

The funeral took place next morning. Then, after the ceremony, the father-in-law and the daughter-in-law found themselves alone in the farmhouse with the child.

It was the usual dinner hour. She lighted the fire, made some soup and placed the plates on the table, while the old man sat on the chair waiting without appearing to look at her. When the meal was ready she bawled in his ear—

"Come, daddy, you must eat." He rose up, took his seat at the end of the table, emptied his soup bowl, masticated his bread and butter, drank his two glasses of cider and then took himself off.

It was one of those warm days, one of those enjoyable days when life ferments, pulsates, blooms all over the surface of the soil.

Old Amable pursued a little path across the fields. He looked at the young wheat and the young oats, thinking that his son was now under the earth, his poor boy! He walked along wearily, dragging his legs after him in a limping fashion. And, as he was all alone in the plain, all alone under the blue sky, in the midst of the growing crops, all alone with the larks which he saw hovering above his head, without hearing their light song, he began to weep as he proceeded on his way.

Then he sat down beside a pond and remained there till evening, gazing at the little birds that came there to drink. Then, as the night was falling, he returned to the house, supped without saying a word and climbed up to his loft. And his life went on as in the past. Nothing was changed, except that his son Cesaire slept in the cemetery.

What could he, an old man, do? He could work no longer; he was now good for nothing except to swallow the soup prepared by his daughter-in-law. And he ate it in silence, morning and evening, watching with an eye of rage the little boy also taking soup, right opposite him, at the other side of the table. Then he would go out, prowl about the fields after the fashion of a vagabond, hiding behind the barns where he would sleep for an hour or two as if he were afraid of being seen and then come back at the approach of night.

But Celeste's mind began to be occupied by graver anxieties. The farm needed a man to look after it and cultivate it. Somebody should be there always to go through the fields, not a mere hired laborer, but a regular farmer, a master who understood the business and would take an interest in the farm. A lone woman could not manage the farming, watch the price of corn and direct the sale and purchase of cattle. Then ideas came into her head, simple practical ideas, which she had turned over in her head at night. She could not marry again before the end of the year, and it was necessary at once to take care of pressing interests, immediate interests.

Only one man could help her out of her difficulties, Victor Lecoq, the father of her child. He was strong and understood farming; with a little money in his pocket he would make an excellent cultivator. She was aware of his skill, having known him while he was working on her parents' farm.

So one morning, seeing him passing along the road with a cart of manure, she went out to meet him. When he perceived her, he drew up his horses and she said to him as if she had met him the night before:

"Good-morrow, Victor—are you quite well, the same as ever?"

He replied:

"I'm quite well, the same as ever—and how are you?"

"Oh, I'd be all right, only that I'm alone in the house, which bothers me on account of the farm."

Then they remained chatting for a long time, leaning against the wheel of the heavy cart. The man every now and then lifted up his cap to scratch his forehead and began thinking, while she, with flushed cheeks, went on talking warmly, told him about her views, her plans; her projects for the future. At last he said in a low tone:

"Yes, it can be done."

She opened her hand like a countryman clinching a bargain and asked:

"Is it agreed?"

He pressed her outstretched hand.

"'Tis agreed."

"It's settled, then, for next Sunday?"

"It's settled for next Sunday"

"Well, good-morning, Victor."

"Good-morning, Madame Houlbreque."

PART III

This particular Sunday was the day of the village festival, the annual festival in honor of the patron saint, which in Normandy is called the assembly.

For the last eight days quaint-looking vehicles in which live the families of strolling fair exhibitors, lottery managers, keepers of shooting galleries and other forms of amusement or exhibitors of curiosities whom the peasants call "wonder-makers" could be seen coming along the roads drawn slowly by gray or sorrel horses.

The dirty wagons with their floating curtains, accompanied by a melancholy-looking dog, who trotted, with his head down, between the wheels, drew up one after the other on the green in front of the town hall. Then a tent was erected in front of each ambulant abode, and inside this tent could be seen, through the holes in the canvas, glittering things which excited the envy or the curiosity of the village youngsters.

As soon as the morning of the fete arrived all the booths were opened, displaying their splendors of glass or porcelain, and the peasants on their way to mass looked with genuine satisfaction at these modest shops which they saw again, nevertheless, each succeeding year.

Early in the afternoon there was a crowd on the green. From every neighboring village the farmers arrived, shaken along with their wives and children in the two-wheeled open chars-a-bancs, which rattled along, swaying like cradles. They unharnessed at their friends' houses and the farmyards were filled with strange-looking traps, gray, high, lean, crooked, like long-clawed creatures from the depths of the sea. And each family, with the youngsters in front and the grown-up ones behind, came to the assembly with tranquil steps, smiling countenances and open hands, big hands, red and bony, accustomed to work and apparently tired of their temporary rest.

A clown was blowing a trumpet. The barrel-organ accompanying the carrousel sent through the air its shrill jerky notes. The lottery-wheel made a whirring sound like that of cloth tearing, and every moment the crack of the rifle could be heard. And the slow-moving throng passed on quietly in front of the booths resembling paste in a fluid condition, with the motions of a flock of sheep and the awkwardness of heavy animals who had escaped by chance.

The girls, holding one another's arms in groups of six or eight, were singing; the youths followed them, making jokes, with their caps over their ears and their blouses stiffened with starch, swollen out like blue balloons.

The whole countryside was there—masters, laboring men and women servants.

Old Amable himself, wearing his old-fashioned green frock coat, had wished to see the assembly, for he never failed to attend on such an occasion.

He looked at the lotteries, stopped in front of the shooting galleries to criticize the shots and interested himself specially in a very simple game which consisted in throwing a big wooden ball into the open mouth of a mannikin carved and painted on a board.

Suddenly he felt a tap on his shoulder. It was Daddy Malivoire, who exclaimed:

"Ha, daddy! Come and have a glass of brandy."

And they sat down at the table of an open-air restaurant.

They drank one glass of brandy, then two, then three, and old Amable once more began wandering through the assembly. His thoughts became slightly confused, he smiled without knowing why, he smiled in front of the lotteries, in front of the wooden horses and especially in front of the killing game. He remained there a long time, filled with delight, when he saw a holiday-maker knocking down the gendarme or the cure, two authorities whom he instinctively distrusted. Then he went back to the inn and drank a glass of cider to cool himself. It was late, night came on. A neighbor came to warn him:

"You'll get back home late for the stew, daddy."

Then he set out on his way to the farmhouse. A soft shadow, the warm shadow of a spring night, was slowly descending on the earth.

When he reached the front door he thought he saw through the window which was lighted up two persons in the house. He stopped, much surprised, then he went in, and he saw Victor Lecoq seated at the table, with a plate filled with potatoes before him, taking his supper in the very same place where his son had sat.

And he turned round suddenly as if he wanted to go away. The night was very dark now. Celeste started up and shouted at him:

"Come quick, daddy! Here's some good stew to finish off the assembly with."

He complied through inertia and sat down, watching in turn the man, the woman and the child. Then he began to eat quietly as on ordinary days.

Victor Lecoq seemed quite at home, talked from time to time to Celeste, took up the child in his lap and kissed him. And Celeste again served him with food, poured out drink for him and appeared happy while speaking to him. Old Amable's eyes followed them attentively, though he could not hear what they were saying.

When he had finished supper (and he had scarcely eaten anything, there was such a weight at his heart) he rose up, and instead of ascending to his loft as he did every night he opened the gate of the yard and went out into the open air.

When he had gone, Celeste, a little uneasy, asked:

"What is he going to do?"

Victor replied in an indifferent tone:

"Don't bother yourself. He'll come back when he's tired."

Then she saw after the house, washed the plates and wiped the table, while the man quietly took off his clothes. Then he slipped into the dark and hollow bed in which she had slept with Cesaire.

The yard gate opened and old Amable again appeared. As soon as he entered the house he looked round on every side with the air of an old dog on the scent. He was in search of Victor Lecoq. As he did not see him, he took the candle off the table and approached the dark niche in which his son had died. In the interior of it he perceived the man lying under the bed clothes and already asleep. Then the deaf man noiselessly turned round, put back the candle and went out into the yard.

Celeste had finished her work. She put her son into his bed, arranged everything and waited for her father-in-law's return before lying down herself.

She remained sitting on a chair, without moving her hands and with her eyes fixed on vacancy.

As he did not come back, she murmured in a tone of impatience and annoyance:

"This good-for-nothing old man will make us burn four sous' worth of candles."

Victor answered from under the bed clothes:

"It's over an hour since he went out. We ought to see whether he fell asleep on the bench outside the door."

"I'll go and see," she said.

She rose up, took the light and went out, shading the light with her hand in order to see through the darkness.

She saw nothing in front of the door, nothing on the bench, nothing on the dung heap, where the old man used sometimes to sit in hot weather.

But, just as she was on the point of going in again, she chanced to raise her eyes toward the big apple tree, which sheltered the entrance to the farmyard, and suddenly she saw two feet—two feet at the height of her face belonging to a man who was hanging.

She uttered terrible cries:

"Victor! Victor! Victor!"

He ran out in his shirt. She could not utter another word, and turning aside her head so as not to see, she pointed toward the tree with her outstretched arm.

Not understanding what she meant, he took the candle in order to find out, and in the midst of the foliage lit up from below he saw old Amable hanging high up with a stable-halter round his neck.

A ladder was leaning against the trunk of the apple tree.

Victor ran to fetch a bill-hook, climbed up the tree and cut the halter. But the old man was already cold and his tongue protruded horribly with a frightful grimace.

VOLUME X.

THE CHRISTENING

"Well doctor, a little brandy?"

"With pleasure."

The old ship's surgeon, holding out his glass, watched it as it slowly filled with the golden liquid. Then, holding it in front of his eyes, he let the light from the lamp stream through it, smelled it, tasted a few drops and smacked his lips with relish. Then he said:

"Ah! the charming poison! Or rather the seductive murderer, the delightful destroyer of peoples!

"You people do not know it the way I do. You may have read that admirable book entitled L'Assommoir, but you have not, as I have, seen alcohol exterminate a whole tribe of savages, a little kingdom of negroes—alcohol calmly unloaded by the barrel by red-bearded English seamen.

"Right near here, in a little village in Brittany near Pont-l'Abbe, I once witnessed a strange and terrible tragedy caused by alcohol. I was spending my vacation in a little country house left me by my father. You know this flat coast where the wind whistles day and night, where one sees, standing or prone, these giant rocks which in the olden times were regarded as guardians, and which still retain something majestic and imposing about them. I always expect to see them come to life and start to walk across the country with the slow and ponderous tread of giants, or to unfold enormous granite wings and fly toward the paradise of the Druids.

"Everywhere is the sea, always ready on the slightest provocation to rise in its anger and shake its foamy mane at those bold enough to brave its wrath.

"And the men who travel on this terrible sea, which, with one motion of its green back, can overturn and swallow up their frail barks—they go out in the little boats, day and night, hardy, weary and drunk. They are often drunk. They have a saying which says: 'When the bottle is full you see the reef, but when it is empty you see it no more.'

"Go into one of their huts; you will never find the father there. If you ask the woman what has become of her husband, she will stretch her arms out over the dark ocean which rumbles and roars along the coast. He remained, there one night, when he had had too much to drink; so did her oldest son. She has four more big, strong, fair-haired boys. Soon it will be their time.

"As I said, I was living in a little house near Pont-l'Abbe. I was there alone with my servant, an old sailor, and with a native family which took care of the grounds in my absence. It consisted of three persons, two sisters and a man, who had married one of them, and who attended to the garden.

"A short time before Christmas my gardener's wife presented him with a boy. The husband asked me to stand as god-father. I could hardly deny the request, and so he borrowed ten francs from me for the cost of the christening, as he said.

"The second day of January was chosen as the date of the ceremony. For a week the earth had been covered by an enormous white carpet of snow, which made this flat, low country seem vast and limitless. The ocean appeared to be black in contrast with this white plain; one could see it rolling, raging and tossing its waves as though wishing to annihilate its pale neighbor, which appeared to be dead, it was so calm, quiet and cold.

"At nine o'clock the father, Kerandec, came to my door with his sister-in-law, the big Kermagan, and the nurse, who carried the infant wrapped up in a blanket. We started for the church. The weather was so cold that it seemed to dry up the skin and crack it open. I was thinking of the poor little creature who was being carried on ahead of us, and I said to myself that this Breton race must surely be of iron, if their children were able, as soon as they were born, to stand such an outing.

"We came to the church, but the door was closed; the priest was late.

"Then the nurse sat down on one of the steps and began to undress the child. At first I thought there must have been some slight accident, but I saw that they were leaving the poor little fellow naked completely naked, in the icy air. Furious at such imprudence, I protested:

"'Why, you are crazy! You will kill the child!'

"The woman answered quietly: 'Oh, no, sir; he must wait naked before the Lord.'

"The father and the aunt looked on undisturbed. It was the custom. If it were not adhered to misfortune was sure to attend the little one.

"I scolded, threatened and pleaded. I used force to try to cover the frail creature. All was in vain. The nurse ran away from me through the snow, and the body of the little one turned purple. I was about to leave these brutes when I saw the priest coming across the country, followed by the sexton and a young boy. I ran towards him and gave vent to my indignation. He showed no surprise nor did he quicken his pace in the least. He answered:

"'What can you expect, sir? It's the custom. They all do it, and it's of no use trying to stop them.'

"'But at least hurry up!' I cried.

"He answered: 'But I can't go any faster.'

"He entered the vestry, while we remained outside on the church steps. I was suffering. But what about the poor little creature who was howling from the effects of the biting cold.

"At last the door opened. He went into the church. But the poor child had to remain naked throughout the ceremony. It was interminable. The priest stammered over the Latin words and mispronounced them horribly. He walked slowly and with a ponderous tread. His white surplice chilled my heart. It seemed as though, in the name of a pitiless and barbarous god, he had wrapped himself in another kind of snow in order to torture this little piece of humanity that suffered so from the cold.

"Finally the christening was finished according to the rites and I saw the nurse once more take the frozen, moaning child and wrap it up in the blanket.

"The priest said to me: 'Do you wish to sign the register?'

"Turning to my gardener, I said: 'Hurry up and get home quickly so that you can warm that child.' I gave him some advice so as to ward off, if not too late, a bad attack of pneumonia. He promised to follow my instructions and left with his sister-in-law and the nurse. I followed the priest into the vestry, and when I had signed he demanded five francs for expenses.

"As I had already given the father ten francs, I refused to pay twice. The priest threatened to destroy the paper and to annul the ceremony. I, in turn, threatened him with the district attorney. The dispute was long, and I finally paid five francs.

"As soon as I reached home I went down to Kerandec's to find out whether everything was all right. Neither father, nor sister-in-law, nor nurse had yet returned. The mother, who had remained alone, was in bed, shivering with cold and starving, for she had had nothing to eat since the day before.

"'Where the deuce can they have gone?' I asked. She answered without surprise or anger, 'They're going to drink something to celebrate: It was the custom. Then I thought, of my ten francs which were to pay the church and would doubtless pay for the alcohol.

"I sent some broth to the mother and ordered a good fire to be built in the room. I was uneasy and furious and promised myself to drive out these brutes, wondering with terror what was going to happen to the poor infant.

"It was already six, and they had not yet returned. I told my servant to wait for them and I went to bed. I soon fell asleep and slept like a top. At daybreak I was awakened by my servant, who was bringing me my hot water.

"As soon as my eyes were open I asked: 'How about Kerandec?'

"The man hesitated and then stammered: 'Oh! he came back, all right, after midnight, and so drunk that he couldn't walk, and so were Kermagan and the nurse. I guess they must have slept in a ditch, for the little one died and they never even noticed it.'

"I jumped up out of bed, crying:

"'What! The child is dead?'

"'Yes, sir. They brought it back to Mother Kerandec. When she saw it she began to cry, and now they are making her drink to console her.'

"'What's that? They are making her drink!'

"'Yes, sir. I only found it out this morning. As Kerandec had no more brandy or money, he took some wood alcohol, which monsieur gave him for the lamp, and all four of them are now drinking that. The mother is feeling pretty sick now.'

"I had hastily put on some clothes, and seizing a stick, with the intention of applying it to the backs of these human beasts, I hastened towards the gardener's house.

"The mother was raving drunk beside the blue body of her dead baby. Kerandec, the nurse, and the Kermagan woman were snoring on the floor. I had to take care of the mother, who died towards noon."

The old doctor was silent. He took up the brandy-bottle and poured out another glass. He held it up to the lamp, and the light streaming through it imparted to the liquid the amber color of molten topaz. With one gulp he swallowed the treacherous drink.

THE FARMER'S WIFE

Said the Baron Rene du Treilles to me:

"Will you come and open the hunting season with me at my farm at Marinville? I shall be delighted if you will, my dear boy. In the first place, I am all alone. It is rather a difficult ground to get at, and the place I live in is so primitive that I can invite only my most intimate friends."

I accepted his invitation, and on Saturday we set off on the train going to Normandy. We alighted at a station called Almivare, and Baron Rene, pointing to a carryall drawn by a timid horse and driven by a big countryman with white hair, said:

"Here is our equipage, my dear boy."

The driver extended his hand to his landlord, and the baron pressed it warmly, asking:

"Well, Maitre Lebrument, how are you?"

"Always the same, M'sieu le Baron."

We jumped into this swinging hencoop perched on two enormous wheels, and the young horse, after a violent swerve, started into a gallop, pitching us into the air like balls. Every fall backward on the wooden bench gave me the most dreadful pain.

The peasant kept repeating in his calm, monotonous voice:

"There, there! All right all right, Moutard, all right!"

But Moutard scarcely heard, and kept capering along like a goat.

Our two dogs behind us, in the empty part of the hencoop, were standing up and sniffing the air of the plains, where they scented game.

The baron gazed with a sad eye into the distance at the vast Norman landscape, undulating and melancholy, like an immense English park, where the farmyards, surrounded by two or four rows of trees and full of dwarfed apple trees which hid the houses, gave a vista as far as the eye could see of forest trees, copses and shrubbery such as landscape gardeners look for in laying out the boundaries of princely estates.

And Rene du Treilles suddenly exclaimed:

"I love this soil; I have my very roots in it."

He was a pure Norman, tall and strong, with a slight paunch, and of the old race of adventurers who went to found kingdoms on the shores of every ocean. He was about fifty years of age, ten years less perhaps than the farmer who was driving us.

The latter was a lean peasant, all skin and bone, one of those men who live a hundred years.

After two hours' travelling over stony roads, across that green and monotonous plain, the vehicle entered one of those orchard farmyards and drew up before in old structure falling into decay, where an old maid-servant stood waiting beside a young fellow, who took charge of the horse.

We entered the farmhouse. The smoky kitchen was high and spacious. The copper utensils and the crockery shone in the reflection of the hearth. A cat lay asleep on a chair, a dog under the table. One perceived an odor of milk, apples, smoke, that indescribable smell peculiar to old farmhouses; the odor of the earth, of the walls, of furniture, the odor of spilled stale soup, of former wash-days and of former inhabitants, the smell of animals and of human beings combined, of things and of persons, the odor of time, and of things that have passed away.

I went out to have a look at the farmyard. It was very large, full of apple trees, dwarfed and crooked, and laden with fruit which fell on the grass around them. In this farmyard the Norman smell of apples was as strong as that of the bloom of orange trees on the shores of the south of France.

Four rows of beeches surrounded this inclosure. They were so tall that they seemed to touch the clouds at this hour of nightfall, and their summits, through which the night winds passed, swayed and sang a mournful, interminable song.

I reentered the house.

The baron was warming his feet at the fire, and was listening to the farmer's talk about country matters. He talked about marriages, births and deaths, then about the fall in the price of grain and the latest news about cattle. The "Veularde" (as he called a cow that had been bought at the fair of Veules) had calved in the middle of June. The cider had not been first-class last year. Apricots were almost disappearing from the country.

Then we had dinner. It was a good rustic meal, simple and abundant, long and tranquil. And while we were dining I noticed the special kind of friendly familiarity which had struck me from the start between the baron and the peasant.

Outside, the beeches continued sighing in the night wind, and our two dogs, shut up in a shed, were whining and howling in an uncanny fashion. The fire was dying out in the big fireplace. The maid-servant had gone to bed. Maitre Lebrument said in his turn:

"If you don't mind, M'sieu le Baron, I'm going to bed. I am not used to staying up late."

The baron extended his hand toward him and said: "Go, my friend," in so cordial a tone that I said, as soon as the man had disappeared:

"He is devoted to you, this farmer?"

"Better than that, my dear fellow! It is a drama, an old drama, simple and very sad, that attaches him to me. Here is the story:

"You know that my father was colonel in a cavalry regiment. His orderly was this young fellow, now an old man, the son of a farmer. When my father retired from the army he took this former soldier, then about forty; as his servant. I was at that time about thirty. We were living in our old chateau of Valrenne, near Caudebec-en-Caux.

"At this period my mother's chambermaid was one of the prettiest girls you could see, fair-haired, slender and sprightly in manner, a genuine soubrette of the old type that no longer exists. To-day these creatures spring up into hussies before their time. Paris, with the aid of the railways, attracts them, calls them, takes hold of them, as soon as they are budding into womanhood, these little sluts who in old times remained simple maid-servants. Every man passing by, as recruiting sergeants did formerly, looking for recruits, with conscripts, entices and ruins them —these foolish lassies—and we have now only the scum of the female sex for servant maids, all that is dull, nasty, common and ill-formed, too ugly, even for gallantry.

"Well, this girl was charming, and I often gave her a kiss in dark corners; nothing more, I swear to you! She was virtuous, besides; and I had some respect for my mother's house, which is more than can be said of the blackguards of the present day.

"Now, it happened that my man-servant, the ex-soldier, the old farmer you have just seen, fell madly in love with this girl, perfectly daft. The first thing we noticed was that he forgot everything, he paid no attention to anything.

"My father said incessantly:

"'See here, Jean, what's the matter with you? Are you ill?'

"He replied:

"'No, no, M'sieu le Baron. There's nothing the matter with me.'

"He grew thin; he broke glasses and let plates fall when waiting on the table. We thought he must have been attacked by some nervous affection, and sent for the doctor, who thought he could detect symptoms of spinal disease. Then my father, full of anxiety about his faithful man-servant, decided to place him in a private hospital. When the poor fellow heard of my father's intentions he made a clean breast of it.

"'M'sieu le Baron'

"'Well, my boy?'

"'You see, the thing I want is not physic.'

"'Ha! what is it, then?'

"'It's marriage!'

"My father turned round and stared at him in astonishment.

"'What's that you say, eh?'

"'It's marriage."

"'Marriage! So, then, you jackass, you're to love.'

"'That's how it is, M'sieu le Baron.'

"And my father began to laugh so immoderately that my mother called out through the wall of the next room:

"'What in the world is the matter with you, Gontran?'

"He replied:

"'Come here, Catherine.'

"And when she came in he told her, with tears in his eyes from sheer laughter, that his idiot of a servant-man was lovesick.

"But my mother, instead of laughing, was deeply affected.

"'Who is it that you have fallen in love with, my poor fellow?' she asked.

"He answered without hesitation:

"'With Louise, Madame le Baronne.'

"My mother said with the utmost gravity: 'We must try to arrange this matter the best way we can.'

"So Louise was sent for and questioned by my mother; and she said in reply that she knew all about Jean's liking for her, that in fact Jean had spoken to her about it several times, but that she did not want him. She refused to say why.

"And two months elapsed during which my father and mother never ceased to urge this girl to marry Jean. As she declared she was not in love with any other man, she could not give any serious reason for her refusal. My father at last overcame her resistance by means of a big present of money, and started the pair of them on a farm—this very farm. I did not see them for three years, and then I learned that Louise had died of consumption. But my father and mother died, too, in their turn, and it was two years more before I found myself face to face with Jean.

"At last one autumn day about the end of October the idea came into my head to go hunting on this part of my estate, which my father had told me was full of game.

"So one evening, one wet evening, I arrived at this house. I was shocked to find my father's old servant with perfectly white hair, though he was not more than forty-five or forty-six years of age. I made him dine with me, at the very table where we are now sitting. It was raining hard. We could hear the rain battering at the roof, the walls, and the windows, flowing in a perfect deluge into the farmyard; and my dog was howling in the shed where the other dogs are howling to-night.

"All of a sudden, when the servant-maid had gone to bed, the man said in a timid voice:

"'M'sieu le Baron.'

"'What is it, my dear Jean?'

"'I have something to tell you.'

"'Tell it, my dear Jean.'

"'You remember Louise, my wife.'

"'Certainly, I remember her.'

"'Well, she left me a message for you.'

"'What was it?'

"'A—a—well, it was what you might call a confession.'

"'Ha—and what was it about?'

"'It was—it was—I'd rather, all the same, tell you nothing about it—but I must—I must. Well, it's this—it wasn't consumption she died of at all. It was grief—well, that's the long and short of it. As soon as she came to live here after we were married, she grew thin; she changed so that you wouldn't know her, M'sieu le Baron. She was just as I was before I married her, but it was just the opposite, just the opposite.

"'I sent for the doctor. He said it was her liver that was affected—he said it was what he called a "hepatic" complaint—I don't know these big words, M'sieu le Baron. Then I bought medicine for her, heaps on heaps of bottles that cost about three hundred francs. But she'd take none of them; she wouldn't have them; she said: "It's no use, my poor Jean; it wouldn't do me any good." I saw well that she had some hidden trouble; and then I found her one time crying, and I didn't know what to do, no, I didn't know what to do. I bought her caps, and dresses, and hair oil, and earrings. Nothing did her any good. And I saw that she was going to die. And so one night at the end of November, one snowy night, after she had been in bed the whole day, she told me to send for the cure. So I went for him. As soon as he came—'

"'Jean,' she said, 'I am going to make a confession to you. I owe it to you, Jean. I have never been false to you, never! never, before or after you married me. M'sieu le Cure is there, and can tell you so; he knows my soul. Well, listen, Jean. If I am dying, it is because I was not able to console myself for leaving the chateau, because I was too fond of the young Baron Monsieur Rene, too fond of him, mind you, Jean, there was no harm in it! This is the thing that's killing me. When I could see him no more I felt that I should die. If I could only have seen him, I might have lived, only seen him, nothing more. I wish you'd tell him some day, by and by, when I am no longer here. You will tell him, swear you, will, Jean—swear it—in the presence of M'sieu le Cure! It will console me to know that he will know it one day, that this was the cause of my death! Swear it!'

"'Well, I gave her my promise, M'sieu It Baron, and on the faith of an honest man I have kept my word.'

"And then he ceased speaking, his eyes filling with tears.

"Good God! my dear boy, you can't form any idea of the emotion that filled me when I heard this poor devil, whose wife I had killed without suspecting it, telling me this story on that wet night in this very kitchen.

"I exclaimed: 'Ah! my poor Jean! my poor Jean!'

"He murmured: 'Well, that's all, M'sieu le Baron. I could not help it, one way or the other—and now it's all over!'

"I caught his hand across the table, and I began to weep.

"He asked, 'Will you come and see her grave?' I nodded assent, for I couldn't speak. He rose, lighted a lantern, and we walked through the blinding rain by the light of the lantern.

"He opened a gate, and I saw some crosses of black wood.

"Suddenly he stopped before a marble slab and said: 'There it is,' and he flashed the lantern close to it so that I could read the inscription:

"'TO LOUISE HORTENSE MARINET,

"'Wife of Jean-Francois Lebrument, Farmer,

"'SHE WAS A FAITHFUL WIFE. GOD REST HER SOUL.'

"We fell on our knees in the damp grass, he and I, with the lantern between us, and I saw the rain beating on the white marble slab. And I thought of the heart of her sleeping there in her grave. Ah! poor heart! poor heart! Since then I come here every year. And I don't know why, but I feel as if I were guilty of some crime in the presence of this man who always looks as if he forgave me."

THE DEVIL

The peasant and the doctor stood on opposite sides of the bed, beside the old, dying woman. She was calm and resigned and her mind quite clear as she looked at them and listened to their conversation. She was going to die, and she did not rebel at it, for her time was come, as she was ninety-two.

The July sun streamed in at the window and the open door and cast its hot flames on the uneven brown clay floor, which had been stamped down by four generations of clodhoppers. The smell of the fields came in also, driven by the sharp wind and parched by the noontide heat. The grass-hoppers chirped themselves hoarse, and filled the country with their shrill noise, which was like that of the wooden toys which are sold to children at fair time.

The doctor raised his voice and said: "Honore, you cannot leave your mother in this state; she may die at any moment." And the peasant, in great distress, replied: "But I must get in my wheat, for it has been lying on the ground a long time, and the weather is just right for it; what do you say about it, mother?" And the dying old woman, still tormented by her Norman avariciousness, replied yes with her eyes and her forehead, and thus urged her son to get in his wheat, and to leave her to die alone.

But the doctor got angry, and, stamping his foot, he said: "You are no better than a brute, do you hear, and I will not allow you to do it, do you understand? And if you must get in your wheat today, go and fetch Rapet's wife and make her look after your mother; I will have it, do you understand me? And if you do not obey me, I will let you die like a dog, when you are ill in your turn; do you hear?"

The peasant, a tall, thin fellow with slow movements, who was tormented by indecision, by his fear of the doctor and his fierce love of saving, hesitated, calculated, and stammered out: "How much does La Rapet charge for attending sick people?" "How should I know?" the doctor cried. "That depends upon how long she is needed. Settle it with her, by Heaven! But I want her to be here within an hour, do you hear?"

So the man decided. "I will go for her," he replied; "don't get angry, doctor." And the latter left, calling out as he went: "Be careful, be very careful, you know, for I do not joke when I am angry!" As soon as they were alone the peasant turned to his mother and said in a resigned voice: "I will go and fetch La Rapet, as the man will have it. Don't worry till I get back."

And he went out in his turn.

La Rapet, old was an old washerwoman, watched the dead and the dying of the neighborhood, and then, as soon as she had sewn her customers into that linen cloth from which they would emerge no more, she went and took up her iron to smooth out the linen of the living. Wrinkled like a last year's apple, spiteful, envious, avaricious with a phenomenal avarice, bent double, as if she had been broken in half across the loins by the constant motion of passing the iron over the linen, one might have said that she had a kind of abnormal and cynical love of a death struggle. She never spoke of anything but of the people she had seen die, of the various kinds of deaths at which she had been present, and she related with the greatest minuteness details which were always similar, just as a sportsman recounts his luck.

When Honore Bontemps entered her cottage, he found her preparing the starch for the collars of the women villagers, and he said: "Good-evening; I hope you are pretty well, Mother Rapet?"

She turned her head round to look at him, and said: "As usual, as usual, and you?" "Oh! as for me, I am as well as I could wish, but my mother is not well." "Your mother?" "Yes, my mother!" "What is the matter with her?" "She is going to turn up her toes, that's what's the matter with her!"

The old woman took her hands out of the water and asked with sudden sympathy: "Is she as bad as all that?" "The doctor says she will not last till morning." "Then she certainly is very bad!" Honore hesitated, for he wanted to make a few preparatory remarks before coming to his proposition; but as he could hit upon nothing, he made up his mind suddenly.

"How much will you ask to stay with her till the end? You know that I am not rich, and I can not even afford to keep a servant girl. It is just that which has brought my poor mother to this state—too much worry and fatigue! She did the work of ten, in spite of her ninety-two years. You don't find any made of that stuff nowadays!"

La Rapet answered gravely: "There are two prices: Forty sous by day and three francs by night for the rich, and twenty sous by day and forty by night for the others. You shall pay me the twenty and forty." But the, peasant reflected, for he knew his mother well. He knew how tenacious of life, how vigorous and unyielding she was, and she might last another week, in spite of the doctor's opinion; and so he said resolutely: "No, I would rather you would fix a price for the whole time until the end. I will take my chance, one way or the other. The doctor says she will die very soon. If that happens, so much the better for you, and so much the worse for her, but if she holds out till to-morrow or longer, so much the better for her and so much the worse for you!"

The nurse looked at the man in astonishment, for she had never treated a death as a speculation, and she hesitated, tempted by the idea of the possible gain, but she suspected that he wanted to play her a trick. "I can say nothing until I have seen your mother," she replied.

"Then come with me and see her."

She washed her hands, and went with him immediately.

They did not speak on the road; she walked with short, hasty steps, while he strode on with his long legs, as if he were crossing a brook at every step.

The cows lying down in the fields, overcome by the heat, raised their heads heavily and lowed feebly at the two passers-by, as if to ask them for some green grass.

When they got near the house, Honore Bontemps murmured: "Suppose it is all over?" And his unconscious wish that it might be so showed itself in the sound of his voice.

But the old woman was not dead. She was lying on her back, on her wretched bed, her hands covered with a purple cotton counterpane, horribly thin, knotty hands, like the claws of strange animals, like crabs, half closed by rheumatism, fatigue and the work of nearly a century which she had accomplished.

La Rapet went up to the bed and looked at the dying woman, felt her pulse, tapped her on the chest, listened to her breathing, and asked her questions, so as to hear her speak; and then, having looked at her for some time, she went out of the room, followed by Honore. Her decided opinion was that the old woman would not last till night. He asked: "Well?" And the sick-nurse replied: "Well, she may last two days, perhaps three. You will have to give me six francs, everything included."

"Six francs! six francs!" he shouted. "Are you out of your mind? I tell you she cannot last more than five or six hours!" And they disputed angrily for some time, but as the nurse said she must go home, as the time was going by, and as his wheat would not come to the farmyard of its own accord, he finally agreed to her terms.

"Very well, then, that is settled; six francs, including everything, until the corpse is taken out."

And he went away, with long strides, to his wheat which was lying on the ground under the hot sun which ripens the grain, while the sick-nurse went in again to the house.

She had brought some work with her, for she worked without ceasing by the side of the dead and dying, sometimes for herself, sometimes for the family which employed her as seamstress and paid her rather more in that capacity. Suddenly, she asked: "Have you received the last sacraments, Mother Bontemps?"

The old peasant woman shook her head, and La Rapet, who was very devout, got up quickly:

"Good heavens, is it possible? I will go and fetch the cure"; and she rushed off to the parsonage so quickly that the urchins in the street thought some accident had happened, when they saw her running.

The priest came immediately in his surplice, preceded by a choir boy who rang a bell to announce the passage of the Host through the parched and quiet country. Some men who were working at a distance took off their large hats and remained motionless until the white vestment had disappeared behind some farm buildings; the women who were making up the sheaves stood up to make the sign of the cross; the frightened black hens ran away along the ditch until they reached a well-known hole, through which they suddenly disappeared, while a foal which was tied in a meadow took fright at the sight of the surplice and began to gallop round and round, kicking cut every now and then. The acolyte, in his red cassock, walked quickly, and the priest, with his head inclined toward one shoulder and his square biretta on his head, followed him, muttering some prayers; while last of all came La Rapet, bent almost double as if she wished to prostrate herself, as she walked with folded hands as they do in church.

Honore saw them pass in the distance, and he asked: "Where is our priest going?" His man, who was more intelligent, replied: "He is taking the sacrament to your mother, of course!"

The peasant was not surprised, and said: "That may be," and went on with his work.

Mother Bontemps confessed, received absolution and communion, and the priest took his departure, leaving the two women alone in the suffocating room, while La Rapet began to look at the dying woman, and to ask herself whether it could last much longer.

The day was on the wane, and gusts of cooler air began to blow, causing a view of Epinal, which was fastened to the wall by two pins, to flap up and down; the scanty window curtains, which had formerly been white, but were now yellow and covered with fly-specks, looked as if they were going to fly off, as if they were struggling to get away, like the old woman's soul.

Lying motionless, with her eyes open, she seemed to await with indifference that death which was so near and which yet delayed its coming. Her short breathing whistled in her constricted throat. It would stop altogether soon, and there would be one woman less in the world; no one would regret her.

At nightfall Honore returned, and when he went up to the bed and saw that his mother was still alive, he asked: "How is she?" just as he had done formerly when she had been ailing, and then he sent La Rapet away, saying to her: "To-morrow morning at five o'clock, without fail." And she replied: "To-morrow, at five o'clock."

She came at daybreak, and found Honore eating his soup, which he had made himself before going to work, and the sick-nurse asked him: "Well, is your mother dead?" "She is rather better, on the contrary," he replied, with a sly look out of the corner of his eyes. And he went out.

La Rapet, seized with anxiety, went up to the dying woman, who remained in the same state, lethargic and impassive, with her eyes open and her hands clutching the counterpane. The nurse perceived that this might go on thus for two days, four days, eight days, and her avaricious mind was seized with fear, while she was furious at the sly fellow who had tricked her, and at the woman who would not die.

Nevertheless, she began to work, and waited, looking intently at the wrinkled face of Mother Bontemps. When Honore returned to breakfast he seemed quite satisfied and even in a bantering humor. He was decidedly getting in his wheat under very favorable circumstances.

La Rapet was becoming exasperated; every minute now seemed to her so much time and money stolen from her. She felt a mad inclination to take this old woman, this, headstrong old fool, this obstinate old wretch, and to stop that short, rapid breath, which was robbing her of her time and money, by squeezing her throat a little. But then she reflected on the danger of doing so, and other thoughts came into her head; so she went up to the bed and said: "Have you ever seen the Devil?" Mother Bontemps murmured: "No."

Then the sick-nurse began to talk and to tell her tales which were likely to terrify the weak mind of the dying woman. Some minutes before one dies the Devil appears, she said, to all who are in the death throes. He has a broom in his hand, a saucepan on his head, and he utters loud cries. When anybody sees him, all is over, and that person has only a few moments longer to live. She then enumerated all those to whom the Devil had appeared that year: Josephine Loisel, Eulalie Ratier, Sophie Padaknau, Seraphine Grospied.

Mother Bontemps, who had at last become disturbed in mind, moved about, wrung her hands, and tried to turn her head to look toward the end of the room. Suddenly La Rapet disappeared at the foot of the bed. She took a sheet out of the cupboard and wrapped herself up in it; she put the iron saucepan on her head, so that its three short bent feet rose up like horns, and she took a broom in her right hand and a tin pail in her left, which she threw up suddenly, so that it might fall to the ground noisily.

When it came down, it certainly made a terrible noise. Then, climbing upon a chair, the nurse lifted up the curtain which hung at the bottom of the bed, and showed herself, gesticulating and uttering shrill cries into the iron saucepan which covered her face, while she menaced the old peasant woman, who was nearly dead, with her broom.

Terrified, with an insane expression on her face, the dying woman made a superhuman effort to get up and escape; she even got her shoulders and chest out of bed; then she fell back with a deep sigh. All was over, and La Rapet calmly put everything back into its place; the broom into the corner by the cupboard the sheet inside it, the saucepan on the hearth, the pail on the floor, and the chair against the wall. Then, with professional movements, she closed the dead woman's large eyes, put a plate on the bed and poured some holy water into it, placing in it the twig of boxwood that had been nailed to the chest of drawers, and kneeling down, she fervently repeated the prayers for the dead, which she knew by heart, as a matter of business.

And when Honore returned in the evening he found her praying, and he calculated immediately that she had made twenty sows out of him, for she had only spent three days and one night there, which made five francs altogether, instead of the six which he owed her.

THE SNIPE

Old Baron des Ravots had for forty years been the champion sportsman of his province. But a stroke of paralysis had kept him in his chair for the last five or six years. He could now only shoot pigeons from the window of his drawing-room or from the top of his high doorsteps.

He spent his time in reading.

He was a good-natured business man, who had much of the literary spirit of a former century. He worshipped anecdotes, those little risque anecdotes, and also true stories of events that happened in his neighborhood. As soon as a friend came to see him he asked:

"Well, anything new?"

And he knew how to worm out information like an examining lawyer.

On sunny days he had his large reclining chair, similar to a bed, wheeled to the hall door. A man servant behind him held his guns, loaded them and handed them to his master. Another valet, hidden in the bushes, let fly a pigeon from time to time at irregular intervals, so that the baron should be unprepared and be always on the watch.

And from morning till night he fired at the birds, much annoyed if he were taken by surprise and laughing till he cried when the animal fell straight to the earth or, turned over in some comical and unexpected manner. He would turn to the man who was loading the gun and say, almost choking with laughter:

"Did that get him, Joseph? Did you see how he fell?" Joseph invariably replied:

"Oh, monsieur le baron never misses them."

In autumn, when the shooting season opened, he invited his friends as he had done formerly, and loved to hear them firing in the distance. He counted the shots and was pleased when they followed each other rapidly. And in the evening he made each guest give a faithful account of his day. They remained three hours at table telling about their sport.

They were strange and improbable adventures in which the romancing spirit of the sportsmen delighted. Some of them were memorable stories and were repeated regularly. The story of a rabbit that little Vicomte de Bourril had missed in his vestibule convulsed them with laughter each year anew. Every five minutes a fresh speaker would say:

"I heard 'birr! birr!' and a magnificent covey rose at ten paces from me. I aimed. Pif! paf! and I saw a shower, a veritable shower of birds. There were seven of them!"

And they all went into raptures, amazed, but reciprocally credulous.

But there was an old custom in the house called "The Story of the Snipe."

Whenever this queen of birds was in season the same ceremony took place at each dinner. As they worshipped this incomparable bird, each guest ate one every evening, but the heads were all left in the dish.

Then the baron, acting the part of a bishop, had a plate brought to him containing a little fat, and he carefully anointed the precious heads, holding them by the tip of their slender, needle-like beak. A lighted candle was placed beside him and everyone was silent in an anxiety of expectation.

Then he took one of the heads thus prepared, stuck a pin through it and stuck the pin on a cork, keeping the whole contrivance steady by means of little crossed sticks, and carefully placed this object on the neck of a bottle in the manner of a tourniquet.

All the guests counted simultaneously in a loud tone—

"One-two-three."

And the baron with a fillip of the finger made this toy whirl round.

The guest to whom the long beak pointed when the head stopped became the possessor of all the heads, a feast fit for a king, which made his neighbors look askance.

He took them one by one and toasted them over the candle. The grease sputtered, the roasting flesh smoked and the lucky winner ate the head, holding it by the beak and uttering exclamations of enjoyment.

And at each head the diners, raising their glasses, drank to his health.

When he had finished the last head he was obliged, at the baron's orders, to tell an anecdote to compensate the disappointed ones.

Here are some of the stories.

THE WILL

I knew that tall young fellow, Rene de Bourneval. He was an agreeable man, though rather melancholy and seemed prejudiced against everything, was very skeptical, and he could with a word tear down social hypocrisy. He would often say:

"There are no honorable men, or, at least, they are only relatively so when compared with those lower than themselves."

He had two brothers, whom he never saw, the Messieurs de Courcils. I always supposed they were by another father, on account of the difference in the name. I had frequently heard that the family had a strange history, but did not know the details. As I took a great liking to Rene we soon became intimate friends, and one evening, when I had been dining with him alone, I asked him, by chance: "Are you a son of the first or second marriage?" He grew rather pale, and then flushed, and did not speak for a few moments; he was visibly embarrassed. Then he smiled in the melancholy, gentle manner, which was peculiar to him, and said:

"My dear friend, if it will not weary you, I can give you some very strange particulars about my life. I know that you are a sensible man, so I do not fear that our friendship will suffer by my I revelations; and should it suffer, I should not care about having you for my friend any longer.

"My mother, Madame de Courcils, was a poor little, timid woman, whom her husband had married for the sake of her fortune, and her whole life was one of martyrdom. Of a loving, timid, sensitive disposition, she was constantly being ill-treated by the man who ought to have been my father, one of those boors called country gentlemen. A month after their marriage he was living a licentious life and carrying on liaisons with the wives and daughters of his tenants. This did not prevent him from having three children by his wife, that is, if you count me in. My mother said nothing, and lived in that noisy house like a little mouse. Set aside, unnoticed, nervous, she looked at people with her bright, uneasy, restless eyes, the eyes of some terrified creature which can never shake off its fear. And yet she was pretty, very pretty and fair, a pale blonde, as if her hair had lost its color through her constant fear.

"Among the friends of Monsieur de Courcils who constantly came to her chateau, there was an ex-cavalry officer, a widower, a man who was feared, who was at the same time tender and violent, capable of the most determined resolves, Monsieur de Bourneval, whose name I bear. He was a tall, thin man, with a heavy black mustache. I am very like him. He was a man who had read a great deal, and his ideas were not like those of most of his class. His great-grandmother had been a friend of J. J. Rousseau's, and one might have said that he had inherited something of this ancestral connection. He knew the Contrat Social, and the Nouvelle Heloise by heart, and all those philosophical books which prepared in advance the overthrow of our old usages, prejudices, superannuated laws and imbecile morality.

"It seems that he loved my mother, and she loved him, but their liaison was carried on so secretly that no one guessed at its existence. The poor, neglected, unhappy woman must have clung to him in despair, and in her intimacy with him must have imbibed all his ways of thinking, theories of free thought, audacious ideas of independent love; but being so timid she never ventured to speak out, and it was all driven back, condensed, shut up in her heart.

"My two brothers were very hard towards her, like their father, and never gave her a caress, and, accustomed to seeing her count for nothing in the house, they treated her rather like a servant. I was the only one of her sons who really loved her and whom she loved.

"When she died I was seventeen, and I must add, in order that you may understand what follows, that a lawsuit between my father and mother had been decided in my mother's favor, giving her the bulk of the property, and, thanks to the tricks of the law, and the intelligent devotion of a lawyer to her interests, the right to make her will in favor of whom she pleased.

"We were told that there was a will at the lawyer's office and were invited to be present at the reading of it. I can remember it, as if it were yesterday. It was an imposing scene, dramatic, burlesque and surprising, occasioned by the posthumous revolt of that dead woman, by the cry for liberty, by the demands of that martyred one who had been crushed by our oppression during her lifetime and who, from her closed tomb, uttered a despairing appeal for independence.

"The man who believed he was my father, a stout, ruddy-faced man, who looked like a butcher, and my brothers, two great fellows of twenty and twenty-two, were waiting quietly in their chairs. Monsieur de Bourneval, who had been invited to be present, came in and stood behind me. He was very pale and bit his mustache, which was turning gray. No doubt he was prepared for what was going to happen. The lawyer double-locked the door and began to read the will, after having opened, in our presence, the envelope, sealed with red wax, of the contents of which he was ignorant."

My friend stopped talking abruptly, and rising, took from his writing-table an old paper, unfolded it, kissed it and then continued: "This is the will of my beloved mother:

"'I, the undersigned, Anne Catherine-Genevieve-Mathilde de

Croixluce, the legitimate wife of Leopold-Joseph Gontran de Councils

sound in body and mind, here express my last wishes.

"I first of all ask God, and then my dear son Rene to pardon me for

the act I am about to commit. I believe that my child's heart is

great enough to understand me, and to forgive me. I have suffered

my whole life long. I was married out of calculation, then

despised, misunderstood, oppressed and constantly deceived by my husband.

"'I forgive him, but I owe him nothing.

"'My elder sons never loved me, never petted me, scarcely treated me as a mother, but during my whole life I did my duty towards them, and I owe them nothing more after my death. The ties of blood cannot exist without daily and constant affection. An ungrateful son is less than, a stranger; he is a culprit, for he has no right to be indifferent towards his mother.

"'I have always trembled before men, before their unjust laws, their inhuman customs, their shameful prejudices. Before God, I have no longer any fear. Dead, I fling aside disgraceful hypocrisy; I dare to speak my thoughts, and to avow and to sign the secret of my heart.

"'I therefore leave that part of my fortune of which the law allows me to dispose, in trust to my dear lover, Pierre-Germer-Simon de Bourneval, to revert afterwards to our dear son Rene.

"'(This bequest is specified more precisely in a deed drawn up by a notary.)

"'And I declare before the Supreme Judge who hears me, that I should have cursed heaven and my own existence, if I had not found the deep, devoted, tender, unshaken affection of my lover; if I had not felt in his arms that the Creator made His creatures to love, sustain and console each other, and to weep together in the hours of sadness.

"'Monsieur de Courcils is the father of my two eldest sons; Rene, alone, owes his life to Monsieur de Bourneval. I pray the Master of men and of their destinies, to place father and son above social prejudices, to make them love each other until they die, and to love me also in my coffin.

"'These are my last thoughts, and my last wish.

"'MATHILDE DE CROIXLUCE.'"

"Monsieur de Courcils had risen and he cried:

"'It is the will of a madwoman.'

"Then Monsieur de Bourneval stepped forward and said in a loud, penetrating voice: 'I, Simon de Bourneval, solemnly declare that this writing contains nothing but the strict truth, and I am ready to prove it by letters which I possess.'

"On hearing that, Monsieur de Courcils went up to him, and I 'thought that they were going to attack each other. There they stood, both of them tall, one stout and the other thin, both trembling. My mother's husband stammered out: 'You are a worthless wretch!' And the other replied in a loud, dry voice: 'We will meet elsewhere, monsieur. I should have already slapped your ugly face and challenged you long since if I had not, before everything else, thought of the peace of mind during her lifetime of that poor woman whom you caused to suffer so greatly.'

"Then, turning to me, he said: 'You are my son; will you come with me? I have no right to take you away, but I shall assume it, if you are willing to come with me: I shook his hand without replying, and we went out together. I was certainly three parts mad.

"Two days later Monsieur de Bourneval killed Monsieur de Courcils in a duel. My brothers, to avoid a terrible scandal, held their tongues. I offered them and they accepted half the fortune which my mother had left me. I took my real father's name, renouncing that which the law gave me, but which was not really mine. Monsieur de Bourneval died three years later and I am still inconsolable."

He rose from his chair, walked up and down the room, and, standing in front of me, said:

"Well, I say that my mother's will was one of the most beautiful, the most loyal, as well as one of the grandest acts that a woman could perform. Do you not think so?"

I held out both hands to him, saying:

"I most certainly do, my friend."

WALTER SCHNAFFS' ADVENTURE

Ever since he entered France with the invading army Walter Schnaffs had considered himself the most unfortunate of men. He was large, had difficulty in walking, was short of breath and suffered frightfully with his feet, which were very flat and very fat. But he was a peaceful, benevolent man, not warlike or sanguinary, the father of four children whom he adored, and married to a little blonde whose little tendernesses, attentions and kisses he recalled with despair every evening. He liked to rise late and retire early, to eat good things in a leisurely manner and to drink beer in the saloon. He reflected, besides, that all that is sweet in existence vanishes with life, and he maintained in his heart a fearful hatred, instinctive as well as logical, for cannon, rifles, revolvers and swords, but especially for bayonets, feeling that he was unable to dodge this dangerous weapon rapidly enough to protect his big paunch.

And when night fell and he lay on the ground, wrapped in his cape beside his comrades who were snoring, he thought long and deeply about those he had left behind and of the dangers in his path. "If he were killed what would become of the little ones? Who would provide for them and bring them up?" Just at present they were not rich, although he had borrowed when he left so as to leave them some money. And Walter Schnaffs wept when he thought of all this.

At the beginning of a battle his legs became so weak that he would have fallen if he had not reflected that the entire army would pass over his body. The whistling of the bullets gave him gooseflesh.

For months he had lived thus in terror and anguish.

His company was marching on Normandy, and one day he was sent to reconnoitre with a small detachment, simply to explore a portion of the territory and to return at once. All seemed quiet in the country; nothing indicated an armed resistance.

But as the Prussians were quietly descending into a little valley traversed by deep ravines a sharp fusillade made them halt suddenly, killing twenty of their men, and a company of sharpshooters, suddenly emerging from a little wood as large as your hand, darted forward with bayonets at the end of their rifles.

Walter Schnaffs remained motionless at first, so surprised and bewildered that he did not even think of making his escape. Then he was seized with a wild desire to run away, but he remembered at once that he ran like a tortoise compared with those thin Frenchmen, who came bounding along like a lot of goats. Perceiving a large ditch full of brushwood covered with dead leaves about six paces in front of him, he sprang into it with both feet together, without stopping to think of its depth, just as one jumps from a bridge into the river.

He fell like an arrow through a thick layer of vines and thorny brambles that tore his face and hands and landed heavily in a sitting posture on a bed of stones. Raising his eyes, he saw the sky through the hole he had made in falling through. This aperture might betray him, and he crawled along carefully on hands and knees at the bottom of this ditch beneath the covering of interlacing branches, going as fast as he could and getting away from the scene of the skirmish. Presently he stopped and sat down, crouched like a hare amid the tall dry grass.

He heard firing and cries and groans going on for some time. Then the noise of fighting grew fainter and ceased. All was quiet and silent.

Suddenly something stirred, beside him. He was frightfully startled. It was a little bird which had perched on a branch and was moving the dead leaves. For almost an hour Walter Schnaffs' heart beat loud and rapidly.

Night fell, filling the ravine with its shadows. The soldier began to think. What was he to do? What was to become of him? Should he rejoin the army? But how? By what road? And he began over again the horrible life of anguish, of terror, of fatigue and suffering that he had led since the commencement of the war. No! He no longer had the courage! He would not have the energy necessary to endure long marches and to face the dangers to which one was exposed at every moment.

But what should he do? He could not stay in this ravine in concealment until the end of hostilities. No, indeed! If it were not for having to eat, this prospect would not have daunted him greatly. But he had to eat, to eat every day.

And here he was, alone, armed and in uniform, on the enemy's territory, far from those who would protect him. A shiver ran over him.

All at once he thought: "If I were only a prisoner!" And his heart quivered with a longing, an intense desire to be taken prisoner by the French. A prisoner, he would be saved, fed, housed, sheltered from bullets and swords, without any apprehension whatever, in a good, well-kept prison. A prisoner! What a dream:

His resolution was formed at once.

"I will constitute myself a prisoner."

He rose, determined to put this plan into execution without a moment's delay. But he stood motionless, suddenly a prey to disturbing reflections and fresh terrors.

Where would he make himself a prisoner and how? In What direction? And frightful pictures, pictures of death came into his mind.

He would run terrible danger in venturing alone through the country with his pointed helmet.

Supposing he should meet some peasants. These peasants seeing a Prussian who had lost his way, an unprotected Prussian, would kill him as if he were a stray dog! They would murder him with their forks, their picks, their scythes and their shovels. They would make a stew of him, a pie, with the frenzy of exasperated, conquered enemies.

If he should meet the sharpshooters! These sharpshooters, madmen without law or discipline, would shoot him just for amusement to pass an hour; it would make them laugh to see his head. And he fancied he was already leaning against a wall in-front of four rifles whose little black apertures seemed to be gazing at him.

Supposing he should meet the French army itself. The vanguard would take him for a scout, for some bold and sly trooper who had set off alone to reconnoitre, and they would fire at him. And he could already hear, in imagination, the irregular shots of soldiers lying in the brush, while he himself, standing in the middle of the field, was sinking to the earth, riddled like a sieve with bullets which he felt piercing his flesh.

He sat down again in despair. His situation seemed hopeless.

It was quite a dark, black and silent night. He no longer budged, trembling at all the slight and unfamiliar sounds that occur at night. The sound of a rabbit crouching at the edge of his burrow almost made him run. The cry of an owl caused him positive anguish, giving him a nervous shock that pained like a wound. He opened his big eyes as wide as possible to try and see through the darkness, and he imagined every moment that he heard someone walking close beside him.

After interminable hours in which he suffered the tortures of the damned, he noticed through his leafy cover that the sky was becoming bright. He at once felt an intense relief. His limbs stretched out, suddenly relaxed, his heart quieted down, his eyes closed; he fell asleep.

When he awoke the sun appeared to be almost at the meridian. It must be noon. No sound disturbed the gloomy silence. Walter Schnaffs noticed that he was exceedingly hungry.

He yawned, his mouth watering at the thought of sausage, the good sausage the soldiers have, and he felt a gnawing at his stomach.

He rose from the ground, walked a few steps, found that his legs were weak and sat down to reflect. For two or three hours he again considered the pros and cons, changing his mind every moment, baffled, unhappy, torn by the most conflicting motives.

Finally he had an idea that seemed logical and practical. It was to watch for a villager passing by alone, unarmed and with no dangerous tools of his trade, and to run to him and give himself up, making him understand that he was surrendering.

He took off his helmet, the point of which might betray him, and put his head out of his hiding place with the utmost caution.

No solitary pedestrian could be perceived on the horizon. Yonder, to the right, smoke rose from the chimney of a little village, smoke from kitchen fires! And yonder, to the left, he saw at the end of an avenue of trees a large turreted chateau. He waited till evening, suffering frightfully from hunger, seeing nothing but flights of crows, hearing nothing but the silent expostulation of his empty stomach.

And darkness once more fell on him.

He stretched himself out in his retreat and slept a feverish sleep, haunted by nightmares, the sleep of a starving man.

Dawn again broke above his head and he began to make his observations. But the landscape was deserted as on the previous day, and a new fear came into Walter Schnaffs' mind—the fear of death by hunger! He pictured himself lying at full length on his back at the bottom of his hiding place, with his two eyes closed, and animals, little creatures of all kinds, approached and began to feed on his dead body, attacking it all over at once, gliding beneath his clothing to bite his cold flesh, and a big crow pecked out his eyes with its sharp beak.

He almost became crazy, thinking he was going to faint and would not be able to walk. And he was just preparing to rush off to the village, determined to dare anything, to brave everything, when he perceived three peasants walking to the fields with their forks across their shoulders, and he dived back into his hiding place.

But as soon as it grew dark he slowly emerged from the ditch and started off, stooping and fearful, with beating heart, towards the distant chateau, preferring to go there rather than to the village, which seemed to him as formidable as a den of tigers.

The lower windows were brilliantly lighted. One of them was open and from it escaped a strong odor of roast meat, an odor which suddenly penetrated to the olfactories and to the stomach of Walter Schnaffs, tickling his nerves, making him breathe quickly, attracting him irresistibly and inspiring his heart with the boldness of desperation.

And abruptly, without reflection, he placed himself, helmet on head, in front of the window.

Eight servants were at dinner around a large table. But suddenly one of the maids sat there, her mouth agape, her eyes fixed and letting fall her glass. They all followed the direction of her gaze.

They saw the enemy!

Good God! The Prussians were attacking the chateau!

There was a shriek, only one shriek made up of eight shrieks uttered in eight different keys, a terrific screaming of terror, then a tumultuous rising from their seats, a jostling, a scrimmage and a wild rush to the door at the farther end. Chairs fell over, the men knocked the women down and walked over them. In two seconds the room was empty, deserted, and the table, covered with eatables, stood in front of Walter Schnaffs, lost in amazement and still standing at the window.

After some moments of hesitation he climbed in at the window and approached the table. His fierce hunger caused him to tremble as if he were in a fever, but fear still held him back, numbed him. He listened. The entire house seemed to shudder. Doors closed, quick steps ran along the floor above. The uneasy Prussian listened eagerly to these confused sounds. Then he heard dull sounds, as though bodies were falling to the ground at the foot of the walls, human beings jumping from the first floor.

Then all motion, all disturbance ceased, and the great chateau became as silent as the grave.

Walter Schnaffs sat down before a clean plate and began to eat. He took great mouthfuls, as if he feared he might be interrupted before he had swallowed enough. He shovelled the food into his mouth, open like a trap, with both hands, and chunks of food went into his stomach, swelling out his throat as it passed down. Now and then he stopped, almost ready to burst like a stopped-up pipe. Then he would take the cider jug and wash down his esophagus as one washes out a clogged rain pipe.

He emptied all the plates, all the dishes and all the bottles. Then, intoxicated with drink and food, besotted, red in the face, shaken by hiccoughs, his mind clouded and his speech thick, he unbuttoned his uniform in order to breathe or he could not have taken a step. His eyes closed, his mind became torpid; he leaned his heavy forehead on his folded arms on the table and gradually lost all consciousness of things and events.

The last quarter of the moon above the trees in the park shed a faint light on the landscape. It was the chill hour that precedes the dawn.

Numerous silent shadows glided among the trees and occasionally a blade of steel gleamed in the shadow as a ray of moonlight struck it.

The quiet chateau stood there in dark outline. Only two windows were still lighted up on the ground floor.

Suddenly a voice thundered:

"Forward! nom d'un nom! To the breach, my lads!"

And in an instant the doors, shutters and window panes fell in beneath a wave of men who rushed in, breaking, destroying everything, and took the house by storm. In a moment fifty soldiers, armed to the teeth, bounded into the kitchen, where Walter Schnaffs was peacefully sleeping, and placing to his breast fifty loaded rifles, they overturned him, rolled him on the floor, seized him and tied his head and feet together.

He gasped in amazement, too besotted to understand, perplexed, bruised and wild with fear.

Suddenly a big soldier, covered with gold lace, put his foot on his stomach, shouting:

"You are my prisoner. Surrender!"

The Prussian heard only the one word "prisoner" and he sighed, "Ya, ya, ya."

He was raised from the floor, tied in a chair and examined with lively curiosity by his victors, who were blowing like whales. Several of them sat down, done up with excitement and fatigue.

He smiled, actually smiled, secure now that he was at last a prisoner.

Another officer came into the room and said:

"Colonel, the enemy has escaped; several seem to have been wounded. We are in possession."

The big officer, who was wiping his forehead, exclaimed: "Victory!"

And he wrote in a little business memorandum book which he took from his pocket:

"After a desperate encounter the Prussians were obliged to beat a retreat, carrying with them their dead and wounded, the number of whom is estimated at fifty men. Several were taken prisoners."

The young officer inquired:

"What steps shall I take, colonel?"

"We will retire in good order," replied the colonel, "to avoid having to return and make another attack with artillery and a larger force of men."

And he gave the command to set out.

The column drew up in line in the darkness beneath the walls of the chateau and filed out, a guard of six soldiers with revolvers in their hands surrounding Walter Schnaffs, who was firmly bound.

Scouts were sent ahead to reconnoitre. They advanced cautiously, halting from time to time.

At daybreak they arrived at the district of La Roche-Oysel, whose national guard had accomplished this feat of arms.

The uneasy and excited inhabitants were expecting them. When they saw the prisoner's helmet tremendous shouts arose. The women raised their 10 arms in wonder, the old people wept. An old grandfather threw his crutch at the Prussian and struck the nose of one of their own defenders.

The colonel roared:

"See that the prisoner is secure!"

At length they reached the town hall. The prison was opened and Walter Schnaffs, freed from his bonds, cast into it. Two hundred armed men mounted guard outside the building.

Then, in spite of the indigestion that had been troubling him for some time, the Prussian, wild with joy, began to dance about, to dance frantically, throwing out his arms and legs and uttering wild shouts until he fell down exhausted beside the wall.

He was a prisoner-saved!

That was how the Chateau de Charnpignet was taken from the enemy after only six hours of occupation.

Colonel Ratier, a cloth merchant, who had led the assault at the head of a body of the national guard of La Roche-Oysel, was decorated with an order.

AT SEA

The following paragraphs recently appeared in the papers:

"Boulogne-Sur-Mer, January 22.—Our correspondent writes:

"A fearful accident has thrown our sea-faring population, which has suffered so much in the last two years, into the greatest consternation. The fishing smack commanded by Captain Javel, on entering the harbor was wrecked on the rocks of the harbor breakwater.

"In spite of the efforts of the life boat and the shooting of life lines from the shore four sailors and the cabin boy were lost.

"The rough weather continues. Fresh disasters are anticipated."

Who is this Captain Javel? Is he the brother of the one-armed man?

If the poor man tossed about in the waves and dead, perhaps, beneath his wrecked boat, is the one I am thinking of, he took part, just eighteen years ago, in another tragedy, terrible and simple as are all these fearful tragedies of the sea.

Javel, senior, was then master of a trawling smack.

The trawling smack is the ideal fishing boat. So solidly built that it fears no weather, with a round bottom, tossed about unceasingly on the waves like a cork, always on top, always thrashed by the harsh salt winds of the English Channel, it ploughs the sea unweariedly with bellying sail, dragging along at its side a huge trawling net, which scours the depths of the ocean, and detaches and gathers in all the animals asleep in the rocks, the flat fish glued to the sand, the heavy crabs with their curved claws, and the lobsters with their pointed mustaches.

When the breeze is fresh and the sea choppy, the boat starts in to trawl. The net is fastened all along a big log of wood clamped with iron and is let down by two ropes on pulleys at either end of the boat. And the boat, driven by the wind and the tide, draws along this apparatus which ransacks and plunders the depths of the sea.

Javel had on board his younger brother, four sailors and a cabin boy. He had set sail from Boulogne on a beautiful day to go trawling.

But presently a wind sprang up, and a hurricane obliged the smack to run to shore. She gained the English coast, but the high sea broke against the rocks and dashed on the beach, making it impossible to go into port, filling all the harbor entrances with foam and noise and danger.

The smack started off again, riding on the waves, tossed, shaken, dripping, buffeted by masses of water, but game in spite of everything; accustomed to this boisterous weather, which sometimes kept it roving between the two neighboring countries without its being able to make port in either.

At length the hurricane calmed down just as they were in the open, and although the sea was still high the captain gave orders to cast the net.

So it was lifted overboard, and two men in the bows and two in the stern began to unwind the ropes that held it. It suddenly touched bottom, but a big wave made the boat heel, and Javel, junior, who was in the bows directing the lowering of the net, staggered, and his arm was caught in the rope which the shock had slipped from the pulley for an instant. He made a desperate effort to raise the rope with the other hand, but the net was down and the taut rope did not give.

The man cried out in agony. They all ran to his aid. His brother left the rudder. They all seized the rope, trying to free the arm it was bruising. But in vain. "We must cut it," said a sailor, and he took from his pocket a big knife, which, with two strokes, could save young Javel's arm.

But if the rope were cut the trawling net would be lost, and this net was worth money, a great deal of money, fifteen hundred francs. And it belonged to Javel, senior, who was tenacious of his property.

"No, do not cut, wait, I will luff," he cried, in great distress. And he ran to the helm and turned the rudder. But the boat scarcely obeyed it, being impeded by the net which kept it from going forward, and prevented also by the force of the tide and the wind.

Javel, junior, had sunk on his knees, his teeth clenched, his eyes haggard. He did not utter a word. His brother came back to him, in dread of the sailor's knife.

"Wait, wait," he said. "We will let down the anchor."

They cast anchor, and then began to turn the capstan to loosen the moorings of the net. They loosened them at length and disengaged the imprisoned arm, in its bloody woolen sleeve.

Young Javel seemed like an idiot. They took off his jersey and saw a horrible sight, a mass of flesh from which the blood spurted as if from a pump. Then the young man looked at his arm and murmured: "Foutu" (done for).

Then, as the blood was making a pool on the deck of the boat, one of the sailors cried: "He will bleed to death, we must bind the vein."

So they took a cord, a thick, brown, tarry cord, and twisting it around the arm above the wound, tightened it with all their might. The blood ceased to spurt by slow degrees, and, presently, stopped altogether.

Young Javel rose, his arm hanging at his side. He took hold of it with the other hand, raised it, turned it over, shook it. It was all mashed, the bones broken, the muscles alone holding it together.

He looked at it sadly, reflectively. Then he sat down on a folded sail and his comrades advised him to keep wetting the arm constantly to prevent it from mortifying.

They placed a pail of water beside him, and every few minutes he dipped a glass into it and bathed the frightful wound, letting the clear water trickle on to it.

"You would be better in the cabin," said his brother. He went down, but came up again in an hour, not caring to be alone. And, besides, he preferred the fresh air. He sat down again on his sail and began to bathe his arm.

They made a good haul. The broad fish with their white bellies lay beside him, quivering in the throes of death; he looked at them as he continued to bathe his crushed flesh.

As they were about to return to Boulogne the wind sprang up anew, and the little boat resumed its mad course, bounding and tumbling about, shaking up the poor wounded man.

Night came on. The sea ran high until dawn. As the sun rose the English coast was again visible, but, as the weather had abated a little, they turned back towards the French coast, tacking as they went.

Towards evening Javel, junior, called his comrades and showed them some black spots, all the horrible tokens of mortification in the portion of the arm below the broken bones.

The sailors examined it, giving their opinion.

"That might be the 'Black,'" thought one.

"He should put salt water on it," said another.

They brought some salt water and poured it on the wound. The injured man became livid, ground his teeth and writhed a little, but did not exclaim.

Then, as soon as the smarting had abated, he said to his brother:

"Give me your knife."

The brother handed it to him.

"Hold my arm up, quite straight, and pull it."

They did as he asked them.

Then he began to cut off his arm. He cut gently, carefully, severing al the tendons with this blade that was sharp as a razor. And, presently, there was only a stump left. He gave a deep sigh and said:

"It had to be done. It was done for."

He seemed relieved and breathed loud. He then began again to pour water on the stump of arm that remained.

The sea was still rough and they could not make the shore.

When the day broke, Javel, junior, took the severed portion of his arm and examined it for a long time. Gangrene had set in. His comrades also examined it and handed it from one to the other, feeling it, turning it over, and sniffing at it.

"You must throw that into the sea at once," said his brother.

But Javel, junior, got angry.

"Oh, no! Oh, no! I don't want to. It belongs to me, does it not, as it is my arm?"

And he took and placed it between his feet.

"It will putrefy, just the same," said the older brother. Then an idea came to the injured man. In order to preserve the fish when the boat was long at sea, they packed it in salt, in barrels. He asked:

"Why can I not put it in pickle?"

"Why, that's a fact," exclaimed the others.

Then they emptied one of the barrels, which was full from the haul of the last few days; and right at the bottom of the barrel they laid the detached arm. They covered it with salt, and then put back the fish one by one.

One of the sailors said by way of joke:

"I hope we do not sell it at auction."

And everyone laughed, except the two Javels.

The wind was still boisterous. They tacked within sight of Boulogne until the following morning at ten o'clock. Young Javel continued to bathe his wound. From time to time he rose and walked from one end to the other of the boat.

His brother, who was at the tiller, followed him with glances, and shook his head.

At last they ran into harbor.

The doctor examined the wound and pronounced it to be in good condition. He dressed it properly and ordered the patient to rest. But Javel would not go to bed until he got back his severed arm, and he returned at once to the dock to look for the barrel which he had marked with a cross.

It was emptied before him and he seized the arm, which was well preserved in the pickle, had shrunk and was freshened. He wrapped it up in a towel he had brought for the purpose and took it home.

His wife and children looked for a long time at this fragment of their father, feeling the fingers, and removing the grains of salt that were under the nails. Then they sent for a carpenter to make a little coffin.

The next day the entire crew of the trawling smack followed the funeral of the detached arm. The two brothers, side by side, led the procession; the parish beadle carried the corpse under his arm.

Javel, junior, gave up the sea. He obtained a small position on the dock, and when he subsequently talked about his accident, he would say confidentially to his auditors:

"If my brother had been willing to cut away the net, I should still have my arm, that is sure. But he was thinking only of his property."

MINUET

Great misfortunes do not affect me very much, said John Bridelle, an old bachelor who passed for a sceptic. I have seen war at quite close quarters; I walked across corpses without any feeling of pity. The great brutal facts of nature, or of humanity, may call forth cries of horror or indignation, but do not cause us that tightening of the heart, that shudder that goes down your spine at sight of certain little heartrending episodes.

The greatest sorrow that anyone can experience is certainly the loss of a child, to a mother; and the loss of his mother, to a man. It is intense, terrible, it rends your heart and upsets your mind; but one is healed of these shocks, just as large bleeding wounds become healed. Certain meetings, certain things half perceived, or surmised, certain secret sorrows, certain tricks of fate which awake in us a whole world of painful thoughts, which suddenly unclose to us the mysterious door of moral suffering, complicated, incurable; all the deeper because they appear benign, all the more bitter because they are intangible, all the more tenacious because they appear almost factitious, leave in our souls a sort of trail of sadness, a taste of bitterness, a feeling of disenchantment, from which it takes a long time to free ourselves.

I have always present to my mind two or three things that others would surely not have noticed, but which penetrated my being like fine, sharp incurable stings.

You might not perhaps understand the emotion that I retained from these hasty impressions. I will tell you one of them. She was very old, but as lively as a young girl. It may be that my imagination alone is responsible for my emotion.

I am fifty. I was young then and studying law. I was rather sad, somewhat of a dreamer, full of a pessimistic philosophy and did not care much for noisy cafes, boisterous companions, or stupid girls. I rose early and one of my chief enjoyments was to walk alone about eight o'clock in the morning in the nursery garden of the Luxembourg.

You people never knew that nursery garden. It was like a forgotten garden of the last century, as pretty as the gentle smile of an old lady. Thick hedges divided the narrow regular paths,—peaceful paths between two walls of carefully trimmed foliage. The gardener's great shears were pruning unceasingly these leafy partitions, and here and there one came across beds of flowers, lines of little trees looking like schoolboys out for a walk, companies of magnificent rose bushes, or regiments of fruit trees.

An entire corner of this charming spot was in habited by bees. Their straw hives skillfully arranged at distances on boards had their entrances—as large as the opening of a thimble—turned towards the sun, and all along the paths one encountered these humming and gilded flies, the true masters of this peaceful spot, the real promenaders of these quiet paths.

I came there almost every morning. I sat down on a bench and read. Sometimes I let my book fall on my knees, to dream, to listen to the life of Paris around me, and to enjoy the infinite repose of these old-fashioned hedges.

But I soon perceived that I was not the only one to frequent this spot as soon as the gates were opened, and I occasionally met face to face, at a turn in the path, a strange little old man.

He wore shoes with silver buckles, knee-breeches, a snuff-colored frock coat, a lace jabot, and an outlandish gray hat with wide brim and long-haired surface that might have come out of the ark.

He was thin, very thin, angular, grimacing and smiling. His bright eyes were restless beneath his eyelids which blinked continuously. He always carried in his hand a superb cane with a gold knob, which must have been for him some glorious souvenir.

This good man astonished me at first, then caused me the intensest interest. I watched him through the leafy walls, I followed him at a distance, stopping at a turn in the hedge so as not to be seen.

And one morning when he thought he was quite alone, he began to make the most remarkable motions. First he would give some little springs, then make a bow; then, with his slim legs, he would give a lively spring in the air, clapping his feet as he did so, and then turn round cleverly, skipping and frisking about in a comical manner, smiling as if he had an audience, twisting his poor little puppet-like body, bowing pathetic and ridiculous little greetings into the empty air. He was dancing.

I stood petrified with amazement, asking myself which of us was crazy, he or I.

He stopped suddenly, advanced as actors do on the stage, then bowed and retreated with gracious smiles, and kissing his hand as actors do, his trembling hand, to the two rows of trimmed bushes.

Then he continued his walk with a solemn demeanor.

After that I never lost sight of him, and each morning he began anew his outlandish exercises.

I was wildly anxious to speak to him. I decided to risk it, and one day, after greeting him, I said:

"It is a beautiful day, monsieur."

He bowed.

"Yes, sir, the weather is just as it used to be."

A week later we were friends and I knew his history. He had been a dancing master at the opera, in the time of Louis XV. His beautiful cane was a present from the Comte de Clermont. And when we spoke about dancing he never stopping talking.

One day he said to me:

"I married La Castris, monsieur. I will introduce you to her if you wish it, but she does not get here till later. This garden, you see, is our delight and our life. It is all that remains of former days. It seems as though we could not exist if we did not have it. It is old and distingue, is it not? I seem to breathe an air here that has not changed since I was young. My wife and I pass all our afternoons here, but I come in the morning because I get up early."

As soon as I had finished luncheon I returned to the Luxembourg, and presently perceived my friend offering his arm ceremoniously to a very old little lady dressed in black, to whom he introduced me. It was La Castris, the great dancer, beloved by princes, beloved by the king, beloved by all that century of gallantry that seems to have left behind it in the world an atmosphere of love.

We sat down on a bench. It was the month of May. An odor of flowers floated in the neat paths; a hot sun glided its rays between the branches and covered us with patches of light. The black dress of La Castris seemed to be saturated with sunlight.

The garden was empty. We heard the rattling of vehicles in the distance.

"Tell me," I said to the old dancer, "what was the minuet?"

He gave a start.

"The minuet, monsieur, is the queen of dances, and the dance of queens, do you understand? Since there is no longer any royalty, there is no longer any minuet."

And he began in a pompous manner a long dithyrambic eulogy which I could not understand. I wanted to have the steps, the movements, the positions, explained to me. He became confused, was amazed at his inability to make me understand, became nervous and worried.

Then suddenly, turning to his old companion who had remained silent and serious, he said:

"Elise, would you like—say—would you like, it would be very nice of you, would you like to show this gentleman what it was?"

She turned eyes uneasily in all directions, then rose without saying a word and took her position opposite him.

Then I witnessed an unheard-of thing.

They advanced and retreated with childlike grimaces, smiling, swinging each other, bowing, skipping about like two automaton dolls moved by some old mechanical contrivance, somewhat damaged, but made by a clever workman according to the fashion of his time.

And I looked at them, my heart filled with extraordinary emotions, my soul touched with an indescribable melancholy. I seemed to see before me a pathetic and comical apparition, the out-of-date ghost of a former century.

They suddenly stopped. They had finished all the figures of the dance. For some seconds they stood opposite each other, smiling in an astonishing manner. Then they fell on each other's necks sobbing.

I left for the provinces three days later. I never saw them again. When I returned to Paris, two years later, the nursery had been destroyed. What became of them, deprived of the dear garden of former days, with its mazes, its odor of the past, and the graceful windings of its hedges?

Are they dead? Are they wandering among modern streets like hopeless exiles? Are they dancing—grotesque spectres—a fantastic minuet in the moonlight, amid the cypresses of a cemetery, along the pathways bordered by graves?

Their memory haunts me, obsesses me, torments me, remains with me like a wound. Why? I do not know.

No doubt you think that very absurd?

THE SON

The two old friends were walking in the garden in bloom, where spring was bringing everything to life.

One was a senator, the other a member of the French Academy, both serious men, full of very logical but solemn arguments, men of note and reputation.

They talked first of politics, exchanging opinions; not on ideas, but on men, personalities in this regard taking the predominance over ability. Then they recalled some memories. Then they walked along in silence, enervated by the warmth of the air.

A large bed of wallflowers breathed out a delicate sweetness. A mass of flowers of all species and color flung their fragrance to the breeze, while a cytisus covered with yellow clusters scattered its fine pollen abroad, a golden cloud, with an odor of honey that bore its balmy seed across space, similar to the sachet-powders of perfumers.

The senator stopped, breathed in the cloud of floating pollen, looked at the fertile shrub, yellow as the sun, whose seed was floating in the air, and said:

"When one considers that these imperceptible fragrant atoms will create existences at a hundred leagues from here, will send a thrill through the fibres and sap of female trees and produce beings with roots, growing from a germ, just as we do, mortal like ourselves, and who will be replaced by other beings of the same order, like ourselves again!"

And, standing in front of the brilliant cytisus, whose live pollen was shaken off by each breath of air, the senator added:

"Ah, old fellow, if you had to keep count of all your children you would be mightily embarrassed. Here is one who generates freely, and then lets them go without a pang and troubles himself no more about them."

"We do the same, my friend," said the academician.

"Yes, I do not deny it; we let them go sometimes," resumed the senator, "but we are aware that we do, and that constitutes our superiority."

"No, that is not what I mean," said the other, shaking his head. "You see, my friend, that there is scarcely a man who has not some children that he does not know, children—'father unknown'—whom he has generated almost unconsciously, just as this tree reproduces.

"If we had to keep account of our amours, we should be just as embarrassed as this cytisus which you apostrophized would be in counting up his descendants, should we not?

"From eighteen to forty years, in fact, counting in every chance cursory acquaintanceship, we may well say that we have been intimate with two or three hundred women.

"Well, then, my friend, among this number can you be sure that you have not had children by at least one of them, and that you have not in the streets, or in the bagnio, some blackguard of a son who steals from and murders decent people, i.e., ourselves; or else a daughter in some disreputable place, or, if she has the good fortune to be deserted by her mother, as cook in some family?

"Consider, also, that almost all those whom we call 'prostitutes' have one or two children of whose paternal parentage they are ignorant, generated by chance at the price of ten or twenty francs. In every business there is profit and loss. These wildings constitute the 'loss' in their profession. Who generated them? You—I—we all did, the men called 'gentlemen'! They are the consequences of our jovial little dinners, of our gay evenings, of those hours when our comfortable physical being impels us to chance liaisons.

"Thieves, marauders, all these wretches, in fact, are our children. And that is better for us than if we were their children, for those scoundrels generate also!

"I have in my mind a very horrible story that I will relate to you. It has caused me incessant remorse, and, further than that, a continual doubt, a disquieting uncertainty, that, at times, torments me frightfully.

"When I was twenty-five I undertook a walking tour through Brittany with one of my friends, now a member of the cabinet.

"After walking steadily for fifteen or twenty days and visiting the Cotes-du-Nord and part of Finistere we reached Douarnenez. From there we went without halting to the wild promontory of Raz by the bay of Les Trepaases, and passed the night in a village whose name ends in 'of.' The next morning a strange lassitude kept my friend in bed; I say bed from habit, for our couch consisted simply of two bundles of straw.

"It would never do to be ill in this place. So I made him get up, and we reached Andierne about four or five o'clock in the evening.

"The following day he felt a little better, and we set out again. But on the road he was seized with intolerable pain, and we could scarcely get as far as Pont Labbe.

"Here, at least, there was an inn. My friend went to bed, and the doctor, who had been sent for from Quimper, announced that he had a high fever, without being able to determine its nature.

"Do you know Pont Labbe? No? Well, then, it is the most Breton of all this Breton Brittany, which extends from the promontory of Raz to the Morbihan, of this land which contains the essence of the

Breton manners, legends and customs. Even to-day this corner of the country has scarcely changed. I say 'even to-day,' for I now go there every year, alas!

"An old chateau laves the walls of its towers in a great melancholy pond, melancholy and frequented by flights of wild birds. It has an outlet in a river on which boats can navigate as far as the town. In the narrow streets with their old-time houses the men wear big hats, embroidered waistcoats and four coats, one on top of the other; the inside one, as large as your hand, barely covering the shoulder-blades, and the outside one coming to just above the seat of the trousers.

"The girls, tall, handsome and fresh have their bosoms crushed in a cloth bodice which makes an armor, compresses them, not allowing one even to guess at their robust and tortured neck. They also wear a strange headdress. On their temples two bands embroidered in colors frame their face, inclosing the hair, which falls in a shower at the back of their heads, and is then turned up and gathered on top of the head under a singular cap, often woven with gold or silver thread.

"The servant at our inn was eighteen at most, with very blue eyes, a pale blue with two tiny black pupils, short teeth close together, which she showed continually when she laughed, and which seemed strong enough to grind granite.

"She did not know a word of French, speaking only Breton, as did most of her companions.

"As my friend did not improve much, and although he had no definite malady, the doctor forbade him to continue his journey yet, ordering complete rest. I spent my days with him, and the little maid would come in incessantly, bringing either my dinner or some herb tea.

"I teased her a little, which seemed to amuse her, but we did not chat, of course, as we could not understand each other.

"But one night, after I had stayed quite late with my friend and was going back to my room, I passed the girl, who was going to her room. It was just opposite my open door, and, without reflection, and more for fun than anything else, I abruptly seized her round the waist, and before she recovered from her astonishment I had thrown her down and locked her in my room. She looked at me, amazed, excited, terrified, not daring to cry out for fear of a scandal and of being probably driven out, first by her employers and then, perhaps, by her father.

"I did it as a joke at first. She defended herself bravely, and at the first chance she ran to the door, drew back the bolt and fled.

"I scarcely saw her for several days. She would not let me come near her. But when my friend was cured and we were to get out on our travels again I saw her coming into my room about midnight the night before our departure, just after I had retired.

"She threw herself into my arms and embraced me passionately, giving me all the assurances of tenderness and despair that a woman can give when she does not know a word of our language.

"A week later I had forgotten this adventure, so common and frequent when one is travelling, the inn servants being generally destined to amuse travellers in this way.

"I was thirty before I thought of it again, or returned to Pont Labbe.

"But in 1876 I revisited it by chance during a trip into Brittany, which I made in order to look up some data for a book and to become permeated with the atmosphere of the different places.

"Nothing seemed changed. The chateau still laved its gray wall in the pond outside the little town; the inn was the same, though it had been repaired, renovated and looked more modern. As I entered it I was received by two young Breton girls of eighteen, fresh and pretty, bound up in their tight cloth bodices, with their silver caps and wide embroidered bands on their ears.

"It was about six o'clock in the evening. I sat down to dinner, and as the host was assiduous in waiting on me himself, fate, no doubt, impelled me to say:

"'Did you know the former proprietors of this house? I spent about ten days here thirty years ago. I am talking old times.'

"'Those were my parents, monsieur,' he replied.

"Then I told him why we had stayed over at that time, how my comrade had been delayed by illness. He did not let me finish.

"'Oh, I recollect perfectly. I was about fifteen or sixteen. You slept in the room at the end and your friend in the one I have taken for myself, overlooking the street.'

"It was only then that the recollection of the little maid came vividly to my mind. I asked: 'Do you remember a pretty little servant who was then in your father's employ, and who had, if my memory does not deceive me, pretty eyes and fresh-looking teeth?'

"'Yes, monsieur; she died in childbirth some time after.'

"And, pointing to the courtyard where a thin, lame man was stirring up the manure, he added:

"'That is her son.'

"I began to laugh:

"'He is not handsome and does not look much like his mother. No doubt he looks like his father.'

"'That is very possible,' replied the innkeeper; 'but we never knew whose child it was. She died without telling any one, and no one here knew of her having a beau. Every one was hugely astonished when they heard she was enceinte, and no one would believe it.'

"A sort of unpleasant chill came over me, one of those painful surface wounds that affect us like the shadow of an impending sorrow. And I looked at the man in the yard. He had just drawn water for the horses and was carrying two buckets, limping as he walked, with a painful effort of his shorter leg. His clothes were ragged, he was hideously dirty, with long yellow hair, so tangled that it looked like strands of rope falling down at either side of his face.

"'He is not worth much,' continued the innkeeper; 'we have kept him for charity's sake. Perhaps he would have turned out better if he had been brought up like other folks. But what could one do, monsieur? No father, no mother, no money! My parents took pity on him, but he was not their child, you understand.'

"I said nothing.

"I slept in my old room, and all night long I thought of this frightful stableman, saying to myself: 'Supposing it is my own son? Could I have caused that girl's death and procreated this being? It was quite possible!'

"I resolved to speak to this man and to find out the exact date of his birth. A variation of two months would set my doubts at rest.

"I sent for him the next day. But he could not speak French. He looked as if he could not understand anything, being absolutely ignorant of his age, which I had inquired of him through one of the maids. He stood before me like an idiot, twirling his hat in his knotted, disgusting hands, laughing stupidly, with something of his mother's laugh in the corners of his mouth and of his eyes.

"The landlord, appearing on the scene, went to look for the birth certificate of this wretched being. He was born eight months and twenty-six days after my stay at Pont Labbe, for I recollect perfectly that we reached Lorient on the fifteenth of August. The certificate contained this description: 'Father unknown.' The mother called herself Jeanne Kerradec.

"Then my heart began to beat rapidly. I could not utter a word, for I felt as if I were choking. I looked at this animal whose long yellow hair reminded me of a straw heap, and the beggar, embarrassed by my gaze, stopped laughing, turned his head aside, and wanted to get away.

"All day long I wandered beside the little river, giving way to painful reflections. But what was the use of reflection? I could be sure of nothing. For hours and hours I weighed all the pros and cons in favor of or against the probability of my being the father, growing nervous over inexplicable suppositions, only to return incessantly to the same horrible uncertainty, then to the still more atrocious conviction that this man was my son.

"I could eat no dinner, and went to my room.

"I lay awake for a long time, and when I finally fell asleep I was haunted by horrible visions. I saw this laborer laughing in my face and calling me 'papa.' Then he changed into a dog and bit the calves of my legs, and no matter how fast I ran he still followed me, and instead of barking, talked and reviled me. Then he appeared before my colleagues at the Academy, who had assembled to decide whether I was really his father; and one of them cried out: 'There can be no doubt about it! See how he resembles him.' And, indeed, I could see that this monster looked like me. And I awoke with this idea fixed in my mind and with an insane desire to see the man again and assure myself whether or not we had similar features.

"I joined him as he was going to mass (it was Sunday) and I gave him five francs as I gazed at him anxiously. He began to laugh in an idiotic manner, took the money, and then, embarrassed afresh at my gaze, he ran off, after stammering an almost inarticulate word that, no doubt, meant 'thank you.'

"My day passed in the same distress of mind as on the previous night. I sent for the landlord, and, with the greatest caution, skill and tact, I told him that I was interested in this poor creature, so abandoned by every one and deprived of everything, and I wished to do something for him.

"But the man replied: 'Oh, do not think of it, monsieur; he is of no account; you will only cause yourself annoyance. I employ him to clean out the stable, and that is all he can do. I give him his board and let him sleep with the horses. He needs nothing more. If you have an old pair of trousers, you might give them to him, but they will be in rags in a week.'

"I did not insist, intending to think it over.

"The poor wretch came home that evening frightfully drunk, came near setting fire to the house, killed a horse by hitting it with a pickaxe, and ended up by lying down to sleep in the mud in the midst of the pouring rain, thanks to my donation.

"They begged me next day not to give him any more money. Brandy drove him crazy, and as soon as he had two sous in his pocket he would spend it in drink. The landlord added: 'Giving him money is like trying to kill him.' The man had never, never in his life had more than a few centimes, thrown to him by travellers, and he knew of no destination for this metal but the wine shop.

"I spent several hours in my room with an open book before me which I pretended to read, but in reality looking at this animal, my son! my son! trying to discover if he looked anything like me. After careful scrutiny I seemed to recognize a similarity in the lines of the forehead and the root of the nose, and I was soon convinced that there was a resemblance, concealed by the difference in garb and the man's hideous head of hair.

"I could not stay here any longer without arousing suspicion, and I went away, my heart crushed, leaving with the innkeeper some money to soften the existence of his servant.

"For six years now I have lived with this idea in my mind, this horrible uncertainty, this abominable suspicion. And each year an irresistible force takes me back to Pont Labbe. Every year I condemn myself to the torture of seeing this animal raking the manure, imagining that he resembles me, and endeavoring, always vainly, to render him some assistance. And each year I return more uncertain, more tormented, more worried.

"I tried to have him taught, but he is a hopeless idiot. I tried to make his life less hard. He is an irreclaimable drunkard, and spends in drink all the money one gives him, and knows enough to sell his new clothes in order to get brandy.

"I tried to awaken his master's sympathy, so that he should look after him, offering to pay him for doing so. The innkeeper, finally surprised, said, very wisely: 'All that you do for him, monsieur, will only help to destroy him. He must be kept like a prisoner. As soon as he has any spare time, or any comfort, he becomes wicked. If you wish to do good, there is no lack of abandoned children, but select one who will appreciate your attention.'

"What could I say?

"If I allowed the slightest suspicion of the doubts that tortured me to escape, this idiot would assuredly become cunning, in order to blackmail me, to compromise me and ruin me. He would call out 'papa,' as in my dream.

"And I said to myself that I had killed the mother and lost this atrophied creature, this larva of the stable, born and raised amid the manure, this man who, if brought up like others, would have been like others.

"And you cannot imagine what a strange, embarrassed and intolerable feeling comes over me when he stands before me and I reflect that he came from myself, that he belongs to me through the intimate bond that links father and son, that, thanks to the terrible law of heredity, he is my own self in a thousand ways, in his blood and his flesh, and that he has even the same germs of disease, the same leaven of emotions.

"I have an incessant restless, distressing longing to see him, and the sight of him causes me intense suffering, as I look down from my window and watch him for hours removing and carting the horse manure, saying to myself: 'That is my son.'

"And I sometimes feel an irresistible longing to embrace him. I have never even touched his dirty hand."

The academician was silent. His companion, a tactful man, murmured: "Yes, indeed, we ought to take a closer interest in children who have no father."

A gust of wind passing through the tree shook its yellow clusters, enveloping in a fragrant and delicate mist the two old men, who inhaled in the fragrance with deep breaths.

The senator added: "It is good to be twenty-five and even to have children like that."

THAT PIG OF A MORIN

"Here, my friend," I said to Labarbe, "you have just repeated those five words, that pig of a Morin. Why on earth do I never hear Morin's name mentioned without his being called a pig?"

Labarbe, who is a deputy, looked at me with his owl-like eyes and said: "Do you mean to say that you do not know Morin's story and you come from La Rochelle?" I was obliged to declare that I did not know Morin's story, so Labarbe rubbed his hands and began his recital.

"You knew Morin, did you not, and you remember his large linen-draper's shop on the Quai de la Rochelle?"

"Yes, perfectly."

"Well, then. You must know that in 1862 or '63 Morin went to spend a fortnight in Paris for pleasure; or for his pleasures, but under the pretext of renewing his stock, and you also know what a fortnight in Paris means to a country shopkeeper; it fires his blood. The theatre every evening, women's dresses rustling up against you and continual excitement; one goes almost mad with it. One sees nothing but dancers in tights, actresses in very low dresses, round legs, fat shoulders, all nearly within reach of one's hands, without daring, or being able, to touch them, and one scarcely tastes food. When one leaves the city one's heart is still all in a flutter and one's mind still exhilarated by a sort of longing for kisses which tickles one's lips.

"Morin was in that condition when he took his ticket for La Rochelle by the eight-forty night express. As he was walking up and down the waiting-room at the station he stopped suddenly in front of a young lady who was kissing an old one. She had her veil up, and Morin murmured with delight: 'By Jove what a pretty woman!'

"When she had said 'good-by' to the old lady she went into the waiting-room, and Morin followed her; then she went on the platform and Morin still followed her; then she got into an empty carriage, and he again followed her. There were very few travellers on the express. The engine whistled and the train started. They were alone. Morin devoured her with his eyes. She appeared to be about nineteen or twenty and was fair, tall, with a bold look. She wrapped a railway rug round her and stretched herself on the seat to sleep.

"Morin asked himself: 'I wonder who she is?' And a thousand conjectures, a thousand projects went through his head. He said to himself: 'So many adventures are told as happening on railway journeys that this may be one that is going to present itself to me. Who knows? A piece of good luck like that happens very suddenly, and perhaps I need only be a little venturesome. Was it not Danton who said: "Audacity, more audacity and always audacity"? If it was not Danton it was Mirabeau, but that does not matter. But then I have no audacity, and that is the difficulty. Oh! If one only knew, if one could only read people's minds! I will bet that every day one passes by magnificent opportunities without knowing it, though a gesture would be enough to let me know her mind.'

"Then he imagined to himself combinations which conducted him to triumph. He pictured some chivalrous deed or merely some slight service which he rendered her, a lively, gallant conversation which ended in a declaration.

"But he could find no opening, had no pretext, and he waited for some fortunate circumstance, with his heart beating and his mind topsy-turvy. The night passed and the pretty girl still slept, while Morin was meditating his own fall. The day broke and soon the first ray of sunlight appeared in the sky, a long, clear ray which shone on the face of the sleeping girl and woke her. She sat up, looked at the country, then at Morin and smiled. She smiled like a happy woman, with an engaging and bright look, and Morin trembled. Certainly that smile was intended for him; it was discreet invitation, the signal which he was waiting for. That smile meant to say: 'How stupid, what a ninny, what a dolt, what a donkey you are, to have sat there on your seat like a post all night!

"'Just look at me, am I not charming? And you have sat like that for the whole night, when you have been alone with a pretty woman, you great simpleton!'

"She was still smiling as she looked at him; she even began to laugh; and he lost his head trying to find something suitable to say, no matter what. But he could think of nothing, nothing, and then, seized with a coward's courage, he said to himself:

"'So much the worse, I will risk everything,' and suddenly, without the slightest warning, he went toward her, his arms extended, his lips protruding, and, seizing her in his arms, he kissed her.

"She sprang up immediately with a bound, crying out: 'Help! help!' and screaming with terror; and then she opened the carriage door and waved her arm out, mad with terror and trying to jump out, while Morin, who was almost distracted and feeling sure that she would throw herself out, held her by the skirt and stammered: 'Oh, madame! oh, madame!'

"The train slackened speed and then stopped. Two guards rushed up at the young woman's frantic signals. She threw herself into their arms, stammering: 'That man wanted—wanted—to—to—' And then she fainted.

"They were at Mauze station, and the gendarme on duty arrested Morin. When the victim of his indiscreet admiration had regained her consciousness, she made her charge against him, and the police drew it up. The poor linen draper did not reach home till night, with a prosecution hanging over him for an outrage to morals in a public place." II

"At that time I was editor of the Fanal des Charentes, and I used to meet Morin every day at the Cafe du Commerce, and the day after his adventure. he came to see me, as he did not know what to do. I did not hide my opinion from him, but said to him: 'You are no better than a pig. No decent man behaves like that.'

"He cried. His wife had given him a beating, and he foresaw his trade ruined, his name dragged through the mire and dishonored, his friends scandalized and taking no notice of him. In the end he excited my pity, and I sent for my colleague, Rivet, a jocular but very sensible little man, to give us his advice.

"He advised me to see the public prosecutor, who was a friend of mine, and so I sent Morin home and went to call on the magistrate. He told me that the woman who had been insulted was a young lady, Mademoiselle Henriette Bonnel, who had just received her certificate as governess in Paris and spent her holidays with her uncle and aunt, who were very respectable tradespeople in Mauze. What made Morin's case all the more serious was that the uncle had lodged a complaint, but the public official had consented to let the matter drop if this complaint were withdrawn, so we must try and get him to do this.

"I went back to Morin's and found him in bed, ill with excitement and distress. His wife, a tall raw-boned woman with a beard, was abusing him continually, and she showed me into the room, shouting at me: 'So you have come to see that pig of a Morin. Well, there he is, the darling!' And she planted herself in front of the bed, with her hands on her hips. I told him how matters stood, and he begged me to go and see the girl's uncle and aunt. It was a delicate mission, but I undertook it, and the poor devil never ceased repeating: 'I assure you I did not even kiss her; no, not even that. I will take my oath to it!'

"I replied: 'It is all the same; you are nothing but a pig.' And I took a thousand francs which he gave me to employ as I thought best, but as I did not care to venture to her uncle's house alone, I begged Rivet to go with me, which he agreed to do on condition that we went immediately, for he had some urgent business at La Rochelle that afternoon. So two hours later we rang at the door of a pretty country house. An attractive girl came and opened the door to us assuredly the young lady in question, and I said to Rivet in a low voice: 'Confound it! I begin to understand Morin!'

"The uncle, Monsieur Tonnelet, subscribed to the Fanal, and was a fervent political coreligionist of ours. He received us with open arms and congratulated us and wished us joy; he was delighted at having the two editors in his house, and Rivet whispered to me: 'I think we shall be able to arrange the matter of that pig of a Morin for him.'

"The niece had left the room and I introduced the delicate subject. I waved the spectre of scandal before his eyes; I accentuated the inevitable depreciation which the young lady would suffer if such an affair became known, for nobody would believe in a simple kiss, and the good man seemed undecided, but he could not make up his mind about anything without his wife, who would not be in until late that evening. But suddenly he uttered an exclamation of triumph: 'Look here, I have an excellent idea; I will keep you here to dine and sleep, and when my wife comes home I hope we shall be able to arrange matters:

"Rivet resisted at first, but the wish to extricate that pig of a Morin decided him, and we accepted the invitation, and the uncle got up radiant, called his niece and proposed that we should take a stroll in his grounds, saying: 'We will leave serious matters until the morning.' Rivet and he began to talk politics, while I soon found myself lagging a little behind with 'the girl who was really charming—charming—and with the greatest precaution I began to speak to her about her adventure and try to make her my ally. She did not, however, appear the least confused, and listened to me like a person who was enjoying the whole thing very much.

"I said to her: 'Just think, mademoiselle, how unpleasant it will be for you. You will have to appear in court, to encounter malicious looks, to speak before everybody and to recount that unfortunate occurrence in the railway carriage in public. Do you not think, between ourselves, that it would have been much better for you to have put that dirty scoundrel back in his place without calling for assistance, and merely to change your carriage?' She began to laugh and replied: 'What you say is quite true, but what could I do? I was frightened, and when one is frightened one does not stop to reason with one's self. As soon as I realized the situation I was very sorry, that I had called out, but then it was too late. You must also remember that the idiot threw himself upon me like a madman, without saying a word and looking like a lunatic. I did not even know what he wanted of me.'

"She looked me full in the face without being nervous or intimidated and I said to myself: 'She is a queer sort of girl, that: I can quite see how that pig Morin came to make a mistake,' and I went on jokingly: 'Come, mademoiselle, confess that he was excusable, for, after all, a man cannot find himself opposite such a pretty girl as you are without feeling a natural desire to kiss her.'

"She laughed more than ever and showed her teeth and said: 'Between the desire and the act, monsieur, there is room for respect.' It was an odd expression to use, although it was not very clear, and I asked abruptly: 'Well, now, suppose I were to kiss you, what would you do?' She stopped to look at me from head to foot and then said calmly: 'Oh, you? That is quite another matter.'

"I knew perfectly well, by Jove, that it was not the same thing at all, as everybody in the neighborhood called me 'Handsome Labarbe'—I was thirty years old in those days—but I asked her: 'And why, pray?' She shrugged her shoulders and replied: 'Well! because you are not so stupid as he is.' And then she added, looking at me slyly: 'Nor so ugly, either: And before she could make a movement to avoid me I had implanted a hearty kiss on her cheek. She sprang aside, but it was too late, and then she said: 'Well, you are not very bashful, either! But don't do that sort of thing again.'

"I put on a humble look and said in a low voice: 'Oh, mademoiselle! as for me, if I long for one thing more than another it is to be summoned before a magistrate for the same reason as Morin.'

"'Why?' she asked. And, looking steadily at her, I replied: 'Because you are one of the most beautiful creatures living; because it would be an honor and a glory for me to have wished to offer you violence, and because people would have said, after seeing you: "Well, Labarbe has richly deserved what he has got, but he is a lucky fellow, all the same."'

"She began to laugh heartily again and said: 'How funny you are!' And she had not finished the word 'funny' before I had her in my arms and was kissing her ardently wherever I could find a place, on her forehead, on her eyes, on her lips occasionally, on her cheeks, all over her head, some part of which she was obliged to leave exposed, in spite of herself, to defend the others; but at last she managed to release herself, blushing and angry. 'You are very unmannerly, monsieur,' she said, 'and I am sorry I listened to you.'

"I took her hand in some confusion and stammered out: 'I beg your pardon. I beg your pardon, mademoiselle. I have offended you; I have acted like a brute! Do not be angry with me for what I have done. If you knew—' I vainly sought for some excuse, and in a few moments she said: 'There is nothing for me to know, monsieur.' But I had found something to say, and I cried: 'Mademoiselle, I love you!'

"She was really surprised and raised her eyes to look at me, and I went on: 'Yes, mademoiselle, and pray listen to me. I do not know Morin, and I do not care anything about him. It does not matter to me the least if he is committed for trial and locked up meanwhile. I saw you here last year, and I was so taken with you that the thought of you has never left me since, and it does not matter to me whether you believe me or not. I thought you adorable, and the remembrance of you took such a hold on me that I longed to see you again, and so I made use of that fool Morin as a pretext, and here I am. Circumstances have made me exceed the due limits of respect, and I can only beg you to pardon me.'

"She looked at me to see if I was in earnest and was ready to smile again. Then she murmured: 'You humbug!' But I raised my hand and said in a sincere voice (and I really believe that I was sincere): 'I swear to you that I am speaking the truth,' and she replied quite simply: 'Don't talk nonsense!'

"We were alone, quite alone, as Rivet and her uncle had disappeared down a sidewalk, and I made her a real declaration of love, while I squeezed and kissed her hands, and she listened to it as to something new and agreeable, without exactly knowing how much of it she was to believe, while in the end I felt agitated, and at last really myself believed what I said. I was pale, anxious and trembling, and I gently put my arm round her waist and spoke to her softly, whispering into the little curls over her ears. She seemed in a trance, so absorbed in thought was she.

"Then her hand touched mine, and she pressed it, and I gently squeezed her waist with a trembling, and gradually firmer, grasp. She did not move now, and I touched her cheek with my lips, and suddenly without seeking them my lips met hers. It was a long, long kiss, and it would have lasted longer still if I had not heard a hm! hm! just behind me, at which she made her escape through the bushes, and turning round I saw Rivet coming toward me, and, standing in the middle of the path, he said without even smiling: 'So that is the way you settle the affair of that pig of a Morin.' And I replied conceitedly: 'One does what one can, my dear fellow. But what about the uncle? How have you got on with him? I will answer for the niece.' 'I have not been so fortunate with him,' he replied.

"Whereupon I took his arm and we went indoors." III

"Dinner made me lose my head altogether. I sat beside her, and my hand continually met hers under the tablecloth, my foot touched hers and our glances met.

"After dinner we took a walk by moonlight, and I whispered all the tender things I could think of to her. I held her close to me, kissed her every moment, while her uncle and Rivet were arguing as they walked in front of us. They went in, and soon a messenger brought a telegram from her aunt, saying that she would not return until the next morning at seven o'clock by the first train.

"'Very well, Henriette,' her uncle said, 'go and show the gentlemen their rooms.' She showed Rivet his first, and he whispered to me: 'There was no danger of her taking us into yours first.' Then she took me to my room, and as soon as she was alone with me I took her in my arms again and tried to arouse her emotion, but when she saw the danger she escaped out of the room, and I retired very much put out and excited and feeling rather foolish, for I knew that I should not sleep much, and I was wondering how I could have committed such a mistake, when there was a gentle knock at my door, and on my asking who was there a low voice replied: 'I'

"I dressed myself quickly and opened the door, and she came in. 'I forgot to ask you what you take in the morning,' she said; 'chocolate, tea or coffee?' I put my arms round her impetuously and said, devouring her with kisses: 'I will take—I will take—'

"But she freed herself from my arms, blew out my candle and disappeared and left me alone in the dark, furious, trying to find some matches, and not able to do so. At last I got some and I went into the passage, feeling half mad, with my candlestick in my hand.

"What was I about to do? I did not stop to reason, I only wanted to find her, and I would. I went a few steps without reflecting, but then I suddenly thought: 'Suppose I should walk into the uncle's room what should I say?' And I stood still, with my head a void and my heart beating. But in a few moments I thought of an answer: 'Of course, I shall say that I was looking for Rivet's room to speak to him about an important matter,' and I began to inspect all the doors, trying to find hers, and at last I took hold of a handle at a venture, turned it and went in. There was Henriette, sitting on her bed and looking at me in tears. So I gently turned the key, and going up to her on tiptoe I said: 'I forgot to ask you for something to read, mademoiselle.'

"I was stealthily returning to my room when a rough hand seized me and a voice—it was Rivet's—whispered in my ear: 'So you have not yet quite settled that affair of Morin's?'

"At seven o'clock the next morning Henriette herself brought me a cup of chocolate. I never have drunk anything like it, soft, velvety, perfumed, delicious. I could hardly take away my lips from the cup, and she had hardly left the room when Rivet came in. He seemed nervous and irritable, like a man who had not slept, and he said to me crossly:

"'If you go on like this you will end by spoiling the affair of that pig of a Morin!'

"At eight o'clock the aunt arrived. Our discussion was very short, for they withdrew their complaint, and I left five hundred francs for the poor of the town. They wanted to keep us for the day, and they arranged an excursion to go and see some ruins. Henriette made signs to me to stay, behind her parents' back, and I accepted, but Rivet was determined to go, and though I took him aside and begged and prayed him to do this for me, he appeared quite exasperated and kept saying to me: 'I have had enough of that pig of a Morin's affair, do you hear?'

"Of course I was obliged to leave also, and it was one of the hardest moments of my life. I could have gone on arranging that business as long as I lived, and when we were in the railway carriage, after shaking hands with her in silence, I said to Rivet: 'You are a mere brute!' And he replied: 'My dear fellow, you were beginning to annoy me confoundedly.'

"On getting to the Fanal office, I saw a crowd waiting for us, and as soon as they saw us they all exclaimed: 'Well, have you settled the affair of that pig of a Morin?' All La Rochelle was excited about it, and Rivet, who had got over his ill-humor on the journey, had great difficulty in keeping himself from laughing as he said: 'Yes, we have managed it, thanks to Labarbe: And we went to Morin's.

"He was sitting in an easy-chair with mustard plasters on his legs and cold bandages on his head, nearly dead with misery. He was coughing with the short cough of a dying man, without any one knowing how he had caught it, and his wife looked at him like a tigress ready to eat him, and as soon as he saw us he trembled so violently as to make his hands and knees shake, so I said to him immediately: 'It is all settled, you dirty scamp, but don't do such a thing again.'

"He got up, choking, took my hands and kissed them as if they had belonged to a prince, cried, nearly fainted, embraced Rivet and even kissed Madame Morin, who gave him such a push as to send him staggering back into his chair; but he never got over the blow; his mind had been too much upset. In all the country round, moreover, he was called nothing but 'that pig of a Morin,' and that epithet went through him like a sword-thrust every time he heard it. When a street boy called after him 'Pig!' he turned his head instinctively. His friends also overwhelmed him with horrible jokes and used to ask him, whenever they were eating ham, 'Is it a bit of yourself?' He died two years later.

"As for myself, when I was a candidate for the Chamber of Deputies in 1875, I called on the new notary at Fousserre, Monsieur Belloncle, to solicit his vote, and a tall, handsome and evidently wealthy lady received me. 'You do not know me again?' she said. And I stammered out: 'Why—no—madame.' 'Henriette Bonnel.' 'Ah!' And I felt myself turning pale, while she seemed perfectly at her ease and looked at me with a smile.

"As soon as she had left me alone with her husband he took both my hands, and, squeezing them as if he meant to crush them, he said: 'I have been intending to go and see you for a long time, my dear sir, for my wife has very often talked to me about you. I know—yes, I know under what painful circumstances you made her acquaintance, and I know also how perfectly you behaved, how full of delicacy, tact and devotion you showed yourself in the affair—' He hesitated and then said in a lower tone, as if he had been saying something low and coarse, 'in the affair of that pig of a Morin.'"

SAINT ANTHONY

They called him Saint Anthony, because his name was Anthony, and also, perhaps, because he was a good fellow, jovial, a lover of practical jokes, a tremendous eater and a heavy drinker and a gay fellow, although he was sixty years old.

He was a big peasant of the district of Caux, with a red face, large chest and stomach, and perched on two legs that seemed too slight for the bulk of his body.

He was a widower and lived alone with his two men servants and a maid on his farm, which he conducted with shrewd economy. He was careful of his own interests, understood business and the raising of cattle, and farming. His two sons and his three daughters, who had married well, were living in the neighborhood and came to dine with their father once a month. His vigor of body was famous in all the countryside. "He is as strong as Saint Anthony," had become a kind of proverb.

At the time of the Prussian invasion Saint Anthony, at the wine shop, promised to eat an army, for he was a braggart, like a true Norman, a bit of a, coward and a blusterer. He banged his fist on the wooden table, making the cups and the brandy glasses dance, and cried with the assumed wrath of a good fellow, with a flushed face and a sly look in his eye: "I shall have to eat some of them, nom de Dieu!" He reckoned that the Prussians would not come as far as Tanneville, but when he heard they were at Rautot he never went out of the house, and constantly watched the road from the little window of his kitchen, expecting at any moment to see the bayonets go by.

One morning as he was eating his luncheon with the servants the door opened and the mayor of the commune, Maitre Chicot, appeared, followed by a soldier wearing a black copper-pointed helmet. Saint Anthony bounded to his feet and his servants all looked at him, expecting to see him slash the Prussian. But he merely shook hands with the mayor, who said:

"Here is one for you, Saint Anthony. They came last night. Don't do anything foolish, above all things, for they talked of shooting and burning everything if there is the slightest unpleasantness, I have given you warning. Give him something to eat; he looks like a good fellow. Good-day. I am going to call on the rest. There are enough for all." And he went out.

Father Anthony, who had turned pale, looked at the Prussian. He was a big, young fellow with plump, white skin, blue eyes, fair hair, unshaven to his cheek bones, who looked stupid, timid and good. The shrewd Norman read him at once, and, reassured, he made him a sign to sit down. Then he said: "Will you take some soup?"

The stranger did not understand. Anthony then became bolder, and pushing a plateful of soup right under his nose, he said: "Here, swallow that, big pig!"

The soldier answered "Ya," and began to eat greedily, while the farmer, triumphant, feeling he had regained his reputation, winked his eye at the servants, who were making strange grimaces, what with their terror and their desire to laugh.

When the Prussian had devoured his soup, Saint Anthony gave him another plateful, which disappeared in like manner; but he flinched at the third which the farmer tried to insist on his eating, saying: "Come, put that into your stomach; 'twill fatten you or it is your own fault, eh, pig!"

The soldier, understanding only that they wanted to make him eat all his soup, laughed in a contented manner, making a sign to show that he could not hold any more.

Then Saint Anthony, become quite familiar, tapped him on the stomach, saying: "My, there is plenty in my pig's belly!" But suddenly he began to writhe with laughter, unable to speak. An idea had struck him which made him choke with mirth. "That's it, that's it, Saint Anthony and his pig. There's my pig!" And the three servants burst out laughing in their turn.

The old fellow was so pleased that he had the brandy brought in, good stuff, 'fil en dix', and treated every one. They clinked glasses with the Prussian, who clacked his tongue by way of flattery to show that he enjoyed it. And Saint Anthony exclaimed in his face: "Eh, is not that superfine? You don't get anything like that in your home, pig!"

From that time Father Anthony never went out without his Prussian. He had got what he wanted. This was his vengeance, the vengeance of an old rogue. And the whole countryside, which was in terror, laughed to split its sides at Saint Anthony's joke. Truly, there was no one like him when it came to humor. No one but he would have thought of a thing like that. He was a born joker!

He went to see his neighbors every day, arm in arm with his German, whom he introduced in a jovial manner, tapping him on the shoulder: "See, here is my pig; look and see if he is not growing fat, the animal!"

And the peasants would beam with smiles. "He is so comical, that reckless fellow, Antoine!"

"I will sell him to you, Cesaire, for three pistoles" (thirty francs).

"I will take him, Antoine, and I invite you to eat some black pudding."

"What I want is his feet."

"Feel his belly; you will see that it is all fat."

And they all winked at each other, but dared not laugh too loud, for fear the Prussian might finally suspect they were laughing at him. Anthony, alone growing bolder every day, pinched his thighs, exclaiming, "Nothing but fat"; tapped him on the back, shouting, "That is all bacon"; lifted him up in his arms as an old Colossus that could have lifted an anvil, declaring, "He weighs six hundred and no waste."

He had got into the habit of making people offer his "pig" something to eat wherever they went together. This was the chief pleasure, the great diversion every day. "Give him whatever you please, he will swallow everything." And they offered the man bread and butter, potatoes, cold meat, chitterlings, which caused the remark, "Some of your own, and choice ones."

The soldier, stupid and gentle, ate from politeness, charmed at these attentions, making himself ill rather than refuse, and he was actually growing fat and his uniform becoming tight for him. This delighted Saint Anthony, who said: "You know, my pig, that we shall have to have another cage made for you."

They had, however, become the best friends in the world, and when the old fellow went to attend to his business in the neighborhood the Prussian accompanied him for the simple pleasure of being with him.

The weather was severe; it was freezing hard. The terrible winter of 1870 seemed to bring all the scourges on France at one time.

Father Antoine, who made provision beforehand, and took advantage of every opportunity, foreseeing that manure would be scarce for the spring farming, bought from a neighbor who happened to be in need of money all that he had, and it was agreed that he should go every evening with his cart to get a load.

So every day at twilight he set out for the farm of Haules, half a league distant, always accompanied by his "pig." And each time it was a festival, feeding the animal. All the neighbors ran over there as they would go to high mass on Sunday.

But the soldier began to suspect something, be mistrustful, and when they laughed too loud he would roll his eyes uneasily, and sometimes they lighted up with anger.

One evening when he had eaten his fill he refused to swallow another morsel, and attempted to rise to leave the table. But Saint Anthony stopped him by a turn of the wrist and, placing his two powerful hands on his shoulders, he sat him down again so roughly that the chair smashed under him.

A wild burst of laughter broke forth, and Anthony, beaming, picked up his pig, acted as though he were dressing his wounds, and exclaimed: "Since you will not eat, you shall drink, nom de Dieu!" And they went to the wine shop to get some brandy.

The soldier rolled his eyes, which had a wicked expression, but he drank, nevertheless; he drank as long as they wanted him, and Saint Anthony held his head to the great delight of his companions.

The Norman, red as a tomato, his eyes ablaze, filled up the glasses and clinked, saying: "Here's to you!". And the Prussian, without speaking a word, poured down one after another glassfuls of cognac.

It was a contest, a battle, a revenge! Who would drink the most, nom d'un nom! They could neither of them stand any more when the liter was emptied. But neither was conquered. They were tied, that was all. They would have to begin again the next day.

They went out staggering and started for home, walking beside the dung cart which was drawn along slowly by two horses.

Snow began to fall and the moonless night was sadly lighted by this dead whiteness on the plain. The men began to feel the cold, and this aggravated their intoxication. Saint Anthony, annoyed at not being the victor, amused himself by shoving his companion so as to make him fall over into the ditch. The other would dodge backwards, and each time he did he uttered some German expression in an angry tone, which made the peasant roar with laughter. Finally the Prussian lost his temper, and just as Anthony was rolling towards him he responded with such a terrific blow with his fist that the Colossus staggered.

Then, excited by the brandy, the old man seized the pugilist round the waist, shook him for a few moments as he would have done with a little child, and pitched him at random to the other side of the road. Then, satisfied with this piece of work, he crossed his arms and began to laugh afresh.

But the soldier picked himself up in a hurry, his head bare, his helmet having rolled off, and drawing his sword he rushed over to Father Anthony.

When he saw him coming the peasant seized his whip by the top of the handle, his big holly wood whip, straight, strong and supple as the sinew of an ox.

The Prussian approached, his head down, making a lunge with his sword, sure of killing his adversary. But the old fellow, squarely hitting the blade, the point of which would have pierced his stomach, turned it aside, and with the butt end of the whip struck the soldier a sharp blow on the temple and he fell to the ground.

Then he, gazed aghast, stupefied with amazement, at the body, twitching convulsively at first and then lying prone and motionless. He bent over it, turned it on its back, and gazed at it for some time. The man's eyes were closed, and blood trickled from a wound at the side of his forehead. Although it was dark, Father Anthony could distinguish the bloodstain on the white snow.

He remained there, at his wit's end, while his cart continued slowly on its way.

What was he to do? He would be shot! They would burn his farm, ruin his district! What should he do? What should he do? How could he hide the body, conceal the fact of his death, deceive the Prussians? He heard voices in the distance, amid the utter stillness of the snow. All at once he roused himself, and picking up the helmet he placed it on his victim's head. Then, seizing him round the body, he lifted him up in his arms, and thus running with him, he overtook his team, and threw the body on top of the manure. Once in his own house he would think up some plan.

He walked slowly, racking his brain, but without result. He saw, he felt, that he was lost. He entered his courtyard. A light was shining in one of the attic windows; his maid was not asleep. He hastily backed his wagon to the edge of the manure hollow. He thought that by overturning the manure the body lying on top of it would fall into the ditch and be buried beneath it, and he dumped the cart.

As he had foreseen, the man was buried beneath the manure. Anthony evened it down with his fork, which he stuck in the ground beside it. He called his stableman, told him to put up the horses, and went to his room.

He went to bed, still thinking of what he had best do, but no ideas came to him. His apprehension increased in the quiet of his room. They would shoot him! He was bathed in perspiration from fear, his teeth chattered, he rose shivering, not being able to stay in bed.

He went downstairs to the kitchen, took the bottle of brandy from the sideboard and carried it upstairs. He drank two large glasses, one after another, adding a fresh intoxication to the late one, without quieting his mental anguish. He had done a pretty stroke of work, nom de Dieu, idiot!

He paced up and down, trying to think of some stratagem, some explanations, some cunning trick, and from time to time he rinsed his mouth with a swallow of "fil en dix" to give him courage.

But no ideas came to him, not one.

Towards midnight his watch dog, a kind of cross wolf called "Devorant," began to howl frantically. Father Anthony shuddered to the marrow of his bones, and each time the beast began his long and lugubrious wail the old man's skin turned to goose flesh.

He had sunk into a chair, his legs weak, stupefied, done up, waiting anxiously for "Devorant" to set up another howl, and starting convulsively from nervousness caused by terror.

The clock downstairs struck five. The dog was still howling. The peasant was almost insane. He rose to go and let the dog loose, so that he should not hear him. He went downstairs, opened the hall door, and stepped out into the darkness. The snow was still falling. The earth was all white, the farm buildings standing out like black patches. He approached the kennel. The dog was dragging at his chain. He unfastened it. "Devorant" gave a bound, then stopped short, his hair bristling, his legs rigid, his muzzle in the air, his nose pointed towards the manure heap.

Saint Anthony, trembling from head to foot, faltered:

"What's the matter with you, you dirty hound?" and he walked a few steps forward, gazing at the indistinct outlines, the sombre shadow of the courtyard.

Then he saw a form, the form of a man sitting on the manure heap!

He gazed at it, paralyzed by fear, and breathing hard. But all at once he saw, close by, the handle of the manure fork which was sticking in the ground. He snatched it up and in one of those transports of fear that will make the greatest coward brave he rushed forward to see what it was.

It was he, his Prussian, come to life, covered with filth from his bed of manure which had kept him warm. He had sat down mechanically, and remained there in the snow which sprinkled down, all covered with dirt and blood as he was, and still stupid from drinking, dazed by the blow and exhausted from his wound.

He perceived Anthony, and too sodden to understand anything, he made an attempt to rise. But the moment the old man recognized him, he foamed with rage like a wild animal.

"Ah, pig! pig!" he sputtered. "You are not dead! You are going to denounce me now—wait—wait!"

And rushing on the German with all the strength of leis arms he flung the raised fork like a lance and buried the four prongs full length in his breast.

The soldier fell over on his back, uttering a long death moan, while the old peasant, drawing the fork out of his breast, plunged it over and over again into his abdomen, his stomach, his throat, like a madman, piercing the body from head to foot, as it still quivered, and the blood gushed out in streams.

Finally he stopped, exhausted by his arduous work, swallowing great mouthfuls of air, calmed down at the completion of the murder.

As the cocks were beginning to crow in the poultry yard and it was near daybreak, he set to work to bury the man.

He dug a hole in the manure till he reached the earth, dug down further, working wildly, in a frenzy of strength with frantic motions of his arms and body.

When the pit was deep enough he rolled the corpse into it with the fork, covered it with earth, which he stamped down for some time, and then put back the manure, and he smiled as he saw the thick snow finishing his work and covering up its traces with a white sheet.

He then stuck the fork in the manure and went into the house. His bottle, still half full of brandy stood on the table. He emptied it at a draught, threw himself on his bed and slept heavily.

He woke up sober, his mind calm and clear, capable of judgment and thought.

At the end of an hour he was going about the country making inquiries everywhere for his soldier. He went to see the Prussian officer to find out why they had taken away his man.

As everyone knew what good friends they were, no one suspected him. He even directed the research, declaring that the Prussian went to see the girls every evening.

An old retired gendarme who had an inn in the next village, and a pretty daughter, was arrested and shot.

LASTING LOVE

It was the end of the dinner that opened the shooting season. The Marquis de Bertrans with his guests sat around a brightly lighted table, covered with fruit and flowers. The conversation drifted to love. Immediately there arose an animated discussion, the same eternal discussion as to whether it were possible to love more than once. Examples were given of persons who had loved once; these were offset by those who had loved violently many times. The men agreed that passion, like sickness, may attack the same person several times, unless it strikes to kill. This conclusion seemed quite incontestable. The women, however, who based their opinion on poetry rather than on practical observation, maintained that love, the great passion, may come only once to mortals. It resembles lightning, they said, this love. A heart once touched by it becomes forever such a waste, so ruined, so consumed, that no other strong sentiment can take root there, not even a dream. The marquis, who had indulged in many love affairs, disputed this belief.

"I tell you it is possible to love several times with all one's heart and soul. You quote examples of persons who have killed themselves for love, to prove the impossibility of a second passion. I wager that if they had not foolishly committed suicide, and so destroyed the possibility of a second experience, they would have found a new love, and still another, and so on till death. It is with love as with drink. He who has once indulged is forever a slave. It is a thing of temperament."

They chose the old doctor as umpire. He thought it was as the marquis had said, a thing of temperament.

"As for me," he said, "I once knew of a love which lasted fifty-five years without one day's respite, and which ended only with death." The wife of the marquis clasped her hands.

"That is beautiful! Ah, what a dream to be loved in such a way! What bliss to live for fifty-five years enveloped in an intense, unwavering affection! How this happy being must have blessed his life to be so adored!"

The doctor smiled.

"You are not mistaken, madame, on this point the loved one was a man. You even know him; it is Monsieur Chouquet, the chemist. As to the woman, you also know her, the old chair-mender, who came every year to the chateau." The enthusiasm of the women fell. Some expressed their contempt with "Pouah!" for the loves of common people did not interest them. The doctor continued: "Three months ago I was called to the deathbed of the old chair-mender. The priest had preceded me. She wished to make us the executors of her will. In order that we might understand her conduct, she told us the story of her life. It is most singular and touching: Her father and mother were both chair-menders. She had never lived in a house. As a little child she wandered about with them, dirty, unkempt, hungry. They visited many towns, leaving their horse, wagon and dog just outside the limits, where the child played in the grass alone until her parents had repaired all the broken chairs in the place. They seldom spoke, except to cry, 'Chairs! Chairs! Chair-mender!'

"When the little one strayed too far away, she would be called back by the harsh, angry voice of her father. She never heard a word of affection. When she grew older, she fetched and carried the broken chairs. Then it was she made friends with the children in the street, but their parents always called them away and scolded them for speaking to the barefooted child. Often the boys threw stones at her. Once a kind woman gave her a few pennies. She saved them most carefully.

"One day—she was then eleven years old—as she was walking through a country town she met, behind the cemetery, little Chouquet, weeping bitterly, because one of his playmates had stolen two precious liards (mills). The tears of the small bourgeois, one of those much-envied mortals, who, she imagined, never knew trouble, completely upset her. She approached him and, as soon as she learned the cause of his grief, she put into his hands all her savings. He took them without hesitation and dried his eyes. Wild with joy, she kissed him. He was busy counting his money, and did not object. Seeing that she was not repulsed, she threw her arms round him and gave him a hug—then she ran away.

"What was going on in her poor little head? Was it because she had sacrificed all her fortune that she became madly fond of this youngster, or was it because she had given him the first tender kiss? The mystery is alike for children and for those of riper years. For months she dreamed of that corner near the cemetery and of the little chap. She stole a sou here and, there from her parents on the chair money or groceries she was sent to buy. When she returned to the spot near the cemetery she had two francs in her pocket, but he was not there. Passing his father's drug store, she caught sight of him behind the counter. He was sitting between a large red globe and a blue one. She only loved him the more, quite carried away at the sight of the brilliant-colored globes. She cherished the recollection of it forever in her heart. The following year she met him near the school playing marbles. She rushed up to him, threw her arms round him, and kissed him so passionately that he screamed, in fear. To quiet him, she gave him all her money. Three francs and twenty centimes! A real gold mine, at which he gazed with staring eyes.

"After this he allowed her to kiss him as much as she wished. During the next four years she put into his hands all her savings, which he pocketed conscientiously in exchange for kisses. At one time it was thirty sons, at another two francs. Again, she only had twelve sous. She wept with grief and shame, explaining brokenly that it had been a poor year. The next time she brought five francs, in one whole piece, which made her laugh with joy. She no longer thought of any one but the boy, and he watched for her with impatience; sometimes he would run to meet her. This made her heart thump with joy. Suddenly he disappeared. He had gone to boarding school. She found this out by careful investigation. Then she used great diplomacy to persuade her parents to change their route and pass by this way again during vacation. After a year of scheming she succeeded. She had not seen him for two years, and scarcely recognized him, he was so changed, had grown taller, better looking and was imposing in his uniform, with its brass buttons. He pretended not to see her, and passed by without a glance. She wept for two days and from that time loved and suffered unceasingly.

"Every year he came home and she passed him, not daring to lift her eyes. He never condescended to turn his head toward her. She loved him madly, hopelessly. She said to me:

"'He is the only man whom I have ever seen. I don't even know if another exists.' Her parents died. She continued their work.

"One day, on entering the village, where her heart always remained, she saw Chouquet coming out of his pharmacy with a young lady leaning on his arm. She was his wife. That night the chair-mender threw herself into the river. A drunkard passing the spot pulled her out and took her to the drug store. Young Chouquet came down in his dressing gown to revive her. Without seeming to know who she was he undressed her and rubbed her; then he said to her, in a harsh voice:

"'You are mad! People must not do stupid things like that.' His voice brought her to life again. He had spoken to her! She was happy for a long time. He refused remuneration for his trouble, although she insisted.

"All her life passed in this way. She worked, thinking always of him. She began to buy medicines at his pharmacy; this gave her a chance to talk to him and to see him closely. In this way, she was still able to give him money.

"As I said before, she died this spring. When she had closed her pathetic story she entreated me to take her earnings to the man she loved. She had worked only that she might leave him something to remind him of her after her death. I gave the priest fifty francs for her funeral expenses. The next morning I went to see the Chouquets. They were finishing breakfast, sitting opposite each other, fat and red, important and self-satisfied. They welcomed me and offered me some coffee, which I accepted. Then I began my story in a trembling voice, sure that they would be softened, even to tears. As soon as Chouquet understood that he had been loved by 'that vagabond! that chair-mender! that wanderer!' he swore with indignation as though his reputation had been sullied, the respect of decent people lost, his personal honor, something precious and dearer to him than life, gone. His exasperated wife kept repeating: 'That beggar! That beggar!'

"Seeming unable to find words suitable to the enormity, he stood up and began striding about. He muttered: 'Can you understand anything so horrible, doctor? Oh, if I had only known it while she was alive, I should have had her thrown into prison. I promise you she would not have escaped.'

"I was dumfounded; I hardly knew what to think or say, but I had to finish my mission. 'She commissioned me,' I said, 'to give you her savings, which amount to three thousand five hundred francs. As what I have just told you seems to be very disagreeable, perhaps you would prefer to give this money to the poor.'

"They looked at me, that man and woman,' speechless with amazement. I took the few thousand francs from out of my pocket. Wretched-looking money from every country. Pennies and gold pieces all mixed together. Then I asked:

"'What is your decision?'

"Madame Chouquet spoke first. 'Well, since it is the dying woman's wish, it seems to me impossible to refuse it.'

"Her husband said, in a shamefaced manner: 'We could buy something for our children with it.'

"I answered dryly: 'As you wish.'

"He replied: 'Well, give it to us anyhow, since she commissioned you to do so; we will find a way to put it to some good purpose.'

"I gave them the money, bowed and left.

"The next day Chouquet came to me and said brusquely:

"'That woman left her wagon here—what have you done with it?'

"'Nothing; take it if you wish.'

"'It's just what I wanted,' he added, and walked off. I called him back and said:

"'She also left her old horse and two dogs. Don't you need them?'

"He stared at me surprised: 'Well, no! Really, what would I do with them?'

"'Dispose of them as you like.'

"He laughed and held out his hand to me. I shook it. What could I do? The doctor and the druggist in a country village must not be at enmity. I have kept the dogs. The priest took the old horse. The wagon is useful to Chouquet, and with the money he has bought railroad stock. That is the only deep, sincere love that I have ever known in all my life."

The doctor looked up. The marquise, whose eyes were full of tears, sighed and said:

"There is no denying the fact, only women know how to love."

PIERROT

Mme. Lefevre was a country dame, a widow, one of these half peasants, with ribbons and bonnets with trimming on them, one of those persons who clipped her words and put on great airs in public, concealing the soul of a pretentious animal beneath a comical and bedizened exterior, just as the country-folks hide their coarse red hands in ecru silk gloves.

She had a servant, a good simple peasant, called Rose.

The two women lived in a little house with green shutters by the side of the high road in Normandy, in the centre of the country of Caux. As they had a narrow strip of garden in front of the house, they grew some vegetables.

One night someone stole twelve onions. As soon as Rose became aware of the theft, she ran to tell madame, who came downstairs in her woolen petticoat. It was a shame and a disgrace! They had robbed her, Mme. Lefevre! As there were thieves in the country, they might come back.

And the two frightened women examined the foot tracks, talking, and supposing all sorts of things.

"See, they went that way! They stepped on the wall, they jumped into the garden!"

And they became apprehensive for the future. How could they sleep in peace now!

The news of the theft spread. The neighbor came, making examinations and discussing the matter in their turn, while the two women explained to each newcomer what they had observed and their opinion.

A farmer who lived near said to them:

"You ought to have a dog."

That is true, they ought to have a dog, if it were only to give the alarm. Not a big dog. Heavens! what would they do with a big dog? He would eat their heads off. But a little dog (in Normandy they say "quin"), a little puppy who would bark.

As soon as everyone had left, Mme. Lefevre discussed this idea of a dog for some time. On reflection she made a thousand objections, terrified at the idea of a bowl full of soup, for she belonged to that race of parsimonious country women who always carry centimes in their pocket to give alms in public to beggars on the road and to put in the Sunday collection plate.

Rose, who loved animals, gave her opinion and defended it shrewdly. So it was decided that they should have a dog, a very small dog.

They began to look for one, but could find nothing but big dogs, who would devour enough soup to make one shudder. The grocer of Rolleville had one, a tiny one, but he demanded two francs to cover the cost of sending it. Mme. Lefevre declared that she would feed a "quin," but would not buy one.

The baker, who knew all that occurred, brought in his wagon one morning a strange little yellow animal, almost without paws, with the body of a crocodile, the head of a fox, and a curly tail—a true cockade, as big as all the rest of him. Mme. Lefevre thought this common cur that cost nothing was very handsome. Rose hugged it and asked what its name was.

"Pierrot," replied the baker.

The dog was installed in an old soap box and they gave it some water which it drank. They then offered it a piece of bread. He ate it. Mme. Lefevre, uneasy, had an idea.

"When he is thoroughly accustomed to the house we can let him run. He can find something to eat, roaming about the country."

They let him run, in fact, which did not prevent him from being famished. Also he never barked except to beg for food, and then he barked furiously.

Anyone might come into the garden, and Pierrot would run up and fawn on each one in turn and not utter a bark.

Mme. Lefevre, however, had become accustomed to the animal. She even went so far as to like it and to give it from time to time pieces of bread soaked in the gravy on her plate.

But she had not once thought of the dog tax, and when they came to collect eight francs—eight francs, madame—for this puppy who never even barked, she almost fainted from the shock.

It was immediately decided that they must get rid of Pierrot. No one wanted him. Every one declined to take him for ten leagues around. Then they resolved, not knowing what else to do, to make him "piquer du mas."

"Piquer du mas" means to eat chalk. When one wants to get rid of a dog they make him "Piquer du mas."

In the midst of an immense plain one sees a kind of hut, or rather a very small roof standing above the ground. This is the entrance to the clay pit. A big perpendicular hole is sunk for twenty metres underground and ends in a series of long subterranean tunnels.

Once a year they go down into the quarry at the time they fertilize the ground. The rest of the year it serves as a cemetery for condemned dogs, and as one passed by this hole plaintive howls, furious or despairing barks and lamentable appeals reach one's ear.

Sportsmen's dogs and sheep dogs flee in terror from this mournful place, and when one leans over it one perceives a disgusting odor of putrefaction.

Frightful dramas are enacted in the darkness.

When an animal has suffered down there for ten or twelve days, nourished on the foul remains of his predecessors, another animal, larger and more vigorous, is thrown into the hole. There they are, alone, starving, with glittering eyes. They watch each other, follow each other, hesitate in doubt. But hunger impels them; they attack each other, fight desperately for some time, and the stronger eats the weaker, devours him alive.

When it was decided to make Pierrot "piquer du mas" they looked round for an executioner. The laborer who mended the road demanded six sous to take the dog there. That seemed wildly exorbitant to Mme. Lefevre. The neighbor's hired boy wanted five sous; that was still too much. So Rose having observed that they had better carry it there themselves, as in that way it would not be brutally treated on the way and made to suspect its fate, they resolved to go together at twilight.

They offered the dog that evening a good dish of soup with a piece of butter in it. He swallowed every morsel of it, and as he wagged his tail with delight Rose put him in her apron.

They walked quickly, like thieves, across the plain. They soon perceived the chalk pit and walked up to it. Mme. Lefevre leaned over to hear if any animal was moaning. No, there were none there; Pierrot would be alone. Then Rose, who was crying, kissed the dog and threw him into the chalk pit, and they both leaned over, listening.

First they heard a dull sound, then the sharp, bitter, distracting cry of an animal in pain, then a succession of little mournful cries, then despairing appeals, the cries of a dog who is entreating, his head raised toward the opening of the pit.

He yelped, oh, how he yelped!

They were filled with remorse, with terror, with a wild inexplicable fear, and ran away from the spot. As Rose went faster Mme. Lefevre cried: "Wait for me, Rose, wait for me!"

At night they were haunted by frightful nightmares.

Mme. Lefevre dreamed she was sitting down at table to eat her soup, but when she uncovered the tureen Pierrot was in it. He jumped out and bit her nose.

She awoke and thought she heard him yelping still. She listened, but she was mistaken.

She fell asleep again and found herself on a high road, an endless road, which she followed. Suddenly in the middle of the road she perceived a basket, a large farmer's basket, lying there, and this basket frightened her.

She ended by opening it, and Pierrot, concealed in it, seized her hand and would not let go. She ran away in terror with the dog hanging to the end of her arm, which he held between his teeth.

At daybreak she arose, almost beside herself, and ran to the chalk pit.

He was yelping, yelping still; he had yelped all night. She began to sob and called him by all sorts of endearing names. He answered her with all the tender inflections of his dog's voice.

Then she wanted to see him again, promising herself that she would give him a good home till he died.

She ran to the chalk digger, whose business it was to excavate for chalk, and told him the situation. The man listened, but said nothing. When she had finished he said:

"You want your dog? That will cost four francs." She gave a jump. All her grief was at an end at once.

"Four francs!" she said. "You would die of it! Four francs!"

"Do you suppose I am going to bring my ropes, my windlass, and set it up, and go down there with my boy and let myself be bitten, perhaps, by your cursed dog for the pleasure of giving it back to you? You should not have thrown it down there."

She walked away, indignant. Four francs!

As soon as she entered the house she called Rose and told her of the quarryman's charges. Rose, always resigned, repeated:

"Four francs! That is a good deal of money, madame." Then she added: "If we could throw him something to eat, the poor dog, so he will not die of hunger."

Mme. Lefevre approved of this and was quite delighted. So they set out again with a big piece of bread and butter.

They cut it in mouthfuls, which they threw down one after the other, speaking by turns to Pierrot. As soon as the dog finished one piece he yelped for the next.

They returned that evening and the next day and every day. But they made only one trip.

One morning as they were just letting fall the first mouthful they suddenly heard a tremendous barking in the pit. There were two dogs there. Another had been thrown in, a large dog.

"Pierrot!" cried Rose. And Pierrot yelped and yelped. Then they began to throw down some food. But each time they noticed distinctly a terrible struggle going on, then plaintive cries from Pierrot, who had been bitten by his companion, who ate up everything as he was the stronger.

It was in vain that they specified, saying:

"That is for you, Pierrot." Pierrot evidently got nothing.

The two women, dumfounded, looked at each other and Mme. Lefevre said in a sour tone:

"I could not feed all the dogs they throw in there! We must give it up."

And, suffocating at the thought of all the dogs living at her expense, she went away, even carrying back what remained of the bread, which she ate as she walked along.

Rose followed her, wiping her eyes on the corner of her blue apron.

A NORMANDY JOKE

It was a wedding procession that was coming along the road between the tall trees that bounded the farms and cast their shadow on the road. At the head were the bride and groom, then the family, then the invited guests, and last of all the poor of the neighborhood. The village urchins who hovered about the narrow road like flies ran in and out of the ranks or climbed up the trees to see it better.

The bridegroom was a good-looking young fellow, Jean Patu, the richest farmer in the neighborhood, but he was above all things, an ardent sportsman who seemed to take leave of his senses in order to satisfy that passion, and who spent large sums on his dogs, his keepers, his ferrets and his guns. The bride, Rosalie Roussel, had been courted by all the likely young fellows in the district, for they all thought her handsome and they knew that she would have a good dowry. But she had chosen Patu; partly, perhaps, because she liked him better than she did the others, but still more, like a careful Normandy girl, because he had more crown pieces.

As they entered the white gateway of the husband's farm, forty shots resounded without their seeing those who fired, as they were hidden in the ditches. The noise seemed to please the men, who were slouching along heavily in their best clothes, and Patu left his wife, and running up to a farm servant whom he perceived behind a tree, took his gun and fired a shot himself, as frisky as a young colt. Then they went on, beneath the apple trees which were heavy with fruit, through the high grass and through the midst of the calves, who looked at them with their great eyes, got up slowly and remained standing, with their muzzles turned toward the wedding party.

The men became serious when they came within measurable distance of the wedding dinner. Some of them, the rich ones, had on tall, shining silk hats, which seemed altogether out of place there; others had old head-coverings with a long nap, which might have been taken for moleskin, while the humblest among them wore caps. All the women had on shawls, which they wore loosely on their back, holding the tips ceremoniously under their arms. They were red, parti-colored, flaming shawls, and their brightness seemed to astonish the black fowls on the dung-heap, the ducks on the side of the pond and the pigeons on the thatched roofs.

The extensive farm buildings seemed to be waiting there at the end of that archway of apple trees, and a sort of vapor came out of open door and windows and an almost overpowering odor of eatables was exhaled from the vast building, from all its openings and from its very walls. The string of guests extended through the yard; but when the foremost of them reached the house, they broke the chain and dispersed, while those behind were still coming in at the open gate. The ditches were now lined with urchins and curious poor people, and the firing did not cease, but came from every side at once, and a cloud of smoke, and that odor which has the same intoxicating effect as absinthe, blended with the atmosphere. The women were shaking their dresses outside the door, to get rid of the dust, were undoing their cap-strings and pulling their shawls over their arms, and then they went into the house to lay them aside altogether for the time. The table was laid in the great kitchen that would hold a hundred persons; they sat down to dinner at two o'clock; and at eight o'clock they were still eating, and the men, in their shirt-sleeves, with their waistcoats unbuttoned and with red faces, were swallowing down the food and drink as if they had been whirlpools. The cider sparkled merrily, clear and golden in the large glasses, by the side of the dark, blood-colored wine, and between every dish they made a "hole," the Normandy hole, with a glass of brandy which inflamed the body and put foolish notions into the head. Low jokes were exchanged across the table until the whole arsenal of peasant wit was exhausted. For the last hundred years the same broad stories had served for similar occasions, and, although every one knew them, they still hit the mark and made both rows of guests roar with laughter.

At one end of the table four young fellows, who were neighbors, were preparing some practical jokes for the newly married couple, and they seemed to have got hold of a good one by the way they whispered and laughed, and suddenly one of them, profiting by a moment of silence, exclaimed: "The poachers will have a good time to-night, with this moon! I say, Jean, you will not be looking at the moon, will you?" The bridegroom turned to him quickly and replied: "Only let them come, that's all!" But the other young fellow began to laugh, and said: "I do not think you will pay much attention to them!"

The whole table was convulsed with laughter, so that the glasses shook, but the bridegroom became furious at the thought that anybody would profit by his wedding to come and poach on his land, and repeated: "I only say-just let them come!"

Then there was a flood of talk with a double meaning which made the bride blush somewhat, although she was trembling with expectation; and when they had emptied the kegs of brandy they all went to bed. The young couple went into their own room, which was on the ground floor, as most rooms in farmhouses are. As it was very warm, they opened the window and closed the shutters. A small lamp in bad taste, a present from the bride's father, was burning on the chest of drawers, and the bed stood ready to receive the young people.

The young woman had already taken off her wreath and her dress, and she was in her petticoat, unlacing her boots, while Jean was finishing his cigar and looking at her out of the corners of his eyes. Suddenly, with a brusque movement, like a man who is about to set to work, he took off his coat. She had already taken off her boots, and was now pulling off her stockings, and then she said to him: "Go and hide yourself behind the curtains while I get into bed."

He seemed as if he were about to refuse; but at last he did as she asked him, and in a moment she unfastened her petticoat, which slipped down, fell at her feet and lay on the ground. She left it there, stepped over it in her loose chemise and slipped into the bed, whose springs creaked beneath her weight. He immediately went up to the bed, and, stooping over his wife, he sought her lips, which she hid beneath the pillow, when a shot was heard in the distance, in the direction of the forest of Rapees, as he thought.

He raised himself anxiously, with his heart beating, and running to the window, he opened the shutters. The full moon flooded the yard with yellow light, and the reflection of the apple trees made black shadows at their feet, while in the distance the fields gleamed, covered with the ripe corn. But as he was leaning out, listening to every sound in the still night, two bare arms were put round his neck, and his wife whispered, trying to pull him back: "Do leave them alone; it has nothing to do with you. Come to bed."

He turned round, put his arms round her, and drew her toward him, but just as he was laying her on the 'bed, which yielded beneath her weight, they heard another report, considerably nearer this time, and Jean, giving way to his tumultuous rage, swore aloud: "Damn it! They will think I do not go out and see what it is because of you! Wait, wait a few minutes!" He put on his shoes again, took down his gun, which was always hanging within reach against the wall, and, as his wife threw herself on her knees in her terror, imploring him not to go, he hastily freed himself, ran to the window and jumped into the yard.

She waited one hour, two hours, until daybreak, but her husband did not return. Then she lost her head, aroused the house, related how angry Jean was, and said that he had gone after the poachers, and immediately all the male farm-servants, even the boys, went in search of their master. They found him two leagues from the farm, tied hand and foot, half dead with rage, his gun broken, his trousers turned inside out, and with three dead hares hanging round his neck, and a placard on his chest with these words: "Who goes on the chase loses his place."

In later years, when he used to tell this story of his wedding night, he usually added: "Ah! as far as a joke went it was a good joke. They caught me in a snare, as if I had been a rabbit, the dirty brutes, and they shoved my head into a bag. But if I can only catch them some day they had better look out for themselves!"

That is how they amuse themselves in Normandy on a wedding day.

FATHER MATTHEW

We had just left Rouen and were galloping along the road to Jumieges. The light carriage flew along across the level country. Presently the horse slackened his pace to walk up the hill of Cantelen.

One sees there one of the most magnificent views in the world. Behind us lay Rouen, the city of churches, with its Gothic belfries, sculptured like ivory trinkets; before us Saint Sever, the manufacturing suburb, whose thousands of smoking chimneys rise amid the expanse of sky, opposite the thousand sacred steeples of the old city.

On the one hand the spire of the cathedral, the highest of human monuments, on the other the engine of the power-house, its rival, and almost as high, and a metre higher than the tallest pyramid in Egypt.

Before us wound the Seine, with its scattered islands and bordered by white banks, covered with a forest on the right and on the left immense meadows, bounded by another forest yonder in the distance.

Here and there large ships lay at anchor along the banks of the wide river. Three enormous steam boats were starting out, one behind the other, for Havre, and a chain of boats, a bark, two schooners and a brig, were going upstream to Rouen, drawn by a little tug that emitted a cloud of black smoke.

My companion, a native of the country, did not glance at this wonderful landscape, but he smiled continually; he seemed to be amused at his thoughts. Suddenly he cried:

"Ah, you will soon see something comical—Father Matthew's chapel. That is a sweet morsel, my boy."

I looked at him in surprise. He continued:

"I will give you a whiff of Normandy that will stay by you. Father Matthew is the handsomest Norman in the province and his chapel is one of the wonders of the world, nothing more nor less. But I will first give you a few words of explanation.

"Father Matthew, who is also called Father 'La Boisson,' is an old sergeant-major who has come back to his native land. He combines in admirable proportions, making a perfect whole, the humbug of the old soldier and the sly roguery of the Norman. On his return to Normandy, thanks to influence and incredible cleverness, he was made doorkeeper of a votive chapel, a chapel dedicated to the Virgin and frequented chiefly by young women who have gone astray . . . . He composed and had painted a special prayer to his 'Good Virgin.' This prayer is a masterpiece of unintentional irony, of Norman wit, in which jest is blended with fear of the saint and with the superstitious fear of the secret influence of something. He has not much faith in his protectress, but he believes in her a little through prudence, and he is considerate of her through policy.

"This is how this wonderful prayer begins:

"'Our good Madame Virgin Mary, natural protectress of girl mothers in this land and all over the world, protect your servant who erred in a moment of forgetfulness . . .'

"It ends thus:

"'Do not forget me, especially when you are with your holy spouse, and intercede with God the Father that he may grant me a good husband, like your own.'

"This prayer, which was suppressed by the clergy of the district, is sold by him privately, and is said to be very efficacious for those who recite it with unction.

"In fact he talks of the good Virgin as the valet de chambre of a redoubted prince might talk of his master who confided in him all his little private secrets. He knows a number of amusing anecdotes at his expense which he tells confidentially among friends as they sit over their glasses.

"But you will see for yourself.

"As the fees coming from the Virgin did not appear sufficient to him, he added to the main figure a little business in saints. He has them all, or nearly all. There was not room enough in the chapel, so he stored them in the wood-shed and brings them forth as soon as the faithful ask for them. He carved these little wooden statues himself—they are comical in the extreme—and painted them all bright green one year when they were painting his house. You know that saints cure diseases, but each saint has his specialty, and you must not confound them or make any blunders. They are as jealous of each other as mountebanks.

"In order that they may make no mistake, the old women come and consult Matthew.

"'For diseases of the ear which saint is the best?'

"'Why, Saint Osyme is good and Saint Pamphilius is not bad.' But that is not all.

"As Matthew has some time to spare, he drinks; but he drinks like a professional, with conviction, so much so that he is intoxicated regularly every evening. He is drunk, but he is aware of it. He is so well aware of it that he notices each day his exact degree of intoxication. That is his chief occupation; the chapel is a secondary matter.

"And he has invented—listen and catch on—he has invented the 'Saoulometre.'

"There is no such instrument, but Matthew's observations are as precise as those of a mathematician. You may hear him repeating incessantly: 'Since Monday I have had more than forty-five,' or else 'I was between fifty-two and fifty-eight,' or else 'I had at least sixty-six to seventy,' or 'Hullo, cheat, I thought I was in the fifties and here I find I had had seventy-five!'

"He never makes a mistake.

"He declares that he never reached his limit, but as he acknowledges that his observations cease to be exact when he has passed ninety, one cannot depend absolutely on the truth of that statement.

"When Matthew acknowledges that he has passed ninety, you may rest assured that he is blind drunk.

"On these occasions his wife, Melie, another marvel, flies into a fury. She waits for him at the door of the house, and as he enters she roars at him:

"'So there you are, slut, hog, giggling sot!'

"Then Matthew, who is not laughing any longer, plants himself opposite her and says in a severe tone:

"'Be still, Melie; this is no time to talk; wait till to-morrow.'

"If she keeps on shouting at him, he goes up to her and says in a shaky voice:

"'Don't bawl any more. I have had about ninety; I am not counting any more. Look out, I am going to hit you!'

"Then Melie beats a retreat.

"If, on the following day, she reverts to the subject, he laughs in her face and says:

"'Come, come! We have said enough. It is past. As long as I have not reached my limit there is no harm done. But if I go, past that I will allow you to correct me, my word on it!'"

We had reached the top of the hill. The road entered the delightful forest of Roumare.

Autumn, marvellous autumn, blended its gold and purple with the remaining traces of verdure. We passed through Duclair. Then, instead of going on to Jumieges, my friend turned to the left and, taking a crosscut, drove in among the trees.

And presently from the top of a high hill we saw again the magnificent valley of the Seine and the winding river beneath us.

At our right a very small slate-covered building, with a bell tower as large as a sunshade, adjoined a pretty house with green Venetian blinds, and all covered with honeysuckle and roses.

"Here are some friends!" cried a big voice, and Matthew appeared on the threshold. He was a man about sixty, thin and with a goatee and long, white mustache.

My friend shook him by the hand and introduced me, and Matthew took us into a clean kitchen, which served also as a dining-room. He said:

"I have no elegant apartment, monsieur. I do not like to get too far away from the food. The saucepans, you see, keep me company." Then, turning to my friend:

"Why did you come on Thursday? You know quite well that this is the day I consult my Guardian Saint. I cannot go out this afternoon."

And running to the door, he uttered a terrific roar: "Melie!" which must have startled the sailors in the ships along the stream in the valley below.

Melie did not reply.

Then Matthew winked his eye knowingly.

"She is not pleased with me, you see, because yesterday I was in the nineties."

My friend began to laugh. "In the nineties, Matthew! How did you manage it?"

"I will tell you," said Matthew. "Last year I found only twenty rasieres (an old dry measure) of apricots. There are no more, but those are the only things to make cider of. So I made some, and yesterday I tapped the barrel. Talk of nectar! That was nectar. You shall tell me what you think of it.

Polyte was here, and we sat down and drank a glass and another without being satisfied (one could go on drinking it until to-morrow), and at last, with glass after glass, I felt a chill at my stomach. I said to Polyte: 'Supposing we drink a glass of cognac to warm ourselves?' He agreed. But this cognac, it sets you on fire, so that we had to go back to the cider. But by going from chills to heat and heat to chills, I saw that I was in the nineties. Polyte was not far from his limit."

The door opened and Melie appeared. At once, before bidding us good-day, she cried:

"Great hog, you have both of you reached your limit!"

"Don't say that, Melie; don't say that," said Matthew, getting angry. "I have never reached my limit."

They gave us a delicious luncheon outside beneath two lime trees, beside the little chapel and overlooking the vast landscape. And Matthew told us, with a mixture of humor and unexpected credulity, incredible stories of miracles.

We had drunk a good deal of delicious cider, sparkling and sweet, fresh and intoxicating, which he preferred to all other drinks, and were smoking our pipes astride our chairs when two women appeared.

They were old, dried up and bent. After greeting us they asked for Saint Blanc. Matthew winked at us as he replied:

"I will get him for you." And he disappeared in his wood shed. He remained there fully five minutes. Then he came back with an expression of consternation. He raised his hands.

"I don't know where he is. I cannot find him. I am quite sure that I had him." Then making a speaking trumpet of his hands, he roared once more:

"Meli-e-a!"

"What's the matter?" replied his wife from the end of the garden.

"Where's Saint Blanc? I cannot find him in the wood shed."

Then Melie explained it this way:

"Was not that the one you took last week to stop up a hole in the rabbit hutch?"

Matthew gave a start.

"By thunder, that may be!" Then turning to the women, he said:

"Follow me."

They followed him. We did the same, almost choking with suppressed laughter.

Saint Blanc was indeed stuck into the earth like an ordinary stake, covered with mud and dirt, and forming a corner for the rabbit hutch.

As soon as they perceived him, the two women fell on their knees, crossed themselves and began to murmur an "Oremus." But Matthew darted toward them.

"Wait," he said, "you are in the mud; I will get you a bundle of straw."

He went to fetch the straw and made them a priedieu. Then, looking at his muddy saint and doubtless afraid of bringing discredit on his business, he added:

"I will clean him off a little for you."

He took a pail of water and a brush and began to scrub the wooden image vigorously, while the two old women kept on praying.

When he had finished he said:

"Now he is all right." And he took us back to the house to drink another glass.

As he was carrying the glass to his lips he stopped and said in a rather confused manner:

"All the same, when I put Saint Blanc out with the rabbits I thought he would not make any more money. For two years no one had asked for him. But the saints, you see, they are never out of date."

VOLUME XI.

THE UMBRELLA

Mme. Oreille was a very economical woman; she knew the value of a centime, and possessed a whole storehouse of strict principles with regard to the multiplication of money, so that her cook found the greatest difficulty in making what the servants call their market-penny, and her husband was hardly allowed any pocket money at all. They were, however, very comfortably off, and had no children; but it really pained Mme. Oreille to see any money spent; it was like tearing at her heartstrings when she had to take any of those nice crown-pieces out of her pocket; and whenever she had to spend anything, no matter how necessary it might be, she slept badly the next night.

Oreille was continually saying to his wife:

"You really might be more liberal, as we have no children, and never spend our income."

"You don't know what may happen," she used to reply. "It is better to have too much than too little."

She was a little woman of about forty, very active, rather hasty, wrinkled, very neat and tidy, and with a very short temper.

Her husband frequently complained of all the privations she made him endure; some of them were particularly painful to him, as they touched his vanity.

He was one of the head clerks in the War Office, and only stayed on there in obedience to his wife's wish, to increase their income which they did not nearly spend.

For two years he had always come to the office with the same old patched umbrella, to the great amusement of his fellow clerks. At last he got tired of their jokes, and insisted upon his wife buying him a new one. She bought one for eight francs and a half, one of those cheap articles which large houses sell as an advertisement. When the men in the office saw the article, which was being sold in Paris by the thousand, they began their jokes again, and Oreille had a dreadful time of it. They even made a song about it, which he heard from morning till night all over the immense building.

Oreille was very angry, and peremptorily told his wife to get him a new one, a good silk one, for twenty francs, and to bring him the bill, so that he might see that it was all right.

She bought him one for eighteen francs, and said, getting red with anger as she gave it to her husband:

"This will last you for five years at least."

Oreille felt quite triumphant, and received a small ovation at the office with his new acquisition.

When he went home in the evening his wife said to him, looking at the umbrella uneasily:

"You should not leave it fastened up with the elastic; it will very likely cut the silk. You must take care of it, for I shall not buy you a new one in a hurry."

She took it, unfastened it, and remained dumfounded with astonishment and rage; in the middle of the silk there was a hole as big as a six-penny-piece; it had been made with the end of a cigar.

"What is that?" she screamed.

Her husband replied quietly, without looking at it:

"What is it? What do you mean?"

She was choking with rage, and could hardly get out a word.

"You—you—have—burned—your umbrella! Why—you must be—mad! Do you wish to ruin us outright?"

He turned round, and felt that he was growing pale.

"What are you talking about?"

"I say that you have burned your umbrella. Just look here."

And rushing at him, as if she were going to beat him, she violently thrust the little circular burned hole under his nose.

He was so utterly struck dumb at the sight of it that he could only stammer out:

"What-what is it? How should I know? I have done nothing, I will swear. I don't know what is the matter with the umbrella."

"You have been playing tricks with it at the office; you have been playing the fool and opening it, to show it off!" she screamed.

"I only opened it once, to let them see what a nice one it was, that is all, I swear."

But she shook with rage, and got up one of those conjugal scenes which make a peaceable man dread the domestic hearth more than a battlefield where bullets are raining.

She mended it with a piece of silk cut out of the old umbrella, which was of a different color, and the next day Oreille went off very humbly with the mended article in his hand. He put it into a cupboard, and thought no more of it than of some unpleasant recollection.

But he had scarcely got home that evening when his wife took the umbrella from him, opened it, and nearly had a fit when she saw what had befallen it, for the disaster was irreparable. It was covered with small holes, which evidently proceeded from burns, just as if some one had emptied the ashes from a lighted pipe on to it. It was done for utterly, irreparably.

She looked at it without a word, in too great a passion to be able to say anything. He, also, when he saw the damage, remained almost dumfounded, in a state of frightened consternation.

They looked at each other, then he looked at the floor; and the next moment she threw the useless article at his head, screaming out in a transport of the most violent rage, for she had recovered her voice by that time:

"Oh! you brute! you brute! You did it on purpose, but I will pay you out for it. You shall not have another."

And then the scene began again, and after the storm had raged for an hour, he at last was able to explain himself. He declared that he could not understand it at all, and that it could only proceed from malice or from vengeance.

A ring at the bell saved him; it was a friend whom they were expecting to dinner.

Mme. Oreille submitted the case to him. As for buying a new umbrella, that was out of the question; her husband should not have another. The friend very sensibly said that in that case his clothes would be spoiled, and they were certainly worth more than the umbrella. But the little woman, who was still in a rage, replied:

"Very well, then, when it rains he may have the kitchen umbrella, for I will not give him a new silk one."

Oreille utterly rebelled at such an idea.

"All right," he said; "then I shall resign my post. I am not going to the office with the kitchen umbrella."

The friend interposed.

"Have this one re-covered; it will not cost much."

But Mme. Oreille, being in the temper that she was, said:

"It will cost at least eight francs to re-cover it. Eight and eighteen are twenty-six. Just fancy, twenty-six francs for an umbrella! It is utter madness!"

The friend, who was only a poor man of the middle classes, had an inspiration:

"Make your fire assurance pay for it. The companies pay for all articles that are burned, as long as the damage has been done in your own house."

On hearing this advice the little woman calmed down immediately, and then, after a moment's reflection, she said to her husband:

"To-morrow, before going to your office, you will go to the Maternelle Assurance Company, show them the state your umbrella is in, and make them pay for the damage."

M. Oreille fairly jumped, he was so startled at the proposal.

"I would not do it for my life! It is eighteen francs lost, that is all. It will not ruin us."

The next morning he took a walking-stick when he went out, and, luckily, it was a fine day.

Left at home alone, Mme. Oreille could not get over the loss of her eighteen francs by any means. She had put the umbrella on the dining-room table, and she looked at it without being able to come to any determination.

Every moment she thought of the assurance company, but she did not dare to encounter the quizzical looks of the gentlemen who might receive her, for she was very timid before people, and blushed at a mere nothing, and was embarrassed when she had to speak to strangers.

But the regret at the loss of the eighteen francs pained her as if she had been wounded. She tried not to think of it any more, and yet every moment the recollection of the loss struck her painfully. What was she to do, however? Time went on, and she could not decide; but suddenly, like all cowards, on making a resolve, she became determined.

"I will go, and we will see what will happen."

But first of all she was obliged to prepare the umbrella so that the disaster might be complete, and the reason of it quite evident. She took a match from the mantelpiece, and between the ribs she burned a hole as big as the palm of her hand; then she delicately rolled it up, fastened it with the elastic band, put on her bonnet and shawl, and went quickly toward the Rue de Rivoli, where the assurance office was.

But the nearer she got, the slower she walked. What was she going to say, and what reply would she get?

She looked at the numbers of the houses; there were still twenty-eight. That was all right, so she had time to consider, and she walked slower and slower. Suddenly she saw a door on which was a large brass plate with "La Maternelle Fire Assurance Office" engraved on it. Already! She waited a moment, for she felt nervous and almost ashamed; then she walked past, came back, walked past again, and came back again.

At last she said to herself:

"I must go in, however, so I may as well do it sooner as later."

She could not help noticing, however, how her heart beat as she entered. She went into an enormous room with grated doors all round it, and above them little openings at which a man's head appeared, and as a gentleman carrying a number of papers passed her, she stopped him and said timidly: "I beg your pardon, monsieur, but can you tell me where I must apply for payment for anything that has been accidentally burned?"

He replied in a sonorous voice:

"The first door on the left; that is the department you want."

This frightened her still more, and she felt inclined to run away, to put in no claim, to sacrifice her eighteen francs. But the idea of that sum revived her courage, and she went upstairs, out of breath, stopping at almost every other step.

She knocked at a door which she saw on the first landing, and a clear voice said, in answer:

"Come in!"

She obeyed mechanically, and found herself in a large room where three solemn gentlemen, all with a decoration in their buttonholes, were standing talking.

One of them asked her: "What do you want, madame?"

She could hardly get out her words, but stammered: "I have come—I have come on account of an accident, something—".

He very politely pointed out a seat to her,

"If you will kindly sit down I will attend to you in a moment."

And, returning to the other two, he went on with the conversation.

"The company, gentlemen, does not consider that it is under any obligation to you for more than four hundred thousand francs, and we can pay no attention to your claim to the further sum of a hundred thousand, which you wish to make us pay. Besides that, the surveyor's valuation—"

One of the others interrupted him:

"That is quite enough, monsieur; the law courts will decide between us, and we have nothing further to do than to take our leave." And they went out after mutual ceremonious bows.

Oh! if she could only have gone away with them, how gladly she would have done it; she would have run away and given up everything. But it was too late, for the gentleman came back, and said, bowing:

"What can I do for you, madame?"

She could scarcely speak, but at last she managed to say:

"I have come-for this."

The manager looked at the object which she held out to him in mute astonishment.

With trembling fingers she tried to undo the elastic, and succeeding, after several attempts, she hastily opened the damaged remains of the umbrella.

"It looks to me to be in a very bad state of health," he said compassionately.

"It cost me twenty francs," she said, with some hesitation.

He seemed astonished. "Really! As much as that?"

"Yes, it was a capital article, and I wanted you to see the condition it is in."

"Yes, yes, I see; very well. But I really do not understand what it can have to do with me."

She began to feel uncomfortable; perhaps this company did not pay for such small articles, and she said:

"But—it is burned."

He could not deny it.

"I see that very well," he replied.

She remained open-mouthed, not knowing what to say next; then, suddenly recollecting that she had left out the main thing, she said hastily:

"I am Mme. Oreille; we are assured in La Maternelle, and I have come to claim the value of this damage."

"I only want you to have it re-covered," she added quickly, fearing a positive refusal.

The manager was rather embarrassed, and said: "But, really, madame, we do not sell umbrellas; we cannot undertake such kinds of repairs."

The little woman felt her courage reviving; she was not going to give up without a struggle; she was not even afraid any more, and said:

"I only want you to pay me the cost of repairing it; I can quite well get it done myself."

The gentleman seemed rather confused.

"Really, madame, it is such a very small matter! We are never asked to give compensation for such trivial losses. You must allow that we cannot make good pocket-handkerchiefs, gloves, brooms, slippers, all the small articles which are every day exposed to the chances of being burned."

She got red in the face, and felt inclined to fly into a rage.

"But, monsieur, last December one of our chimneys caught fire, and caused at least five hundred francs' damage; M. Oreille made no claim on the company, and so it is only just that it should pay for my umbrella now."

The manager, guessing that she was telling a lie, said, with a smile:

"You must acknowledge, madame, that it is very surprising that M. Oreille should have asked no compensation for damages amounting to five hundred francs, and should now claim five or six francs for mending an umbrella."

She was not the least put out, and replied:

"I beg your pardon, monsieur, the five hundred francs affected M. Oreille's pocket, whereas this damage, amounting to eighteen francs, concerns Mme. Oreille's pocket only, which is a totally different matter."

As he saw that he had no chance of getting rid of her, and that he would only be wasting his time, he said resignedly:

"Will you kindly tell me how the damage was done?"

She felt that she had won the victory, and said:

"This is how it happened, monsieur: In our hall there is a bronze stick and umbrella stand, and the other day, when I came in, I put my umbrella into it. I must tell you that just above there is a shelf for the candlesticks and matches. I put out my hand, took three or four matches, and struck one, but it missed fire, so I struck another, which ignited, but went out immediately, and a third did the same."

The manager interrupted her to make a joke.

"I suppose they were government matches, then?"

She did not understand him, and went on:

"Very likely. At any rate, the fourth caught fire, and I lit my candle, and went into my room to go to bed; but in a quarter of an hour I fancied that I smelt something burning, and I have always been terribly afraid of fire. If ever we have an accident it will not be my fault, I assure you. I am terribly nervous since our chimney was on fire, as I told you; so I got up, and hunted about everywhere, sniffing like a dog after game, and at last I noticed that my umbrella was burning. Most likely a match had fallen between the folds and burned it. You can see how it has damaged it."

The manager had taken his cue, and asked her: "What do you estimate the damage at?"

She did not know what to say, as she was not certain what value to put on it, but at last she replied:

"Perhaps you had better get it done yourself. I will leave it to you."

He, however, naturally refused.

"No, madame, I cannot do that. Tell me the amount of your claim, that is all I want to know."

"Well, I think that—Look here, monsieur, I do not want to make any money out of you, so I will tell you what we will do. I will take my umbrella to the maker, who will re-cover it in good, durable silk, and I will bring the bill to you. Will that suit you, monsieur?"

"Perfectly, madame; we will settle it so. Here is a note for the cashier, who will repay you whatever it costs you."

He gave Mme. Oreille a slip of paper, who took it, got up and went out, thanking him, for she was in a hurry to escape lest he should change his mind.

She went briskly through the streets, looking out for a really good umbrella maker, and when she found a shop which appeared to be a first-class one, she went in, and said, confidently:

"I want this umbrella re-covered in silk, good silk. Use the very best and strongest you have; I don't mind what it costs."

BELHOMME'S BEAST

The coach for Havre was ready to leave Criquetot, and all the passengers were waiting for their names to be called out, in the courtyard of the Commercial Hotel kept by Monsieur Malandain, Jr.

It was a yellow wagon, mounted on wheels which had once been yellow, but were now almost gray through the accumulation of mud. The front wheels were very small, the back ones, high and fragile, carried the large body of the vehicle, which was swollen like the belly of an animal. Three white horses, with enormous heads and great round knees, were the first things one noticed. They were harnessed ready to draw this coach, which had something of the appearance of a monster in its massive structure. The horses seemed already asleep in front of the strange vehicle.

The driver, Cesaire Horlaville, a little man with a big paunch, supple nevertheless, through his constant habit of climbing over the wheels to the top of the wagon, his face all aglow from exposure to the brisk air of the plains, to rain and storms, and also from the use of brandy, his eyes twitching from the effect of constant contact with wind and hail, appeared in the doorway of the hotel, wiping his mouth on the back of his hand. Large round baskets, full of frightened poultry, were standing in front of the peasant women. Cesaire Horlaville took them one after the other and packed them on the top of his coach; then more gently, he loaded on those containing eggs; finally he tossed up from below several little bags of grain, small packages wrapped in handkerchiefs, pieces of cloth, or paper. Then he opened the back door, and drawing a list from his pocket he called:

"Monsieur le cure de Gorgeville."

The priest advanced. He was a large, powerful, robust man with a red face and a genial expression. He hitched up his cassock to lift his foot, just as the women hold up their skirts, and climbed into the coach.

"The schoolmaster of Rollebose-les-Grinets."

The man hastened forward, tall, timid, wearing a long frock coat which fell to his knees, and he in turn disappeared through the open door.

"Maitre Poiret, two seats."

Poiret approached, a tall, round-shouldered man, bent by the plow, emaciated through abstinence, bony, with a skin dried by a sparing use of water. His wife followed him, small and thin, like a tired animal, carrying a large green umbrella in her hands.

"Maitre Rabot, two seats."

Rabot hesitated, being of an undecided nature. He asked:

"You mean me?"

The driver was going to answer with a jest, when Rabot dived head first towards the door, pushed forward by a vigorous shove from his wife, a tall, square woman with a large, round stomach like a barrel, and hands as large as hams.

Rabot slipped into the wagon like a rat entering a hole.

"Maitre Caniveau."

A large peasant, heavier than an ox, made the springs bend, and was in turn engulfed in the interior of the yellow chest.

"Maitre Belhomme."

Belhomme, tall and thin, came forward, his neck bent, his head hanging, a handkerchief held to his ear as if he were suffering from a terrible toothache.

All these people wore the blue blouse over quaint and antique coats of a black or greenish cloth, Sunday clothes which they would only uncover in the streets of Havre. Their heads were covered by silk caps at high as towers, the emblem of supreme elegance in the small villages of Normandy.

Cesaire Horlaville closed the door, climbed up on his box and snapped his whip.

The three horses awoke and, tossing their heads, shook their bells.

The driver then yelling "Get up!" as loud as he could, whipped up his horses. They shook themselves, and, with an effort, started off at a slow, halting gait. And behind them came the coach, rattling its shaky windows and iron springs, making a terrible clatter of hardware and glass, while the passengers were tossed hither and thither like so many rubber balls.

At first all kept silent out of respect for the priest, that they might not shock him. Being of a loquacious and genial disposition, he started the conversation.

"Well, Maitre Caniveau," said he, "how are you getting along?"

The enormous farmer who, on account of his size, girth and stomach, felt a bond of sympathy for the representative of the Church, answered with a smile:

"Pretty well, Monsieur le cure, pretty well. And how are you?"

"Oh! I'm always well and healthy."

"And you, Maitre Poiret?" asked the abbe.

"Oh! I'd be all right only the colzas ain't a-goin' to give much this year, and times are so hard that they are the only things worth while raisin'."

"Well, what can you expect? Times are hard."

"Hub! I should say they were hard," sounded the rather virile voice of Rabot's big consort.

As she was from a neighboring village, the priest only knew her by name.

"Is that you, Blondel?" he said.

"Yes, I'm the one that married Rabot."

Rabot, slender, timid, and self-satisfied, bowed smilingly, bending his head forward as though to say: "Yes, I'm the Rabot whom Blondel married."

Suddenly Maitre Belhomme, still holding his handkerchief to his ear, began groaning in a pitiful fashion. He was going "Oh-oh-oh!" and stamping his foot in order to show his terrible suffering.

"You must have an awful toothache," said the priest.

The peasant stopped moaning for a minute and answered:

"No, Monsieur le cure, it is not the teeth. It's my ear-away down at the bottom of my ear."

"Well, what have you got in your ear? A lump of wax?"

"I don't know whether it's wax; but I know that it is a bug, a big bug, that crawled in while I was asleep in the haystack."

"A bug! Are you sure?"

"Am I sure? As sure as I am of heaven, Monsieur le cure! I can feel it gnawing at the bottom of my ear! It's eating my head for sure! It's eating my head! Oh-oh-oh!" And he began to stamp his foot again.

Great interest had been aroused among the spectators. Each one gave his bit of advice. Poiret claimed that it was a spider, the teacher, thought it might be a caterpillar. He had already seen such a thing once, at Campemuret, in Orne, where he had been for six years. In this case the caterpillar had gone through the head and out at the nose. But the man remained deaf in that ear ever after, the drum having been pierced.

"It's more likely to be a worm," said the priest.

Maitre Belhomme, his head resting against the door, for he had been the last one to enter, was still moaning.

"Oh—oh—oh! I think it must be an ant, a big ant—there it is biting again. Oh, Monsieur le cure, how it hurts! how it hurts!"

"Have you seen the doctor?" asked Caniveau.

"I should say not!"

"Why?"

The fear of the doctor seemed to cure Belhomme. He straightened up without, however, dropping his handkerchief.

"What! You have money for them, for those loafers? He would have come once, twice, three times, four times, five times! That means two five-franc pieces, two five-franc pieces, for sure. And what would he have done, the loafer, tell me, what would he have done? Can you tell me?"

Caniveau was laughing.

"No, I don't know. Where are you going?"

"I am going to Havre, to see Chambrelan."

"Who is Chambrelan?"

"The healer, of course."

"What healer?"

"The healer who cured my father."

"Your father?"

"Yes, the healer who cured my father years ago."

"What was the matter with your father?"

"A draught caught him in the back, so that he couldn't move hand or foot."

"Well, what did your friend Chambrelan do to him?"

"He kneaded his back with both hands as though he were making bread! And he was all right in a couple of hours!"

Belhomme thought that Chambrelan must also have used some charm, but he did not dare say so before the priest. Caniveau replied, laughing:

"Are you sure it isn't a rabbit that you have in your ear? He might have taken that hole for his home. Wait, I'll make him run away."

Whereupon Caniveau, making a megaphone of his hands, began to mimic the barking of hounds. He snapped, howled, growled, barked. And everybody in the carriage began to roar, even the schoolmaster, who, as a rule, never ever smiled.

However, as Belhomme seemed angry at their making fun of him, the priest changed the conversation and turning to Rabot's big wife, said:

"You have a large family, haven't you?"

"Oh, yes, Monsieur le cure—and it's a pretty hard matter to bring them up!"

Rabot agreed, nodding his head as though to say: "Oh, yes, it's a hard thing to bring up!"

"How many children?"

She replied authoritatively in a strong, clear voice:

"Sixteen children, Monsieur le cure, fifteen of them by my husband!"

And Rabot smiled broadly, nodding his head. He was responsible for fifteen, he alone, Rabot! His wife said so! Therefore there could be no doubt about it. And he was proud!

And whose was the sixteenth? She didn't tell. It was doubtless the first. Perhaps everybody knew, for no one was surprised. Even Caniveau kept mum.

But Belhomme began to moan again:

"Oh-oh-oh! It's scratching about in the bottom of my ear! Oh, dear, oh, dear!"

The coach just then stopped at the Cafe Polyto. The priest said:

"If someone were to pour a little water into your ear, it might perhaps drive it out. Do you want to try?"

"Sure! I am willing."

And everybody got out in order to witness the operation. The priest asked for a bowl, a napkin and a glass of water, then he told the teacher to hold the patient's head over on one side, and, as soon as the liquid should have entered the ear, to turn his head over suddenly on the other side.

But Caniveau, who was already peering into Belhomme's ear to see if he couldn't discover the beast, shouted:

"Gosh! What a mess! You'll have to clear that out, old man. Your rabbit could never get through that; his feet would stick."

The priest in turn examined the passage and saw that it was too narrow and too congested for him to attempt to expel the animal. It was the teacher who cleared out this passage by means of a match and a bit of cloth. Then, in the midst of the general excitement, the priest poured into the passage half a glass of water, which trickled over the face through the hair and down the neck of the patient. Then the schoolmaster quickly twisted the head round over the bowl, as though he were trying to unscrew it. A couple of drops dripped into the white bowl. All the passengers rushed forward. No insect had come out.

However, Belhomme exclaimed: "I don't feel anything any more." The priest triumphantly exclaimed: "Certainly it has been drowned." Everybody was happy and got back into the coach.

But hardly had they started when Belhomme began to cry out again. The bug had aroused itself and had become furious. He even declared that it had now entered his head and was eating his brain. He was howling with such contortions that Poirat's wife, thinking him possessed by the devil, began to cry and to cross herself. Then, the pain abating a little, the sick man began to tell how it was running round in his ear. With his finger he imitated the movements of the body, seeming to see it, to follow it with his eyes: "There is goes up again! Oh—oh—oh—what torture!"

Caniveau was getting impatient. "It's the water that is making the bug angry. It is probably more accustomed to wine."

Everybody laughed, and he continued: "When we get to the Cafe Bourbeux, give it some brandy, and it won't bother you any more, I wager."

But Belhomme could contain himself no longer; he began howling as though his soul were being torn from his body. The priest was obliged to hold his head for him. They asked Cesaire Horlaville to stop at the nearest house. It was a farmhouse at the side of the road. Belhomme was carried into it and laid on the kitchen table in order to repeat the operation. Caniveau advised mixing brandy and water in order to benumb and perhaps kill the insect. But the priest preferred vinegar.

They poured the liquid in drop by drop this time, that it might penetrate down to the bottom, and they left it several minutes in the organ that the beast had chosen for its home.

A bowl had once more been brought; Belhomme was turned over bodily by the priest and Caniveau, while the schoolmaster was tapping on the healthy ear in order to empty the other.

Cesaire Horlaville himself, whip in hand, had come in to observe the proceedings.

Suddenly, at the bottom of the bowl appeared a little brown spot, no bigger than a tiny seed. However, it was moving. It was a flea! First there were cries of astonishment and then shouts of laughter. A flea! Well, that was a good joke, a mighty good one! Caniveau was slapping his thigh, Cesaire Horlaville snapped his whip, the priest laughed like a braying donkey, the teacher cackled as though he were sneezing, and the two women were giving little screams of joy, like the clucking of hens.

Belhomme had seated himself on the table and had taken the bowl between his knees; he was observing, with serious attention and a vengeful anger in his eye, the conquered insect which was twisting round in the water. He grunted, "You rotten little beast!" and he spat on it.

The driver, wild with joy, kept repeating: "A flea, a flea, ah! there you are, damned little flea, damned little flea, damned little flea!" Then having calmed down a little, he cried: "Well, back to the coach! We've lost enough time."

DISCOVERY

The steamer was crowded with people and the crossing promised to be good. I was going from Havre to Trouville.

The ropes were thrown off, the whistle blew for the last time, the whole boat started to tremble, and the great wheels began to revolve, slowly at first, and then with ever-increasing rapidity.

We were gliding along the pier, black with people. Those on board were waving their handkerchiefs, as though they were leaving for America, and their friends on shore were answering in the same manner.

The big July sun was shining down on the red parasols, the light dresses, the joyous faces and on the ocean, barely stirred by a ripple. When we were out of the harbor, the little vessel swung round the big curve and pointed her nose toward the distant shore which was barely visible through the early morning mist. On our left was the broad estuary of the Seine, her muddy water, which never mingles with that of the ocean, making large yellow streaks clearly outlined against the immense sheet of the pure green sea.

As soon as I am on a boat I feel the need of walking to and fro, like a sailor on watch. Why? I do not know. Therefore I began to thread my way along the deck through the crowd of travellers. Suddenly I heard my name called. I turned around. I beheld one of my old friends, Henri Sidoine, whom I had not seen for ten years.

We shook hands and continued our walk together, talking of one thing or another. Suddenly Sidoine, who had been observing the crowd of passengers, cried out angrily:

"It's disgusting, the boat is full of English people!"

It was indeed full of them. The men were standing about, looking over the ocean with an all-important air, as though to say: "We are the English, the lords of the sea! Here we are!"

The young girls, formless, with shoes which reminded one of the naval constructions of their fatherland, wrapped in multi-colored shawls, were smiling vacantly at the magnificent scenery. Their small heads, planted at the top of their long bodies, wore English hats of the strangest build.

And the old maids, thinner yet, opening their characteristic jaws to the wind, seemed to threaten one with their long, yellow teeth. On passing them, one could notice the smell of rubber and of tooth wash.

Sidoine repeated, with growing anger:

"Disgusting! Can we never stop their coming to France?"

I asked, smiling:

"What have you got against them? As far as I am concerned, they don't worry me."

He snapped out:

"Of course they don't worry you! But I married one of them."

I stopped and laughed at him.

"Go ahead and tell me about it. Does she make you very unhappy?"

He shrugged his shoulders.

"No, not exactly."

"Then she—is not true to you?"

"Unfortunately, she is. That would be cause for a divorce, and I could get rid of her."

"Then I'm afraid I don't understand!"

"You don't understand? I'm not surprised. Well, she simply learned how to speak French—that's all! Listen.

"I didn't have the least desire of getting married when I went to spend the summer at Etretat two years ago. There is nothing more dangerous than watering-places. You have no idea how it suits young girls. Paris is the place for women and the country for young girls.

"Donkey rides, surf-bathing, breakfast on the grass, all these things are traps set for the marriageable man. And, really, there is nothing prettier than a child about eighteen, running through a field or picking flowers along the road.

"I made the acquaintance of an English family who were stopping at the same hotel where I was. The father looked like those men you see over there, and the mother was like all other Englishwomen.

"They had two sons, the kind of boys who play rough games with balls, bats or rackets from morning till night; then came two daughters, the elder a dry, shrivelled-up Englishwoman, the younger a dream of beauty, a heavenly blonde. When those chits make up their minds to be pretty, they are divine. This one had blue eyes, the kind of blue which seems to contain all the poetry, all the dreams, all the hopes and happiness of the world!

"What an infinity of dreams is caused by two such eyes! How well they answer the dim, eternal question of our heart!

"It must not be forgotten either that we Frenchmen adore foreign women. As soon as we meet a Russian, an Italian, a Swede, a Spaniard, or an Englishwoman with a pretty face, we immediately fall in love with her. We enthuse over everything which comes from outside—clothes, hats, gloves, guns and—women. But what a blunder!

"I believe that that which pleases us in foreign women is their accent. As soon as a woman speaks our language badly we think she is charming, if she uses the wrong word she is exquisite and if she jabbers in an entirely unintelligible jargon, she becomes irresistible.

"My little English girl, Kate, spoke a language to be marvelled at. At the beginning I could understand nothing, she invented so many new words; then I fell absolutely in love with this queer, amusing dialect. All maimed, strange, ridiculous terms became delightful in her mouth. Every evening, on the terrace of the Casino, we had long conversations which resembled spoken enigmas.

"I married her! I loved her wildly, as one can only love in a dream. For true lovers only love a dream which has taken the form of a woman.

"Well, my dear fellow, the most foolish thing I ever did was to give my wife a French teacher. As long as she slaughtered the dictionary and tortured the grammar I adored her. Our conversations were simple. They revealed to me her surprising gracefulness and matchless elegance; they showed her to me as a wonderful speaking jewel, a living doll made to be kissed, knowing, after a fashion, how to express what she loved. She reminded me of the pretty little toys which say 'papa' and 'mamma' when you pull a string.

"Now she talks—badly—very badly. She makes as many mistakes as ever—but I can understand her.

"I have opened my doll to look inside—and I have seen. And now I have to talk to her!

"Ah! you don't know, as I do, the opinions, the ideas, the theories of a well-educated young English girl, whom I can blame in nothing, and who repeats to me from morning till night sentences from a French reader prepared in England for the use of young ladies' schools.

"You have seen those cotillon favors, those pretty gilt papers, which enclose candies with an abominable taste. I have one of them. I tore it open. I wished to eat what was inside and it disgusted me so that I feel nauseated at seeing her compatriots.

"I have married a parrot to whom some old English governess might have taught French. Do you understand?"

The harbor of Trouville was now showing its wooden piers covered with people.

I said:

"Where is your wife?"

He answered:

"I took her back to Etretat."

"And you, where are you going?"

"I? Oh, I am going to rest up here at Trouville."

Then, after a pause, he added:

"You have no idea what a fool a woman can be at times!"

THE ACCURSED BREAD

Daddy Taille had three daughters: Anna, the eldest, who was scarcely ever mentioned in the family; Rose, the second girl, who was eighteen, and Clara, the youngest, who was a girl of fifteen.

Old Taille was a widower and a foreman in M. Lebrument's button manufactory. He was a very upright man, very well thought of, abstemious; in fact, a sort of model workman. He lived at Havre, in the Rue d'Angouleme.

When Anna ran away from home the old man flew into a fearful rage. He threatened to kill the head clerk in a large draper's establishment in that town, whom he suspected. After a time, when he was told by various people that she was very steady and investing money in government securities, that she was no gadabout, but was a great friend of Monsieur Dubois, who was a judge of the Tribunal of Commerce, the father was appeased.

He even showed some anxiety as to how she was getting on, and asked some of her old friends who had been to see her, and when told that she had her own furniture, and that her mantelpiece was covered with vases and the walls with pictures, that there were clocks and carpets everywhere, he gave a broad contented smile. He had been working for thirty years to get together a wretched five or six thousand francs. This girl was evidently no fool.

One fine morning the son of Touchard, the cooper, at the other end of the street, came and asked him for the hand of Rose, the second girl. The old man's heart began to beat, for the Touchards were rich and in a good position. He was decidedly lucky with his girls.

The marriage was agreed upon, and it was settled that it should be a grand affair, and the wedding dinner was to be held at Sainte-Adresse, at Mother Jusa's restaurant. It would cost a lot certainly, but never mind, it did not matter just for once in a way.

But one morning, just as the old man was going home to luncheon with his two daughters, the door opened suddenly, and Anna appeared. She was well dressed and looked undeniably pretty and nice. She threw her arms round her father's neck before he could say a word, then fell into her sisters' arms with many tears and then asked for a plate, so that she might share the family soup. Taille was moved to tears in his turn and said several times:

"That is right, dear, that is right."

Then she told them about herself. She did not wish Rose's wedding to take place at Sainte-Adresse—certainly not. It should take place at her house and would cost her father nothing. She had settled everything and arranged everything, so it was "no good to say any more about it—there!"

"Very well, my dear! very well!" the old man said; "we will leave it so." But then he felt some doubt. Would the Touchards consent? But Rose, the bride-elect, was surprised and asked: "Why should they object, I should like to know? Just leave that to me; I will talk to Philip about it."

She mentioned it to her lover the very same day, and he declared it would suit him exactly. Father and Mother Touchard were naturally delighted at the idea of a good dinner which would cost them nothing and said:

"You may be quite sure that everything will be in first-rate style."

They asked to be allowed to bring a friend, Madame Florence, the cook on the first floor, and Anna agreed to everything.

The wedding was fixed for the last Tuesday of the month.

After the civil formalities and the religious ceremony the wedding party went to Anna's house. Among those whom the Tailles had brought was a cousin of a certain age, a Monsieur Sauvetanin, a man given to philosophical reflections, serious, and always very self-possessed, and Madame Lamondois, an old aunt.

Monsieur Sautevanin had been told off to give Anna his arm, as they were looked upon as the two most important persons in the company.

As soon as they had arrived at the door of Anna's house she let go her companion's arm, and ran on ahead, saying: "I will show you the way," and ran upstairs while the invited guests followed more slowly; and, when they got upstairs, she stood on one side to let them pass, and they rolled their eyes and turned their heads in all directions to admire this mysterious and luxurious dwelling.

The table was laid in the drawing-room, as the dining-room had been thought too small. Extra knives, forks and spoons had been hired from a neighboring restaurant, and decanters stood full of wine under the rays of the sun which shone in through the window.

The ladies went into the bedroom to take off their shawls and bonnets, and Father Touchard, who was standing at the door, made funny and suggestive signs to the men, with many a wink and nod. Daddy Taille, who thought a great deal of himself, looked with fatherly pride at his child's well-furnished rooms and went from one to the other, holding his hat in his hand, making a mental inventory of everything, and walking like a verger in a church.

Anna went backward and forward, ran about giving orders and hurrying on the wedding feast. Soon she appeared at the door of the dining-room and cried: "Come here, all of you, for a moment," and as the twelve guests entered the room they saw twelve glasses of Madeira on a small table.

Rose and her husband had their arms round each other's waists and were kissing each other in every corner. Monsieur Sauvetanin never took his eyes off Anna.

They sat down, and the wedding breakfast began, the relations sitting at one end of the table and the young people at the other. Madame Touchard, the mother, presided on the right and the bride on the left. Anna looked after everybody, saw that the glasses were kept filled and the plates well supplied. The guests evidently felt a certain respectful embarrassment at the sight of all the sumptuousness of the rooms and at the lavish manner in which they were treated. They all ate heartily of the good things provided, but there were no jokes such as are prevalent. at weddings of that sort; it was all too grand, and it made them feel uncomfortable. Old Madame Touchard, who was fond of a bit of fun, tried to enliven matters a little, and at the beginning of the dessert she exclaimed: "I say, Philip, do sing us something." The neighbors in their street considered that he had the finest voice in all Havre.

The bridegroom got up, smiled, and, turning to his sister-in-law, from politeness and gallantry, tried to think of something suitable for the occasion, something serious and correct, to harmonize with the seriousness of the repast.

Anna had a satisfied look on her face, and leaned back in her chair to listen, and all assumed looks of attention, though prepared to smile should smiles he called for.

The singer announced "The Accursed Bread," and, extending his right arm, which made his coat ruck up into his neck, he began.

It was decidedly long, three verses of eight lines each, with the last line and the last but one repeated twice.

All went well for the first two verses; they were the usual commonplaces about bread gained by honest labor and by dishonesty. The aunt and the bride wept outright. The cook, who was present, at the end of the first verse looked at a roll which she held in her hand, with streaming eyes, as if it applied to her, while all applauded vigorously. At the end of the second verse the two servants, who were standing with their backs to the wall, joined loudly in the chorus, and the aunt and the bride wept outright.

Daddy Taille blew his nose with the noise of a trombone, and old Touchard brandished a whole loaf half over the table, and the cook shed silent tears on the crust which she was still holding.

Amid the general emotion Monsieur Sauvetanin said:

"That is the right sort of song; very different from the nasty, risky things one generally hears at weddings."

Anna, who was visibly affected, kissed her hand to her sister and pointed to her husband with an affectionate nod, as if to congratulate her.

Intoxicated by his success, the young man continued, and unfortunately the last verse contained words about the "bread of dishonor" gained by young girls who had been led astray. No one took up the refrain about this bread, supposed to be eaten with tears, except old Touchard and the two servants. Anna had grown deadly pale and cast down her eyes, while the bridegroom looked from one to the other without understanding the reason for this sudden coldness, and the cook hastily dropped the crust as if it were poisoned.

Monsieur Sauvetanin said solemnly, in order to save the situation: "That last couplet is not at all necessary"; and Daddy Taille, who had got red up to his ears, looked round the table fiercely.

Then Anna, her eyes swimming in tears, told the servants in the faltering voice of a woman trying to stifle her sobs, to bring the champagne.

All the guests were suddenly seized with exuberant joy, and all their faces became radiant again. And when old Touchard, who had seen, felt and understood nothing of what was going on, and pointing to the guests so as to emphasize his words, sang the last words of the refrain:

"Children, I warn you all to eat not of that bread," the whole company, when they saw the champagne bottles, with their necks covered with gold foil, appear, burst out singing, as if electrified by the sight:

"Children, I warn you all to eat not of that bread."

THE DOWRY

The marriage of Maitre Simon Lebrument with Mademoiselle Jeanne Cordier was a surprise to no one. Maitre Lebrument had bought out the practice of Maitre Papillon; naturally, he had to have money to pay for it; and Mademoiselle Jeanne Cordier had three hundred thousand francs clear in currency, and in bonds payable to bearer.

Maitre Lebrument was a handsome man. He was stylish, although in a provincial way; but, nevertheless, he was stylish—a rare thing at Boutigny-le-Rebours.

Mademoiselle Cordier was graceful and fresh-looking, although a trifle awkward; nevertheless, she was a handsome girl, and one to be desired.

The marriage ceremony turned all Boutigny topsy-turvy. Everybody admired the young couple, who quickly returned home to domestic felicity, having decided simply to take a short trip to Paris, after a few days of retirement.

This tete-a-tete was delightful, Maitre Lebrument having shown just the proper amount of delicacy. He had taken as his motto: "Everything comes to him who waits." He knew how to be at the same time patient and energetic. His success was rapid and complete.

After four days, Madame Lebrument adored her husband. She could not get along without him. She would sit on his knees, and taking him by the ears she would say: "Open your mouth and shut your eyes." He would open his mouth wide and partly close his eyes, and he would try to nip her fingers as she slipped some dainty between his teeth. Then she would give him a kiss, sweet and long, which would make chills run up and down his spine. And then, in his turn, he would not have enough caresses to please his wife from morning to night and from night to morning.

When the first week was over, he said to his young companion:

"If you wish, we will leave for Paris next Tuesday. We will be like two lovers, we will go to the restaurants, the theatres, the concert halls, everywhere, everywhere!"

She was ready to dance for joy.

"Oh! yes, yes. Let us go as soon as possible."

He continued:

"And then, as we must forget nothing, ask your father to have your dowry ready; I shall pay Maitre Papillon on this trip."

She answered:

"All right: I will tell him to-morrow morning."

And he took her in his arms once more, to renew those sweet games of love which she had so enjoyed for the past week.

The following Tuesday, father-in-law and mother-in-law went to the station with their daughter and their son-in-law who were leaving for the capital.

The father-in-law said:

"I tell you it is very imprudent to carry so much money about in a pocketbook." And the young lawyer smiled.

"Don't worry; I am accustomed to such things. You understand that, in my profession, I sometimes have as much as a million about me. In this manner, at least we avoid a great amount of red tape and delay. You needn't worry."

The conductor was crying:

"All aboard for Paris!"

They scrambled into a car, where two old ladies were already seated.

Lebrument whispered into his wife's ear:

"What a bother! I won't be able to smoke."

She answered in a low voice

"It annoys me too, but not an account of your cigar."

The whistle blew and the train started. The trip lasted about an hour, during which time they did not say very much to each other, as the two old ladies did not go to sleep.

As soon as they were in front of the Saint-Lazare Station, Maitre Lebrument said to his wife:

"Dearie, let us first go over to the Boulevard and get something to eat; then we can quietly return and get our trunk and bring it to the hotel."

She immediately assented.

"Oh! yes. Let's eat at the restaurant. Is it far?"

He answered:

"Yes, it's quite a distance, but we will take the omnibus."

She was surprised:

"Why don't we take a cab?"

He began to scold her smilingly:

"Is that the way you save money? A cab for a five minutes' ride at six cents a minute! You would deprive yourself of nothing."

"That's so," she said, a little embarrassed.

A big omnibus was passing by, drawn by three big horses, which were trotting along. Lebrument called out:

"Conductor! Conductor!"

The heavy carriage stopped. And the young lawyer, pushing his wife, said to her quickly:

"Go inside; I'm going up on top, so that I may smoke at least one cigarette before lunch."

She had no time to answer. The conductor, who had seized her by the arm to help her up the step, pushed her inside, and she fell into a seat, bewildered, looking through the back window at the feet of her husband as he climbed up to the top of the vehicle.

And she sat there motionless, between a fat man who smelled of cheap tobacco and an old woman who smelled of garlic.

All the other passengers were lined up in silence—a grocer's boy, a young girl, a soldier, a gentleman with gold-rimmed spectacles and a big silk hat, two ladies with a self-satisfied and crabbed look, which seemed to say: "We are riding in this thing, but we don't have to," two sisters of charity and an undertaker. They looked like a collection of caricatures.

The jolting of the wagon made them wag their heads and the shaking of the wheels seemed to stupefy them—they all looked as though they were asleep.

The young woman remained motionless.

"Why didn't he come inside with me?" she was saying to herself. An unaccountable sadness seemed to be hanging over her. He really need not have acted so.

The sisters motioned to the conductor to stop, and they got off one after the other, leaving in their wake the pungent smell of camphor. The bus started tip and soon stopped again. And in got a cook, red-faced and out of breath. She sat down and placed her basket of provisions on her knees. A strong odor of dish-water filled the vehicle.

"It's further than I imagined," thought Jeanne.

The undertaker went out, and was replaced by a coachman who seemed to bring the atmosphere of the stable with him. The young girl had as a successor a messenger, the odor of whose feet showed that he was continually walking.

The lawyer's wife began to feel ill at ease, nauseated, ready to cry without knowing why.

Other persons left and others entered. The stage went on through interminable streets, stopping at stations and starting again.

"How far it is!" thought Jeanne. "I hope he hasn't gone to sleep! He has been so tired the last few days."

Little by little all the passengers left. She was left alone, all alone. The conductor cried:

"Vaugirard!"

Seeing that she did not move, he repeated:

"Vaugirard!"

She looked at him, understanding that he was speaking to her, as there was no one else there. For the third time the man said:

"Vaugirard!"

Then she asked:

"Where are we?"

He answered gruffly:

"We're at Vaugirard, of course! I have been yelling it for the last half hour!"

"Is it far from the Boulevard?" she said.

"Which boulevard?"

"The Boulevard des Italiens."

"We passed that a long time ago!"

"Would you mind telling my husband?"

"Your husband! Where is he?"

"On the top of the bus."

"On the top! There hasn't been anybody there for a long time."

She started, terrified.

"What? That's impossible! He got on with me. Look well! He must be there."

The conductor was becoming uncivil:

"Come on, little one, you've talked enough! You can find ten men for every one that you lose. Now run along. You'll find another one somewhere."

Tears were coming to her eyes. She insisted:

"But, monsieur, you are mistaken; I assure you that you must be mistaken. He had a big portfolio under his arm."

The man began to laugh:

"A big portfolio! Oh, yes! He got off at the Madeleine. He got rid of you, all right! Ha! ha! ha!"

The stage had stopped. She got out and, in spite of herself, she looked up instinctively to the roof of the bus. It was absolutely deserted.

Then she began to cry, and, without thinking that anybody was listening or watching her, she said out loud:

"What is going to become of me?"

An inspector approached:

"What's the matter?"

The conductor answered, in a bantering tone of voice:

"It's a lady who got left by her husband during the trip."

The other continued:

"Oh! that's nothing. You go about your business."

Then he turned on his heels and walked away.

She began to walk straight ahead, too bewildered, too crazed even to understand what had happened to her. Where was she to go? What could she do? What could have happened to him? How could he have made such a mistake? How could he have been so forgetful?

She had two francs in her pocket. To whom could she go? Suddenly she remembered her cousin Barral, one of the assistants in the offices of the Ministry of the Navy.

She had just enough to pay for a cab. She drove to his house. He met her just as he was leaving for his office. He was carrying a large portfolio under his arm, just like Lebrument.

She jumped out of the carriage.

"Henry!" she cried.

He stopped, astonished:

"Jeanne! Here—all alone! What are you doing? Where have you come from?"

Her eyes full of tears, she stammered:

"My husband has just got lost!"

"Lost! Where?"

"On an omnibus."

"On an omnibus?"

Weeping, she told him her whole adventure.

He listened, thought, and then asked:

"Was his mind clear this morning?"

"Yes."

"Good. Did he have much money with him?"

"Yes, he was carrying my dowry."

"Your dowry! The whole of it?"

"The whole of it—in order to pay for the practice which he bought."

"Well, my dear cousin, by this time your husband must be well on his way to Belgium."

She could not understand. She kept repeating:

"My husband—you say—"

"I say that he has disappeared with your—your capital—that's all!"

She stood there, a prey to conflicting emotions, sobbing.

"Then he is—he is—he is a villain!"

And, faint from excitement, she leaned her head on her cousin's shoulder and wept.

As people were stopping to look at them, he pushed her gently into the vestibule of his house, and, supporting her with his arm around her waist, he led her up the stairs, and as his astonished servant opened the door, he ordered:

"Sophie, run to the restaurant and get a luncheon for two. I am not going to the office to-day."

THE DIARY OF A MADMAN

He was dead—the head of a high tribunal, the upright magistrate whose irreproachable life was a proverb in all the courts of France. Advocates, young counsellors, judges had greeted him at sight of his large, thin, pale face lighted up by two sparkling deep-set eyes, bowing low in token of respect.

He had passed his life in pursuing crime and in protecting the weak. Swindlers and murderers had no more redoubtable enemy, for he seemed to read the most secret thoughts of their minds.

He was dead, now, at the age of eighty-two, honored by the homage and followed by the regrets of a whole people. Soldiers in red trousers had escorted him to the tomb and men in white cravats had spoken words and shed tears that seemed to be sincere beside his grave.

But here is the strange paper found by the dismayed notary in the desk where he had kept the records of great criminals! It was entitled: WHY?

20th June, 1851. I have just left court. I have condemned Blondel to death! Now, why did this man kill his five children? Frequently one meets with people to whom the destruction of life is a pleasure. Yes, yes, it should be a pleasure, the greatest of all, perhaps, for is not killing the next thing to creating? To make and to destroy! These two words contain the history of the universe, all the history of worlds, all that is, all! Why is it not intoxicating to kill?

25th June. To think that a being is there who lives, who walks, who runs. A being? What is a being? That animated thing, that bears in it the principle of motion and a will ruling that motion. It is attached to nothing, this thing. Its feet do not belong to the ground. It is a grain of life that moves on the earth, and this grain of life, coming I know not whence, one can destroy at one's will. Then nothing—nothing more. It perishes, it is finished.

26th June. Why then is it a crime to kill? Yes, why? On the contrary, it is the law of nature. The mission of every being is to kill; he kills to live, and he kills to kill. The beast kills without ceasing, all day, every instant of his existence. Man kills without ceasing, to nourish himself; but since he needs, besides, to kill for pleasure, he has invented hunting! The child kills the insects he finds, the little birds, all the little animals that come in his way. But this does not suffice for the irresistible need to massacre that is in us. It is not enough to kill beasts; we must kill man too. Long ago this need was satisfied by human sacrifices. Now the requirements of social life have made murder a crime. We condemn and punish the assassin! But as we cannot live without yielding to this natural and imperious instinct of death, we relieve ourselves, from time to time, by wars. Then a whole nation slaughters another nation. It is a feast of blood, a feast that maddens armies and that intoxicates civilians, women and children, who read, by lamplight at night, the feverish story of massacre.

One might suppose that those destined to accomplish these butcheries of men would be despised! No, they are loaded with honors. They are clad in gold and in resplendent garments; they wear plumes on their heads and ornaments on their breasts, and they are given crosses, rewards, titles of every kind. They are proud, respected, loved by women, cheered by the crowd, solely because their mission is to shed human blood; They drag through the streets their instruments of death, that the passer-by, clad in black, looks on with envy. For to kill is the great law set by nature in the heart of existence! There is nothing more beautiful and honorable than killing!

30th June. To kill is the law, because nature loves eternal youth. She seems to cry in all her unconscious acts: "Quick! quick! quick!" The more she destroys, the more she renews herself.

2d July. A human being—what is a human being? Through thought it is a reflection of all that is; through memory and science it is an abridged edition of the universe whose history it represents, a mirror of things and of nations, each human being becomes a microcosm in the macrocosm.

3d July. It must be a pleasure, unique and full of zest, to kill; to have there before one the living, thinking being; to make therein a little hole, nothing but a little hole, to see that red thing flow which is the blood, which makes life; and to have before one only a heap of limp flesh, cold, inert, void of thought!

5th August. I, who have passed my life in judging, condemning, killing by the spoken word, killing by the guillotine those who had killed by the knife, I, I, if I should do as all the assassins have done whom I have smitten, I—I—who would know it?

10th August. Who would ever know? Who would ever suspect me, me, me, especially if I should choose a being I had no interest in doing away with?

15th August. The temptation has come to me. It pervades my whole being; my hands tremble with the desire to kill.

22d August. I could resist no longer. I killed a little creature as an experiment, for a beginning. Jean, my servant, had a goldfinch in a cage hung in the office window. I sent him on an errand, and I took the little bird in my hand, in my hand where I felt its heart beat. It was warm. I went up to my room. From time to time I squeezed it tighter; its heart beat faster; this was atrocious and delicious. I was near choking it. But I could not see the blood.

Then I took scissors, short-nail scissors, and I cut its throat with three slits, quite gently. It opened its bill, it struggled to escape me, but I held it, oh! I held it—I could have held a mad dog—and I saw the blood trickle.

And then I did as assassins do—real ones. I washed the scissors, I washed my hands. I sprinkled water and took the body, the corpse, to the garden to hide it. I buried it under a strawberry-plant. It will never be found. Every day I shall eat a strawberry from that plant. How one can enjoy life when one knows how!

My servant cried; he thought his bird flown. How could he suspect me? Ah! ah!

25th August. I must kill a man! I must—

30th August. It is done. But what a little thing! I had gone for a walk in the forest of Vernes. I was thinking of nothing, literally nothing. A child was in the road, a little child eating a slice of bread and butter.

He stops to see me pass and says, "Good-day, Mr. President."

And the thought enters my head, "Shall I kill him?"

I answer: "You are alone, my boy?"

"Yes, sir."

"All alone in the wood?"

"Yes, sir."

The wish to kill him intoxicated me like wine. I approached him quite softly, persuaded that he was going to run away. And, suddenly, I seized him by the throat. He looked at me with terror in his eyes—such eyes! He held my wrists in his little hands and his body writhed like a feather over the fire. Then he moved no more. I threw the body in the ditch, and some weeds on top of it. I returned home, and dined well. What a little thing it was! In the evening I was very gay, light, rejuvenated; I passed the evening at the Prefect's. They found me witty. But I have not seen blood! I am tranquil.

31st August. The body has been discovered. They are hunting for the assassin. Ah! ah!

1st September. Two tramps have been arrested. Proofs are lacking.

2d September. The parents have been to see me. They wept! Ah! ah!

6th October. Nothing has been discovered. Some strolling vagabond must have done the deed. Ah! ah! If I had seen the blood flow, it seems to me I should be tranquil now! The desire to kill is in my blood; it is like the passion of youth at twenty.

20th October. Yet another. I was walking by the river, after breakfast. And I saw, under a willow, a fisherman asleep. It was noon. A spade was standing in a potato-field near by, as if expressly, for me.

I took it. I returned; I raised it like a club, and with one blow of the edge I cleft the fisherman's head. Oh! he bled, this one! Rose-colored blood. It flowed into the water, quite gently. And I went away with a grave step. If I had been seen! Ah! ah! I should have made an excellent assassin.

25th October. The affair of the fisherman makes a great stir. His nephew, who fished with him, is charged with the murder.

26th October. The examining magistrate affirms that the nephew is guilty. Everybody in town believes it. Ah! ah!

27th October. The nephew makes a very poor witness. He had gone to the village to buy bread and cheese, he declared. He swore that his uncle had been killed in his absence! Who would believe him?

28th October. The nephew has all but confessed, they have badgered him so. Ah! ah! justice!

15th November. There are overwhelming proofs against the nephew, who was his uncle's heir. I shall preside at the sessions.

25th January. To death! to death! to death! I have had him condemned to death! Ah! ah! The advocate-general spoke like an angel! Ah! ah! Yet another! I shall go to see him executed!

10th March. It is done. They guillotined him this morning. He died very well! very well! That gave me pleasure! How fine it is to see a man's head cut off!

Now, I shall wait, I can wait. It would take such a little thing to let myself be caught.

The manuscript contained yet other pages, but without relating any new crime.

Alienist physicians to whom the awful story has been submitted declare that there are in the world many undiscovered madmen as adroit and as much to be feared as this monstrous lunatic.

THE MASK

There was a masquerade ball at the Elysee-Montmartre that evening. It was the 'Mi-Careme', and the crowds were pouring into the brightly lighted passage which leads to the dance ball, like water flowing through the open lock of a canal. The loud call of the orchestra, bursting like a storm of sound, shook the rafters, swelled through the whole neighborhood and awoke, in the streets and in the depths of the houses, an irresistible desire to jump, to get warm, to have fun, which slumbers within each human animal.

The patrons came from every quarter of Paris; there were people of all classes who love noisy pleasures, a little low and tinged with debauch. There were clerks and girls—girls of every description, some wearing common cotton, some the finest batiste; rich girls, old and covered with diamonds, and poor girls of sixteen, full of the desire to revel, to belong to men, to spend money. Elegant black evening suits, in search of fresh or faded but appetizing novelty, wandering through the excited crowds, looking, searching, while the masqueraders seemed moved above all by the desire for amusement. Already the far-famed quadrilles had attracted around them a curious crowd. The moving hedge which encircled the four dancers swayed in and out like a snake, sometimes nearer and sometimes farther away, according to the motions of the performers. The two women, whose lower limbs seemed to be attached to their bodies by rubber springs, were making wonderful and surprising motions with their legs. Their partners hopped and skipped about, waving their arms about. One could imagine their panting breath beneath their masks.

One of them, who had taken his place in the most famous quadrille, as substitute for an absent celebrity, the handsome "Songe-au-Gosse," was trying to keep up with the tireless "Arete-de-Veau" and was making strange fancy steps which aroused the joy and sarcasm of the audience.

He was thin, dressed like a dandy, with a pretty varnished mask on his face. It had a curly blond mustache and a wavy wig. He looked like a wax figure from the Musee Grevin, like a strange and fantastic caricature of the charming young man of fashion plates, and he danced with visible effort, clumsily, with a comical impetuosity. He appeared rusty beside the others when he tried to imitate their gambols: he seemed overcome by rheumatism, as heavy as a great Dane playing with greyhounds. Mocking bravos encouraged him. And he, carried away with enthusiasm, jigged about with such frenzy that suddenly, carried away by a wild spurt, he pitched head foremost into the living wall formed by the audience, which opened up before him to allow him to pass, then closed around the inanimate body of the dancer, stretched out on his face.

Some men picked him up and carried him away, calling for a doctor. A gentleman stepped forward, young and elegant, in well-fitting evening clothes, with large pearl studs. "I am a professor of the Faculty of Medicine," he said in a modest voice. He was allowed to pass, and he entered a small room full of little cardboard boxes, where the still lifeless dancer had been stretched cut on some chairs. The doctor at first wished to take off the mask, and he noticed that it was attached in a complicated manner, with a perfect network of small metal wires which cleverly bound it to his wig and covered the whole head. Even the neck was imprisoned in a false skin which continued the chin and was painted the color of flesh, being attached to the collar of the shirt.

All this had to be cut with strong scissors. When the physician had slit open this surprising arrangement, from the shoulder to the temple, he opened this armor and found the face of an old man, worn out, thin and wrinkled. The surprise among those who had brought in this seemingly young dancer was so great that no one laughed, no one said a word.

All were watching this sad face as he lay on the straw chairs, his eyes closed, his face covered with white hair, some long, falling from the forehead over the face, others short, growing around the face and the chin, and beside this poor head, that pretty little, neat varnished, smiling mask.

The man regained consciousness after being inanimate for a long time, but he still seemed to be so weak and sick that the physician feared some dangerous complication. He asked: "Where do you live?"

The old dancer seemed to be making an effort to remember, and then he mentioned the name of the street, which no one knew. He was asked for more definite information about the neighborhood. He answered with a great slowness, indecision and difficulty, which revealed his upset state of mind. The physician continued:

"I will take you home myself."

Curiosity had overcome him to find out who this strange dancer, this phenomenal jumper might be. Soon the two rolled away in a cab to the other side of Montmartre.

They stopped before a high building of poor appearance. They went up a winding staircase. The doctor held to the banister, which was so grimy that the hand stuck to it, and he supported the dizzy old man, whose forces were beginning to return. They stopped at the fourth floor.

The door at which they had knocked was opened by an old woman, neat looking, with a white nightcap enclosing a thin face with sharp features, one of those good, rough faces of a hard-working and faithful woman. She cried out:

"For goodness sake! What's the matter?"

He told her the whole affair in a few words. She became reassured and even calmed the physician himself by telling him that the same thing had happened many times. She said: "He must be put to bed, monsieur, that is all. Let him sleep and tomorrow he will be all right."

The doctor continued: "But he can hardly speak."

"Oh! that's just a little drink, nothing more; he has eaten no dinner, in order to be nimble, and then he took a few absinthes in order to work himself up to the proper pitch. You see, drink gives strength to his legs, but it stops his thoughts and words. He is too old to dance as he does. Really, his lack of common sense is enough to drive one mad!"

The doctor, surprised, insisted:

"But why does he dance like that at his age?"

She shrugged her shoulders and turned red from the anger which was slowly rising within her and she cried out:

"Ah! yes, why? So that the people will think him young under his mask; so that the women will still take him for a young dandy and whisper nasty things into his ears; so that he can rub up against all their dirty skins, with their perfumes and powders and cosmetics. Ah! it's a fine business! What a life I have had for the last forty years! But we must first get him to bed, so that he may have no ill effects. Would you mind helping me? When he is like that I can't do anything with him alone."

The old man was sitting on his bed, with a tipsy look, his long white hair falling over his face. His companion looked at him with tender yet indignant eyes. She continued:

"Just see the fine head he has for his age, and yet he has to go and disguise himself in order to make people think that he is young. It's a perfect shame! Really, he has a fine head, monsieur! Wait, I'll show it to you before putting him to bed."

She went to a table on which stood the washbasin a pitcher of water, soap and a comb and brush. She took the brush, returned to the bed and pushed back the drunkard's tangled hair. In a few seconds she made him look like a model fit for a great painter, with his long white locks flowing on his neck. Then she stepped back in order to observe him, saying: "There! Isn't he fine for his age?"

"Very," agreed the doctor, who was beginning to be highly amused.

She added: "And if you had known him when he was twenty-five! But we must get him to bed, otherwise the drink will make him sick. Do you mind drawing off that sleeve? Higher-like that-that's right. Now the trousers. Wait, I will take his shoes off—that's right. Now, hold him upright while I open the bed. There—let us put him in. If you think that he is going to disturb himself when it is time for me to get in you are mistaken. I have to find a little corner any place I can. That doesn't bother him! Bah! You old pleasure seeker!"

As soon as he felt himself stretched out in his sheets the old man closed his eyes, opened them closed them again, and over his whole face appeared an energetic resolve to sleep. The doctor examined him with an ever-increasing interest and asked: "Does he go to all the fancy balls and try to be a young man?" "To all of them, monsieur, and he comes back to me in the morning in a deplorable condition. You see, it's regret that leads him on and that makes him put a pasteboard face over his own. Yes, the regret of no longer being what he was and of no longer making any conquests!"

He was sleeping now and beginning to snore. She looked at him with a pitying expression and continued: "Oh! how many conquests that man has made! More than one could believe, monsieur, more than the finest gentlemen of the world, than all the tenors and all the generals."

"Really? What did he do?"

"Oh! it will surprise you at first, as you did not know him in his palmy days. When I met him it was also at a ball, for he has always frequented them. As soon as I saw him I was caught—caught like a fish on a hook. Ah! how pretty he was, monsieur, with his curly raven locks and black eyes as large as saucers! Indeed, he was good looking! He took me away that evening and I never have left him since, never, not even for a day, no matter what he did to me! Oh! he has often made it hard for me!"

The doctor asked: "Are you married?"

She answered simply: "Yes, monsieur, otherwise he would have dropped me as he did the others. I have been his wife and his servant, everything, everything that he wished. How he has made me cry— tears which I did not show him; for he would tell all his adventures to me—to me, monsieur—without understanding how it hurt me to listen."

"But what was his business?"

"That's so. I forgot to tell you. He was the foreman at Martel's—a foreman such as they never had had—an artist who averaged ten francs an hour."

"Martel?—who is Martel?"

"The hairdresser, monsieur, the great hairdresser of the Opera, who had all the actresses for customers. Yes, sir, all the smartest actresses had their hair dressed by Ambrose and they would give him tips that made a fortune for him. Ah! monsieur, all the women are alike, yes, all of them. When a man pleases their fancy they offer themselves to him. It is so easy—and it hurt me so to hear about it. For he would tell me everything—he simply could not hold his tongue—it was impossible. Those things please the men so much! They seem to get even more enjoyment out of telling than doing.

"When I would see him coming in the evening, a little pale, with a pleased look and a bright eye, would say to myself: 'One more. I am sure that he has caught one more.' Then I felt a wild desire to question him and then, again, not to know, to stop his talking if he should begin. And we would look at each other.

"I knew that he would not keep still, that he would come to the point. I could feel that from his manner, which seemed to laugh and say: 'I had a fine adventure to-day, Madeleine.' I would pretend to notice nothing, to guess nothing; I would set the table, bring on the soup and sit down opposite him.

"At those times, monsieur, it was as if my friendship for him had been crushed in my body as with a stone. It hurt. But he did not understand; he did not know; he felt a need to tell all those things to some one, to boast, to show how much he was loved, and I was the only one he had to whom he could talk-the only one. And I would have to listen and drink it in, like poison.

"He would begin to take his soup and then he would say: 'One more, Madeleine.'

"And I would think: 'Here it comes! Goodness! what a man! Why did I ever meet him?'

"Then he would begin: 'One more! And a beauty, too.' And it would be some little one from the Vaudeville or else from the Varietes, and some of the big ones, too, some of the most famous. He would tell me their names, how their apartments were furnished, everything, everything, monsieur. Heartbreaking details. And he would go over them and tell his story over again from beginning to end, so pleased with himself that I would pretend to laugh so that he would not get angry with me.

"Everything may not have been true! He liked to glorify himself and was quite capable of inventing such things! They may perhaps also have been true! On those evenings he would pretend to be tired and wish to go to bed after supper. We would take supper at eleven, monsieur, for he could never get back from work earlier.

"When he had finished telling about his adventure he would walk round the room and smoke cigarettes, and he was so handsome, with his mustache and curly hair, that I would think: 'It's true, just the same, what he is telling. Since I myself am crazy about that man, why should not others be the same?' Then I would feel like crying, shrieking, running away and jumping out of the window while I was clearing the table and he was smoking. He would yawn in order to show how tired he was, and he would say two or three times before going to bed: 'Ah! how well I shall sleep this evening!'

"I bear him no ill will, because he did not know how he was hurting me. No, he could not know! He loved to boast about the women just as a peacock loves to show his feathers. He got to the point where he thought that all of them looked at him and desired him.

"It was hard when he grew old. Oh, monsieur, when I saw his first white hair I felt a terrible shock and then a great joy—a wicked joy—but so great, so great! I said to myself: 'It's the end-it's the end.' It seemed as if I were about to be released from prison. At last I could have him to myself, all to myself, when the others would no longer want him.

"It was one morning in bed. He was still sleeping and I leaned over him to wake him up with a kiss, when I noticed in his curls, over his temple, a little thread which shone like silver. What a surprise! I should not have thought it possible! At first I thought of tearing it out so that he would not see it, but as I looked carefully I noticed another farther up. White hair! He was going to have white hair! My heart began to thump and perspiration stood out all over me, but away down at the bottom I was happy.

"It was mean to feel thus, but I did my housework with a light heart that morning, without waking him up, and, as soon as he opened his eyes of his own accord, I said to him: 'Do you know what I discovered while you were asleep?'

"'No.'

"'I found white hairs.'

"He started up as if I had tickled him and said angrily: 'It's not true!'

"'Yes, it is. There are four of them over your left temple.'

"He jumped out of bed and ran over to the mirror. He could not find them. Then I showed him the first one, the lowest, the little curly one, and I said: 'It's no wonder, after the life that you have been leading. In two years all will be over for you.'

"Well, monsieur, I had spoken true; two years later one could not recognize him. How quickly a man changes! He was still handsome, but he had lost his freshness, and the women no longer ran after him. Ah! what a life I led at that time! How he treated me! Nothing suited him. He left his trade to go into the hat business, in which he ate up all his money. Then he unsuccessfully tried to be an actor, and finally he began to frequent public balls. Fortunately, he had had common sense enough to save a little something on which we now live. It is sufficient, but it is not enormous. And to think that at one time he had almost a fortune.

"Now you see what he does. This habit holds him like a frenzy. He has to be young; he has to dance with women who smell of perfume and cosmetics. You poor old darling!"

She was looking at her old snoring husband fondly, ready to cry. Then, gently tiptoeing up to him, she kissed his hair. The physician had risen and was getting ready to leave, finding nothing to say to this strange couple. Just as he was leaving she asked:

"Would you mind giving me your address? If he should grow worse, I could go and get you."

THE PENGUINS' ROCK

This is the season for penguins.

From April to the end of May, before the Parisian visitors arrive, one sees, all at once, on the little beach at Etretat several old gentlemen, booted and belted in shooting costume. They spend four or five days at the Hotel Hauville, disappear, and return again three weeks later. Then, after a fresh sojourn, they go away altogether.

One sees them again the following spring.

These are the last penguin hunters, what remain of the old set. There were about twenty enthusiasts thirty or forty years ago; now there are only a few of the enthusiastic sportsmen.

The penguin is a very rare bird of passage, with peculiar habits. It lives the greater part of the year in the latitude of Newfoundland and the islands of St. Pierre and Miquelon. But in the breeding season a flight of emigrants crosses the ocean and comes every year to the same spot to lay their eggs, to the Penguins' Rock near Etretat. They are found nowhere else, only there. They have always come there, have always been chased away, but return again, and will always return. As soon as the young birds are grown they all fly away, and disappear for a year.

Why do they not go elsewhere? Why not choose some other spot on the long white, unending cliff that extends from the Pas-de-Calais to Havre? What force, what invincible instinct, what custom of centuries impels these birds to come back to this place? What first migration, what tempest, possibly, once cast their ancestors on this rock? And why do the children, the grandchildren, all the descendants of the first parents always return here?

There are not many of them, a hundred at most, as if one single family, maintaining the tradition, made this annual pilgrimage.

And each spring, as soon as the little wandering tribe has taken up its abode an the rock, the same sportsmen also reappear in the village. One knew them formerly when they were young; now they are old, but constant to the regular appointment which they have kept for thirty or forty years. They would not miss it for anything in the world.

It was an April evening in one of the later years. Three of the old sportsmen had arrived; one was missing—M. d'Arnelles.

He had written to no one, given no account of himself. But he was not dead, like so many of the rest; they would have heard of it. At length, tired of waiting for him, the other three sat down to table. Dinner was almost over when a carriage drove into the yard of the hotel, and the late corner presently entered the dining room.

He sat down, in a good humor, rubbing his hands, and ate with zest. When one of his comrades remarked with surprise at his being in a frock-coat, he replied quietly:

"Yes, I had no time to change my clothes."

They retired on leaving the table, for they had to set out before daybreak in order to take the birds unawares.

There is nothing so pretty as this sport, this early morning expedition.

At three o'clock in the morning the sailors awoke the sportsmen by throwing sand against the windows. They were ready in a few minutes and went down to the beach. Although it was still dark, the stars had paled a little. The sea ground the shingle on the beach. There was such a fresh breeze that it made one shiver slightly in spite of one's heavy clothing.

Presently two boats were pushed down the beach, by the sailors, with a sound as of tearing cloth, and were floated on the nearest waves. The brown sail was hoisted, swelled a little, fluttered, hesitated and swelling out again as round as a paunch, carried the boats towards the large arched entrance that could be faintly distinguished in the darkness.

The sky became clearer, the shadows seemed to melt away. The coast still seemed veiled, the great white coast, perpendicular as a wall.

They passed through the Manne-Porte, an enormous arch beneath which a ship could sail; they doubled the promontory of La Courtine, passed the little valley of Antifer and the cape of the same name; and suddenly caught sight of a beach on which some hundreds of seagulls were perched.

That was the Penguins' Rock. It was just a little protuberance of the cliff, and on the narrow ledges of rock the birds' heads might be seen watching the boats.

They remained there, motionless, not venturing to fly off as yet. Some of them perched on the edges, seated upright, looked almost like bottles, for their little legs are so short that when they walk they glide along as if they were on rollers. When they start to fly they cannot make a spring and let themselves fall like stones almost down to the very men who are watching them.

They know their limitation and the danger to which it subjects them, and cannot make up their minds to fly away.

But the boatmen begin to shout, beating the sides of the boat with the wooden boat pins, and the birds, in affright, fly one by one into space until they reach the level of the waves. Then, moving their wings rapidly, they scud, scud along until they reach the open sea; if a shower of lead does not knock them into the water.

For an hour the firing is kept up, obliging them to give up, one after another. Sometimes the mother birds will not leave their nests, and are riddled with shot, causing drops of blood to spurt out on the white cliff, and the animal dies without having deserted her eggs.

The first day M. d'Arnelles fired at the birds with his habitual zeal; but when the party returned toward ten o'clock, beneath a brilliant sun, which cast great triangles of light on the white cliffs along the coast he appeared a little worried, and absentminded, contrary to his accustomed manner.

As soon as they got on shore a kind of servant dressed in black came up to him and said something in a low tone. He seemed to reflect, hesitate, and then replied:

"No, to-morrow."

The following day they set out again. This time M, d'Arnelles frequently missed his aim, although the birds were close by. His friends teased him, asked him if he were in love, if some secret sorrow was troubling his mind and heart. At length he confessed.

"Yes, indeed, I have to leave soon, and that annoys me."

"What, you must leave? And why?"

"Oh, I have some business that calls me back. I cannot stay any longer."

They then talked of other matters.

As soon as breakfast was over the valet in black appeared. M. d'Arnelles ordered his carriage, and the man was leaving the room when the three sportsmen interfered, insisting, begging, and praying their friend to stay. One of them at last said:

"Come now, this cannot be a matter of such importance, for you have already waited two days."

M. d'Arnelles, altogether perplexed, began to think, evidently baffled, divided between pleasure and duty, unhappy and disturbed.

After reflecting for some time he stammered:

"The fact is—the fact is—I am not alone here. I have my son-in-law."

There were exclamations and shouts of "Your son-in-law! Where is he?"

He suddenly appeared confused and his face grew red.

"What! do you not know? Why—why—he is in the coach house. He is dead."

They were all silent in amazement.

M. d'Arnelles continued, more and more disturbed:

"I had the misfortune to lose him; and as I was taking the body to my house, in Briseville, I came round this way so as not to miss our appointment. But you can see that I cannot wait any longer."

Then one of the sportsmen, bolder than the rest said:

"Well, but—since he is dead—it seems to me that he can wait a day longer."

The others chimed in:

"That cannot be denied."

M. d'Arnelles appeared to be relieved of a great weight, but a little uneasy, nevertheless, he asked:

"But, frankly—do you think—"

The three others, as one man, replied:

"Parbleu! my dear boy, two days more or less can make no difference in his present condition."

And, perfectly calmly, the father-in-law turned to the undertaker's assistant, and said:

"Well, then, my friend, it will be the day after tomorrow."

A FAMILY

I was to see my old friend, Simon Radevin, of whom I had lost sight for fifteen years. At one time he was my most intimate friend, the friend who knows one's thoughts, with whom one passes long, quiet, happy evenings, to whom one tells one's secret love affairs, and who seems to draw out those rare, ingenious, delicate thoughts born of that sympathy that gives a sense of repose.

For years we had scarcely been separated; we had lived, travelled, thought and dreamed together; had liked the same things, had admired the same books, understood the same authors, trembled with the same sensations, and very often laughed at the same individuals, whom we understood completely by merely exchanging a glance.

Then he married. He married, quite suddenly, a little girl from the provinces, who had come to Paris in search of a husband. How in the world could that little thin, insipidly fair girl, with her weak hands, her light, vacant eyes, and her clear, silly voice, who was exactly like a hundred thousand marriageable dolls, have picked up that intelligent, clever young fellow? Can any one understand these things? No doubt he had hoped for happiness, simple, quiet and long-enduring happiness, in the arms of a good, tender and faithful woman; he had seen all that in the transparent looks of that schoolgirl with light hair.

He had not dreamed of the fact that an active, living and vibrating man grows weary of everything as soon as he understands the stupid reality, unless, indeed, he becomes so brutalized that he understands nothing whatever.

What would he be like when I met him again? Still lively, witty, light-hearted and enthusiastic, or in a state of mental torpor induced by provincial life? A man may change greatly in the course of fifteen years!

The train stopped at a small station, and as I got out of the carriage, a stout, a very stout man with red cheeks and a big stomach rushed up to me with open arms, exclaiming: "George!" I embraced him, but I had not recognized him, and then I said, in astonishment: "By Jove! You have not grown thin!" And he replied with a laugh:

"What did you expect? Good living, a good table and good nights! Eating and sleeping, that is my existence!"

I looked at him closely, trying to discover in that broad face the features I held so dear. His eyes alone had not changed, but I no longer saw the same expression in them, and I said to myself: "If the expression be the reflection of the mind, the thoughts in that head are not what they used to be formerly; those thoughts which I knew so well."

Yet his eyes were bright, full of happiness and friendship, but they had not that clear, intelligent expression which shows as much as words the brightness of the intellect. Suddenly he said:

"Here are my two eldest children." A girl of fourteen, who was almost a woman, and a boy of thirteen, in the dress of a boy from a Lycee, came forward in a hesitating and awkward manner, and I said in a low voice: "Are they yours?" "Of course they are," he replied, laughing. "How many have you?" "Five! There are three more at home."

He said this in a proud, self-satisfied, almost triumphant manner, and I felt profound pity, mingled with a feeling of vague contempt, for this vainglorious and simple reproducer of his species.

I got into a carriage which he drove himself, and we set off through the town, a dull, sleepy, gloomy town where nothing was moving in the streets except a few dogs and two or three maidservants. Here and there a shopkeeper, standing at his door, took off his hat, and Simon returned his salute and told me the man's name; no doubt to show me that he knew all the inhabitants personally, and the thought struck me that he was thinking of becoming a candidate for the Chamber of Deputies, that dream of all those who bury themselves in the provinces.

We were soon out of the town, and the carriage turned into a garden that was an imitation of a park, and stopped in front of a turreted house, which tried to look like a chateau.

"That is my den," said Simon, so that I might compliment him on it. "It is charming," I replied.

A lady appeared on the steps, dressed for company, and with company phrases all ready prepared. She was no longer the light-haired, insipid girl I had seen in church fifteen years previously, but a stout lady in curls and flounces, one of those ladies of uncertain age, without intellect, without any of those things that go to make a woman. In short, she was a mother, a stout, commonplace mother, a human breeding machine which procreates without any other preoccupation but her children and her cook-book.

She welcomed me, and I went into the hall, where three children, ranged according to their height, seemed set out for review, like firemen before a mayor, and I said: "Ah! ah! so there are the others?" Simon, radiant with pleasure, introduced them: "Jean, Sophie and Gontran."

The door of the drawing-room was open. I went in, and in the depths of an easy-chair, I saw something trembling, a man, an old, paralyzed man. Madame Radevin came forward and said: "This is my grandfather, monsieur; he is eighty-seven." And then she shouted into the shaking old man's ears: "This is a friend of Simon's, papa." The old gentleman tried to say "good-day" to me, and he muttered: "Oua, oua, oua," and waved his hand, and I took a seat saying: "You are very kind, monsieur."

Simon had just come in, and he said with a laugh: "So! You have made grandpapa's acquaintance. He is a treasure, that old man; he is the delight of the children. But he is so greedy that he almost kills himself at every meal; you have no idea what he would eat if he were allowed to do as he pleased. But you will see, you will see. He looks at all the sweets as if they were so many girls. You never saw anything so funny; you will see presently."

I was then shown to my room, to change my dress for dinner, and hearing a great clatter behind me on the stairs, I turned round and saw that all the children were following me behind their father; to do me honor, no doubt.

My windows looked out across a dreary, interminable plain, an ocean of grass, of wheat and of oats, without a clump of trees or any rising ground, a striking and melancholy picture of the life which they must be leading in that house.

A bell rang; it was for dinner, and I went downstairs. Madame Radevin took my arm in a ceremonious manner, and we passed into the dining-room. A footman wheeled in the old man in his armchair. He gave a greedy and curious look at the dessert, as he turned his shaking head with difficulty from one dish to the other.

Simon rubbed his hands: "You will be amused," he said; and all the children understanding that I was going to be indulged with the sight of their greedy grandfather, began to laugh, while their mother merely smiled and shrugged her shoulders, and Simon, making a speaking trumpet of his hands, shouted at the old man: "This evening there is sweet creamed rice!" The wrinkled face of the grandfather brightened, and he trembled more violently, from head to foot, showing that he had understood and was very pleased. The dinner began.

"Just look!" Simon whispered. The old man did not like the soup, and refused to eat it; but he was obliged to do it for the good of his health, and the footman forced the spoon into his mouth, while the old man blew so energetically, so as not to swallow the soup, that it was scattered like a spray all over the table and over his neighbors. The children writhed with laughter at the spectacle, while their father, who was also amused, said: "Is not the old man comical?"

During the whole meal they were taken up solely with him. He devoured the dishes on the table with his eyes, and tried to seize them and pull them over to him with his trembling hands. They put them almost within his reach, to see his useless efforts, his trembling clutches at them, the piteous appeal of his whole nature, of his eyes, of his mouth and of his nose as he smelt them, and he slobbered on his table napkin with eagerness, while uttering inarticulate grunts. And the whole family was highly amused at this horrible and grotesque scene.

Then they put a tiny morsel on his plate, and he ate with feverish gluttony, in order to get something more as soon as possible, and when the sweetened rice was brought in, he nearly had a fit, and groaned with greediness, and Gontran called out to him:

"You have eaten too much already; you can have no more." And they pretended not to give him any. Then he began to cry; he cried and trembled more violently than ever, while all the children laughed. At last, however, they gave him his helping, a very small piece; and as he ate the first mouthful, he made a comical noise in his throat, and a movement with his neck as ducks do when they swallow too large a morsel, and when he had swallowed it, he began to stamp his feet, so as to get more.

I was seized with pity for this saddening and ridiculous Tantalus, and interposed on his behalf:

"Come, give him a little more rice!" But Simon replied: "Oh! no, my dear fellow, if he were to eat too much, it would harm him, at his age."

I held my tongue, and thought over those words. Oh, ethics! Oh, logic! Oh, wisdom! At his age! So they deprived him of his only remaining pleasure out of regard for his health! His health! What would he do with it, inert and trembling wreck that he was? They were taking care of his life, so they said. His life? How many days? Ten, twenty, fifty, or a hundred? Why? For his own sake? Or to preserve for some time longer the spectacle of his impotent greediness in the family.

There was nothing left for him to do in this life, nothing whatever. He had one single wish left, one sole pleasure; why not grant him that last solace until he died?

After we had played cards for a long time, I went up to my room and to bed; I was low-spirited and sad, sad, sad! and I sat at my window. Not a sound could be heard outside but the beautiful warbling of a bird in a tree, somewhere in the distance. No doubt the bird was singing in a low voice during the night, to lull his mate, who was asleep on her eggs. And I thought of my poor friend's five children, and pictured him to myself, snoring by the side of his ugly wife.

SUICIDES

To Georges Legrand.

Hardly a day goes by without our reading a news item like the following in some newspaper:

"On Wednesday night the people living in No. 40 Rue de——-, were awakened by two successive shots. The explosions seemed to come from the apartment occupied by M. X——. The door was broken in and the man was found bathed in his blood, still holding in one hand the revolver with which he had taken his life.

"M. X——was fifty-seven years of age, enjoying a comfortable income, and had everything necessary to make him happy. No cause can be found for his action."

What terrible grief, what unknown suffering, hidden despair, secret wounds drive these presumably happy persons to suicide? We search, we imagine tragedies of love, we suspect financial troubles, and, as we never find anything definite, we apply to these deaths the word "mystery."

A letter found on the desk of one of these "suicides without cause," and written during his last night, beside his loaded revolver, has come into our hands. We deem it rather interesting. It reveals none of those great catastrophes which we always expect to find behind these acts of despair; but it shows us the slow succession of the little vexations of life, the disintegration of a lonely existence, whose dreams have disappeared; it gives the reason for these tragic ends, which only nervous and high-strung people can understand.

Here it is:

"It is midnight. When I have finished this letter I shall kill myself. Why? I shall attempt to give the reasons, not for those who may read these lines, but for myself, to kindle my waning courage, to impress upon myself the fatal necessity of this act which can, at best, be only deferred.

"I was brought up by simple-minded parents who were unquestioning believers. And I believed as they did.

"My dream lasted a long time. The last veil has just been torn from my eyes.

"During the last few years a strange change has been taking place within me. All the events of Life, which formerly had to me the glow of a beautiful sunset, are now fading away. The true meaning of things has appeared to me in its brutal reality; and the true reason for love has bred in me disgust even for this poetic sentiment: 'We are the eternal toys of foolish and charming illusions, which are always being renewed.'

"On growing older, I had become partly reconciled to the awful mystery of life, to the uselessness of effort; when the emptiness of everything appeared to me in a new light, this evening, after dinner.

"Formerly, I was happy! Everything pleased me: the passing women, the appearance of the streets, the place where I lived; and I even took an interest in the cut of my clothes. But the repetition of the same sights has had the result of filling my heart with weariness and disgust, just as one would feel were one to go every night to the same theatre.

"For the last thirty years I have been rising at the same hour; and, at the same restaurant, for thirty years, I have been eating at the same hours the same dishes brought me by different waiters.

"I have tried travel. The loneliness which one feels in strange places terrified me. I felt so alone, so small on the earth that I quickly started on my homeward journey.

"But here the unchanging expression of my furniture, which has stood for thirty years in the same place, the smell of my apartments (for, with time, each dwelling takes on a particular odor) each night, these and other things disgust me and make me sick of living thus.

"Everything repeats itself endlessly. The way in which I put my key in the lock, the place where I always find my matches, the first object which meets my eye when I enter the room, make me feel like jumping out of the window and putting an end to those monotonous events from which we can never escape.

"Each day, when I shave, I feel an inordinate desire to cut my throat; and my face, which I see in the little mirror, always the same, with soap on my cheeks, has several times made me weak from sadness.

"Now I even hate to be with people whom I used to meet with pleasure; I know them so well, I can tell just what they are going to say and what I am going to answer. Each brain is like a circus, where the same horse keeps circling around eternally. We must circle round always, around the same ideas, the same joys, the same pleasures, the same habits, the same beliefs, the same sensations of disgust.

"The fog was terrible this evening. It enfolded the boulevard, where the street lights were dimmed and looked like smoking candles. A heavier weight than usual oppressed me. Perhaps my digestion was bad.

"For good digestion is everything in life. It gives the inspiration to the artist, amorous desires to young people, clear ideas to thinkers, the joy of life to everybody, and it also allows one to eat heartily (which is one of the greatest pleasures). A sick stomach induces scepticism unbelief, nightmares and the desire for death. I have often noticed this fact. Perhaps I would not kill myself, if my digestion had been good this evening.

"When I sat down in the arm-chair where I have been sitting every day for thirty years, I glanced around me, and just then I was seized by such a terrible distress that I thought I must go mad.

"I tried to think of what I could do to run away from myself. Every occupation struck me as being worse even than inaction. Then I bethought me of putting my papers in order.

"For a long time I have been thinking of clearing out my drawers; for, for the last thirty years, I have been throwing my letters and bills pell-mell into the same desk, and this confusion has often caused me considerable trouble. But I feel such moral and physical laziness at the sole idea of putting anything in order that I have never had the courage to begin this tedious business.

"I therefore opened my desk, intending to choose among my old papers and destroy the majority of them.

"At first I was bewildered by this array of documents, yellowed by age, then I chose one.

"Oh! if you cherish life, never disturb the burial place of old letters!

"And if, perchance, you should, take the contents by the handful, close your eyes that you may not read a word, so that you may not recognize some forgotten handwriting which may plunge you suddenly into a sea of memories; carry these papers to the fire; and when they are in ashes, crush them to an invisible powder, or otherwise you are lost—just as I have been lost for an hour.

"The first letters which I read did not interest me greatly. They were recent, and came from living men whom I still meet quite often, and whose presence does not move me to any great extent. But all at once one envelope made me start. My name was traced on it in a large, bold handwriting; and suddenly tears came to my eyes. That letter was from my dearest friend, the companion of my youth, the confidant of my hopes; and he appeared before me so clearly, with his pleasant smile and his hand outstretched, that a cold shiver ran down my back. Yes, yes, the dead come back, for I saw him! Our memory is a more perfect world than the universe: it gives back life to those who no longer exist.

"With trembling hand and dimmed eyes I reread everything that he told me, and in my poor sobbing heart I felt a wound so painful that I began to groan as a man whose bones are slowly being crushed.

"Then I travelled over my whole life, just as one travels along a river. I recognized people, so long forgotten that I no longer knew their names. Their faces alone lived in me. In my mother's letters I saw again the old servants, the shape of our house and the little insignificant odds and ends which cling to our minds.

"Yes, I suddenly saw again all my mother's old gowns, the different styles which she adopted and the several ways in which she dressed her hair. She haunted me especially in a silk dress, trimmed with old lace; and I remembered something she said one day when she was wearing this dress. She said: 'Robert, my child, if you do not stand up straight you will be round-shouldered all your life.'

"Then, opening another drawer, I found myself face to face with memories of tender passions: a dancing-pump, a torn handkerchief, even a garter, locks of hair and dried flowers. Then the sweet romances of my life, whose living heroines are now white-haired, plunged me into the deep melancholy of things. Oh, the young brows where blond locks curl, the caress of the hands, the glance which speaks, the hearts which beat, that smile which promises the lips, those lips which promise the embrace! And the first kiss-that endless kiss which makes you close your eyes, which drowns all thought in the immeasurable joy of approaching possession!

"Taking these old pledges of former love in both my hands, I covered them with furious caresses, and in my soul, torn by these memories, I saw them each again at the hour of surrender; and I suffered a torture more cruel than all the tortures invented in all the fables about hell.

"One last letter remained. It was written by me and dictated fifty years ago by my writing teacher. Here it is:

"'MY DEAR LITTLE MAMMA:

"'I am seven years old to-day. It is the age of reason. I take advantage of it to thank you for having brought me into this world.

"'Your little son, who loves you

"'ROBERT.'

"It is all over. I had gone back to the beginning, and suddenly I turned my glance on what remained to me of life. I saw hideous and lonely old age, and approaching infirmities, and everything over and gone. And nobody near me!

"My revolver is here, on the table. I am loading it . . . . Never reread your old letters!"

And that is how many men come to kill themselves; and we search in vain to discover some great sorrow in their lives.

AN ARTIFICE

The old doctor sat by the fireside, talking to his fair patient who was lying on the lounge. There was nothing much the matter with her, except that she had one of those little feminine ailments from which pretty women frequently suffer—slight anaemia, a nervous attack, etc.

"No, doctor," she said; "I shall never be able to understand a woman deceiving her husband. Even allowing that she does not love him, that she pays no heed to her vows and promises, how can she give herself to another man? How can she conceal the intrigue from other people's eyes? How can it be possible to love amid lies and treason?"

The doctor smiled, and replied: "It is perfectly easy, and I can assure you that a woman does not think of all those little subtle details when she has made up her mind to go astray.

"As for dissimulation, all women have plenty of it on hand for such occasions, and the simplest of them are wonderful, and extricate themselves from the greatest dilemmas in a remarkable manner."

The young woman, however, seemed incredulous.

"No, doctor," she said; "one never thinks until after it has happened of what one ought to have done in a critical situation, and women are certainly more liable than men to lose their head on such occasions:"

The doctor raised his hands. "After it has happened, you say! Now I will tell you something that happened to one of my female patients, whom I always considered an immaculate woman.

"It happened in a provincial town, and one night when I was asleep, in that deep first sleep from which it is so difficult to rouse us, it seemed to me, in my dreams, as if the bells in the town were sounding a fire alarm, and I woke up with a start. It was my own bell, which was ringing wildly, and as my footman did not seem to be answering the door, I, in turn, pulled the bell at the head of my bed, and soon I heard a banging, and steps in the silent house, and Jean came into my room, and handed me a letter which said: 'Madame Lelievre begs Dr. Simeon to come to her immediately.'

"I thought for a few moments, and then I said to myself: 'A nervous attack, vapors; nonsense, I am too tired.' And so I replied: 'As Dr. Simeon is not at all well, he must beg Madame Lelievre to be kind enough to call in his colleague, Monsieur Bonnet.' I put the note into an envelope and went to sleep again, but about half an hour later the street bell rang again, and Jean came to me and said: 'There is somebody downstairs; I do not quite know whether it is a man or a woman, as the individual is so wrapped up, but they wish to speak to you immediately. They say it is a matter of life and death for two people.' Whereupon I sat up in bed and told him to show the person in.

"A kind of black phantom appeared and raised her veil as soon as Jean had left the room. It was Madame Berthe Lelievre, quite a young woman, who had been married for three years to a large a merchant in the town, who was said to have married the prettiest girl in the neighborhood.

"She was terribly pale, her face was contracted as the faces of insane people are, occasionally, and her hands trembled violently. Twice she tried to speak without being able to utter a sound, but at last she stammered out: 'Come—quick—quick, doctor. Come—my—friend has just died in my bedroom.' She stopped, half suffocated with emotion, and then went on: 'My husband will be coming home from the club very soon.'

"I jumped out of bed without even considering that I was only in my nightshirt, and dressed myself in a few moments, and then I said: 'Did you come a short time ago?' 'No,' she said, standing like a statue petrified with horror. 'It was my servant—she knows.' And then, after a short silence, she went on: 'I was there—by his side.' And she uttered a sort of cry of horror, and after a fit of choking, which made her gasp, she wept violently, and shook with spasmodic sobs for a minute: or two. Then her tears suddenly ceased, as if by an internal fire, and with an air of tragic calmness, she said: 'Let us make haste.'

"I was ready, but exclaimed: 'I quite forgot to order my carriage.' 'I have one,' she said; 'it is his, which was waiting for him!' She wrapped herself up, so as to completely conceal her face, and we started.

"When she was by my side in the carriage she suddenly seized my hand, and crushing it in her delicate fingers, she said, with a shaking voice, that proceeded from a distracted heart: 'Oh! if you only knew, if you only knew what I am suffering! I loved him, I have loved him distractedly, like a madwoman, for the last six months.' 'Is anyone up in your house?' I asked. 'No, nobody except those, who knows everything.'

"We stopped at the door, and evidently everybody was asleep. We went in without making any noise, by means of her latch-key, and walked upstairs on tiptoe. The frightened servant was sitting on the top of the stairs with a lighted candle by her side, as she was afraid to remain with the dead man, and I went into the room, which was in great disorder. Wet towels, with which they had bathed the young man's temples, were lying on the floor, by the side of a washbasin and a glass, while a strong smell of vinegar pervaded the room.

"The dead man's body was lying at full length in the middle of the room, and I went up to it, looked at it, and touched it. I opened the eyes and felt the hands, and then, turning to the two women, who were shaking as if they were freezing, I said to them: 'Help me to lift him on to the bed.' When we had laid him gently on it, I listened to his heart and put a looking-glass to his lips, and then said: 'It is all over.' It was a terrible sight!

"I looked at the man, and said: 'You ought to arrange his hair a little.' The girl went and brought her mistress' comb and brush, but as she was trembling, and pulling out his long, matted hair in doing it, Madame Lelievre took the comb out of her hand, and arranged his hair as if she were caressing him. She parted it, brushed his beard, rolled his mustaches gently round her fingers, then, suddenly, letting go of his hair, she took the dead man's inert head in her hands and looked for a long time in despair at the dead face, which no longer could smile at her, and then, throwing herself on him, she clasped him in her arms and kissed him ardently. Her kisses fell like blows on his closed mouth and eyes, his forehead and temples; and then, putting her lips to his ear, as if he could still hear her, and as if she were about to whisper something to him, she said several times, in a heartrending voice:

"'Good-by, my darling!'

"Just then the clock struck twelve, and I started up. 'Twelve o'clock!' I exclaimed. 'That is the time when the club closes. Come, madame, we have not a moment to lose!' She started up, and I said:

"'We must carry him into the drawing-room.' And when we had done this, I placed him on a sofa, and lit the chandeliers, and just then the front door was opened and shut noisily. 'Rose, bring me the basin and the towels, and make the room look tidy. Make haste, for Heaven's sake! Monsieur Lelievre is coming in.'

"I heard his steps on the stairs, and then his hands feeling along the walls. 'Come here, my dear fellow,' I said; 'we have had an accident.'

"And the astonished husband appeared in the door with a cigar in his mouth, and said: 'What is the matter? What is the meaning of this?' 'My dear friend,' I said, going up to him, 'you find us in great embarrassment. I had remained late, chatting with your wife and our friend, who had brought me in his carriage, when he suddenly fainted, and in spite of all we have done, he has remained unconscious for two hours. I did not like to call in strangers, and if you will now help me downstairs with him, I shall be able to attend to him better at his own house.'

"The husband, who was surprised, but quite unsuspicious, took off his hat, and then he took his rival, who would be quite inoffensive for the future, under the arms. I got between his two legs, as if I had been a horse between the shafts, and we went downstairs, while his wife held a light for us. When we got outside I stood the body up, so as to deceive the coachman, and said: 'Come, my friend; it is nothing; you feel better already I expect. Pluck up your courage, and make an effort. It will soon be over.' But as I felt that he was slipping out of my hands, I gave him a slap on the shoulder, which sent him forward and made him fall into the carriage, and then I got in after him. Monsieur Lelievre, who was rather alarmed, said to me: 'Do you think it is anything serious?' To which I replied: 'No,' with a smile, as I looked at his wife, who had put her arm into that of her husband, and was trying to see into the carriage.

"I shook hands with them and told my coachman to start, and during the whole drive the dead man kept falling against me. When we got to his house I said that he had become unconscious on the way home, and helped to carry him upstairs, where I certified that he was dead, and acted another comedy to his distracted family, and at last I got back to bed, not without swearing at lovers."

The doctor ceased, though he was still smiling, and the young woman, who was in a very nervous state, said: "Why have you told me that terrible story?"

He gave her a gallant bow, and replied:

"So that I may offer you my services if they should be needed."

DREAMS

They had just dined together, five old friends, a writer, a doctor and three rich bachelors without any profession.

They had talked about everything, and a feeling of lassitude came over them, that feeling which precedes and leads to the departure of guests after festive gatherings. One of those present, who had for the last five minutes been gazing silently at the surging boulevard dotted with gas-lamps, with its rattling vehicles, said suddenly:

"When you've nothing to do from morning till night, the days are long."

"And the nights too," assented the guest who sat next to him. "I sleep very little; pleasures fatigue me; conversation is monotonous. Never do I come across a new idea, and I feel, before talking to any one, a violent longing to say nothing and to listen to nothing. I don't know what to do with my evenings."

The third idler remarked:

"I would pay a great deal for anything that would help me to pass just two pleasant hours every day."

The writer, who had just thrown his overcoat across his arm, turned round to them, and said:

"The man who could discover a new vice and introduce it among his fellow creatures, even if it were to shorten their lives, would render a greater service to humanity than the man who found the means of securing to them eternal salvation and eternal youth."

The doctor burst out laughing, and, while he chewed his cigar, he said:

"Yes, but it is not so easy to discover it. Men have however crudely, been seeking for—and working for the object you refer to since the beginning of the world. The men who came first reached perfection at once in this way. We are hardly equal to them."

One of the three idlers murmured:

"What a pity!"

Then, after a minute's pause, he added:

"If we could only sleep, sleep well, without feeling hot or cold, sleep with that perfect unconsciousness we experience on nights when we are thoroughly fatigued, sleep without dreams."

"Why without dreams?" asked the guest sitting next to him.

The other replied:

"Because dreams are not always pleasant; they are always fantastic, improbable, disconnected; and because when we are asleep we cannot have the sort of dreams we like. We ought to dream waking."

"And what's to prevent you?" asked the writer.

The doctor flung away the end of his cigar.

"My dear fellow, in order to dream when you are awake, you need great power and great exercise of will, and when you try to do it, great weariness is the result. Now, real dreaming, that journey of our thoughts through delightful visions, is assuredly the sweetest experience in the world; but it must come naturally, it must not be provoked in a painful, manner, and must be accompanied by absolute bodily comfort. This power of dreaming I can give you, provided you promise that you will not abuse it."

The writer shrugged his shoulders:

"Ah! yes, I know—hasheesh, opium, green tea—artificial paradises. I have read Baudelaire, and I even tasted the famous drug, which made me very sick."

But the doctor, without stirring from his seat, said:

"No; ether, nothing but ether; and I would suggest that you literary men should use it sometimes."

The three rich bachelors drew closer to the doctor.

One of them said:

"Explain to us the effects of it."

And the doctor replied:

"Let us put aside big words, shall we not? I am not talking of medicine or morality; I am talking of pleasure. You give yourselves up every day to excesses which consume your lives. I want to indicate to you a new sensation, possible only to intelligent men—let us say even very intelligent men—dangerous, like everything else that overexcites our organs, but exquisite. I might add that you would require a certain preparation, that is to say, practice, to feel in all their completeness the singular effects of ether.

"They are different from the effects of hasheesh, of opium, or morphia, and they cease as soon as the absorption of the drug is interrupted, while the other generators of day dreams continue their action for hours.

"I am now going to try to analyze these feelings as clearly as possible. But the thing is not easy, so facile, so delicate, so almost imperceptible, are these sensations.

"It was when I was attacked by violent neuralgia that I made use of this remedy, which since then I have, perhaps, slightly abused.

"I had acute pains in my head and neck, and an intolerable heat of the skin, a feverish restlessness. I took up a large bottle of ether, and, lying down, I began to inhale it slowly.

"At the end of some minutes I thought I heard a vague murmur, which ere long became a sort of humming, and it seemed to me that all the interior of my body had become light, light as air, that it was dissolving into vapor.

"Then came a sort of torpor, a sleepy sensation of comfort, in spite of the pains which still continued, but which had ceased to make themselves felt. It was one of those sensations which we are willing to endure and not any of those frightful wrenches against which our tortured body protests.

"Soon the strange and delightful sense of emptiness which I felt in my chest extended to my limbs, which, in their turn, became light, as light as if the flesh and the bones had been melted and the skin only were left, the skin necessary to enable me to realize the sweetness of living, of bathing in this sensation of well-being. Then I perceived that I was no longer suffering. The pain had gone, melted away, evaporated. And I heard voices, four voices, two dialogues, without understanding what was said. At one time there were only indistinct sounds, at another time a word reached my ear. But I recognized that this was only the humming I had heard before, but emphasized. I was not asleep; I was not awake; I comprehended, I felt, I reasoned with the utmost clearness and depth, with extraordinary energy and intellectual pleasure, with a singular intoxication arising from this separation of my mental faculties.

"It was not like the dreams caused by hasheesh or the somewhat sickly visions that come from opium; it was an amazing acuteness of reasoning, a new way of seeing, judging and appreciating the things of life, and with the certainty, the absolute consciousness that this was the true way.

"And the old image of the Scriptures suddenly came back to my mind. It seemed to me that I had tasted of the Tree of Knowledge, that all the mysteries were unveiled, so much did I find myself under the sway of a new, strange and irrefutable logic. And arguments, reasonings, proofs rose up in a heap before my brain only to be immediately displaced by some stronger proof, reasoning, argument. My head had, in fact, become a battleground of ideas. I was a superior being, armed with invincible intelligence, and I experienced a huge delight at the manifestation of my power.

"It lasted a long, long time. I still kept inhaling the ether from my flagon. Suddenly I perceived that it was empty."

The four men exclaimed at the same time:

"Doctor, a prescription at once for a liter of ether!"

But the doctor, putting on his hat, replied:

"As to that, certainly not; go and let some one else poison you!"

And he left them.

Ladies and gentlemen, what is your opinion on the subject?

SIMON'S PAPA

Noon had just struck. The school door opened and the youngsters darted out, jostling each other in their haste to get out quickly. But instead of promptly dispersing and going home to dinner as usual, they stopped a few paces off, broke up into knots, and began whispering.

The fact was that, that morning, Simon, the son of La Blanchotte, had, for the first time, attended school.

They had all of them in their families heard talk of La Blanchotte; and, although in public she was welcome enough, the mothers among themselves treated her with a somewhat disdainful compassion, which the children had imitated without in the least knowing why.

As for Simon himself, they did not know him, for he never went out, and did not run about with them in the streets of the village, or along the banks of the river. And they did not care for him; so it was with a certain delight, mingled with considerable astonishment, that they met and repeated to each other what had been said by a lad of fourteen or fifteen who appeared to know all about it, so sagaciously did he wink. "You know—Simon—well, he has no papa."

Just then La Blanchotte's son appeared in the doorway of the school.

He was seven or eight years old, rather pale, very neat, with a timid and almost awkward manner.

He was starting home to his mother's house when the groups of his schoolmates, whispering and watching him with the mischievous and heartless eyes of children bent upon playing a nasty trick, gradually closed in around him and ended by surrounding him altogether. There he stood in their midst, surprised and embarrassed, not understanding what they were going to do with him. But the lad who had brought the news, puffed up with the success he had met with already, demanded:

"What is your name, you?"

He answered: "Simon."

"Simon what?" retorted the other.

The child, altogether bewildered, repeated: "Simon."

The lad shouted at him: "One is named Simon something—that is not a name—Simon indeed."

The child, on the brink of tears, replied for the third time:

"My name is Simon."

The urchins began to laugh. The triumphant tormentor cried: "You can see plainly that he has no papa."

A deep silence ensued. The children were dumfounded by this extraordinary, impossible, monstrous thing—a boy who had not a papa; they looked upon him as a phenomenon, an unnatural being, and they felt that hitherto inexplicable contempt of their mothers for La Blanchotte growing upon them. As for Simon, he had leaned against a tree to avoid falling, and he remained as if prostrated by an irreparable disaster. He sought to explain, but could think of nothing-to say to refute this horrible charge that he had no papa. At last he shouted at them quite recklessly: "Yes, I have one."

"Where is he?" demanded the boy.

Simon was silent, he did not know. The children roared, tremendously excited; and those country boys, little more than animals, experienced that cruel craving which prompts the fowls of a farmyard to destroy one of their number as soon as it is wounded. Simon suddenly espied a little neighbor, the son of a widow, whom he had seen, as he himself was to be seen, always alone with his mother.

"And no more have you," he said; "no more have you a papa."

"Yes," replied the other, "I have one."

"Where is he?" rejoined Simon.

"He is dead," declared the brat, with superb dignity; "he is in the cemetery, is my papa."

A murmur of approval rose among the little wretches as if this fact of possessing a papa dead in a cemetery had caused their comrade to grow big enough to crush the other one who had no papa at all. And these boys, whose fathers were for the most part bad men, drunkards, thieves, and who beat their wives, jostled each other to press closer and closer, as though they, the legitimate ones, would smother by their pressure one who was illegitimate.

The boy who chanced to be next Simon suddenly put his tongue out at him with a mocking air and shouted at him:

"No papa! No papa!"

Simon seized him by the hair with both hands and set to work to disable his legs with kicks, while he bit his cheek ferociously. A tremendous struggle ensued between the two combatants, and Simon found himself beaten, torn, bruised, rolled on the ground in the midst of the ring of applauding schoolboys. As he arose, mechanically brushing with his hand his little blouse all covered with dust, some one shouted at him:

"Go and tell your papa."

Then he felt a great sinking at his heart. They were stronger than he was, they had beaten him, and he had no answer to give them, for he knew well that it was true that he had no papa. Full of pride, he attempted for some moments to struggle against the tears which were choking him. He had a feeling of suffocation, and then without any sound he commenced to weep, with great shaking sobs. A ferocious joy broke out among his enemies, and, with one accord, just like savages in their fearful festivals, they took each other by the hand and danced round him in a circle, repeating as a refrain:

"No papa! No papa!"

But suddenly Simon ceased sobbing. He became ferocious. There were stones under his feet; he picked them up and with all his strength hurled them at his tormentors. Two or three were struck and rushed off yelling, and so formidable did he appear that the rest became panic-stricken. Cowards, as the mob always is in presence of an exasperated man, they broke up and fled. Left alone, the little fellow without a father set off running toward the fields, for a recollection had been awakened in him which determined his soul to a great resolve. He made up his mind to drown himself in the river.

He remembered, in fact, that eight days before, a poor devil who begged for his livelihood had thrown himself into the water because he had no more money. Simon had been there when they fished him out again; and the wretched man, who usually seemed to him so miserable, and ugly, had then struck him as being so peaceful with his pale cheeks, his long drenched beard, and his open eyes full of calm. The bystanders had said:

"He is dead."

And some one had said:

"He is quite happy now."

And Simon wished to drown himself also, because he had no father, just like the wretched being who had no money.

He reached the water and watched it flowing. Some fish were sporting briskly in the clear stream and occasionally made a little bound and caught the flies flying on the surface. He stopped crying in order to watch them, for their maneuvers interested him greatly. But, at intervals, as in a tempest intervals of calm alternate suddenly with tremendous gusts of wind, which snap off the trees and then lose themselves in the horizon, this thought would return to him with intense pain:

"I am going to drown myself because I have no papa."

It was very warm, fine weather. The pleasant sunshine warmed the grass. The water shone like a mirror. And Simon enjoyed some minutes of happiness, of that languor which follows weeping, and felt inclined to fall asleep there upon the grass in the warm sunshine.

A little green frog leaped from under his feet. He endeavored to catch it. It escaped him. He followed it and lost it three times in succession. At last he caught it by one of its hind legs and began to laugh as he saw the efforts the creature made to escape. It gathered itself up on its hind legs and then with a violent spring suddenly stretched them out as stiff as two bars; while it beat the air with its front legs as though they were hands, its round eyes staring in their circle of yellow. It reminded him of a toy made of straight slips of wood nailed zigzag one on the other; which by a similar movement regulated the movements of the little soldiers fastened thereon. Then he thought of his home, and then of his mother, and, overcome by sorrow, he again began to weep. A shiver passed over him. He knelt down and said his prayers as before going to bed. But he was unable to finish them, for tumultuous, violent sobs shook his whole frame. He no longer thought, he no longer saw anything around him, and was wholly absorbed in crying.

Suddenly a heavy hand was placed upon his shoulder, and a rough voice asked him:

"What is it that causes you so much grief, my little man?"

Simon turned round. A tall workman with a beard and black curly hair was staring at him good-naturedly. He answered with his eyes and throat full of tears:

"They beat me—because—I—I have no—papa—no papa."

"What!" said the man, smiling; "why, everybody has one."

The child answered painfully amid his spasms of grief:

"But I—I—I have none."

Then the workman became serious. He had recognized La Blanchotte's son, and, although himself a new arrival in the neighborhood, he had a vague idea of her history.

"Well," said he, "console yourself, my boy, and come with me home to your mother. They will give you—a papa."

And so they started on the way, the big fellow holding the little fellow by the hand, and the man smiled, for he was not sorry to see this Blanchotte, who was, it was said, one of the prettiest girls of the countryside, and, perhaps, he was saying to himself, at the bottom of his heart, that a lass who had erred might very well err again.

They arrived in front of a very neat little white house.

"There it is," exclaimed the child, and he cried, "Mamma!"

A woman appeared, and the workman instantly left off smiling, for he saw at once that there was no fooling to be done with the tall pale girl who stood austerely at her door as though to defend from one man the threshold of that house where she had already been betrayed by another. Intimidated, his cap in his hand, he stammered out:

"See, madame, I have brought you back your little boy who had lost himself near the river."

But Simon flung his arms about his mother's neck and told her, as he again began to cry:

"No, mamma, I wished to drown myself, because the others had beaten me —had beaten me— because I have no papa."

A burning redness covered the young woman's cheeks; and, hurt to the quick, she embraced her child passionately, while the tears coursed down her face. The man, much moved, stood there, not knowing how to get away.

But Simon suddenly ran to him and said:

"Will you be my papa?"

A deep silence ensued. La Blanchotte, dumb and tortured with shame, leaned herself against the wall, both her hands upon her heart. The child, seeing that no answer was made him, replied:

"If you will not, I shall go back and drown myself."

The workman took the matter as a jest and answered, laughing:

"Why, yes, certainly I will."

"What is your name," went on the child, "so that I may tell the others when they wish to know your name?"

"Philip," answered the man:

Simon was silent a moment so that he might get the name well into his head; then he stretched out his arms, quite consoled, as he said:

"Well, then, Philip, you are my papa."

The workman, lifting him from the ground, kissed him hastily on both cheeks, and then walked away very quickly with great strides. When the child returned to school next day he was received with a spiteful laugh, and at the end of school, when the lads were on the point of recommencing, Simon threw these words at their heads as he would have done a stone: "He is named Philip, my papa."

Yells of delight burst out from all sides.

"Philip who? Philip what? What on earth is Philip? Where did you pick up your Philip?"

Simon answered nothing; and, immovable in his faith, he defied them with his eye, ready to be martyred rather than fly before them. The school master came to his rescue and he returned home to his mother.

During three months, the tall workman, Philip, frequently passed by La Blanchotte's house, and sometimes he made bold to speak to her when he saw her sewing near the window. She answered him civilly, always sedately, never joking with him, nor permitting him to enter her house. Notwithstanding, being, like all men, a bit of a coxcomb, he imagined that she was often rosier than usual when she chatted with him.

But a lost reputation is so difficult to regain and always remains so fragile that, in spite of the shy reserve of La Blanchotte, they already gossiped in the neighborhood.

As for Simon he loved his new papa very much, and walked with him nearly every evening when the day's work was done. He went regularly to school, and mixed with great dignity with his schoolfellows without ever answering them back.

One day, however, the lad who had first attacked him said to him:

"You have lied. You have not a papa named Philip."

"Why do you say that?" demanded Simon, much disturbed.

The youth rubbed his hands. He replied:

"Because if you had one he would be your mamma's husband."

Simon was confused by the truth of this reasoning; nevertheless, he retorted:

"He is my papa, all the same."

"That can very well be," exclaimed the urchin with a sneer, "but that is not being your papa altogether."

La Blanchotte's little one bowed his head and went off dreaming in the direction of the forge belonging to old Loizon, where Philip worked. This forge was as though buried beneath trees. It was very dark there; the red glare of a formidable furnace alone lit up with great flashes five blacksmiths; who hammered upon their anvils with a terrible din. They were standing enveloped in flame, like demons, their eyes fixed on the red-hot iron they were pounding; and their dull ideas rose and fell with their hammers.

Simon entered without being noticed, and went quietly to pluck his friend by the sleeve. The latter turned round. All at once the work came to a standstill, and all the men looked on, very attentive. Then, in the midst of this unaccustomed silence, rose the slender pipe of Simon:

"Say, Philip, the Michaude boy told me just now that you were not altogether my papa."

"Why not?" asked the blacksmith,

The child replied with all innocence:

"Because you are not my mamma's husband."

No one laughed. Philip remained standing, leaning his forehead upon the back of his great hands, which supported the handle of his hammer standing upright upon the anvil. He mused. His four companions watched him, and Simon, a tiny mite among these giants, anxiously waited. Suddenly, one of the smiths, answering to the sentiment of all, said to Philip:

"La Blanchotte is a good, honest girl, and upright and steady in spite of her misfortune, and would make a worthy wife for an honest man."

"That is true," remarked the three others.

The smith continued:

"Is it the girl's fault if she went wrong? She had been promised marriage; and I know more than one who is much respected to-day, and who sinned every bit as much."

"That is true," responded the three men in chorus.

He resumed:

"How hard she has toiled, poor thing, to bring up her child all alone, and how she has wept all these years she has never gone out except to church, God only knows."

"This is also true," said the others.

Then nothing was heard but the bellows which fanned the fire of the furnace. Philip hastily bent himself down to Simon:

"Go and tell your mother that I am coming to speak to her this evening." Then he pushed the child out by the shoulders. He returned to his work, and with a single blow the five hammers again fell upon their anvils. Thus they wrought the iron until nightfall, strong, powerful, happy, like contented hammers. But just as the great bell of a cathedral resounds upon feast days above the jingling of the other bells, so Philip's hammer, sounding above the rest, clanged second after second with a deafening uproar. And he stood amid the flying sparks plying his trade vigorously.

The sky was full of stars as he knocked at La Blanchotte's door. He had on his Sunday blouse, a clean shirt, and his beard was trimmed. The young woman showed herself upon the threshold, and said in a grieved tone:

"It is ill to come thus when night has fallen, Mr. Philip."

He wished to answer, but stammered and stood confused before her.

She resumed:

"You understand, do you not, that it will not do for me to be talked about again."

"What does that matter to me, if you will be my wife!"

No voice replied to him, but he believed that he heard in the shadow of the room the sound of a falling body. He entered quickly; and Simon, who had gone to bed, distinguished the sound of a kiss and some words that his mother murmured softly. Then, all at once, he found himself lifted up by the hands of his friend, who, holding him at the length of his herculean arms, exclaimed:

"You will tell them, your schoolmates, that your papa is Philip Remy, the blacksmith, and that he will pull the ears of all who do you any harm."

On the morrow, when the school was full and lessons were about to begin, little Simon stood up, quite pale with trembling lips:

"My papa," said he in a clear voice, "is Philip Remy, the blacksmith, and he has promised to pull the ears of all who does me any harm."

This time no one laughed, for he was very well known, was Philip Remy, the blacksmith, and was a papa of whom any one in the world would have been proud.

VOLUME XII.

THE CHILD

Lemonnier had remained a widower with one child. He had loved his wife devotedly, with a tender and exalted love, without a slip, during their entire married life. He was a good, honest man, perfectly simple, sincere, without suspicion or malice.

He fell in love with a poor neighbor, proposed and was accepted. He was making a very comfortable living out of the wholesale cloth business, and he did not for a minute suspect that the young girl might have accepted him for anything else but himself.

She made him happy. She was everything to him; he only thought of her, looked at her continually, with worshiping eyes. During meals he would make any number of blunders, in order not to have to take his eyes from the beloved face; he would pour the wine in his plate and the water in the salt-cellar, then he would laugh like a child, repeating:

"You see, I love you too much; that makes me crazy."

She would smile with a calm and resigned look; then she would look away, as though embarrassed by the adoration of her husband, and try to make him talk about something else; but he would take her hand under the table and he would hold it in his, whispering:

"My little Jeanne, my darling little Jeanne!"

She sometimes lost patience and said:

"Come, come, be reasonable; eat and let me eat."

He would sigh and break off a mouthful of bread, which he would then chew slowly.

For five years they had no children. Then suddenly she announced to him that this state of affairs would soon cease. He was wild with joy. He no longer left her for a minute, until his old nurse, who had brought him up and who often ruled the house, would push him out and close the door behind him, in order to compel him to go out in the fresh air.

He had grown very intimate with a young man who had known his wife since childhood, and who was one of the prefect's secretaries. M. Duretour would dine three times a week with the Lemonniers, bringing flowers to madame, and sometimes a box at the theater; and often, at the end of the dinner, Lemonnier, growing tender, turning towards his wife, would explain: "With a companion like you and a friend like him, a man is completely happy on earth."

She died in childbirth. The shock almost killed him. But the sight of the child, a poor, moaning little creature, gave him courage.

He loved it with a passionate and sorrowful love, with a morbid love in which stuck the memory of death, but in which lived something of his worship for the dead mother. It was the flesh of his wife, her being continued, a sort of quintessence of herself. This child was her very life transferred to another body; she had disappeared that it might exist, and the father would smother it in with kisses. But also, this child had killed her; he had stolen this beloved creature, his life was at the cost of hers. And M. Lemonnier would place his son in the cradle and would sit down and watch him. He would sit this way by the hour, looking at him, dreaming of thousands of things, sweet or sad. Then, when the little one was asleep, he would bend over him and sob.

The child grew. The father could no longer spend an hour away from him; he would stay near him, take him out for walks, and himself dress him, wash him, make him eat. His friend, M. Duretour, also seemed to love the boy; he would kiss him wildly, in those frenzies of tenderness which are characteristic of parents. He would toss him in his arms, he would trot him on his knees, by the hour, and M. Lemonnier, delighted, would mutter:

"Isn't he a darling? Isn't he a darling?"

And M. Duretour would hug the child in his arms and tickle his neck with his mustache.

Celeste, the old nurse, alone, seemed to have no tenderness for the little one. She would grow angry at his pranks, and seemed impatient at the caresses of the two men. She would exclaim:

"How can you expect to bring a child up like that? You'll make a perfect monkey out of him."

Years went by, and Jean was nine years old. He hardly knew how to read; he had been so spoiled, and only did as he saw fit. He was willful, stubborn and quick-tempered. The father always gave in to him and let him have his own way. M. Duretour would always buy him all the toys he wished, and he fed him on cake and candies. Then Celeste would grow angry and exclaim:

"It's a shame, monsieur, a shame. You are spoiling this child. But it will have to stop; yes, sir, I tell you it will have to stop, and before long, too."

M. Lemonnier would answer, smiling:

"What can you expect? I love him too much, I can't resist him; you must get used to it."

Jean was delicate, rather. The doctor said that he was anaemic, prescribed iron, rare meat and broth.

But the little fellow loved only cake and refused all other nourishment; and the father, in despair, stuffed him with cream-puffs and chocolate eclairs.

One evening, as they were sitting down to supper, Celeste brought on the soup with an air of authority and an assurance which she did not usually have. She took off the cover and, dipping the ladle into the dish, she declared:

"Here is some broth such as I have never made; the young one will have to take some this time."

M. Lemonnier, frightened, bent his head. He saw a storm brewing.

Celeste took his plate, filled it herself and placed it in front of him.

He tasted the soup and said:

"It is, indeed, excellent."

The servant took the boy's plate and poured a spoonful of soup in it. Then she retreated a few steps and waited.

Jean smelled the food and pushed his plate away with an expression of disgust. Celeste, suddenly pale, quickly stepped forward and forcibly poured a spoonful down the child's open mouth.

He choked, coughed, sneezed, spat; howling, he seized his glass and threw it at his nurse. She received it full in the stomach. Then, exasperated, she took the young shaver's head under her arm and began pouring spoonful after spoonful of soup down his throat. He grew as red as a beet, and he would cough it up, stamping, twisting, choking, beating the air with his hands.

At first the father was so surprised that he could not move. Then, suddenly, he rushed forward, wild with rage, seized the servant by the throat and threw her up against the wall stammering:

"Out! Out! Out! you brute!"

But she shook him off, and, her hair streaming down her back, her eyes snapping, she cried out:

"What's gettin' hold of you? You're trying to thrash me because I am making this child eat soup when you are filling him with sweet stuff!"

He kept repeating, trembling from head to foot:

"Out! Get out-get out, you brute!"

Then, wild, she turned to him and, pushing her face up against his, her voice trembling:

"Ah!—you think-you think that you can treat me like that? Oh! no. And for whom?—for that brat who is not even yours. No, not yours! No, not yours—not yours! Everybody knows it, except yourself! Ask the grocer, the butcher, the baker, all of them, any one of them!"

She was growling and mumbling, choked with passion; then she stopped and looked at him.

He was motionless livid, his arms hanging by his sides. After a short pause, he murmured in a faint, shaky voice, instinct with deep feeling:

"You say? you say? What do you say?"

She remained silent, frightened by his appearance. Once more he stepped forward, repeating:

"You say—what do you say?"

Then in a calm voice, she answered:

"I say what I know, what everybody knows."

He seized her and, with the fury of a beast, he tried to throw her down. But, although old, she was strong and nimble. She slipped under his arm, and running around the table once more furious, she screamed:

"Look at him, just look at him, fool that you are! Isn't he the living image of M. Durefour? just look at his nose and his eyes! Are yours like that? And his hair! Is it like his mother's? I tell you that everyone knows it, everyone except yourself! It's the joke of the town! Look at him!"

She went to the door, opened it, and disappeared.

Jean, frightened, sat motionless before his plate of soup.

At the end of an hour, she returned gently, to see how matters stood. The child, after doing away with all the cakes and a pitcher full of cream and one of syrup, was now emptying the jam-pot with his soup-spoon.

The father had gone out.

Celeste took the child, kissed him, and gently carried him to his room and put him to bed. She came back to the dining-room, cleared the table, put everything in place, feeling very uneasy all the time.

Not a single sound could be heard throughout the house. She put her ear against's her master's door. He seemed to be perfectly still. She put her eye to the keyhole. He was writing, and seemed very calm.

Then she returned to the kitchen and sat down, ready for any emergency. She slept on a chair and awoke at daylight.

She did the rooms as she had been accustomed to every morning; she swept and dusted, and, towards eight o'clock, prepared M. Lemonnier's breakfast.

But she did not dare bring it to her master, knowing too well how she would be received; she waited for him to ring. But he did not ring. Nine o'clock, then ten o'clock went by.

Celeste, not knowing what to think, prepared her tray and started up with it, her heart beating fast.

She stopped before the door and listened. Everything was still. She knocked; no answer. Then, gathering up all her courage, she opened the door and entered. With a wild shriek, she dropped the breakfast tray which she had been holding in her hand.

In the middle of the room, M. Lemonnier was hanging by a rope from a ring in the ceiling. His tongue was sticking out horribly. His right slipper was lying on the ground, his left one still on his foot. An upturned chair had rolled over to the bed.

Celeste, dazed, ran away shrieking. All the neighbors crowded together. The physician declared that he had died at about midnight.

A letter addressed to M. Duretdur was found on the table of the suicide. It contained these words:

"I leave and entrust the child to you!"

A COUNTRY EXCURSION

For five months they had been talking of going to take luncheon in one of the country suburbs of Paris on Madame Dufour's birthday, and as they were looking forward very impatiently to the outing, they rose very early that morning. Monsieur Dufour had borrowed the milkman's wagon and drove himself. It was a very tidy, two-wheeled conveyance, with a cover supported by four iron rods, with curtains that had been drawn up, except the one at the back, which floated out like a sail. Madame Dufour, resplendent in a wonderful, cherry colored silk dress, sat by the side of her husband.

The old grandmother and a girl sat behind them on two chairs, and a boy with yellow hair was lying at the bottom of the wagon, with nothing to be seen of him except his head.

When they reached the bridge of Neuilly, Monsieur Dufour said: "Here we are in the country at last!" and at that signal his wife grew sentimental about the beauties of nature. When they got to the crossroads at Courbevoie they were seized with admiration for the distant landscape. On the right was Argenteuil with its bell tower, and above it rose the hills of Sannois and the mill of Orgemont, while on the left the aqueduct of Marly stood out against the clear morning sky, and in the distance they could see the terrace of Saint-Germain; and opposite them, at the end of a low chain of hills, the new fort of Cormeilles. Quite in the distance; a very long way off, beyond the plains and village, one could see the sombre green of the forests.

The sun was beginning to burn their faces, the dust got into their eyes, and on either side of the road there stretched an interminable tract of bare, ugly country with an unpleasant odor. One might have thought that it had been ravaged by a pestilence, which had even attacked the buildings, for skeletons of dilapidated and deserted houses, or small cottages, which were left in an unfinished state, because the contractors had not been paid, reared their four roofless walls on each side.

Here and there tall factory chimneys rose up from the barren soil. The only vegetation on that putrid land, where the spring breezes wafted an odor of petroleum and slate, blended with another odor that was even less agreeable. At last, however, they crossed the Seine a second time, and the bridge was a delight. The river sparkled in the sun, and they had a feeling of quiet enjoyment, felt refreshed as they drank in the purer air that was not impregnated by the black smoke of factories nor by the miasma from the deposits of night soil. A man whom they met told them that the name of the place was Bezons. Monsieur Dufour pulled up and read the attractive announcement outside an eating house: Restaurant Poulin, matelottes and fried fish, private rooms, arbors, and swings.

"Well, Madame Dufour, will this suit you? Will you make up your mind at last?"

She read the announcement in her turn and then looked at the house for some time.

It was a white country inn, built by the roadside, and through the open door she could see the bright zinc of the counter, at which sat two workmen in their Sunday clothes. At last she made up her mind and said:

"Yes, this will do; and, besides, there is a view."

They drove into a large field behind the inn, separated from the river by the towing path, and dismounted. The husband sprang out first and then held out his arms for his wife, and as the step was very high Madame Dufour, in order to reach him, had to show the lower part of her limbs, whose former slenderness had disappeared in fat, and Monsieur Dufour, who was already getting excited by the country air, pinched her calf, and then, taking her in his arms, he set her on the ground, as if she had been some enormous bundle. She shook the dust out of the silk dress and then looked round to see in what sort of a place she was.

She was a stout woman, of about thirty-six, full-blown, and delightful to look at. She could hardly breathe, as her corsets were laced too tightly, and their pressure forced her superabundant bosom up to her double chin. Next the girl placed her hand on her father's shoulder and jumped down lightly. The boy with the yellow hair had got down by stepping on the wheel, and he helped Monsieur Dufour to lift his grandmother out. Then they unharnessed the horse, which they had tied to a tree, and the carriage fell back, with both shafts in the air. The men took off their coats and washed their hands in a pail of water and then went and joined the ladies, who had already taken possession of the swings.

Mademoiselle Dufour was trying to swing herself standing up, but she could not succeed in getting a start. She was a pretty girl of about eighteen, one of those women who suddenly excite your desire when you meet them in the street and who leave you with a vague feeling of uneasiness and of excited senses. She was tall, had a small waist and large hips, with a dark skin, very large eyes and very black hair. Her dress clearly marked the outlines of her firm, full figure, which was accentuated by the motion of her hips as she tried to swing herself higher. Her arms were stretched upward to hold the rope, so that her bosom rose at every movement she made. Her hat, which a gust of wind had blown off, was hanging behind her, and as the swing gradually rose higher and higher, she showed her delicate limbs up to the knees each time, and the breeze from her flying skirts, which was more heady than the fumes of wine, blew into the faces of the two men, who were looking at her and smiling.

Sitting in the other swing, Madame Dufour kept saying in a monotonous voice:

"Cyprian, come and swing me; do come and swing me, Cyprian!"

At last he went, and turning up his shirt sleeves, as if undertaking a hard piece of work, with much difficulty he set his wife in motion. She clutched the two ropes and held her legs out straight, so as not to touch the ground. She enjoyed feeling dizzy at the motion of the swing, and her whole figure shook like a jelly on a dish, but as she went higher and higher; she became too giddy and was frightened. Each time the swing came down she uttered a piercing scream, which made all the little urchins in the neighborhood come round, and down below, beneath the garden hedge, she vaguely saw a row of mischievous heads making various grimaces as they laughed.

When a servant girl came out they ordered luncheon.

"Some fried fish, a rabbit saute, salad and dessert," Madame Dufour said, with an important air.

"Bring two quarts of beer and a bottle of claret," her husband said.

"We will have lunch on the grass," the girl added.

The grandmother, who had an affection for cats, had been running after one that belonged to the house, trying to coax it to come to her for the last ten minutes. The animal, who was no doubt secretly flattered by her attentions, kept close to the good woman, but just out of reach of her hand, and quietly walked round the trees, against which she rubbed herself, with her tail up, purring with pleasure.

"Hello!" suddenly exclaimed the young man with the yellow hair, who was wandering about. "Here are two swell boats!" They all went to look at them and saw two beautiful canoes in a wooden shed; they were as beautifully finished as if they had been ornamental furniture. They hung side by side, like two tall, slender girls, in their narrow shining length, and made one wish to float in them on warm summer mornings and evenings along the flower-covered banks of the river, where the trees dip their branches into the water, where the rushes are continually rustling in the breeze and where the swift kingfishers dart about like flashes of blue lightning.

The whole family looked at them with great respect.

"Oh, they are indeed swell boats!" Monsieur Dufour repeated gravely, as he examined them like a connoiseur. He had been in the habit of rowing in his younger days, he said, and when he had spat in his hands—and he went through the action of pulling the oars—he did not care a fig for anybody. He had beaten more than one Englishman formerly at the Joinville regattas. He grew quite excited at last and offered to make a bet that in a boat like that he could row six leagues an hour without exerting himself.

"Luncheon is ready," the waitress said, appearing at the entrance to the boathouse, and they all hurried off. But two young men had taken the very seats that Madame Dufour had selected and were eating their luncheon. No doubt they were the owners of the sculls, for they were in boating costume. They were stretched out, almost lying on the chairs; they were sun-browned and their thin cotton jerseys, with short sleeves, showed their bare arms, which were as strong as a blacksmith's. They were two strong, athletic fellows, who showed in all their movements that elasticity and grace of limb which can only be acquired by exercise and which is so different to the deformity with which monotonous heavy work stamps the mechanic.

They exchanged a rapid smile when they saw the mother and then a glance on seeing the daughter.

"Let us give up our place," one of them said; "it will make us acquainted with them."

The other got up immediately, and holding his black and red boating cap in his hand, he politely offered the ladies the only shady place in the garden. With many excuses they accepted, and that it might be more rural, they sat on the grass, without either tables or chairs.

The two young men took their plates, knives, forks, etc., to a table a little way off and began to eat again, and their bare arms, which they showed continually, rather embarrassed the girl. She even pretended to turn her head aside and not to see them, while Madame Dufour, who was rather bolder, tempted by feminine curiosity, looked at them every moment, and, no doubt, compared them with the secret unsightliness of her husband. She had squatted herself on ground, with her legs tucked under her, after the manner of tailors, and she kept moving about restlessly, saying that ants were crawling about her somewhere. Monsieur Dufour, annoyed at the presence of the polite strangers, was trying to find a comfortable position which he did not, however, succeed in doing, and the young man with the yellow hair was eating as silently as an ogre.

"It is lovely weather, monsieur," the stout lady said to one of the boating men. She wished to be friendly because they had given up their place.

"It is, indeed, madame," he replied. "Do you often go into the country?"

"Oh, only once or twice a year to get a little fresh air. And you, monsieur?"

"I come and sleep here every night."

"Oh, that must be very nice!"

"Certainly it is, madame." And he gave them such a practical account of his daily life that it awakened afresh in the hearts of these shopkeepers who were deprived of the meadows and who longed for country walks, to that foolish love of nature which they all feel so strongly the whole year round behind the counter in their shop.

The girl raised her eyes and looked at the oarsman with emotion and Monsieur Dufour spoke for the first time.

"It is indeed a happy life," he said. And then he added: "A little more rabbit, my dear?"

"No, thank you," she replied, and turning to the young men again, and pointing to their arms, asked: "Do you never feel cold like that?"

They both began to laugh, and they astonished the family with an account of the enormous fatigue they could endure, of their bathing while in a state of tremendous perspiration, of their rowing in the fog at night; and they struck their chests violently to show how hollow they sounded.

"Ah! You look very strong," said the husband, who did not talk any more of the time when he used to beat the English. The girl was looking at them sideways now, and the young fellow with the yellow hair, who had swallowed some wine the wrong way, was coughing violently and bespattering Madame Dufour's cherry-colored silk dress. She got angry and sent for some water to wash the spots.

Meanwhile it had grown unbearably hot, the sparkling river looked like a blaze of fire and the fumes of the wine were getting into their heads. Monsieur Dufour, who had a violent hiccough, had unbuttoned his waistcoat and the top button of his trousers, while his wife, who felt choking, was gradually unfastening her dress. The apprentice was shaking his yellow wig in a happy frame of mind, and kept helping himself to wine, and the old grandmother, feeling the effects of the wine, was very stiff and dignified. As for the girl, one noticed only a peculiar brightness in her eyes, while the brown cheeks became more rosy.

The coffee finished, they suggested singing, and each of them sang or repeated a couplet, which the others applauded frantically. Then they got up with some difficulty, and while the two women, who were rather dizzy, were trying to get a breath of air, the two men, who were altogether drunk, were attempting gymnastics. Heavy, limp and with scarlet faces they hung or, awkwardly to the iron rings, without being able to raise themselves.

Meanwhile the two boating men had got their boats into the water, and they came back and politely asked the ladies whether they would like a row.

"Would you like one, Monsieur Dufour?" his wife exclaimed. "Please come!"

He merely gave her a drunken nod, without understanding what she said. Then one of the rowers came up with two fishing rods in his hands, and the hope of catching a gudgeon, that great vision of the Parisian shopkeeper, made Dufour's dull eyes gleam, and he politely allowed them to do whatever they liked, while he sat in the shade under the bridge, with his feet dangling over the river, by the side of the young man with the yellow hair, who was sleeping soundly.

One of the boating men made a martyr of himself and took the mother.

"Let us go to the little wood on the Ile aux Anglais!" he called out as he rowed off. The other boat went more slowly, for the rower was looking at his companion so intently that by thought of nothing else, and his emotion seemed to paralyze his strength, while the girl, who was sitting in the bow, gave herself up to the enjoyment of being on the water. She felt a disinclination to think, a lassitude in her limbs and a total enervation, as if she were intoxicated, and her face was flushed and her breathing quickened. The effects of the wine, which were increased by the extreme heat, made all the trees on the bank seem to bow as she passed. A vague wish for enjoyment and a fermentation of her blood seemed to pervade her whole body, which was excited by the heat of the day, and she was also disturbed at this tete-a-tete on the water, in a place which seemed depopulated by the heat, with this young man who thought her pretty, whose ardent looks seemed to caress her skin and were as penetrating and pervading as the sun's rays.

Their inability to speak increased their emotion, and they looked about them. At last, however, he made an effort and asked her name.

"Henriette," she said.

"Why, my name is Henri," he replied. The sound of their voices had calmed them, and they looked at the banks. The other boat had passed them and seemed to be waiting for them, and the rower called out:

"We will meet you in the wood; we are going as far as Robinson's, because Madame Dufour is thirsty." Then he bent over his oars again and rowed off so quickly that he was soon out of sight.

Meanwhile a continual roar, which they had heard for some time, came nearer, and the river itself seemed to shiver, as if the dull noise were rising from its depths.

"What is that noise?" she asked. It was the noise of the weir which cut the river in two at the island, and he was explaining it to her, when, above the noise of the waterfall, they heard the song of a bird, which seemed a long way off.

"Listen!" he said; "the nightingales are singing during the day, so the female birds must be sitting."

A nightingale! She had never heard one before, and the idea of listening to one roused visions of poetic tenderness in her heart. A nightingale! That is to say, the invisible witness of her love trysts which Juliet invoked on her balcony; that celestial music which it attuned to human kisses, that eternal inspirer of all those languorous romances which open an ideal sky to all the poor little tender hearts of sensitive girls!

She was going to hear a nightingale.

"We must not make a noise," her companion said, "and then we can go into the wood, and sit down close beside it."

The boat seemed to glide. They saw the trees on the island, the banks of which were so low that they could look into the depths of the thickets. They stopped, he made the boat fast, Henriette took hold of Henri's arm, and they went beneath the trees.

"Stoop," he said, so she stooped down, and they went into an inextricable thicket of creepers, leaves and reed grass, which formed an undiscoverable retreat, and which the young man laughingly called "his private room."

Just above their heads, perched in one of the trees which hid them, the bird was still singing. He uttered trills and roulades, and then loud, vibrating notes that filled the air and seemed to lose themselves on the horizon, across the level country, through that burning silence which weighed upon the whole landscape. They did not speak for fear of frightening it away. They were sitting close together, and, slowly, Henri's arm stole round the girl's waist and squeezed it gently. She took that daring hand without any anger, and kept removing it whenever he put it round her; without, however, feeling at all embarrassed by this caress, just as if it had been something quite natural, which she was resisting just as naturally.

She was listening to the bird in ecstasy. She felt an infinite longing for happiness, for some sudden demonstration of tenderness, for the revelation of superhuman poetry, and she felt such a softening at her heart, and relaxation of her nerves, that she began to cry, without knowing why. The young man was now straining her close to him, yet she did not remove his arm; she did not think of it. Suddenly the nightingale stopped, and a voice called out in the distance:

"Henriette!"

"Do not reply," he said in a low voice; "you will drive the bird away."

But she had no idea of doing so, and they remained in the same position for some time. Madame Dufour had sat down somewhere or other, for from time to time they heard the stout lady break out into little bursts of laughter.

The girl was still crying; she was filled with strange sensations. Henri's head was on her shoulder, and suddenly he kissed her on the lips. She was surprised and angry, and, to avoid him, she stood up.

They were both very pale when they left their grassy retreat. The blue sky appeared to them clouded and the ardent sun darkened; and they felt the solitude and the silence. They walked rapidly, side by side, without speaking or touching each other, for they seemed to have become irreconcilable enemies, as if disgust and hatred had arisen between them, and from time to time Henriette called out: "Mamma!"

By and by they heard a noise behind a bush, and the stout lady appeared, looking rather confused, and her companion's face was wrinkled with smiles which he could not check.

Madame Dufour took his arm, and they returned to the boats, and Henri, who was ahead, walked in silence beside the young girl. At last they got back to Bezons. Monsieur Dufour, who was now sober, was waiting for them very impatiently, while the young man with the yellow hair was having a mouthful of something to eat before leaving the inn. The carriage was waiting in the yard, and the grandmother, who had already got in, was very frightened at the thought of being overtaken by night before they reached Paris, as the outskirts were not safe.

They all shook bands, and the Dufour family drove off.

"Good-by, until we meet again!" the oarsmen cried, and the answer they got was a sigh and a tear.

Two months later, as Henri was going along the Rue des Martyrs, he saw Dufour, Ironmonger, over a door, and so he went in, and saw the stout lady sitting at the counter. They recognized each other immediately, and after an interchange of polite greetings, he asked after them all.

"And how is Mademoiselle Henriette?" he inquired specially.

"Very well, thank you; she is married."

"Ah!" He felt a certain emotion, but said: "Whom did she marry?"

"That young man who accompanied us, you know; he has joined us in business."

"I remember him perfectly."

He was going out, feeling very unhappy, though scarcely knowing why, when madame called him back.

"And how is your friend?" she asked rather shyly.

"He is very well, thank you."

"Please give him our compliments, and beg him to come and call, when he is in the neighborhood."

She then added: "Tell him it will give me great pleasure."

"I will be sure to do so. Adieu!"

"Do not say that; come again very soon."

The next year, one very hot Sunday, all the details of that adventure, which Henri had never forgotten, suddenly came back to him so clearly that he returned alone to their room in the wood, and was overwhelmed with astonishment when he went in. She was sitting on the grass, looking very sad, while by her side, still in his shirt sleeves, the young man with the yellow hair was sleeping soundly, like some animal.

She grew so pale when she saw Henri that at first he thought she was going to faint; then, however, they began to talk quite naturally. But when he told her that he was very fond of that spot, and went there frequently on Sundays to indulge in memories, she looked into his eyes for a long time.

"I too, think of it," she replied.

"Come, my dear," her husband said, with a yawn. "I think it is time for us to be going."

ROSE

The two young women appear to be buried under a blanket of flowers. They are alone in the immense landau, which is filled with flowers like a giant basket. On the front seat are two small hampers of white satin filled with violets, and on the bearskin by which their knees are covered there is a mass of roses, mimosas, pinks, daisies, tuberoses and orange blossoms, interwoven with silk ribbons; the two frail bodies seem buried under this beautiful perfumed bed, which hides everything but the shoulders and arms and a little of the dainty waists.

The coachman's whip is wound with a garland of anemones, the horses' traces are dotted with carnations, the spokes of the wheels are clothed in mignonette, and where the lanterns ought to be are two enormous round bouquets which look as though they were the eyes of this strange, rolling, flower-bedecked creature.

The landau drives rapidly along the road, through the Rue d'Antibes, preceded, followed, accompanied, by a crowd of other carriages covered with flowers, full of women almost hidden by a sea of violets. It is the flower carnival at Cannes.

The carriage reaches the Boulevard de la Fonciere, where the battle is waged. All along the immense avenue a double row of flower-bedecked vehicles are going and coming like an endless ribbon. Flowers are thrown from one to the other. They pass through the air like balls, striking fresh faces, bouncing and falling into the dust, where an army of youngsters pick them up.

A thick crowd is standing on the sidewalks looking on and held in check by the mounted police, who pass brutally along pushing back the curious pedestrians as though to prevent the common people from mingling with the rich.

In the carriages, people call to each other, recognize each other and bombard each other with roses. A chariot full of pretty women, dressed in red, like devils, attracts the eyes of all. A gentleman, who looks like the portraits of Henry IV., is throwing an immense bouquet which is held back by an elastic. Fearing the shock, the women hide their eyes and the men lower their heads, but the graceful, rapid and obedient missile describes a curve and returns to its master, who immediately throws it at some new face.

The two young women begin to throw their stock of flowers by handfuls, and receive a perfect hail of bouquets; then, after an hour of warfare, a little tired, they tell the coachman to drive along the road which follows the seashore.

The sun disappears behind Esterel, outlining the dark, rugged mountain against the sunset sky. The clear blue sea, as calm as a mill-pond, stretches out as far as the horizon, where it blends with the sky; and the fleet, anchored in the middle of the bay, looks like a herd of enormous beasts, motionless on the water, apocalyptic animals, armored and hump-backed, their frail masts looking like feathers, and with eyes which light up when evening approaches.

The two young women, leaning back under the heavy robes, look out lazily over the blue expanse of water. At last one of them says:

"How delightful the evenings are! How good everything seems! Don't you think so, Margot?"

"Yes, it is good. But there is always something lacking."

"What is lacking? I feel perfectly happy. I don't need anything else."

"Yes, you do. You are not thinking of it. No matter how contented we may be, physically, we always long for something more—for the heart."

The other asked with a smile:

"A little love?"

"Yes."

They stopped talking, their eyes fastened on the distant horizon, then the one called Marguerite murmured: "Life without that seems to me unbearable. I need to be loved, if only by a dog. But we are all alike, no matter what you may say, Simone."

"Not at all, my dear. I had rather not be loved at all than to be loved by the first comer. Do you think, for instance, that it would be pleasant to be loved by—by—"

She was thinking by whom she might possibly be loved, glancing across the wide landscape. Her eyes, after traveling around the horizon, fell on the two bright buttons which were shining on the back of the coachman's livery, and she continued, laughing: "by my coachman?"

Madame Margot barely smiled, and said in a low tone of voice:

"I assure you that it is very amusing to be loved by a servant. It has happened to me two or three times. They roll their eyes in such a funny manner—it's enough to make you die laughing! Naturally, the more in love they are, the more severe one must be with them, and then, some day, for some reason, you dismiss them, because, if anyone should notice it, you would appear so ridiculous."

Madame Simone was listening, staring straight ahead of her, then she remarked:

"No, I'm afraid that my footman's heart would not satisfy me. Tell me how you noticed that they loved you."

"I noticed it the same way that I do with other men—when they get stupid."

"The others don't seem stupid to me, when they love me."

"They are idiots, my dear, unable to talk, to answer, to understand anything."

"But how did you feel when you were loved by a servant? Were you—moved—flattered?"

"Moved? no, flattered—yes a little. One is always flattered to be loved by a man, no matter who he may be."

"Oh, Margot!"

"Yes, indeed, my dear! For instance, I will tell you of a peculiar incident which happened to me. You will see how curious and complex our emotions are, in such cases.

"About four years ago I happened to be without a maid. I had tried five or six, one right after the other, and I was about ready to give up in despair, when I saw an advertisement in a newspaper of a young girl knowing how to cook, embroider, dress hair, who was looking for a position and who could furnish the best of references. Besides all these accomplishments, she could speak English.

"I wrote to the given address, and the next day the person in question presented herself. She was tall, slender, pale, shy-looking. She had beautiful black eyes and a charming complexion; she pleased me immediately. I asked for her certificates; she gave me one in English, for she came, as she said, from Lady Rymwell's, where she had been for ten years.

"The certificate showed that the young girl had left of her own free will, in order to return to France, and the only thing which they had had to find fault in her during her long period of service was a little French coquettishness.

"This prudish English phrase even made me smile, and I immediately engaged this maid.

"She came to me the same day. Her name was Rose.

"At the end of a month I would have been helpless without her. She was a treasure, a pearl, a phenomenon.

"She could dress my hair with infinite taste; she could trim a hat better than most milliners, and she could even make my dresses.

"I was astonished at her accomplishments. I had never before been waited on in such a manner.

"She dressed me rapidly and with a surprisingly light touch. I never felt her fingers on my skin, and nothing is so disagreeable to me as contact with a servant's hand. I soon became excessively lazy; it was so pleasant to be dressed from head to foot, and from lingerie to gloves, by this tall, timid girl, always blushing a little, and never saying a word. After my bath she would rub and massage me while I dozed a little on my couch; I almost considered her more of a friend than a servant.

"One morning the janitor asked, mysteriously, to speak to me. I was surprised, and told him to come in. He was a good, faithful man, an old soldier, one of my husband's former orderlies.

"He seemed to be embarrassed by what he had to say to me. At last he managed to mumble:

"'Madame, the superintendent of police is downstairs.'

"I asked quickly:

"'What does he wish?'

"'He wishes to search the house.'

"Of course the police are useful, but I hate them. I do not think that it is a noble profession. I answered, angered and hurt:

"'Why this search? For what reason? He shall not come in.'

"The janitor continued:

"'He says that there is a criminal hidden in the house.'

"This time I was frightened and I told him to bring the inspector to me, so that I might get some explanation. He was a man with good manners and decorated with the Legion of Honor. He begged my pardon for disturbing me, and then informed me that I had, among my domestics, a convict.

"I was shocked; and I answered that I could guarantee every servant in the house, and I began to enumerate them.

"'The janitor, Pierre Courtin, an old soldier.'

"'It's not he.'

"'A stable-boy, son of farmers whom I know, and a groom whom you have just seen.'

"'It's not he.'

"'Then, monsieur, you see that you must be mistaken.'

"'Excuse me, madame, but I am positive that I am not making a mistake.

"As the conviction of a notable criminal is at stake, would you be so kind as to send for all your servants?"

"At first I refused, but I finally gave in, and sent downstairs for everybody, men and women.

"The inspector glanced at them and then declared:

"'This isn't all.'

"'Excuse me, monsieur, there is no one left but my maid, a young girl whom you could not possibly mistake for a convict.'

"He asked:

"'May I also see her?'

"'Certainly.'

"I rang for Rose, who immediately appeared. She had hardly entered the room, when the inspector made a motion, and two men whom I had not seen, hidden behind the door, sprang forward, seized her and tied her hands behind her back.

"I cried out in anger and tried to rush forward to defend her. The inspector stopped me:

"'This girl, madame, is a man whose name is Jean Nicolas Lecapet, condemned to death in 1879 for assaulting a woman and injuring her so that death resulted. His sentence was commuted to imprisonment for life. He escaped four months ago. We have been looking for him ever since.'

"I was terrified, bewildered. I did not believe him. The commissioner continued, laughing:

"'I can prove it to you. His right arm is tattooed.'

"'The sleeve was rolled up. It was true. The inspector added, with bad taste:

"'You can trust us for the other proofs.'

"And they led my maid away!

"Well, would you believe me, the thing that moved me most was not anger at having thus been played upon, deceived and made ridiculous, it was not the shame of having thus been dressed and undressed, handled and touched by this man—but a deep humiliation—a woman's humiliation. Do you understand?"

"I am afraid I don't."

"Just think—this man had been condemned for—for assaulting a woman. Well! I thought of the one whom he had assaulted—and—and I felt humiliated—There! Do you understand now?"

Madame Margot did not answer. She was looking straight ahead, her eyes fastened on the two shining buttons of the livery, with that sphinx-like smile which women sometimes have.

ROSALIE PRUDENT

There was a real mystery in this affair which neither the jury, nor the president, nor the public prosecutor himself could understand.

The girl Prudent (Rosalie), servant at the Varambots', of Nantes, having become enceinte without the knowledge of her masters, had, during the night, killed and buried her child in the garden.

It was the usual story of the infanticides committed by servant girls. But there was one inexplicable circumstance about this one. When the police searched the girl Prudent's room they discovered a complete infant's outfit, made by Rosalie herself, who had spent her nights for the last three months in cutting and sewing it. The grocer from whom she had bought her candles, out of her own wages, for this long piece of work had come to testify. It came out, moreover, that the sage-femme of the district, informed by Rosalie of her condition, had given her all necessary instructions and counsel in case the event should happen at a time when it might not be possible to get help. She had also procured a place at Poissy for the girl Prudent, who foresaw that her present employers would discharge her, for the Varambot couple did not trifle with morality.

There were present at the trial both the man and the woman, a middle-class pair from the provinces, living on their income. They were so exasperated against this girl, who had sullied their house, that they would have liked to see her guillotined on the spot without a trial. The spiteful depositions they made against her became accusations in their mouths.

The defendant, a large, handsome girl of Lower Normandy, well educated for her station in life, wept continuously and would not answer to anything.

The court and the spectators were forced to the opinion that she had committed this barbarous act in a moment of despair and madness, since there was every indication that she had expected to keep and bring up her child.

The president tried for the last time to make her speak, to get some confession, and, having urged her with much gentleness, he finally made her understand that all these men gathered here to pass judgment upon her were not anxious for her death and might even have pity on her.

Then she made up her mind to speak.

"Come, now, tell us, first, who is the father of this child?" he asked.

Until then she had obstinately refused to give his name.

But she replied suddenly, looking at her masters who had so cruelly calumniated her:

"It is Monsieur Joseph, Monsieur Varambot's nephew."

The couple started in their seats and cried with one voice—"That's not true! She lies! This is infamous!"

The president had them silenced and continued, "Go on, please, and tell us how it all happened."

Then she suddenly began to talk freely, relieving her pent-up heart, that poor, solitary, crushed heart—laying bare her sorrow, her whole sorrow, before those severe men whom she had until now taken for enemies and inflexible judges.

"Yes, it was Monsieur Joseph Varambot, when he came on leave last year."

"What does Mr. Joseph Varambot do?"

"He is a non-commissioned officer in the artillery, monsieur. Well, he stayed two months at the house, two months of the summer. I thought nothing about it when he began to look at me, and then flatter me, and make love to me all day long. And I let myself be taken in, monsieur. He kept saying to me that I was a handsome girl, that I was good company, that I just suited him—and I, I liked him well enough. What could I do? One listens to these things when one is alone—all alone—as I was. I am alone in the world, monsieur. I have no one to talk to—no one to tell my troubles to. I have no father, no mother, no brother, no sister, nobody. And when he began to talk to me it was as if I had a brother who had come back. And then he asked me to go with him to the river one evening, so that we might talk without disturbing any one. I went—I don't know—I don't know how it happened. He had his arm around me. Really I didn't want to—no—no—I could not—I felt like crying, the air was so soft —the moon was shining. No, I swear to you—I could not—he did what he wanted. That went on three weeks, as long as he stayed. I could have followed him to the ends of the world. He went away. I did not know that I was enceinte. I did not know it until the month after—"

She began to cry so bitterly that they had to give her time to collect herself.

Then the president resumed with the tone of a priest at the confessional: "Come, now, go on."

She began to talk again: "When I realized my condition I went to see Madame Boudin, who is there to tell you, and I asked her how it would be, in case it should come if she were not there. Then I made the outfit, sewing night after night, every evening until one o'clock in the morning; and then I looked for another place, for I knew very well that I should be sent away, but I wanted to stay in the house until the very last, so as to save my pennies, for I have not got very much and I should need my money for the little one."

"Then you did not intend to kill him?"

"Oh, certainly not, monsieur!"

"Why did you kill him, then?"

"It happened this way. It came sooner than I expected. It came upon me in the kitchen, while I was doing the dishes. Monsieur and Madame Varambot were already asleep, so I went up, not without difficulty, dragging myself up by the banister, and I lay down on the bare floor. It lasted perhaps one hour, or two, or three; I don't know, I had such pain; and then I pushed him out with all my strength. I felt that he came out and I picked him up.

"Ah! but I was glad, I assure you! I did all that Madame Boudin told me to do. And then I laid him on my bed. And then such a pain griped me again that I thought I should die. If you knew what it meant, you there, you would not do so much of this. I fell on my knees, and then toppled over backward on the floor; and it griped me again, perhaps one hour, perhaps two. I lay there all alone— and then another one comes—another little one—two, yes, two, like this. I took him up as I did the first one, and then I put him on the bed, the two side by side. Is it possible, tell me, two children, and I who get only twenty francs a month? Say, is it possible? One, yes, that can be managed by going without things, but not two. That turned my head. What do I know about it? Had I any choice, tell me?

"What could I do? I felt as if my last hour had come. I put the pillow over them, without knowing why. I could not keep them both; and then I threw myself down, and I lay there, rolling over and over and crying until I saw the daylight come into the window. Both of them were quite dead under the pillow. Then I took them under my arms and went down the stairs out in the vegetable garden. I took the gardener's spade and I buried them under the earth, digging as deep a hole as I could, one here and the other one there, not together, so that they might not talk of their mother if these little dead bodies can talk. What do I know about it?

"And then, back in my bed, I felt so sick that I could not get up. They sent for the doctor and he understood it all. I'm telling you the truth, Your Honor. Do what you like with me; I'm ready."

Half of the jury were blowing their noses violently to keep from crying. The women in the courtroom were sobbing.

The president asked her:

"Where did you bury the other one?"

"The one that you have?" she asked.

"Why, this one—this one was in the artichokes."

"Oh, then the other one is among the strawberries, by the well."

And she began to sob so piteously that no one could hear her unmoved.

The girl Rosalie Prudent was acquitted.

REGRET

Monsieur Saval, who was called in Mantes "Father Saval," had just risen from bed. He was weeping. It was a dull autumn day; the leaves were falling. They fell slowly in the rain, like a heavier and slower rain. M. Saval was not in good spirits. He walked from the fireplace to the window, and from the window to the fireplace. Life has its sombre days. It would no longer have any but sombre days for him, for he had reached the age of sixty-two. He is alone, an old bachelor, with nobody about him. How sad it is to die alone, all alone, without any one who is devoted to you!

He pondered over his life, so barren, so empty. He recalled former days, the days of his childhood, the home, the house of his parents; his college days, his follies; the time he studied law in Paris, his father's illness, his death. He then returned to live with his mother. They lived together very quietly, and desired nothing more. At last the mother died. How sad life is! He lived alone since then, and now, in his turn, he, too, will soon be dead. He will disappear, and that will be the end. There will be no more of Paul Saval upon the earth. What a frightful thing! Other people will love, will laugh. Yes, people will go on amusing themselves, and he will no longer exist! Is it not strange that people can laugh, amuse themselves, be joyful under that eternal certainty of death? If this death were only probable, one could then have hope; but no, it is inevitable, as inevitable as that night follows the day.

If, however, his life had been full! If he had done something; if he had had adventures, great pleasures, success, satisfaction of some kind or another. But no, nothing. He had done nothing, nothing but rise from bed, eat, at the same hours, and go to bed again. And he had gone on like that to the age of sixty-two years. He had not even taken unto himself a wife, as other men do. Why? Yes, why was it that he had not married? He might have done so, for he possessed considerable means. Had he lacked an opportunity? Perhaps! But one can create opportunities. He was indifferent; that was all. Indifference had been his greatest drawback, his defect, his vice. How many men wreck their lives through indifference! It is so difficult for some natures to get out of bed, to move about, to take long walks, to speak, to study any question.

He had not even been loved. No woman had reposed on his bosom, in a complete abandon of love. He knew nothing of the delicious anguish of expectation, the divine vibration of a hand in yours, of the ecstasy of triumphant passion.

What superhuman happiness must overflow your heart, when lips encounter lips for the first time, when the grasp of four arms makes one being of you, a being unutterably happy, two beings infatuated with one another.

M. Saval was sitting before the fire, his feet on the fender, in his dressing gown. Assuredly his life had been spoiled, completely spoiled. He had, however, loved. He had loved secretly, sadly, and indifferently, in a manner characteristic of him in everything. Yes, he had loved his old friend, Madame Sandres, the wife of his old companion, Sandres. Ah! if he had known her as a young girl! But he had met her too late; she was already married. Unquestionably, he would have asked her hand! How he had loved her, nevertheless, without respite, since the first day he set eyes on her!

He recalled his emotion every time he saw her, his grief on leaving her, the many nights that he could not sleep, because he was thinking of her.

On rising in the morning he was somewhat more rational than on the previous evening.

Why?

How pretty she was formerly, so dainty, with fair curly hair, and always laughing. Sandres was not the man she should have chosen. She was now fifty-two years of age. She seemed happy. Ah! if she had only loved him in days gone by; yes, if she had only loved him! And why should she not have loved him, he, Saval, seeing that he loved her so much, yes, she, Madame Sandres!

If only she could have guessed. Had she not guessed anything, seen anything, comprehended anything? What would she have thought? If he had spoken, what would she have answered?

And Saval asked himself a thousand other things. He reviewed his whole life, seeking to recall a multitude of details.

He recalled all the long evenings spent at the house of Sandres, when the latter's wife was young, and so charming.

He recalled many things that she had said to him, the intonations of her voice, the little significant smiles that meant so much.

He recalled their walks, the three of them together, along the banks of the Seine, their luncheon on the grass on Sundays, for Sandres was employed at the sub-prefecture. And all at once the distinct recollection came to him of an afternoon spent with her in a little wood on the banks of the river.

They had set out in the morning, carrying their provisions in baskets. It was a bright spring morning, one of those days which intoxicate one. Everything smells fresh, everything seems happy. The voices of the birds sound more joyous, and-they fly more swiftly. They had luncheon on the grass, under the willow trees, quite close to the water, which glittered in the sun's rays. The air was balmy, charged with the odors of fresh vegetation; they drank it in with delight. How pleasant everything was on that day!

After lunch, Sandres went to sleep on the broad of his back. "The best nap he had in his life," said he, when he woke up.

Madame Sandres had taken the arm of Saval, and they started to walk along the river bank.

She leaned tenderly on his arm. She laughed and said to him: "I am intoxicated, my friend, I am quite intoxicated." He looked at her, his heart going pit-a-pat. He felt himself grow pale, fearful that he might have looked too boldly at her, and that the trembling of his hand had revealed his passion.

She had made a wreath of wild flowers and water-lilies, and she asked him: "Do I look pretty like that?"

As he did not answer—for he could find nothing to say, he would have liked to go down on his knees—she burst out laughing, a sort of annoyed, displeased laugh, as she said: "Great goose, what ails you? You might at least say something."

He felt like crying, but could not even yet find a word to say.

All these things came back to him now, as vividly as on the day when they took place. Why had she said this to him, "Great goose, what ails you? You might at least say something!"

And he recalled how tenderly she had leaned on his arm. And in passing under a shady tree he had felt her ear brushing his cheek, and he had moved his head abruptly, lest she should suppose he was too familiar.

When he had said to her: "Is it not time to return?" she darted a singular look at him. "Certainly," she said, "certainly," regarding him at the same time in a curious manner. He had not thought of it at the time, but now the whole thing appeared to him quite plain.

"Just as you like, my friend. If you are tired let us go back."

And he had answered: "I am not fatigued; but Sandres may be awake now."

And she had said: "If you are afraid of my husband's being awake, that is another thing. Let us return."

On their way back she remained silent, and leaned no longer on his arm. Why?

At that time it had never occurred to him, to ask himself "why." Now he seemed to apprehend something that he had not then understood.

Could it?

M. Saval felt himself blush, and he got up at a bound, as if he were thirty years younger and had heard Madame Sandres say, "I love you."

Was it possible? That idea which had just entered his mind tortured him. Was it possible that he had not seen, had not guessed?

Oh! if that were true, if he had let this opportunity of happiness pass without taking advantage of it!

He said to himself: "I must know. I cannot remain in this state of doubt. I must know!" He thought: "I am sixty-two years of age, she is fifty-eight; I may ask her that now without giving offense."

He started out.

The Sandres' house was situated on the other side of the street, almost directly opposite his own. He went across and knocked at the door, and a little servant opened it.

"You here at this hour, Saval! Has some accident happened to you?"

"No, my girl," he replied; "but go and tell your mistress that I want to speak to her at once."

"The fact is madame is preserving pears for the winter, and she is in the preserving room. She is not dressed, you understand."

"Yes, but go and tell her that I wish to see her on a very important matter."

The little servant went away, and Saval began to walk, with long, nervous strides, up and down the drawing-room. He did not feel in the least embarrassed, however. Oh! he was merely going to ask her something, as he would have asked her about some cooking recipe. He was sixty-two years of age!

The door opened and madame appeared. She was now a large woman, fat and round, with full cheeks and a sonorous laugh. She walked with her arms away from her sides and her sleeves tucked up, her bare arms all covered with fruit juice. She asked anxiously:

"What is the matter with you, my friend? You are not ill, are you?"

"No, my dear friend; but I wish to ask you one thing, which to me is of the first importance, something which is torturing my heart, and I want you to promise that you will answer me frankly."

She laughed, "I am always frank. Say on."

"Well, then. I have loved you from the first day I ever saw you. Can you have any doubt of this?"

She responded, laughing, with something of her former tone of voice.

"Great goose! what ails you? I knew it from the very first day!"

Saval began to tremble. He stammered out: "You knew it? Then . . ."

He stopped.

She asked:

"Then?"

He answered:

"Then—what did you think? What—what—what would you have answered?"

She broke into a peal of laughter. Some of the juice ran off the tips of her fingers on to the carpet.

"What?"

"I? Why, you did not ask me anything. It was not for me to declare myself!"

He then advanced a step toward her.

"Tell me—tell me . . . . You remember the day when Sandres went to sleep on the grass after lunch . . . when we had walked together as far as the bend of the river, below . . ."

He waited, expectantly. She had ceased to laugh, and looked at him, straight in the eyes.

"Yes, certainly, I remember it."

He answered, trembling all over:

"Well—that day—if I had been—if I had been—venturesome—what would you have done?"

She began to laugh as only a happy woman can laugh, who has nothing to regret, and responded frankly, in a clear voice tinged with irony:

"I would have yielded, my friend."

She then turned on her heels and went back to her jam-making.

Saval rushed into the street, cast down, as though he had met with some disaster. He walked with giant strides through the rain, straight on, until he reached the river bank, without thinking where he was going. He then turned to the right and followed the river. He walked a long time, as if urged on by some instinct. His clothes were running with water, his hat was out of shape, as soft as a rag, and dripping like a roof. He walked on, straight in front of him. At last, he came to the place where they had lunched on that day so long ago, the recollection of which tortured his heart. He sat down under the leafless trees, and wept.

A SISTER'S CONFESSION

Marguerite de Therelles was dying. Although she was only fifty-six years old she looked at least seventy-five. She gasped for breath, her face whiter than the sheets, and had spasms of violent shivering, with her face convulsed and her eyes haggard as though she saw a frightful vision.

Her elder sister, Suzanne, six years older than herself, was sobbing on her knees beside the bed. A small table close to the dying woman's couch bore, on a white cloth, two lighted candles, for the priest was expected at any moment to administer extreme unction and the last communion.

The apartment wore that melancholy aspect common to death chambers; a look of despairing farewell. Medicine bottles littered the furniture; linen lay in the corners into which it had been kicked or swept. The very chairs looked, in their disarray, as if they were terrified and had run in all directions. Death—terrible Death—was in the room, hidden, awaiting his prey.

This history of the two sisters was an affecting one. It was spoken of far and wide; it had drawn tears from many eyes.

Suzanne, the elder, had once been passionately loved by a young man, whose affection she returned. They were engaged to be married, and the wedding day was at hand, when Henry de Sampierre suddenly died.

The young girl's despair was terrible, and she took an oath never to marry. She faithfully kept her vow and adopted widow's weeds for the remainder of her life.

But one morning her sister, her little sister Marguerite, then only twelve years old, threw herself into Suzanne's arms, sobbing: "Sister, I don't want you to be unhappy. I don't want you to mourn all your life. I'll never leave you—never, never, never! I shall never marry, either. I'll stay with you always—always!"

Suzanne kissed her, touched by the child's devotion, though not putting any faith in her promise.

But the little one kept her word, and, despite her parents' remonstrances, despite her elder sister's prayers, never married. She was remarkably pretty and refused many offers. She never left her sister.

They spent their whole life together, without a single day's separation. They went everywhere together and were inseparable. But Marguerite was pensive, melancholy, sadder than her sister, as if her sublime sacrifice had undermined her spirits. She grew older more quickly; her hair was white at thirty; and she was often ill, apparently stricken with some unknown, wasting malady.

And now she would be the first to die.

She had not spoken for twenty-four hours, except to whisper at daybreak:

"Send at once for the priest."

And she had since remained lying on her back, convulsed with agony, her lips moving as if unable to utter the dreadful words that rose in her heart, her face expressive of a terror distressing to witness.

Suzanne, distracted with grief, her brow pressed against the bed, wept bitterly, repeating over and over again the words:

"Margot, my poor Margot, my little one!"

She had always called her "my little one," while Marguerite's name for the elder was invariably "sister."

A footstep sounded on the stairs. The door opened. An acolyte appeared, followed by the aged priest in his surplice. As soon as she saw him the dying woman sat up suddenly in bed, opened her lips, stammered a few words and began to scratch the bed-clothes, as if she would have made hole in them.

Father Simon approached, took her hand, kissed her on the forehead and said in a gentle voice:

"May God pardon your sins, my daughter. Be of good courage. Now is the moment to confess them—speak!"

Then Marguerite, shuddering from head to foot, so that the very bed shook with her nervous movements, gasped:

"Sit down, sister, and listen."

The priest stooped toward the prostrate Suzanne, raised her to her feet, placed her in a chair, and, taking a hand of each of the sisters, pronounced:

"Lord God! Send them strength! Shed Thy mercy upon them."

And Marguerite began to speak. The words issued from her lips one by one—hoarse, jerky, tremulous.

"Pardon, pardon, sister! pardon me! Oh, if only you knew how I have dreaded this moment all my life!"

Suzanne faltered through her tears:

"But what have I to pardon, little one? You have given me everything, sacrificed all to me. You are an angel."

But Marguerite interrupted her:

"Be silent, be silent! Let me speak! Don't stop me! It is terrible. Let me tell all, to the very end, without interruption. Listen. You remember—you remember—Henry—"

Suzanne trembled and looked at her sister. The younger one went on:

"In order to understand you must hear everything. I was twelve years old—only twelve—you remember, don't you? And I was spoilt; I did just as I pleased. You remember how everybody spoilt me? Listen. The first time he came he had on his riding boots; he dismounted, saying that he had a message for father. You remember, don't you? Don't speak. Listen. When I saw him I was struck with admiration. I thought him so handsome, and I stayed in a corner of the drawing-room all the time he was talking. Children are strange—and terrible. Yes, indeed, I dreamt of him.

"He came again—many times. I looked at him with all my eyes, all my heart. I was large for my age and much more precocious than—any one suspected. He came often. I thought only of him. I often whispered to myself:

"'Henry—Henry de Sampierre!'

"Then I was told that he was going to marry you. That was a blow! Oh, sister, a terrible blow—terrible! I wept all through three sleepless nights.

"He came every afternoon after lunch. You remember, don't you? Don't answer. Listen. You used to make cakes that he was very fond of—with flour, butter and milk. Oh, I know how to make them. I could make them still, if necessary. He would swallow them at one mouthful and wash them down with a glass of wine, saying: 'Delicious!' Do you remember the way he said it?

"I was jealous—jealous! Your wedding day was drawing near. It was only a fortnight distant. I was distracted. I said to myself: 'He shall not marry Suzanne—no, he shall not! He shall marry me when I am old enough! I shall never love any one half so much.' But one evening, ten days before the wedding, you went for a stroll with him in the moonlight before the house—and yonder—under the pine tree, the big pine tree—he kissed you—kissed you—and held you in his arms so long—so long! You remember, don't you? It was probably the first time. You were so pale when you came back to the drawing-room!

"I saw you. I was there in the shrubbery. I was mad with rage! I would have killed you both if I could!

"I said to myself: 'He shall never marry Suzanne—never! He shall marry no one! I could not bear it.' And all at once I began to hate him intensely.

"Then do you know what I did? Listen. I had seen the gardener prepare pellets for killing stray dogs. He would crush a bottle into small pieces with a stone and put the ground glass into a ball of meat.

"I stole a small medicine bottle from mother's room. I ground it fine with a hammer and hid the glass in my pocket. It was a glistening powder. The next day, when you had made your little cakes; I opened them with a knife and inserted the glass. He ate three. I ate one myself. I threw the six others into the pond. The two swans died three days later. You remember? Oh, don't speak! Listen, listen. I, I alone did not die. But I have always been ill. Listen—he died—you know—listen—that was not the worst. It was afterward, later—always—the most terrible—listen.

"My life, all my life—such torture! I said to myself: 'I will never leave my sister. And on my deathbed I will tell her all.' And now I have told. And I have always thought of this moment—the moment when all would be told. Now it has come. It is terrible—oh!—sister—

"I have always thought, morning and evening, day and night: 'I shall have to tell her some day!' I waited. The horror of it! It is done. Say nothing. Now I am afraid—I am afraid! Oh! Supposing I should see him again, by and by, when I am dead! See him again! Only to think of it! I dare not—yet I must. I am going to die. I want you to forgive me. I insist on it. I cannot meet him without your forgiveness. Oh, tell her to forgive me, Father! Tell her. I implore you! I cannot die without it."

She was silent and lay back, gasping for breath, still plucking at the sheets with her fingers.

Suzanne had hidden her face in her hands and did not move. She was thinking of him whom she had loved so long. What a life of happiness they might have had together! She saw him again in the dim and distant past-that past forever lost. Beloved dead! how the thought of them rends the heart! Oh! that kiss, his only kiss! She had retained the memory of it in her soul. And, after that, nothing, nothing more throughout her whole existence!

The priest rose suddenly and in a firm, compelling voice said:

"Mademoiselle Suzanne, your sister is dying!"

Then Suzanne, raising her tear-stained face, put her arms round her sister, and kissing her fervently, exclaimed:

"I forgive you, I forgive you, little one!"

COCO

Throughout the whole countryside the Lucas farn, was known as "the Manor." No one knew why. The peasants doubtless attached to this word, "Manor," a meaning of wealth and of splendor, for this farm was undoubtedly the largest, richest and the best managed in the whole neighborhood.

The immense court, surrounded by five rows of magnificent trees, which sheltered the delicate apple trees from the harsh wind of the plain, inclosed in its confines long brick buildings used for storing fodder and grain, beautiful stables built of hard stone and made to accommodate thirty horses, and a red brick residence which looked like a little chateau.

Thanks for the good care taken, the manure heaps were as little offensive as such things can be; the watch-dogs lived in kennels, and countless poultry paraded through the tall grass.

Every day, at noon, fifteen persons, masters, farmhands and the women folks, seated themselves around the long kitchen table where the soup was brought in steaming in a large, blue-flowered bowl.

The beasts-horses, cows, pigs and sheep-were fat, well fed and clean. Maitre Lucas, a tall man who was getting stout, would go round three times a day, overseeing everything and thinking of everything.

A very old white horse, which the mistress wished to keep until its natural death, because she had brought it up and had always used it, and also because it recalled many happy memories, was housed, through sheer kindness of heart, at the end of the stable.

A young scamp about fifteen years old, Isidore Duval by name, and called, for convenience, Zidore, took care of this pensioner, gave him his measure of oats and fodder in winter, and in summer was supposed to change his pasturing place four times a day, so that he might have plenty of fresh grass.

The animal, almost crippled, lifted with difficulty his legs, large at the knees and swollen above the hoofs. His coat, which was no longer curried, looked like white hair, and his long eyelashes gave to his eyes a sad expression.

When Zidore took the animal to pasture, he had to pull on the rope with all his might, because it walked so slowly; and the youth, bent over and out of breath, would swear at it, exasperated at having to care for this old nag.

The farmhands, noticing the young rascal's anger against Coco, were amused and would continually talk of the horse to Zidore, in order to exasperate him. His comrades would make sport with him. In the village he was called Coco-Zidore.

The boy would fume, feeling an unholy desire to revenge himself on the horse. He was a thin, long-legged, dirty child, with thick, coarse, bristly red hair. He seemed only half-witted, and stuttered as though ideas were unable to form in his thick, brute-like mind.

For a long time he had been unable to understand why Coco should be kept, indignant at seeing things wasted on this useless beast. Since the horse could no longer work, it seemed to him unjust that he should be fed; he revolted at the idea of wasting oats, oats which were so expensive, on this paralyzed old plug. And often, in spite of the orders of Maitre Lucas, he would economize on the nag's food, only giving him half measure. Hatred grew in his confused, childlike mind, the hatred of a stingy, mean, fierce, brutal and cowardly peasant.

When summer came he had to move the animal about in the pasture. It was some distance away. The rascal, angrier every morning, would start, with his dragging step, across the wheat fields. The men working in the fields would shout to him, jokingly:

"Hey, Zidore, remember me to Coco."

He would not answer; but on the way he would break off a switch, and, as soon as he had moved the old horse, he would let it begin grazing; then, treacherously sneaking up behind it, he would slash its legs. The animal would try to escape, to kick, to get away from the blows, and run around in a circle about its rope, as though it had been inclosed in a circus ring. And the boy would slash away furiously, running along behind, his teeth clenched in anger.

Then he would go away slowly, without turning round, while the horse watched him disappear, his ribs sticking out, panting as a result of his unusual exertions. Not until the blue blouse of the young peasant was out of sight would he lower his thin white head to the grass.

As the nights were now warm, Coco was allowed to sleep out of doors, in the field behind the little wood. Zidore alone went to see him. The boy threw stones at him to amuse himself. He would sit down on an embankment about ten feet away and would stay there about half an hour, from time to time throwing a sharp stone at the old horse, which remained standing tied before his enemy, watching him continually and not daring to eat before he was gone.

This one thought persisted in the mind of the young scamp: "Why feed this horse, which is no longer good for anything?" It seemed to him that this old nag was stealing the food of the others, the goods of man and God, that he was even robbing him, Zidore, who was working.

Then, little by little, each day, the boy began to shorten the length of rope which allowed the horse to graze.

The hungry animal was growing thinner, and starving. Too feeble to break his bonds, he would stretch his head out toward the tall, green, tempting grass, so near that he could smell, and yet so far that he could not touch it.

But one morning Zidore had an idea: it was, not to move Coco any more. He was tired of walking so far for that old skeleton. He came, however, in order to enjoy his vengeance. The beast watched him anxiously. He did not beat him that day. He walked around him with his hands in his pockets. He even pretended to change his place, but he sank the stake in exactly the same hole, and went away overjoyed with his invention.

The horse, seeing him leave, neighed to call him back; but the rascal began to run, leaving him alone, entirely alone in his field, well tied down and without a blade of grass within reach.

Starving, he tried to reach the grass which he could touch with the end of his nose. He got on his knees, stretching out his neck and his long, drooling lips. All in vain. The old animal spent the whole day in useless, terrible efforts. The sight of all that green food, which stretched out on all sides of him, served to increase the gnawing pangs of hunger.

The scamp did not return that day. He wandered through the woods in search of nests.

The next day he appeared upon the scene again. Coco, exhausted, had lain down. When he saw the boy, he got up, expecting at last to have his place changed.

But the little peasant did not even touch the mallet, which was lying on the ground. He came nearer, looked at the animal, threw at his head a clump of earth which flattened out against the white hair, and he started off again, whistling.

The horse remained standing as long as he could see him; then, knowing that his attempts to reach the near-by grass would be hopeless, he once more lay down on his side and closed his eyes.

The following day Zidore did not come.

When he did come at last, he found Coco still stretched out; he saw that he was dead.

Then he remained standing, looking at him, pleased with what he had done, surprised that it should already be all over. He touched him with his foot, lifted one of his legs and then let it drop, sat on him and remained there, his eyes fixed on the grass, thinking of nothing. He returned to the farm, but did not mention the accident, because he wished to wander about at the hours when he used to change the horse's pasture. He went to see him the next day. At his approach some crows flew away. Countless flies were walking over the body and were buzzing around it. When he returned home, he announced the event. The animal was so old that nobody was surprised. The master said to two of the men:

"Take your shovels and dig a hole right where he is."

The men buried the horse at the place where he had died of hunger. And the grass grew thick, green and vigorous, fed by the poor body.

DEAD WOMAN'S SECRET

The woman had died without pain, quietly, as a woman should whose life had been blameless. Now she was resting in her bed, lying on her back, her eyes closed, her features calm, her long white hair carefully arranged as though she had done it up ten minutes before dying. The whole pale countenance of the dead woman was so collected, so calm, so resigned that one could feel what a sweet soul had lived in that body, what a quiet existence this old soul had led, how easy and pure the death of this parent had been.

Kneeling beside the bed, her son, a magistrate with inflexible principles, and her daughter, Marguerite, known as Sister Eulalie, were weeping as though their hearts would break. She had, from childhood up, armed them with a strict moral code, teaching them religion, without weakness, and duty, without compromise. He, the man, had become a judge and handled the law as a weapon with which he smote the weak ones without pity. She, the girl, influenced by the virtue which had bathed her in this austere family, had become the bride of the Church through her loathing for man.

They had hardly known their father, knowing only that he had made their mother most unhappy, without being told any other details.

The nun was wildly-kissing the dead woman's hand, an ivory hand as white as the large crucifix lying across the bed. On the other side of the long body the other hand seemed still to be holding the sheet in the death grasp; and the sheet had preserved the little creases as a memory of those last movements which precede eternal immobility.

A few light taps on the door caused the two sobbing heads to look up, and the priest, who had just come from dinner, returned. He was red and out of breath from his interrupted digestion, for he had made himself a strong mixture of coffee and brandy in order to combat the fatigue of the last few nights and of the wake which was beginning.

He looked sad, with that assumed sadness of the priest for whom death is a bread winner. He crossed himself and approaching with his professional gesture: "Well, my poor children! I have come to help you pass these last sad hours." But Sister Eulalie suddenly arose. "Thank you, father, but my brother and I prefer to remain alone with her. This is our last chance to see her, and we wish to be together, all three of us, as we—we—used to be when we were small and our poor mo—mother——"

Grief and tears stopped her; she could not continue.

Once more serene, the priest bowed, thinking of his bed. "As you wish, my children." He kneeled, crossed himself, prayed, arose and went out quietly, murmuring: "She was a saint!"

They remained alone, the dead woman and her children. The ticking of the clock, hidden in the shadow, could be heard distinctly, and through the open window drifted in the sweet smell of hay and of woods, together with the soft moonlight. No other noise could be heard over the land except the occasional croaking of the frog or the chirping of some belated insect. An infinite peace, a divine melancholy, a silent serenity surrounded this dead woman, seemed to be breathed out from her and to appease nature itself.

Then the judge, still kneeling, his head buried in the bed clothes, cried in a voice altered by grief and deadened by the sheets and blankets: "Mamma, mamma, mamma!" And his sister, frantically striking her forehead against the woodwork, convulsed, twitching and trembling as in an epileptic fit, moaned: "Jesus, Jesus, mamma, Jesus!" And both of them, shaken by a storm of grief, gasped and choked.

The crisis slowly calmed down and they began to weep quietly, just as on the sea when a calm follows a squall.

A rather long time passed and they arose and looked at their dead. And the memories, those distant memories, yesterday so dear, to-day so torturing, came to their minds with all the little forgotten details, those little intimate familiar details which bring back to life the one who has left. They recalled to each other circumstances, words, smiles, intonations of the mother who was no longer to speak to them. They saw her again happy and calm. They remembered things which she had said, and a little motion of the hand, like beating time, which she often used when emphasizing something important.

And they loved her as they never had loved her before. They measured the depth of their grief, and thus they discovered how lonely they would find themselves.

It was their prop, their guide, their whole youth, all the best part of their lives which was disappearing. It was their bond with life, their mother, their mamma, the connecting link with their forefathers which they would thenceforth miss. They now became solitary, lonely beings; they could no longer look back.

The nun said to her brother: "You remember how mamma used always to read her old letters; they are all there in that drawer. Let us, in turn, read them; let us live her whole life through tonight beside her! It would be like a road to the cross, like making the acquaintance of her mother, of our grandparents, whom we never knew, but whose letters are there and of whom she so often spoke, do you remember?"

Out of the drawer they took about ten little packages of yellow paper, tied with care and arranged one beside the other. They threw these relics on the bed and chose one of them on which the word "Father" was written. They opened and read it.

It was one of those old-fashioned letters which one finds in old family desk drawers, those epistles which smell of another century. The first one started: "My dear," another one: "My beautiful little girl," others: "My dear child," or: "My dear (laughter)." And suddenly the nun began to read aloud, to read over to the dead woman her whole history, all her tender memories. The judge, resting his elbow on the bed, was listening with his eyes fastened on his mother. The motionless body seemed happy.

Sister Eulalie, interrupting herself, said suddenly:

"These ought to be put in the grave with her; they ought to be used as a shroud and she ought to be buried in it." She took another package, on which no name was written. She began to read in a firm voice: "My adored one, I love you wildly. Since yesterday I have been suffering the tortures of the damned, haunted by our memory. I feel your lips against mine, your eyes in mine, your breast against mine. I love you, I love you! You have driven me mad. My arms open, I gasp, moved by a wild desire to hold you again. My whole soul and body cries out for you, wants you. I have kept in my mouth the taste of your kisses—"

The judge had straightened himself up. The nun stopped reading. He snatched the letter from her and looked for the signature. There was none, but only under the words, "The man who adores you," the name "Henry." Their father's name was Rene. Therefore this was not from him. The son then quickly rummaged through the package of letters, took one out and read: "I can no longer live without your caresses." Standing erect, severe as when sitting on the bench, he looked unmoved at the dead woman. The nun, straight as a statue, tears trembling in the corners of her eyes, was watching her brother, waiting. Then he crossed the room slowly, went to the window and stood there, gazing out into the dark night.

When he turned around again Sister Eulalie, her eyes dry now, was still standing near the bed, her head bent down.

He stepped forward, quickly picked up the letters and threw them pell-mell back into the drawer. Then he closed the curtains of the bed.

When daylight made the candles on the table turn pale the son slowly left his armchair, and without looking again at the mother upon whom he had passed sentence, severing the tie that united her to son and daughter, he said slowly: "Let us now retire, sister."

A HUMBLE DRAMA

Meetings that are unexpected constitute the charm of traveling. Who has not experienced the joy of suddenly coming across a Parisian, a college friend, or a neighbor, five hundred miles from home? Who has not passed a night awake in one of those small, rattling country stage-coaches, in regions where steam is still a thing unknown, beside a strange young woman, of whom one has caught only a glimpse in the dim light of the lantern, as she entered the carriage in front of a white house in some small country town?

And the next morning, when one's head and ears feel numb with the continuous tinkling of the bells and the loud rattling of the windows, what a charming sensation it is to see your pretty neighbor open her eyes, startled, glance around her, arrange her rebellious hair with her slender fingers, adjust her hat, feel with sure hand whether her corset is still in place, her waist straight, and her skirt not too wrinkled.

She glances at you coldly and curiously. Then she leans back and no longer seems interested in anything but the country.

In spite of yourself, you watch her; and in spite of yourself you keep on thinking of her. Who is she? Whence does she come? Where is she going? In spite of yourself you spin a little romance around her. She is pretty; she seems charming! Happy he who . . . Life might be delightful with her. Who knows? She is perhaps the woman of our dreams, the one suited to our disposition, the one for whom our heart calls.

And how delicious even the disappointment at seeing her get out at the gate of a country house! A man stands there, who is awaiting her, with two children and two maids. He takes her in his arms and kisses as he lifts her out. Then she stoops over the little ones, who hold up their hands to her; she kisses them tenderly; and then they all go away together, down a path, while the maids catch the packages which the driver throws down to them from the coach.

Adieu! It is all over. You never will see her again! Adieu to the young woman who has passed the night by your side. You know her no more, you have not spoken to her; all the same, you feel a little sad to see her go. Adieu!

I have had many of these souvenirs of travel, some joyous and some sad.

Once I was in Auvergne, tramping through those delightful French mountains, that are not too high, not too steep, but friendly and familiar. I had climbed the Sancy, and entered a little inn, near a pilgrim's chapel called Notre-Dame de Vassiviere, when I saw a queer, ridiculous-looking old woman breakfasting alone at the end table.

She was at least seventy years old, tall, skinny, and angular, and her white hair was puffed around her temples in the old-fashioned style. She was dressed like a traveling Englishwoman, in awkward, queer clothing, like a person who is indifferent to dress. She was eating an omelet and drinking water.

Her face was peculiar, with restless eyes and the expression of one with whom fate has dealt unkindly. I watched her, in spite of myself, thinking: "Who is she? What is the life of this woman? Why is she wandering alone through these mountains?"

She paid and rose to leave, drawing up over her shoulders an astonishing little shawl, the two ends of which hung over her arms. From a corner of the room she took an alpenstock, which was covered with names traced with a hot iron; then she went out, straight, erect, with the long steps of a letter-carrier who is setting out on his route.

A guide was waiting for her at the door, and both went away. I watched them go down the valley, along the road marked by a line of high wooden crosses. She was taller than her companion, and seemed to walk faster than he.

Two hours later I was climbing the edge of the deep funnel that incloses Lake Pavin in a marvelous and enormous basin of verdure, full of trees, bushes, rocks, and flowers. This lake is so round that it seems as if the outline had been drawn with a pair of compasses, so clear and blue that one might deem it a flood of azure come down from the sky, so charming that one would like to live in a but on the wooded slope which dominates this crater, where the cold, still water is sleeping. The Englishwoman was standing there like a statue, gazing upon the transparent sheet down in the dead volcano. She was straining her eyes to penetrate below the surface down to the unknown depths, where monstrous trout which have devoured all the other fish are said to live. As I was passing close by her, it seemed to me that two big tears were brimming her eyes. But she departed at a great pace, to rejoin her guide, who had stayed behind in an inn at the foot of the path leading to the lake.

I did not see her again that day.

The next day, at nightfall, I came to the chateau of Murol. The old fortress, an enormous tower standing on a peak in the midst of a large valley, where three valleys intersect, rears its brown, uneven, cracked surface into the sky; it is round, from its large circular base to the crumbling turrets on its pinnacles.

It astonishes the eye more than any other ruin by its simple mass, its majesty, its grave and imposing air of antiquity. It stands there, alone, high as a mountain, a dead queen, but still the queen of the valleys stretched out beneath it. You go up by a slope planted with firs, then you enter a narrow gate, and stop at the foot of the walls, in the first inclosure, in full view of the entire country.

Inside there are ruined halls, crumbling stairways, unknown cavities, dungeons, walls cut through in the middle, vaulted roofs held up one knows not how, and a mass of stones and crevices, overgrown with grass, where animals glide in and out.

I was exploring this ruin alone.

Suddenly I perceived behind a bit of wall a being, a kind of phantom, like the spirit of this ancient and crumbling habitation.

I was taken aback with surprise, almost with fear, when I recognized the old lady whom I had seen twice.

She was weeping, with big tears in her eyes, and held her handkerchief in her hand.

I turned around to go away, when she spoke to me, apparently ashamed to have been surprised in her grief.

"Yes, monsieur, I am crying. That does not happen often to me."

"Pardon me, madame, for having disturbed you," I stammered, confused, not knowing what to say. "Some misfortune has doubtless come to you."

"Yes. No—I am like a lost dog," she murmured, and began to sob, with her handkerchief over her eyes.

Moved by these contagious tears, I took her hand, trying to calm her. Then brusquely she told me her history, as if no longer ably to bear her grief alone.

"Oh! Oh! Monsieur—if you knew—the sorrow in which I live—in what sorrow.

"Once I was happy. I have a house down there—a home. I cannot go back to it any more; I shall never go back to it again, it is too hard to bear.

"I have a son. It is he! it is he! Children don't know. Oh, one has such a short time to live! If I should see him now I should perhaps not recognize him. How I loved him? How I loved him! Even before he was born, when I felt him move. And after that! How I have kissed and caressed and cherished him! If you knew how many nights I have passed in watching him sleep, and how many in thinking of him. I was crazy about him. When he was eight years old his father sent him to boarding-school. That was the end. He no longer belonged to me. Oh, heavens! He came to see me every Sunday. That was all!

"He went to college in Paris. Then he came only four times a year, and every time I was astonished to see how he had changed, to find him taller without having seen him grow. They stole his childhood from me, his confidence, and his love which otherwise would not have gone away from me; they stole my joy in seeing him grow, in seeing him become a little man.

"I saw him four times a year. Think of it! And at every one of his visits his body, his eye, his movements, his voice his laugh, were no longer the same, were no longer mine. All these things change so quickly in a child; and it is so sad if one is not there to see them change; one no longer recognizes him.

"One year he came with down on his cheek! He! my son! I was dumfounded —would you believe it? I hardly dared to kiss him. Was it really he, my little, little curly head of old, my dear; dear child, whom I had held in his diapers or my knee, and who had nursed at my breast with his little greedy lips—was it he, this tall, brown boy, who no longer knew how to kiss me, who seemed to love me as a matter of duty, who called me 'mother' for the sake of politeness, and who kissed me on the forehead, when I felt like crushing him in my arms?

"My husband died. Then my parents, and then my two sisters. When Death enters a house it seems as if he were hurrying to do his utmost, so as not to have to return for a long time after that. He spares only one or two to mourn the others.

"I remained alone. My tall son was then studying law. I was hoping to live and die near him, and I went to him so that we could live together. But he had fallen into the ways of young men, and he gave me to understand that I was in his way. So I left. I was wrong in doing so, but I suffered too much in feeling myself in his way, I, his mother! And I came back home.

"I hardly ever saw him again.

"He married. What a joy! At last we should be together for good. I should have grandchildren. His wife was an Englishwoman, who took a dislike to me. Why? Perhaps she thought that I loved him too much.

"Again I was obliged to go away. And I was alone. Yes, monsieur.

"Then he went to England, to live with them, with his wife's parents. Do you understand? They have him—they have my son for themselves. They have stolen him from me. He writes to me once a month. At first he came to see me. But now he no longer comes.

"It is now four years since I saw him last. His face then was wrinkled and his hair white. Was that possible? This man, my son, almost an old man? My little rosy child of old? No doubt I shall never see him again.

"And so I travel about all the year. I go east and west, as you see, with no companion.

"I am like a lost dog. Adieu, monsieur! don't stay here with me for it hurts me to have told you all this."

I went down the hill, and on turning round to glance back, I saw the old woman standing on a broken wall, looking out upon the mountains, the long valley and Lake Chambon in the distance.

And her skirt and the queer little shawl which she wore around her thin shoulders were fluttering tike a flag in the wind.

MADEMOISELLE COCOTTE

We were just leaving the asylum when I saw a tall, thin man in a corner of the court who kept on calling an imaginary dog. He was crying in a soft, tender voice: "Cocotte! Come here, Cocotte, my beauty!" and slapping his thigh as one does when calling an animal. I asked the physician, "Who is that man?" He answered: "Oh! he is not at all interesting. He is a coachman named Francois, who became insane after drowning his dog."

I insisted: "Tell me his story. The most simple and humble things are sometimes those which touch our hearts most deeply."

Here is this man's adventure, which was obtained from a friend of his, a groom:

There was a family of rich bourgeois who lived in a suburb of Paris. They had a villa in the middle of a park, at the edge of the Seine. Their coachman was this Francois, a country fellow, somewhat dull, kind-hearted, simple and easy to deceive.

One evening, as he was returning home, a dog began to follow him. At first he paid no attention to it, but the creature's obstinacy at last made him turn round. He looked to see if he knew this dog. No, he had never seen it. It was a female dog and frightfully thin. She was trotting behind him with a mournful and famished look, her tail between her legs, her ears flattened against her head and stopping and starting whenever he did.

He tried to chase this skeleton away and cried:

"Run along! Get out! Kss! kss!" She retreated a few steps, then sat down and waited. And when the coachman started to walk again she followed along behind him.

He pretended to pick up some stones. The animal ran a little farther away, but came back again as soon as the man's back was turned.

Then the coachman Francois took pity on the beast and called her. The dog approached timidly. The man patted her protruding ribs, moved by the beast's misery, and he cried: "Come! come here!" Immediately she began to wag her tail, and, feeling herself taken in, adopted, she began to run along ahead of her new master.

He made her a bed on the straw in the stable, then he ran to the kitchen for some bread. When she had eaten all she could she curled up and went to sleep.

When his employers heard of this the next day they allowed the coachman to keep the animal. It was a good beast, caressing and faithful, intelligent and gentle.

Nevertheless Francois adored Cocotte, and he kept repeating: "That beast is human. She only lacks speech."

He had a magnificent red leather collar made for her which bore these words engraved on a copper plate: "Mademoiselle Cocotte, belonging to the coachman Francois."

She was remarkably prolific and four times a year would give birth to a batch of little animals belonging to every variety of the canine race. Francois would pick out one which he would leave her and then he would unmercifully throw the others into the river. But soon the cook joined her complaints to those of the gardener. She would find dogs under the stove, in the ice box, in the coal bin, and they would steal everything they came across.

Finally the master, tired of complaints, impatiently ordered Francois to get rid of Cocotte. In despair the man tried to give her away. Nobody wanted her. Then he decided to lose her, and he gave her to a teamster, who was to drop her on the other side of Paris, near Joinville-le-Pont.

Cocotte returned the same day. Some decision had to be taken. Five francs was given to a train conductor to take her to Havre. He was to drop her there.

Three days later she returned to the stable, thin, footsore and tired out.

The master took pity on her and let her stay. But other dogs were attracted as before, and one evening, when a big dinner party was on, a stuffed turkey was carried away by one of them right under the cook's nose, and she did not dare to stop him.

This time the master completely lost his temper and said angrily to Francois: "If you don't throw this beast into the water before—to-morrow morning, I'll put you out, do you hear?"

The man was dumbfounded, and he returned to his room to pack his trunk, preferring to leave the place. Then he bethought himself that he could find no other situation as long as he dragged this animal about with him. He thought of his good position, where he was well paid and well fed, and he decided that a dog was really not worth all that. At last he decided to rid himself of Cocotte at daybreak.

He slept badly. He rose at dawn, and taking a strong rope, went to get the dog. She stood up slowly, shook herself, stretched and came to welcome her master.

Then his courage forsook him, and he began to pet her affectionately, stroking her long ears, kissing her muzzle and calling her tender names.

But a neighboring clock struck six. He could no longer hesitate. He opened the door, calling: "Come!" The beast wagged her tail, understanding that she was to be taken out.

They reached the beach, and he chose a place where the water seemed deep. Then he knotted the rope round the leather collar and tied a heavy stone to the other end. He seized Cocotte in his arms and kissed her madly, as though he were taking leave of some human being. He held her to his breast, rocked her and called her "my dear little Cocotte, my sweet little Cocotte," and she grunted with pleasure.

Ten times he tried to throw her into the water and each time he lost courage.

But suddenly he made up his mind and threw her as far from him as he could. At first she tried to swim, as she did when he gave her a bath, but her head, dragged down by the stone, kept going under, and she looked at her master with wild, human glances as she struggled like a drowning person. Then the front part of her body sank, while her hind legs waved wildly out of the water. Finally those also disappeared.

Then, for five minutes, bubbles rose to the surface as though the river were boiling, and Francois, haggard, his heart beating, thought that he saw Cocotte struggling in the mud, and, with the simplicity of a peasant, he kept saying to himself: "What does the poor beast think of me now?"

He almost lost his mind. He was ill for a month and every night he dreamed of his dog. He could feel her licking his hands and hear her barking. It was necessary to call in a physician. At last he recovered, and toward the 2nd of June his employers took him to their estate at Biesard, near Rouen.

There again he was near the Seine. He began to take baths. Each morning he would go down with the groom and they would swim across the river.

One day, as they were disporting themselves in the water, Francois suddenly cried to his companion: "Look what's coming! I'm going to give you a chop!"

It was an enormous, swollen corpse that was floating down with its feet sticking straight up in the air.

Francois swam up to it, still joking: "Whew! it's not fresh. What a catch, old man! It isn't thin, either!" He kept swimming about at a distance from the animal that was in a state of decomposition. Then, suddenly, he was silent and looked at it: attentively. This time he came near enough to touch, it. He looked fixedly at the collar, then he stretched out his arm, seized the neck, swung the corpse round and drew it up close to him and read on the copper which had turned green and which still stuck to the discolored leather: "Mademoiselle Cocotte, belonging to the coachman Francois."

The dead dog had come more than a hundred miles to find its master.

He let out a frightful shriek and began to swim for the beach with all his might, still howling; and as soon as he touched land he ran away wildly, stark naked, through the country. He was insane!

THE CORSICAN BANDIT

The road ascended gently through the forest of Aitone. The large pines formed a solemn dome above our heads, and that mysterious sound made by the wind in the trees sounded like the notes of an organ.

After walking for three hours, there was a clearing, and then at intervals an enormous pine umbrella, and then we suddenly came to the edge of the forest, some hundred meters below, the pass leading to the wild valley of Niolo.

On the two projecting heights which commanded a view of this pass, some old trees, grotesquely twisted, seemed to have mounted with painful efforts, like scouts sent in advance of the multitude in the rear. When we turned round, we saw the entire forest stretched beneath our feet, like a gigantic basin of verdure, inclosed by bare rocks whose summits seemed to reach the sky.

We resumed our walk, and, ten minutes later, found ourselves in the pass.

Then I beheld a remarkable landscape. Beyond another forest stretched a valley, but a valley such as I had never seen before; a solitude of stone, ten leagues long, hollowed out between two high mountains, without a field or a tree to be seen. This was the Niolo valley, the fatherland of Corsican liberty, the inaccessible citadel, from which the invaders had never been able to drive out the mountaineers.

My companion said to me: "This is where all our bandits have taken refuge?"

Ere long we were at the further end of this gorge, so wild, so inconceivably beautiful.

Not a blade of grass, not a plant-nothing but granite. As far as our eyes could reach, we saw in front of us a desert of glittering stone, heated like an oven by a burning sun, which seemed to hang for that very purpose right above the gorge. When we raised our eyes towards the crests, we stood dazzled and stupefied by what we saw. They looked like a festoon of coral; all the summits are of porphyry; and the sky overhead was violet, purple, tinged with the coloring of these strange mountains. Lower down, the granite was of scintillating gray, and seemed ground to powder beneath our feet. At our right, along a long and irregular course, roared a tumultuous torrent. And we staggered along under this heat, in this light, in this burning, arid, desolate valley cut by this torrent of turbulent water which seemed to be ever hurrying onward, without fertilizing the rocks, lost in this furnace which greedily drank it up without being saturated or refreshed by it.

But, suddenly, there was visible at our right a little wooden cross sunk in a little heap of stones. A man had been killed there; and I said to my companion.

"Tell me about your bandits."

He replied:

"I knew the most celebrated of them, the terrible St. Lucia. I will tell you his history.

"His father was killed in a quarrel by a young man of the district, it is said; and St. Lucia was left alone with his sister. He was a weak, timid youth, small, often ill, without any energy. He did not proclaim vengeance against the assassin of his father. All his relatives came to see him, and implored of him to avenge his death; he remained deaf to their menaces and their supplications.

"Then, following the old Corsican custom, his sister, in her indignation carried away his black clothes, in order that he might not wear mourning for a dead man who had not been avenged. He was insensible to even this affront, and rather than take down from the rack his father's gun, which was still loaded, he shut himself up, not daring to brave the looks of the young men of the district.

"He seemed to have even forgotten the crime, and lived with his sister in the seclusion of their dwelling.

"But, one day, the man who was suspected of having committed the murder, was about to get married. St. Lucia did not appear to be moved by this news, but, out of sheer bravado, doubtless, the bridegroom, on his way to the church, passed before the house of the two orphans.

"The brother and the sister, at their window, were eating frijoles, when the young man saw the bridal procession going by. Suddenly he began to tremble, rose to his feet without uttering a word, made the sign of the cross, took the gun which was hanging over the fireplace, and went out.

"When he spoke of this later on, he said: 'I don't know what was the matter with me; it was like fire in my blood; I felt that I must do it, that, in spite of everything, I could not resist, and I concealed the gun in a cave on the road to Corte.

"An hour later, he came back, with nothing in his hand, and with his habitual air of sad weariness. His sister believed that there was nothing further in his thoughts.

"But when night fell he disappeared.

"His enemy had, the same evening, to repair to Corte on foot, accompanied by his two groomsmen.

"He was walking along, singing as he went, when St. Lucia stood before him, and looking straight in the murderer's face, exclaimed: 'Now is the time!' and shot him point-blank in the chest.

"One of the men fled; the other stared at, the young man, saying:

"'What have you done, St. Lucia?' and he was about to hasten to Corte for help, when St. Lucia said in a stern tone:

"'If you move another step, I'll shoot you in the leg.'

"The other, aware of his timidity hitherto, replied: 'You would not dare to do it!' and was hurrying off when he fell instantaneously, his thigh shattered by a bullet.

"And St. Lucia, coming over to where he lay, said:

"'I am going to look at your wound; if it is not serious, I'll leave you there; if it is mortal I'll finish you off."

"He inspected the wound, considered it mortal, and slowly reloading his gun, told the wounded man to say a prayer, and shot him through the head.

"Next day he was in the mountains.

"And do you know what this St. Lucia did after this?

"All his family were arrested by the gendarmes. His uncle, the cure, who was suspected of having incited him to this deed of vengeance, was himself put in prison, and accused by the dead man's relatives. But he escaped, took a gun in his turn, and went to join his nephew in the brush.

"Next, St. Lucia killed, one after the other, his uncle's accusers, and tore out their eyes to teach the others never to state what they had seen with their eyes.

"He killed all the relatives, all the connections of his enemy's family. He slew during his life fourteen gendarmes, burned down the houses of his adversaries, and was, up to the day of his death, the most terrible of all the bandits whose memory we have preserved."

The sun disappeared behind Monte Cinto and the tall shadow of the granite mountain went to sleep on the granite of the valley. We quickened our pace in order to reach before night the little village of Albertaccio, nothing but a pile of stones welded into the stone flanks of a wild gorge. And I said as I thought of the bandit:

"What a terrible custom your vendetta is!"

My companion answered with an air of resignation:

"What would you have? A man must do his duty!"

THE GRAVE

The seventeenth of July, one thousand eight hundred and eighty-three, at half-past two in the morning, the watchman in the cemetery of Besiers, who lived in a small cottage on the edge of this field of the dead, was awakened by the barking of his dog, which was shut up in the kitchen.

Going down quickly, he saw the animal sniffing at the crack of the door and barking furiously, as if some tramp had been sneaking about the house. The keeper, Vincent, therefore took his gun and went out.

His dog, preceding him, at once ran in the direction of the Avenue General Bonnet, stopping short at the monument of Madame Tomoiseau.

The keeper, advancing cautiously, soon saw a faint light on the side of the Avenue Malenvers, and stealing in among the graves, he came upon a horrible act of profanation.

A man had dug up the coffin of a young woman who had been buried the evening before and was dragging the corpse out of it.

A small dark lantern, standing on a pile of earth, lighted up this hideous scene.

Vincent sprang upon the wretch, threw him to the ground, bound his hands and took him to the police station.

It was a young, wealthy and respected lawyer in town, named Courbataille.

He was brought into court. The public prosecutor opened the case by referring to the monstrous deeds of the Sergeant Bertrand.

A wave of indignation swept over the courtroom. When the magistrate sat down the crowd assembled cried: "Death! death!" With difficulty the presiding judge established silence.

Then he said gravely:

"Defendant, what have you to say in your defense?"

Courbataille, who had refused counsel, rose. He was a handsome fellow, tall, brown, with a frank face, energetic manner and a fearless eye.

Paying no attention to the whistlings in the room, he began to speak in a voice that was low and veiled at first, but that grew more firm as he proceeded.

"Monsieur le President, gentlemen of the jury: I have very little to say. The woman whose grave I violated was my sweetheart. I loved her.

"I loved her, not with a sensual love and not with mere tenderness of heart and soul, but with an absolute, complete love, with an overpowering passion.

"Hear me:

"When I met her for the first time I felt a strange sensation. It was not astonishment nor admiration, nor yet that which is called love at first sight, but a feeling of delicious well-being, as if I had been plunged into a warm bath. Her gestures seduced me, her voice enchanted me, and it was with infinite pleasure that I looked upon her person. It seemed to me as if I had seen her before and as if I had known her a long time. She had within her something of my spirit.

"She seemed to me like an answer to a cry uttered by my soul, to that vague and unceasing cry with which we call upon Hope during our whole life.

"When I knew her a little better, the mere thought of seeing her again filled me with exquisite and profound uneasiness; the touch of her hand in mine was more delightful to me than anything that I had imagined; her smile filled me with a mad joy, with the desire to run, to dance, to fling myself upon the ground.

"So we became lovers.

"Yes, more than that: she was my very life. I looked for nothing further on earth, and had no further desires. I longed for nothing further.

"One evening, when we had gone on a somewhat long walk by the river, we were overtaken by the rain, and she caught cold. It developed into pneumonia the next day, and a week later she was dead.

"During the hours of her suffering astonishment and consternation prevented my understanding and reflecting upon it, but when she was dead I was so overwhelmed by blank despair that I had no thoughts left. I wept.

"During all the horrible details of the interment my keen and wild grief was like a madness, a kind of sensual, physical grief.

"Then when she was gone, when she was under the earth, my mind at once found itself again, and I passed through a series of moral sufferings so terrible that even the love she had vouchsafed to me was dear at that price.

"Then the fixed idea came to me: I shall not see her again.

"When one dwells on this thought for a whole day one feels as if he were going mad. Just think of it! There is a woman whom you adore, a unique woman, for in the whole universe there is not a second one like her. This woman has given herself to you and has created with you the mysterious union that is called Love. Her eye seems to you more vast than space, more charming than the world, that clear eye smiling with her tenderness. This woman loves you. When she speaks to you her voice floods you with joy.

"And suddenly she disappears! Think of it! She disappears, not only for you, but forever. She is dead. Do you understand what that means? Never, never, never, not anywhere will she exist any more. Nevermore will that eye look upon anything again; nevermore will that voice, nor any voice like it, utter a word in the same way as she uttered it.

"Nevermore will a face be born that is like hers. Never, never! The molds of statues are kept; casts are kept by which one can make objects with the same outlines and forms. But that one body and that one face will never more be born again upon the earth. And yet millions and millions of creatures will be born, and more than that, and this one woman will not reappear among all the women of the future. Is it possible? It drives one mad to think of it.

"She lived for twenty-years, not more, and she has disappeared forever, forever, forever! She thought, she smiled, she loved me. And now nothing! The flies that die in the autumn are as much as we are in this world. And now nothing! And I thought that her body, her fresh body, so warm, so sweet, so white, so lovely, would rot down there in that box under the earth. And her soul, her thought, her love—where is it?

"Not to see her again! The idea of this decomposing body, that I might yet recognize, haunted me. I wanted to look at it once more.

"I went out with a spade, a lantern and a hammer; I jumped over the cemetery wall and I found the grave, which had not yet been closed entirely; I uncovered the coffin and took up a board. An abominable odor, the stench of putrefaction, greeted my nostrils. Oh, her bed perfumed with orris!

"Yet I opened the coffin, and, holding my lighted lantern down into it I saw her. Her face was blue, swollen, frightful. A black liquid had oozed out of her mouth.

"She! That was she! Horror seized me. But I stretched out my arm to draw this monstrous face toward me. And then I was caught.

"All night I have retained the foul odor of this putrid body, the odor of my well beloved, as one retains the perfume of a woman after a love embrace.

"Do with me what you will."

A strange silence seemed to oppress the room. They seemed to be waiting for something more. The jury retired to deliberate.

When they came back a few minutes later the accused showed no fear and did not even seem to think.

The president announced with the usual formalities that his judges declared him to be not guilty.

He did not move and the room applauded.

The Grave appeared in Gil Blas, July 29, 1883, under the signature

of "Maufrigneuse."

VOLUME XIII.

OLD JUDAS

This entire stretch of country was amazing; it was characterized by a grandeur that was almost religious, and yet it had an air of sinister desolation.

A great, wild lake, filled with stagnant, black water, in which thousands of reeds were waving to and fro, lay in the midst of a vast circle of naked hills, where nothing grew but broom, or here and there an oak curiously twisted by the wind.

Just one house stood on the banks of that dark lake, a small, low house inhabited by Uncle Joseph, an old boatman, who lived on what he could make by his fishing. Once a week he carried the fish he caught into the surrounding villages, returning with the few provisions that he needed for his sustenance.

I went to see this old hermit, who offered to take me with him to his nets, and I accepted.

His boat was old, worm-eaten and clumsy, and the skinny old man rowed with a gentle and monotonous stroke that was soothing to the soul, already oppressed by the sadness of the land round about.

It seemed to me as if I were transported to olden times, in the midst of that ancient country, in that primitive boat, which was propelled by a man of another age.

He took up his nets and threw the fish into the bottom of the boat, as the fishermen of the Bible might have done. Then he took me down to the end of the lake, where I suddenly perceived a ruin on the other side of the bank a dilapidated hut, with an enormous red cross on the wall that looked as if it might have been traced with blood, as it gleamed in the last rays of the setting sun.

"What is that?" I asked.

"That is where Judas died," the man replied, crossing himself.

I was not surprised, being almost prepared for this strange answer.

Still I asked:

"Judas? What Judas?"

"The Wandering Jew, monsieur," he added.

I asked him to tell me this legend.

But it was better than a legend, being a true story, and quite a recent one, since Uncle Joseph had known the man.

This hut had formerly been occupied by a large woman, a kind of beggar, who lived on public charity.

Uncle Joseph did not remember from whom she had this hut. One evening an old man with a white beard, who seemed to be at least two hundred years old, and who could hardly drag himself along, asked alms of this forlorn woman, as he passed her dwelling.

"Sit down, father," she replied; "everything here belongs to all the world, since it comes from all the world."

He sat down on a stone before the door. He shared the woman's bread, her bed of leaves, and her house.

He did not leave her again, for he had come to the end of his travels.

"It was Our Lady the Virgin who permitted this, monsieur," Joseph added, "it being a woman who had opened her door to a Judas, for this old vagabond was the Wandering Jew. It was not known at first in the country, but the people suspected it very soon, because he was always walking; it had become a sort of second nature to him."

And suspicion had been aroused by still another thing. This woman, who kept that stranger with her, was thought to be a Jewess, for no one had ever seen her at church. For ten miles around no one ever called her anything else but the Jewess.

When the little country children saw her come to beg they cried out: "Mamma, mamma, here is the Jewess!"

The old man and she began to go out together into the neighboring districts, holding out their hands at all the doors, stammering supplications into the ears of all the passers. They could be seen at all hours of the day, on by-paths, in the villages, or again eating bread, sitting in the noon heat under the shadow of some solitary tree. And the country people began to call the beggar Old Judas.

One day he brought home in his sack two little live pigs, which a farmer had given him after he had cured the farmer of some sickness.

Soon he stopped begging, and devoted himself entirely to his pigs. He took them out to feed by the lake, or under isolated oaks, or in the near-by valleys. The woman, however, went about all day begging, but she always came back to him in the evening.

He also did not go to church, and no one ever had seen him cross himself before the wayside crucifixes. All this gave rise to much gossip:

One night his companion was attacked by a fever and began to tremble like a leaf in the wind. He went to the nearest town to get some medicine, and then he shut himself up with her, and was not seen for six days.

The priest, having heard that the "Jewess" was about to die, came to offer the consolation of his religion and administer the last sacrament. Was she a Jewess? He did not know. But in any case, he wished to try to save her soul.

Hardly had he knocked at the door when old Judas appeared on the threshold, breathing hard, his eyes aflame, his long beard agitated, like rippling water, and he hurled blasphemies in an unknown language, extending his skinny arms in order to prevent the priest from entering.

The priest attempted to speak, offered his purse and his aid, but the old man kept on abusing him, making gestures with his hands as if throwing; stones at him.

Then the priest retired, followed by the curses of the beggar.

The companion of old Judas died the following day. He buried her himself, in front of her door. They were people of so little account that no one took any interest in them.

Then they saw the man take his pigs out again to the lake and up the hillsides. And he also began begging again to get food. But the people gave him hardly anything, as there was so much gossip about him. Every one knew, moreover, how he had treated the priest.

Then he disappeared. That was during Holy Week, but no one paid any attention to him.

But on Easter Sunday the boys and girls who had gone walking out to the lake heard a great noise in the hut. The door was locked; but the boys broke it in, and the two pigs ran out, jumping like gnats. No one ever saw them again.

The whole crowd went in; they saw some old rags on the floor, the beggar's hat, some bones, clots of dried blood and bits of flesh in the hollows of the skull.

His pigs had devoured him.

"This happened on Good Friday, monsieur." Joseph concluded his story, "three hours after noon."

"How do you know that?" I asked him.

"There is no doubt about that," he replied.

I did not attempt to make him understand that it could easily happen that the famished animals had eaten their master, after he had died suddenly in his hut.

As for the cross on the wall, it had appeared one morning, and no one knew what hand traced it in that strange color.

Since then no one doubted any longer that the Wandering Jew had died on this spot.

I myself believed it for one hour.

THE LITTLE CASK

He was a tall man of forty or thereabout, this Jules Chicot, the innkeeper of Spreville, with a red face and a round stomach, and said by those who knew him to be a smart business man. He stopped his buggy in front of Mother Magloire's farmhouse, and, hitching the horse to the gatepost, went in at the gate.

Chicot owned some land adjoining that of the old woman, which he had been coveting for a long while, and had tried in vain to buy a score of times, but she had always obstinately refused to part with it.

"I was born here, and here I mean to die," was all she said.

He found her peeling potatoes outside the farmhouse door. She was a woman of about seventy-two, very thin, shriveled and wrinkled, almost dried up in fact and much bent but as active and untiring as a girl. Chicot patted her on the back in a friendly fashion and then sat down by her on a stool.

"Well mother, you are always pretty well and hearty, I am glad to see."

"Nothing to complain of, considering, thank you. And how are you, Monsieur Chicot?"

"Oh, pretty well, thank you, except a few rheumatic pains occasionally; otherwise I have nothing to complain of."

"So much the better."

And she said no more, while Chicot watched her going on with her work. Her crooked, knotted fingers, hard as a lobster's claws, seized the tubers, which were lying in a pail, as if they had been a pair of pincers, and she peeled them rapidly, cutting off long strips of skin with an old knife which she held in the other hand, throwing the potatoes into the water as they were done. Three daring fowls jumped one after the other into her lap, seized a bit of peel and then ran away as fast as their legs would carry them with it in their beak.

Chicot seemed embarrassed, anxious, with something on the tip of his tongue which he could not say. At last he said hurriedly:

"Listen, Mother Magloire—"

"Well, what is it?"

"You are quite sure that you do not want to sell your land?"

"Certainly not; you may make up your mind to that. What I have said I have said, so don't refer to it again."

"Very well; only I think I know of an arrangement that might suit us both very well."

"What is it?"

"Just this. You shall sell it to me and keep it all the same. You don't understand? Very well, then follow me in what I am going to say."

The old woman left off peeling potatoes and looked at the innkeeper attentively from under her heavy eyebrows, and he went on:

"Let me explain myself. Every month I will give you a hundred and fifty francs. You understand me! suppose! Every month I will come and bring you thirty crowns, and it will not make the slightest difference in your life—not the very slightest. You will have your own home just as you have now, need not trouble yourself about me, and will owe me nothing; all you will have to do will be to take my money. Will that arrangement suit you?"

He looked at her good-humoredly, one might almost have said benevolently, and the old woman returned his looks distrustfully, as if she suspected a trap, and said:

"It seems all right as far as I am concerned, but it will not give you the farm."

"Never mind about that," he said; "you may remain here as long as it pleases God Almighty to let you live; it will be your home. Only you will sign a deed before a lawyer making it over to me; after your death. You have no children, only nephews and nieces for whom you don't care a straw. Will that suit you? You will keep everything during your life, and I will give you the thirty crowns a month. It is pure gain as far as you are concerned."

The old woman was surprised, rather uneasy, but, nevertheless, very much tempted to agree, and answered:

"I don't say that I will not agree to it, but I must think about it. Come back in a week, and we will talk it over again, and I will then give you my definite answer."

And Chicot went off as happy as a king who had conquered an empire.

Mother Magloire was thoughtful, and did not sleep at all that night; in fact, for four days she was in a fever of hesitation. She suspected that there was something underneath the offer which was not to her advantage; but then the thought of thirty crowns a month, of all those coins clinking in her apron, falling to her, as it were, from the skies, without her doing anything for it, aroused her covetousness.

She went to the notary and told him about it. He advised her to accept Chicot's offer, but said she ought to ask for an annuity of fifty instead of thirty, as her farm was worth sixty thousand francs at the lowest calculation.

"If you live for fifteen years longer," he said, "even then he will only have paid forty-five thousand francs for it."

The old woman trembled with joy at this prospect of getting fifty crowns a month, but she was still suspicious, fearing some trick, and she remained a long time with the lawyer asking questions without being able to make up her mind to go. At last she gave him instructions to draw up the deed and returned home with her head in a whirl, just as if she had drunk four jugs of new cider.

When Chicot came again to receive her answer she declared, after a lot of persuading, that she could not make up her mind to agree to his proposal, though she was all the time trembling lest he should not consent to give the fifty crowns, but at last, when he grew urgent, she told him what she expected for her farm.

He looked surprised and disappointed and refused.

Then, in order to convince him, she began to talk about the probable duration of her life.

"I am certainly not likely to live more than five or six years longer. I am nearly seventy-three, and far from strong, even considering my age. The other evening I thought I was going to die, and could hardly manage to crawl into bed."

But Chicot was not going to be taken in.

"Come, come, old lady, you are as strong as the church tower, and will live till you are a hundred at least; you will no doubt see me put under ground first."

The whole day was spent in discussing the money, and as the old woman would not give in, the innkeeper consented to give the fifty crowns, and she insisted upon having ten crowns over and above to strike the bargain.

Three years passed and the old dame did not seem to have grown a day older. Chicot was in despair, and it seemed to him as if he had been paying that annuity for fifty years, that he had been taken in, done, ruined. From time to time he went to see the old lady, just as one goes in July to see when the harvest is likely to begin. She always met him with a cunning look, and one might have supposed that she was congratulating herself on the trick she had played him. Seeing how well and hearty she seemed he very soon got into his buggy again, growling to himself:

"Will you never die, you old hag?"

He did not know what to do, and he felt inclined to strangle her when he saw her. He hated her with a ferocious, cunning hatred, the hatred of a peasant who has been robbed, and began to cast about for some means of getting rid of her.

One day he came to see her again, rubbing his hands as he did the first time he proposed the bargain, and, after having chatted for a few minutes, he said:

"Why do you never come and have a bit of dinner at my place when you are in Spreville? The people are talking about it, and saying we are not on friendly terms, and that pains me. You know it will cost you nothing if you come, for I don't look at the price of a dinner. Come whenever you feel inclined; I shall be very glad to see you."

Old Mother Magloire did not need to be asked twice, and the next day but one, as she had to go to the town in any case, it being market day, she let her man drive her to Chicot's place, where the buggy was put in the barn while she went into the house to get her dinner.

The innkeeper was delighted and treated her like a lady, giving her roast fowl, black pudding, leg of mutton and bacon and cabbage. But she ate next to nothing. She had always been a small eater, and had generally lived on a little soup and a crust of bread and butter.

Chicot was disappointed and pressed her to eat more, but she refused, and she would drink little, and declined coffee, so he asked her:

"But surely you will take a little drop of brandy or liqueur?"

"Well, as to that, I don't know that I will refuse." Whereupon he shouted out:

"Rosalie, bring the superfine brandy—the special—you know."

The servant appeared, carrying a long bottle ornamented with a paper vine-leaf, and he filled two liqueur glasses.

"Just try that; you will find it first rate."

The good woman drank it slowly in sips, so as to make the pleasure last all the longer, and when she had finished her glass, she said:

"Yes, that is first rate!"

Almost before she had said it Chicot had poured her out another glassful. She wished to refuse, but it was too late, and she drank it very slowly, as she had done the first, and he asked her to have a third. She objected, but he persisted.

"It is as mild as milk, you know; I can drink ten or a dozen glasses without any ill effects; it goes down like sugar and does not go to the head; one would think that it evaporated on the tongue: It is the most wholesome thing you can drink."

She took it, for she really enjoyed it, but she left half the glass.

Then Chicot, in an excess of generosity, said:

"Look here, as it is so much to your taste, I will give you a small keg of it, just to show that you and I are still excellent friends." So she took one away with her, feeling slightly overcome by the effects of what she had drunk.

The next day the innkeeper drove into her yard and took a little iron-hooped keg out of his gig. He insisted on her tasting the contents, to make sure it was the same delicious article, and, when they had each of them drunk three more glasses, he said as he was going away:

"Well, you know when it is all gone there is more left; don't be modest, for I shall not mind. The sooner it is finished the better pleased I shall be."

Four days later he came again. The old woman was outside her door cutting up the bread for her soup.

He went up to her and put his face close to hers, so that he might smell her breath; and when he smelt the alcohol he felt pleased.

"I suppose you will give me a glass of the Special?" he said. And they had three glasses each.

Soon, however, it began to be whispered abroad that Mother Magloire was in the habit of getting drunk all by herself. She was picked up in her kitchen, then in her yard, then in the roads in the neighborhood, and she was often brought home like a log.

The innkeeper did not go near her any more, and, when people spoke to him about her, he used to say, putting on a distressed look:

"It is a great pity that she should have taken to drink at her age, but when people get old there is no remedy. It will be the death of her in the long run."

And it certainly was the death of her. She died the next winter. About Christmas time she fell down, unconscious, in the snow, and was found dead the next morning.

And when Chicot came in for the farm, he said:

"It was very stupid of her; if she had not taken to drink she would probably have lived ten years longer."

BOITELLE

Father Boitelle (Antoine) made a specialty of undertaking dirty jobs all through the countryside. Whenever there was a ditch or a cesspool to be cleaned out, a dunghill removed, a sewer cleansed, or any dirt hole whatever, he way always employed to do it.

He would come with the instruments of his trade, his sabots covered with dirt, and set to work, complaining incessantly about his occupation. When people asked him then why he did this loathsome work, he would reply resignedly:

"Faith, 'tis for my children, whom I must support. This brings me in more than anything else."

He had, indeed, fourteen children. If any one asked him what had become of them, he would say with an air of indifference:

"There are only eight of them left in the house. One is out at service and five are married."

When the questioner wanted to know whether they were well married, he replied vivaciously:

"I did not oppose them. I opposed them in nothing. They married just as they pleased. We shouldn't go against people's likings, it turns out badly. I am a night scavenger because my parents went against my likings. But for that I would have become a workman like the others."

Here is the way his parents had thwarted him in his likings:

He was at the time a soldier stationed at Havre, not more stupid than another, or sharper either, a rather simple fellow, however. When he was not on duty, his greatest pleasure was to walk along the quay, where the bird dealers congregate. Sometimes alone, sometimes with a soldier from his own part of the country, he would slowly saunter along by cages containing parrots with green backs and yellow heads from the banks of the Amazon, or parrots with gray backs and red heads from Senegal, or enormous macaws, which look like birds reared in hot-houses, with their flower-like feathers, their plumes and their tufts. Parrots of every size, who seem painted with minute care by the miniaturist, God Almighty, and the little birds, all the smaller birds hopped about, yellow, blue and variegated, mingling their cries with the noise of the quay; and adding to the din caused by unloading the vessels, as well as by passengers and vehicles, a violent clamor, loud, shrill and deafening, as if from some distant forest of monsters.

Boitelle would pause, with wondering eyes, wide-open mouth, laughing and enraptured, showing his teeth to the captive cockatoos, who kept nodding their white or yellow topknots toward the glaring red of his breeches and the copper buckle of his belt. When he found a bird that could talk he put questions to it, and if it happened at the time to be disposed to reply and to hold a conversation with him he would carry away enough amusement to last him till evening. He also found heaps of amusement in looking at the monkeys, and could conceive no greater luxury for a rich man than to own these animals as one owns cats and dogs. This kind of taste for the exotic he had in his blood, as people have a taste for the chase, or for medicine, or for the priesthood. He could not help returning to the quay every time the gates of the barracks opened, drawn toward it by an irresistible longing.

On one occasion, having stopped almost in ecstasy before an enormous macaw, which was swelling out its plumes, bending forward and bridling up again as if making the court curtseys of parrot-land, he saw the door of a little cafe adjoining the bird dealer's shop open, and a young negress appeared, wearing on her head a red silk handkerchief. She was sweeping into the street the corks and sand of the establishment.

Boitelle's attention was soon divided between the bird and the woman, and he really could not tell which of these two beings he contemplated with the greater astonishment and delight.

The negress, having swept the rubbish into the street, raised her eyes, and, in her turn, was dazzled by the soldier's uniform. There she stood facing him with her broom in her hands as if she were bringing him a rifle, while the macaw continued bowing. But at the end of a few seconds the soldier began to feel embarrassed at this attention, and he walked away quietly so as not to look as if he were beating a retreat.

But he came back. Almost every day he passed before the Cafe des Colonies, and often he could distinguish through the window the figure of the little black-skinned maid serving "bocks" or glasses of brandy to the sailors of the port. Frequently, too, she would come out to the door on seeing him; soon, without even having exchanged a word, they smiled at one another like acquaintances; and Boitelle felt his heart touched when he suddenly saw, glittering between the dark lips of the girl, a shining row of white teeth. At length, one day he ventured to enter, and was quite surprised to find that she could speak French like every one else. The bottle of lemonade, of which she was good enough to accept a glassful, remained in the soldier's recollection memorably delicious, and it became a custom with him to come and absorb in this little tavern on the quay all the agreeable drinks which he could afford.

For him it was a treat, a happiness, on which his thoughts dwelt constantly, to watch the black hand of the little maid pouring something into his glass while her teeth laughed more than her eyes. At the end of two months they became fast friends, and Boitelle, after his first astonishment at discovering that this negress had as good principles as honest French girls, that she exhibited a regard for economy, industry, religion and good conduct, loved her more on that account, and was so charmed with her that he wanted to marry her.

He told her his intentions, which made her dance with joy. She had also a little money, left her by, a female oyster dealer, who had picked her up when she had been left on the quay at Havre by an American captain. This captain had found her, when she was only about six years old, lying on bales of cotton in the hold of his ship, some hours after his departure from New York. On his arrival in Havre he abandoned to the care of this compassionate oyster dealer the little black creature, who had been hidden on board his vessel, he knew not why or by whom.

The oyster woman having died, the young negress became a servant at the Colonial Tavern.

Antoine Boitelle added: "This will be all right if my parents don't oppose it. I will never go against them, you understand, never! I'm going to say a word or two to them the first time I go back to the country."

On the following week, in fact, having obtained twenty-four hours' leave, he went to see his family, who cultivated a little farm at Tourteville, near Yvetot.

He waited till the meal was finished, the hour when the coffee baptized with brandy makes people more open-hearted, before informing his parents that he had found a girl who satisfied his tastes, all his tastes, so completely that there could not exist any other in all the world so perfectly suited to him.

The old people, on hearing this, immediately assumed a cautious manner and wanted explanations. He had concealed nothing from them except the color of her skin.

She was a servant, without much means, but strong, thrifty, clean, well-conducted and sensible. All these things were better than money would be in the hands of a bad housewife. Moreover, she had a few sous, left her by a woman who had reared her, a good number of sous, almost a little dowry, fifteen hundred francs in the savings bank. The old people, persuaded by his talk, and relying also on their own judgment, were gradually weakening, when he came to the delicate point. Laughing in rather a constrained fashion, he said:

"There's only one thing you may not like. She is not a white slip."

They did not understand, and he had to explain at some length and very cautiously, to avoid shocking them, that she belonged to the dusky race of which they had only seen samples in pictures at Epinal. Then they became restless, perplexed, alarmed, as if he had proposed a union with the devil.

The mother said: "Black? How much of her is black? Is the whole of her?"

He replied: "Certainly. Everywhere, just as you are white everywhere."

The father interposed: "Black? Is it as black as the pot?"

The son answered: "Perhaps a little less than that. She is black, but not disgustingly black. The cure's cassock is black, but it is not uglier than a surplice which is white."

The father said: "Are there more black people besides her in her country?"

And the son, with an air of conviction, exclaimed: "Certainly!"

But the old man shook his head.

"That must be unpleasant."

And the son:

"It isn't more disagreeable than anything else when you get accustomed to it."

The mother asked:

"It doesn't soil the underwear more than other skins, this black skin?"

"Not more than your own, as it is her proper color."

Then, after many other questions, it was agreed that the parents should see this girl before coming; to any decision, and that the young fellow, whose, term of military service would be over in a month, should bring her to the house in order that they might examine her and decide by talking the matter over whether or not she was too dark to enter the Boitelle family.

Antoine accordingly announced that on Sunday, the 22d of May, the day of his discharge, he would start for Tourteville with his sweetheart.

She had put on, for this journey to the house of her lover's parents, her most beautiful and most gaudy clothes, in which yellow, red and blue were the prevailing colors, so that she looked as if she were adorned for a national festival.

At the terminus, as they were leaving Havre, people stared at her, and Boitelle was proud of giving his arm to a person who commanded so much attention. Then, in the third-class carriage, in which she took a seat by his side, she aroused so much astonishment among the country folks that the people in the adjoining compartments stood up on their benches to look at her over the wooden partition which divides the compartments. A child, at sight of her, began to cry with terror, another concealed his face in his mother's apron. Everything went off well, however, up to their arrival at their destination. But when the train slackened its rate of motion as they drew near Yvetot, Antoine felt: ill at ease, as he would have done at a review when; he did not know his drill practice. Then, as he; leaned his head out, he recognized in the distance: his father, holding the bridle of the horse harnessed to a carryall, and his mother, who had come forward to the grating, behind which stood those who were expecting friends.

He alighted first, gave his hand to his sweetheart, and holding himself erect, as if he were escorting a general, he went to meet his family.

The mother, on seeing this black lady in variegated costume in her son's company, remained so stupefied that she could not open her mouth; and the father found it hard to hold the horse, which the engine or the negress caused to rear continuously. But Antoine, suddenly filled with unmixed joy at seeing once more the old people, rushed forward with open arms, embraced his mother, embraced his father, in spite of the nag's fright, and then turning toward his companion, at whom the passengers on the platform stopped to stare with amazement, he proceeded to explain:

"Here she is! I told you that, at first sight, she is not attractive; but as soon as you know her, I can assure you there's not a better sort in the whole world. Say good-morning to her so that she may not feel badly."

Thereupon Mere Boitelle, almost frightened out of her wits, made a sort of curtsy, while the father took off his cap, murmuring:

"I wish you good luck!"

Then, without further delay, they climbed into the carryall, the two women at the back, on seats which made them jump up and down as the vehicle went jolting along the road, and the two men in front on the front seat.

Nobody spoke. Antoine, ill at ease, whistled a barrack-room air; his father whipped the nag; and his mother, from where she sat in the corner, kept casting sly glances at the negress, whose forehead and cheekbones shone in the sunlight like well-polished shoes.

Wishing to break the ice, Antoine turned round.

"Well," said he, "we don't seem inclined to talk."

"We must have time," replied the old woman.

He went on:

"Come! Tell us the little story about that hen of yours that laid eight eggs."

It was a funny anecdote of long standing in the family. But, as his mother still remained silent, paralyzed by her emotion, he undertook himself to tell the story, laughing as he did so at the memorable incident. The father, who knew it by heart brightened at the opening words of the narrative; his wife soon followed his example; and the negress herself, when he reached the drollest part of it, suddenly gave vent to a laugh, such a loud, rolling torrent of laughter that the horse, becoming excited, broke into a gallop for a while.

This served to cement their acquaintance. They all began to chat.

They had scarcely reached the house and had all alighted, when Antoine conducted his sweetheart to a room, so that she might take off her dress, to avoid staining it, as she was going to prepare a nice dish, intended to win the old people's affections through their stomachs. He drew his parents outside the house, and, with beating heart, asked:

"Well, what do you say now?"

The father said nothing. The mother, less timid, exclaimed:

"She is too black. No, indeed, this is too much for me. It turns my blood."

"You will get used to it," said Antoine.

"Perhaps so, but not at first."

They went into the house, where the good woman was somewhat affected at the spectacle of the negress engaged in cooking. She at once proceeded to assist her, with petticoats tucked up, active in spite of her age.

The meal was an excellent one, very long, very enjoyable. When they were taking a turn after dinner, Antoine took his father aside.

"Well, dad, what do you say about it?"

The peasant took care never to compromise himself.

"I have no opinion about it. Ask your mother."

So Antoine went back to his mother, and, detaining her behind the rest, said:

"Well, mother, what do you think of her?"

"My poor lad, she is really too black. If she were only a little less black, I would not go against you, but this is too much. One would think it was Satan!"

He did not press her, knowing how obstinate the old woman had always been, but he felt a tempest of disappointment sweeping over his heart. He was turning over in his mind what he ought to do, what plan he could devise, surprised, moreover, that she had not conquered them already as she had captivated himself. And they, all four, walked along through the wheat fields, having gradually relapsed into silence. Whenever they passed a fence they saw a countryman sitting on the stile, and a group of brats climbed up to stare at them, and every one rushed out into the road to see the "black" whore young Boitelle had brought home with him. At a distance they noticed people scampering across the fields just as when the drum beats to draw public attention to some living phenomenon. Pere and Mere Boitelle, alarmed at this curiosity, which was exhibited everywhere through the country at their approach, quickened their pace, walking side by side, and leaving their son far behind. His dark companion asked what his parents thought of her.

He hesitatingly replied that they had not yet made up their minds.

But on the village green people rushed out of all the houses in a flutter of excitement; and, at the sight of the gathering crowd, old Boitelle took to his heels, and regained his abode, while Antoine; swelling with rage, his sweetheart on his arm, advanced majestically under the staring eyes, which opened wide in amazement.

He understood that it was at an end, and there was no hope for him, that he could not marry his negress. She also understood it; and as they drew near the farmhouse they both began to weep. As soon as they had got back to the house, she once more took off her dress to aid the mother in the household duties, and followed her everywhere, to the dairy, to the stable, to the hen house, taking on herself the hardest part of the work, repeating always: "Let me do it, Madame Boitelle," so that, when night came on, the old woman, touched but inexorable, said to her son: "She is a good girl, all the same. It's a pity she is so black; but indeed she is too black. I could not get used to it. She must go back again. She is too, too black!"

And young Boitelle said to his sweetheart:

"She will not consent. She thinks you are too black. You must go back again. I will go with you to the train. No matter—don't fret. I am going to talk to them after you have started."

He then took her to the railway station, still cheering her with hope, and, when he had kissed her, he put her into the train, which he watched as it passed out of sight, his eyes swollen with tears.

In vain did he appeal to the old people. They would never give their consent.

And when he had told this story, which was known all over the country, Antoine Boitelle would always add:

"From that time forward I have had no heart for anything—for anything at all. No trade suited me any longer, and so I became what I am—a night scavenger."

People would say to him:

"Yet you got married."

"Yes, and I can't say that my wife didn't please me, seeing that I have fourteen children; but she is not the other one, oh, no—certainly not! The other one, mark you, my negress, she had only to give me one glance, and I felt as if I were in Heaven."

A WIDOW

This story was told during the hunting season at the Chateau Baneville. The autumn had been rainy and sad. The red leaves, instead of rustling under the feet, were rotting under the heavy downfalls.

The forest was as damp as it could be. From it came an odor of must, of rain, of soaked grass and wet earth; and the sportsmen, their backs hunched under the downpour, mournful dogs, with tails between their legs and hairs sticking to their sides, and the young women, with their clothes drenched, returned every evening, tired in body and in mind.

After dinner, in the large drawing-room, everybody played lotto, without enjoyment, while the wind whistled madly around the house. Then they tried telling stories like those they read in books, but no one was able to invent anything amusing. The hunters told tales of wonderful shots and of the butchery of rabbits; and the women racked their brains for ideas without revealing the imagination of Scheherezade. They were about to give up this diversion when a young woman, who was idly caressing the hand of an old maiden aunt, noticed a little ring made of blond hair, which she had often seen, without paying any attention to it.

She fingered it gently and asked, "Auntie, what is this ring? It looks as if it were made from the hair of a child."

The old lady blushed, grew pale, then answered in a trembling voice: "It is sad, so sad that I never wish to speak of it. All the unhappiness of my life comes from that. I was very young then, and the memory has remained so painful that I weep every time I think of it."

Immediately everybody wished to know the story, but the old lady refused to tell it. Finally, after they had coaxed her for a long time, she yielded. Here is the story:

"You have often heard me speak of the Santeze family, now extinct. I knew the last three male members of this family. They all died in the same manner; this hair belongs to the last one. He was thirteen when he killed himself for me. That seems strange to you, doesn't it?

"Oh! it was a strange family—mad, if you will, but a charming madness, the madness of love. From father to son, all had violent passions which filled their whole being, which impelled them to do wild things, drove them to frantic enthusiasm, even to crime. This was born in them, just as burning devotion is in certain souls. Trappers have not the same nature as minions of the drawing-room. There was a saying: 'As passionate as a Santeze.' This could be noticed by looking at them. They all had wavy hair, falling over their brows, curly beards and large eyes whose glance pierced and moved one, though one could not say why.

"The grandfather of the owner of this hair, of whom it is the last souvenir, after many adventures, duels and elopements, at about sixty-five fell madly in love with his farmer's daughter. I knew them both. She was blond, pale, distinguished-looking, with a slow manner of talking, a quiet voice and a look so gentle that one might have taken her for a Madonna. The old nobleman took her to his home and was soon so captivated with her that he could not live without her for a minute. His daughter and daughter-in-law, who lived in the chateau, found this perfectly natural, love was such a tradition in the family. Nothing in regard to a passion surprised them, and if one spoke before them of parted lovers, even of vengeance after treachery, both said in the same sad tone: 'Oh, how he must have suffered to come to that point!' That was all. They grew sad over tragedies of love, but never indignant, even when they were criminal.

"Now, one day a young man named Monsieur de Gradelle, who had been invited for the shooting, eloped with the young girl.

"Monsieur de Santeze remained calm as if nothing had happened, but one morning he was found hanging in the kennels, among his dogs.

"His son died in the same manner in a hotel in Paris during a journey which he made there in 1841, after being deceived by a singer from the opera.

"He left a twelve-year-old child and a widow, my mother's sister. She came to my father's house with the boy, while we were living at Bertillon. I was then seventeen.

"You have no idea how wonderful and precocious this Santeze child was. One might have thought that all the tenderness and exaltation of the whole race had been stored up in this last one. He was always dreaming and walking about alone in a great alley of elms leading from the chateau to the forest. I watched from my window this sentimental boy, who walked with thoughtful steps, his hands behind his back, his head bent, and at times stopping to raise his eyes as if he could see and understand things that were not comprehensible at his age.

"Often, after dinner on clear evenings, he would say to me: 'Let us go outside and dream, cousin.' And we would go outside together in the park. He would stop quickly before a clearing where the white vapor of the moon lights the woods, and he would press my hand, saying: 'Look! look! but you don't understand me; I feel it. If you understood me, we should be happy. One must love to know!' I would laugh and then kiss this child, who loved me madly.

"Often, after dinner, he would sit on my mother's knees. 'Come, auntie,' he would say, 'tell me some love-stories.' And my mother, as a joke, would tell him all the old legends of the family, all the passionate adventures of his forefathers, for thousands of them were current, some true and some false. It was their reputation for love and gallantry which was the ruin of every one of these men; they gloried in it and then thought that they had to live up to the renown of their house.

"The little fellow became exalted by these tender or terrible stories, and at times he would clap his hands, crying: 'I, too, I, too, know how to love, better than all of them!'

"Then, he began to court me in a timid and tender manner, at which every one laughed, it was, so amusing. Every morning I had some flowers picked by him, and every evening before going to his room he would kiss my hand and murmur: 'I love you!'

"I was guilty, very guilty, and I grieved continually about it, and I have been doing penance all my life; I have remained an old maid—or, rather, I have lived as a widowed fiancee, his widow.

"I was amused at this childish tenderness, and I even encouraged him. I was coquettish, as charming as with a man, alternately caressing and severe. I maddened this child. It was a game for me and a joyous diversion for his mother and mine. He was twelve! think of it! Who would have taken this atom's passion seriously? I kissed him as often as he wished; I even wrote him little notes, which were read by our respective mothers; and he answered me by passionate letters, which I have kept. Judging himself as a man, he thought that our loving intimacy was secret. We had forgotten that he was a Santeze.

"This lasted for about a year. One evening in the park he fell at my feet and, as he madly kissed the hem of my dress, he kept repeating: 'I love you! I love you! I love you! If ever you deceive me, if ever you leave me for another, I'll do as my father did.' And he added in a hoarse voice, which gave me a shiver: 'You know what he did!'

"I stood there astonished. He arose, and standing on the tips of his toes in order to reach my ear, for I was taller than he, he pronounced my first name: 'Genevieve!' in such a gentle, sweet, tender tone that I trembled all over. I stammered: 'Let us return! let us return!' He said no more and followed me; but as we were going up the steps of the porch, he stopped me, saying: 'You know, if ever you leave me, I'll kill myself.'

"This time I understood that I had gone too far, and I became quite reserved. One day, as he was reproaching me for this, I answered: 'You are now too old for jesting and too young for serious love. I'll wait.'

"I thought that this would end the matter. In the autumn he was sent to a boarding-school. When he returned the following summer I was engaged to be married. He understood immediately, and for a week he became so pensive that I was quite anxious.

"On the morning of the ninth day I saw a little paper under my door as I got up. I seized it, opened it and read: 'You have deserted me and you know what I said. It is death to which you have condemned me. As I do not wish to be found by another than you, come to the park just where I told you last year that I loved you and look in the air.'

"I thought that I should go mad. I dressed as quickly as I could and ran wildly to the place that he had mentioned. His little cap was on the ground in the mud. It had been raining all night. I raised my eyes and saw something swinging among the leaves, for the wind was blowing a gale.

"I don't know what I did after that. I must have screamed at first, then fainted and fallen, and finally have run to the chateau. The next thing that I remember I was in bed, with my mother sitting beside me.

"I thought that I had dreamed all this in a frightful nightmare. I stammered: 'And what of him, what of him, Gontran?' There was no answer. It was true!

"I did not dare see him again, but I asked for a lock of his blond hair. Here—here it is!"

And the old maid stretched out her trembling hand in a despairing gesture. Then she blew her nose several times, wiped her eyes and continued:

"I broke off my marriage—without saying why. And I—I always have remained the—the widow of this thirteen-year-old boy." Then her head fell on her breast and she wept for a long time.

As the guests were retiring for the night a large man, whose quiet she had disturbed, whispered in his neighbor's ear: "Isn't it unfortunate to, be so sentimental?"

THE ENGLISHMAN OF ETRETAT

A great English poet has just crossed over to France in order to greet Victor Hugo. All the newspapers are full of his name and he is the great topic of conversation in all drawing-rooms. Fifteen years ago I had occasion several times to meet Algernon Charles Swinburne. I will attempt to show him just as I saw him and to give an idea of the strange impression he made on me, which will remain with me throughout time.

I believe it was in 1867 or in 1868 that an unknown young Englishman came to Etretat and bought a little but hidden under great trees. It was said that he lived there, always alone, in a strange manner; and he aroused the inimical surprise of the natives, for the inhabitants were sullen and foolishly malicious, as they always are in little towns.

They declared that this whimsical Englishman ate nothing but boiled. roasted or stewed monkey; that he would see no one; that he talked to himself hours at a time and many other surprising things that made people think that he was different from other men. They were surprised that he should live alone with a monkey. Had it been a cat or a dog they would have said nothing. But a monkey! Was that not frightful? What savage tastes the man must have!

I knew this young man only from seeing him in the streets. He was short, plump, without being fat, mild-looking, and he wore a little blond mustache, which was almost invisible.

Chance brought us together. This savage had amiable and pleasing manners, but he was one of those strange Englishmen that one meets here and there throughout the world.

Endowed with remarkable intelligence, he seemed to live in a fantastic dream, as Edgar Poe must have lived. He had translated into English a volume of strange Icelandic legends, which I ardently desired to see translated into French. He loved the supernatural, the dismal and grewsome, but he spoke of the most marvellous things with a calmness that was typically English, to which his gentle and quiet voice gave a semblance of reality that was maddening.

Full of a haughty disdain for the world, with its conventions, prejudices and code of morality, he had nailed to his house a name that was boldly impudent. The keeper of a lonely inn who should write on his door: "Travellers murdered here!" could not make a more sinister jest. I never had entered his dwelling, when one day I received an invitation to luncheon, following an accident that had occurred to one of his friends, who had been almost drowned and whom I had attempted to rescue.

Although I was unable to reach the man until he had already been rescued, I received the hearty thanks of the two Englishmen, and the following day I called upon them.

The friend was a man about thirty years old. He bore an enormous head on a child's body—a body without chest or shoulders. An immense forehead, which seemed to have engulfed the rest of the man, expanded like a dome above a thin face which ended in a little pointed beard. Two sharp eyes and a peculiar mouth gave one the impression of the head of a reptile, while the magnificent brow suggested a genius.

A nervous twitching shook this peculiar being, who walked, moved, acted by jerks like a broken spring.

This was Algernon Charles Swinburne, son of an English admiral and grandson, on the maternal side, of the Earl of Ashburnham.

He strange countenance was transfigured when he spoke. I have seldom seen a man more impressive, more eloquent, incisive or charming in conversation. His rapid, clear, piercing and fantastic imagination seemed to creep into his voice and to lend life to his words. His brusque gestures enlivened his speech, which penetrated one like a dagger, and he had bursts of thought, just as lighthouses throw out flashes of fire, great, genial lights that seemed to illuminate a whole world of ideas.

The home of the two friends was pretty and by no means commonplace. Everywhere were paintings, some superb, some strange, representing different conceptions of insanity. Unless I am mistaken, there was a water-color which represented the head of a dead man floating in a rose-colored shell on a boundless ocean, under a moon with a human face.

Here and there I came across bones. I clearly remember a flayed hand on which was hanging some dried skin and black muscles, and on the snow-white bones could be seen the traces of dried blood.

The food was a riddle which I could not solve. Was it good? Was it bad? I could not say. Some roast monkey took away all desire to make a steady diet of this animal, and the great monkey who roamed about among us at large and playfully pushed his head into my glass when I wished to drink cured me of any desire I might have to take one of his brothers as a companion for the rest of my days.

As for the two men, they gave me the impression of two strange, original, remarkable minds, belonging to that peculiar race of talented madmen from among whom have arisen Poe, Hoffmann and many others.

If genius is, as is commonly believed, a sort of aberration of great minds, then Algernon Charles Swinburne is undoubtedly a genius.

Great minds that are healthy are never considered geniuses, while this sublime qualification is lavished on brains that are often inferior but are slightly touched by madness.

At any rate, this poet remains one of the first of his time, through his originality and polished form. He is an exalted lyrical singer who seldom bothers about the good and humble truth, which French poets are now seeking so persistently and patiently. He strives to set down dreams, subtle thoughts, sometimes great, sometimes visibly forced, but sometimes magnificent.

Two years later I found the house closed and its tenants gone. The furniture was being sold. In memory of them I bought the hideous flayed hand. On the grass an enormous square block of granite bore this simple word: "Nip." Above this a hollow stone offered water to the birds. It was the grave of the monkey, who had been hanged by a young, vindictive negro servant. It was said that this violent domestic had been forced to flee at the point of his exasperated master's revolver. After wandering about without home or food for several days, he returned and began to peddle barley-sugar in the streets. He was expelled from the country after he had almost strangled a displeased customer.

The world would be gayer if one could often meet homes like that.

> This story appeared in the "Gaulois," November 29, 1882. It was the original sketch for the introductory study of Swinburne, written by Maupassant for the French translation by Gabriel Mourey of "Poems and Ballads."

MAGNETISM

It was a men's dinner party, and they were sitting over their cigars and brandy and discussing magnetism. Donato's tricks and Charcot's experiments. Presently, the sceptical, easy-going men, who cared nothing for religion of any sort, began telling stories of strange occurrences, incredible things which, nevertheless, had really occurred, so they said, falling back into superstitious beliefs, clinging to these last remnants of the marvellous, becoming devotees of this mystery of magnetism, defending it in the name of science. There was only one person who smiled, a vigorous young fellow, a great ladies' man who was so incredulous that he would not even enter upon a discussion of such matters.

He repeated with a sneer:

"Humbug! humbug! humbug! We need not discuss Donato, who is merely a very smart juggler. As for M. Charcot, who is said to be a remarkable man of science, he produces on me the effect of those story-tellers of the school of Edgar Poe, who end by going mad through constantly reflecting on queer cases of insanity. He has authenticated some cases of unexplained and inexplicable nervous phenomena; he makes his way into that unknown region which men are exploring every day, and unable always to understand what he sees, he recalls, perhaps, the ecclesiastical interpretation of these mysteries. I should like to hear what he says himself."

The words of the unbeliever were listened to with a kind of pity, as if he had blasphemed in an assembly of monks.

One of these gentlemen exclaimed:

"And yet miracles were performed in olden times."

"I deny it," replied the other: "Why cannot they be performed now?"

Then, each mentioned some fact, some fantastic presentiment some instance of souls communicating with each other across space, or some case of the secret influence of one being over another. They asserted and maintained that these things had actually occurred, while the sceptic angrily repeated:

"Humbug! humbug! humbug!"

At last he rose, threw away his cigar, and with his hands in his pockets, said: "Well, I also have two stories to tell you, which I will afterwards explain. Here they are:

"In the little village of Etretat, the men, who are all seafaring folk, go every year to Newfoundland to fish for cod. One night the little son of one of these fishermen woke up with a start, crying out that his father was dead. The child was quieted, and again he woke up exclaiming that his father was drowned. A month later the news came that his father had, in fact, been swept off the deck of his smack by a billow. The widow then remembered how her son had woke up and spoken of his father's death. Everyone said it was a miracle, and the affair caused a great sensation. The dates were compared, and it was found that the accident and the dream were almost coincident, whence they concluded that they had happened on the same night and at the same hour. And there is a mystery of magnetism."

The story-teller stopped suddenly.

Thereupon, one of those who had heard him, much affected by the narrative, asked:

"And can you explain this?"

"Perfectly, monsieur. I have discovered the secret. The circumstance surprised me and even perplexed me very much; but you see, I do not believe on principle. Just as others begin by believing, I begin by doubting; and when I cannot understand, I continue to deny that there can be any telepathic communication between souls; certain that my own intelligence will be able to explain it. Well, I kept on inquiring into the matter, and by dint of questioning all the wives of the absent seamen, I was convinced that not a week passed without one of them, or one of their children dreaming and declaring when they woke up that the father was drowned. The horrible and continual fear of this accident makes them always talk about it. Now, if one of these frequent predictions coincides, by a very simple chance, with the death of the person referred to, people at once declare it to be a miracle; for they suddenly lose sight of all the other predictions of misfortune that have remained unfulfilled. I have myself known fifty cases where the persons who made the prediction forgot all about it a week after wards. But, if, then one happens to die, then the recollection of the thing is immediately revived, and people are ready to believe in the intervention of God, according to some, and magnetism, according to others."

One of the smokers remarked:

"What you say is right enough; but what about your second story?"

"Oh! my second story is a very delicate matter to relate. It happened to myself, and so I don't place any great value on my own view of the matter. An interested party can never give an impartial opinion. However, here it is:

"Among my acquaintances was a young woman on whom I had never bestowed a thought, whom I had never even looked at attentively, never taken any notice of.

"I classed her among the women of no importance, though she was not bad-looking; she appeared, in fact, to possess eyes, a nose, a mouth, some sort of hair—just a colorless type of countenance. She was one of those beings who awaken only a chance, passing thought, but no special interest, no desire.

"Well, one night, as I was writing some letters by my fireside before going to bed, I was conscious, in the midst of that train of sensuous visions that sometimes pass through one's brain in moments of idle reverie, of a kind of slight influence, passing over me, a little flutter of the heart, and immediately, without any cause, without any logical connection of thought, I saw distinctly, as if I were touching her, saw from head to foot, and disrobed, this young woman to whom I had never given more that three seconds' thought at a time. I suddenly discovered in her a number of qualities which I had never before observed, a sweet charm, a languorous fascination; she awakened in me that sort of restless emotion that causes one to pursue a woman. But I did not think of her long. I went to bed and was soon asleep. And I dreamed.

"You have all had these strange dreams which make you overcome the impossible, which open to you double-locked doors, unexpected joys, tightly folded arms?

"Which of us in these troubled, excising, breathless slumbers, has not held, clasped, embraced with rapture, the woman who occupied his thoughts? And have you ever noticed what superhuman delight these happy dreams give us? Into what mad intoxication they cast you! with what passionate spasms they shake you! and with what infinite, caressing, penetrating tenderness they fill your heart for her whom you hold clasped in your arms in that adorable illusion that is so like reality!

"All this I felt with unforgettable violence. This woman was mine, so much mine that the pleasant warmth of her skin remained in my fingers, the odor of her skin, in my brain, the taste of her kisses, on my lips, the sound of her voice lingered in my ears, the touch of her clasp still clung to me, and the burning charm of her tenderness still gratified my senses long after the delight but disillusion of my awakening.

"And three times that night I had the same dream.

"When the day dawned she haunted me, possessed me, filled my senses to such an extent that I was not one second without thinking of her.

"At last, not knowing what to do, I dressed myself and went to call on her. As I went upstairs to her apartment, I was so overcome by emotion that I trembled, and my heart beat rapidly.

"I entered the apartment. She rose the moment she heard my name mentioned; and suddenly our eyes met in a peculiar fixed gaze.

"I sat down. I stammered out some commonplaces which she seemed not to hear. I did not know what to say or do. Then, abruptly, clasping my arms round her, my dream was realized so suddenly that I began to doubt whether I was really awake. We were friends after this for two years."

"What conclusion do you draw from it?" said a voice.

The story-teller seemed to hesitate.

"The conclusion I draw from it—well, by Jove, the conclusion is that it was just a coincidence! And then—who can tell? Perhaps it was some glance of hers which I had not noticed and which came back that night to me through one of those mysterious and unconscious —recollections that often bring before us things ignored by our own consciousness, unperceived by our minds!"

"Call it whatever you like," said one of his table companions, when the story was finished; "but if you don't believe in magnetism after that, my dear boy, you are an ungrateful fellow!"

A FATHER'S CONFESSION

All Veziers-le-Rethel had followed the funeral procession of M. Badon-Leremince to the grave, and the last words of the funeral oration pronounced by the delegate of the district remained in the minds of all: "He was an honest man, at least!"

An honest man he had been in all the known acts of his life, in his words, in his examples, his attitude, his behavior, his enterprises, in the cut of his beard and the shape of his hats. He never had said a word that did not set an example, never had given an alms without adding a word of advice, never had extended his hand without appearing to bestow a benediction.

He left two children, a boy and a girl. His son was counselor general, and his daughter, having married a lawyer, M. Poirel de la Voulte, moved in the best society of Veziers.

They were inconsolable at the death of their father, for they loved him sincerely.

As soon as the ceremony was over, the son, daughter and son-in-law returned to the house of mourning, and, shutting themselves in the library, they opened the will, the seals of which were to be broken by them alone and only after the coffin had been placed in the ground. This wish was expressed by a notice on the envelope.

M. Poirel de la Voulte tore open the envelope, in his character of a lawyer used to such operations, and having adjusted his spectacles, he read in a monotonous voice, made for reading the details of contracts:

My children, my dear children, I could not sleep the eternal sleep in peace if I did not make to you from the tomb a confession, the confession of a crime, remorse for which has ruined my life. Yes, I committed a crime, a frightful, abominable crime.

I was twenty-six years old, and I had just been called to the bar in Paris, and was living the life off young men from the provinces who are stranded in this town without acquaintances, relatives, or friends.

I took a sweetheart. There are beings who cannot live alone. I was one of those. Solitude fills me with horrible anguish, the solitude of my room beside my fire in the evening. I feel then as if I were alone on earth, alone, but surrounded by vague dangers, unknown and terrible things; and the partition that separates me from my neighbor, my neighbor whom I do not know, keeps me at as great a distance from him as the stars that I see through my window. A sort of fever pervades me, a fever of impatience and of fear, and the silence of the walls terrifies me. The silence of a room where one lives alone is so intense and so melancholy It is not only a silence of the mind; when a piece of furniture cracks a shudder goes through you for you expect no noise in this melancholy abode.

How many times, nervous and timid from this motionless silence, I have begun to talk, to repeat words without rhyme or reason, only to make some sound. My voice at those times sounds so strange that I am afraid of that, too. Is there anything more dreadful than talking to one's self in an empty house? One's voice sounds like that of another, an unknown voice talking aimlessly, to no one, into the empty air, with no ear to listen to it, for one knows before they escape into the solitude of the room exactly what words will be uttered. And when they resound lugubriously in the silence, they seem no more than an echo, the peculiar echo of words whispered by ones thought.

My sweetheart was a young girl like other young girls who live in

Paris on wages that are insufficient to keep them. She was gentle, good, simple. Her parents lived at Poissy. She went to spend several days with them from time to time.

For a year I lived quietly with her, fully decided to leave her when I should find some one whom I liked well enough to marry. I would make a little provision for this one, for it is an understood thing in our social set that a woman's love should be paid for, in money if she is poor, in presents if she is rich.

But one day she told me she was enceinte. I was thunderstruck, and saw in a second that my life would be ruined. I saw the fetter that I should wear until my death, everywhere, in my future family life, in my old age, forever; the fetter of a woman bound to my life through a child; the fetter of the child whom I must bring up, watch over, protect, while keeping myself unknown to him, and keeping him hidden from the world.

I was greatly disturbed at this news, and a confused longing, a criminal desire, surged through my mind; I did not formulate it, but I felt it in my heart, ready to come to the surface, as if some one hidden behind a portiere should await the signal to come out. If some accident might only happen! So many of these little beings die before they are born!

Oh! I did not wish my sweetheart to die! The poor girl, I loved her very much! But I wished, possibly, that the child might die before I saw it.

He was born. I set up housekeeping in my little bachelor apartment, an imitation home, with a horrible child. He looked like all children; I did not care for him. Fathers, you see, do not show affection until later. They have not the instinctive and passionate tenderness of mothers; their affection has to be awakened gradually, their mind must become attached by bonds formed each day between beings that live in each other's society.

A year passed. I now avoided my home, which was too small, where soiled linen, baby-clothes and stockings the size of gloves were lying round, where a thousand articles of all descriptions lay on the furniture, on the arm of an easy-chair, everywhere. I went out chiefly that I might not hear the child cry, for he cried on the slightest pretext, when he was bathed, when he was touched, when he was put to bed, when he was taken up in the morning, incessantly.

I had made a few acquaintances, and I met at a reception the woman who was to be your mother. I fell in love with her and became desirous to marry her. I courted her; I asked her parents' consent to our marriage and it was granted.

I found myself in this dilemma: I must either marry this young girl whom I adored, having a child already, or else tell the truth and renounce her, and happiness, my future, everything; for her parents, who were people of rigid principles, would not give her to me if they knew.

I passed a month of horrible anguish, of mortal torture, a month haunted by a thousand frightful thoughts; and I felt developing in me a hatred toward my son, toward that little morsel of living, screaming flesh, who blocked my path, interrupted my life, condemned me to an existence without hope, without all those vague expectations that make the charm of youth.

But just then my companion's mother became ill, and I was left alone with the child.

It was in December, and the weather was terribly cold. What a night!

My companion had just left. I had dined alone in my little

dining-room and I went gently into the room where the little one was asleep.

I sat down in an armchair before the fire. The wind was blowing, making the windows rattle, a dry, frosty wind; and I saw trough the window the stars shining with that piercing brightness that they have on frosty nights.

Then the idea that had obsessed me for a month rose again to the surface. As soon as I was quiet it came to me and harassed me. It ate into my mind like a fixed idea, just as cancers must eat into the flesh. It was there, in my head, in my heart, in my whole body, it seemed to me; and it swallowed me up as a wild beast might have. I endeavored to drive it away, to repulse it, to open my mind to other thoughts, as one opens a window to the fresh morning breeze to drive out the vitiated air; but I could not drive it from my brain, not even for a second. I do not know how to express this torture. It gnawed at my soul, and I felt a frightful pain, a real physical and moral pain.

My life was ruined! How could I escape from this situation? How could I draw back, and how could I confess?

And I loved the one who was to become your mother with a mad passion, which this insurmountable obstacle only aggravated.

A terrible rage was taking possession of me, choking me, a rage that verged on madness! Surely I was crazy that evening!

The child was sleeping. I got up and looked at it as it slept. It was he, this abortion, this spawn, this nothing, that condemned me to irremediable unhappiness!

He was asleep, his mouth open, wrapped in his bed-clothes in a crib beside my bed, where I could not sleep.

How did I ever do what I did? How do I know? What force urged me on? What malevolent power took possession of me? Oh! the temptation to crime came to me without any forewarning. All I recall is that my heart beat tumultuously. It beat so hard that I could hear it, as one hears the strokes of a hammer behind a partition. That is all I can recall—the beating of my heart!
In my head there was a strange confusion, a tumult, a senseless disorder, a lack of presence of mind. It was one of those hours of bewilderment and hallucination when a man is neither conscious of his actions nor able to guide his will.

I gently raised the coverings from the body of the child; I turned them down to the foot of the crib, and he lay there uncovered and naked.

He did not wake. Then I went toward the window, softly, quite softly, and I opened it.

A breath of icy air glided in like an assassin; it was so cold that I drew aside, and the two candles flickered. I remained standing near the window, not daring to turn round, as if for fear of seeing what was doing on behind me, and feeling the icy air continually across my forehead, my cheeks, my hands, the deadly air which kept streaming in. I stood there a long time.

I was not thinking, I was not reflecting. All at once a little cough caused me to shudder frightfully from head to foot, a shudder that I feel still to the roots of my hair. And with a frantic movement I abruptly closed both sides of the window and, turning round, ran over to the crib.

He was still asleep, his mouth open, quite naked. I touched his legs; they were icy cold and I covered them up.

My heart was suddenly touched, grieved, filled with pity, tenderness, love for this poor innocent being that I had wished to kill. I kissed his fine, soft hair long and tenderly; then I went and sat down before the fire.

I reflected with amazement with horror on what I had done, asking myself whence come those tempests of the soul in which a man loses all perspective of things, all command over himself and acts as in a condition of mad intoxication, not knowing whither he is going—like a vessel in a hurricane.

The child coughed again, and it gave my heart a wrench. Suppose it should die! O God! O God! What would become of me?

I rose from my chair to go and look at him, and with a candle in my hand I leaned over him. Seeing him breathing quietly I felt reassured, when he coughed a third time. It gave me such a shock tat I started backward, just as one does at sight of something horrible, and let my candle fall.

As I stood erect after picking it up, I noticed that my temples were bathed in perspiration, that cold sweat which is the result of anguish of soul. And I remained until daylight bending over my son, becoming calm when he remained quiet for some time, and filled with atrocious pain when a weak cough came from his mouth.

He awoke with his eyes red, his throat choked, and with an air of suffering.

When the woman came in to arrange my room I sent her at once for a doctor. He came at the end of an hour, and said, after examining the child:

"Did he not catch cold?"

I began to tremble like a person with palsy, and I faltered:

"No, I do not think so."

And then I said:

"What is the matter? Is it serious?"

"I do not know yet," he replied. "I will come again this evening."

He came that evening. My son had remained almost all day in a condition of drowsiness, coughing from time to time. During the night inflammation of the lungs set in.

That lasted ten days. I cannot express what I suffered in those interminable hours that divide morning from night, right from morning.

He died.

And since—since that moment, I have not passed one hour, not a single hour, without the frightful burning recollection, a gnawing recollection, a memory that seems to wring my heart, awaking in me like a savage beast imprisoned in the depth of my soul.

Oh! if I could have gone mad!

M. Poirel de la Voulte raised his spectacles with a motion that was peculiar to him whenever he finished reading a contract; and the three heirs of the defunct looked at one another without speaking, pale and motionless.

At the end of a minute the lawyer resumed:

"That must be destroyed."

The other two bent their heads in sign of assent. He lighted a candle, carefully separated the pages containing the damaging confession from those relating to the disposition of money, then he held them over the candle and threw them into the fireplace.

And they watched the white sheets as they burned, till they were presently reduced to little crumbling black heaps. And as some words were still visible in white tracing, the daughter, with little strokes of the toe of her shoe, crushed the burning paper, mixing it with the old ashes in the fireplace.

Then all three stood there watching it for some time, as if they feared that the destroyed secret might escape from the fireplace.

A MOTHER OF MONSTERS

I recalled this horrible story, the events of which occurred long ago, and this horrible woman, the other day at a fashionable seaside resort, where I saw on the beach a well-known young, elegant and charming Parisienne, adored and respected by everyone.

I had been invited by a friend to pay him a visit in a little provincial town. He took me about in all directions to do the honors of the place, showed me noted scenes, chateaux, industries, ruins. He pointed out monuments, churches, old carved doorways, enormous or distorted trees, the oak of St. Andrew, and the yew tree of Roqueboise.

When I had exhausted my admiration and enthusiasm over all the sights, my friend said with a distressed expression on his face, that there was nothing left to look at. I breathed freely. I would now be able to rest under the shade of the trees. But, all at once, he uttered an exclamation:

"Oh, yes! We have the 'Mother of Monsters'; I must take you to see her."

"Who is that, the 'Mother of Monsters'?" I asked.

"She is an abominable woman," he replied, "a regular demon, a being who voluntarily brings into the world deformed, hideous, frightful children, monstrosities, in fact, and then sells them to showmen who exhibit such things.

"These exploiters of freaks come from time to time to find out if she has any fresh monstrosity, and if it meets with their approval they carry it away with them, paying the mother a compensation.

"She has eleven of this description. She is rich.

"You think I am joking, romancing, exaggerating. No, my friend; I am telling you the truth, the exact truth.

"Let us go and see this woman. Then I will tell you her history."

He took me into one of the suburbs. The woman lived in a pretty little house by the side of the road. It was attractive and well kept. The garden was filled with fragrant flowers. One might have supposed it to be the residence of a retired lawyer.

A maid ushered us into a sort of little country parlor, and the wretch appeared. She was about forty. She was a tall, big woman with hard features, but well formed, vigorous and healthy, the true type of a robust peasant woman, half animal, and half woman.

She was aware of her reputation and received everyone with a humility that smacked of hatred.

"What do the gentlemen wish?" she asked.

"They tell me that your last child is just like an ordinary child, that he does not resemble his brothers at all," replied my friend. "I wanted to be sure of that. Is it true?"

She cast on us a malicious and furious look as she said:

"Oh, no, oh, no, my poor sir! He is perhaps even uglier than the rest. I have no luck, no luck!

"They are all like that, it is heartbreaking! How can the good God be so hard on a poor woman who is all alone in the world, how can He?" She spoke hurriedly, her eyes cast down, with a deprecating air as of a wild beast who is afraid. Her harsh voice became soft, and it seemed strange to hear those tearful falsetto tones issuing from that big, bony frame, of unusual strength and with coarse outlines, which seemed fitted for violent action, and made to utter howls like a wolf.

"We should like to see your little one," said my friend.

I fancied she colored up. I may have been deceived. After a few moments of silence, she said in a louder tone:

"What good will that do you?"

"Why do you not wish to show it to us?" replied my friend. "There are many people to whom you will show it; you know whom I mean."

She gave a start, and resuming her natural voice, and giving free play to her anger, she screamed:

"Was that why you came here? To insult me? Because my children are like animals, tell me? You shall not see him, no, no, you shall not see him! Go away, go away! I do not know why you all try to torment me like that."

She walked over toward us, her hands on her hips. At the brutal tone of her voice, a sort of moaning, or rather a mewing, the lamentable cry of an idiot, came from the adjoining room. I shivered to the marrow of my bones. We retreated before her.

"Take care, Devil" (they called her the Devil); said my friend, "take care; some day you will get yourself into trouble through this."

She began to tremble, beside herself with fury, shaking her fist and roaring:

"Be off with you! What will get me into trouble? Be off with you, miscreants!"

She was about to attack us, but we fled, saddened at what we had seen. When we got outside, my friend said:

"Well, you have seen her, what do you think of her?"

"Tell me the story of this brute," I replied.

And this is what he told me as we walked along the white high road, with ripe crops on either side of it which rippled like the sea in the light breeze that passed over them.

"This woman was one a servant on a farm. She was an honest girl, steady and economical. She was never known to have an admirer, and never suspected of any frailty. But she went astray, as so many do.

"She soon found herself in trouble, and was tortured with fear and shame. Wishing to conceal her misfortune, she bound her body tightly with a corset of her own invention, made of boards and cord. The more she developed, the more she bound herself with this instrument of torture, suffering martyrdom, but brave in her sorrow, not allowing anyone to see, or suspect, anything. She maimed the little unborn being, cramping it with that frightful corset, and made a monster of it. Its head was squeezed and elongated to a point, and its large eyes seemed popping out of its head. Its limbs, exaggeratedly long, and twisted like the stalk of a vine, terminated in fingers like the claws of a spider. Its trunk was tiny, and round as a nut.

"The child was born in an open field, and when the weeders saw it, they fled away, screaming, and the report spread that she had given birth to a demon. From that time on, she was called 'the Devil.'

"She was driven from the farm, and lived on charity, under a cloud. She brought up the monster, whom she hated with a savage hatred, and would have strangled, perhaps, if the priest had not threatened her with arrest.

"One day some travelling showmen heard about the frightful creature, and asked to see it, so that if it pleased them they might take it away. They were pleased, and counted out five hundred francs to the mother. At first, she had refused to let them see the little animal, as she was ashamed; but when she discovered it had a money value, and that these people were anxious to get it, she began to haggle with them, raising her price with all a peasant's persistence.

"She made them draw up a paper, in which they promised to pay her four hundred francs a year besides, as though they had taken this deformity into their employ.

"Incited by the greed of gain, she continued to produce these phenomena, so as to have an assured income like a bourgeoise.

"Some of them were long, some short, some like crabs-all bodies-others like lizards. Several died, and she was heartbroken.

"The law tried to interfere, but as they had no proof they let her continue to produce her freaks.

"She has at this moment eleven alive, and they bring in, on an average, counting good and bad years, from five to six thousand francs a year. One, alone, is not placed, the one she was unwilling to show us. But she will not keep it long, for she is known to all the showmen in the world, who come from time to time to see if she has anything new.

"She even gets bids from them when the monster is valuable."

My friend was silent. A profound disgust stirred my heart, and a feeling of rage, of regret, to think that I had not strangled this brute when I had the opportunity.

I had forgotten this story, when I saw on the beach of a fashionable resort the other day, an elegant, charming, dainty woman, surrounded by men who paid her respect as well as admiration.

I was walking along the beach, arm in arm with a friend, the resident physician. Ten minutes later, I saw a nursemaid with three children, who were rolling in the sand. A pair of little crutches lay on the ground, and touched my sympathy. I then noticed that these three children were all deformed, humpbacked, or crooked; and hideous.

"Those are the offspring of that charming woman you saw just now," said the doctor.

I was filled with pity for her, as well as for them, and exclaimed: "Oh, the poor mother! How can she ever laugh!"

"Do not pity her, my friend. Pity the poor children," replied the doctor. "This is the consequence of preserving a slender figure up to the last. These little deformities were made by the corset. She knows very well that she is risking her life at this game. But what does she care, as long as he can be beautiful and have admirers!"

And then I recalled that other woman, the peasant, the "Devil," who sold her children, her monsters.

AN UNCOMFORTABLE BED

One autumn I went to spend the hunting season with some friends in a chateau in Picardy.

My friends were fond of practical jokes. I do not care to know people who are not.

When I arrived, they gave me a princely reception, which at once awakened suspicion in my mind. They fired off rifles, embraced me, made much of me, as if they expected to have great fun at my expense.

I said to myself:

"Look out, old ferret! They have something in store for you."

During the dinner the mirth was excessive, exaggerated, in fact. I thought: "Here are people who have more than their share of amusement, and apparently without reason. They must have planned some good joke. Assuredly I am to be the victim of the joke. Attention!"

During the entire evening every one laughed in an exaggerated fashion. I scented a practical joke in the air, as a dog scents game. But what was it? I was watchful, restless. I did not let a word, or a meaning, or a gesture escape me. Every one seemed to me an object of suspicion, and I even looked distrustfully at the faces of the servants.

The hour struck for retiring; and the whole household came to escort me to my room. Why?

They called to me: "Good-night." I entered the apartment, shut the door, and remained standing, without moving a single step, holding the wax candle in my hand.

I heard laughter and whispering in the corridor. Without doubt they were spying on me. I cast a glance round the walls, the furniture, the ceiling, the hangings, the floor. I saw nothing to justify suspicion. I heard persons moving about outside my door. I had no doubt they were looking through the keyhole.

An idea came into my head: "My candle may suddenly go out and leave me in darkness."

Then I went across to the mantelpiece and lighted all the wax candles that were on it. After that I cast another glance around me without discovering anything. I advanced with short steps, carefully examining the apartment. Nothing. I inspected every article, one after the other. Still nothing. I went over to the window. The shutters, large wooden shutters, were open. I shut them with great care, and then drew the curtains, enormous velvet curtains, and placed a chair in front of them, so as to have nothing to fear from outside.

Then I cautiously sat down. The armchair was solid. I did not venture to get into the bed. However, the night was advancing; and I ended by coming to the conclusion that I was foolish. If they were spying on me, as I supposed, they must, while waiting for the success of the joke they had been preparing for me, have been laughing immoderately at my terror. So I made up my mind to go to bed. But the bed was particularly suspicious-looking. I pulled at the curtains. They seemed to be secure.

All the same, there was danger. I was going perhaps to receive a cold shower both from overhead, or perhaps, the moment I stretched myself out, to find myself sinking to the floor with my mattress. I searched in my memory for all the practical jokes of which I ever had experience. And I did not want to be caught. Ah! certainly not! certainly not! Then I suddenly bethought myself of a precaution which I considered insured safety. I caught hold of the side of the mattress gingerly, and very slowly drew it toward me. It came away, followed by the sheet and the rest of the bedclothes. I dragged all these objects into the very middle of the room, facing the entrance door. I made my bed over again as best I could at some distance from the suspected bedstead and the corner which had filled me with such anxiety. Then I extinguished all the candles, and, groping my way, I slipped under the bed clothes.

For at least another hour I remained awake, starting at the slightest sound. Everything seemed quiet in the chateau. I fell asleep.

I must have been in a deep sleep for a long time, but all of a sudden I was awakened with a start by the fall of a heavy body tumbling right on top of my own, and, at the same time, I received on my face, on my neck, and on my chest a burning liquid which made me utter a howl of pain. And a dreadful noise, as if a sideboard laden with plates and dishes had fallen down, almost deafened me.

I was smothering beneath the weight that was crushing me and preventing me from moving. I stretched out my hand to find out what was the nature of this object. I felt a face, a nose, and whiskers. Then, with all my strength, I launched out a blow at this face. But I immediately received a hail of cuffings which made me jump straight out of the soaked sheets, and rush in my nightshirt into the corridor, the door of which I found open.

Oh, heavens! it was broad daylight. The noise brought my friends hurrying into my apartment, and we found, sprawling over my improvised bed, the dismayed valet, who, while bringing me my morning cup of tea, had tripped over this obstacle in the middle of the floor and fallen on his stomach, spilling my breakfast over my face in spite of himself.

The precautions I had taken in closing the shutters and going to sleep in the middle of the room had only brought about the practical joke I had been trying to avoid.

Oh, how they all laughed that day!

A PORTRAIT

"Hello! there's Milial!" said somebody near me. I looked at the man who had been pointed out as I had been wishing for a long time to meet this Don Juan.

He was no longer young. His gray hair looked a little like those fur bonnets worn by certain Northern peoples, and his long beard, which fell down over his chest, had also somewhat the appearance of fur. He was talking to a lady, leaning toward her, speaking in a low voice and looking at her with an expression full of respect and tenderness.

I knew his life, or at least as much as was known of it. He had loved madly several times, and there had been certain tragedies with which his name had been connected. When I spoke to women who were the loudest in his praise, and asked them whence came this power, they always answered, after thinking for a while: "I don't know—he has a certain charm about him."

He was certainly not handsome. He had none of the elegance that we ascribe to conquerors of feminine hearts. I wondered what might be his hid den charm. Was it mental? I never had heard of a clever saying of his. In his glance? Perhaps. Or in his voice? The voices of some beings have a certain irresistible attraction, almost suggesting the flavor of things good to eat. One is hungry for them, and the sound of their words penetrates us like a dainty morsel. A friend was passing. I asked him: "Do you know Monsieur Milial?"

"Yes."

"Introduce us."

A minute later we were shaking hands and talking in the doorway. What he said was correct, agreeable to hear; it contained no irritable thought. The voice was sweet, soft, caressing, musical; but I had heard others much more attractive, much more moving. One listened to him with pleasure, just as one would look at a pretty little brook. No tension of the mind was necessary in order to follow him, no hidden meaning aroused curiosity, no expectation awoke interest. His conversation was rather restful, but it did not awaken in one either a desire to answer, to contradict or to approve, and it was as easy to answer him as it was to listen to him. The response came to the lips of its own accord, as soon as he had finished talking, and phrases turned toward him as if he had naturally aroused them.

One thought soon struck me. I had known him for a quarter of an hour, and it seemed as if he were already one of my old friends, that I had known all about him for a long time; his face, his gestures, his voice, his ideas. Suddenly, after a few minutes of conversation, he seemed already to be installed in my intimacy. All constraint disappeared between us, and, had he so desired, I might have confided in him as one confides only in old friends.

Certainly there was some mystery about him. Those barriers that are closed between most people and that are lowered with time when sympathy, similar tastes, equal intellectual culture and constant intercourse remove constraint—those barriers seemed not to exist between him and me, and no doubt this was the case between him and all people, both men and women, whom fate threw in his path.

After half an hour we parted, promising to see each other often, and he gave me his address after inviting me to take luncheon with him in two days.

I forgot what hour he had stated, and I arrived too soon; he was not yet home. A correct and silent domestic showed me into a beautiful, quiet, softly lighted parlor. I felt comfortable there, at home. How often I have noticed the influence of apartments on the character and on the mind! There are some which make one feel foolish; in others, on the contrary, one always feels lively. Some make us sad, although well lighted and decorated in light-colored furniture; others cheer us up, although hung with sombre material. Our eye, like our heart, has its likes and dislikes, of which it does not inform us, and which it secretly imposes on our temperament. The harmony of furniture, walls, the style of an ensemble, act immediately on our mental state, just as the air from the woods, the sea or the mountains modifies our physical natures.

I sat down on a cushion-covered divan and felt myself suddenly carried and supported by these little silk bags of feathers, as if the outline of my body had been marked out beforehand on this couch.

Then I looked about. There was nothing striking about the room; every-where were beautiful and modest things, simple and rare furniture, Oriental curtains which did not seem to come from a department store but from the interior of a harem; and exactly opposite me hung the portrait of a woman. It was a portrait of medium size, showing the head and the upper part of the body, and the hands, which were holding a book. She was young, bareheaded; ribbons were woven in her hair; she was smiling sadly. Was it because she was bareheaded, was it merely her natural expression? I never have seen a portrait of a lady which seemed so much in its place as that one in that dwelling. Of all those I knew I have seen nothing like that one. All those that I know are on exhibition, whether the lady be dressed in her gaudiest gown, with an attractive headdress and a look which shows that she is posing first of all before the artist and then before those who will look at her or whether they have taken a comfortable attitude in an ordinary gown. Some are standing majestically in all their beauty, which is not at all natural to them in life. All of them have something, a flower or, a jewel, a crease in the dress or a curve of the lip, which one feels to have been placed there for effect by the artist. Whether they wear a hat or merely their hair one can immediately notice that they are not entirely natural. Why? One cannot say without knowing them, but the effect is there. They seem to be calling somewhere, on people whom they wish to please and to whom they wish to appear at their best advantage; and they have studied their attitudes, sometimes modest, Sometimes haughty.

What could one say about this one? She was at home and alone. Yes, she was alone, for she was smiling as one smiles when thinking in solitude of something sad or sweet, and not as one smiles when one is being watched. She seemed so much alone and so much at home that she made the whole large apartment seem absolutely empty. She alone lived in it, filled it, gave it life. Many people might come in and converse, laugh, even sing; she would still be alone with a solitary smile, and she alone would give it life with her pictured gaze.

That look also was unique. It fell directly on me, fixed and caressing, without seeing me. All portraits know that they are being watched, and they answer with their eyes, which see, think, follow us without leaving us, from the very moment we enter the apartment they inhabit. This one did not see me; it saw nothing, although its look was fixed directly on me. I remembered the surprising verse of Baudelaire:

And your eyes, attractive as those of a portrait.

They did indeed attract me in an irresistible manner; those painted eyes which had lived, or which were perhaps still living, threw over me a strange, powerful spell. Oh, what an infinite and tender charm, like a passing breeze, like a dying sunset of lilac rose and blue, a little sad like the approaching night, which comes behind the sombre frame and out of those impenetrable eyes! Those eyes, created by a few strokes from a brush, hide behind them the mystery of that which seems to be and which does not exist, which can appear in the eyes of a woman, which can make love blossom within us.

The door opened and M. Milial entered. He excused himself for being late. I excused myself for being ahead of time. Then I said: "Might I ask you who is this lady?"

He answered: "That is my mother. She died very young."

Then I understood whence came the inexplicable attraction of this man.

THE DRUNKARD

The north wind was blowing a hurricane, driving through the sky big, black, heavy clouds from which the rain poured down on the earth with terrific violence.

A high sea was raging and dashing its huge, slow, foamy waves along the coast with the rumbling sound of thunder. The waves followed each other close, rolling in as high as mountains, scattering the foam as they broke.

The storm engulfed itself in the little valley of Yport, whistling and moaning, tearing the shingles from the roofs, smashing the shutters, knocking down the chimneys, rushing through the narrow streets in such gusts that one could walk only by holding on to the walls, and children would have been lifted up like leaves and carried over the houses into the fields.

The fishing smacks had been hauled high up on land, because at high tide the sea would sweep the beach. Several sailors, sheltered behind the curved bottoms of their boats, were watching this battle of the sky and the sea.

Then, one by one, they went away, for night was falling on the storm, wrapping in shadows the raging ocean and all the battling elements.

Just two men remained, their hands plunged deep into their pockets, bending their backs beneath the squall, their woolen caps pulled down over their ears; two big Normandy fishermen, bearded, their skin tanned through exposure, with the piercing black eyes of the sailor who looks over the horizon like a bird of prey.

One of them was saying:

"Come on, Jeremie, let's go play dominoes. It's my treat."

The other hesitated a while, tempted on one hand by the game and the thought of brandy, knowing well that, if he went to Paumelle's, he would return home drunk; held back, on the other hand, by the idea of his wife remaining alone in the house.

He asked:

"Any one might think that you had made a bet to get me drunk every night. Say, what good is it doing you, since it's always you that's treating?"

Nevertheless he was smiling at the idea of all this brandy drunk at the expense of another. He was smiling the contented smirk of an avaricious Norman.

Mathurin, his friend, kept pulling him by the sleeve.

"Come on, Jeremie. This isn't the kind of a night to go home without anything to warm you up. What are you afraid of? Isn't your wife going to warm your bed for you?"

Jeremie answered:

"The other night I couldn't find the door—I had to be fished out of the ditch in front of the house!"

He was still laughing at this drunkard's recollection, and he was unconsciously going toward Paumelle's Cafe, where a light was shining in the window; he was going, pulled by Mathurin and pushed by the wind, unable to resist these combined forces.

The low room was full of sailors, smoke and noise. All these men, clad in woolens, their elbows on the tables, were shouting to make themselves heard. The more people came in, the more one had to shout in order to overcome the noise of voices and the rattling of dominoes on the marble tables.

Jeremie and Mathurin sat down in a corner and began a game, and the glasses were emptied in rapid succession into their thirsty throats.

Then they played more games and drank more glasses. Mathurin kept pouring and winking to the saloon keeper, a big, red-faced man, who chuckled as though at the thought of some fine joke; and Jeremie kept absorbing alcohol and wagging his head, giving vent to a roar of laughter and looking at his comrade with a stupid and contented expression.

All the customers were going away. Every time that one of them would open the door to leave a gust of wind would blow into the cafe, making the tobacco smoke swirl around, swinging the lamps at the end of their chains and making their flames flicker, and suddenly one could hear the deep booming of a breaking wave and the moaning of the wind.

Jeremie, his collar unbuttoned, was taking drunkard's poses, one leg outstretched, one arm hanging down and in the other hand holding a domino.

They were alone now with the owner, who had come up to them, interested.

He asked:

"Well, Jeremie, how goes it inside? Feel less thirsty after wetting your throat?"

Jeremie muttered:

"The more I wet it, the drier it gets inside."

The innkeeper cast a sly glance at Mathurin. He said:

"And your brother, Mathurin, where's he now?"

The sailor laughed silently:

"Don't worry; he's warm, all right."

And both of them looked toward Jeremie, who was triumphantly putting down the double six and announcing:

"Game!"

Then the owner declared:

"Well, boys, I'm goin' to bed. I will leave you the lamp and the bottle; there's twenty cents' worth in it. Lock the door when you go, Mathurin, and slip the key under the mat the way you did the other night."

Mathurin answered:

"Don't worry; it'll be all right."

Paumelle shook hands with his two customers and slowly went up the wooden stairs. For several minutes his heavy step echoed through the little house. Then a loud creaking announced that he had got into bed.

The two men continued to play. From time to time a more violent gust of wind would shake the whole house, and the two drinkers would look up, as though some one were about to enter. Then Mathurin would take the bottle and fill Jeremie's glass. But suddenly the clock over the bar struck twelve. Its hoarse clang sounded like the rattling of saucepans. Then Mathurin got up like a sailor whose watch is over.

"Come on, Jeremie, we've got to get out."

The other man rose to his feet with difficulty, got his balance by leaning on the table, reached the door and opened it while his companion was putting out the light.

As soon as they were in the street Mathurin locked the door and then said:

"Well, so long. See you to-morrow night!"

And he disappeared in the darkness.

Jeremie took a few steps, staggered, stretched out his hands, met a wall which supported him and began to stumble along. From time to time a gust of wind would sweep through the street, pushing him forward, making him run for a few steps; then, when the wind would die down, he would stop short, having lost his impetus, and once more he would begin to stagger on his unsteady drunkard's legs.

He went instinctively toward his home, just as birds go to their nests. Finally he recognized his door, and began to feel about for the keyhole and tried to put the key in it. Not finding the hole, he began to swear. Then he began to beat on the door with his fists, calling for his wife to come and help him:

"Melina! Oh, Melina!"

As he leaned against the door for support, it gave way and opened, and Jeremie, losing his prop, fell inside, rolling on his face into the middle of his room, and he felt something heavy pass over him and escape in the night.

He was no longer moving, dazed by fright, bewildered, fearing the devil, ghosts, all the mysterious beings of darkness, and he waited a long time without daring to move. But when he found out that nothing else was moving, a little reason returned to him, the reason of a drunkard.

Gently he sat up. Again he waited a long time, and at last, growing bolder, he called:

"Melina!"

His wife did not answer.

Then, suddenly, a suspicion crossed his darkened mind, an indistinct, vague suspicion. He was not moving; he was sitting there in the dark, trying to gather together his scattered wits, his mind stumbling over incomplete ideas, just as his feet stumbled along.

Once more he asked:

"Who was it, Melina? Tell me who it was. I won't hurt you!"

He waited, no voice was raised in the darkness. He was now reasoning with himself out loud.

"I'm drunk, all right! I'm drunk! And he filled me up, the dog; he did it, to stop my goin' home. I'm drunk!"

And he would continue:

"Tell me who it was, Melina, or somethin'll happen to you."

After having waited again, he went on with the slow and obstinate logic of a drunkard:

"He's been keeping me at that loafer Paumelle's place every night, so as to stop my going home. It's some trick. Oh, you damned carrion!"

Slowly he got on his knees. A blind fury was gaining possession of him, mingling with the fumes of alcohol.

He continued:

"Tell me who it was, Melina, or you'll get a licking—I warn you!"

He was now standing, trembling with a wild fury, as though the alcohol had set his blood on fire. He took a step, knocked against a chair, seized it, went on, reached the bed, ran his hands over it and felt the warm body of his wife.

Then, maddened, he roared:

"So! You were there, you piece of dirt, and you wouldn't answer!"

And, lifting the chair, which he was holding in his strong sailor's grip, he swung it down before him with an exasperated fury. A cry burst from the bed, an agonizing, piercing cry. Then he began to thrash around like a thresher in a barn. And soon nothing more moved. The chair was broken to pieces, but he still held one leg and beat away with it, panting.

At last he stopped to ask:

"Well, are you ready to tell me who it was?"

Melina did not answer.

Then tired out, stupefied from his exertion, he stretched himself out on the ground and slept.

When day came a neighbor, seeing the door open, entered. He saw Jeremie snoring on the floor, amid the broken pieces of a chair, and on the bed a pulp of flesh and blood.

THE WARDROBE

As we sat chatting after dinner, a party of men, the conversation turned on women, for lack of something else.

One of us said:

"Here's a funny thing that happened to me on, that very subject." And he told us the following story:

One evening last winter I suddenly felt overcome by that overpowering sense of misery and languor that takes possession of one from time to time. I was in my own apartment, all alone, and I was convinced that if I gave in to my feelings I should have a terrible attack of melancholia, one of those attacks that lead to suicide when they recur too often.

I put on my overcoat and went out without the slightest idea of what I was going to do. Having gone as far as the boulevards, I began to wander along by the almost empty cafes. It was raining, a fine rain that affects your mind as it does your clothing, not one of those good downpours which come down in torrents, driving breathless passers-by into doorways, but a rain without drops that deposits on your clothing an imperceptible spray and soon covers you with a sort of iced foam that chills you through.

What should I do? I walked in one direction and then came back, looking for some place where I could spend two hours, and discovering for the first time that there is no place of amusement in Paris in the evening. At last I decided to go to the Folies-Bergere, that entertaining resort for gay women.

There were very few people in the main hall. In the long horseshoe curve there were only a few ordinary looking people, whose plebeian origin was apparent in their manners, their clothes, the cut of their hair and beard, their hats, their complexion. It was rarely that one saw from time to time a man whom you suspected of having washed himself thoroughly, and his whole make-up seemed to match. As for the women, they were always the same, those frightful women you all know, ugly, tired looking, drooping, and walking along in their lackadaisical manner, with that air of foolish superciliousness which they assume, I do not know why.

I thought to myself that, in truth, not one of those languid creatures, greasy rather than fat, puffed out here and thin there, with the contour of a monk and the lower extremities of a bow-legged snipe, was worth the louis that they would get with great difficulty after asking five.

But all at once I saw a little creature whom I thought attractive, not in her first youth, but fresh, comical and tantalizing. I stopped her, and stupidly, without thinking, I made an appointment with her for that night. I did not want to go back to my own home alone, all alone; I preferred the company and the caresses of this hussy.

And I followed her. She lived in a great big house in the Rue des Martyrs. The gas was already extinguished on the stairway. I ascended the steps slowly, lighting a candle match every few seconds, stubbing my foot against the steps, stumbling and angry as I followed the rustle of the skirt ahead of me.

She stopped on the fourth floor, and having closed the outer door she said:

"Then you will stay till to-morrow?"

"Why, yes. You know that that was the agreement."

"All right, my dear, I just wanted to know. Wait for me here a minute, I will be right back."

And she left me in the darkness. I heard her shutting two doors and then I thought I heard her talking. I was surprised and uneasy. The thought that she had a protector staggered me. But I have good fists and a solid back. "We shall see," I said to myself.

I listened attentively with ear and mind. Some one was stirring about, walking quietly and very carefully. Then another door was opened and I thought I again heard some one talking, but in a very low tone.

She came back carrying a lighted candle.

"You may come in," she said.

She said "thou" in speaking to me, which was an indication of possession. I went in and after passing through a dining room in which it was very evident that no one ever ate, I entered a typical room of all these women, a furnished room with red curtains and a soiled eiderdown bed covering.

"Make yourself at home, 'mon chat'," she said.

I gave a suspicious glance at the room, but there seemed no reason for uneasiness.

As she took off her wraps she began to laugh.

"Well, what ails you? Are you changed into a pillar of salt? Come, hurry up."

I did as she suggested.

Five minutes later I longed to put on my things and get away. But this terrible languor that had overcome me at home took possession of me again, and deprived me of energy enough to move and I stayed in spite of the disgust that I felt for this association. The unusual attractiveness that I supposed I had discovered in this creature over there under the chandeliers of the theater had altogether vanished on closer acquaintance, and she was nothing more to me now than a common woman, like all the others, whose indifferent and complaisant kiss smacked of garlic.

I thought I would say something.

"Have you lived here long?" I asked.

"Over six months on the fifteenth of January."

"Where were you before that?"

"In the Rue Clauzel. But the janitor made me very uncomfortable and I left."

And she began to tell me an interminable story of a janitor who had talked scandal about her.

But, suddenly, I heard something moving quite close to us. First there was a sigh, then a slight, but distinct, sound as if some one had turned round on a chair.

I sat up abruptly and asked.

"What was that noise?"

She answered quietly and confidently:

"Do not be uneasy, my dear boy, it is my neighbor. The partition is so thin that one can hear everything as if it were in the room. These are wretched rooms, just like pasteboard."

I felt so lazy that I paid no further attention to it. We resumed our conversation. Driven by the stupid curiosity that prompts all men to question these creatures about their first experiences, to attempt to lift the veil of their first folly, as though to find in them a trace of pristine innocence, to love them, possibly, in a fleeting memory of their candor and modesty of former days, evoked by a word, I insistently asked her about her earlier lovers.

I knew she was telling me lies. What did it matter? Among all these lies I might, perhaps, discover something sincere and pathetic.

"Come," said I, "tell me who he was."

"He was a boating man, my dear."

"Ah! Tell me about it. Where were you?"

"I was at Argenteuil."

"What were you doing?"

"I was waitress in a restaurant."

"What restaurant?"

"'The Freshwater Sailor.' Do you know it?"

"I should say so, kept by Bonanfan."

"Yes, that's it."

"And how did he make love to you, this boating man?"

"While I was doing his room. He took advantage of me."

But I suddenly recalled the theory of a friend of mine, an observant and philosophical physician whom constant attendance in hospitals has brought into daily contact with girl-mothers and prostitutes, with all the shame and all the misery of women, of those poor women who have become the frightful prey of the wandering male with money in his pocket.

"A woman," he said, "is always debauched by a man of her own class and position. I have volumes of statistics on that subject. We accuse the rich of plucking the flower of innocence among the girls of the people. This is not correct. The rich pay for what they want. They may gather some, but never for the first time."

Then, turning to my companion, I began to laugh.

"You know that I am aware of your history. The boating man was not the first."

"Oh, yes, my dear, I swear it:"

"You are lying, my dear."

"Oh, no, I assure you."

"You are lying; come, tell me all."

She seemed to hesitate in astonishment. I continued:

"I am a sorcerer, my dear girl, I am a clairvoyant. If you do not tell me the truth, I will go into a trance sleep and then I can find out."

She was afraid, being as stupid as all her kind. She faltered:

"How did you guess?"

"Come, go on telling me," I said.

"Oh, the first time didn't amount to anything.

"There was a festival in the country. They had sent for a special chef, M. Alexandre. As soon as he came he did just as he pleased in the house. He bossed every one, even the proprietor and his wife, as if he had been a king. He was a big handsome man, who did not seem fitted to stand beside a kitchen range. He was always calling out, 'Come, some butter —some eggs—some Madeira!' And it had to be brought to him at once in a hurry, or he would get cross and say things that would make us blush all over.

"When the day was over he would smoke a pipe outside the door. And as I was passing by him with a pile of plates he said to me, like that: 'Come, girlie, come down to the water with me and show me the country.' I went with him like a fool, and we had hardly got down to the bank of the river when he took advantage of me so suddenly that I did not even know what he was doing. And then he went away on the nine o'clock train. I never saw him again."

"Is that all?" I asked.

She hesitated.

"Oh, I think Florentin belongs to him."

"Who is Florentin?"

"My little boy."

"Oh! Well, then, you made the boating man believe that he was the father, did you not?"

"You bet!"

"Did he have any money, this boating man?"

"Yes, he left me an income of three hundred francs, settled on Florentin."

I was beginning to be amused and resumed:

"All right, my girl, all right. You are all of you less stupid than one would imagine, all the same. And how old is he now, Florentin?"

She replied:

"He is now twelve. He will make his first communion in the spring."

"That is splendid. And since then you have carried on your business conscientiously?"

She sighed in a resigned manner.

"I must do what I can."

But a loud noise just then coming from the room itself made me start up with a bound. It sounded like some one falling and picking themselves up again by feeling along the wall with their hands.

I had seized the candle and was looking about me, terrified and furious. She had risen also and was trying to hold me back to stop me, murmuring:

"That's nothing, my dear, I assure you it's nothing."

But I had discovered what direction the strange noise came from. I walked straight towards a door hidden at the head of the bed and I opened it abruptly and saw before me, trembling, his bright, terrified eyes opened wide at sight of me, a little pale, thin boy seated beside a large wicker chair off which he had fallen.

As soon as he saw me he began to cry. Stretching out his arms to his mother, he cried:

"It was not my fault, mamma, it was not my fault. I was asleep, and I fell off. Do not scold me, it was not my fault."

I turned to the woman and said:

"What does this mean?"

She seemed confused and worried, and said in a broken voice:

"What do you want me to do? I do not earn enough to put him to school! I have to keep him with me, and I cannot afford to pay for another room, by heavens! He sleeps with me when I am alone. If any one comes for one hour or two he can stay in the wardrobe; he keeps quiet, he understands it. But when people stay all night, as you have done, it tires the poor child to sleep on a chair.

"It is not his fault. I should like to see you sleep all night on a chair—you would have something to say."

She was getting angry and excited and was talking loud.

The child was still crying. A poor delicate timid little fellow, a veritable child of the wardrobe, of the cold, dark closet, a child who from time to time was allowed to get a little warmth in the bed if it chanced to be unoccupied.

I also felt inclined to cry.

And I went home to my own bed.

THE MOUNTAIN POOL

Saint Agnes, May 6.

MY DEAR FRIEND:

You asked me to write to you often and to tell you in particular about the things I might see. You also begged me to rummage among my recollections of travels for some of those little anecdotes gathered from a chance peasant, from an innkeeper, from some strange traveling acquaintance, which remain as landmarks in the memory. With a landscape depicted in a few lines, and a little story told in a few sentences you think one can give the true characteristics of a country, make it living, visible, dramatic. I will try to do as you wish. I will, therefore, send you from time to time letters in which I will mention neither you nor myself, but only the landscape and the people who move about in it.

And now I will begin.

Spring is a season in which one ought, it seems to me, to drink and eat the landscape. It is the season of chills, just as autumn is the season of reflection. In spring the country rouses the physical senses, in autumn it enters into the soul.

I desired this year to breathe the odor of orange blossoms and I set out for the South of France just at the time that every one else was returning home. I visited Monaco, the shrine of pilgrims, rival of Mecca and Jerusalem, without leaving any gold in any one else's pockets, and I climbed the high mountain beneath a covering of lemon, orange and olive branches.

Have you ever slept, my friend, in a grove of orange trees in flower? The air that one inhales with delight is a quintessence of perfumes. The strong yet sweet odor, delicious as some dainty, seems to blend with our being, to saturate us, to intoxicate us, to enervate us, to plunge us into a sleepy, dreamy torpor. As though it were an opium prepared by the hands of fairies and not by those of druggists.

This is a country of ravines. The surface of the mountains is cleft, hollowed out in all directions, and in these sinuous crevices grow veritable forests of lemon trees. Here and there where the steep gorge is interrupted by a sort of step, a kind of reservoir has been built which holds the water of the rain storms.

They are large holes with slippery walls with nothing for any one to grasp hold of should they fall in.

I was walking slowly in one of these ascending valleys or gorges, glancing through the foliage at the vivid-hued fruit that remained on the branches. The narrow gorge made the heavy odor of the flowers still more penetrating; the air seemed to be dense with it. A feeling of lassitude came over me and I looked for a place to sit down. A few drops of water glistened in the grass. I thought that there was a spring near by and I climbed a little further to look for it. But I only reached the edge of one of these large, deep reservoirs.

I sat down tailor fashion, with my legs crossed under me, and remained there in a reverie before this hole, which looked as if it were filled with ink, so black and stagnant was the liquid it contained. Down yonder, through the branches, I saw, like patches, bits of the Mediterranean gleaming so that they fairly dazzled my eyes. But my glance always returned to the immense somber well that appeared to be inhabited by no aquatic animals, so motionless was its surface. Suddenly a voice made me tremble. An old gentleman who was picking flowers—this country is the richest in Europe for herbalists—asked me:

"Are you a relation of those poor children, monsieur?"

I looked at him in astonishment.

"What children, monsieur?"

He seemed embarrassed and answered with a bow:

"I beg your pardon. On seeing you sitting thus absorbed in front of this reservoir I thought you were recalling the frightful tragedy that occurred here."

Now I wanted to know about it, and I begged him to tell me the story.

It is very dismal and very heart-rending, my dear friend, and very trivial at the same time. It is a simple news item. I do not know whether to attribute my emotion to the dramatic manner in which the story was told to me, to the setting of the mountains, to the contrast between the joy of the sunlight and the flowers and this black, murderous hole, but my heart was wrung, all my nerves unstrung by this tale which, perhaps, may not appear so terribly harrowing to you as you read it in your room without having the scene of the tragedy before your eyes.

It was one spring in recent years. Two little boys frequently came to play on the edge of this cistern while their tutor lay under a tree reading a book. One warm afternoon a piercing cry awoke the tutor who was dozing and the sound of splashing caused by something falling into the water made him jump to his feet abruptly. The younger of the children, eight years of age, was shouting, as he stood beside the reservoir, the surface of which was stirred and eddying at the spot where the older boy had fallen in as he ran along the stone coping.

Distracted, without waiting or stopping to think what was best to do, the tutor jumped into the black water and did not rise again, having struck his head at the bottom of the cistern.

At the same moment the young boy who had risen to the surface was waving his stretched-out arms toward his brother. The little fellow on land lay down full length, while the other tried to swim, to approach the wall, and presently the four little hands clasped each other, tightened in each other's grasp, contracted as though they were fastened together. They both felt the intense joy of an escape from death, a shudder at the danger past.

The older boy tried to climb up to the edge, but could not manage it, as the wall was perpendicular, and his brother, who was too weak, was sliding slowly towards the hole.

Then they remained motionless, filled anew with terror. And they waited.

The little fellow squeezed his brother's hands with all his might and wept from nervousness as he repeated: "I cannot drag you out, I cannot drag you out." And all at once he began to shout, "Help! Help!" But his light voice scarcely penetrated beyond the dome of foliage above their heads.

They remained thus a long time, hours and hours, facing each other, these two children, with one thought, one anguish of heart and the horrible dread that one of them, exhausted, might let go the hands of the other. And they kept on calling, but all in vain.

At length the older boy, who was shivering with cold, said to the little one: "I cannot hold out any longer. I am going to fall. Good-by, little brother." And the other, gasping, replied: "Not yet, not yet, wait."

Evening came on, the still evening with its stars mirrored in the water. The older lad, his endurance giving out, said: "Let go my hand, I am going to give you my watch." He had received it as a present a few days before, and ever since it had been his chief amusement. He was able to get hold of it, and held it out to the little fellow who was sobbing and who laid it down on the grass beside him.

It was night now. The two unhappy beings, exhausted, had almost loosened their grasp. The elder, at last, feeling that he was lost, murmured once more: "Good-by, little brother, kiss mamma and papa." And his numbed fingers relaxed their hold. He sank and did not rise again . . . . The little fellow, left alone, began to shout wildly: "Paul! Paul!" But the other did not come to the surface.

Then he darted across the mountain, falling among the stones, overcome by the most frightful anguish that can wring a child's heart, and with a face like death reached the sitting-room, where his parents were waiting. He became bewildered again as he led them to the gloomy reservoir. He could not find his way. At last he reached the spot. "It is there; yes, it is there!"

But the cistern had to be emptied, and the proprietor would not permit it as he needed the water for his lemon trees.

The two bodies were found, however, but not until the next day.

You see, my dear friend, that this is a simple news item. But if you had seen the hole itself your heart would have been wrung, as mine was, at the thought of the agony of that child hanging to his brother's hands, of the long suspense of those little chaps who were accustomed only to laugh and to play, and at the simple incident of the giving of the watch.

I said to myself: "May Fate preserve me from ever receiving a similar relic!" I know of nothing more terrible than such a recollection connected with a familiar object that one cannot dispose of. Only think of it; each time that he handles this sacred watch the survivor will picture once more the horrible scene; the pool, the wall, the still water, and the distracted face of his brother-alive, and yet as lost as though he were already dead. And all through his life, at any moment, the vision will be there, awakened the instant even the tip of his finger touches his watch pocket.

And I was sad until evening. I left the spot and kept on climbing, leaving the region of orange trees for the region of olive trees, and the region of olive trees for the region of pines; then I came to a valley of stones, and finally reached the ruins of an ancient castle, built, they say, in the tenth century by a Saracen chief, a good man, who was baptized a Christian through love for a young girl. Everywhere around me were mountains, and before me the sea, the sea with an almost imperceptible patch on it: Corsica, or, rather, the shadow of Corsica. But on the mountain summits, blood-red in the glow of the sunset, in the boundless sky and on the sea, in all this superb landscape that I had come here to admire I saw only two poor children, one lying prone on the edge of a hole filled with black water, the other submerged to his neck, their hands intertwined, weeping opposite each other, in despair. And it seemed as though I continually heard a weak, exhausted voice saying: "Good-by, little brother, I am going to give you my watch."

This letter may seem rather melancholy, dear friend. I will try to be more cheerful some other day.

A CREMATION

Last Monday an Indian prince died at Etretat, Bapu Sahib Khanderao Ghatay, a relation of His Highness, the Maharajah Gaikwar, prince of Baroda, in the province of Guzerat, Presidency of Bombay.

For about three weeks there had been seen walking in the streets about ten young East Indians, small, lithe, with dark skins, dressed all in gray and wearing on their heads caps such as English grooms wear. They were men of high rank who had come to Europe to study the military institutions of the principal Western nations. The little band consisted of three princes, a nobleman, an interpreter and three servants.

The head of the commission had just died, an old man of forty-two and father-in-law of Sampatro Kashivao Gaikwar, brother of His Highness, the Gaikwar of Baroda.

The son-in-law accompanied his father-in-law.

The other East Indians were called Ganpatrao Shravanrao Gaikwar, cousin of His Highness Khasherao Gadhav; Vasudev Madhav Samarth, interpreter and secretary; the slaves: Ramchandra Bajaji, Ganu bin Pukiram Kokate, Rhambhaji bin Fabji.

On leaving his native land the one who died recently was overcome with terrible grief, and feeling convinced that he would never return he wished to give up the journey, but he had to obey the wishes of his noble relative, the Prince of Baroda, and he set out.

They came to spend the latter part of the summer at Etretat, and people would go out of curiosity every morning to see them taking their bath at the Etablissment des Roches-Blanches.

Five or six days ago Bapu Sahib Khanderao Ghatay was taken with pains in his gums; then the inflammation spread to the throat and became ulceration. Gangrene set in and, on Monday, the doctors told his young friends that their relative was dying. The final struggle was already beginning, and the breath had almost left the unfortunate man's body when his friends seized him, snatched him from his bed and laid him on the stone floor of the room, so that, stretched out on the earth, our mother, he should yield up his soul, according to the command of Brahma.

They then sent to ask the mayor, M. Boissaye, for a permit to burn the body that very day so as to fulfill the prescribed ceremonial of the Hindoo religion. The mayor hesitated, telegraphed to the prefecture to demand instructions, at the same time sending word that a failure to reply would be considered by him tantamount to a consent. As he had received no reply at 9 o'clock that evening, he decided, in view of the infectious character of the disease of which the East Indian had died, that the cremation of the body should take place that very night, beneath the cliff, on the beach, at ebb tide.

The mayor is being criticized now for this decision, though he acted as an intelligent, liberal and determined man, and was upheld and advised by the three physicians who had watched the case and reported the death.

They were dancing at the Casino that evening. It was an early autumn evening, rather chilly. A pretty strong wind was blowing from the ocean, although as yet there was no sea on, and swift, light, ragged clouds were driving across the sky. They came from the edge of the horizon, looking dark against the background of the sky, but as they approached the moon they grew whiter and passed hurriedly across her face, veiling it for a few seconds without completely hiding it.

The tall straight cliffs that inclose the rounded beach of Etretat and terminate in two celebrated arches, called "the Gates," lay in shadow, and made two great black patches in the softly lighted landscape.

It had rained all day.

The Casino orchestra was playing waltzes, polkas and quadrilles. A rumor was presently circulated among the groups of dancers. It was said that an East Indian prince had just died at the Hotel des Bains and that the ministry had been approached for permission to burn the body. No one believed it, or at least no one supposed that such a thing could occur so foreign was the custom as yet to our customs, and as the night was far advanced every one went home.

At midnight, the lamplighter, running from street to street, extinguished, one after another, the yellow jets of flame that lighted up the sleeping houses, the mud and the puddles of water. We waited, watching for the hour when the little town should be quiet and deserted.

Ever since noon a carpenter had been cutting up wood and asking himself with amazement what was going to be done with all these planks sawn up into little bits, and why one should destroy so much good merchandise. This wood was piled up in a cart which went along through side streets as far as the beach, without arousing the suspicion of belated persons who might meet it. It went along on the shingle at the foot of the cliff, and having dumped its contents on the beach the three Indian servants began to build a funeral pile, a little longer than it was wide. They worked alone, for no profane hand must aid in this solemn duty.

It was one o'clock in the morning when the relations of the deceased were informed that they might accomplish their part of the work.

The door of the little house they occupied was open, and we perceived, lying on a stretcher in the small, dimly lighted vestibule the corpse covered with white silk. We could see him plainly as he lay stretched out on his back, his outline clearly defined beneath this white veil.

The East Indians, standing at his feet, remained motionless, while one of them performed the prescribed rites, murmuring unfamiliar words in a low, monotonous tone. He walked round and round the corpse; touching it occasionally, then, taking an urn suspended from three slender chains, he sprinkled it for some time with the sacred water of the Ganges, that East Indians must always carry with them wherever they go.

Then the stretcher was lifted by four of them who started off at a slow march. The moon had gone down, leaving the muddy, deserted streets in darkness, but the body on the stretcher appeared to be luminous, so dazzlingly white was the silk, and it was a weird sight to see, passing along through the night, the semi-luminous form of this corpse, borne by those men, the dusky skin of whose faces and hands could scarcely be distinguished from their clothing in the darkness.

Behind the corpse came three Indians, and then, a full head taller than themselves and wrapped in an ample traveling coat of a soft gray color, appeared the outline of an Englishman, a kind and superior man, a friend of theirs, who was their guide and counselor in their European travels.

Beneath the cold, misty sky of this little northern beach I felt as if I were taking part in a sort of symbolical drama. It seemed to me that they were carrying there, before me, the conquered genius of India, followed, as in a funeral procession, by the victorious genius of England robed in a gray ulster.

On the shingly beach the four bearers halted a few moments to take breath, and then proceeded on their way. They now walked quickly, bending beneath the weight of their burden. At length they reached the funeral pile. It was erected in an indentation, at the very foot of the cliff, which rose above it perpendicularly a hundred meters high, perfectly white but looking gray in the night.

The funeral pile was about three and a half feet high. The corpse was placed on it and then one of the Indians asked to have the pole star pointed out to him. This was done, and the dead Rajah was laid with his feet turned towards his native country. Then twelve bottles of kerosene were poured over him and he was covered completely with thin slabs of pine wood. For almost another hour the relations and servants kept piling up the funeral pyre which looked like one of those piles of wood that carpenters keep in their yards. Then on top of this was poured the contents of twenty bottles of oil, and on top of all they emptied a bag of fine shavings. A few steps further on, a flame was glimmering in a little bronze brazier, which had remained lighted since the arrival of the corpse.

The moment had arrived. The relations went to fetch the fire. As it was barely alight, some oil was poured on it, and suddenly a flame arose lighting up the great wall of rock from summit to base. An Indian who was leaning over the brazier rose upright, his two hands in the air, his elbows bent, and all at once we saw arising, all black on the immense white cliff, a colossal shadow, the shadow of Buddha in his hieratic posture. And the little pointed toque that the man wore on his head even looked like the head-dress of the god.

The effect was so striking and unexpected that I felt my heart beat as though some supernatural apparition had risen up before me.

That was just what it was—the ancient and sacred image, come from the heart of the East to the ends of Europe, and watching over its son whom they were going to cremate there.

It vanished. They brought fire. The shavings on top of the pyre were lighted and then the wood caught fire and a brilliant light illumined the cliff, the shingle and the foam of the waves as they broke on the beach.

It grew brighter from second to second, lighting up on the sea in the distance the dancing crest of the waves.

The breeze from the ocean blew in gusts, increasing the heat of the flame which flattened down, twisted, then shot up again, throwing out millions of sparks. They mounted with wild rapidity along the cliff and were lost in the sky, mingling with the stars, increasing their number. Some sea birds who had awakened uttered their plaintive cry, and, describing long curves, flew, with their white wings extended, through the gleam from the funeral pyre and then disappeared in the night.

Before long the pile of wood was nothing but a mass of flame, not red but yellow, a blinding yellow, a furnace lashed by the wind. And, suddenly, beneath a stronger gust, it tottered, partially crumbling as it leaned towards the sea, and the corpse came to view, full length, blackened on his couch of flame and burning with long blue flames:

The pile of wood having crumbled further on the right the corpse turned over as a man does in bed. They immediately covered him with fresh wood and the fire started up again more furiously than ever.

The East Indians, seated in a semi-circle on the shingle, looked out with sad, serious faces. And the rest of us, as it was very cold, had drawn nearer to the fire until the smoke and sparks came in our faces. There was no odor save that of burning pine and petroleum.

Hours passed; day began to break. Toward five o'clock in the morning nothing remained but a heap of ashes. The relations gathered them up, cast some of them to the winds, some in the sea, and kept some in a brass vase that they had brought from India. They then retired to their home to give utterance to lamentations.

These young princes and their servants, by the employment of the most inadequate appliances succeeded in carrying out the cremation of their relation in the most perfect manner, with singular skill and remarkable dignity. Everything was done according to ritual, according to the rigid ordinances of their religion. Their dead one rests in peace.

The following morning at daybreak there was an indescribable commotion in Etretat. Some insisted that they had burned a man alive, others that they were trying to hide a crime, some that the mayor would be put in jail, others that the Indian prince had succumbed to an attack of cholera.

The men were amazed, the women indignant. A crowd of people spent the day on the site of the funeral pile, looking for fragments of bone in the shingle that was still warm. They found enough bones to reconstruct ten skeletons, for the farmers on shore frequently throw their dead sheep into the sea. The finders carefully placed these various fragments in their pocketbooks. But not one of them possesses a true particle of the Indian prince.

That very night a deputy sent by the government came to hold an inquest. He, however, formed an estimate of this singular case like a man of intelligence and good sense. But what should he say in his report?

The East Indians declared that if they had been prevented in France from cremating their dead they would have taken him to a freer country where they could have carried out their customs.

Thus, I have seen a man cremated on a funeral pile, and it has given me a wish to disappear in the same manner.

In this way everything ends at once. Man expedites the slow work of nature, instead of delaying it by the hideous coffin in which one decomposes for months. The flesh is dead, the spirit has fled. Fire which purifies disperses in a few hours all that was a human being; it casts it to the winds, converting it into air and ashes, and not into ignominious corruption.

This is clean and hygienic. Putrefaction beneath the ground in a closed box where the body becomes like pap, a blackened, stinking pap, has about it something repugnant and disgusting. The sight of the coffin as it descends into this muddy hole wrings one's heart with anguish. But the funeral pyre which flames up beneath the sky has about it something grand, beautiful and solemn.

MISTI

I was very much interested at that time in a droll little woman. She was married, of course, as I have a horror of unmarried flirts. What enjoyment is there in making love to a woman who belongs to nobody and yet belongs to any one? And, besides, morality aside, I do not understand love as a trade. That disgusts me somewhat.

The especial attraction in a married woman to a bachelor is that she gives him a home, a sweet, pleasant home where every one takes care of you and spoils you, from the husband to the servants. One finds everything combined there, love, friendship, even fatherly interest, bed and board, all, in fact, that constitutes the happiness of life, with this incalculable advantage, that one can change one's family from time to time, take up one's abode in all kinds of society in turn: in summer, in the country with the workman who rents you a room in his house; in winter with the townsfolk, or even with the nobility, if one is ambitious.

I have another weakness; it is that I become attached to the husband as well as the wife. I acknowledge even that some husbands, ordinary or coarse as they may be, give me a feeling of disgust for their wives, however charming they may be. But when the husband is intellectual or charming I invariably become very much attached to him. I am careful if I quarrel with the wife not to quarrel with the husband. In this way I have made some of my best friends, and have also proved in many cases the incontestable superiority of the male over the female in the human species. The latter makes all sorts of trouble-scenes, reproaches, etc.; while the former, who has just as good a right to complain, treats you, on the contrary, as though you were the special Providence of his hearth.

Well, my friend was a quaint little woman, a brunette, fanciful, capricious, pious, superstitious, credulous as a monk, but charming. She had a way of kissing one that I never saw in any one else— but that was not the attraction—and such a soft skin! It gave me intense delight merely to hold her hands. And an eye—her glance was like a slow caress, delicious and unending. Sometimes I would lean my head on her knee and we would remain motionless, she leaning over me with that subtle, enigmatic, disturbing smile that women have, while my eyes would be raised to hers, drinking sweetly and deliciously into my heart, like a form of intoxication, the glance of her limpid blue eyes, limpid as though they were full of thoughts of love, and blue as though they were a heaven of delights.

Her husband, inspector of some large public works, was frequently away from home and left us our evenings free. Sometimes I spent them with her lounging on the divan with my forehead on one of her knees; while on the other lay an enormous black cat called "Misti," whom she adored. Our fingers would meet on the cat's back and would intertwine in her soft silky fur. I felt its warm body against my cheek, trembling with its eternal purring, and occasionally a paw would reach out and place on my mouth, or my eyelid, five unsheathed claws which would prick my eyelids, and then be immediately withdrawn.

Sometimes we would go out on what we called our escapades. They were very innocent, however. They consisted in taking supper at some inn in the suburbs, or else, after dining at her house or at mine, in making the round of the cheap cafes, like students out for a lark.

We would go into the common drinking places and take our seats at the end of the smoky den on two rickety chairs, at an old wooden table. A cloud of pungent smoke, with which blended an odor of fried fish from dinner, filled the room. Men in smocks were talking in loud tones as they drank their petits verres, and the astonished waiter placed before us two cherry brandies.

She, trembling, charmingly afraid, would raise her double black veil as far as her nose, and then take up her glass with the enjoyment that one feels at doing something delightfully naughty. Each cherry she swallowed made her feel as if she had done something wrong, each swallow of the burning liquor had on her the affect of a delicate and forbidden enjoyment.

Then she would say to me in a low tone: "Let us go." And we would leave, she walking quickly with lowered head between the drinkers who watched her going by with a look of displeasure. And as soon as we got into the street she would give a great sigh of relief, as if we had escaped some terrible danger.

Sometimes she would ask me with a shudder:

"Suppose they, should say something rude to me in those places, what would you do?" "Why, I would defend you, parbleu!" I would reply in a resolute manner. And she would squeeze my arm for happiness, perhaps with a vague wish that she might be insulted and protected, that she might see men fight on her account, even those men, with me!

One evening as we sat at a table in a tavern at Montmartre, we saw an old woman in tattered garments come in, holding in her hand a pack of dirty cards. Perceiving a lady, the old woman at once approached us and offered to tell my friend's fortune. Emma, who in her heart believed in everything, was trembling with longing and anxiety, and she made a place beside her for the old woman.

The latter, old, wrinkled, her eyes with red inflamed rings round them, and her mouth without a single tooth in it, began to deal her dirty cards on the table. She dealt them in piles, then gathered them up, and then dealt them out again, murmuring indistinguishable words. Emma, turning pale, listened with bated breath, gasping with anxiety and curiosity.

The fortune-teller broke silence. She predicted vague happenings: happiness and children, a fair young man, a voyage, money, a lawsuit, a dark man, the return of some one, success, a death. The mention of this death attracted the younger woman's attention. "Whose death? When? In what manner?"

The old woman replied: "Oh, as to that, these cards are not certain enough. You must come to my place to-morrow; I will tell you about it with coffee grounds which never make a mistake."

Emma turned anxiously to me:

"Say, let us go there to-morrow. Oh, please say yes. If not, you cannot imagine how worried I shall be."

I began to laugh.

"We will go if you wish it, dearie."

The old woman gave us her address. She lived on the sixth floor, in a wretched house behind the Buttes-Chaumont. We went there the following day.

Her room, an attic containing two chairs and a bed, was filled with strange objects, bunches of herbs hanging from nails, skins of animals, flasks and phials containing liquids of various colors. On the table a stuffed black cat looked out of eyes of glass. He seemed like the demon of this sinister dwelling.

Emma, almost fainting with emotion, sat down on a chair and exclaimed:

"Oh, dear, look at that cat; how like it is to Misti."

And she explained to the old woman that she had a cat "exactly like that, exactly like that!"

The old woman replied gravely:

"If you are in love with a man, you must not keep it."

Emma, suddenly filled with fear, asked:

"Why not?"

The old woman sat down familiarly beside her and took her hand.

"It was the undoing of my life," she said.

My friend wanted to hear about it. She leaned against the old woman, questioned her, begged her to tell. At length the woman agreed to do so.

"I loved that cat," she said, "as one would love a brother. I was young then and all alone, a seamstress. I had only him, Mouton. One of the tenants had given it to me. He was as intelligent as a child, and gentle as well, and he worshiped me, my dear lady, he worshiped me more than one does a fetish. All day long he would sit on my lap purring, and all night long on my pillow; I could feel his heart beating, in fact.

"Well, I happened to make an acquaintance, a fine young man who was working in a white-goods house. That went on for about three months on a footing of mere friendship. But you know one is liable to weaken, it may happen to any one, and, besides, I had really begun to love him. He was so nice, so nice, and so good. He wanted us to live together, for economy's sake. I finally allowed him to come and see me one evening. I had not made up my mind to anything definite; oh, no! But I was pleased at the idea that we should spend an hour together.

"At first he behaved very well, said nice things to me that made my heart go pit-a-pat. And then he kissed me, madame, kissed me as one does when they love. I remained motionless, my eyes closed, in a paroxysm of happiness. But, suddenly, I felt him start violently and he gave a scream, a scream that I shall never forget. I opened my eyes and saw that Mouton had sprung at his face and was tearing the skin with his claws as if it had been a linen rag. And the blood was streaming down like rain, madame.

"I tried to take the cat away, but he held on tight, scratching all the time; and he bit me, he was so crazy. I finally got him and threw him out of the window, which was open, for it was summer.

"When I began to bathe my poor friend's face, I noticed that his eyes were destroyed, both his eyes!

"He had to go to the hospital. He died of grief at the end of a year. I wanted to keep him with me and provide for him, but he would not agree to it. One would have supposed that he hated me after the occurrence.

"As for Mouton, his back was broken by the fall, The janitor picked up his body. I had him stuffed, for in spite of all I was fond of him. If he acted as he did it was because he loved me, was it not?"

The old woman was silent and began to stroke the lifeless animal whose body trembled on its iron framework.

Emma, with sorrowful heart, had forgotten about the predicted death—or, at least, she did not allude to it again, and she left, giving the woman five francs.

As her husband was to return the following day, I did not go to the house for several days. When I did go I was surprised at not seeing Misti. I asked where he was.

She blushed and replied:

"I gave him away. I was uneasy."

I was astonished.

"Uneasy? Uneasy? What about?"

She gave me a long kiss and said in a low tone:

"I was uneasy about your eyes, my dear."

> Misti appeared in. Gil Blas of January 22, 1884, over the signature of "MAUFRIGNEUSE."

MADAME HERMET

Crazy people attract me. They live in a mysterious land of weird dreams, in that impenetrable cloud of dementia where all that they have witnessed in their previous life, all they have loved, is reproduced for them in an imaginary existence, outside of all laws that govern the things of this life and control human thought.

For them there is no such thing as the impossible, nothing is improbable; fairyland is a constant quantity and the supernatural quite familiar. The old rampart, logic; the old wall, reason; the old main stay of thought, good sense, break down, fall and crumble before their imagination, set free and escaped into the limitless realm of fancy, and advancing with fabulous bounds, and nothing can check it. For them everything happens, and anything may happen. They make no effort to conquer events, to overcome resistance, to overturn obstacles. By a sudden caprice of their flighty imagination they become princes, emperors, or gods, are possessed of all the wealth of the world, all the delightful things of life, enjoy all pleasures, are always strong, always beautiful, always young, always beloved! They, alone, can be happy in this world; for, as far as they are concerned, reality does not exist. I love to look into their wandering intelligence as one leans over an abyss at the bottom of which seethes a foaming torrent whose source and destination are both unknown.

But it is in vain that we lean over these abysses, for we shall never discover the source nor the destination of this water. After all, it is only water, just like what is flowing in the sunlight, and we shall learn nothing by looking at it.

It is likewise of no use to ponder over the intelligence of crazy people, for their most weird notions are, in fact, only ideas that are already known, which appear strange simply because they are no longer under the restraint of reason. Their whimsical source surprises us because we do not see it bubbling up. Doubtless the dropping of a little stone into the current was sufficient to cause these ebullitions. Nevertheless crazy people attract me and I always return to them, drawn in spite of myself by this trivial mystery of dementia.

One day as I was visiting one of the asylums the physician who was my guide said:

"Come, I will show you an interesting case."

And he opened the door of a cell where a woman of about forty, still handsome, was seated in a large armchair, looking persistently at her face in a little hand mirror.

As soon as she saw us she rose to her feet, ran to the other end of the room, picked up a veil that lay on a chair, wrapped it carefully round her face, then came back, nodding her head in reply to our greeting.

"Well," said the doctor, "how are you this morning?"

She gave a deep sigh.

"Oh, ill, monsieur, very ill. The marks are increasing every day."

He replied in a tone of conviction:

"Oh, no; oh, no; I assure you that you are mistaken."

She drew near to him and murmured:

"No. I am certain of it. I counted ten pittings more this morning, three on the right cheek, four on the left cheek, and three on the forehead. It is frightful, frightful! I shall never dare to let any one see me, not even my son; no, not even him! I am lost, I am disfigured forever."

She fell back in her armchair and began to sob.

The doctor took a chair, sat down beside her, and said soothingly in a gentle tone:

"Come, let me see; I assure you it is nothing. With a slight cauterization I will make it all disappear."

She shook her head in denial, without speaking. He tried to touch her veil, but she seized it with both hands so violently that her fingers went through it.

He continued to reason with her and reassure her.

"Come, you know very well that I remove those horrid pits every time and that there is no trace of them after I have treated them. If you do not let me see them I cannot cure you."

"I do not mind your seeing them," she murmured, "but I do not know that gentleman who is with you."

"He is a doctor also, who can give you better care than I can."

She then allowed her face to be uncovered, but her dread, her emotion, her shame at being seen brought a rosy flush to her face and her neck, down to the collar of her dress. She cast down her eyes, turned her face aside, first to the right; then to the left, to avoid our gaze and stammered out:

"Oh, it is torture to me to let myself be seen like this! It is horrible, is it not? Is it not horrible?"

I looked at her in much surprise, for there was nothing on her face, not a mark, not a spot, not a sign of one, nor a scar.

She turned towards me, her eyes still lowered, and said:

"It was while taking care of my son that I caught this fearful disease, monsieur. I saved him, but I am disfigured. I sacrificed my beauty to him, to my poor child. However, I did my duty, my conscience is at rest. If I suffer it is known only to God."

The doctor had drawn from his coat pocket a fine water-color paint brush.

"Let me attend to it," he said, "I will put it all right."

She held out her right cheek, and he began by touching it lightly with the brush here and there, as though he were putting little points of paint on it. He did the same with the left cheek, then with the chin, and the forehead, and then exclaimed:

"See, there is nothing there now, nothing at all!"

She took up the mirror, gazed at her reflection with profound, eager attention, with a strong mental effort to discover something, then she sighed:

"No. It hardly shows at all. I am infinitely obliged to you."

The doctor had risen. He bowed to her, ushered me out and followed me, and, as soon as he had locked the door, said:

"Here is the history of this unhappy woman."

Her name is Mme. Hermet. She was once very beautiful, a great coquette, very much beloved and very much in-love with life.

She was one of those women who have nothing but their beauty and their love of admiration to sustain, guide or comfort them in this life. The constant anxiety to retain her freshness, the care of her complexion, of her hands, her teeth, of every portion of body that was visible, occupied all her time and all her attention.

She became a widow, with one son. The boy was brought up as are all children of society beauties. She was, however, very fond of him.

He grew up, and she grew older. Whether she saw the fatal crisis approaching, I cannot say. Did she, like so many others, gaze for hours and hours at her skin, once so fine, so transparent and free from blemish, now beginning to shrivel slightly, to be crossed with a thousand little lines, as yet imperceptible, that will grow deeper day by day, month by month? Did she also see slowly, but surely, increasing traces of those long wrinkles on the forehead, those slender serpents that nothing can check? Did she suffer the torture, the abominable torture of the mirror, the little mirror with the silver handle which one cannot make up one's mind to lay down on the table, but then throws down in disgust only to take it up again in order to look more closely, and still more closely at the hateful and insidious approaches of old age? Did she shut herself up ten times, twenty times a day, leaving her friends chatting in the drawing-room, and go up to her room where, under the protection of bolts and bars, she would again contemplate the work of time on her ripe beauty, now beginning to wither, and recognize with despair the gradual progress of the process which no one else had as yet seemed to perceive, but of which she, herself, was well aware. She knows where to seek the most serious, the gravest traces of age. And the mirror, the little round hand-glass in its carved silver frame, tells her horrible things; for it speaks, it seems to laugh, it jeers and tells her all that is going to occur, all the physical discomforts and the atrocious mental anguish she will suffer until the day of her death, which will be the day of her deliverance.

Did she weep, distractedly, on her knees, her forehead to the ground, and pray, pray, pray to Him who thus slays his creatures and gives them youth only that he may render old age more unendurable, and lends them beauty only that he may withdraw it almost immediately? Did she pray to Him, imploring Him to do for her what He has never yet done for any one, to let her retain until her last day her charm, her freshness and her gracefulness? Then, finding that she was imploring in vain an inflexible Unknown who drives on the years, one after another, did she roll on the carpet in her room, knocking her head against the furniture and stifling in her throat shrieks of despair?

Doubtless she suffered these tortures, for this is what occurred:

One day (she was then thirty-five) her son aged fifteen, fell ill.

He took to his bed without any one being able to determine the cause or nature of his illness.

His tutor, a priest, watched beside him and hardly ever left him, while Mme. Hermet came morning and evening to inquire how he was.

She would come into the room in the morning in her night wrapper, smiling, all powdered and perfumed, and would ask as she entered the door:

"Well, George, are you better?"

The big boy, his face red, swollen and showing the ravages of fever, would reply:

"Yes, little mother, a little better."

She would stay in the room a few seconds, look at the bottles of medicine, and purse her lips as if she were saying "phew," and then would suddenly exclaim: "Oh, I forgot something very important," and would run out of the room leaving behind her a fragrance of choice toilet perfumes.

In the evening she would appear in a decollete dress, in a still greater hurry, for she was always late, and she had just time to inquire:

"Well, what does the doctor say?"

The priest would reply:

"He has not yet given an opinion, madame."

But one evening the abbe replied: "Madame, your son has got the small-pox."

She uttered a scream of terror and fled from the room.

When her maid came to her room the following morning she noticed at once a strong odor of burnt sugar, and she found her mistress, with wide-open eyes, her face pale from lack of sleep, and shivering with terror in her bed.

As soon as the shutters were opened Mme. Herrnet asked:

"How is George?"

"Oh, not at all well to-day, madame."

She did not rise until noon, when she ate two eggs with a cup of tea, as if she herself had been ill, and then she went out to a druggist's to inquire about prophylactic measures against the contagion of small-pox.

She did not come home until dinner time, laden with medicine bottles, and shut herself up at once in her room, where she saturated herself with disinfectants.

The priest was waiting for her in the dining-room. As soon as she saw him she exclaimed in a voice full of emotion:

"Well?"

"No improvement. The doctor is very anxious:"

She began to cry and could eat nothing, she was so worried.

The next day, as soon as it was light, she sent to inquire for her son, but there was no improvement and she spent the whole day in her room, where little braziers were giving out pungent odors. Her maid said also that you could hear her sighing all the evening.

She spent a whole week in this manner, only going out for an hour or two during the afternoon to breathe the air.

She now sent to make inquiries every hour, and would sob when the reports were unfavorable.

On the morning of the eleventh day the priest, having been announced, entered her room, his face grave and pale, and said, without taking the chair she offered him:

"Madame, your son is very ill and wishes to see you."

She fell on her knees, exclaiming:

"Oh, my God! Oh, my God! I would never dare! My God! My God! Help me!"

The priest continued:

"The doctor holds out little hope, madame, and George is expecting you!"

And he left the room.

Two hours later as the young lad, feeling himself dying, again asked for his mother, the abbe went to her again and found her still on her knees, still weeping and repeating:

"I will not . . . . I will not. . . . I am too much afraid . . . . I will not. . . ."

He tried to persuade her, to strengthen her, to lead her. He only succeeded in bringing on an attack of "nerves" that lasted some time and caused her to shriek.

The doctor when he came in the evening was told of this cowardice and declared that he would bring her in himself, of her own volition, or by force. But after trying all manner of argument and just as he seized her round the waist to carry her into her son's room, she caught hold of the door and clung to it so firmly that they could not drag her away. Then when they let go of her she fell at the feet of the doctor, begging his forgiveness and acknowledging that she was a wretched creature. And then she exclaimed: "Oh, he is not going to die; tell me that he is not going to die, I beg of you; tell him that I love him, that I worship him. . ."

The young lad was dying. Feeling that he had only a few moments more to live, he entreated that his mother be persuaded to come and bid him a last farewell. With that sort of presentiment that the dying sometimes have, he had understood, had guessed all, and he said: "If she is afraid to come into the room, beg her just to come on the balcony as far as my window so that I may see her, at least, so that I may take a farewell look at her, as I cannot kiss her."

The doctor and the abbe, once more, went together to this woman and assured her: "You will run no risk, for there will be a pane of glass between you and him."

She consented, covered up her head, and took with her a bottle of smelling salts. She took three steps on the balcony; then, all at once, hiding her face in her hands, she moaned: "No . . . no . . . I would never dare to look at him . . . never. . . . I am too much ashamed . . . too much afraid . . . . No . . . I cannot."

They endeavored to drag her along, but she held on with both hands to the railings and uttered such plaints that the passers-by in the street raised their heads. And the dying boy waited, his eyes turned towards that window, waited to die until he could see for the last time the sweet, beloved face, the worshiped face of his mother.

He waited long, and night came on. Then he turned over with his face to the wall and was silent.

When day broke he was dead. The day following she was crazy.

THE MAGIC COUCH

The Seine flowed past my house, without a ripple on its surface, and gleaming in the bright morning sunlight. It was a beautiful, broad, indolent silver stream, with crimson lights here and there; and on the opposite side of the river were rows of tall trees that covered all the bank with an immense wall of verdure.

The sensation of life which is renewed each day, of fresh, happy, loving life trembled in the leaves, palpitated in the air, was mirrored in the water.

The postman had just brought my papers, which were handed to me, and I walked slowly to the river bank in order to read them.

In the first paper I opened I noticed this headline, "Statistics of Suicides," and I read that more than 8,500 persons had killed themselves in that year.

In a moment I seemed to see them! I saw this voluntary and hideous massacre of the despairing who were weary of life. I saw men bleeding, their jaws fractured, their skulls cloven, their breasts pierced by a bullet, slowly dying, alone in a little room in a hotel, giving no thought to their wound, but thinking only of their misfortunes.

I saw others seated before a tumbler in which some matches were soaking, or before a little bottle with a red label.

They would look at it fixedly without moving; then they would drink and await the result; then a spasm would convulse their cheeks and draw their lips together; their eyes would grow wild with terror, for they did not know that the end would be preceded by so much suffering.

They rose to their feet, paused, fell over and with their hands pressed to their stomachs they felt their internal organs on fire, their entrails devoured by the fiery liquid, before their minds began to grow dim.

I saw others hanging from a nail in the wall, from the fastening of the window, from a hook in the ceiling, from a beam in the garret, from a branch of a tree amid the evening rain. And I surmised all that had happened before they hung there motionless, their tongues hanging out of their mouths. I imagined the anguish of their heart, their final hesitation, their attempts to fasten the rope, to determine that it was secure, then to pass the noose round their neck and to let themselves fall.

I saw others lying on wretched beds, mothers with their little children, old men dying of hunger, young girls dying for love, all rigid, suffocated, asphyxiated, while in the center of the room the brasier still gave forth the fumes of charcoal.

And I saw others walking at night along the deserted bridges. These were the most sinister. The water flowed under the arches with a low sound. They did not see it . . . they guessed at it from its cool breath! They longed for it and they feared it. They dared not do it! And yet, they must. A distant clock sounded the hour and, suddenly, in the vast silence of the night, there was heard the splash of a body falling into the river, a scream or two, the sound of hands beating the water, and all was still. Sometimes, even, there was only the sound of the falling body when they had tied their arms down or fastened a stone to their feet. Oh, the poor things, the poor things, the poor things, how I felt their anguish, how I died in their death! I went through all their wretchedness; I endured in one hour all their tortures. I knew all the sorrows that had led them to this, for I know the deceitful infamy of life, and no one has felt it more than I have.

How I understood them, these who weak, harassed by misfortune, having lost those they loved, awakened from the dream of a tardy compensation, from the illusion of another existence where God will finally be just, after having been ferocious, and their minds disabused of the mirages of happiness, have given up the fight and desire to put an end to this ceaseless tragedy, or this shameful comedy.

Suicide! Why, it is the strength of those whose strength is exhausted, the hope of those who no longer believe, the sublime courage of the conquered! Yes, there is at least one door to this life we can always open and pass through to the other side. Nature had an impulse of pity; she did not shut us up in prison. Mercy for the despairing!

As for those who are simply disillusioned, let them march ahead with free soul and quiet heart. They have nothing to fear since they may take their leave; for behind them there is always this door that the gods of our illusions cannot even lock.

I thought of this crowd of suicides: more than eight thousand five hundred in one year. And it seemed to me that they had combined to send to the world a prayer, to utter a cry of appeal, to demand something that should come into effect later when we understood things better. It seemed to me that all these victims, their throats cut, poisoned, hung, asphyxiated, or drowned, all came together, a frightful horde, like citizens to the polls, to say to society:

"Grant us, at least, a gentle death! Help us to die, you who will not help us to live! See, we are numerous, we have the right to speak in these days of freedom, of philosophic independence and of popular suffrage. Give to those who renounce life the charity of a death that will not be repugnant nor terrible."

I began to dream, allowing my fancy to roam at will in weird and mysterious fashion on this subject.

I seemed to be all at once in a beautiful city. It was Paris; but at what period? I walked about the streets, looking at the houses, the theaters, the public buildings, and presently found myself in a square where I remarked a large building; very handsome, dainty and attractive. I was surprised on reading on the facade this inscription in letters of gold, "Suicide Bureau."

Oh, the weirdness of waking dreams where the spirit soars into a world of unrealities and possibilities! Nothing astonishes one, nothing shocks one; and the unbridled fancy makes no distinction between the comic and the tragic.

I approached the building where footmen in knee-breeches were seated in the vestibule in front of a cloak-room as they do at the entrance of a club.

I entered out of curiosity. One of the men rose and said:

"What does monsieur wish?"

"I wish to know what building this is."

"Nothing more?"

"Why, no."

"Then would monsieur like me to take him to the Secretary of the Bureau?"

I hesitated, and asked:

"But will not that disturb him?"

"Oh, no, monsieur, he is here to receive those who desire information."

"Well, lead the way."

He took me through corridors where old gentlemen were chatting, and finally led me into a beautiful office, somewhat somber, furnished throughout in black wood. A stout young man with a corporation was writing a letter as he smoked a cigar, the fragrance of which gave evidence of its quality.

He rose. We bowed to each other, and as soon as the footman had retired he asked:

"What can I do for you?"

"Monsieur," I replied, "pardon my curiosity. I had never seen this establishment. The few words inscribed on the facade filled me with astonishment, and I wanted to know what was going on here."

He smiled before replying, then said in a low tone with a complacent air:

"Mon Dieu, monsieur, we put to death in a cleanly and gentle—I do not venture to say agreeable manner those persons who desire to die."

I did not feel very shocked, for it really seemed to me natural and right. What particularly surprised me was that on this planet, with its low, utilitarian, humanitarian ideals, selfish and coercive of all true freedom, any one should venture on a similar enterprise, worthy of an emancipated humanity.

"How did you get the idea?" I asked.

"Monsieur," he replied, "the number of suicides increased so enormously during the five years succeeding the world exposition of 1889 that some measures were urgently needed. People killed themselves in the streets, at fetes, in restaurants, at the theater, in railway carriages, at the receptions held by the President of the Republic, everywhere. It was not only a horrid sight for those who love life, as I do, but also a bad example for children. Hence it became necessary to centralize suicides."

"What caused this suicidal epidemic?"

"I do not know. The fact is, I believe, the world is growing old. People begin to see things clearly and they are getting disgruntled. It is the same to-day with destiny as with the government, we have found out what it is; people find that they are swindled in every direction, and they just get out of it all. When one discovers that Providence lies, cheats, robs, deceives human beings just as a plain Deputy deceives his constituents, one gets angry, and as one cannot nominate a fresh Providence every three months as we do with our privileged representatives, one just gets out of the whole thing, which is decidedly bad."

"Really!"

"Oh, as for me, I am not complaining."

"Will you inform me how you carry on this establishment?"

"With pleasure. You may become a member when you please. It is a club."

"A club!"

"Yes, monsieur, founded by the most eminent men in the country, by men of the highest intellect and brightest intelligence. And," he added, laughing heartily, "I swear to you that every one gets a great deal of enjoyment out of it."

"In this place?"

"Yes, in this place."

"You surprise me."

"Mon Dieu, they enjoy themselves because they have not that fear of death which is the great killjoy in all our earthly pleasures."

"But why should they be members of this club if they do not kill themselves?"

"One may be a member of the club without being obliged for that reason to commit suicide."

"But then?"

"I will explain. In view of the enormous increase in suicides, and of the hideous spectacle they presented, a purely benevolent society was formed for the protection of those in despair, which placed at their disposal the facilities for a peaceful, painless, if not unforeseen death."

"Who can have authorized such an institution?"

"General Boulanger during his brief tenure of power. He could never refuse anything. However, that was the only good thing he did. Hence, a society was formed of clear-sighted, disillusioned skeptics who desired to erect in the heart of Paris a kind of temple dedicated to the contempt for death. This place was formerly a dreaded spot that no one ventured to approach. Then its founders, who met together here, gave a grand inaugural entertainment with Mmes. Sarah Bernhardt, Judic, Theo, Granier, and twenty others, and Mme. de Reske, Coquelin, Mounet-Sully, Paulus, etc., present, followed by concerts, the comedies of Dumas, of Meilhac, Halevy and Sardon. We had only one thing to mar it, one drama by Becque which seemed sad, but which subsequently had a great success at the Comedie-Francaise. In fact all Paris came. The enterprise was launched."

"In the midst of the festivities! What a funereal joke!"

"Not at all. Death need not be sad, it should be a matter of indifference. We made death cheerful, crowned it with flowers, covered it with perfume, made it easy. One learns to aid others through example; one can see that it is nothing."

"I can well understand that they should come to the entertainments; but did they come to . . . Death?"

"Not at first; they were afraid."

"And later?"

"They came."

"Many of them?"

"In crowds. We have had more than forty in a day. One finds hardly any more drowned bodies in the Seine."

"Who was the first?"

"A club member."

"As a sacrifice to the cause?"

"I don't think so. A man who was sick of everything, a 'down and out' who had lost heavily at baccarat for three months."

"Indeed?"

"The second was an Englishman, an eccentric. We then advertised in the papers, we gave an account of our methods, we invented some attractive instances. But the great impetus was given by poor people."

"How do you go to work?"

"Would you like to see? I can explain at the same time."

"Yes, indeed."

He took his hat, opened the door, allowed me to precede him, and we entered a card room, where men sat playing as they, play in all gambling places. They were chatting cheerfully, eagerly. I have seldom seen such a jolly, lively, mirthful club.

As I seemed surprised, the secretary said:

"Oh, the establishment has an unheard of prestige. All the smart people all over the world belong to it so as to appear as though they held death in scorn. Then, once they get here, they feel obliged to be cheerful that they may not appear to be afraid. So they joke and laugh and talk flippantly, they are witty and they become so. At present it is certainly the most frequented and the most entertaining place in Paris. The women are even thinking of building an annex for themselves."

"And, in spite of all this, you have many suicides in the house?"

"As I said, about forty or fifty a day. Society people are rare, but poor devils abound. The middle class has also a large contingent."

"And how . . . do they do?"

"They are asphyxiated . . . very slowly."

"In what manner?"

"A gas of our own invention. We have the patent. On the other side of the building are the public entrances—three little doors opening on small streets. When a man or a woman present themselves they are interrogated. Then they are offered assistance, aid, protection. If a client accepts, inquiries are made; and sometimes we have saved their lives."

"Where do you get your money?"

"We have a great deal. There are a large number of shareholders. Besides it is fashionable to contribute to the establishment. The names of the donors are published in Figaro. Then the suicide of every rich man costs a thousand francs. And they look as if they were lying in state. It costs the poor nothing."

"How can you tell who is poor?"

"Oh, oh, monsieur, we can guess! And, besides, they must bring a certificate of indigency from the commissary of police of their district. If you knew how distressing it is to see them come in! I visited their part of our building once only, and I will never go again. The place itself is almost as good as this part, almost as luxurious and comfortable; but they themselves . . . they themselves!!! If you could see them arriving, the old men in rags coming to die; persons who have been dying of misery for months, picking up their food at the edges of the curbstone like dogs in the street; women in rags, emaciated, sick, paralyzed, incapable of making a living, who say to us after they have told us their story: 'You see that things cannot go on like that, as I cannot work any longer or earn anything.' I saw one woman of eighty-seven who had lost all her children and grandchildren, and who for the last six weeks had been sleeping out of doors. It made me ill to hear of it. Then we have so many different cases, without counting those who say nothing, but simply ask: 'Where is it?' These are admitted at once and it is all over in a minute."

With a pang at my heart I repeated:

"And . . . where is it?"

"Here," and he opened a door, adding:

"Go in; this is the part specially reserved for club members, and the one least used. We have so far had only eleven annihilations here."

"Ah! You call that an . . . annihilation!"

"Yes, monsieur. Go in."

I hesitated. At length I went in. It was a wide corridor, a sort of greenhouse in which panes of glass of pale blue, tender pink and delicate green gave the poetic charm of landscapes to the inclosing walls. In this pretty salon there were divans, magnificent palms, flowers, especially roses of balmy fragrance, books on the tables, the Revue des Deuxmondes, cigars in government boxes, and, what surprised me, Vichy pastilles in a bonbonniere.

As I expressed my surprise, my guide said:

"Oh, they often come here to chat." He continued: "The public corridors are similar, but more simply furnished."

In reply to a question of mine, he pointed to a couch covered with creamy crepe de Chine with white embroidery, beneath a large shrub of unknown variety at the foot of which was a circular bed of mignonette.

The secretary added in a lower tone:

"We change the flower and the perfume at will, for our gas, which is quite imperceptible, gives death the fragrance of the suicide's favorite flower. It is volatilized with essences. Would you like to inhale it for a second?"

"'No, thank you," I said hastily, "not yet . . . ."

He began to laugh.

"Oh, monsieur, there is no danger. I have tried it myself several times."

I was afraid he would think me a coward, and I said:

"Well, I'll try it."

"Stretch yourself out on the 'endormeuse.'"

A little uneasy I seated myself on the low couch covered with crepe de Chine and stretched myself full length, and was at once bathed in a delicious odor of mignonette. I opened my mouth in order to breathe it in, for my mind had already become stupefied and forgetful of the past and was a prey, in the first stages of asphyxia, to the enchanting intoxication of a destroying and magic opium.

Some one shook me by the arm.

"Oh, oh, monsieur," said the secretary, laughing, "it looks to me as if you were almost caught."

But a voice, a real voice, and no longer a dream voice, greeted me with the peasant intonation:

"Good morning, m'sieu. How goes it?"

My dream was over. I saw the Seine distinctly in the sunlight, and, coming along a path, the garde champetre of the district, who with his right hand touched his kepi braided in silver. I replied:

"Good morning, Marinel. Where are you going?"

"I am going to look at a drowned man whom they fished up near the Morillons. Another who has thrown himself into the soup. He even took off his trousers in order to tie his legs together with them." his trousers in order to tie his legs together with them."

CPSIA information can be obtained at www.ICGtesting.com
Printed in the USA
BVOW04s0953120815

413035BV00004B/54/P

9 781595 478764